CAESAREA

JERUSALEM

ALEXANDRIA

DEC 2015

CAPTIVITY

György Spiró

CAPTIVITY

Translated from the Hungarian
by Tim Wilkinson

RESTLESS BOOKS
BROOKLYN, NEW YORK

ISBN: 978-1-63206-049-5

Translation of *The Book of Enoch* used here follows the text in
From the Apocrypha and Pseudepigrapha of the Old Testament by R.H. Charles
(Oxford: The Clarendon Press, 1913)

Cover design by Rodrigo Corral
Endpaper artwork by Mauricio Diaz

Ellison, Stavans, and Hochstein LP
232 3rd Street, Suite A111
Brooklyn, NY 11215

www.restlessbooks.com
publisher@restlessbooks.com

This translation was made possible with the support of Gabor and Zsuzsa Bojar.

Text designed and set in FF Tibere by Tetragon, London, UK
Printed in the United States

CAPTIVITY

I

FROM ROME TO JERUSALEM

"YOU'RE SETTING OFF FOR JERUSALEM THE DAY AFTER TOMORROW!"

Uri woke with a start.

His father was standing over him.

Uri raised himself up on his rags, picked up the scroll that had slipped from his hand to the floor, and looked up apologetically from where he was sitting. An awkward smile played across his lips, as it did whenever he was caught doing something, and he always was caught, even if it wasn't anything bad.

His father fidgeted a bit in the gloomy nook, the gray February afternoon throwing light from the yard on his stern bearded features, his prominent cheekbones, his deeply set eyes; the little square thrown onto the wall happened to be gleaming just above Uri's disheveled, greasy hair. His father was standing there somberly, no longer looking at him but gazing at the yard. He turned on his heels and pushed aside the carpet that hung over the doorway, so forcefully that it conveyed his deep-seated disgust at his son, at his own position, with Creation in general.

Uri had not yet fully regained consciousness; he was merely ashamed of what his father had caught him doing: falling asleep while reading. He had a habit of taking a nap in the afternoon, and even though he had nothing to do and was quite free to withdraw to his hovel and go to sleep whenever he wanted, he felt guilty about it nevertheless. It was as if reading were a penance, a humiliating duty, for some ancient sin that he had not even committed. Yet he liked reading; it was the only thing that he really liked to do.

Scroll in hand, he got up to his feet, stretched his aching back, turned his head around and cracked his neck, shrugged his shoulders repeatedly, bent down, then gazed out the window.

Uri shivered in the damp and chilly darkness of Rome in early February. Images from his dreams were still drifting around in his mind, sinking ever deeper like fish burrowing into the Tiber's mud and merging with the murky halos in the yard. The dream cannot have been altogether disagreeable, because a pleasant feeling lingered, a hopeful image, though there was no point trying

9

to recall it. It was as though his real living was done in his dreams. There were people sauntering around in the yard, but too far off to recognize; he saw them only in blurred outline. At this hour of the day they were probably women, because the menfolk were still going about their business.

Uri had poor eyes.

His leg was bad too. Ever since he was small, walking hurt his feet and ankles. His back usually hurt also. His right hip had turned out bigger than the left, but it was his eyes that were plagued worst of all; he was very near-sighted. It had not always been so. Up to the age of ten or eleven he had been able to do all the things the other boys his age could do, but at some point he dropped out of their games, moved less assuredly, squinted, and leaned ever closer to the scroll when he read. It had not bothered him at first, coming on so gradually that he had barely noticed; it was just that he often had headaches.

Eusebius, the teacher who took care of him and ten or fifteen other boys in the house of prayer (that was what the community paid him for), told Joseph that, in his opinion, Uri had poor eyesight. Joseph had protested: no one in his family had poor eyesight, his son included. The teacher just shook his head. Joseph's first-born was his only son, his wife had not become pregnant again after the second girl was born, so the teacher realized that Joseph was in a difficult position.

That evening his father had interrogated him.

"Is it true that you don't see well?" he asked pointedly.

He walked over to the farthest corner in the main room and asked how many fingers he was holding up. The main room was not all that big, but even so, the hand was a long way off, and it was dim as well. The oil lamp was barely flickering, but it gave off a lot of fumes, and that too was bothersome. Uri sighed and chose at random, "Two." From the silence that followed, he could tell that he had guessed wrong.

That was when relations with his father started to go downhill.

He had always been the precious boy, the only whole person Joseph had managed to sire. He was the favorite. His father had been proud that his son knew how to read and write before other boys his age; he had boasted about him and had also started instructing him in the logic of business, as if he were already an adult.

His father repeated the experiment half a year later. Uri confessed then that he could not see how many fingers his father was holding up.

"Because you don't want to see!" Joseph had shouted angrily.

That sentence had haunted Uri ever since.

From that point on, his father avoided him. He did not want to see that his son could not see. Doctors claimed that dried gum from the balsam tree had a beneficial effect on cataracts and shortsightedness, and as Joseph had once traded in, among other things, balsam and dates, and was at that moment still receiving them in shipments from Judaea, he instructed Uri to place over his eyes every evening a poultice soaked in a watery solution of powdered balsam gum. Uri diligently applied the compresses and was nauseated by the smell of the balsam, but his eyesight did not improve. Another six months, and Uri still could not see how many fingers his father was showing. Joseph hinted that he should stop with the poultices, since balsam was expensive.

Uri was relieved and also despondent.

He could read all right; indeed, if he screwed his eyes up tight he could even see farther away as well, and if he looked through a funneled hand he could even see for quite a distance, albeit only over a tiny area, but honestly quite a long distance. He tried that out a lot when he was alone, because, bit by bit, he retreated to the little hovel, rarely even stepping out into the courtyard, which he could see quite well, everything being so close. He would stare out at the yard through the cracks between his fingers, which also helped him to see the far-off corners.

It was a spacious courtyard, impossible to tell where it ended; in truth it had neither beginning nor end.

Houses on the far side of the Tiber—the Transtiberim in Latin, though the Jewish population referred to it simply as Far Side, as if they were looking back at themselves with pity from somewhere else, from the true Rome, even a bit disparagingly—had originally been built contiguous with their yards. They had formed a single elongated, complex, erratic, winding system of dwellings and alleys on the old-time Far Side. Because the Jews constructed their houses as they had in Palestine, with the windows and doorways opening only onto the inner courtyard, all that existed to the outside world was an interconnected wall. As a result, what had come into existence was an endless, seemingly impervious single-story zigzagging system of fortifications, spiked at irregular intervals with strong gates, both secretive and exotic to anyone not familiar with this part of the Transtiberim. Yet it was well known that the Jews lived a wretched existence: leprous Jews would beg around the Porta Capena, at the beginning of the Appian Way, for all to see, and many found themselves in that part of town, given that the main gateway to commerce on the southern side of the city was outside the nearby Via Ostiensis. Produce was cheaper there than around the Forum, so half of Rome shopped there. It would also have been obvious that haggard people with stooped backs swarmed around with their pitchers, bearded and in worn sandals and frayed togas: they were going for drinking water because the aqueducts supplied Far Side with polluted water, good for nothing more than irrigation, if at all. Requests had been made from one generation to the next, but they were not granted better water by the city, and in districts that were blessed with a better water supply, outsiders had to pay the locals good money for what the latter received free of charge. The water of the Tiber was drinkable in theory, but the Jews considered it unclean, especially when, from time to time, it overflowed with corpses, so they did not drink it or even wash with it. They preferred water from cisterns, and there were some benighted souls who, obeying the religious precepts of their ancestors more strictly than most, considered water from any other district impure, so their families were also prohibited from using it. There might well have been something to it, though, because the water in those lead pipes left a grayish scum on the children's skin, who turned out slower and dimmer than the others.

Lepers, incidentally, were treated decently; they were not expelled from the community but had a fairly spacious pen designated as their dwelling place, minimal rations were provided, and they counted on tzedakah, or charitable funds, or at least on a charity bowl of victuals for immediate relief, which even the most destitute and needy visitors can count on from a Jewish community anywhere. But because lepers were impure, their family was not allowed direct contact and could only shout to them from a distance, and the afflicted were obliged to smash to pieces the single-use clay vessels provided to them by the community, and, to the great delight of pottery merchants, to bury the pieces three feet underground. That aside, they were free to move around, even go beyond the walls of the Jewish quarter to beg like any other sick person. They too were obliged to go to the house of prayer, but not only were priests forbidden to touch them, they were not even supposed to see them, lest they become unclean themselves, so the lepers had to stand throughout the services in a dark corner that was walled off by planks; they arrived earlier than the priest and left well after. Because there were so few priests, their cleanliness was safeguarded by the most ancient and stringent regulations. As descendants of Aaron, they were sent from Judaea to Rome for the more important festivals to confer blessings, and afterward they would return to Jerusalem. In the course of time they also sent out a few Levites, who could not themselves become priests but could act as priests' assistants: it was they who blew the shofar, they who did the singing and played the music, they who collected the taxes. The ritual butchers and slaughterers also came from their ranks, so there were more of them in Rome than there were priests.

Apart from their religious activities, the priestly families and Levites had no say in the life of a community. Unlike back East, the rich and respected families in Rome did not cede important decisions, so many of Rome's Levites asked to be sent back to Jerusalem, and the Roman municipal administration was only too happy to oblige. In their place, others came from the ranks of the lower priesthood and the lower Levites (for it seems that, even there, not everything went so swimmingly for all priests and Levites), and after a bit of administrative maneuvering they were generally allowed into Rome, especially if wealthy Jewish families vouched for their subsistence. The officials of the magistracy could breathe easily, because they would not be obliged to hand out free grain to the newcomers and their families. After all, people like that arrived with family; indeed, that was largely the point of leaving the Holy City and traveling out to the impure Diaspora. But after a few weeks or months, they would get fed up with the climate in Rome and go back to Jerusalem; then either somebody else would be sent to replace them or not. In time, a few Levite families settled down and got rich, mostly through the ritually pure oil and wine that they imported from Judaea and Galilee.

Rome's non-Jews were not very interested, to tell the truth, in how the population on the right side of the Tiber lived.

There were many small ethnic enclaves in Rome, and outsiders had no awareness into them, and the Jewish enclave was not among the larger and most important ones either: in a city of around one million, it accounted for no more than thirty or forty thousand, the majority of them the gradually liberated progeny of the slaves who were sporadically carried off to Rome. They did have synagogues, however, twelve of them, one of which was on the Appian Way, where they also had an underground cemetery, a catacomb. Counting on eventual resurrection as they did, they did not incinerate their dead like the foolish Latini. Seven of the prayer houses were along the road to Ostia alone, the thoroughfare by which goods delivered by sea reached Rome by land.

The first of the temples, named for Marcus Agrippa, the Roman potentate who had given patronage to the Jews, was built almost a century before and was still standing. Although Uri's family did not go there, Joseph had shown it to his young boy, telling him the tale of the first convoy of Jewish captives who refused to work until the Roman slaveholders accepted the Sabbath as the slaves' day of rest; they would follow the law laid down by their religion at all costs, and they wanted their own temple. A number of them were killed on account of those demands, but even still the rest would not relent. Uri clapped his hands in delight at hearing this, and he resolved to be that brave if ever needed.

He also rejoiced when his father related that the lords had paired their males and females off to boost the ranks of their slaves, but the Jewish men would only go along with it if any non-Jewish women with whom they were designated to multiply first converted to Judaism. Later on, to simplify matters, women were imported from the Jewish part of the empire. Herod the Great, king of the Jews and a friend of Marcus Agrippa's, established good relations with Emperor Augustus and managed to finagle permission to ship women in to Rome. There were prostitutes and thieves and women with the clap among them, but they were Jewish and there was no need to bother converting them.

Shipping them cost money, however, his father recounted, and that is something that no state power likes. Herod the Great and Emperor Augustus realized that, and before long this fount of women dried up.

Under Roman law, the descendants of slaves were supposed to inherit their master's religion, but the Jews were unwilling to propagate on those terms, so an exception had to be made. Non-Jewish slaves were not granted the same concessions, so they loathed the Jews, which was nothing new; ever since Alexander the Great conquered the East, non-Jews who lived there had always resented the Jews and the special treatment that they demanded, appealing each time to prerogatives that they had won under Persian rule. It was one thing if they all fell, Greeks and Jews alike, under foreign—Persian—dominion, but another thing altogether if the Jews came under Greek sway but for centuries refused to accept it. Since both the Greeks and the Jews had fallen under Roman dominion, the Jews regarded Rome as a Babylon, paying it homage in practice more zealously than did the Greeks. The female slaves, incidentally, were glad to turn Jewish: they knew that Jews, unlike Greeks or Romans, would never abandon a child. There were even some male slaves who converted, calculating that the Jewish communities would contribute to their manumission, and there were indeed some cases of Jewish converts freed in this manner. The only thing that may have given them pause was circumcision, a painful procedure for an adult, and not without danger. The women, though, were not threatened with clitoral resection, since the Roman Jews did not demand it, so there were droves of Syrian, Greek, Arab, Abyssinian, Egyptian, German, Gallic, Hispanic, Thracian, Illyrian, and female slaves of other origins who became Jewish in Rome, to the greater glory of the One and Only God, giving birth to Jewish children in the zigzag ghetto of Far Side. And since the Transtiberim—which was not even fenced in at that time, already considered part of the city by government bodies, albeit unofficially—was inhabited not only by Jews but also by people of various conquered nations, for the surplus daughters who became Jewish converts it was often only a matter of moving a few houses away, so they were even able to visit their parental households, should they so wish. Not that they had much wish to: their non-Jewish families were generally more than happy to be rid of them, and they made that quite clear. In any case, the women became part of the husband's family forever, with no ties of any kind to their parents' family—on that score, Roman and Jewish laws were in accord. A girl who converted to the bosom of the One and Only God could only be thankful that her parents had not cast her out as prey for wolves or men, or strangled her at birth.

That is how a Jewish Diaspora took root in the capital of the empire.

Joseph considered it an injustice that he must live on foreign soil, as technically speaking everyone who did not live in the Holy Land was unclean, and that was a blemish no water could wash away. But, then, it was not the first time this had happened in Jewish history, he said, and he pointed out to Uri that the Roman Jews were much better off than those back home, as they well knew it; they acted rather like a sizable permanent legation in Rome, and if they traded shrewdly, and Rome and Jewry were bounded by ever more threads, as was predestined by necessity, they were only doing what the Creator had seemingly intended them to do.

The winding interior courtyard had originally been a single labyrinthine system. Fortification had arisen spontaneously in the open space—although the wealthiest, as is the custom wherever Mammon is master, were separated from the communal yard with high walls and indeed had special guards to protect them—may money be cursed eternally—especially now, because an ever increasing number of Rome's Jews were rich, and an even greater number were getting poorer. There might have even been a connection of sorts between the two phenomena.

The original Far Side stood right in the center of the Jewish quarter, with new houses built around it, but in recent years rich entrepreneurs had started building multistory tenement blocks. Joseph feared that, one of these days, their own ramshackle shed would be cleared away, along with the small huts around it, and replaced by four- or five-story buildings. That is what had happened in the non-Jewish areas immediately next to Far Side, where Egyptians, Syrians, and Greeks from Asia Minor lived just as wretchedly as most Jews, and they went around the Jewish area just as comfortably as in their own.

The reason the yards had become a single, capricious, erratic space was because, on holy days, Jews were not allowed to wander more than two thousand cubits from their home. A cubit measured roughly forty-five centimeters, but it might be somewhat longer or shorter depending on the size of the forearm, since a cubit was the measure from the elbow to the fingertips. In other words, on holy days Jews were not supposed to go more than a meager half-mile from their home.

And the Jews had lots of holy days, starting with the four main festivals every year, each of which lasted for quite a few days. Then there was the Sabbath, each week from sundown Friday to sundown Saturday. Even then, people wanted to go more than two thousand cubits, which is only a few hundred paces. They wanted to visit neighbors, to chat and gossip, none of which is prohibited on a holy day as long as no work is being done. Chitchat is hardly working, as the Creator himself is well aware, and he no doubt jabbers with his archangels, since everyone knows he got his own work done in six days. So people joined their yards together, which meant that they were able to cover not two thousand but ten thousand cubits, festival or not, without leaving their own yard, or at least that was what they told their Creator, who had to accept the perfection of their reasoning. This is how the Law was outwitted by the Jews of Rome, much like the other approximately five million Jews in the world at the time; that is to say, they adhered to the Law because they respected it to the letter.

A special ordinance was laid down on this crafty sanction, a joint ruling, with various fine subclauses, one pertaining to Rome. It stipulated that the one-time Far Side counted as a single courtyard, and people were allowed to do within it anything they would do in their own home, even on the Sabbath or during festivals. There was fierce debate over whether the ruling also applied to new housing constructed outside the walls of Far Side, with some arguing that the whole of Jerusalem counted as one combined courtyard, and it was permitted to deliver certain things within it, even on the Sabbath, whereas others opposed, saying that Rome was not a Jewish city, nor was Transtiberim (or Traseteberin, as they generally pronounced it in those days, with the nasal before the "s" disappearing and the word clipped, the end result being the "Trastevere," the name by which this district would still be known two thousand years later). The whole of Rome was unclean, Far Side too, according to those who sought a return to the basic principles of the faith, themselves being impure, just like every Jew in the Diaspora. But be that as it may, the inhabitants of the old Far Side continued to reap the benefit of the blessed ruling.

In this labyrinth of a yard that was Far Side, there was no need to resort to that pious deceit that almost every Jew in Judaea committed, before the holy day began, by setting out a meal two thousand cubits away to signal that this was the boundary of a household, so when the holy day was in force they were permitted to go a further two thousand cubits from those provisions. This way, too, they were adhering to the Law—whichever suited them. That trick could not be employed in Rome, because any food left out would have been instantly stolen. The outside world corrupts the inner; intensive Jewish society was wrecked by pantheistic (hence godless) Roman society, and lamentations could be wallowed in on that account. It was typical Latin stupidity that their first emperor was still under the misapprehension that Jews eat nothing on the Sabbath, as if it were a day of fasting! Even after decades this was still raising eyebrows among Rome's Jews, who prayed on the Sabbath in their houses of prayer and listened to interpretations of the Torah and the scriptures of the prophets, but the essence was nevertheless the communal meal, the costs of which were covered by the communal tax. Festal food could not be skimpy; there had to be meat and wine on the menu, likewise vegetables and fruit, to say nothing of unleavened bread. Poor families would have very little to eat for the rest of the week, but on the Sabbath they could eat their fill, and for free, through the good offices of the community.

The rationale, therefore, for this singular form of architecture may have been primarily religious—to be more specific, an injunction against death by starvation—but neither was the fortified structure entirely irrational.

When the Emperor Tiberius decided, fifteen years before, that adherents to the cult of Isis and the Jewish faith should clear out of Rome, the Roman mob got wind of the news and tried to lay siege to this mysterious system of walls, but because they had no grasp of the whole, they were unable to force their way in. The Jews defended themselves by firing arrows and throwing javelins from the flat rooftops.

They had to leave their homes in Rome all the same, with Joseph fleeing with his wife and three-year-old Uri.

They withdrew to the hill village of Ariccia, twenty miles from Rome, to a stable with a leaky roof. Joseph cleaned out the manure and plowed, his wife strewed straw and litter, and Uri spent the whole day chasing poultry. But six months later, thanks to the kindly Roman notable who was their patron, the freed Joseph being a client, the father and family were able to return to their ransacked, wrecked home.

Apart from the four thousand unmarried Jewish men who were called up for military service and taken off to Sardinia, supposedly to ward off gangs of robbers—though the climate and homesickness finished more of them off—virtually all of the Jews with families drifted back, bit by bit; in total, a couple of hundred were killed by the robbers in the country, and the Emperor Tiberius was no longer issuing such strict edicts.

The houses were repaired, the furnishings slowly made good. Not that there was much to replace, given how poor the Jews of Rome already were.

Uri recalled almost nothing about being dragged away for the first time—only the smell of chicken droppings, his father placing him on his shoulders and carrying him long distances, which felt so good that he would dream about it even now, at the age of seventeen. In his dream, he wished he would wake up to see his father standing above him, saying, "Come on, my boy, hop on my shoulders again."

All that had remained of the temporary exile was that his mother, Sarah, would still cry out from time to time at the memory of an elegant utensil she had once owned. It had been tucked away and not returned by the non-Jewish freemen, also clients of their patron. She would moan on and on about that. The truth is that several of them had been honest enough to hand back the valuables that had been deposited with them, and to this day the family still ate out of such vessels, as the father would sometimes note, though that did not hinder Sarah in her lamentations.

These days, his father no longer looked up, but dourly spooned in his food. If he ever looked at his wife, at the repulsive sight of her kerchief-covered head, profound disgust shot from his eyes: it was not the thieves he hated, but her. And he held his tongue. Divorce was difficult for a Jew in Rome: there were so few of them. Divorce was easy in Judaea, and that was not just hearsay but written law: If anyone found another woman more beautiful than his wife, that was, in itself, sufficient grounds for divorce. A man could divorce, and he could even drive his wife away if she undressed, which was not prohibited between a married couple on certain occasions. But then, Judaea was not a border castle for Jewry but the body of the nation, and all sorts of things were possible there. In Rome, Jews could marry their cousins, unlike the Latini, because their numbers were scant. In Judaea and Galilee it counted as incest and was forbidden. On the other hand, a Roman widow was under no obligation to marry her dead husband's brother, which was still compulsory in Palestine.

Uri's father never spoke about that half year of privation. The story went around that the whole exile was caused by four vile, thieving Jews who, by some means, were able to win over Fulvia, wife of Saturninus, the senator, and to wheedle cash from her to purchase costly carpets for the Temple in Jerusalem. They absconded with the money, of course, and an incensed Fulvia reported this to the emperor, and Tiberius in turn flew into a rage.

From other variations that Uri heard, however, he suspected it was only a pretext for expelling the Jews from Rome, on account of Germanicus.

Germanicus, the famous general, was a nephew and adopted son of the emperor's, but Tiberius took offense at him and packed him off to the Eastern provinces. Germanicus had made the mistake of setting off from Syria to Alexandria, even though Egypt was a no-go area for all Romans of any rank, seeing that Egypt, as every street urchin in Rome knew, was Rome's bread basket; it was the source of the free grain, of which Jews who had been granted citizenship also partook. Anyone who disturbed Egypt would bring serious famine down on Rome. Anthony had been the last to try it, but his navy was defeated at Actium by Octavian, who became the Emperor Augustus. He then prohibited Roman senators and legionnaires from visiting Egypt. Tiberius must have presumed that Germanicus, passing through Judaea, had cut a deal with the Jews living there that they would stand by him if a war were to break out with Egypt. Indeed, it is quite certain that this was his thinking. Otherwise, why not expel Egyptians, who lived separately from the Jews in Transtiberim, along with the Jews? Germanicus, subsequently, was fatally poisoned. The rumor was that the emperor had dismissed the previous governor of Judaea, Valerius Gratus, for meeting with Germanicus, although it would have been difficult for him not to meet with the emperor's adopted son when he was wandering around Judaea. The matter was of little importance, one governor being much the same as another viewed from Rome. But this particular event did become noteworthy because the emperor waited seven years before relieving Gratus, which was not a sign of forgetfulness but rather, according to political analysts, precisely the opposite: he never forgot and sooner or later would take vengeance for sure. It was unusual, by the way, for Emperor Tiberius to replace procurators and prefects, choosing rather to leave them in place on the principle that "a well-fed tick sucks less blood than a hungry one."

It may well be, though, that the previous prefect got mixed up somehow in the Sejanus affair.

Agrippina the Elder is another oft-cited example. She was Germanicus's very popular widow who, fourteen years after her husband died, was starved to death by Tiberius. It wasn't like that, interjects another political commentator: banished to the island of Pandataria, Agrippina went on a hunger strike, a centurion poked out one of her eyes, then she was force-fed, on Tiberius's orders, but incompetently, and that's what caused her death. What does it matter? She was murdered. The Jews are just as up on Roman gossip as any other nation, and they have just as many worthy political commentators.

Uri was interested in history; all tales with twists and turns interested him, and he read countless works of Greek and Latin authors in his little alcove. There he was left alone and could spend the whole day musing and piecing things together.

The images he saw in his waking dreams were sharp and bright, almost palpable. Imagination is a great thing, if someone has it.

He could read Greek, because their neighbors in the Jewish quarter had Greek as their mother tongue, and most Jewish boys in Rome answered to a Greek name. They brought it from Palestine, where Hellenization had proved most successful in the area of language, and they had passed it on to their successors in Rome. Cultured Latini spoke more polished Greek, but this was also Greek; Jews spoke the same Greek as the Greeks themselves, it was impossible to tell them apart from their pronunciation.

Joseph and his family were exceptional in that they also spoke Aramaic at home, which was related to Hebrew, the original but by then extinct language of the Holy Scriptures. There was a somewhat calculated dimension to this: Joseph had the view that as long as it was necessary to do business with commercial agents who spoke only Aramaic, his children should learn it too.

Rome's Jews had, for some time, spoken neither Aramaic nor Hebrew, and the Hebrew texts had been translated into Greek for the congregation in the house of prayer. A Greek translation of the Old Testament was already in existence: the Septuagint, which seventy-two scholars translated in seventy-two days on the island of Pharos in Alexandria about two centuries before. At home, left to themselves, everyone would read aloud from this Greek Torah. It was not permitted to recite the Holy Scriptures by heart, lest one commit the grave error of misremembering a text and saying something other than what was written; that might have unforeseen consequences for the whole of Creation. In the house of prayer, on the other hand, Hebrew texts were translated impromptu in front of the assembled community, and of course a person was not forbidden to learn by heart that day's reading from the Septuagint, provided he pretend to understand the Hebrew and translate from that.

It did not occur to Uri as a child that his mother's knowledge of Aramaic was somehow unusual, and that other mothers spoke better Greek than she did. It was only as an adolescent that he reflected on the fact that his mother was called Sarah, which was a name, as he was well aware by then, often bestowed on proselytized women who had converted to the Jewish faith. By that time, however, he was not on good terms with his father, so he did not ask if Sarah was Jewish by birth, and there was no way he was going to ask his mother, with whom he had never had a good relationship. She took such care to abide strictly by the religion of her husband and son.

If Sarah was not originally Jewish—as her religious overzealousness suggested, because fresh coverts were always that way—then she must have been born a slave and Joseph must have emancipated her. Given Joseph's business acumen, he would have chosen a slave girl who spoke Aramaic, which meant she would have come from Syria or Babylon. Uri assumed that his father, who had been orphaned at a young age, could not have been prosperous enough to land a Jewish girl, for even if he had waived a dowry he would not have been much of a catch, and so he had been obliged to marry a slave girl. Under the laws of Palestine, this meant that he, Uri, as the son of a proselytized slave girl, would be of very lowly status over there in the Old Country, because his mother's descent would apply to him too. He might not be a slave or new convert, and he would count as an Israelite, but one of the least esteemed. It was a stroke of luck to have been born a Jew in Rome, where only the paternal lineage was taken into account.

For Uri, learning Latin was not easy.

The young people of the Jewish quarter spoke only a broken Latin; they rarely crossed over to the other bank of the Tiber, where Rome itself lay. They contented themselves with the frenetic life of Far Side, and they could get by perfectly well with their native Greek any time they ventured over. Even the non-Jewish inhabitants of Far Side spoke Greek, or else they spoke a language that no else understood.

The Jews had a habit of writing Latin with Greek letters, which came readily to them. They learned the Hebrew alphabet as well, of course, which they called Assyrian lettering, so that they would at least be able to read the Sh'ma for themselves in their daily prayers and, when necessary, the psalms, if called upon in the house of prayer. Occasionally elements of all three alphabets would be mixed up in a single sentence, even a single word. Uri was fond of that sort of mixture, and he did not transpose Latin or Greek texts into Hebrew lettering out of negligence or ignorance or even just for fun. He devised abbreviations in all three languages for himself, to copy things more quickly if he was loaned a particularly interesting scroll for a few days. He would omit vowels or diacritical marks, so that his shorthand was legible to no one apart from himself, and a few months later, not even himself. He would write pure Hebrew texts with the left hand from right to left, Greek and Latin with the right hand from left to right, and he had no idea why that was. He was amazed when he discovered, from a scroll, that systems of Latin and Greek shorthand already existed; others had invented them just like him; he happily learned those too.

Gaius Theodorus. When he was small, he had first written down his official name this way, then as Uriel, which means "the Lord is my light," was only used within the family; no one else knew what he was called at home.

Officially, his father was not Joseph either, but Lucius Ioses.

Gaius was the forename of their patron, while Joseph had adopted Lucius from the patron's father, who had freed Joseph's father. That was the custom; the forenames of Jewish freemen, which was often the only name they had, was the same as their patron's, as a result of which the Jews of Rome had primarily Latin and, second of all, Greek names and virtually none had a Semitic name. The very fact that Joseph's father gave him a Semitic name is significant; he found slavery hard to endure and longed to be in Palestine, though he had never seen it, as he too was a slave born in Rome, and indeed his father before him.

The Jews of Rome, then, had Latin and Greek names, but they were still Jews; they did not eat unkosher food, they observed the Sabbath and the festivals, and they prayed sedulously and in accordance with the rules.

If ever he was not reading or copying, by screwing up his unaided eyes Uri could see roughly as far as three doors along in the zigzagged, crisscross yard, and between his fingers up to six or seven doors along. He wanted to have keen eyesight, as his father's remark had cut him to the quick and still rankled; there were times when, trying his eyes out in the morning, he may have seen more clearly, perhaps, but by evening he had to conclude that he was still not seeing well enough.

Not long before, he had fabricated a contraption for himself out of a wooden board that could rest on the ridge of the nose, so that he did not have to look through his fingers all the time: he bored two small holes to look through, and when he was wearing it on his nose and looking through the holes he did get a nice, if very restricted, view. The view was nice because everything was sharper and more stable, relatively speaking, than when he simply peeked through his forefinger and thumb; in fact, it was just as good as when he looked through the splayed fingers of both hands held in front of his eyes.

The plank had the extra advantage that it could be held in place with just one hand, but he dared not show himself outside his own hovel with the nose-board, because people would have laughed. Indeed, he did not even dare to stand close to the window, with the device on his nose or not, because it was known throughout the yard, just like everything was known, that he was in the habit of hanging around and gazing out; in fact he was mocked on that account, and even his father had told him to lay off: "Spying is despicable," was what he said, so Uri would spend long periods of time loafing deep in his alcove, as far as he could get from the window, and he hoped no one outside could make him out in the gloom. There was a story told about a weak-eyed but rich Latini who was able to see everything clearly by skillfully holding a ground diamond before his eyes and looking through it. But Uri had never encountered anything of the kind; indeed, he had never seen a gemstone at all.

He feared going totally blind.

Blindness was not common in the labyrinthine yard, and anyone who went blind did not roam around outside, but people could sometimes be heard saying that this person or that had been struck down in that manner by the wrath of the Lord. Blind people, unless they were trachomatous, were not segregated; they were not regarded as unclean, merely unfortunate. Uri brooded for days and weeks and months on end about whether the Lord had marked him to be blind, or if it was simply a case of his having so much else to do that he was not paying attention, or maybe even Satan, or more likely Fate, intervening to cause this affliction. Uri held an assortment of Judeo-Latin-Greek notions about it because he had read a lot. What he really did not understand was why he had not been born blind from the outset, if that was his fate. Had the Lord changed his mind after he was already underway? What sort of considerations could be driving Him? he wondered. Uri raked through the memories of his childhood but could not identify a single transgression so massive that he would have to be inexorably blinded on its account; when he looked back, even with the best will in the world toward the Lord, he could find nothing in his actions.

The most obvious explanation was also the boldest: the Lord did not concern Himself with anyone, even His Chosen People; all that had been entrusted to Him was the task of the Creation and getting the stone tablets delivered by Moses to His people. That explanation was not something that came from any original thinking on Uri's part; the Lord Almighty was cast in the same terms collectively by the Zadokite sect of Roman Jews, also called the Sadducees, who accepted only the five books of Moses and nothing else, nothing handed down in the oral tradition, and that was also the official position of the high priests in Jerusalem: the Creator had generously created the world, and mankind as part of it, that it should exist, but He had no further say thereafter; everyone was free to do with his life as he wished, within the bounds of the Law, though naturally anyone who broke the Law would be smitten down.

Man lived as best he could, then died, and there was no Hell, no Heaven, the way the primitive Jews imagined over there in Palestine; there was no transmigration of souls, as the primitive Pharisees also believed, as no one rises up from the dead, or only after the coming of the Messiah, but that was still a long way off. "We have not suffered enough yet to be forcibly washed," his father had said once, as had gullible Palestinian Jewish "people of the land," the spiritually impoverished *am ha'aretz*, with their purblind, narrow-minded, and pernicious notions, which commercial travelers returning to Rome's Jewish quarter from Palestine would often recall, disapprovingly, with a shudder.

Uri, in his hovel, spent a lot of time mulling over resurrection, coming to the conclusion that if the Creator had just a touch of compassion He would make resurrection possible, and he, Uri, would meet with many fair, clever, and wise people who had lived before he was born, and would also live after he was dead, and they would carry on a timeless discourse, rich in ideas, in a fragrant and radiant space without time, after the Last Judgment, where bodies become weightless and painless, and human bodies that had been restored by magic would float and fly even without wings, as he pictured himself doing in his most delightful dreams as, so to speak, a foretaste of existence after the Last Judgment. It was rational, even natural, for that to be so, because if there were no resurrection with Judgment Day and the end of time, an individual's life would not have the slightest meaning at all.

Uri passed his time either with his eyes screwed up, gazing out at the life of the yard, happy at least that he could see at all, or else he read.

He did not need to be instructed in anything; he would have been able to instruct others, but he had no desire to do so, even though his father had asked him. If he did not count as a fully able-bodied man, let the community draw at least some use from him, and anyway teachers were paid, which was not a point to be sneezed at. His teacher, Eusebius, who was fond of Uri and rated his abilities highly, had also encouraged him, but in vain: Uri hated anything to do with the community.

Others could see well, he couldn't.

Others did not have a head and feet and back that ached with pain.

Others were able to chew well, whereas he could only chew on the right side, because the teeth on the left side did not clench and had started to come loose, which was a sign that he was going to lose them. It was terrible, on the other hand, that the permanent incisors projected so far forward that he could not close his mouth properly, though admittedly they allowed him to whistle superbly through the gap that could be formed with his tongue, and sometimes people would greatly admire that, but he would rather have had normal teeth.

Other boys the same age were not going bald, as he had been since sixteen.

Others were not born freaks, as he was. It might not have been visible to everyone, but that is what he felt like, and that is what he became.

It was not solely on account of his physical problems, however, that he shut himself away in his hovel.

Around five years ago, when his eyesight had been better, not long after his bar mitzvah—his ceremonial initiation into manhood by the synagogue—he often went on strolls on the other side of the Tiber. In Rome, Jews could go wherever they pleased, and Uri, thanks to his grandfather, who had scraped together the money from his work as a slave to pay for his manumission, got married, begot a son, then died straight after—thanks to him, the grandson, Uri, had been born a Roman citizen.

Jewish though he was, he was a Roman citizen with full rights, so he did not pay the taxes that were imposed on non-Romans and non-Italians. Indeed, he was given money by Rome: through his patron's intervention, he was awarded the *tessera*, which he was entitled to under the law since the age of fourteen, although the magistrate was perfectly able to string this out for years if some big shot did not snap at them. He had drilled a hole in the small lead token and wore it hidden under his tunic, slung low on his neck so it would not be stolen, and he would feel for it compulsively at frequent intervals.

If he showed it at the biggest distribution center on the Campus Martius, he would receive the monthly ration of grain that was due to paupers of unemployed Roman freedmen, the libertines who were capable only of begetting children—plebeians, as they were also called. Meat he would obtain on the right side of the Tiber, at home, as on the other side it was not possible to procure kosher meat; that was also where he drew the wine ration. A few taverns on that side let it be known that they also held stocks of kosher food and drink, but the public was banned from those taverns by the Roman gerousia or synedrion, or Sanhedrin as it was called in Judaea, the council which met at irregular intervals to decide on the affairs of the various congregations, as it had an interest in seeing that one and all purchased the produce of the official Transtiberian Jewish slaughtermen, and should only drink wine that was sold by the powerful Jewish wine victualers of Rome. It was possible to make an even bigger profit on wine than on meat because drinking wine was compulsory on feast days; wine victualers also sold the two-handled flasks, fired from white clay and freed of impurities, from which the wine was supposed to be drunk. Romans, both Jews and non-Jews alike, drank a lot of wine because wine did not loosen the bowels, whereas water often did. Somehow, the same victualers who shipped pure olive oil from Palestine to the Roman communities, as the use of Italian oil was judged a capital offense, upheld time and time again by the leadership of the congregations, given that substantial numbers of wine and oil importers were to be found among the elders of this collective leadership.

Uri self-righteously consumed a good deal less of the ration than he was entitled by its regulators, so that he too, along with his father, could consider himself a breadwinner. On the days his ration was to be handed to him, the whole family would be with him, which is to say his father, mother, and two sisters; together they would all carry their allotment back home. The wealthier among them would go with a handcart; the rest would take sacks and wicker baskets, because a handcart was too expensive. At times like that, Uri was happy that, through chance, thanks to a grandfather he had never seen, he was able to help his family. His father had also never seen his own father, because Joseph had been just a few months old when Thaddeus died at the age of twenty-five—five years earlier than the average life span for a slave (those long years of hard labor he had sweat out to pay his redemption bond cannot have done his health any good).

If a Jew was scheduled to receive his monthly grain ratio on a Saturday, or a Jewish feast day, he was allowed, under one of the still-active decrees of Augustus Caesar, of blessed memory, to go pick it up on a Monday, or whenever the holiday ended; the decree had not been repealed by Tiberius, even after he had expelled the Jews. There were Jews with a tessera who had kept a low profile in the vicinity of Rome during those months, but brazenly stole back into the City. The municipal administrators, long faced, had to dispense their allocation, because without an order of exclusion they were obliged to do so. There were some banished Jews, it was said, who threatened to bring a lawsuit against the reluctant official, and in the end the official had given way, even though he could have called out the sentinels to arrest the hectoring Jew. The world was crazy; it always had been, and it would remain so until the coming of the Messiah.

In truth, Joseph could have been a Roman citizen himself, because three children of his had been born there, and Augustus's decree that the parents of three children should be awarded citizenship was still in effect. Uri had tried to persuade his father to apply for citizenship, on account of his children; he would no doubt be granted it with his patron's intervention, which would mean that he too could have a tessera.

Joseph, however, was unwilling to do that.

Things are fine the way they are, Joseph said. Uri kept nagging until his father finally said he would rather work for the money, because some very big issue might come up one day, some really important business, and he would call for Gaius Lucius's assistance on that, but until that happened he did not want to pester him, lest they resent him for asking unnecessary favors.

Uri saw that it was no use arguing and never brought the matter up again. He wondered what the very big business might be. Did his father fear another expulsion?

Often Uri would take a stroll on his own over to the far bank of the Tiber to Rome, the "true Rome," and gaze around. He made his way there from beyond the river. For some strange reason, the Jews always lived beyond some river or other; their very names—the Hebrew, one from beyond the river—said as much. In Babylon they had also lived on the far bank of the Euphrates, before they were allowed to head home, to the West.

He sauntered around and stared out with nothing to do, being unfit for physical labor. People finally gave up on him when the congregation's members persuaded Joseph to try him out as a roofer: that was easy work. Uri was acrophobic, though, with no head for heights, and on the very first day of work he fell off and broke his right arm. The arm healed, and in any case his left arm was fortunately the nimbler one; he already wrote Hebrew and Aramaic with the left hand, and now he took the opportunity to learn to write Greek and Latin with it, as well. Ever since that accident, his father was left in peace.

Then Joseph came up with limeburning, also a good profession, but Uri rebelled and started yelling: not only would he not be a limeburner, he would never be a glassblower either, he would rather die. That shook Joseph, who had himself started out as a glassblower, or rather as a goldsmith, because Jews were the only ones in the Roman Empire who were able to blow glass around figures of filigree gold thread, and without another word he left his son to rant on for a few minutes longer, jumping up and down and even threatening to sign on as a longshoreman.

He was not serious about that; with his aching legs and lousy back he would not have lasted a day lugging those loads. Aside from tanning, that was the lowliest work a Jew would undertake. The pay was bad, but if you had a tessera it was possible to sustain a family with several children on the handouts and the extra income from dock work. That was to say nothing about pilfering a bit of the cargo when the supervisor was not watching, and he would not be looking, so long as he also got a share of the swag.

In principle, a Jewish worker was not supposed, on religious grounds, to steal from a Jewish consignment, but a non-Jewish one was fair game. It might be hard to tell, though, what came from Jews in Judaea or Alexandria and what had not. Anyway, goods were no longer Jewish if they were not destined for a Jew; the destination would taint them. Wages were low, families were big, and necessity teaches a man to steal; the Lord Almighty does not support those things, but they were deaf to the Word of the Lord; to harm those who deny Him can be construed as a divine action. The Jewish longshoreman, therefore, filched as much as the rest, as much as they were able. Besides, how many had already filched from a consignment while it was en route! And that was nothing compared to those who deviously pushed up the prices. No shortage of them, to be sure!

All the same, even among Jews, to be a docker was a lowly profession. Because they also had to unload impure goods, even the priests got a taste to expedite purification, although no one got around the dues for ritual bathing, which did not exist in Palestine, and even in Rome there was not a mikveh, a ritual bath, in every house of prayer.

The goods were taken up the Tiber from Ostia by skiffs and flat-bottomed lighters, bringing goods day and night, colliding as if they were wrestling one another, with a small trade war raging for landing spots. On both banks of the Tiber, as the loading and unloading went on day and night, inns and brothels prospered. Everyone was drunk on shore and on the boats, Jews and non-Jews alike, and there was no way of knowing who was what, because they all yelled and swore in Greek. It is true that block and tackle devices had been introduced on the docks, but the bulk of freight handling nevertheless proceeded by hand. Bales were unloaded and lugged to be swallowed by the enormous city without a trace and then discharged into the sewers, which likewise flowed into the Tiber. No wonder the Jews took care not to drink from it, and, as for washing, they never washed in it, and during epidemics the dockers were segregated.

Infectious diseases were diagnosed in Palestine according to a well-known formula: if on three successive days three corpses out of a community of five hundred were carried off three separate times, then it was the plague. If fewer, then it was not the plague and there was no need to impose quarantine. At times like that, the poor in some congregations would deny they had corpses, so that breadwinners could keep working, and only later would they report a death. The archisynagogoses took a strong stance against this, as did Levites, who were well-paid experts at burial. An uproar would arise over this every other day or so, as would be expected anywhere that persons lived surrounded by other persons, bound together.

Joseph made one last try to obtain a man's work for his son.

The post of grammateus had fallen vacant in their community.

The grammateus was a scribe, a notary and secretary, the archisynagogos's right-hand man, a man of influence, because he was in a position to whisper or suggest anything to a community leader at any time; he could be of some use and also do a great deal of harm. Fortunatus, the previous grammateus, had been ill and forgetful when he died, but nevertheless many members of the congregation had accompanied his body to the catacomb, located on the Appian Way. Joseph and Uri too had been present at the burial ceremony at the terraced entrance to the cemetery, which resembled a tiny, semicircular amphitheater.

A Jewish assembly like this was not large by Roman standards, and if one of its number should die, the five or six hundred menfolk, a small town's worth, would be there at his burial, and it was also permitted for women and children to attend, because in Rome women were of virtually equal rank to men, unlike in Palestine, where women were of no account.

The route was a long one, not because of the distance, for there could have been no more than three or four stadia, a mile or so, between Far Side and the cemetery, which lay just beyond the city gate, but because it was necessary to stop seven times on the way, first at the Jewish bridge, the Pons Cestius, as the section on the near side of the island was officially known, or the Pons Fabricius, farther away; at each stop, someone, each time a different person, seven times over, would expound at length on the virtues of the deceased.

Not that the burial was notable for this, but in the congregation that day there also happened to be a priest from Jerusalem by the name of Philippos. He was spending Passover in Rome, and he was staying until Shavuot, or Pentecost, and since he was there, he thought he would bless the people on the occasion of the burial. A priestly blessing was a big deal, because that blessing could only be said by a priest; Uri too would get a chill every time it was recited at some big feast by a suitable person, a descendant of Aaron. Philippos was not permitted anywhere near the body. Not only was he forbidden to see the tumbrel that carried the corpse; it was not even supposed to cast its shadow on him because it would have made him unclean. Philippos blessed the mourners in the crescent entryway to the cemetery, likewise speaking highly of the deceased, expressing hope that a general resurrection was not far away, so that the living and the dead would not be deprived of each other's company for long. He read out the prayer, those present wept and said amen, then they shepherded the priest away and only pulled the tumbril into the cemetery once Philippos was long gone. The body, wrapped in white shroud, was carried through the gate by the Levite attendants, who had been gazing off and leaning listlessly on their spades during the speech. Members of the family rent their garments as they entered the gate to see into the niche where the body was placed, onto which vault or rectangular hollow scooped into the stone of the catacomb wall they should place the thin marble plate they had brought along with them, on which stood just the name,

29

Fortunatus, and that he had lived sixty-four years and been a grammateus. Fortunatus's eldest son went down with the Torah scroll, tucking his head into his shoulders to pass under the low entrance, the other family members held a lit torch and oil lamps so they could see anything in the underground passages.

Joseph made an unexpected request at this point: that Uri only return to the catacomb when he, the father, was buried, but never again. He asked that Sarah and the girls stay outside. He also asked that nothing be put on the sepulchral plaque apart from a menorah; no name, no age, nothing else. Let no bird be painted or engraved on the plaque, nor shofar, nor wine flask, no lulav, no etrog—nothing.

Uri was shaken that his father was speaking about death.

Not much later, he realized that his father had marked him to step into Fortunatus's shoes, and wanted to prepare him mentally.

His father's emotional blackmail felt demeaning and sneaky, but he had nothing against a notary's work. It was a cushy job; there was no need to spend all day, every day in the house of prayer; the only bad thing was that you were the servant of the archisynagogos and could not talk back.

An archisynagogos was not a priest but a layperson who had a position of esteem in the congregation, on account of his wealth, for instance, and he was generally elected to look after communal affairs for a five-year term. Annianus, the current archisynagogos, was an uptight, hysterical man, and difficult to get along with. On the other hand, a grammateus was well paid, twice as much as a teacher and four times as much as a limeburner. True, a glassblower was much better paid, and the more shrewd merchants made even more, but a grammateus was a good prospect and could take his pick of the girls. By the time he was twenty, virtually every Jewish young man in Rome was married, so Uri still had a year. As a grammateus he would have free choice of single girls older than twelve, and there were lots of those, and every father dreaded that his daughter would remain a spinster. Uri loathed the thought of marriage, but he conceded that it was a fate he could not escape. For days he was thrilled to have his choice among potential brides; he would cast a leisurely eye over girls, sizing up their charms, and at nights he would have such terrible dreams that he would have to quickly rinse out his tunic in the morning. Neither Sarah nor Joseph made any remark about the tunic that was left out to dry on the line, as if they had not noticed.

One evening Joseph announced furiously that Honoratus wanted to put up his idiot son of sixteen for the post of grammateus, even though he could barely write and knew no other language but Greek, and could not count either. Honoratus was a rich and influential man, the owner of three tenement buildings in the Syrian quarter, and his wife was a cousin of the banker Tullius Basileus. The only sort of person who might knock Honoratus's son off his perch was someone like Uri.

Uri said nothing, just nodded. Gaudentius, the son, was so dumb that he stood no chance of getting the job as grammateus.

Joseph smiled happily, taking Uri's silence as a sign of agreement. He left no stone unturned; yet it was still the idiot who was named grammateus, with the favor of Annianus.

Uri relaxed. Being a notary for a hysterical archisynagogos was not such a great deal; marriage could also wait.

Then two months later, Gaudentius, Honoratus's idiot son, died unexpectedly, having lived just sixteen years, two months, and three days, as was nicely engraved on his sepulchral plaque. Uri, in his cubbyhole, said prayers for him; he genuinely felt sorry for the blockhead and could not help it if, by the grace of the Lord, he had been seen as good-for-nothing in life.

Joseph took a new lease on life and once again started to pay visits to influential members of the assembly.

Then the influential members of the assembly, on Annianus's advice, decided that the next son born to Honoratus should be the grammateus, and, until that son was conceived and born, let the post be discharged by others, who would relieve one another every three months. Joseph was assured that Uri was highly placed on the list of substitutes, even if he was blind as a bat. Joseph had a few salty words of his own, as a result of which Gaius Theodorus, son of Lucius Ioses, was removed from the list. From that point on, Uri was left in peace and out of harm's way, and when he was not reading in his alcove, he sauntered over to the true Rome.

There was much he saw and heard, and he would gladly have reported on these rambles to his father, but his father avoided talking with him. He would gladly have reported on them to his friends, but he had no friends. He was mocked on account of his physical defects, hated because he wrote, read, and calculated better than them and even so did not work.

He would have carried on with these pleasant, solitary wanderings for the rest of his life, scraping by on handouts from the state and his patron, dipping into books, parasitically, carefree and undemanding, had something not happened.

Unexpectedly, from one day to the next, unrest broke out over the way the Praetorian prefect Sejanus was deposed for his despotic rule as the plenipotentiary representative of Tiberius Caesar, who was living on the island of Capri (that is to say, his rule over the Latin wealthy was despotic; he did not trouble Jews, because they were simply of no interest to him). Many people were seized, and the entire leadership bodyguard was replaced; indeed, they had already been hacked to pieces. Uri happened to be poking around the street of goldsmiths, the Via Sacra, near the Forum, because he liked looking at jewelry, when people started shouting and he was carried along with the crowds to the foot of the Gemonian Stairs, where the dead bodies had been laid out for public display. That was where he saw a corpse for the first time in his life, and not just one but a dozen or more, and more than one of them without a head. Uri wanted to run off, but the crowd would not permit that; indeed, he was jostled into the front row, right in front of the soldiers who were shoving the crowd back, just as the executioner and his assistants dragged an adolescent boy and a girl of about ten years old over to the steps by their hair. Both had long fair hair, perfect for dragging.

A cry went up from the crowd.

Uri was standing near the stairs, so he had a good view.

The executioner went for the boy first, who wisely chose not to protest, and with one blow his head tumbled down.

The girl, by contrast, wailed and pleaded: she did not dispute that she had committed some sort of crime and should be punished as a child would lawfully be punished, but she never committed a capital offense and did not deserve to lose her head.

Silence fell; the executioner hesitated.

People in the crowd bawled:

"It is forbidden to put a virgin to death!"

That was true; Uri himself was familiar with Roman law, having studied it out of his own sheer diligence, because his people were only instructed in Jewish law, at their own request and in keeping with the obliging decree of the great Augustus. Not a particularly wise decision, Uri thought to himself more than a few times, unless Augustus had cunningly wanted to ensure that no Jew could ever become a lawyer.

The executioner thought for a moment before unfastening his toga. He whipped out his member from under his loincloth and kneaded it with his right hand until it became erect. He had a large tool, half a cubit long, the glans hiding the foreskin and the whole prong looking like a horizontal long-stalked mushroom cap. The soldiers set about the girl, ripping her dress off, wrestling her down, and spreading her spindly legs apart. The executioner knelt down and slammed home his member. The young girl screeched. To a rhythmic clap from the crowd, the executioner gradually sped up his movements, his buttocks flashing white, until he roared out, trembled, threw his head back, and gasped. He pulled his tool out of the girl; it was bloodied, and he showed it off proudly to the front row of the crowd, like a triumphant army commander, the still-erect bloodied member in his right hand, his left hand pointing at it. The crowd roared with laughter, then the executioner picked up his sword and began stabbing drunkenly at the girl's body. He slashed indiscriminately until shreds were all that was left of her, and these were then tossed and kicked onto the steps, among the others corpses.

The crowd, which until that point had egged him on enthusiastically, now fell silent. That was a bit too much, even for the Roman plebes. The executioner sensed the change in mood, swiftly wrapped his toga back in place, and raced off with his assistants.

Mutely, glumly, the crowd started to disperse. There was one beggar who even climbed the steps and started to abuse a headless corpse, as the remaining soldiers hastily threw the bodies into the Tiber.

Uri was drenched in sweat, shivering, his heart hammering, dizzy, the sweat stinging his eyes, his stomach heaving. He had wanted to avert his eyes throughout but found himself unable. There were cries of "Wait, they're bringing Sejanus's wife now. Let's see her mourning," but he took to his heels and ran as fast as he could. On his way he vomited onto his own legs. He could not remember which bridge he crossed, whether it was the Pons Aemilius or the Jewish bridge, because both led to the Jewish quarter. He huddled up in his alcove and did not budge from his place for weeks.

Nor indeed could he have shown himself, because the Elders prohibited it.

Somebody had seen him on the bridge, running home, filthy and panting, and reported it. The Elders assembled and called in his father. Joseph argued that Uri had reached the age of maturity, was unable to work, and could go wherever he pleased. The Elders, of whom there were seventy to faithfully mirror the Sanhedrin in Jerusalem, gathered together very rarely, only on the most vital matters, its membership being made up of the heads of eminent families in the city's various congregations. After protracted debate, they came to the conclusion that anyone who went around in places where reprisals were raging in these grave days and weeks was putting the entire Jewish community of Rome under threat.

"We must not get mixed up in it," they declared. "That is a matter for the Latini, we have nothing to do with it, and we should never cross their minds.

Your son put us all at risk, albeit unintentionally. He is not to leave your house until we send word."

Joseph had no choice but to acquiesce.

Following this contretemps, he exchanged a few words with his son. He explained that while others went across the river, they had not been punished with house arrest; it was typical because, as he noted, "We are the indigenous ones here, not them, and we shall never be forgiven for that."

He never asked what Uri had seen of the upheavals in Rome, the true one.

Uri held his peace. He had already been instructed as a young boy that many tensions were mounting in Rome's Jewish community, that a fierce rivalry was going on between the first wave of settlers in the city, and those who came after.

The first settlers were descendant from those who had arrived in Rome with the earliest convoys of Jewish captives. They were hauled from Judaea in the year Pompeius Magnus seized Jerusalem. It was not Pompey who took them captive, however, but Aulus Gabinius, who massacred three thousand Jews who had been fighting alongside the Jewish prince, Alexander, while he took another three thousand captive. Though painful to admit, there were also Jewish soldiers who fought against the co-religionists, on the orders of Aristobulus, Alexander's brother, who was on the side of the Roman mercenaries. Herod the Great's subsequent rise to power occurred in much the same way, with Roman help, with Jews again butchering tens of thousands of fellow Jews.

Uri's great-great-grandfather was one of the three thousand whom Gabinius had carried off.

Compared with them, the thirty thousand whom Cassius took prisoner not much later, when he marched into Judaea from Syria and took Taricheae, counted as mere novices in Rome, though just a fraction of them reached Rome, the great bulk of them having been sold off or died en route.

Even newer waves had arrived at Rome five, ten, twenty, and thirty years later, ever newer ones, as a result of Herod the Great's carnage. Because the newcomers came to make up the majority, they had appropriated the leading posts of fledgling organization of Jewish life in Rome from the old hands. His father complained bitterly as if he had personally had an important position snatched from him, though it was from his great-grandfather and grandfather, who, slaves though they were, had fought for the right to their own prayer house, and the slave women by whom they produced offspring should convert to Judaism. Joseph had inherited neither wealth nor office from his forebears. Uri was tired of these laments, and even more so because these tensions, which had arisen three or four generations before him, showed no sign of burning out.

He could not understand why the "old hands" were so proud to boast that they had spent more years in "Roman captivity"; to his way of thinking, his ancestors had been lucky that they had, only by chance, avoided the subsequent bloodshed in Palestine. If Gabinius had not taken prisoner his great-great-grandfather, he himself more than likely would never have been conceived.

Even now the "old hands" would provoke the "new boys" by calling them the spawns of robbers and thieves, which they would fervently dispute, often shedding blood on that account. Yet everyone knew that the thieves had been sold off abroad as slaves by Herod the Great, with most ending up in Rome due to the chronic shortage of slave labor. Until then it had been the law among the Jews that thieves could be kept in servitude no more than six years, and even then only domestically, serving Jews, and they were obliged to pay back four times the value of the stuff that had been misappropriated.

Apart from thieves, Herod the Great had also sold bandits off as slaves, and in truth it was next to impossible to puzzle out what crimes these late-arriving Jews had committed to get them shipped off to Rome.

The "old hands" would use the argument to this day that they were the progeny of Jewish freedom fighters, in contrast to the "new boys," who were the offspring of common convicted criminals, Jewish scum. Uri had his doubts about that. Alexander had recruited warriors against his own brother; it was a Jewish civil war in which Rome had, of course, been keen to have a say, and the Jewish state had come off worst that time. It was not much to Uri's liking to create freedom fighters from people who had happened to end up on the losing side, but he preferred not to advertise that; nor did he share with anyone his question that if the forebears of the "old hands" were indeed freedom fighters who struggled against Rome, why were they, the proud descendants, so pleased they were finally granted Roman civil rights? On the other hand, he was frankly amazed to discover that the entire Jewish colony living in Rome was considered traitors in the old country. What did those lunatics want? A new war of the Maccabees? Against Rome, even though Rome was doing the Jews no harm?

When he was five or six, Uri had thought long and hard about one particular story. A person is still a genius when just six; only later on did he become dull, he thought in his cubbyhole when he read about it.

When Pompey laid siege to Jerusalem, the city was reinforced mightily, with the Jews demolishing the bridge that connected the Temple courtyard to the town so that the Roman besiegers could not use it. Only there was no wall to the north, where a ravine ran, which the defenders believed could not be filled in. Pompey started work on filling it in all the same, with the Jews dismantling from above; whatever Pompey threw up, the Jews set alight, and so it went on for five days. But then the Sabbath came around, when it is forbidden to undertake any military maneuver unless to ward off a direct attack. There was no direct attack, Pompey was not stupid, so the Jews peacefully offered sacrifices for the Sabbath, all the Jewish defenders occupied themselves with the day of rest and did not tear down the ramparts that Pompey had erected. The Romans duly broke through on the next day. That was how Jerusalem fell.

This business was cited to children in Rome's Jewish quarter, the descendants of slaves, as a superb example of faithful devotion: "Better Jerusalem should fall, but keep true to the Law," they would say, and tears would come to the teachers' eyes, and all those who bequeathed the glorious memory to their descendants would shed tears, the descendants, too, valiantly shedding tears. Uri did not shed tears; the heretical thought came to his mind that perhaps it would have been better to breach the Torah and demolish the rampart Pompey had thrown up that day, then under the influence of propitiatory sacrifices, their One and only Lord would surely have forgiven them, His Chosen People, sooner or later. No doubt there were others to whom the same thought occurred, but they did not voice that opinion; Uri learned early on that it was not imperative to reveal everything that came to his mind. He said something of the sort once to his father, who heard what he was saying, because Uri still had good eyesight at the time; Joseph shook his head but did not rebuke him. Which suggested that his father had also given some thought to this sad episode.

The terror and turmoil passed, Uri's house arrest was lifted, and he was again free to wander, which he did. The Jews escaped any physical reprisals, while most of the filthy rich Roman elite was executed and their fortunes confiscated for the state coffers, which is to say Tiberius's private imperial coffers. But for Uri, Rome, the true Rome, had lost its allure.

Still, it was a distinctly good time to be Jewish in Rome, and not a good time to be a senator or a knight; it was good to be poor, and not so good to be rich, because anyone might be condemned, have his fortune taken and be put to death, with any denunciation given credence. There was no reason to accuse the poor, and they pulled through, unless they were made to bear witness against their patron on the rack. Although in principle it was only permissible to torture a slave, not a freedman, the law on this was widely disregarded. The retribution had been methodical, people in the true Rome later recalled, when they dared to speak; everyone had already been outlawed in advance in Sejanus's heyday; Sejanus had shed blood freely in Rome for years, so nobody had the least pity for him or his family or his friends when Tiberius finally rid the City of him.

Everyone spoke their mind. Horror stories circulated and were embellished ever more richly. Romans had time; they did not work but gossiped and enjoyed the fact that it was possible for them to live a quiet life gratis there, in the storied center of world power. Tiberius stayed on the island of Capri; he had not returned to Rome once, running the global empire from Capri through his cronies.

The Jews lived their own lives. Joseph continued to trade, and his patron, Gaius Lucius, had managed to squeak through also, even though he was rich, very rich. His servants said that once he had invited over all the people he thought might have designs on his money; he entertained them lavishly and explained to them that it was not they who would profit from his fortune but Tiberius, and he offered them a decent monthly remittance, to the end of their days, if they did not denounce him. True or not, the main thing is that no one ever did denounce him.

Uri went over to the true Rome less and less often, closing himself up in his nook, reading scrolls in all sorts of languages, and dreaded the thought of ever again seeing those milk-white, rapidly moving buttocks, or that little girl's bleeding abdomen and eviscerated guts, or to experience the sordid cravings evoked by that ever-present ghost.

Uri dreaded going to sleep; he had no desire to dream.

He had to go to sleep sometime, however, sometimes by night, sometimes by day. That is when he saw the ghosts, and he also saw other terrifying images in his makeshift resting place, thrown together as it was from rags and tatters; he dared not look his father in the eye, dared not look his mother and sisters in the eyes. All that showed was a troubled half-smile, which disgusted his father; he too must have been acquainted with the horrifying power of dreams.

Meanwhile Uri studied the Scriptures diligently, and he figured he was not sinning the way that Onan had done. He was not responsible for his dreams; the Creator was responsible for them. The Creator wanted all things, including evil and tormenting dreams, but the Creator was good, because the scenes in his dreams were clear and sharp, his eyesight in his dreams was good, and that too was the Creator's will. Maybe the Creator wanted him, a Chosen one, to see Evil, to see Satan. He may have ruined his eyes but he had a purpose: so that Uri would study more scrupulously. Study the Holy Writ. The Writings.

Studying the Holy Writ was a very Jewish notion, but not studying The Writings. Many Writings existed in Rome at that time; anyone who wanted could get hold of them, and Uri wanted to; but only one Holy Writ was the Lord's, or else none of them.

Uri collected works in Greek and Latin. Some of the goods he got through the tessera, and whatever the family did not need he would sell across the way and buy scrolls with the money. He would rather have gone without food, although at home he showed up for his share of meals, so there was no actual need to go hungry, which made it easy. He was a visitor to the splendid public libraries, where one did not have to pay much to enter, and it was possible to read all afternoon. Secretly he hoped that his father would forbid him to read, to study heathen writings, to read all the Greek and Latin poets and philosophers, but his father did not forbid him, although he must have had his suspicions about what his son was reading. He did not forbid him to do anything; he gave up on him.

Disowned him without ever saying so.

Simply because his eyesight had degenerated.

He begot me faultily, was the thought that often came to Uri's mind; he was sloppy in begetting me, didn't pay enough attention, and now he blames me.

Yet it was not just Uri; no better a job had been done in begetting his younger sisters either. The older of them, Hermione, was stupid, while the smaller had been born bright, but she coughed continually, snorted, and was breathless. Her hacking coughs at night would wake everybody up, and her whining drove them crazy.

However, Uri was least affected: he slept on his own in his alcove, shivering under the window, while his father and mother slept with the two girls in the main room, where there was also a fireplace for cooking. Uri thought it was no mystery why no children had not been added to the family. It was a relief, because it meant that there would be no little brother, who, if he were healthy, would stand to inherit everything if his father disowned him officially for his bad eyes. As it was, he would inherit everything, however decrepit he might be.

That small recess of four by five cubits, separated by a flimsy, rotting partition and a shoddy carpet from his sweaty parents and clammy sisters was an exceptional gift, he would have to admit, that he would never have come by had he been healthy. It was a prison cell, but a voluntary one—freedom itself.

He tossed and turned restlessly on his bed in that alcove for nights on end, an acidic sting constantly creeping into his throat, and if he eventually drifted off he would be haunted by abominable images and wake up choking, coughing, gasping for air because the sour spit would find its way into his lungs. He had nobody to cry out to, only the Lord, for whom he would gladly have been a priest, although he could not for lots of reasons, his physical ailments among them. Any one of his miseries was enough to disqualify him from the priesthood, but most of all it was that he did not descend from Aaron's clan. His ancestors were anonymous Jewish grubbers of the land whom a blustering Alexander once press-ganged into military service. They had been taken prisoner by the Romans, just two years short of a century ago. He had no one to cry out to; even the Lord never answered his prayers. But that little cubbyhole of four by five cubits was an exceptional gift; nobody came in, he could read, dream, or ruminate to his heart's content, peer out the window every now and then, and that too was life of a sort, and no doubt pleasing to the Lord, if he had created it.

He peered out the window, flexed his aching back, and it was then that he remembered something his father had said shortly before:

"You're setting off for Jerusalem the day after tomorrow!"

JERUSALEM, FOR LORD'S SAKE!

Me, of all people!

He huddled back on his rags and carefully set the scroll he was holding, a work written by a Syrian peripatetic philosopher who had become fashionable in Italia, onto the floor of packed earth, turned away from the window, and stared in front of him.

My father must love me after all, was the first clear thought to enter his head. He finagled a trip to Jerusalem for me! He can bother himself with me after all!

It was such a good feeling that tears sprang to Uri's eyes.

Jerusalem! Home! Where the Temple is!

Since there was a Temple and a Diaspora, the entrance of every synagogue faced Jerusalem; it was toward Jerusalem that everyone looked who stood on a bimah, the pulpit from which the Torah is read. It was toward Jerusalem that all Jews everywhere in the world bowed when they said their prayers at home; he too bowed toward Jerusalem, to the southeast, when he said his prayers three times daily, his back to the north-facing window, in the left-hand corner beside the carpet that covered the door opening, where he did nothing else. Or rather, he did: he stared out the window from there. He could not stare out from anywhere else if he did not want to be noticed, but this corner had enormous power as a result of the prayers that had been performed there, and it mattered not that no one else knew: it was enough that he knew, and it was the Lord's duty, even though He did not concern himself much with human affairs, to see that he, Uri, did nothing with his wretched life other than to bring it to the Lord's attention that he existed. Should the Lord happen, one day, to peek into this nook.

He would be the first person in the family to go to Jerusalem since his great-great-grandfather had been dragged off to Italia. The attention of the indifferent Lord must have drifted toward him, finally!

His father had not reached Jerusalem, nor his grandparents, nor his great-grandparents, nor his great-great-grandparents, nobody he knew or had been told about, no one among the names he had been obliged to repeat since he was a toddler, so that the tribal memory was not lost. There were many dozens of names of dead people that he had to include in his prayers every single day.

Rome was only the center of the wide world. Jerusalem belonged to the Lord: the center of the Jewish world, the Holy City of the Chosen People, and therefore, because there was one Lord, the center of the whole Creation. That was where he was going to go.

It was an unexpected gift, all the more so because he had never asked for it, never longed for it.

He needed to think this through.

His father, whom he had supposed, stupidly and spitefully, did not care about him and would happily exchange him for a child in perfect health, had now presented him with the greatest gift that a Diaspora Jew could be given: to be sent to Jerusalem.

His conscience now began to prick at him. Why had he not asked the Lord to guide him back to Jerusalem? What sort of halfheartedness had gripped him, one of the Chosen People, so that this had not so much as entered his mind? Why had he been so content to be born in Rome and to live there?

Nonetheless, the main thing about the joy that was arising slowly and spreading to his every atom was "Father loves me after all."

Uri was sitting under the window, facing the middle of the tiny room, brooding over things as he stared into the air before him. It was the beginning of February now. If all went well, he could reach Jerusalem in early April... Just in time for Passover, perhaps! He might be in Jerusalem for Passover!

He shivered: he understood it now.

His father had arranged for him to join the delegation that would be taking the offering of First Fruits—the Holy Money, the aparkhai.

He was going to Jerusalem with the delegation!

The Jews celebrated three major festivals each year, and by the Roman calendar Passover, the spring festival, was the first, when the autumn sowing would be ripening. This was the Feast of the Unleavened Bread; that is what the ancestors took with them when, under the direction of Moses, they were delivered from enslavement in Egypt. This was the festival for which all Jews, wherever they might be living, sent their sacrifices, or tithes, to Jerusalem. Anyone living up to three days' walk from Jerusalem would take their own offering, whether of meat or grain or fruit; those who lived farther away would send it via their elected representatives; and those who lived very far from Jerusalem, like the Roman Jews—they also included, for instance, those living in Babylon or Parthia, on the Greek islands or in Egypt—would send a monetary redemption for the offering of First Fruits. The obligatory sacrifices of animals and grain could be exchanged for money at any time, but in such cases it was necessary to pay one fifth more than the officially established price for a sacrificial animal or produce.

The Roman Jews sent money to Jerusalem once a year, for Passover; a monetary redemption, and not just because crops would go moldy on the way but because the Roman Jews had little to do with agricultural production, and what little they did produce would be used to provide for their own Levites. They only had small gardens in which to grow anything at all, because the Jews of Rome were not permitted to own farmland, either within the city limits or beyond. Even a Roman citizen with full rights was not allowed to farm in Rome or in the vicinity of the city if he was a Jew; land could only belong to the community, and even that had to be beyond the city wall—the cemetery. Far Side itself did not belong to the Jews but to the state—that was the law. They had outgrown the cemetery on the Appian Way, and it could not easily be extended. Negotiations were in progress with the magistrates to open another cemetery somewhere; the municipal office was currently offering the Via Nomentana, which could not be farther away, whereas the Jewish magistrates were asking for a plot on nearby Monteverde, so a tug of war was underway.

The sacrificial money was taken to Jerusalem by an elected delegation. It was a large amount of money, so the undertaking was not without danger; there had been instances when those carrying it had been robbed and slaughtered, after which the Roman Jews would collect the money all over again and send it the following Passover. The aparchai covered a per capita tax of half a shekel (or didrachma, which meant two drachmas or two denarii) plus any voluntary donations. Jewish men between twenty and fifty were happy to pay the half shekel of tax, because he was either one of the Lord's Chosen People or not, but if he was, then he could count his blessings.

The configuration of the delegation was arrived at through wise deliberation.

The entire Jewish population, all five million who happened to be alive then, was in principle divided into twenty-four portions, just like the priesthood in Jerusalem. So too was the Jewish population in Rome divided into twenty-four, with a strict rotation observed for every single religious duty. Each clan was entitled to provide, every twenty-four years, one of the money carriers headed for the festival of Passover. Precise accounts had been kept in Rome for ninety-eight years now; the only accounts more precise were the priestly records of the their own line of descent, in which the household and offspring of every priest was recorded. A priest could only marry a female descendant of a priest, and that had to be proven irrefutably with documents. Had the journey not been risky, they would of course not keep so strictly to the rotation, and, naturally, it would have been only wealthiest families that were always filling up the delegation.

Uri did not know, and neither did the residents of Far Side, how many members made up a delegation of this sort. The Elders also gave out no information when a delegation would be setting off, or from where. Of course anyone who badly wished to could find out, because there were unmistakable early warning signs, but keeping secrets has its own magic and even busybodies did not pry needlessly; it was a sacred matter, best no one knew about it in advance. Better, in any case, because there was no way of knowing what sort of evildoers might crop up: Satan was never idle, so there was no need to tip off malefactors who might report to our enemies.

Those who had returned from a trip to Jerusalem could tell their tales.

People would congregate in the yard, in some open part of the baffling labyrinth and listen with pride to how exquisite the Temple in Jerusalem was, construction of which had been started by Herod the Great and was still going on, with twenty-five thousand laborers continually at work on it.

Amazing adventures; narrow escapes from mortal danger, vicious pirate attacks, robberies, and miraculous releases—these would be recounted by the returnees, who could now spin stories as they had, after all, admirably delivered the money and would not have to do it again for at least another twenty-three years. They would tell of Judaea's miraculous climate, the incomparable flavors of the foods, the amazing moral character and courage of the Jews over there, the wondrous beauty of the women over there, the matchless treasures of the Homeland, but also the alarming, barbaric, superstitious, and incurable mental disorders that one encountered among the Jews of Palestine that the Jewish enclave in Rome, thank the Lord, been spared to the present day and thus, it was to be hoped, to the end of time.

Uri too had listened, mouth agape, to such accounts, and although it did cross his mind from time to time to wonder why, if that distant land was so miraculous, not a single member of the delegation ever stayed behind in Judaea but had always scurried back, helter-skelter, to despised, heathen, unclean Rome and eat the sour bread of the exile, but he always reproached himself for his bad faith and would add another Sh'ma or two to his evening prayers, and might sometimes even add a Torah verse.

I'm going to be a delegate, an astounded Uri murmured to himself happily.

He remembered then that someone from his family had already been a member of a delegation, just five years before. He would not be the first, after all, to return home. Odd that he had forgotten. He must not ascribe any particular importance to the mission if he had forgotten that.

It was a third cousin by the name of Siculus Sabinus, a blacksmith, whom Uri knew only distantly and whose house he had never visited. He was a strapping oaf of a guy who was asked in vain to describe what he had seen. All he could report was that there had been enough to eat, but even so, ever since, he got more orders than before due to his celebrity. The pilgrimage had been worth it from a business angle. It was a good profession anyway; he could bank it just making shackles, getting plenty of orders from the true Rome because there was a shortage of slaves, what with the dearth of wars, and as a result the masters were even less pleased if one did escape, so they fettered them with ever more ingenious shackles.

Siculus belonged to his extended family, and because he had been to Jerusalem five years before, if the rotation rule was applied strictly, no one else from the family could go for Passover for another nineteen years. Yet someone was going anyway: him.

Something did not add up here.

Joseph had to make a huge sacrifice to get his son squeezed into a delegation of this kind. Life would toss out any rulebook, however strict, if the Creator so willed, but then why would the Creator have so badly wanted his father to finagle this trip, not so long after Siculus Sabinus's mission, the family connection ignored?

Uri was not on cordial terms with the Elders. They were very well aware that Uri was lettered and erudite, and that if he so wished, he could put anyone in the synagogue to shame; he never did, but he could have, and for that alone they detested him. They never exchanged courtesies with him in the way they did with others. Others with poor eyesight—he was far from the only one, of course—were coddled and spoiled, but not him. Maybe they were waiting for him to turn to them, to seek their support as the weak will do, but he did not do that. Maybe they were waiting for him to transfer to one of their congregations; in theory, the heads of congregations did not poach believers from one another, but they would be delighted if something like that were to transpire. There is at least a drop of vanity in everyone, archisynagogoses more than most; they could outdo even actors. Uri was familiar with a few actors by sight, even though he never went to the theater over there, because they still lived in the Jewish quarter, and he knew that they were actors at all times and incapable of speaking in a natural voice, they never stopped orating in orotund tones. But the moment the leaders of a house of prayer put on their festive fineries, the way they strutted around, the way they held their limbs during prayers, the way they flaunted and carried themselves... It was as if they were the sole repositories of the faith, yet they were not even priests.

Clans were extended enough that someone else could be selected to go in his place, if the time had come, and Uri had no doubt that none in the leading circles of Rome's Jews would hold him in high regard.

Why is my father sending me to Jerusalem? How did he manage that?

HE HAD TO GET UP EARLY THE NEXT DAY, HE AND HIS FATHER BEING expected at their patron's place; they had to put in an appearance every other morning. As one of the equestrian order, Gaius Lucius kept track of the presence of each of his past slaves and their offspring, keeping a list of those who were missing, and if there were no pressing reason for the absence, he would withdraw his patronage. It was not a good thing for a client to be given the boot by his patron, because that meant being passed over for a great many critically important favors.

Like all wealthy Romans, Gaius Lucius held an official morning reception, a salutation, every day, but he had so many personal dependents—clients, that is—he was obliged to split them into two groups, otherwise they would not all have fit in the house.

Uri was unable to sleep all night. His tunic was soaked through with sweat; a cold wind had been blowing in through the window, but he hopelessly wrapped himself in his rags as he shivered.

He had no desire to see the world, no desire to accomplish a glorious mission, no desire to reach Jerusalem; he would have preferred to stay in his alcove forever.

He would be unable to stand the footslog. If his companions got way ahead of him, he would never see them again, what with his bad eyes; he would go the wrong way, fall victim to robbers and murderers.

He would not withstand the starvation; would not be able to stand the foreign food, would develop deadly runs, be carried off by the plague, catch leprosy, perish in a malarial fever; he could not hold his ground if they came under attack; he would be at the mercy of foreign hordes; he would be captured and sold into slavery.

He was going to have to declare himself unfit for the journey.

He tried to imagine standing before his father and saying this.

He could see his father flying into an uncontrollable rage and disinheriting him. That disinheritance would be made public, the community would withdraw their support from him, he would be officially cast out, which would be announced in the temple, and he would waste away from hunger and thirst and perish in a garbage dump.

In the depths of his soul, Uri almost yearned to be disinherited. It occurred to him that he would at last be free to live in the true Rome. He would enter service as a scribe for some rich man and scrape out a lonely existence like that until the end of his days. There was no need to die of starvation in Rome; that was unusual even among the destitute. He could take the tessera with him—a rotten trick maybe, but it was possible. He would never go back to the Jewish quarter, not even to pray. A Jew could pray on his own and still remain a Jew, though he would have to find nine others who were similarly disinherited to share the prayers on the Sabbath and feast days. He would send the customary tithe regularly to Transtiberim, and the Lord would have nothing to reproach him for. This was his chance to free himself from the whole kit and caboodle, his mother and his sisters; get free of his father, who did not love him anyway. All he had to do was stand in front of his father and say: I'm not going.

He cowered on his bed, his stomach ached. He pulled up his legs, linked his arms around his knees, and rocked back and forth, wordlessly, softly humming a sort of prayer; he was scared of traveling and, most of all, of what suddenly came to mind.

His heart was pounding from the terrible darkness of the freedom that seemed to be in the offing, and as his belly cramped he retched a sour vomit. As he mopped up the ejecta, easing his mental torment by occupying himself physically, he came to the decision, knowing that there was in fact no need for him to decide. He rubbed down his sweating body with the bedding and fled back into the customary logic.

No, it was not possible to reject the delegacy once the Elders conferred it, and it must have been conferred on him if his father had announced that decision. Why would they have said it directly to him anyway? He was only nineteen and had not yet paid half a shekel in dues; there was still a year to go before he reached full maturity. If he reached it, if he managed somehow to struggle back to Rome, next year would be the first time he paid the half-shekel tax. Until then he would not have the full status of an adult, though he had been initiated into manhood at his bar mitzvah. A few days ago his father had paid the half-shekel tax they had been collecting since the fifteenth of Adar, as synagogues were doing

45

throughout the Diaspora; then the treasurer would count up the money, as in other congregations. The obligatory dues paid by all adult Roman Jewish males between twenty and fifty years of age was collected, coins were changed. They would pay back, too, the money crammed into big sacks by servants and carried off somewhere where the chief treasurer would re-count it and have the small change swapped for coins of greater value. Uri had accompanied his father to the house of prayer and seen the treasurer. He did not imagine that this year he personally would be carrying that money, and the monetary equivalent of ample other produce, to Jerusalem.

To reject this honor would be the grossest form of desecration of the faith, and Uri had no desire to desecrate the faith; he merely did not want to be a delegate. For all that, he could still remain a good Jew and wash his feet, say his prayers, and respect the laws.

To try explaining that, however, would be fruitless.

A commission like this was the greatest possible honor; it raised the prestige of the commissioned, a major injection of moral capital, which might even be exchanged for small coins. People would hustle and bustle, scramble, and even pay for an honor like this, albeit mostly to no avail, because it was necessary to comply with the rotation principle.

That principle might not have been laid out in the books of Moses, an oral tradition, like much else which had become customary since then. But it was strong all the same and it had to be admitted that rotation was now a highly venerable practice, with people living by it even in Jerusalem, so the Roman Jewish community also had to respect it. The Elders of Rome did not much care for Jerusalem's families of high priests, because Herod the Great had brought them in from Babylon, having exterminated every last one of the old families. By then there was already a Jewish Diaspora in Rome, and the leadership of the time decided that they would not accept the new rulings of half-Jewish Herod the Great's damned high priests. They had done so since then, of course, but the rotation principle had been decided on some time before Herod the Great's massacres, and that principle was alive in Rome as well.

Refuse a favor from the Elders, when they had flouted the rotation principle on his behalf? Inconceivable.

He sank into a feverish light sleep.

He was in bad shape when his father stepped into the alcove.

Uri hurriedly put a toga-like sheet over his sweat-stained tunic and pulled sandals on his feet. He must have cut an even more pitiful figure than usual, because a look of disgust appeared on his father's face.

Why is he sending me to Jerusalem, agonized Uri, and followed his father out of the cubbyhole. His stomach rumbled miserably after the sleepless night. "The whole thing feels wrong for me," he wanted to shout and wake up the still-slumbering Jewish quarter.

In front of the house, they dangled their feet in a brass pot of stagnant rainwater before sitting down on a small bench to towel off with a damp cloth and quickly recite the Sh'ma. A parchment with biblical texts was always on hand when Jews set off on longer journeys, as they would bind a pair of small black leather boxes containing the scrolls with leather thongs to the forehead or left arm. Of course, if they were expecting to be back by the evening, they would usually not bother; only those who ostentatiously sought to draw attention to their Jewishness wore it everywhere and at all times, in which case it would be on the forehead, but many only wore it under their cloak, on the arm, if they were traveling. Uri was not in the habit of wearing a phylactery, though admittedly he had never left Rome before. The Ten Commandments were also hanging from a door post, in a mezuzah, at the entrance to the house. In Rome it did not matter if a Jew did or did not wear a sign of his faith demonstratively on his forehead, as there were so many odd sights in Rome—so many kinds of dress, cults, skin pigments, hair colors, and madness—that non-Jews paid no mind.

His father pressed a small basket into his hand.

He too was carrying one.

The sportula was for carrying the goods the clients could pick up free of charge during breakfast at their patron's home. In Rome every plebeian, Jews included, would go around the whole day long with one of these; Jews frequently carried one woven from wicker and lined with straw to hold anything they purchased or found on the way, or they used it to take anything they wished to sell to market. No one knew the origins of the custom, perhaps from the old country, although those who returned declared that the people back home did not go around with baskets on their arms. The straw-lined basket originally served to keep food warm on a Sabbath, only that made no sense in Rome during winter and people forgot its purpose; if a custom is not recorded in a must-read matter, it loses its sense, and yet this still lingered.

Gaius Lucius personally saw to it that the sportulas of his clients were duly crammed to bursting when they departed, and if he thought one was not, he would have his servants fill them with more food and more drink while he chuckled benevolently. He wanted to be agreeable, whatever the cost. He must have something weighing on his soul, Uri surmised when he was around ten, but then he forgot ever thinking such a thing about his kindly patron.

Uri had first visited his patron fourteen years earlier, at the age of five. Gaius Lucius, the equestrian, had received him pleasantly, pinching his cheek and patting Joseph on the back—a custom he had stuck with ever since. Uri would brace himself with a respectful grin any time the great man reached toward his face. The knight had put on twice the weight in the meantime, developing a huge, flabby, oily body with vast jowls, which, together with the swollen rolls of his neck, set his ruddy features in a rotund frame like a scarf of fat, yet he wore togas made from the costliest silks and muslins, like a rich woman, having a wardrobe of several hundred of these, changing them at least five or six times a day, putting a fresh one on after every bath. It so happened that in the year Uri was born, the emperor Tiberius had banned the wearing of muslin or silk by men, but they had gone on doing so. A huge edifice with four large basins for bathing belonged to Gaius Lucius's house, staffed with highly qualified slaves to massage and oil him and his guests. Before he acquired his taste for silk, his togas were of wool and canvas, never being willing to don cloths that had been laundered by fullers; he had a man whose exclusive job it was to procure for him three or four new togas every day. Used, furled togas would be given to clients and servants or else sold off by his stewards.

Uri abhorred silk and muslin, perhaps because a significant amount passed into the great man's possession thanks to his father's good offices, but perhaps most of all because they were mainly fabrics for women who bedecked their bodies in silk and muslin to show it off.

For a long time Joseph traded in much the same goods as others; he picked up handicraft goods, traded in timber, dates, and balsam and sold them on for a slight but guaranteed profit. Gaius Lucius demanded that his manumitted former slaves stay in touch, not just through the free gifts he distributed with breakfasts but also in a business sense, and to that extent he was also practicing philanthropy, because he could always be relied upon for orders, though at the same time he also limited their freedom by determining what articles they should deal in. He considered himself to be a decent man, treating his slaves well and acting no differently toward freedmen, as if he had never taken a penny of redemption money from them for their patent of release, though that had to be scraped together over twenty or thirty years from the small change that the knight gave them daily; granted, though, they did not have to pay for their board and lodging, and he did not starve them.

"You are my true family," the knight would say every morning in the big new atrium that he had built for hosting the salutation, raising his hands dramatically to the heavens and saying a prayer for his clients. His wife and two sons would smile awkwardly because they too were obliged to show up every day for these assemblies; hundreds must have seen that Gaius Lucius was loathed by his wife and sons. In the new atrium stood the statues of the household gods, the lares and penates, the busts and masks of his ancestors. He had commissioned them from the very best Greek sculptors, being able to afford them.

Gaius Lucius had become an exceedingly rich man over the decades, and in all truth he should be a senator by now; indeed, he had been asked to join the Assembly of the Fathers, or Council of Elders, but he preferred to squander his fortune on his clients, banquets, and organizing festive games, and he put nothing aside apart from four or five thousand sesterces that he invested each year in property in the neighborhood of Rome.

As a child Uri had heard, with his own ears, Gaius Lucius tell his father, "I suspect you could make more, Joseph, if you were to import silk and muslin. I'm a ready buyer for any amount."

This was no stray whim or polite request but a direct order. Joseph had gone pale and nodded; he had wandered around the house at a loss for days on end.

Even Uri had picked up enough rudimentary business sense to know that bringing silk and muslin in from the East was a risky enterprise. The two fine textiles had become immensely fashionable in Rome, where senators and knights who had accumulated fabulous wealth would pay any money at all to pamper themselves and their family; but if a consignment went wrong on a long journey, the investment would be lost, and extremely large amounts had to be tied up in importing these rare materials. The Silk Road stretched from distant China and India, leading back through Abyssinia in Africa or Parthia, via Asia and Asia Minor, among the lands of wild tribes, so that brigands would leave caravans untouched it was necessary to pay off the tribal leaders, of whom there was a great profusion, with the borders of the territory for any one tribe changing every ten or twenty miles, it was said. On top of which the local agents might either hand over the money or else purloin it, and in the latter case the silk would go no farther. Goods that were produced in the provinces in any case fetched a price one hundred times more in Rome, but the price of muslin or silk might be as much as tens of thousands more, so huge were the distances, the risk, and the whims of fashion. The shippers were canny enough to give the impression that they were carrying other merchandise, so the silk and muslin were rolled up and hidden in the most unlikely places, sometimes even swallowed and then excreted at the final destination, but even so, it was worth it: the price would be a multiple of what it would have been if they had swallowed the same weight of gold. They would swallow gold too, for that matter, and much else besides to

49

fool both official and unofficial customs inspectors, who would impose duties on honest, innocent commercial travelers, on the assumption that even if a merchant did not swallow gold or gemstones or silk, he could have. As a result, it was better to swallow it anyway.

Uri could understand his father's fears, but he also grasped that Gaius Lucius did not seek anything that was out of the question. A large population of Jews lived at one of the stations in Parthia along the Silk Road; they had not returned from Babylon to Judaea with the rest and, through the Jews of Palestine and Egypt, stayed in touch with Rome via Alexandria, and there were also Jews living in that other great eastern port, Antioch, the capital city of Syria, carrying on trade from there. The commercial links were solid, had been established within Jewry centuries before, even war being unable to disrupt it. Trading is always vital; at most, there may be a time when it is necessary to deliver weapons in place of pots, cosmetics, pans, and comestibles.

Joseph had no desire for big profits; for his whole life he had been a considerate negotiator, striving for cordial relations with each link in the commercial chain, near and far, believing this to be a long-term investment.

There was just one time he attempted to be an innovator, which was when he saw at his patron's place a vase of unbreakable glass; whatever one threw at it just dented, like an inflated bladder, the favorite plaything of emperors and children, and one could always hammer it back to its original shape. It was of Roman manufacture, and it was easy to make contact with the glassmaker. Jews were averse to these vases of unbreakable glass, or vitrum flexile as it was called, even though they had never seen one, with the idea that it was impure, but there would be plenty of opportunity to supply them to the likes of rich men like Gaius Lucius. Joseph paid a visit to the inventor, who was none other than the engineer who a few years before had restored a collapsed old colonnade; he had reinforced the pedestals, wrapped the other parts in wool, bound them with cord, and had them hauled back into place using winches and a lot of manpower. He had been granted a large sum of money by Tiberius as a reward. For some reason, he had also been banished from Rome. Joseph reached an agreement with him on distributing the unbreakable glass when an example of one of the vases was shown to Tiberius. The emperor conjectured that the invention would lead to a steep devaluation of earthenware and golden pots, had the arrogant inventor tracked down and executed, and also banned manufacture of the unbreakable glass. There was a danger that all of the inventor's acquaintances would likewise be hunted down and put to death on the off chance that they knew the secret of the glass's manufacture. Joseph had to ask for the assistance of the Elders of the synagogue in effacing any trace of his connection with the inventor. The Elders had heard that the executed inventor was a Jew, and considered that was more than likely, given that glassblowing was a Jewish craft, so it was also in their interests that Judaism should come out of this awkward business with clean hands. There was no way of knowing what the Elders did, but in any event, neither Joseph nor the community was harassed on account of the unbreakable glass vase, and even the inventor's name was forgotten as time passed.

Uri still had good eyesight when Gaius Lucius urged his father to go into silk and muslin, and being a precocious child he was not surprised when his father let him in on his doubts. Who else would he share them with if not his only son? Joseph had been uneasy yet sober in his assessment. He knew nothing about the details of the silk trade as up till then he had been concerned with quite different sorts of merchandise, but he assumed that with silk, as was generally the case with other articles from far away, there would be at least two big outfits engaged in it, with one of them being almost certainly Arab. He also assumed that the Jewish and Arab mafias would have come to an agreement some time, and that agreement was periodically renewed because there was no break in the supply of silk and muslin to Rome, although the amounts that were made available were fairly modest in spite of the huge demand—no doubt deliberately to hold the price up. That alone was indicative of some sort of gang involvement. It went without saying that he would choose the Jewish bunch, but that had the disadvantage that he, being an anonymous merchant among the Roman freedmen, carried no prestige among the Jews, and as silk was such a massive business you could be quite sure that leaders in Parthia, Syria, Judaea, and Alexandria were up to their neck in it, and those were people who would never have the time of day for the likes of him.

The Arab tribes were a different matter. Presumably, the Jews of Antioch and Alexandria had contact with these non-Jewish tribes, but the Greeks of Antioch and Alexandria would also have a cut of the business, by virtue of the fierce Greco-Judaic commercial rivalry. So what if it was somehow possible to become a link in the non-Jewish chain? How else than with money?

That was Joseph's other big idea after the unbreakable glass vase of painful memory. He methodically haunted the premises of Greek, Syrian, Abyssinian, and Arab traders in Rome, strolling with his son over the bridge and wandering with him around the city, because it was not so easy to track anyone down given that streets had no names and houses were not numbered.

Joseph would offer immediate cash in return for a negligible and, initially, almost certainly loss-making stake in the silk business. Some, having a sound capital base, rejected the idea out of hand, but some were takers because they happened to be short on money, or maybe they were inherently greedy. There were any number of strange homes that Uri visited with his father, coming across peculiar modes of life and odd customs, and that was when the conviction grew in him that it paid to speak with everyone in his own tongue. Uri knew only Aramaic and Greek at that time, like his father, though it would not have hurt to know Arabic and Egyptian as well. A deal would be done not just for profit—Uri appreciated that even as a child—but at least as much, if not more, for the fun of it and for the sake of camaraderie.

In the course of those visits he became acquainted with the use of an abacus, those frames with several rows above each other in which would be placed pebbles; by sliding them one could make incredibly swift calculations. Uri was quicker than his father to arrive at the principle by which it worked, with the lowest row being used for single units, the next for tens, the one above that for hundreds, and so on, and this made it possible to add, subtract, multiply, and divide very speedily, without looking. Being based on the decimal system, the abacus represented local values, though that was not quite how it was put at the time. Back home Uri traced his own abacus on the ground; pebbles and twigs could always be found, and he was proud that sometimes his father, when he got tired of calculating, would trudge out into the yard and ask him to work some calculation or other. The Jews incidentally would also use letters of the Greek alphabet for making calculations, with alpha as one, beta as two, gamma as three, delta as four, and so on, so it was far from easy to perform addition, subtraction, multiplication, and division, squaring or extracting the square root with the long strings of letters this involved. Uri wanted to explain the exceedingly simple principle on which the device worked to the other children and their teacher, but they did not so much as listen: the abacus was not a Jewish custom.

His father would negotiate anxiously, doggedly, with determination, his counterparts chattering in leisurely fashion, relishing the chance to talk, whether they were inclined to reach agreement or not. They would willingly pass time with idle gossip, dismissing the serious details of a business deal with a flamboyant sweep of the hand, regaling Joseph and his son countless items of Roman tittle-tattle with quiet snickering, a gleeful giggling, or glorious guffawing, slapping their knee, marveling at life's oddities. They would be plied with food and drink, which his father would usually decline but they would insist Uri had to drink; as a child it was not unusual for him to stagger drunkenly out of the tenements, private palaces, and shacks.

In the end it cost Joseph close to one hundred thousand sesterces to get into the silk business.

That was a staggeringly large sum of money if one considers that the annual income for a prefect running a province would be just two and a half times that, or that with a fortune of four times that a person could procure a knighthood. The one hundred thousand sesterces was not Joseph's own money, as he never had a significant amount of working capital, the family scraping by on a few coppers and the sportula before Uri got the tessera. Part of the money was loaned at forty-percent interest by Roman-Jewish bankers (usurious rates like that were strictly forbidden, of course, under both Roman and Jewish law), and partly obtained from Gaius Lucius at an annual interest of no more than ten percent, which was two percent less than the official Roman bank rate.

Joseph lost weight, the furrows around his eyes sank and turned blue, he did not sleep for nights on end, just paced around in the yard and prayed to the Lord that the winds would favor him and his ships not sink (the ships themselves were insured, it was true, the shipping companies being rich, but in general the cargoes were not, with the merchants taking the risk), and he also prayed that the Arabs and the Egyptians and Greeks of Alexandria, the whole treacherous bunch, would stick to their agreements, to say nothing of those far-off tribes, their very names unknown to him, who would transport the goods along the sides of great mountains and desert country somewhere in Tibet, between China and India, and also that the Jewish mafia would not pay him any mind and spare him the curses of the Jewish Elders of Rome. There were attempts to do so, it later turned out, but because a fair number of the Jewish Elders of Rome had close links with Jewish bankers, indeed more than a few were themselves bankers, it was not in their interests to ruin Joseph, so they smoothed things over in anticipation of that forty-percent interest.

When the loan was due, Joseph did not have enough money to pay off both the Jews and the equestrian. He asked Gaius Lucius for a period of grace and a loan of a further thirty-thousand sesterces, which was granted, and from that and his earnings he paid off the Jewish banks, and it was only at the end of the third year that he was able to pay back his outstanding debt to Gaius Lucius. Until then, all he did was suffer and worry. He could not breathe easily for a single day, for the moment that the Jewish bankers pocketed the loan he had paid back, along with the interest, Joseph's temporary protection came to an end and the Jewish silk mafia instantly leeched him. They demanded a cut of the trade, even though Joseph had already made a deal with the Arabs. He asked them too for a grace period, and after admitting the debt to Gaius Lucius, he was thereafter obliged to pay the Jews fifteen percent on every consignment, which meant that he barely made anything on the silk. Nobody believed him, of course; they thought he was rolling in it and was only so thrifty in the way he lived with his own family to hoodwink others. Admittedly, from that point on they did not pester him any longer, indeed there were even cases where his extortive co-religionists would take care of things when a particular shipment was held up.

Joseph struggled for years until he hit on a third route and had the silk delivered secretly from Parthia via Greece and Dalmatia, over dry land the whole way to avoid shipwrecks and even letting the proverbially unreliable Illyrians in on the business. Doing deals with the Illyrians was at least as calamitous as the worst storm at sea, but if a few shipments yearly by some miracle made it through, then it was worth it. The adolescent Uri was also let in on the plan, being sworn to secrecy, because he was taking a big risk if the news ever reached the ears of the Elders or the other Jewish merchants. The trade must have worked, to some extent, because from then on Joseph slept much more soundly at night.

It occurred to Joseph around that time that what should be imported from China was not the silk itself, but the plant from which those incredibly gossamer fibers were made. He started to poke around, but the Arab and Greek merchants simply laughed at him; he was not the first to come up with the idea, but the Chinese guarded the secret of the plant so closely that no one had yet managed to see it, and anyone who tried to get too close was killed for their trouble. There was a tale that a mad Syrian merchant from Antioch had tried to make silk from the threads of spiders, but he had not succeeded and in utter misery he had slashed his wrists; he left two million drachmas for his fatherless children. Multiplied by four that gives how many sesterces? Eight million! Even in talenta that was a staggering amount of $333\frac{1}{3}$.

The knight was satisfied with the quality of the silk and muslin delivered by Joseph, and he even had his slave girls dress in these lavish materials, putting on short muslin robes to whip up his desires and those of honored guests. There was also a rise in the number of progeny among the slaves. It struck Uri that his grandfather was not necessarily descended from a Jewish father; Tadeus, the grandpa who had emancipated himself from slavery, might have been a bastard child, a mamzer, illegitimate. It could even be, Uri shuddered, that I am a third cousin to Gaius Lucius; maybe that is why he is so pleasant to all his former slaves and their offspring, because he suspects they might be his own blood relatives. When he tried to raise the topic with his father, all Joseph said was merely, "Slave folk are well advised not to speculate too much." I'm half-Latin, half-Persian, and that's how I came to be Jewish, Uri thought when he was around ten; there's even a bit of me that is Etruscan, because Gaius Lucius figured on having some Etruscan ancestry.

Wise are the peoples that, in slavery, trace descent through the female line, concluded Uri when he was a child. There were such peoples in Rome, but the Jews were not among them. Uri was still glad that patriarchy was in force: he was horrified by his ugly and grumpy mother, much as his father was, and he did not love her, even though she was occasionally overcome by fits of affection and would slobber hysterically all over him with kisses, even when he was a teenager. He loved only his father, who gave up on him because his eyesight went bad.

So, early in the morning Joseph and Uri set off from home for the patron's place, in their right hands an empty sportula to be crammed full, and they held their peace. The daily ration in a sportula could be exchanged for money, with a basketful being worth twenty-five asses, but the clients of Gaius Lucius waived that opportunity because they were able to stuff a basket with food that was worth a good deal more. The knight's clients were in fact the objects of general envy, with many applying to be taken on as protégés, since a client was free to have more than one patron, and they would hold out promises of all sorts of return services, but the eques would turn all offers away, saying that he had no wish for any other clients other than the progeny of slaves who had served his ancestors. Mostly people did not know quite what lay behind this, but Joseph did, and he told Uri once: Gaius Lucius was not born to his father's wife, because she was barren, but to a German slave girl. It was a big secret that Gaius Lucius learned from the lips of his dying father, Lucius. It would have been possible for Lucius to adopt the child born to the slave girl, and the child could still have inherited everything, but he felt there was more security in keeping it a secret. Gaius Lucius, of course, could have reacted by hating the offspring of slaves, said Joseph; indeed that would have been the natural thing, but as it happened he did not respond that way. Uri was perplexed by what his father said, but even more by the way he said it; he must know something about souls. So there is still Germanic blood in me, Uri supposed; perhaps that is why I have a shock of sandy hair.

His father trudged somberly, grave thoughts clouding his brow. Judging from his red-ringed, gummy eyes, he also had gotten no sleep the previous night. Uri would have liked to express his gratitude; some tasteful words of thanks to his father would have been for arranging his journey to Jerusalem, but the words escaped him. He was afraid of traveling.

They passed wordlessly over the bridge. The island was basically uninhabited, because floods frequently inundated it, so it provided optimal conditions for trees, shrubs, and, above all, mosquitoes to proliferate luxuriantly. A few centuries before, a temple to Aesculapius had been built to the south and its ruins still existed, but one would hardly say any healing power radiated from them. Uri had often felt an urge to climb down the gig stone flags of the old steps in the middle of the bridge and pitch a small tent to live quietly within the dense screen of vegetation. He even imagined catching fish in the river and eating them, but he was forced to recognize that even there he would not be on his own: vagabonds would install themselves on the island whenever it was not flooded, and they were in the habit of greeting intruders with a sharp blade.

They walked wordlessly next to each other, northeastward, toward the murkily dawning, mysterious, true Rome, among the huge blocks of its theaters, baths, and palaces looming darkly among the palm trees on the other side.

There were still many who slept on the banks of the river, even in winter. Some were wrapped in blankets, some not. Compared to these indigent beggars, they, the inhabitants of the wretched Jewish world of Transtiberim, counted as well-to-do; at least they had roofs over their heads.

Uri would have shared that reflection as well with his father, but they were not in that sort of mood.

His father was morose as he walked, never looking at his son, beset by onerous worries. Uri suspected that it was on his account, but he found it incomprehensible: almost as if his father did not know intuitively that he was unsuitable for such a trip. Why would he want it, all the same? To do him a favor, the biggest he could do? Or was it his way of getting rid of him?

That was how they walked in the true, sleeping, auroral Rome, the two of them, father and son, making their way to their rich patron, the fat Gaius Lucius, who lived at the foot of Capitoline Hill. There was almost no one among the Jews of the world, except the lucky and rich Alexandrian Jews, who would not have envied them on their patron's account.

By the time they reached Gaius Lucius's house, all Rome was on its feet, with everybody dashing to greet whatever patron outranked them: equites hurrying to senators, even the senators themselves hurrying to reach the consul at his breakfast, and there were even panting clients who had followed their patrons to the Forum, to some court case or other hearing. The city woke from one minute to the next; it became noisy and dusty, even though the sun had barely risen above the horizon.

THERE WERE ALREADY A DOZEN OR SO CLIENTS HANGING AROUND THE knight at the court. Joseph came to a stop at the entrance, with Uri halting beside him.

The tables in the new atrium, built not long ago, were laden with food, and there were twenty-two of them, all told, in the enormous space. Delicacies of every imaginable kind graced the tables. It was possible to eat standing up, or one could recline on carpets and eat that way; everyone was free to race around, push, and scramble to fill his sportula with food and drink. Musicians had already struck up at one end of the atrium.

Jews were forbidden from partaking of some of this bounty: they were not supposed to consume meat or wine in such a place, but they were able to stuff their baskets with fruits, berries, and smoked or raw fish. Joseph had taught Uri not to participate in the scrum; he might pick and choose from what was left, it did not matter if the sportula was not entirely filled.

Every other day, Joseph and Uri placed sufficient victuals in their baskets to supply the family with food for two days. This included the twenty-five asses' worth of free food in each sportula, on top of which there was the sustenance received for the past five years from Uri's tessera.

Then again, they had substantial expenses. The rent they paid for their house to the Jewish community was high, even though Uri's grandfather had built it with his own bare hands, and had even paid off the plot of land where it stood, while Joseph had rebuilt it with his own bare hands after they returned from the expulsion. That tax was all the more curious since the ground on which Far Side was built never passed into Jewish hands; Rome's administrators set greater value than any sky-high rent that could be raked in by word of command on being able to expel the newcomers any time they wished without having to worry about lawsuits. The real money was made by the Levite butchers who charged brazenly extortionate prices for supplying and preparing kosher meat, and by merchants who dealt in pure olive oil and wine.

Other patrons treated their clients haughtily, seating them at separate tables and serving them food and drink of lower quality than they themselves consumed. Gaius Lucius was wont to say that his clients should not flatter him to get better fare; flatter him if they wished, but even in their dreams they would not be able to imagine better fare.

Joseph and Uri would always set aside fruits and fish dishes that Sarah and the girls liked; they would only think of their own stomachs if there was space left in the baskets and anything left on the tables. Joseph in particular would never take anything that he truly relished: he was born a hedonist, and this is how he would mortify the flesh. He would overlook it if Uri placed a delicacy in the basket, but Uri would feel his gaze, and in more recent years he too chose the more mediocre foodstuffs for himself. He would look enviously at the non-Jewish clients savoring crabs, snails, and shellfish; unfortunately, any creature that had its bony frame on the outside and did not have scales or fins was ritually unclean in Jewish eyes.

Had Gaius Lucius not been so generous, Joseph and his family would have gone hungry.

A price had to be paid for that gift; every other morning they had to make conversation with the other clients and the slaves who had not yet been able to manumit themselves, or else—and this was most common—had not the slightest intention of purchasing their freedom. They were not held back from freedom by their long years of scrimping so much as by seeing that freedom was burdensome, irritating; it meant solitude and independent decision-making, and they preferred leaving their fate to the whims of their lords and masters. An emancipated slave did not automatically become a Roman citizen, a civis Romanus, merely a metoikos, a tolerated foreigner. Even a son did not acquire full rights of citizenship, including the tessera and its guarantee of gratis food rations; that was only granted to grandchildren. Uri sometimes imagined that he had been born a slave, and he caught himself thinking that this would not have been so bad; he would be given lighter work, reasonable for his poor eyesight, bad back, and bad legs—cleaning up or cooking, for instance—and in his spare time he could recline on a couch in some corner or other and read to his heart's content. He would do everything that he did as a freedman, and yet better; he would no longer feel the pangs of conscience that whatever he was doing was not quite right—in other words, he was not making anything of his freedom.

It was no pleasure to chat with these narrow-minded simpletons, to nod approvingly at their opinions and hosanna their sagacity. One had to feign cordiality, lest they take umbrage, lest their jealousy and envy be provoked, because other clients and slaves, if nothing else, could do harm: whisper this or that into Gaius Lucius's ear and suddenly they were no longer welcome at the grand man's tables. Uri had seen that sort of thing more than once by now.

It was best to appear gray in this colorful mob—stupid and harmless. Much as back home, on Far Side, among the Jews.

Ever since Joseph had become the silk purveyor to the court of knight Gaius Lucius, other clients and the older slaves never missed an opportunity to pester him for tiny, insignificant, negligible sums of money, as a token of the years of servitude they had shared with his father, Thaddeus, the many, many years of shared suffering, and also in requital for purported support and assistance given many years ago. They too, like the Jews, supposed that Joseph was rolling in money, but keeping it quiet. Gaius Lucius himself was not loath to encourage that impression, as he would proudly announce that he had talked Joseph into importing silk for him, and within two weeks Joseph had done so. It was not true, but it sounded good and served to boost the prestige of Gaius Lucius that he had such a talented client.

Hitherto the silk had hindered jealous clients, and the even more jealous acquaintances among the slaves—friends—from being able to harm him: Gaius Lucius valued highly the services that Joseph had rendered him, and even more highly that he could boast to other dignitaries about being blessed with a Jewish client who had such business expertise. As long as Gaius Lucius took delight in this ridiculous tale, trotted out a hundred times and more by now, they could never put a knife in Joseph, and everyone was well aware of that; but the moment Gaius Lucius hinted that he was would wear linen or wool, starting tomorrow, there would be wretched times ahead for Joseph and his family.

Joseph withdrew into a corner and did his best to make himself as inconspicuous as possible; Uri stood beside him and, eyes blinking, stared into thin air. They were waiting until Gaius Lucius worked his way around to them. Uri would have made a start on filling his sportula, but his father growled; Uri stopped, and Joseph shook his head. Uri did not understand but shrugged his shoulders and waited beside him.

Accompanied by a gaggle of clients, the knight, freshly bathed, freshly shaven, and clothed in one of his marvelous silk togas of shifting color, smiled benevolently at them.

"Ah! My dear Joseph! Uri, my dear boy!" he declared, pulling them in to embrace them. He prided himself on knowing the names of all his clients without fail, and not just the office they filled but also the nickname by which they were called within the family, and he never had to resort to the help of nomenclatures—that is, slaves who prompted him with the names.

Unbearable wafts of rare salves swirled around them, with Uri picking out balsam among the scents, which he particularly loathed—not because it was a product from Judaea but simply because his eyes did not tolerate it.

His father departed from custom in announcing to the parting knight, "Sire, my son will be absent from your hearth for several months: he is setting off for Jerusalem tomorrow."

Gaius Lucius swung around in surprise:

"Jerusalem, indeed? That is a long way off."

"He is being sent there for the big feast," his father carried on.

"That's as it should be," said Gaius Lucius, and turned away to move on.

"Sire!" Joseph addressed the knight again. Gaius Lucius, now astonished and fast running out of patience, turned back once more. "May I ask you, Sire, not to mention this to anyone else; my son's trip is of a confidential nature. He is making the trip for the feast of Passover."

"Yes, of course," Gaius Lucius said distractedly, and it was clear that he had no idea what Passover was, and that he was dithering for a second before asking, but seeing the pack that was with him, he chose to go onward. Joseph's request was superfluous: the knight had already forgotten the whole thing.

Uri kept quiet. He had inferred correctly that he was going to be a delegate, that's what his father had said. His father also kept quiet, but then he spoke:

"Bring him a gift—most definitely! Some unusual specialty. Don't forget!"

"I won't," said Uri.

Some people stepped up to Joseph. Uri respectfully greeted them, and on Joseph's face appeared a smile of forced attentiveness, as always when he had to speak to people with whom he had no business. It started off with household gossip, with servants and clients earnestly expounding and Joseph smiling, nodding, and feigning interest. Uri could see from his face that he was very tense; it must be something serious, he supposed. What is he worried about, and why do I have to go to Jerusalem?

A plump, jovial, slit-eyed, bald man joined the group. Uri looked across at him with loathing: this was Pancharius, also one of Gaius Lucius's freedmen, a slave-trader. Unwanted children—especially girls, who were worthless, but also a good numbers of boys—would be turned out of families by Romans, Italians, all kinds of peoples, with only the Germanic races and Jews forbidding this. That is how the unwanted progeny of wealthy citizens, equites, and senators became slaves and never learned about their true descent. Ever since peace reigned in the world, because Augustus had abandoned further invasions and set his sights on maintaining the imperium's borders, a policy that Tiberius, his son-in-law and successor, had wisely adhered to, prisoners of vanquished peoples no longer flowed into Rome like Uri's ancestors of old had; indeed, people were now even willing to pay parents money for surplus children.

Pancharius slapped Joseph familiarly on the shoulder, but before he could utter a word Joseph growled at Uri, hurried over to the nearest table, opened his sportula, and started to pack food into it. Uri followed his example. Joseph, atypically for him, crammed food indiscriminately into his sportula; Uri tried to be a bit more selective and went over to a nearby table to pick some fruit, but his father went after him and grabbed him by the arm.

"Let's go," he said.

Uri squeezed a couple of dried figs into the basket and followed his father.

The guards at the entrance gazed at them in astonishment; on such occasions no one left this early.

In the street Joseph almost broke into a run so that Uri, who had become used to idleness, had a hard job keeping up and panted. Joseph came to a halt, wheeled around to face his son and, staring into the distance past his ear, announced, "The day before yesterday, Agrippa sent for me and saw me. He told me he had heard that several years ago I scraped together a few hundred thousand sesterces. He asked me to scrape together for him two hundred thousand sesterces as a matter of urgency."

Joseph fell silent; Uri, feeling dizzy, held his peace.

Agrippa!

Agrippa was a notorious individual, a grandson of Herod the Great, a favorite of the senators—he would invite them to his carousals where he would scatter gifts around. Indeed, the emperor was in the habit of having him as his guest on the island of Capri.

"So what did you say?" Uri queried.

"What could I say?"

"So what happened?"

"I scraped it together. I handed it over to him yesterday morning."

The world went into a dizzy spin around Uri.

His father had run up an immense debt. Who could say when Agrippa would pay off the loan, and how much interest would have accumulated by then on the money that his father had borrowed. No doubt the loan that was given to Joseph would have a fancy high-interest tag attached to it; his father would be paying off the capital and the interest on it to the end of his days, and the family would do without.

"Agrippa asked the bankers for a loan, but they refused; after some deliberation they suggested me, and that's when he sent me word. No one would dare have asked Agrippa to pay interest; they are too scared of him, but me they are not scared of."

Uri shivered.

"How much is the interest?"

"Twenty percent."

They might well have crewed the interest even higher, but even so it was a full eight percent above the officially allowed rate.

"I suppose it wouldn't be possible," Uri started off, "to ask the knight for the money...?"

"No!" Joseph groaned and threw a sad glance at his son. "A reputable man doesn't do things like that."

He ought to ask for a loan from Gaius Lucius at ten percent interest and use that to pay off the bankers, but his father had already taken the hint. Uri blushed: the idea must have crossed his father's mind, he could guess what Uri had been intending to say: "And I'm disreputable! It's Agrippa who's disreputable, always in debt!"

They fell silent. The whole thing was unbelievable.

"I don't know who your companions on the trip will be," Joseph said, "but they'll know about the loan, and they aren't going to like you for it. Be prepared for the very worst."

After a short pause, he added, "I can't help it, son. I had no choice."

Uri wanted to say that Agrippa should have been given what he wanted, otherwise he would have his revenge, but he did not even bother because he saw that his father was paying no attention to him.

Joseph sat on the ground and, hunched over, started nibbling on a date. Uri took a seat beside him, and it ran through his mind that his father must have asked Agrippa in return that his son be made a delegate. Agrippa must have sent a message to the Elders and they quickly forgot that someone from the same clan had gone to Jerusalem no more than five years before. Agrippa was a big wheel, and bankers feared him.

My father does love me, after all!

That encouraged him, so he dipped into his sportula and took out a fig.

Passersby did not so much as glance at them; two Jews sitting in the street, even if they were ripping each other apart, were not a cause of any interest. Yet something major had happened, Uri considered: his father had just reconciled with his son.

"Did he say when he would give it back?"

"It doesn't matter. What's more important for you is to figure out how you are going to persist."

His father must be aware that he would rather stay home.

"Never let yourself become stuck-up," Joseph said. "Even if you know better than others, keep quiet about it. Better for people to think that you are stupid. They hate you anyway, so don't give them any reason to show it."

It was the voice of old times, when he had still seen clearly, and his father had treated him as a friend.

They chewed silently.

"It's a big thing, getting the chance to go to Jerusalem," said Joseph. "That is something I shall certainly never do."

URI DID NOT DARE SLEEP, HE WAS AFRAID HE WOULD NOT WAKE IN TIME; but he must have dropped off anyway, because his father shook him awake.

His first thought was the tessera, which he must not forget to hand over to his father, since it could be transferred, but his father muttered that he had already passed it on the previous evening. Uri clutched at his neck: the tessera was not there. Then a memory drifted back of those hours before he had gone to bed: he had handed over the lead token as if he were making a last will and testament.

As he tugged on his loincloth under his tunic in the dark, the thought running through his head was that the tessera was worth more without him than with him.

His father draped his gown over him. Uri protested, but his father squeezed his shoulder. It was a seamless, rectangular outer garment of cloth with a blue braided tassel dangling in approved fashion at each of the four corners. Uri had not owned a gown before; Joseph would get another for himself. If he could spare the money.

Outside, they dipped their feet in the brass bowl, dried them, splashed a bit of water onto themselves, or rather onto their clothes, then, bowing to the southeast, recited a Sh'ma. Uri did not take the teffilin off his forehead and set it back on the ground, but wound it around his left hand, after which Joseph placed his right hand on Uri's head by way of a blessing. They stood like that for a moment and then Joseph went back in the house and pulled back the curtain over the entrance. Uri looked at the curtain, touched the mezuzah affixed to the door post; tears sprang into his eyes, but he quickly turned away and set off.

I am going to Jerusalem, after all. To Him in His Land.

He tried to be happy.

There were five standing in front of old Simeon's house; they were purple in the moonlight. Barely had Uri reached them when they were joined by a seventh.

"I will be your leader," said a tall, middle-aged man. "Matthew's my name. I live in Ostia. To date I have taken five delegations to Jerusalem. You must do whatever I tell you to."

The six of them murmured consent.

Matthew then handed out the packages lying by the house. He said this was the community's gift and reminded them emphatically that anything durable would have to be given back on their return, so they should take care. The cloth sacks were not large or especially heavy. Uri tapped his and felt some sort of jug, then rounder forms, fruit perhaps, and a matzo biscuit cracked between his fingers.

"I have the money for travel expenses," Matthew announced. "I'll be the one who pays at the inns, at customs, for wagons, and for the ship. When we get back, I shall have to account for everything, and anything that is left, I shall have to hand back."

It was on the tip of Uri's tongue to ask who would be carrying the loads of money that had been collected by the Jews of Rome for the feast, and to whom they'd be delivered, but he swallowed the question. The others did not ask either.

Maybe they do not know quite how much money they were delivering, but without any doubt it was a huge fortune. Worth slaughtering them for.

Matthew slung his sack on his back and set off. The rest picked up their luggage and followed.

They went out through the gate; the two guards blinked sleepily after them before locking the gate again.

Beside him strong, seasoned men stepped with buoyant strides. He was the youngest, the least worthy, the weakest. How long would his legs hold up?

Being a lefty, he carried his sack on his right shoulder, bouncing it up from time to time to get a sense of its weight and to guess whether it was him carrying the money. It would have to come to hundreds of talenta, and that would have to weigh a great deal. His sack was not heavy, though, so he could not be carrying it.

Were they going to take turns?

Had it been divided up between them?

Lifting his sack, he estimated that it could not weigh more than thirty Roman libra—twenty pounds, say. Sixty to seventy-five pounds was the weight of the food that he and his father used to lug back home as the ration issued on his tessera. He wondered how many sesterces might fit into a sack, or rather how many denarii, or silver pennies, each of which was worth four sesterces? Say they were carrying a total of twenty thousand denarii between the seven of them, which would mean that he was perhaps carrying one seventh of that. One denarius would weigh $1/84$ of a libra, and his sack did not weigh more than twenty or twenty-eight pounds. That meant he might be carrying two and a half to three thousand denarii.

But where would that be?

There had to be some tried-and-true method, Uri supposed, and he marched on, completely immersed in his calculations. They were surely not making a futile trip in this, the 3,760th year *anno mundi*, from the creation of the world.

Up till then, the offering had always reached Jerusalem, for even when it was robbed, it was collected anew and delivered later. It had gone this way for ninety-eight years, since the first Jews landed up in Rome; a sacrifice was supposedly sent, in accordance with tradition, already in the first year, and that was surely true. It must have been a small sum, no more than a few hundred asses altogether, but it was saved at the expense of their stomachs, collected, and sent off. They themselves were unable to go: their ears were pierced and they lived their life in chains, but non-Jews could be persuaded to take it—for money. They paid and sent the money, and have every year since then. More and more, as things began to take a turn for the better for the Jews in Rome, and for a fair amount of time, they had been carrying the money themselves, with official permission.

By now they were walking over into the true Rome. Uri did not turn around to glance at the Jewish quarter on the far side, since all he would have seen anyway was fuzzy blotches.

At the Circus Maximus they swung southward. These were all familiar streets; Uri would never have imagined the day would come that he would pass that way in such an official capacity.

They tramped silently, like people who were on an important mission.

They left Rome by the Porta Capena. Wagons laden with produce were by then already creaking their way in toward the markets.

They came to a halt at the beginning of the Appian Way, at the Jewish house of prayer near the cemetery.

"Let's take a rest," Matthew said. "Anyone who wants breakfast may eat."

"May we open the sacks now?" one man asked. Uri took a squint: he was a strong man with a thick, black beard.

"They are yours," Matthew said. "A present from the community."

Uri nibbled on a matzo; that was his favorite, and some days that was all he ate, because matzos were able to sop up the acid that would well up in his stomach.

"Let's move off now!" asserted a thickset man.

"Our goal is not to walk ourselves into the ground," said Matthew. "We shall have plenty of chances to walk. Just wait."

They were silent and ate.

"Where shall we get water?" asked the thickset man.

"There will be water everywhere we stop," said Matthew. "Wine as well."

The day was dawning. More and more wagons appeared in the street.

Along the Appian Way came an empty wagon with two oxen in harness. Matthew got to his feet and waved; the wagon stopped.

Matthew climbed on next to the driver at the front; the other six clambered onto the back. The wagon turned and set off in a southerly direction.

THE BEATING OF URI'S HEART BEGAN TO SLACKEN WHEN HE WEDGED HIS sack under his back. Everybody was silent, and Uri did not dare give the once-over to the companions with whom he would be confined for months on the long journey. He gazed at the countryside; he could see the roadside cypresses fairly clearly but not buildings and plants that were more than 100 or 150 paces away. For him they were a blur of greenish, yellowish, and brownish blots, and the sky above, as it was February, a clear blue. Uri peered through narrow eyes, more with the left one because he saw better through that, using the right eye more for reading and inspecting small objects.

They jolted along on the wagon without a word. Uri regained his composure; the trip might be tedious and without incident, and if his companions were not talkative and did not pester him unnecessarily, he might be able to put up with them. The signs suggested that they too were awed to take part in this sacrosanct journey. Uri felt a twinge of conscience: his father had paid out two hundred thousand sesterces so he could jolt along on this wagon now, and even so, he was not truly glad. He made up his mind that he was going to be glad.

It was hard to control his outrage when he realized that his father had loaned Agrippa roughly two and a half times as much money as the total offering of Rome's Jews that they were bringing to Jerusalem.

Better not to think about it.

He jolted along on the wagon and became sleepy.

He had the sense of being enclosed in a husk: nearby things that he could readily see were, so to speak, pressed onto his body by a fabric of colored blotches, and because there was nothing of interest in the visible world, he was in the end in the grip of a hazy trust that there would be an opportunity in the course of the long journey to reflect as he did in his little recess back at home, although without having his treasured scrolls at hand, but then the bulk of those were already committed to memory. Beyond the cage of the visible world, inside the space of these thoughts, he was filled with a sense of the security that slaves feel: he had no cares for anything, his companions would take care of him and defend him, and it seemed that he would not even be forced to chitchat with them, which was something he detested.

After all, he was the exception, he had done nothing to deserve the distinction; his companions had no doubt all done something that merited membership in the official festive delegation to Jerusalem, in adherence to the rotation principle of the Elders, in consultation with the archisynagogoses of the individual assemblies and taking their recommendations on board, or else modifying them—who could know exactly what went on in the rare sessions of the Roman Sanhedrin—had decided on these individuals, obviously with good reason; better that he spoke with them as little as possible so that his own unsuitability, both spiritual and physical, should not come too soon to light.

As Uri jolted along on the wagon with his taciturn companions, staring at the trees as they slowly retreated (the oxen pulled the wagon no faster than they would have been able to walk), and as these trees assumed ever more uncertain outlines in the distance, it dawned on him that even after his eyesight had deteriorated he had still been able to move around confidently in the true Rome and also in the labyrinthine, interconnecting inner yard of Far Side, because he could project memorized images onto the present so that he knew exactly what was where, and he only got confused in the real Rome if he was unable to find a building that had once stood but had burned down or been dismantled and another built in its place. In those cases, he would walk around the place a number of times to make a mental note of it. Now, though, these were all new places of which he had no memories or any notion, and he had to reach the sad conclusion that, indeed, someone else ought to have been sent on this big journey instead. He was not even going to see the splendor of the Second Temple in Jerusalem, not even if he was allowed to get close to it, to be sure, not even if he was allowed to stand directly beside the altar stone that is said to be situated right in front of the Temple. To be allowed close to the altar is a huge blessing; the scrimmage is fierce, and only the true elect are admitted into the small space. They might admit a delegation from Rome, perhaps, but even then maybe only the leader.

But then if I have ended up in this group, transporting money to Jerusalem, let me see that famous altar and the wondrous Temple from close to, he thought with an effort, because he did not suppose that the prospect of being able to see the Temple and the altar would fill him with any joy. However little he wanted to see, it crossed his mind that it was still possible to turn back.

Just get off the wagon and start off northward, toward Rome. It was not far. Or else he could wait for the night and take off when the others were asleep, not returning to Rome but seeking out a town and selling himself into slavery (that sort of thing was not uncommon), and, if he was in luck, even denying being a Jew. After all, they did not necessarily check if slaves had circumcised penises.

He shuddered at such thoughts, and it occurred to him that similar thoughts had already crossed his mind. He prayed silently that something utterly different should come to mind.

What came to mind was that he held Rome dearer than he would ever have thought. He was assailed by homesickness even though they were not yet far away. The future horrified him; with every hour, every day, he would be more distant from his home.

Over there, in the true Rome, exteriors were the most important; the fools attached everything to appearances, not to the vital. That would be what would bring them down; the Creator was not going to tolerate the intolerable to the end of time. But at least Uri felt that over there, in the true Rome, he was treated as an adult.

He could gaze at all the peoples that flocked to Rome from all parts of the world, slink right up close to give them a thorough lookover, and get close enough to know how their breath smells. There was every kind of man from ebony black through deep and light yellow to milk-white, costume of every kind; in certain squares and alleys there was a massive throng, an incredible bustle, and there were buildings and statues on the grand scale. Uri looked everything over from very close up to see it well, he even sniffed at the stonework and felt all over the walls, strolling around evenly and methodically, until he had registered in his head all of Rome, that enormous, magical city of one million people, along with all its smells and every tiny, barely palpable protrusion.

He knew the alleys where it was worth looking up every second or third step because it was likely that scraps or other filth would be tossed out onto the heads of those below; he knew which alleys cart drivers liked to careen, flattening passersby; he knew where brothels flourished and passersby might be knifed for no particular reason. There was one street in the Saepta, near where Roman citizens voted in the Campus Martius, that he never got to visit in the course of his rambles, because once upon a time an Illyrian giant, strong as an ox and in a quarrelsome mood, had unexpectedly attacked and almost strangled him. Uri was lucky that a military tribune happened to be going that way with his escort, and they had rescued him.

In the real Rome, his mongrel character faded into insignificance among the many hundreds of thousands of freakish people. At first sight he did not even look to be a mongrel; there were large numbers of people who were even more of a mess—sick, maimed, ulcerated, wounded, veteran legionnaires, and useless, cast-off slaves with missing limbs, wailing and begging for alms at every turn. He became acquainted with that bank of the Tiber and was witness to many things that his Jewish contemporaries were denied because, being intact, they were preoccupied with life on Far Side and did not have time to wander around in the true Rome. He, however, could wander; his father never asked what he was doing with his time, nor did anyone else.

Being a Roman citizen with full rights, he was entitled to enter into conversation with all sorts of people in the true Rome, and he tried to speak with everybody in their own mother tongue. These were wonderful language lessons, and one did not even have to pay for them. Over there, he thrived, shone, played roles, bluffed; he was just one of Rome's malingering plebeians. Back home, withdrawn in his shack, he was a pariah among the Jews because of his poor eyesight, his bad legs and back, not fit for physical labor. Among Jews he was nobody, yet in the true Rome he was a man of equal rank to whom, should he speak, people would listen just like anyone else, and they would pay as little notice to his opinion as they did anyone else's. At home, he did not dare offer an opinion about anything; over there, however, he chattered, passed judgments, held forth and butted in on any conversation. He had a Jewish self, and he acquired a Roman self; both sides would have been amazed to see him in the other milieu. But that they did not see.

He never denied, if asked, that he was Jewish, but nothing was made of it. "A Jew's just like everybody else, only crazier" was the general, patronizing view of atheistic Jews and their unfounded arrogance that placed their one god above all the other gods. There was nothing hostile in that view; it was more disdainful indulgence, something that amused others. In this enormous city, citizens had gotten used to a great variety of peoples who found ways to get by in the world, and every one of them, without exception, was in Rome, with its comic superstitions and ludicrous customs. Where lanky Germanic people who barely spoke broken Latin were the emperor's best Praetorian Guards; where philosophers descending from everywhere discoursed only in Greek, not Latin; where splendid delegations arrived from all parts of the world; where countless deposed kings were preparing to claim their throne and loafed around with their populous families; where a statue of the gods of every conquered people stood in the Forum—all except the Jewish God, the Unrepresentable One. A single Roman Jew with full civil rights counted little and raised no passions.

The only thing Uri was ashamed about was the begging of the grubby, barefooted Jewish children running around the true Rome in gangs of four and five.

The children were coached by adults—former beggar children themselves, well schooled in the psychology of prospective donors—in what they should say in Latin and Greek, how to surround a wealthy gentleman or lady and plead aggressively, and how to look even more destitute than they were. These adults would then collect the day's take from the children. Any upstanding Jew was appalled by the practice, but the Elders did not forbid it, with some no doubt raking off a share of the income; names were flung around, often baselessly, of those who supposedly profited from the children.

When it became clear that Uri had bad eyesight, Joseph had also been approached to have his son tail after the indigent children as an overseer, so that they would not hide away the money that they had begged, but his father had chased them out of the house with cries of outrage. Uri knew precisely which of the idle Jews over there were keeping an eye on the gangs of beggar children. That was the one time he gave thanks for his bad eyesight, because when the Elders called his father in on account of his scandalous behavior, he could invoke his son's shortsightedness and say that he had been so enraged by the suggestion because he thought they were poking fun of a well-known defect. On that occasion, no punishment had been inflicted on Joseph.

Maybe being a boss to children back home in Rome was better than being jolted along toward the unknown, he thought to himself now.

He watched Matthew's back at length as he sat beside the wagoner. He was a sturdy, broad-shouldered man of middle age with sharp, sunburned features, thick, light-brown hair, and blue eyes, as Uri had already noticed at daybreak. It must be good to be strong like him, accustomed to traveling.

The silence must have been too protracted for Matthew's taste, as he partly swung around and started speaking.

He begged forgiveness for rudely interrupting his companions' sacred meditations, but he felt it was incumbent on him, as their leader, to give a short account of his life and therefore their commander, as it were, on this journey. It was a matter of regret that the delegation to Jerusalem from the community of Jewish congregations was not being led by a man of Roman citizenship; he was merely a citizen of the Italian provinces, but the Elders had found that this was the safe solution, and up till now that had in fact been so: on the occasions he had led the journey, no harm had come to them.

He lived in Ostia, as he had said before. He was proud of the town, and at least two thousand out of a population of approximately twenty thousand were Jewish. They had a house of prayer and a public bath next door, everything they needed, and there were also private baths in or next to the houses of the richer citizens.

There were a great variety of peoples living in this important seaport, the importance of which would only grow; in it there was a sanctuary to Isis and a sanctuary to the renowned Magna Mater, to Cybele, mother of the gods, and to many other Eastern deities, like Mithras, what would be expected in a port town. But it was his fervent hope that a Jewish house of prayer would eventually be built that people from distant lands would flock to admire.

The Latini in Ostia had exquisite baths, a magnificent stadium, an amphitheater that held four thousand spectators, a substantial records office, the houses of the wealthier citizens, some of the houses of Jews also, had hypocaust heating systems, and some of these were on two floors, provided with an ample balcony where it was possible to sit outside in the evening. He did not say it to boast, but his house was one of them; it had been completed not even six months ago; it is true that it was situated outside the town walls. On the sea coast to the southeast of the town itself that extramural territory—and incidentally he had not had to pay the municipal administration for it, or to be more exact, the land did not belong to the town, but he had asked for a written document, which he received, to the effect that he was permitted to build on it—would be worth something one day, perhaps even more than a plot inside the town. Previously he had lived in a tenement with his children, but they had outgrown the two rooms of that apartment and, over his wife's protestations, he had put all the money he had saved into this villa; so far no one had attacked the house or robbed it. Not far from the house were two mausoleums and the Bona Dea sanctuary, which were likewise outside the Porta Marina. The new mausoleum had been consecrated not long before, but he had personally known the individual to whom it had been erected, the famed C. Cartilius Poplicola, slayer of the pirates who had once tried to ransack all the ships in the harbor but had all come to a bad end. Poplicola, the new mausoleum's occupant who had passed away to an eternal peace, had been a dignified old man in his final years, who had loved company and threw large banquets; he, Matthew, had visited him on two occasions and could also say that both times Poplicola had stroked his face with his hand because in the twilight of his years he had gone completely blind.

Uri shuddered.

Ostia's chief attraction, Matthew continued, was its public toilet, the forica, with its dozens of marble seats ornamented with statues and mural mosaics. Lots of people took shits there at any given time, all sorts of people, side by side and opposite one another, drinking, eating, chatting, making jokes, reading out loudly to each other. It was a pretty place from the outside too; if ever they went that way they should seek it out, because as far as he was aware there was no facility like it in Rome.

His wife, a good-natured soul, had given him six children. Three of the four sons had by now grown up and were sailing on ships. He himself was now in his second decade on active duty in the Jewish fleet, initially as a sailor, later as captain, and he was used to issuing orders, which is why he asked for his companions to excuse him in advance for any occasional curtness or harshness in his dealings with them; that was not due to lack of respect, merely his mind, toughened by necessity, because in the end an officer could not feel compassion if he had to direct a galley of rowing slaves. He had shipped goods most frequently to Alexandria, or else from Alexandria to Caesarea and later, to avoid paying excise in Alexandria and Egypt, he had sailed with Judaean produce straight from Caesarea to Ostia; many times he had freighted from Alexandria to Ostia and back, and sometimes also found himself going to the Greek islands as well.

Given that he had a thorough knowledge of the hazards of the port of Ostia, the high command of the Jewish fleet had asked him to settle there for good as the agent, pilot, and warehouseman for the Jewish fleet. Once he had agreed, he had taken up the posting with the speedy consent of the Roman authorities. As a person who had already settled in Ostia many, many years before, he had instantly been granted Italian citizenship and had not even had to pay for it.

Anyway, this now was the fifth time that he had led a delegation to Jerusalem, and he felt it necessary to give them a few pieces of information.

The Torah scroll was in his possession.

He had a letter with the seal of the municipal administration in his possession to the effect that he, Matthew, citizen of Ostia, and five companions were traveling on an important mission, and the Roman powers-that-be were obliged to assist and support him and his companions wherever they were.

At this point he turned to Uri and explained reluctantly that the document did not speak of six companions because Gaius Theodorus had only been added to the delegation at the last moment and there had not been time to get the safe-conduct rewritten, not that this would cause any problems, he was quite sure of that; excise men would simply be glad that there was an extra traveler to charge for. On occasions like this, they would ask for extra money, of course, though it was usually possible to haggle that down a bit.

Uri felt a numbing chill in the region of his stomach, but he forced a smile to his lips and nodded.

He was also in possession, Matthew continued, of the money that the Elders had voted to cover the costs of the delegation; that had been the case with each of his trips, and as a rule it had been spent down to the last penny; his accounts for the amount had hitherto been accepted without question, even though the Elders were somehow amazingly well informed how much things cost outside Rome.

The route, he went on, had been properly prepared. Safe places where they would be given quarters had been arranged. They would be spending their nights alternately at private houses and at hostelries as long as they were on Italian soil, though on occasion it might be outdoors, under the open sky, but only if weather permitted; it was not one of their aims to drag themselves in sickness to Jerusalem. They would land in Sicily at Messina—or Messana, as the Romans called it—then, after another dry-land journey, they would set sail from the port of Siracusa for Caesarea, near the Greek islands, whence they would take the military road to Jerusalem. Experience had shown that this was the safest and the second-shortest course, and if nothing cropped up en route, they might even cover it in as little as six weeks, but, just to be on the safe side, they always allowed an extra two weeks over and above that. One of those weeks was made up of Sabbaths, of course, when they would not be doing any traveling; the route was so devised that they would be spending the Sabbaths, wherever possible, with Jewish families who welcomed delegations and would be glad to celebrate with them.

The question might be raised, he added, why they would not be traveling by sea from Ostia to Caesarea, since that would be the simplest route and even quicker than he had outlined, if the wind was favorable, and in the spring it did tend to be favorable indeed. Well, the thing was that the boats that plied directly between Ostia and Judaea were overloaded with produce and were not really in a position to carry passengers as well, or else they were only willing to do so at sky-high prices, despite being well aware of the importance of this delegation, such that it wasn't worth it to the Roman community. From Ostia it was possible to travel with a Greek or Latin boat to Alexandria, and from there by a Jewish ship to Judaea, but then there was a bigger risk of something untoward happening to them, and that way excise would have to be paid at Alexandria, an extortionate amount, and even then there was no guarantee that they would not be held up in the harbor for days or possibly weeks.

Finally, he expressed his conviction that it would be a good trip, and he gave his thanks to the Creator for being able to travel with such excellent companions, whom the Elders had plainly selected for this exalted task not without good reason.

Uri blushed.

Now that Matthew had finished his introduction, the others livened up and plied him with many questions.

First, a thickset man inquired as to whether Jews also frequented the public privy. On receiving an affirmative response, he became indignant at the sacrilege: only the Creator had the right to see his elect naked or in a shameful position, and a Jew shitting was absolutely no concern of non-Jews. Neither Matthew nor the others saw fit to respond to these qualms. The thickset man shook his head and growled a profanity. Uri could not even begin to imagine what his occupation might be.

Many of the questions pertained to the harbor at Ostia, with the strong, black-bearded man showing the most interest in it. Matthew said that the harbor, at the mouth of the Tiber, lay in an unfortunate position, exposed to the prevailing western winds, and the shore was not suitable to allow the bigger boats to take shelter during storms. That was a problem that had not existed in previous centuries, when boats were smaller and shallower, but nowadays they were so big that the port's sole advantage was its proximity to Rome, no more than twenty miles. Deep-drafted craft were no longer able to pass up the Tiber; everything had to be shipped onto small vessels, which were tossed around dangerously by the waves, so that a great many accidents occurred as a result of smaller boats smashing against the sides of the big ships. The southward orientation of Puteoli's harbor, in a gulf protected from the winds, was undoubtedly more fortunate, but he was quite certain that Ostia, once its harbor was rebuilt, would best Puteoli simply because it was much closer to Rome.

He had seen plans for how the harbor ought to be rebuilt, how the sea bottom should be excavated, what kinds of breakwaters should be constructed and where they should be located in the coastal waters, but these would be very costly operations and, in his view, the emperor, to whom the plans had been shown, was unlikely to commit himself to them. Private entrepreneurs would not finance that sort of work, as the payoff was too long-term—one or two generations, some had calculated—so the Roman state would have to put up the money. The plans would come to nothing until the day a very big storm broke up the entire fleet that were anchored off the harbor entrance, and they went down, together with their cargoes of grain, bringing Rome to the brink of starvation. Then they would get serious about rebuilding the harbor, in his view, but only then. True, he added with a laugh, it was in his interest that the harbor was not modernized, because there would be a call for experienced pilots only; he made his living from the deficiencies of Ostia's harbor.

The black-bearded man asked if those reconstruction plans were accessible somewhere. Matthew said that he had seen them in the home of a Latin acquaintance of his, who had them on loan from the local public records office.

A soft question was then raised as to whether the wagoner was deaf, at which Matthew laughed before replying: No way! A deaf cart-driver cost a lot, with the wealthy paying as much as twenty thousand sesterces for one, but since drivers had to be relieved along the way, it would be quite impossible to engage that many deaf cart-drivers. But they should feel free to talk aloud in his presence, and that of those who would follow, because the cart-drivers were hardly in a position to pass on whatever information they had gleaned to the relieving cart-driver as they did not have enough time: they had to turn back immediately.

The conversation was conducted in Greek, and the delegation had every reason to suppose that the wagoner knew at least a smattering of Greek, but he did not react to this exchange in any way and instead dozed on the box.

It did occur to Uri that maybe it was not they who were carrying the sacrificial money but another group, and by another route, less conspicuous than them; they were nothing more than bait. Because it was written all over them that they were Jews—not so much their clothing but because they were not permitted to shave, unlike Romans, who since the end of the republic had forsaken beards so that hordes of plebeians and slaves made a living out of barbering.

Another question was raised as to whether the leader was carrying any object that qualified as a weapon. Matthew shook his head no. Experience had shown that it was more hazardous to travel with a weapon than without. "Those that take the sword shall perish with the sword," Matthew quoted the proverb, adding that anyone who traveled with an armed escort was unnecessarily inviting attention from evil-minded parties.

By that point they had covered a good few miles along the Appian Way, on which military sentries were posted every three miles—not that there was any need for them, as there had been no war on Italian soil since the time of Hannibal, but it did no harm if everybody saw that in Rome a military dictatorship held sway. Pedestrians, soldiers, and carters showed up on the road every now and then, but they did not give so much as a glance at a wagon loaded with Jews. Uri marveled at how well the road was built; considering that they were plodding along on a wagon drawn by oxen, he might even have been able to read, had he brought any scrolls with him. He regretted that he had not thought of that in the excitement, but then he realized that the others would take it the wrong way if he were to immerse himself in reading; they might well suppose that he held them in contempt and sought conversation only with a person who was cleverer than they were—the author.

He had never been outside Rome before, and the endless strip of the Appian Way fascinated him. The others must have been feeling much the same, because one of them—Iustus was his name, he had introduced himself—remarked that his father, when he had been in slavery as a youngster, had worked in road gangs and never tired of declaring what painstaking work they had carried out. Uri squinted at him through narrowed eyes, and it struck him that this was someone he already knew by sight: he belonged to the same congregation. He was a small, weedy, quarrelsome person, uneducated and limited. One did not need much culture to be a road-maker; it was the sort of trade that strapping young guys went in for, but plainly Iustus had been driven to it because he was stupid. Maybe he was employed as a gang leader or purchasing agent. I'm at least as fit for the journey as him, Uri thought to himself with relief. Then he was struck by the unpleasant thought that Iustus might very well be acquainted with Joseph and, should the occasion arise over the coming days, might take the chance to spread gossip about him to the others.

Iustus related that a road would first be marked out by spade in accordance with the surveyors' directions: the earth would be tamped down, a trench would be dug on both the right- and left-hand sides to drain the rain, because if the rain froze, it would crack the road; then the surface would be covered with two layers of stone flags, the gaps being filled with a material they called cement, which was composed of three parts gravel and one part lime mortar. The best limestone comes from Puteoli, but it did not always work out; gravel is sprinkled evenly on the flags—something to which special attention is paid—then a further layer of flags is laid on top of that, with the gaps filled with gravel, all of it stuffed down in such a way that it should have a little camber to both left and right, again to ensure that the rain runs off. The flagstones are hacked out by slaves in the quarries and transported from there ready for use, stacked on top of each other.

"Where is this Puteoli?" the black-beard queried.

"Off to the south," said Iustus. "It's a big port, one hundred and forty-three stadia from Rome."

"We won't be stopping," said Matthew, "but we'll be passing by."

Iustus went on to relate that his father had put on a tremendous amount of muscle with the road construction, but there came a time when he badly strained his back while working and from then on, for the rest of his days, he was only able to get around with a stick. As his master could not sell him, he let him emancipate himself inexpensively. "So, my father sired me with his stick," declared Iustus, in rather poor taste.

If it was only Iustus's father who gained his freedom, then he cannot be a Roman citizen himself, Uri figured. Were all the rest citizens? he wondered. Not that the authorities were particularly interested which people left Rome for Jerusalem, but he was still somewhat comforted by the thought that there was someone in the delegation who was legally of lesser worth than himself.

Going south, they stopped at a hostelry, not so much to eat as to have a drink, wash their feet, and pray. A Jewish male, wherever he might be, had to wash his hands and feet and pray three times a day. Matthew brought out a big brass bowl from the inn, drew water into it from the well, then set the bowl on the ground. His companions stretched their backs, massaged their feet, and one by one followed Matthew in stepping to the bowl, fully clothed, dabbling hands and feet in the water, then stepping out. Uri, being the youngest, went last and so, by way of ritually washing himself, dabbled in everyone else's filth. They then turned to the southeast and, after affixing the tefillin, a leather box with straps attached and a portion of the Pentateuch inside on rolled-up parchment, to the forehead or left arm, they prayed for a while with repeated bowing. Matthew emptied a cupful of fresh water into their jugs, and they drank water; they each had a bulky jug, one of those crudely finished articles sold by the dozen and surprisingly heavy given how little water they held. Uri had no difficulty imagining himself drinking from something a bit more genteel. Matthew took the brass bowl back and climbed up onto the box while they clambered onto the wagon, stuffed the phylacteries and jugs back into their sacks, and set off again.

Uri broke off a piece of matzo and started to chew it, because the middle of his chest had started to hurt, and a bit of matzo was always good for that. Now even Matthew held his peace, maybe even dozed off, but Uri was ruminating on whether he too should introduce himself, and he could not make out why, after Matthew had introduced himself, his other companions, with one exception, had not introduced themselves in turn, as would have been proper. Or had the Elders already told Matthew about the people who were traveling with him? If so, what could they have said about Uri? He feared that his companions knew one another, even though they had given no sign of it, but they had plenty of time to get acquainted even if they belonged to different congregations, they were grown-up working men after all, but they did not know him, by sight at most; they probably did not even know that he was Joseph's son. Well, Iustus would tell them, and no doubt ply them with baseless lies.

He regretted that his father had not gone with him to the meeting-place and helped him get acquainted with his companions. Could it have been his father's way of showing that he trusted him and was treating him as an adult, or on the contrary, conveying that his fate was of no interest? But then, if the latter were the case, he would not have given him all that advice, and he would not have wakened him at dawn, even before it had started to get light. It occurred to Uri that this had been the second night running his father had been sleepless, and he felt a twinge of remorse; his own nocturnal torments did not cross his mind.

His head drooping, he jolted on until he suddenly awoke to the fact that they had stopped. Matthew jumped down freshly and happily.

"I do love traveling in February," he declared. "It's still possible to get around by daylight, unlike the journeys to the other feasts. In the summer months, you are guaranteed to fry."

They had turned in to a hostelry, where they greeted Matthew as a familiar figure. They rinsed hands and feet in a brass bowl, prayed again, then sat down at a long table, and before long were served with food: freshly baked fish, with bread and wine. The innkeeper was Latinian, but he knew precisely what he could serve to Jews: Uri ate the fish and the bread, but he offered the wine to the others because he only drank water. That statement was received with silence, though nothing insulting had been intended. Matthew, picking up on the sudden tension, took the wine from him with thanks and downed it.

Uri had figured they would be spending the night at the hostelry, but that was not what happened: their sacks on the ox-drawn wagon were shifted onto an ass-drawn trap, and after relieving themselves and praying anew, they set off on foot, still headed south. Matthew drove the ass while walking beside the trap; the others dawdled along in its wake.

Before long, Uri's legs began to hurt, and he carried on with clenched teeth. The basalt rocks of the highway felt atrociously hard and unyielding. He had no desire to lose touch with the others, who, it seemed, were used to physical burdens and marched along effortlessly, but all the same he fell a few paces behind. He was wrapped up in his own cares and it was only after a fair amount of time had elapsed that he noticed his companions, in knots of two or three, had stepped up to Matthew at the front and were engaging in quiet conversations with him. When this happened a third time, he noticed that they were casting sly looks his way after falling back slightly from Matthew. He quickened his pace, even though both his feet were now hurting and his back was aching too. They are whispering about me, he thought.

He made an effort to reduce the pain and throbbing to a dull tingling, looking up to the sky where instead of shining stars he saw only dim, overlapping, gleaming circles and the moon, a larger and broader patch than in his boyhood days, with an indefinite, blurred outline, and he made a silent supplication to his Creator, asking him what his plan had been in leading him on this journey. Why did you not send someone else on this dark, deserted road, my Lord?

Matthew suddenly stopped, handed the traces over to Iustus and waited for Uri.

"Are you still up to it?" he asked.

"I can take it," Uri said.

"We'll go on a bit more before we call it a day and get some sleep."

"I can take it," Uri said.

They carried on without a word, Matthew treading by his side.

"I don't want to offend you," Matthew said finally, "but no one can figure out why your family picked you for this journey."

"I don't know either," said Uri.

"Never mind," said Matthew. "You'll get stronger along the way."

"No doubt," said Uri.

They walked on.

Uri noticed that three or four of his companions were treading closer than they had been before. He thought it was a good opportunity to introduce himself. Speaking as if he were only seeking to inform, he reported that he was the son of the merchant Joseph, his mother was named Sarah, and he had two younger sisters; he did not know what else he could say about himself.

"So, your father," the black-beard started, "he's the one who delivers silk to Agrippa, too, is that right?"

That disconcerted Uri even more.

"I don't know; I have no knowledge of my father's business affairs."

That assertion was met with a reproachful growl. That was not the answer he was supposed to give; he should have been working for his father long before now.

"I know that is not how it ought to be," he pleaded, "but my eyesight's not good..."

"Trading doesn't require good eyes, only a brain," the thickset one declared.

That was true but no comfort to Uri.

"So you know nothing about your father's affairs," Matthew summed up.

He may simply have been trying to end an unproductive and embarrassing conversation, but Uri sensed in his words a note of scorn, and he was anxious to make a good impression on such a strong and determined man.

"What I do know is that my father raised a lot of money for Agrippa."

That announcement was received in silence. Uri gathered that everybody knew about the loan, probably more than he did.

"And so," said black-beard, "that is why Agrippa persuaded the Elders to let you come with us?"

Uri said nothing. He could not be blamed for this unsolicited, awkward privilege. They probably think we are currying favor with Agrippa, he thought, and that we pay off everybody, even though we are penniless—but then no one would believe that.

"I have never seen Agrippa," he said bitterly, "but perhaps he heard from someone that I know a lot of languages."

As soon as he said it he realized that he had made an even bigger mistake than before. Right at the start of the journey, he had already committed the one error that his father had warned him against: flaunting his knowledge when he should have been keeping quiet about it.

The thickset one seized the opportunity. "Let's see now. Which languages do you speak?"

There was no going back, so Uri reeled them off. There was a stony silence as they trudged after the ass trap.

"There's no point in learning Egyptian and Hebrew; a complete waste of time," said Matthew. "And Latin is not a necessity either. Greek is spoken everywhere. Aramaic could come in handy if you plan to roam around in the country, but there won't be time for that now: as soon as the feast comes to an end we shall be heading back."

As an ex-seaman, Matthew obviously spoke a number of languages, but for him that was a matter of course and so of no value. I failed to win his sympathy, Uri concluded, and that rankled; he would have liked to have that strong and resolute man on his side. Instead, I have given the others a reason to hate me.

He walked with gritted teeth, his head bowed down to make clear there was no point asking more questions. The others drew away, then Matthew pushed ahead also and took the reins back from Iustus, who had proven expert in road construction. Because it really was him, the stonemason and house-builder, Uri had meanwhile assured himself that this—the one to whom Matthew had temporarily handed the reins—was the same as the Iustus whose grandfather had reported to Gaius Lucius's father that Uri's grandfather had been stealing when his grandfather had never stolen anything. That was something his father had told him once.

He was half-asleep by the time Matthew called a halt, unharnessed the donkey and tethered it to a tree. They took from their sacks the tefillin, bound it to their forehead or arm, said a prayer while facing southeast, then lay down, each placing his sack beneath his head. There was no water with which to rinse hands and feet, so they rubbed them with soil instead, as that was considered clean. No one asked Matthew if he had aimed for this coppice deliberately or had failed to reach the intended hostelry. It was on my account that progress was so slow, Uri reflected; that is not going to make them like me any better.

He had almost fallen asleep when he noticed that the others were whispering with Matthew. They're talking about me; they want to get rid of me. I'm the problem.

So what?

THE FIRST INN THEY STAYED IN WAS SMALL AND RAMSHACKLE BUT reasonably clean; there were six men idling in togas, sitting next to one another on a bench. The group took seats next to them. Uri wearily wiggled his toes; he had slogged on manfully, eating little and drinking little, as his stomach could not take much. His companions must have seen that he was suffering without a word of complaint, trying to keep up.

His companions eyed the men suspiciously; Uri blinked in their direction but could see nothing remarkable. Even if they were robbers, they were quiet. Then, to his surprise, the men began speaking with women's voices. He narrowed his eyes: the togaed individuals were women, but they wore their togas the same way men did in Rome. Uri was amazed, since in Rome the women went around in tunics with long sleeves, so this was evidently the fashion in the provinces.

Uri would have kept on looking, but his companions were there too and it would not do to stare openly. By now Uri had the feeling that they had warmed toward him a bit; in fact, they were even striking up conversations with him.

By now he had gotten to know their names.

One of them, a muscular, proud man by the name of Alexandros, was a merchant; he was acquainted with Joseph, he said, and had a high opinion of him, which pleased Uri greatly.

Another answered to the name of Valerius and was a hyperetes, or assistant to the archisynagogos, not as a grammateus but as maintenance man, which essentially meant he was a cleaner. Although a nobody and a nothing, he was still the only person in the delegation with a religious occupation. Uri had never come across him before; Valerius's services were done for the Hebrew temple, which was located a long way from the temple to which Uri went, because it stood on the Via Aurelia, outside the city wall, to the west of the center of Far Side. People who used the Hebrew temple spoke Greek. A couple of generations ago the language of the divine service was perhaps Hebrew or Aramaic, from which the name for the house of prayer might have derived, designating it as a position beyond the river, because the Greek "Hebraios" comes from Aramaic "ibrhay" or Hebrew "ibrhi⁻," meaning "from beyond the river."

The strong, black-bearded one was called Plotius and said he was a joiner. He mostly kept silent, but Uri would have been glad to hear more from him.

The thickset little busybody was a teacher by the name of Hilarus. No surprise that he was teacher; it's their job to find fault with everything and everybody. Uri was just thankful his own teacher had been nothing like that.

Anyway, Uri did not dare scrutinize the women, but he did notice what while waiting for their supper his companions, strong adult males that they were, were gaping at them and, all except Matthew and Plotius, fidgeting restlessly on the bench. It struck Uri that marriage does not efface all traces of sexual desire. The Lord knows, he intoned noiselessly, what specters and hideous urges still await me in life!

They were still dining when four Latinian youths dropped into the hostelry. Judging from their clothes and jewels, they must have been rich; maybe they were headed to the country house of one of their fathers, but they hitched their horses in front of the inn. On entering the premises, they weighed the situation and sat down next to the wilting damsels, who livened up, and while the Jews stared into their plates as they chewed, they took drinks. When the Jews had finished the meal, the four youths and six women went upstairs.

By then even Uri had comprehended that these women were professionals. He knew from his reading that whatever takes place in a hostelry does not count as marital infidelity in a court of law. He kept quiet, and so did his companions. From upstairs a sound of tittering, periodic screaming, rhythmic panting, pounding, and creaking of the floor could be heard.

Uri had encountered prostitutes before in Rome while going around his favorite part of the city, the Subura, with ladies in short sleeveless tunics sometimes accosting him and offering to take care of him for two or three asses; the whores in Rome were proverbially dirt-cheap, there being too many of them. Uri always retreated panic-stricken, precisely because, thanks to his father's good nature, he would always have enough money on his person to pay for their services. He had no money on him now, thank the Lord, so he was in no place to proposition the worthy ladies, were he to be seized by a momentary madness.

They slept in a warehouse, packed together on the ground. For a long time Uri could not get to sleep, listening to the snores and wheezing of his companions and imagining what might be going on upstairs in the inn.

Naked men and women were not unknown sights to him, Roman statuary not exactly being prudish. Paintings in the public library also depicted fauns and nymphs who had nothing on, and the painter had not given Helen too many clothes either, portraying her virtually naked at the side of a Paris with a conspicuous hard-on.

Uri feared sexuality and yearned in equal measure for a woman to initiate him at last. Hanging around in the true Rome, he could hardly shield his eyes from open displays and depictions of sexuality. There were statues of humans, murals of naked nymphs also, in the houses of even rich Roman Jews—not that Uri saw them, as he had no access to such places, but there was talk all over Far Side about it being possible for Jews to purchase with impunity a sarcophagus portraying a nude Venus or Poseidon in specialist shops run by non-Jews, and Levite cemetery attendants would raise no objections. The Elders of Rome took the view that portrayals of man or beast were prohibited only on hilltops, because there they might be worshiped as idols, whereas anywhere else was permitted. Sarah was always happy to inveigh against this disgusting, barbaric custom any time she brought food and drink and clean clothes to a weary Joseph when he got back home, as were a wife's duties, after all. Uri too understood that the Torah contained a general prohibition against portrayals of both man and beasts, and he simply could not make his mind up whether to support the written Law or the spoken Word in his soul.

When the weather was good, which it was for eight or nine months in the year, benches would be set up on the street, and it was possible to gaze at the bustle for hours on end, and there were few bigger amusements going in the Rome of those days. Sitting in a Roman tavern, Uri would look at the women and try to imagine what kinds of children he would father with each, and how.

He was attracted by the darker-skinned, wild-looking women from far-off lands, Ethiopians especially. They were tall and slender, and they wore their decorative veils with grace, not walking so much as gliding on their long legs, walking along the street as if they were carrying themselves on their own palanquin, even though their ears were pierced. Uri used to daydream about one day converting an Ethiopian woman like that to the Jewish faith, purchasing her out of slavery, and her bringing a cartload of children into the world by him, to the greater glory of the Lord.

There was barely a tavern in Rome in which women did not sit around next to the men; these women were likewise professional, and Uri might avert his gaze, but he could not stop his ears from hearing their puerile suggestions. His command of Latin grew superbly in the process. It was also quite usual for erotic drawings by well-versed hands to appear on house walls, and it was impossible not to see these; they would even desecrate the walls of villas on the Capitoline from time to time, though graffiti like that vanished quickly, as they were washed off by the sentinels. Non-Jewish plebeians with whom Uri was on good terms in the true Rome related that the best paintings were to be found in the thermal springs, always offering some new instruction, and female staff would even demonstrate a desired position with a guest, albeit not cheaply. Uri considered himself lucky that, being Jewish, he was not allowed to frequent such baths, though he was dying to try everything out.

It was late when he finally got to sleep, almost daybreak, and he found it near impossible to get up for the morning prayer. When he wanted to get the matzo from his sack he could not find it at first, and he was alarmed that it might have shaken out somewhere en route, but then he found it, though it was broken up.

Someone had been through the sack.

The pleasant feelings of the previous day evaporated.

They didn't trust him; they were suspicious.

But what could they have been looking for in a sack that had been given him by Matthew? They could see that, apart from his father's cast-off cloak, he had arrived with nothing.

After the morning prayer they ate a hearty breakfast to fortify themselves from the journey ahead; the women were languishing in place, while the rich Roman youngsters had taken off. Still, it was not how they looked after group sex that concerned Uri, but only the dreadful emptiness of his belly into which he crammed the food. His companions chatted merrily and even spoke to him pleasantly enough; they did not notice that his mood had altered.

Before the start—there was again a trap to carry the luggage, this time with two donkeys, which meant they would be walking—Uri went up to Matthew and declared gloomily:

"Someone's been through my sack."

Matthew cast a glance at him. There was no sympathy in the look but also no malice.

"Was anything taken?" he asked.

"No," Uri replied, surprised.

"Well, then, no harm came of it," Matthew replied, and turned away.

Uri was disconsolate. He would have liked to take after this group of strong men, to please them; he had no trouble accepting Matthew as a leader and mentor, but for some reason they were suspicious of him. His father was right: they bore him malice from the outset, and all because his wretched father had been put in a worse position than ever before by Agrippa's request. And he could not even tell them; they wouldn't believe him anyway.

He worried away as they walked; on account of that, he did not feel his legs hurting him so much. He no longer looked at the countryside; it was just boring evergreen cypresses everywhere, gentle slopes, hills, withered over-wintering vines, dormant crops, leafless woodlands, and every twenty-five stadia a post where the wealthy could change horses but their group could not drop in, not because it was forbidden but just because everything was more expensive. Uri no longer wondered about anything; he did not blink, just mulled things over bitterly.

Then it occurred to him: what if his sack had not been tampered with deliberately? They all looked the same, after all; maybe someone had mistaken it for their own.

That thought was comforting.

No doubt that is what happened, but he suspected his companions of searching through his sack, and, worse, had made the mistake of relaying that to Matthew. He would have to beg their pardon at the first suitable opportunity.

This was the first time since setting off that he had cheered up.

Life was glorious after all! He was walking in Italia on an important mission, among excellent companions, to Jerusalem—a wretched little Roman Jew, his sandals tied together and slung around his neck, the only one of the group who was barefoot, because sandals were expensive, one needed to take care of them.

Matthew was right; he would toughen up on the journey. Already the walking was easier; his body was already toughening up, the soles of his feet becoming callused. More than likely his eyesight was also improving.

He gazed at the many intermittent points of light against the outlines of the roadside trees: the bare branches would be covered by marvelous green foliage by the time they, having fulfilled their noble mission several months from now, would walk back this way.

THEIR PROGRESS WAS SLOWER THAN MATTHEW HAD PLANNED, BECAUSE sunset on the first Friday, the onset of the Sabbath, overtook them in open country.

They had left the paved road by then; they did not have a trap with them, and so, sacks slung on shoulder, they trailed after Matthew up hill and down dale; he, it seemed, was thoroughly familiar with the zigzag route to be taken to avoid costly excise payments in the towns.

They said the Sabbath evening prayers under a tree in full leaf, and on this occasion Matthew read out relevant passages from the Torah scroll he from his sack. It was small, but the crowns of the two wooden staves on which the scroll was rolled were ornamented, maybe that too a gift from the Elders in Rome.

Matthew asked Uri to interpret from Greek to Aramaic. Uri blushed; he had never before been picked for such a distinction, and he was amazed to be asked to interpret to Aramaic, of all languages, which, aside from Matthew, none of the others understood. But then again, to interpret from the Torah was a sublime task, whatever the circumstances.

In the more prosperous synagogues, a designated leader would read the Pentateuch text, sentence by sentence, in Hebrew, and another designated adult male, likewise held in high repute, a different person every Sabbath and feast day, would interpret the text sentence by sentence into Greek. In poorer houses of prayers in the provinces, so it was said, there was only a Torah in Greek and no need to interpret. The faithful would only say the "Amen" along with the leader.

Uri interpreted the Greek passages of the Septuagint into Aramaic, even though everyone spoke Greek as their native tongue. With prompts from Matthew, the companions dutifully said the "Amens" in the appropriate places. Uri interpreted fluently and elegantly; his face was burning, he was proud of himself. Matthew, who obviously spoke Aramaic, gave him no plaudits, then, when they began nibbling the matzos and preparing for a day of rest, he said— because one was permitted to speak, just not to work—on Sunday they would see the house where they were supposed to pass the night.

"We'll call in," he said, "in case anyone is worried about us."

For Uri this was the first Sabbath in his life that he had celebrated away from home. He woke up early, said his prayers, rinsed down his feet with dew, dried them on his toga, and used his fingernails to burst the blisters and peel off the thickened skin. It was more a kind of nonchalant and light-hearted picking, rather than with serious corrective intent, as any medication, including self-medication, was forbidden on the Sabbath. It was lucky that the ground was dewy, though religion saw to it that a son of the chosen people would be able to wash his feet even were dew lacking, because there was always going to be soil.

The Lord God had taken good care to insert a day of rest after six days of labor; God well understood that a person can stick out six days on foot but would not take a seventh.

He went off to relieve himself, and he saw that his stool was blood-flecked. His rectum had been itching and throbbing for days, perhaps from all the walking. His father suffered from bouts of colic, especially when he was helplessly worrying about an uncertain business matter.

Uri was delighted by the bloody stool.

He felt that the common ailment brought him closer to his distant father, who would likewise be observing the Sabbath back at home; right now he must be setting off with Sarah and the girls for the house of prayer where upon the Sabbath morning the members of the congregation would collectively listen to the prayer, men and women together and with them any children able to walk. There were stories that in Judaea women were given a place separate from the men; Uri did not understand the need for this degrading differentiation. If the opportunity arose, he would ask Matthew about it someday.

He lolled on the grass the whole day long; it was nice and warm. He extracted the jug from the sack—he had just come to the end of the matzos and had long since polished off the fruit—and placed it under his back; he wrapped his father's poor old cloak around himself, giving thanks to Joseph for begetting him, and stared at the skies. Up above, confused, multiple outlines blotched bluish, whitish, and grayish-blue, blurring into one another, unpredictably. Beyond that was Heaven, to which, at the end of his days, if he had worthily stood his ground down here below, he would hopefully ascend, there to meet with all the dear souls of his relations. That may have been a Greek idea originally, but the Jews had also adopted it, and quite rightly too; it was very reassuring.

The others in the delegation strolled around, chatted in twos and threes, but they did not go far, as that would have counted as traveling, which of course was forbidden on the Sabbath; they did not move farther than the tree under which the Torah had been read. No one spoke to him, but that did not bother Uri now; the Lord had seen well that on the seventh day one ought to rest. He must have seen the heavy toils of slaves in Egypt and wanted to give them too a reason for rejoicing on the seventh day. Uri exercised his feet; they hurt, but there was something ecstatic even in that. His rectum did not hurt now that he was lying down: it seemed as if the pain had departed from him also, along with the tainted blood.

He was surrounded by countryside of Edenic intactness, charming hills and moors, woods and fields, the glorious land of Campania, and needless to say there was a babbling brook nearby, as they had to drink and ritually bathe; God knew just where to conjure up a brook.

The whole of Italia was not yet cultivated; a vast amount of land was left fallow and belonged either to nobody or to the emperor, which came to the same thing. These hills had perhaps never been cultivated, with only sheep or goats sometimes grazing as they strayed in that direction. These were the sorts of landscapes about which verses were dashed off by bucolic Latin poets who developed an eye for the countryside because they lived in crowded cities.

Uri's soul was filled, as he lay there, with cheerfulness and an unfocused yearning. At that moment he was at peace with the created world, with the

87

Creator, and specifically because he very much wanted to experience right now the future for which he was predestined. Travel would play a part in it, as a matter of course, for how else would he have ended up where he was? Because he had done nothing wrong, he felt now that the trip to Jerusalem was in fact a gift.

The Lord wanted him to break free at last from his pagan reading matter, to grow up, and to see the Temple, which few in the Diaspora had the chance to see, and for his faith to be strengthened. Uri was one of the chosen people, however wretched he might consider himself to be. How could he not be one of the Lord's chosen people too if he was one of those, everywhere in the world this morning, who had listened to the same passages from the Torah that not long before he had interpreted to Aramaic?

No one at all passed that way, only the birds flitted around and twittered, but even if someone had come by and seen seven men in tunics—they had taken off the outer garments, it was so warm; spring had arrived early that year—he would not suspect how happy they were.

Non-Jews have no idea, thought Uri, what a joy this was. For all the sufferings that the Lord has visited on his chosen people, it was nonetheless they who were His chosen people: they were worth more than all the rest simply by virtue of existing. That knowledge gave security; that knowledge was the guarantee that everything was fine and would continue to be fine no matter what bad things had happened or ever would happen. When the Messiah, who might become the Anointed Priest of all people but would be Jewish all the same, came, he, Uri, along with his people, would ascend among the privileged into Sublime Eternity.

He had a foretaste of that fine, celestial eternity right now, as his legs were aching less and his rectum was not cramping.

They got to the house they should have reached a day and a half earlier at daybreak on Sunday, but that kind of delay did not count for anything on a journey of this length, Matthew assured them.

Four houses stood on the settlement, surrounded by tall stone walls, and nothing outside gave any sign that Jews lived in one of the houses; it was just the same sort of house as the others. Uri mused how the Lord God and his servants, the angels, would not know which door to knock on when the time came, but then it occurred to him that they were able to recognize a soul, they could see through walls and bodies and faith, and were that not so they would make some serious errors, but that was impossible.

The residents of the house welcomed them with relief; they had been anxious on their account.

It was a big family, with three grandparents, two parents, eight children from adults down to a small infant: five sons and three daughters. They could not own land in their own right, it was true, they only rented, but they kept a lot of sheep, the children taking them out to pasture, whereas they would drive any who met requirements to the harbor a day's walk away, and from there they would be taken by ship to Ostia and Jewish butchers in Rome.

Which harbor was that? Dicaearchia, naturally.

Uri asked how far that was from Rome.

Plotius stared in wonder.

"We've told you once already," he replied.

Uri still did not understand.

"It's what the Latini call Puteoli," said Plotius. "No doubt because of all the little wells. It was founded by the Greeks and it still has many Greek inhabitants."

Uri was overcome with shame.

"I know that," he said, blushing. "Foul-smelling hot springs in that area, it's supposed to be medicinal... Cicero used to own a property there..."

The homeowners told them that they themselves sheared the sheep, and they spun the wool themselves; they were able to get a good price for the yarn; in one of the rooms was an enormous wooden contrivance, a weaving loom. Obviously, the young girls spun the yarn; their mother had taught them how. On the kitchen wall, hung up on hooks by their handles, was a row of long daggers in the event that they needed to defend themselves, but they had never had to do so as yet.

They were prepared to receive the delegation and had baked enough matzos to last the whole week: they barely fit into the sacks. They also handed out wine in skins that were tied off and sealed with wax.

They prayed together then breakfasted together.

During the meal, Uri recited a passage of Latin verse from memory:

Of old, when Titus Tatius ruled the land, the Sabine women
Tended their land and never themselves.
Among them the hale and hearty, good mother, seated on a high bench
Quickly wove the raw thread with her dexterous fingers,
While her daughter closed the flock in the sheep-fold,
She herself laid billets on the brushwood fire.

The residents of the house laughed nervously before it dawned on Uri that they did not speak Latin.

Though a couple of his companions might have had a smattering, there was little chance that they knew whom the poem was by, and they stayed silent.

Uri laughed apologetically, his ears reddening.

That too had been unnecessary.

The next day the delegation got up and started off again.

Life must be good for them, the thought went through Uri's head. It disappointed him that he had not spoken with a single member of the family in the course of the evening.

Everyone had been shouting, talking all at once, cutting one another off, laughing, joking, nudging. They were used to everyone yelling, otherwise no one would have paid attention, and they were a bit deaf as a result, which particularly appealed to Uri. Life must be good for them, he thought, the dank gloom, the tense quiet of his own home in mind.

One day I am going to have family like that, he resolved. He also resolved that if he made it to the altar of the Temple in Jerusalem, he would make a solemn vow to that effect, cost what it may, because one had to pay for a vow there.

His good cheer gradually dissipated as the walking continued. His rectum was at times seized by cramps, and his feet also gave the occasional pang.

He tried to think back on the good that the Sabbath had brought, but a dark suspicion came over him: Matthew might well have asked him to interpret the text into Aramaic as a test, a chance for him to fail. After all, none of the party apart from Matthew spoke Aramaic; he had not believed that Uri spoke other languages.

But I said that I did, Uri reflected despondently, so why did he not believe me?

THE WALKING WAS TEDIOUS AND HARD; URI WOULD HAVE LIKED SOMEthing to read while they progressed.

For instance, the *Acta Diurna*.

The day's *Acta Diurna* was something he read habitually at his patron's house while the others gorged themselves like pigs; a reader enjoyed a measure of protection, with idiots being less likely to pester him with chatter. At the age of five, he had already pounced on this handwritten daily newspaper, several copies of which were delivered to Gaius Lucius by entrepreneurs who specialized in copying and distribution. In the paper were Senate proceedings, laws passed, court decisions, and all sorts of other official announcements—and Uri adored it. Gaius Lucius noticed the boy's passion for reading and proclaimed that one copy was to be reserved solely and exclusively for Uri. That had been forgotten over the years, of course, but Uri still scanned the day's Acta Urbis virtually every other day and, if still available, the previous day's, the imperial decrees, the actions taken by the municipal administration, any news about the foundations run by the wealthy, the marriage notices and the deaths, because everything was in that newspaper, the first in the world, that there ought to be, with only the sports news missing, which Uri did not understand. If he were to edit the *Acta*, then he would publish daily reports on the competitions that were going on in the stadium, which would boost the circulation many times over. There were also times that he was angry because the hand of the copyist that day was careless, and the paper was barely legible or teeming with spelling errors.

While he was living in Rome, it seemed that the *Acta Diurna* spoke about him. Or so he felt, at least, even though the news was always reporting on important people he had never seen and was never going to see. Still, what was written about had happened in Rome and related to Rome—in other words, to him, too, as a Roman citizen. But now he had left Rome and was getting ever farther away from it, and the relevance of the Acta Urbis to his current location was zero. Uri walked despondently; there was no sense in moving farther from Rome when he wanted nothing more than to be back home.

But then the sea—that was a big deal.

He saw it for the very first time when they arrived in Rhegium to take the boat to Messana across the narrow straits that Homer referred to as Scylla and Charybdis.

It was not the actual sea, because Sicily appeared as a nearby massif off in the distance, the sea really just a large lake, but all the same it was a mighty stretch of water. As they waited for the boat, Uri paddled in the shallow and, despite the winter, still fairly warm water, gawking at the wriggling fish as he bent over its surface. His companions also took a dip; they said the midday prayers and got out quickly, dried themselves on their cloaks, and dressed. Uri stayed; he felt a yearning to set out on the sea and to merge into this mighty stretch of water, to be carried off, but he controlled himself, and anyway he could not swim, as was the case with virtually everyone in those days; so he just gazed in wonder at the miraculous fish and the luxuriant aquatic plants in the completely transparent water and hummed to himself. He was undisturbed that his companions on dry land might laugh at him; he was not out to earn their favor. He did not presume that they liked him, but they had gotten used to his presence, and he did not irritate them. He had lost weight through the rigors of traveling, his body becoming leaner and stringier, the untimely rolls of fat dropping from his hips and belly;

it had been days since an acrid sourness had oozed up from his stomach, even the slight irritation in his throat had stopped. A thick layer of skin had formed on the soles of his feet, and his ankles, which had hurt him since he was a small child, were inured to the suffering and did not ache anymore.

As they alighted from the ferry onto the shore they met two Jews who were headed from Sicily to the Italian mainland. Seeing they were also Jewish, they greeted them and demanded with eyes burning that they should repent immediately. They spoke brusquely, holding forth on the now-imminent end of time, which had already begun in Caesarea, and that the Lord's wishes were now evident to one and all: He wanted the end...

But what had happened in Caesarea anyway?

Talking over one another, they explained that the prefect of Caesarea had apparently tried to smuggle some sort of military insignia into Jerusalem at night. He smuggled them into the palace on gilded shields, whereupon the people of Caesarea demonstrated for six days in front of the palace and then occupied the stadium. The prefect had sent in soldiers, who threw themselves to the ground with their arms outstretched and pleaded for death because they could not stand to see such lawlessness, so the prefect got scared, dismissed them, and removed the shields from Jerusalem.

"That's the beginning! Strew ashes on your heads!" one of them cried out before they leapt onto the ferry.

It was amusing to watch these bulky, uniformly bearded and bald-headed men stir their short stumps. There was no reason to rush; they had only just started offloading the ferry, so it would take a good hour or two before the boat set back off. But those two wanted to be on board as early as possible; they were in a hurry.

The travelers watched them blankly. They could not take the return trip just to hear more about the details; they would have had to pay again for boarding the boat.

Matthew guffawed.

"Stark raving mad!" he said.

His companions joined in laughing.

Alexandros had heard that in Judaea, and especially in Galilee, many people these days were awaiting the Last Judgment; false prophets were claiming, with those exact same piercing eyes, that the Messiah was due any day now; their followers were wandering around the two provinces offering purification before the imminent Last Judgment, anointing people with oil or dunking them in water or fasting for weeks in penitence.

"Instead of doing something," he added disparagingly.

"Harmless blockheads," was Matthew's comment. "There was a prophet in Galilee once who made rain during a drought and brought about cures by setting his hands on people. He was stoned in Jerusalem for his troubles, just after Passover, but it was before I was born and the rains didn't come after all."

"That must have been Honi," said Plotius. "He would draw a circle around himself at times of drought and would not step outside it until it rained. He fasted inside the circle, the others outside it, and they would encourage each other... I once met his grandson, he was also named Honi; people thought he was also a miracle worker, and with every drought they would hound him to step inside a circle too, but he did not want to stand in a circle; he was not a sorcerer, he would snarl and hide in the outhouse, and he would not come out for days on end..."

They laughed.

"I have heard exactly the same about a man by the name of Onias," Alexandros said.

"That's the one," Matthew clarified. "In Greek it's Onias; in Aramaic, Honi."

They chartered seven donkeys in the harbor after paying one sestertius per head in municipal duties.

It was no easy matter to bargain with the excise men, because apart from the capital tax they demanded two and a half percent of the value of the luggage. It was useless to say they had nothing of value; not only did they make them unpack the sacks, they also searched their persons. The excise men even examined the tefillin. The tax collectors also examined the cheap and crude clay water jugs, unwilling to believe that this was all they had. When they saw that there really was nothing else, they demanded a further three sesterces per head, but it was impossible to know why. Matthew haggled that down to one sestertius each, and then they could set off.

Matthew laughed: the excise men had not noticed that only six names were on the safe-conduct, and he winked at Uri. Uri did not wink back; he was still unhappy about his name not being on the safe-conduct.

They saw nothing of Messana, that charming little town.

This particular mode of transport was even less comfortable than walking, Uri soon found; his delicate behind was not made for an ass's lumpy back. They rode the donkeys in single file, and as they tried to keep their feet off the ground and steer clear of roadside trees and rocks, they swapped theories about the inhabitants of Judaea and Galilee.

Uri figured that Matthew the boatman, Plotius the joiner, and Alexandros the merchant were all somewhat conversant in Judaean affairs, and the rest as clueless as himself. Apart from vague family myths, he had no idea what life was like and what people believed in Judaea and Galilee.

Alexandros knew the name of the present prefect; he was called Pilatus. He had held the office for nine years, and in those years had quarreled with the Jew just once, when he tried to build a new aqueduct in Jerusalem and had asked for money from the Temple's treasury. The new aqueduct was not built because most of the community had protested, and the high priest did not dare defy them.

"They held demonstrations on the Temple Square," Alexandros confirmed. "The soldiers allegedly attacked the crowd and slaughtered many protesters, but I have not met anyone who was there that evening. It's not customary to slaughter in the Temple Square," he went on. "There is not enough room for a crowd anyway—not near the tabernacle, in any case. I've never managed; it's guarded dearly."

"It's been guarded so tightly," chipped in Valerius, assistant to the archisynagogos, "ever since the Samaritans scattered human ashes around to desecrate the altar."

"When was that?" Uri inquired.

"A long time back," Valerius replied.

"Ten years before the Jews were driven out of Rome," said Matthew. "There was a huge outcry; it was hard to keep some people from overrunning Samaria."

Uri figured this must have been seven years before he was born.

Matthew recounted that Pilatus had embarked upon a major construction project as soon as he was appointed. In Caesarea, it was he who built the sanctuary dedicated to the emperor Tiberius, the Tiberium as it was called, and laying the foundation stone was his first official act. The group could soon see for themselves, he said. It was a massive building, and splendid indeed by Hellenistic standards. He also related that the prefect had wanted a stadium built in Jerusalem also, under the Temple Mount, but the Sanhedrin dissuaded him.

"Whereupon the Sanhedrin," he added with a laugh, "went ahead and built one, and no one protested against that... Not that it would have been possible, because it was converted from a hippodrome by Herod, and they adjusted to that... It is not used very much for anything; there are Greeks living there. It's used to house people during festivals, so it serves that purpose."

He was asked if he had met this Pilatus personally.

He had met him, and more than once; he was a meticulously cautious, straight-talking, easy-mannered man, who wouldn't hurt a fly.

"It is completely out of the question," asserted Matthew, "to think he would try to sneak Roman military standards into Jerusalem."

"Maybe he is unaware that it's forbidden for Jews," Hilarus guessed.

"How could he not know!" Matthew spluttered. "He's been kicking his heels in Judaea for nine years; he knows exactly what is allowed and what's not."

Silence fell. Maybe it would be better, Uri thought, if he does not know our laws, if what those flaming-eyed men said was true.

"I saw him once in Rome," said Alexandros. "Before he was appointed prefect. He was there when I was meeting several of my clients. They told me he was interested in Palestine; he wanted to trade with that part of the world, because he was a knight of the equestrian order."

"An equestrian," Matthew confirmed.

"A knight of the equestrian becoming a prefect?" Uri queried.

"Judaea is a province of the third rank," said Matthew. "Being a knight is sufficient to be sent there."

"As far as I recall," Alexandros continued, "he was not ignorant about our affairs, but that's as it should be, if Tiberius named him prefect. It's a fair bet there were other candidates."

Matthew snorted. Uri saw that he was glancing toward him as he laughed—as if the laughter were directed against him. He did not understand; he shook off his doubts, he had been needlessly oversensitive before.

There was a lull as they rode the donkeys silently, heavy with worry.

"They're lunatics, that's what they are," Matthew broke the silence. "Nothing happened in Caesarea, and nothing forbidden was taken into Jerusalem. They are looking for something to get excited about. Sailors on my ships tell yarns after an uneventful voyage; each one has seen a dozen sirens, and Pluto himself visits them in the company of Proserpina. Judaeans arriving in Ostia have praised the moderation of the present governor. He never meddles and he doesn't try to steal any more than is feasible. Obviously he has business dealings with the high priests; otherwise why would he be prefect in the first place? He must have lined his pockets a fair bit over nine years. Business is booming, so why spoil it? He was only looking to do good with the aqueduct; he was in the right, and not the rabble."

"He wanted to steal from the Temple's treasures," snapped the teacher, Hilarus.

"So what?" Matthew retorted. "That's where they hold the Judaean state wealth. It would have been built for our benefit, wouldn't it? Why shouldn't we give money for a new aqueduct? There is never water for the crowds for feast days! As delegates, we will get water, but what about them? They shove their way into creeks to wash, and then you can't drink the water for weeks! It's Hell on Earth in the Valley of Hinnom... Then it takes weeks more to clear the filth... The

Temple builders are detailed for the job, and meanwhile work on the Temple comes to a stop... Then, before you know, it's time for the next feast and it starts all over again... Not that it isn't marvelous to see that throng," he added dutifully, with an ambivalence that made Uri feel suddenly sick.

Plotius chimed in:

"There's nothing wrong with people in Judaea and Galilee, aside from a few nutcases. Those madmen did not even speak the governor's name. If you ask me, they've probably never seen or even heard of him! What's a good governor when you don't even know his name? They don't know it because things are peaceful; there's been peace for a good while, thanks be to the Lord. People have gotten used to it, and that is just fine with them. You'll soon see for yourselves..."

"No one has a problem with the prefect," Matthew added after a short pause, and then fell silent.

Uri thought he understood what Matthew had meant: the problem was actually with the high priests. And indeed there was a problem. The Hasmoneans had been producing high priests for generations, since Herod the Great had massacred their predecessors. It was not they who killed the families of the previous high priests, it is true, but they had been the beneficiaries of that awful crime, and the people did not forget it. And if they had not forgotten it in Rome, then they certainly hadn't in Judaea.

They soon forgot the two mad Jews and trotted on their way, their backsides bruised, their legs numb.

For Uri, traveling no longer scared him. He could take it, and he stuck it out to the end. By the time he got home, toughened up, a real man, he would kiss his father on the hand for paying for this journey.

ALL OF A SUDDEN, THEY CAUGHT SIGHT OF A TALL, SMOLDERING MOUN-tain to the right; this was Etna. They saw the smoke for three days. Matthew said this was nothing compared to the tabernacle in Jerusalem, they would see. Plotius nodded; it was really that thick. Valerius was all for climbing to the peak, and Alexandros was also game, but the rest overruled them. Uri was also not in the mood to make any needless effort. The soles of his feet had hardened—he continued to carry his sandals slung around his neck—but his feet hurt. Still, they had to walk a few hours each day to give the donkeys some rest, otherwise they would get stubborn; as Matthew said, an ass has brains, and if it sees men going about with a load on their necks, then it wouldn't mind so much doing the same for a few hours. Plotius told a story about an ass that went around reared up on two legs like a man; it could even bray out a few intelligible words, and his companions were flabbergasted, but then Plotius let the cat out of the bag by laughing too soon.

They avoided Catina, as they had no wish to pay duties.

In Syracusa, on the other hand, they paid the duty at the city gate. Matthew knew full well that there were places along the partly ruined city wall where it was possible to scramble over, but it was better not to tempt fate, in case the local guards happened to make their patrol right then.

The urban duties there were also one sestertius per head, but Matthew now had to pay five sesterces per sack; he argued in vain that the practice was illegal, because personal baggage was duty free.

"Of course it's duty free," grinned the chief excise officer as his armed minions rummaged assiduously though their sacks. "Another five sesterces per head, I make it."

"Religious accessories are exempt," Matthew insisted when the soldiers started tinkering with the phylacteries, making them unclean in the process; the thongs would have to be dipped into water later.

"Jugs, however, are subject to taxation," the excise man said.

"They're worth no more than two asses each, and two and a half percent of that is negligible, even if you calculate in quadrans," Matthew asserted.

"Nevertheless," said the excise man. "It still comes to five sesterces per head."

"Then we'll smash them," Matthew said stubbornly. "They're not worth anything anyway. Look, you can see, they're just rough, clunky objects; we can buy replacements later."

The customs officer was not concerned in the least.

"Then you can pay tax on the shards," he said. "And there will be an additional fee of five sesterces per head for clean up."

With a scowl, Matthew got out the leather pouch from under his cloak and counted the money out into the outstretched hand of the customs chief, who laughed and gave him a friendly pat on the shoulder.

Uri once again started ruminating on where they might be keeping the untold amount of cash they were supposedly carrying to Jerusalem for Passover. There was no money anywhere to be seen. Maybe others were carrying it and had arrived a long time ago. Or else there was a sack rolled up around Matthew's body, under his tunic. He did not understand why Matthew had argued with the excise man, as the customs officials were in the habit of frisking people. It couldn't be around his back anyway; when they had taken their dip in the sea at Messana he had been wearing nothing but a loincloth.

It occurred to Uri in retrospect that the customs officials in Syracusa had not examined the letter of safe-conduct either. Matthew had been proven right; it did not matter that only six delegates, not seven, were listed.

He was excited and disappointed all at the same time. From the crumbling city wall, this did not seem like the magnificent town that Archimedes had defended with his splendid inventions and where, while doodling in the dust, he had been knifed in the back by an idiot. Where was the spot? he wondered. Had anyone put up a memorial tablet?

The donkeys were returned. The local operator of the donkey-hire business, a Cretan scoundrel, wouldn't accept the animals, claiming they were in poor condition, but he could be persuaded by a fairly stiff extra payment, which Matthew bargained down by half. Some debate arose among the companions as to why it was necessary to turn in the donkeys, and to make an additional payment when they had already paid once; after all, they could have just left them unclaimed at the harbor—that was the consensus. Matthew, for his part, began to yell at them for the first time on the journey: he had connections with the firm that went back decades, and however crooked they might be, he could not leave the donkeys to their fate, as that would not fetch the price of a nettle patch. If he did that, they would rent anything to him again, and they would give him a bad name in Italia and throughout the East.

The plan was to sail the next day, but two of the departures had been nixed on account of a couple of storms, and there were others who had made it there earlier. Matthew cursed, but there was nothing he could do about it; he had no luck bribing the harbor authority that booked the passengers, for they were quite happy to take his money but were unable to secure a ship. So after going to great lengths, he rented a warehouse for the night.

They slept on the bare ground with rats, mice, fleas, mosquitoes, and other living creatures for company, but at least they had a roof over their heads. They had to leave the store the next morning, because three shiploads were expected from Alexandria. No matter how much Matthew howled at the representatives of the port authority, they were not going to travel that day either, and were obliged to find somewhere to spend another night.

Matthew found a cheap basement, but Valerius, the hyperetes, was unhappy with it and haughtily stalked off, leaving his sack behind in a huff. Consequently Hilarus, the teacher, also declared that he would not spend another night in the shit—he wasn't just anyone, he was a teacher. He tossed his sack over his shoulder and started off, but Matthew unexpectedly socked him on the jaw, took the sack, and sat down on it. Not sure what else to do, the rest just lingered around the enormous harbor, where life went on as normal and no one took the least notice of them.

"You're not going to go mutinous on me," Matthew yelled. "Anyone who mutinies, I'll kill!"

Hilarus, weeping, wiped his nose and asked, "Why did you let him go? Why did you let him go?"

"Because I'll lodge a complaint against him back home," Matthew continued to yell. "And they'll kick him out of the synagogue so fast his feet won't touch the ground!"

Uri would have liked to side with Matthew, that resolute and staunch man whom he had admired up until then, even though they had barely spoken. He, the weak kid, would have liked to defend the strong man, only he had no idea what to say or do in this situation, so he too just faltered mutely, at a loss.

Hilarus acquiesced and stayed. They trudged into the cellar, locking the door behind them with a great many chains (the locks and chains were fortuitously lying in a corner, as if waiting for them), and then went off to eat.

On Matthew's suggestion, everyone took his jug along to fill with wine later. Led by Matthew, who knew perfectly well how to handle an unruly crew and blessed power of a decent meal, they traipsed into a tavern—grubby though it might have been, packed with whores and hideous characters from any number of harbors on the Great Sea, the wine was good—after which they went to the market, bought some fish and drank more wine, before having their jugs filled and heading out to the pier to keep drinking. They got tighter than Uri ever imagined was possible, any more than he expected that one day he would puke in the sea. He did that at Syracusa, however; Iustus, the stonemason, held his forehead. Blessed be Syracusa forever, Amen! Even if there was nowhere for them to bake the fish, so by the morning it stank and had to be thrown away.

They woke up with splitting headaches in that basement, the cellar of a formerly rich man's burnt-out villa, where a vinegary fluid was leaking from buckled containers, as it probably had been for years, when Valerius returned contritely. His face and neck were covering by angry red scratches and bites. Matthew acknowledged him with a nod and then went off to the harbor to plot a passage for them somehow; they agreed to meet on the pier.

They locked up the basement and went off to the pier, where a tall lighthouse stood; at the top was a small chamber where flares burned constantly, and, according to the locals, inside the tower was a spiral staircase. As they waited, they struck up a conversation with some other idlers, who gradually let on that the reason for the delays was probably more serious than a mere storm: the

Greeks were having their way with the Jewish fleet's gullible new local representative (the previous one had been replaced, maybe because he filched too much). The harbor's military commander, a centurion, favored the Greeks; the Jews had obviously not greased his palm sufficiently.

The Jews were having some trouble nowadays—that was the general view of the Latini, Greeks, Syrians, Gauls, and Spaniards. When asked why, they answered with incredible stories about a revolt in Caesarea and some sort of uprising in Jerusalem. About how the Jews in Jerusalem had clashed, they said, with a Roman legion and made off with their battle standards, which were now under guard at Temple, in the innermost shrine. And how the Jews had wanted to stone the Roman prefect at a chariot race in Caesarea, and the prefect barely escaped with his life. Syracusa's Greeks and Latini and Syrians and Arabs and Abyssinians and others regaled them with these and other ridiculous stories.

The Jews could not take Roman military banners into the Temple in Jerusalem. Just one person, the high priest, was allowed in the innermost sanctum at all, and even he only once a year, on Yom Kippur, the Day of Atonement, which was in the autumn, whereas now it was almost spring. It was just as farfetched to imagine that the Jews would want to stone the governor at a chariot race in the stadium; besides, the guards would have clearly been able to see the stones in the spectators' hands. All the same, these rumors were unsettling; something had undoubtedly happened in Judaea, and that was exactly where they were headed.

When Matthew found them at the lighthouse, they began to grill him on what he knew. Matthew admitted that the delay was probably not caused by reported storms; no Jewish ships had arrived in recent days from the port of Caesarea, even though the sea was calm, as the Greek boats that had called in at Caesarea could attest; and it was, indeed, true that the Jewish fleet had a new local representative, the old one had been replaced and the new man was rather feeble, but the military commander was not biased toward the Greeks, and anyway he, Matthew, had already bribed him twice; and how was a Roman centurion supposed to put Jewish ships ahead of the Greeks if none had called in for days now?

"Wouldn't we be better off on a Greek ship?" Iustus asked.

That was not such a bad idea; more than a few Greek ships had set off for Caesarea over the past two days, with two of them calling in at Crete. But Matthew still shook his head. The Greeks were asking exorbitant fares, and then there was the risk of getting robbed en route. They needed to find a Jewish boat; no Jews would not dare to fleece once they found out this was the delegation.

"Do you mean that if we weren't, then they would?" Uri inquired.

"We're no worse than other pirate peoples," Matthew replied in a superior tone.

They all laughed, and when it was time for the noonday prayer, they all beseeched the Lord to finally send a few Jewish ships to dock in Syracusa.

Three boats did arrive soon after, but these were from Alexandria, and they were going back there; two were Greek and one Jewish. They talked with the Greek sailors. They had also heard about a furor in Jerusalem, but they thought it was highly unlikely that the local governor had ordered Roman army standards to be taken into the Temple Square. The Jewish protest would follow immediately, as he was well aware; more likely, it was an overzealous regimental commander. Several of them had heard that someone resembling Tiberius had also been taken into the Temple. Others disputed that; apparently the Jews had written a letter to Tiberius about the matter, or at least the Jewish high priest in Alexandria had done so, the president of the Alexandrian Sanhedrin, the council of Elders, Alexander the gerusiarch and also alabarchos. It was also reported that Alexander, the head of the Jews in Alexandria, said that the emperor would almost certainly reprimand the prefect, maybe even relieve him of his office, because he was not prepared to see the Pax Romana threatened in the provinces. The Alexandrian Jewish sailors spoke highly of Alexander, whereas the priestly clans of Jerusalem were worthless, an opinion they made clear, although not in so many words. The Roman delegation also grasped from the Alexandrian Jews that they should feel shame that their city didn't have a house of prayer like the Basilica in Alexandria, which rivaled the Temple in Jerusalem—not that their co-religionists from Alexandria mentioned a single word about it. But as far as thinking goes, they were almost certainly thinking that—so surmised the Roman Jews. Plotius fancied he knew for sure that Alexander did not stem from a priestly family but was a descendant of common Jewish slaves who had settled in Egypt, so he was not rightfully entitled to the title of priest: a gerusiarch and alabarchos, yes, but in no way a priest. These Greeks were ignorant.

"What's an alabarchos?" queried Iustus.

"The customs and excise chief," Plotius answered.

Matthew tried to persuade the seemingly sympathetic Jewish captain to sail back to Alexandria via Caesarea, offering quite a substantial sum of money, but the captain spread his arms in a gesture of powerlessness: he sailed on a timetable, and he could not account for the four-day delay that such a detour would cause. It wouldn't work, even if he could pick up a valuable cargo at Caesarea:

there was room on the ship, but Judaea produced nothing that would be worth taking to Alexandria.

Matthew disputed that, whereupon the captain inquired why there was no regular boat traffic between Caesarea and Alexandria.

In Matthew's opinion it was the excise rates in Alexandria, which were outrageously high and were exacted impudently on ships coming from Judaea.

The captain, being an Alexandrian Jewish patriot, held the view that this was proper; he had visited Jerusalem, and the two-drachma toll that they collected from every pilgrim was typical of the brazen extortion in Jerusalem. They made their living from fleecing pilgrims; a fee of two drachmas that was also collected for using a vessel of clean water, a mikveh, as though smaller coins were not in circulation over there, and anyone who is proven not to have ritually cleansed themselves for six days, which means twelve drachmas, is not permitted to enter Temple Square. Lodgings were also overpriced, because cheap rooms had to be booked at least a year in advance, and that was not possible for a sailor. Food was cheap, no argument there, but on the other hand it was lousy.

The indignant captain proposed that they come with him to Alexandria, and go from there over dry land to Judaea; he would take them on his ship cheaply, and the next day at that. Uri was keen to see the marvelous city of Alexandria, but Matthew did not take up the opportunity; in his view the delay would undermine their mission, and moreover he had never made the journey from Alexandria to Judaea by foot, nor did he wish to. He had no wish to ride a camel, and anyway he would not take the responsibility, because he had met people who had completed the journey with extreme difficulty and had come within a hair's breadth of death. The Nile was unnavigable close to Alexandria. They needed to get to Nicopolis somehow and board a ship there. They would have to disembark at Thmuis and go east on foot. It was inconceivable that they would not pass through Heracleopolis and Pelusium, yet excise dues in those cities were undoubtedly high. Only at Pelusium would they be able to ford the Nile, and that was where the desert began; even at a forced march, it would take eight to ten days over arid land to reach Gaza—that is, if they did not die of thirst. Only a well-equipped military unit on iron rations or a major commercial caravan could take on the overland route from Alexandria to Judaea, not a delegation a few strong that was just delivering money.

Iustus was amazed that a navigable channel between the Nile and the port of Alexandria had not been constructed already.

"If even the Pharaohs did not build one," Plotius ventured, "there can be only one reason."

"And what would that be?" Iustus asked.

The others snickered, Uri included, because they knew the answer: it would have cost too much even for the Pharaohs who built the pyramids. Iustus took offense and spoke to no one for the rest of the day.

Alexandros maintained that the Pharaohs had the money to make the Nile navigable up to the seacoast, but they did not want to make it easy for their enemies, by capturing the seacoast, to penetrate into the heart of the country. It was an opinion that surprised Uri, and he looked pensively at Alexandros, the merchant.

The next day, Matthew went off early "to arrange matters"; the other six knocked around aimlessly on the pier. Hilarus, the teacher, took the line that they too ought to do something because, to their shame, they were going to miss Passover in Jerusalem.

Matthew is a great man, but he ought to be pressing harder for us to set sail, he thought.

In Plotius's opinion, they had only lost three days, and, since they had set off early, they were still safely within their two-week margin of error, even allowing for six Sabbaths altogether.

Hilarus proposed that they choose from among themselves a deputy leader who would give orders when Matthew was not around.

Alexandros, being a seasoned traveler, immediately volunteered, with Iustus taking his side. Valerius recommended Hilarus. Everyone now turned expectantly to Uri, and he sought eye contact with Plotius, who was staring into the distance.

The tension between them suddenly mounted; Uri did not understand it. If he were to come out for Hilarus or Alexandros, Plotius could do nothing to block the selection of a deputy leader besides plumping for the other, in which case there would be a tie and nothing would happen. But then why choose a deputy leader when he would have no more idea where to start than any of the others? Besides, Matthew would turn up soon anyway.

Plotius broke the silence: he announced that he was going off to think until the evening. Hilarus started yelling about what would happen if a ship were suddenly ready to leave; where would Plotius be found?

"There will be no ship ready to go by evening," said Plotius, "because even if a boat arrives, it will have to be unloaded then loaded, and it will not leave before tomorrow morning."

On that note, he left and walked off along the pier toward town.

They looked at Uri for the decisive vote. He sighed and said that he too wanted to think it over, and he hurried after Plotius.

Plotius was strolling slowly, as if he had been waiting. When Uri caught up, he nodded. They vanished together among the houses.

"It's remarkable how many morons there are in the world," Plotius declared as they passed through an alley. "One can't give them their way on everything, but it's best not to pick fights with them either. They can't help being morons; the Creator, in His infinite wisdom, wills it so."

Uri was amazed to hear such a thing from Plotius, the joiner, who had barely spoken a single word the entire trip, yet Plotius was speaking directly to him, who had likewise held his tongue for the most part.

They took a seat at the back of a tavern; they did not settle down on the street, like the locals, because the sun was shining fiercely. Plotius did not mince words. He came straight out and asked Uri how he managed to get himself squeezed into the delegation as a supernumerary at the last minute.

Uri told him frankly that the whole thing was a gift that his father had extracted from Agrippa in return for an immense loan, but he was glad about it because it suggested that his father still considered him his son, even though he had poor eyesight and was useless at everything. Plotius nodded. He had noticed that Uri did not see well but thought he could still make it as a joiner. Then Uri told the story about falling off the roof on his first day of work, at which Plotius chortled: only someone trying very hard would fall off. Uri protested, but Plotius brushed that aside. The mind knows what we want better than we do.

Plotius ordered wine and set down a pitcher, and again Uri protested: he didn't drink. Plotius urged him on, so Uri took a sip. The wine tasted good; it was heavily honeyed.

"Have you got your own money?" Uri asked with surprise.

"Everybody has some," Plotius admitted, "except you."

Uri pondered for a moment, then he asked what Plotius had meant when he called him the supernumerary.

"The decision is made weeks in advance," he said, "as to who will be in the delegation. Not a word was said about you till the very last moment. We couldn't really figure out why a feeble young boy had been foisted on us."

Uri quietly sipped he wine.

"This is a dangerous mission," Plotius declared. "Never mind getting there, but on the way back we shall be carrying a lot more money. Enough to make it really worth killing for."

"What do you mean?"

"Just that going there we are only taking sacrificial money, but going back we shall be taking the money that our Elders use to grease the palms of the Roman authorities to give rights of Roman or Italian citizenship to the rich of Judaea. They come through too!"

Uri was dumbfounded.

It was not the Romans who distributed citizenship rights to the inhabitants of the provinces; members of the Sanhedrin in Jerusalem and their families were legally excluded from the circle of potential Roman citizens. In principle, a subject of Judaea or Galilee could never become a Roman or Italian citizen, and that went for Syrians and Egyptians as well.

Yet there was a way nonetheless—and how else but with money!

How else but with money. That was the expression his father had used when he was obliged to enter the silk business.

Only half of their mission was exalted, then, and the smaller half at that, it appeared.

But how did the joiner know all this?

Uri gulped his wine and stayed quiet. It did not enter his mind to ask if they really were taking the sacrificial money as Plotius says, where it could actually be.

The joiner had a good profession: he could work anywhere at all in Rome outside the Jewish quarter, and because houses often burned down, there was always work and it paid decently as well. It was this prospect of a bright future with which his father had tried to persuade him to become a roofer, it being easier than joinery; it involved no more than placing tiles or slates onto and alongside each other. Plotius must have picked up several languages in the course of his work, as his employers might belong to any nation, so he must have heard all kinds of things along the way. He might be on good terms with individual Roman Elders, including bankers, having worked for them; these days huge houses were being built just to be rented out.

"Do all the others know about this?" Uri asked.

"I suspect they do," said Plotius. "We get a small commission; after all, we earn it. We'll be nicely paid off."

Uri said nothing, just sipped his wine.

Plotius broke out in laughter.

"It's not what you would call nice," he admitted, "but if a delegation is carrying money over there, why let it go back empty-handed? On top of which we also have a safe-conduct."

"Who gives us the money, then?"

"It doesn't matter," said Plotius. "One day someone will come from the prefect with a fair-sized sack that jingles. We won't be hard to spot, even in that colossal mass of people. We are an important delegation."

"Why from the prefect?"

"Because he has been getting a taste too."

Uri pondered: so that's how it went.

"Have you done similar work before?" he quizzed.

"No, but I've heard that's the way it's done."

"So does the person in question also hand over a list of who is to be granted citizenship in Rome?"

"I very much doubt something like that gets put down in writing. They'll tell the names to someone with a good memory, and he'll register them; there won't be many names to learn—twenty or thirty at most."

"I've got a good memory," Uri said with pride. "If I read something once, then I have it down perfectly, word for word."

"You're exactly the sort I would expect that from," said Plotius.

Uri picked up a note of sarcasm in his tone and felt a trifle ashamed of himself. Boasting again. Fat good it was his father warning him.

He appreciated Plotius's candor. Maybe the Lord had arranged this delay in Syracusa so that Uri would finally learn something about his companions.

He would have liked to ask a few other things about the whole setup but he did not dare. Plotius guessed what he was thinking.

"The carriers to Rome do not usually give the names of anyone except those who have actually paid," he said. "It's not possible to squeeze in anyone who has not paid. That sort of thing comes to light sooner or later, and the consequences would be serious. There's a tariff for everything; you can't gain citizenship free of charge. Just think how lucky we are; we acquired Roman citizenship because it was tossed our way when we were kind enough to be born."

Uri nodded in agreement. He really had been lucky; he had to thank his grandfather, who perished in the effort to free himself for his grandson, whom he never saw, to become a Roman with full rights of citizenship.

"So Judaean Jews who are full Roman citizens and therefore no longer taxed can move to Italia without hindrance," he deduced wisely.

"That's not the point," said Plotius. "They still have to pay all the Jewish taxes, and they cannot leave the province that they have been living in up till now without special permission, but they do escape the control of the Sanhedrin and fall under Roman jurisdiction. The Jewish authority has no powers over them; it cannot even arrest them but has to turn to the prefect responsible for the matter, who is a long way away. The Roman municipal administration sends the prefect the official list of new Roman and Italian citizens if they happened to live in Judaea; from that moment they cannot be touched by Jewish courts. That is what the real point is, because that is a legal security that does not otherwise exist in Judaea. That is priceless."

Uri was astounded.

"There was a time once in Jerusalem," Plotius continued, "when I was arraigned, and not to get hauled up before the Sanhedrin I had to prove that I was a Roman citizen. I told them, and they were so scared they backed right off, did not dare lay a finger on me, though they kept me under close observation and I was unable to leave the city. So I wrote to the prefect in Caesarea, and they got an answer two and a half weeks later that I genuinely was a Roman citizen. Letters between Caesarea and Rome get a response in a fortnight because of the state diplomatic bag. As a result the Jews were forced to leave me alone."

"What were you accused of?"

"I don't recall," said Plotius.

Uri had the sense to let it go at that.

Then Plotius said something else to which Uri did not pay any attention at the time, adding with a smile, "The mail in Rome is slower than the Jewish. News gets from Jerusalem to Antioch in a day and a half at most, because it is passed on by beacons on hilltops; it might take only a day, but one is best advised to avoid Samaria, because those scum light interfering flares to make it impossible to read messages."

It felt good to idle about in the dark at the back of the tavern; Uri could dimly see colorful figures moving past on the sunlit street, many carrying the same sort of sportulas as they did in Rome, which indicated that here there were likewise patrons and clients, just fewer of them; they were the spitting image of the sportulas in Rome. Evidently Rome dictated the fashions—something that filled Uri with pride. There, inside, he looked at Plotius's cheerful, mocking, deeply lined face over a thick, unkempt, black beard. He could see that nearby face well, and because he could make it out well, to him it felt familiar. If he did not know he was a Jew and Plotius were to shave his face, anyone might easily take it to be the profile of a Roman noble, complete with dignified aquiline nose in the middle. His baldness was utterly Roman in character. It would be worth having him sit as a model for a bust of a Latin patrician; more than likely there had been patrician blood flowing in the veins of his slave grandfather or great-grandfather.

The wine loosened Uri's reticence, and he asked Plotius about his trade.

Plotius recounted that he earned his living as a joiner. It did not pay badly; indeed, after a commission in Jerusalem a few years ago he had been hired to build villas for the rich in the Roman style, and he accepted because he had learned all the house-building tricks of the trade back at home, in Rome. In recent times massive new villas had been going up in the center of Jerusalem; they were so big and splendid that they vied with the best in Rome, and not a few of them were graced by his own handiwork; he would show Uri later. Well-off Jews were willing to pay to be able to display their wealth in the city center, above all in the fashionable upper city, rather than on the outskirts. *Homo novus*, the lot of them, he added contemptuously. He had spent years building villas in Jerusalem, being passed on by personal recommendation from one satisfied customer to the next, and they did pay handsomely, whereas he hardly spent anything because the cost of living in Jerusalem was incredibly low, as compared with Rome.

"Are they rich merchants?"

"No," said Plotius. "Landowners."

Vast latifundia—estates—had come into existence in Judaea over the past decade or two since peace had been secured, because the first-born sons who had inherited land were generally unable to come to terms with the other siblings about how that land should be divided, so generally the land would be sold and the money split up, with everyone getting very little, as a result of which they would move into town and become homeless plebs; for that reason the supply of land had swollen so much that it was only possible to sell at prices well below its true value. In other words, the same thing was happening in Judaea as in Italia, the only difference being that in Palestine the land was communal in principle; that is, it was supposed to be redistributed every fifty years, but that had long not been the case, and as a result there was even more ownerless land in Palestine ripe for stealing.

Anyone who had any capital to invest put it into land, including the families of the high priests, even though in principle they were forbidden to do so. They did not buy in their own names, but the land was nevertheless theirs; by now three quarters of Judaea was the personal property of members of families of the high priests, and they sold bits of this on at huge premiums to others, including Romans, even though it was not permitted to sell any part of the Holy Land to non-Jews. Then again, land was supposed to be left fallow for one year in seven to let it recover, but nobody did that.

"There's not one law that is not transgressed in Judaea," asserted Plotius. "That's true in Rome too: every law is transgressed if people can get away with it, but it's even easier for them to get away with it in Judaea."

Uri inquired why Plotius did not stay in Judaea if things were going so well for him. Had his family called him back, perhaps?

"I've got a wife and I also have a son—Plotius Fortunatus, he's called. But I don't see them often, and I don't miss them very much," said Plotius. "They have gotten used to the fact that this is my line of work, it's not they who are the reason. The fact is that Judaea is of no interest; Jerusalem is a hole. It is said that the Temple will be magnificent when it's ready, but that's just tripe; there is nothing to see of it, it's been surrounded by scaffolding for decades. The crowds that flock there during festivals are just appalling, to say nothing of the infectious diseases they carry! Jerusalem is tedious; there's nothing to do, just a bunch of whores—and those are all wretched: even they are no pleasure at all. Even the Transtiberim is more interesting than Jerusalem, where nothing ever happens or ever will!"

"It did now."

Plotius gestured dismissively.

"Protests are always going on, especially around feast days, when any number of crazies flood into the city, but then the Jewish watchmen easily deal with them. I don't know if mercenaries really did take military standards into the Temple, but even if they did, the stink was raised in Caesarea, not in Jerusalem, and that's a Greek town, not ours, never will be, for all that Jews make up the majority who reside there these days."

"All the same, the boats are not sailing for some reason," Uri offered.

"There are other times they don't sail either," said Plotius. "Twice already I have spent weeks in Syracusa waiting for a boat and almost died of boredom. There are not many items of Jewish produce that are worth shipping to Italia. Dates you can get elsewhere, and balsam is not something that sells in big amounts; wood is about all that's worth trading. Whole forests are being felled in Palestine for Rome; they tend to ship the timber to Judaea, and they don't like ships coming over here empty. So they wait there until a cargo of some sort is finally collected. Or enough people collected."

Uri did not understand, and Plotius was somewhat surprised that he had to explain this too:

"Spies. They're important people, and they have money. They come from Syria, Babylon, Armenia—wherever. They carry military and commercial information. We're important as well, because we shall be carrying a big sum of money on the return journey. It will be easy finding a boat to Caesarea for the return journey: we'll have enough money to make it worth the captain's while even with an empty hold. Here in Syracusa there are lots of goods to pack in, and he will be happy making the trip back because they're things that people will buy in Judaea. But if there happens to be no Jewish ship in the harbor here, we shan't be able to persuade anyone to take us. What are they going to bring back?

Nothing. Any timber that has accumulated there will be picked up eventually by our boat: it will take time for the next forest to be felled."

Uri mused.

"Could it be that we won't make it to Judaea in time?"

"Never fear!" assured Plotius. "From Caesarea we'll be able to make it to Jerusalem in four days, even crawling on our bellies, it's only two hundred stadia or so. Something is bound to come along sooner or later."

Uri cogitated; this fellow impressed him. He went on to ask, "What made you become a member of the delegation?"

Plotius did not reply immediately.

"I've got things to do in Judaea," he said finally. "And you'll be paying for my trip—you Roman Jews, I mean."

"And how did that work out? Did you apply to the archisynagogos, and he put your name forward?"

Plotius laughed.

"No, it doesn't go like that... I started by knocking on the doors of the rich people in my congregation... I made it in their interest... There's the rotation thing, isn't there, and even though I had not yet been a delegate, some individuals from my family had been, and not so long ago either... I made it onto the list at the last moment, maybe even later than you... I promised them something by way of business."

So there was someone else who had been squeezed in as an afterthought, not just him; maybe most of them had. So they have no reason to be hostile toward me, Uri realized with relief.

They got back to the pier that evening; their companions were all there, Matthew included. They were right in the middle of an excited discussion. Matthew had located a boat repairer who had a bireme standing ready and waiting in his shipyard, and its owner would only be coming two weeks later to pick it up, until which time the boat was free to come and go between Syracusa and Caesarea. The boat master was secretly inclined to make the boat available and would even ask to be paid for the return trip, because even so he would be better off than if the boat—it was not his anyway—sat in the docks; he was even ready to rustle up free of charge the oarsmen and officers needed, though of course they would need to be paid both ways by the delegation. He was, however, asking for a deposit: half the value of the boat, which of course he would hand back when they got to Syracusa on the return journey.

"I have no vote in this," Matthew announced. "I have no interest in the matter. You lot decide."

There were two extreme factions, one represented by Hilarus, the other by Alexandros, who contended with each other. Hilarus was supported by Valerius, and Alexandros by Iustus, just like that morning.

Hilarus was of the opinion that the offer should be accepted, but the deposit should be whittled down and a legally watertight contract established. Alexandros, however, felt that this was all nonsense: what was meant by "a legally watertight contract" anyway? There was no such thing as entering an unassailable contract over the use of an inanimate object if the underwriting party was not the owner.

Hilarus said that one had to understand the ship repairer; he probably knew that the boat was insured for half its value. The master was only asking for what he would get if the boat was wrecked and he could claim that the boat had sunk, or it had not gotten back in time, or it had been stolen. Anyway it fell within the allowed expenditure, he asserted. He looked inquiringly at Matthew, who shook his head to signal not only that he was not voting but also that he was not prepared to offer any information about the delegation's financial standing either.

Alexandros outlined what would happen if the officers and slaves recruited by the master builder understood nothing about sailing, which there was every chance of:

"The only ones who will do any rowing in rough seas are us, the seven of us, twenty-four hours a day, and long before we ran the ship aground and drowned as it went down, our hearts—by the grace of the Lord—would burst."

Uri shuddered.

Hilarus for his part believed that was also nonsense. If the captain proved unsuitable, Matthew would take over command; after all, that was his expertise. He again looked at Matthew, who again shook his head. Hilarus added, "We're just as capable of dishing out lashes as any officer!"

Uri shuddered. He had not the slightest wish to lash out at sculling slaves.

Valerius and Iustus offered affirmative or opposing grunts but no opinions.

All looked at Plotius.

It's almost as if I were not even here, Uri thought sullenly to himself.

Plotius deliberated.

"What's the boat like?" he queried.

"It looks up to the job," said Matthew.

"And if we were to buy it, would we be able to sell it?"

Uri did not grasp what Plotius was driving at, but the others understood.

"That's it!" Hilarus exclaimed. "We buy it here, take it across and sell it there for a decent profit."

"Fair enough, but to whom?" Matthew asked.

There was silence.

"Let's say we buy it," Matthew said. "That's a good idea. The master ship builder will sell it cheaper than the owner would; the master will make up some tale for the latter and recover some damages for him, and even so he will make a bundle on it without having to do a lick of work. That's fine so far. Even the owner doesn't make out badly, because it's far from certain that he really did insure it for half its value. The world is full of fake shipping calamities: insurers have a hard time proving that fraud had a hand in them; the owner not only gets the full value from the insurer, but even makes a profit on it—the payoff he gets from the master. That too is fair enough. It is also possible that the proprietor and the master are in collusion against the insurer: let them make a bit, and let the insurers lose out, the jerks. We get it across somehow or other—that too is fair enough. But who exactly is going to purchase it from us in Caesarea?"

Silence.

"There must be someone," said Hilarus despondently. The teacher was longing for a big adventure, and it pained him that nothing would come of it.

"You haven't so much as asked Uri," said Plotius.

The others stared at him, and Uri flushed. Nobody gave a cordial look; he had to say something.

"I don't know a thing about boats," Uri protested. "I don't know anything about most things. I'm deeply sorry that someone worthier than me did not come with you instead of me."

"The Lord created everyone worthy," said Plotius. "He created the brute ignorant animals because He had a purpose with them. It is not for us to guess the Creator's reasons but to accept His disposals. So what do you have to say?"

He would have to say something after all.

"Isn't there anyone over there for whom a ship like that would come in handy?" he ventured. "The Jewish navy perhaps..."

"No doubt they would be happy to take one as a free gift," Matthew nodded vigorously. "They might even purchase it, albeit at a rock-bottom price. It's not just that—there's no way I could account for a loss like that, I could not even fiddle my way around it."

Silence.

"What about the Romans?" Uri ventured.

Matthew snorted, and the others joined in the laughter.

"The Romans would take the boat over well and good," Plotius explained. "But they would clap us in irons on the grounds that we had stolen it, and they'd hand us over to the Sanhedrin to pass sentence. No one among the Jerusalem Elders would come to our defense; we would be rowing in chains till the end of our days."

Uri flared up:

"But we're the delegation! We have safe conduct! We're Roman citizens!"

Plotius stepped up to him and patted him on the shoulder.

"Dear boy, the Sanhedrin nurtures extremely good relations with the Romans," he said. "And so it should. That's what peace is, the Lord be praised. Naturally, a few people would hotfoot it from Rome to Judaea on our behalf, and the beloved members of our families would never forsake us, and they would protest till they were blue in the face in every forum that the Sanhedrin had no power of jurisdiction over Roman citizens, and our loved ones would be able to prove that sooner or later, after which the Roman authorities would move Heaven and Earth to have us tracked down; that would take half a year, a year, or even more; and by the time they found us we would long since have croaked in a galley boat, maybe the very one that we offered for purchase to the Romans."

Uri still did not give up:

"The Sanhedrin cannot pass judgment on Roman citizens! You yourself said so!"

Plotius groaned.

"Dear boy, the Sanhedrin is stuffed with the high priest's placemen. The high priest is appointed by the Roman prefect, and he can replace him whenever he likes without even having to give a justification. In matters that are not religious the high priest dances whatever jig the prefect whistles, and his placemen dance in turn to his whistle. You don't seriously believe that the high priest would not take seriously thousands of sesterces from the Romans to keep quiet about them filching a ship with Jewish owners? He'd get the full price of the boat—maybe even more."

"But that's corruption!" Hilarus explained.

"In plain Latin," Matthew nodded his agreement.

They fell silent. Plotius next said, turning to Uri but with the others paying close attention:

"For all that, I am wholeheartedly in full support of whoever is the current high priest in Jerusalem and the Sanhedrin, whatever mischief they might get up to, because they are better by far than those madmen who impair their authority and threaten the peace, our faith, and the very existence of the Jewish people with their muddy ideas and sick notions."

THEY EXAMINED THE BOAT IN QUESTION THE NEXT DAY, BUT THEY HAD to admit that it was too large for them, and postponed any decision for another day on the off chance that something would happen. They had to move out of the basement, but they found a deserted building that was in ruins beside the crumbling city wall, and cleared out the ground floor. It was none too secure a place, but it cost nothing and was close to the harbor. They decided that three of them would stay "at home" at all times, and the others would keep an eye on movements and staying up to date.

As he went around the city Uri marveled at how such a significant port could be in such a state of neglect. It was not just that the city wall had collapsed in many places; most of the shrines could have done with a major overhaul.

He came to a halt in front of a papyrus notice stuck to one of the walls.

Matthew also came to a halt.

It was an announcement that the famous Makedonios would be appearing tomorrow at the amphitheater and expounding his theses in person.

Uri became very excited.

"I've got two of his works back at home," he said. "He's witty. It would be good to listen to him."

Matthew said nothing.

"It costs eight asses at the theater," Uri said. "That's what is written here."

"I can see," said Matthew. "Not exactly cheap."

"Wouldn't it be a good idea to go and hear him?"

Matthew goggled at him. Uri could see that he was astounded even though there was no rule to forbid a Jew from listening to a non-Jewish philosopher expounding his theses; after all, he was not a priest of some strange rite.

"I'd like to listen to him," Uri persisted stubbornly.

"Well, then, listen," said Matthew, and resumed walking.

Uri hurried after him.

"I have no money," he said. "Lend me eight asses. I'll give it back in Rome."

Matthew stopped, reached under his toga, pulled out the little pouch that he carried tied to his back, took out a sestertius, and offered it to Uri.

Uri hesitated.

"Take it!" said Matthew. "One day you'll come to my place in Ostia and you'll invite me out to drink a jar of wine in the best tavern."

Uri thanked him and took the coin from him.

He prayed that a ship would not come just yet. The prayer was heard, and in the afternoon of the following day he handed the money over to the guards at the entrance to the amphitheater and waited for the change. The guards shoved him on, and he was also pushed from behind by others who were seeking to enter, so he was obliged to carry on. Given that one sestertius was worth sixteen asses, he had lost eight asses—and that would have come in handy. He would have fastened it to his loincloth and not spent it, happy in the knowledge that he could do so any time.

There were thirty rows running around the amphitheater. Uri had arrived early so as to be able to take a seat in one of the front rows because from farther back there was no chance of his being able to see the speaker. He hoped he would come close to the audience. The amphitheater was not quite full, but still there was a decent audience, and Uri was relieved to note that there were some other Jews among them. He would make a note of that to Matthew, who seemed to disapprove of his interest in pagan philosophy.

In the center of the space enclosed by the semicircles stood a platform assembled from planks, at the back of which were five steps leading up to it, so the speaker would step up there, perhaps on account of the acoustics. If Uri were to sit a few rows higher, he would be able to see over the landscape to the sea—at least its blueness, if not the horizon. But he wanted a seat near the podium.

It was a pleasant early spring afternoon. A small group appeared in the arena, four men carrying a lectica on which the philosopher was seated. His bald brow was adorned with a wreath of laurels. He was a burly, red-haired man, as Uri could see clearly from the second row, because the litter was carried around past the first row, and the philosopher waved happily to the spectators, who shouted words of encouragement toward him as if they were attending a chariot race. Servants hurried behind, including a scampering manikin.

His physician, people in the crowd commented, goes with him everywhere and if necessary will even open a vein while he is orating. An outstanding doctor; learned his craft at the feet of Celsus, no less.

Uri looked on disappointedly as the burly philosopher, supported by two servants, made his way with great difficulty up the steps to the platform. Even though the folds of the toga were nicely arranged on the ground, somehow it still sat badly on him, pushed out on both sides by his huge misshapen hips. On the basis of the scrolls, Uri had pictured someone with quite a different exterior: a tall, angular figure with sharp features, a pointed nose, irreverently flashing eyes. This man had a turned-up nose and drooping eyes. Admittedly, Socrates also had a totally deformed head; his pug-nosed bust stood in the Capitoline along with all the other Greek greats, whose exteriors were similarly unprepossessing with the sole exception of the dashing Euripides.

The crowd was noisy; a small table was placed on the platform next to the philosopher and an amphora, which may well have contained wine. The servants stood in a semicircle at the back, sunk into reverent immobility; the physician hung around next to the platform. The philosopher raised his right hand; a hush fell on the crowd. Then the philosopher spoke, his deep, sonorous voice filling the space.

He started with a humorous subject: a crocodile wanted to be a man and asked the camel, being a servant to man, what the distinguishing feature of human existence was, so the camel enumerates them and goes on to advise the crocodile on how to be a camel, because that was only one step away from being a man. After the second or third sentence, Uri had the vague feeling that he had already encountered the text—indeed, knew it by heart. The people in the audience chortled with glee as they followed the twists and turns in the witty but rather undemanding text, until Uri realized that he had read the tale among several other works of a similar kind in a scroll by another author. He hoped he was mistaken, but then he saw in his mind's eye the scroll itself, and he could even recall where in the scroll the words were placed.

The philosopher delivered the text as if it were one of his own compositions. Uri looked around at the heedlessly chuckling audience.

Plagiarism: the philosopher had pilfered another philosopher's text. He had not even taken the trouble to write a new one, or at least declaim one of his own older texts.

That grieved Uri. When the orator, having reaped his well-earned success, bowed deeply to ovation, took a sip of his wine, and again raised an arm to request silence to strike up on a new subject, it came as no surprise to Uri that he was also familiar with this tale. It concerned another philosopher's happy-go-lucky make-believe composition about a cobbler who pretends to be Zeus to win over his friend's wife, and how the virtuous lady asks Zeus for his assistance, and thus the lady partakes of divine love.

The unsuspecting audience laughed, with the females (there were rich, bejeweled ladies seated among the spectators in the company of their husbands or lovers) demurely gasping a bit at the more indelicate runs of the story, but no protests were to be heard. Uri felt a strong urge to stand up on behalf of the plundered authors and to thunder against the thief, but he controlled himself and watched scornfully at the way the fat man who called himself a philosopher managed to play in his one person the various roles. Not that he was bad at ham-acting: while portraying the female character he even wiggled his hips, simpered and whined in a falsetto tone.

Grown-up men and women enjoyed the infantile stories—grown-ups but utter morons nonetheless.

Uri trailed home despondently. He had wasted sixteen asses, which were not even his, on a shameful farce. He brought to mind the two works of the philosopher he had just seen and considered that they were good, despite his newly found, jaundiced distaste. They were not comparable with his great works but there was in them a certain seriousness, a dignity, a loftiness of the mind. It was terrible that a serious philosopher had to earn a living as a buffoon, filching texts from others.

He made an attempt to guess how much the philosopher might have earned that afternoon. The thirty rows had been roughly two thirds full, and one row seated about 150 people, so there must have been something like three thousand there. Fifteen hundred sesterces. There would have been expenses, like the hire of the theater, and who knows what that would have been: say one third of that, then of course there was the pay of his permanent attendants, which again was hard to assess. The lectica was obviously hired locally; the physician was certainly expensive, and each one of the servants probably cost more to maintain per day than his whole family in Rome.

So, the wretched thief cannot have earned all that big a sum of money if he had to support so many hangers-on. How much would be left for him personally? Not more than two hundred sesterces. Uri's family could live off of that for months, of course, but it was still a measly remuneration.

He wondered how the clown planned his tours of the Italian provinces. Quite possibly he would make an appearance in some other town every three or four days. In prosperous towns maybe he not only glittered in the amphitheater but was also invited into the homes of the well-off. There were plenty of wealthy people in Syracusa, judging by the villas; who knows, maybe he would be bowing and scraping in private houses tomorrow, and make more from that than he did in the theater. Maybe he even declaimed more serious texts on such occasions.

It was not the sort of thing that Plato or Aristotle went in for.

Uri felt obliged the next day to report to Matthew on the philosopher's performance. He honestly confessed to having been disappointed that the philosopher had ripped off the works of others.

"I enjoyed it," said Matthew.

Uri was staggered.

"I was sitting in the back row," said Matthew. "His voice carried clearly that far off. I saw you sitting in the second row; you kept turning around to look at the audience."

He's watching me, Uri thought. Following and watching me. What does he think I am, then? Some sort of spy who had a secret rendezvous with someone in Syracusa's amphitheater?

"I tried to catch up with you in the crowd," said Matthew, "but I got stuck at the exit, and by the time I managed to push through you were nowhere to be seen."

Uri sighed. Once again he had supposed the worst of someone when in reality there had indeed been a big scrimmage on the way out.

IN THE END, A SHIP DID ARRIVE FROM JUDAEA, DOCKING ON FRIDAY afternoon, two or three hours before sunset and the onset of the Sabbath. Valerius happened to be keeping watch at the harbor; he announced that he had already managed to reach an agreement with the captain, who said that he would pick them up at first light on Sunday and would be setting off back to Caesarea. Matthew was none too pleased to have the glory of securing the boat stolen from him; Valerius was elated and described in detail the bireme on which they would be sailing. Uri was astounded at the rich nautical vocabulary Valerius commanded because he had never before so much as heard reference to the various types of masts and sails. Evidently shipping must be a mania for Valerius, assistant to an archisynagogos, and Uri asked him as well whether he had ever sailed before. Valerius replied that yes, he had; a few days ago he had sailed on a ferry from Italia to Sicily. But just wait, just wait, he said, his eyes glittering like a crackpot. Uri was less sanguine: it would take only a stray little storm for them to find themselves on the bottom of the sea. Now that a boat had turned up, he would most willingly have turned back.

The Judaean boat was anchored some two to three hundred feet from the shore, and the huge logs the boat had carried were hauled aloft by an enormous 100- to 120-foot-high pulley rig and lowered onto the smaller craft that had been sculled out to unload the cargo. Matthew said that the reason the boat did not come closer to the shore was so that slaves should not throw themselves into the water and swim off—not that there was much chance of that, seeing as they were chained together, but it did no harm to be careful.

Uri had been struck by the fact that only slaves were working on the boats and on the shore, albeit under the supervision of a few slave drivers, and he even said as much.

Iustus, who had been keeping watch with Valerius, laughed.

"Pity you didn't see the sailors jumping ashore," he said, "and the hurry they were in! Racing to be sure that the Sabbath should fall with them in a safe place."

Matthew also laughed, though he had not even seen them.

"They will be celebrating next door to us," he said.

Half an hour before the onset of the Sabbath, they arrived at the sawmill to which Matthew led them.

Right up till the sun set, the slaves—whole families: fathers, mothers, and children—ceaselessly rotated, around and around, a huge ribbed wheel, to which a second wheel with a horizontal axis was transversely engaged; a strap attached to the thickened far end of its axle turned a massive circular saw. Others were sawing logs from the new consignment into rectangular planks: a trunk would be tugged onto a table with a slot cut into one end, and at the halfway point the saw would then bite into the wood with a buzzing and howl and split off the surplus bits, which a further detachment of slaves were occupied with chopping up. Uri had seen horses going around in circles in mills and was rather surprised not to see even one such beast here until Hilarus tipped him off that it was cheaper to keep slaves fed than it was to buy fodder for horses.

The logs were seasoned in Judaea because the climate was favorable there; it was not worth trying to work wood that was still wet because later on it would warp and buckle, and not just the builder but also the supplier would be sued on that account if it led to the collapse of a multistory building, an almost weekly occurrence in Rome, as Plotius explained. Besides being able to sell at a higher price when the timber had been processed, cutting it into planks also had the advantage that it was possible to stack more of them together on the next ship that was heading northward, continued Aaron, the sawmill's owner who had invited them.

"That would be a nice trick," quipped Matthew, "if trees grew naturally with rectangular trunks."

"I wouldn't be too thrilled," Aaron retorted, "because then I would have to look for a less lucrative trade for myself."

Uri was amazed that even the sawdust was collected in sacks, but Matthew explained that this was also transported to Rome, where it was scattered on the mud in front of the houses of the rich. Uri was amazed at that as well: did that too come from Judaea? He had often seen sawdust being scattered on the mud in Rome but never imagined that a day would come when he had something to do with it.

Sawdust was not much cheaper than wooden beams, Matthew noted; every last scrap of the forests felled in Judaea was turned to profitable use. He himself had transported a huge amount of timber in his own work. When they got to Judaea he would point out the locations of the forests that had been felled in recent decades; due to the dearth of trees the soil was being blown away by the wind and rocks were now jutting out of the ground. On the other hand, what is one supposed to do if there is no demand for much else in the way of exports from Judaea?

"Dates, for example," Uri stated.

"Up till now it was possible," said Matthew, "but in recent times they have also been planting them in Italia, unfortunately."

The slaves left off work at sunset on the dot to resume at first light on Sunday. They withdrew to a large barn-like building a bit like a stables in which they all lived and where they too celebrated their own Sabbath. They were not chained, but their ears were pierced, and, judging by the stone wall of at least ten feet in height, Uri had not the slightest doubt that they were not able to escape. At the sole gate two sentries, shield and spear in hand, stood on guard; they were not Jews and therefore allowed to do duty on the Sabbath.

Uri brooded on why he felt such twinges of conscience over a Jewish mill-owner keeping Jewish slaves. In Rome the Jews had all been liberated, and they had not been replaced by new slaves from Palestine; peace had reigned for decades. How come these Jews had become slaves despite that?

He questioned Plotius.

"They were unable to pay their debts," said Plotius, "so they sold themselves, along with their families."

Uri shuddered.

"Their thinking is," Plotius went on, "it is better if the family stays together, and also that they will be better off in a Jewish establishment. That is not always the case."

Uri imagined having to trundle, with his father and sisters, a ribbed wheel around and around for hours at a time, and he felt dizzy. But it was not every day that a shipment of timber arrived at Syracusa; maybe it was not only on the Sabbath that they had a chance to rest.

He felt badly that he had also failed to greet the slaves, even though they too belonged to the household. There was always tomorrow evening, of course.

Aaron owned a true Italian house—huge and with all the trimmings: an atrium, kitchen, bedrooms, and two big pools in the garden, one for ritual bathing (they too were free to take a dip in it, each of them being given a clean loincloth to cover his genitals), whereas in the second swam gorgeous fish of various shapes and sizes. Non-Jewish slaves (there were also some of them) took care of them throughout the night, as the Sabbath restrictions did not apply to them. The house was plumbed for sewage disposal, with the privies, as in richer Roman villas, built to allow for flushing with water. Uri spent three longish spells perched on the oval pottery seats there over the course of the evening, examining the walls of the latrines, tiled to the ceiling as they were with Solomon's seals—Stars of David, some called them—the bare soles of his feet pleasantly warmed by the floor tiles—under-floor heating by hypocaust had been installed in all the rooms.

Aaron was a middle-aged man of nondescript appearance, more than content with his lot in life. Two sons of his also spent the Sabbath there; as young adults they already had their own houses and were engaged in other trades even though they were not yet married. Uri had the feeling that they looked down on the delegation's members: they were a long way from Rome, and they had precious little to do with it; they were successful businessmen from a good Syracusan family, and the Roman Jewish community was of no significance for them. Uri would not be surprised to find that they had never read a single scroll in their life, and if they had been present in the amphitheater they would certainly have been unaware that the orator was declaiming works by others. They looked happy.

Aaron proposed that they cast lots to be "king of the wine," or toastmaster—a suggestion to which the company enthusiastically assented, though Uri had no idea what that office might entail.

They threw a pair of dice, which, as an implement of a game of chance, was forbidden to Jews not only on a Sabbath but at any time. However, seeing that it was only being used to draw lots, no prohibition applied. After several rounds, Valerius emerged as the winner. The hyperetes was so elated at his luck that he leapt around and clapped his hands ecstatically like a child. Uri could only watch in wonder.

The non-Jewish servants brought in an enormous bronze dish, filled it with water, brought out several more large dishes and a good dozen amphorae, then set out ornamental murrhine glasses before them on the table.

Valerius instructed the servants to mix the wine and water in a fifty-fifty ratio. The big vessels—punchbowls, as they were called—were filled with equal quantities of wine and water, and from these the drinks were measured out with a large ladle through a funnel into each person's drinking glass.

At that point Aaron announced that it was time to say prayers.

They started with the first of the two classes of blessings, because the second type could only be uttered by a priest, then they said the Sh'ma and the seven obligatory blessings for the Sabbath, and finally the kiddush, which is recited over a cup of wine in private houses to consecrate the Sabbath.

Valerius then ordered everyone to down the glass in one and then he would get the next.

They did his bidding.

From then on it was Valerius who stipulated the proportions in which the wine and water were to be mixed, and how often they should drink. His orders had to be complied with, given that he was the wine king. There was no Law, written or unwritten, that said anything about the office of wine king, and therefore it was allowed to comply with the wine king on the Sabbath.

It was likewise allowed to converse and sit around in the garden while drinking. Uri kept casting stealthy glances at the large building looming in the dark behind the high stone wall, where the sailors were celebrating their Sabbath. He noticed that the others also looked over there from time to time. Oil lamps glowed behind the curtains in the tiny windows, much as they did on the table that had been set out in the garden on their side, and at times a sound like the meowing of cats was audible. Maybe they had a menorah in the rooms over there, because in their garden there was a massive, cast-bronze menorah on a marble plinth, with all seven of its candles burning.

"They're screwing," Aaron said.

The rest laughed.

It then began to glimmer in Uri's mind what the dark, two-story building next door might be.

All the same, he asked, and indeed it was: Syracusa's Jewish brothel.

That was what the sailors had been hurrying to.

The proprietor of the brothel was Jewish, Aaron related, and the women who lived there were Jewish as well, around three dozen of them—or at least so people say, because he personally had never seen them. He chortled, and his sons gave him looks as disgusted as those Gaius Lucius's sons gave him in Rome. Except that there was no wife present, and nobody asked if she was still alive, had died, or been driven away by Aaron.

The harlots came from Judaea and Galilee, recounted Aaron, and constantly at that; if any fled or died, the gap was immediately filled, because the demand was very high. There were short girls, tall ones, slim ones, and fat ones, girls with large bosoms and others with small bosoms, skinny thighs or fat thighs, broad-hipped or narrow-hipped, red-haired or black-haired, short-haired or long-haired girls; some could dance, others might play the harp, some could read out loud very nicely, and others were completely dumb, but each and every one was well versed in the arts of lovemaking. Divorced wives, unmarried girls who had been knocked up by mercenaries, girls who had been abandoned or anathematized, women, raped virgins, expectant grandmothers, pickpockets, madwomen, women cursed by magic spells—one and all of them unfortunate females who would long ago have given up the ghost had they not found their way here, where they had a roof over their head and food to eat, and none too bad at that, and plenty enough of it too. They not only received Jewish clients, but Jewish sailors were always preferred and were given discounts, because the proprietor strictly observed religious commandments in all things at all times.

A hush fell; they sipped their wine and strove not to take a peek in the direction of the dark, two-story house lowering at the end of the garden, past the pools, past the high wall, but the place where, Uri sensed, they all, himself included, longed to be.

"On the Sabbath, even fallen women are not supposed to work, if they're Jewish," Uri piped up.

Iustus and Hilarus endorsed that vigorously: they thought it was outrageous, an unpardonable sin to force women to work on the Sabbath and, worse still, by a Jew, even if they were whores.

Uri looked at Plotius, but the latter said nothing. Valerius shook his head and ordered a new round in a mix of one-third to two-thirds, the larger part being wine.

"It's not as if they are working," Matthew said, and he snorted with laughter. "On the Sabbath married couples have a duty to live a married life."

"That's right, but those women are not married! They're lousy whores!" declared teacher Hilarus.

"But they are married," Matthew rejoined with a mischievous chuckle. "That's the custom here in Syracusa." At which he turned to Aaron: "Correct me if I've got that wrong..."

"No, you've got it right," Aaron said with a grin on his face.

"Well, anyway, I've been told that sailors can drop into the brothel at any time, and they will be served forthwith. If it so happens that they arrive on the Sabbath, because the wind was against them, or the oarsmen mutinied, or pirates wanted to grapple with the ship and had to be beaten off, then they will be heartily welcome on production of a standard marriage certificate, and on these the only blank that is left is for the client's name; the girls' names are entered sure enough, only those of the men are missing. The form is quickly completed as soon as the man chooses a woman; the owner of the brothel personally blesses all the newly married couples, and they are free to couple lawfully the whole night long. They spend the Sabbath like any God-fearing Jew, and because they are married it is even obligatory for them to couple. Then on the Sabbath evening, when the sun goes down and the Sabbath comes to a close, they enter the appropriate names into the standard religious document, both sign it, and thereafter they may consider themselves as divorced under the Law—and all perfectly legally."

"How hypocritical!" expostulated Uri.

"Why's that?" Matthew asked. "They do genuinely get married, but nowhere does it say how many times a Jew may contract marriage. And they do genuinely get divorced. It's all done in accordance with the Law. I've seen a bill of marriage—not just one either, because some people collect them. Usually they are burned—the real married ones burn them anyway, so the paper will not be found on them by chance. No proof is left in the brothel. The Lord God sees anyway what he must see, and up till now He has not interfered once; not brought down a pestilence on the house, or an earthquake, and no tidal wave has carried it off, though it's been operating for quite a while."

"When I first came here," said Aaron, "it was already here, and that was nearly twenty years ago."

That bore thinking about. The Lord bestowed on the Jews laws that were full of holes. Equally, that might, of course, be a matter for rejoicing.

"This Syracusan brothel is the most humane I've ever heard of," said Plotius unexpectedly. "The owner has brought in the rule that the men do not pay up front but upon leaving, and pay precisely what the wench says, her status for the evening of the Sabbath indeed being that of a freshly divorced wife. The women are not beaten up here, because any woman who is beaten will declare, purely out of vengeance, a staggeringly large sum, and if the blighter does not have that much, the proprietor recovers it from the rest: nobody is allowed to leave until everyone has paid. There are brutes of servants who can get anybody to cough up, but that is not needed, because anyone going in is clear about the rules. Apparently there have been cases when the woman asked for nothing, but those are just legends, of course; any owner would instantly dismiss a woman like that."

They supped more wine; by now there was little water in it.

"Cornelius, the proprietor," said Aaron, "is just as much a father of the synagogue—Pater synagogue—as I am. He offered it a mosaic floor (ten thousand sesterces, it cost), and not as the proprietor of a brothel, but as a merchant. After all, he does trade as well. The community accepted the gift."

"Has it ever happened," an overwrought Uri queried, "that a marriage was not dissolved by the evening of the next day?"

Neither Aaron nor Matthew nor Plotius had yet heard of such a miracle.

Hilarus strenuously disapproved of a mockery being made of the sanctity of married life in a brothel, and he was of the opinion that it was the duty of jurists to hunt out objections to such cases.

Plotius snorted: there were no jurists, only priests and believers. Interpreters of the law were noxious beings, because they did not take their stance on the ground of the Pentateuch of Moses but set themselves up as religious experts upon their own authority without having been granted any sort of legitimacy by the Lord.

Uri was amazed at the ferocity of the fires in the eyes of Plotius, who had himself just been expounding a law that certainly had not been revealed by God. Maybe it had been put forward to Him at some time, but He had not yet gotten around to endorsing it because once He did, it became doctrine.

Aaron had a more indulgent attitude toward the secessionists, the name used for the masters, of whom there were many over there in Palestine, and who had been instructing the population for at least one hundred years. They had acquired prestige with their advice and interpretations of law, and they had seats in the Sanhedrin—admittedly only in a minority. Their legal counsel was called upon in Jerusalem and other cities alike to adjudicate on complex cases.

"So, what does one of those masters advise in this case?" Uri was curious.

"I don't know," Aaron said, "but I can imagine tough debates went on in the Sanhedrin about prostitution. Not that they had any outcome: there is complete silence about prostitution. As if it did not exist. Yet they too are Jews, and there are scads of them over there."

"That's not quite true," Iustus interjected. "A courtesan, like an exciseman, is disqualified from testifying in a court of law, not even in her own case. A regulation has been passed against them."

"True," said Aaron, "but anyone who uses a courtesan is allowed to give witness; he suffers no penalty, even though he is not sleeping with his wife. He is sinning, but he is not punished for that. What else would you call that but confusion? There are some masters over there who take the side of the courtesans, pleading for compassion to be shown toward them because they are not allowed to partake of the *tzedakah* or charity-box; or in other words, they are unable to quit the business or else they would die. It's a vicious circle, but the high priests have never said a single word about it up till now."

"Is there a priest here in Syracusa at all?" Hilarus inquired.

"Sometimes there is," said Aaron. "There's one who usually comes for a few days from across the sea. He shuttles. It just so happens that he's here right now; you will meet him in the house of prayer tomorrow morning. But he'll soon be off again; his family lives in Jerusalem, close to the fire. That is where the sacrificial meals are given out; they never come over. He has something like eight children, if I'm not mistaken..."

"And what has he got to say about this disgraceful practice?" Hilarus asked, gesturing with his head toward the neighboring building.

"Nothing at all," Aaron laughed. "What should he say? Forbid sailors from sleeping with a woman after they have spent weeks cooped up at sea? Tell them to switch to brotherly love? Hardly! Apart from anything else, that would be a grave sin he was proclaiming. So he holds his tongue. Though I don't know," he added, "how much he gets, or from whom, for holding his tongue. In the final analysis, he would be within his rights to call down a curse on the place, but he has never done so. Though I also don't know whether anyone has paid him to lay a curse on the house."

"So, what happens when the Sabbath overtakes a ship at sea?" Uri asked. "Do the slaves lay off rowing? Do the sailors stop climbing the masts?"

"That's a quite different situation," Matthew responded. "There is a threat to life, so they are allowed to work. In such cases the law of the exception pertains, according to which man does not exist for the Sabbath, but the Sabbath exists for man."

"It doesn't say that in the Torah," said Uri.

"But it's there in our tradition," said Matthew.

"All but two short of one hundred years ago it was not there," persisted Uri. "When Pompey occupied Jerusalem, the Jews did nothing, because it was the Sabbath; they didn't defend the City by pulling down the rampart the same day. It can't be all that ancient a tradition, even if it has been added since. But then where is it written down?"

"It's written down all right," observed Plotius. "I've seen hefty collections of laws in Judaea and Galilee, more than one of them containing not the word of the Torah but subsequent laws that are based on the Torah. They are guarded in stout, locked chests, and they are of such value that not just anybody can consult them. I asked how much one would have to pay for something like that, and they looked at me as if I were insane: they are so precious that they have no price, they can't be bought and sold; they are passed as a bequest from a master to his favorite pupil, to his first-born son, or to his brother. The new laws cannot be recorded in principle, as there are numerous instances where they conflict with the laws of the Torah; in short, these collections of laws do not officially exist. But all the same, in practice even those who have never seen such a book stick to these collections of legal cases. If the designated judges have to adjudicate on a complex case and in the end are at a loss what to do, they send envoys with the questions to the masters who are familiar with these collections. Naturally even they only know them through hearsay, as is permitted—though of course they have never seen anything of the like. Perish the thought! Of course, on getting the advice, the judges pass judgment according to their own discretion because there is no necessity to reach a judgment according to a nonexistent book of laws, but oddly enough in most cases they do reach them. It is what in Rome is called the law of precedence."

Could this be the deficient legal security in Judaea of which Plotius had spoken?

They were now drinking the pure wine that Valerius, the wine king, had now ordered for their throats, and their consciousness became so weighed down that the next day none of them awoke in time, and they did not go to the house of prayer and did not take part in holy worship on that Sabbath.

"It's only the meal you need to feel sorry about," said Aaron, placing a wet towel around his head as a compress. "I contributed to acquiring it and it must have been celestial. On the other hand, you were let off having to listen to the sermon. Our priest is long-winded and boring in teaching virtue. He hardly ever lets anyone else get a word in edgewise; stupid, the poor man, but what can we do..."

It was good that a Torah was kept on hand for such cases, and from that they could read what was due to be read on the Sabbath. Anyone was allowed to read what was designated so long as they were among a community of at least ten men. There were precisely ten of them, including Aaron and his sons, so there was no need for them to pray together with the slaves. Matthew quickly unrolled the Greek Torah scroll and read out what had to be read, and at least they were sober enough by then to say the "Amens" in the right places.

Wherever a quorum of ten Jews are together, God is present; to be more precise, the Shechinah, or Divine immanence, is present in everyone, and for that reason the place is holy. Thus, the house of the owner of the sawmill had become holy simply by virtue of their male presence—at least as holy as the house of prayer itself. Indeed, they were even able to take a dip in the basin again before prayers, whereas in the house of prayer the faithful would only have been able to dip their hands in a bowl of water placed there for that purpose, and perhaps splash a little water casually on themselves. They too were able to partake of a big meal, which after all is the very essence of the Sabbath, because the Omnipotent arranged that on the seventh day even Jews who might have been starving until then should finally have access to food that was adequate to man.

Uri ruminated on whether the nearby brothel did not also become a holy place on the Sabbath. There were almost certainly ten men in the building who were praying right then in the prescribed fashion. Maybe most of them were even present together with Cornelius and his family for the regular Sabbath service in the house of prayer, and also said the "Amens" in the right places, and overate at the free meal. Maybe they even took along with them yesterday's wives, whom they would be divorcing that day; for after all women and children were of equal rank, it was just that they only had to say the Sh'ma twice, once in the morning and once in the evening.

The sailors and wenches were beyond reproach: they observed the law.

It was a wise ordinance of the Lord that the Torah was the centerpiece of the religion rather than the house of prayer in which it was read out from. Since the Diaspora came into existence it is permissible to read from the Torah anywhere if ten men were present, and there would usually be that many assembled.

As a result, they did not meet with the shuttling priest, who had nothing to say on the matter of the brothel but was all the more a windbag on other matters, or with the local Jewish beggars who would overrun the courtyards and gardens of prayer houses in excessive numbers on such occasions (just as they did the sur-roundings of synagogues in Rome). Still, when all is said and done, and in spite of sleeping through the Sabbath service in the house of prayer, they too, worthy members of the Jewish delegation from Rome, observed the law nonetheless.

AT FIRST LIGHT ON SUNDAY THE SHIP WAS LOADED, ALONG WITH THE galley slaves, with all sorts of precious cargo, half of which were luxury goods that the rich of Judaea craved, their wives especially: oils, paints, and balms with which it was the latest fad to daub the body in Italia; caskets of jewels; small mir-rors; little jars. There were also medicinal herbs guaranteed to cure all manner of ills, either moist in barrels that kept them fresh or in sacks, dried and powdered: rejuvenating salves, aperients to loosen constipated bowels, emollients to calm loose bowels, remedies to inhibit hair loss or counter balding, potions to regrow split nails or banish pimples and warts—all in copious quantities.

The other half of the cargo consisted of Sicilian wine and sizable sacks of almonds. Before now, Uri would have been unable to conceive of that amount of almonds. He had eaten them once before: the roast fish at his bar mitzvah had a thin sprinkling of roasted almonds.

Uri himself also carried a number of smaller parcels over the plank onto the skiff that plied between the ship anchored in the bay and the shore; squint-ing sideways, he marveled meanwhile at the slaves, who, without a word of complaint, carried barrel after barrel, their eyes dull, apathetic, as if they were oxen or mules driving a mill. When they had finished, they seated themselves in comfort, insofar as their chains permitted; they were chained together in groups of ten, thanks to the newfangled Roman decimal system, which the Jews of Judaea had also adopted, so it seemed the chain gang was an Italian product. It was obviously more comfortable if the shackles were not unfastened when they prayed. Uri got to thinking whether it was pleasing to the Lord to be prayed to by people who had been clapped in irons, although of course He must have gotten used to that sort of thing down the millennia.

The slave driver and his assistant arrived and doled out the rations into small dishes, which were produced from under their leather-belted tunics. The slaves slurped greedily and dug into their food with dirty hands. Uri wondered what he would do if he had been born a slave; he would die of hunger if he could not wash his hands.

I didn't say goodbye to Aaron's slaves, it crossed Uri's mind, and he felt an unpleasant twinge in the pit of his stomach. What must they have thought of the delegation? What had his grandfather, Thaddeus the slave, thought of masters?

When the sailors, sleepily, tottering, put in an appearance, the captain, who had not been with them at the brothel but had celebrated the Sabbath together with the slaves and some of the slave drivers, issued the order to set sail. Uri wondered if a wench had been rowed out to the boat for him, or maybe he had a male lover among the slaves.

The travelers were dead tired by the time they came to say dawn prayers, bowing to the prow of the boat in a southeasterly direction, or, rather, more to the east. The stem had an odd appearance; the curved beams on the two sides were arched gracefully toward each other and upward, as if seeking each other out proudly at the front, yet they met merely in a stubby, thick stump. Uri gazed at the stump with tightly screwed eyes before gradually realizing that a figure-head of some kind must once have been placed there, a god or goddess, as was customary on Roman ships, but when it was bought by Jews they had it sawed off. They circumcised the ship, thought Uri sardonically, before chiding himself.

The ship had been late, waiting for a consignment of balsam that had not arrived in time for some reason. They had also been waiting for a substantial cargo from Galilee, and things from there were always delayed; people there were never in a hurry. The timber had been loaded a long time ago, but balsam now fetched a high price, so it was worth waiting for it.

The captain had also heard about there being a demonstration of some sort at the stadium in Caesarea, but that had not been organized by local Jews; they were very sober-minded and calm and had nothing to do with it. These were people from Jerusalem, not in the hundreds or thousands, just a few dozen angry vagabonds; they had come to no harm and had gone home peacefully. That was not the reason for their being late; it was because the balsam had not arrived.

The ship was pervaded with the aroma of balsam. Nauseated by it, Uri tried vainly to rid his nostrils of the smell. Their quarters were in the belly of the ship, but the dreadful stench there proved, if anything, even more penetrating, so he went up on deck at the stern, sat down with his back against the wall of the bridge, and went to sleep, seated in the open air.

He woke up to find his hands were freezing and felt a tickle. He grabbed and got a yelp in response. He opened his eyes to see a squat, short-legged, short-coated, odd-looking, long-snouted, light brown dog leap away. It came to a stop about three feet away and watched expectantly. Its legs were not just stubby but also bowed, and its long tail whisked right and left. Uri had not had much to do with animals, having at most had to chase away cats, of which there were a great abundance in Rome; a few of the residents of Far Side had kept goats and sheep, out of respect for tradition, but only a few, because there was nowhere to graze them.

"He's called Remus," said in Aramaic a sailor who had just shinned down one of the masts.

"So was his mother Romulus?" Uri quipped back good-naturedly, now that he could speak in his family's secret tongue.

The sailor didn't get it, however, and he shook his head and vanished.

Uri clucked at the dog and called out its name, whereupon the dog wagged its tail even more enthusiastically, padded over toward Uri, and looked at him even more expectantly. Uri slowly opened the hand that had been licked and stroked him. The dog allowed him, indeed pushed his muzzle vigorously under Uri's hand so that he would go on stroking him; not being able to do so himself because of his short legs.

Until the time for prayers came around again, Uri stroked the sleeping dog nestled in his lap.

Remus was not the only dog on board; there were eight or nine of them, the precise number varying depending on which sailor was asked. They were used to hunt any rats and mice that pillaged the freight. All were short-bodied, long-nosed dogs that could wriggle through gaps—the smaller the dog, the better. In fact, they were hunting dogs, specially bred by the Romans and very useful, because they did not have to be fed, only allowed to work and be given water now and then.

Wherever Uri went, Remus was sure to follow. He formed the view that the dog knew him better than his human companions, recognizing that he was a reliable and affectionate person. Or did loneliness have its own aura? Was that what the dog smelled?

Countless leather bottles of water, along with dried figs, salted raw fish, smoked fish, and dried fish had been stocked for the crew and passengers, along with several hundred pounds of unleavened bread, baked in thicker portions than matzos generally were. Uri grew tired of the monotonous diet by the first evening; they were taking water to sea, taking fish to sea. It seemed the Creation had not been devised to absolute perfection.

With a favorable northwesterly wind to fill the sails, they forged eastward and later northeastward. The captain said that in the spring it was always better going from Syracusa to Caesarea than the reverse. The slaves, who rowed on the lower level of the bireme, the upper level left empty, were being given a break. Uri looked down on them. They were lying, chained to each other, naked in the gloom of the ship's belly. Light and air they got from above, from where they could be reached by clambering down a ladder, except that the ladder was pulled up right then. It was only let down when the armed slave drivers took victuals down to them, with the ladders being pulled up after them once they'd scrambled up with the vessels of excrement. One of the slave drivers was always down there with them to control the rhythm of the rowing; he was now resting alongside them—that being his occupation right then. Slave drivers were relieved, not so the slaves.

The long oars had been drawn in. There were something like forty down below. One of the drivers noticed that Uri was looking at the slaves with interest and straightaway began explaining to him in Greek that the oars that were located on the upper bank were much longer, and there were twenty of them.

"We rarely use them," he said, "because it's harder to row with them. They're saved for big storms, and then they are not to move the ship forward but to stabilize it. That is when the best oarsmen are directed to the upper level."

He was a bald-pated, muscular man, who was beginning to get paunchier from leading a comfortable life. Uri found the heavy jowls and chops, the sycophantic currying of favor, distasteful, but he was grateful that here was someone from whom he could gain information.

"How does one become a slave driver?" he asked.

The man was surprised.

"You need merit and a dose of luck," he said.

"Could a more profitable, less dangerous occupation not be an option?"

The driver was astonished at first, but then he had a moment of realization and broke into a broad grin.

"I'm happy to be a slave driver, sir. Before that I worked in the galley down below for eight years."

Uri looked at the reclining bodies below.

The slave driver was also a slave, only he had been promoted to leader.

The driver stood humbly waiting for any further questions, bending forward intently to catch even Uri's sighs.

"Are they lashed?" Uri queried, indicating them below with a nod.

"Yes," said the driver. "The language of the scourge is all they understand."

"Were you beaten?"

"And how! It was the only language I understood."

"And did you hate the people who beat you?"

"You bet! And they hate me now that I have become a slave driver. But while I was a galley slave I paid no thought to the possibility that those who were my slave drivers hated me. Now I know they did, because I also hate them. That's how it has to be, otherwise I wouldn't be able to lash them."

Uri turned away and looked out to sea with narrowed eyes. It was a steely blue with white flecks. Somewhere far off glistened the green-brownish colors of a line blurring the horizon, like a mosaic studded with granules—that might be dry land. They were not yet far from the shore.

"We hug closely to the coast of Italia to start with," said the driver politely, "then we cut across and sail by the Dalmatian coast to the Greek islands until we touch Crete, after which we sail on farther to the Syrian coast, where we veer left. If we get a favorable wind we won't stop till we get to Crete. Three weeks for the whole voyage, if not less."

Uri looked at the driver's ear—or rather the piercing in it, which had closed. I should have spotted it earlier, he thought.

The slave driver's presence was onerous but at the same time disturbing.

"Were you born a slave?" he asked.

"No, not at all, sir," the driver protested. "We Jews, don't you know, are not born slaves."

Uri, shamefaced, stayed silent. He had no idea how things were in Judaea.

"I had a family, even had work," the slave driver said. "I was a carpenter, but the devil got into me, and I killed my wife and her mother; I smashed their brains in with a hatchet. I also wanted to kill my children, the devil had such a hold on me, but I was wrestled to the ground. The court sentenced me to servitude for life. Though they would have been entitled to have me stoned to death. I'm grateful to the court, sir, because they spared my life, though of course I have the added punishment that until the end of my days I shall grieve my unhappy little ones, six of them altogether, who are left to fend for themselves in the world without mother and father..."

Uri was nauseated to hear the slave driver's willing confession, though he had no idea quite why. Maybe the tone in which the man had told the tale was somehow disgusting.

"When you became a slave did it not enter your mind to kill yourself?"

The driver was brought up short, surprised by the question.

"No, sir," he said after a pause. "It never entered my mind. I was possessed by the devil. He did what I did, not me. I can't help it, sir. It was the demon that they punished, not me. The demon has left me since then, I have the feeling, but I am being punished because I let him take hold of me... That's my crime, sir: I was not watching out for the devil, and allowed him into my soul."

Uri looked at the slave driver's troubled eye. He was looking into the distance past Uri's unpierced ears.

"You know that you will never be able to be free," said Uri. "Is it worth living in slavery?"

"I don't know, sir," said the driver, his voice recovered. "A person doesn't think; he lives."

"Something must keep you going, all the same," Uri insisted.

"That could be, sir. Indeed, it very likely does. But as far as killing myself is concerned, there wouldn't have been the means to do so. But then again, it didn't even enter my head. When the slave drivers started to lash, and they started at once so that I'd know my place, all that I had in my mind was that one day I would be a slave driver. I would be a slave driver and repay with interest. Not to them, that's not possible, but to the oarsmen. And I pay it back now. Yes, sir, that's how it was. And that's how it has turned out, sir."

Uri screwed his eyes up. The slave driver was standing in front of him. If I were to slap him across the face, thought Uri, no one would chide me, and he wouldn't dare hit me back.

Strange.

Both of us are identical creatures of God, and yet not the same. What exactly did the Creator have in mind?

"That is what drives them as well," the driver said, gesturing down toward the slaves with his head. "You can't row year in, year out, without a person wanting something. They want to become drivers—all of them! If not now, then next year, in ten years, twenty years. Because being a slave driver is good: better to beat than be beaten. To thrash someone is freedom itself, sir. Anyone who doesn't want that, and doesn't want it hard enough, is dead in a few weeks—even the strongest of men, if he does not want at any cost to become a slave driver. If the spirit of revenge does not live in him."

Uri turned away again and looked at the sea. If he looked to the left, he could still see the greenish-brown spots of the coast, and if he looked to the right, the steely blue of the sea. Who would ever suppose that at the far end of the endless expanse of water lay Africa?

They had been sailing for a day and a half when, to their left, on the far-off shore huge lights flared up and the sounds of muffled clamor reached them. The companions gathered on the port side of the deck and gazed toward the shore. Uri also stared, his eyes screwed up, through the fingers of one hand. He was not concerned that in addition to his companions the sailors could also see how shortsighted he was. Uri saw a mass of little colored fireflies in the distance, with the small circlets of light touching one another.

"Today is the anniversary of shipping," said Matthew touchingly. "Today's the eighth of March."

"Pity we didn't stay in Syracusa for another few days," Plotius ventured. "We might have seen some real wonders."

Uri was not the only one who did not know about the anniversary of shipping; neither did Hilarus and Iustus, though Valerius, the hyperetes, did know.

"It's not customary to set sail till the eighth of March," he said, "unless it's in an emergency."

"All year round, in other words," Matthew laughed. "Commercial shipping is under way the whole winter."

"Ah, but they don't carry passengers," Valerius countered. "And that's still hazardous from now right up till the twenty-seventh of May, when the Pleiades rise into the sky. One can sail safely from then until Arcturus rises..."

"On September the twenty-fourth," said Matthew.

"Yes, on September the twenty-fourth the equinoctial gales blow in, on the fifth of October rain-bringing Capricorn rises, and around October thirteenth you have Taurus, the bull. In November, the Pleiades go down, and that marks the end of the sailing year."

"Military galleys and rapid gunboats run all year," noted Plotius.

"At least one thing is true out of all that," said Matthew with a smile. "On the eighth of March, in every town along the coast they will be celebrating the anniversary of shipping. In Syracusa on these occasions there are usually gladiatorial contests, they hold chariot races, and performances are staged in the amphitheater," and here he turned to Uri, "the place where the amusing philosopher spoke. One eighth of March I saw a play in that theater; they were performing a comedy of some sort. Quite immoral it was, and much else besides—dances that it is not seemly to relate... I did indeed see some real wonders..."

They all looked with longing toward the coast, where immense lights must have been burning if they could see them, and real wonders were no doubt happening among the celebrating throng.

"So why did we set sail when it was still perilous to do so?" Hilarus asked in alarm.

"That's right," said Plotius gravely. "Over the last two days there was every chance of our being wrecked. It's a miracle we're still alive."

They laughed at Hilarus's jitters, Uri included.

"Will we be following the coastline all the way?" Iustus asked, perhaps in the hope that if the ship were wrecked he would somehow manage to flounder ashore.

"All the way," said Uri. "Down the Dalmatian coast, by the Greek islands, with only a halt in Crete en route to the Syrian coast."

There was a brief silence while Plotius and Matthew gazed out at the shore. Uri regretted having spoken.

"But that's an immense detour!" exclaimed Iustus. "Why aren't we going by the African coast via Malta?"

"That's the usual way with a bireme," said Matthew.

THEY LEFT ITALIA AT HYDRIS, AND WITH A FAVORABLE WIND THEY crossed the Adriatic in a day and a half. Uri's mind was set at rest that they would again be navigating close to the safe shore.

He could see that Matthew and Plotius had warmed to each other; they spoke at length. He could also see that the others regarded them with jealousy and whenever possible would step up to them to have a word. They wanted to suck up and form a triumvirate with Matthew and Plotius, Uri reflected as he stroked the dog.

The storm caught them by the Greek islands. Uri was standing on the deck and was amazed because the clouds were as yet a long way off when the captain began bawling, and Matthew yelled in turn, ordering him to get down quick into the rowing area.

Brawny slaves shimmied up the ladder onto the upper rowing bank on the command of the drivers, who quickly unchained them. It seemed all men became equal in a storm, and there was no reason to fear escapes. The slaves' places were taken by the members of the delegation and a few sailors who were not needed to furl the sails, as the others were taking care of that. Alexandros was the only one of the delegation who went up to the upper bank, saying that he was a good oarsman. Uri was astonished, but on looking at Alexandros's gigantic back, he must have been telling the truth. Might it be that he was an escaped slave rather than a real merchant?

Uri was given a right-hand oar, Iustus beside him a left-hand one. Before them the huge backs of slaves strained; behind them were seated Hilarus and Plotius. The slave driver who had been supervising the rowing up till then also clambered up onto the upper bank of oarsmen and Matthew took over directing the rhythm. He started in good voice and at a good tempo; the oars were still in the slaves' hands for a brief moment, after which they immediately followed his commands.

"Let's change places," Uri panted to Iustus after the first few pulls.

"No way," said Iustus determinedly, even though he was right-handed and the change would have been welcome for him as well. Uri did not try again.

He felt something warm hit against his feet. He looked, and it was Remus, the dog. It was whimpering, but Uri could not stroke it; he needed both hands to hold the oar.

The handle of the oar was slippery with the sweat of one of the slaves who had clambered into the upper bank. The oar was pushed through a gap in the hull left expressly for this purpose and dipped into the sea; a thick leather strap was threaded through a hole drilled through the oar close to the handle, with the strap fastened to a beam in the rowing chamber so that it would not fall into the water if the rower lost his grip.

Uri tried to row in the same rhythm as the others, but it was more than likely that he was just paddling air (he was unable to see the blade of the oar, there being no porthole in the rowing chamber), as it went remarkably easily. Then all of a sudden he felt a huge wrench on his arms, shoulders, and neck; a wave had caught the oar, and the oar slipped out of his grip, obliging him to stand up in the pitching boat to retrieve it. Shamefaced, he sat back down in his place. Matthew said nothing, having other things to think of: he was in command.

Over the next hour and a half the squall lasted, the oar was wrenched out of his hands more than a few times, but Hilarus and Iustus were not much better oarsmen. Valerius fared better than them; his only trouble was that he was sick.

Uri was barely able to dip his oar in the water, just threshing with it, and yet he was soon dog-tired nonetheless. When the squall had blown through and the boat was rocking peacefully, allowing the slaves to take a rest, Uri lay flat out on the floor. The boat rolled in one place, the sails having yet to be hoisted; the slaves and sailors on the upper bank were also resting; at that moment moving on was not the important thing; what mattered was for them to recover. They finally clambered down from the upper level, and Uri ought to have gotten up, but he was unable to move. His companions left him to climb the ladder to the deck, but Uri did not have the strength and simply lay on his side. Matthew leaned over him.

"You weren't rowing," he informed him scathingly. "I was watching."

Matthew also climbed up the ladder.

They're going to pull the ladder up, and I'll be left here among the slaves, it passed through Uri's head.

And indeed, on reaching the top Matthew pulled the ladder up. He was laughing mischievously, Uri could see.

The slaves were going to tear him limb from limb, devour him.

Then the ladder was let down again, though not by Matthew: the head slave driver had to climb down.

"Wait!" Uri bawled, gathered all his strength to pick himself to his feet and, limbs trembling, struggled up to the deck.

Once there he almost tumbled back down into the depths when he looked back for the dog; it was nowhere to be seen.

He retched a sour liquid onto the slippery deck. The skin over his whole body ached; his heart was pounding at a horrifying rate.

Down below, the slaves were being shackled to one another again.

"You stood your ground just great," he heard Matthew's derisive voice. "All of you."

Why does he hate me so much? Uri asked himself disconsolately.

HE SCOURED THE WET, SLIPPERY DECK FORLORNLY; IT WOULD SOON DRY if the sun continued to shine this brightly. He noticed an opening between the planks, a hatch cover of some sort, which had been completely lifted back; up till then everything had been shut. He stopped, bent down, and took a look into the small cabin.

He saw the captain from above, recognizing him from the big bald head; he knelt and bent over. Peering into the dimness, he could make out a gleaming statuette about three feet in height standing on a little table, with the captain bowing to it.

Uri was stupefied: what was a Jewish captain doing praying to an idol?

He held his breath and tried to bend closer in such a way that he did not block the sunlight. The captain sensed that someone was watching and glanced up. Uri was aghast and slid back, but the captain was in an extremely good mood that the ship had pulled through, and he shouted out, "Come down, whoever you are!"

Uri scrambled down the ladder.

"He saved us," the captain said, indicating the statuette.

A snake was wrapped seven times around a standing male body, his head reminiscent of a lion's. Wings sprouted from the man's shoulders, his left hand held a globe on which ran two intersecting lines, and his right hand held a knife.

"The Celestial Lord," said the captain. "He saved us. Twenty times or more he has saved me; my father, more than fifty times!"

He offered Uri a drink, which was strong and stung his throat. The captain, just glad to have someone to talk to, didn't look to see who it was.

That was how Uri learned about Mithras, who killed the bull and whom pirates and astronomers on Rhodes and in Tarsus worshiped as the Celestial Lord.

The captain was from Tarsus, and his father had been a pirate, or rather not so much a pirate as a sailor, except that the Cilician king's regular navy was considered by the Romans to be a pirate fleet, and anything that could be plundered, they plundered, just the same as the Roman pirates with whom they competed and, every now and then, would come into conflict. In the end they were taken over by the Romans when they conquered their land, and from then onward they had been valued as commercial seamen.

The captain's father had also been both an adept astrologer and a captain. He had reached the fourth degree or rank of the mysteries of Mithras but had been unable to advance, because he did not have the appropriate knowledge to do so; initiates were highly erudite people, astrologers all, and they knew everything, and they had ancient clay tablets and papyri from long ago, and they even knew, so his father related, that one time long ago the vernal and autumnal equinoxes were in Taurus, but Mithras decided to displace them to later in the year, and that had been a thousand years ago and more. The sages kept calculating when the equinoxes would be precessed back in Taurus, because if Mithras had displaced them, then he would also replace them, and that is when the initiatory state would set in. That duration was called an Age, and everyone had a different opinion about how long that lasted, how many thousands of years. Mithras was a great lord, in other words, who had conjured the North Star precisely to the north, because, so said the sages, it had not been situated there before, but Mithras wanted mankind to orient by this readily located bright star so that people would be able to sail in certainty.

These and other things were related by the captain to Uri, who found it hard to follow even half of it.

Uri wondered what the Creator said about Mithras's activities, given that this suggested he was able to move fixed stars around.

The captain said that naturally God was unique and eternal; he was Jewish, like his father before him, but a Great Force had begun to operate after the creation of the stars, the sun, and the moon, and if that was able to operate, then it was not counter to the Creator's intention, may His name be blessed. The Creator was in fact depicted as the sun, to which Mithras, lion-headed and firmament-mitered, humbly sacrificed. After some hesitation, the captain added that in these depictions the Sun-Creator was generally shown as being the same height as Mithras, who was actually also Perseus, because he had come from the Persians, but then he was not the only Jew in Tarsus who had Mithras to thank when he or a member of his family had stayed alive after a storm.

From then on Uri would occasionally climb down to see the captain, who would relate to him marvelous things about Mithras, the lord of the Upper and Lower Firmament, who was powerful enough to move the constellations. He decided that when he got back to Rome he would inquire with believers in Mithraism there to find out where one could find written traces of these splendid tales.

AROUND TWO WEEKS LATER THEY REACHED HARBOR ON CRETE.

Uri did not go on shore with the rest. Crete was of no interest: a rocky island, houses of white stone, and men who somehow made a living there. Plotius tried to tempt him by saying that Cretan Jews were most hospitable, and exceedingly rich, but Uri simply shrugged his shoulders.

Prior to that, Matthew and Plotius, who had sailed that way more than a few times, had enumerated the names of all the totally identical, rocky, desolate islands and the settlements on them. They would be helped out sometimes by Alexandros, who, being a merchant, had also often passed that way. Uri was amazed, because Roman merchants were not known for traveling. Some lines from Homer came to Uri's mind, and he quietly intoned them. On these Greek islands, according to these lines, the gods and demigods were born, and immortal heroes roamed. Even with his eyes screwed up, however, he saw little: white rocks, some green, and in the distance some darker spots, which had an equal chance of being either tall mountains or clouds.

They were tied up for a whole day at Phalasarna, a port on the coast of western Crete. The slaves stowed away agricultural produce in the still-empty spaces of the hold, whereas Uri stroked the dog and talked to him, the dog occasionally looking as if he almost understood.

"Remus," Uri would say, and the dog vigorously and happily wagged his tail. He at least recognized his own name.

"Uri," he would say, pointing to himself. The dog would vigorously and happily wag his tail at this too, though judging from the dimming of his eyes Uri could see that he did not grasp the meaning. What a stupid dog! It could only love.

What sense is there in a dog's life? What sense is there in a human life? What does the Creator want with us?

As he passed by, the captain would cast disapproving glances at them, the man sitting on the desk and the dog nestling on his lap. But he said nothing. Uri was one of the delegates from Rome, an important man; an idiot, but he could cause problems for the captain if he wanted to. The sailors that had stayed on the ship would tease him, sometimes in Greek, sometimes in Aramaic, "Your brood will be dogs," but Uri paid them no attention.

He was a little disappointed that they had not stopped in Herakleion or Miletus, even though they were headed for Rhodes, where he too might disembark. But he had not disembarked even in Ithaca, where they had also stopped for half a day. He did not consider it to be his duty to retrace Odysseus's steps, and anyway it was far from certain that this Ithaca was the Ithaca of the Odyssey, as was confirmed by Valerius, the armchair mariner, who had been seasick all the way: Homer's Ithaca probably lay farther north, on the island of Levkas.

Uri understood less and less what he was doing on the ship. What would he do in Jerusalem? If his father had been looking to do him a favor, why had he not sent him to Athens? Knowing his son's passion for reading, it might at least have occurred to him that Uri would be able to bury himself in the libraries there and listen to the academics. Besides, there were also Jews in Athens; he could live among them.

Or why not send me to Alexandria? The most enchanting city in the world—everyone knows.

His companions returned to the ship so drunk they could barely stand. Even Matthew and Plotius, the two men whose respect Uri most wanted to win, were reeling commendably. He did not censure them; it was more a case of his being ashamed that he had not gotten drunk with them.

There's going to be a time when I get really drunk, he resolved. Much drunker than when I was sick in the sea at Syracusa.

AFTER RHODES AND CYPRUS, THE NEXT STOP WAS SIDON, WHERE PART of the produce—some three quarters of the almonds—was unloaded. Uri asked where the almonds would be taken to, and Matthew gaped in astonishment.

"The whole lot ought to have been offloaded here," he explained, enunciating deliberately so that Uri might understand, "but the captain lied that the price had gone up in the meantime, and he had only received what the merchant had given him in advance. The captain would sell off the remaining one quarter somewhere else; that was pure profit for him. The merchants yelled at him for a while, and the captain yelled back. All sides ended up pleased with themselves, but it was the merchants who broke off first; that was the custom, and it was calibrated into the calculations."

In Tyre the cosmetics were unloaded. Here there were more prosperous towns, said Matthew, more so than any in Syria, Galilee, Samaria, and Judaea—Jerusalem and Caesarea excepted, of course.

None of them is wealthier than Rome, thought Uri, the Roman citizen, to himself.

They advanced southward right along the coast.

One week before Passover they arrived at Caesarea. It had once been called Pyrgos Stratonos, or Straton's Tower. It had been reconstructed by Herod the Great, and he naturally had renamed it for the emperor, said Valerius, well informed as ever and happy that his stomach was no longer going to trouble him.

They were left with plenty of time to cover the two hundred stadia to Jerusalem, Matthew said cheerfully. He was thankful that the long sea voyage had reached an end and they were able to rest for a few days. Uri picked up on everyone's sense of relief that Matthew was such an experienced seaman. Though maybe it was precisely on that account that Uri was surprised: he had never sensed any danger, even during the squall, but then he had been preoccupied with rowing, so he had no time to be alarmed. He entertained a boundless youthful confidence in his Creator, who had clearly marked him out for something if he was helping him stay alive and did not wish him to perish young.

Uri was made conscious by his companions' shouts that they were now able to see it. They were all assembled on the port side of the ship. What they could pick out in the distance was already big enough for Uri to make out if he screwed up his eyes: a huge, round, gleaming white building on a hilltop.

"The Temple of Augustus," said Matthew. "In front of it stand statues of Augustus and the Roman wolves. A colonnade all around! And dazzling inside as well: it's vast, gets its light through round apertures from above. That too was built by Herod the Great, when Augustus forgave him for having earlier been in Mark Antony's service."

The harbor looked big. Plotius estimated that it was exactly the same size as that of Piraeus. "No, bigger!" insisted Valerius. He also noted that the harbor area was known separately as Sebastos, which was the Greek for Caesar Augustus.

Matthew chuckled: he had met some Jews from Rome who mixed up the harbor area of Caesarea with the town of Sebaste in Galilee, little knowing that Herod the Great had rebuilt the latter on the site of the town of Samaria, which had been razed to the ground by the Jews.

The harbor was truly capacious, suitable for accommodating an entire flotilla. The entrance to the harbor faced north, as in Caesarea northerly winds were the most uncommon. There was a continuous, high stone ledge that protected it somewhat from the African southerlies, which carried sand that covered everything.

On reaching the port, they saw to the port side a large, round tower, set on a wide rectangular pedestal; this was the Caesarea lighthouse and could only be approached by sea in a small boat. As it was daytime, no fire was burning on the uppermost level. The mole was two hundred feet wide, Matthew told them. Herod the Great had built it, as he had the whole town, in just twelve years. It had cost a horrendous amount, with the construction materials—the stone and marble—being brought from far off, along with the engineers. The mole rested on gigantic blocks of rock sunk twenty cubits deep and were on average fifty feet long by eighteen feet wide by nine feet high. The southern breakwater, a stone wall interrupted periodically by towers, ran off as far as they could see to starboard. Before either of the breakwaters was built, Herod had the bay dredged, so that the sandbanks disappeared and no longer presented a danger to shipping, though the dredging still had to be carried out again at intervals.

The tallest and most splendid tower was a scaled-down copy of the Pharos of Alexandria. It bore the name of Augustus's son, Drusus, who had died young, and was known as the Druseion, Matthew explained. They were able to wonder at this truly impressive edifice as they drew nearer. It was square and comprised thirteen plus three levels. Seamen coming from far overseas would be put up in the Druseion, said Matthew. He had never resided there, sad to say, but he had visited it many times. It had four separate staircases, one on each face, and in the atrium there was a garden, and shops selling anything imaginable. The prostitutes were installed on the eighth floor, though women were very pricey there—at least that was what foreign sailors had told him. The Pharos in Alexandria also has thirteen floors in its lower block, Matthew went on, but its upper is even taller, of six floors, and above that there is yet another tower in which the light burns. It may well be that Herod had intended to copy the whole thing, but ran out of money by the time he had gotten around to constructing the upper levels of the Druseion. The tower marked the start, on the shore, of a long and broad promenade, visible even from where they were, which was bordered by palaces, all built from polished marble, above which stands the temple of Augustus with its two statues, visible from much farther away and to which a long, broad set of steps led from the harbor.

"When the Druseion was opened," said Matthew, "Herod the Great tried to persuade Augustus to make the trip here, but all to no avail."

"It's also worth having a look at what's belowground," said Plotius. "The sewers are so wide and tall, and the chambers that have been fashioned within them are so big that one could hold banquets in them when the tide is out. They have been built in parallel with an interconnecting cross-passage so that rainwater and sewage can flow easily; the sea comes in at high water and on the ebb all the filth is washed away. There is no need for power to clean it.

Alexandros displayed a lively interest in the sewage canals; he wished to see them if that were possible.

Plotius told them that the Romans had completed the system, doubling the width of a section of the aqueduct constructed by Herod because the population had grown and there was a growing demand for water. The seven-mile aqueduct was an incredible engineering feat; it rested on arches that were something like five hundred feet high, and at one place a tunnel bored through a hill and into the city. Over the entire seven miles from spring to city, unobservable to the eye, it sloped slightly downward, without a single hitch; it could hardly be believed that Herod had been able to get this constructed in the first place, and that the Romans were later able to double its capacity, also without a hitch.

Uri noted that when it came down to it, in the end, all aqueducts worked on the same principle, and there were some in Rome that ran even higher aboveground.

"Sure," Plotius retorted angrily, "but those were not built in the lethargic and imprecise East!"

A devil got into Uri:

"But the pyramids are said to be incredibly precise in their construction. Doesn't Egypt count as the East?"

Plotius waved that aside in annoyance.

Just opposite the harbor entrance, and thus at its southernmost point, at the foot of the stadium, there was an enormous theater that opened northward, toward the sea, Matthew said, and from its highest point it was possible to see a long way, so there was no barge that would not be spotted from at least twenty or thirty stadia away. It held fifteen thousand people. Pilate had recently replaced its old plaster flooring with marble.

"That's exactly how Ostia should be built," Matthew sighed. "Herod the Great had the money; Augustus and Tiberius didn't..."

"But Herod the Great murdered and robbed on an unimaginable scale," Alexandros observed. "That is how he got the money. I have no wish for the Romans to get a splendid harbor at that sort of price."

"All the same, it's ridiculous," said Matthew.

Uri did quietly wonder to himself whether Herod the Great had actually murdered any more than Tiberius was said to have. To start with, he had done his murdering through the Praetorian prefect Sejanus, then he had gotten a new Praetorian prefect, Macro, to murder Sejanus and his followers. It was said that Tiberius used force to induce the wealthy to draw up their last will and testament in his favor, so it was more than likely that he had enough money to build a harbor if he wanted.

Matthew outlined that he was putting his trust in Pilate receiving them in Herod's palace; it might be a matter of luck, but Pilate had already received one delegation that he'd led some six years ago. He had rarely met a Roman who was more agreeable, polite, tactful, or knowledgeable about Jewish affairs, but the important thing was the palace: an immense and glittering building that stood at the southern end of the city on a promontory that ran into the sea, directly above it. It was 240 cubits in length by 130 in breadth, and in the middle it had a pool surrounded by splendid colonnades, one of the columns bearing the names of all the Roman prefects to date, in Greek as well as Latin, and a list of their merits. That was the residence of all the prefects, Pilate too, and he seldom went to Jerusalem; it was a truly marvelous building. It would be nice to see it again inside.

"Can boats be moored by the palace?" Alexandros inquired.

Matthew paused to think. He had not seen a boat over in that direction, but there seemed to be no reason why not. He looked at Alexandros with some amazement.

"Why? Do you want to deliver something directly to the palace?" he asked with a grin.

Alexandros shook his head; he was just interested.

"No doubt Herod sited his palace," chipped in Plotius, "in a place that he would be able to escape from by ship, if need be, so as to avoid a possible naval blockade of the harbor."

Uri did not understand what had put such a sharp edge to the tone of Plotius's voice. Matthew must also have sensed something of the kind because he abandoned his attempt to sketch the history of the town and stared fixedly at the shore.

Uri was glad they had arrived, but he was unable to say goodbye to the dog. He searched and called, but Remus was nowhere to be seen; maybe he had hidden away somewhere in grief. Uri was astonished that he should almost come to crying over a dopey dog.

When they stepped from the gangplank to the shore, Matthew knelt and kissed the ground, which at this point was composed of slabs of marble. Uri hesitated but on seeing that the others did the same, he kneeled down likewise, though he did not kiss the slab, jut touched it with the tip of his nose. Hilarus and Alexandros shed tears, and even Valerius was moved, wiping his nose on his shawl.

A toll of six sesterces per head had to be paid to the Greek exciseman. Matthew had forewarned them that these were not like the Greeks in Italia, with whom it was possible to joke along; these Greeks hated Jews. It mattered not that Jews were multiplying faster than the Greeks; the city was still not truly theirs.

It was typical that the largest house of prayer stood on a plot of land belonging to a Greek merchant, who would not sell the plot. There was no way of compelling him to do so. It had not raised any problems, but whenever he was approached with a new proposal to sell it, he threatened instantly to build on the neighboring plots, because those also belonged to him, and he could block access to the house of prayer. The concept of easement was familiar enough in Caesarea and Judaea, but it was not exactly clear how large it should be; it would not be helpful if the Greek landowner left only an alleyway for the Jewish faithful.

"It's Alexandria writ small," Alexandros declared derisively, perhaps hinting at the Greco-Jewish rivalry there, but perhaps also because it was conspicuous how bereft the oversize harbor was of ships.

Plotius remarked that less than half the inhabitants of Alexandria were Jewish, so the comparison did not quite stand, to which Alexandros rejoined that if there were more Jews in Caesarea, then it was high time they forced the Greeks out, but Matthew held that to be foolish because the Greeks would take their revenge on all the Jewish minorities living in Syrian towns. Hilarus tried to put a stop to the senseless squabbling by repeating again and again that they had arrived, they had arrived.

Uri lazily wondered, as they walked over from the mole to the promenade fringed with all the grand buildings, what he would need to do to prevail on his companions to make the return leg of the trip via Alexandria. Maybe the ship would cost more, but it was a shorter route, so part of the extra expense could be recovered.

Caesarea was packed with magnificent buildings, vast palaces and villas, constructed in the finest of Greek styles—a miniature Rome with parks, a theater, a stadium, baths. The town's location was favorable, and over the city rose a mountainside dotted with attractive big buildings. The harbor surpassed that of Syracusa—smaller perhaps, but orderly and clean. Well-tended date palms and cypresses, planted and pruned to uniform shape, bordered the promenade, which also had a stretch on which lulav and etrog were being grown for Sukkot. Uri could scarcely believe his eyes; he peered, went closer, and stared until tears came. Up till then he had only seen a lulav, with its long, slender branches dense with small leaves, or etrog, with its fruits, in painted images or ritual carvings, placed next to a menorah or shofar. So these plants really did exist! On the fifth day after Yom Kippur, the Day of Atonement, on the fifteenth day of Tishri, comes the festival of thanksgiving, when the autumn harvest is celebrated in Palestine; then lulav branches and etrog lemons have to be taken into the Temple, traditionally, but not in the houses of prayer across the Diaspora, partly because they are not native elsewhere, but also because there is but one Temple, the one in Jerusalem. Word had it that only the Jews of Alexandria were unwilling to acknowledge this, and therefore they carried lulav branches and etrog lemons into their largest house of prayer, the Basilica.

They had to pass a huge temple. Mounted atop a tall stone pillar at the top of the steps in front of its Doric columns was a huge marble statue of a person who was identifiably the emperor Tiberius. The statue was at least as high as the one of Augustus in Rome.

"The Tiberium," said Matthew. "It took five years to construct. Pilate started building it the moment he was appointed, bringing the plans with him from Rome. The site had been picked out in advance, and a lot of expensive villas had to be demolished to make way for it, and the owners were given a considerable amount in compensation, albeit none too readily, as the lawsuits dragged on for years. Inside the edifice there are statues of Julius Caesar and Augustus, as well as Jupiter, Venus, and Priapus. There was also one of Sejanus, but when he was disgraced Pilate had his head smashed."

"The torso has been put in storage," Plotius snickered. "Malicious tongues say it is waiting for the next emperor. It only needs a new head to be carved and joined on."

Uri went closer to the temple while his companions stopped and watched impatiently. He walked up the steps and around the statue.

The colossus was at least sixty feet high. From below all he could see clearly was Tiberius's jutting jaw, which blocked out his nose and other features. The sculptor, whoever it was, had fashioned an enormous, pugilistic chin for the figure. In Rome there were numerous busts of the ruling emperor, so Uri looked on him as almost a personal acquaintance; nevertheless there were not all that many depictions of him, as early in his reign he had forbidden statues of himself to be raised. Later he did give up on the ban, but sculptors worked slowly and had to fulfill commissions from cities all over Italia.

Uri searched for the edges of the marble blocks that had been fit together, but these had either been so well finished they were hidden, or else they were too high up for him to see clearly, so even from close up the statue seemed to him to have been carved from a single block. That could not possibly be the case, however. He wondered how much a statue of that size cost. The marble alone must have cost a great deal, to say nothing of the transport.

He stopped at the top of the steps and looked back toward the harbor.

Streets laid out in straight lines, carefully planned buildings, marble, gilded roofs, blinding white colonnades. He blinked hard and squinted through a crack in his fingers.

It was a cold, unfriendly town. No alleyways, or random narrowings and widenings. It was a planned city; it did not live.

"You'll have time later to gape at everything," Matthew called out angrily, when Uri got back to the group. "Let's go! People are waiting for us."

There were few people in the streets; they were not hurrying. Peace reigned on all sides, and boredom. Nothing in this sleepy, pretty town suggested that disturbances of public order had taken place a few weeks before. The messengers had exaggerated as usual.

They clambered up the mountain, with Uri's companions also stopping every now and then to look back at the harbor. They went by gardens with rich, dense vegetation screened behind high stone walls in the depths of which no doubt lurked immense villas that were obliterated from sight by the wall and the vegetation. By the entrances to several of the villas there were sentry cabins for the guards. In his belly, Uri sensed a strange emptiness; there was something threatening in the Roman prefect's seat of residence that he had not felt elsewhere. The fate of the Jewish people could not have been too good under Herod the Great, who had conceived the town.

The hillside was not completely deserted, with laden carts creaking their way up and here and there a pedestrian carrying something on his back or head. But the artificial miniature city, named after Caesar Augustus, stood out in such a sharp contrast to everything that they had seen up till then on the route, and most especially with Rome, that Uri wished, more than ever before, that he was anywhere but where he happened to be.

"We'll be there any time now," Matthew panted, "but if you want we'll climb a bit higher up to the peak, because from there you can pick out Jerusalem."

Hilarus and Iustus ran on ahead, with the rest trudging on behind toward the top of the hill. They stopped. Matthew pointed to the east rather than southward. The weather was clear, with the sun shining on their backs, and Uri deduced from the whoops of his companions that they could genuinely see it. He turned in the same direction but saw nothing but an endless twinkling blur of blue and green.

"Can you see it?" an exultant Valerius inquired of him. "The Temple!"

"I can see," said Uri.

He couldn't see it.

It was time to pray. Matthew poured water from his jug into a bronze dish, and one after the other they rinsed their hands, got out their paraphernalia, affixed the phylacteries to their upper arms or foreheads, turned toward Jerusalem, and bobbing forward and backward said the Sh'ma: "Hear, O Israel: the Lord our God, the Lord is One." It seemed to Uri that Israel was not listening; there was no one passing nearby. He rebuked himself for the thought; he was in the Holy Land after all. Valerius, Hilarus, and Iustus prostrated themselves with outstretched arms, while the others prayed standing up. Alexandros was weeping, but Uri felt nothing. He thought of his father: would he feel anything himself were he here?

They made their way down the mountain.

"You didn't see it, did you," said Plotius.

"Yes, I did," Uri rebutted him angrily.

Plotius uttered a soft reproving gurgle, confidentially, so it would not have reached the others. Uri gritted his teeth; he is hurting me, but at least he's watching. The insult did not please him, but the attention did.

The stone wall at the gate they halted at was covered with vines. Matthew rang a bell to announce their arrival. They waited. Matthew rang again, but there was no response.

"There must be servants around," he said, troubled.

They might have been there, but either they did not hear or they did not want to open the gate. Alexandros, Hilarus, Valerius, and Iustus in turn pounded on the gate—all to no avail.

"Where are we going to stay?" Plotius queried, and, leaning against the wall, he put down his sack on the ground.

"With Simon the Magus," Matthew replied. "He's an important man. Physician to the prefect's wife."

"Oh!" was Plotius's response. They waited to see if he was going to say anything else, but he did not speak, so it became no clearer whether he knew him. They lay down on the western side of the wall, the sun shining strongly on them.

Matthew made excuses: he knew that Simon still lived there; he had been renting the gorgeous residence ever since he had become a confidant of the prefect's wife. He had not been notified that Simon might have moved; he had also stayed with him on his last two trips, the last time not six months ago, in the month of Tishri, when he had led a delegation for the Day of Atonement. He would know if anything had happened to him. But if he had moved nevertheless, then they would go back to the harbor, because he had an acquaintance there, the secretary to the representative of the Jewish fleet, who had sailed with him for years; he was certain that he'd be able to put them up at his place.

"Never fear," said Matthew. "You'll have a roof over your heads."

They still had a bit of unleavened bread, so they snacked on that, and they still had some water from the boat, which they drank, and went on slumbering at the foot of the wall.

Uri cogitated on what sort of delegation Matthew might have been leading to Jerusalem six months ago. Money was not taken for Yom Kippur, only for Passover. There must be a continuous exchange of information and business between Jerusalem and Rome. Strange that his father had never spoken about it.

When the sun had sunk below the sea in the west, they turned again to Jerusalem and said their prayers.

Matthew paced restlessly.

They sat, backs propped up on the wall, gazing, out of sorts and wordless.

It crossed Uri's mind that it would be no bad thing if the mission were to end at this point; if he could go straight back to the harbor and set sail on the first ship that was setting off for Alexandria.

On his own.

He would install himself in that famous big library, which Julius Caesar had put to the torch seventy-six years before with the loss of untold millennia of irreplaceable manuscripts, clay tablets, petroglyphs, and scrolls of parchment and cloth. It was rumored, though, that everything possible had since been replaced, and more than one Roman Jew able to offer manuscripts of value to the library in Alexandria had enriched himself. The whole stock was continuously being recollected, and although it was impossible to replace every single item, the rebuilt library of Alexandria once again counted as the world's richest library.

He would read the works to which he could not gain access in Rome.

In his head there was a long list of the titles of works that absolutely had to be read, mainly mathematical works, the existence of which he had gleaned from public libraries in Rome, which did not hold the works themselves, only references to them. Once he had read those, he would get on a boat that was running from Alexandria to Ostia, finally get back to Rome and home, and lie around in Rome's damp, cool, miasmic, leprous, malarial air, resting his throbbing head, his sore midriff, and his aching back, and when his father stepped in to upbraid him for something, he could start telling him what he had read, and his father would seat himself on his couch and listen entranced as he had never done before. He, Uri, would be inspired by the spirit and mentality of all the authors he had read, whose works had seeped into him, become one with his blood, and his father would be touched at last by the vast, prodigious human knowledge that emanated from his own son. His spirit, bogged down as it was in mundane cares, would be uplifted. Joseph rarely read, not having the time for it, but Uri was sure that these works would be of assistance to his cruelly fated father.

Down in the harbor a lavish display of lights went up, the brightest of which was the Pharos of Caesarea.

Matthew began talking about the Pharos of Alexandria, which stood at the entrance to the royal harbor.

"That is a sight to behold!" he said. "Hundreds of ships at anchor on both sides, some of them monstrously large: I once saw an Achaean quinquereme. You can hardly get a boat in there, it's always jam-packed. If a mariner has no reliable contacts in the city and cannot drop the 'right' name, he may find himself kept waiting for weeks on the water. Dozens of craft make the rounds with pilots and excisemen between the harbor and the ships at anchor, and if the captain does not pay them unconscionable sums of money (since like everyone else they too work to fill their own pockets), then he will find his ship is constantly put to the bottom of the list until he sees sense or rows over to the city and raises the credit from a banker..."

It would have been good to hear more about Alexandria, but all of a sudden some servants with laden baskets on their heads appeared on the steeply sloping street. At first all that could be seen were the wobbling baskets and only after that the heads. They were followed by a few armed men, and behind them came eight slaves bearing an ornate palanquin up the hill. A litter borne by eight slaves was a rare enough sight even in Rome, where even the wealthy made do with four. It was set down at the gate as gently as if they were transporting eggs, and out of it descended a tousled, black-bearded, rotund figure, balding and with graying hair and bushy eyebrows and wearing an exquisitely draped toga.

This was Simon the Magus.

Their host had made his arrival. They got to their feet to greet him.

Simon offered no excuses; after all, they might just as easily have arrived a day or two earlier or later. He just nodded by way of welcome, greeted Matthew in Aramaic as an old acquaintance and embraced him too, though without a smile on his face. The gate was opened and they were finally able to go in.

They made their way through a splendid, well-kept garden to the stone house, which was larger than that of the proprietor of the sawmill in Syracusa.

Room was made for them in an enormous chamber somewhat like an atrium. They were given wood benches to rest their backs on, and on those were mattresses spread with fine linen. They took a dip in a sumptuous tiled pool, prayed, and then gathered for supper, by which time Simon had also changed, putting on a clean tunic. His hair and beard were uncombed and he was pop-eyed with weariness.

They were served a meal of countless dishes, among them a great variety of meats (Simon knew that having been on a ship, they had eaten no meat for weeks) and fine wines. They fell on the food and ate with gusto, whereas Simon the Magus took only small bites of everything.

Uri looked around; there was nothing to suggest that the person dwelling in the house was a physician.

Simon started speaking Greek with them, but he struggled with the declension of words and the mysteries of the aorist tense, so after a few glasses he switched to Aramaic. He spoke with an easily recognizable Galilean accent. Matthew spoke Aramaic, and now it was suddenly revealed that Plotius spoke it perfectly; not surprising, thought Uri, given that he had spent quite a few years in Judaea, though he found it peculiar that he had not made this clear before. So Plotius too was also testing my Aramaic that Sabbath when I interpreted the reading, he thought.

Hilarus spoke Hebrew, so he was able to follow what the host was saying, more or less, and for the benefit of Iustus, Valerius, and Alexandros, a Jewish servant interpreted from Aramaic to Greek—perfectly, as far as Uri could tell.

Simon tried to banter, but he wasn't suited to play the role of man of the world, as he was quite obviously unable to set his worries aside, and although no one asked him, he began to talk about them.

He had gotten back to the house so late because he had been trying to call in the outstanding debts of his creditors, and that was no easy matter. He had been concentrating almost exclusively on that for several weeks, and he had been forced to realize that lenders took a much bigger risk than he would ever have imagined. He had been poor for all of his days; he had limped the length and breadth of Galilee as an itinerant sorcerer, curing where he was asked and seeing very little in the way of money as he generally worked for room and board until, by a stroke of luck, Pilate, having heard about the cures he had achieved, sent for him and asked him to restore his sickly wife to health. He did indeed manage to help the lady recover, and he had been given a large amount of money by a grateful Pilate, after which he had gone away and for a few weeks had resumed his healing work in the villages of Galilee, until Pilate's men caught up with him and called him to the palace, where the condition of Pilate's spouse had taken a turn for the worse. A few days of speaking to the lady once more brought an improvement; Pilate had retained his services, and since then had very generously supported him financially. It now seemed that the curative effect was no longer working; he would not be able to keep his job much longer, and he wanted to be sure that the money he had saved was in a secure place. He did not regret having to leave this beautiful house: he had been content in stables and sties, and in fact greatly missed the smells of the land and livestock; he missed the country people, who were more appreciative than the rich, even when they could barely pay him, not even in kind, if they had nothing. But if he had come by money, better it should not go astray.

Matthew advised Simon the Magus to invest his money in land; it was cheap now but prices were certain to rise. Plotius recommended something else: buy a share in a well-run bank, and he would then have a share of the bank's profits, in proportion to the capital that had been put in, with the money accumulating much faster than if it were simply earning interest.

Simon the Magus shook his head: he was a bit old-fashioned and had no head for working out compound interest; indeed, he was not interested, he just wanted to put his money in the safest place, and that was the treasury of the Temple in Jerusalem. It was so well guarded that he could be sure the money would not go astray. Plotius conceded that he was right; as far as he was informed, private fortunes were also stored there, but then the treasury did not pay out any interest. That didn't matter, said Simon the Magus, as long as the money was in a safe place.

Anyway, he had recently been trying to call in his outstanding debts, and to be sure he was sorry now that earlier on he had given loans at usurious rates, because if the interest had been lower he would have gotten the money back long ago. He had all the promissory notes; they were drawn up in three copies in the presence of two witnesses, as they should be, with a copy going to him, a second to the debtor, and a third to the records office in Caesarea, by the Druseion, but then again a records office could be torched at any time, or a promissory note filched and the debtor's own copy destroyed, and then the money was as good as gone.

"The Temple's treasury is safe, because the Jews will never let that be torched," said Simon the Magus. "If I choose, I can reclassify a part of the money as a donation, and then I shall be putting into effect a deed that is genuinely pleasing to God, and who knows, maybe even the priests will leave me be and not try to curse me two or three times a year for helping the sick and driving out their demons."

Uri was happy he could understand every word: how lucky he was that his mother tongue was Aramaic, and Greek only his father's language.

He would never have thought that a sorcerer would have problems like that—exactly the same as any businessman. But there had been gossip about sorcerers back in Rome; they were good for nothing beyond the laying on of hands, it was said, and they cast dubious spells instead of studying Celsus.

"Has Pilate's wife's illness gotten worse?" asked Matthew. "Are you afraid that you'll be kicked out?"

"She's no worse than earlier," said Simon the Magus. "She's dogged by being chronically unloved, which breaks out in various forms on and in her body. I am able to converse with her, listen to her; I am a friend, a well-wisher, her spiritual adviser, but I am not her husband. She has no children, her relatives are a long way away, she can't confide in the servants, her husband is preoccupied and restless, and the initial charm of my sympathy for her, which made her improvement so spectacular early on, has since disappeared. She has grown accustomed to me and has relapsed. I, in my turn, have grown accustomed to her; her ailments bore me. I know her too well, and for that very reason I can't think of anything to say. She needs a new doctor—anyone, just not me. Someone in whom she can place unbounded trust. Healing is anyway mostly a question of faith. Pilate is a wise man; he knows that, but I am not waiting for him to terminate the arrangement."

Uri listened in amazement. An intelligent man, this sorcerer. He might be a sorcerer, but he speaks like a philosopher. Maybe there will be surprises in store for me on the trip, after all.

"Are you also a healer for Pilate?" Plotius asked.

"No," the Magus answered. "He has a Roman physician, and rightly so. He lets Pilate's blood, controls his diet, prescribes the order in which baths should be taken. That's what Pilate believes in, and who am I to undermine that belief? Me, a Jew. As far as his wife is concerned, he was able to admit that Greek medicine had been a washout, but that is not so for himself. I would not have taken him on anyway; I'm not crazy, I'm used to dealing with rural Jews and have no idea what troubles high-ranking Romans. Mediocre as the salves and pills of a Latin doctor may be, he certainly knows better than me what makes Pilate's belly gripe. More than that, I have striven all along to know as little as possible about him: any time that his wife began to gossip about him I interrupted her and asked her not to go on. I'm sure she would have told this to her husband and in doing so I earned his confidence more than by my initial success in curing his wife. Well, it's from there that I got this villa." He gestured around him. "Anyway, it's not actually mine, I only rent it. I don't want property of my own; I never did have my own house, and I don't intend to either. It only brings trouble."

The members of the delegation carried on eating and drinking in silence. Except for Matthew, they were surprised by the magus; they had not imagined a Galilean quack would be anything like this. Matthew also kept quiet as he ate, but Uri could see that a serenely sardonic sparkle of triumph was glinting in his eyes.

Uri had never before met a man who was so forthright in the way he expressed himself. Roman Jews kept those kinds of ideas to themselves, if they thought them at all; they would never say them out loud. Was the Magus not afraid that someone might inform on him? He must be very sure of himself, and especially about Pilate's affection for him.

"So, Pilate is restless nowadays?" Alexandros finally inquired in Greek.

"It would seem so," Simon the Magus replied in Greek. "He was already wound up before the demonstration, though. Previously, he only sent a courier once or twice a week to Rome or Antioch, but in recent weeks it has been five or six, and there are as many coming the other way. I don't know what's afoot, but something must have happened in Rome."

The delegates looked at one another. What on Earth could have happened in Rome? There had been nothing when they set off. The state couriers made the trip more rapidly than their delegation: with fresh remounts at relay stations, they were able to cover the Rome–Naples route in five days; then if they sailed straight via Alexandria to Caesarea, they might be able to make that in two weeks, though that was not significantly faster. It was unlikely anything had happened in Rome, because the news would have reached them in Syracusa through some loudmouthed courier on one of the ships plying the Ostia–Syracusa route; after all, news of the demonstration in Caesarea had already reached them in Messina.

Matthew asked about what had actually happened two weeks back.

Simon related that a crowd of a few hundred had come from Jerusalem and demonstrated for days in front of Pilate's palace. Leaning out of the window, without regard for possible arrows or javelins, Pilate had politely asked them to go home, but they stayed. He could have had them dispersed by his soldiers, as there were three cohorts and an *ala*, a division, stationed in the barracks at Caesarea, but he did not; indeed, he issued the order that not a single hair be harmed on the head of any Jew, and he tried to bring the raving lunatics to their senses, telling them that the military insignia that had been taken into the palace in Jerusalem were not images, merely inscriptions with the names of the emperor Tiberius and himself, and anyway the standards had been furled when they were taken up into the tower of Phasael that Herod had built in the Upper City, as they had always done, ever since a Roman governor resided there. Nobody had taken any exception to that previously, so he was of the opinion that it was perfectly in line with Jewish law to carry them in like that.

Pilate's arguments were to no avail, however; the crowd had been stirred up against him.

Then the Jews had marched to the stadium, and there they were surrounded by an armed detachment. What else were they supposed to do? The Jews had thrown themselves to the ground and demanded to be executed, but then Pilate had arrived in great haste. He ordered the soldiers to leave the stadium and told the Jews that, though it was a grave affront to imperial dignity, in the interests of keeping the peace he would have the military insignia withdrawn. That is what happened, and not a single hair on anyone's head was harmed. The malcontents trooped home, and it's been peaceful since then.

"Is it true that a letter of complaint was sent to Tiberius?" Matthew asked.

"I've heard rumors of the kind, but I don't know for a fact. Allegedly Tiberius wrote back immediately and chided Pilate. But then that's only gossip; Pilate's couriers aren't in the habit of opening his correspondence."

"So, it's been peaceful since then?" Alexandros asked.

"Yes, peaceful," said the Magus, but shook his head to show a lack of conviction. "Except for people: the numbers of crazy people grow by the day. I haven't visited Jerusalem or been around the two counties for months. The time has come for me to leave this nice, cool villa behind; time to do what I can for the crazy people whose troubles I can sense and recognize. Here I have only one crazy person entrusted to me, and I can do nothing for her any longer."

After a short pause he added, "It's been peaceful for too long. A second generation has grown up now that has not seen war. From what I see, people can't stand peace, because when left in peace there's time to think—and that is painful. There's as much deception and lying as ever, but now there is time to get caught up in it. Injustice may be a slow-killing poison, but it does kill. Left in peace, the soul becomes crippled—in war, only the body. It will come to war sooner or later. The Creator planted it in us; somehow the soul must want it that way."

Alexandros livened up, his eyes flashing:

"And what does the Lord want?"

Simon the Magus look wearily at him.

"The Lord God let us choose for ourselves what sort of trouble to get into with each other and ourselves," he said, now slipping back into Aramaic. "'Thou shalt love thy neighbor as thyself,' He said. All interpreters of the Law also say it: 'Do not do unto your neighbor what you would not do unto yourself.' That is the Great Commandment, the Last Word, on which even the schools of Hillel and Shammai agree. Nobody in their right mind can expect anyone who does not love himself to love his neighbor."

THAT WAS THE MOST COMFORTABLE OF ALL THEIR LODGINGS SO FAR, and Matthew allowed them to wander around as they wished during the day.

"But be back by nightfall," he ordered. "I don't know when we will be moving on. We have a whole week to get there."

He also added, "Don't take anything with you; everything must stay here."

That "everything" meant the sack, which contained nothing except a jug, tefillin, and a cloak.

"There are not enough berths in Jerusalem," Plotius explained to Uri. "Many hundreds of thousands make pilgrimage for the feast, often more than a million, and it is not easy to find accommodation, even though we are privileged persons. The later we arrive, the happier they will be; it doesn't matter if we make a nuisance of ourselves here until the last minute."

Uri was delighted that at last he would be left alone and could ramble on his own. Maybe Matthew would manage to arrange an audience with Pilate for them. Pilate himself was of no great interest: Gaius Lucius must be wealthier than him, a provincial governor was no big deal, but if he happened to be there, he would quite like to see Herod's palace from the inside.

He got to the vicinity of the palace. It was a vast edifice, as imposing from the outside as Matthew had described it. There was little chance of being able to inspect it from the inside; Simon the Magus was preoccupied with calling in the money that was owed to him, but without him Matthew could not present himself to the palace saying that they had an audience with the prefect. They were an important delegation, but not so far as Pilate was concerned.

No trace of preparation for the feast could be picked up among the Jews in Caesarea. Of course, for them it was simple: it was enough for them to set off four days beforehand. Matthew wasn't making much effort to make contact with the Jews of Caesarea; they wouldn't be able to offer them a more pleasant or comfortable place to stay than Simon's. There they were given an ample breakfast, and the suppers were marvelous; the table in the dining room was permanently laid and the servants saw to it that they should instantly be given fresh food and drink whether they appeared on their own or with several of the others. Even so, Uri was starving during the day; he had not an as to call his own. He had not the slightest idea what the money here was worth, nor had he even seen any, as he was unable to sit out on the terrace of a tavern to have food or a drink.

In the evenings his companions talked mostly about money. Plotius and Matthew would attempt to explain how much each coin was worth. From the second evening onward that became a daily task for them before going to bed; Uri would lie on his couch, listening to them, perceiving their disputes over exchange rates as a monotonous psalmody. Stupendous amounts of money were in circulation, it turned out, virtually all the denominations that had ever been minted within the field of attraction of the Great Sea, and the exchange between these was impossibly complicated. "Tetradrachma, sela, shekel, sacred shekel, ordinary shekel, dinar. Tropaik, asper, ma'ah, tresith, pondion, issar, prutah, zuz, mina, shekel, dupondius, zuz, mina, shekel, dupondius, drachma, drachma, drachma, dinar, prutah, lepton," Uri crooned to himself on the couch the names of the coins that he heard, and as he drifted into sleep these magic words droned on of their own accord. The one conversion factor that he registered was that one lepton was worth one eighth of an as, or in other words half a quadrans. It amused him that the smallest coin in Rome also had a half counterpart here, though even a Roman pleb like himself did not measure value in quadrans back home but in asses, and it particularly tickled him that this tiny coin, a lepton, had two names, its Semitic name being the prutah. He had taken note of that because his companions were constantly teasing Hilarus to tell them how many prutah made a lepton, and every time the teacher would give them some other figure for the exchange rate, never realizing that it was the same coin.

It pained Uri that in Syracusa he had been so brazenly robbed of half a sestertius: never again will I be such a numbskull, he vowed keenly.

Early on in the morning all his companions would leave the house, so Uri supposed he could not stay either. Each set off alone and also arrived alone. Uri did not ask them what the devil they were up to; he would have a good feed in the morning and until the evening would stroll aimlessly, hungry and thirsty.

He had seen a house of prayer, a fair-sized building; even the largest synagogue in Rome was not that big. Maybe that was the one that stood on the Greek's plot of land. He would have gone in, but it was closed. There were a lot of Jews living there, so why was their house of prayer closed? Was there another one? He asked a Greek, and of course there was another. Uri followed his directions and walk there. That too was closed.

That evening he questioned the others. Matthew explained.

"In Palestine houses of prayer are only left open on market days. Mondays and Thursdays are the market days; that is when peasants come in from the villages, bringing their produce, and if they are able to sell anything, they buy themselves something. That is also when they would visit the house of prayer, if they were going that way—not to pray, mind you, but to litigate. That would cost them, so they would take home less money than they had come with, even if they managed to sell something. The Jews of Palestine adore litigation. The courts hold their sessions in the refectory of the house of prayer, hearing cases late into the evening. The houses of prayers are open on the Sabbath as well, of course, but on those days only the members of the local congregation would eat supper there because, being the Sabbath, peasants are not allowed into the city."

"Here Monday and Thursday are also days of fasting for pious Jews," Plotius said. "They abstain from eating until sunset, if I understand it right. Our forbears made a wise decision lest peasants, on the pretext of litigating or praying, should demand free meals in the towns."

Uri felt tempted to sit through a whole day of court cases, but then he decided he'd prefer to wander aimlessly in the harbor area on the off chance that some more interesting diversion would arise.

He noticed a poster. It advertised two events: the theatrical performance of a play by the poet Agathon, which would have been of interest, and an appearance by the famous philosopher Makedonios, who would be speaking in the interval between chariot races.

The very man he had heard in Syracusa.

He must have set off from Syracusa a few days before them and then, after visiting several towns, arrived here after them. Would he be plagiarizing this time too, Uri wondered, or finally reading his own work?

Uri was unfamiliar with Agathon's dramas, but he been interested in the strange author ever since reading that Aristotle had criticized his plays for breaking all the rules. There has to be something to them if Aristotle loathed them so. Definitely something to be seen.

That was all well and good, but what, he wondered, would the philosopher be saying in the interval between chariot races?

The two events were at the same time on the same day. Which should he choose? Whichever he wouldn't have to pay for, the free one: he had no desire to ask for another loan.

He made inquiries in the harbor, and found that both productions were free.

There was also a proletariat in Caesarea, Uri concluded. It was just that, at first, he couldn't figure out why there were no crowds of ordinary people out and about on the streets, strolling, gossiping, and acting big like back at home, in Rome. Then he finally realized why this delightfully built town was so dead: there were no dockworkers bustling in the port, no trade. Even a city like this, devised by cool heads, would burst with life if there were poor folks chatting and making a fuss somewhere in it.

He decided to go to the stadium; maybe he would get a chance to see Agathon's work back in Rome.

It was early in the afternoon, the weather was glorious. A large proportion of the crowd streaming toward the edifice was made up of soldiers. They were not carrying weapons but they were in uniform. They marched under the leadership of their officers, with the civilians, most of them Jewish, respectfully making way for them.

Two entrances led into the U-shaped structure, and after passing through one of the vomitoria one reached a corridor separating the upper and lower stands. A separate set of steps led to each vomitorium to divide the crowd into smaller groups before they made their way into the auditorium. Uri was enchanted by the inscription that was set above the entrance passageways: VOMITORIUM I, VOMITORIUM II, and so on, as if some enormous force were regurgitating the unsavory crowd into the auditorium through these openings.

When he reached the auditorium, through the third vomitorium from the north, Uri realized he would have had a fine view out to sea if his eyesight had been any good. He would gladly have climbed up into the upper section, but he decided to find a place as low down as possible so that he could at least see something. The soldiers raced into the upper tribune; they were eagle-eyed, that was how they had been picked. Civilians took the seats next to Uri in the lower sector.

The stadium had a paved floor but was thickly covered in sawdust. Centered between the northward-pointing arms of the U was a platform running north to south, about three feet high and eight or nine feet wide, on top of which notables and the judges of the chariot race would obviously be seated. The truncated pyramid of marble that indicated the turnaround in the course was placed at the northern end of the platform; the four positions that made up the starting line were placed at the southern end.

It became clear why the soldiers had raced to the upper tribune, and the upper rows at that: the platform partially obscured the upper, western, section of the track from the view of spectators in the lower tribune.

The theater lying immediately south of the stadium had a number of ancillary buildings tacked on to it: a water tower, stables, and dressing rooms, as well as two entrances that were closed to the public and concealed by two high walls. It was through these that the competitors would later drive their chariots to the starting line.

Uri seemed to recall that it was in the stadium at Caesarea that the Jews from Jerusalem had protested against Pilate.

He shuddered.

This was the stadium.

Only a few weeks before, the Jewish protesters had lain down in this sawdust-strewn arena and demanded that their heads be cut off.

He looked around, peering with narrowed eyes.

Spectators were pouring in peacefully through the vomitoria, hungry for spectacle; not one of them had any memory of the unrest.

Those two risible characters they had encountered in Messina would have reached Rome by now and would be proclaiming to Far Side at large about the monstrous things that were happening in Caesarea. No doubt there would be some who gave credence to their reports, who became alarmed, and who plied the message bearers with food and drink.

Once he got back home he would tell his father; let him be amused.

As Uri peered around he pondered the strategic considerations that may well have played a part in choosing the location for the stadium; it stood right by the seashore, just like Herod's palace, and could likewise function secretly as a mooring place for military craft. Herod the Great could not have put much faith in his hold on power if he had built as many as three secret harbors, Uri reflected; and then for decades on end he had ruled without any trouble, murdering notable Jews by the thousand, not to mention members of his own family, including his adored wife and all his sons.

There were fifteen rows in the upper stands, and the same number in the lower. How many could be packed into each of those rows? Around five hundred, he guessed, which came to fifteen or twenty thousand in total. Nothing when compared with the capacity of the Circus Maximus in Rome, which held some 180,000. Uri's stomach knotted. He felt lost among the unfamiliar soldiers and civilians, much more so than he had in Syracusa, perhaps because that had at least still been in Italia, home. Here he looked around with a Roman sense of superiority: what had fallen to his lot was more, bigger, and better. Not that he would have dared set foot in the Circus Maximus; he had just heard about it and passed it many a time. He vowed that once he reached home, he would attend the Circus Maximus. He was a Roman citizen; he was entitled to.

The stadium had not filled up completely; it must have been about three quarters full. The spectators yelled to one another and to the vendors, who prowled along the corridor separating the upper and lower tribunes with their big baskets, shouting themselves hoarse as they sold wine, pancakes, olives pickled in wine vinegar, honey, and knick-knacks. Alexandros must be right: half of the town's population was Jewish. He must have been here a few times before, thought Uri; odd, though, that a merchant should be a traveler himself.

All of a sudden, Alexandros himself popped up nearby, looking for a good seat. Uri was flabbergasted; it was as if he had just conjured him. But he was delighted as well, and he hollered at the top of his voice until Alexandros heard him. It was not delight that registered on his face so much as perplexity before he decided to break into a grin, and, pulling himself past the legs of others, he sat down next to Uri. His neighbors grumbled and squeezed to make room.

"I'd never have figured you as one for the Circus," Alexandros said.

"I'm not," said Uri. "I'm here for the philosopher."

Alexandros was unaware that a philosopher was on the program; all he knew about was chariot races and wrestling.

"But of course!" he said. "You were also in the amphitheater in Syracusa on account of some philosopher."

Uri was again flabbergasted: how did he know that?

"Matthew said."

Uri fell silent. Was his every move being discussed by his companions? Alexandros twisted his head around, studying the soldiers sitting in the upper tribune.

"They get everything free," he said cryptically. "Even the wine. Civilians have to pay."

The indignation came as a surprise to Uri.

"In a few days they too will be in Jerusalem," said Alexandros. "All three cohorts and the whole ala."

"What gives you that idea?"

"Everyone knows."

"Have you been to Jerusalem before?"

"No, but everyone knows that all four cohorts and the ala have to be there, along with the prefect, for the four big feasts. Caesarea falls empty on these occasions. If anyone wants to occupy it, this is the time to do it."

"Why so many soldiers in Jerusalem?"

"They're frightened of us," said Alexandros, with an evil laugh. "Scared stiff, the wretches. If we were united in our will, we would rise up and hurl them out from the top row, and they would all fall down dead."

Uri thought it best to say nothing, so he turned toward the wall, separated from the race track by railings on both sides; on the steps constructed at the south end of this the notables were starting to file up. They were greeted with loud acclamation by the soldiers in the upper tribune, and in turn they waved and bowed as if they were actors.

"Big nobodies," said Alexandros. "Local quaestors and aediles."

I've been traveling for a month and a half with my companions, thought Uri, yet I know nothing at all about them. What does he mean by their being frightened "of us"? Who are "we" anyway? Alexandros and me? Who else is "one of us"?

The preparations for the chariot race lasted for ages, deliberately dragged out with all sorts of hocus pocus, and while the spectators were now cheering for the four colors (green seemed to be the most popular, as it was in Rome, with the soldiers uniformly banking on that, whereas the Jewish citizens, from the noise, went more for blue), Uri, for the sake of having something to say, asked Alexandros if he minded going with him later if he was able to arrange to see the sewer.

"I've already seen it," said Alexandros. After a short pause, he added, "It really is a magnificent construction. Every building is connected, the biggest of them with drains ten to twenty cubits across. It's possible to go around the whole town down there; with a good map one always knows which building one happens to be passing beneath."

"Are there maps like that?"

"Yes, in diagram form. They were needed for its construction and now for maintenance; it is checked regularly, as it needs to be."

"And is there a sewer under the stadium?"

"Certainly. The latrines are beneath us. As long as you hold your nose, you can crawl up a drainage channel into whichever sector you choose. The rainwater ditch is also connected. See? It runs all along the side of the arena, and there, next to the wall, is the gutter from the two sides. The stables are also connected. The city spent more on what's down below than on what can be seen up top. That tall water tower on the left, that's the stadium's own special water tower. Look there! On the top of the wall, next to the place of honor is the fountain. It works, too, because it is at a lower height than the water tower... All the important buildings have their own water towers, haven't you noticed? But there is just one aqueduct... You can't stand sentries alongside it every ten paces; that would require many tens of thousands of them, and they can't afford that many..."

A man who is as strong as a bull, allegedly a merchant, comes here from Rome, the city of sewers and aqueducts, and that is what interests him. What, in God's name, is Alexandros a merchant in? He has never spoken about that. And from what is there a need to defend an aqueduct made of stone that is ten to fifteen cubits wide and runs at the height of five or six men? Surely not from us?

Uri felt no urge to demolish this superb aqueduct.

A colossal din arose: to the south, the quadrigas—two-wheeled chariots with teams of four horses abreast—appeared, with their drivers standing in them. They drove to their starting positions and turned there. The four chariots, one for each color, stood for the start. Bets were being laid, with agents of the local betting office flitting around between rows, handing out tessera, the precise nature of which remained a mystery to Uri, with the names of drivers and horses flying back and forth. The lunacy had begun.

"It's a dangerous course," Alexandros said excitedly, panting in Uri's ear, his nostrils quivering. "There's room for at most three and half chariots; they were stingy. Blood will flow, mark my word!"

Uri peered and blinked. He would not have ventured a guess at how many chariots fit alongside each other on the track; Alexandros must be a seasoned race-goer. The starter, with an orange kerchief aloft in his right hand, appeared at the starting line; the crowd roared. When he dropped the kerchief to the ground, with a theatrical flair, the gates at the four start positions were yanked up by a servant by means of a pulley contraption, and the cutthroat contest began. Before the kerchief hit the ground they were already hurtling.

By the end of the first half-circuit the left-side wheel of one of the chariots got caught on the pyramid that marked the turn, the chariot had toppled over and another had driven over it, leaving two horses lying with broken legs and one of the charioteers lying on his side, head bleeding, the other was limping, trying to escape by hopping toward the ditch on one leg. Servants scurried to clear the smashed chariots out of the way of the two chariots left in the race, and they paid no attention to the drivers. The two remaining chariots popped into view from behind the wall and again hurtled from left to right along the length nearest the stands; veering sharply to avoid the horses lying across the track, they came within a hair's breadth of colliding. The crowd raged. The two chariots galloped for seven complete circuits, and the green colored driver won—as it happened, the one for whom the bulk of the crowd had been rooting.

Everyone was yelling; those next to Uri jumped to their feet. The victorious chariot driver took a victory lap; people whistled and clapped and clamored. The winner staggered up to the wall and was garlanded with a wreath. The limping driver inched his way from right to left to the starting line and then vanished through a doorway, to whistling and jeering. The bloody-headed one lay unconscious next to the wall; he was just left there. The second-place driver was sobbing as he drove his panting horses toward the starting line and then disappeared onto the path that led to the stables.

In the second race, one of the chariots overturned and broke apart immediately. The horses stopped, the chariot was unhitched, and they were led back to the starting line, with the driver sprinting off to let the remaining three chariots speed along without obstruction. The man with the bleeding head from the first race was only carried off after the winner of the second race had been announced; he too was whistled at, though he could have heard little of it.

It was then the wrestlers' turn to enter from the left; they clambered up onto the southern end of the partitioning wall, where cordons had been set up on either side to keep them from falling off, while still leaving spectators on both sides a good view. The combatants were not armed and wore loincloths. Blows, holds, kicks, or bites of any kind were allowed; a match was over when one of the contestants conceded. The winner got up and beat his chest at length, aiming kicks at the opponent who was lying on the ground, every kick acknowledged with rapturous hoots from the crowd. The winner bowed toward the notables and the public at large before ambling down the steps toward the stables. The loser left in the same direction; on reaching the arena he sank to all fours and squirmed away, wiggling his hindquarters to gales of laughter and applause from the public.

Next came two athletes, who likewise proceeded along the wall, this time right by the notables, one balancing on the forehead of the other before clambering up a long pole like a monkey and balancing on one arm. He posed there for minutes on end without anything happening. The bored public, busy chomping, slurping, and gossiping, only cried out when the lower equilibrist knocked the pole off his forehead. The athlete who had been poised on one arm gracefully flew through the air and, after performing two and a half somersaults, managed miraculously to land on his feet in the sawdust, take a step or two, then bow. Applause, ovation. The two athletes scampered off.

Then the dignitaries sitting atop the wall got to their feet, marched to the steps, and began to file down. Only then did the greatest pandemonium so far break out, as they were celebrated as if they had carried out quite exceptional feats of arms. Then they too left, along with their retinues, and headed off in the direction of the stables, with the masses rising to their feet in acclamation.

"Is that it? Is it the interval now? What happened?" Uri inquired uncomprehendingly.

"If you ask me," Alexandros said in some excitement, "it's the women's turn now..."

No one came. They had to wait. The public exulted. But then from over by the starting line ten women shrouded in veils trotted in, raced up the steps, and came to a stop in the middle of the wall.

A gaggle of musicians then ambled in, also from the direction of the starting line, playing percussion and wind instruments. The women started to dance, casting their veils to the ground, strutted around in mantles, cast the mantles off, danced in breast-bands and loincloths, then they discarded their breast-bands, and the public went wild, calling out colorfully, while the swaying women undid their loincloths and discarded those too, leaving them stark naked to perform their provocative dance—at the very end writhing as they lay on their backs. The public erupted. The dance over, the performers gathered their veils, draped them over themselves, and ran down the steps to the left, toward the stables. Applause. The musicians slowly plodded off after them, while servants ran in to gather the other discarded garments. One of the boys got a vigorous round of applause for dangling one of the loincloths before his nose, sniffing theatrically, and then draping it between his legs and making a jerky motion with it as he ran off.

Alexandros fumed.

"They didn't wrestle," he said in disappointment—though that was more to himself.

Uri didn't understand who was supposed to have wrestled: the servants or the women.

An intermission followed. The notables reappeared, mounted the steps in dignified fashion, and resumed their seats. The procession was again accompanied by jubilation, the public being grateful that beforehand, by their absence, they had allowed what would otherwise have been a prohibited item in the program. Uri understood well enough: the local dignitaries could not watch immoral acts like that, only the plebs could do that.

He was discomposed. That was the very first time he had seen living female bosoms—twenty of them at that. True, he had barely seen them; his unflagging goggling had been to little avail, though he had seen enough to spot that they were quite varied, with even the individual units of a pair differing. A female crotch was another matter, but the one he saw had been bleeding, and in his dreams it was encircled by disemboweled guts. He would be having no dreams, good or bad, about these particular bosoms.

Following that, arriving from the direction of the stables and accompanied by several of his retinue, the philosopher stepped up onto the wall from the left. The same one, indeed, whom Uri had seen in Syracusa. Now he wore white stars on a silk mantle of dark blue, with a wreath of laurels adorning his brow. This time the short physician stopped at the foot of the steps and gazed up.

Makedonios shook hands with one of the notables and bowed deeply to one of the ladies sitting there on high before turning to bow to the spectators. He was greeted just like the chariot drivers, athletes, and women. He downed a tumbler of wine before beginning to declaim in a ringing voice that was as clearly audible as it had been in Syracusa.

He told exactly the same two stories as before, changing not a single word.

The soldiers guffawed, taking pleasure at each shoddy twist like little boys, interjecting. He was even more successful than at Syracusa, applauded almost as warmly as the naked women; their earlier triumph had obviously rubbed off on him. The philosopher gratefully made repeated bows, then, joined by his physician and a servant, he took a place at the top of the wall to watch the high point in the program: a final match in which the two earlier winners were pitted against each other. Both started in green, clearly on the principle that a green had to win; the soldiers would have that pleasure, thought Uri, and he was forced to conclude that this was hardly pure chance. Evenly matched, each won a round, leaving the third to decide the competition. The one who came second in the final contest struck his head repeatedly on the ground, threw his arms to the sky, and lashed his horses to get a laugh from the public.

They were just acting, performing a predetermined dance; they too were buffoons. The philosopher was a buffoon, so were the local dignitaries. Who knows, maybe even the chariot spills had been arranged in advance to add an element of suspense. The horse's legs, it now occurred to Uri, were obviously insured.

Except during the number with the dancing girls, Alexandros kept scouring the auditorium with his gaze, an expression of somber attention on his face. It's not me he's spying on, Uri thought, but everyone here.

On the way out, they lost each other, though it was true that they had not agreed to part together. Uri thought for a brief moment before jumping over the ditch between the auditorium and the arena, and addressed the philosopher, who was wheezing his way down the steps from the wall.

He was the only one to approach the philosopher as the crowd thronged around the victorious charioteer to touch his tunic's ornately edged hem. The competitor's bodyguards pushed the fans farther back, and there was much gloating when two of them eventually plopped into the ditch, though they too had a laugh.

Uri congratulated him on the two highly amusing stories, and he stammered out the titles of the philosopher's works with which he was already familiar. The philosopher came to a halt; the physician and a servant holding a fan idled impatiently as these signs of interest on Uri's part were not to their taste. A faint smile appeared on the philosopher's face as Uri mentioned the titles.

"I wrote those a long time ago," he said with a dismissive gesture, and proudly drew himself up. "Nowadays it's not possible to get acclaim for writing those sorts of works: they're too good. The signs of decay are dreadful. That is the only word I can use, young friend: dreadful."

Uri made no reference to the fact that he had heard exactly the same stolen tales before in Syracusa, asking instead where the philosopher's itinerary would be taking him. The sage told him that he would be traveling northward, with audiences waiting impatiently in Sidon and Damascus, and once there he would organize the rest of the tour. From that Uri took it that he had started off from Alexandria.

"From Sicily I took a boat to Africa," the philosopher recounted. "I had appearances in Leptis and Cyrene, but Alexandria was not one of the stops... There are too many so-called thinkers there; it's just impossible to attract an audience. Even a Plato or Aristotle would be whistled off the stage these days; the public has been mollycoddled, and also hardened: the fashion is for their own primitive local favorites."

Uri asked what work he had in progress.

"Not a single thing has come to my mind for years," said the philosopher woefully. "I have forgotten even the things I once wrote. I wasn't able to find a wealthy sponsor; I have to keep traveling all the time, even though I loathe doing that. I was not too clever in arranging my fate."

Uri wagged his head in disbelief.

"There you have it. In Rome I am known even to the Jews," the philosopher sighed happily. "Who would have believed it! Perhaps a time will come when I make an appearance even in Rome itself... It must be twenty years since I went that way... I had a major success there. But those were the days when there was still culture, erudition in the world..."

Uri trudged slowly among the civilians toward the town center. The soldiers, formed into detachments, made faster progress; the nailed soles of their boots struck the pavement hard, and they disappeared in the direction of the barracks, which had been built here, as throughout the empire, outside the city walls as a precautionary measure.

Uri had the feeling that as a Jew who paid taxes to the Romans in Judaea, he too had been robbed. He thought about how much was collected from each Jew in Rome in poll taxes and the tariffs on produce, out of which these free shows were paid for. He had heard back home that dues here were self-assessed, with the newborn and dead only being reported every fourteenth year. But how high a percentage was the tax? He would ask when the occasion arose.

He cautiously inspected the Jews trudging by, not noticing that he was staring at them. Apart from feeling cheated, he had nothing in common with them. Yet our religion is the same, Uri thought uncertainly; we are one race, the chosen people.

The charming family with whom they had spent the night in Campania, near Puteoli, came to mind. The many children who shouted happily at one another; the loom; the sheep. God willing, I shall pay them a visit again, he resolved.

He decided to make a solemn promise on the matter. He was amazed how close he now was to the Temple, where that vow was due. Only he could not imagine how he would pay for the sacrificial dove that was necessary for such a vow.

THE DAYS OF WAITING DRAGGED ON; URI RAMBLED AROUND TOWN ON his own while his companions disappeared early in the morning, declining his requests to go with them. What important business did they have in Caesarea?

He saw Plotius occasionally in the distance; there were not too many men in this neck of the woods who had such thick, coal-black beards or graying, bald-pated heads. He kept his eyes peeled as he gazed at the harbor; Plotius was drinking on tavern terraces and absorbed in conversation with old men. For the most part, they were Jews, though there were some Greeks as well. Antique buzzards with decrepit features and bodies—not the kind who would be building palaces for themselves. What, he wondered, might Plotius the builder be inquiring about?

One evening he decided to ask him. After prayers and supper, Plotius set off by himself to one of the bowers in the garden, and Uri went to join him. Plotius stopped and waited for him, as he had two weeks previously at the harbor in Syracusa.

"You saw me with the Elders, didn't you?" Plotius asked.

Uri swallowed deeply. Plotius must have good eyes if he had spotted Uri.

"Yes."

"Fair enough," Plotius said, and sat down on a bench in a vine arbor. Uri sat down next to him. It was warm, the sun had just set. Plotius reeked of wine; he had spent the day plying the old men with drink.

"It was the reason I wanted at all costs to be a member of the delegation," Plotius said. "Even though the last time I was here I was falsely denounced and barely managed to get the hell out of here... I was accused of theft. Me! All I can say is take good care of yourself in this part of the world... Anyway, I came because the harbor of Caesarea interests me."

He paused, waiting for this to sink in. Uri just ogled.

"You must remember: Matthew talked about how hazardous the harbor at Ostia was; that it ought to be reconstructed..."

"I remember."

"Well, I'm looking to rebuild it."

Uri still did not get it.

"That, my friend, is a big deal!" said Plotius. "There's millions to be made from it. Some emperor is bound to want to do it sometime. Puteoli is a long way from Rome; Ostia is near. Ostia is the future. There's just one difficulty: saltwater corrodes cement... But it may well be that Herod the Great's engineers found a way around this—right here. They discovered a way of making a concrete that hardens in seawater, only the method has been forgotten. The builders were Latini, invited here by Herod. I followed up on them in Italia: they died long ago, but there are still a few people living who worked on the construction of the harbor with their own hands. I'm trying to learn from them what materials were used."

Uri brightened. He had liked Plotius from the start, and now he knew why: he was a man with a goal. He wanted to make money, a lot of it. That was a worthy ambition.

"Did you learn anything?"

"Not much," Plotius said. "I probed very discreetly, of course, tangentially. 'Don't make yourself noticeable in the eyes of authority'—that's a wise Judaean proverb to be found in the secret books of the law... I have found out that rocks carved in squares were framed with wood, submerged in the sea, and the gaps were filled out with some kind of sand... The wood rotted, but the sand in the wooden molds hardened... It's said that two centuries ago the harbor of Cosa in Italia was built in exactly the same way. I've been to Cosa, however, and that harbor is ruined. This marine concrete as it is called will not last two hundred years, but four or five decades—most certainly if Caesarea's harbor is still standing, and, as you can see, it is standing... That's more than enough for any emperor. The word is that some volcanic ash was brought in from Italia; a few of the old boys maintain it was called puteolanum... Two of them gave the Latin name even though they don't speak a word of Latin... Maybe it comes from around Puteoli; it could be the ash from one of the eruptions of Vesuvius. But there must have been some other material mixed in—something, on being exposed to the salt of the sea, works with the volcanic ash to become stronger than rock in the seawater... I can't find out anything, though, about this other material..."

He fell silent. Matthew came up and sat down with them in the arbor.

"Am I disturbing anything?" he asked.

"Not at all," said Plotius. "I was just explaining to Gaius that it's my wish to rebuild the harbor at Ostia."

"So I've heard," said Matthew. "The old buzzards have been telling me that you were grilling them about the secret of concrete that sets in water."

Plotius laughed.

"Before long the whole of Rome is going to know about my secret plans!" he declared merrily.

"From me they won't," said Matthew. "But rest assured that there is no way that the work will be awarded to you. There is too much money at stake. It'll be won by huge bribes; they'll pay off the entire senate, the Praetorian Guard, the emperor... You're a pipsqueak in this game."

"But what if I know the secret of concrete that binds on contact with water alone?"

"Then they'll drag it from you and throw you into the Tiber!"

Plotius thought that over.

Uri was not sure if he should be happy to be here. Was this perhaps the right time to stand up and go so that they could talk more freely?

"What do you think?" Matthew asked suddenly.

"Me?" Uri asked.

"Yes, you!" said Matthew.

"I have no grasp of that sort of thing."

"But your father's an influential man," said Matthew. "He knows well enough how to land a good line of business. The bigger the investment, the more you can pinch. That's why it pays to work on as big an investment as possible. Building harbors is just like trading in silk behind everyone else's back; for example, taking the trouble with the Illyrians to bring it through Dalmatia..."

Uri clammed up. These people were privy to all his father's secrets, and if they wanted, they could ruin him. But they didn't know his father too well, because he didn't steal; he worked hard for his money.

"So what did they say? Where the material comes from? Puteoli?" Matthew asked. "How far is that from Rome?"

"I have no idea," said Plotius.

"One hundred and forty-three stadia," interjected Uri.

"Really?"

"According to Iustus," said Uri.

"That material was on someone's property then, and that property must belong to somebody today," said Matthew. "Herod the Great would have paid informers; he had the money. You are not going to have that sort of money, my dear Plotius. You'll never get near that material."

Plotius held his tongue.

"I'll give you a sure tip," said Matthew. "Build a synagogue in Ostia! The land on the seashore is mine... I've already got four exquisite Greek columns for it; all that's left is to rustle up a building around them... I want a house of prayer bigger than the one at Delos!"

There was a mad gleam in Matthew's eyes.

"Don't tell me you've planted four small columns in the garden of your house," Plotius retorted, "and watered them, and now they're sprouting like palm trees!"

"They're not standing, because they were on their sides when I dug them up in my garden," said Matthew. "The shore is sandy, so it's easy for things to get buried. It was pure fluke that I managed to procure them without paying a penny. Turns out that a consignment of columns had arrived from Greece, but the customer who placed the order went bust shortly beforehand. He killed his family, and then himself. The captain was able to dump about thirty of them at half price but was still left with four. He didn't want to take them back, they took up a lot of room, and he was in a hurry, so he didn't have time to rustle up a buyer. So I told him: I'll take them off your hands. He gave them to me for free; all I had to do was pay for their removal. I buried them in front of my house."

"How tall are they?"

"Twelve cubits, plus two feet on account of the capitals."

"You don't say!" said Plotius.

A servant came out from the house to ask if they wanted anything. Matthew asked for some wine.

"They're made of the finest marble," Matthew said.

"So where are you going to put them in your synagogue?" Plotius asked.

"Does it matter? The main thing is that it should be at least as big as the house of prayer at Delos."

The servant brought a jug of wine and three delicate glasses.

Matthew poured a glass for Uri as well. There was a fire in Matthew's eyes; he was drunk in advance on the idea of his prayer-house-to-be.

"Mosaic floor," he continued. "Circles of stone benches... Wonderful murals... A mikveh... Near the sea, as it should be... A well can be dug... The water will run from the cistern into the kitchen..."

"What kitchen?" Plotius inquired.

"It will have a hostel for Jewish seamen. At present there is nowhere for them to eat and sleep; they have to be put up at private houses, six or seven to a room. It's like trying to sleep in the belly of a ship. My house of prayer will be their house of prayer, so they won't even have to go into town. They'll need something to eat, so we shall cook for them for a modest fee, and not just on the Sabbath. Plenty of sailors, plenty of small payments—a huge return."

"Is that the reason you built your villa outside the town wall? So you could have a house of prayer near at hand?"

"That's right!" said Matthew. "And once it's built I shall be the archisynagogos."

"If I build it, I shall be the archisynagogos," said Plotius. "That's the condition, apart from the fee, which of course is priceless."

They laughed and quaffed the wine.

"I'm serious," said Matthew. "It's a fantastic business, but a realistic one."

"So how will you finance it?" Plotius quizzed.

"I throw in the four columns," said Matthew. "Each of them is worth several thousand sesterces. The rest will be raised by Jewish seamen; it's for them that it will be built. I'll milk the Jews of Ostia as well; after all, it will be theirs as well. There has been just one congregation in Ostia so far; now there'll be two."

"It won't come together just from that," said Plotius. "To say nothing of the fact that it's not going to be in their interest to create another congregation."

"As soon as we get to Jerusalem, I'm going to have a word with the high priest; I'll get him to make a donation from the treasury."

"Complete nonsense," said Plotius. "The priests have never given backing to the construction of synagogues. Each and every house of prayer that is built detracts from the weight of the Temple, and thereby their own weight too."

"It's worth a try anyway."

They drank the wine. Uri was touched that they were speaking so openly in front of him. It meant that they accepted him and considered him a grown man.

Plotius sketched in the air.

"Let's say we have the southeastern wall here, facing Jerusalem. That is the entrance... You have to go straight, into the house of prayer... The bimah is opposite the entrance... That needs a platform with benches around it... Where am I going to put your columns? Over the bimah? The sanctum is here, opposite the entrance... On the left or the right is a big hall for the school and the court..."

"On the left," said Matthew firmly.

"Why?" Plotius asked.

"Because that way it will fit in, due to the seashore."

"It's all the same to me," said Plotius. "Let the other hall be on the right... But then if the four pillars are so attractive, then you need to be able to see them from the sanctum and from the second hall... Shall we place the columns right between them?"

"Let's," said Matthew.

"But then what kind of roof am I going to build? Are you going to have these idiotic columns, which are two and a half stories high, punching through the roof?"

"Let the whole roof be as high as the columns."

"Are you out of your mind? I've never seen a synagogue that tall. Twelve cubits and two feet?"

"That's what will be good about it," said Matthew. "Ours will be the tallest."

"You're a maniac, Matthew!" said Plotius admiringly.

"That's me," said Matthew. "And I'm going to get the money together. I'll tap the Jews in Rome as well." At this he turned to Uri: "Your father too. A lot more of them as well."

Uri kept quiet.

"Agrippa will also give," said Matthew. "I'll wring something out of him."

"If Agrippa is going to be involved," said Plotius, "that's when I get out. A dirty swine if ever I saw one!"

"He's never short of a penny."

"To bribe senators and the emperor, but he's never given a red cent to the Jews. He wants to be king of a Greater Israel bigger than his grandfather's was."

"Agrippa will never be a king," Matthew asserted. "Too many people loathe him."

"But the Jews of Alexandria want that," said Plotius. "Nothing is too dear for them... They couldn't care less whether Agrippa stirs up the am ha'aretz, those wretched ignoramuses, throughout Judaea!"

"He won't stir them up," said Matthew. "He can't even speak to them; he doesn't speak a word of Aramaic."

"His agents will do that for him," said Plotius. "The man's sick in the head. He wants to be greater than any Jewish king so far... We've gone to the grave for that more than a few times already. The last time was when his grandfather ruined us. Agrippa give money for a house of prayer in Ostia? He wants Judaea along with Galilee; nothing else is of interest to him."

Uri felt awkward. It was all very well their heaping abuse on Agrippa so openly in front of him, but he had to say something.

"My thanks that you speak openly in my presence," Uri declared.

After a short pause, Matthew spoke.

"What of it?"

"I know that you know my father gave him money, and he asked in return that I should come with you... But my father had no money... He borrowed it from bankers at an interest rate of twenty percent... Agrippa had asked the bankers for the money, they wouldn't give it but sent him around to my father, who was in no position to say no..."

Silence.

Matthew laughed.

"Agrippa will spend that on a single supper," he said. "The bird species does not exist whose tongues he would not have served up in a pâté."

"Were you there?" asked Plotius.

"No," said Matthew, "but I know someone who was."

Uri felt dizzy.

The rat had squandered that gigantic sum of money on a single meal!

Plotius turned to Uri.

"A singularly clear-headed merchant like your father is not in the habit of departing from his senses. He's counting on a high position falling into your lap when Agrippa becomes king. The loan will be paid back if Greater Israel is awarded to Agrippa by the emperor. It's a big risk, but your father will have considered it worth taking."

"My father is not like that! No way are we Agrippa's agents!"

The other two sipped their wine. Uri did not drink.

"Here everybody is someone's agent," Matthew declared in an amiable tone. "Any ass can deliver money. Not one person made his way into this delegation by chance; each and every one of us is an important person."

Uri was enraged.

"All right, then! Out with it!" he yelled. "Who is an agent for whom? Let's hear it!"

Matthew and Plotius were shaken; they had not expected this.

"I'll tell you," said Matthew quietly. "But don't shout because the others can hear. Should I say?"

Plotius shrugged his shoulders.

"At least I'll also get to find out."

Matthew hesitated, then he too shrugged his shoulders.

"Valerius was pushed into the delegation by the archisynagogos. He has a pile of contracts with him; his boss is buying land in Judaea... The sellers will sign, Valerius will take the papers back, and the money will be sent to the sellers with the next delegation... Valerius is making nothing on it, but he will be allowed to keep his job; he'll be a hyperetes to the end of his days—instead of becoming a sailor and getting to spew his guts out..."

He snickered, then carried on:

"Hilarus bought jewels in Caesarea. They're cheap here, you see, but ever since then he's been petrified that his sack will be stolen."

"Have you looked in his sack?" Uri asked.

"Sure."

"What about mine? Have you searched that too?" Uri asked determinedly.

"That too. Is anything missing?"

"Nothing." Uri felt the wine rise up in his stomach. "So what were you looking for?"

"A letter from Agrippa."

Uri was aghast.

"That's logical," Plotius tried to smooth things over. "You were put into the delegation at Agrippa's request; you're his agent."

"It's not like that," Uri exclaimed. "There was never any letter of any kind on me!"

"No, there wasn't," Matthew confirmed. "I didn't know then what a good memory you had."

Uri shook his head. He did not understand.

"One hundred and forty-three stadia," Plotius prompted him helpfully.

"What about one hundred and forty-three stadia?"

"The distance of Puteoli from Rome," said Plotius. "You heard it just once, and you registered it. You weren't even paying any attention. I asked the question as if I didn't know; Iustus gave the answer, and Matthew immediately changed the subject. If there was anything you would be expected to forget, it would have been that. But just a moment ago you told us how many stadia Puteoli is from Rome. Agrippa made a good choice of courier."

"I'm sorry!" Uri whispered, jumped to his feet and vomited into the bushes. He wiped his mouth and, gritting his teeth, took his seat again.

They had been spying on him all along, testing him. Let them just carry on.

"I'm listening, Matthew. And Alexandros?"

"A noxious beast," said Matthew. "He wanted to be a Roman legionary, only they didn't take him because he's a Jew. Out of spite, now he wants to become a Jewish military leader and trounce the whole Roman Empire—by himself. Right now he is buying up weapons from legionaries; the Jews are hiding them in caves to rise up in rebellion later on..."

"What legionaries?" Uri asked.

"Members of the Sebaste non-Jewish cohort," said Plotius patiently. "They report that their weapons, unfortunately, have been mislaid, and they get replacements at no charge. Spears, swords, knives—whatever... They're paid a per diem of thirty-nine asses, or nine hundred sesterces a year, because the Roman state picks up the tab for their provisions and their weapons, but then it deducts the costs of these from their salaries, so in the end they earn less than a Roman plebe does with his sportula full of food worth twenty-five asses, and he doesn't have to do anything for it but kill time, much like you! And then you have your tessera on top, which they don't! So as an unemployed Roman plebeian, you earn twice as much as they do—and they have drills, are deployed whenever there is an earthquake anywhere, or a fire to be fought. They are not allowed to have a family, and they serve for decades on end, the fools, before being resettled, with a minimal pension, somewhere a long way off so they will not rise up in rebellion! No wonder they wheel and deal and steal whenever they get the chance. The state pays again and again for lost weapons, but it does not charge the legionaries, because the state is stupid, and its dopey bookkeeping officials don't do any thinking for it! Alexandros is not the first to trade in black-market weapons. Judaea is full of caves, and they're all full to bursting with weapons. The mercenaries sell them cheaply, and the Jews buy heaps of them. Nowadays the only ones who use them are their co-religionists who are highway robbers, but that brute Alexandros is making strenuous preparations to be a Rome-bashing Jewish military leader! And there are many more like him!"

Uri kept quiet and digested that.

"Iustus is keeping tabs on me," Matthew said with a laugh. "There hasn't been a delegation yet that did not have its spy. But then he's not going to have anything to report—unless he reports on you. You're in the same congregation, if I'm not mistaken."

"We are," said Uri. "I know already why Plotius came... So, Matthew, what about you?"

Matthew took a little sip of the wine.

"My obsession is the house of prayer in Ostia... It's hard to see how I can go wrong when it gets built. I'll take small charges from the hostelry guests, and even smaller ones from the court officials for the use of the hall, and very little indeed for the school to function, but all of those small charges will add up, and everyone in the town will come to my house of prayer sooner or later, that's for sure. I shall be the first archisynagogos ever who manages to make money from the post. But peace is needed for Jews to be able to build. The Pax Romana, praise be, is a necessary thing, and praise be to Julius Caesar for conceiving it... Mark my words: I'll do anything—anything at all—to make sure crazy Jews will not threaten the peace."

"That's how I feel as well," said Plotius.

Uri's stomach was gripped by a new round of cramps.

"I also need peace," he said hoarsely, "to read, because for me nothing else is of interest. I can recite to you the whole of Greek and Latin literature by heart. No one is using me to pass messages to anyone: I swear by Everlasting God who is One that this is the truth."

After a brief hush, Plotius added, "Amen."

ALL OF A SUDDEN, SIMON THE MAGUS DEPARTED FOR JERUSALEM, LEAVing a letter in which he wished them a continued pleasant stay in his house. He had taken some of the servants with him; the rest were left at their disposal. Presumably he had called in all his demands and was hastening to place the money in the Temple's treasury.

The companions returned together late that evening. Uri had seen nothing of the kind until then; previously they had reached home individually, albeit not so late. They were not in a happy state of mind.

They took their seats in the garden for supper. Hilarus roundly abused the Jews of Alexandria. A stuck-up, brainless bunch; they had money to burn but did not give a hoot for Jewry.

Matthew and Plotius held their tongues.

"The bastards didn't even invite us for a meal," said Alexandros.

It turned out that the companions had been at the Druseion that day with the delegation traveling from Alexandria to Jerusalem, who'd had the money to rent the most expensive suites of rooms in that miraculous edifice but had not offered the companions a thing, parting after some empty courtesies and marching off to the most expensive of the lighthouse's restaurants, though not without making sure that the Jews from Rome should happen to catch them doing just that.

It must have been humiliating in the extreme.

"They're delivering a hundred and thirty-three times as much money as us," said Matthew dryly.

"How much is that?" Uri asked, flabbergasted.

"One hundred talents, near enough," said Matthew. "Of course, that includes taxes from the whole of Egypt, not just the Jews of Alexandria..."

How in God's name did they carry such so much money? Uri made a quick count: that must be at least 122 pounds of gold! What were they taking it by? A caravan of camels?

Uri was glad that he had not experienced the arrogance of the rich.

It then occurred to him that he was the only one they had not taken with them. That was not nice of them. So, his companions had conspired against him. Even though he had sworn he was carrying no message from Agrippa to anyone, they did not believe him. Not even Plotius or Matthew—nobody.

It occurred to him that maybe the fact that he was not doing business deals with the locals in itself looked fishy. The way their minds worked, what possible reason could there be other than that he, Agrippa's spy, was superbly well paid and had no need to get involved in trifling business deals.

Let it be over! Let them reach Jerusalem, hand over the money, get through the festival, and return to Rome as soon as possible.

"Pity the Magus did not speak to the prefect," said Hilarus once the mudslinging at the Jews of Alexandria had been exhausted. "He's never going to receive us."

Iustus endorsed that: it would have been nice to look at the palace. Maybe there would be a chance on the return leg.

"It's possible to get in," Alexandros supposed. "It's possible to clamber up from the sewage system..."

"Don't make the mistake of thinking they don't guard it," said Plotius grimly. "A good job they do! If they didn't guard it, I'd have words with them."

Alexandros laughed scornfully.

Uri took that to mean that Alexandros had inspected the entire sewage system to find out how it would be possible to launch an attack against the more important buildings. This fellow was surely insane.

They sat, sipping their wine, the conversation returning once again to coins and prices in Caesarea. How cheap everything was here in comparison with Rome; a length of linen cost so-and-so much in this shop, so-and-so much in another, though it was not of the same quality; the wine here was more tart; the lamb in the tavern at the harbor was more tender than it was back at the Tiberium.

Long-forgotten tastes were reawakened on Uri's palate, not so much the flavors of wine and lamb but of the matzo that he had eaten in boyhood, when his father had still considered him a colleague, teaching him about mark-ups on commodities and how to steer clear of forgeries of high-quality goods. These prices were for children; they couldn't be taken seriously. The only things to be taken seriously were works of art. But it would have been better, perhaps, had his eyes not deteriorated and had he read nothing other than the Holy Scriptures, and he too had been interested in prices.

After prayers and supper they sat in a vine arbor at the highest point of the garden's steeply sloping ground, from which they could look down on the house itself. The long table was sumptuously laden with all imaginable seafood dishes that could be considered kosher, which is to say many fishes but no crabs, snails, or shellfish. Who, Uri wondered, could have decided that, and when, because there is not a word in the Pentateuch about why fish with external bony skeletons are placed among the calcareous shellfish, and are not kosher, which ones are exceptionally kosher, and what is the difference between the skeletons? What makes a skeleton bony and what makes it a shell? If the Creator had created man in such a way that an external armor held him in place from the outside, with his flesh on the inside, would such a man not be Jewish on principle? Putting himself, in his imagination, in the shoes of the Creator, Uri pictured for himself tortoise-men and snake-men and bird-men, and the soporific conversation that was carried on among his companions about prices did not penetrate his consciousness.

The western horizon over the sea was flushed; the sun had set just a few minutes before. The tops of the larger buildings in the harbor area could be seen between the palms and cypresses, the high towers almost in their entirety. Lights glimmered in the tiny windows of the uppermost levels of the Druseion. There must be people dwelling there, living and making love, right then. That might be the Alexandrian delegation carousing.

Not that we ourselves are not carousing, Uri admitted even-handedly to himself; indeed, those Jews were paying for themselves in the Druseion, whereas we are getting free board and lodging. Perhaps we are getting the better deal.

Then he reminded himself that there was no "we."

He was excluded from that community. And if he thought over what Matthew had said about the motives of their fellows, everyone—with the possible exception of an alliance between Matthew and Plotius—was out for himself. The delegation was not a community, but why would it need to become one? The community was hateful; its members were keeping watch, spying on each other, accusing each other of infringing on principles that were thought of as common, reporting on those infringements, even condemning each other to death. Uri very much hoped that he would never see a single one of his companions again once their mission was over.

Then it occurred to him that they were, indeed, a community, bearing all the characteristics of such, and it could even be that he, the one whom everyone was spying on, was as a matter of fact was the cohesive glue of this community, the proof of that being precisely the fact that they had not taken him—him alone—with them today to the Druseion. They competed with each other, collaborated, kept an eye on each other, but they had just one common enemy: himself. That would make him the most important member of the delegation, he concluded, and the reason they did not take me with them is because the Alexandrians support Agrippa, on whose behalf they think I am spying.

That was a startling idea, and he dismissed it straightaway by telling himself that he would think it over with a clearer head at some later time.

The fires were burning in the Caesarean Pharos; even Uri was able dimly to make out its glow. The gilded roofs of the temple of Augustus and the Tiberium were also visible, gleaming rubicund in the twilight. In the garden field crickets stridulated and birds chirped; it was a warm spring evening—a peaceful, quiet sense of well-being prevailed. Uri examined the scenery through a small gap between his fingers; it now seemed to him even more improbable than ever that he happened to be right where he was.

The mission to Jerusalem would be coming to an end in a few days' time, and they would be setting off for home. He still did not know who was carrying the money. Perhaps the smallest and dimmest of them all: Hilarus or Iustus. Or maybe me.

But it is definitely not in my sack.

Was it not possible that Matthew had handed it over to Simon the Magus, and that is why he had gone on ahead? He had an armed escort; it would be safer with him. Back in Rome he had heard recently—though he had not paid much attention—that bankers anywhere would give money on any letter of credit that had been duly stamped and signed. What if Matthew were bearing a letter of credit like that, and he had given it to Simon, who would then change it for money and deposit it at the treasury?

Uri exercised his feet and kneaded his back. His stomach had stopped cramping a few days back, thanks to the walks and the plentiful, tasty repasts. The painful dispute between Matthew and Plotius had passed without consequences; it seemed if anything to have shown them in a more sympathetic light. True, they had said nothing about going to meet the Alexandrian delegation, he had been left out of that, but at the same time he had also been let off the communal humiliation. He wanted to feel at ease and carefree; he was at peace with the world, because he wanted to be at peace with it.

"In all truth, it's you who ought to be speaking to Pilate, no?" Hilarus asked unexpectedly.

Uri looked around to see whom Hilarus was addressing, but Hilarus was looking intently at him.

"What was that? Me, speak to whom, about what?"

"You ought to be speaking to Pilate, or have I got that wrong?" Hilarus repeated his question.

Uri had no idea what this was about.

"What would I say to him?" he asked.

"I have no idea: that's for you to know," said Hilarus.

Everyone paused. Uri looked around at them; there was not a trace of goodwill in their eyes. Uri shuddered.

"The first time I heard the name was after setting off on this trip," said Uri. "Before that I had no idea who the prefect of Judaea was. What am I supposed to speak to him about?"

"How would I know? It's you who knows," Hilarus said. "You just skulk around the town, staring at women's naked breasts all day long."

Everything was still.

Uri did not look at Alexandros. He'd obviously blabbed that I was at the stadium. Somehow it doesn't count that he was also there; all that matters is that I was there. Why should that be?

"You keep spying on me all the time," Uri let fly. "Why's that? Are you going to tell me, at long last, why?"

They stared mutely.

"What makes you think that anyone is spying on you?" Matthew asked soothingly, gently, commiseratingly, paternally.

What a hypocrite, my God.

Uri got up, picked up his goblet of wine, and went into the house. He sat down on his bed and stared into the darkness.

Why do they not believe me?

FROM THEN ON, URI SLEPT OUTSIDE IN THE GARDEN. HE SPENT FRIDAY evening praying with the group and the Jewish servants, after which he left. For the whole Sabbath he said nothing to them, nor they to him. He ate when they had finished and avoided their company, and they avoided his. He wandered around the garden and fretted. I'm the victim of some diabolical mistake, he thought; they don't believe a word I tell them.

It won't be long before this torment comes to an end; next Friday evening is the start of Passover. We have to arrive on Thursday at the latest because—so he had heard—no one would be allowed into the city on Friday. That means they would have to set off no later than Monday at daybreak, maybe even on Sunday evening. Just one more night, Uri thought, and we will be on our way.

They looked through his bag once more. The tefillin had been stuffed into the jug, which had been empty for days now. It had never occurred to him to stuff anything into the jug, least of all his phylactery. They must have wanted him to see that they had searched it. Was it Matthew or one of the others?

He said nothing. One of them is threatening me, he thought; he's made up some lie about me to the others, and they believed him. But what could that be?

He brooded over what could be eating Hilarus. They had not exchanged a single word on the trip. But they had been rowing next to each other during the squall. Hilarus had been looking at his back. But he had not looked back even once, so he had not seen the fear, if there was any, on his face. He might be annoyed on account of that, but this much? And anyway, it was not Hilarus who had puked, but Valerius, the armchair seaman.

The more time I spend with them, the less I know them.

It crossed his mind that he should turn to Plotius for advice, who had spoken with him warmly and paternally in Syracusa, and had added an "Amen" when he had sworn that he was telling the truth. But something held Uri back. Not even Plotius had come to his defense when Hilarus came out with that nonsense earlier, though Plotius should have known better.

Can he really know, though?

Not so sure.

Who am I, after all?

He tried to examine himself from the outside. A young man, reddish beard, prematurely balding, who squinted, his eyes screwed up to slits, his back bowed, his chin receding and lopsided, the nose protuberant. Although he had lost weight on the way, he had not lost his modest potbelly or his double chin. He wriggled when seated because either his rectum or his back was causing him some discomfort; he walked clumsily, waddling; apparently he talked in his sleep, shouting and arguing; he had a constantly runny nose and was always clearing his throat. Not exactly an edifying spectacle, he concluded. But then what bad was there to see in such a preposterous figure?

Me—Agrippa's agent? Come on! Surely they can't seriously suppose that an ambitious grandson of Herod would entrust an important message to such a wretched stripling.

The Creator created me the way that I am, and He left it to me to make what I can of my endowments. I shall harden my soul, endure the indignity; be strong like nobody before.

"We're hitting the road!" said Matthew.

He was standing over him in the garden and looking down just like his father had done in Rome, at home, two months earlier.

Uri scrambled to his feet, but by the time he could thank him for the wake-up call Matthew had gone back to the house.

It was daybreak on Sunday. Uri shivered as he raked the dew from his greasy hair with his frozen fingers.

They would reach Jerusalem on Wednesday, Thursday at the latest. They had already covered distances like that in Italia, and just as fast. A good thing that the days were longer in spring and summer than winter. And now they would also have a highway under their feet.

THE CAESAREA-JERUSALEM ROAD WAS WELL CONSTRUCTED, WIDER THAN the Appian Way. But there was a dark aspect to the overly broad thoroughfare:

its builders understood that it was surrounded by a province that was not exactly peaceful. The reason it had been built was so that Roman legionaries might quickly march along it along to quell any Jewish rebellion; there was plenty of room for a big army, even for war chariots. Yet it was constructed in peaceful times, and the peace had held ever since, for many decades now, and Jewish leaders, wherever they might live, were doing all they could to keep the peace forever.

There was going to be war. Everyone was counting on that, even though it was peacetime; the builders of the military road had counted on war decades before. Simon the Magus could also see it coming and was doing what he could to save his money while he could.

At the edge of the road lolled women in scanty dresses made up in the Egyptian style. Their faces were daubed white, with their eyebrows picked out in dark paint and their lips red. Even Uri could see their features as they were standing no more than three or four feet away. He estimated the distance between the women as thirty to forty cubits; every one of them, old or young, had a half-crazed look about her. Some stood motionless, like resigned statues; others swayed, their legs apart, or whistled; others mechanically licked the corners of their mouths, or wiggled their backsides, or even pulled out their breasts to display. The travelers pretended not to notice. Uri assumed that some people were skimming off the top of whatever the women made, just as much of the profit his father made from silk was raked off. The reason the whores were allowed to live, as was his father in Rome, was because they made money for someone; the moment they ceased to be of use, they would be disposed of.

It would be good to talk about this with Joseph, but it was something that could not be discussed.

He couldn't tell his father that he was being treated like a prostitute. No, that wasn't the right word. He couldn't tell his father that he was a slave.

The good thing about thoughts is that one can chew on them for a prolonged period, which made walking more tolerable. He was again carrying his sandals around his neck, and the bare, hardened soles of his feet tramped the military road from Caesarea to Jerusalem. His ankle became sore much sooner than it had in Italia, on account of the rough ground, he supposed, or as a result of the week of inactivity in Caesarea.

When they set out, the seven of them were the only ones walking on the road, but as the day went on they encountered ever more people on the way to Jerusalem, to the festivities. For these people, however, there was no need to set out so early: they lived more than three days' walking distance from the Temple. Nowhere had it been set down in writing, but since the time of Herod the Great, the notorious marathon distance—twenty-four stadia—had been customarily regarded as one day's walking distance, the notion adopted in the rich towns of Palestine and Syria along with the quinquennial Olympic games. The members of the delegation managed to cover a daily average of one and a half times that much, but then they were, so to speak, professional walkers, and apart from small sacks they were carrying nothing else, no animals, baggage, week's provisions, or infants.

By noon the innocuous crowd had proliferated, swelling to a group of several hundred Jews; people from nearby villages had taken to the military road to avoid the bumps of unpaved paths with their traps, carts, and barrows.

They could not be asked for road tolls now that they were on their way to a festival, Uri supposed, gaining an insight into the logic of the Pax Romana.

Families and clans walked together, and they carried with them everything that was intended for sacrifice at the Temple. Wheels creaked under carts loaded with plant and animal offerings. There were baskets on the heads of the womenfolk, smaller baskets on the heads of the children, also containing sacrificial offerings.

They marched along in their finest clothes, singing psalms, with the psalms intermingling and a cacophony of sounds arising. For many even the finest clothes were rags, the best sandals, bare feet. Their skin was ulcerated, their bodies scrawny. The oxen pulling the carts were also scraggly, their bones very nearly poking through their hides. The bellies of the countless small children were swollen over their skinny thighs, the bellies of the cattle, donkeys, and camels similarly swollen. This was poverty that Uri had never seen in Italia or Rome.

Could this be my people?

He looked at the shuffling old folks and the small barefoot brats that kept straying off. Already, at six or seven years of age, children had to go to the festivities in Jerusalem; the smallest, the infants of one or two years of age, traveled on their fathers' backs, and he envied them: he too had hung on to his father's neck when they had fled, and he had been the family's only child.

He looked at the solemn heads of families, swathed in their gowns, the women covering their faces; a procession the likes of which it was impossible to imagine in Rome, even though there one could find almost anything imaginable. There, every Jew went to his own synagogue for Passover, and he would have a hearty lunch. Here, there was a mass pilgrimage, and families, so it seemed, took along with them not just the sacrificial offerings but their entire wealth, including all their cattle, their tents as well, either on their backs or on carts, fearing perhaps that anything left at home would be filched. In front and at the back of the carts were tethered horses, foals, oxen, and cattle, with the poultry thrown into the carts themselves; these could not all be sacrificial animals, it was just that they dared not leave them at home, unguarded, in the village—otherwise they would be stolen by robbers, Jewish and non-Jewish alike, so they took with them to Jerusalem their entire fortunes, everything, and then, once the festival was over, they would drive them back home again, or at least as many of the cattle, children, and old people who were still alive after the major effort. This migration back and forth occurred at least three times a year, as if the settled Jewish peasants were returning to their ancestral nomadic lifestyle three times a year; as if wandering were in their blood and the festivals had been codified merely to give free rein to this primitive instinct.

In the autumn, for the Day of Atonement, the holiest feast in the Jewish calendar, there must be even bigger crowds on the move in Judaea. The Feast of Booths, harvest festival, and feast of thanksgiving is called Sukkot for the hastily erected bivouacs, roofed with straw; these were still being carried and would be set up somewhere. Only the name given to this feast is Passover, the spring festival commemorating, in part, the deliverance of Moses and his people and, in part, the ripening of the early-winter sowing of barley.

So many tents and tent poles were being carried that Uri was convinced that tent-making must be the best of all trades in Palestine.

Where would this vast mass of people pitch their tents? he wondered. Hardly in the city, for that was surely paved; indeed, he seemed to recall it being said that the paving of the city had been in constant progress since the time of Herod the Great. This continuously growing throng of people was surely going to camp outside the city during the three most important days of the festival, with many spending the entire week under a tent. There were a couple of half-holidays in between the feast days, but the crowd would still be there, close to Jerusalem, and only then would it set off for home.

He looked at the faces, and with few exceptions they struck him as foreign.

Among them were many faces that he had not encountered in Rome, either among the Jews or the inhabitants of the true Rome. They resembled, most of all, Arabs, Egyptians, Numidians, Ethiopians, and Abyssinians. If the men had not been wearing gowns over their heads, or there had been no kerchief covering the women's heads, and in some cases a veil as well, he would have had a tough time recognizing them as Jews. The Jews in Rome were not like these; there the Jews were Roman.

They spoke either Greek or Aramaic, and it was only the psalms that were in Hebrew. They sang it inaccurately, garbling words, mixing up word endings;

they did not understand the psalms, warbling them in a plaintive drawl, just as they had heard them from their parents. Perhaps it was the essence that one did not need to understand the psalms, just croon and mumble them under his breath in a nonsense language. One has to speak to God, Uri supposed, in a language that has no sense; maybe He understood that. The Lord was hardly going to fool around with meaningful words; He had too many things to worry about, what with all existing worlds being entrusted to Him, not just our earthly world. There must be a fair amount of trouble in the heavenly world as well, with the angels squabbling, to say nothing of the devils, those curious puppets of God whom He had created—after all, He had created everything—to have someone to worry about when He was bored. Maybe He inspired the embrace of bad causes deemed necessary so that men would not castigate Him on their account; maybe the devils were just like Sejanus had been, and the Lord God just like the emperor Tiberius. The Lord was not paying attention to us, and if He hears anything at all, He hears only a querulous, chanting song; but then if He was almighty, He would understand that.

This ever-swelling mass moving in the same direction was unsettling. Uri looked to the front where his feet were falling, then he moved across to the edge of the roadside beyond the ditch, which was less hard going. Plotius and Matthew were already walking there; they too must have felt their ankles aching.

Uri looked at his feet so as not to trip on a clod of earth and sprain his ankle; he avoided weathered roots and stinging weeds, and not to have to think about the world around him, he recalled mathematical problems that had given him trouble when he tried to figure them out in his recess, and which even his teacher had been unable to solve because he was weak on matters of arithmetic and geometry.

Uri puzzled over the formula for generating a prime number of any size. It was a senseless, abstract puzzle, there being no practical reason for a person to look for an integer that is not divisible by any other integer apart from by one and itself, which was why it was a good problem. When, in the afternoon, he got weary of thinking and started to feel that if he carried on thinking any longer he was going to drive himself crazy, he posed himself another task, which was to look for another perfect number aside from six, the integer that was already known, which had the property of being equal to the sum of all its possible factors—in that case: one, two, and three.

All at once, horsemen appeared behind them and bellowed something; horns rasped, the crowd pulled off the road and stopped. Even the carts came to a standstill, though they could not easily pull off the way. Soldiers jabbed people with their spears, motioning them to step aside into the ditch next to the road. Many carts got stuck, some overturned and the produce spilled onto the ground. No one moved; they would scrape it together later on.

A great number of cavalry came along. The Caesarean division, Uri heard someone say. The leading horseman proudly carried an enormous Roman eagle. Uri was standing right at the edge of the road, so he got a good look at both the eagle and the division's standard. The horsemen carried spears, with swords at their waists; they were seated on their mounts not so much dashingly as alertly, as if they were going into battle and the crowd surrounding them was not the civilian population of a friendly allied province but rather a bloodthirsty enemy to be wiped out, longing to grab hold of their military insignia. If they had indeed been recruited from Caesarea, these horsemen were local non-Jewish inhabitants, whom, for simplicity's sake, the Jews referred to as Greeks, though they were actually neither Greeks nor Romans but a motley population united solely by being non-Jewish and hating Jews.

Uri thought it better to pull back farther from the road in case he were to be run into by a carelessly brandished sword. If he, a Roman citizen, were accidentally to be cut down by a cavalryman domiciled in Judaea, the latter would pay with his life. The very thought of that was so comical that he was moved to laugh out loud. Peasants glowered at him with surly looks. Uri choked back the laughter and moved on; they quite likely thought he was laughing at them.

Behind the cavalry came a unit of infantry in ranks of six, marching extremely briskly, one of the cohorts. Only foot soldiers are able to move that rapidly; they were even quicker than the delegation. At their head marched their centurion, armored from head to toe, sweat running down his thighs.

"The Caesarean infantry, so Pilate will be somewhere behind," said Alexandros, licking his lips.

The horses of the vanguard, a squadron, had detached from the ala, peeled back, and got off the highway so as to give free passage to the infantry; they would gallop ahead later on to clear the way.

They were dawdling near a military outpost, with four legionaries standing to attention before the sentry cabin. At other times it was no doubt they who collected the tolls.

The entire cohort went through, the heels of their boots ringing hard on the basalt paving, then a palanquin came into view, with horsemen bearing spears and shields trotting directly before and after.

It was carried by eight bearers, just like Simon the Magus's litter, except these were taller and stronger: Uri guessed they might be as much as seven feet tall. They were all clothed in white tunics with a squarely twisted embroidered pattern on the hem and running uniformly at the double. Even though no one was giving any commands, the palanquin was traveling in a perfect horizontal line on their shoulders; they must be professional bearers.

It was not possible to see into the curtained window.

Inside the litter sat Pilate, the prefect. He could sleep or read, even write letters if he wished. Who knows: maybe his high-strung spouse was traveling with him.

Enchanted, Uri watched the litter bearers. They had splendid, strong bodies, like the most perfect Greek statues, and they were not even sweating or panting from the running. Their upper arms were as bulky as one of Uri's thighs, their thighs three times bulkier, their calves as big as many people's backsides, but their own rumps were small, their stomachs flat, their chests like barrels. Their hair was closely cropped, their faces clean-shaven. On their feet were the highest-quality leather boots money could buy. They looked straight ahead, contemptuous of the population that was clearing the way for them, well aware of their great importance.

Uri would very much have loved to be more like them: as brawny, as handsome, as brainless.

"They're the pick of Sebaste and Tiberias," Matthew whispered. "The parents get a small fortune for them. The boys train from the age of ten, and any who don't make the grade are posted as regular soldiers. The youngest litter bearers are eighteen years old; by the time they are twenty-four they are replaced, and posted to a cohort. When they are thirty they can be discharged, and pensioned off as elite legionaries. Jews are not permitted to be taken on."

"They quickly turn to flab," said Alexandros disdainfully. "Most do not make it to thirty-five. Not gladiator material."

Pilate's palanquin was whisked away. In its wake a seemingly endless army streamed speedily by in ranks of six: the other two cohorts. Ahead of the troops, on horseback, rode their centurion and his escort, carrying a curious standard with a Roman eagle perched atop a menorah.

"Are they Greeks as well?" Uri inquired, finding it rather odd.

"Are you kidding!" Alexandros said. "Samaritan Jews from the Sebaste region is what they are... They loathe us at least as much as the Greeks do."

"The officers are Greeks," said Plotius softly. "It's only the grunts who are Samaritan Jews... They don't normally allow them to mix with the Greek cohorts because they are constantly brawling. Their camps are kept separated..."

"Where is Sebaste anyway?" Uri asked.

"Where Samaria once stood. Herod Antipas built it on the ruins of the old capital... When he made Tiberias, instead of Sepphoris, the metropolis of Galilee..."

"Tiberias was built on a cemetery," said Alexandros disdainfully. "All the inhabitants are unclean..."

"Herod Antipas is far from stupid," said Plotius. "The old elite would not have moved from Sepphoris to an unclean city, anyone could have figured that out, so Herod Antipas was obliged to set up a new elite. That was how he got rid of the old guard, with hypocritical regrets for the reasons they were unwilling to serve him..."

Plotius guffawed.

A covered chariot drawn by four horses, cavalry around it, now appeared.

"Pilate's household gods," Matthew whispered. "He takes them wherever he goes, even though his ancestors were not high-born; he married into a knightly order."

They stood and watched the chariot creaking along.

"This year Pilate is going to Jerusalem earlier than usual," Matthew muttered to himself. "Very early."

There must be some trouble in Judaea after all, that suggested.

A huge crowd was now waiting at the edge of the road for the mercenaries to pass by so that they too could return to the military road.

For a long time yet legionaries in full armor strode by, their boots tramping rhythmically.

The crowd mutely watched them march past; even the children fell silent. The delegation from Rome likewise remained still.

Our people, and our allied army. Our people forced off the road by our army.

Upturned carriages were then righted; the livestock and cultivated crops were reloaded, swept together, or tossed back by the handful into intact sacks. The womenfolk sewed torn sacks with the needles and flax they kept at hand. The children picked up a few kernels of grain in their grubby little hands and proudly dropped those too into the sacks before turning back to look for more. It looks as though they will get the grain milled somewhere close to Jerusalem, Uri reflected, and they will eat it too, because grain like that is impure from a priest's perspective.

The legs of spavined donkeys and asses were examined by elderly men, their injuries fixed with the aid of broken-off branches and cord; the animals that could not be treated were hoisted onto a cart; they could not be used as sacrificial animals, because they were not sound and the Levites would not accept such an animal, but the travelers would eat those themselves communally during the festival, and that is how they would be accounted for back home, each and every one. Their fellow pilgrims would back them in avowing that everything had happened the way they told it.

The mass reoccupied the military road, but the stillness lasted a long time, with even the small children realizing that now was not the time for their screams.

But then the singing did of course sound again, perhaps coming from tribes that were only now taking to the road and had not seen the passage of the army, though it is also possible that those who had been pushed into the ditch and onto the field had resumed their song.

Whatever might happen at any time, it was good to sing psalms.

IT CAME ABOUT SPONTANEOUSLY WHEN THE MASS CAME TO A STANDSTILL to wash their hands and pray; perhaps the old sensed the time more keenly than the young. The delegates too yielded to the mass sense of time: when the crowd halted, so did they; when the crowd sprinkled themselves with water, so Matthew sprinkled the delegates; when the crowd prayed, so did they. When their own water ran out, they rinsed their hands with soil at the roadside, like the others, just as they had done once in Campania. Here, however, it was holy land, the Homeland, and therefore automatically clean from a ritual point of view.

There was about this crowd of many, many thousands something uplifting and at the same time frightening. Something impersonal. Uri felt that he had become no more than an ant-sized part of the throng, and he was unsure what to make of that. He was looking out of its head from the inside, but it was also as if he were watching from above, like an eagle. He had a bird's eye view of himself too, and he was just as tiny as everyone else, yet it was also not like that, because the throng was not looking at itself from above. Young and old, men and women were sunk in themselves, praying and treading onward. Passover in Rome was nothing like this. There it was small and intimately domestic.

Uri caught himself looking at the vast throng through the eyes of a non-Jewish Roman, as if he were an idle traveler, gazing with interest at the peoples of far-off foreign lands but having nothing to do with what was happening. As if he were not walking among them but seated comfortably in a litter, looking in amazement and with haughty disdain at the throng of people down below. As if he were the prefect and had not curtained off the window of his carriage but were looking out with interest over those whom he ruled, gazing at the corruption, decomposition, and disgusting decay to which children and the elderly, men and women, animals and plants were subjected, and deriving a titillating pleasure from voluptuously inspecting the kinds of ulcers that covered their bodies, what sort of rags they were going around in. Not as if a large portion of Roman Jews were not gravely ill; not as if the Roman plebeians in general did not suffer from countless maladies. Disease, though, seems to be a concomitant of life, almost a fundamental condition, but Uri could not recall from his days in Rome, in either its Jewish or non-Jewish quarters, seeing quite so many seriously misshapen faces. The eyes of the Roman Jews had not gleamed, even on holidays, in such a fashion.

Uri gazed at them as if he had been sent to spy on them.

These people were enthusiastic. They were marching along, going up to the Temple in Jerusalem! In Rome no one enthused about anything, skeptical Jewish descendants of slaves least of all. To be a Jew in Rome meant objectivity: it was bad for everyone, but worst of all, hallelujah, for us, praise be to the Lord for that. One could see, from here in the Holy Land, that while to be a Jew in Rome was a hundred times better, even at times better than for the Latini, who had good reason to be terrified when power changed hands.

Uri was not boundlessly glad to be making his way to Jerusalem with his painful leg and throbbing back. I don't believe, he now acknowledged to himself, that the Lord dwells in the most secret sanctum of the Temple in Jerusalem; He dwells nowhere, He does not have human form, He does not need to dwell anywhere, He is All, He is the Creation, who created His very self because He wanted to do so, and He sees Himself in us in moderation and indeed sometimes, no doubt, with sorrow. He dwells just as much in Rome as anywhere else.

These people, however, seemed really to believe that He dwelled in the Temple, and that by reaching Jerusalem they would be able to come into His direct presence. They would not, no one can. Perhaps one day the Anointed One, the Messiah, who will descend among us from His right hand to raise us mercifully and set us beside the Lord. The Messiah is certainly there; He belongs there by necessity. But until the Messiah comes, God is present in all places where Jews are present, indeed even in those places where there are no Jews, for, after all, He is God of all men, of all created beings; non-Jews simply do not know it. But it will become known to them. It will become known to non-Jewish servants of the post houses who, standing in front of the buildings and masking their cowardice with grins—though one would think they might have gotten used to it by now—are trembling at the great might of this throng as it wends its way, singing peacefully. They dread that the peaceful throng will all at once turn savage; that is their fear. It will become known to the whores, posted at regular distances along the road, and when the Messiah arrives they too will be relieved of their terrible service. It will become known to the soldiers posted to the sentry cabins; they likewise are afraid. They may be non-Jews, but God is also their only god, only they do not yet know it. The Messiah will free them, too, from all their troubles. One can see from their terrified eyes that they sense His immanent earthly presence, the Shechinah, this all-pervading, all-permeating female spirit, only they fear it as yet. They do not know that they should rejoice.

Uri was assailed by an uncomfortable feeling of being unable to truly rejoice. As if he were not a Jew, though he had been born one of the chosen people. It was a sin to be unable to rejoice sufficiently at this, but he felt that God had inflicted this sin as a diversion: he had become, so he felt, the eye of the Almighty, who was all-seeing. With his poor eyes, to report to Him. So that he might be a spy for the Messiah, who all at once would appear, praying, supplicating, singing to himself softly.

He, the Lord himself, sent me here to spy, and he may be reading my thoughts even now. It may be that He does not see what I see, but my thoughts reach up to Him.

At one of the mass hand-washings he pictured how they might have performed the communal washings in the Jordan conducted by John, whom Herod Antipas had arrested, imprisoned, and for some reason put to death.

Vague rumors regarding those mass bathings had reached Rome, the Jews there just shaking their heads, as though they could not understand. Why immerse oneself completely in the Jordan? It was more than enough to wash hands and feet before saying one's prayers, and one's hands before each meal, and one could take a dip perfectly well in the foot-deep water of a mikveh. But even a mikveh was not absolutely necessary; the Roman mikvehs were not intended for total immersion of the body, it was only possible to wash the hands and feet, as the Torah prescribes. What was the point of going beyond what the Torah wisely and moderately prescribes?

That John the Baptist, as he was called, in fact had done nothing, Uri reflected. He was at the place where the masses, longing to be pure, had gotten in the habit of immersing themselves in the Jordan. The throng had been in rapture, and they had outdone what was prescribed by the faith. Those people must have been very sick, just like the crowd now, and they greatly wished to be cleansed of the spiritual torments that were hobbling them so hopelessly. John discerned that and put himself at the head of that rapture—as if he had hit upon it. Absurd! If a river were standing in their path right now, the people would swarm into it to clean themselves and reach Jerusalem in that condition. I too could do with a nice cool bath, Uri thought, wiping the sweat once more with the palm of his hand from his brow and the back of his neck.

I ought to ask Simon the Magus about this; he is a Galilean, like the Baptist. Maybe he knew him personally since it was not long ago that he was executed—perhaps less than a year. It's a pity Simon had gone on ahead to sort out his filthy financial affairs in time, before the festival begins.

AT FIRST IT WAS JUST THE SMOKE THAT THEY SAW, ONLY LATER DID THEY glimpse the City.

It was impossible not to see the smoke; even Uri could see it. It was a cloud like any other, but one that narrowed to an increasingly thin streak as it neared the ground, as if the cloud were hanging over the City attached to an umbilical cord. The cloud could also be pictured inversely: God had created it above the City and He was lowering himself in an attenuating emanation of double paraboloid shape, honoring the City by choosing it as the spot at which to do so.

The smoke of burning flesh on the altar stone rises thinly, only then to disperse. The high, ashlar fireplace stands in the square before the Temple. It is possible to reach the top by stairs, it is said; it is up there that the pyre burns, to there that the parts of the carcasses dismembered by the Levites are carried and roasted. All day long, from dawn to dusk, the priests elected for service that day cremate the sacrificial animals, the flesh and skin of which are due, according to complex laws, either only to the priests themselves, or to members of the priestly families as well, with the Levites also receiving certain parts.

Uri was very much hoping that he would soon be standing near the altar stone, close enough to make a thorough inspection so as to be able to describe it to his father back home.

The smoke lay darkly and with firm contours directly above the horizon, and although no smell carried this far, the throng was intoxicated by the spectacle.

Jewry was doing God a favor by incinerating those countless cattle as His comestibles (the priests eat them, yes, but all the same it may as well be the Lord Himself who consumes them via the stomachs of His adherents), and a well-fed God will forgive His chosen people their sins, and leave them to live and multiply.

Jews were treading across the hills and meadows everywhere in the neighborhood of the City, many hundreds of thousands of people, to arrive in the City on time, although it was only Wednesday afternoon. Since they had started on Sunday at daybreak, in their great haste the delegates had been covering almost fifty stadia a day, two marathons daily. They would easily get there by sunset on Thursday and they, the privileged, would be admitted at one of the city gates.

The city wall itself could now be made out, and also visible was the roof of Herod's palace, or, to be more precise, the tips of the extremely high towers that had been built next to it, as well as the roof of the Temple, and more than a few other tall edifices: the tower of Phasael, they said, the palace of the high priests. They incandesced in the searing light, a light that Uri too could see; to his eyes they blurred into one, which meant that these palaces on two hills must be close to one another. This was a small city; even a fraction of this throng would never fit in.

Matthew explained that, with Jewry being divided into twenty-four parts, people were allowed entry into the City by the rotation principle, and it was decided by a further complicated process of drawing lots which tribes were entitled to enter Temple Square, and which of its courts, in a given year. The results were known to the guards at the city gates, and they would let inside only the people who had been chosen. The leaders of the tribes carried tablets of marble or clay or scrolls of papyrus to identify themselves, and after thorough scrutiny of these documents, the guards would direct them this way or that. Priority was given to anyone who had not yet visited Jerusalem, or had only done so a long time ago. But anyone who saw the smoke, even though he was stranded outside the city wall, had satisfied the aim of the pilgrimage and would live in the knowledge that he too had seen the City and the Temple.

"You are sure we will get in?" Hilarus inquired anxiously.

"Quite sure," said Matthew. "I've got our letter of safe-conduct."

They came to a stop; people were clustering together. Matthew signaled that they were to stick closely to him. They slowly shuffled ahead for hours on end. Uri's feet, back, and neck were aching; he had gotten used to walking, not dawdling.

The reason they had come to a standstill was that a chain of Jewish guardians of the law were stationed seven or eight cubits apart on the meadow, among the well-tended gardens and tiny houses. They were checking individuals and families at random, in some cases searching through their baggage or clothes.

"They're looking for daggers," Matthew explained.

"Is that normal?" Hilarus asked.

"No."

Others could not pass while the check was in progress. True, the crowd could easily have brushed the guardians of the law aside, but the thought did not even arise. People stood and shuffled ahead like sheep. If the guards said they had to wait, then wait they would; that was one of the concomitants of a feast, of joy. For Passover was a joyful celebration, the feast of unleavened bread (the deliverance from slavery in Egypt) and of the first crop in spring. This vast crowd of people had gathered to rejoice and make merry, and that meant cheerfully enduring the burdens that accompany joy.

The strapping guardians of law and order doggedly picked and chose from the throng; Uri studied their work through narrowed eyes. Each inspection took a long time, and Uri was able to guess which people would be beckoned over. Among the poor it was the healthier-looking ones who would be subjected to a search, especially if they were raggedly dressed; among the better-off it was those who appeared more impatient than usual; among the women, the agitated ones; and among the children, the more disciplined. There was a method to this selection that testified to a knowledge of human psychology, though Uri still did not quite grasp why they should expect holidaymakers of conspiring to upset public order in Judaea. The ones who were frisked were suspected—obviously without any foundation—of murderous intent. He recalled something Plotius had said in Syracusa: there was no legal protection in Judaea, which was precisely why so many wanted to win Roman or Italian citizenship.

Eventually they too reached the line of guardians of the law. One of them, fair-haired and young, gave them a once-over before nodding his head to indicate that they could move ahead.

Matthew stepped up to him, took out the letter of safe-conduct, and said something.

The fair-haired Jew flicked his eyes down at the safe-conduct, then looked up at Matthew.

"Which one?"

Matthew pointed to Uri.

Strong hands seized Uri under the armpits, and whisked him off behind the police cordon. Uri found it amusing that he was able to beat the air with his legs, he even laughed out. He was hit on the head. Everything went black: that much he could still see, and he was amazed that such things could also exist.

II

JUDAEA

HIS HEAD ACHED, BUT THE COLD WAS WORSE. HE SHIVERED, CURLED UP, and noted that he was lying on a thin layer of straw on a stone floor. He opened his eyes.

It was mostly dark in the high, vaulted chamber. Two robust figures were seated on the stone, legs drawn up, backs to the wall, looking at him.

"What's this?" Uri asked in Greek.

"Prison," one of the figures replied in Aramaic.

Uri hauled himself up onto all fours, stretched his limbs, and wiggled his neck. Nothing broken. The nape of the neck ached a lot, but dully.

The builder had left a gap of a palm's width to admit light very high up between the ashlar blocks. On the left wall, next to the wall opposite the slit, he spotted a wooden door with iron bands that could obviously only be opened from the outside. Uri stood up and inspected the slit; it had been cut into the middle of the wall, directly below the arch of the vault. As was his habit back home, he knocked on the wall, even smelled it. Blocks stacked beneath the slit were smaller than on the other walls, and moreover the wall only stretched up to the vault. The gaps between the stones had been liberally filled with a cement-like material, the mortar having trickled down before drying. It was quite possible it was laid later than the rest.

He tapped on all the other walls as well. All along the base of the wall opposite the slit there was a protuberance on which one could sit. Nearly rectangular ashlars of identical height had been placed next to one another, the gaps being plugged with gravel and earth.

What on Earth might the cell have been before it was converted into a prison?

He sat down and took a better look at the two figures. They were young men with coarse features; even seated it was clear that they were strong. Both were wearing tunics and cloaks, which was why they had been able to rest their backs on the cold wall. Where was his own cloak? It was in the sack. His father's cloak. He regretted not having that.

"How long have I been here?" he asked in Aramaic.

"You were brought in the evening."

Uri looked up. Beams of light were playing at the top of the wall above the door, but only above the door, grazing the wall diagonally, the rest being left in shadow.

"Is it morning now?"

"It will be noon soon."

The slit must be facing east, or rather northeast.

Uri rubbed his belly.

"Do they feed you here?"

"You slept through breakfast. Next will be supper."

"Just great!" said Uri.

He tested his eyes one after the other, but his sight had gotten no better from the blow. But it hadn't gotten worse either.

He felt relief. He was only grateful when he thought of Matthew, who had informed on him and gotten him thrown in prison. I'm now in the right place for me, he considered, and laughed out loud.

The two figures exchanged looks.

The whole thing was now clear to Uri.

There would have been time before they left Rome to have his name added to the safe-conduct; after all, Plotius had said he was brought into the delegation even later, yet they had managed to get his name included. It was only Uri's name that had been missing. Matthew had not so much as mentioned his name to the magistrate on the day before they had set off, as that was his last chance to declare that he would be traveling with six companions, not five. Plotius's name had been added to the list even though it was only decided later that he would be coming. He, Uri, had been added to the list two days before, at Agrippa's request, yet even so Matthew had not reported that; he could have done so at the time he was making the arrangements for Plotius. He had not.

Matthew must have planned in advance that he was going to inform on Agrippa's presumed spy when he got to Jerusalem.

As a matter of fact, he had said so beforehand, in Caesarea, that evening when they had drunk wine together with Plotius. Of course, he had not been explicit, but Plotius had almost certainly understood. Plotius had also known what was going to happen, but he had said nothing—obviously because he agreed.

It did not pain Uri that he had been betrayed by precisely the two men he had thought most highly of among his companions.

I'm not suited for a delegation like this, he thought. Even prison is better; at least my position is clear-cut.

Uri realized that he was not afraid; he was quite sure he'd get out, and didn't think that he was in true peril. There were adventures in store for him beyond his wildest dreams. How many Jews in Rome could tell a story of having been imprisoned in Jerusalem, of all places?

Uri laughed out loud.

He would no longer have to feel awkward among staid people of tawdry character and dubious intentions, prompted by petty political and venal commercial calculations.

I shall never again be a member of any delegation, he decided; no power on Earth can compel me.

He was glad that his instincts had not deserted him; he had sensed all along that something was wrong. He would have liked to think that he was simply imagining things, but he wasn't. On the contrary, he had always sensed what he should have done.

I am perfectly sound.

He breathed deeply. The back of his neck ached, but he still felt strong. He would tell his father that he had grown up overnight: that was what had just happened to him.

"What's typical here? Are prisoners interrogated at all, or just left to rot?" Uri inquired brightly.

There was a short pause before the one sitting under the slit spoke.

"Where are you from?"

"Rome."

"You don't say! Pay attention, then. A sentence has to be passed, so you get a hearing. The first thing to do is say this and that, you did nothing wrong, quite the opposite in fact, then someone weighs in with the accusations, and if there are any witnesses, they are heard, then the members of the court of law, the Beth Din, come to a verdict. In the villages three judges are enough, and in the towns it can be anything up to twenty-three, and verdicts have to be reached by a majority vote of at least two. The verdicts are given from the youngest, at the end of each row, to the oldest in the middle. While that is going on, you have to stand facing them, your hair has grown long out of remorse, and you are grieving, and you stand there penitently, your head hung low, even if you have pleaded innocence. If anyone has spoken on your behalf, they can say another word before the verdict is reached, but anyone who was a witness against you cannot speak again. After that, they cast votes. If you are acquitted, you are immediately released, but if you are condemned, they do not pronounce the verdict right then, only the next day... But if the next day is a holiday or the Sabbath, then only after that."

"I don't get it," said Uri. "If three judges are enough, how do you get a verdict with a majority of three?"

"You don't, in that case," the other said. "The verdict is either unanimous or else they call in two more and from that point the two-vote majority applies."

"Twenty-three judges?" asked Uri. "Even in a small town?"

"The towns are not that small!" said the one sitting under the slit, affronted. "Any place with five hundred adult males counts as a town! That means at least fifteen hundred or two thousand inhabitants, though likely much more! The towns are not so small here."

A local patriot, Uri thought cheerily.

"Are there that many judges in a town?" he asked. "Or are some of them lawyers as well? Sometimes prosecuting, sometimes defending?"

The other two did not understand, so Uri tried to describe what was meant by prosecuting and defending counsels and by a judge. Gradually they caught on.

"There's nothing like that here," said the one sitting under the slit. "There are men—tailors, cooks, joiners, tentmakers, robbers, thieves, that sort of thing." He laughed at his own wit before carrying on.

"If they need you to try a case, the master sends for you. And you go to the house of prayer to try the case. If there is no two-vote majority, they keep on calling people until there is. But twenty-three is the most, and if a verdict is still not reached, then the case is referred to the Great Sanhedrin—that's here, above where we are now... But even they do not always sit together; they too start with three members, and so on, all the way up to seventy-one. It's not usual to bring cases here, though; the two-vote majority system works locally, sooner or later."

"I've never heard of a case that could not be settled locally," said the one seated closer.

"And this master, the elder of the juridical tribunal... where does he get the right to call others in to pass judgment? Is he the archisynagogos?"

That was a term that meant nothing to them, so Uri explained that he was thinking of the leading member of the congregation of a house of prayer. They shook their heads.

"He's the master, that's all there is to it!"

"Does he make a living from doing that?" Uri asked.

"Not at all!" said the one sitting under the slit. "He's not allowed to take money for teaching, sitting in judgment, or giving advice. He has an occupation, though, as a tiller of the soil or limeburner or furniture maker... That's why he is a master..."

"Or he robs and steals," said the other.

They both laughed.

This really was another world.

"Have your cases already been heard?"

"Not yet," said the one sitting under the slit.

"Mine hasn't either," said the other.

"When will they be?"

The one sitting under the slit looked up toward the light.

"Well, either right away, today, or else after Passover."

"If not today, then it will be more than a week, next Monday, in eleven days' time. The days for juridical sessions are Mondays and Thursdays. There are no other days."

In other words, it was the same in Jerusalem as in the country, with a court being convened only on market days. If they did not come to hear a case by sunset today, Thursday, then they would not be able to do so on Monday either, on account of Passover, nor on the following Thursday, because that was also a half-holiday, on which it was forbidden to sit in judgment. There was a lot that could be done on half-holidays that was not permitted on full holidays—burying the dead, for instance, or healing the sick, but not sitting in judgment.

He did not like the idea of killing time here for eleven days. Better they come today. Let everything be settled, then he could go home to Rome, though he did not yet know how. Of course, as long as they gave him something to eat, even eleven days would be tolerable in the end, too.

"What are you in for?" asked the one sitting under the slit.

"I did nothing," said Uri, and he gave another laugh. "You're not going to believe it, but nothing at all."

"You're right, we don't believe it," said the other.

"Never mind," said Uri. "Gaius Theodorus is my name."

The other two remained silent. Uri shrugged his shoulders.

"So why are you here?"

"We're innocent," the one sitting under the slit said sardonically. "But we're accused of robbery."

How droll: I've fallen in among thieves. And they can't even rob me of anything, because I have nothing!

"That's quite a serious charge," said Uri.

"Are you kidding?" said the other. "The most they can sentence us to is four or five years of slavery, and when that's over, we will be released without having to pay a bond for our manumission. We're not petty thieves, but robbers!"

"That is to say, we're being made out to be robbers," the one sitting under the slit added. "But they'll have to prove it!"

Uri thought he could not have heard that properly, or maybe they had a different way with words, so he asked what they supposed the difference was between a robber and a thief.

They looked at each other in amazement. All the same, the one sitting under the slit then took it upon himself to explain, with considerate shouting and syllabifying so that even Uri would understand: a thief stole, whereas a robber took something away by force.

So Uri had heard right.

"A robber is given a lighter sentence than a thief?" he asked in astonishment.

The two looked at each other again.

"Are you Jewish in any way at all?"

"Yes, of course."

"Then you must be slow," said the one who was seated closer, sighing before launching into an explanation. "A thief does not just steal; he offends the Eternal One by hiding himself from His countenance. He does evil on the sly, seeking to hide his evil deeds from the Lord. A robber, on the other hand, attacks from the front, and he does not offend the Almighty, because he does not hide from Him! A thief's crime is therefore more serious!"

A fine, clear, religious exposition, thought Uri; the laws here really are different.

In Rome a robber would receive the death penalty, whereas a thief would be sentenced to a few years or eternal servitude, and there were two grades at that: he might remain a slave on Far Side or else he might be sold off in Italia, in Puteoli for example, where there is a famous slave market because human cargo is put into its harbor from every part of the empire.

If the offender were a Jew who was a Roman citizen, the Jewish jurisdiction in principle had to run the more serious punishments by a Roman court of law, but in practice the Curia would give the nod to any Jewish verdict; it had plenty to do as it was. The Latini tended to approve even sentences of death, and if, every now and then, an appeal was heard, neither defendant nor witnesses were recalled; the decision was a formality and invariably upheld the judgment. The superfluous right of appeal was reserved by Curia, on the other hand, and there were cases where they might want to save a person sentenced to death for political reasons—because he was of great interest to an influential senator, even to the emperor himself, being a favorite actor, lover, or something of the kind—then the Curia would dig in its heels until it had been given an appropriate bribe.

"What can a thief expect here?" Uri inquired.

"He is sentenced to death."

That must be a newfangled law.

As he had learned it in Rome, a thief was obliged to reimburse four times the value of the stolen object, and once he had done that, he was set free. On the orders of Herod the Great, thieves were sold off as slaves and so a crowd of Jewish thieves, the "new ones," had found their way to Rome. But the Roman prefects had put an end to that practice when Herod died.

"I once saw the execution of a thief," said the man who was seated nearer. "Not a pretty sight."

"Was he stoned?" asked the one sitting under the slit.

"No, burned alive."

The man who was seated closer related the incident with relish. Every one of the villagers, even women and children, had assembled to watch; they were summoned to learn from it. The smith boiled up iron in a pan over an enormous fire, and when the iron was flowing, the bound thief had a scarf tied around his neck and pulled from both ends. He was strong and lasted a fair time without air, but he eventually gave out and opened his mouth wide, gasping for air. Well, it was then that the smith's assistant poured the scalding iron into his gullet, made him drink it up until he burned. With white-hot metal pouring out through the holes in his burst-open chest and belly. The thief was still alive, but he was unable to shout out because he no longer had a throat; he was just writhing and burning from the inside out, with the scarf-pullers keeping hold from the two sides until the whole thing became a trickling live metal statue.

Uri shuddered.

"What if he hadn't opened his mouth?"

"He would have choked," the man who was seated nearer said. "But because the sentence was burning, not strangling, they would have forced the corpse's mouth open and filled it with molten iron."

"I can't say I would be too happy to be burned alive," the one sitting under the slit pondered. "I'd rather be strangled."

"That's not good either," the other opined. "If done ineptly, that can drag on for a long time."

"Stoning to death as well," the one sitting under the slit. "They can pelt and pelt, but you're still alive. Better to be strangled."

"The best of all," said the one seated more closely, "is if they chop off your head with a sword—a moment and it's over."

"That's the foreign-style execution," the one sitting under the slit scoffed. "No Edomite execution for me, thank you. I don't want the angels having to search for the head that's rolled away from my body when the time comes for resurrection; they're quite capable of not noticing that they've stuck it onto the wrong body—a whore's, say. No, thank you: I'd rather be strangled!"

Strange place, this Judaea; Jerusalem too must be a strange place. Uri smiled: he was there, though, even if he had seen nothing of it.

"Where is this prison exactly?" he asked.

"The high priests have their dwellings above us," said the man sitting beneath the slit, indicating with his head the vaulting of the ceiling. "We're being put up in a fair-sized building, to be sure. They don't have it much better than us, now that we share residences," he gave a hollow laugh.

"Where is this palace? In the Temple Square?"

"No, it's in the Upper City. The Temple is nearby, to the northeast of here... Count five hundred steps and you're there."

Uri gazed up at the slit of a window, and he saw a tiny, faded-blue slice of the sky; the sun was no longer shining in. Even these affable rogues knew which way was northeast, and when the time comes for evening prayers that is the direction in which they would bow. From now on, neither would he have to bow toward Jerusalem when it came to prayer-time, because he was right there in the very middle, but toward the Temple just five hundred paces away.

"These were shops right here, where we are sitting," said the one seated more closely, as he got to his feet to walk around. He was tall and powerfully built; he might easily have gotten a position in the Jewish police—indeed, had it not been for his Jewishness, even among Pilate's litter bearers. "They rented the premises at a high rate from the high priests, but then the traders moved to the market square in front of Herod's palace, because they could earn more there, both they and the high priests. There were more people. As a result something had to be done with the premises, and that is how it had become a prison."

"It's easier for them like this," said the man sitting beneath the slit, and he too got up. He was not short but seemed a little on the pudgy side.

"Most recently the Sanhedrin has been sitting upstairs. The defendants don't have to be escorted very far; better for them if we're right here, underneath, in a shared building. There's no need for a whole troop to take us all the way out to the Xystus, with us being sneaky enough to make a break for it along the way."

Uri's stomach rumbled. He had eaten nothing for a whole day now, and he could also use a chance to relieve himself. He looked around.

"Over there," the plump one said, pointing to a corner opposite the door.

A broad-brimmed pitcher covered with a square slab of marble was standing there, the skewed slab indicating that it was not empty. Uri took the trouble to turn around and, pulling up his tunic with one hand and clutching his loosened loincloth with the other, finally managed to squat in such a way that the protruding excrement of the others would not rub off anywhere on him. He squatted with his back to the other prisoners, who just laughed at him. Maybe it would be best, he thought, if they were to hear me today.

Hours passed. It was getting dark outside.

"There you have it, boys," said the plump one, sitting back down under the slit. "We're going to be taking a shit in each other's shit for another eleven days."

The door opened and two guards entered; the one with a blazing torch in his hand stayed by the door, the other set two dishes down on the ground. In one dish there was some food, in the other water. The lankier rogue jumped toward the pitcher to hand it over to the guard, but he gestured: "Not now." The guards left and locked the door.

Outside it became almost pitch-dark, though it was still just possible to make out that the two rogues were dabbling their hands in the dish of water before turning toward the pitcher and, bowing, saying the Sh'ma for that evening. Uri sprinkled water on his hand and said it with them. The pitcher happened to be to the northeast.

The two rogues then knelt down next to the dish and sniffed the food, like a dog would. They made a face and shook their heads before crouching back on their heels and cramming a chunk of the rations into their mouths. Uri did not move until they had finished and scrambled away from the dish. He then clambered to the dish, smelt it likewise, then prodded it with a forefinger. It was some sort of flatbread. He licked his finger: perhaps with a trace amount of honey in it, it was not something he had ever eaten before. He did not eat much, because they did not leave him a lot.

He scooped up some water with the palm of a hand and drank it.

In all truth, now was the time one ought really to sit down to supper.

It was the eve of Seder. They ought to have been given lamb like the rest of the Jewish world.

Of course, it could be that there had been a few morsels but the two rogues had polished them off.

He could see nothing; blindness must be something like this. He was alarmed.

"Can you see anything?" he asked.

"How the devil are we supposed to see, stupid, when it's dark!" said the one sitting under the slit.

Uri's mind was set at rest.

He was roused from his sleep by the rattling of keys. The door opened, and between two torchbearing guards two others led in, by the arms, an older, heavier man; the torches fluttered in the draft, and shadows flickered across the prisoner's face and tunic. One of the guards then cut through with his dagger the cord that was pinning the fat man's arms behind his back, then they left. Uri looked quickly to the side; his companions were still seated in their places. The new captive stood, not looking anywhere in particular. He was balding, and his bedraggled, graying beard was unkempt. He stood barefoot. The door was shut, and it became even darker than it had been previously. Nothing was said. The scanty straw rustled quietly under the new prisoner's feet, then he took a seat next to Uri and sighed deeply.

"They won't even let a man sleep," said the one sitting under the slit.

There was a silence; the new prisoner breathed heavily.

"Did they beat you up?" asked the man sitting under the slit.

"No," replied the new prisoner. He had a pleasant, deep voice, and although he spoke softly, it seemed loud.

"Let's get some rest, then," said the man to Uri's right.

There was a silence; all four of them were awake.

"What are you in for?" asked the man sitting under the slit.

"Causing a disturbance," said the new prisoner. He must be Galilean, judging by his accent.

There was a silence.

"Not a big enough disturbance, sadly," he added after a pause.

"Why are we not sleeping?" said the other irately.

"You go on and sleep; we're talking," said the man sitting under the slit. "What disturbance was that, then?"

"We went up onto Temple Mount, the women's court, on Tuesday, to buy turtledoves, and I saw that they were cheating people. I told them not to, but they just carried on. So I tipped a few tables over."

There was a silence.

"So where have they been banging you up since Tuesday?" the man sitting under the slit asked.

"Nowhere. We were allowed to leave. We live outside the city."

"I don't get it. So they didn't even arrest you on Tuesday?"

"No, we went back the next day, and they were still cheating, and again I told them not to, but they just carried on. The guards then came over, we had a discussion, and then we went home. It was only today, in the evening, that they came to where we live, and I told the others to scatter, but it wasn't them they were after; they only caught me."

"I don't get it," said the other, the one to Uri's right. "They went looking for you afterward to arrest you? Why didn't they take you into custody straight-away?"

"I have no idea," said the new prisoner.

"It can't have been that much of a fuss," said the one sitting under the slit, "because our police take you in straightaway for much less, especially on Temple Square. There, just one word out of place is enough. They get bonuses for making arrests there, especially around feast days—a per capita sum, I'm telling you."

"What do you mean by cheating?" Uri inquired.

"Obviously he's referring to the way the moneychangers charge more than a kalubon to exchange currencies."

"What's that?" Uri asked.

"That's the moneychangers' fee: a silver ma'ah," said the one sitting under the slit. "A sixth of a zuz. Do you know how much a zuz is?"

"No, I don't."

The robbers were getting worked up; there were sounds of shifting about.

"A zuz is half a shekel, which to say a dinar or an Attic drachma, or in other words four sesterces... A silver ma'ah is two pondions... Now, then," the one sitting under the slit asked, "how many sesterces to a kalubon, kid?"

Uri made an effort to calculate it, but he got mixed up.

"Give it to him in prutahs, that's the smallest copper coin," said the other. "Something like that would certainly be in the damn fool's hand... Thirty-two prutahs... That's a kalubon."

"A prutah is also called a lepton, that much I do know," said Uri, proud of himself.

"So far you haven't set hands on anything else, you wretch," the one seated in the middle weighed in scornfully.

"So anyway, how many sesterces is that?" the man seated under the slit asked again.

"I have no idea."

The two robbers guffawed; they could hardly get over the fact that someone might not be able to do the math.

"Two-thirds," said the new prisoner.

There was a slight pause.

"That's right," said the one sitting under the slit, annoyed that his little game had been brought to an end.

No one said a word.

"Why? What do they charge instead?" Uri inquired.

"In some cases," said the one sitting under the slit, "it may be as much as seven or eight pondions! I've even seen them go for seven or eight tresiths, and the stupid klutzes don't even notice! They're from the villages, and they're clueless! Just so you know, you moron: one ma'ah is just two pondions and three-quarters of a tresith. Instead of taking one sixth of a zuz, they may pull in as much as three quarters of a zuz! Four times as much! The fools keep coming; they know nothing about what things are worth, just the same as you; the peasants never handle any money except at times like this, so they get swindled out of a fortune!"

"Half the profits are handed on by the moneychangers to the high priests," said the other, who, to judge from the rustling, was sitting up. "Of course they cheat, but it's the high priests who cheat the worst, the damned foreigners!"

"They even cheat over the doves," the new prisoner chipped in. "For a dove bought to redeem a lamb, they ask double the price, even though that is prohibited. I told them they should only be charging a flat fee, but it did no good." His voice sounded tired and resigned. "They brazenly leech on people's faith. And the wretched people hand over what little money they have, because at all events they have to have two turtledoves to make an offering..."

"That's the third tithe of turtledoves," said the other sarcastically. "That's what it's known as, and that too finds its way into the pockets of the high priests... They're the biggest thieves of all, the high priests! That's also why they live here, over the prison... They know this is the right place for them, together with us. They're bigger villains than us; that's why their rooms are bigger too!"

They fell silent. Uri regretted that he had never had any Palestinian money in his hands, and he had paid no attention in Caesarea when his companions had been arguing over the value of the local coins. At least now he had learned that one ma'ah is two thirds of a sestertius; if the chance were to arise, he would tell them.

He broke into a smile. Now he was unlikely to be seeing much more of them, thanks be to the Lord!

"Have you come from Galilee?" the one sitting under the slit asked.

"Yes," replied the new prisoner, starting up from his doze.

"Do you pay taxes there too?"

"Yes, we do."

"There you go! So you voluntarily changed money on account of the sacrificial doves, so it's actually forbidden to charge you a kalubon! You should be getting money changed for free! Free! Didn't you realize?"

"No, I didn't," said the new prisoner wearily.

"The brazen cheek of it!" the one sitting under the slit exclaimed. "The dirty, low-down scum! But they never get tossed in the can like us, because they grease the palms of the high priests! The dirtbags!"

Uri woke at daybreak. The new prisoner was quietly praying, bowing in a kneeling position toward the pitcher. The other two prisoners were both sleeping with faces to the wall, their cloaks pulled over their heads. Uri was shivering; he had no cloak, and his waist, back, and shoulders were aching. The new prisoner had no cloak either, only a tunic of white linen, but he showed no signs of being cold; perhaps prayer was keeping him warm. He looked at Uri while praying. The older man was just a pace away, his face clearly visible in the dawn light. His tousled hair and beard were turning gray, and he had gentle eyes, clear, pale, maybe gray, set in a puffy face; he must have been a handsome man at one time. He is almost the same age as my father, Uri thought, and smiled at him. The new prisoner nodded back and went on with his prayers.

The door then opened, and in came the two guards. They yanked the coverings off the sleepers, held a torch close to each man's face, and finally stopped in front of the new prisoner. He got to his feet; each guard took him by an arm and they led him out. The door was bolted again from outside.

"Let's get back to sleep," said the man lying to Uri's right, and rolled back to face the wall.

LATER IN THE MORNING, THEY WERE GIVEN FRESH WATER AND MATZOS, and also at last they took the pitcher out. The man sitting under the slit tried to teach Uri the values of all the currencies that were in use in Palestine, but Uri soon got bored; he was never going to have any money in this land. The rogues asked him how much he had been making in Rome, and how he had gotten there. Uri explained that he was a member of the delegation bringing money from Rome, and the robbers shut up for a long time at that.

"So you're a Roman citizen, then?" the other man, the lankier one, asked.

"Yes, I am," said Uri.

"Why didn't you tell them?" the other exclaimed. "Jews are not allowed to arrest you!"

"I didn't exactly have a chance to discuss the matter," said Uri. "They banged me on the head."

"Tell the guards when they come in this evening," the man sitting under the slit advised. "They're going to be petrified and take you straight off to a better place, better than this."

Uri shook his head. He did not hold out much hope of any favors being done for him; Matthew, the head of the delegation, had been the one who informed on him. But he would somehow weather the ten days among these likable robbers. He would ask for a cloak.

It must have been around the second hour of the day when the door opened and five soldiers came in. They halted in front of the two robbers, who scrambled to their feet.

"Out with you," ordered one of the soldiers.

"But it's Friday," protested the lanky one. "There's no court hearing on a Friday."

"Out with you," the soldier repeated, prodding them with the tip of his spear.

The door then closed so swiftly that Uri did not get a chance to ask for a cloak, or to take leave of his cell mates.

He was now left alone in the cell.

He stood up, and began to move around.

He would ask not only for a cloak but also for something to read. He would manage well enough here; it did not matter if no one was brought in on account of the feast. During the two months since they had set out, he had no time on his own to read. He pondered on what scroll he should ask for, and whether they would bring it, but in the end it did not matter: anything so long as it was lengthy.

As it grew dark a guard brought the empty pitcher, along with water and two good-sized blocks of matzo. Uri got to his feet.

"Excuse me, sir, but I have no cloak... and I'd like something to read."

The guard stared in amazement.

"No one reads here," he said, and went out.

Uri grew dejected. This was going to make it a long ten days, so he made up his mind to recite from memory the *Iliad* or the *Aeneid*. He liked the *Iliad* above all.

He heard a dreadful horn blast. He froze; it was as if a fatally wounded lion had roared in his ear. What could that be? Surely a shofar did not sound like that? Had Passover started?

No one came in until Monday morning. Then he gave up the struggle. He was going almost mad every time he was unable to recall how a line went: he could see the letters in front of him, but it seemed as though precisely the lines in question had been deleted out of some sort of spite. It seemed his memory was not as good as he had supposed.

On Tuesday some kind of cloak was tossed to him, and he instantly wrapped it around himself; he felt feverish and was coughing. His gums were bleeding, his stool was bloodstained, and his stomach ached. He needed to take life more easily, he thought; I should not be worrying when I'm innocent.

On Wednesday he decided to do physical exercises as the Greeks did. There were several Greek-style gymnasiums in Rome; it was possible to look into the garden through the fence. Uri had kept his eyes peeled, sometimes peering through the cracks between his fingers, staring at how rich Roman youths ran around and stooped. Now here was an opportunity to strengthen his body; there was plenty of time. He toiled away until the evening, doing every exercise several hundred times, overdoing it so much that he spent the whole of Thursday just lying flat on his back.

Just three days to go, he thought on Friday morning; on Monday they will come for me and take me out of here. Whatever crime they suspect me of, they are not going to leave me here at state expense. He was still coughing, but his temperature had gone down.

On Friday afternoon he was given meat, decently roasted lamb. That and a pitcher—and in this one there was wine! He was able to celebrate the Sabbath in befitting fashion, albeit alone. That had to be a good sign: they had not forgotten him and did not want him to get totally run down.

Together with the meat they also brought dates, figs, and grapes, and those had even been washed. He also got some freshly baked barley bread instead of that sticky pap! Uri determined that this must be three days' rations, the three whole days of the festival, and so it proved to be: for two and a half days nobody came in. On Sunday evening, the guard set down a nice, big dish of fruit and said, "They will be coming for you tonight."

He took away the pitcher and did not bring another in its place.

At last.

He walked up and down the cell, tapping the walls. He wanted to imprint the place on his memory so as never to forget it. He summoned up the conversations that he had conducted with the robbers and the new prisoner so as not to forget them either. He was somewhat surprised at the affection in which he held them, even going so far as to have developed a fondness for this gloomy, cool cell. It had been his dwelling place in Jerusalem, he reflected, with a twinge of emotion.

Outside, evening was drawing in. All of a sudden the shofar sounded; to him it sounded as if it was coming from very close by. It had to be from the roof of the Temple that it was blown: it gave a terrible, raucous, penetrating noise.

That marked the end of Passover.

That night they came for him. He was not bound but led by the elbows from both sides. They went up a story to the first floor; torches burned on the walls. They reached a long, wide corridor, and the decorative marble floor under the bare soles of his feet felt warm; it was heated. He was led into a room with a real window, so he peered out into the dark with his eyes narrowed on the off chance that he might be able to see a bit of the city, but the guards turned him around. They let go of him and went away.

Uri found himself in front of a youngish man in military garb; he must have been a high-ranking officer, and he looked stern. A few soldiers, who might well be subalterns, were loitering farther off.

"Give him a good scrubbing," the high-ranking officer said, "and a decent rub with oils."

Silence fell. The commanding officer stepped a little closer and started to sniff. Uri bit his lip to stop himself from laughing.

"Not too foul," he declared. "Get him straightened up, but nothing to eat, mind you!"

He swung around on his heels and strode off.

Uri was led back out into the corridor. They went down another flight of stairs and reached a lovely interior garden decorated with Greek columns and stocked with carefully tended plants; that too was lit by torches. There was a door on one side, and they entered. Uri's nostrils were assailed by the odor of steaming water. He breathed a deep sigh of relief.

The waist-high water in the basin, which was lined with marble mosaics, was tepid, and he took great pleasure in being able to take a dip again in the nude. Around the basin lounged sleepy soldiers whose features he could not make out due to the distance and the steam, but they were of no interest anyway. He floated on the surface of the water. The ceiling of the baths block was lined with slates of transparent crystal, and Uri could make out a dim twinkle of faint stars.

He was left to enjoy it for a while, but then a whistle shrilled. Uri climbed out; he was swathed in a white sheet and rubbed down, then led into a room next door, and his limbs and body were massaged with oils. That was something Uri had never previously experienced; he was amazed at how pleasant it was. His hair was also sleeked with oil and his scalp was massaged vigorously before the nails of his fingers and toes were attended to, being carefully polished with a coarse, granular material. When they were done with that, he was taken into the next hall, where he was also able to take a dip in a pool of water; it was cold, and he was not permitted to soak for very long. With another whistle he was ordered out, rubbed down once more in a thick white blanket of fine wool, and escorted back to the first room, where he again had oil smeared over him, this one with a different scent from the first.

An elderly officer inspected the results, with Uri standing there naked. The officer walked around him as if he were a statue. He nodded and went away. Uri was then slipped into a crisp, fragrant, newly laundered tunic and over it a toga, a real toga like the ones worn by Roman patricians. Uri would never have been able to drape the single sheet of the garment into complicated folds on his own, but that was the task of practiced hands, finishing up with one end of the toga being put into his right hand to grasp. Like a statue of the emperor Augustus, that's how I look, thought Uri. He was given a pair of sandals of the finest leather for his feet, with the straps delicately laced around his ankles, hardly being pulled at all when they were knotted.

This time it was a younger officer who scrutinized the result, tugged the toga a little higher, slung the end to point to the side on Uri's right arm so that he only had to grip the rolled-up tip in his fist.

"Walk about a bit," the officer said in Aramaic.

Uri did what was bidden.

"Straighten up!" the officer said.

Uri drew himself up and walked around like that. It was hard to believe that a pair of sandals could be so comfortable.

"Wait here, you lot, until we come," the officer said before going off.

Uri was left there, done up, dolled up, and generally made ready in the company of five soldiers. Rank-and-file soldiers, he supposed, gazing at them with screwed-up eyes until all at once he noticed a young, fair-haired man.

He was the one to whom Matthew had shown the safe-conduct. Uri looked defiantly at him, and he turned away.

He recognized me too, Uri thought.

"Where are you going to take me?" he asked.

He got no reply. Uri nodded. It had been a silly question; it would become clear soon enough.

His stomach rumbled. However much he asked for something to eat, though, the high-ranking officer had forbidden that he be given anything.

It was then that the officer who had smelled him reappeared. The others all saluted like Roman soldiers, though this was the Jewish army, the Jerusalem division. It's Rome that sets the fashion in everything, thought Uri, the Roman citizen. He almost broke into a laugh, so grotesque was the whole business he was being put through; true, many big adventures would be in store for him.

The officer set off out of the room; the five soldiers stepped up alongside Uri and marched him out into the yard, then onward.

HE WAS AWAITED BY A PALANQUIN WITH FOUR SLAVES AMID A TEAM OF torchbearers, and he was ordered to get into the litter. He turned around inquiringly but was pushed forward. Someone opened the door of the litter, and Uri, head bowed, had to scramble in. He barely had time to find a place to seat himself when, all of a sudden, there was a lurch as the litter was picked up. With that, they were on their way.

There was a drumming of hooves from both sides. Not only was the palanquin itself magnificent, it also had a guard of honor.

The window of the litter was curtained. Uri pulled back one of the curtains but all he found behind it was a wooden board; it was not possible to look out of the litter. He grunted in irritation; now was the first time he had become impatient since he had been knocked out. I shall never see Jerusalem, he thought to himself.

He was carried for a while, and then the litter was again set down on the ground. The horses also halted.

"Make way for the Sagan!" he heard the cry.

The litter was lifted up again and carried onward. The escort of a clattering hooves did not accompany them any farther.

Sagan?

That young high-ranking officer had been the Sagan, or *strategos*, no less! The Levite commander of Jerusalem, head of twenty-four divisions who at every sacrifice stood at the altar at the right hand of the high priest and handed him the Torah scroll! The captain of the Temple guard! The bodyguard! The highest secular Jewish potentate!

The strategos himself had smelled him all over with his own nose!

The litter must conceal some VIP if the strategos were proceeding at the head of the procession.

Who are they mistaking me for?

The litter was set down and the door opened. Uri climbed out and drew himself up. He strove to grip the end of the toga less tightly in his right hand. Torchbearers surrounded him. The strategos glanced at him, then turned away.

They were standing at the entrance gate to some palace, with a multitude of guards on both sides. Uri came to notice that the palace was made up of two conjoint wings.

"To Pilate, for dinner!" announced the strategos before turning around and setting off. The empty litter was picked up and carried behind him, with the escort also setting off in its wake. The boots drummed loud; Uri looked down and saw that he was standing on marble slabs.

He looked around him. Off to his right was a stone wall at a man's height and before it a long and graceful row of Greek-style columns lit by torches. Above it were sky-scraping bastions, exceedingly high, three of them, one after the other. He turned back and discerned the outlines of a massive palace. What could it be?

He was shoved from behind and found himself obliged to enter a gate.

THEY TOOK AN IMPRESSIVE MARBLE STAIRCASE UPWARD; MASSES OF BIG torches lit the way and they passed a larger-than-man-sized statue—Apollo perhaps—at the turn in the stairs.

If they were leading him to Pilate, then this must be the palace of Herod the Great, where the governor lived when he was in Jerusalem. And one of the three towers that he had seen outside was no doubt the tower of Phasael, named by Herod after his younger brother, but what were the other two called? Let's see, he had read about that. Yes, that was it: Hippicus and Mariamne! The first was one of Herod's friends, the other a wife before he had her killed. Forty, thirty, and twenty cubits high, but which was which? Yet that too was something he knew...

Fragments of thoughts, pages that he had read, whizzed through his mind; he tried to compose himself. He would have to be careful, to keep his wits about him. This was not the time to be deliberating about that sort of thing. It had been interesting to sample the life of a prisoner, but why get oneself put back in prison when there was no need?

At the top of the stairs they came to a standstill in front of a huge oak door decorated with gold leaves. Servants on each side held it open.

Uri entered. The door was closed behind him.

He could see a long, uncovered table, a hand's span in thickness, and a great many low, ornamental couches. There were big torches burning around the walls. On the table were some gigantic ornamental candles. Three people turned toward him; they were reclining on one side at the left end of the table, and they were looking at him. Uri was unable to pick out their faces.

He stopped and bowed deeply.

GYÖRGY SPIRÓ

"Come here, come!" he heard Matthew's voice say.

Uri gritted his teeth, drew himself up and headed toward them before coming to a standstill at a respectful distance.

"Stretch yourself out here, next to me!" a gruff voice declared, also in Greek. It was a bald, clean-shaven, burly man, wearing a tunic and with gleaming rings on his fingers; he smiled.

Uri made his way around the end of the table and sat down at the place that had been indicated. He looked up. Matthew returned his gaze, visibly uneasy. Uri nodded with a smile. Matthew also smiled, and he nodded back. Could that have been a wink? Uri glanced at the head of the table. An elderly, white-haired, bearded man was reclining on his side; he was in an ornamental, Eastern-style garment and bareheaded. Uri gave him a bow of acknowledgment, and the elderly man nodded back.

"There's no need for me to introduce Matthew," the plump man said. "Apart from him, at the head of the table is a good friend of mine, the king of Galilee, who is likewise curious about you, my dear Gaius."

Uri kept a hold on himself.

At the head of the table was reclining Herod Antipas and next to him Pontius Pilate, the prefect of Judaea.

Herod Antipas was one of the sons of Herod the Great, and by virtue of that an uncle of Agrippa's. He would have to watch out.

"It is a deep honor for me to be allowed into such distinguished company," he managed to declare in a calm tone of voice.

"Just recline in comfort," said Pilate. "I'm not going to quiz you on what you did over the feast days. I hope that you had a chance to rest yourself after the travails of your long journey. Unfortunately, I had many pressing matters to attend to. Passover is no holiday for me; I have to keep working even then, even harder than at other times, so it is only now that I am in a position to receive you. I hope your appetite will be whetted with strictly kosher food, given that there are three Jews present, and I, the sole non-Jew as always, will gladly accommodate to your customs."

Uri set himself down, resting on one elbow like the other guests. It was an uncomfortable body position. He could not imagine how he was going to be able to eat like that; he was used to eating while squatting on his heels on the floor.

Servants brought a large gold bowl and set it down in front of Herod Antipas. He dabbled both hands in it, being followed by Matthew then Pilate and Uri, and they all dried their hands on table napkins. These were very fine, white cloths with curlicues of the same material embroidered into them. Uri took a close look at his own; there were no figures as such on it, just lines that twisted in on themselves so that nothing figurative would be seen. Pilate obviously used Jewish napkins.

Antipas stood up and turned toward the far end of the table; Matthew also got up and turned in the same direction. Uri also got up to turn toward the Temple, though he sacrilegiously glanced around to see where the pitcher might be. Pilate, still reclining, had lowered his head and immersed himself in thought so as not to disturb them. The three Jews—the king of Galilee, the pilot from Ostia, and the young Roman citizen—said the Sh'ma and then settled back in their places.

It came to Uri's mind that in principle they were not supposed to eat as guests of a non-Jew or else they would become impure. But then there were many times en route that they had eaten at non-Jewish places, though the innkeepers invariably asserted that they served entirely kosher food and drink. Moreover, the Diaspora itself was unclean in principle and yet there were Jews living all over the world. Here, at the very heart of sacred and pure Jerusalem, all the ambiguities of Diaspora existence converged in a palace that had been built by half-Jewish Herod the Great and usurped by a non-Jew.

Servants came and poured wine into their goblets of murrhine glass. These were even bigger crystal goblets than in the Syracusan sawmill, each holding three or four units of wine.

"To your good health, my friends!" Pilate raised his glass. "Your good health, my fine Gaius Theodorus!"

Uri raised the full goblet, but it was too heavy for his weak arm, and his hand trembled. He tasted the wine as he reclined, but just a sip, and he took great care not to spill it on himself. A person can easily get drunk on an empty stomach. He needed to keep his wits about him; there was no watering down the wine here!

No, I had not been mistaken for somebody else. Matthew had told them all about me, including some things that were not true.

Salads and fruits on huge, marvelous bowls were brought in by servants, who then withdrew.

"I love eating," said Pilate. "It's no use my wife constantly prattling on about how I'm putting on weight all the time, my way of life is unhealthy, and I hardly exercise. I'm well aware of those things, but what am I to do when I can't stand dieting?"

"It's better to start a meal with pickled greens, salads, and the like before starting on meat, whether roasted or cooked," Uri declared quite unexpectedly, as if he were reading it out.

He did not look across to the other side of the table, but he could tell that Matthew was surprised.

"How true!" exclaimed Pilate. "Celsus advises the same. As well as moderation. Sadly, though, I am going to be unable to resist all the many kinds of meat dishes this evening, and I would not advise that for you either, my dear Gaius. I'd love to be as slim as you are again! To be able to gorge myself without worries, because I still eat now, only uneasily! And I am often tormented by stomachaches."

"That might well be due to the southern wind and spring," Uri said by way of chatting, turning toward Pilate. "Celsus says that spring is the time for the onset of illnesses associated with the movement of humors..." He could almost see the text of the scroll of Celsus's writings before his eyes, and, not even noticing that he'd switched to Latin, he went on: "Eyes stream, piles bleed, the digestive canal becomes inflamed, gallstones, dementia, angina, and nosebleeds all may arise, the tonsils become angry... Disorders of the joints and tendons are more common... As far as losing weight is concerned, one should bathe in saline hot water..."

A silence fell. Uri looked around. Matthew was looking at him aghast; Antipas also looked stony-faced. Uri felt a sudden sense of shame.

"My apologies for speaking," he said in Greek.

"You did well to say it!" Pilate vigorously approved. "My own doctor also swears by Celsus, although of course he has adopted some procedures from Cassius and Erasistratus... He gets his annual fee of eighty thousand sesterces on the dot on the first day of January... It's a lot, I know, but good physicians today cost a lot; the emperor's physician gets three hundred thousand a year and finds even that too little, so I'm told, even though he does nothing, the lucky dog, because Tiberius has enjoyed excellent health all his livelong days and is in superb condition even now, I hear... I, on the other hand, overeat and, to be honest, there are times when I use an emetic, to be sure, even though Asclepiades does not advise it..."

"He was not in favor of purgation either," Uri commented again, "whereas Celsus says that it is useful if you have to void strong medicaments... Though of course he does agree that it's not good when it is employed for luxury's sake."

Matthew was still looking aghast. All he had ever seen in the young man was a tongue-tied, narrow-minded Jew, and now out of this had blossomed a loquacious Roman lazybones. Matthew shook his head in disbelief.

"Now, then, my dear Gaius," said Pilate, turning his entire body to the left to see for himself, "what do you think about fever?"

"I am no physician, prefect... I've only read a thing or two and learned it..." He again quoted in Latin: "According to Celsus, fever is often the body's way of defending itself, however odd that may seem."

"Superb!" Pilate exclaimed. "My dear Matthew, I'm positively delighted by your delegate!"

"He's a clever lad," said Matthew.

Uri could sense the warning in his voice.

"So, let's eat," said Pilate, taking some of the salad greens and fruits.

There was a big murrhine dish and a tastefully fashioned silver spoon in front of everyone. Uri took for himself some of the fruit, and in doing so his eye was caught by the shiny, mirror-smooth tabletop surface on which the torches on the walls were mirrored. Never before had he seen veining as gorgeous as that; there were wonderful whorls in it, which in places coalesced in pink-colored peacock eyes. His eyes ranged over the whole surface; it had been made from a single slab of wood. It must have been worth a fortune.

"I've always had a partiality for Jews," said Pilate. "Among them are so many clever, truly wise men. When I was getting ready to come to Judaea, I started to learn about the foundations of the Jewish faith; I was astonished at how expedient and humane your commandments are. I don't share the widespread view in Rome that superstition is harmful; it can't be if it has helped keep an entire people in existence for two thousand years."

Uri had the feeling that Pilate was speaking sincerely, though of course it was perfectly possible to lie in a serious, sober voice. After all, politicians were the best of actors. But then, why say it if he did not mean it?

They feasted on salad greens and fruits; it was all fresh and appetizing. There was silence apart from the crunching made by their teeth. There was something else that was also there from which everyone took only a tiny portion. What could that have been? Marsh mallow leaves maybe?

Pilate pushed the dish away, whereupon Matthew followed suit, Uri too. Antipas took yet another small portion.

Servants jumped forward and changed the plates for new ones. Only now did Uri notice that the servants were all bearded; Jewish servants were serving up the food so that it would not become impure.

A great profusion of fish dishes came next. They had been braised whole: gigantic fishes of various species, all with scales and fins as specified by Jewish law. One servant, the scissorer, used a few deft movements of a flat spoon to fillet out the spine, while a second used a small knife to lop off the fish heads, and a third cut off the fins. The servants then vanished.

"Fish dishes are of moderate heaviness, Celsus asserts," said Pilate. "We should not take too much of it, is my recommendation, because a miraculous peppered veal escalopes and a fantastic marinated mutton roast still awaits, if I am not mistaken."

Uri saw before his eyes the text by Celsus: "The heaviest of them, which is salted, is for example the mackerel." He kept quiet; he hadn't the faintest idea what a mackerel looked like, and in any case the fish here were braised rather than salted.

He often went to the fish market in Rome; he loved the smell of fish, which revolted many, and he saw all kinds of marvelous sea creatures, arthropods, cephalopods, and shellfish, though he did not know the names of any of them and never asked since he could not eat them anyway.

He sensed that Matthew was moaning in satisfaction, and not at the sight of the fish, but because this time Uri had not spoken. He looked up; Matthew was gazing at the fish, it seemed he gave a nod.

We are in league, Matthew and I, Uri thought. The same Matthew that had me knocked on the head and carted off to prison. Interesting.

"I can particularly recommend those handsome little brutes," Pilate said, pointing with a spoon at one of the dishes. "Barbel, that is."

Uri shuddered.

"Someone once sent something of the kind to the emperor Tiberius," said Uri, "and he ordered that they would do better to put it up for auction; he made a wager, saying he would be amazed if Apicius or Publius Octavius, those famed gourmands, did not snap it up... As best I know, Octavius won out. He paid five thousand sesterces for it..."

"There's not much you don't know, my dear Gaius!" Pilate cried out contentedly. "That's very good! How did that information get to you?"

"It was a story that went around the markets in Rome."

"Poor Apicius," said Pilate. "He cut open his veins in the end..."

"Not for that reason, though," yapped Herod Antipas, "but because he spent hundreds of millions on banquets, and when he grasped that he had only ten million left, he resolved that he did not want to live in poverty!"

Everyone tittered, Uri too. While he laughed he saw himself from outside. What a comfy stooge I've become, he thought.

Everyone took some fish—Antipas a lot, Pilate lashings of them, Matthew very little, and Uri even less. He modestly avoided the mullet even though Pilate encouraged him to try it: a fish only cost three thousand.

"Yes, indeed!" said Pilate. "Our own modest repast is nothing compared with the banquets that are thrown over the water! Lucullus knew what to do! When Cicero and Pompey dropped in on him without prior notice one day, he had a dinner served out straightaway that cost two thousand sesterces! Then there's the wealthy advocate Quintus Hortensius, whose fishponds alone were worth three million sesterces! Then again, the dinners given by Maecenas! Fancy plying his guests with asses' flesh!" Pilate chuckled. "Apicius had the geese stuffed with figs and dished up, roast, like that... I'm going to try that out one of these days. The mullet was served with a fish-liver sauce, which sounds intriguing... Pasties of the tongues of flamingos, peacocks, and nightingales— that's the sort of thing Vitellius adores, he was telling me not long ago... Here we are, friends: garum sauce, all four kinds. Dip the fish in it! All the ingredients are kosher; they are all based on olive oil, ground pepper, wine, and honey, all clean... There's watery, olive, vinegary, and wine-flavored. I get them brought in from a factory in Sparturia, five hundred sesterces per congius... I gave explicit instructions that they were to be made with Jewish oil, which is ten times more expensive than the non-Jewish oil... But then, as I say, what are our meals compared with those of the true hedonists! Nowadays Agrippa too spends two hundred thousand on a single supper, so I hear... He even gets them to prepare cinnamon gravy, even though it's better as an unguent than a condiment."

Uri listened, feeling not a scrap of eagerness; he finished cleaning a portion of fish with his spoon, dunked it with his fingers in the sauce and dabbled it around a bit before placing it in his mouth.

"First-rate!" he declared enthusiastically.

"They're all sea fish," said Pilate, "since Jews consider the sea cleaner than the rivers, though those too are pure, have I got that right?"

"That's quite right, prefect," said Matthew.

"There are hardly any bones in these," said Pilate, "because bones, I have to tell you, they're one thing I hate. I hate all superfluous difficulties, and that includes with food. There are difficulties as it is. There are plenty of people in Rome who look askance at my nurturing such good relations with Jews. I always hit it off excellently with your people. Whatever tensions may have arisen, it was never a fault on my part, nor, I hasten to add, on the part of the Jews! All the tensions came from Rome. Thanks be to my gods, and to your one and only Everlasting Lord, up till now I have always managed to repair the damage, and I very much hope it will stay that way."

Pilate pushed his plate away from him, with Matthew immediately doing the same. Uri put another piece of fish in his mouth, though he did not dip it in garum first. Antipas helped himself to another large portion of the mullet and started to eat. There was a hush as everybody waited patiently until Antipas had finished. When he had swallowed the last mouthful, he too pushed his plate away.

Three quarters of the food served in the fish dishes had been left behind. Who was going to eat that? Was it going to be thrown out?

Servants jumped, and no sooner had the fish course disappeared than the three roast meats were there in front of them. Steaming away, they smelled dangerously tempting. New plates were set out.

I'm dining with a king and a prefect. This is not going to end well.

"It infuriates me," said Pilate before anyone could help themselves, "that people should want to come between me and your people. I'm a disciplined person, thanks be to my gods, and to your one and only Everlasting Lord, and so far I have not fallen for any provocation. I come from a lowly background; I learned to discipline myself, and to the present day I have not forgotten that. It will not be through any doing of mine that I lose this post. The emperor is free to relieve me of my office, but let him do so to appoint me to a higher post. In the case of the viaduct, for instance, it was in your general interest, but I stepped back. I also did not allow myself to be provoked when those few dozen dimwitted fanatics were whipped up by a blatant lie to rush to Caesarea and protest in front of my palace; not a hair on their heads was harmed. Passover this year was more tense than usual, and I had to fear that a further provocation was stewing. I had to put an end to that, so I had three Jewish common criminals crucified. Let people see that I can also be hard-nosed, and that even my patience has its limits. Caiaphas the high priest was also concerned that dubious elements wanted to use the feast as a cover for public unrest, and he handed them over to me. They died; anyone who wanted could watch, anyone else could hear. I am only sorry that I had to make an example of them, but it seems the Jews drew the right lesson."

Pilate now served himself a helping of meat.

"Every Jew knows that I am supporting the building of the city wall to the north out of my personal fortune, even though the emperor is more against it than for it. Now that's not something I would do if I wanted a confrontational policy, is it? Why build you a wall if I only want to batter it down? I only sought to do good with the aqueduct, the stadium, and everything else I proposed! Any time Jews protested, I withdrew; peace is more important. But I can't step back all the time! I have no intention of making it a regular practice to interfere in matters under the authority of the Jewish courts; I have neither right nor time to do so. This, though, was an exceptional situation. Let no one in Rome or Judaea make the mistake of supposing that I, whom they have only ever known as soft-hearted and agreeable, cannot put my foot down when necessary."

Herod Antipas grabbed a portion from one of the roasts and put it on his plate. Matthew and Uri did likewise.

"My friend King Herod Antipas agrees," said Pilate.

"Absolutely," muttered Antipas as he ate.

"His presence here right now," Pilate continued, "is highly esteemed and means a lot to me. We share this splendid palace now, and news of that will reach the ears of the powers that be soon enough, if it has not done so already. Our letters are not always answered, but they will understand our present coexistence. The Roman political rabble-rousers who would love to bring my name into disrepute and turn the emperor against me are on the wrong track. Peace and quiet reign in Judaea, and ever shall do so. The close alliance between the king of Judaea and the governor of Galilee is the guarantee."

"There's also endless plotting against me," grumbled Antipas, staring gloomily straight ahead. "Ignorant people are continually needling me; I'm even driven to make war on my own ex-father-in-law! That is something I have no appetite for. My neighbors are being incited from Rome against me, Rome's loyal ally; that's going on all the time. The neighboring provinces would be peaceful forever were it not for the internal politicking in Rome that sets them against each other."

"I can assure you, prefect—" Matthew began, but Pilate cut in, turning to Uri.

"Did you bring a message from Agrippa? If so, what? And to whom?"

Uri had been waiting for the question.

Matthew's breathing on the other side of the table audibly quickened.

"Yes," said Uri nonchalantly. "His message to the high priest was that he would leave him in office if he could be king."

A silence fell.

Matthew's breathing broke off.

Antipas snorted.

Pilate grunted then fell silent.

The silence persisted.

Uri reached for a plate, took a nice veal escalope and set it on his plate. Only then did he look up.

Matthew was looking at Pilate with a horrified expression on his face, Antipas was grinding his teeth. Uri squinted to the right. Pilate smiled a rueful smile then laughed it off.

"Well, what do you expect? Stands to reason! Let's eat."

When the dinner had ended, Pilate patted Uri on the shoulder.

"I hope that went down well, dear Gaius."

"I've never eaten so many delicacies in my life!"

"That's what I like to hear."

Matthew and Uri were led down to the front of the palace. They were standing in Temple Square, but it was dark, almost nothing could be seen; the moon was barely shining.

"Stay there!" said a soldier.

Matthew waited until the soldier had moved away before asking:

"Did you really bring a message?"

Uri burst out laughing.

"Whatever I say, you won't believe it."

Matthew slowly nodded. There was silence.

"You won't believe me either," he said gravely, "but I saved your life. I had you jailed, that's true, but I told the prefect that you were probably carrying a message from Agrippa. The reason you were not executed is I said you knew something they needed to know. People who know nothing are crucified. I said you knew something important; I saved your life, do you hear?"

Uri shivered.

He was lying. I'm a Roman citizen; that's why I was released.

Yet what if that wasn't the reason after all?

A litter with four bearers appeared; it was tiny and ramshackle. They beckoned to Matthew and he got in. The litter was picked up and they set off.

A squadron was left with Uri in front of Herod's palace.

"Let's go!" an officer ordered.

Uri made his way alongside the colonnade, in the middle of a procession of soldiers dangling lowered weapons. He was able to take a peek at the hall behind in the light of the torches; under some vaults were a table and chairs, others were empty. He heard a drumming from above and looked up; soldiers were patrolling on the roof of the colonnade. He saw to the right the big palace that had attracted his attention on arrival: that must be the Hasmoneans' palace. It was less ornamented than Herod's palace. He spotted behind it a tall, dark, flat-roofed building that was separated from the palace by a wall at least eight cubits high. What could that be, he wondered.

They reached the end of the colonnade and left the square by a gate. A massive citadel with four towers stood before them, and they marched along one of its walls. The Antonia Fortress! Which meant that the flat-roofed building had to be the Temple!

THEY MARCHED THROUGH A GATE. THREE SOLDIERS ACCOMPANIED URI some five floors up a staircase, quite probably in one of the four towers. There he had to go through a door, which was then locked on him.

A terracotta lamp was burning in the room, one exactly like the lamps in use in Rome. There was a couch with a blanket, a copper bowl, a pitcher containing water, another containing wine, a tumbler, and a fruit dish with dried figs, dried dates, and raisins. The room had a window, but high up and not so much a window as an embrasure that had been left between stones at regular intervals to let air into the room or to fire arrows out from. It was a windy night, as could be felt even in the room. This too was a prison, only higher class.

I'm in the Antonia, he said to himself in some amazement.

The fort had been built by Herod the Great and was named after Herod's patron, Mark Antony. It could have been renamed, given that Mark Antony had been defeated by Octavian, who then became the emperor Augustus, but since Herod also managed to find favor with the latter, he did not do that. It was said that Augustus respected fidelity—or maybe the matter was of no interest to him.

Uri poured some water into the bowl, washed his hands and face, and as on each occasion since he had been placed under arrest, he prayed without being able to put on a phylactery. He also did not know which way was east, so he picked one of the corners at random and, bowing in that direction, recited the Sh'ma.

He begged his Lord that it would not come out that he had lied.

Now, after the fact, he broke out in a cold sweat.

The matter was not at an end.

In the morning he would be brought in front of the high priest and would have to repeat what he had said. He would have to lie again once he had started, because if he were to tell the truth, which was that no message had been entrusted to him, then he would be asked why he had lied to Pilate. That too was a sin—maybe an even bigger one. It was not impossible that Agrippa would drop by this way, he would be led in front of him, and Agrippa would be flabbergasted: he had never seen this person in his life! Fair enough, thought Uri, but then I could say that the message had been passed on by my father, and he in turn had been told by someone else whom he thought was one of Agrippa's people... No, that's no good. I mustn't get my father mixed up in this; he has enough worries as it is.

For a few seconds he thought he was losing his mind: if so many people believed it, maybe he had been entrusted with a message after all, only he had forgotten. Why else would he have found his way into the delegation? He had hardly understood that before, and now he understood it even less. He racked his brain but he had no recollection of anybody entrusting him with anything at all, and his father had most certainly said nothing.

Was such a thing as torture practiced in Jerusalem? Why wouldn't it be? He would not be able to withstand it, but they would not believe whatever he yelled out in pain, and would go on torturing him.

It was not a good sign that they were going to keep holding him in prison.

But then it was a good sign that this was a comfortable prison.

Maybe they supposed he was one of Agrippa's important people, and they did not know what to do with him until he had been asked. But if asked about him, Agrippa would just dismiss the business, saying he had no knowledge of such a person, which would mean at best losing his head: one chop was all it took. An exchange of letters between Rome and Caesarea would take two weeks... Did that mean he had just two weeks left of his life?

He ran over the dinner again in his memory and came to the conclusion that he had not made any missteps. Pilate had struck him as being honest; Matthew had been amazed, of course; and all three of them had believed that Agrippa had sent that message to the high priest. Why wouldn't they have believed it if Agrippa really were the sort of person Matthew and Plotius had painted? It could be that Agrippa really had sent a message through one of them; who knows, it could well be literally the one that in his misery he had made up.

He pondered what might have prompted him to say that. He did not rehearse an answer, only that he would be asked that. He had improvised and been believed, so if they had believed him, he might be capable of improvising a truth.

But why did I improvise precisely that?

There was no fathoming the workings of the human brain. He found that he was able to justify the answer that he had given retroactively: Rome would always leave local leaders in power as long as they pledged their allegiance, because it took the view that if they acquired authority, then they must be suitable people with the right local connections. Rome would only parley with rebels if it wished to overturn the local powers.

Uri's belly grumbled. He had eaten very little, not wishing to overtax his stomach after fasting. He felt tempted to take some fruit from the bowl, but it crossed his mind that it may have been poisoned. But then again, why poison him if they presumed that he knew something? Only people who know nothing are killed... Cruel, but appropriate. What if they thought that he knew more? What if they wanted to knock it out of him?

He decided to stick with the lie for the time being. If he were to be confronted by Agrippa, he would say that it was the only way he could think of to hang on to his life. Perhaps he would be forgiven.

Life is cheap here. In Rome too, of course. Suddenly, it came to Uri's mind: Surely it was not those two amiable scoundrels and that third prisoner, the scandalizer, whom Pilate had crucified. It can't have been. Those were surely not capital offenses with which they were charged; scandal was most certainly not. And anyway their court hearings could not have been held yet. It must have been others who were executed; they had been taken to another prison.

He really could not imagine that his chance fellow prisoners—whom he had very little chance to get to know properly—might no longer be among the ranks of the living.

It was only around daybreak that he eventually dozed off to sleep; the blanket was warm and soft, and he bundled up snugly in it.

He awoke some time before noon. He washed his hands and feet, prayed, took some of the fruit, and drank some wine with a little water. The whole thing seemed like an improbable dream. How had he ended up here, in this room of all rooms, in Jerusalem of all places?

The guards came. They led him out to a corridor and down some stairs. He was led into a room, and the escort stepped back to the wall and closed the door. Uri blinked. The light was beating in through a wide, tall window. There were three men seated in the room on one side of a table opposite him, their backs to the light. Uri bowed and moved closer to them. On his way, he recognized the strategos. He was seated between two elderly men who were not wearing priest's garb. Uri felt relieved: the high priest was not one of them because he was not permitted to show himself in non-priestly apparel. It then crossed his mind that the high priest would hardly be entering the Antonia anyway.

"Gaius Theodorus!" the strategos spoke in Aramaic, turning toward the elderly men in turn. "Native of Rome, nineteen years of age: you came with the Roman delegation. You were carrying a message from Agrippa to the high priest." He looked at Uri. "You said last night to the prefect that Agrippa's message was that he would leave Caiaphas in office if he could be king. Is that right?"

Uri sighed.

"Yes," he said.

There was a slight pause.

"If the high priest is called Caiaphas," he added uncertainly.

There was another pause.

The strategos nodded.

"Is that why you became a member of the delegation?" the man sitting to the right of the strategos asked. There was nothing pointed or accusatory in the question.

"It is," Uri said.

"How come you speak Aramaic?" asked the other elderly man.

"That's my mother's native tongue. That's what we speak at home."

"Are you a Roman citizen?" the man asked.

"Yes, I am."

Silence fell. The two elderly men shook their heads.

"If you're a Roman citizen," declared the strategos, "then we are unable to hear your case. In the national interest, we shall nevertheless have to check if you have been telling the truth. If not, and it proves that you truly are a Roman citizen, we shall hand you over to Rome to make its ruling."

One of the elderly men quietly asked something, and the strategos faltered.

"When did you arrive in Jerusalem?" he asked Uri.

"Before Passover... Wednesday perhaps."

The strategos nodded and turned toward the elderly man.

"A week has gone by; he can be regarded as pure."

The elderly man also nodded.

"You will be led out now," said the strategos. "Wait your turn."

Uri had been about to say that he would confess to everything as long as they did not torture him, but by then they were already pushing him outside. They stopped in the corridor. The two guards stood next to him but did not take him by the arms. They waited. So did Uri.

From Uri's right, a thin man was dragged along, held by the arms by two guards. They stopped at the door, opened it, led him in, then shut the door.

Uri closed his eyes and went over the hearing again, only opening his eyes when it had ended. At that point the man was brought out. Those two guards likewise stopped, with the man between them looking at his feet and panting.

Yet another man was brought in from the right by two guards. The procedure was the same. Uri closed his eyes and once more went over the hearing, and when that was done this man was also brought out.

If that's a court hearing, thought Uri, they get through their cases fast.

There were eight other prisoners besides Uri and sixteen guards by the time the strategos came out of the room, the two elderly men behind him. The strategos went to the left down the corridor, with the guards and the accused setting off after him.

They reached the end of the palace; the light hit Uri's eyes. Below him was a drop of several stories deep. He grew dizzy. He threw a glance backward. On the third floor of the citadel they had stepped out onto the top of the double colonnade, which surrounded the Temple. The columns of white marble were covered with cedar planks. He looked up at the fortress. He could see a tower at each of the four corners, the eastern and southern ones being taller than the other two.

He turned to the front, southward. On his right there was a parapet on the top of the colonnade, guarding the outer edge, but not one for the inner edge, and the parapet was not high anyway, reaching the hips, so one might easily fall off. He had a sudden empty feeling in his stomach, and even though the top of the colonnade was not particularly narrow, fifteen or twenty cubits perhaps, he still felt dizzy. They would have to go the length of the stone-flagged ledge. He peered to the front, narrowing his eyes; the colonnade led past the mass of the Temple and met at the end, at right angles, with an enormous, very long colonnade that was two stories high; the upper level, which must have been the royal stoa, was narrower than the lowers. Around the middle of the colonnade, down on the right, a bridge: that must be the viaduct there had been so much dispute about, which connected the Upper City with Temple Square.

They moved slowly; Uri looked to his left and gazed at the huge, scaffolded edifice of the Temple. It was an odd, T-shaped structure, the farther block to the east being taller than the western limb pointed toward them, which had lower wings on both sides. Smoke was rising above the Temple; meat was being burned, sacrifices being made even at this time. The altar stone could not be seen from the wall; it was concealed by the giant building. The parts of the T-shaped building that were not scaffolded dimly gleamed white and yellow. As they got closer Uri could see that the enormous stone blocks were faced in some places with marble plates, in others with gold sheets. Presumably similar trim was going to be applied to the whole, and that was the reason for the scaffolding. He noticed the same sort of parapet on the flat roof of the T-shaped building as on the top of their own colonnade: it was of crenellated stone, perhaps so that soldiers would be able to shoot arrows downward if need be.

The Temple was a fortress, and that was why it was so massive and tall—maybe as much as one hundred cubits from its foundations. Buildings as imposing as this were not erected in Rome; the buildings on Capitoline Hill were much lower.

An empty space lay to the north of the Temple, toward the Antonia, with no more than a few people wandering in it. What might that be?

He nudged in the side the prisoner next to him, and indicated the square with his head.

"It belongs to the Gentiles," said the sullen man.

In other words, that was the part that non-Jews could enter if they wished to observe the central edifice of the Jewish faith; they were not allowed elsewhere.

Uri was walking in the middle of the row, as far as he could get from the two edges of the ledge. When he looked to the right, there, beyond the viaduct, at the end of a long fortified wall stood Herod's palace, where he had eaten dinner yesterday evening. He could see the two wings of the building, and was surprised at how tall the three towers at the northern end were, the most westerly of them being the tallest. All three towers seemed to have house-like structures on their tops, with windows and roof gardens. He was screwing up his eyes because he was unable to make them out well, with the white marble towers glistening fiercely in the strong sunlight. Someone else should be here, someone who can see, he thought. He looked back to the left, then again to the right. He was able to see that the Temple was higher than even the tallest of the towers. It may well be a regulation, he thought.

From the top of the colonnade he could also vaguely discern that the Temple esplanade was itself divided into a number of sections, and between these ran bulky brick and stone walls, higher than a man and of varied design. Uri cupped both hands in front of his eyes; the guard let him. On the eastern half of the large, paved square that was not built on and situated toward the Antonia, north of the Temple, skinned animal carcasses hung on hooks from huge columns. That was therefore the slaughterhouse, and it was from there that the hunks of the sacrificial offerings were taken to put on the top of the altar. Uri peered; he could see nothing to the east beyond the far colonnade, only peacefully leafing hillocks with trees and gardens. That was presumably the Valley of Hinnom, running between the hills and Temple Mount; it was from there that sacrificial animals were taken to the slaughterer's bench. Somewhere down there would have to be the hand-over place where the Levite slaughterers inspected the sacrificial animals and any that did not prove to be intact would be rejected. That must be unpleasant, Uri considered: what was the procedure to be followed in such a case? It had to be redeemed with money, for an extra fifth over its value? Or bring a replacement animal later if one did not have that much money? How did it go?

To the right, a glorious colonnade ran from Herod's palace toward the next construction, the Hasmoneans' palace. It was a dark, plain building; he could not see it very well because of the sun shining in his eyes, but that palace was not encased with white marble, that was for sure.

They clambered up onto a two-cubit high platform, proceeding over the top of the gate above the viaduct. Uri dared not look down; one of the prisoners quietly said, "The Sanhedrin!" Uri took a grip on himself and looked down; he could see a quadrangular building pasted onto the base of the viaduct. Could that really be where the Great Sanhedrin held its sessions? The Hall of Hewn Stones? This building, the Xystus? He did not dare ask. His previous fellow prisoners had said that the Sanhedrin was no longer holding its sessions there.

Blinking, he searched for where the palace of the high priest, where he had been imprisoned, might be, but he could not see through the rooftops, and in any case he would not have recognized it. The Upper City was heavily built up; only the highest buildings stood out. Uri could not see a single straight road; the alleyways meandered capriciously, with huts standing next to huge houses. Here it was as if Far Side and true Rome had been jumbled up together. It was strange to see into gardens from the top of the wall; in some he saw glinting mirrors, water basins. The wealthy had their own mikvehs.

The top of the long, wide colonnade that rested on the high ramparts of the Upper City was likewise flat, with an exit from the first floor of Herod's palace opening directly onto it. There seemed to be people strolling about on top of the colonnade right now, just like the evening before: yes, mercenaries, each with a spear in his right hand. No doubt the famous "right-handers." Perhaps they were keeping an eye on the Upper City market square to intervene if they spotted any cheating at the stalls of the traders. Yet it was not here that his fellow prisoner had overturned tables but in the Temple Square, in the women's court, to the left.

Uri stopped to look back. It was possible to walk on the top of the city wall from Herod's palace to the top of the colonnades ringing the Temple Mount and the Antonia Fortress, which also had an exit opening onto it—the one that had spat them out. Several divisions of soldiers would fit onto the top of the colonnade, which spanned three sides of the Temple Mount, and that was not counting the broad roof of the royal stoa's lower level. It was quite certain that one could also walk there along the wall; Herod the Great would not have been driven solely by a desire for extravagance when he had the colonnades put up.

"They're watching us," Uri heard from the row.

A few of the prisoners looked right, toward Herod's palace. Uri could see figures moving around the small structures in front of the palace. Stalls? Was that the Upper City market? Yesterday evening he had seen nothing. Could it be that it was a movable market and everyone covered his handcart and stall for the night?

Uri's fellow accused lowered their heads, some even screening their face with a hand or arm; they had spotted that some were peeking up from down below, about a stadion away, at the procession as it marched along the top of the wall. Sharp eyes they had.

They dropped back to the level of the colonnade's top and walked toward the next entrance to Temple Mount, at the corner of its southern wall. Far below them was a long, broad flight of steps, broken at intervals by rest areas, with little dwellings in the valley glued to the right of its wall.

They now reached a flight of steps going down on the left of the colonnade to Temple Square. It was narrow and steep, but it had a stone handrail; only one person at a time could use it. Uri grasped the stone and clambered down, held between two guards, until he finally felt himself on the ground. He breathed a heavy sigh of relief. He could see opposite him, held up by high columns, the inner, western side of the monumental royal stoa, but he was given no time to gaze, because the guards pushed him toward the Temple.

They tramped across a large, empty, rectangular square, with the shadow thrown by the royal stoa reaching as far as the middle. Under their feet was rough paving, not marble like in front of Herod's palace; they then went up fourteen steps and proceeded between low, chest-high stone balusters. Sunk into the middle of the square were two broad stairs that led downward, the way being decorated with stone tracery; obviously it was possible to get out from under the royal stoa by way of an underground passage into the open air to the south. That way lay the Acra, and past it the Lower City, where the poor people lived.

Another five steps took them to the inner wall surrounding the Temple. The entrance facing them seemed surprisingly narrow; two by two they were just able to pass.

They found themselves in another rectangular square, with colonnades built onto the wall on the right with moving figures. The structure, flanked on two sides, looked like a tiny fortification, with guards standing sentry before its closed bronze gate; the gate was low and single-leafed. What could that be?

People, some of them women, were standing, bowing their heads in prayer, kneeling, walking about. All were nicely dressed, their faces serious and uplifted. They looked sternly at the prisoners. There were some conspicuous raggedly dressed beggars rummaging around, some with both legs missing. One of the latter sped his mutilated trunk over toward them in a bounding sprint, his highly muscular arms supported on enormous palms, until one of the guards growled at him, whereupon he departed just as hastily. Here it was adults who did the begging, not children as in Rome. Vendors vegetated by their handcarts. In one, living turtledoves, tethered to a cord by the legs, cowered motionless, unable to control only the trembling of their heads.

"The women's chamber," Uri heard from the line.

In other words, women could only come in this far if they were Jewish—and they were not sick or menstruating.

The text of a description of the women's chamber was summoned up before Uri's mind's eye. The treasury ought to be somewhere around here, but where? Surely it was not that tiny building with the narrow entrance. All that untold wealth of money, jewels, and golden and silver dishes about which legends had been told would not fit in there. Could this be where Simon the Magus had brought his money? Or was that structure just the entrance that led down to the treasure chamber, which was actually hidden in the depths of the Temple Mount? It was said that natural caves and man-made tunnels lay under the Temple Mount and led outside to beyond the city wall.

A few steps in a semicircular arc led to the next, hefty gate. The wall must have been some forty cubits high, with a steep, narrow staircase leading up from the left-hand side to the top, and there Uri saw several women lingering. What could they be looking at, he wondered. As he saw wisps of smoke rising over the other side of the wall, he knew at once that the altar was in the Chamber of the Israelites; women were not permitted to enter there at all, but it seemed they were not forbidden from watching the cremation of offerings from the top of the wall.

They went up the semicircle of steps, fifteen in all. Uri looked up. He was standing in front of a vastly high and wide, two-winged bronze gate, decorated with studs of solid silver and gold. Each of the bronze handles set into each wing of the gate, with the united efforts of four guards being needed to pull them open.

And the sound! This was the famous Temple gate whose creaking could be heard as far away as Jericho!

He saw the altar.

A rectangular structure fifteen to twenty cubits high, and at its base some fifty cubits high but narrowing higher up, with a ramp on the left leading to its top. That was made from gigantic ashlar blocks, with the angles of the gates being twisted into the shape of ram's horns. At the top a man was continually bending over, incinerating the meat: the duty priest. People stood around, praying.

The other accused burst out in tears.

Uri shuddered.

He was able to see it after all. A Jew who was able to get to the inner space of the Temple was privileged; unhappy millions died without ever getting the chance to see it.

They were escorted off to the left, to the southern side of the altar, where they had to stand. There was a silence, then the slow creaking again: the bronze gate was being closed. Uri gazed at the altar, just ten steps away from him. It was made of gigantic, undressed slabs of rock. No other materials were used; they must have spent ages selecting and fitting the stones.

The sun was shining from behind, but as luck would have it, they were standing in the shade at the foot of the wall in front of the arcade.

The strategos sauntered off to the left before coming to a standstill between the entrance to the Temple and the altar, where an enormous metal basin was resting on the ground. That must be the golden laver in which the priests made their ritual washing. Uri screwed his eyes: the gold was dark and did not glitter, as it was in the shade.

Uri looked up at the Temple. From there, at its foot, all that could be seen was how massive it was.

Several steps led up to the gate, which was hidden by scaffolding. The two elderly men who had conducted his hearing were standing by the southeast corner, face to face with the strategos, who was looking east. Up above, on the altar of holocausts, the white-garbed priest was incinerating meat, possibly the legs of cattle. Thin wisps of smoke rose, not the dense clouds of the sacrifice for the feast, which could be seen from as far off as the fields, but ordinary, everyday fumes. Down below, three Levites were hard at work preparing the next hunks of meat to be burned, sprinkling them with oil. The slaughterer's benches, which Uri had noticed as soon as they stepped out of the Antonia, were separated by a wall from the innermost courtyard, though this was not as high as the one screening the Court of the Israelites from the outside world. Uri saw the marble columns on which the carcasses were hanging; they were slung up by the legs, and he could see down them as far as the middle of the thighs, the lower legs being obscured by the wall. These were offerings to sacrifice to the Lord; he would not go hungry today, that was for sure.

The elderly men produced a stylus and wax tablet from under their mantles.

Uri was standing in the middle of the row of accused. It almost made him laugh out loud: he was standing in the very center of Judaism as a prisoner. Some crazy dream this was.

The strategos beckoned. Someone on the left end of the row was pushed forward, and he cried out. The accused made his way to the right of the elderly men and stopped. One of them gave a sign, and the prisoner stepped with trembling legs over a knee-high marble barrier, which, as Uri only now noticed, completely encircled the altar and the Temple and within which no one else was standing except the three Levites who were assisting the priest from the ground; even the strategos and the two elderly judges were standing outside it.

The men watching the ceremony exclaimed in consternation, while there were gasps from the women staring from the top of the wall on the right.

The prisoner moved groggily, proceeding by the southeastern corner of the altar, then turned northward and disappeared behind the altar, only to reappear a short time later from behind it, his head hung low, on the northwestern side, going past the strategos, though himself still inside the barrier, turning again at that corner and coming again before the other prisoners, made another circuit of the altar, by now sobbing and, though scarcely able to move, carrying on. The two elderly men looked on fiercely. When he came in front of the strategos at the end of the third circuit, the latter raised a hand. The accused halted, stepped back over the barrier and staggered toward the two guards, who seized him and set him back in the row.

The two elderly men wrote something onto their wax tablets.

The next accused man made a theatrical job of doing the same thing. Uri peered, not understanding anything. He could not see the faces very well, but he could hear the sobbing and could also see that they staggered as they made the circuit. Are we rehearsing penitence here?

In this case the strategos raised his hand after the fifth circuit, and his guards took the accused back to the row.

Uri counted: an aging man made the most laps around the altar—seven in all. He then stopped, the strategos stepped up to him, looked at him in the eyes for a lengthy time, and then gave a signal; only then did the guards lead him back to the row.

The two elderly men again scored a few lines onto their wax tablets.

When Uri's turn came, he stepped forward of his own accord, not waiting to be pushed. He stepped over the barrier, he heard the groans and gasps, he went around the altar happy at having the chance to inspect it up close. On the northern side small green items of something or other were visible between the stones—moss perhaps. He was also able now to look at the Temple's gate: there were no leaves! And the frame of the door was a dark metal like bronze, though it was really supposed to be gold. The decoration on it was not as sumptuous as that on the bronze gate to the Court of the Israelites. Inside was a gloomy space in which a further gate could be made out, with curtains hanging down in the gateway, embroidered floor-length curtains of blue, white, scarlet, and purple: scarlet being since time immemorial a symbol of fire; white, of earth; blue, of the air; and purple, of the sea. The eagle knocked down in the last days of Herod the Great was not over the gate; bold Jews had somehow climbed up onto the roof of the Temple and slid down from there on a rope—that was how they knocked down the eagle, and they had paid for it with their lives. Uri looked up: he could not imagine dangling on a rope there. The chamber behind the inner gate was dark, with no window or opening anywhere. In that chamber there must be a table with a costly menorah, a seven-armed candlestick of gold, and incense burners, though he could not see them while he was passing by. That outer sanctum in turn opened into an inner sanctum, the Holy of Holies, in which there was nothing; the Ark of the Covenant had vanished at the time of the destruction of the First Temple, when Nebuchadnezzar sacked the whole of Jerusalem; and when the Jews rebuilt the Temple several decades later, the Ark was no longer there, and the emptiness in the Holy of Holies was a reminder of this. Uri ought to have been able to see the door to the inner sanctuary, but the curtains prevented him. In there was a gate of gold, as everyone knew, decorated with man-size gold bunches of grapes. He would have liked to stop and inspect the inside of the Temple, to step a little closer, for, after all, he was inside that magic barrier, but he had a feeling that this was not the right occasion. He passed by the gold laver, in which water was glistening. He looked up and saw that he was standing to the right of the strategos, who was watching him. Uri passed in front of him with his head held high, turned left, and reached the note-taking elderly men; he did not look at them but started on a new circuit.

He made seven circuits, and in doing so had a good peek at the Temple's scaffolding, the altar of holocausts and the priest who was officiating up there, the Levites, the inner curtains—in short, everything that his peering eyes were able to make out as he went by. Uri was about to start an eighth circuit when he noticed from the protests of the two elderly men that something had happened. He looked back and saw that the strategos's hand was raised. Uri stopped. The strategos stepped closer to the barrier and gazed at his face. Uri returned the stare. How young he is! He can only be five or six years older than me, and look what a high position he holds already. There was something strange about his face, his eyes perhaps. Yes, that was it! He had not noticed it before, but the strategos had gray eyes.

The two elderly men also stepped nearer and stopped. One made a motion with his head that Uri interpreted as meaning that he should step out, so he stepped back over the marble barrier, stopped, and looked at them. They had kindly faces with alert eyes; one had brown eyes, the other was swarthy, almost black, and their gray beards were tidy. The thinner of the two had an exceedingly lined face, with a long scar on his right cheek that went down to his neck. The other had a double chin but a distinguished bearing. They gazed at Uri's face as if they were looking at a miracle; involuntarily, Uri smiled at them, at which the elderly men's eyes flickered.

The strategos barked something out. The guards stepped up to Uri and to his great amazement did not set him back in the row but escorted him away toward the bronze gate in the eastern wall.

From there Uri could see little of what was happening to the other accused. They too circled the altar a few times, but none of them as many as seven times. Uri was standing opposite the altar and the east side of the Temple that loomed high behind it. With his eyes narrowed, and through the slits between his fingers, he made another attempt to estimate their size. He then looked at the men, who were standing excitedly and fixedly watching the accused as they circled the altar. Nobody looked at him, perhaps because he was standing close to them and they did not wish to stare intrusively.

When all the accused had gone around the altar, the strategos and the two elderly men sauntered over to the bronze gate, where the guards led the accused. They seemed to be somewhat relieved, no longer weeping and shrieking aloud, only sniveling. What Uri read from their faces was resignation and exhaustion.

As he went past, the strategos took another look at his face. Uri nodded, and the strategos snatched his gaze away in confusion, moving on further.

They retraced the same route that they had come by back to the Antonia. Uri now felt more secure in walking on top of the colonnades; he was right at the back of the line, with two guards behind him.

They halted in the corridor, with the others going on before finally disappearing at the turn at the end.

The strategos, with the two elderly men behind, approached Uri. They looked at him with amazement.

"We ask you to excuse us," said the strategos, "but we had to follow the correct procedure. Until a decision is reached on your case, you will be extended our hospitality, and not in any way as a prisoner. I can promise that the decision will be made soon; after that you may move around as you choose in Judaea."

Uri was relieved. He did not understand why the strategos had asked his forgiveness, but as far as he was concerned, that was not the important thing.

"When is my delegation going back to Rome?" he asked.

The strategos, who was already about to move on, looked back.

"They set off this morning," he said. "You could not go with them in view of the investigation."

"So when can I go after them? Maybe I shall be able to catch up with them while they wait for a boat in Caesarea..."

The strategos hesitated before coming out with it:

"You will not be able to go after them for the time being. It's a dangerous trip for someone on his own, and we have no spare people to accompany you. I've already promised you that a decision will soon be reached."

"You will come to no harm," the double-chinned elderly man spoke. "A few weeks more and you will be able to travel back to Rome. Meanwhile, life here is also interesting."

They withdrew. Uri looked at the guards.

"What was that all about?" he asked.

The guards did not answer.

THIS TIME HE WAS TAKEN TO A CHARMING SMALL ROOM, WHICH HAD a Roman-style couch, with an expensive Oriental carpet as a cover, and a nice little table. The conspicuously narrow window started at chest height and, to judge from the way the light was falling, looked to the east, not toward Temple Square. Uri looked through the window, leaned out, and narrowed his eyes.

He had expected to have a view of Jerusalem and Temple Square, but all he could see was the inner court of the Antonia Fortress. He was looking from the first floor, and even the parts of the building situated between the high towers were some five stories high. The inner court was entirely paved; for all Uri's squinting there was nobody and nothing to see down there. The windows were small, as if built like that for the purpose of firing arrows.

He did not have long to wait; guards came and took him out to the corridor. They went down to the ground floor, where he was shown into a room.

A young Jew clothed in a cloak was seated at a table, looking as if he either were a hunchback or simply had a negligent way of holding himself.

"My greetings, Gaius Theodorus!" he said in Greek. "Take a seat."

Uri sat down on a stool opposite the table. How young he is, thought Uri, only three or four years older than me, if I'm not mistaken.

"I am pleased to be able to inform you," the man went on in a neutral official tone, "that the high priests appreciate and are disposed to accept your request that, like your nostalgic fellow men of the Diaspora, you would like to become more thoroughly acquainted with Judaea, the land of your ancestors, and you wish to stay here for a while. They have designated as your place of residence a village, Beth Zechariah by name, which has an exceptionally pleasant climate, snuggled in attractive hilly country. You will set off today with two escorts."

"I never asked for that favor," said Uri. "I want to go home to Rome!"

"That is perilous on your own," the young man replied calmly. "The delegation has already set off; we would not like you to risk your safety on your own."

"In other words, I'm being exiled!" Uri exclaimed.

"There is no such punishment in Jewish law," the man declared. "We have no such thing as the *aquae et ignis interdictio*, or banishment, and anyway no one has passed sentence on you. How could we? You're a Roman citizen, and only a Roman court can bring charges against you."

"Yet that is precisely what you've done just now!"

"I'm not passing sentence, simply chatting with you. And rest assured, I'm a Roman citizen myself."

"What about my interrogation?"

"That was not a court hearing but a logging of information. The main thing is that on the lie detector test you proved innocent."

Uri was aghast.

"You stood your ground on what you had asserted!" said the young man, not without a certain amount of respect. "No red spots broke out on your face. That's rarely the case; they usually appear even on those who are innocent."

Uri's heart beat massively; he took a deep breath and rapidly exhaled.

If he had known that beforehand, he was quite sure that red spots would have covered his whole body as he circled the altar. He already felt his face was burning.

There was a silence. Uri gathered himself.

"I would like to speak with Pilate!"

"That, unfortunately, will not be possible. The prefect set off back to Caesarea this morning."

"But that's where I want to go!"

"We have no one to escort you there."

"Is someone going to escort me to that village?"

"To there—yes, certainly."

Uri pondered.

"May I write a letter to my father?" he inquired.

"You may," said the young man, "but there's no point: in Rome the delegates will relate to him what has happened. What happened is that you were captivated by the spell of the Holy Land and you decided to spend a few months among us. Elderly men in the Diaspora willingly resettle here to make this their grave, but there are also a fair number of young people—more than we know where to put them. There is nothing special about your request, or at most only that your case was brought to the front of the queue for a decision, and a favorable one at that. I'm not a native of Jerusalem either, and I had to petition to be allowed to live near the Temple; I had to wait years for the permit. Consider yourself lucky, Gaius Theodorus."

The young man's words were meant to be taken sarcastically, but the tone of his voice was not. Uri looked at him and stared, and it was then he noticed: he was sitting there in front of him but he could not register the man's features, as if he were faceless—perhaps because he was seeking to fuse with his office. His look is screened off, he's not looking at me, the person, but looking at a task. Uri strained to see. He was a black-haired, cross-eyed man with an olive complexion.

"My father needs me back home," said Uri in desperation. "He's a merchant, and I'm his only son."

"You can also establish commercial links here that will be advantageous for your family," said the official, and got to his feet. He must have had short legs, because he hardly became any taller. "It's a plus that you speak Aramaic. The strategos wishes you an edifying stay in Judaea, Gaius Theodorus."

THEY TREKKED NORTHWARD ON THE ROAD TO DAMASCUS, WITH URI IN the middle and on either side a young, well-built civilian swathed in a cloak.

One had a spear, the other a sword in his hand, and on their feet were the sort of sandals worn by the Jewish police, but they were rather shabby, and the cloaks were far from new. Uri still had tied to his ankles the well-made spruce sandals that he had been given before the dinner with Pilate. He stopped, as did the guards. He kneeled down and undid the knots, slipped the sandals off, then slung them, tied together, around his neck before straightening up. The guards cast lackluster glances at the sandals but said nothing. They moved on.

They held steadily northward. Uri looked back toward Jerusalem, but it was now covered by the bright green contours of mountains and hills. I didn't see much of it, he thought to himself, but that little was not without its excitements. The guards said that they were passing through Bezetha, the New City, though Uri did not see much of that either, except that shacks and shiny new dwellings of the wealthy were mixed together, showing that Plotius had been right. Uri saw not one straight street.

The walking did him good. In prison his muscles had gotten out of trim, and the thickened soles that had been built up on his feet by sustained exercise had begun to thin. Once he got back to Rome he would walk a few hours every day, and he would never get into the habit of sitting around on tavern terraces.

They trekked steadily north on the road to Damascus, which was not a paved Roman road but a dusty dirt road that had been tamped down by carts, oxen, asses, camels, and people. Uri visualized the map of Palestine that he had seen on the scrolls of Strabo. To their east now lay the River Jordan, and they were making their way toward Samaria. He even asked if they were going to escort him into Samaria, but they were astonished by his denseness.

"We can't go there! They would kill us," one of them said, the spearsman on his right. He had rugged features and a protruding nose.

The centuries-old strife between these two people still held. The Samaritans were also Jews and took the local Israelite women as their wives and converted them. But for centuries now there had been no love lost with other Jews, and they did not pay tithes to the Temple in Jerusalem; indeed, they had built their own separate temple on Mount Gerizim, which a few generations before had been pulled down by John Hyrcanus, of the Hasmonean Dynasty, who were ethnarchs of Judaea, and since the death of Archelaus, a son of Herod the Great, the Samaritans, along with the people of Judaea, had been living under Roman suzerainty.

"Can one tell where the border lies?" Uri asked.

"Sure you can," said the spearsman, keeping a straight face. "The moment you notice that you're dead, you already crossed it."

Not everyone here was a complete dolt, not even if they were rogues or policemen disguised in civilian cloaks.

They left the dirt road and now proceeded along paths. Uri saw terraced farmland, with people spaced apart from one another, bending over; he could not make out whether they were men or women, only that they were bent over between strips of grain; some were shorter than the others, perhaps children. They were harvesting some kind of cereal. In places where the grain had been reaped the stalks were collected into bundles, bound up either by themselves or with straw. Yes, they were harvesting! This was when they would have to harvest, since Passover, after all, was a holiday that celebrated the ripening of the crop sown in the winter. On the second day of Passover, an omer of barley was offered in the Temple to signal that grains from the new harvest could be consumed, as marked by the baking of unleavened barley bread on the day after the Passover. So that was the odd-tasting bread he had been given in prison after the other prisoners had been taken away.

"That's barley, isn't it?" he asked.

The sword-carrying guard snorted sardonically. They had been sparing in doling out his eyes, as his were little more than slits. Perhaps he did not see well either, and all the screwing up of the eyes had finally left its mark on his eyelids.

"And some wheat as well, isn't there?" Uri asked hopefully. In Rome all they ever ate was wheat bread; that was what he was used to.

"It sure is," marveled the spearsman. "It will be ripe is six weeks' time—that's what the Shavuot is about. They start to reap the barley in the Nisan, the first month of spring, wheat toward the end of Iyyar, and both of them in Sivan, the third month."

That was good news. Uri was able to tramp on with his mind at ease.

They were passing near some flat-roofed, mud-brick houses, which must be some kind of village. Uri could only see a door to the dwellings, so maybe there were windows that looked onto an inner yard, rather like in the old Far Side, a few remaining tumbledown cottages of which had still been standing when Uri was a small boy. Some of the mud-brick houses stood on their own, whereas others had been built onto one another. The gardens were not fenced off, with date trees, fig trees, and vines growing, along with a few plants that Uri had not seen before. In most of the gardens there was a cistern; out of some of these ran earthenware pipes, perhaps for irrigation.

In some gardens, between the fruit trees and vine stocks, there were wooden dolls on which rags fluttered in the breeze.

"What are they?" Uri asked.

"Scarecrows," said the spearsman.

Uri did not understand.

"The birds come along and eat everything," said the spearsman. "But if they spot a human, they are frightened off. They think those dolls are people!" he said, and chuckled at the birds' stupidity.

"It does no harm if real people scare them off from time to time," said the swordsman. "Otherwise they get used to the dolls and work out that it's a trick. Birds are not totally stupid, ravens in particular; scarecrows like that are no protection against them."

"Or against locusts," said the spearsman. "I've seen a swarm of migratory locusts. There's no pestilence worse than that. By the time you can count to six, they will have stripped everything bare. They even go for your eyes to check if those are edible too."

"Only if they're famished," said the swordsman. "If they are not as hungry, they don't swarm and hardly eat anything. People usually have an idea when the hunger is setting in, so they make the harvest early in anticipation. In periods of drought a watch is kept for locusts with fires. It is possible to pick up a signal a day and a half beforehand when a migration is imminent. Then the whole village will race and pick everything, just as the locusts do—so people are themselves the locusts!" the swordsman laughed. "Worse! There are fools who clear off things that a locust will not touch! Things that are not yet ripe they cook, leave to ripen, boil, and reboil... At such times there will be no bread won from the barley, but beer... And not raisins from the grapes, but wine—and sour wine at that, no matter how much honey you add."

"It's just as well that jackals and lions only eat meat," the spearsman ventured, "or there would be nothing left for humans."

Uri inquired if there really were lions in Judaea.

"There are," replied the spearsman. "They live in the Jordan Valley. They need water, but they can range out to here. It's not a good idea to wander around in this part of the world on your own and without a weapon."

"Robbers are a bigger threat," the swordsman declared. "A lion will not attack two or three people, because it knows they will be armed, but that won't stop a robber."

"But only," said the spearsman, "if they aren't informed in advance that the group should be left untouched."

"Are there many robbers here?" Uri inquired in some consternation.

"You bet!" said the spearsman. "There are many caves out this way, so yes, there are. But there's no need to be afraid, because they have been forewarned that we are coming."

Uri shook his head; he did not find that funny. The guards were no doubt exaggerating. They could hardly be so important that any self-respecting, dutiful, law-abiding robber bands should be given notice of them. And anyway how was that done?

All the same, he asked if they had encountered robbers before.

The swordsman grunted. The spearsman, after a brief pause, said with a deadpan face, "Every day."

Uri laughed.

They obtained permission to stay in a barn for the night and were given water, bread, and figs that had been dried the previous year. Without even bothering to see who was providing the hospitality, Uri fell asleep as if he had been clubbed on the head.

They rose at daybreak; Uri was barely able to stand on his legs; his feet, thighs, and backside all ached, having fallen out of practice with walking. It went through his head that it was Tuesday. They took water from a wooden bowl to wash their hands, before turning to the south to bow and recite the Sh'ma. Both the guards had a tefillah, the small wooden box being held on the left arm under their cloaks, but Uri was still without one; his own phylactery right now was in the sack that was being taken back by his fellow delegates. The two guards prayed for longer than Uri did, which indicated to him that they were probably adding some extra text. He listened carefully but did not understand what they were muttering. They drank water and ate barley bread, which was just like what he had eaten in prison, and then they were on their way.

At noon they rested under a palm tree. By then it was already baking hot, and over the last hour Uri had walked using his arms to protect his head. His guards draped over their heads woolen shawls, which until then they had tied around their waists.

"There's going to be a drought this year," said the swordsman, staring at the brilliant blue sky as he lay. "Everything is going to burn, and we're going to go hungry."

"The rains should have come by now," said the spearsman, nodding. "We're between Nisan and Iyyar, and there has been not a drop of rain."

Uri tried to guess where he would be when famine broke out in Palestine. He was amazed to find that he now had no destination, no object in life was left for him; he was no longer rebelling against destiny, sweeping him toward his unknown future. He looked at the countryside, to the extent that he saw anything, and the countryside that happened to be around him right then was no more real than the Rome that he had left two and a half months previously. The guards were pleasant men, the rascals in prison had been pleasant men, Pilate had been a pleasant man, but had red spots appeared on his face while he was jogging around the altar then he might not be alive. The whole thing was improbable; it was impossible to sense the weight of anything.

The sun was still beating down strongly when the guards got up and set off.

"It's not far now," the spearsman said by way of encouragement.

The sun had begun to go down by the time they reached a cluster of buildings. It was made up of mud-brick dwellings, with no girding wall.

The guards came to a halt.

"This is it," said the spearsman. "Look for a master carpenter called Jehuda ben Mordecai. He already knows about you."

"Aren't you going any farther?" asked Uri.

"No, we have to hurry back," said the spearsman. "Our greetings to Jehuda and his household. Peace be with you."

"Peace be with you," repeated the swordsman.

"Wait a moment," said Uri, and unslung the sandals from around his neck. "Take these."

His escorts were startled. They exchanged glances. The spearsman, touched by the gesture, sniffled.

"Our thanks, but which one of us should wear them?"

"If you sell off your worn sandals," said Uri, "you'll be able to buy a new pair, then both of you will get new footwear."

They gave that some hard thought. The spearsman took the sandals in his hands, examined them, and nodded. The swordsman also took them in his hands, inspected them, even sniffed at them.

"There's nothing to be afraid of with them," he said to Uri. "They're not as wicked as they pretend to be. I was a peasant myself."

Uri wished them peace too and set off toward the mud-brick houses. He looked back; they were standing and watching. Uri waved, and they waved back.

Uri came to a stop amid the mud-brick dwellings. There was not a soul around. He turned back around, but the two escorts were gone.

CRAFTSMAN JEHUDA BEN MORDECAI WAS A BURLY, STRONG MAN, AND his smell was strong too, penetrating, like his voice; he was unable to speak quietly, only in a bellow.

"You're the one they sent me?" he shouted out from the gloom when Uri stepped over the threshold, ducking because the doorpost was low. "How puny you are! I'm not going to get much that's of any use out of you! Call yourself a joiner? Why, you can't so much as lift a beam."

Uri let his eyes become accustomed to the dark. There was a tiny window cut into the wall on the side that overlooked the yard, too small for even a child to wriggle through, possibly to prevent thieves from entering.

"Tell me, kid: what do they call you?" Jehuda ben Mordecai yelled.

Uri introduced himself, giving his official Latin name.

"Gaius!" thundered Jehuda in vexation. "Gaius, with Theodorus to go with it! All bad cometh from Edom, don't you know that?"

The Edomites refused to allow Moses and the children of Israel passage through their land on their way to Canaan; they had to go around Edom and struggle over the River Jordan. But how long ago had that been? Two thousand years. The later Edomites were traditional descendants of Esau, and they deliberately vexed the Jews, being a kindred people, until the Arabs overran them, then the Nabataeans, after which they reassimilated to Judaism. Herod the Great was half-Edomite. Was it him that Master Jehuda was insulting? Why would he be?

"So, what do you want from me?" demanded Jehuda.

Uri shifted from foot to foot.

"Well, you'd better come with me, dopey Theo, and I'll show you where you'll sleep!"

Jehuda scrambled to his feet from the bed on which he had been lying, snorted, and squeezed past Uri out of the house.

Uri trotted after him. Jehuda aimed a few kicks at the chickens pecking around in the yard and cursed them. He stopped in front of a henhouse.

"Sling the chickens out," he bellowed. "They'll get on well enough out here! But don't get the idea they'll thank you for it!"

Uri looked at the coop. Was that going to be his quarters from now on? It was so small that he could not even climb in. A very odd sense of humor this master had. He looked around. There was a big barn opposite the house at the end of the yard; it had a big door through which even a cart could pass, and there was a ladder leaning against the wall up which one could clamber to the loft.

"I'm not giving you that!" Jehuda declared firmly. "That's where my workshop is! I'll show you, you misfit! I don't show this to just anyone, so consider yourself honored!"

Jehuda stormed ahead, Uri following.

In the barn stood a group of uncompleted tables and chairs with pleated straw seats, around a crude workbench on which lay iron and bronze tools and nails. The floor had wood shavings tamped down into it. Leaning against one wall were adzes and planks.

"Splendid, aren't they?" Jehuda asked Uri.

Uri mumbled something.

"Masters like me," Jehuda said with evident satisfaction, "don't make a living from explaining the law; we have honest occupations that pay their way, and anyone who does not have an honest occupation is in no position to explain the law! We're not priests! How is it in Edom?"

Uri did not know how matters stood in Edom of yore.

"Who explained the law to your people?" asked Jehuda.

"Where?" Uri asked.

"Back in Rome, you half-wit!"

"In Rome we have teachers to explain it," said Uri.

"Teachers!" roared Jehuda scornfully. "Teachers indeed!"

Jehuda stalked out of the barn, Uri in his wake. They stopped in the yard. Jehuda turned to face Uri and gave him a once-over. Dissatisfied with the sight, he shook his head. He sniffed the air.

"You stink!" he declared.

Uri lifted his arms and smelled.

"Maybe," he said.

"There'll be times when you stink much worse," said Jehuda, satisfied now. "Stink as bad as my slaves, I'll have you working that hard! Have no fear!"

Uri just stood there, his stomach rumbling, and cursed Judaea, Jerusalem, and all of Palestine to Hell and high water, blessed be the Eternal One.

Jehuda set off back to the house. Uri trailed after him, but Jehuda turned around, a vicious smirk on his face.

"Yours is the henhouse!" he declared roundly. "But if any harm comes to one of my hens, I'll flay you alive!"

At that he stormed into the house, leaving Uri in the yard.

Not the most cordial of welcomes.

It grew dark, and finally there was a cooler breeze. The chickens pecked. Uri contemplated the coop. If he had Remus, the dog from the ship, with him, he would be able to offer him a marvelous supper.

He crawled into the coop on all fours. The chicks inside did not know what to make of him but just gazed fixedly; they had not learned that man was to be feared. Uri began to bark, and the chickens finally made a panic-stricken escape outside. When Uri settled himself on his belly and stretched out, his legs stuck out, but it was better to lie on his front, pressing his stomach, which was grumbling for food.

The devil take it all.

HE WOKE UP FREEZING COLD AND FAMISHED. IN PRISON AT LEAST HE had been given something to eat; it was not always better to be free as a bird.

It was still dark, with a big stillness all around except for some animals whining in the distance. They were screeching and yelping at regular intervals, one after the other, and then falling silent. Might they be jackals?

Uri backed out of the henhouse still on his stomach, sat up, and looked at the night sky. He saw multiple shiny sparkles above him: the stars.

Where there are hens, there must also be eggs, he thought.

Flat on his belly, he wriggled back into the coop and felt around. Finally, he found a nest with three eggs in it.

Jehuda had said nothing about eggs, only his chickens. An egg was not a hen.

He picked up one of the eggs, the one on his right, picked out two small holes in the shell with a canine, one on top and one on the bottom, the way his father had instructed him, then sucked out and swallowed the contents raw. Magnificent food! He then polished off the other two eggs similarly.

His stomach and his whole being could now be at ease. I had better make good use of this until I feel hungry again. He ordered himself to fall asleep.

ON WEDNESDAY MORNING JEHUDA BEN MORDECAI PULLED HIM OUT OF the henhouse by the ankles.

It was only outside that Uri woke up, and then only partly. Daylight, he confirmed, and at that rolled onto his side, curled up, and tried to fall asleep again.

Master Jehuda knelt and poked his head into the henhouse. By now Uri was paying attention. Jehuda was squirming his massive shoulders, powerful back, and substantial backside rather like a boa that has just swallowed an elephant. He backed out again and sat up.

"Where are the eggs?" he asked severely.

"I ate them," said Uri with some pride.

Jehuda's face went purple.

"You pay for those," he demanded.

"I'll pay," said Uri flippantly.

"The price is four prutahs a piece," yelled Jehuda.

"That's four leptons," said Uri with a knowing air.

Jehuda stared in astonishment.

"Let's see the money, then," he muttered.

"I have nothing," admitted Uri. "I can't pay."

Jehuda was flabbergasted. There was a hush.

"You have no money?" he asked in a slightly lowered voice.

"None," said Uri. "I've had not a coin since I set off on this journey."

The master digested this answer. He looked Uri up and down as he sat there in the chicken droppings.

Master Jehuda then got up, dusted himself down, and stood over Uri, who was still seated. He thought further, and Uri also scrambled to his feet. Jehuda posed the question again softly.

"You don't have any money?"

"None," Uri confirmed. "I have my entire fortune on me as I stand here."

Master Jehuda pondered hard and long. Uri could not discern what his host might be deliberating.

"The quarters you can have free," Master Jehuda declared eventually, indicating the coop with a nod of the head. "But there'll be no food."

"Fair enough," said Uri.

"You can take from the pe'ah and the water barrel," said Jehuda, "but leave it at that. You'll get nothing from me!"

Jehuda nodded with great conviction at his own words, as if he were sanctioning a law, before starting off.

Uri piped up after him.

"What's the pe'ah?"

Jehuda came to a standstill, turned around, and shook his head as if he were trying to get rid of a sudden deafness.

"You don't know what the pe'ah is?"

"No, I don't," said Uri.

Master Jehuda again gave some thought.

"Feel free to take the gleanings, whatever there is," he said finally, as if he were pronouncing a particularly weighty judgment, then went into his house.

GLEANINGS, GLEANINGS—THAT SOUNDED VAGUELY FAMILIAR, BUT WHAT were they?

Gleanings... gleanings!

All at once a scroll sprang into Uri's mind's eye, and there was the word, near the beginning of the Book of Ruth.

In Bethlehem, Ruth, the widowed Moabite who had converted to Judaism, together with her mother-in-law, Naomi, also a widow, gathered among sheaves on the field after the reapers, and she roasted half an ephah of barley. In that way Ruth did not starve to death, and she became the wife of Boaz, a kinsman of Naomi's who had let Ruth glean in his field. And Ruth bore him a son, who was nursed by Naomi, and they called him by the name Obed, who was later the father of Jesse, who was the father of David. So Ruth was the great-grandmother of David, greatest of the kings of the Jews.

The word in Rome was that in Palestine they were awaiting the coming of a Messiah from the house of David.

Uri looked about him. Various mysterious-looking wooden implements were lying around the yard—no doubt tools for gardening. Not far from the house stood two circular brass cisterns. Uri took a handful of water and washed his face, then drank. It crossed his mind that there would come a time when he would have to pay even for that. As noon was approaching, he said the morning prayer. If one had no phylactery and on it the little box holding the law, it was permissible as a last resort to recite it from memory, but one had to take care not to add or omit any words. Uri was now saying the prayer for the umpteenth time from memory; he was well used to it by now, though he had never done it in Rome.

He left the yard and stood hesitantly among the houses. It was warm. He sniffed at his tunic, dirtied with chicken droppings. It was a good thing that he had left the fine ceremonial toga at the Antonia in his haste when he was taken before the judges, because if he had been wearing that, that too would have been spattered with chicken droppings.

The nearby fields all belonged to the village, and plainly they would have been sown with barley and wheat, so it didn't matter where he began. He kept looking back and narrowing his eyes, trying to memorize the rhythm of the mud-brick cottages' rooftops so that he would be able to find his way back to the coop without having to ask for directions.

The village lay in a valley, with gardens and plowed fields sloping—now gently, now steeply—as far as the woods.

There were many out at work on the fields. Uri stopped, screwed his eyes and peered through his fingers.

The field of barley was divided into several plots. On some, reaping was happening, while others were already reaped, and on others again the heads of grain were still bobbing untouched in the easterly breeze. All the same, the many small plots were clearly not all be of barley, because he noticed other kinds of heads of grain nodding in the breeze. Perhaps wheat... Barley and wheat alongside each other... Uri had a dim recollection that in Rome people who could not have sown or reaped for generations spoke about it being a mistake to sow a single kind of grain in a field, nor more than two; in other words, there had to be two kinds, with a space being left between them.

On one of the plots a strange contraption was doing the reaping. A figure wrapped head to toe in a cloak—a woman maybe—squatted on a seat rigged between two large stone wheels and tugged the traces of a pair of oxen drawing it along from the front. Making slow progress, it left strips in the soil behind it. An odd base of planks was fastened to its bottom in a similar way to how gemstones were worn around the necks of high priests. It crossed Uri's mind that he was never going to see the high priest's ceremonial garb or the gemstones around his neck. Was this something his companions from Rome might have seen at Passover? he wondered. Had they also stood next to the altar? Or was it just he, Uri, who had been party to that privilege, albeit with some delay? He gave a snort of laughter.

Farther off, men wielding sickles in their right hands chopped off heads of grain they held with their left hands, keeping hold of the stalks as they threw down the heads and moved on, stooping over as if they were in labor, only to grab more handfuls of heads of grain. When they could collect a whole armful of stalks in their left arm, they tied the bundle before throwing it down and moving on to gather more ears in the left hand, cut them away from the stems, and drop the heads on the ground.

Uri stood there and studied.

Gleanings could only be picked up from the places where the grain had already been taken away, but that was where the ox-drawn contraption was plowing. He needed to walk on.

He headed northward on the slopes of the hill.

He saw four men on one harvested plot, each of them with a pair of oxen harnessed to a wooden yoke. They held in their left hands a draft-pole that stuck back from the yoke and in their right hands the handles of two solid but crooked shafts, which were attached to each other and pushing into the soil. Uri went closer. Fitted to the bottom of the longer shaft was a metal plate shaped with a pointed tip, which shoveled the soil to the side.

So that was what a scratch plow looked like.

The men were plowing. Uri could not work it out. If winter was the season for sowing, why were they plowing now, after the harvest had been reaped?

A man approached him, a scarf on his head and a staff in one hand.

"What are you looking for?" he asked.

"I want to glean," said Uri.

"That's not permitted. Clear off!"

"I'm staying as the guest of Master Jehuda ben Mordecai," Uri proclaimed. "He advised me to glean."

"So you're Theo, the one who arrived yesterday?" asked the man in astonishment.

"That's me," Uri confirmed.

"And Master Jehuda told you to glean?" he continued incredulously.

"That's what he said."

The man pondered for a time and meanwhile kept brushing flies from his face; he smelled of dung, which must have been attracting them. I must smell too, Uri thought, because he also had flies buzzing around him.

"Well, if that's what he said, I suppose you'd better glean," the man finally came out with. "Only mind you don't get in the way."

"Which is a part where I can pick gleanings?" Uri asked.

"The parts that we've already gathered," said the man before wheeling around and walking off.

Uri remained standing. The man went up to one of the plowmen, and they proceeded together for a distance before, all at once, he rapped the plowman's hand with his staff. The plowman winced, pushed the plowshare deeper in the earth with his right hand, struggling and in pain, with the man walking beside him for a while, then coming to a standstill, turning away, and looking around to see whose hand needed to be rapped next.

That must be some sort of supervisor, Uri thought. A driver. I wonder if the workers are all slaves.

Uri sauntered over to an already harvested plot on which no one was working. He looked at the ground and squatted. Here and there on the soil, among the bundles of straw, lay some grains of barley and a miserable head or two. Was that the sort of thing he was meant to gather? How much to half a measure, an ephah or bushel? That was a lot—thirty-three pounds. Ruth cannot have had an easy time of it.

As he lolled on his back, Uri figured that he would be able to live comfortably on a twentieth of that, if he had something to collect it in, something to mill it with, as well as water and yeast to make it rise into a dough to knead, and then a vessel in which to roast it.

His mother had often baked wheat bread at home since that was cheaper than buying from a baker; Uri had seen how she did it, and as a small child he too had eagerly kneaded the dough. It was an enjoyable experience, giving the fingers a sense of pleasure. Back home, they had a basket in which to carry the flour home from the market; there was also water and yeast, a molding board, a vessel, oil if the dough were used to make flatbread, and a small clay oven in the yard. If they were baking leavened bread the oven had to be heated separately with extra wood, which Uri was happy to cut.

He could use his loincloth to carry the grain; he didn't really need it, as it was so hot.

But then a whole day would be taken up in gathering a twentieth of a bushel, and it would take another two or three days to acquire yeast, water, a molding board and vessel, and he would not be able to do that on an empty stomach.

Perhaps I would be best advised to toast the grain like Ruth; then it did not need water or yeast. But where would he do that?

He heard a low whir of voices and raised himself on one elbow.

Two decrepit crones in tattered clothes were sliding on their knees toward him, gathering fallen heads of grain into a small linen sack; they did not bother with single grains. They had unprepossessing, wrinkled features, with straggling strands of hair slipping out from under their headscarf. They looked a lot like each other; either they must have been sisters or old age and destitution had made them similar. It could just be, however, that this was a mother and daughter who had reached the same stage in life.

They looked at Uri as he reclined, and their eyes were vacant. There was no sign of surprise or fright; they just looked and slid on farther on their knees, gathering up the heads of grain. They had a right to the pe'ah.

A modern-day Ruth and Naomi, thought Uri. Or else I have dropped in a millennium earlier.

That thought had a lot of appeal.

His belly may have been aching, but he sat up and broke out into a loud laugh. The crones gave a start, pausing on all fours with their backsides pointed at Uri, but they did not turn around and look back; they were frozen still for a moment before they resumed inching forward as if nothing had happened. Like the chickens last night, they were not at all scared of him. Uri looked on them, delighted with the idea that they could look back on many, many generations of this simple, scanty existence.

What one saw here was something very ancient, something that could not be experienced in Rome. Maybe it had been worth the trip after all.

He also decided that he was not going to collect the gleanings; he would work. That had to pay something.

He stood up and peered, looking for the supervisor. He didn't see him, but never mind, someone would set him on the right track.

After some indecisiveness, the supervisor took him on as a day laborer. Theo would not be given any money, but he would get lunch, though he would have to work for it until sunset.

He spent until the sun went down among women and children, binding the stalks that had been thrown on the ground into larger bundles, or sheaves as he learned they were called. The work required no expertise, but it was tiring. He noticed that the stalks cut up his palms and not those of the women. Perhaps they looked down on him, he imagined, because he was the only man among them, but he shrugged his shoulders: let them! Early that afternoon he really did get lunch like everyone else: two slices of barley bread dipped in vinegar. Two servants brought around the dish of vinegar, while a third sliced the bread as evenly as possible and, after dipping it in the vinegar, handed it to the next one.

Uri wolfed down the first slice he was given in just five bites. He burped loudly, and for a few seconds he felt content. He took the second slice more slowly and came to the conclusion that this was food he detested: it burned his tongue, his throat, and his stomach. He managed slowly to force it down but resolved that next time he would ask them not to dip the bread in vinegar. But how did the others cope with living off it from sunup to sundown?

By the time they finished work it was completely dark. Uri could see nothing at all, but he was guided by the women's voices and exhalations as he stumbled home among them. The moon was out and shining to some extent, which was enough for them to see; without them Uri would have spent the night out in the field.

He felt an urge to defecate but did not dare to move aside, because by the time he was done they would be far away and he would never catch up.

Uri asked if they worked for their supper. At first they did not understand, and Uri thought he must be pronouncing the words incorrectly, but it wasn't that: the question was meaningless. Of course they worked for dinner, they replied, when they finally grasped Uri's question after the umpteenth time of being asked. Money? No, they did not get any money. The menfolk, yes; they received a daily wage and lunch. Bread and vinegar? Bread and vinegar. Nothing else? No, of course not; bread and vinegar was what they got.

"What sort of person is Master Jehuda ben Mordecai?" Uri inquired when they were close to the village, by now having to fight with all his might to hold back his bowels.

The women said nothing. A few of the girls gave evil laughs but said nothing either. Better I hadn't asked, but then he put another question to them anyway.

"Is he a man of great knowledge?"

They were walking quietly in the dark into the village.

One of the women said, "He's the master."

The women then vanished among the mud-brick dwellings. Uri squatted and felt that he was spilling his guts onto the ground, with all his excrement voided in one fell swoop.

He could scarcely see a thing but nevertheless found his way to his host's home at the first try. I'm not a lost person, he muttered under his breath and with some triumph, as he flailed with one hand to throw the chickens out of the coop to make room for himself to lie prone, flat on his belly, in their place.

ON THURSDAY HE WOKE OF HIS OWN ACCORD AT DAYBREAK. HE DID NOT wait for Jehuda to pull him out by the ankles but wriggled out backward, drank from the cistern, quickly gabbled the Sh'ma, and set off for the fields.

I'm even more soiled with chicken droppings than ever, he thought. Beelzebub, the lord of the flies, will find me not by sight but by smell alone; he was very pleased with himself at this new insight.

The supervisor told him that one of the plowmen had gotten sick and he should replace him.

"But I have no idea how to plow," protested Uri glumly.

"You'll learn," said the supervisor.

He led Uri over to one of the pairs of oxen and showed him how the plowstaff should be held so that the plowshare bit into the soil, how the protruding end of the yoke should be grasped with the left hand, how the oxen were to be induced to start by thrusting it forward. The supervisor had a tough job stopping the oxen once they had set off, having to yell and pull back the yoke for a considerable time before they finally came to a stop.

"Right, now you," said the supervisor.

Uri sat down behind the plow, grasped the stilt with his right hand and the beam with his left.

"That's it," the supervisor said encouragingly.

"Just a moment," said Uri. "What pay do I get?"

"Your lunch," said the supervisor.

"The men get pay as well," Uri notified him knowledgeably.

"You're not a man yet, Theo," said the supervisor matter-of-factly.

Uri allowed the answer to sink in. There was some truth in it, as he had not yet paid half a shekel in taxes that year; that would only come next year, when he would be twenty years old.

"Fair enough," he said, "but I ask that my bread not be dipped in vinegar."

The supervisor pondered. He was plunged into thought for a long time, which suggested that the request was no simple matter.

"That's not possible," he declared finally, almost reluctantly. "The vinegar goes with it."

Uri groaned quietly, then, with his left hand, pushed the rod on the yoke. The oxen did not respond, so Uri moved the rod more vigorously. The oxen reared.

"Shove the plow into the soil!" the supervisor yelled.

The pull from the oxen was so powerful that Uri all but fell flat on his face.

Uri tried to press the plowstaff down, and his right shoulder was wrenched, almost dislocating it.

"Shove down!" the supervisor shouted, striking Uri on the right hand with his staff.

The oxen, confused, began tossing their heads into each other and bellowing. They tried to run in opposite directions, and there was a tremendous crack; the plowstaff slipped out of Uri's hand and fell on its side.

The supervisor howled and left.

Uri lay on the ground; his right arm was throbbing. He licked it; it was salty. He tried to move it but could not. He felt it swelling and puffing up; there would be no plowing with that arm that day. A sharp pain ran through his right shoulder; no plowing with that one either.

The plowmen gathered around and wailed.

"The yoke's broken! The yoke's broken!"

Uri sat up. His right hand was swollen, bleeding, and he was unable to move his right shoulder. He looked in amazement at the assembled throng of men and women screeching, "The yoke's broken! The yoke's broken!"

The same wail went up in Master Jehuda's house from an elderly woman when Uri was helped in, a wet compress wrapped around his hand and shoulder. He was laid down on Jehuda's own bed: "The yoke's broken! The yoke's broken!"

By then Uri was heartily sick of the whole thing, and he said as much.

"It will be fixed..."

The response was a general shrieking. The room full of servants, plowmen, and sheaf-binding women now set up a panicked cry: "Fix the yoke? Fix the yoke?"

Master Jehuda drove them away from his house with his yelling.

The only one left screeching about the yoke was the old woman. Master Jehuda began belaboring her with his fists and with great difficulty removed her from the room.

He seated himself, disheveled, sweating, panting, next to Uri on the edge of the bed, which sank under his weight, sending shooting pains through Uri's shoulder.

"That's big trouble you've brought, Theo!" Jehuda said disconsolately. "Big trouble you've brought on us!"

"I only wanted to plow to be able to eat," Uri responded angrily. "I'm hungry!"

"I'll give you something to eat," said Jehuda, "but the yoke, the yoke!"

"They'll repair it," said Uri.

Master Jehuda cried out. Uri sat up on the bed and looked in amazement: the massive body of the man was shuddering as he sobbed.

"It's forbidden to repair a yoke!" he cried out. "That's big trouble you've brought on us, Theo! There's going to be a drought because you've broken a yoke. An easterly wind has been blowing up till now as it is, and now it's sure to keep blowing until the autumn! The yoke's broken! The yoke's broken!"

OXEN WERE HELD IN SUCH ESTEEM IN JUDAEA THAT WHENEVER ANY OF them turned wild and gored a man to death, not only the owner but also the oxen itself had to be present, chewing the cud, when it was sentenced; it was forbidden to sit in judgment in the absence of the ox in question, and if it was not there, then the hearing had to be postponed. That was what Uri learned as his hand and shoulder were being poulticed. He also learned that it was never permissible to repair a broken yoke and that although a wooden yoke was more fragile it was not permissible to employ a durable yoke made of metal, as it would signify eternal slavery, which should not be inveighed against either man or beast, blessed be the Almighty, who set this into law. It may not be written down, so one wouldn't find it in the Torah, but it was the tradition dictated by the Eternal One, the protector of enslaved people and animals, blessed be He for this forever. The crack when the yoke broke undoubtedly reached the all-hearing ear of the Everlasting Lord, no doubt deaf to many prayers, and He was angry that men were tormenting his animals, and that was why as a punishment he will send a drought to the land of his chosen people. On account of that crack there would be drought and famine throughout Judaea and maybe even Galilee too!

This was all explained by Master Jehuda, who had been driven from his own bed and was obliged to sleep in the bed of the screeching old woman, who was his lawfully wedded wife, while Uri recuperated. The two beds had been put some way away from each other, although in Palestine, in principle, or so it was claimed in Rome, husband and wife were supposed to share the same bed. Maybe there was a different custom in Judaea, or perhaps the two of them had long not been a true man and wife.

The shoulder hurt, it was true (the puffiness and bruising of the hand had started to subside), but Uri still took great delight in stretching himself out on the hard couch and gazing through the tiny window overlooking the yard at the blue and green lights glinting outside as his stomach peacefully made music. He was given food: leavened bread, which at his request was not dipped in vinegar, along with greens and fruit and even wine—only raisin wine, admittedly, but it tasted good. The Lord might be justifiably angry about the yoke breaking, but not at Uri.

He was treated like an uncommonly welcome guest whose very presence was seen as an honor.

Uri inferred that it was for purposes of instruction that Master Jehuda had let him go hungry for two days when he first arrived, but it was not his business to roast his guest over a slow fire and eat him. There was something forced about his solicitude; he smiled and joked more than Uri would have allowed himself had he been in the same position. Might he be acting under instructions, he speculated, but then when, and from whom?

Uri was well aware that he had been banished to this village despite the fact that no punishment of the sort existed in Judaea; on this, the living puppet in Jerusalem must have been right. Still, Uri did not understand how a message would have gotten from Jerusalem to the master, unless, perhaps, his escorts had dropped in after they had parted with Uri. That, however, was not very likely, as Uri had quickly located Jehuda's place, and there was no sign that his escorts had been there before him.

This evening marks the onset of the Sabbath, he mused. He would certainly not be asked to work tomorrow, by Sunday even his shoulder might be better, and it was rather unlikely that he would be entrusted with plowing anymore.

On the Sabbath two weeks ago he had been alone in the prison; the two rogues who were charged with robbery and the third man had been taken away. He had been alone in the prison cell for one week, and he had not known that he would be dining with the prefect. Now here he was, lying in a godforsaken Judaean village, the name of which he did not know; the hunchbacked official had told him, but it had not registered and now he was being looked after well even though he had committed a capital offense by breaking the yoke and because of him there would be a drought this year. He was damned if he could understand any of it.

There were occasions when time intensified; at others it stood still for years on end or barely trickled ahead. He could not say what had happened in this or that year in Rome since Sejanus and his children had been executed, but over these past three weeks in Judaea time had intensified, Uri concluded, and he strongly sensed that with every particle of his being, though he was well aware that time in Judaea, here in the country, had been standing still for centuries and millennia, and would do so forever; whatever might happen in Rome or the capital city of the next empire, sowing and reaping would be done the same way here.

Jehuda turned up at noon, puffing as he took a seat at the table, beside which there was a small bench. The elderly woman was cooking at the fireplace, while Jehuda peered in Uri's direction.

"You'll get lunch if you can get up," Jehuda said.

"It's not my legs that hurt," said Uri, dragging himself to his feet and across to the table.

"Sit down, then—here, next to me," said Jehuda, so Uri sat down there.

"Are you good at anything at all?" Jehuda inquired.

"That would be hard to say."

"You must have been included in that delegation for some reason," Jehuda exclaimed.

"I know a few languages," said Uri.

Jehuda pondered that hard.

"For what purpose?" he finally asked.

"Well, so I can read this and that," said Uri hesitantly.

"Except for the Torah there's no need to read," Jehuda declared. "All a person needs is there. Or do you hold a different view?"

"Yes, all a person needs is in the Torah," Uri let it go at that, nodding enthusiastically. "A person only reads anything else to see what kinds of errors also exist, and if one wishes to convince someone that all a person needs is in the Torah; it's better to know in advance what sort of silliness he is going to utter. It's easier to refute arguments if one knows them in advance."

Jehuda knitted his brow, chewing that answer over for some time. His spouse set down before them large earthenware plates with large helpings of noodles with raisins before returning to the fireplace. Jehuda was still chewing on Uri's words, and Uri was glad that Jehuda clearly had no sense of humor.

"There's no need to convince people," Jehuda announced at last. "Not everyone needs to belong to the Lord's chosen people; there are enough of us as it is. Nor is there any need to engage them in conversation."

"Indeed, there are enough of us," Uri nodded, "though there are not enough of us in the Diaspora; we are surrounded by non-Jews..."

"That's why you're unclean, you dirty people," said Jehuda. "Though even if all the people in the Diaspora were Jewish, you would still be unclean because you don't live where we do."

"We envy you for that, Master," said Uri respectfully. "I now envy myself for being able to be here among you."

Jehuda smiled at that.

"That's all right."

Jehuda got up, twisted the strings of his tefillin around his forehead, tying them at the back of his head so that they hung down onto his shoulders. He glanced at Uri.

"Where's your tefillin?"

"My companions have taken it back to Rome."

"You mean you haven't even got a tefillin?" the master snorted. "Woman! A tefillin for the child!"

The master's spouse went out of the room. Jehuda looked around the room, where in one corner there were blankets lying around among other odds and ends.

"Woman!" thundered Jehuda.

The woman came back with a phylactery in one hand, which he put down on the table.

"Sew some tzitzits onto one of the blankets right away! The child doesn't even have a gown!"

"Now?" the woman wailed out. "I'm right in the middle of cooking lunch!"

"No cooking, get sewing, and no lip!"

The woman did not answer but went across to the corner and started rummaging among the blankets.

"So anyway, tell me," Jehuda sat back on the bench, "were you important delegates there at the altar at Passover?"

Uri also took a seat. Better to tell the truth, though it may not be necessary to talk about every last detail.

"I wasn't there," he said, "but it's possible that the rest were."

"And why weren't you there? Did they think you were too young? Or there wasn't enough room?"

"Well, that might have been the reason..."

"I've never stood by the altar myself," said Jehuda. "Our turn never came... though I'm past forty-five now! Casting lots, rotation, fairness? Come on! They're all fiddling there, in the Sanhedrin! Fiddling! Every year we trudge there and back three times over, and our turn still doesn't come!"

"That's hardly fair," Uri asserted.

"It's awful!" Jehuda declared. "But it's a good thing you didn't stand next to the altar, because our crowd would have hated you for it! As it is they are just going to feel sorry for you, you wretch, for having to live in Edom, that odious, abominable hellhole."

Uri nodded. Edom was their way of saying Rome. That's what they called it here, and they cursed it—that was all right. If anyone reported them for abusing Rome, they would say it wasn't true, because they'd only mentioned Edom, not Rome. Cunning.

Master Jehuda did not know I was in prison. Better to deny it anyway; it was not possible to lock up a member of the Roman delegation in prison, but if that was what had happened, one must pretend that it hadn't.

The woman came with the blanket onto the corners of which she had sewn fringes, one of the threads of which was blue as convention demanded. Jehuda took it from her, inspected it thoroughly, then nodded.

"Right."

The woman put an earthenware dish in front of them on the table.

Jehuda stood up. The woman went back to the fireplace.

Uri also got to his feet and grasped the tefillin with his left hand; there was a leather box on it as there should have been. He put it down.

"I can't wind it into place," he said. "My shoulder hurts."

"Woman!" Jehuda yelled so loudly that the mud-brick cottage shook.

The woman left the fireplace and came over to them.

"Wash your hands, then put the tefillin on his forehead!"

The woman hesitated.

"What's wrong?" Jehuda yelled.

"I haven't been in the mikveh yet," the woman said quietly.

Jehuda kept quiet.

If his wife was unclean, then she could not put the tefillin on him.

Uri understood that if she touched it when she was unclean, then the tefillin would not be clean either. That was bound to be a source of complications.

It was. Jehuda shooed the women off to the mikveh. Naturally there was a mikveh in the village—a real double mikveh, in the garden of one of the farmers. It was communal, not his own, but he was still responsible for looking after it. A frequent check was made on the state of the mikveh, above all by Master Jehuda, who was also tasked with doing so.

"What's a double mikveh?" Uri asked.

Master Jehuda's eyes twinkled as he explained.

A double mikveh consisted of two basins, and it was possible to immerse oneself completely in one of them—that's what the water was for. One did not immerse themselves in the other mikveh, and it was filled with water brought by the womenfolk from far away. Whenever the purity of the mikveh for immersion was in doubt, it was possible to transfer the contents of the clean water basin to it through a tube. A tenth of the water from the clean one bestowed cleanliness on the whole of the other; that was the tradition.

In Jerusalem, of course, there were no double mikvehs, only single ones. Which is to say that they could not be clean, to be sure. Of course, people believed they were clean, the miserable wretches. There wasn't a really clean mikveh to be had in Jerusalem, but then again it was not necessary, because all Jerusalem was considered clean. Pilgrims to Jerusalem would do their ritual ablutions in those filthy mikvehs, and they had to purify themselves for a week in those before being allowed to step onto Temple Square. In Jerusalem there would be a great pushing and shoving around the mikvehs every Wednesday and Friday, when ritual immersion was obligatory.

Something clicked for Uri upon learning this.

"When I was taken to Temple Square, they asked me beforehand when I had arrived, and their minds were set at rest when they heard that I had been in the land for over a week..."

Master Jehuda nodded.

"All pilgrims have to purify themselves for a week, and for that period they are not permitted to step into Temple Square. Until then, they have to stay somewhere and eat something. That's what Jerusalem makes its living from—foreign tourists... For one week, pilgrims spend their money—a handsome amount..."

Master Jehuda roared with laughter.

Uri broke into a smile.

"But you people from this village don't need to get there a week before a holiday," he said, "because you're not pilgrims."

Master Jehuda was pleased to hear that his guest had finally grasped the essential point.

"No, we don't need to," he confirmed. "Syrian Jews also do not have to. It is said that Antioch is like a suburb of Jerusalem, which makes us near enough to also be considered clean, provided we stay within the law in other respects. Which mikveh did you use for ritual bathing in Jerusalem?"

Uri weighed his reply.

"We weren't given a name."

"Still, where was it? I'm familiar with the City."

"Somewhere in the lower town, it was..."

"It could have been in the Acra... What did it look like from outside?"

"My eyes are not good, master," Uri said. "I can only see well up to an arm's length."

Jehuda sighed.

"So, that too!"

Uri nodded in commiseration; he sympathized with the master for having such an impossible individual charged to his care.

Master Jehuda contemplated, even farted in his efforts, before speaking.

"I'll take you sometime to a neighboring village. There's a man who's blind as a bat there."

Uri waited for Master Jehuda to go on, but something else came to Jehuda's mind.

"Do you go to a mikveh to bathe yourselves over there in Edom?"

Uri hesitated.

Better not to lie, he thought.

"There are not many mikvehs," he confessed. "We wash our hands and feet then sprinkle ourselves with water..."

"There are some big heathen baths, so I've been told," said Master Jehuda.

"There are," Uri admitted, "but we don't go to them."

This delighted the master so much that he personally, after washing his own hands, washed the phylactery in the outside cistern. He then grasped it by one thong and whirled it around in huge circles in the air, warbling benedictory phrases as he did so that it should dry. He tied it onto Uri's forehead with his own hands, nicely arranging the straps in front and on Uri's shoulders, thus making the three letters: the first was already written in the leather box, twice at that, and that was the letter shin; the second letter, a dalet, was formed by the knot at the back; and the two straps in front formed the third letter, a yod, with the three favored points together neatly proclaiming "ShDaY," which is to say "Shaddai," or "Almighty."

It was not quite the same in Rome, where two tefillin had to be worn in principle, one attached to the forehead, the other to the upper left arm, and the yod was formed by the knot of the tefillin tied to the arm. When traveling, though, everyone had just one tefillah, but that was permissible in an emergency, which travel counted as.

That was the purpose of a phylactery: anyone wearing those three letters himself becomes almighty, just like the Eternal One.

"She needed to go to a mikveh in any case," said Jehuda, offering excuses for his wife, "only I bundled her off a bit earlier than I had to. It's difficult with women, who are only semi-human. Are you married yet, kid?"

"No, I'm not."

"Be very careful whom you wed—very, very careful!"

Uri promised that he would be very careful.

They stood in front of the table. Jehuda turned toward the east—he feels he is in Jerusalem, Uri observed, and likewise turned to the east—and with repeated bows and in a chanting tone very loudly started to pray. He did not take out the piece of parchment in the tefillin, so Uri did not do so either; after all, in Judaea it was not obligatory to read the Sh'ma.

Uri also prayed, reciting the Sh'ma from memory. He again finished first, with Jehuda continuing and chanting a few benedictions that Uri recognized, as well as a few passages that he had never heard before, one being about the Messiah coming from the house of David, while the next one went "Give us this day tomorrow's bread."

Uri mused on that. It was not possible to eat tomorrow's bread today, so this bread was not actual bread but food for the soul. The saying no doubt related to the End of Days, when the Messiah would arrive, and that must be connected with the former.

It was quite possible that the guards and the prisoners in the prison had recited the same sentences, only back then his ear had not yet fully adjusted to hearing Aramaic, and they had mumbled it softly.

On reaching the end of the prayer, Jehuda sat back down, and Uri sat down beside him.

"You people in Edom, that accursed, unclean place, do you only recite the Sh'ma before the arrival of the Shabbat Queen?"

"Yes."

"May the Almighty raze Edom to the ground, and with it all the ungodly!" declared Jehuda, and he thereupon began eating the challah.

They polished off the loaf of bread, drinking wine with it, Jehuda knocking back four cups in a row, Uri just one.

"Don't you all in Edom, may the Almighty raze it to the ground—don't you ever drink?"

"Not a lot," said Uri, blushing.

Jehuda scornfully looked him over.

"It shows, you puny lot!"

By the time his wife had gotten back from taking the ritual immersion, Jehuda was hungry again. She protested that the meat would have been ready long before if she had not had to break off to go early to the mikveh, but that did not stop Jehuda from reprimanding her once more.

After he stuffed himself with meat, Uri went back to lying on the couch. He burped and farted contentedly, feeling that he had never been safer since leaving Rome.

A lot of people crowded into the room as evening drew in, all Master Jehuda's household—domestics and outdoor servants—along with guests from the village who had come together in the master's house to greet the Sabbath, the arrival of the Sabbath Queen, in a fitting manner and, as it emerged, also to sleep there. Master Jehuda must be an important man if they came to his place on Friday evening and he didn't have to go anywhere else.

Uri lay on the bed, squinting around at them in the lamplight. There was no menorah in the room, just ten oil lamps that smoked and gave off an unpleasant odor as they burned away. Uri secretly reviled the Lord for afflicting him with poor vision, because he could not see the faces of all the many people too well, though this would have been an excellent opportunity to scrutinize the village's inhabitants. They were eating and drinking, but Uri was not hungry and did not get up. A few people noticed him and moved toward him and looked him over with curiosity; Uri smiled.

The hubbub and dim lighting were soporific, and he plunged into a deep sleep.

"WAKE UP!" MASTER JEHUDA HOLLERED. "LET'S GET OFF TO THE HOUSE of prayer!"

Uri opened his eyes. He moved his right shoulder: it hardly hurt now.

No end of people were stirring in the master's room; there were some two dozen men, women, and children sleeping on the floor, the air was thick with the fumes of candles and human exhalations; their reek was unfamiliar, Uri realized, as they were from nearby villages. The whiff given off by people there was different; he had become accustomed to the smell of his village.

After prayers and a snatched breakfast of a few bites, he found himself in front of the house.

Virtually the entire population of the village, several dozen men, women, and children had assembled there, some strangers having slept overnight, from Friday evening to the Sabbath holiday, at other houses, because there must have been around one hundred souls there in all.

Master Jehuda patted some cheeks, and slapped the behinds of some girls and women, then set off.

Uri trudged along in the middle of the crowd.

There were vessels sitting on the road at the village boundary. Here everyone stopped, broke off a piece of matzo, took some fresh green figs—Uri took some too—then moved on, because, while on Friday evening they could travel as far as they wished, from when the sun went down until sunset on the Sabbath they could go no more than two thousand cubits, and the house of prayer lay farther than that from their villages than it did from this village. The reason why the food had been set down at the edge of the village before the onset of the Sabbath was to mark it as their household's boundary, so by that reasoning the synagogue must lie within a distance of two thousand cubits of this point.

It seemed there was not such a big difference between here and the Roman Far Side after all.

They went over the plowed field in single file on a scarcely noticeable track between plots. Uri noted that the heads of grain had been left standing in a row along the edges of the already harvested plots, and he even went so far as to ask why they were so sloppy in their work. The middle-aged man who was tramping in front of him, also barefoot, looked back in astonishment.

"That's on account of the pe'ah," he said.

"But doesn't the pe'ah consist of fallen heads that have been left?" Uri asked.

"No," said the man. "They've just been accidentally dropped, but it is not permitted to reap the edge of a field on account of the poor."

"The pe'ah is the sixtieth part," said the man behind Uri. "But that's not easy to work out..."

"We count on the master to make a decision if there is any dispute about the size of the pe'ah," said the one in front. "It is not all the same if the grain is in one plot or two, because if it's in two plots then a pe'ah only has to be left on one..."

"Not always," said the one behind Uri, and he started to list exceptions.

Uri was unable to follow the debate upon which they went into a passionate discussion of the finer legal points of the pe'ah.

They were treading in each other's footsteps between the plots. Uri kept a constant check that he did not place his feet on the stubbly patches. It was a good thing they were not going any faster; in Judaea everything was slower than in Italia. These people were not even walking at a stadium or a stadium and a half in an hour.

"Don't you leave a pe'ah in Edom?" later asked a younger man who came up on Uri's footsteps.

"As it just so happens," said Uri, "we don't leave one because we can't; we don't own any land."

With that, the dispute over the riddles of the pe'ah ceased. There was a silence. Even some people who were walking farther away stopped talking.

"You have no land?" the one who was walking in front finally asked, having come to a halt and so forced Uri to do the same, whereupon the entire line that was behind came to a halt.

"No, we don't."

"That's impossible!"

"We don't own any land," Uri persisted. "It's not allowed."

"A curse on ruddy Bozrah!" the man standing behind him exclaimed.

A few more also cursed. Uri was now thoroughly confused. Bozrah had been the capital city of Edom many, many centuries ago, but why ruddy? Perhaps Edom meant "red" in Semitic languages.

"If you have no land, what do you make a living from?"

Uri sighed.

"We trade," he said. "We have artisans, craftsmen, builders, dockers, scribes..."

"Handicrafts, we've also got them," said a gruff voice from behind. "Jerusalem is overflowing with master craftsmen, the best in the world! But one can't live without land. Land is life itself!"

"What do you people eat anyway?" another voice asked.

"Whatever we buy, I suppose," said Uri.

"You... you mean you buy your food?"

That piece of news went right down the line: those Edomites pay money to buy food for themselves, they pay money to buy food for themselves, they pay money to buy food for themselves!

Unbelievable.

"Where do you buy the food?"

"In shops, at the market..."

This was so peculiar that people began to laugh. In shops, at the market!

"And how much does a measure of wheat cost in ruddy Bozrah?"

Uri was stumped; he did not know. With his tessera he got the grain free of charge, enough for the whole family, but he felt that this was better left unsaid; people just would not understand. They would not understand the whole Roman system.

"Something like six sesterces," he said uncertainly.

"How much is that in zuz?" could be heard simultaneously from several quarters.

Uri sighed. He tried to recall what those pleasant plunderers had said in prison and replied at random, "One zuz."

There was a big gasp of consternation.

"One zuz! One zuz for a single ephah in Edom! One whole zuz for a single ephah in bloody Bozrah!"

"You're out of your minds," declared the gruff voice from behind. "You're paying twenty times more than you ought to!"

Uri gave a growl of accordance and nodded; he did not consider it his duty to acquaint them with the mysteries of the retail trade, especially when he was not entirely clear himself.

"You don't produce any grain?" someone asked.

"No, we don't."

That was too much for them; they could not understand it at all.

Somebody started guessing how grain might reach Edom. Uri just smiled.

"The grain comes from Egypt," he said. "That's what the whole of Rome eats."

More gasps.

From Egypt? But they don't pay any attention to how things are baled. You can be sure moisture gets in, and that makes it unclean! Uri went on the defensive; there were quite a lot of Jews living in Rome, and they kept to the rules of purity. They only ate kosher meat; they cooked with Jewish oil, and the forefathers had been very scrupulous in ruling what a Roman Jew could and could not eat. If they had decided generations back that wheat from Egypt was edible, then it could not be unclean.

The climate of opinion around Uri grew antagonistic. Everybody in the Diaspora was unclean—there was your proof! It had now turned out to be unequivocally true as far as Edom was concerned.

It would have been better to have said nothing at all, Uri reflected.

The peasants had not come out of Egypt all that long ago, but we Roman Jews did a very long time ago, he recognized.

He needed to invent something quickly.

"That is the case," he said loudly so everyone could hear. "We Roman Jews eat wheat grown by Jews in Egypt, and it undergoes strict inspections..."

It did no harm to make that up, because the position was already rather embarrassing. As they began to digest the announcement, the anger subsided.

There were cries from the front asking what the matter was, why they had stopped. People at the back started to shove forward, and the line started to move again.

"Why don't you all rise up in revolt?" someone asked. "It's a shame you're treated like that!"

A prolonged, highly detailed storm of abuse against Edom ensued. People forgot about Uri and the original topic of discussion, thanks be to the Eternal One.

THE SYNAGOGUE WAS LOCATED IN THE NEXT VILLAGE.

People also arrived from other villages, and they all stood around in front of the small, mud-brick, straw-thatched building, chatting in gratifying and leisurely fashion. There were many hundreds of people—men, women, and children; the young and the aged; the poor and the well-off. Not even a tiny fraction of that crowd would fit into the house of prayer.

Like that million-strong mass in Jerusalem.

In front of the synagogue stood long, crudely built tables on which food had been laid out, covered with white tablecloths, the Sabbath meal that every Jew who was a guest of the house of prayer was given for free. It was the same as in Rome, only there the members of the congregation would sit inside a building. Uri was curious about how they would go about praying in Judaea.

They went about it in such a way that the Torah scroll, which normally resided in the house of prayer, was brought outside, and the readings were made from it in the open air. No one went into the house, no particular group was favored, and everyone said an "amen" at the end of the verses. The prayer leader, a young man, did not give a priestly blessing, suggesting that there might also be a shortage of priests in the Judaean countryside. Perhaps that was why the masters were important, Uri guessed; something of the priestly vocation's intermediary role was shifted onto them, though they were not allowed to recite the prayers reserved for priests, give blessings, or dress in white.

Children kicked up a racket and women chattered as the communal prayer went ahead, giving the service a refreshingly relaxed, vital character. The prayer leader read in Hebrew from the Torah the part prescribed for that week, and an elderly man translated every two or three sentences into Aramaic so that the whole congregation could understand. Uri strained to hear what the elderly man was saying in the hubbub, and he was not such a bad interpreter; he had no scroll in his hands, but he must have prepared for the entire week, because it sounded as if he were chanting a text he had memorized perfectly. All the same, the prayer leader also had no faith that the crowd was paying attention, and he had to flutter a kerchief to signal to the congregated throng when they had to say "amen." The crowd watched for the kerchief, yet they themselves did not pray, only said the "amens."

After the reading, the prayer leader tagged on a sort of explanation, and that did not need interpretation, as he said it in Aramaic. The young man, four or five years older than Uri at most, was not exactly an imaginative individual; he expounded on how anything that is lost is not lost forever, and what dies does not die forever. Someone in the crowd commented that his mother had died recently; he no doubt had her in mind.

Right then, on track to complete the reading of the Torah by the autumn and start once more amid the Simchat Torah festivities, they happened to be at the Book of Samuel, the bit that anyone who happened to be paying attention could hear was about the Ark in which the Lord's covenant with His people is kept was stolen by the Philistines but subsequently sent back in fulfillment of the Lord's will.

The Philistines stole the Ark of the Covenant from Shiloh at a time when the Jews still held the Ark in the Tabernacle, but, by a miracle, it was returned seven months later, so they retrieved this most ancient and holy box, in which the Tablets of Stone with the Ten Commandments handed down to Moses were kept, along with a few other precious articles, and on whose golden lid, in principle, the Almighty was seated and conversed with those who entered the sanctum. King David then took it to Jerusalem, and his successor Solomon built the First Temple, in the inner sanctum of which the Ark stood until it later disappeared.

Uri wondered whether others also wondered if the Ark might still be preserved somewhere. The Ark of the Covenant was not in the inner sanctum of the Second Temple, into which he had been unable to see, and that was why the Holy of Holies, the place that even the high priest could only enter once a year to testify to the Ark's exalted absence, was empty. Uri seemed to recollect reading somewhere that Jeremiah once took the Ark and the Tabernacle and buried them in a cave on Mount Nebo, hiding the way to the place even from his own companions, and he also vaguely recalled reading that Josiah had hidden the Ark in the caves under Temple Mount. The important thing was that it had been missing ever since.

It would be an extraordinary and major event if it were to turn up; people would be greatly excited to see it.

Between "amens," Master Jehuda joked with his friends, still speaking loudly. It was largely due to him that the prayer leader's text was inaudible; he simply outshouted the young man, and Uri had a suspicion that this was for the purpose of showing that he, and no one else, was master around these parts, even if he was not leading the prayers.

The children ran around, with mothers trying—by occasionally rapping knuckles—to dissuade them from reaching out from under the white tablecloths and pinching wedges of the special festive bread. The dogs were not exactly respectful of the solemn occasion either, because, perhaps following the lead of the children, they raced around and barked in a manner that was quite unworthy of Jewish dogs.

When the communal service closed with the reciting of the Sh'ma, the prayer leader, accompanied by two elderly men, took the Torah back into the house of prayer, where he placed it back in its cupboard. He then came out and washed his hands in a bowl held out to him into which something was sprinkled, though Uri had no idea why he would do this and, indeed, asked.

"He was made unclean by touching the Torah scroll," several around him said, quite at a loss to understand why anyone would ask.

"Unclean—from the Torah?"

Uri was astounded. Back home in Rome it was necessary to wash hands *before* picking up a Torah scroll.

It was an interesting way of looking at things, he reflected—to believe that a holy book might make a person unclean. Maybe that came from experience long forgotten by Roman Jews.

He inquired what was sprinkled in the bowl.

The answer was the ashes of a red deer doe's remains, which are best for cleaning off fat.

Uri was staggered. Red deer does were mentioned in the Books of Moses, and symbolic ashes were used in Rome as well when they got to that point during the reading of the Torah, but here people in Judaea truly lived by the written word! Time stood still here.

The prayer leader drank a sip of wine, whereupon everyone jumped for the flasks of wine, poured some out for themselves and one another—women and children too. The flasks were drained in an instant.

That was also when the white tablecloths were taken off and everyone, whether standing or moving around, started eating. The food was barley bread, baked from the newly harvested grain, and it was dipped into vessels of vinegar and enormous dishes of salt, of which there was at least one per table. There were also greens on the tables, including some that Uri had never seen before. Once the bread was gone, the faithful resigned themselves to eating these. There was no meat because there was not much of that and it came only with the major feasts. Uri did well to grab two thick slices of bread, and he did not dunk them in vinegar but most certainly in the salt, and he took several helpings of the greens, which were not too popular.

He was left behind when it came to the wine, however, for which he did not begrudge the others. It was true that it was compulsory to drink some wine on the Sabbath, but it quickly ran out in the crush, so he did not commit a sin. He looked around all the same to check if anyone had spotted that he was not drinking, as he suspected that these nice people were nevertheless quite capable of upbraiding him for sinning and that Master Jehuda would impose the due penalty, but fortunately—thank goodness—no one was bothering about that.

The assembly, several hundred strong, that had gathered for the Sabbath from nearby villages was merry, and they were merry for the same reason Uri was: they would not have to work that day—plus they also got free food and drink. Uri noticed that freemen and slaves were eating together, with no essential difference between them on this occasion; in the end, Uri supposed, that was the main point of the holiday, and that was especially the sense of Passover, which, it was true, had passed, but on its first day the counting of the Omer, which lasted for fifty days until Shavuot, had begun and had now reached the fourteenth day. All those many tribes which eventually became the Israelites had been delivered out of slavery in Egypt, and it was no bad thing to remind oneself of that; let the slaves also enjoy being free for one single day a week, the Sabbath.

Passover was still close, and the residents of the nearby villages stood around Uri and compared their experiences on the pilgrimage to Jerusalem.

Everyone in that part of the world was required to make the trip, as it lay within two days' walk, and all had in fact made the trip and they could not get over relating the marvelous experiences they had two short weeks before.

On the way there, someone had gotten a thorn in their foot and was unable to get it out, so it had festered, and on the way back it had been cut open with a knife, though the festival was still going, or to be more specific it was a half-holiday, whereupon a dispute had arisen over whether it was permissible to cut the wound open on a half-holiday. What carried the argument was the notion that by the time the festival reached its very end the whole leg might go gangrenous and the individual would die. How he had screamed! It turned one's stomach. Of course he was all right now, or rather not entirely, because last week a plow ran into his other foot, and *that* had festered, but he'd had it cut open too, and by the day before yesterday he was plowing again.

Another drank too much wine and fell into a cistern, and he floundered around for a long time before they were able to pull him out, because the wells in Jerusalem are very deep. He had wailed and cursed and lamented just like the prophet Jeremiah when he was cast into a cistern (or maybe it was a dungeon, because the princes were not too fond of him), and he was only hauled out much later, as had been the case with that drunk ten days ago.

That was something that could amuse people endlessly, and different bits of the story had to be repeated time and time again.

The older men teased the girls, having seen that they were attracted to the young priest who had guided them to the valley. Though they also found out that he was unwed, the girls balked at the very idea of becoming a priest's wife; a priest could never marry a girl who was not from a priestly family, and thus no son of theirs could ever be a priest, either. They wouldn't think of bringing ruin on that handsome priest, just so long as he had a wife who came from a priestly family, be she ever so ugly, old, and shrewish, with hairs sticking out of her ears, nose, and rear.

People had a good laugh at that too.

They compared notes on who had stayed where in Jerusalem during the festivities.

The villagers had made camp for ten days on end either in the Kidron Valley or in the Valley of Hinnom, and they did not even try to get into the City, as they knew there would not be room for them anyway and the guards would have chased them away because the people of this whole surrounding district were not entitled to pass inside the city walls.

Manasseh, said somebody else, had stood in Temple Square some twenty years before.

There were a lot of people who knew Manasseh, who was famous precisely for the fact that he had once stood by the altar in front of the Temple. Many indeed asked how he was getting on, and whether he was here; he was somewhere around here, just earlier they'd seen him down a whole flask of wine in one go. He already had seven grandchildren, five of whom were boys, so Manasseh was a happy man—though a few screws were coming loose as he aged.

Uri's thoughts also strayed back to how he and the rest of the delegation had fed two weeks ago on the military highway on the way from Caesarea to Jerusalem, and what his thoughts had been about the throng striving to get to Jerusalem. It had been foreign rabble as far as he was concerned, one big mass; he had no idea that the individuals in the crowd might have names, or that also walking among them had been one called Manasseh, who had once stood by the altar at which his tribe's animal sacrifices had been burned and who had seven grandchildren. Uri took a strong liking to this Manasseh who was now going soft in the head, and he wished to have the chance of meeting him one day.

I have already stood on Temple Square, it crossed Uri's mind. How people would envy me if I told them.

Master Jehuda stepped over to him, leading an old man by the hand.

"Here he is," Jehuda exclaimed triumphantly, letting go of the old man's hand. "Talk to each other!"

At that he left them.

There was silence. The old man blinked; Uri greeted him politely and stayed quiet.

"So, you're that weak-sighted kid from Edom?" the old man inquired.

Uri muttered something in reply.

"Blessed be your weak-sightedness, Theo," said the old man, and he stretched out a hand, found Uri's face, and stroked it.

Uri stood there petrified.

"Thank you," he said.

"Give thanks to the Almighty, son," the old man said, and leaned closer to Uri's face. He narrowed his eyes to slits to see better.

Is that how I screw up my eyes? Uri wondered in horror.

"Aren't you happy with yourself, lad?" the old man asked.

"Not always," said Uri cautiously.

"That's a mistake. I've been blessed by the Almighty, and so have you, only you don't yet know it. Because I didn't see well, I couldn't sow or plow, so I learned how to read instead. I read a lot, and that made me clever, and other people sensed that and used to come to me from the village for advice. They still come from distant villages, and I can help them, because I've read a lot and thought a lot, and I gained prestige. That was what the Lord wanted from me, and I understood it in time. People love me, lad, and they will love you too, because the Lord wanted you to be weak-sighted. Be thankful, son!"

Tears came to Uri's eyes. He grasped the weak-sighted old man's hand and kissed it. The old man was surprised and gave Uri a searching look straight in the eyes from close up.

"You don't see all that badly," he determined somehow, and at that lost interest. Nevertheless, he shook his head and said, "Be proud, son, that you too were created for life for a short while. I ask you now to accompany me back to the table, because I would like to eat a bit more."

Uri linked arms with the old man, guided him to a table, handed him a plate of fruit, and the old man started nibbling. Uri looked at his wrinkled face, his happy features, then, without a word, stepped quickly away.

Until late in the afternoon people were taking snacks, and there was no end to the jabbering, but there was nothing else to do until someone evidently gave word that the feast there, in front of the small house of prayer, had come to an end, because the inhabitants of the different villages swiftly separated and set off in various directions back home, chanting psalms.

"How about it?" bellowed Master Jehuda exultantly. "Are there Sabbaths as superb as that back where you come from?"

"No, there aren't," answered Uri with conviction.

THEY BECAME RECONCILED TO THE NOTION THAT URI WAS UNFIT FOR any sort of agricultural work.

He would not have to plow again, the Lord preserve us; it was enough that Theo had brought just one drought on Judaea in one year, it was said, but Uri, with his sharpened sense of hearing, concluded from something in their voices that they did not consider the breaking of the yoke to be as serious a sin as they had originally said, and it seemed that they were not seeking to blame him entirely for the drought which was indubitably persisting.

Jehuda consulted with a few of the wealthier landowners, and they decided that Uri should continue to bind sheaves with the women.

He had to hold in his right hand a short-handled sickle, which had a twisted blade with backward-set teeth on it. In his left hand he grasped the heads of grain and brushed the kernels from them. He was clumsy in doing it, having to brush five or six times until the majority of the grains had fallen to the ground, together with a fair bit of the rest of the ear. That was when it dawned on Uri that he ought to do things the other way around, with the sickle in his left hand and the heads of grain in his right. He tried this new way, but he was immediately jumped on: that was not permitted, it was not the way to do it.

Uri lowered his arms dejectedly; if a person was not allowed to be left-handed in Judaea, then he was not going to work.

The work supervisor, who treated him like a delicate, fragile vessel, suggested he bunch smaller sheaves into bigger ones, but Uri was still slow.

In that case he'd better lug the sheaves.

Uri's back and waist ached, so he went to tell the driver, who, whether he liked it or not, was obliged to assign him to work with the women who took care of sweeping up the grain.

Uri suspected that the supervisor reported back to Master Jehuda every evening what he had gotten him to do (in short, nothing) and Master Jehuda would approve any new suggestion from the supervisor.

The sweeping-up went better. All that had to be done was to sweep together the dried grains, pack them into sacks, and carry them off on a cart or on their backs to a threshing floor at the outskirts of the village, where the grain was shaken out. The sacks were taken back to the fields, because there were not enough sacks but a lot of grain to be transported.

This was the *goren*, the threshing ground, and it had to be at least fifty cubits beyond the outskirts of any town or village. Uri gazed around and asked where this village's outskirts were, as he could not see any boundary. The women tittered: the village's limits were imaginary, and this threshing ground was exactly fifty cubits from them. The fence around the threshing ground was formed by prickly bushes so that when the wind picked up, it would catch the grain; this was one reason why the threshing ground could not be located in a high and open place.

They related the story—"that was when you were not yet with us"—of how they would wet the ground first with water then set oxen loose to tamp the soil down solidly. They would repeat the wetting for several days, and the oxen would tamp the ground for several days, and, as he could see, the consistency was just fine.

They would then set to scattering the grain around with spades.

The grains were covered with husks and other bits of chaff. Uri found it hard to envisage how the grains would be picked out from a sea of what looked like debris. All the same, he too turned back with the others to pack more of it into the sacks.

They were treading a good, thick heap of crop by the time a strange treadmill appeared on the threshing ground one fine day. Uri recalled that he had seen something of the kind on the very first day: a plank drag contraption on two stone wheels, drawn by a pair of oxen, which left a trail after it. Now he was able to see one close up and from underneath. The plank was not very wide, about two feet or so, and another plank, some two or three times as long and studded irregularly with basaltic rocks, was fixed under the axle of the stone wheels. The women said the device was called a *morag*, or a threshing board. The supervisor, who seemingly could not do enough to make good the damage caused by the stick blow he had meted out previously, declared proudly that this was an instrument used by Jews alone in the world and unknown anywhere else. Threshing was done elsewhere too, of course, but in such a way as the Arabs, for instance, did it, with the oxen being driven around on the heads of grain, whereas in Syrian villages a stick was used to beat out the grain from the chaff, as of course was the case in Judaea with lighter grains, but a morag was something that could only be found in Judaea, and what a wonderful device it was too, being Jewish.

Uri watched as the oxen set off on the carpet of grain, with the rocks set under the plank tearing into the heap and, as Uri saw when he bent over, most of the grains dropping away from the husks.

The ox-drawn sledge would be passed slowly two or three times over the crop, then it was taken out to the fields, because it could also be used where the ground was firm.

However, Uri could still not see how the grain was going to be picked out.

"It is left like this," said the supervisor, "while we wait for a wind."

Uri put heads of grain into sacks for three days, and his back was getting used to the work by the time the wind picked up. It was noon. Everyone left the field and hurried toward the threshing ground. By the time they got there the threshing floor was full of people, each beating away with a wide, flat, wooden-handled bronze shovel called a *mizreh*.

Women and men alike had begun digging into the heap of grain, swiftly lifting the mizreh above their heads to toss the crop into the air.

The crop rose in the breeze to rain down on their heads and get caught up in their hair, and they sneezed and laughed as they bent down to scoop up another shovelful of the crop into the air.

Uri also picked up a mizreh and did likewise. He too sneezed, spat chaff from his lips, blew the straw and grains from his nose.

By the time they had finished, the breeze had also died down, but by then they were surrounded largely by grain, the heavier parts, as the breeze had blown away the lighter husks and chaff.

That's clever, Uri thought.

The supervisor asked Uri if he wanted to be one of the guards; if he did, he would not have to fill any more sacks.

Uri agreed.

He did not have to fill any more sacks or do any more flailing; he could sleep by day, and when evening drew in he would stroll out with a few men to the threshing ground, staying there with them until a new day dawned, when they would be replaced by some elderly women who, though she might not be able to withstand even the weakest of robbers, could, on the other hand, unleash horrific screams, which were more effective.

A crop that size was worth stealing, he came to understand the first night, so the grain needed to be guarded every night from now on until the wheat was milled.

"Who would steal it?" Uri asked.

"Robbers," he was told in some wonder, as if he were being instructed on a widely known natural phenomenon.

Uri was interested in robbers, but he had no desire to say anything publicly on the subject. Were there any in that area? They were to be found anywhere caves existed, and caves were to be found everywhere. Anywhere the Creator, blessed be the Eternal One, had let slip an opportunity to make a cave, robbers would gouge a lair out for themselves. They too need to eat, so they steal.

"Are they entitled to the pe'ah?" asked Uri.

Anyone who was needy could take from the pe'ah, and robbers, let's be honest, are needy. They are not wealthy, because if they were they would be bankers in Jerusalem.

They could laugh at that.

"Can't we steal from it?" Uri queried further.

The men were astonished. Well, the riddled grain was measured, hadn't Uri seen? No. Well, anyway it was a separate team of men engaged to do that; the grain they were guarding right now had been measured, and tomorrow or the day after would be taken away to a barn and guarded there. A new lot of the freshly reaped grain would be brought here, and when that had been flailed and winnowed, that too would have to be guarded. So it would go to the end of the reaping season in Av, or even Elul.

That process could be shortened, Uri supposed, if all the plots were harvested at the same time, and naturally also sown at the same time in the winter. He even said as much, but they did not understand what he was going on about. Uri repeated it, adding that they would gain a bunch of time in the summer and could occupy themselves with something else.

That was not allowed, they said in alarm. It was prohibited to sow all the seeds at the same time! If some calamity were to befall the crop, then it would all be lost. The sowing was spread over two months for that reason, and the reaping over two or three months, but it had never been the case that all of the sown seed had been lost, thanks be to the Everlasting Lord, who had enjoined that it was prohibited to sow all the seeds at once.

Uri then inquired what sort of people his companions were, and they in turn recounted all the ways to get engaged in plowing or the other agricultural jobs there were for those who had no land, or were slaves, or were not firstborn sons, or had been obliged to sell their father's land because the family failed to hit on a decent way to share it out after he died.

Many men went to Jerusalem in search of work, but there was no work in Jerusalem. It was impossible to find employment among the building works on the Temple as those jobs were inherited; there were around twenty thousand men working there, but it had been impossible for generations now to gain admittance to that sort of work. The Temple building workers were even paving the streets now, that was the latest fad, and it was impossible on that account even to obtain a job as a street paver. There were not many being taken on by the Jewish police force, because their pay was too high, and anyway the police did not do a thing; all they did was supervise in Temple Square and sometimes beat people up, and that was only when the three big feast days came around. Otherwise they just sunned themselves.

The craftsmen who sold mementos during the holidays were not taking people on either, and even if they could one could not rent a room in Jerusalem if you had not been a house owner for generations—though you could make a tidy sum from that during the holidays.

There were many men who went to Jerusalem despite all that. Many preferred begging and sleeping out in the streets to being robbers. They were tolerated when they used what they made begging to pay off the police, but they still kept getting kicked out of the City. Those wretches had finally lost touch with the land, even though it was both the Holy Land and holy in being meant for agriculture, even if it had not long belonged to the Jews.

Uri asked if the lands were redistributed every fifty years as the laws of Moses required. One of the guards that day was an old man who had lived for seventy years, and he said that there had been no redistribution yet, and he did not expect to see one either, even if he lived another seventy years.

None of Uri's fellow guards owned any land; they were all peasants but landless. The well-off landowners did not need to watch crops by night.

Master Jehuda was also landless, he was informed, because he was a tenant, but he didn't cultivate his land himself; he sublet it, which he was free to do. Master Jehuda was a good man—and a very learned man, because he was able to explain the laws. He railed nicely against usurers, and he was right to do so because usurers and tax collectors were the wickedest people on Earth, even if they were Jews.

Master Jehuda also lent out money, noted someone in the darkness, when a cloud just happened to be covering the moon.

Yes, he lent out money, that was true, came the answer, also in the dark, but only for low interest, and Master Jehuda himself had explained not long ago that this was allowed under the laws.

A protracted dispute started over whether Master Jehuda was *aris*, a tenant, or *hokker*, a landlord, since it made a big difference. An aris only rented the land for a year or two, and he passed on a portion of the crop, usually half, to the landlord. A hokker, on the other hand, rented the land under terms whereby he did not pay the landowner a certain fraction of the crop but rather a fixed amount of money that was stipulated in advance in the contract.

In the long run, someone said, it was all the same, because the good and the bad years canceled each other out, although it might matter in the short term.

Yes, but then Master Jehuda had been renting land for a long time.

Indeed, but there was no way of knowing from whom.

It turned out that in fact the night watchmen had no clue whose land they were working on for the bread and vinegar.

They did agree, though, that Master Jehuda could not be a *sokker*, who paid a money rental for a short tenancy.

Then, among the guards, some were *sattels*, who contracted for a season for half of the crop but also took on the job of night watchman because they would return to their big family after the spring sowing and do nothing until the next spring.

A *sakkir*, also to be found among the guards, lived on leasehold land in a small shack. He also received board through the goodwill of the supervisor and a sum of money when he left. The extremes of the contracts were one week and seven years, but normally it would be for three years, especially if the person was unmarried. Another guard had not married either, but he was older than thirty and would never have a family of his own. Uri took a look at him at dawn; he had no more than two teeth left in his mouth and ground his bread soaked in vinegar with his gums.

There was not one *ikker*, a farmer, among Uri's companions, but all the more *po'els*, that is, journeymen, working for a day's pay. The po'els did not tire of repeating to Uri that if he worked as a po'el, he would be obliged to receive the wage in advance, which was four or five leptons, or, if he could drive a hard bargain, as much as seven leptons a day, on top of which they were obliged to give him bread—one and a half slices.

One of their number was an older man, who had managed to find wives for his sons and husbands for all but one of his daughters. He had sold what property he owned—a decent-sized piece of land with four plots of barley and three of wheat—then leased it back from the new owner. There would have been no other way for him to find the dowry for his daughters and give some support to his sons in starting their new, independent lives; even his house was not his own.

"Whom does it belong to?" Uri asked.

"I don't know," said the old man. "The person who bought it from me sold it straightaway, but I'm still paying him and he's paying the new owner. I asked who that was, but he wouldn't say. Perhaps it's a priest in Jerusalem who will later sell it to the Edomites."

"Your sons will recover your land for you," someone said in the dark. "They'll drive out the foreigners and recover it!"

"If only they would!" the old man said gloomily. "It was my father's land, Jewish land. If only they would recover it!"

Uri's companions were in tattered rags and hungry, just like him.

There was no bread for the night's work, nothing at all, and they would get only two leptons in the morning when the women relieved them. That had become a tradition, and that was what they said to Uri again and again each morning, as if this were the first time he'd heard it; the women could scream loudly if they were attacked by robbers, and it was easier to chase robbers by day.

Uri then asked how Master Jehuda made his livelihood.

The question received uncertain responses. Carpenter, yes, he had been that, but for a long time all the work had been done by his assistants, and he was rather tight-fisted about paying them, which was within his rights because he was the master. He was a well-to-do man as he rented land and employed people to cultivate it; he personally did not work, because he was the personification of the law. A good master he was too, because he was good at administering justice.

"Is the master really a judge?" Uri asked.

"Most certainly he is. What else would he be?"

"And there's no priest out this way?"

Again they did not understand what he was asking at first, but eventually they caught on.

There was no priest within three days' walking distance; the only priests were in Jerusalem, but there were many thousands of them.

There had been priests out in the country in the olden days, but then they had seen very little of their share of tithe paid for the priesthood, the sacrificial offering from the harvest, which was all collected in Jerusalem, so it was better for the priests to move closer, since the tithe was what they fed on, and the offspring of priestly families went up from the country to Jerusalem, and now only the odd token priest remained in the provinces.

But even when they were there, not all of them were in a good position. There were starving priests in Jerusalem too, because their share of the sacrificial offerings was decided by drawing lots, and that lottery was always open to dispute. The high priests, along with their favorites, took their cut, and everyone else got what was left; it was hard living on scraps.

This arrangement was not against the masters' interest anyway; in the country it was the master craftsmen who passed judgment, and anyone who was literate could be a prayer leader. In the country it was the masters who led the people; the priests did so only in Jerusalem, and even there, to be sure, the big masters still have considerable prestige, because they were also to be found in the Great Council.

283

"Is Master Jehuda in the habit of leading the prayers?" Uri was curious. His companions could not recall ever having heard him leading the prayers, but then that was not his business. Let him explain the law and pass judgments in accordance with it. There were a great many lawsuits in Judaea; Master Jehuda had a difficult job keeping up, which was why he was so restless and roared all the time. Responsibility lay heavily on his shoulders; he had put on weight to bear it. That was why his sons had fled to far-off areas, all of them marrying in Transjordan. Master Jehuda's sons had left him because they could not stand his temper tantrums.

It was good being able to spend the nights among the guards, wrapped up in warm blankets. Sweltering as it was by day, the nights were cool. The dew at dawn surprised Uri to the point that he would lick it from the bushes, he was so taken with the idea that the Everlasting Lord brought forth moisture even in such torrid weather.

It was also good that at last he was able to do exactly the same thing, in exactly the same way, and as well as the others. Any idiot, any am ha'aretz, can keep an overnight vigil, of course, but Uri did it even better; he never dropped off to sleep, whereas from time to time the others did. But then again, they were not looking to do a better job of something that any fool could do.

Uri was expecting to be questioned about Rome and the big, wide world, and to have to answer lots of questions about which he had no clue, but that didn't happen; people took note of the fact that Uri had been born in Rome and also lived there, and the information had spread around that the Jews in Rome bought everything in shops, which the peasants had trouble coming to terms with, but Uri was asked about nothing else.

Or rather, he was asked if he had spoken with the emperor.

It was a word that they uttered somewhat dubiously, and it occurred to Uri that perhaps they might not even know who the present emperor was by name. Indeed, from the standpoint of a Roman Jew it made no difference either. Whoever the emperor was, he ruled over them.

He told them that he had not spoken to the emperor.

The Judaean peasants shook their heads in disapproval.

An emperor's role was to get to know his subjects, hear their complaints, and take good suggestions to heart. He should not step into the Lord's shoes and have statues made of him or his image minted on coins.

Uri pointed out that the peasants were not allowed to see a high priest eye-to-eye, but that was different, they said: a high priest was not an emperor.

Uri maintained doggedly that they hadn't seen the prefect either.

A prefect was only a prefect; he didn't count.

"But the emperor is your emperor too," said Uri, "and you also haven't seen him."

"He's not our emperor but theirs."

"Whose is that?"

"The Edomites."

"I see. So, what about me? Does that make me a full-fledged Edomite?" Uri tried to pin them down.

That proved a trickier question than they initially thought, and two nights was not enough to get to the bottom of it. After all, Theo was Jewish just like them, but then he was also living among the sinful Edomites who were enemies of the Israelites. This made Theo sinful because he was unclean and lived among the unclean.

"Except he is here in Judaea right now. Is he sinful here?"

"Here he's not sinful because he is cleansed among us."

"And if he goes back, then what?"

"Then he becomes unclean again."

"Is everyone in the Diaspora unclean, even if they keep their faith?"

Opinions on that were exceedingly divided, but most of them thought that he would indeed be unclean. Every Jew should reside in the dwelling place of his ancestors. The Eternal One had given them Canaan, and everyone was under an obligation to fight dispersal in his own way. If that could not be while he was alive, then he should certainly return to the Holy Land after death.

Their advice to Uri was not to go back to Rome; he was in a good place here. No one who farmed the land starved to death; he also received two slices of bread, though he hardly did anything, and he should appreciate that. He could also drink free wine every Sabbath, and if he were to learn how to plow eventually, he would get daily wages, no small amount at that, and within half a year he'd be able to buy himself a pair of sandals. If he was looking to start a family, he could do that; he was the right age, and there were heaps of girls here who were just ready for the picking.

They warned him not to miss out on the next time they had to take their tents to Jerusalem, on the High Holy Day of Yom Kippur, the Day of Atonement, and the days that follow—a long holiday that everyone from the neighborhood attended right through to the end. He should go up onto the Mount of Olives, where the marriageable girls danced every day and anyone could pick and choose to his heart's content.

Girls would be dressed up very nicely for the occasion, having sewn the white linen dresses themselves. Girls from the neighborhood all danced there at the beginning of autumn—even those whose fathers kept them hidden at home all year, either because they were exceedingly pretty creatures, the apples of their fathers' watchful eyes, or because they were shamefully hideous. But at Sukkot, the Festival of Booths, all the girls danced up there at the Mount of Olives, pretty and ugly alike, and that is somewhere Theo really should visit, they said. He wouldn't come back empty-handed, they'd guarantee it.

There, in that peaceful Judaean night, Uri very much longed to look at the girls on the Mount of Olives, though he had no idea where it was located in relation to his prison cell and the Antonia. He longed to take his pick among the girls and to satisfy his duties to married life not just on Fridays but on every single blessed day that the Lord gave them.

He asked them if they had chosen brides for themselves on the Mount of Olives.

No, not them, but lots had.

"Which of you are married, anyway?" he inquired.

A few were, but most were unmarried. One needed a lot of money to start a family, but Theo could do that because his father would surely send him money from Edom.

Uri did not feel it was his duty to enlighten them as to his family's financial situation, as they wouldn't understand in any case.

It became clear that many rich Roman Jewish heads of families gave financial support to family members left behind in Judaea, even if the fathers or grandfathers had never even seen them. The shores and provinces of the Great Sea were interwoven with far-reaching, invisible family spider's webs, and Uri was not in the least surprised when he was told that there were even people in nearby villages who, being the relatives of prosperous Jews living in the Parthian Empire, sometimes quite unexpectedly received an allowance of one kind or another from Babylon. It wasn't unusual for even the most learned masters who specialized in this sort of thing to be unable to disentangle their precise ties of kinship, yet all the same these unexpected gifts arrived from afar.

It was among these uneducated and illiterate peasants keeping watch over the crop by night that Uri came across a marvel with an exceptionally good memory. He was unable to say how old he was, and he too was called Simon, like the magus, and he had not left the village even once in his life. But he was able to retain every single thing he had ever heard; his memory was unable to delete a single thing. That was how the Everlasting Lord had created him, and the wretched creature was totally satisfied with his lot. He was a short, bald, pot-bellied, lazy man, with lots of laughter lines under his eyes. Whatever subject was under discussion he was able to string together such a multiplicity of anecdotes, with explanations tagged on, that his companions just couldn't stop laughing. Simon had no liking for keeping vigil, but then he did not like to plow either; he preferred not to eat for days, or else he gleaned and roasted the grain somewhere. He had no family and no place to live.

Uri dared quietly to ask this Simon the name of the village whose hospitality he happened to be enjoying.

"Beth Zechariah," said Simon.

That was what the hunchback had said, wasn't it!

"It's quite a famous village," declared the homeless, roofless Simon. "When the Hasmoneans revolted, Judah Maccabee, the son of Mattathias, made an alliance with the Romans, occupied Jerusalem, and raised a new altar, but Antiochus Epiphanes, at the head of an army of fifty thousand foot soldiers, five thousand horsemen, and one hundred elephants, invaded Judaea from Syria, occupied Bethsura, and razed it, leaving no trace, and it was right here, in the defile where Beth Zechariah lies, that Antiochus clashed with Judah and his forces. And Judah's younger brother, Eleazar ben Mattathias, singled out the biggest of the elephants, supposing that it was on the back of this one that King Antiochus was seated. He wounded the elephant from below, in the belly, and it collapsed, burying Eleazar beneath it. It was not on this elephant, however, that Antiochus was seated but a common soldier, as a trick. The Jews lost the battle too, and Antiochus went on to occupy Jerusalem, but he was not in a position to do much, as his food ran out, so he trailed back to Syria. Judah Maccabee could not handle the opportunity, and he fell in another battle, and the next of his bothers, Jonathan the Hasmonean, was also killed..."

"When was all this?" Uri asked.

"A long time ago."

"Is there any trace of that battle?"

"There is."

"Have they found the bones of men and elephants?"

"No," said the homeless Simon. "Those turned into earth, to grass, to trees, and to barley. We have been eating them ever since, and we are living—that's the trace."

Uri would have been happy to carry on as night watchman until reaping was over, but it got to the ears of Master Jehuda that Uri was deriving pleasure from chatting with the others, and to stop him asking any more questions he ordered that Uri stop working as a guard.

The supervisor put him on a day shift, against his better judgment. Uri was assigned the task of driving the birds off a rather large field.

It did not go well.

In addition to Uri's efforts, there were scarecrows set up on poles in the field, but there was no wind to make them flap, and the birds were no longer startled by them.

On the first day Uri raced across the field assiduously whenever he spotted a bird, and the birds would take to the air, settle on a tree, and wait. The moment Uri sat down, the birds swooped down on the field to pick seeds. Uri would run after them, the birds would fly up, settle on a tree again, and wait.

Uri was dog-tired before noon.

He sat on the harvested field and watched the birds feeding. The birds, impudent creatures, dared to get close and peck. Uri searched for stones and threw them, but not a single one hit.

The vague outlines of a human shape could be seen moving around a neighboring field as well, so Uri got to his feet and worked his way over. The scarecrow on that field was a small boy of maybe seven or eight.

He had a slingshot, and around him were the carcasses of something like eight birds.

Uri inquired where a slingshot could be obtained. The boy took fright, thinking Uri wanted to take his, but Uri reassured him that was not his intention, so the boy told him that everyone made his own.

"What happens to these birds, then?" he asked.

"They get eaten by other birds," the boy said.

"Not us?"

"These are unclean."

The boy went off to get near another bird with the slingshot.

Why, though, was he collecting the carcasses of the birds he had shot down? Did he perchance get something like a prutah each for them? Did someone check?

Uri lounged, and occasionally lobbed a stone at the birds, of which they took not the slightest notice. Any bird that dared to hop closer, he inspected more thoroughly. How hideous they were, when it came down to it, but then again, how free. He stretched out on the ground, closed his eyes, and waited for them to come over and tear his liver out. He would never have imagined he could so hate these living creatures, though it was not hate so much as envy.

That evening he said to Master Jehuda that the job was not going well; he was not a seven-year-old boy, he should be given something else to do. Master Jehuda said morosely that he would think about it.

He came up with the idea that Uri should riddle grain.

It was the supervisor who imparted the decision, and Uri was not pleased; he took exception to the fact that it was not Master Jehuda who had communicated this personally. Uri was by this point sleeping in the barn with the master's chairs and tables, where the master's assistants sawed and trimmed off with adzes the excess wood and produced joints and dovetails. The master looked in from time to time to check that they were working, so he would have had plenty of chances to speak with Uri.

But who knows, maybe this would be another adventure. He did not know how to do the riddling, and so far he had spoken little to the womenfolk; perhaps they might have the odd thing or two to say. It might be interesting.

Riddling was done not just by married women but also by young girls. They began at first light and continued until the sun went down. Lamps and oil were expensive, so they did not work in the evenings, even during the harvest period.

The riddling was done at the edge of the threshing ground. Even after it had been threshed and winnowed, the grain still contained debris. In the next step, *kevarah*, women sat and shook a round sieve with fiber mesh attached to its bottom. The grains would fall down through the gaps, and the debris left on the surface would then be skimmed off and set aside to be mixed with straw to make fodder, or else pounded in a mortar and mixed into animal dung. With any remaining chaff that was saved, it could be used for laying fires.

A use was found, therefore, for everything that the Everlasting Lord had given man to use.

But this was not the end; the grain would be sieved several times before it was taken off, and after it had been ground (that, too, was women's work), it was jiggled through finer and finer sieves—so went the riddling.

Uri would never have thought that there could be so much involved in turning grain into flour.

When the supervisor led Uri to join them, saying that he should be given a sieve, the women hardly glanced up before going on with their riddling.

Uri lifted the sieve, finding it to be heavier than he would have imagined, and watched how the women riddled.

They weren't too attractive, he ascertained, and they all wore scarves so their heads would not be baked by the sun. The women hummed unself-consciously, swaying a little back and forth as they sat, picking out the chaff, scooping up a fresh palmful of grain onto the sieve, swirling it, shaking it, and again picking out the bits of muck...

An awful job, Uri thought: to do that the whole day long could drive a person mad.

Either the women were mad, or else they had gotten used to it from doing it since they were little; they did it without complaining, singing softly to themselves. They only let up in the early afternoon, when the lunch arrived: two thin slices of barley bread, which the servants dunked in vinegar before handing over.

Pitchers of water were also brought, which the women, one after another, took deep drafts from before setting aside to drink from later on.

Uri, being a man, was not offered any water.

He accepted the bread dipped in vinegar; he had come to the realization that the vinegar was good, after all, for warding off feelings of thirst.

By then he had begun to feel as if his shoulder and upper arm were going to break off and his back disintegrate. His legs went to sleep from all the sitting, and he could no longer feel them.

He gritted his teeth and suffered wordlessly, sieving until the sun went down.

These women were veritable Goliaths, and he the David who had not been given a sling; a sieving David. It would be no surprise if even these women had a laugh at his expense.

The cereal grew in one big heap beside the women, the discards in another. But in Uri's case there were just two small heaps.

The dwindling sun was ruddy in the sky when the women finished their work; Uri too. The women shoveled the grain into sacks and put a canvas sheet knotted at the edges over the dross so that it would not be blown away by the wind. Uri was unable to shovel; indeed, he could barely get to his feet. Sieving was worse than anything he had been pestered into doing before.

No one spoke to him the whole day long, and the women said very little even to one another, given that a man was among them.

He staggered back to the barn and dropped down. He did not get his supper because by then he was deep asleep.

The next day at dawn, one of Master Jehuda's assistants shook him awake, and he set off for the threshing ground. He was going to have to stick it out, he thought. He had asked about breakfast, whereupon the assistant, a spotty-faced youth, scoffed, "Later, out there, with the women."

He loathes me. But why would that be? He carries out better work than I have. What does it matter here if I am a Roman citizen?

He mused on what the countless Roman citizens would say if they were obliged to sieve the day long for their food. There was little doubt they would rise up and the emperor would fall.

He picked up his sieve, plunged one hand into the grain, sprinkled it onto the sieve, and began to joggle it.

There were still pains shooting through his right shoulder; his legs developed pins and needles and went dead almost instantly. It was only early in the morning; when would it get to the evening?

Uri sieved away with his teeth gritted, though he did ask himself why he had to suffer every indignity without saying a word. Anyone else in his position would have rebelled long, long ago. Rebellion was fair enough, but what form might it take here?

I ought to escape, he conjectured.

He knew where from, but where would he escape to?

Back to Rome? Yes, but how?

Roving on his own, exposed to attack from any quarter?

He would be caught, taken back to Jerusalem, and thrown in prison again.

What have you meted out on me, O Righteous Everlasting One, and for what reason?

It seemed implausible that he would be able to continue sitting among strange women in Judaea, shaking a stupid, round object all day long simply because they did so.

He then noticed that he was humming quietly.

The women were in fact praying all the time! And now I am praying too!

The finding astonished him.

Perhaps this was the origin of psalms—this appalling joggling. The psalms may have been wordless to begin with, and it was only later that they were given lyrics. The Eternal One, the One and Only Lord, had not understood words, but he could have listened to chanting. It was obligatory for the Eternal One once he had offered an alliance with the people. I, who am a member of the Everlasting Lord's chosen people, meet that alliance by renewing it day after day; let Him now do the same.

"That's not the way to do it!" Uri heard.

The voice signaled that it was one of the more elderly women who had addressed him; he could not see her face, as it was obscured by her scarf.

"Then how?"

"More circular movements."

The woman carried on sieving. Uri watched. She performed broad movements, so that grains dropped through over the entire surface of the screen. Uri looked down before his feet. His own pile was small because the grains were able to riddle through his sieve only at the center, whereas the diameter of the pile in front of the woman's feet was indeed wider.

Uri groaned.

He was being called on to make an even bigger effort when even as things were his arms were almost falling off! The real place for these women was in a circus; they would make a much more skillful job of choking lions than the gladiators did.

Uri put down his sieve and sat there, motionless.

I'm not a slave, he thought. If I'm going to be kept as a slave, they're going to have to strike me down. That's enough of this.

He cast a stealthy glance to both sides. The women were waggling their sieves. From this comes the bread that sustains us; from this comes the sacrificial bread on which the Almighty is sustained when it is incinerated on the altar on high days and its smoke rises up to Him.

His stomach rumbled when it came to mind that he had been late when he reached the threshing ground and missed breakfast. He looked around. There was no sign that the women had been given anything: not a crumb to be seen. They would be bringing it later.

He felt ashamed.

These women, they were just as much the Lord's creatures as he was. And they shake their sieves, and their arms are also falling off, but they keep on shaking. Their lives were terrible. That was something those lazy night watchmen who kept dozing off, to whose number he had been privileged to belong for a few days, had said nothing about. Why not?

He picked up his sieve, plunged one hand into the grain, sprinkled it onto the sieve and began to joggle it.

And hummed.

May the Lord hear what He had created. Look down and see and be ashamed.

IT IS NOT EASY TO CATCH THE MOMENT WHEN A COMMUNITY ACCEPTS A person. When he looks back, of course, it is possible to tell that he has been accepted, but it is hard to reconstruct the crucial event. Uri's hunch was that it was the moment during the second day of riddling when, having defiantly put down his sieve, he raised it up again. Right then, he was accepted by the women as one of them. They disregarded the fact that the Everlasting Lord had created him as a man, which is to say, an enemy. From that moment on he was considered to be a female, one of them. A slave.

Uri was wrong, however; he was not yet accepted then, only the next day.

What happened at daybreak that day was that Uri, tormented by the pains in his back and shoulders, with teeth gritted, set to the sieving, and he sieved and sieved, but somehow it went even worse than before: there was almost no debris left on the net of the sieve but all the more flax among the grain on the ground. Uri disconsolately waggled the wretched device around, making no progress.

The women and girls next to him were so engrossed in their own work that they were not even humming; they shook their sieves, but in silence.

That silence was suspicious to Uri. He looked at them, puzzled, but their faces were now even better veiled by their shawls. The sun was still low in the sky; it was warm but not yet scorching. There was no sense in the girls and women covering their heads in the morning. He had covered his own head the day before with a mantle (a hand-me-down that Master Jehuda had given him) but had been late in doing it, as by then the crown of his head was already sunburned.

Uri looked at the sieve sitting on his lap, then lifted it up close to his eyes.

The fiber mesh seemed different: the holes were larger. Uri made a careful inspection to see what was making it seem so. He discovered that every other strand had been removed, indeed in some places even two successive fibers. The fibers were pinned to the side of a wooden frame that had been bent into a circle. The pins were still in place, but some of them had been pried loose and the threads pulled out. Any debris would fall through the sieve, rendering his labors completely useless.

He looked up. The women were engrossed in their work.

Uri laughed out loud, chortling ever more whole-heartedly. Some person or persons had devoted yesterday evening to playing a trick on him. Before his eyes emerged a picture of an assiduous woman who had spent part of her night pulling strands out of his sieve instead of sleeping. Perhaps others had also been present and looked on eagerly, even helping with advice as to how many strands to pull out—the idea of not just every other one could have occurred to someone. There have not been many times when I was deemed worthy of that much attention, he thought, and roared with laughter.

All of a sudden, every single girl and woman also broke out laughing, and there must have been around three dozen of them too. The whole gathering chuckled happily.

A woman then got to her feet and brought Uri a new sieve. He thanked her, took it, checked that it was good, and, with difficulty choking back his laughter, resumed work.

One lunchtime several days later, Uri asked what would have happened if he had not laughed at the trick but instead had run to the supervisor and told on them. You would have had a hard time of it among us, came the answer.

It was a pleasant, gray-haired lady who responded; her face was wrinkled, but she still had her good looks, especially her deep-blue eyes. Uri greatly regretted that she was not twenty years younger, or he was not twenty years older, because they would have made a handsome pair, the two of them, but the Lord had other plans, blessed be He.

The day it happened, though, Uri carried on sieving, but at noon, when they were chomping on their lunch (all of the more elderly ones doing so toothlessly), it was she who said to Uri, "There's no point in your riddling with us, Theo. We'll do your work; you'd do better keeping us amused."

"Fair enough," said Uri, "but what should I do?"

"Tell us stories," the woman said.

"What stories should I tell? Nothing interesting has ever happened to me."

"Not stories about yourself but about the big wide world, and the afterlife."

Uri pondered. He could find things to say about the world, but the afterlife was another matter!

"In our country, in Edom," he said, "people don't concern themselves much with the afterlife... They know nothing about it."

"Others do, however," said the lady. "We have scrolls, only we can't read them. Men occasionally try to make them out, but they don't have the time; they are tired out by the evening when they might be able to read. They'd rather curl up and snore. People say you can read. Read out the scrolls to us, and we'll work in the meantime."

"Is that permitted, then?" Uri inquired.

Several voices clamored loudly that it was not forbidden, so it was allowed. They would perform Uri's work; the supervisor could hardly object.

That was a bargain Uri was happy to enter. He would never have thought that scrolls existed in a godforsaken village such as this. What could they be?

That day he went on riddling, but the next morning one of the women thrust a thick scroll into his hands. Years ago, it had been left in the village by a wandering prophet, whom Master Jehuda had driven away in a great hurry, because he was proclaiming exactly what Master Jehuda did when inspired. The woman said that there had once been a time when her husband had tried reading out short passages to her, but he had gotten bored with that: reading did not come easily to him, and it had been impossible to persuade him to carry on. Yet the scroll concerned the one thing that was of paramount concern to people: what happens to us after we die.

The scroll must have passed through many hands, as the edges of the parchment were frayed. Uri carefully blew the dust off his sieve, and placed the scroll in that.

"I'd like to wash my hands," he said. "I don't want to smudge it."

Two women jumped up and brought Uri pitchers of drinking water to pour onto Uri's hands. That was significant, drinking water being in such short supply, but the women's thirst for knowledge was greater than their bodily thirst. Uri asked them to take great care in pouring it out: slowly and just a little. That was how he rinsed his hands.

His tunic was mucky, and he could not dry his hands on it, so he dangled them and let them dry like that. When they were dry, he carefully took the scroll out of the sieve.

He sat down on the ground, blown-clean sieve in lap, scroll in hand. It was not as hefty as a Torah but it was as bulky as some of Ovid's shorter works. It was not rolled onto a stick, just around itself. He threaded his left fist into the empty center of the roll and with his right hand he cautiously, delicately pulled the sheet to the right, only just enough so that he would be able to read the two columns in which the copyists had transcribed the first page. He looked at the text: it was upside down and in Greek. He rewound it and now poked his right fist into the scroll's central gap and pulled it out with his left hand, then just when the scroll was about to roll itself onto his left arm, he grasped it at the bottom, between the left index finger and thumb, and pulled it gingerly, gently, leaving it to rewind on the left side of its own accord.

To begin he read slowly, hesitantly, having to get accustomed to the lettering, the omissions, and the language, which, though it was Greek, was an old Greek, with Hebrew words cropping up every now and then. The author of the Greek text must have translated it from the Hebrew, and any words that he did not know he had left in his mother tongue. He had become accustomed to this by the time he had reached the fourth or fifth page; anything he could not decipher he eked out from his imagination. If the ensuing sentences contradicted his guesswork, he went back and reread it and retranslated it to Aramaic as best he could. The riddling women did not make any reproving remarks on his jumping back in the text or his corrections; they were glad the reading helped them forget their physically punishing and soul-destroying work.

URI WAS HOLDING THE BOOK OF ENOCH, HE ASCERTAINED FROM THE very first sentence.

He had heard of the existence of such a scroll, but not one person in Rome had a copy of it, or if they did, they were not admitting it, and it was the sort of work that the City's public librarians never collected.

> These are the words of the blessing of Enoch, wherewith he blessed the Elect and righteous, who will be living in the Day of Tribulation, when all the wicked and godless are to be removed...

Enoch begat Methuselah and lived 365 years, no less, as it states in the fifth chapter of Genesis. His father was Jared, who had lived 162 years before he begot Enoch. Like Elijah, Enoch was transported to Heaven in a chariot of fire. He may not even have died and was assumed to Heaven by the Lord in such a manner anyone witnessing it would have died. According to the Torah, his son Methuselah lived 187 years. He was Noah's grandfather. The passage in question being found very near the beginning of the First Book of Moses, it is read out in every single Jewish prayer house on the first Sabbath of every year, not long after one year's reading of the Torah is completed and an immediate ceremonial beginning is made to reading it out again.

Uri was helped in the translation by the fact that the Septuagint, the Greek translation of the Torah made in Alexandria, was also in use in Rome; there it was not necessary to translate the Torah into the vernacular because everyone was familiar with the Greek Torah, and there was only the odd household that kept a Hebrew Torah. On the other hand, the Ten Commandments on the parchment scroll in the mezuzah affixed to the doorpost of every house, as well as in the tiny scroll in the little leather box of every tefillin, were always written in Hebrew.

It occurred to Uri that he had never given any thought before as to what it must be like to live to 365—as many years as there were days in a year by the Roman calendar. Other Jews cannot have found much to get hung up on with that number: that was what was stated in the Torah, and even if it was a fairy tale, it was a true one and there was no need to give it further thought.

> The Holy Great One will come forth from His dwelling, and the Everlasting Lord will tread upon the earth, even on Mount Sinai, and appear in the strength of His might from the heaven of heavens. And all shall be smitten with fear, and the Watchers shall quake. And great fear and trembling shall seize them unto the ends of the earth... And the earth

shall be wholly rent asunder, and all that is upon the earth shall perish, and there shall be a judgment upon all men. But with the righteous He will make peace and will protect the Elect.

Uri read with great trouble, and although the riddling women did not ask him for any correction, he had to retranslate the opening passage to make more sense of it.

He was not in a position to notice, struggling as he was, that it was not the sense of what he was saying so much as his deep, pleasantly ringing bass-baritone voice. Its meaningless music helped the women in their work and swathed their minds in a soothing warmth. It was the voice of a man, who might still be little more than a child, but nevertheless that of a man, not the eternal chirrup of riddling women.

Uri read and translated extemporaneously what was written in the chapter concerning angels:

> And it came to pass, when the children of men had multiplied, that in those days were born unto them beautiful and comely daughters. And the angels, the children of Heaven, saw and lusted after them... And Semjaza was their leader... And they were in all two hundred; who descended in the days of Jared on the summit of Mount Hermon, and they called it Mount Hermon, because they had sworn and bound themselves by mutual imprecations upon it. And these are the names of their leaders: Samlazaz, their leader, Araklba, Rameel, Kokablel, Tamlel, Ramlel, Danel, Ezeqeel, Baraqijal, Asael, Armaros, Batarel, Ananel, Zaqlel, Samsapeel, Satarel, Turel, Jomjael, Sariel. These are their decarchs...

Uri came to a stop. The women went on swirling their sieves.

He asked if they understood the meaning of the word *Decarch*, which he did not know how to translate into Aramaic. They didn't, so he paraphrased the sentence, saying that these were the names of the leaders of each group of ten men. The women nodded with an air of exasperation and waited for him to continue; they had no great wish to understand the exact details of the tale.

That unsettled Uri, who would have liked to give an accurate translation, if any at all. This is where he had the feeling that something more was at work between the women and himself than the translation of a story. But then he was reluctant to go into that, so he went on.

> And all the others, together with them, took unto themselves wives, and each chose for himself one, and they began to go in unto them and to defile themselves with them, and they taught them charms and enchantments, and the cutting of roots, and made them acquainted with plants. And they became pregnant, and they bore great giants, whose height was three thousand ells, who consumed all the acquisitions of men. And when men could no longer sustain them, the giants turned against them and devoured mankind. And they began to sin against birds, and beasts, and reptiles, and fish, and to devour one another's flesh, and drink the blood...

Uri stopped and looked up. The women went on riddling; they were waiting for him to continue. They did not appear to have been shocked by all the monstrosities—the monstrosities in the story, not those in real life. After all, human beings do not normally devour one another's flesh and drink their blood, though they were perfectly capable of imagining these things.

Uri went on.

> And Azazel taught men to make swords, and knives, and shields, and breastplates, and made known to them the metals of the earth and the art of working them, and bracelets, and ornaments, and the use of antimony, and the beautifying of the eyelids, and all kinds of costly stones, and all coloring tinctures...

At this the women perked up, and they asked questions about what those might have been, but Uri plowed on implacably.

> And there arose much godlessness, and they committed fornication, and they were led astray, and became corrupt in all their ways. Semjaza taught enchantments, and root-cuttings, Armaros the resolving of enchantments, Baraqijal taught astrology, Kokabel the constellations, Ezeqeel the knowledge of the clouds, Araqiel the signs of the earth, Shamsiel the signs of the sun, and Sariel the course of the moon. And as men perished, they cried, and their cry went up to Heaven...

Uri glanced up and saw that the women were expecting him to continue, shuttling their sieves impatiently.

The writer who had pieced the book together was not over-endowed with talent and inspiration, Uri reflected. After all, he could not even remember whom he had listed just before as leaders of the groups of ten. He went on translating, seeing that this was what had been asked for, and it was better than riddling or sifting.

> And then Michael, Uriel, Raphael, and Gabriel looked down from Heaven, and they saw much blood being shed upon the earth, and all lawlessness being wrought upon the earth, and they spake unto the Lord... Then said the Most High, the Holy and Great One spake, and sent Uriel to the son of Lamech, and said to him: "Go to Noah and tell him in my name, 'Hide thyself!' and reveal to him the end that is approaching: that the whole earth be destroyed, and a deluge is about to come upon the whole earth, and destroy all that is on it. And now instruct him that he may escape and his seed may be preserved for all the generations of the world."

Uri stopped again. Uriel was his own nickname: it was a jolt to see it written down, and suddenly the text acquired a new relevance. He hoped the name would appear again. He went on.

> And again the Lord said to Raphael: "Bind Azazel hand and foot, and cast him into the darkness: and make an opening in the desert, which is in Dudael, and cast him therein. And place upon him rough and jagged rocks, and cover him with darkness, and let him abide there forever, and cover his face that he may not see light. And on the day of the great judgment he shall be cast into the fire. And heal the earth which the angels have corrupted, and proclaim the healing of the earth, that they may heal the plague, and that all the children of men may not perish through all the secret things that the Watchers have disclosed and have taught their sons. And the whole earth has been corrupted through the works that were taught by Azazel: to him ascribe all sin."

Uri raised his eyes. He did not grasp what the text was driving at, but the women must have done so rather better because they assiduously carried on with their riddling while waiting for him to resume. The women wore scarves for good reason; by now the sun was high in the sky, Uri's own head was being burned, and he was parched. There was a hush. One of the women looked up, removed her own scarf and handed it to Uri.

"You'll get a touch of the sun," Uri said.

"I can pull my robe up over my head," the woman said, and did just that. Uri gratefully knotted the scarf onto his head before carrying on reading the senseless text. It was still better than riddling.

> And to Gabriel said the Lord: "Proceed against the bastards and the reprobates, and against the children of fornication, and destroy the children of fornication and the children of the Watchers from amongst men, and cause them to go forth: send them one against the other that they may destroy each other in battle..." And the Lord said unto Michael: "Go, bind Semjaza and his associates who have united themselves with women so as to have defiled themselves with them in all their uncleanness. And when their sons have slain one another, and they have seen the destruction of their beloved ones, bind them fast for seventy generations in the valleys of the earth, till the day of their judgment and of their consummation, till the judgment that is forever and ever is consummated."

Uri read and translated the whole day long, and for the whole of the week he recounted the scroll, which the owner had asked be returned to her every evening but then gave back each day. By the time Uri, his head reeling, had reached the end, the women asked him to read it again, but now to try a bit harder.

Starting again from the beginning, Uri strove to couch the antiquated language into more everyday Aramaic. The women were amazed that a scroll might be construed in more than one way and recalled details from his halting first effort, which they asked him to recite. Uri tried to explain that the text had been written many generations ago, and meanwhile the Greek language had changed, as Aramaic had, but they could not understand; it was the language they had been handed down by their parents, and they in turn by their parents, and it was the same language. Uri did not push the matter further; he chose to let it spread in the village that Theo was a strange marvel: he could read something once, but not a second time.

The riddling and sifting women—for by then they had done the sifting, which was the final phase of the winnowing process, begun after the grain had been brought back from the mill, and they were riddling the newly threshed grain as it came in—nonetheless enjoyed the tale more the second time around, and when Uri reached the end again, they begged him to read it a third time. By then the supervisor himself was in the habit of hanging around; at first he had merely turned up more often on the pretext of checking the work, but in the end he would perch among them and, enthralled, listen to the adventures of Enoch. Uri had a shrewd suspicion that the plowmen were quite pleased that things had turned out that way, and would repay him for his service when the occasion arose, because during those days, thanks to him, they were spared the rigors of the supervisor's stick.

Another thing also happened.

One day a frail young girl was riddling with her sieve next to Uri. Uri noticed she was radiant in some manner but did not pay it any attention; that evening, however, the girl took off her headscarf, and Uri suddenly felt a deep-seated, tingling pang in his chest. Never before had he seen such loveliness. She had an oval little face, close-knit black eyebrows, long, jet-black hair, dark-brown eyes, a snub nose, nicely arched lips, slim arms, slender wrists, and long, thin fingers. Uri propped his head on his elbows and just gazed, spellbound. The girl sensed it, took one triumphant glance at him from under those black brows, and burst out laughing.

Uri averted his gaze in shame. The spectacle had consumed his entire inner being. He began to fume, because in casting his mind back he distinctly recalled that he had been entranced by the young girl the whole day long. Why was it only now that she was acting as if she had just noticed him?

That night Uri tossed restlessly, unable to sleep, his body no longer drained by work. He would have preferred to sleep but couldn't; in a half-sleeping state he relived the Book of Enoch.

It's not such a bad idea at all, he mused, if every time women were expecting offspring they could see the rotten end that awaited their children and mourn them in advance with their sighs, and their pleas for mercy would be in vain.

It was all very well that Enoch took pity upon the guardian angels mixing with the children of men, and he went off, sat down at the waters of Dan and wrote out their petition. That's practically Homeric, Uri thought, to read this petition in the presence of the Lord of Heaven till he fell asleep—not the Lord but Enoch himself, the author of the petition! Someone finds himself in the presence of the Lord, reads his petition to the Lord and meanwhile falls asleep!

In his dream, visions fell down upon Enoch, apocalyptic visions. That's pretty good as well, Uri thought, and he could see before his eyes the letters, which he had already gone through twice, but even more so the scene that lay behind them, colorful and sharp, and which the writer also saw, it would seem, being able, like Uri, to think pictorially.

In Enoch's vision, clouds invited him and a mist summoned him, lightning hastened him, and the winds lifted him upward; that is how he was borne into Heaven. He reached a wall built of crystals and surrounded by tongues of fire. Enoch went into the tongues of fire and reached a large house with walls or crystal, tessellated floor of crystal, and groundwork all of crystal. Its ceiling was like the paths of the stars, illuminated by lightning flashes, and between them were fiery cherubim, and a flaming fire surrounded the walls, and its portals blazed with fire. And Enoch entered that house, and it was hot as fire and cold as ice. (The author of the scroll must also have been in lands that were farther north than Palestine, Uri supposed in his more prosaic earthly fashion.) And in that house there was a second house, an even greater one built of flames of fire, and in it stood a lofty throne with wheels looking like the shining sun and cherubim. On the throne was seated the Great Glory, and His raiment shone more brightly than the sun and was whiter than any snow. None of the angels could enter that house or behold Him. Ten thousand times ten thousand stood waiting for His orders before Him, who could do anything.

Enoch was also standing there, and the Lord railed against the degenerate angels who had lain with women, saying:

> As for the spirits of Heaven, in Heaven shall be their dwelling, but as for the spirits of the earth which were born upon the earth, on the earth shall be their dwelling. And the spirits of the giants afflict, oppress, destroy, attack, do battle, and work destruction on the earth until the day of the great judgment in which the age shall be consummated.

And the Lord bade Enoch to say to them, "You have no peace."

So much for Heaven as far as the scroll was concerned.

Uri contemplated what more might be added but there wasn't anything. Heaven, it seemed, was not too interesting.

All the more so the earth and the Underworld.

> And they brought me to a place in which those who were there were like flaming fire, and, when they wished, they appeared as men.

Uri recollected that sentence precisely; he had translated it at first sight, and only then had he thought about it.

Man as a fire—not bad. Man as a thing—not bad. Things that could assume human form if they wished. That sort of thing could be read about neither in Greek nor Roman poetry. The person who wrote down the Book of Enoch must have known a thing or two about men. Plato would have been delighted to listen, might have even given its philosophy a once-over.

I too am a flaming fire, Uri reflected. What is so different about being human?

I saw the great rivers and came to the great river and to the great darkness, and went to the place where every flesh walks.

What sort of river was that? What kind of place was that, where every flesh walks? Human flesh?

And I saw a deep abyss, with columns of heavenly fire, and among them I saw columns of fire fall, which were beyond measure alike toward the height and toward the depth. And beyond that abyss I saw a place which had no firmament of the heaven above, and no firmly founded earth beneath it. There was no water upon it, and no birds, but it was a waste and horrible place. I saw there seven stars like great burning mountains, and to me, when I inquired regarding them. The angel said, "This place is the end of Heaven and Earth; this has become a prison for the stars and the host of Heaven. And the stars which roll over the fire are they which have transgressed the commandment of the Lord in the beginning of their rising, because they did not come forth at their appointed times. And He was wroth with them, and bound them till the time when their guilt should be consummated—even for ten thousand years."

Uri liked the idea of the Lord punishing the reluctant stars.

And there was in it four hollow places, deep and wide and very smooth. How smooth are the hollow places and deep and dark to look at. Then Raphael answered, one of the holy angels who was with me, and said unto me, "These hollow places have been created for this very purpose, that the spirits of the souls of the dead should assemble therein, yet that all the souls of the children of men should assemble here. And these places have been made to receive them till the day of their judgment and till the great judgment." I saw a dead man crying, and his voice went forth to Heaven and he cried. And Raphael said: "This is the spirit which went forth from Abel, whom his brother Cain slew, and he cries against him till his seed is destroyed from the face of the earth..."

He can cry for ages, thought Uri.

Enoch then came to the Garden of Righteousness and he saw from afar many very great, beautiful, glorious, and magnificent trees, and the Tree of Knowledge, whose holy fruit they eat and know great wisdom.

> "This," said Raphael, the holy angel, who was with Enoch: "This is the tree of which thy old father and thy aged mother, who were your ancestors, have eaten, and they learned wisdom and their eyes were opened, and they knew that they were naked, and they were driven out of the garden."

Uri was reclining, half-asleep. It was the first time in many months that he had come across letters; he was tired out by the task of translating.

Since he had been compelled to live away from Rome and his books, he had hardly missed exerting any mental effort, and now, in this godforsaken village, here was this prophetic, vision-packed ancient scroll in Greek. An odd coincidence, as if the Lord were guiding him back to his original path.

Never before had he read anything so slowly and scrupulously, so the listeners could fully absorb the material. There were not many scrolls in Judaea—the Torah and a few scrolls of the Psalms certainly. The text struck him more deeply here, precisely because there was nothing else. The more tightly the writing is rationed, the greater the effect it has.

He had been sleeping badly ever since he was forced into employment as a reader. But now the reason he could not sleep was because he saw the little girl, her pretty face, the slender neck, the eyebrows that almost ran together above her nose, the fine dark hairs on her arms and also on her legs. A woman for all that! Uri groaned. A raging emptiness was worrying his insides. A horribly happy torment.

He was apprehensive about getting up the next day. If he translated the scroll once again for the women, was he also going to return to the sieve?

He wished the scroll were longer.

The Eternal One was merciful to him, though; the scroll was in the woman's hands again, and he was asked to read it through yet again, but now starting from the point that concerned the Lord of Spirits, because they had taken a great liking to that bit.

Uri muttered a prayer of thanksgiving as he peered around in search of the young girl. He did not see her, however, so he sighed and went on to read out the Vision of Wisdom seen by Enoch, the son of Jared, the son of Mahalalel, the son of Cainan, the son of Enos, the son of Seth, the son of Adam. On reading and translating it this time, he discovered that this part might well be of more recent origin than the rest. Here there were only Greek words, not any Hebrew. Maybe that meant the scroll was not the work of a single author.

Deepening his already sonorous voice even further, Uri almost crooned through this reading, directing it at the young girl, even though she was not present.

> And when the Righteous One shall appear before the eyes of the righteous, whose elect works hang upon the Lord of Spirits, and light shall appear to the righteous and the elect who dwell on the earth. Where then will be the dwelling of the sinners, and where the resting place of those who have denied the Lord of Spirits? It had been good for them if they had not been born. When the secrets of the righteous shall be revealed and the sinners judged, and the godless driven from the presence of the righteous and elect, from that time those that possess the earth shall no longer be powerful and exalted, and they shall not be able to behold the face of the holy, for the Lord of Spirits has caused His light to appear on the face of the holy, righteous, and elect. Then shall the kings and the mighty perish and be given into the hands of the righteous and holy. And thenceforward none shall seek for themselves mercy from the Lord of Spirits, for their life is at an end.

So taken were the vengeful women by this passage that Uri was obliged to read it out for a fourth time. They even stopped riddling, and kept nodding and calling out: "Yes, that's how it will be; that's exactly right." The more prudent, being fearful of this prophecy, asked him to carry on.

He was unable to do so because one of the women, Rachel by name, said that she had seen the skies open and an angel had descended to take action against the powerful. Rachel had deep-set eyes and looked intently for long periods in one direction. All her limbs were withered. The other women, though, backed her up; what Rachel had said was true, because she had already told them as much earlier. Rachel also related that in her dream she had been visited by the same Gabriel Enoch encountered. Gabriel had spoken of huge rats, but Rachel could not fully understand why, and the angel had not come again to explain further. Still, it was quite certain that he would because she had heard his voice, albeit only briefly, when she was wide awake.

Another woman, Anna, told of how when she was young, when her mother was dying, a prophet had spoken to her about the heavens, and how up there her mother would lie on soft feather bedding and the boils would disappear from her back, and the gangrene of her legs would heal. The boils had disappeared since then, because that had been many, many years ago, and in her dreams she would see her mother on the other side, and she was completely healthy, even more sound than when she had been living in this world.

Others corroborated her claims.

"When our dead relatives visit us in our dreams they are unscathed, and Master Jehuda said that this was no mere chance, because if we were good and our souls were clean, then we would win a vision of Heaven; that was our reward for our obedience. On these occasions we were able to see our loved ones after the Day of Judgment, for which every dead person readies himself in great haste. It is necessary to be ready by the time everybody is reborn. Everybody will be as they were in the prime of life, may the Eternal One be blessed for not resurrecting anyone who is ill, as that would be a great and unjust cruelty! Surely the Lord could not want that. 'If we were not good and our souls were shackled by our evil actions,' said Master Jehuda, 'then we see nothing, or only horrors.' And we must listen to what our dead relatives say. Their chatter may seem meaningless, but they know very well what they are saying. We just have to try hard to understand."

Others said they had seen demons exorcised from the bodies of sick people. They were exceedingly vile—hairy, with tails, hooves, and teeth like wild beasts'.

They told him that in Jerusalem many were overcome each year by a wonderful dream in which they would bathe in the Hinnom during the feast days. It was well known that the long-lost Ark of the Covenant was not in fact lost but there, wisely concealed in the bed of the river before our ancestors went to Babylon, and to this day the Eternal One was in that submerged ark. He sent dreams to his believers through the rays of the sun, and the faithful who truly observed the law dreamed the truth. They owned very little and could not sacrifice very much, but they had love for the Lord in their hearts, so they observed the law; that was what counted, not the size of the sacrifice. The wandering prophets had already told them as much when they had come here to console them, and they had surely been right.

The more sober-minded among the women asked Uri to continue; they were not curious about the dreams of common people but Enoch's dreams. Uri resumed.

And it shall come to pass in those days that elect and holy children will descend from the high Heaven, and their seed will become one with the seed of the children of men...

"That of their daughters," someone said.

"It says 'children' here," said Uri.

"Does that mean women descend and become one with our husbands?"

"That I don't know," said Uri. "I'm only translating what is written here."

The women began to argue about what the holy children who would descend from Heaven, the angels, might be. Were they boys or girls? The scroll's owner considered that some paired with boys, others girls, depending on their own gender. An aging, stringy women said with a wheeze that devils were all male and angels all female, as could be seen on Earth. Some young women protested that they had come across a brood of women possessed by devils of both genders. A portly, loud woman reminded them that when a sorcerer had healed an unhinged Judith and successfully exorcised her demon, he said that she had a male devil in her.

"What sort of cure was that? She went and died!"

"Yes, but only six months later, and it's not certain the healing helped at all."

"Most certainly it is! Everyone dies from being cured. It's best not to cure anyone but to pray for them."

Here was something they could all agree on: praying always helped, while medical treatment only seldom did, and even then it was not certain that the treatment was what had done it.

The supervisor came up and the women started to wriggle the sieves assiduously, whereas Uri carried on. The supervisor lay down on one side, supporting his head on his arm. He popped a grain of barley into his mouth and began to chew it.

And there I saw One who had a head of days, and his head was white like wool, and with him was another being whose countenance had the appearance of a man, and his face was full of graciousness, like one of the holy angels. I asked the angel who went with me and showed me all the hidden things, concerning that Son of Man, who he was, and whence he was. And he answered and said unto me, "This is the Son of Man with whom dwelleth righteousness, and who revealeth all the treasures of that which is hidden. Because the Lord of Spirits hath chosen him, and whose lot hath the preeminence before the Lord of

Spirits in uprightness for ever. And this Son of Man whom thou hast seen shall raise up the kings and the mighty from their seats, and he shall loosen the reins of the strong and break the teeth of the sinners. And he shall put down the kings from their thrones and kingdoms because they do not extol and praise Him, nor humbly acknowledge whence the kingdom was bestowed upon them. And he shall put down the countenance of the strong, and shall fill them with shame, and darkness shall be their dwelling, and worms shall be their bed..."

Silence reigned, except for a heaving of sighs.

And in that place I saw the fountain of righteousness, which was inexhaustible. And around it were many fountains of wisdom, and all the thirsty drank of them and were filled with wisdom. And their dwellings were with the righteous and holy and elect. And at that hour that Son of Man was named in the presence of the Lord of Spirits, and his name before the Head of Days... He shall be a staff to the righteous whereon to stay themselves and not fall, and he shall be the light of the Gentiles and the hope of those who are troubled of heart... For this reason hath he been chosen and hidden before Him, before the creation of the world and for evermore...

At this point the supervisor asked what the Son of Man was called.

Uri said that the text did not give any name.

"It should, though," some said.

Uri replied that he only read and translated, and he did not know. He added that even he did not understand every word.

He was not clear how the Son of Man was formed before the creation of the world, and by whom. Did that mean there was another Creator and another Creation, that our Lord's Creation had been torn down and rebuilt, and all that remained of the old was the Son of Man? And he had been in danger of being stricken down by God for a long time, and our Everlasting had only now forgiven him for existing? And had the Lord, who formed everything, also given a part in that formation to Mithras, who spans the stars every thousand years and is thus a second Creator beside the Creator? And could that second Creator perchance have been named the Son of Man in the text?

No one answered the questions, nor did they understand them. They had not heard about Mithras, and they did not wish to, simply because they had not previously heard about him. Another name would have been too much, as would another Creator. They were quite content with the One who punishes and to whom they had to make sacrifices to appease.

Uri set aside those thoughts for the night and carried on with the story his audience could not get enough of.

> In these days, downcast in countenance shall the kings of the earth have become, and the strong who possess the land because of the works of their hands, for on the day of their anguish and affliction they shall not be able to save themselves... Because the Elect One standeth before the Lord of Spirits, and his glory is for ever and ever, and his might unto all generations... On the day of affliction on which evil shall have been treasured up against the sinners. And the righteous shall be victorious in the name of the Lord of Spirits... And in those days shall the earth also give back that which has been entrusted to it, and Sheol also shall give back that which it has received. And Hell shall give back that which it owes. For in those days the Elect One shall arise, and he shall choose the righteous and holy from among them, for the day has drawn nigh that they should be saved... And in those days shall the mountains leap like rams, and the hills also shall skip like lambs satisfied with milk...

It was a treat for him to say, and a treat for them to hear, that Enoch knew for sure there would be a resurrection.

Not for everyone, however!

> There mine eyes saw a deep valley with open mouths, and all who dwell on the earth and sea and islands shall bring to him gifts and presents and tokens of homage, but that deep valley shall not become full. And their hands commit lawless deeds, and the sinners devour all whom they lawlessly oppress, yet the sinners shall be destroyed before the face of the Lord of Spirits, and they shall be banished from the face of His earth, and they shall perish for ever and ever. For I saw all the angels of punishment abiding there and preparing all the instruments of Satan. And I asked the angel of peace who went with me, "For whom are they preparing these instruments?" And he said unto me, "They prepare these for the kings and the mighty of this earth, that they may thereby be destroyed." And I looked and turned to another part of the earth, and saw there a deep valley with burning fire.

And they brought the kings and the mighty, and began to cast them into this deep valley. And there mine eyes saw how they made these their instruments, iron chains of immeasurable weight. And I asked the angel of peace who went with me, "For whom are these chains being prepared?" And he said unto me, "These are being prepared for the hosts of Azazel, so that they may take them and cast them into the abyss of complete condemnation, and they shall cover their jaws with rough stones as the Lord of Spirits commanded... And in those days he will open all the chambers of waters above the heavens and of the fountains which are beneath the earth. And all the waters shall be joined with the waters. That which is above the heavens is the masculine, and the water which is beneath the earth is the feminine. And in those days the angels shall return and hurl themselves to the east upon the Parthians and Medes. They shall stir up the kings, so that a spirit of unrest shall come upon them, and they shall rouse them from their thrones, that they may break forth as lions from their lairs, and as hungry wolves among their flocks. And they shall go up and tread under foot the land of His elect ones. And the land of His elect ones shall be before them a threshing-floor and a highway. But the city of my righteous shall be a hindrance to their horses. They shall begin to fight among themselves, and their right hand shall be strong against themselves. A man shall not know his brother, nor a son his father or his mother, till there be no number of the corpses through their slaughter. And their punishment be not in vain. In those days Sheol shall open its jaws, and they shall be swallowed up therein. And their destruction shall be at an end; Sheol shall devour the sinners in the presence of the elect."

That part was greatly to the taste of the bloodthirsty women, and even more so was Enoch's proclamation.

"Woe to those who build their houses with sin; for from all their foundations shall they be overthrown, and by the sword shall they fall. And those who acquire gold and silver in judgment suddenly shall perish. Woe to you, ye rich, for ye have trusted in your riches, and from your riches shall ye depart, because ye have not remembered the Most High in the days of your riches. For ye have acquired it all in unrighteousness, and ye shall be given over to a great curse. And in those days in one place the fathers together with their sons shall be smitten, and brothers one with another shall fall in death, till the streams flow with their blood... From dawn till sunset they shall slay one another. And the horse shall walk up to the breast in the blood of sinners, and the chariot shall be submerged to its height... I tell you, ye sinners, ye are content to eat and drink, and rob and sin, and strip men naked, and acquire wealth and see good days... And although ye sinners say, 'All our sins shall not be searched out and be written down,' nevertheless the hosts of Heaven shall write down all your sins every day!"

The supervisor, who'd seemingly abandoned his old habit of hitting them hard with his stick, gave a nod, and the women sighed in agreement. They persevered in the sifting, satisfied that, according to the scroll, the Day of Judgment was nigh and that they were the Lord's chosen people. They were the righteous because they had nothing; they would remain alive, and their dead would all be resurrected by the Everlasting Lord. In the meantime, it was necessary to put food on the table until that happened.

Uri, tired of reading, lay on his back in the field, and had to keep wiping his watering eyes; the women meanwhile did his work. He got up and began to walk around, his way of taking a break. He was looking for the young girl, but all the women wore a shawl on their head and he couldn't find her. His efforts in vain, he set himself down again, rolled onto his front, pulled his gown over his head and fell asleep like Enoch before the face of the Lord.

THAT EVENING MASTER JEHUDA CAME TO SEE HIM IN THE WORKSHOP. By then Uri had just eaten supper (the assistants had given him fresh milk and soft challah bread); he sat up on the rush matting and burped.

Puffing, Master Jehuda took a seat.

"If you can deal with reading so well, no doubt you can write too," he said sarcastically.

"Yes, I can," said Uri.

"Well, then, you'd better write for me from now on."

Master Jehuda looked around at the workshop, half-finished tables and chairs lying scattered all around. He shook his head; it truly was untidy, but he said nothing. Uri did not say anything either. It is not to my host's liking that I entertain the womenfolk; I'm being banned from their company and shall never see the girl again.

Laboriously, Master Jehuda got to his feet, swaying as he stood. He was very fat; his legs could hardly support him. Comfort is not good for one.

Uri politely got up.

"How long am I to stay with you, Master?" he asked.

Master Jehuda turned the answer over before responding.

"I don't know," he said in an unexpected burst of honesty. "They'll let me know sometime."

"Will a delegation be coming from Jerusalem to you regarding my case?" Uri queried. "Could I truly be such an important person?"

"Delegation? What are you talking about? They use fires to signal—like before you arrived."

"You mean, you knew in advance that I was coming?"

"We always know if someone is being sent to us. We find out everything about him."

"Have you been sent guests before, then?"

"It's happened."

"Can letters of the alphabet also be transmitted in the fire?"

"Every letter can, but there are also old signals, certain combinations of words... I don't understand how it works, what the fire-watchers do."

Uri let his mind stray. He had a vague idea that somebody, somewhere, had once talked about messaging with fire. Would that have been in Syracusa?

"Does the news spread quickly?" he asked.

"Yes, quickly. It takes two or three days to reach Antioch from Alexandria."

Syracusa again came to Uri's mind; yes, it was there it was mentioned. Plotius had spoken about it. Where could he be now, Uri wondered.

Master Jehuda set off out of the barn.

"Master, do you think I could be a fire-watcher?"

Jehuda turned around and shook his head.

"No, you couldn't. It's one of those hereditary occupations like that of the Levites."

URI BECAME THE MASTER'S NOTARY, AND HE WAS FORCED TO CONCLUDE that the master did do some work every now and then, even if it was not much to his liking.

He used to see petitioners in the morning, before lunch, with magistrates and witnesses dropping by on Mondays and Thursdays. That particular village did not hold fairs, but they still kept to the same law-days as the rest of Palestine.

Everyone would take off their sandals at the threshold as a mark of respect and enter the house barefoot. Uri now had no sandals, but he would still scratch the sole of one foot with the other before entering.

On those days, the young men of the village would walk off to the synagogue, where they held the Sabbath ceremony. There they learned the elements of calligraphy from a teacher who came over from four villages away and whose pay was pooled by the communities of seven villages (seven being a magic number). Unlike in Rome, girls were not taught reading or writing or arithmetic; they were destined for work in the fields and house, so it was better they remained stupid. The Creator, blessed be His name, preserve us from argumentative women.

People came to the master's place on days besides the Sabbath, of course, and not just on fair-days. They came at the most varied times of day, for advice of all kinds. Uri now understood that Jehuda did not see them all simply out of good humor; it was his responsibility as master. People came with questions relating to matters of health and purity to which even Uri knew the answer, but then there were more complex issues concerning purity that he had never so much as heard about before.

For the most part the visitors came on matters of lawsuits or to make a report against someone. People would inform on a neighbor for eating unclean food, or stealing, or brawling, or for talking unkindly about others, or not sleeping with his wife on the night of the Sabbath, for not washing their hands before prayers. They would squeal on their wives for using foul language or burning the food, and they complained about their children and mothers-in-law and fathers-in-law and everyone else.

The master would listen to them as he quietly dozed, then politely request them to bring at least two witnesses the next time. For the most part that would take away an informer's desire for vengeance, and only a fraction of them would return with two witnesses. But then not many days later the same people would drop by again with something else, and the master would again listen to them; that was his job as a master. Uri's initially caustic stance on squealing gradually altered: informing was a way of life, and in general it had no consequences, and the complainers usually suspected as much when they set about elaborately framing their complaints. When Roman Jews whispered in the ear of some powerful rich man, it would have serious consequences.

On Mondays and Thursdays the master would be joined by two men who were spared having to work in the fields those two days. It was always the same two Uri saw, both middle-aged, brawny men, Esdras and Johanen. They and the master constituted the three-man court of law.

Years ago, they had been elected by the rest to serve as judges alongside the master, and all the signs indicated people were happy with them. They must have had some sort of demon residing in them to be able to sit by the master's side and pass judgment every Monday and Thursday for years on end. They received no emolument of any sort, judges being disqualified from receiving pay for their work, and even suffered a direct loss because for those two days they were unable to work on their land. Having their own lands is what gave them their prestige. Others did the work for them on law-days, but they forswore personally supervising their workforce in favor of working on the community's behalf, whatever loss it might entail.

On some law-days they might have nothing to do; they would sit in the shade, snacking on the challah baked by the master's wife, sipping wine and scratching, the master dispensing pearls of wisdom. But there would be other occasions they were called on to make decisions on two or three matters, in which case they would have to deliberate hard, with their brows furrowed in deep thought. The master's wife served the challah and wine but otherwise was not to be seen; she had no right to participate. The closing of the day's affairs was dinner, the master's wife serving it with a surly look, slapping it down and departing. Master Jehuda, Esdras, Johanen, and Uri would consume the food and drink, then the two magistrates would leave and Master Jehuda would ask Uri what he thought—whether they had done well in sorting out that day's business, and whether they had served the law in a manner that was pleasing to the Lord—and would sit smugly as Uri told him that they had.

It was around this time, toward the end of the day, that the assistants would come to the house and give an account of what they had done that day, whether they had finished this or that chair or couch or table, whether they had managed to sell it, and to whom, which adze or knife had become blunted and whether they had been able to whet it anew. It was never news of major matters that they reported, but it was always embellished and made to sound important, and Master Jehuda took pleasure in the details.

The people who requested advice or were in litigation were also interested in the tiny details. Uri never ceased to be amazed at the questions. To whom does fruit hanging over a fence from a tree on the other side belong? To whom does water situated on the boundary line between two properties belong? Whose duty was it to repair the cistern? Who should pay the cost of a broken vase, a slave's owner or the slave himself? Was it permissible to slaughter a neighbor's stray chicken? What punishment was due to a slave boy who fell asleep while watching a flock and let a sheep go missing? What was the owner's liability?

But then there were also some more serious issues with which the judges might wrestle for weeks.

The three of them were charged with determining whether a firstborn animal brought before them was ritually pure and flawless and therefore fit to be handed over to the priests as a sacrificial offering.

Three of them were needed because none of them was a kosher butcher. A firstborn lamb, calf, chick, or any other clean animal species would be carefully examined: the ears to check they were not damaged, likewise the mouth and nose; the legs to check whether they were broken, and the tail too; the eyes to ensure they were not dropsical or inflamed and the white had not infiltrated the black of the pupil, which was an imperfection (though not the other way around because any color was allowed to infiltrate white, white being clean). Uri's presence inspired them to conduct even more thorough investigations than usual.

There was one religious matter that they pondered on for a long time.

A man by the name of Ezekiel had died unexpectedly, but his widowed wife, Martha, mother of three sons and many daughters, did not wish to marry her deceased husband's elder brother, Thomas, which she would normally be obliged to do by the rules of levirate marriage unless she underwent the ceremony of *halizah*.

"Such a thing still exists?" Uri asked.

Yes and no, he was told. It still existed under the law, but was not common by tradition. Still, custom had to defer to the law, seeing as the Lord had commanded that two people who did not desire each other's bodies should not be united. Out of that there would be no proliferation. The Creator had commanded that people should multiply, and that command took priority over the levirate, which was compulsory of course, but except for when a woman was infertile, since then she had no value to the Lord.

In such a case, Master Jehuda explained, the usual practice was for the wife to take the brother-in-law's left sandal and publicly spit in front of him as a sign that she did not wish to enter a levirate marriage. Because her dead husband's family could not tolerate such humiliation, by this coarse act she would extricate herself from their ownership and return to her father's family. Even if her father had long since died, her male relatives were obliged to accept her under their ownership, a woman being a man's property through the wish of the Lord, who also subordinated the beasts to man. The same would happen if a dead man's brother did not wish to marry the widow, Master Jehuda explained, except in that case the brother would take off the dead man's sandal and spit in front of the widow and the halizah would be in force.

However, in this case, Thomas, the elder brother, was unwilling to validate the halizah, saying that his younger brother had wished to dissolve his marriage bond and had gone as far as having a bill, a get, written out and signed by two witnesses. The widow had hidden it but he had somehow found it. The woman ought to be regarded as divorced, he argued, and the removal of the sandal and the spitting should be regarded as invalid.

Jehuda said that they would give some thought to the matter, and Thomas left. He was a swarthy, vigorous man with dark eyes and a menacing gait.

All four of them carefully studied the divorce instrument. It was scrawled in Aramaic, but still legible.

It was the first time Uri had seen a divorce bill.

"What do you make of it?" Jehuda inquired.

Uri shrugged his shoulders.

"A divorce bill has to contain the signatures of the husband and two witnesses and to state what it is, for what purpose, and when it was written," said Jehuda.

"Those things are all present," said Uri.

"It's a forgery," Johanen declared roundly.

"I believe so too," Master Jehuda said. "But then what proof do we have?"

"Thomas is always lying," said Johanen, "even when he is not speaking."

Esdras confirmed this.

The two magistrates had no great liking for Thomas, Uri had to conclude, and he waited with some curiosity to see if they would dismiss the dubious evidence on that account.

They established, however, that the ketubah did figure in the text.

The ketubah was the marriage document recording the husband's obligations to his wife and what she is entitled to so as not to be left destitute in the case of a divorce. It was a form of contract also made in Rome which often gave the people who dwelt on Far Side reason to gossip for weeks on end about which women had received how much money upon being divorced. Reading that in this case the ketubah concerned land, Uri asked what the custom was in Judaea.

Master Jehuda gave a mischievous laugh.

"Among us, a ketubah can only ever be about land," he said. "There's the issue! So?"

Esdras and Johanen scanned the letter of divorce once more but could find nothing odd about it.

"You're all blind," Master Jehuda declared with a superior air. "It says here that the woman is to receive a land area equal to seventeen qabs of grain and a stretch of orchard equal to four qabs. What do you make of that, then?"

They still saw nothing wrong with that.

"Right, then," said the master, taking a deep breath, his face shining and eyes glinting as slyly as any Roman lawyer's, before launching into his explanation. "They had three sons. The eldest inherits twice as much as the other two, which makes four parts, two of which go to the firstborn son. It says here the deceased man owned fields equal to sixty-five qabs plus five qabs of orchard. As far as the field area is concerned, you have to subtract the seventeen qabs that are owed to the woman from the sixty-five qabs, leaving forty-eight qabs. The eldest son will get twenty-four, and the other two, twelve each. That's all in order, because then everyone gets more than nine qabs, the minimum required. However, if the mother gets four qabs of the orchard, that will leave the three sons altogether one qab. The obligatory minimum portion of an inheritance is half a qab of orchard; one is not allowed to bequeath any less than that! Ezekiel must have been fully aware of the size of his property. He could not have bequeathed to Martha a stretch of orchard equal to four qabs, because in so doing that would have left only one qab over, and splitting that into four half-qab portions just cannot be done! Under the law Martha could only have been due three qabs; then at least the sons would have been left two qabs, of which one qab was due to the firstborn and a half a qab each to the other two. But that's not what is written here, so it's invalid!"

Esdras and Johanen just gazed stupidly, while Uri did the math in his head.

"That's true," he said. "But maybe the man made a mistake in his calculations."

"In principle, he could have," Master Jehuda nodded. "In such cases the power is vested in us to correct a bill of divorce and to get it signed by him and the witnesses. But he's dead now, and it's useless for us to alter it. So what are we to do?"

Master Jehuda's manner of proceeding was to tease things out by posing questions; he had no other approach.

Esdras and Johanen had no idea; Uri mulled it over.

"I have no idea," he announced.

"That's it!" exclaimed Master Jehuda. "That's it! We have to hear the woman out! Didn't that ever occur to you?"

Uri bit his lip; that had not occurred to him. He was being put to shame by a bumbling, blaring, blustering master craftsman! He fumed.

Master Jehuda sent a servant to the widow with a message, and she appeared on the next law-day. She was a sad woman dressed in mourning clothes like any elderly widow, though her sons were still minors and she could not have been more than twenty-five years old. She said that her husband had never wanted to divorce her; that was merely a lie constructed by his elder brother, who, she was now hearing, wanted to marry her even though they had never been able to stand each other. She didn't understand what this might be about. She herself had never seen the bill of divorce.

Master Jehuda sent away Martha, the widow, and summoned the two alleged witnesses to the letter. One had the features of a mouse, the other of a rat; Uri shuddered when he saw them. They were both in rags and stank to high heaven.

Both asserted that Ezekiel had dictated the bill of divorce in their presence and that they had signed it in front of him when he was still alive (the date was on it). They had also been present when he handed it to his wife.

Jehuda dismissed them.

"So?" he asked.

In Esdras's opinion Martha had been telling the truth, while in Johanen's opinion that was not necessarily the case.

Uri then asked when a bill of divorce became valid.

"That's a good question," Master Jehuda nodded. "According to the sage Hillel a bill of divorce becomes effective when the woman receives and reads it and understands she is again free to marry. But according to his colleague Shammai it is valid if it is simply read out in front of her."

"The two witnesses were bribed," said Uri. "Only I don't understand why."

"That's it!" exclaimed Master Jehuda. "Let's assume Ezekiel did not want a divorce. The elder brother would then be obliged to marry his younger brother's widow, in which case all the property would be his. Thomas knew, though, that Martha would be unwilling to marry him after her husband's death and would quite certainly go through with the ceremony of halizah. In that case he would get nothing. However, with a forged bill of divorce, which can't be proven to have been drawn up after the event, the relation between mother and sons would be destabilized. The forged bill of divorce would raise discord, one or more three of the sons flees to Thomas to be kept under his guardianship, and he, together with them, composes a last will and testament containing the inheritance to which they are entitled. Until they have reached the age of majority, he administers it and derives the benefit, with only the very little the law provides going to the widow. She is wiped out, and he accomplishes his aim. No doubt he was attracted to Martha, who was very good-looking when she was young, but even then she did not wish to share his bed, so this was his way of getting revenge!"

Uri was astounded as he listened to the master: the beast knew a thing or two after all! Uri was none too pleased in realizing it.

"Martha was a pretty girl when she was twelve," Master Jehuda nodded, lost in reverie. Esdras and Johanen nodded along too. They gave thanks to the Lord for creating something of beauty; if only he had created it to last just a tiny bit longer! Uri imagined the black-haired young girl, who could not be much older than Martha had been when she was still entrancing. In another fifteen years she too would be an ancient hag.

"So, what should we do to prevent this disgraceful deed?" the master asked.

Uri thought a bit before answering.

"It seems likely, I know, that the bill of divorce was forged, but let's pretend that it's genuine. The woman spits in front of her brother-in-law and no longer has to become his wife. We ratify the ownership of the land but amend the bit that relates to the orchard. Instead of four qabs she'll get three."

"That we can't amend!" screeched Master Jehuda. "Only the head of the family can do that, which in this case means the dead man's older brother, Thomas. There is no brother older than him, only younger brothers, and the father is no longer alive."

They fell silent. It was no easy matter sitting in judgment in Rome, where one couldn't tell who was the head of a clan, and evidently it wasn't easy here either, even if everybody had known everybody else since birth.

"One thing we can do," said Master Jehuda after some rumination. "We drum up two witnesses who swear they saw Thomas, the elder brother, forging the bill of divorce. Then it's two witnesses' word against two—and all four are lying. There's no way for one side to disprove the other. It will cost the widow a bit, but it will be worth it. After hearing the false witnesses we will decide that the bill of divorce is genuine, but faulty and thus null. Since the deceased is not in a position to rewrite it, it's as if it did not exist. We will not request that the head of the family correct it; that's not a requirement. The woman will not insist on it; she spits in front of him, so she'll be left to live in peace with her sons and daughters."

A sage man was Jehuda; he was not a master for no reason.

Slow-talking Johanen nodded respectfully and kept on nodding until he noticed that he was in fact shaking his head. With great difficulty he formulated his objection, which was, "If the bill of divorce is faulty, it ought to be amended."

"It doesn't need to be," said Master Jehuda, turning purple.

"Yes, we need to," persisted Johanen.

Everyone looked at Esdras, who was not just slow of speech but slow in his thinking. He cogitated long and hard before shaking his head. Master Jehuda jumped up irately and, quite spryly considering his bulk, raced around the room.

"You can't mean that we should ask Master Joshua, can you?" he bellowed.

Esdras prepared himself to give a slow nod, at which point the matter suddenly took on an unexpected new complexion. As it was explained to Uri, it would be necessary to see Master Joshua in the seventh village for him to give an opinion.

Uri suspected that there were no warm feelings between Jehuda and Joshua: both were masters and the authority of their respective villages, so what reason would they have to respect each other?

The issue then came up of whom to send to see Master Joshua.

The two elected magistrates were unwilling to go; it was quite enough that they were already losing their Mondays and Thursdays during the harvest.

Johanen put forward a few names, but Master Jehuda did not believe any of them were suitable, at which Johanen took offense. Uri inferred that he had recommended various relatives or their sons.

Esdras, out of slowness and for safety's sake, had no recommendations. Jehuda looked at Uri.

"I can go," he said. "But give me someone to go with who knows the way."

He was glad at the prospect of at last getting free of the village. Other villages might be no better, but at least he would be away from this one.

Master Jehuda, however, decided that Uri could not go.

"You've been placed under my care," he said, with something that almost resembled affection. "I couldn't bear it if any harm were to befall you on the way."

Uri protested that no harm would befall him, but Master Jehuda was unbending. Of course, Uri thought gloomily; he's my jailer, that's what he was instructed by the fire signals. He's frightened I'll make my escape.

In the end, they sent someone else, with whom Uri was not acquainted; he was a young man but already married, and he spent a long time in whispered conversation with Jehuda in a corner before eventually setting off. He returned two days later, and again there was a lengthy whispered conversation with Master Jehuda.

On the next law-day, when at dawn people reluctantly trudged off toward the house of prayer, clay tablets under their arms, Uri stood in front of the house, watching them, and Master Jehuda greeted the two elected magistrates with a transfigured countenance.

"I've got the solution!" he exclaimed jubilantly.

They ate challah, sipped wine, and the master expounded. He announced with some sorrow that the messenger's trip had proved fruitless. Master Joshua had provided no advice of any use, even though he did possess a lot of the oral tradition in written form. Still, the Teaching did not have to be in written form so long as it was in heads and hearts, Master Jehuda declared. He nodded in agreement with himself and the two elected magistrates enthusiastically joined him.

The Eternal One, Jehuda made known, did not wish for this complex affair to remain unresolved, and while the messenger was talking with Master Joshua, who had no ideas to offer, the Creator had divulged to Jehuda the solution to the problem in a dream.

The bill of divorce was original; there could be no doubt about that, and there was no need to call in new witnesses. An error had been committed when it came to transferring the orchard portion of the property, and that error could be attributed to the fact that Ezekiel, may he rest in peace, had not been of sound mind when he dictated the ketubah. If he had not been of sound mind when he made the list of his wealth, then it was reasonable to suppose he did not wish to divorce either, since Martha had been a faithful wife, as anyone would be able to attest. On those grounds, then, the whole bill of divorce was null and void.

Jehuda went on. "Martha is lucky that Thomas miscalculated. Only the Eternal One could have clouded his mind when he muddled up the details of the orchard, just as it is the Creator dictating our judgment, blessed be His name."

Master Jehuda had made a wise decision; the parties were able to acquiesce to it, and it satisfied Uri's sense of justice. Still he would gladly have sought out that Master Joshua in the seventh village to ask him whether it was true that no ideas had occurred to him—along the lines, say, of Ezekiel not being of fully sound mind. He also considered whether partial judgments based on preconceptions were reached in all matters that were even just a tiny bit complicated.

MASTER JOSHUA'S NAME CAME UP AGAIN SOON ENOUGH.

Uri woke up one morning to find Master Jehuda standing gravely over him.

"Did I oversleep?" asked Uri in a panic, and sat up.

Master Jehuda shook his head.

"No, you didn't oversleep, but for a week starting today you cannot sleep in the barn."

"What did I do?" asked Uri, a little irritated.

"You didn't do anything," said Master Jehuda. "That's an order, though. You are going to sleep in my room for a week, starting today."

Uri scratched his head; the change was not much to his liking.

Since it was not a law-day, he was free to gaze at the slow, leisurely puttering of the assistant cabinetmakers, an agreeable activity given that it was blazing hot outside. It must be tough out in the fields right now. When the day drew to a close he went into the master's place.

The master was reclining on his bed and staring at the ceiling. His wife sat by the window, sewing something in the dark. They had not yet lit a lamp.

When she saw Uri, she jumped up, furiously snatched a blanket, and clattered out of the house.

"Have I done something to offend her?" Uri queried.

"She offended you, the guest, for leaving without showing you any hospitality!"

Uri still didn't understand. Jehuda sat up.

"Master Joshua," he said, "big brains that he is, explains the law by saying that a menstruating woman need not sleep separately, but tradition makes it absolutely clear that a women should sleep for a week outside the house because she's unclean! Master Joshua is stirring women up against us! It has driven my wife mad as well; at this time in the month she rages outside in the barn for a week! The custom is quite clear, though, and she knows it full well!" He then added confidentially, "Master Joshua, big brains that he is, uses his explanations of the law against me, but I can see through his game!"

Uri felt uneasy and did not have a single pleasant dream the whole week. Meanwhile, he had to listen to Master Jehuda's infernal snoring from the other bed.

He did not see why Master Jehuda had to banish his wife for a week when they didn't even share a bed.

As far as they knew in Rome, married partners in Palestine shared beds.

Master Jehuda's wife might be glad that she was able to sleep outside in the barn, Uri thought. At least it was quiet there. Why had she stormed out so angrily?

URI TOOK NOTES IN MASTER JEHUDA'S HOUSE UP TILL SHAVUOT, WHICH fell on the sixth of Sivan, fifty days after the first day of Passover, which also marked when reaping of the wheat began. Because the gathering of the barley was still in progress, every hand was needed, Uri's included.

Shavuot was a splendid festival, the ending of the Feast of Weeks. Flowers would be gathered to decorate the houses, wine would be drunk, and prayers said. People would go in procession to the shul, sing psalms, and listen to readings of the Torah, which would invariably include the Ten Commandments. The passages would be explained by prayer leaders, the masters among them.

Work was still an urgent matter, and people got up at daybreak the next day for the harvest. Uri was put to work gathering the ears of grain, bending down like any of the women, a serrated blade in his right hand. His back ached but he did not complain.

The women wanted to hear the Book of Enoch from him all over again, but anything they did not understand they would ask to have explained, taking it for granted that Uri had a much better understanding (after all, he was the one reading it). I've become Enoch's priest, Uri realized. The scroll was not there, but Uri was able to recite it from memory. When they asked about the large house built of crystals, he shared the vision that had come to his mind upon reading it, which differed from what the women imagined. He did not believe in the existence of angels but was obliged to give an account at particularly great length, given that the Book of Enoch passed on very little information about them. He spoke about the archangel Uriel, who radiated light but was unaware that inside him was the eternal flame of a sanctuary lamp. It was something he had made up, and it pleased the women.

He noticed that in the fields he was improvising ever more audacious tales. When he became wary of this and hesitated, the women pleaded with him until he felt bound to continue. Merged into the Book of Enoch were embellished and modified Greek and Roman fables. Uri astonished himself with how readily the storytelling went. There were times when he came to a standstill, because sometimes he too had to work and lost his breath, but the women would not stop urging him to continue. Uri once suggested someone else continue, it wasn't so difficult, and provoked a general outcry. The women were convinced that Uri had already read secret chapters of the Book of Enoch back in Babylon (Why Babylon? Wasn't Edom their name for Rome? Uri asked himself) and that it was his duty to share that knowledge with them. So Uri always picked it up again. Somehow, whenever he had to repeat a story he had already told and got to the first sentence, a picture would come to him, and he would begin telling the women about that picture. The picture would then come to life, and all he had to do was to relate what was transpiring before his mind's eye, as if the image actually existed but he were the only one who saw it and had to describe it for the blind. When they questioned him on where he took the stories from, Uri himself would fib that back home in Babylon he had indeed read and heard other bits of the Book of Enoch. That would set their minds at rest, but Uri became uneasy. There was something sinful about his telling stories as if he were reading, and although he did not believe in devils, it was still a bit like having Satan dictate what he said.

When he was not telling tales, Uri would peer around as he bent over, searching from the side of his eyes for the lovely young girl. Finally he spotted her. She was balancing a pitcher on her head, so she must have been assigned to water-carrying duties; she smiled at him and moved on. Uri was again bewitched by those two dense, almost contiguous eyebrows. He asked what the girl's name was, and after some hesitation the women told him: Miriam. A daughter of Master Jehuda's slaves, and herself a slave, like all her older sisters and brothers.

Constantly, awake and in his dreams, he saw a vision of the lovely girl before his eyes. His entire inside pulsated, became a throbbing, exasperating, blissful torment as he began to think about how he could purchase her. He made inquiries as to what the price of a slave was. In Rome the starting price was eight hundred sesterces, or roughly the price of a cow, but it might go as high as one hundred thousand for an expert at some task. The women could make nothing of prices in sesterces, but they did know that the price of an agricultural slave laborer was forty zuz.

Uri's heart sank. Forty zuz, or 160 sesterces, was no small amount, even in Rome.

It then became clear that this was the price for an adult male slave; women cost only half that. Uri breathed a sigh of relief. He tried to calculate how many days he would have to work as a journeyman in Judaea to scrape together the twenty zuz or eighty sesterces needed to buy the lovely young girl for himself.

A good worker in Jerusalem might earn one denarius per day, he was told when he asked about—not so different from Rome, where one could make around four sesterces. For twenty days' wages in Jerusalem it was possible to buy a woman, but in the countryside even an experienced journeyman would not make one tenth the going rate in Jerusalem. So, it would be worth getting a job as a worker in Jerusalem, if only he could find a way of somehow getting back there. For the time being, however, he had to work unpaid for his lunch of bread dipped in vinegar, which he now ate just the same as the rest. Although it still upset his stomach, the vinegar did help quench his thirst in the hellish heat, and there was not enough water for all the girls with pitchers on their heads to serve the harvesters.

Get a laboring job in Jerusalem!

The supervisor, who remained on friendly terms with Uri and missed no chance to greet him when he checked up on the reaping women, said that he too had gained work as a laborer in Jerusalem, working as a paver on the roads for one denarius per day. He'd almost had to pay more for his bread and board, so he had returned to the village. Jerusalem was an expensive city. Most of the workers had no home to go to and slept like beggars out on the streets, where they were often robbed of whatever money they had. A man could consider himself lucky if he managed to save twenty or thirty zuz in a year.

A whole year's work to earn the money to free a slave girl? Not so impossible.

Rome vanished from his consciousness; the only thing in the world was the present—the monotonous reality of barley and wheat fields, Judaea, nothing else. Uri suspected that he was starting to lose his senses, but he did not really care. He dreamed of having a family of his own. The young girl would bear him many children while he plowed and harvested, or learned about carpentering, and to the end of his days he would live here with the girl, who would never age. It was as if it were not the days of his exile he was spending in this village, as if his exile could not come to an end, ever.

Uri lay out in the field whenever he could during the lunch break, which was not long, and gazed at the sky.

The firmament was different here, so too were the spirits with which man was surrounded; the past, present, and future were different, the religion too, than they were in Rome. Uri was overcome by different images, different stories. Enoch was a living presence here, whereas in Rome it was Plato and Ovid. Enoch did not understand Plato, nor vice versa, but both were present where they were valid. Nothing valid in the Jewish quarter of Rome pertained here, whereas the Roman Jews had no awareness of Enoch.

How could that be?

The Eternal One must have been fed up with Uri's infantile dreams because one morning he cut his left hand on a head of grain. It was bleeding heavily and the women advised him to go home to Master Jehuda, who had an herbal infusion that quelled bleeding.

Clutching the two bleeding fingers of his left hand with his right hand, Uri trudged back home from the fields. It was a route he knew well by now. He entered the house and stood there blinking. After the blinding outside light he could hardly see anything, hearing only a grunting and high-pitched shriek. The master's wife was the one he saw first, sitting under the window and sewing something assiduously. The sounds emanated from over by the bed. Uri stepped closer and saw his prostrate master, who was fat but had surprisingly spindly legs that stuck out naked from underneath his rolled-up shirt. On his belly, unclothed, was the lovely young girl, riding him in a seated position, her long black hair let down and cascading. The master grunted while the young girl screamed and rode, and the master's wife sewed.

Uri was so scared he couldn't move. The master noticed someone had come in, and as he lay there he took a sideways glance at Uri and broke into a grin.

"Pretty little creature, isn't she? No one could claim this is a goat!" he exclaimed, giving the girl's naked behind a hefty whack and laughing uproariously. "If I'm in need of hands to work for me, I make them myself!"

The master's wife glanced at Uri. In her eyes was a look of profound, blank loathing that encompassed everything living and lifeless—a curse. The young girl continued to ride on the master's belly, oblivious.

Uri turned on his heels and ran out of the house. He raced over to the poultry yard and shooed the hens from one of the coops. Wings flapping, they scattered in panic. He crawled in and, flat on his stomach, hands clutched to his head, cried tears of anger.

HE HAD TO BREAK FREE.

He was a Roman citizen; no one could force him to carry out slave labor in Judaea. He had not been sentenced for anything by any court of law. Everything that had been carried out against him over these months was illegal.

He would set off in any direction and just keep on going. The main thing was to get away from here.

The thought put him in a cheerful frame of mind. Things had become boring here anyway; new adventures awaited. Whether he would manage to get back to Rome at all was subject to doubt. But then what was home? Rome was a long way away, and the nineteen years that he had been obliged to live there had not been particularly pleasant. There was a world beyond Rome and Judaea.

Two days later he went out to the fields and waited until breakfast was brought. He ate the slice of bread dunked in vinegar, drank long drafts of water from a pitcher set in front of him by an elderly woman, put down his sickle, and slowly set off. No one looked after him, assuming he had something to attend to and would be back later.

Uri walked northward. The harvest was in progress all around, and the sun was blazing hot. Uri pulled his mantle over his head and kept walking. He was headed toward Samaria, where they hated the Jews of Judaea and did not pay tithes to the Temple in Jerusalem, but he was not a Judaean Jew; he was a Roman citizen with a mind of his own.

Around midday he decided to lie down and rest. What was the point in hurrying when he didn't even know where he was going?

Sleep overcame him under a fig tree. The foliage of fig trees throw impenetrable, thick, marvelous shadows, may the Eternal One be blessed for creating them. It was late in the afternoon when he awoke.

He opened his eyes and could see human legs around him. He looked at the legs. They were all barefooted except for a single pair in sandals.

Uri sat up and studied the sandals before looking up.

There were seven dour male faces looking down at him. Two of them seemed familiar—he had been harvesting with them during the previous weeks—but he had never seen the others. He inspected the individual wearing the sandals more thoroughly, and the man inspected Uri back. Uri somehow felt he had seen that face before. Yes, that was it! He recalled the spearsman who had accompanied him from Jerusalem to Master Jehuda's place. Uri nodded; it was the spearman's younger brother.

Uri drew his legs up and waited for them to speak, but they remained silent. Uri looked the man in sandals straight in the eyes.

"Those were my sandals once," he said impertinently.

Silence. Then the man in the sandals said, "I know."

Uri was relieved. He clambered to his feet and stood there.

There was silence again.

"You're going to have to go back," the sandaled man said in a friendly tone. "You're the guest of Master Jehuda."

"I don't care to," Uri informed them.

Silence again as the men digested this response. Then the sandaled man, the spearsman's younger brother, said, "You have to. We are here to defend the village. The master requested our help. We help him, and he pays us. We'll escort you back lest there be any trouble."

"I would prefer to stay with you in the caves," Uri declared.

Another silence.

"That's not possible," said the sandaled man apologetically. "Master Jehuda didn't say you could take to the caves, among the robbers. Or was that what he said to you?"

Uri pondered his response. "No, he didn't say that," he admitted.

They set off back to the south.

THEY WERE STURDY FELLOWS, AND THEY CERTAINLY DID NOT GIVE THE appearance of wanting for anything. They were tidily clothed, and no ribs stuck out of their skin. Their tread was surer than that of peasants.

Uri laughed, nodded, and hummed a tune to himself.

It seemed Jerusalem was recruiting its police force from among the robbers, and out here in the country the robbers nurtured close relations with masters and acted as a local police force too. Like the master operating as a faithful representative of the Sanhedrin, they had no other choice. There was no way of escaping; the state was lying in wait behind every bush.

The robbers came to a stop at the edge of the village.

"Go back to Master Jehuda," the man with the sandals advised. "If you try to leave again, we'll catch you again."

Uri nodded.

"My greetings to your brother," he said.

"I'll pass them on. Peace be with you."

"Peace be with you all."

Uri stood at the edge of the village like the spearsman and swordsman had done when, on their arrival at the village two months before, Uri had set off to look for Master Jehuda. He looked back and cordially waved. The robbers stood motionless.

Master Jehuda was gruff in his welcome.

"What do you expect from me?" he growled. Uri knew by now that his demeanor was more acting than genuine emotion. "That I kiss your ass because you were dumped on me? Isn't this good enough for you? Can I help that? What's your problem with me? Why do you want to ruin me?"

"I'm bored," Uri announced. "At least let me return to Jerusalem!"

"Permission has to be granted for that," the master grumbled.

"Get it," Uri, the Roman citizen, urged.

"How am I to get it? From whom?"

"I'm not interested, just get it! Send a fire signal!"

"That costs! Each and every letter is three pondions!"

"So?"

"You pay for it!"

"How can I? You know very well that I have no money. You pay! You give loans at usurious interest rates and bankroll those robbers as your policemen!"

"You still pay, you good-for-nothing!" the master fumed, now with genuine passion.

"Pay yourself, you've got the money!"

"I don't have the slightest intention of paying," the master seethed. "Three pondions for each letter, vowels included! And they don't even send those, the lazy bastards—only the consonants, but they still charge for them! I'm not willing to pay them! Lousy gougers, getting rich at my expense! I'm not letting them pinch my vowels!"

Uri could sense the bile accumulating within himself and did nothing to prevent it. Thoughts of the lovely young girl and her thrilling eyebrows had disappeared, and the throbbing in his insides he had felt each time he saw her had vanished; only a masculine desire for revenge remained, that of a murderer.

I'll have forty other wives, Uri thought, each lovelier than Miriam.

"I'll pay the half-shekel tax now," said Uri scornfully, though quite unexpectedly even for himself.

The master did not understand and became flustered.

"That's only needed at the end of winter," he exclaimed.

"I want to pay it now!" Uri insisted with all the stubbornness of someone who wanted to grow up.

"Impossible! It's collected in Adar!"

"And I'm going to pay in Sivan!" yelled Uri.

There was a lull. Uri took a wicked delight in all this. How on earth would he get half a shekel together now when he hadn't a single prutah to his name? The master, though, did not think of that. He was alarmed. Never before had there been a case of someone wishing to pay the half-shekel tax in the summer. Not ever. The boy was crazy.

"Fair enough," Jehuda said in a conciliatory tone, trying to smile. "You won't work any more. Do whatever you please, but no trying to escape or you'll be brought back anyway. I don't want any scenes. What do you need? Tell me and you'll get it."

Uri kept quiet. There was no way now he would get what he had wanted. She had been taken by Satan, in whom he had never believed before but who existed all the same.

"I want a woman," he whispered.

Master Jehuda was flabbergasted but pricked up his ears.

"What's that you said?" he asked, flushed by keenness to help.

"A woman," Uri said hoarsely.

"A woman?" Master Jehuda repeated and, as Uri could see, was highly relieved. "No problem. You'll get as many women as you want. Which one? Just say, and you'll get her. We've got slave girls growing out of our ears! I'll call them together, all you have to do is point. Free for as long as you stay here."

Uri gave a groan.

"I'll set up the workshop as a dwelling," said Master Jehuda obligingly. "Set it up just fine! Say, half of it... That's quite a lot of space, isn't it? Well, you know yourself... Half. I'll partition it from the workshop with a wall... You'll get a bed and chairs. No more sleeping on the floor. You can lounge around on that comfy bed all day long, and I'll send you the women. As many as you want! Only don't ruin me! I don't deserve that. I've never treated you anything less than well!"

URI WAS ASHAMED TO ASK MASTER JEHUDA FOR A WOMAN, BUT HE accepted the dwelling. In a room separated from the workshop, he could lie on a pallet stuffed evenly and generously with crisply fresh straw, brushing the flies away and feeling extremely miserable. He was free, but he was bored.

He had behaved abominably, in the way that only young men can, and he could not for the life of him understand why Master Jehuda did not take advantage of that. Uri could only draw the conclusion that this fearsome, voracious, loudmouthed, red-haired, fat man, who was held in such high public esteem even far away, was even weaker than he was.

Uri gnashed his teeth. He had to do something or he would go crazy.

I'll be a cabinetmaker, he decided.

Two days later Uri snuck into Master Jehuda's house. He did not find Miriam or the master's wife there. Master Jehuda was sitting hunched over a scroll, his forehead supported by both hands, and seemed mightily care-laden. He looked up.

"I have to anathematize someone!" he declared unhappily. "Dreadful!"

Uri nodded, then announced that he wanted to learn carpentering given that he happened to live in the workshop.

"So learn it," said Master Jehuda irately, as Uri was showing him no sign of sympathy.

So Uri let the assistants know that on Master Jehuda's orders he would become a cabinetmaker, and they should show him all the tricks of the trade.

The assistants were less than pleased; it was a good craft, and the three of them were the only ones who plied it within a radius of a day and a half's walking distance, and now they had to instruct a competitor. However, they did not have the nerve to take a stand against Master Jehuda.

They told him to take a seat in the workshop and watch.

They spent the whole day smoothing down planks of wood. Uri became bored and requested to be allowed to do something himself. They told him there was a spare plane that needed to be sharpened. Uri spent the rest of the time using a piece of hard stone with a milled surface to rub the metal surface. It did not wear away easily, and there was no pleasure in doing it.

The next day the work was no different, and Uri got angry. He noted where there were lamps in the workshop, stole back that night, and by the light of two lamps he took a chair apart to find out how it was assembled. He was unable to put it together again because a joint broke. When the assistants kicked up a fuss about it the next day, Uri cheekily endured it, simply shrugging his shoulders. The chief assistant raced off to make a complaint to Master Jehuda, but he was unwilling to take the twenty paces to the workshop and instead just sent the message that Uri should be instructed in everything if that is what he wanted.

Barely one month later, by the middle of Tammuz, by his own efforts he had produced a nice little table. It did not rock however much it was pushed about, its top was shiny and smooth, and the grain stood out beautifully. No glue or packing material had been used in the joints but it still did not wobble. They told him what it was, one of the better kinds of wood, but Uri did not catch the name. He rubbed his wrists; they had given him the hardest wood just to make him struggle.

"This is my sort of work," he stated happily.

He had to bend down close to the wood to work it, and his close-up vision was brilliant, even better than that of the others. He even noticed tiny fibers in the wood. The Everlasting Lord created me to be a carpenter, he concluded, and he reproached his Creator for not making him aware of this much earlier.

The assistants told him that he might want to give inlay work a try.

Uri did not know what that was. Making sketches with a twig in the dust, they explained that particularly expensive tabletops had parts chiseled away into which the master would set minute strips of other woods in marvelously multicolored designs. They could not show him any examples; tables of that kind were not found in the provinces, only at the homes of the rich in Jerusalem. But there were some tabletops on which fantastic birds and plants were to be seen, all put together from strips of wood and staggeringly expensive.

From discarded bits of wood, Uri cut up strips to be inlaid, paring and shaping them to fit together, concocting attractive patterns the like of which, so the assistants said, no one had done before. Uri could see that this was something he was cut out for.

He enjoyed working with wood, inhaling its fragrance, gazing at the contours of a cut-off butt's edge, taking a long, hard look at the concentric circles of a knot or gnarl. He enjoyed shaping wood with a sharp blade, brushing away the sawdust. He enjoyed these things so much so that he did not really need to think of anything else, not even why he happened to be precisely where he was.

When they showed him, with the aid of the sort of wheel potters use, that it was also possible to mold wood in a similar fashion as clay, using the legs to push a treadle and drive a wheel so that an affixed piece of wood was spun around while a blade, pressed steadily onto the wood, cut shavings off it, Uri felt as overjoyed as the Creator may have felt in forming man from clay.

If only my father knew how this trip to Jerusalem had put a craft in my hands! He'll know someday, and he will be astonished and delighted that his son's poor eyesight is good for something in spite of everything.

"GIZBARIM! GIZBARIM! GIZBARIM!"

That was the cry to which Uri awoke at daybreak one day. He clambered out of the barn. It was still dawn, but people were hurrying out to the fields, women and children included. Uri peered; he could not see the faces but there were so many of them all of a sudden that he had the feeling he had not yet encountered most of them before, small though the village was. Could they be from nearby villages? Had they known beforehand that something was brewing?

One of the assistants who had popped into the barn informed Uri that the train of carts had arrived to take the First Fruits and the First Ripe Fruits to Jerusalem (not the Tithe, which was collected separately and was not being taken now).

"How do you know?"

"They sent a message."

"Did some delegate come?"

"The message was sent by fire signals. This year they're late; they usually come a couple of weeks before Shavuot, but due to the drought, everything has been burning up and the animals are scraggly. They waited in the hope that it would rain."

"When do they normally collect it otherwise?"

"Like I said, a couple of weeks before Shavuot, but the villages out here usually only get a message and then take it into the City themselves. They only come to take it from a lot farther away. They don't collect it from the Transjordan; it is brought voluntarily. There is another gathering in a fortnight or so, before Sukkot..."

The excited assistant ran out of the barn, clean feast-day sandals on his feet.

Uri washed quickly in the yard. It hadn't rained for weeks, and the water was at hand in a pitcher, brought by women from a remote well. He said his prayers, bolted down a slice of dry bread, and hurried after the others.

People were standing in a long chain at the outskirts of the village, so Uri joined them. Girls were carrying pitchers around and splashing water onto people's hands, which they then rubbed together. Uri received a drop and he scrubbed too. He had never seen the people of the village washing their hands before eating or prayers, that being customary only in the Diaspora. The girls had their hair pinned up, and their freshly laundered dresses clung damply to their bodies, rousing Uri's desires. The menfolk were carrying sacks, barrels, and clay pots, with Master Jehuda scurrying excitedly among them. It must be something major brewing if he had gotten up at dawn. Master Jehuda was fussing about the cleanness of earthenware bowls, wiping the dew off them with a white linen cloth.

When he spotted Uri, he explained: "Moisture attracts flies! The uncleanness of mosquitoes will pass, but not that left by flies!" He scurried on, now crying out that lentils would be brought.

Was it lentils they would be eating today? Was that the festive fodder? Lentils had never once been served since Uri had been in the village. It was explained to him that the lentils were used to gauge the purity of grain; dirt smaller than a lentil was acceptable, but anything bigger would make a whole sack of flour unclean, and priests could not eat it. He was reassured that the presence of a lentil was purely symbolic, as there was no chance of a piece of a lentil-sized flyspeck remaining in grain; they took great care of that.

The empty bowls were set down on a blanket on the ground to Uri's left. The sacks and barrels stood to his right. Animals were also driven onto the field, the calves and lambs still stumbling.

No one ate a thing, taking great care that their hands not be dirtied. They stood in the sun in festival mood. A table was set out on the field covered with white tablecloths upon which stood wine and water and a mixing bowl. Master Jehuda smoothed down some invisible creases in the tablecloth. He inspected the wines. He inspected the bowls that had been wiped clean and wiped them a bit more, and he also wiped their outsides, as it was said that flyspecks were common on the outsides.

The *gizbarim*, it turned out, was what the collectors were called; they were the ones who went out into the countryside to collect the First Fruits and the First Ripe Fruits. The Temple had three such treasurers, and these officials took orders from the *katholikin*, or deputy receivers, who, Levites of the high priesthood were also occupied with collecting. On ceremonial occasions, once the population had handed in their ritual offerings in Jerusalem at Sheep Gate by the North Wall, next to the big pool, it was the katholikin who examined everything to check that it was clean and intact so that Levites would have no qualms about consuming it. The priests would get a tenth of this tithe. In principle, a Levite would get ten times more than a priest, but priests had come to Jerusalem from all over Palestine and now there were more of them there than in the olden days.

A priest was coming to us today from Jerusalem! He would give us a blessing too!

There was great joy even as the sun blazed over the thousands of people lying about or standing in line with garments covering their heads. Master Jehuda walked around inspecting everyone with a severe expression on his face, as if he were able to look through them. He suddenly stopped in front of one of the boys.

"When was your uncle buried?" he asked.

"Last week," said the lad.

"Were you present?"

"Of course."

"Who else was there?"

"Well, the whole family..."

Master Jehuda gathered the family together, a dozen or so people, youngsters, old people, women, and children, eventually found themselves standing at the front of the line.

Jehuda stood in such a way that his shadow did not overlap any of their shadows. He gazed at them for a long time before instructing them to leave.

The head of the family, a sturdy red-haired man, protested: a week had gone by since the burial, they had every right to be there. Jehuda did not budge an inch: it was not certain that they had become clean since then—maybe yes, maybe no. The situation was disputable, so they couldn't stay.

Uri saw, because the dispute took place just four paces away, that it took great effort for the burly red-haired man to maintain his self-control before he nodded and set off, the other members of his family glumly in tow. They would not partake of the priest's blessings, the unfortunate people, because the master had decided so.

Jehuda looked at Uri.

"It is just possible that they threw a shadow on the dead man!" he said with a care-laden, conscientious look. "If it did, then they became unclean and a priest should not even see them because the uncleanness of a corpse crosses onto anyone throwing a shadow on it. It may be that they didn't throw a shadow on the deceased, but that's not certain. We can't take that risk."

Master Jehuda moved on, deliberating very hard about what still had to be done so that everything would go perfectly smoothly.

From the distance there was a cry of "Demah! Demah!"

Uri asked what that was.

It was agricultural produce that may or may not have been truly tithed. For safety's sake it would later be tithed anyway, but it could not be used as an offering of either First Fruits or the First Ripe Fruits; it would have to be taken back.

The carts arrived at about midday. The collection in the previous villages must have dragged on. Indeed, people commented disparagingly, they slept all the time.

Eight big ox-drawn carts arrived, one after the other. On the first the priest, a man with a rectangular cropped beard and garbed in a white linen robe, snoozed on the box seat, and a man with a cloak sat beside him. It went along the line of people that he was the Levite deputy receiver, come from Jerusalem, the katholikos. On the last cart lurched eight armed men, one a civilian in black. The other carts were already laden with sacks and cloth-covered pots, with some calves tethered to the back of one of them. On that cart there were also chickens shut up in large cages dopily dozing.

That's odd, thought Uri. *Gizbar* sounded as if it might be a word of Persian origin, and *katholikos* was Greek, of course. Why was there no Hebrew or Aramaic word for a collector?

The carts drew up. Master Jehuda went over to the priest. The priest clambered down from the cart, whereupon Jehuda prostrated himself on the ground. The rest of the crowd kneeled. Holding both arms out before him, the priest said a prayer and pronounced the priestly benediction. Uri, likewise kneeling, looked around. The others, transfigured, were ecstatically on their knees, many weeping for joy. They were blessed for their diligence by the priest through whom they won the blessing of the Lord himself. They had labored hard and long so that the Lord would obtain his victuals; they had earned the benediction. The Levites and the priests would later consume the First Fruits and the First Ripe Fruits on behalf of the Eternal One's consecrated bellies. The chosen among the chosen people.

The katholikos and the armed men also got down. The katholikos seated himself on a barrel. He produced a papyrus, unrolled it, and placed it on a small table set in front of him. Master Jehuda sent over a youngster, who, blushing fiercely, placed the flats of his hands on it so that it would not roll back. The youngster looked around proudly for having been given such an important job. The Levite dipped a goose's quill in a little inkwell dangling at his chest and scratched at the papyrus.

A chair was placed under the priest, who sat down, and an awning was held over his head. The priest's head drooped, perhaps he dropped off to sleep. He had done his bit by giving the benediction, something an ordinary mortal was never allowed to pronounce.

The armed escort was given food and drink. They lay down under a tree and quietly snacked.

The civilian in the black robe did not get down from the last cart. Uri could not see his face clearly and had no idea who he might be.

The katholikos made a sign. The supervisor, who was standing beside the little table with the awning holders, also signaled. At the end of the line closest to the table the people started singing a psalm. Some around Uri joined in, and the singing spread along the row. When it came to an end, people started carrying bowls and sacks to the little table. People standing in the chain passed the sacks from hand to hand, untied them in front of the little table, and poured some of the contents out into each bowl. The katholikos examined the flour—there was both barley and wheat in the sacks—and more was only poured out when he gave a nod.

The crowd went into a new psalm, then another. They would carry on for as long as the hand off was in progress.

Uri sang along in his boredom, his back now aching from all of the standing around. They would spend the whole day here at this rate. He had a strong sense of urgency that he had seen this before, and he knew that he ought to be doing something else now. There was no sense of urgency in the minds of the others; they lived in the holy moment that had just taken place. This was an exalted day, the time they received forgiveness for their sins from the Lord. Uri felt a twinge of guilt for not having the feeling that his sins could be forgiven in such a manner.

The priest was dozing, and no one took any notice. Uri was perplexed both at why he was not livelier and why people were not bothered. The priest had an intermediary function between the Lord and His people, but he seemed not to serve it. A prayer-spouting puppet.

The Levite, on the other hand, was an important person. He was not satisfied with one of the bowls, which in shame, without a word of protest, was then immediately thrown to the side so hard that it broke. He also found fault with the quality of one sack's contents; it was set aside and the opening tied again. Perhaps a fly had gotten into it, or else the deputy receiver had deemed it damp, but whatever the case it would be left behind, to be eaten by the local peasants.

The katholikos beckoned, and Master Jehuda leapt over. A young lad held a bowl in front of the katholikos's nose. He fished out something from a barrel of oil with a stick and gave it a long, hard look. He dug around in the bowl of lentils with the other hand, took out a single lentil, and measured it against whatever the something was. He weighed it over for a long time, then nodded; the barrel could be put on the cart.

The people around Uri breathed a sigh of happiness and redoubled their singing. It had been a long time since any oil they pressed had been considered impure. Uri regretted that hitherto he had not participated in pressing olives.

When the sacks were done with, it was the turn of the fruits. These were carried on plates and placed before the Levite, who examined every single specimen. The feebler ones were set aside. They would be for us to eat, Uri surmised. Yet they had all been cut down with a flint knife, because that was never unclean. However, it was a case not of the flint knife being unclean but rather of the fruit being unclean.

On a sign given by Master Jehuda, the line broke and the singing stopped. The sudden stillness woke the priest, who stepped into a basin of water, dabbled his feet, bent down and splashed water on himself, stepped out of the bowl, and wobbled over to a table with wine and water. He chanted a prayer, and the Levite mixed wine into a glass of water, which the priest drank. This was the signal for the armed men to start drinking and eating, and now those who up until then had just passed the harvest down the chain started eating. The chain had been formed not to make the work easier (after all, one man could have carried the sacks) but so that everybody would have a part to play.

Once lunch was over, it was time for the calves and lambs, which were lying on straw at the foot of the trees. They were sprinkled with water before being led in front of the katholikos, who closely examined each one from its teeth to its hooves, he alone being qualified to do this because he counted as an expert. There were not so many firstborn animals in the village, Beth Zechariah being small. Uri thought there were too many, but then he was reminded that they were also gathering the best animals, not just the firstborn. The examination proceeded slowly, and more than one of the animals was judged faulty. Those animals would be reared and eventually slaughtered; they were good enough for the second tithe, the provender set aside for the villagers themselves to eat during the pilgrimage. The second tithe could be substandard; only the first tithe, which went to the priests and the Levites, had to be perfect.

The katholikos used a paintbrush dipped in red dye to mark the brow or wings of the selected animals and gestured that the owners should take them back into the shade. It was high time too, with the animals panting and near fainting from thirst. From that moment on, the owners were former owners and merely shepherds for the animals, because the priests—which is to say the Eternal One—now owned them.

The civilian in black now got down from the last cart, looking like someone in mourning, and made his way to the table. The soldiers lined up facing the inhabitants. The man in black halted. Silence fell.

"Who's that?" Uri whispered.

"The tax collector."

Animals, sacks of grain, and fruit were set before him, but no one checked their quality. This would go to the Romans in taxes, so it did not matter if it was impure. The tax collector stood there and counted. The sacks were loaded onto the cart, the livestock tethered to the back of the cart. The priest was sleeping or pretending to sleep. The Levite moved into the shade. The rows of people broke up as they gossiped, their backs turned to the tax collector.

"How much is the Edomite tax?" Uri inquired.

One percent of everything was the per capita tax, and one and a half percent the tax on produce. The tax collector was Jewish, and he paid an annual fixed sum to secure the right to collect taxes for Edom. If he happened to pull in more, the margin was his; if it was under, he bore the loss. He was evil, the tax collector, and he standing with the population was of a person in mourning: his testimony would not be accepted, it was forbidden to accept any present from him, and if he gave money to a person, it was forbidden to exchange it. Tax collectors went around the countryside with priests, Levites, and soldiers because they feared popular anger. It was a miracle that people were willing to act as tax collectors at all.

"They ruin the feast for us," people said tartly.

Against sober voices counseling that one ought to render unto Caesar the things that are Caesar's, people complained bitterly about being ruined by Edom's shameless tax collectors.

"How does he know how much needs to be taken in?" Uri asked.

"He just does."

Once a year the heads of households had to go to the tax collector in the nearest town and declare how much of what produce had been cultivated and how many souls there were in their families. That declaration was only checked in very rare instances; there just were not enough tax collectors. In that particular village there had never yet been a check on the Roman tax; no tax inspector would make it out alive if there were, that was for sure. All the same, they paid their taxes honestly to Edom because that was what their leaders demanded, and it was also what was demanded, for instance, by Master Jehuda, and if Master

Jehuda said that they had to pay taxes to Edom, then they paid the tax, because Jehuda was the master.

Children did not have to be declared at birth but only once they reached seven years of age. That had been the case since Edom ruled them, maybe because so many died early in childhood. They did declare them to the priests, though, and if the firstborn was a son, they would immediately pay five sela'im to redeem him, because that son belonged to the Lord (or, in other words, to the priests), and he would have to be purchased back from them. Boys born subsequently would also have to be declared or they would not be circumcised, and girls were also declared. After each and every childbirth, even for a girl, the mother would sacrifice a lamb and a dove, or, if she was very poor, just two doves. Anyone who had no money—five silver sela'im was a huge sum, the equivalent of twenty drachmas!—would have to sign a promissory note that it would be paid as soon as they were able.

"And can a priest relieve a man of that debt?" Uri queried.

"No, that belongs to the Lord. It can never be paid off in crops, only in Tyrian silver."

"The priest can give the money as a present to a poor family if he sees fit," someone commented.

But they were in no mood for explanations; they wanted to grumble. So they carried on grumbling—in hushed tones so that the tax collector could hear, but not the Levite resting in the shade two paces farther away.

As if it were not enough that they had to pay a water fee, even though there was no aqueduct coming their way, all they had were their own cisterns and wells; as if it was not enough that they had to pay a road levy every time they went on a highway, festival periods aside, and there were times when they might have to go to Jerusalem in connection with a lawsuit; as if it was not enough that they had to pay a house tax even though they had put up their shacks with their own bare hands; as if it was not enough that they had to pay a frontier-crossing toll every time they needed to enter a town surrounded by a wall. Some three to four percent of their crop was taken away because the amount paid to the tax collector was more than two and a half percent, and if he was not happy he wouldn't have his say here but would report them straight to Jerusalem, which meant that the high priests would bring some unfavorable decision with regard to the village, such as not allowing them to enter the City on feast days, or pushing them farther back in the hierarchy of the twenty-four tribes so that they would never get to stand next to the altar. So whatever they thought to themselves, they would fill separate wineskins for the tax collector, which would not go toward enhancing the emperor's wealth but his own.

Uri then asked where all the crops and animals ended up. Were they shipped across the Great Sea to Italia?

No, because the present emperor had forbidden it. All the meat and grain had gone bad on the long journey, and since then it had been used locally, sold at the bigger markets. The money received from that was used by the prefect to maintain the soldiers and officials. That tax stayed local.

"We keep our occupiers going," said sage heads.

"In the same way we brought them down on us!" said even sager heads.

Uri made a quick mental calculation. If the Roman tax, including the water levy, the house tax, the road taxes, the frontier-crossing tolls, and the produce were put at five or six percent of the total harvest, that was probably not far off the mark.

He quizzed people about the exact taxes on the Jews of Judaea, and they readily and proudly enumerated them.

They gave the Levites one tenth of everything edible, out of which one tenth went to the priests.

They also put aside another tenth for themselves to cover the three big festivals. They consumed this during the long journeys and in Jerusalem itself, and it was generally insufficient. There had been cases when they had to go hungry and thirsty for two or three days during the walk back home.

When adjudged guilty, they would pay for sacrifices in sin and guilt offerings. That was quite common, to be sure. The Lord created us as sinful beings, but He did not hold any ill will if we duly repented and propitiated Him.

If a wish or vow of ours should be fulfilled, a votive offering would be given, with the breast and right shoulder of the sacrificial animal going to the priests. We would gladly give these because the supplication would be heard by the Eternal One, may He be praised.

The priests received all first fruits and every firstborn male animal, and that was precisely what was being collected now, as Uri could see.

The ground tax was the year's first fruit of the wheat, barley, grapes, figs, pomegranates, olives, and honey. The priests also had a right to the very best of the crop, which was was also being collected that very day. That meant the best of the food that stemmed from any plot of land or tree. Either a person knew himself what was best or else the experts—the masters and supervisors—would draw his attention to it. The most important of these products were the wheat, wine, and oil. One fifteenth of their entire income would be put aside for that purpose, even though nowhere had it been set down in writing and it was not even measured. The heave offering comprised a cake of the first of the dough, which was due on wheat, barley, oats, and rice, and it was not food as such but the offering had to be given in the form of dough, being fixed at one twenty-fourth if it was for private consumption, or one forty-eighth if it was for sale by baker.

A toll had to be paid at the gates of a city to enter.

All adult men paid half a shekel of sacrificial money annually at Passover, which is two drachmas.

They would also have to pay to get coins changed because sacrificial money could not display a graven image of anyone.

To buy two doves they would have to pay the price of three.

A pe'ah was left with everything.

Deductions were made to pay for alms, the tzedakah, the rations that went to the neediest, the disabled, the infirm, and itinerants. This differed from place to place, being whatever the master said.

They paid for the upkeep of the ritual bath.

They paid for the teacher who instructed the children.

They paid for the kosher butchers, the shochets.

Uri mused on how much all that might amount to—no doubt more than half of an average year's income, even though altogether it was not all that much.

But none of that was Roman tax, those were just the Jewish dues, though the Jews were unaware of the fact.

Five percent imperial tax as against at least fifty percent Jewish dues.

It wasn't certain, Uri reflected, that the tax Rome received was worth the trouble. The empire in the provinces was self-sufficient, and what went on was economically rational; in fact Rome was not seeking profits, yet it still aroused hatred in people's souls.

If the imperial tax was assessed on self-declared income, as it was in Rome, Uri went on thinking, then men would not declare even one tenth of their real income, and maybe one would perchance forget all about the age of that seven-year-old child and therefore not pay the poll tax for the child for a year or two more, and if Rome genuinely did not have enough people or means to check the authenticity of the self-declaration, then the Jews of Judaea were barely paying any taxes to Rome.

As if they were not even a province of Rome!

It was a free country, but its inhabitants were unaware.

Rome did not impoverish them; Rome made no money on the Jews.

He sensed that it would not be a good idea to enlighten them; they would stone him. They considered themselves pariahs, oppressed and eviscerated by a foreign power, with their sole enemy Rome, or Edom, no one else.

Barefooted, tattered men, women, and children were standing around next to him. They had no festive clothes to don to observe feast days; these were the same garments they wore on the Sabbath. In Rome even Jewish beggars did not look so strapped and shabby, however hard they might try.

It was necessary for their self-esteem to see the foreign power as being responsible for their misery, yet it was not the cause.

Rome had nevertheless taken something: their pride. It was not a sound policy, which should be brought to the emperor's attention. How could pride be expressed in monetary terms? What unit should be put on it? Half a pride equals two oxen?

The priest looked up at the sky. The day had begun to draw to a close. He asked something of Master Jehuda, who then launched into an enthusiastic explanation. The priest shook his head, and Master Jehuda gesticulated disconsolately, but the priest demurred and dragged himself back up onto his cart.

"He will not be spending the night with us," people around Uri muttered in disappointment.

The katholikos got up onto the box seat, the soldiers clambered onto their cart, the tax collector scrambled onto the last one, and the eight carts moved off onward toward the north. They could collect at one more village before nightfall.

The carts left clouds of dust floating over the dry land. The drought was my fault, it came to Uri's mind. Master Jehuda was lying on the ground on his stomach, his big belly pushing his backside up. The villagers fell to their knees or likewise prostrated themselves. Uri knelt. Another psalm was chanted, with Uri joining in. By now he knew both the Judaean text and the melody. "Give us this day our daily bread," he chanted.

It had been a joyous day. They had partaken of a priestly benediction, the Everlasting Lord had forgiven them for all the sins they had committed since the last priestly benediction, and they could sin again until the next time. Their firstborn and their best livestock as well as their best ripe fruits would end up with the Lord; very few had been found to be imperfect, which was something to be proud of. At the end of it all, that was the sense of this fine day, and the woeful figure of the tax collector was long forgotten.

As in Rome, everybody would be granted forgiveness anyway by going to the bank of a nearby river at the start of Rosh Hashanah and throwing in some object. The sins of the past year would adhere to that object, and the river would carry them away with it, while they would be left, cleansed, on the bank.

These people are not sinners in any case, Uri thought. They have neither time, nor strength, nor money, nor imagination for that.

The festival was not over. That evening, oil lamps were lit, and they all traipsed out to a field at the edge of the village where a bonfire was already crackling. They sang psalms, and the young men began capering. The girls grouped together and giggled as they watched them. The girls did not dance, only the young men, who were also allowed to drink. They pranced around barefoot, in their festive best, waving around sticks and whooping. The elderly reclined, supping, and watched them with forgiving, sage smiles: let them jump around until they drop. Uri was also invited. He was at first reluctant, but he eventually joined in the leaping around. He knew he looked stupid, but he capered determinedly.

There were some villages where people would walk on lit coals, but this was not a Jewish custom. It came from Persia, and it was nothing special: lit coals make no impression on feet with thick soles.

A few days later the Levites' carts again made an appearance, this time for the early summer tithe. Now there were eighteen carts, some already fully laden with produce and poultry, four-footed livestock trotting in their wake.

The people again gathered at the outskirts of the village, driving the animals, lugging open sacks of grain, fruit, and vegetables in large bowls. The law—not the law of Moses but the one in force—told them that "anything edible is to be tithed." They did not bring any firstborn or best animals or the best produce; those had already been allocated and were guarded and nursed, with care being taken that they personally should be able to carry the offering up to Jerusalem for Sukkot, thereby removing the burden of transport from the shoulders of the Levites.

One Levite with a long stick paced in front of the animals and counted them. When he got to every tenth one, he pointed at it with the stick and a second Levite dipped a brush in a bucket of red paint and daubed a sign on the animal's brow or wing. It might happen that an animal would jump impatiently out of line, in which case the Levite would gesture that it should be marked and the counting would start again at one.

The Levite might also do the counting, but then he would have to count in pairs for the rest of the day, Uri learned.

One of the sheep that had been marked raced back among its fellows. There was a mix-up, and the Levite gestured and the sheep next to it was also marked. The mark was washed off with a damp rag from the one that had rejoined the flock. Animals also had rights, they too having been created by the Almighty.

Uri stood in the crowd. This time the mood was not festive, because there was no priest present. He looked at the produce that the village had gathered: grain, shorn fleeces, oxen, cattle, poultry.

It wasn't much. It was a poor village.

Then he looked at the three laden carts and the livestock that were tethered behind them, the tithe that fell due the village at the beginning of summer.

It was a lot.

IT WAS NOT THE WISH OF THE ETERNAL ONE THAT URI SHOULD BECOME proficient in all aspects of carpentry, and around the middle of Av, Master Jehuda summoned him to say that he had received a message from Jerusalem that Uri was to return. There was no knowing why, but Uri was to go now.

The wheat was still being reaped and fruit gathered in. They had already started on the vintage, with the grapes being trampled in big tubs. There really would have been a need for his hands and feet too, Uri thought as he and two others set off back south. He curtly took his leave of the master and even more curtly of the assistants; they were able to breathe a sigh of relief that Uri had finally gone.

I didn't make any friends, Uri concluded, but he was not sure whether he should lament the fact.

He walked with practiced tread and did not converse with his companions; he used a mantle Jehuda had given him to cover his head. Two younger boys accompanied him with great respect and did not dare to address him. His exile must have given off a different impression than Uri imagined.

Master Jehuda had instructed them that Uri was supposed to report to a certain Joseph, son of Nahum, in the Upper City when they got to Jerusalem, and the youths had promised to ask without fail for a written acknowledgment of receipt from this Joseph when Uri was handed over.

They saw traces of abandoned construction work with weeds growing over some parts of it, but there was no city wall to the north. Stunted hedging had been planted all around the City, including the north, not so much on account of possible attacking armies as of fresh arrivals who could be extorted. Everyone had to enter via one of the gates and pay a toll, and even though the hedging was such that it was easy for anyone to step over, a Jew simply did not do that, and the toll would be paid. Uri remembered that from the north the Damascus Gate was the only one through which he could have left the City weeks before, but he was wrong; there was another northern gate, the Jericho Gate, at the beginning of the road leading straight and steeply to the Temple Mount, but they were not headed that way.

Before entering the gate, Uri paused to look back. Hills, downs, fruit trees, all green, all peaceful, all sleepy. He peered as the youths respectfully waited. Earlier they had shouted out that they could see the Temple, and no doubt they did because they were approaching the City along the spine of a high elevation. One of the youths kept asserting that they were now passing over Mount Scopus, which is to say Mount Lookout. Those heading for the festival would pass this way, but they were going on still farther in the Kidron Valley, to the east of the City.

Uri could not see the Temple, try as he might. Perhaps it was a phenomenon like some sort of cloud.

Yet I seem to have better eyesight than ever, Uri mused.

And veritably he could distinguish individual trees and bushes from each other better than before. That was impossible, he thought. Still, in the village he had been able to look at, touch, and smell plants as never before; what from afar continued to be uncertain contours now filled with content. In fact, as he had to recognize, he had been seeing from memory, and he was surprised that such a phenomenon existed.

One of the youths tugged out from under his robe a leather satchel tied to his waist. This was the money. He was hugely relieved when the boy had counted out the toll for the guard, and nothing more remained in the satchel. By then their two days of provender had run out; the two youths would be walking back home without food or drink, but for them two days of hunger was not a great price to pay if they could enter Jerusalem.

His escorts prostrated themselves and wept as they prayed.

Uri was unmoved, but he too knelt and murmured a prayer.

It was approaching noon when they reached the City. People ambled slowly in this residential area of the City. It was a strange hodgepodge of new and older housing, seedy buildings and guarded palaces surrounded by high fences, broad boulevards, and narrow alleyways, and, in its center, ditches separating it from the Antonia Fortress. This was Bezetha, the Jewish name for Kainopolis or New Town, through which Uri had been led by the two guards when they had set off for Beth Zechariah. Uri did not remember a single street or house; he may well have been confused then.

The youths did not dare accost anyone; they were awestruck just to be walking through the Holy City and could only gape in astonishment. Before now they had only reached the neighborhood of Jerusalem, never the City itself. Uri had to make inquiries himself as to whether anyone knew a Joseph ben Nahum. The passersby shook their heads and carried on strolling. Uri by now was hungry and thirsty, since they had finished off the provisions for the journey yesterday evening. On top of that, he wanted to be rid of the youths.

They saw a large market to the left, so they went over to take a look. This could not be the market in the Upper City, Uri realized, as he had seen from the wall that it was situated in the square directly in front of Herod's palace, and here there was no sign of any palace. They started asking vendors where the other market was located and were directed farther south.

They finally got to the Upper City and, upon emerging from the winding alleyways, they kept on southward until they reached the city wall. They proceeded westward beside the wall until they got to a gate. Uri recognized the large building at the southeast corner of the Upper City as the Antonia Fortress, where he had already had the pleasure of being quartered. To the right rose the Temple, its top occasionally visible among the haphazard jumble of streets and houses, as he too could now see, though he still felt nothing. The youths were trembling in their excitement, hardly able to walk, dumbfounded. Uri again asked passersby where the person in question resided, but none knew.

Finally someone came to a halt.

"Joseph ben Nahum?" he repeated.

"Yes."

"He doesn't live here but in the City of David."

"But I was told," Uri said with some irritation, "that I should look for him in the Upper City."

"Well, then you'd better go to the palace of the high priest. That's where the Sanhedrin comes together."

Uri was startled. There were memories tying him to one of the arches of that palace.

"What does he have to do with the Sanhedrin?" Uri asked.

"He's a member," the man said, bowed politely, and went on.

The youths were flabbergasted. Theo, whom they were accompanying, was paying a visit to no less than a member of the Sanhedrin! Uri glanced at them. They would be talking about this for weeks back home, and even next year it would still be a topic of conversation during the reaping and winnowing.

I've become as famous as that dumb Manasseh, Uri thought. He laughed out loud.

Everyone knew the way to the palace of the high priest, though it was far from easy getting there because they repeatedly had to turn left and right in the twisting streets.

Finally a small square opened before them in front of a two-story palace. Uri stopped and looked along the wall at ground level. Yes. Arches carved from ashlars, seven each to the right and to the left of the ornamental gateway. It was here that vendors had set up their stalls before they were moved in front of Herod's palace and the arches were bricked up to create twelve prison cells. Their doors could only be reached from inside, each of them separately. There was just one row of bricks separating them from the square, so if a person shouted from inside, he could be heard outside. Why did it never occur to us to shout?

Something still did not add up. If he was in the cell and facing the door, then the slit window had been high up and to the right, but the windows could not have abutted one another, as there had been fresh air coming in through them.

"I'll only take a moment," he quickly said to the idling youths, and set off along the wall toward the left of the north-facing main entrance.

He turned at the corner of the building and looked up.

At a height of around seven feet was a small vent facing east. The slit window of the corner cell.

That was where he had been imprisoned with the two robbers and the third person and then alone.

There were women walking about in the street, baskets or pitchers in hand. People must have been roaming around like this back then as well; it would have been possible to shout to them, and they would have heard.

He listened to test whether he could hear anything from inside. Maybe there were prisoners in the cell right now. He heard nothing.

Inside they did not know they could be heard. Or else the cell was empty.

But then what could he have said back then to those on the outside? That he was innocent but had been arrested? Even if he had yelled and been heard, what were they supposed to do? They would have quickened their pace in alarm. He was surprised that he had heard no street noise through the window—or was it forbidden to come this way during festivals?

In Rome there was just one prison, the *carcer*, a small, aging building kept purely for show. Although in the provinces of Italia there were workhouses for escaped slaves, robbers, and thieves, all arrested people were held in their own homes. It would have been very odd to have defendants packed into the basement rooms of the palace of the Pontifex Maximus, the chief of the priests, especially given that the Pontifex Maximus for quite some time had been none other than the emperor, who lived on the Palatine (or at least lived there in principle, as Tiberius had for many years been living on the isle of Capri).

Uri strolled back to the elated youths and motioned to them that they should wait before knocking on the palace gate. It was opened, revealing two Jewish soldiers standing sentry. Uri said that he was looking for Joseph ben Nahum.

"Who's looking?"

"Gaius Theodorus from Rome."

There was a lull as some people inside murmured something.

"You can come in," a voice said.

Uri turned around and waved to the youths, who just gawped as they watched him enter and the gate slam behind him.

A guard escorted him without a word along the ground level to the right—the opposite direction from where his former cell lay. Uri heaved a sigh of relief. The corridor received light from an inner space to the left; a well-trimmed garden with tall trees, clipped bushes, and fountains. He then found himself in a small room with a window cut high up in the wall, reminiscent of his old cell, and the guard shut the door.

Joseph ben Nahum was a gaunt, elderly gentleman, each and every hair white, even his eyes were a pale gray that was almost white. There were a number of stools and a table on which there were scrolls.

Joseph offered Uri a seat.

"What was it like with Master Jehuda?" he inquired affably.

"Interesting," said Uri frankly. "I would find it hard to say what exactly I learned in the village, but I don't have the feeling it was a waste of time."

"Splendid," said Joseph. "We have not placed any pilgrims with him so far, but that seems to indicate that we might do so in the future."

Uri kept quiet; it was not his place to raise any objections to this honor.

Joseph also fell silent, and Uri sensed that he was hesitating.

He thought back to the young official who three months ago, in the Antonia Fortress, had directed him to Master Jehuda. He could not recall any of the man's features. He glanced at Joseph's face; this one he would be able to recollect in the future.

"We are well aware, dear Gaius, that you wish to return to Rome, but until the opportunity to do so arises, you might place your knowledge and experience at our disposal. We would be extremely grateful."

"First of all I want to go to Alexandria," Uri said, surprising even himself.

Joseph nodded thoughtfully.

"Yes, we can assist with that," he said.

"It's something I really want," Uri said in excitement.

"I'll do what I can," Joseph declared.

It's not certain that he's an enemy, Uri thought. The white-haired man appealed to him, but caution was no bad thing.

"What was the trip from Rome like?" Joseph queried.

Uri was staggered. How far back that now seemed!

"Easier than I imagined," Uri replied. "We didn't drown in the sea, we weren't slaughtered by highwaymen, we didn't die of hunger even once."

Joseph laughed.

"Lots of people come from Rome for Rosh Hashanah," he said. "You could go back with them. Until then we'll place you in a pilgrim group. We were thinking it would be good for you to be with the Babylonians. They've got a nice place, and they're hospitable."

Uri considered the proposal.

"Don't the Jews from Alexandria have a guesthouse?" he asked.

"They do," said Joseph, "but we would still suggest the Babylonians."

"I'd be seen as a spy and ostracized!" Uri exclaimed. "I don't want to live in any community! I don't want to know anything about anybody!"

Silence reigned.

Joseph looked straight at Uri, who pursed his lips.

"If you're not going to live in a community, where you get free food and board," said Joseph cordially, "then you'll have to earn your keep."

"Fine," said Uri.

"What skills do you have?"

Uri pondered before giving his answer.

"I learned to be quite a good cabinetmaker with Master Jehuda," he said. "But I don't know if people here are looking for furniture-makers. I don't want to be a roofer, that's for sure, because I get dizzy."

Joseph ruminated on that.

"I know about just one builder who might be looking for a cabinetmaker," he said, "but before I send you over there, I'll have to ask if I'm allowed to do that."

"Where do they make those decisions?" Uri inquired in all innocence.

"At higher levels," Joseph replied, not without a touch of malice.

So the lunacy carries on, Uri thought to himself. They still believe I'm somebody important.

"All right, then," said Joseph. "Until a decision is made you'll stay at my place as a guest."

"I'm grateful, master."

Joseph froze. Uri fell silent; he was convinced that he was sitting opposite a Pharisee master: there was something both of Simon the Magus and Jehuda about Joseph ben Nahum. Joseph returned a rueful gaze before nodding.

THE BOYS FROM THE VILLAGE WERE GIVEN A STAMPED ACKNOWLEDG-ment of receipt and, in accordance with Master Jehuda's instruction, immediately set off back to Beth Zechariah. Uri found himself thinking that he would be quite glad to be going along with them. He gazed after them before going back through the gates of the high priest's palace.

He waited in a room on the ground floor until Joseph, worthy member of the Sanhedrin that he was, had finished his work. His accent was Galilean, Uri concluded in thinking back, and that surprised him somewhat. He was given water and fruit. The door was shut; Uri opened it once while he was waiting and looked out into the corridor, but no one was on guard. Joseph ben Nahum trusted him.

With a torch-carrying guard to accompany them, they walked down into Acra, the Lower City.

In the evening light they went along alleyways crammed with people, Master Joseph sunk in thought, Uri looking around him.

The bereft slept out on the streets, curled up in little piles like garbage set outside the houses. They had no belongings apart from the clothes they wore, and their stomachs rumbled even in their sleep, while up above, on both sides of the alley, the rich, oblivious to them, took the air and drank, shouting merrily across to one another from roof terraces ornamented with tubs of plants. Also sipping wine were their small children, who had been granted the unparalleled Jewish luck to have been born in the City; they too yelled and screeched merrily, the rich of the future, who did not have the stomach to look down onto the alleyway. The two shores of Sodom and Gomorrah, Uri reflected, and between them Sheol.

The homeless held their hands out lazily, without conviction, and did not look up at them. Perhaps they had done all the begging they could get out of themselves for that day, or else they could see it was rather unlikely that anyone escorted by a guard with a torch would be of a generous disposition.

Joseph took care not to step on them.

They passed through a gate under the Romanesque aqueduct that ran southward beside the inner city wall, then they turned north along the far side of the wall before descending a set of steps into the valley and climbing up the opposite hill. Uri asked what the valley was called.

"It's the Tyropoeon, the Valley of the Cheesemakers," Joseph said.

"And that is what the aqueduct bridges over?"

"Yes, only more to the north."

They proceeded among small, old, rickety houses, through alleyways that could barely be called roads. It was a district much to Uri's liking.

"It reminds me of Far Side," he said, "only that's flat."

"I've never been to Rome," said Joseph.

"It's interesting, though."

They ambled on. Joseph displayed to Uri no further interest in the empire's capital city.

"I live on my own in the house," he said. "My family does not live with me."

The torchbearer halted outside one of the houses, and they entered, whereupon the torchbearer bowed, wished them a good evening, and set off back to the Upper City.

They were greeted by an elderly servant, and Joseph asked for the supper. A back room led off from the front one, and behind the back room was a small garden with a foot-deep basin and a table surrounded by benches. The servant set on the table a terracotta oil lamp of precisely the kind that was in use in Rome. On the roofs of the small white houses that encircled the garden like a wall, neighbors, whole families with children, were perched, drinking and calling across to one another. As soon as the lamp was lit on the table, they greeted Joseph, and he in turn wished them a good evening. The roof of Joseph's house was also flat, but there was no ladder propped up against the wall.

"Is this the City of David?" Uri asked.

"It only borders it," said Joseph. "This is the lower part of Acra; we're not far from the Essene Gate and the Pool of Siloam. It's only possible to reach the City of David in a circle, because the old wall is still standing. There is a fine basin of water next to the Siloam. At times like now, when no festival is on, one can immerse in it."

Uri suspected that Joseph did not wish to share the garden basin with him, but no matter.

"Can I go to Temple Square?" he asked all of a sudden.

"What, now?"

"Not now, but by day."

"You can go now, as it's open until midnight, but you won't see very much of it."

"I saw it once, but I'd like another look. Do I need to be cleansed for a week beforehand?"

"You don't have to," Joseph said. "You've been cleansed by being in Judaea."

The servant brought two plates, one with bread, the other with greens. He also fetched a pitcher of wine and two earthenware cups.

"Thank you," said Joseph.

"Thank you," said Uri.

The servant went back into the house. Joseph got up and sprinkled some water from the basin on himself, then turned north and waited. Uri likewise sprinkled water from the basin on himself and turned north. Joseph had the shorter prayer because Uri spoke the prayer as he had learned in Beth Zechariah. Joseph stood quietly until Uri had finished, then resumed his seat on the bench. Uri sat beside him.

"Did you also say the part about 'Give us this day our daily bread'?" Joseph inquired.

"That's how I learned it in the village," said Uri. "I thought that was the way everyone in Judaea said the Sh'ma."

"Not everybody," said Joseph. "Only people who believe the end is nigh."

"And you don't?"

"The end is equally nigh at all times. I am one with those who believe the end may come at any time."

Joseph picked from the plates.

The food was good to eat, the wine good to drink—a light, slightly acidic wine to which they added no water—and it was good to hear the voices of the chattering neighbors.

"What was your trade in Galilee?" Uri inquired.

"I was a glassblower," answered Joseph.

"That's a good trade."

"Good, but it doesn't pay as much as in Italia."

"How did you become a master?"

Joseph gave it some thought.

"I don't rightly know," he said. "It sort of happened that way. People seemed to trust in me."

"Did you do any healing?"

"I'm not a magus," said Joseph. "I have too little faith to heal people."

Uri waited to see if the pleasant but serious man was going to ask him a thing or two, but he didn't. Either I'm of no interest to him, Uri mused, or he already knows too much about me. He hesitated to bring up the matter of Agrippa and confess that it was out of error that he had been seen as some sort of messenger. He made up his mind that if Joseph asked, he would be frank, but he would not bring it up himself. Joseph did not ask him, however.

Once they had finished the wine, Joseph said, "I'm trying to persuade them that it would be better if you had some work. Feel free to wander around the city, but don't leave because you'll only have to pay a toll to get back in."

"I won't leave," said Uri, and laughed. "Anyway, I have no money."

"Do you want some?"

"No, thank you."

"As a loan—to be repaid when you start earning money."

"No, thank you, all the same. I can manage fine without—assuming, that is, that I can have meals here."

"You eat as much as you want here. Just speak to Solomon, the servant. You'll have to yell, though, because he's hard of hearing."

"And my eyesight is poor," said Uri. "He's old, I'm young—we complement each other."

Joseph bade him a good night and went into the house. Uri sat out in the garden for a while, waiting until the neighbors climbed down from their roofs.

What business does Joseph have with knowing that my eyesight is bad? Why did I tell him? To show that I'm no longer ashamed?

URI GOT UP EARLY THE NEXT MORNING AND WENT INTO THE CITY. HE was surprised at how small it was.

Jerusalem was living its normal everyday life, not swarming with hundreds of thousands of pilgrims. A seaside town in Italia would be much the same with the passing of summer: sleepy, unhurried, dead.

The Roman mercenaries were not patrolling atop the colonnades but were standing about chatting in front of Herod's palace, the palace of the Hasmoneans and the Antonia Fortress. The market in the Upper City was full of stalls where sleepy vendors sold doves and every manner of jug, household article, and soil in small vessels: the holy soil of Judaea for pilgrims from distant lands, who, even when there were no holidays would still crop up from time to time. Few moneychangers were serving; they had mostly withdrawn under the arcades, where they blathered with the soldiers. Uri was mobbed by beggars and had a hard time getting rid of them. It did him no good saying he didn't have anything to give them because they simply didn't believe him, leaving Uri no alternative but to make a run for it. Nowhere, though, did he come across the legless beggar who raced around on his hands.

He found it odd that he was quite free to enter Temple Square. The bored Jewish police idled under the colonnades and paid no attention to the altar, where the duty priest made the burned offerings. Inscribed in Greek and Latin on the superb Corinthian brass gates separating Temple Square from the Women's Court was the warning that entry was forbidden for non-Jews. Through the Temple gates Uri could see no more of the interior than he had the first time, in fact less, because he was not allowed to step over the marble railing. He might have done so when the guards were not looking, for the minute of so that it would take until they noticed, but it never so much as entered his mind to do that.

Although he remembered an even bigger edifice, the Temple was still enormous. It was completely surrounded by scaffolding, but he saw hardly anyone at work; the few workers were just tinkering around. Levites were again lounging around the altar, carrying blocks of wood, or washing their hands in the golden bowl. They took exsanguinated, boned pieces of meat from the slaughterer's bench to the altar, sprinkled blood around, and sprayed the flesh with oil.

Uri stood on the south side of the altar. Three months before he had stood in the shadow of the wall, but now the sun shone on his head. It was later in the day and almost midsummer. The harvest was in full swing in Judaea. The paving burned the bare soles of his feet.

Not so long ago he had stood here as a suspect, and he had been made to walk seven times around the altar. Now he was again standing there, but at his own liberty.

There was no sign anywhere that in this holy place it was customary to force accused individuals to circle around the altar.

It was quiet and no one was pestering him. It was almost as if the two episodes of standing around had not happened in the same world. Maybe the episode three months ago was not even congruent with itself. Uri was certainly not the same person who had set off from Rome five months ago.

There were a few pilgrims, a couple of women accompanied by a group of men, standing atop the gate and piously watching the incineration, but most were either hanging around and chatting on the shaded, northerly side of the Temple or listening under similarly shaded arcades to the orations of prophets with bushy beards and blazing eyes. The lazy guards gave scant heed to the preaching and didn't give the impression of wishing to censor the words of the ardent orators. That was a wise practice, Uri acknowledged; if anything could be aired, then nothing had any weight. Still, it was curious that incitement was allowed in the immediate proximity of the Temple, the very center of the Judaic faith. Uri listened to the preachers, and it was not too much to say that the word incitement was unfitting; the lamentations of Jeremiah could be heard from the lips of speakers with impassioned eyes the whole day long.

One was tenacious in his hate-filled ranting about doom, disaster, and punishment of evil, but his incandescent, repetitive, and unimaginative words, like those of the rest, were lost in the prattling of his audience and the pandemonium of the other preachers. Uri was curious as to how long the speaker would be able to keep up the tedious tide. He got hoarse by noon, but he was no hoarser by the evening; he just kept on and on and incessantly on. Uri recognized the accomplishment, but he was alone. The preacher did indeed glance at him from time to time, but he did not notice that Uri spent the whole afternoon listening to him; it was not people to whom he wished to communicate something, but the Lord.

Also idling in Temple Square were individuals of scholarly air who expounded quietly and at length, backing up their statements with arguments. They explained the law to those standing around, many of them young men. Uri was surprised at how many men of leisure were loitering about, despite it being the time of day when most people should have been working. They would have been better plowing or plucking grapes! He then came to his senses and was amused by his own neophyte peasant consciousness.

There was a surplus of priests in Jerusalem. They were easily differentiated from everyone else by the white robes and the fact that they haughtily held their noses high. There cannot have been any fewer Levites either; indeed, there had to be even more of them if only a tenth of the tithe they received went to the priests, but they had no distinguishing dress. At first Uri shuddered at the very sight of priests' robes, just as he had in Rome, where priests were rarely to be seen, but here there were so many priestly garments that Uri's shuddering quickly abated.

What might be going on in his head, I wonder, Uri had pondered whenever he saw a priest. The priests in Rome were menacing to look at, and Uri expected to be struck dead any time he glimpsed one. A priest's robes also seemed to Uri to be part of the Creator's robes, and to touch them would be fatal. He would never dare speak to them, ever. He had thought that priests were in direct contact with the Lord Almighty and might address him any time they chose and get an instant answer. But with there being as many priests as there were here in Jerusalem, the Creator could not possibly speak to each and every one at the same time. What was going on in their heads must be more interesting than that.

Priests loitered on their own or in groups all over the City, and, not being on duty, they were unhurried, bored, and talkative. Uri did not accost any of them, though he would have been quite interested to know if the portion they were entitled to from the sacrificial offerings provided enough for them and their families. He vaguely recalled someone somewhere saying that some priestly families were on the verge of starving.

He could not be very Jewish if his soul was untouched by even the slightest feeling of joy to be able to spend time in Jerusalem. The youths, his companions, had wept. Good for them.

He was tormented by misgivings; that must be the cause of his strange state of mind.

He was being kept in Jerusalem, kept in the country, fed and watered as if he were livestock marked for slaughter. People will come along one day and slaughter me, and if my carcass is found to be without blemish, I'll be served up on the altar, my smoke will rise up to the Almighty and the priests will eat me; if my carcass is with blemish, on the other hand, I'll be eaten by ordinary Jews. It would be more reassuring if they were to milk their cows more regularly, but they don't do that.

What am I being kept here for?

That evening Joseph was late in getting home, and Uri had already eaten supper in the garden.

"You haven't been assigned work yet," Joseph said, "but they'll make arrangements soon."

Uri did not ask who the "they" were.

Joseph started to eat, and Uri watched. Eating was clearly not much to Joseph's liking; he seemed tired. He must fulfill some important office in the Sanhedrin, Uri thought.

Uri made up his mind to interrogate him.

"Why is the work on the Temple taking so long? I saw from the harbor at Caesarea that the work there was completed in just a few years, yet that was a vast undertaking—much larger in scale than the construction of the Temple, yet if I'm not mistaken they were started at pretty much the same time."

"Construction on the Temple started earlier," said Joseph.

"Why all the fiddling about?"

"It was completed long, long ago," said Joseph. "They're burnishing the finishing work; it keeps on being knocked down, then relaid... It's marble and gold, expensive."

Uri did not understand.

"It nominally gives work to twenty-five thousand men," said Joseph, "and that is too few. We really ought to be employing and paying a force of one hundred thousand, but that is beyond our capacity. You've seen how many beggars are living here, how many are dying in the streets. They lost their land so they came here; there's no way we have of forbidding it. On what grounds? Before long we'll be able to pave the whole city with them..."

Joseph's voice and mien were weary; this appealed to Uri.

"Freeloaders in Rome get state support," he said. "Me too."

Joseph nodded.

"Rome is wealthy," he said. "Rome has the means to support a few hundred thousand plebeians. We, on the other hand, cannot afford it, though we ought to be supporting at least that many or even more. We're poor, and we're breeding at a breakneck rate."

"Still, a time has to come when the scaffolding is taken down," Uri opined.

"We are doing the best we can to make that sublime and solemn moment fall as far into the future as possible. Before then we'll pave the nearby hills... Then there will be stupendous celebrations; everyone will rejoice except us. What are we going to set about doing with that mass of people? Ever more of them as time goes by! Order them not to reproduce when the Creator Himself encourages them to do precisely that?"

"All the same, is it near the end?"

Joseph broke into a smile.

"At the depth of the soul every generation expects some catastrophe," he said. "People have been preaching about this for centuries, but few fear it. They would like to believe that it will happen in their lifetime and make their period exceptional. They believe that they will avoid death by the skin of their teeth and that the moment of their death will coincide with their resurrection. For my part, I am afraid. It's not that I don't place infinite faith in the Lord who created me, but I'm alarmed at the naïve confidence that people have in this arrangement. It's as if the Lord had not given us the freedom to sort out our own lives for ourselves. If we do it well, He is pleased, and if we do it badly, He is saddened, but He is not in the habit of intervening. I have read the whole of Scriptures; He has never intervened."

This was when Uri came to understand that not everyone here was stupid. Not that Master Jehuda was stupid at all, but Simon the Magus and Joseph ben Nahum saw a lot more than he did.

"Not all masters speak that way," he said.

Joseph shook his head.

357

"What am I master of? It so happened that in my village I was good at my craft, grinding millstones and constructing water-lifting contraptions, and others noticed that I was a better miller than what they were accustomed to and started consulting me about business. As if I were smarter than them! Well, I wasn't, but that's how it was. Out of sheer terror I started reading, in case books had the answers. I didn't notice but before long I was being addressed as master, then I was expected to explain the law, and before long I was a judge... My wife was more cautious. She had married a young miller's son with flour in his eyes and flour in his hair. She had borne children for *him*, not for a master. But am I supposed to turn out of my house anyone who comes seeking my advice? A wretch who is just hopefully standing there? I took speedy leave with my family to settle down in another village that did not have a miller, and there I became a glassblower. But then it all began again."

The man really was a master.

"I wasn't careful enough," said Joseph. "Word about me spread... Men sent by King Antipas tracked me down and brought me before him. He wanted me as a counselor, as he did not have many trained people around him. The old elite had no liking for him, and he had done nothing to raise a new elite for himself. I wasn't willing to accept the position and went back to my village; all I wanted was to work. But people did not let me; they thought I'd rejected the offer because I was holding out for more money. They asked, pleaded, and finally threatened. I wasn't given any peace; they started working on my family... I wasn't firm enough, and in the end I was unable to say no."

Joseph looked at Uri.

"Don't ever let slip what you know—and still less what you don't know—because that knowledge is priceless, and people know that full well."

Uri shivered. A similar sentence had been said to him by another Joseph—his father.

"Don't get noticed. Don't stand out. Don't trust anyone," Joseph said, and averted his eyes. "You'll be used and then thrown away; whether you live or die, it's all the same to them. Be suspicious. If people love you, take an interest in you, caress you, be very afraid. Be especially wary of anyone who takes you into their confidence or to whom you are attached, because that person is also a human being, a selfish, cowardly, opportunist, abject scoundrel. Your enemies are the only ones in whom you will never be disappointed."

Uri sighed. He suspected that he would share no more suppers with Joseph.

THERE WAS, HOWEVER, ONE MORE SHARED SUPPER THE NEXT DAY.

"They approved it," Joseph said, and he seemed to be sincerely pleased.

He told Uri that he would be able to get a job on a nearby building site in the City of David. The walls of the palace were standing and the roofing was ready, but they needed a cabinetmaker, and there was a mosaic floor to be laid. It had been started six months before, a palace for Queen Helena.

"Where is she from, if I may ask?" Uri inquired.

"She's the consort of the king of Adiabene."

Uri did not venture to ask where exactly Adiabene lay. It was most likely a tiny kingdom somewhere in the East, though west of Babylon. He seemed to recall hearing the name before, only he had not taken much notice.

"From Rome's point of view," Joseph said, "it's probably barely noticeable..."

Uri broke out laughing, and even Joseph had to smile.

All at once Uri saw before his eyes lines from a scroll: "The marriageable girls are sold by auction to the bridegrooms, always selling first those who are the more highborn..."

"For just as ablution is customary after touching a corpse," Uri quoted aloud from memory, "so also is it customary after intercourse. And in accordance with a certain oracle the custom of Babylonian women is the have intercourse with a foreigner..."

"I have no idea if it is still the same today," said Joseph, "but around fifty years ago Strabo took the descriptions of others, and they are unlikely to have been all that fresh at the time, but anyway for him the description applied to all the Assyrians, and it was more a fable than a fact."

Uri nodded respectfully. Joseph spoke Greek and was a well-read man.

"Right now King Monobaz is their ruler," Joseph carried on. "A sort of tribal king, but Rome recognized him, and so did the Parthians. His wife, Helena, and their eldest son Izates let it be known not so long ago that they wished to convert to Judaism, but Monobaz did not. As a result the palace where you'll be working is being built for Helena, the Jewish queen, and Izates, the Jewish heir to the throne."

Uri was amazed.

"They converted—to Judaism?"

"What's strange about that?" Joseph commented. "There are plenty of Greeks, too, who convert in Syria, in Hellas, in Macedonia, in Armenia, you name it..."

"But a queen? And the heir to the throne?"

Joseph nodded.

"The story is that a clever merchant by the name of Ananias paid a visit, and he converted them. Only I know of no merchant by that name. I do, however, know a former high priest, the father-in-law of Caiaphas, the present high priest..."

Uri was shocked.

"It's a royal family," said Joseph. "We couldn't refuse. There was one difficulty, however, one that was hard to overcome, which is that Queen Helena was not only King Monobaz's consort but also his older sister."

Uri was even more amazed. Jewish law forbids incestuous marriage between a brother and sister.

"What was the solution?" he asked.

"Helena could not divorce, because then she would no longer be queen," Joseph responded. "But if she were living separately from her husband, then from the moment she converted it was possible to handle her like a divorced woman."

"But what if she did not get a divorce bill?"

"Since Monobaz was not Judaized, he could not be compelled to produce a divorce bill. Helena married her younger brother under the laws of Adiabene before she was converted to Judaism, and by converting she was absolved of all previous sins."

Uri shook his head.

"But it still can't be lawful," he said. "Herod the Great slept with his sister Salomé, but even he didn't dare marry her."

"The interesting case is not Helena. Izates would be willing to get circumcised, and he's the heir to the throne of Adiabene! Just think about it, Gaius: Adiabene will have a Jewish king. The only legitimate Jewish king in the whole world! Antipas is only tetrarch, and so was Philip before him, but Izates will be king—and as a Jew! Rome has assented, although incestuous marriage is also forbidden there."

Uri sipped the wine. Joseph was speaking quietly. From the surrounding rooftops, loudly and all at the same time, neighbors were talking, children shrieking, women laughing; they had little interest in the queen of a small far-off country becoming Jewish.

Large forces are at work, Uri reflected.

If Rome had assented, then that meant the emperor Tiberius had given his assent, and if the reports were true, Agrippa, who wanted to become a Jewish king, had access to him. What Joseph had said suggested that the heir to the throne of Adiabene, a child still, wanted to be circumcised, which would make him Agrippa's rival, and he in turn was supported by Jerusalem against Alexandria, the supporter of Agrippa.

Something still did not add up.

"As far as I know," he said, "Herod the Great had his son Alexander killed, and his sons, Tigranes and Alexander, and their descendants in turn became the kings of Armenia... So Armenia down to the present day is ruled over by a Jewish king..."

Joseph nodded.

"That's true, but then Armenia is a long way away, and it's far from certain that the emperor insists that Herod the Great's descendants should become Jewish kings..."

That applies to Agrippa as well, Uri thought to himself.

It can't be pure chance Joseph is sending me to work on that building site, Uri thought. When I'm brought before Agrippa, I'm supposed to report to him that a big palace is being put up in the City of David for the mother of a future Jewish king.

"Agrippa is well aware of all this," Joseph spoke.

Uri blushed in the dark.

"I'm not a spy," he declared.

"I never thought that you were," said Joseph. "I didn't say it because of that. But the workers know also, so don't be left knowing less than them. The queen and her son will move into the palace on Yom Kippur, since there will be a huge celebration anyway, and then the whole world will know about it. In any case, you won't meet Agrippa before then, because the high priests informed him long ago that he was not welcome in Judaea."

"Does that mean I have to remain in Jerusalem until Yom Kippur?"

"Until then for sure."

They sipped their wine.

"Don't let yourself stand out among the workers," Joseph advised. "Don't be any more diligent than them. Someone will come in the morning, and he will accompany you to see the foreman. It would not do if you were treated like a peasant; you're a Roman citizen, a pilgrim, and a cabinetmaker. They have a hut on the Mount of Olives. Some of the workers live there, the rest sleep in the street in the city. You would do best to sleep in the hut; you have to pay, but it's worth it. Watch your money, though it won't help. The wages are handed out a week in advance; that's the custom. None too clever, I have to say, but one can't do anything to change it; the arrangement evolved when people did not steal. Pay for your supper a week in advance. The owner of the hut runs a good canteen. Use the rest of the money to buy yourself a pair of sandals."

THE FOREMAN HAD A STICK IN HIS HANDS BUT IT SEEMED TOO LONG TO be used for beating people. Uri took it to be a plain old standard-bearing pole. He did not seem pleased that he was being made to take on a cabinetmaker.

"Well, all right, then," he said when Uri's companion, a burly, middle-aged man had repeated that it was the Sanhedrin's wish. "We'll find something for him to do."

The middle-aged man went away, leaving Uri standing in the half-finished building, on the ground floor of which men were seated and sprawled.

"We're waiting for the tiles," said the foreman. "Right now there is no cabinetmaking work. I'll drop a word later on to have you taken onto the payroll. What's your name?"

"Gaius Theodorus," said Uri.

"What kind of name is that?"

"It's Latin. I've come from Rome."

The foreman raised his eyebrows in wonder, then shrugged his shoulders and went off.

Uri looked around at the palace under construction.

The ashlars were marble-lined both inside and out, the basin in the center of the atrium on the ground floor was marble, the staircase marble, the columns marble. On the upper story the larger blocks of stone and the smaller stones that were fit in between them were plastered over. There was a man working in one of the rooms, painting colored birds next to one another on the wall opposite the window. Uri entered to take a closer look. Pots of paint were lined up on the floor, which had not been paved yet. The painter stepped aside so that Uri might admire his work. Extraordinary, man-sized birds bedecked in vibrant colors lined the wall, one next to the other, and they all had something cloddish, oafish, hilariously human in their features. Uri stepped up close to the wall, his nose almost brushing the half-finished, still wet paint.

"Do birds like this exist anywhere?" he inquired.

"Not on your life!" replied the painter self-assuredly. "I make them up!"

The whole wall had a blue and green base with capriciously intertwined plant tendrils, runners, and branches. The enormous birds were fit in at the front of those.

"It's marvelous," said Uri sincerely.

The painter nodded.

"This is the queen's bedroom," he gestured around him.

"Isn't she going to be frightened by these creatures?" Uri asked.

"Not on your life!" said the painter. "I also paint monsters, but these birds are friendly."

Uri asked how many rooms the master would be painting and what sort of figures they would have. Well, there was the queen's bedroom and then there would be three guest rooms. He had been given a free reign in the designs; all they had requested was that he shouldn't paint any improper scenes.

"Mind you, I'm an expert at those, too," he declared. "In Antioch I painted three bordellos from top to bottom. They were very pleased with the result and even gave me a letter of recommendation!"

Uri sniffed the paintings, which had a strange odor. The painter explained what each pigment was made of and where it came from. The purple dye came from Tyre, where the most highly prized mollusks were bred. They also produced many good dyes in other colors, but for some reason the painters from Sidon were the best. Generally speaking, Phoenician painters, stargazers, and land surveyors were highly talented, the master said enthusiastically. He had trained as a surveyor himself and had even visited Tyre, but he had grown tired of computations; they gave him headaches.

When the painter asked what he did, Uri explained that he was a cabinetmaker and had started work that morning.

"There isn't much need for cabinetmaking work," said the painter. "The furniture will be coming from Alexandria."

"One piece or another is bound to get damaged in transit," Uri offered hopefully.

"That may well be possible."

Uri asked if Queen Helena would have to remove all the fine birds from the wall when she became Jewish, or would it be enough to hide them under a curtain, but the painter did not get what he was driving at.

"It's the portrayal of living creatures," said Uri. "That's not allowed for us Jews..."

"That's long dead and buried!" the painter exclaimed, breaking into a laugh. "Rich Jews the world over have been filling their houses with pictures of animals and people since I don't know when! Jewish sarcophaguses are decorated with naked Greek gods. I carved two myself when I was in Antioch, one of Apollo, the other of Dionysus, for good, upstanding Jews who kept to the letter of the law. I wouldn't be a painter if there were no customers for the work, would I?"

This pleasant man was the only one working; the other workers were lolling about or sauntering in the shade of the cool, half-ready palace.

Uri took a seat among them and introduced himself. They grunted by way of a greeting and resumed their small talk.

At midday water and griddle bread were brought out, with a helping for Uri as well.

Nothing happened after lunch either. A couple of workers dozed off, while others went out into the yard and sat down in the shade, where they scribbled figures in the dust. Uri asked them what they were up to.

"As you can see, we're laying down some floors," said a portly, elderly man, and guffawed.

"We're waiting for the mosaic tiles. They're said to be in Caesarea."

Uri said he hoped it would not be long before he got to grips with learning that craft, because he had spent a day learning how to rest. The portly man laughed.

He was called Judas, and he had three younger brothers among the workers. They too seemed intelligent.

Uri introduced himself, saying that he had come from Rome. Judas asked him how well workers got paid over there. Uri had only the daily wages of dockers to go on; skilled workers no doubt earned a lot more. There were no docks in Jerusalem, so that was of no interest to them. They asked him how much he could earn as a cabinetmaker. Uri had to confess that he had picked up cabinetmaking since he had been in Judaea, so he didn't know about it in Rome.

"Whereabouts in Judaea?"

Uri told them about Beth Zechariah and Master Jehuda. Judas and his brothers had never been in that part of the world, though they too were villagers by background and had a thing or two they could relate.

They were peasants, six boys and three girls. Judas was the firstborn, but only in the sense that priests use since their mother had been pregnant when their father was wed to her. He was the sort of firstborn for whom the priests would be paid five Tyrian shekels, but he was not permitted to inherit property on that account, in other words, he wasn't entitled to a double share. A boy like that was considered illegitimate even if the man who had sired him married his mother; a man is a different person as a bachelor than after he has taken a woman as his wife. None of that had mattered as long as their father was alive; they lived and got by working on the land. But their father died after he spiked his foot on a nail. His leg and abdomen had swollen up, and he choked to death, hard as they had prayed for him. Then it had been necessary to split the wealth into seven and a half equal portions (daughters were only due half shares). Those seven and a half equal portions—fifteen portions out of which each of the daughters had gotten one and each son, two—were not enough for anyone's livelihood. In any case, it was prohibited to split land into such tiny portions. They had bickered for a long time until they, four of the brothers, had grown tired and left the village, leasing the land for free to the other two brothers and the three sisters, having made a declaration to that effect to the village's master and two witnesses. When two of the girls had gotten married it had been possible for them to take a dowry. The two boys who stayed behind were now grubbing the land, with their mother and remaining sister cooking for them. They would stay, because that sister was a bit weak in the head and no one would wed her. Things may be tight, but they managed to make a living.

The four elder brothers had learned the carpentry trade and been squeaking by in Jerusalem for ten years now. They had no house, nothing at all, but they thought themselves lucky not to have starved to death. They had worked on putting up the Temple, private houses, and warehouses beyond the city walls, but there were not so many jobs now. It was a good thing that this palace was being put up, and there were rumors that Izates, the princeling from Adiabene, would eventually have his own separate palace; maybe they could get jobs on that.

Uri then asked if, by any chance, they had worked with a Roman by the name of Plotius, because he too was a joiner.

"A big, black-bearded bloke?"

"That's the one!"

Judas nodded. He was a clever man, able to plan houses, and not at all badly, but he had been banished from Jerusalem because he stole.

"Are you sure?" Uri asked.

"No, I'm not sure he stole," said Judas, "but he was driven out anyway. Of course if there had been any proof he would have been in much bigger trouble. True, they wouldn't be able to sell him off as a slave, what with his being a Roman citizen, but people like that are carted off to the prefect in Caesarea. He investigates the matter, and if he finds the charge to be well-founded, then the accused is sent back to Rome and sentenced there."

Uri said that Plotius had not run into any trouble, indeed he had been able to return to Jerusalem as a delegate, which indicated that he hadn't stolen anything after all.

"He might have done some stealing anyway," chipped in one of Judas's brothers. "It all depends who he stole for."

Judas gave a dirty laugh and confirmed that if you were going to steal, it made a big difference whom you paid off.

"The richer they are, the more they steal," he declared. "Jerusalem is well-known for that."

"Just who are the wealthiest ones?" Uri asked.

"Well, the wealthiest ones..." said one of Judas's brothers, winding up for a long discussion.

Nothing happened until late that afternoon, when the foreman appeared, blew a whistle, and raised his stick in the air. The men scrambled to their feet, gathered around him, and walked out of the City of David through one of the city gates. They said that this was the Fountain Gate, that had long been its name, though there was no fountain anywhere near. The foreman tuned southward at the gate, and a few of the men followed. They were going to go through the Essene Gate into the Lower City, but most of them went through the meadow along the Valley of Kidron toward the river. The River Kidron itself was little more than a shallow trickle, with a plank leading over it to the other side.

"There's a lot more water in it in the autumn and spring," said Judas, "just in time for the festivals. But the drought is so bad this year that the river might dry up completely."

Lying about on parched stretches of the riverbed were broken wheels, rusted metal implements, rags, rubbish, leather bags, and animal skeletons—all the things that the celebrating masses had dropped or thrown into the water. It passed through Uri's head that this was the river in which tens of thousands of people yearning to cleanse themselves took a dip.

On the other side of the river they trudged up to the top of the Mount of Olives, proceeding past well-kept gardens, with small houses built of timber and stone dotted about at wide intervals.

They reached one cottage, where one of the workers rapped on the door. An elderly lady looked out before throwing up her hands in astonishment.

"You people already? So early! You should be ashamed, such loafers!"

This was the canteen Joseph had mentioned. Three tables of roughly-hewn timber stood in an unfenced garden. The cistern was empty, so the workers washed their hands in a bowl. They waited for something to happen. Uri grew restless.

"I was told that the week's wages were paid in advance," he said.

They confirmed that indeed they were.

"All the same, I didn't get any pay today," he countered.

"We get paid on Sunday," they said.

Uri tried to work out what day it was. The Sabbath he had spent in the village, so it must be Tuesday or even Wednesday. It was in fact Wednesday. His companions insisted he would get no pay until Sunday, so he shouldn't hold out any other hope. Sunday was the day the cashier came; he wasn't in the habit of coming any other day.

"But I've got no money," said Uri.

They were astonished. How could that be? Uri was in no mood to go into any details and instead asked them what they thought the chances were that the elderly woman would give him supper on credit until Sunday evening. They hemmed and hawed again but gave him no answer.

When the woman brought out plates of bread and cooked meat and placed them on the table, the workers reached for them without saying any prayers or even washing their hands. Uri stepped up to her, politely introduced himself and laid out his difficulty.

"One more hungry mouth to feed! That's all I needed!" she exclaimed in an unfriendly tone. "Pity they didn't warn me in time. It can't be done, it just can't... We make no profit as it is, and now we're expected to pay for being big-hearted!"

On that note she went back indoors to fetch the broiled greens. The aroma assailed Uri's nostrils.

The workers tucked in, with Uri standing by watching.

Judas growled at one of his brothers to give Uri some bread. The brother flared up in anger and went red in the face, but he still tore off a crust and set it down on the table. Uri did not touch the bread and walked farther off.

What Joseph had referred to as a hut might have originally stored tools but had since been renovated. Uri felt quite at home there, as it was not much different from a stable. The workers were still eating outside when Uri rubbed his hands clean on the earthen floor of the hut. Uri turned west, where he suspected the Temple was located, recited the short version of the Sh'ma, lay down on the sparse straw in one corner, and spread out over himself his sole possession, a blanket that Master Jehuda had given him, with fringed tassels along each of the four hems. He lay on one side, his legs drawn up so that the stomach cramps would be less distracting. After all, he had eaten twice that day, breakfast at Joseph's house and then again at noon in the palace under construction. If he did not have to do any work, he would last on one meal a day until Sunday. He would be moving around less and eating a lot. The palace was already connected to a water supply, and he had taken a drink, which tasted fine.

He woke at daybreak to find he was freezing and the air was smoky.

He sat up and searched around in the gloom for his blanket but could not find it. His hand struck a sleeping man, who groaned. He felt in the other direction and again knocked against somebody else. Hunger gnawed at his stomach.

He realized that if he were to go out right now he was unlikely to find a space to fit back into, and outside it might be even colder. At least the smoke was giving a bit of warmth, and anyway he was not going to find the blanket right now. He lay back down and, humming to himself and rocking as if he were praying, managed to slip into a light sleep.

It was morning, and the others had gone out to have breakfast. Uri got up from where he lay prone, and looked for the blanket. He searched the whole hut without coming across it. It had undoubtedly been stolen, and if he had any money, that would have disappeared too. Good thing he had no money. If he had a pair of sandals, those would have been slipped off his feet. Good thing he had no sandals.

He set off after the voices fading into the distance and caught up with them at the plank crossing over the brook. They were engrossed with one another and joked with full bellies; no one spoke to him.

The dark blocks of the city wall, the Temple, the palaces and towers now sparkled with a golden color as the morning sun shone on them from the east, the direction of the Mount of Olives. Uri had trouble mapping out the buildings' boundaries but could see the color well. He was lost in wonder that such a color existed.

The workers did not have to pay at the city gate; they were known to the guards. Uri wormed in among them, his head bowed, and was not noticed.

The foreman arrived at the palace late that morning. Uri stepped up to him, greeted him and asked whether he could be given an advance on his wages.

"Oh, of course," the foreman said. "You weren't here on Sunday..."

The foreman agonized over what to do.

"It's fine by me," said Uri, "if you let drop a word at the canteen to let me eat on credit..."

The foreman shook his head.

"I can't get over there nowadays; I haven't got the time... Ask Judith, the woman who runs it, she's a decent sort, just a bit grumpy. You have to ask nicely, yes, that's the way around it. Don't ask her husband, he doesn't make the decisions, she does."

The foreman was delighted with that plan and gave Uri a friendly pat on the back before rushing off to attend to some urgent matter upstairs.

Uri drank a lot of water those days and chewed his lunch slowly, beginning to suspect he was not really entitled to it.

On Friday afternoon they went back to the hut early, the Sabbath being the Sabbath however you looked at it. They made their prayers to the northwest, the direction in which the Temple was actually located. Uri also received a share of the supper on the Sabbath. This is charity I receive, he thought, like some destitute vagrant. He was not offended, though; he got roast meat for the first time in ages. He again chewed slowly, deliberately, almost cautiously—not too much but not too little either. The wine made him slightly tipsy, and the next morning he slept past the morning prayer.

On Sunday morning he marched cheerfully along with the others toward Fountain Gate, not even trying to avoid the gaze of the gatekeepers, who still did not haul him out from among the others, either because they were not looking in his direction or had already seen him going out.

The cashier arrived in the morning escorted by two guards, though they were carrying no weapons. The cashier squatted in the atrium, opened his case, and took a scroll out. He ticked off the names of those whose wages had been counted. Uri was left at the end. The cashier shut the case, rolled up the scroll, and rose to leave.

"I'm owed as well," said Uri.

The workers looked his way.

"Everyone got theirs," said the cashier.

"I haven't gotten mine yet," said Uri.

"There's no other name on the roll," said the cashier.

Uri saw red. He yelled inarticulately that they would regret this, that he was going to report them, that everyone would be in for it. Even the guards stiffened, uncertain about what to do.

"I'll tell Joseph, the one in the Sanhedrin," bawled Uri. "They can make your lives truly unpleasant, you dolts! This is enough from you all! I've had enough! Enough!"

The workers had fallen silent. The panic-stricken cashier started to make excuses: that was all the money he had been given, nobody had said anything, it was not his fault if somebody was not on the roll.

"Who is responsible?" demanded Uri.

The foreman appeared, having heard the shouting.

Uri tore into him.

"It's your fault. It was up to you to inform people, you scum! You'd better go right now and tell them I've been taken on, and bring me my wages!"

"Come on!" the foreman said mockingly. "It's not as if you moved so much as a speck of dust."

"You go right now," Uri whispered. By now he had grown hoarse. "If you don't, I'll see that you're taken care of! Joseph ben Nahum is not exactly going to thank you!"

At this the foreman was alarmed; his tone changed.

"Why didn't you say so to start with?" he wailed. "You didn't tell me, none of you did... You didn't come with him. How was I supposed to know?"

He turned on the cashier.

"Give him his wages!"

"I can't, I have no more money with me!"

"Never mind," whispered Uri. "You can come back later and bring it then. Gaius Theodorus is my name. Take note of that!"

The foreman wrote down Uri's name, and Uri checked it; he had made three mistakes.

"Correct that," Uri said sternly, pointing out the incorrect letters. "There, there, and there."

The foreman flushed but made the corrections.

"I won't be able to bring it today," the cashier remonstrated. "It's closed already... Tomorrow..."

"I'm not prepared to starve for another day," Uri declared. "I need to pay for the whole week in advance, and to lay down the money today. You'll have to drum up the money from somewhere and come back, because if you don't I'm going to report you. And you too!" he said, turning toward the foreman.

Silence fell. The workers enjoyed the scene quietly.

"Fine," said the foreman. "I'll give you an advance, but then I'm getting it back next week, okay?"

"It's all the same to me," said Uri, "as long as I get my wages!"

The cashier and his two escorts departed, and the foreman took a pile of coins out of his pouch and counted them, bemoaning why Gaius Theodorus had not spoken up in time. He had a huge amount of respect for Joseph ben Nahum and the whole Sanhedrin and the higher-ups! Why didn't Gaius Theodorus speak up before this?

He pressed the coins into Uri's palm.

At least he registered my name, reflected Uri as he stuffed the coins into his loincloth.

The foreman had urgent business to attend to, so he hurried off. The workmen chortled. Uri sat back down, leaned his back against a wall and looked at the fountain, which was now operating. The sculpture portrayed fish clinging to each other like a bunch of grapes, with the water spurting from the topmost fish.

Judas took a seat beside him.

"You've got a big mouth," he said. "I'd never have thought so from the look of you."

"It *was* big," Uri croaked.

Judas laughed.

"How much money were you given?"

"I don't know," he answered. "My wages for the week."

"And how much is that?" Judas asked.

The others gathered around, sitting or stretching out.

Uri tried to recollect what they had said about this back in Beth Zechariah.

"A drachma a day," is what came to mind.

The workers laughed.

"Only the very best get that much," one of them said.

"I'm a very good worker," Uri whispered with conviction.

That raised a laugh.

"So, how much did you get?" Judas pushed. "Let's see."

Uri stood up and took the coins from his loincloth. The workers tittered. Uri spread out the small change, a mix of silver and coppers. He had no idea what they were or what they were worth. He arranged the identical ones next to each other.

Judas slowly counted them up, doing a careful job as he had nothing else to do.

"Three ma'ahs, one tropik, two tresiths, twelve issars, two aspers, four pondions, one hundred and twelve prutahs..." He looked up. "Do you think that's about seven drachmas?"

The workers were quickly rolling on the ground with laughter; a couple of them traced out the numbers in the dust and became absorbed in adding them up.

"Half a zuz, plus half a zuz, plus a quarter zuz, plus a half zuz, plus two fifths of a zuz, plus one third of a zuz, plus roughly three fifths of a zuz... That can't come to more than three zuz, man!"

Uri sat again; the workers crowed.

"One drachma is how many zuz?" Uri asked, his ears starting to redden.

The workers roared with laughter, still rolling on the ground. Even the painter popped his head out from the upper floor, curious to find out what everyone found so amusing.

"One drachma is how many zuz? Lord Almighty! You're asking how many zuz in a drachma?"

Naturally, one drachma was one zuz, and the foreman had handed over less than half of Uri's weekly wage! Menachem had dipped into his pouch and unerringly handed over half! Menachem wouldn't make a mistake with something like that! He has a good feel for it; he's had plenty of practice!

After they had amused themselves, Judas fished a piece of papyrus out from somewhere and wrote down the more important exchange rates for Uri to memorize. Uri thanked him and bundled the coins back into his loincloth.

They had laughed at him, but not all that much; they had accepted him, because he had dared to speak up.

THE BREAKFAST, SUPPER, AND LUNCH, WHICH JUDITH ALSO DELIVERED to the workers, cost altogether two-fifths of a zuz per day, and the use of the room, another one-fifth per day. She took all of the money Uri had, did some lengthy calculations in her head, and gave back some of it, not a lot.

"So you have money after all!" she said, raising her index finger. "I knew it, you dark horse!"

Uri stuffed the remaining coins back into his loincloth.

Two days later unsightly, itchy red spots covered his testicles and the bases of his thighs. He and wealth did not get along well, he concluded. Early the next morning, while the others were still sleeping, he scratched a place for the coins in the ground, not far from the big holes that had been dug as a privy at the bottom of the garden. He hoped the money was not going to be made irretrievably unclean. He washed the loincloth thoroughly and hung it out on a tree branch so that it would be dry by evening. That was a mistake, because come evening the loincloth was gone. Never mind, he told himself; at least it won't chafe my balls.

He was paid the next week's wages in full. He had seen other workers shoving off without anyone caring, so, without asking for permission to leave work, he went that same day to the Upper City market, where he bought himself a new loincloth and a new pouch. He put the money in the pouch and tied it to his waist under his long shirt. There was a long stretch along the row of stalls selling second-hand goods; he looked around, thinking that this was probably where his tasseled blanket had ended up not so long ago. He didn't see that particular one, but he did see others; however, he did not buy one, there being no point as it was now so warm at night. He did buy an ointment for every imaginable skin complaint; it did not come from laserpicium, because that was unknown in this part of the world, but it was not balsam either: he had smelled it. It was sold in small jars, five tresiths a jar, which was expensive, because that was five-eighths of a zuz, as he now knew, but he could allow himself the expense. He put a jar in his pouch and strolled contentedly back to the City of David.

That evening he paid for all the coming week's meals and added what was left, which now came to a tidy sum, to the coins he had already stashed. He was delighted to have come across such a safe bank in the land of Judaea. If he ever met Simon the Magus again, he would recommend it.

Uri spent a lot of time sitting on the upper floor, gazing at the activities of Hiskiyya, the painter, while the other workers on the ground floor fretted or, in the Roman style, played games of chance, which are forbidden to Jews. Hiskiyya had by now finished with the queen's bedroom and had begun on Izates's room. There was no one pushing him; he just liked working. Uri asked if he might try his hand at painting one of the figures, but the painter was unwilling to let him. Uri tried arguing that if he messed anything up, Master Hiskiyya would be able to correct it easily, but the painter insisted that it was wrong to waste costly pigments. The next day Uri appeared with a piece of papyrus and some chalk, which he had bought in the nearer market in the Lower City; he asked if he might copy the figures the master had already painted. Hiskiyya permitted it, so Uri stepped up close to the wall, squatted, drew, stood up, stepped close to the wall, squatted back down, drew... He spent the rest of the day contentedly doing that.

"Well, I never!" Hiskiyya said that afternoon, wagging his head. "That's not bad at all... Pity about your being semi-blind, because you could have made a wonderful painter..."

Uri would have been happy to go on drawing, but the Almighty again had other plans in store for him than his making progress in that craft. The next day the sheets of mosaic for which they had been waiting for weeks finally arrived.

The crates, lying in straw and themselves lined inside with straw, were lifted carefully from the big carts. There were sixteen long, bulky crates, four on each cart. The foreman jumped around nervously, watching each crate get opened. A count was made, noted by the foreman, of the marvelous square-shaped, painted, and fired tiles and the smaller bits that would have to be laid around them to make the pattern. Once that had been done, all the pieces were carefully placed back in the crates.

The foreman signed a papyrus to indicate that he had received the crates and their contents were without loss, after which the unloaded carts clattered off.

The foreman divided the workers into watches to stand guard. It would not do to leave the readily transportable and valuable tiles there as they had done with the marble blocks before they had been built into the palace; it would have taken more than a whole night to lift those. Uri would be on the first watch in the evening. He was not pleased, as it meant that they would have to go without supper that day, and in the days to come there would be little opportunity to make that up: Old Ma Judith, such a decent woman, was not going to give them more. He was glad, on the other hand, that Menachem had put him on the same watch as Judas and his brothers.

Uri was relieved when Judas sent one of the brothers off to buy supper for them all.

That evening, by the light of the oil lamps, they were eating warm griddle bread with a delicious goat's milk cheese accompanied by wine when Menachem turned up in the company of two torchbearers. He politely wished them all a pleasant meal, then said something to the torchbearers, who picked up one of the crates and carried it out of the atrium. Uri did not understand what was going on, but Judas and his brothers went on eating, so he did too. Before long two torchbearers reappeared and carried off another crate; Menachem wished them a good evening, then he too went off. A cart could be heard creaking outside, then silence fell.

"What was that about?" Uri asked.

"He was just checking whether we were on guard," said Judas. "It wouldn't look good if any of the mosaics were to be stolen."

"And so?"

"We were on guard."

One of his brothers could not hold in his peals of laughter.

"But they carried off two crates of them!"

"Sure they did. Look, Gaius, any site you can't steal from is a site where no building will take place."

Uri absorbed that answer.

"But won't those two crates be missed?" he responded.

"No," said Judas, "because the shortage will be made up by slipping in a bit more cement along the walls to make it look like it was the design from the start. It will still look very imposing."

Uri probed a little further, asking about where Menachem had taken the crates, and who he had sold them to."

"It'll be a place he's had a long time now," one of the brothers concluded. "Menachem is the foreman on more than one site. He's also stolen marble and sheets of silver from here without it ever being noticed."

Uri was beginning to grasp what sort of crimes Plotius had been accused of.

"That's nothing," Judas suggested. "A drop in the sea, and if one thinks about it, there's no Jew harmed. The small palace is going up at the expense of the king of Adiabene, and it will decorate the city of Jerusalem, and those two crates will also go toward the decoration of a house in Jerusalem. The only ones who are harmed are the people of Adiabene, but so far as they are concerned it doesn't matter what exactly their king fritters away their taxes on because he's going to fritter them away in any case."

At this the three younger brothers also perked up.

"This is not the way to organize a really grand theft," said Gedaliah, the youngest. "Let's just suppose, purely for the sake of theory, that the priests wanted to steal. That can never happen, and there's no record of such a thing ever happening, but just suppose."

"So, let's suppose," said Uri, now curious.

"Let's also suppose that the high priests wanted to steal," Gedaliah continued. "Not that they ever did such a thing! It would never even cross their minds, but purely for the supposition's sake."

"Purely a supposition," said Uri. "But how would a high priest steal?"

"By stealing the Almighty Lord's property, that's how," said Judas. "They would set up a system like this. To start with, the priests would receive the meat—all sacrificial offerings, with rules on which parts belonged to the Levites and which to the priests, which could only be eaten in the Temple and which outside, which could go to their immediate families, and which to their in-laws."

"The thing is, though, all the animals that make up the priesthood's property, before sacrifice, are held by herdsmen in pens on the nearby hills. If one of those animals got injured, then it would no longer be immaculately pure and could not be placed on the altar as a sacrificial offering, but the priests are free to do with it what they wanted. They could eat it or sell the meat; it didn't matter now because it belonged not to the Lord but to the priests."

"Let's just suppose that this is actually the practice. It would mean everyone in Jerusalem could guzzle themselves to death with meat, while in the provinces they'd be left without even enough for feast days."

The tale accorded fully with Uri's experiences. In the countryside they rarely ate meat, and there was little even for festivals, whereas people here, even they themselves, had plenty. He had seen meat being sold in the market, kept cool by goatskin bags of cold water—lots of meat, almost like in Rome. He had also seen live poultry and wondered how that could be.

He still did not fully understand how the system worked, so they explained.

"A sacrificial animal belongs either to the Lord or to the priests," Judas said. "It was pure when brought into the process. Otherwise it would never have been picked out in the countryside, and the authorities would not have allowed it to cross the border into Jerusalem. Any declaration about the animal made by the priests is invalid because they are the owners, and the word of an owner, according to the law, is null and void. It is a fine law, a wise law; our predecessors were experienced men for setting down the law, blessed be their names. The word of a herdsman, by contrast, is acceptable by law, because he is not the animals' owner. A fine law that too, a wise law. After all, why would anyone who was not the owner lie? Only, like any law, this too leaves some room for play. Shepherds, for instance, might swear that a ewe stepped in a ditch, and that was how its leg came to be broken, and that testimony would have to be accepted because a shepherd is not the owner of the livestock entrusted to his care, and from that moment on the priests are free to do with it what they wish."

"But then who would instruct a shepherd as to what sort of statement he needed to make?" Judas asked with a malicious laugh. "A priest, of course. Let us say that an animal designated by a priest has its leg broken by the shepherd, hitting it in just the right spot with his staff, it immediately becomes imperfect just on that account. Or he cuts its nose, clips a bit from the ears, after which the butchers examine it and declare—for what else can they do?—that the animal has become unclean, and right away the animal is off to the market, and the priest makes money on it. He gives the shepherd a few prutahs, the butcher a few ma'ahs, but the real profit is the priest's. Or rather: would be. He has to give a few zuz to the high priests, who head the whole shady business and do the bookkeeping. In that way it would be possible for Jerusalem to be choking in meat in while the peasants all around die of starvation."

Only hypothetically, of course, added Yoram, another of the brothers, because nothing like that had ever happened, and Uri must have seen with his own eyes that people ate less meat than in the countryside.

"Oh, indeed!" Uri affirmed. "I was quite surprised myself!"

Judas's brothers said that if indeed things were like that, then no city in the world would be more sinful than Jerusalem because everything the Ten Commandments forbids is sinful, and those who were the Law's foremost servants would be committing sin first of all. It would be a miracle if rebellion did not break out on account of such ungodliness. But then there was little chance of that, with Jews being so law-abiding, and the peasants did not know what was going on. Even if they were told about it by excited rebels with wild, burning eyes, they would not believe it, so pure were their souls. It was divine luck that this was purely hypothetical and that no high priest or ordinary priest, no butcher or shepherd would do such a thing, at least not in Judaea.

LAYING MOSAIC TILES WAS TIRING, BACKBREAKING WORK—HARD ON the knees but interesting all the same.

Setting the ready-made square or hexagonal sheets of mosaics alongside one another did not take any effort in itself, but to produce nice designs from the small pieces of stone was an exciting challenge, and Uri kept on badgering Menachem until he allowed Uri to join in this part of the work. He enjoyed choosing among the small, colored, square-cut chips of stone and fitting them alongside each other, smoothing some of them down to fit with the rest. Uri loved fiddling around and now he had free reign. The picture to be laid out was outlined by the painter, but he left the workers to their own devices and would only look at the end result.

Judas was quite right: the two stolen crates of tiles went unnoticed.

Uri now understood why mosaic-laying was such an expensive business; it involved the work of a huge number of people—people to hack out the variously colored stones, others to cut them down to small fragments, people to cut them into squares, people to transport them, people to sketch a design, people to lay them out... He recalled the huge number of splendid mosaics that he had seen in Rome and could not understand why he had never given this thought until now.

He had gotten used to Judith's grouching and even made the acquaintance of her fat husband, who spent all day lying around the house and praying. His fellow workers had accepted him as if he had been living among them for years, working on the outer cladding of the Temple; they no longer stole from him and had even forgiven him for the sin of having been born in the unclean Diaspora. They had no interest in Rome; that was a long way away, whereas they could relate many tales about Jerusalem. They told stories about lodging houses where their sandals were swiped from off their feet while they slept, how they had been short-changed by foremen who were much more villainous than Menachem, how the puffed-up rich had treated them like slaves, even though they were free men, all their ancestors had been, as far back as family memories went, which was many generations back. It had crossed their minds to leave the city and join up with some band of robbers, though they had given up on that idea; it was only certain tribes that had traditionally occupied themselves with robbery, so they could only be underlings at best.

It would be nice if they could make money from smuggling, but having been born in the middle of Judaea they had no contacts with the Jews of the Parthian empire, so they had discarded that idea too. For a few years they had toyed with joining a community of the devout, which would have certain advantages, like being sure they would never die from starvation, but they would have no freedom of movement and be subject to the will of a leader. There were many such pious communities all over the place, with families in every town who made their living out of being more devout than a high priest. There were times when people would not speak to one another for weeks on end because that was what the leader had ordered. They might not be able to step outside the house for weeks or be allowed to establish contact with women outside the community. They helped one another everywhere, but they looked down on those who were less zealous. Judas and his brothers preferred to knock around as workers in Jerusalem.

Uri looked forward to Rosh Hashanah and the immense throng that would arrive for the long series of festivals. It would surely be interesting to observe how people celebrated at the city he had become an inhabitant of by chance. This was a time, said the workers, when it was possible to drink a lot and eat a lot, with the break from work lasting for two weeks. However, they had not heard anything about white-garbed brides-to-be for sale dancing on the Mount of Olives. If they didn't know, it must be a fairy tale, Uri concluded.

They went into great detail about the festive garments of the high priest, because they had lived in Jerusalem for so long that most of them had been able to stand by the altar and see him. Even those who had not stood near the altar could visualize the priest's exact appearance, with his breastplate, set with four rows of three small square gemstones each, representing the twelve tribes of Israel. It was as if anyone who happened to be staying anywhere near Jerusalem at the time had seen it with their own eyes.

They also recounted that wicked Edom laid claim to the high priest's vestments the whole year round, storing them in the unclean palace that Herod had built. Only two days before the festivals did the prefect's people hand the garments over to the high priest's representative so that the high priest might don them for sacrifices, and at Passover, as the Law allows, and also for Yom Kippur, which the Law commands. After the festivals the garments would be handed back to the Edomites, thus becoming unclean again. The Sagan's men would have to spend a whole day cleaning it before the high priest could clothe himself. The workers strongly objected to the humiliating practice; even Menachem himself was in agreement.

Uri was never asked about Rome, either by the workers or, for that matter, the peasants in the village, but they still had their own firm ideas about what the Roman Empire was. No question that it was Beelzebub's snare, which the Everlasting Lord permitted; He had a habit of amusing himself by sowing dissent among men and waiting for the good to triumph even without his assistance. The Roman Empire was a test that the Lord had given his chosen people.

He had made it so powerful so that it would be harder for the good ones to vanquish, so that they would brace themselves, strive a little. But Beelzebub would be defeated, the workers were quite convinced of that, and Jews would recover the right to look after the high priest's vestments, and the foreign forces would clear out of the Holy Land at long last. What about the Lord's works in Babylon? There had been just one language until He had confounded all the languages of the earth there, so that the people should no longer understand one another's speech, which highly amused Him. The Tower of Babel fell down and Babylon's power ended, yet the Jews had escaped, thanks to the mercifulness of the Eternal One.

Uri just nodded and did not attempt to point out that the chosen people were not the only ones the Eternal One had put under the yoke of this gigantic empire. Nevertheless, he too had often wondered what the sense was in having a single power rule over the Great Sea and all its coasts and the inner lands—to wit, all the known world, beyond which there was little, not counting the Parthians, India, and China, which were so far away that their existence seemed unfathomable beyond the silk that came from there.

The Creator must have some purpose with the Roman Empire, Uri supposed, but he did not know whether to adopt the standpoint of a Roman or a Judaean Jew. He could not imagine the tens of thousands of Jewish men who lived in Far Side all of a sudden marching off to the Forum and declaring that from that day onward all Rome should worship a single god and all the inhabitants of the empire's seat being converted in one stroke, shattering all idols, and becoming eager servants of an Invisible Lord. Of course, Cicero on one occasion in a lawsuit had spoken of the Jews of Rome as being a nation of rascals. Uri had read the collected speeches the great orator made in tribunals and, now he came to think of it, a hint of fear seemed to be emanating from those contemptuous words, as if the advance of that dirty, loquacious riffraff could be a threat to Rome's integrity. But the Jews were an overwhelmingly poor and humble people in Far Side, and just happy that they were tolerated.

As Uri saw it, he himself was a beneficiary of the power that the workers considered their deadly enemy and against whom they invoked their gravest curses when breathing their solitary prayers. This was now the third occasion when he had sensed how ambiguous his position was as a Roman citizen in Judaea, and if the truth be told, he was also in an ambiguous position as a Jew in Rome. He thought back to what had run through his head while watching the cohorts from Caesarea marching past: our army pushing our people from the road. But then what kind of soldiers were those? There had not been a single Italian or

Roman citizen among them. It was all more complicated than something the Almighty could have created; he had created something beautiful and rational, then it slipped out of his hands.

It was the month of Elul, and Uri hoped that nothing would happen until Rosh Hashanah, at the beginning of next month, on Tishri 1–2, so that he could spend the long festival in Jerusalem. Ten days after Rosh Hashanah, the New Year, came Yom Kippur, the Day of Atonement, the biggest of all the Jewish festivals, and on Tishri 15 would come Sukkot, the Feast of Booths, and that festival would last until Tishri 23, the festival of Simhat Torah, the day of rejoicing in the Law, which would mark the end of a year of weekly Torah readings in the shul, and also the restarting of the cycle. Virtually the whole of Tishri, then, was a festival. By that time it would be September in Rome, and the Jews of Far Side asserted that the weather at Rosh Hashanah was always good for at least ten days, as it was necessary for it to be good on Yom Kippur. His mother too had said it each time August came around, nice and early: "You'll see, the weather will be fine in September, when it gets to Rosh Hashanah." And it had always been fine, and his mother was proud to be Jewish.

The weather was also fine in Jerusalem at Rosh Hashanah, on Tishri 1.

That day no one worked. In the evening a fire was lit in the hut, and they held a communal prayer with an informal family mood. The next morning they rambled down the Mount of Olives and crossed the River Kidron, but this time instead of entering the City through the Fountain Gate they went to the Valley of Hinnom where many people were already strolling ceremoniously. All the workers had taken with them some insignificant tiny article, which they threw into the Hinnom with a murmured prayer. Uri tossed a prutah into the water to carry away with it all his past year's sins. He asked why it was that the Kidron was not good enough as a river for that purpose; the Hinnom had also dried to a brook as the autumn rains had not yet arrived. Their reply was that the Hinnom was the river of the wicked, where children had been sacrificed in Israel's darkest days; the river could not forget this.

That evening it was possible to eat, but the next day was for fasting.

Rosh Hashanah in Jerusalem was a rather somber affair, Uri decided. He was expecting Yom Kippur and Sukkot to be more exciting, but the Almighty cannot have wished for Uri to see a glittering festival in Jerusalem, because on Tishri 4, when they resumed work on the palace, a man came and had a whispered conversation with Menachem, after which Menachem came over to Uri to say the man had come for him.

"Where am I going?" Uri asked.

Menachem did not know, but the man was following instructions from the Sanhedrin and would now accompany Gaius.

"Am I going to come back here?" Uri asked, thinking now of the tidy sum that he had buried under the tree next to the privy.

Neither the messenger nor Menachem had an answer.

He was not even able to take proper leave of his colleagues.

This time they proceeded northward along the Valley of the Cheesemakers and entered a smaller building a bit to the east of the Xystus, which Uri had by now learned used to be where the Sanhedrin had held its sessions. The building was known as the Hall of Hewn Stones, as the judges, all seventy of them, had at one time sat in several semicircular rows around a stone platform reserved for the accused or the petitioner.

Uri was curious to see whether he would be received by Joseph or the hunchback whose name he did not know.

It was a Jewish military officer. He was a middle-aged, stocky man, bald and with strongly protruding eyebrows.

"The reason I asked you to come, Gaius," he said, "is that I would like to make a deal with you. At Rosh Hashanah a delegation will be setting off for Galilee, and I would like you to be a member. You would be passing through Samaria under the leadership of an experienced commander."

Uri held his peace, not knowing what to make of the matter.

"Who would I be representing?" he inquired.

The officer did not understand.

"I'm a Roman citizen," Uri added. "Is Rome sending me?"

"You are a Jew," said the officer, "and you'll represent Judaea, if you prefer. But like I said, we are offering a deal. You are an experienced delegate, and if you return we would reward you by sending you to Alexandria as you wish."

Uri's heart leapt. Alexandria! To swap this dusty provincial small town, sleepy Jerusalem, where nothing ever happened, for the true center of the world!

This meant that Joseph ben Nahum had indeed passed on his request.

"Fair enough," Uri said. "When do we set off?"

"Tomorrow morning."

I won't have time to pick up my money, Uri thought. Never mind.

He was already walking off to the meeting-place in the company of three taciturn Jewish soldiers when he was struck in retrospect by the odd way in which the officer had expressed himself. "*If* you return," he had said, though he might equally have said "*upon* your return."

Samaria was dangerous. Why are we not avoiding it, as those traveling between Galilee and Judaea customarily do? They had time to choose a detour, and maybe we are now taking an urgent message to someone.

And anyway, who's this *we*?

Uri established that he was more thrilled by this new assignment than by spending the whole day laying mosaics in the company of familiar workers, as much as he truly enjoyed that.

I'm an adventurer, he reflected, both remorsefully and proudly.

THEY CUT ACROSS THE SQUARE AT THE TEMPLE, WENT DOWN THE SERpentine path, exited the City through the Jericho gate, and took a northeasterly route. Uri was quite certain that his escort had no idea what kind of mission they were sending him on, so he did not try to interrogate them. That reticence seemed to meet with their approval, as they did not try even once to prod him into saying something.

They came to a rest by a village house that was bigger than usual and had two soldiers on sentry duty in front.

His escort handed him over, took a draft of water, and headed back toward the City.

There were eight mules grazing in the yard. There will be eight of us, including me, Uri reflected. A mule is an elegant beast compared to an ass, appropriate for longer journeys. He was quite sure that his backside was going to get saddlesore over the first few days.

One of the guards ushered him into the house.

There in the gloom sat a throng of people, a mix of soldiers and civilians.

"Pax to you, Gaius Theodorus!" said an officer.

"Pax to you too! Pax to you all!" said Uri.

"He's the last of your companions," said the officer, turning to the civilians. "Gaius Theodorus, young though he may be, is an experienced traveler; he was a member of this year's Roman delegation, and he has spent time as a peasant and a worker in Judaea to cleanse himself."

There was a murmured welcome. The officer did not introduce any of the other members of the delegation to him, and they didn't say anything themselves. Uri had no wish to converse with anybody and spent the night squatting in one corner. During the long trip he would get to know them.

The next morning they went northward on mule-back.

They did not carry any weapons, only a sack with bread, olives, and fruit.

Uri took special note of two figures clothed in white. He at first thought them to be priests, but they did not behave like priests. Their mantles were short, hardly reaching their knobby knees, and they did not give a priestly benediction; indeed, they did not engage in conversation with anyone. Each had a trowel dangling from his belt.

Riding his mule at the back of the procession, Uri saw that his companions, with the exception of the officer, were seated clumsily on their mules. Not experienced travelers, then.

Uri's thighs ached, but he was familiar with the feeling, and by tomorrow they would no longer be aching. His companions would not become acquainted with the feeling until that night, the skin of their behinds broken-skinned and bleeding, but that would also clear up with time. Uri sat rigidly upright; if he were ever to get a crick in his back, as had happened once on an ass in Sicily, his life would be sheer misery for days on end. His back was the one thing he needed to watch out for, nothing else.

They carried on northward, first crossing the road to Damascus, then advancing across fields. It was a journey that Uri was now familiar with, having done it twice before—once to Beth Zechariah and once back, only those times it had been on foot. Even carried by mules they did not make faster headway.

None of the other seven gave any sign of knowing one another, but for all Uri was concerned that did not exclude the possibility that there might be old alliances among them. They exchanged no words, maybe fearing that there might be squealers among them. My companions might just as easily be disagreeable figures who don't know what to do with people, just like me, Uri thought, then chided himself: he knew nothing about his companions, so it was wrong to presume anything about them.

When they rested and ate, Uri reclined on his side and did not touch the smarting calluses that had formed on his thighs; in two days' time they would no longer hurt. The others despondently felt at and squeezed the calluses and blisters on their backsides; as they were close to him, Uri could see them all too well. I rise above them all in traveling, he thought blithely, notwithstanding the fact that he was the second puniest of the lot. He had noticed earlier a young man even punier than himself, with colorless hair and watery eyes, his entire frame in poor condition. The lad took the bruising surprisingly well, however; he may have had an opportunity to ride a mule or ass before. True, his feet did not touch the ground, so there was no need for him to make an effort to keep them lifted. He also had long arms and thin fingers, so what might he be? A pickpocket? He did not look fit for anything else.

Uri scrambled to his feet and went behind the bushes to relieve himself. He heard a noise of something rustling about and looked up. One of the white-garbed men was squatting, while the other was carefully scooping earth over his own turd with a trowel. The other then finished, stood and, started to dig, strewing the earth he dug in a nice little mound over the feces. Both took care, making sure that the shovel did not touch the excrement. Uri could only wonder.

The big heat wave was prevailing, with a dry easterly wind bowing. I brought this on, Uri contemplated. He was waiting for one of his companions to make some comment and curse the east wind, which was associated with drought, but no one said anything. Maybe they were all town dwellers. Uri felt an urge to vilify the east wind if they wouldn't, but he resisted the temptation. I'm school-ing myself not to disclose what I know, he thought, but then he mused that his knowledge of easterly winds was not truly thorough. Some people had told him that this brought drought and he had believed them, but maybe it was not so; he had no personal knowledge of it, so it was better to keep his mouth shut.

The officer stood, mounted his mule, and set off. The others followed with-out a word being said.

As evening drew in, they reached the edge of a village. Uri narrowed his eyes to try and make out whether this was a village he had seen before, but nearly all the villages looked alike. The scattering of houses, the settlement with no wall—that is what made it less than a town. With the officer leading they slowly jogged among the houses, before which old crones and children were seated, staring at them. The officer asked which was the master's house, and they pointed it out.

The master was a short man with a wrinkled face. The officer dismounted from the mule and drew the master to one side. He explained something, slipped a hand under his tunic, and gave a handful of coins to the master, who bowed, accepted the money, and hid it under his tunic in a pouch of some kind.

"Are we going to get something to eat, or maybe even quarters for the night?" asked the scrawny youth.

Uri shook his head but didn't say anything.

We haven't been pestered for two days by robbers, the thought occurred to him, but he hadn't said anything. The day after tomorrow another master will have to be sought out and he too will have to be paid off. It will not be possible to pay him any less than the first, because by then he will know for sure how much his colleague got—if no other way, via message by fire.

Uri's suspicion proved correct; they simply had a drink of water before moving on, and they only stopped when even Uri felt weary. He tethered his mule to a tree, recited the long Judaean version of the Sh'ma, pulled out his loaf of bread, spread his blanket, and lay down on it. He set about his meal with relish, his body pleasantly tired by the travel. The officer watched him, then he too said his prayers, followed by the others.

"Is this where we're going to spend the night?" came a tremulous, horrified voice.

"Yes," said the officer.

"But we might get robbed!"

"No one is going to rob us," said Uri. "Quite the opposite, the robbers will be keeping watch over us as we sleep!"

Whether that was true or not, the next morning all their belongings were still there.

They prayed, had breakfast, and resumed the trekking on muleback.

Uri screwed his eyes up, now beginning to sense that the countryside was familiar, that they were somewhere in the neighborhood of Beth Zachariah.

My village, Uri thought, and he laughed at himself for feeling so emotional about it. He wiped the tears from his eyes with a snicker. What a dolt I am!

He felt a strong temptation to lead the party to Master Jehuda; his companions would be amazed to see that he was on home ground here, and it would do wonders for his prestige. All the same, he decided against doing so: he was not on intimate terms with them, and he was not going to betray to them those whom he regarded as his kinsmen. The thought also ran through his head that Master Jehuda and the others, even the young girl, were part of a long-gone past; it now belonged to somewhere else, locked in the realm of memories. It would not be right to disturb the passage of time; one had to move on.

The officer moved to one side to wait for Uri at the back of the line; the rest kept on trotting northward.

"Have you been around here before?" he asked.

"I have," Uri replied. "But no farther north."

They swayed along beside each other on their mules.

"I'm Aaron," the officer said. "I already introduced myself to the others before you arrived at the house."

The mules trod slowly but surely; there was no need to spur them on.

"These mules are experienced travelers," commented Uri. "Same as me..."

Aaron gave a snort of laughter.

After hesitating a little, Uri asked, "Where are we headed anyway?"

Aaron did not answer immediately but eventually came out with, "Tiberias."

"Why are we not avoiding Samaria?" Uri asked.

Aaron sighed.

"Because that's the order," he said, and promptly moved off to the front.

They proceeded all day, not even stopping for lunch; anyone who felt hungry had to eat on muleback. We're in a hurry, Uri thought. I wonder why.

He did a quick calculation. In four days' time it would be Yom Kippur. Every Jew who lived within three days' traveling distance of Jerusalem would now be preparing to set off. From this area they would reach it in two days. Tomorrow they would be passing through a region from which people were just setting off southward to Jerusalem. It's odd, Uri thought, but we're going in exactly the opposite direction.

He shuddered.

It was the same as the shiver that had gone through him in Rome when he had grasped that he had to reach Jerusalem for Passover, but he did not understand why he was shuddering now. This was not the same kind of journey. He nevertheless felt some presentiment; there was no knowing what it was, but it was unsettling.

The next day they reached the border between Judaea and Samaria. There was nothing marking it, but the party became tenser than they had been up till then, and Aaron was even more taciturn than before, if that was possible. That night he split them up into shifts to stand guard, estimating time from the arc of the moon across the branches of a tree. Uri was allocated to the dawn shift, but he spent much of the night awake thinking. We are creeping along like robbers, he thought. If it was necessary to stand guard, then the safe passage they'd bought from the robbers had expired, so from now on it was other robbers that had to be feared.

He still knew nothing about his traveling companions, merely that the two men in white-tunics consistently buried their excrement under a mound of earth. What could had enticed them into this, he wondered? Did they also long to go to Alexandria? Or were they, perhaps, guilty of some misdemeanor and paying for it by having to take part in this delegation?

In the morning they moved off, still northward.

At the edge of a village they noticed that people were congregating: old people and children, men and women gathered around two carts loaded with animals and produce. They must be setting off for the festival in Jerusalem, Uri thought. Aaron resolutely jogged in front as they took the path leading into the village.

When they were near the group of people, Aaron jumped off his mule.

"Peace be upon you!" he greeted them.

"And upon you!" a few of the people answered.

Uri narrowed his eyes; he could not see the faces clearly.

"For the festival?" Aaron asked.

"Yes, the festival," they replied proudly.

"We'll meet up there," said Aaron.

"We'll meet there!" they replied.

Uri's group carried on northward.

He swayed as he walked, half-asleep when he was suddenly startled into full consciousness.

Those people were setting off southward whereas we are still headed northward. Why, then, had Aaron said that we would meet up with them at the festival? That can't be true!

On the path they encountered a larger group, which was driving livestock and a cart, but they were headed north.

This was already Samaria! These people were not striving to reach Jerusalem but their own ruined shrine in the north, at Mount Gerizim.

Was that where we were headed?

The temple of the Samaritans had once stood on Mount Gerizim, which they had built in defiance of the Temple in Jerusalem that had been demolished. There they had made sacrificial offerings of incinerated meat to appease a wrathful Lord, and before Herod the Great it had been destroyed by John Hyrcanus, then the king of the Jews, and since lain in ruins. However, the Samaritans kept making sacrificial offerings among the ruins even now, and they hated the Jews, with whom they shared a common God and language.

They had difficulty making further progress along the path, continually changing course because of pedestrians, forcing the mules to trample untrodden shrubland, listening to the joyful singsong. Like the Judaeans, the Samaritans chanted psalms; they were taking sacrificial animals and produce to the ruins of their own temple.

These people are not going to harm us, it occurred to Uri; they believe that we too are going to make sacrificial offerings at their temple, that we are not hostile Jews but their brothers.

A cunning dodge, that: a Jew from Judaea could hardly be safer in traveling in Samaria. Presumably we are also saving ourselves a substantial detour on the way to Tiberias.

But what about the way back? Shall we be coming back at the time of the Festival of Booths, like good Samaritans? But traveling is forbidden for them, too, at that time.

By the afternoon every path had become clogged with people, and the mules, unused to such activity, constantly tugged this way and that, balking and coming to a standstill.

These people struck Uri as being happier than those on the road from Caesarea to Jerusalem.

A prophet with a flowing beard went along in the center of one group, yelling hoarsely, with people joining in.

"The Ark of the Covenant!" they shouted.

Aaron held back until he was in step with Uri at the end of the line.

"Move it! We're making progress too slowly. Don't fall behind."

"What are those people shouting?" Uri asked.

"You can hear them yourself," Aaron said, pressing on to the front.

That evening they were unable to find a place for themselves, so they made camp among a throng of people.

A divine miracle has occurred, people kept on saying, joyously, both to themselves and to each other. The Lord has had mercy on us, God is with us, blessed be the Eternal One. They bowed to the north and prayed, saying a short Sh'ma, and they never wearied of proclaiming that those alive right now were joyous because the Ark of the Covenant had turned up. It was a miracle, a miracle! The Almighty had worked a miracle: the Ark of the Covenant had been found!

Uri shuddered.

He had already given some thought to the Ark of the Covenant on the journey. It was as if his thinking about it had caused people to start talking about it. They wielded shovels, sticks, and swords; serious men and shriveled elders and irrational children and wailing women. The Ark of the Covenant was in the depths of Mount Gerizim; the depths of the Holy Mountain were concealing it. It only had to be dug out.

So that was what we were going to do—dig it out!

They prayed and chanted throughout the night; it was impossible to sleep.

By daybreak Uri had formed a clear picture for himself.

The Lord had appeared in a dream to a certain Matthew, a prophet, and informed him that the lost Ark of the Covenant was hidden by Mount Gerizim, and also told him exactly where it was to be sought. Upon awakening Matthew doubted whether he had really spoken with the Lord in his dream, but when he turned his gaze on the mountain he saw a burning bush in its depths at exactly the spot the Lord said the Ark of the Covenant had been buried centuries ago. Matthew raced over and began digging, but he realized that he alone was not equal to the task, and he set to preaching to the populace what the Lord had told him, calling on them to dig alongside him. He had been preaching the words of the Lord for a week now. The Lord was well aware when to announce the secret because the people would be flocking there for the Day of Atonement anyway;

indeed, many had set off earlier than usual. Everyone would dig, and the Ark of the Covenant would be found, and with the Ark of the Covenant, power! Because the Lord is seated on the Ark of the Covenant, and in this way he would raise the Semites of Samaria above all peoples, blessed be His name!

As to what kind of man this Matthew was, no one had anything to say; obviously they did not know him. But the important thing was not so much who this prophet was but that the Lord God had appeared to him in a dream.

Uri, however, was troubled.

He would have been extremely pleased were the Ark of the Covenant to come to light, but he found himself unable to believe it was about to happen. If it had not been located for centuries on end, and why would it now in particular? The peaceful landscape of Judaea and Samaria did not exactly give the impression that Judgment Day was nigh.

No way are we going to Tiberias, it occurred to him. Mount Gerizim had been the destination from the outset.

But why?

He began to calculate.

They had been traveling for four days now. If the vision really had come to Matthew a week ago, as people were saying, then it would have taken at least four days for news of it to reach Jerusalem. Messages could be sent by fire, but that was not usually used for long, complicated messages, as vowels were left out and meanings could easily be misunderstood. It was quite probably a courier who had carried the news. It must have been at least eight days ago, or even earlier, that the courier had arrived in Jerusalem with the news that people were going to search for the Ark of the Covenant at the festival with shovels and swords in the depths of the mountain. We're being sent there to see whether the chest comes to light.

Uri muttered discontentedly to himself that the story was not credible.

There was no chance of the actual chest turning up, Uri thought. Had another chest been fabricated? Had the Samaritans forged one and buried it on the mountain so that it would be found and they could assert ownership and gain the upper hand over other Semites? Even supposing that was the case, why precisely was it us, newcomers to Judaea, who were going to be put in proximity to the chest? What might our task be—to bear witness to the fact that the chest was a fake or, on the contrary, that it was genuine? But then who amongst us would have the courage to bear witness on a matter like that? If that chest came to light the high priest would have to see it, but there is not a priest among us!

We have been sent to Samaria as spies, to spy on those looking for the Ark of the Covenant.

The Samaritans were so joyous that they paid no attention to them. They scarcely even greeted the two in white robes, though they recognized and appreciated that they did not worship toward the Temple in Jerusalem. Aaron had heard the familiar way that the two white-robed men addressed the Samaritans, but he had let it be.

How could it be that men in white robes lived in Judaea and didn't pray toward Jerusalem? Was it not all a single religion? Or was it a single religion that had broken up into several faiths?

Roman Jews, like the priests of Jerusalem, did not believe in a Hereafter or the immortality of souls or the transmigration into a new body, yet Master Jehuda and other masters believed in these things. They still belonged to one religion, however, because they made sacrificial offerings to the Temple. But was anyone who did not make such sacrifices a Jew at all? Was where one paid taxes a criterion of Jewishness? The Jews of Parthia who had stayed in Babylon paid no dues, or like the Roman Jews sent only half a shekel in taxes, yet they were still Jews. What did they believe in?

To believe in an Invisible, One and Only, Everlasting Lord, to see Him, to strive with the Lord, as the name Israel literally means—maybe that is enough to be Jewish. The Eternal One binds His people to Himself with a bond stronger than the Ark of the Covenant: He has the menfolk's prepuces cut off, and that is the mark that shows they are His.

From then on they were surrounded night and day by an intoxicated throng. The Samaritans had not drunk any wine, but they had become inebriated by their own souls, and as far as the eye could see signs of the Divine presence, the Shekinah, His Immanence in the world, the Holy Spirit, appeared in the fields and trees, in the grass and sky.

For the Samaritans this Day of Atonement was more significant than usual. Uri was pleased when he recognized this. Once he got back to Rome, he would recount it all in detail to his father.

They moved with the crowd. The walkers were hemmed onto the narrow tracks as there were no other paths. Stones, clods of earth, and protruding roots cut their unshod feet, and Uri felt a twinge of guilt watching from above on the back of a mule. They made slow progress, adopting the pace of the mass anyway, so Uri got down and walked on among the people. His feet were sore but he did not mind, as the soles would soon be as tough as leather. Aaron saw but did not upbraid him. The two white-robed men noticed and also dismounted, leading their mules by the tether. The others, though, stayed on their mules.

Progress was slow.

"We are Essenes," one of the white-robed men said. "What about you? Where are you from?"

Uri gave a brief outline. The Essenes humphed.

"Was it your people, then, after whom the gate in Jerusalem was named?" Uri asked.

"Our forbears," they answered proudly.

Uri carried on walking with the Essenes, who were greeted gladly by the singing Samaritans attached to the throng.

The day becomes long if a person is walking, and talk is slack until the sun sets. That was how Uri learned that Essenes, of whom he had never heard in Rome, were few in Judaea, perhaps just a few thousand altogether, but had been there for a century now. There were places where they lived in their own houses, with the occasional scattered family member living in a village or town; wherever they were they helped one another and obeyed the commands of their leader. When Uri asked whether they had a single leader in Judaea, they first gave an evasive answer, then confessed that there were several sects of Essenes and several leaders. Many Essenes maintained only frigid relations with those Essenes that still paid dues to the Temple, but they still considered them clean; the Essenes alone had striven for purity in this mire that the Almighty had unleashed on Earth during recent generations. The high priests and even the masters left them alone. Individuals and even whole families could join the Essenes, but it was difficult to gain admission. Newcomers were subject to a trial period, during which it was not permitted to do or, above all, think anything impure. Thoughts could also be impure; indeed, it was mainly thoughts that were impure, stemming as they do from the bowels, and they condemned impurity of thought among themselves. They would regularly recount to each other their thoughts, even their dreams, and the community would discuss them and judge whether they were clean. If not, the leader would impose a punishment on the person who had thought or dreamt it.

They carried a trowel at all times because they were allowed to leave no impurity in their tracks on the face of the earth. They never resorted to arms, although a trowel might be used a weapon if it was whet. They only used it in self-defense, and if it was ever used as a weapon it had to be buried deep in the soil, at least five feet deep, because blood made it impure and would never wash away. Violent use of the trowel had to be confessed to the community, who would judge whether it was legitimate or not. If it wasn't, the leader would mete out a harsh punishment, the harshest of which, for the Essenes as it was for the Jews, was ostracism, even if a follower had attained the highest rank of initiation, the fourth.

Both of the Essenes had attained the second degree, though only after many years, because unfortunately they were not born Essenes. Their leader had nominated them for this delegation in response to the high priest's request for Essene involvement.

Uri felt inclined to live in an Essene community for a while, though he did not admit it, as it would have been a futile wish.

Unclean Samaritans were not to be found among the Essenes, the Essenes said disparagingly, as they walked with the masses toward Mount Gerizim and politely returned the respectful greetings of the unclean Samaritans.

By the second day of advancing through the crowd Uri was singing their psalms softly to himself, having learned the texts; they did not sing many psalms in Rome. Joyfully treading in step with pipes, the Samaritans were carrying their produce northward—wheat, barley, grapes, figs, pomegranates, olives, honey. They said a golden-horned ox decorated with olive branches proceeded at their head, while the women carried fruit in baskets wreathed with laurel leaves on their heads. It was one of the psalms of King David that they sang most often, the thirtieth:

> I will extol thee, O Lord, for thou hast lifted me up, and hast not made my foes to rejoice over me.
>
> O Lord my God, I cried unto thee, and thou hast healed me.
>
> O Lord, thou hast brought up my soul from Sheol; thou hast kept me alive, that I should not go down to the pit.
>
> Sing unto the Lord, O ye saints of his, and give thanks at the remembrance of his holiness.
>
> For his anger endureth but a moment; in his favor is life; weeping may endure for a night, but joy cometh in the morning.
>
> And in my prosperity I said, I shall never be moved.
>
> Lord, by thy favor thou hast made my mountain to stand strong; thou didst hide thy face, and I was troubled.
>
> I cried to thee, O Lord; and unto the Lord I made supplication.

What profit is there in my blood, when I go down to the pit? Shall the dust praise thee? Shall it declare thy truth?

Hear, O Lord, and have mercy upon me; Lord, be thou my helper.

Thou hast turned for me my mourning into dancing: thou hast put off my sackcloth, and girded me with gladness;

To the end that my glory may sing praise to thee, and not be silent, O Lord my God, I will give thanks unto thee for ever.

He switched to a dance rhythm as he hummed the psalms, in the way that the others did, and found out that it was easier to move ahead by dancing and singing in this manner.

One more day, Uri thought to himself as evening drew in, and we shall be reaching the sacred mountain.

They had just set up camp for the night when Aaron, who was standing and looking to the north, called them over to him. He pointed to the distance, up in the sky. Uri didn't see anything, but Uri's companions did, and a great excitement took hold of them. Others looked in the same direction and noticed too.

"Birds," whispered the thin youth, Jehoram.

Uri squinted but could still see nothing.

The sun was peacefully preparing to go down.

People discussed something excitedly, a few cried out, then there were ever more people as a large group arrived running from the north, yelling, "Soldiers! Soldiers! Soldiers!"

The tribes got together, and the elders consulted one another. There was a general commotion, no one lay down to sleep.

Those coming from the north related with sobs that soldiers had attacked and slaughtered the people assembling at the foot of Mount Gerizim. Syrian soldiers, a whole cohort; they had come from the north, from Antioch via Galilee, and encamped peacefully two days ago at the foot of the hill, but then they had unexpectedly set upon the people, striking at will, chopping, lashing. Many had died—children, women, and old people alike.

"Let's push on," said Aaron.

They resumed their northward muleback trek in the gathering twilight, while people streamed past in the opposite direction, shouting, lamenting, raising their hands to the heavens, and cursing.

That night they stretched out farther away from the trail. Aaron again organized them into a duty roster. He ordered a start soon after daybreak the next day, only allowing them a drink from a brook but giving them nothing to eat.

By the morning they reached the village of Tirithana at the foot of the hill.

Several hundred corpses were scattered around, with blood, or something very like it, still oozing from some of them. Fires were smoldering. Children, women, and old people, decapitated, without legs, impaled, all lay motionless, among them mourning relatives kept vigil, whole clans beating their chests, sprinkling ashes on their heads, rocking back and forth as they prayed and rent their garments.

There were no soldiers to be seen.

Aaron went with two men into the village to seek out the elder. Meanwhile the rest sat down. Uri felt a dull empty numbness overcoming his insides. He had no wish to look at the dead bodies, but some force ordered him to look. The women were all dressed in colorful garments; they had been cut down in their finest clothes.

Here and there, wailing mourners raised a dead person aloft to take them to be buried. A crowd tried to carry the body of a small child; everyone wished to get near, jostling and wailing, shaking fists. The mountain loomed on high; Uri narrowed his eyes but couldn't see any ruins, only the clouds above.

An old man was being carried off next to him. A long, white beard flowed down his face, and his eyes were open as if in wonder, even though he was dead.

Farther off, a man who had been split in two lengthwise was now being put back together, his innards stuffed back into his abdomen and the two halves knotted together with cord. A sword blow had landed on his shoulders and split him apart again down to the navel.

Uri shivered; he would have easily vomited had there been anything in his stomach. Aaron knew full well when he did not allow them to eat.

Uri suddenly discovered that even sitting down he was rocking back and forth, quietly intoning a prayer for the spiritual tranquility of the murdered. That made him feel better. He grasped a handful of earth and sprinkled it on his head; the ground was cool, which was gratifying.

Aaron appeared with the two companions.

"We're going back," he declared.

Two mules that had gone lame during the journey were left behind, and they proceeded in turn by muleback and by foot. Aaron hustled them along, almost as if they had been responsible for the murders of those several hundreds.

They spent the Day of Atonement praying in a cave. It occurred to Uri that Aaron had too much local knowledge for it to have been pure chance that they came upon a suitable cave on the way back—and what's more, an uninhabited cave.

URI ENTERED THE HIGH PRIEST'S PALACE IN JERUSALEM FOR A THIRD time, this time along with his companions.

Before that they took a dip in the basin of the bathhouse built on Mount Zion, the water in which was only knee-high. The Essenes said that they, having seen dead bodies, would be going through a cleansing process for another week.

It was only on the third day that the reek, the stench of rotting human flesh, comparable to nothing else, left Uri's nostrils.

They were now led to the upper level, where they entered a chamber. Someone came and took Aaron away with him.

They waited.

Uri wondered whether Joseph ben Nahum was here in the palace. What did he know about the mission?

They waited and held their peace.

Eventually a short old man in a blue robe and white tunic appeared, supported by two men, Aaron and the hunchbacked, narrow-eyed man who had sent Uri to Beth Zachariah.

All the others prostrated themselves, and Uri quickly followed.

The old man made a sign of blessing with his right hand and took a seat on a bench. The other two remained standing. Uri's fellows got to their feet, as did he.

Aaron then spoke.

"The high priest Ananias has honored us by welcoming us in person."

Uri squinted. So this was the high priest who was no longer a high priest but father-in-law to the present high priest, as someone had said.

Aaron carried on.

"It is Ananias's wish that as a sign of reaching agreement on the text that is to be read out you all subscribe to it with your signatures."

The young man unrolled the scroll in his hands and started to read in Greek.

Without being asked, Jehoram, the scrawny youth, interpreted fluently into Aramaic. Not a pickpocket, then, but an interpreter. So he had been the spy among us, the Sanhedrin's man.

The text read that they, the members of a festival delegation from Judaea heading for Mount Gerizim, on the morning of the day of the festival in the village of Tirithana were eyewitnesses of an attack by the Judaean cohort on a celebrating throng misled by the false prophet. Several hundred people had been slain.

That was exactly what Uri was able to hear in Aramaic as well; the youth interpreted it accurately.

But we were not eyewitnesses, and the cohort was not Judaean but Syrian.

"Are you in accord?" the high priest asked.

"I'm in accord," said Aaron.

He stepped over to the small table on which the hunchbacked young man had placed the scroll and wrote his name on it with a quill, the inkpot held by the young man.

Everyone else, the Essenes included, went over and added their names in turn.

Uri was the penultimate; only Jehoram, who politely stepped aside, would follow him. It did cross Uri's mind what would happen if he were to speak out and ask that the text be corrected because it was a lie as it stood. What would happen? He would be clapped in prison and would never reach Alexandria, that's what would happen.

They needed several witnesses, preferably people belonging to different sects, and they clearly considered a Roman with full rights of citizenship to be important.

Uri dipped the quill's nib in ink and wrote his own name in Greek letters under the others.

So did Jehoram.

The high priest got to his feet.

"Thank you, my sons. May the blessings of the Eternal One be upon you."

He recited a priestly benediction, his right hand raised toward them, his fingers splayed, then left the chamber on the arm of the young man.

"I, too, thank you," said a relieved Aaron. "You may pick up your rewards on the ground floor. Jehoram will lead you there."

III

ALEXANDRIA

"MOST HIGH ETERNAL ONE!"

The words escaped Uri's lips as he first glimpsed the harbor of Alexandria through the bluish-violet gemstone he was holding to his left eye.

He had received the flat, circular stone, polished and set in a silver mounting, from the captain, who used it mainly at night when viewing the stars for long periods. One day, at around dawn, Uri had asked if he could try and placed it over his left eye—that was the stronger one—and he was amazed at how sharply he could see with it. All at once the odors of Far Side, that he had smelled as a child, when his eyesight had been good, filled his nostrils. Tears came to his eyes, and Uri resolved that either in Alexandria or back home in Rome he would learn how gemstones are polished.

The captain laughed: he was used to hearing expressions of that sort from the lips of those who caught their first glimpse of Alexandria from the sea.

On the right was the Pharos, much like the tower in Jerusalem in which Uri had lived for several months, except bulkier and topped by a statue of Zeus Soter; on the left, opposite the small island of Antipharos, was another promontory on which sat gardens and a palace. The proper name for it was Antirhodes, the captain related; it had been given that name around three centuries ago, when Rhodes had still had a larger harbor than Alexandria's. A row of enormous palaces, each more magnificent that the last, rose to ever-greater heights along the shoreline. Alexandria might not have been built on hills like Rome, but so far as Uri could see Rome could never rival Alexandria: the banks of the Tiber were nothing in comparison to this huge harbor.

Around them, no end of deep- and shallow-draught boats—monoreme galleys, biremes, and triremes—waited to dock, bobbed gracefully or ponderously, almost perilously close to one another, surrounded by barges and rafts, the diminutive craft of pilots and scullers. On the docks, all crammed with boats, goods were loaded and offloaded amidst the endless bustle of crowds, pack camels, mules, handcarts, carriages.

"Most High Eternal One!"

As if he were a native Alexandrian citizen, the Judaean captain proudly pointed out the landmarks: "The palace of Cleopatra is to the right, easily recognized by the two tall obelisks of Cleopatra's Needles. Cleopatra VII had started work on the building next to it, but it was completed as the Sebasteion a temple of Caesar Augustus. And that unfinished, yawning edifice was to become the temple of Arsinoë, with a roof made from lodestone so that an iron statute of Isis-Arsinoë should hover in the air above it. That was the plan at least, but the magnet turned out not to be powerful enough and the statue was stored somewhere in the palace, waiting for an engineer to work out a solution. That building with the elongated, transparent roof is the Emporion, the largest customs and excise office in the Greek world, where anything produced, grown, or manufactured by peoples around the Great Sea can be purchased cheaply. To the left of that are baths, then farther on, toward the sea and farther to the right, left of that north-pointing horseshoe of a stadium and past the line of hills, is the royal palace, and past the outer palace you can pick out the roof of the Mouseion, or Musaeum, in one wing of which is the old Great Library. That tall building beyond to the right is the Serapeion, or Serapeum, the temple of Serapis, on a hill in the town of Rhakotis. Atop the hill with corkscrew paths around it, that's the Paneion, the temple of Pan, in the middle of the Gymnasium gardens. It is worth making the trip to the top—you'll get a marvelous panoramic view of the whole of the city. Next to that—a little to the left, though you can't see it from here—is the Square Stoa, with an observatory at the top; that's not far from the Greek market, officially the Forum Augusti, though no one ever calls it anything but the marketplace."

With the assistance of the pilot (with whom the captain turned out to be acquainted—perhaps part of the reason why they were able to jump ahead of many ships that had been anchored outside the harbor for days on end) they maneuvered their way into the old harbor from the north, and Uri—who never once took the gemstone from his eye—felt that this spectacle was worth all the painful, tiring and humiliating adventures that he had gone through.

"This is my sort of town," he said to the captain before stepping ashore.

The captain laughed:

"It's everyone's sort of town."

On shore stood a knot of cantankerous excisemen; the captain cheerily waved at one of them and headed over.

"He came with me," said the captain, pointing to Uri. "Let him through."

"He has to pay the excise," said the exciseman severely.

"Give it a rest," said the captain. "I've brought your wife a nice muslin shawl:

light as a feather with mauve and blue nymphs on it. With that wrapped around her waist, you can be sure you'll at last get a hard-on."

The exciseman looked around.

"Well, all right!" he said. "You know where, this afternoon. But not a word to the wife!"

Uri got off scot-free.

He gratefully took leave of the captain, noting that the Greeks in Caesarea had hardly been any pleasanter. The captain guffawed:

"He wasn't a Greek but a Jew like me and you."

The second authority, the border patrol, Uri did not manage to evade. The captain had warned him of this right at the start of the voyage: anyone who wanted to spend more than twenty days in Alexandria had to make an application on arrival, then go back to the harbor five days later to get the permit; until then one would be given a temporary residence permit. The captain had also said that the office, which had been operating now for two hundred years, had spent each of those two hundred years carefully but begrudgingly giving out permits, lest the city be overrun by even larger numbers of peasants. As a result, the permit might not be ready even after five days—at best one might get a renewed five-day temporary residence permit. It would do no harm, then, to find in the city a sponsor whom the authorities respected and at whose request they would issue a residence permit for a more prolonged period; although it was possible to lie low there for a month or two (it being a big city with a million or so inhabitants), anyone caught without a permanent residence permit would be expelled, but not before being beaten and stripped of everything of value as if they were stolen goods.

"Find yourself a sponsor" was the captain's prudent advice. He embraced Uri and went off on his own business toward the docks.

Uri found himself at the end of a long line supervised by a group of listlessly sweating soldiers, among callous-handed, shabbily dressed Egyptian and Greek workers who had returned to pick up permits—not, as became clear from their conversations, for the first time. Elderly people and children jostled and yelled (the young children howling), and the sun was scorching and uncomfortable. The Egyptians also spoke Greek, though at times they would use incomprehensible words; quite possibly they had come from nearby villages in search of work as dockers. They looked askance at Uri, since he was on his own. A few poor Jews from Palestine, just as shabbily dressed, spoke Aramaic, but Uri did not enter into conversation with them.

It took a long time for Uri to get to an official, by which time he was hungry and thirsty.

The official in the alcove before which applicants had to pass mopped his perspiring, bald pate.

"We're done for this morning," announced the official. "I'm off for lunch."

"No you are not!" exclaimed Uri, slapping down a drachma on the counter.

"Well, all right," said the official, shaking his head in disgruntlement and breathing heavily. "Why are there so many of you today?"

Once Gaius Theodorus had declared himself to be a Roman citizen, he issued a small piece of papyrus granting a five-day temporary residence permit; his name was written in Greek lettering in the empty space.

"Come back in five days," the official said in friendly fashion.

"And what if it's not ready then?"

"There are too many of you," said the official. "That's not our fault."

Uri stood on the shore. There was a great coming and going; people of many races and nationalities were prowling around, bustling about, or strolling over the paving of marble mosaics in the Roman style. There was no way of telling who among them might be Greek, Jewish, Macedonian, Egyptian, or whatever: Jewish-looking faces passed by, though they wore no beards; there were also blond, bearded, curly-haired Greeks, some in richly ornamented tunics, others in nondescript garb, a few even in white, though they did not look like priests. A few extremely attractive brown-skinned women, maybe Indian, accosted him with invitations to lunch with them, but Uri shook his head to decline: he did not feel free to accept, though he had a sense that he would soon lose his virginity, Alexandria being a superb place for that purpose, as for every other—that he did not just feel but knew for sure.

Here even middling buildings were taller than the tallest tenement blocks in Rome, or even the Temple of Jupiter on the Capitoline, and they were built close next together; plots of land must be expensive. Uri comprehended right away the city's matchless planning: the Ptolemies had established parallel streets, so the city consisted of a grid, the whole being planned out in advance but so generously that the huge jumble of buildings of various styles from various ages made the otherwise rigid network lively, rich, and homely. Uri was surprised that he did not feel that the gigantic buildings were about to topple over him and crush him, but he soon worked it out as he strolled eastward along the harbor: it was because of the sheer multitude of people teeming at the foot of the buildings. A person does not look up if he can behold all of this colorful, captivating life at eye level. Taverns, guesthouses, state edifices and tenements—the chaotic stuff of life. Rome would never be like this.

Uri thought of Matthew, who wanted to erect a synagogue in Ostia, on the shoreline, and who had already visited Alexandria and had talked about it. His words, of course, were inadequate to give one the real flavor of the place, from which Uri inferred that Matthew was counting on Ostia becoming Rome's main port, a city that might one day grow into a miniature Alexandria. Not a bad gamble at all to build on the seashore in Ostia: land prices would be boosted many times over. Alexandria's only major drawback was the dense system of canals that threaded through it: the waters stank, the skiffs plying them moved through what was little more than sewage water.

He was headed for the Delta district, the city's Jewish quarter; he needed to find the Basilica, where he was supposed to hand over to a responsible individual a calculation regarding the timing of Rosh Hashanah. While still in Jerusalem he had asked how he would be able to find the place, and they had just smiled: there was no chance of missing the palatial building with its double colonnade.

He made his way eastward along the seashore in the direction of the chain of hills which shut in the Great Harbor on the east, and beyond which lay the buildings of the royal palace; the Delta quarter was over that way, south of the palace, he was told by those he asked along the way. He was now confident in addressing anybody, no longer ashamed if there was something he did not know. Tiny shrines, palaces surrounded by enormous peristyles, villas, and apartment blocks succeeded one another, and he noticed that there were more stone houses, and fewer of brick (let alone gimcrack timber structures), than in Rome. This was a city that would never crumble away, nor would it ever burn down.

It was early afternoon, yet even so the sunshine couldn't manage to make its way to pavement level, whether by the east-west or north-south streets: so tall were most of the buildings that a comfortable shade prevailed, and Uri saw only a blinding whiteness if he looked up toward the tops of the marble-clad edifices.

From the summit of a promontory—no doubt the famed Lochias—he was able to look down upon the Royal Harbor of Cape Lochias, kept segregated from the Great Harbor by a sparkling stone causeway. Two small, tranquilly rocking biremes were anchored in it, one most likely the prefect's, the other belonging to his bodyguard, should they ever need to flee. But then there was no reason for anyone to flee. Who, he wondered idly, was the prefect of Alexandria and Egypt? Not that it made a lot of difference. Someone of equestrian rank, that he knew for sure; Augustus himself, when he defeated Egypt, had decreed that no senator would be allowed to set foot in Alexandria or Egypt, and so it had been ever since.

He had grown peckish so he decided to take a seat in a hostelry; it was a luxury he could afford since—for the first time in his life—he still had enough money left over. I'm a dignified traveler, he told himself, and would have smiled had there not already been a smile on his face from the moment that he'd glimpsed the city's grandiose outline from aboard the ship through that crystal.

He stepped through the low entrance, which was separated from the street not by a door but a thin curtain, and sat down at a table. It was a hostelry comparable with a classy Roman tavern, on a whitewashed wall was a menu, written in Greek, of the all the day's dishes, along with their prices. Uri converted from Egyptian drachmas to Syrian drachmas and discovered that the place was very cheap. A plump woman emerged from the back to ask what the guest would like to eat, and Uri requested fish. The woman then started to enumerate all the different sorts of fish they had, until Uri interrupted her: he had no idea about all of these varieties, but did they have any barbel? Naturally. How much is that? Barbel is not exactly cheap, to be frank: five drachmas for half a cubit, poached or fried in oil, served up with all kinds of sauces. Uri thought he had heard wrongly, but the woman repeated it.

Nowhere else in the world could one get barbel so cheaply.

Uri accordingly ordered the barbel; a girl placed a jug of wine in front of him and a jug of water and a nice-looking copper dish to use as a mixing vessel. Uri protested: he had not ordered any wine.

"It's included in the price," the girl said.

Uri cautiously slopped some wine into the mixing vessel then, to be on the safe side, poured in a larger portion of water, scooped some of that with a ladle into a drinking jar, and carefully sipped it. It had a divine flavor. In moderation now, Uri reasoned with himself: no getting plastered until I've completed my mission.

The plump woman brought the poached barbel, and Uri was horrified: it was an enormous helping.

"That's more than half a cubit! It must be more like a cubit and a half!"

"It doesn't matter," said the woman. "It costs the same."

"Is it clean?" Uri asked suspiciously.

The woman laughed.

"We're in the Delta. Everything here is kosher; if it wasn't we might as well pack up and leave. Jews come all the time; they sniff and grumble, but no one has ever faulted our food."

Uri set about the fish. They gave him a broad, flat, thin knife, which made it easy to dissect the meat from the backbone. Uri turned the fish around in his mouth: even a man like Pilate seldom had the chance to eat fish as good as that.

Poor Pilate.

It was not even three weeks ago, on the Thursday before Passover, that the prefect had been brought out, bound, from Herod's palace as Vitellius, the imperial legate and governor of Syria in person, read out his sentence in Greek so that everyone might understand: on account of the slaughter at Mount Gerizim, Pilate was to be sent to Rome for the judiciary there to pass sentence on him.

Anyone brought out from his palace in chains could hardly count on a rosy future.

The Jews around Uri had been jubilant, not particularly at losing Pilate (because that meant the relatives of the massacred Samaritans were receiving moral redress, and they cared even less for that), but because Lucius Vitellius, for the first time since the Roman occupation had begun, had restored custody of the high priest's vestments and had abolished the poll tax throughout Judaea. Vitellius was applauded and cheered, and the emperor was also enthusiastically hailed. With great fuss, and in full view of the populace, the high priest's ceremonial garb was brought out of the Antonia fortress—the crowd delirious with joy and praying as they fell to their knees and prostrated themselves—and handed over to the *strategos's* men as if it were made of fragile glass. Pilate, bound, had stood mute and motionless between his guards; he looked nowhere, staring calmly ahead; but no one paid any heed to him as they followed the passage of the priestly garments, which were carried away by tall stalwarts of the Jewish police force toward the palace of the high priest. Vitellius then appointed Marcellus the new provisional prefect, but they paid him no attention either, however much he puffed out his chest.

It went through Uri's head that it was a smart move to abolish a tax which there was no means of collecting in any case. In a few years another governor of Syria would come along, he would be the boss of whoever would by then be prefect of Judaea, and he would reintroduce the same poll tax, which they would be just as unable to collect.

Uri lunched deliberately, with great pleasure, watched by the woman from a distance, and when she saw that he had sated his immediate hunger pangs she took a seat at his table.

"If the gentleman were to honor us at least once a week, then we could come to an arrangement on the price."

"Marvelous," growled Uri, and he dunked the next morsel in what looked very much like a garum sauce, which was extremely garlicky.

"Will the gentleman be staying in Alexandria for long?" the woman wanted to know.

"I very much hope so," said Uri.

"This is a decent town," said the woman. "It doesn't matter who is what, or what you were born as. We're Hellenes, for example, but we have a good life here, among the Hebrews. No one cares what god you worship. It's a decent town, though the competition is cutthroat. My husband and I started next to the Gymnasium, but that's no way to make a living: there are so many places to eat. It's good here, though; one can hang on here."

Uri drank half the wine, but he could not manage even one third of the barbel. It was a long time since his belly had last groaned so contentedly; his blood seemed to be bubbling, and his head felt heavier by the minute.

"The gentleman can take a nap," said the woman. "We've got a room for that purpose with a nice big bed for two in it."

Uri was unable to make up his mind. He still had some time, having arrived a day earlier than expected because the wind had been favorable, but on the other hand he wanted the reassurance of having fulfilled his mission, so he shook his head. He paid in Attican drachmas and the woman gave the change in Egyptian drachmas, so he automatically ran a mental check, but the woman had not cheated him.

Uri asked the way to the Jewish Basilica.

It was four blocks away.

It would, indeed, have been hard to miss.

The Basilica was, in effect, an enormous market hall, though it had no roof. There were long double rows of columns three stories high, with gorgeous Greek capitals; over the two rows of columns there were strips of roofing, but the vast rectangular space between the columns was open to the sky. The edifice did not have an entrance as such—it was possible, in principle, to pass between the columns at any point, though in most places the stall keepers had blocked free circulation. Anything grown or made by all the peoples around the Great Sea could be purchased here; compared with this, the Upper Market in Jerusalem—the biggest in the city—was just a village jumble sale. Uri could not imagine what might be in the Emporium if all manner of goods were already to be had here. And on the main street in the middle of the city there was supposedly an even bigger market—the biggest in the Greek world.

In the inner space of the tidy rectangular covered walkway, which was paved with sheets of ornamental marble, there stood a timber platform on which lay costly carpets. To the east and west of the platform stood rows of stone benches with gilded edges: Uri counted seventy-two rows. He nodded: there were supposed to be that many, because there had been seventy-two translators of the Bible into Greek, working right here, in Alexandria, three centuries ago. Uri looked at the bronze plaques that were fastened to the outside stone benches. In each row places were reserved for Jews of different occupations. All that was inscribed on the end of the first row of benches looking east was *alabarkhos*. That must be some very elevated rank indeed.

Bronze plaques? Uri was suspicious and leaned a bit closer. The bronze plaques were gold. Uri shuddered. What lavishness, and coupled to such trust! Anyone might pry off one of the plaques, and if he managed to get away with it, he would be rich for the rest of his life. And it was left here unguarded! This city of Alexandria was quite a strange place.

Then he spotted the armchairs standing by the northern entrance, and he went closer. He was dumbfounded: the armchairs too were solid gold. He counted them: seventy-one. He did not dare try to move the one that his hand was touching, because there were people coming and going around the Basilica, but he would not have been surprised if the chairs were fixed to the ground.

He had heard in Jerusalem that Jews also prayed in this Basilica, in addition to many hundreds of synagogues that were scattered throughout all parts of Alexandria (because Jews lived not just in the Delta, the fourth district, but also in the other four districts as well). Uri looked over the eastern double stoa, or colonnade, to see where there might be an ark or cabinet in which Torah scrolls might be kept, but he saw no fixture that might have served that purpose. Maybe it was delivered here on Friday evening and for any feast days. That would mean the platform in the center of the stoa acted as the bimah, the "elevated place" from which the Torah readings were made. To hold divine services outdoors, under the open sky, was a fine, even sublime idea. He looked at the interior space and estimated that each row of stone benches might hold as many as a hundred people, which would come to 7,200, plus there was a lot of free space between the benches and the columns, while lots of people would also fit in between columns, so several tens of thousands of Jews might cram in if need be, assuming the poorer ones stood, of course. He felt a strong urge to take a seat in the middle of the first row of stone benches to the west of the rostrum, but not now—later on when a divine service was in progress. I'm going to win that right for myself, Uri vowed; it was his duty to conquer Alexandria.

He would have been more than ready to make a votive offering, but that was only possible at the Temple in Jerusalem, whereas here there was only a Basilica—a marketplace which could also be used as a house of prayer.

Scattered here and there on the rows of benches were small knots of Jews discussing various things, either doing business or gossiping in unhurried, contented fashion; around them women were chatting, their faces not made up, while children were running around freely and kicking up a racket. Whoever had power and prestige in Alexandria stood closer to the head of the Jewish populace than the priests in Jerusalem, to say nothing of the Roman Jews.

Under one of the arches a group of master jewelers had set out their merchandise; Uri went over and immersed himself in the sight. One master and his assistants were producing settings, the silver for which was heated up over the flame of a small oil lamp and bent with tweezers; the gemstones, standing nearby in a small container, must already have been cut. Anyone with the nerve could have snatched up a few of the sparkling gems and run off into the crowd, yet nevertheless no one stooped to this level, and the masters seemed to have no apprehensions on that score. Uri looked at them, and once again the thought crossed his mind that this would be a craft worth learning: it suited him better than cabinetmaking or laying stone floors. Who could know? Perhaps he might somehow get the chance.

In the end, he asked where he might find the stargazer Heraclitos.

On the third try, he was informed that the Jewish stargazers resided on the island of Pharos—that was where their synagogue stood, and anyone on the island would be able to tell him which building that was, and anyway it had a massive marble menorah over its entrance; Uri should go back to the harbor along the Heptastadion, to the island, you couldn't go wrong. It wasn't far, nothing in Alexandria was. He would reach it by evening.

Holy Moses, Uri sighed as he passed under the bridge at the southern end of the Heptastadion, the causeway that separated Alexandria's two harbors, connecting the island of Pharos to the mainland. If I could only lay my hands on a shack in this wonderful city!

Stepping onto the causeway, he could see skiffs heavily laden with goods being rowed out of the Great Harbor into the Western Harbor, the port of Eunostos, through the seawater channel that ran under the tightly curved stone bridge at the Heptastadion's northern end, nearly a mile away. The traffic was dense, with boatmen bawling at one another and occasionally even colliding or clashing with their oars. There was also traffic in the opposite direction, with all kinds of bales being moved from the Western Harbor into the Great Harbor. Boats, skiffs and other watercraft also plied a broad channel that fed from the southwest into the Western Harbor, which to Uri's squinting assessment was a great deal larger than the Great Harbor. Might that be the channel that connected Lake Mareotis to the Western Harbor? No doubt. But he could not see the lake itself, since the tall edifices rising toward the south blocked off his view of the horizon.

The stargazers' house stood at the western tip of the island. A temporary, timber lighthouse tower was situated nearby; the captain had told him that morning that a new Pharos, much bigger than the old, was to be built but that the city did not yet have the financing for it. How was it possible, Uri had wondered, that a city like this did not have sufficient money? The captain had just laughed: Every third person in a city might well be rolling in it, and every second person able to buy up the whole lot, all the same a city might still be poverty-stricken.

The fires were not yet burning in the interim Pharos; it was still early evening. Uri could not understand why the house of the Jewish astronomers had been constructed next to the Pharos, of all structures, as the fires surely interfered with their examinations of the firmament. On the ship even the few small torches that lit the deck at night interfered with the examinations of the heavens by the captain, who was well versed in the mysteries of the cult of Mithras. Uri came to realize, however, that the of the Jewish astronomers had settled in first, and it was only afterward that the timber lighthouse had gone up.

Uri had his fill of astronomers.

When he had returned from Samaria and drawn his reward of 120 zuz—the tidy sum they had each received for the lie that Pilate's soldiers had been responsible for the massacre—it happened to be a half-holiday after Rosh Hashanah and before the Day of Atonement. He had tried to arrange his departure along with the Alexandrian delegation immediately after Sukkot, but he wasn't allowed anywhere near them; the Alexandrian delegates went around under strong-armed protection and cut themselves off from beggars and petitioners. Offices resumed work only after Sukkot, but so slowly that he needed something to do until they go around to him, so he asked where he might find a library, but they couldn't grasp what he was after: there were no public libraries in Jerusalem, and the office did not have any private libraries at its disposal. They suggested that he move in with the stargazers in the tower of Phasael, as they buried themselves in books for sure.

That is how Uri found himself where the stargazers lived, at the top of the tower of Phasael, at ninety cubits high the tallest structure in Jerusalem and built as a copy of the Pharos in Alexandria.

The astronomers did not concern themselves with him, beyond simply taking note that he was present. In any case they did little or nothing, spending the whole day eating, drinking, basking in the sun, and spinning yarns. On top of the tallest tower in the city they were invisible from below due to the projecting balcony that ran all around its lip. Uri found a few interesting books and became immersed in a volume of Eratosthenes. He delved for months on end into the secrets of trigonometry as his quarters were free, even his board, and he spent hardly anything of the 120 zuz. He rarely went down into the city, living in the tower of Phasael much as he had done in his cubbyhole in Rome.

When he got tired of reading, he went up to the balcony at the top of the tower, and there he would always find people just looking around. He slowly worked out that these stargazers were not astronomers as such—they were more interested in what was going on down below than up above. From the top of the tower of Phasael even Uri, squinting, could see the square by the Temple and the squares of the Upper City—everything. It was only gradually that the realization dawned: these stargazers were lookouts.

He could see from up above that people were also walking atop the Temple. Also lookouts.

Those other lookouts were under observation from the tower of Phasael, who made sure that they were alert in keeping a lookout.

The Lord must have a lot to see when, from time to time, he looks down as Supreme Guard on his holy city. But there is no one keeping a check on Him.

Uri was eventually dispatched to Alexandria as carrier of the calculations of the New Year, but the arrangements were so slapdash that he was only able set off a good few days later than were strictly needed to make the voyage from Jerusalem to Alexandria. If he had not chanced to find a boat in Gaza, crewed by the remaining Phoenicians, and if they had not been granted favorable winds, with the prevailing north-westerlies getting up a bit earlier than usual that spring—he would certainly have been late. It did occur to him en route to wonder whether the stargazers in Jerusalem had caused the delay not just through simple negligence but because they explicitly *wanted* him to be late.

I've grown up, Uri reflected for the umpteenth time on his journey: I no longer necessarily ascribe good intentions to people.

There were a dozen or so astronomers sitting around at ground level, beside the timber Pharos, that slim, flat-topped, five-story building. They were eating and drinking, gossiping, and drawing leisurely lines on rolls of papyrus.

The Heraclitos in question was not the great Greek philosopher but a Jewish astronomer, elderly, graying, and in Hellenic style wearing no beard and garbed in a white tunic.

Uri hauled out from under his own tunic the leather cylinder in which the New Year calculations of the astronomers in Jerusalem were rolled up.

"About time!" said Heraclitos. "Here at last."

Uri protested that they had been late in dispatching him, that wasn't his fault, and he had gotten here a day early nonetheless.

"That's them all over, the dolts," said Heraclitos without any animosity. "Couriers are deliberately sent off late just to play us for suckers."

"So what happens if a moon courier is late?" Uri asked.

"Nothing," replied Heraclitos, taking the papyrus out of the case, unrolling it, glancing at it, nodding and pushing it back into the leather box. "They're not the only ones who can do calculations. There's not a new moon anywhere in the world that was missed on account of those dolts in Jerusalem. There were new moons long before there any Jews, even before the Egyptians learned to compute."

"Then what's the point of sending couriers?"

"Tradition, and we bow to that. It's one of the ways we have of expressing our loyal devotion to the Temple, which is ninety percent sustained by the dues we pay."

Uri was crestfallen; his heroic efforts to get there in time had been pointless. He wasn't so important a person that they had been seeking to put him personally in an awkward situation by the crafty dodge of deliberately delaying his departure. They were continually seeking ways of humiliating Alexandria, which merely laughed off the infantile trick.

Heraclitos made a sign, a young man stood up, took the leather case and vanished with it through a door.

"We'll file it," said Heraclitos. "Deep underneath us is a cellar where we keep all the calculations, going back three hundred years, but there are also earlier ones, the oldest of them nine hundred years old and more. In a couple of hundred years or so someone will have to think about expanding it a bit."

Heraclitos's dry, self-assured humor appealed to Uri, but it was not an appropriate time to laugh.

Heraclitos sat back on a bench where others were in the process of measuring something on a papyrus.

Uri remained standing.

What next?

Heraclitos looked up.

"Do you need us to sign an acknowledgment of receipt?" he queried.

"I'm not going back to Jerusalem," Uri said. "I was allowed to leave on the understanding that I was not expected to return. I want to stay here."

Heraclitos made a disdainful, commiserative grimace and turned away.

There was silence; Uri was still standing until one of the younger men took pity on him.

"No one is allowed to settle down here, don't you know that? The city is overcrowded; we are not in a position to support immigrants, and those coming from Palestine are particularly unwelcome."

"But I'm a Roman citizen," said Uri.

Heraclitos looked up and now inspected Uri properly for the first time as a human individual, sizing him up from head to toe, but he was not satisfied with the result and puckered his brow.

"What's your name?" he asked.

"Gaius Theodorus."

Heraclitos shook his head in disbelief. The other astronomers now also looked up. There was silence as Heraclitos went on:

"Not the son of Ioses Lucius, in person?"

Uri stiffened: how did he know that?

"Actually... yes."

"So tell me: what is your father famous for?"

It then hit Uri.

"For having me as his son!"

"And what's his son famous for?"

"For being one of the apostles who took the sacrificial tithe money from Rome to Jerusalem."

Heraclitos whooped in joy and bounded up.

"Why didn't you say so from the start, you hare-brain? We were just about to ask you to leave!"

The elderly, graying, highly respectable man leapt on Uri and embraced him.

The other astronomers also got to their feet, came over to Uri with great respect and, one after the other, gave him a solemn, ceremonial embrace, kissing his cheek on both sides of the face. Uri didn't know what to make of this and tolerated the embraces; his hands were free and he knew that he ought to return the embraces, but he just couldn't do it.

The young man returned meanwhile to the room and stopped in utter amazement.

"It's him!" Heraclitos shouted to him jubilantly. "He's finally here! Gaius Theodorus, Agrippa's courier! Take him straightaway to Philo!"

Uri was shaking all over. This must be another dream. He didn't know what to think.

"Philo?" he asked faintly. "The philosopher?"

"The same," shouted Heraclitos. "He has been waiting for you most eagerly!"

HE WAS NOT TAKEN TO PHILO RIGHT AWAY, BECAUSE EVENING HAD COME, and Philo did not receive guests during evenings: he was accustomed to doing his writing then.

Philo lived on the banks of Lake Mareotis, a few hours' travel west of Alexandria; it was possible to reach the place at night if you had torchbearers to accompany you, but that was pointless. In any case a whole party was about to set off for the tavern; wouldn't Uri tag along? Some one would take him to see Philo the next morning.

All fifteen of them went to the Alpha; not one was missed back home, even though several of them had families. Their wives had grown accustomed to the fact that their husbands did not spend the nights with them, and usually not the daylight hours either. The astronomers' pay was not so great—they could have earned a great deal more working as merchants. That was not the reason why the wives forgave them, or their in-laws had considered them good catches in the first place. Rather, all of them had been schooled at the Gymnasium, which meant that they had been given military training and in the process had won Alexandrian citizenship rights, which could otherwise only be extended to Greeks and exempted them from the electoral tax usually imposed on Jews. Uri didn't inquire any further about that; he find out later on, once he was allowed to put down roots.

They asked Uri about Jerusalem, and it turned out that none of them had ever been there, nor did they ever intend to go there: the Jewish stargazers of Alexandria were not big fans of pilgrimages, preferring to gossip. They knew precisely which hostelry they were headed for, but on the way they would pop into one inn or another for a drink or two. They did not give Uri a chance to say much at all about Jerusalem, because they grew more interested in Rome, though when Uri outlined how Far Side was arranged, they cut in to say that Rome wasn't really of interest either. Uri was dumbfounded: they showed as little interest in anything else as the peasants in Judaea. Of course, the stargazers justified their outlook: if Mark Antony had been victorious, and there had been every chance that he would have, Rome would now be a province of Alexandria, and if one of the emperors had an ounce of sense, he would have transferred the seat of the empire to Alexandria—that was where the real money was, trade, and there was no Senate here to make life difficult.

It was an unexpected point of view, but he did not have time to ruminate on it because he had to concentrate on not getting hopelessly drunk before they even reached the hostelry for which they were aiming. He did not truly register the fact that one of the astronomers had raised the point that since Cleopatra had not been too fond of Jews, things would not have gone so well for them even if Mark Antony had been victorious.

In the end, they did not end up at the hostelry they had spoken of, but one that was closer, and also very good, on a broad avenue which even in the evening was packed with crowds of promenading people as if it were daytime, and small shops, in which one could get anything, were still open. There was no need for them to order anything because dishes and wine were continually brought to the big, round table, even without being asked for, the moment anything was polished off. Heraclitos was given beer because that's what he preferred. He didn't have to order that either: he was well known there. They sat in an inner, closed-off garden in a circle under fragrant thuja trees, surrounded by knots of young and old people, Greeks, Jews, Somalis, Ethiopians, Hindus, and peoples of who-knows-what origin. Perhaps Egyptians were the only ones not to be found among them, but that was because the Copts by that time were resting under their own roofs. Torches and sturdy candles provided illumination, along with oil lamps, which were bigger than Jewish lamps and ingeniously designed so that in each one the oil fed nine different flames—an old trick, to be sure, maybe as old as the menorah. There were also musicians trilling away, beating drums and fiddling on strings. Uri was appreciative of the fact that they could perch their backsides on chairs and did not have to eat Roman-style, reclining to one side.

He also took a bit of everything without asking if it was pure, because the Jewish stargazers were eating it, and they must know. He was a bit surprised, it was true, because one thing they served up was seafood, and the astronomers enthusiastically dunked these delicious marvels in garum sauce, and when he finally asked, they pooh-poohed it, with Heraclitos saying that anything coming from the sea was pure. They reassured him that, as Jews, they would not be brought anything uncooked; they took great care with that, so he could eat without any worries.

Uri didn't know how they managed to get back to the island of Pharos; obviously along the Heptastadion as there was no other way, but that had somehow slipped his memory by the time he woke up the following morning in a little room upstairs. He burped contentedly then quickly had to look for a privy. The one he found on the ground floor had a window overlooking the sea; Uri spent a fair time on the throne, for good reason, but the view was also fascinating: even with his poor eyesight he could see the immense sailing ships bobbing in the Western Harbor.

What a city this is, Most High Eternal One! What a city!

He was also treated to breakfast, and offered sips of decent wine to counter any hangover, before he was sent on his way.

Hippolytos, who accompanied him, was the same young man who had taken the roll down to the archive the previous day.

As they walked to the west, Hippolytos related that Philo rarely stayed in the city, at the palace of his younger brother, Alexander, the alabarch, because he preferred the quiet of the countryside, where he was better able to concentrate on his writing. Philo had a big and splendid house, it wasn't far away, no more than four or five hours' walk, but Philo had the feeling that he was living in the country, and that allowed his mind to calm itself. He was in the habit of throwing big parties there, and sometimes as many as a hundred guests would arrive on horseback or ass. But the house was so big and there were so many outbuildings belonging to it that even that number, along with their mounts, could be easily accommodated.

Hippolytos recounted with a laugh that virtually all those with a deep attachment to the land were the descendants of Jews who sometime in the past, many generations ago, had been carried off as slaves into Egypt. The Ptolemies had crammed them into border fortresses to protect the frontiers of the state, and they had graciously given them land instead of food and pay, of course—let them make their livelihood as best they could, and if they couldn't, then so be it, they'd perish of hunger. Those Jewish slaves of the border fortresses, who were subjugators, oppressors and looters of the indigenous population, had become the first wealthy Jews in Egypt since Moses—mistakenly, as it had turned out for sure in retrospect—had plumped for an exodus from Egypt. There was no richer countryside anywhere else on Earth; the Nile valley, due to its yearly flooding, was the most fertile land anywhere in the world, and the Jews would have saved themselves a world of trouble if, two thousand years ago, they had just calmly sat on their bottoms. Their monotheistic religion would in any case gradually have spread this far, only with fewer conflicts. If things had happened that way, then the conquering Greeks who had overrun the country under Alexander the Great would today be our slaves, Hippolytos declared wistfully.

Uri was captivated by the young astronomer's compact philosophy of history, and asked him whether he was right in believing that by that token anyone among the Jews who was enslaved at the right time and in the right place was favored by fortune. Hippolytos confirmed that this was indeed the case: anyone who remained free on his own land, that he himself had dug, whether he was Jewish or some other Canaanite, would sooner or later be consumed by the hordes which swooped across it.

Uri simply noted the Roman experience: the present-day descendants of the robbers and murderers whom Herod the Great had deported to Italia as a punishment were doing remarkably well for themselves.

Hippolytos nodded: those of us who are doing so remarkably well for themselves and living off the fat of the land are virtually all descendants of the villains who mercilessly pillaged and slaughtered the indigenous population, bringing them under their rule; for that reason, they were not much liked even nowadays in those areas where the locals lived, he added, memories died hard even after hundreds of years, and it was not possible to eradicate legends and myths. But the wretched Copts did not like the Hellenes any better because they too were newcomers; they had arrived with their fire and swords not long before the Jews, and they were at least as villainous as the Hebrews. For the aboriginal workers of the soil it was all the same—whether one was a Hebrew or Hellene, they hated you, and the only place it didn't matter was in Alexandria, where the two equally exploiting forces fleeced each other for profit. In any case, it hardly mattered who was hated by the natives, who more than likely were originally Jewish or from some similarly inferior rabble, since they held no power, were quite incapable of any organized way of life, didn't have the knowhow to manufacture weapons, and were superstitious to boot.

They strolled southward along the bank of the broad north-south canal.

En route, Uri would have liked to inspect the edifices, the vast stadium and everything else that he could see, but he was troubled by a deep-seated disquiet: he had again become a victim of mistaken identity, and that was going to land him in big trouble one of these days.

Here he was liked for precisely the reason he had been loathed in Judaea. Or maybe not loathed, but all the same... Yet there was no foundation in reality for this identification, any more than there had been for the other. What was going to happen when they found out?

And anyway, how come they know about me at all?

They were passing by the rectangular structure of the massive fortress-like Serapeion, tall even though it was only one story high; it must have been near to a stadion long and almost half a stadion wide. Its entrance was set amid Ionic and Corinthian columns facing to the north, toward the sea, being built by Ptolemy III Euergetes, Hippolytos said, and Uri had just nodded, though he had no idea when that ruler had lived. On obelisks standing in front of the temple were a pair of red granite sphinxes and a black granite statue of Apis. This was on the hill of Rhakotis, Hippolytos said, and called Uri's attention to the entrance to the cemetery next to the temple, where there was a statue of jackal-headed Anubis, the interesting feature of which was that the sculptor—whether in mockery or in an attempt to curry favor—had carved him wearing the dress of a Roman centurion. Inside there was also a shrine to Isis, Hippolytos noted, and a number of other smaller shrines such as one to Harpocrates, the Greek rendering of the Egyptian *Har–pa–khered*, meaning "Horus, the child." Now Horus was regarded as being the son of Serapis and Isis, Isis being the wife of Serapis—if Uri was not clear on that point, because some of the characteristics of Osiris had been blended into this Serapis whom the first Ptolemies had dreamed up, yes, along with some of the characteristics of Asclepius, the god of healing, and of Hades as well, of course. There was no special cult of the son, Harpocrates, but Isis, Serapis's consort, was considered to be a savior, who forgave sins, Serapis himself as well—a sacred family trinity of Father, Mother and Son, not that this had any particular religious outgrowth.

The new Great Library was also inside the temple, its stock having been transferred here from Pergamum by Mark Antony and a gift to Cleopatra in return for the volumes that Julius Caesar had committed to the flames.

In a big garden could be seen a statue of Serapis, this new state-proclaimed god who the subjects of the Ptolemies had hastened to worship, sedulously offering sacrifices to him in expression of absolute fidelity to the new Macedonian ruling house that had been planted on them. Nowadays this confected deity was more or less the only one to which the Greeks here offered sacrifices; the Egyptians too, when it comes to that. Ptolemy I Soter had the massive, bearded marble figure, sheaves of grain adorning the locks of his hair and seated on a marble throne, brought over from Sinope, where it was worshiped as Jupiter Dis; every year the Greeks celebrated the arrival of Serapis—in other words, the arrival of the statue—on the twenty-ninth day of August, which also marked the start of the Egyptian New Year. Seated on a smaller throne beside that was his assistant, Pluton, commander of the realm of the dead, with a marble snake coiled around the throne.

Sheets of gold, silver, bronze and marble were affixed all over the temple's ancient exterior walls, and Uri stepped closer: former patients, not one of them still alive, Uri suspected, had carved words of gratitude to Serapis for curing them.

They then walked westward alongside the wall of the old Egyptian necropolis until they reached the city gates. Heading out into the fields, the guards handed each traveler a slip of parchment that they might return to the city without any problems.

"It's easy to get out, hard to get back," said Hippolytos. "That's one thing the Hellenes and Hebrews can agree on."

Uri looked at the city wall, at least eight feet high. It looked old, built of coarse stones, with the trees and shrubs growing out of the cracks locking the structure together rather than splitting it apart. Anyone who wanted to badly enough might climb over it.

The city wall, said Hippolytos, was raised by Ptolemy I Soter, thanks to whom Alexandria was founded as a city. He recounted the legend that as Alexander the Great had himself selected the site, cantering on horseback around a dozen fishing villages that had stood here, and because he had no other means he had dropped his army's entire stores on the field to mark the place. The legend does not say, however, what the soldiers thought of this, but it shows how decent he was, because at that time barbarians were still in the habit of marking out a city's walls in blood—the great warrior might just as easily have had the local people or their livestock slaughtered, using their blood to trace the walls of his city to be in the untouched ground.

That Soter himself must be one of the old kings, Uri thought, ashamed at not knowing anything about Alexandria's history. Never mind: if he were allowed to stay, he would be able to bone up on it.

They moved past extensive, nicely kept gardens attached to the villas of wealthy citizens of the town, and at one place he even saw gravestones. He didn't know what to make of that.

That was the Western Necropolis, one of the old burial grounds. In times gone by the rich of Alexandria were buried in ample, shaded parkland just beyond the city wall, but eventually the living begrudged the dead the fine space they were occupying, and pushed into it while they were still alive. Plots of land here were extremely expensive, whether intended for the living or the dead, Hippolytos explained admiringly. Some people were born here and also happily died here, but Jews were never established in these parts, alive or dead.

"Have you people been expecting me?" Uri finally asked, summoning all his resolve.

"We've heard talk about you," Hippolytos averred respectfully.

"From who was that?"

"That I don't know, but I've heard your name before, and more than once at that. We knew that you had been knocking about in Judaea for a fair time on a mission of some kind... I had also heard your father's name mentioned—his perhaps more than your own. He must be a big wheel in Rome if Agrippa asked him for a loan."

Uri "umm"ed and "aah"ed.

"Here Agrippa asked the alabarch himself for a loan the last time he paid a visit," said Hippolytos. "As best we know, the alabarch also gave him a sizable amount, two hundred thousand drachmas, it's said, or rather not him but his wife, Cypron, but only the first installment, a tenth of it..." Hippolytos snorted ironically. "He handed it over in installments, the latter of which were forwarded to Dikaiarchia for Agrippa to pick up once he got there, and even then only at intervals so that the whole lot could not be picked up in one go to blow on a single dinner... A wise man, Alabarch Alexander, otherwise he wouldn't have the entire tax revenues of the Nile for himself... And your father must be wise man also, Gaius Theodorus."

"On a mission of some kind."

But what on Earth might my mission be?

Uri sensed that Hippolytos would like him to be more forthcoming, but nothing more occurred to Uri. He felt odd that a highly intelligent young man should speaking to him in the most fantastic city in the world; more than that, he had the feeling that Hippolytos wanted to present himself as being even more intelligent than he in fact was. He's another who fancies I'm some potentate, and feels it necessary to sketch for me an entertaining potted history of the Jews of Alexandria. If I utter a word it will immediately show how much of a nonentity I am, but then again it won't be possible for me to keep my trap shut permanently!

Right now they were headed for the house of the most famous living Jewish philosopher... Who is dying to meet me! My father can have had no notion of what he was doing when he had me pushed into that ill-fated delegation!

They were now walking along the shore of Lake Mareotis. Here there were even larger docks, set deep in the water beside the stone moles like the teeth on a comb, as in the Great Harbor, and even more ships bustling about to unload and load. Uri paused and stared. Hippolytos confirmed that internal commerce was greater than the external trade, with all of the goods from India and Persia transferred here to craft that navigated the Nile. Papyrus, frankincense and saffron—Egypt's best known exports—were also brought here, with only a small fraction of that making its way down the canal into the Western Harbor. Uri could also see strange reed-like plants on the shore, and was amazed to learn that these were papyrus. Hippolytos just laughed and reassured him that these were only used to make the poorest quality of papyrus used for packaging and baling. These somewhat smaller and gnarlier plants were also papyrus, though their bark was stripped not for writing on but to chew. If Uri looked a bit closer later on, back in Alexandria, he would see that people were constantly munching, and what they were chewing on was the stripped and crushed bark, which left a pleasant tingle in the gums and was also an aphrodisiac. Jews chewed it too; there was nothing to forbid that in the Scriptures.

They reached a beguilingly pretty fishing village, which Hippolytos declared with pride was the renowned Taposiris, where they held an annual festival of Osiris, always worth the trip because of the beauty contests: Hedylos the epigrammatist had written about these, which were open not only to rosy-cheeked girls but to older women too, who could enter any body parts that remained in good condition, their thighs, say, or their noses. This was not Athens, he added; here spectators were not lured to come to the competitions or theatrical performances by bounties but had to pay—though not a lot—with the cost of food and drink included in the price.

Uri stood and looked at the peaceful village, the boats, their crews placidly stowing their ropes, the unhurried people, the green and blue islets on the lake on which, if he narrowed his eyes in a squint, he could see white villas rising from among trees.

"Philo also has a small house on one of the islets where he grows vines, himself picks and presses the grapes at vintage time, then himself puts the wine aside to ferment," noted Hippolytos. "If ever he tires of creative solitude in the country, that's where he pulls back to. He invites no guests, so only trusted servants accompany him there, and all the scrolls he needs which deal with the mysteries of wine production are packed onto five or six boats. The tales go around that Philo grinds grape stalks and pips into the wine-barrels out of forgetfulness, so the resulting wine is more properly a marc that only he finds drinkable."

Hippolytos's laughter was mocking.

Philo's house in the country, whitewashed on the outside, was very large, and it sat in the midst of a gigantic property, with orchards, stables, forests, fields, with a great number of servants, three of whom escorted the two guests to the atrium.

"The master is working," one of them said deferentially, "and he instructed us that he was not to be disturbed... Nor was he expecting any guests today."

Hippolytos nodded and parked himself on a couch. Uri remained standing and gazed at the circle of Hellenistic statues, sculptures of women, men, and winged beings, fine enough that they would have graced even the old Forum in Rome. All around the walls were colorful depictions of nature, and Uri became self-absorbed, as though the atrium he was standing in was a valley bordered by trees, flowers, and hills. Something of the kind was perhaps also to be found in the bedroom of the emperor Augustus and his wife, as went the gossip in the taverns in Rome from those who had seen them, or just heard about them—there every tree, every blade of grass was as true to nature as if it had been alive, and the mural he found himself gazing at here seemed to have the same realistic depth. Uri thought it amusing: in Rome, ringed by masses of stone it might make sense to feign nature on a wall, but here, where the house was truly standing in the middle of nature?

He stepped closer to one of the walls and examined it thoroughly. He had the distinct feeling that it was a landscape that he had seen before even though he had not seen many murals—actually, he hadn't even seen many landscapes at all, on account of his poor eyesight. How could he be familiar with the picture all the same? It quickly dawned on him that the encircling mural depicted the surroundings of the very house in which he was standing. Lest any inhabitant of the atrium, cut off from the outside world, should forget—among all the other things to which he might be attending—where he happened to be situated.

This is just too extravagant for me. The thought entered Uri's mind. Senseless. They'd do better to cut a window in the wall of the atrium and anyone could gaze outside through that. Cheaper.

Perish the thought, he chided himself. The reason the wealthy had money was to squander it on senseless luxuries.

Two of the servants vanished, leaving the one who stayed there standing respectfully without watching them.

"I've never been here before," said Hippolytos, happily sprawled on the couch. "I've you to thank for this, Gaius Theodorus."

He was also gazing at the mural, examining the length of the four walls, though he could look at it from where he was seated as his eyesight was good. All of a sudden he shrieked:

"This panorama depicts precisely the spot where we are now! Do you see?"

"Yes, I see it."

A short, bald, aged man hastened into the atrium accompanied by one of the servants. He was wearing a simple white tunic and there was a conspicuous flushed quality about his cheeks. Hippolytos leapt to his feet.

"Your Worthiness, Philo..." he began until Philo gestured for him to hold it, and turned to Uri.

"Are you Gaius Theodorus?"

"That's me," said Uri.

Philo rushed over and hugged him. Uri returned the embrace. The great philosopher had slender bones.

"The rest of you can go," Philo said impatiently.

Uri watched sorrowfully as Hippolytos, the young astronomer, who was no doubt a hundred times brighter and more talented than himself, disappointedly trailed out after the servants. Uri called out to him:

"Many thanks for accompanying me, Hippolytos."

"MY DEAR SON, COME—TAKE A SEAT! WHAT CAN I OFFER YOU? TELL ME all! Or rather, take a bath: you'll get a rub-down with oil and get beaten with birch twigs... What do you hanker after? Some wine? Food?"

Uri felt somewhat faint as he took a seat on a couch with a twisting, convoluted ornamental back, made from a beautifully grained wood, not turned on a lathe but handcrafted, he noted as he ran his fingers over it.

"How lovely this is!" broke from his lips.

Philo sat down on the couch next to it with a happy laugh.

"You've got good taste! That is the most expensive seat in the whole room! Rosewood."

"I was a cabinetmaker for a while..."

"Marvelous!" the elderly man clapped in delight. "A cabinetmaker! Terrific!"

Some servants raced at the sound of the clapping. Philo didn't understand what they wanted, but since they were there he gave orders for one thing and another, after which the servants left.

"So, tell me all!"

It was now Uri's turn to laugh out loud.

"What could I possibly tell you that you don't know already? I am deeply honored... I've read your works—at least some of them... But the idea that one day I would get to meet the author is something I never even dreamed of doing."

"So, which of my works have you read?" Philo asked teasingly.

Uri began to list them. Philo was flabbergasted. When Uri got to a work entitled "On the Life of Moses," he interrupted.

"What do you make of that?"

Uri pondered.

The servants at this point brought wine, water and fruit, and they pulled the table between the two couches so that both men might reach.

"I found it a hugely entertaining read," said Uri cautiously. "I have to admit I was startled by the notion behind it—the idea of portraying Moses as an original philosopher, that is to say, and that he is the source of all Greek wisdom and art, even including Homer..."

"You really have read it!"

"Of course I did!" burst from Uri.

"Keep your hair on!" Philo said appeasingly. "Any number of people brag about how cultivated they are, when they aren't."

"I've encountered something of the same," said Uri. "But to get back to Moses, as I said, that stunned me to begin with. But after a while I got used to the notion, and I believe grasped its purpose, which is to show that one sphere of thought can be just as valuable as another, that the one can be derived from the other and vice versa."

"Amazing!"

Philo gazed in astonishment at the young man sitting tensely, uneasily on his most expensive couch. There was nothing special in his outward appearance: myopic gaze, sharply steeled brow, greasy, mousy-brown hair, sunken cheeks yet despite that an incipient double chin under a receding jaw line. His nose was crooked, bending to the right, as did his jaw.

"Did you also speak to Agrippa about philosophy?"

"No," said Uri, and left it at that.

Philo roared with laughter:

"I doubt Agrippa read even three books in his entire life, and half of those will have been lost on him!"

Philo picked up the plate of fruit and offered it to Uri, who took a fig.

"So," Philo resumed, "and do you agree with that line of thinking?"

"I'm not mature enough intellectually to be able to agree with it," said Uri carefully, yet frankly. "My mind has not become as unruffled as yours, a venerable philosopher's."

Philo gave an unforced chuckle.

Uri also laughed out loud.

"Well, there's plenty of time to debate that," said Philo cheerfully. "But I ought to draw your attention to one of my predecessors whose notion I merely developed further in my "Moses," the idea was not mine originally... Have you heard of Artapanus?"

Uri blushed and confessed that he hadn't.

"One of the most significant Jewish thinkers," exclaimed Philo. "Never mind, you'll get around to reading him... but tell me, what happened to you in Judaea? We lost track of you after you set off from Caesarea for Jerusalem."

Uri was astounded but kept that hidden.

"Well," he said, "after that I got pulled into some quite extreme scrapes."

"What happened in Samaria?" Philo asked.

Uri was again astounded: some people had been continually feeding reports about him—and to Alexandria at that. It was staggering.

Uri gave a brief account of the massacre at Mount Gerizim, saying that it had been Vitellius's soldiers who were responsible for the slaying, but Ananias, the former high priest, had gotten the delegation to sign off on a report that blamed Pilate's cohorts for the killing.

"And did you sign?" Philo ask pensively.

"I had no choice," said Uri. "Otherwise it's hard to believe I would be here now."

Philo nodded.

"That we didn't know," he said. "You did well."

"I did well by signing what I knew to be a lie?"

Philo raised his head and stared vacantly into the space above the hills and dales that were painted on the atrium walls.

"You did well," Philo repeated, returning his gaze to Uri. "That was how Vitellius was able to disgrace Pilate. About time too. Were you there when they led him away in chains?"

Uri confirmed that he had been there and seen that. Just as he was present in the exultant throng when Vitellius announced that he was restoring the safeguarding of the high priest's vestments to the Jews.

"That's about as far as their intellectual horizon extends," said Philo ruefully. "As if it matters who looks after the high priest's vestments."

"It was a pity that many hundreds of innocent, jubilant people were slain for the sake of machinations like that," Uri opined.

Philo took a melancholy sip of the wine, not mixing it with water.

"You're right, of course, it was a pity," he said. "A dirty, low-down provocation to use that hired false prophet—what was his alias? Simon, wasn't it? That the Ark of the Covenant has been found! Only in Samaria could the masses be made to swallow that sort of guff... To the best of our knowledge it was the high priest who spun the line to Vitellius, who took the bait... Pilate was cautious, being singularly moderate in his reactions to any provocation, constantly backing down... That, however, was one thing he cannot have counted on... To be saddled with responsibility for a bloody act that he didn't even commit. It's not something for delicate stomachs: it sickens me!"

Uri felt uncomfortable: this was high politics and had nothing to do with him. The Jews of Rome by tradition wisely steered clear of this sort of thing.

"Look, my boy," said Philo. "The high priest and Vitellius came to an agreement that they would have Pilate removed. Antipas in Galilee allowed the

Syrian cohort into Samaria; he had no choice because he did not want to upset Rome—after all, the Syrian legate is the embodiment of Rome. In his shoes Agrippa would have done exactly the same."

Uri nodded, but there was still something he wished to get out.

"Master," he said. "While I was going about among the mutilated corpses on that hillside in Samaria, the dead bodies of women, children, and old people— not all of them had been cleared away and the relatives were still grieving over them—there were some fairly weird sensations at play. The wretched fanatics had gone there simply because they were looking for the Ark of the Covenant... It wasn't they who hit upon the idea, they had been duped there by others... The ruins, the remains of their destroyed temple, are there on the hillside... That was where those who share the same faith as us once used to pray, and it was their co-religionists, the Jews, who destroyed their shrines... All I saw was a cloud over the mountaintop, that must have been the ruins, but I understood why only the worship of idols built at the top of hills is forbidden... a mountaintop is a very big deal indeed... Excuse me if I am still indignant when I speak about this..."

Uri fell silent.

Philo muttered:

"It's not possible to feel sorry for everybody... They were Samaritans..."

"People!"

"You're not a Samaritan."

Uri nodded glumly.

"That's true, I'm a Roman Jew..."

"I understand you, I really do understand," Philo quickly added.

There was a silence.

"Young man that you are," said Philo, smiling with an omniscient air, "you most likely came to like even the peasants of Judaea..."

"Yes, I grew fond of them. They were hosts for me, and they treated me well..."

"I too will be your host: you'll spend the night here."

As a result, Uri spent the night at Philo's, though he did not get a wink of sleep, the guestroom being crammed with scrolls of parchment and tablets, and he was able to burn as many lamps as he wished, so it was with bleary, red eyes that he looked up in the morning, when Philo dropped by to say good morning.

"Didn't you sleep at all?" Philo asked.

"Not really," murmured Uri, drunk from reading.

Philo ran his eyes over the books that were piled up on the table; there must have been a good ten of them, some quite voluminous scrolls.

"And you read all of those?"

"All of them," muttered Uri.

"Can I test you?"

"What's that?"

Philo picked up one of the scrolls, a play, the "Exagoge." He picked out a passage at random and read out aloud: "Aaron: It's not worth going that way, there's nothing there!"

Uri closed his swollen eyelids and half-asleep mumbled: "Moses: How would it not be worth going that way! Over there is the Promised Land..."

Philo put down the scroll.

"You know it off by heart?"

"Certainly," said Uri with a big yawn.

"And you know where it comes from?"

"A Jewish play of some sort. What's the title? Maybe 'Exodus'... Not a particularly good work as the outcome is given from the start, moreover one can have a fair guess what the ending is and that they will reach their goal... It's not possible to turn that subject into a tragedy; the author ought to know..."

"Ezekiel the Poet wrote it, two centuries ago! Is it something you read earlier?"

"Why would I have done that? I'm not going to spend time rereading things that I've already read in Rome... The works here on the table are not available in Rome."

Philo picked his way through the scrolls lying on the table and nodded. Indeed, it was unlikely that a copy would be found in Rome.

"Have you been to libraries there?"

"Of course I have," said Uri. "From the time they open to when they close, from the first to the fifth hour, one can read anything there, on the premises, for free, and it's surprising how much one can read in four hours if one tries..."

Philo looked at the sleepy, red-eyed young man swaying around, almost out cold, on the seat in front of him, and he was genuinely touched.

"Get some sleep now," he said, and he cleared his throat. "I'll give orders that you're not to be disturbed. And that when you wake up, you are to be fed. There's no need to hurry the reading: you'll have plenty of time for that, plenty of time for reading, dear boy."

The old man was almost on the point of tears and hurried out. It was almost as if he were flying, a tiny, airy-boned bird.

He has no child of his own, Uri reflected, and was glad about that.

URI DID NOT UNDERSTAND WHAT WAS HAPPENING TO HIM, BUT HE found he had been accepted in Alexandria.

And not by just any family either, but by the family of Alabarch Alexander, the richest and most influential of all Jewish families in Egypt, and hence in the whole world, the family for whom the very first row of stone benches on the west side of the stoa of the Basilica was reserved.

Alabarch means chief tax collector, the person who collected all the customs duties on goods carried along the Nile and paid these in to the Roman state treasury. All of Egypt had become the private property of the Roman emperor, by edict of the Deified Augustus, when sixty years ago he crushed Mark Antony. Uri could well imagine that the alabarch held on to a tiny bit of it as there was no one to keep a check on him.

The prefect of Egypt, commander in chief of the two Roman armies stationed in the country, had no trouble with them as it was peacetime, but his entire day was taken up by dispensing justice, and acting as the guardian of all rights—an office which had devolved on him from the kings of Egypt by the grace of Augustus—and he did not concern himself with excise matters. He was the alabarch's superior nominally, but not in practice. A twenty-five percent excise was assessed on goods arriving in Egypt from abroad, payable at the port of entry—in other words at Alexandria, Canopus, and Pelusium. The alabarch was not concerned with these as he only exacted internal duties. Uri was amazed that a Jew could be a chief tax collector on all the goods freighted along the Nile, even if it was one who had been granted Greek citizenship rights. In response to which he was told that for two hundred years and more Jewish soldiers had been standing guard along the Nile because the Egyptian kings had judged them more reliable than the Greeks, and the Romans had left things that way: don't fix what isn't broken, a wise dictum.

The stargazers whom he had met at the Basilica—and who wanted to maintain good relations with him because he was now living at the house of Philo, elder brother to the alabarch—related that Alexander had now been in office for fifteen years, to the evident satisfaction of the emperor, ever since Germanicus—a general of whose successes Tiberius, his stepfather, was jealous—had appeared in Alexandria, causing a huge commotion during his short stay of just a few weeks, with throngs of people, Greeks and Jews by turn, holding processions daily to cheer him, in their desire to please him and his wife Agrippina. Germanicus had the state's grain stores opened, and thereby the price of grain across the length and breadth of Egypt plummeted, at which point Germanicus made tracks out of Egypt and back to Syria with his wife and small children, and before too long he was dead, poisoned by Gnaeus Calpurnius Piso, who while the court hearing was in progress took his own life in Rome, yet on the orders of Tiberius, the trial continued as if the accused had been still alive. It was at this juncture that the governor of Egypt at the time relieved the former chief tax collector of his duties, appointing in his stead Alexander, who as it happened had just returned from Rome where he had gone before Germanicus arrived in Alexandria. There might be some connection between the two, smirked the stargazers, and they also related that Emperor Tiberius had unexpectedly granted Germanicus's mother, Antonia, vast lands in Egypt, and Alabarch Alexander—for reasons one can only guess at—had become the estate manager of those lands.

Uri did some quick reasoning: that must have happened around the time when Tiberius had expelled from Rome both the Jews and adherents of Egyptian cults, as a result of which he and his parents had roved around the countryside, with him carried piggyback by his father. Strange that he should be enjoying the hospitality of a family whose lucky star had at the time happened to be in the ascendant. Antonia, Germanicus's mother, must have supplied the emperor with signal services if, after Roman dominion was instituted she alone had been granted private estates in Egypt. Germanicus and Agrippina had been exceedingly popular, and the rumor was still making the rounds that Germanicus had been poisoned either by Piso or someone else. Tiberius subsequently banished the widowed Agrippina and had her murdered on the island of Pandataria. Of the sons of Germanicus only Gaius was still alive, along with three daughters, and Tiberius kept Gaius with him on the island of Capri.

Could it be, by any chance, that Antonia had sacrificed her unguarded son, Germanicus—whom popularity had turned soft in the head—to protect her other son, Claudius, and her grandsons? And had Alexander the alabarch played some role in this?

The astronomers divulged no secrets, telling Uri only things that were common knowledge in Alexandria, but still they were honoring him with their trust, and for that reason alone he sensed they would be expecting some favor in return.

The first Friday evening that he took his seat among the Jews of Alexandria in the double-colonnaded Basilica, on the first row of stone benches to the west(and near the middle of the row at that), opposite the bimah, the very place where he had developed such a hankering to sit the day of his arrival, he found himself seated next to Alabarch Alexander's second son, Tiberius Julius Alexander, who bore the nickname Tija and was just a year older than himself. He almost had to force himself to marvel that it all seemed so natural, the impossibility that he, a good-for-nothing from Far Side in Rome, had been accepted so smoothly and speedily by the most powerful Jewish family in the world.

And people stared: Who is that young man; why have we never seen him before? Uri refrained from looking back, he grew—not exactly eyes, but more an ear on the back of his head—and even if he couldn't quite make out the whispers about him, he understood them well enough: the astronomers must have gossiped, and the rumors had been passed on. There was a big crowd of people for services at the Basilica that evening. Philo was unmarried, and nothing was said about Alexander's wife (maybe she had died or he had driven her away), but on Alexander's right was seated his firstborn son, Marcus, a tall, ash-blond young man; also seated in the front row of stone benches were several collateral female relatives and their husbands, siblings and children. Uri was introduced to them, though he was incapable of registering who was who.

"The leathermakers' Kahal," someone next to Uri had whispered, meaning that a representative of the *koinon* of Jewish leather-dressers was doing the reading from the Septuagint that day. All the crafts in Alexandria were organized into koinon, which in Ptolemaic Egypt was the name for a guild, which just as with the Greeks had their own leaders, notaries, and secretaries, and these were rotated in strict order for officiating at the divine services on Friday evenings and other feast days, just the same way as the tribes of priests and Levites succeeded each other in Jerusalem. Uri was told by an elderly woman from the alabarch's family that lots were not drawn, as in Jerusalem, but rather the order was settled collectively each Rosh Hashanah by democratic deliberation and calculation, with no further arguments for the rest of the year.

It crossed Uri's mind that his father would be listening to that same passage in their modest house of prayer in Rome, and it was quite within the bounds of possibility that a tanner was also reading it out there. Next to the reader, standing ramrod-straight, was a tall man with a solemn expression on his face, the very image of one with a holy mission to do. He held a pale red kerchief in his hand, and when he held the kerchief aloft the ten thousand or so in the assembly said "Amen." That kerchief was necessary, because although the acoustics in the Basilica were good, the tanner's words were nearly impossible to hear beyond the first few rows due to all the rustling.

Few went home after the prayers, with the mass staying in the Basilica. On countless trestles under the roofed sections stood food and drink, and everyone was free to take as much as they cared to. Nobody chided the children who spilled wine or threw food onto the floor, chased and frisked about: a group already chosen would tidy up tomorrow evening. The cost of the spread was covered by a common fund, drawing on compulsory donations from the three-hundred-thousand-strong Alexandrian Jewish community. Uri asked if everyone was present, but of course not: most of the city's Jews would celebrate Friday evening at their own local houses of prayer, scattered across the other four districts of the city, the feasts in these being just as copious.

The stargazers gravitated toward Uri and were delighted—especially Hippolytos—to greet him. Uri was also pleased to see them, though they had little in common to talk about and the conversation grew increasingly tiresome. Uri couldn't manage to slip away—even aged Heraclitos, eminent and funny, would not let him go, pressing after him as he tried to make his way to the next table. Nothing of importance was said, but Uri still sensed that he—a gadabout good-for-nothing—was being fawned over by these agreeable, scholarly men merely because Philo had shown him favor, and he also had the feeling that Philo esteemed by them not on account of his philosophical oeuvre but for being brother to the all-powerful Alabarch Alexander.

Philo's younger brother was a vigorous man, his brow wrinkled by many laughter-lines. Alexander also had supervisory charge of the postal service in Egypt, Uri was later to learn, and thus he was able—should he so desire—to find out what anybody wrote in their letters. He too was a great bibliophile; in Rome, Antonia's lame, deformed boy Claudius, was a bookworm just like Philo, and the two often sent each other bibliographic rarities. By no means incidentally Antonia was close friends with Berenice, the mother of Julius Agrippa, and Claudius had grown up side by side with Julius Agrippa, a grandson of Herod the Great, one of whose names was given after Julius Caesar, the other after Herod the Great's friend, Agrippa, who was so loved by Jews that the largest synagogue in Rome was also named for him.

Alexander was recognized by all as the real leader of the Jews of Alexandria; no major decisions were taken without him. And somehow he, Gaius Theodorus, a nobody from Rome, had won access to this of all families. He would have liked to tell the stargazers that everyone was mistaken: he had been given no important mission by anyone, it was all a misunderstanding, but instead of doing that he just smiled inanely back and started inquiring about the ingredients of some of the unfamiliar dishes of food.

The alabarch's palace was not situated in the Jewish Delta district, but in Beta, the second district. As the inner city of Alexandria was laid out by the Ptolemies according to a regular rectilinear plan, it was divided into five districts, and special Greek councils were convened to arrange the affairs of the districts entrusted to them. They even took pains to reorganize the rural Egyptian populace and all manner of immigrant settlers into invented, artificial tribes, which were named after Greek divinities. Over the centuries, these tribes had gradually come to bear the names of the divinities with such pride—so said Philo—that by now they were all convinced that they were lineal descendants of Artemis, Poseidon or Athene. Greeks had two names officially, their own and that of their god, and in all official documents they were obliged to use both; Jews had only one name, but beside that they had to write that they were Jewish.

The single-story building, which had an extensive floor plan and inside was divided into many spaces, was surrounded by Greek palaces, villas, shrines, and tenement houses and was guarded by the alabarch's own armed men. These had been recruited from among the Nilotic excisemen, and they included Greeks who accepted Judaic eating customs. It would have been impossible to tell which of the members of the alabarch's private army were Jewish and which Greek, they wore exactly the same uniforms and spoke exactly the same way.

Uri would have been curious to know how big the alabarch's annual income was, but all he knew that the tax paid to Rome on produce was two and a half percent of the value, and by custom the alabarch's personal income was the same, though of course out of that he had to pay the excisemen and a lot more besides, as it was more than likely that local and municipal councilors were also paid out of this, so the alabarch did not earn as much from Egypt as Rome did. That said, he earned enough to be rolling in it. Uri found it hard to imagine how the two and a half percent excise duty payable to the alabarch was imposed on goods that flowed down the Nile to the harbors, and he assumed it was not paid in ready cash but in goods, but then those would have to be stored somewhere; yet there were no granaries or slaughterhouses in the inner-city areas of Alexandria; goods destined to be shipped were piled up in warehouses at the docks. The alabarch also had to attend to transport on dry land because the many-branched Nile was not navigable right up to the sea.

This was the domain of the family that had received him into its ranks, and—an even greater asset—he was accepted as a friend by Tija, which is to say Tiberius Julius Alexander, whose full name betrayed the high hope his parents had of him in his career: to be as unwavering as the emperor Tiberius, under whose rule he had been born twenty years ago, but also as clever and wise a general and statesman as Julius Caesar, and as mighty a warlord as Alexander the Great. That was a huge burden to carry, but Tija, so it seemed, effortlessly bore all the grave associations of his name.

Marcus, the alabarch's firstborn son, had been named after Mark Antony, trounced by the emperor Augustus around fifty years before Marcus was born. Plainly had been so named by the alabarch for the sake of the Greeks of Alexandria, who with their contemptuous attitude toward Rome, cherished the memory of Mark Antony and his struggle for Egypt's independence. It was maybe only in the wake of this that the alabarch had entered Roman service. Marcus was a tall, thin, blond, fine-haired boy, with misty blue eyes and a slightly rolling gait, who smiled convivially on all and liked to listen. As Uri could see, Marcus was not on good terms with his younger brother Tija, though he never caught them squabbling. Tija, for his part, pretended that Marcus did not exist; Marcus in return regarded his brother as if he were not even a five-year-old and therefore not worth arguing with. Marcus was rarely to be seen, being preoccupied with the *Boule*, the Jewish Council of Elders, of which he was the youngest member. Uri had no idea what duties might be accomplished by the seventy-two members of the supreme body of Alexandrian Jews, which in principle was drawn from leaders of the strongest guilds and families, but it turned out that they had not held sessions very often since there had been no head since Augustus abolished the office. Marcus most likely functioned as a secretary in a virtually nonexistent council, and did he receive any pay for doing so; he probably busied himself assiduously producing documents. When Uri asked about Marcus's activities Tija derisively shrugged his shoulders.

"He's the firstborn," Tija said, "so it doesn't matter what he does. He's where he is that one of us should be there as well."

Philo did not test Uri any further: the impression he had formed on the first day sufficed for Uri to be loved liked a son, but he was challenged by Tija. There could hardly be a more cultivated, cleverer, wittier or better-looking young man anywhere in the Jewish world. Everything about him was fine: his slender, long face; his Grecian profile; his curly, wiry, blond hair; his straight nose, his thick, sensual lips; his ears, set close to the head; his tall, muscular frame. Uri was astounded that such a being might also be created by the Eternal One. He had no envy, as he once had held for Pilate's brawny litter bearers; this young man was made of different stuff than most men—a person cannot envy a lion or elephant, only his own kind.

Tija set about testing Uri the moment Philo introduced him, which was at the palace in Alexandria. Uri was granted an entire suite of rooms with a bedroom, a separate atrium, baths, and kitchen, and he was free to stay there, he was assured, for as long as he stayed in Alexandria, with no reference made to the duration of that stay. After the first Sabbath was over, Uri mentioned to

Philo that he would have to go back to the harbor for his residence permit, but Philo brushed that aside and sent a servant for the permit, who brought one, too, for three months. Palace servants were also placed at Uri's disposal, but he respectfully declined. Philo smiled, the alabarch shrugged his shoulders; Uri was relieved not to be at the focus of the alabarch's attention, because he was afraid of him. He sensed from Philo's smile that he had for some reason become his favorite, and it was a position he would not lose for the time being; indeed, every cloddish mistake that Uri made would redound to his favor as long as that affection held.

At last—to the extent that he felt he ought to declare it was his intention, after taking a short holiday—he announced that he would have to return to Rome to assist his father make business deals because he would be going back much richer in experience. He would have to admit that he had been of little use to his father... but Philo waved that aside. Your father will get by without you, he's obviously a good merchant.

"Is there something that you know of about him?"

"No," said Philo. "All we know is that he lent money to Agrippa."

"And who told you that?"

"Agrippa in person," said Philo.

While Uri had been in Judaea, Agrippa had appeared in Alexandria and asked to be lent money. Uri had already heard this from the stargazer Hippolytos, and Philo related essentially the same story, adding only that the two hundred thousand drachmas were merely a bridging loan: Agrippa had for years owed the Roman exchequer eight hundred thousand drachmas, and if he did not pay off a chunk then he would not be allowed to set foot on Italian soil, where he was heading at the time; if he were to enter at Dikaiarchia, he would be arrested. He had been given three hundred thousand sesterces by Antonia, it was true, but it seems he squandered that on something else. It was during his sojourn in Alexandria that Agrippa had dropped a reference to a Ioses Lucius in Rome to whom he likewise owed money; he had also mentioned his son, Gaius Theodorus, who had become a member of the delegation that was delivering the holy tribute. Philo tacked on that they had later also heard this from other sources: it did no harm to treat any boastful statement that Agrippa made with some reservation, Philo elucidated, but this time it seems he had told the truth.

Uri wondered whether Agrippa had done anything since then toward repaying his overall debt to the Roman exchequer. Philo seemed to hesitate before reluctantly admitting that yes, in Dikaiarchia Agrippa had been given an interest-free loan of one million drachmas by a Samaritan slave, which he had been able to put toward sorting out his debts, as a result of which it became possible for him to travel to see the emperor on Capri.

Uri did not ask any further questions.

But how could a Samaritan slave have come by such an immense fortune? He couldn't have, otherwise he would not long have been a slave. He must have been a cover for someone else, but Philo wasn't going to say who that was. Maybe it was the alabarch himself. Even the emperor, to whom Agrippa was of importance. Or maybe some senator. When all was said and done, it made no difference.

Tija, anyway, began quizzing him, throwing out questions seemingly arbitrarily, about astronomy, Greek literature, or philosophy or history, listening to Uri's answers for only two or three sentences, by which time Uri's proficiency had become apparent and then switching to another topic. The one area in which he did not pose any questions was Latin literature, and Uri was shrewd enough to ask him—during a lull in the barrage of questions—which particular line in Virgil was Tija's favorite. Tija was speechless: he was not used to being interrogated. Uri loftily brushed that aside, all right, then, what about being so kind as to quote something from Livius's rough translation of the *Odyssey*. Tija started to grow uneasy and began declaiming bits of Greek, but Uri was impertinent enough to signal that he should stop: Latin, if possible. Tija made an attempt to render in Latin hexameters the passage he had just quoted in Greek, but he could not do it without errors, omitting to place a caesura in the line, as Uri was not slow in pointing out. Philo, who had been an earwitness to the exchange, gleefully swooped down on his nephew:

"See, you don't know everything!"

Tija fumed angrily; probably nobody had ever dared to humiliate him in such a fashion. Not that it was a serious humiliation: more in the way of a little teasing, but Tija still turned bright red.

"That's not fair!" he burst out. "He lives in Rome; Latin's his native tongue!"

Uri protested: Greek was his native language too; he had learned Latin through his own industriousness, for at least a third of the Roman populace, if not half, didn't speak a word of Latin, or at best read only graffiti. The Jews there spoke no Latin, as they had no need to.

Philo guffawed; he was enjoying the exchange.

"Gaius is right," he said. "Tiberius can speak excellent Greek, yet for some reason it was Latin that he would have liked to hear everywhere, and he was irate, as long as he was living in Rome, then not even all the senators spoke it!"

He turned to Uri:

"I'll take you on as Tija's instructor in Latin," he declared forthrightly. "He could do with one. At the Gymnasium he almost totally ignores Latin out of sheer arrogance. Read a bit of Cato and a bit of Cicero together and you'll be done with the matter."

After hesitating a moment, Tija decided with a nod of the head to accept. It was an odd smile, more in the way of a grimace. Uri shuddered, but he was glad that by this means, under the pretext of teaching Latin, he would have the chance of officially spending some hours with this prodigy, and that delight dispelled the momentary aversion.

Alabarch Alexander was seldom seen in the palace, attending to his business affairs across the city and along the Nile, whereas Tija kept to his suite of rooms from Friday after dusk until Sunday evening, being a boarder at the Gymnasium. Uri was thus free to read in the palace library or roam around town and in the evening, by the light of a multitude of gorgeous candles, he conversed with Philo, who on weekdays during the daytime would visit the Musaeum's famous Library which Uri himself so longed to do.

It transpired that it was no simple matter to visit the Library. to enter it, one had to be a citizen of Alexandria, and if one were Jewish only those who were Alexandrian Greek citizens could set foot in the sanctum of the Library; it was not enough merely to have rights of residence in Alexandria. An Alexandrian Jew might feel he was a cut better than a metic (a Greek resident alien), but not much.

Philo clarified: an Alexandrian citizen did not pay electoral taxes; these were paid by those who merely had rights of residence in Alexandria, as was the case with most Jews. Citizens who were exempt from paying the electoral tax (and all Greek natives of the city belonged to that category) clung to that privilege and were loath to award rights of Alexandrian citizenship to Jews and other non-Greek nationals. To this day, the peoples living in the villages on the sites on which Alexandria was built—Persians, for instance, who had arrived with the Babylonian invasion, and whose descendants still lived in the city—had not been granted rights of citizenship even though it was the Greeks who had "assimilated," not them. The Jews, whose ancestors had been resident in Alexandria centuries before, had long been fighting to be accepted as Greek citizens by virtue of being born there and had already addressed countless petitions on the matter to both Augustus and Tiberius, but—though it was hard to say why that was so, because the electoral tax amounted to no great sum—assent had been slow in coming. All the same, Alexandrian Jews were not united on the issue, as many preferred to pay the additional tax and stay segregated from the Greeks as members of the Alexandrian Jewish polity, fearing that by coming under the same jurisdiction as the Greeks they would lose their status as God's chosen people.

"How much is the electoral tax?" Uri queried.

Philo, being a Jew with full rights of Greek citizenship, was stumped: he didn't know exactly, but he would make inquiries.

"But then I don't even know the price of eggs at the market," he confessed with a blush. "I've never had to buy anything in person."

Uri felt that the time was ripe for him to mention that he would be happy to buy this or that for himself, but he didn't have a penny to his name. Philo again blushed.

"Don't take it amiss, dear boy. I completely forgot about that... I'll instruct the majordomo to provide you with daily pocket money. How much do you need?"

Uri paused. He could name any price at all: Philo would have no clue as to its value, but decided nonetheless to stick with a small amount, about as much as his tessera would get him in Rome.

"You'll get twice that," said Philo, shaking his head in dissatisfaction with himself.

Still, Uri had to make himself useful for that per diem, a half to two-thirds of which he would put aside each day: during their evening discussions Philo would grill him, pleasantly but methodically. And Uri would have to muster his entire knowledge in responding. The talk ranged from literature to matters of history or philosophy, and sometimes Philo would interrogate Uri about Rome and Judaea, having visited neither. Uri was worried he would start questioning him about Agrippa, but he was spared that, and it suddenly occurred to Uri that they already knew more than enough about Agrippa not to need any information from others.

Tija was present on one occasion when Philo made a strange assertion about Agrippa: that unconscionable, prodigal, giddy, greedy charlatan would someday become the greatest Jewish king there ever was, just wait and see, even greater than Herod the Great.

He even stated his grounds: Agrippa owed people in Rome left, right, and center, not just Jews but also senators, and the only way they would get the money back with interest was if they were to use their united might to make Agrippa king of the Jews. Philo laughed, and Uri could only gape, flabbergasted. Tija added that Antipas too was bidding for Judaea, Samaria, and everything else which had at one time been part of his father's realm to be annexed to Galilee, and there was even some chance he would achieve that, but he was going about it in a very stupid way, because he didn't owe money to anyone in Rome.

Uri was surprised at how Philo, the omniscient great philosopher, was so ill-informed about conditions in Rome and Judaea that he knew virtually nothing about the lives of Rome's Jews, the Judaean countryside, even Jerusalem itself. With a deft, witty choice of words, Uri sketched what he knew. Philo was immensely diverted to learn that a Jewish house of prayer was to be constructed in Ostia purely because someone had by chance, and at no cost, had laid hands on four Greek columns.

"Those Jews!" he shook his head contentedly. "Those Jews!"

Uri had a good mind to give an account of the Jewish bordello in Syracusa, the prison cells that filled the shop premises in the palace of the high-priest, and similar topics, but he checked himself: there was no way of knowing what might provoke Philo, who had perhaps never truly had to come to terms with the practicalities of living.

In exchange, with regard to the lesser-known works of certain individual philosophers, Philo willingly held little lectures, in the manner of the Peripatetic school, pacing up and down the room as Uri slowly braced himself to ask again: how might he, without Alexandrian citizenship, be able to get into the renowned Library so as to be able to read these works. It was not that Philo's explanations were in any way deficient, but he loved the smell, the feel, of parchment and papyrus...

Philo would shake his head: that was no easy matter, Uri was a newcomer, not even a native Alexandrian Jew. Precise records were kept of all the three hundred and some thousand locally born Jews, and copies of these were sent to Jerusalem so that the information would be safe if any harm were to befall the genealogical volumes in Alexandria. Reports were also made on those Jewish citizens of Alexandria who were permitted to enter the library, because a number of those were of priestly descent.

"How might I get to be an Alexandrian citizen?" Uri asked audaciously.

Philo was astonished.

"You want to settle here definitively?"

"Not that," Uri responded diplomatically. "But I very much like this city... It's not that I want to live off you permanently," he added. "Having the pleasure of your family's hospitality cannot last for long, and I would not want to abuse that. I'd be glad to take up some respectable trade and earn my keep... If that's not possible, then I'll go back to my father."

"All right, all right," Philo muttered disconcertedly. "For the time being, though, just stay seated on your bottom, and read... It's no easy matter... There are no more than three or four hundred citizens of Alexandria who have gained Greek citizenship... Just like Rome, Alexandria takes care of itself..."

"But Rome doesn't take care of itself," said Uri, "because all the Jews there are granted citizenship provided the grandfather is a freedman—that's how I too acquired it..."

Philo brightened up.

"Of course! You're a Roman citizen! That means you can visit the library. In principle, Roman citizenship is of a higher class than Alexandrian Greek: anything that is more difficult to obtain at any given place is automatically of a higher class."

Uri was extremely pleased by that flash of inspiration.

Needless to say, this was not quite how things turned out: a Roman citizen needed to obtain special permission to visit the library, Philo was told, and that was hard to get.

"I can understand them," said Philo on the evening of the next day. "They're concerned for their scrolls. And don't think that Alexandrian citizens, the ones who are entitled, flock there in droves to read... Nearly all of them are preoccupied with business. Only a handful of us readers potter around there, and half of us are Jews, the rest professional copyists... There'd be no trouble finding space for you, it's just..."

Uri protested that there was no reason to fear for any scrolls in his hands, he took great care of them.

Philo recounted what the librarians in Alexandria were truly worried about.

Eighty-eight years ago, the book collection was burned by Julius Caesar, and it had been estimated that some four hundred thousand irreplaceable scrolls had thereby been lost. It was not the Library as such that the Revered One had torched, but the timber sheds at the port used for warehousing that caught fire when Caesar, who at the time was residing in the palace next to the Musaeum, was caught by surprise, and his residence came under fire from ships in the harbor. In their pursuit of Pompey, Caesar's navy had driven him into Alexandria, Pompey had been killed, so Caesar had felt he was safe—a mistake. The wing with the Royal Library, which still stands today as part of the Musaeum, just cannot hold many books. Caesar was placed in the fraught position of having to order blazing torches to be hurled against the enemy ships anchored in the harbor, and they were set ablaze, but the fire also spread to the book depots on the shore. When later asked why he had not taken greater care for the books, Caesar is supposed to have quipped: "Why didn't you build your whole city of stone?"

Philo recounted that Isidoros, the present head of the Gymnasium, was in the habit of remarking to Jews, whom he loathed: "The Revered Julius, man of culture, your beloved patron, your idol." Philo himself tended to argue back that he was unaware that Julius Caesar had shown Jews any particular favor, as compared with other groups, to which Isidoros would always enumerate all the people in the entourage first of Caesar then Augustus who had once been Jewish slaves, and the way in which their influence had been exerted to the detriment of Greeks—insignificant snippets of information that Isidoros must have pieced together in a manner befitting more serious matters. It was a waste of time for Philo to expostulate that he did not believe that other peoples had been any less pushy than Jews in the crush around the emperors.

The Musaeum itself had remained intact, but the remaining volumes— around one tenth of the former stock—had been transferred from there to the Serapeion, which was also home to the two hundred thousand scrolls that Mark Antony had brought over from Pergamum as a gift to Cleopatra VII. The inhabitants of Pergamum had been demanding the return of the scrolls ever since, but Alexandria was not disposed to oblige them: a delegation would regularly be sent from Pergamum to Rome to gain an audience with the emperor, and they would pace around with the dozens of other delegations from 101 other nations who were likewise waiting to gain an audience with the emperor, except that the emperor never went to Rome, spending his time continually on Capri, so that after a few weeks or months the delegations, their business unattended to, would go back home, only to try and put the same request again to Rome ten or twelve years later.

The Serapeion was a long way from the harbor, out of range of arrows and ballista. The temple, like the Pyramids, would stand forever, the Greeks avowed, and in Philo's opinion there was something in that. Uri could endorse the idea: a pretty fortification, he had seen it.

"The storerooms in the Serapeion went several floors underground," said Philo. "They were hewn from rock so the books did not get damp. Like all the bigger temples, it too had been designed with fortification in mind but one couldn't help dreading that if a major disaster like a flood were to happen, or the roofing were to catch fire, that library of umpteen hundred thousand volumes, which once more brings together in one place just about everything that is worth reading, will vanish from the face of the earth, and all knowledge will be lost with it. It is not at all certain that it is such a clever idea to hold every important work in one and the same building... Other places have libraries, but the one here is devoted to acquiring, even at disproportionately high expense, the rarities that other places own. Ever since the great conflagration there has been an insane purchasing mania for every piece of writing... Cleopatra VII wanted to turn Alexandria once more into the center of the world of learning; she invited the great scholars of the Greek world, devoted a great deal of money to adding to the Library's acquisitions—which I never tire of approving, even if she did loathe us Jews. But the way it is now, in the place it used to be there are no longer any scrolls at all, and in the place where the scrolls now are... they might well be destroyed along with everything else. It's lucky the city has little money and so only infrequently does it buy scrolls: it prefers to have them copied: that costs less, and the original is then returned to wherever it was being safeguarded... Even so, of course, a lot of scrolls are damaged in the process, some even disappear completely—odd, isn't it, that it's always the most valuable to which this happens?"

Philo also related that Aulus Avilius Flaccus, the prefect of Egypt ("our dear Aulus"), was a genuinely cultivated man who devoted substantial sums out of Roman treasury coffers to acquiring books, obviously with Tiberius's awareness; he also financed the enticement of famous scholars to Alexandria, just as Cleopatra had done, and they came, but still the truly talented rhetoricians headed for Rome as anyone who became successful could make better money there: Rome had great allure for those skilled in legal argumentation.

Uri commented that he would like to read in the library before the next misfortune befell it, and if he could not do so as a Roman citizen, then he would apply for Alexandrian citizenship, except he did not know how to do that.

"There's no way," said Philo.

"I find it hard to believe that there is no back door," said Uri.

He felt a devil was taking hold:

"I'd also like to attend the Gymnasium," he declared. "Anyone who completes that is automatically given rights of citizenship, isn't that so?"

Philo studied Uri's totally unexceptional features with great interest. Uri bent forward to pick a fig for himself.

"So it is, only it's not that easy to get in," said Philo paternally. "The entrance exam is tough: you have to get a distinction in all subjects, most particularly if you are Jewish..."

"God forbid!" said Uri. "I can get distinctions if necessary."

Philo chuckled.

"Have you tried before?" he asked.

"Not yet," said Uri. "I'm sure it would turn out right..."

"The Gymnasium has just two Jewish students altogether," said Philo, growing serious. "Tija is brilliant by any standard, and there's another boy by the name of Apollonos, an extraordinarily gifted orator; his father is a merchant in sesame oil in Memphis. The head could hardly be prevailed on to take even him on. Tija he was forced to enroll, as he had Greek citizenship by birthright after my brother had earned it."

"I'm not scared of failure," said Uri. "If I happen to find myself in Alexandria, I might as well try. In Rome I used to peek through the fence around the Greek Gymnasium, and I used to envy the boys the chance to be there... They played ball games, ran... Not one Jew among them... No one among us ever aspired to enter; it never so much as crossed my mind... I was still a toddler then... I now feel that I may have learned a thing or two through my travels... Thanks to Agrippa, who put me in the delegation."

"And who is going to support you financially?" Philo queried. "The first year costs a packet... The most outstanding are taught free from the second year on, but that goes only for a very few. Who will pay the school fees in the first year, Gaius Theodorus?"

"I'll earn the money," Uri said confidently.

Philo pondered.

"Even then it's not sure they'll take you on... Apollonos has remarkable oratorical gifts, being able to extemporize on any given subject for several hours on end—a real joy to hear..."

Philo snorted with laughter.

"Not long ago I was present at the oratory competition that is run every year on the Gymnasium's grounds and free for anyone who cares to listen... The subject chosen for him was frog's legs... He plunged right into it with a moment's preparation, anything you can think of, from Homer through Sophocles to Aristotle, he mixed in a bit of everything and everybody, citing nonexisting lines from the Iliad, ad-libbed hexameters about the intimate sensual relations of Helen of Troy and the frog. It had the whole audience in stitches... He's an incredibly sharp-witted young man who will almost certainly be granted citizenship."

"I'm still going to apply," said Uri.

Philo shook his head.

"There's nothing to stop you from applying; even a Jew may apply," he said with a troubled look, "but the entrance exam is very stiff. The head in person asks the questions and at best he will admit one of us Jews in a decade... Like that Apollonos... Tija was also there at his entrance exam; Apollonos improvised on the spot a text in couplets about how Moses became a pharaoh through murder, and it was the murdered pharaoh's son who led the Egyptians out of their own land because they could not stand the evil rule of the Jews... In the wilderness on the way there appeared to the pharaoh's son, all of a sudden, some five hundred gods, and they made a collective conversion... So, as they are wending their way toward their new homeland the Egyptians began spreading their polytheism in Canaan and the whole of the Hellenistic world, but to this day they have remained in a minority, poor things, because backward, pagan Judaism still remains in vogue, choking every other faith..."

Philo guffawed, his head rocking in mirth; Uri morosely held his tongue. A clever boy it seemed, that Apollonos; Tija too, as he had already found out. These were people he could not compete with.

"I'd give it a go, all the same," he muttered under his breath.

"What's that?" Philo asked.

"The entrance exam... What does it comprise?"

Philo shook his head.

"I don't know. You'd have to ask Tija... If you very much want to... genuinely very much want to, and if you don't wish to return to Rome as yet, which really would make no sense for the time being, then I could drop a word in Isidoros's ear to pay attention when you apply..."

Philo's eyes misted over as he went on:

"If he takes you on, then I'll pay for you studies..."

"I shall apply," said Uri obstinately. "Any my thanks in advance."

Philo choked back his tears and wagged his head.

"Perhaps it's no handicap if I recommend you," he ruminated. "Isidoros holds my work in esteem... Though I suspect that in his heart of hearts, he detests me too..."

Tija shrugged his shoulders when Uri pumped him about the entrance exam that weekend.

"I didn't have to take it," he said. "I'm a Greek citizen, and Isidoros is under an obligation to my father as every year the Gymnasium receives a nice little sum from us... Apollonos, on the other hand, had to take the exam; out of sixty-six Jewish applicants, he was the only one to be accepted. Ask him."

"Where can I find him?" Uri asked.

"At the Gymnasium, he's a boarder."

"But I won't be allowed in."

"Probably not, I suppose."

"When does he go out?"

"He doesn't make a habit of it."

Uri nodded, and switched instead to asking whether it was not time to make a start of the Latin tuition.

"Get real!" said Tija. "Philo long forgot about the whole business. He has to be told anything five times over before it finally registers with him."

Uri shrugged his shoulders: he had made up his mind that he didn't need any help from Tija.

Tija waited for Uri to insist, and he was surprised that he did nothing of the kind.

"Tell me," Uri finally spoke. "Why are you all being so nice to me?"

They were standing in the atrium, by a shaded, western wall. It was the afternoon of the Sabbath when it was permissible to chat and everything had been prepared for them on the Friday afternoon.

"Your father lent money to Agrippa," said Tija pensively. "So did my father, but only four times as much as your father lent, even though he is umpteen thousand times wealthier. Agrippa sent a message to Jerusalem through you... It must have been an important message, and any of Agrippa's people is our ally."

Uri nodded.

"All the same," he persisted. "What are you supporting me for?"

Tija smiled wryly:

"I have no idea," he said, and he sounded sincere. "Maybe we need a reliable courier. We don't have too many reliable contacts in Rome: the Roman Jews are cowardly, narrow-minded, and they know nothing about Roman politics. Or rather... Maybe we are afraid of you, Gaius Theodorus. You may become a man of importance, just as Agrippa will become king, and you can be sure that he will. It is unusual for someone to be chosen as one of the delegates who carry the money to Jerusalem, and Agrippa explicitly said, I remember it distinctly, that it was on his word that you were taken into the delegation. For some reason, he must have a high regard for you. You were sent ahead to study the situation in Judaea. Your on-the-spot knowledge will be important for him one of these days: he has not really seen anything of Judaea as he was constrained to living on Antipas's favor when he had to vanish from Rome on account of his mounting debts, so he had no time to look around in Judaea. You're a favorite of Agrippa's, and it doesn't matter why. You may or may not be his spy, as my father assumes, and if that's what he assumes, then that's the way it is. Whether you're a sleepwalker or an ignorant novice, you still become what people consider you to be, and you can't do anything about that. It does no harm if the confidant of the future king of the Jewish empire-in-the-making, is, at the same time, under an obligation to us."

Uri's legs began to tremble.

He stepped over to the table on which bowls of fruit were standing, picked up a grapefruit, dug a nail into and began to peel it.

Tija likewise sauntered over, eyed a cluster of grapes and sat down on a couch, ready to switch to serious conversation. There were three couches in the yard, symbolizing a Roman eating-couch, a triclinium.

Nibbling segments of the grapefruit, Uri sat down on another of the couches.

"How big do you figure Agrippa's kingdom will be," he queried impassively.

"Big," was Tija's view. "At least as big as Herod the Great's, maybe even bigger."

"Galilee included?" Uri asked.

"Naturally," said Tija. "Antipas has to be cleared out of the way. One trait that all of Herod the Great's descendants inherited is a love for doing away with one another. Antipas still remains. Herod Philip, the tetrarch of Trachonitis and Gaulanitis, dodged trouble by departing this life; his kingdom was absorbed into Syria, but that can be handed back at any time to a scion of Herod..."

Uri nodded and pushed a further segment into his mouth.

"There was an occasion once," he said wistfully, "when I dined with both Pilate and Antipas, last Passover, in Jerusalem..."

Tija sat up.

"Really?"

"Excellent dinner too," Uri stated matter-of-factly, and continued eating.

Tija was looking at him with narrowed eyes. What could he be thinking? Uri wondered.

"Earlier on they weren't too fond of each other," said Tija. "Antipas is not stupid; he could also angle for Judaea; he would get more out of it than out of Galilee. It's questionable if he realizes that he needs to hook Caligula by some means, but even if he were to try, Agrippa has beaten him to it: he's already there on Capri, and Tiberius has appointed him tutor to Gemellus and Caligula, his joint heirs apparent, whereas Antipas cannot even visit the island."

Uri got to his feet, took a fig from the table, and sat back down.

"Antipas can send couriers to both Tiberius and Caligula," he reasoned. "So he is also able to aspire to Herod the Great's former kingdom; after all, he's his son, Agrippa is only a grandson."

Tija shook his head in silent disagreement.

"Agrippa is the one with friends in Rome, not Antipas," he finally said. "Agrippa has bribed half the Senate, showering gifts on them, inviting them to banquets, providing them with courtesans—and all through loans of money, because before he was out of his teens he had run through the fortune he inherited. I've said it before: the one who gets to be king will be the one with the biggest debts!"

Tija broke out into laughter.

"Both your father and mine, a lot of fathers, have lent money to Agrippa that loose women and putrid strutters of the boards can suck off the limp dicks of the senators of Rome! Antipas can promise them whatever he wants, they'll only believe what their dicks are telling them: it's dicks that pull the strings in the world of the human race."

The viewpoint came as a surprise to Uri.

"So what happens if someone finds a way of having Agrippa poisoned?"

He was amazed at his temerity, but it was out now. Tija did not bat an eyelid.

"Fair enough," he said, "after all, someone has to die. If Tiberius's adopted son, Caligula, is made emperor, then Tiberius's flesh-and-blood grandson will have to die. If Gemellus, the grandson, becomes emperor, then Caligula has to perish. Flaccus, the prefect here in Egypt, is a friend of Macro, prefect of the Praetorian Guard; the two of them together have placed their bet on Gemellus, have been friends with him for years and send him gifts every now and then because Tiberius's blood runs through his veins. Agrippa has bet on Caligula for reasons he knows best, and its he who is there, on Capri, he has the direct experience from which to read the auguries. Flaccus has a sober, smart, political brain and is putting his money on Gemellus, and our Agrippa, the cunning rambler, has gambled on Caligula. We don't know who Antipas has backed already or will back, most likely both of them if it were up to him, only that's not possible: this is a chariot race and you can only place a bet on one color. We've plumped for Agrippa—my father has, at any rate. You've also placed your bet on him, because your father has done the same. In other words, all of us are backing Caligula; we're together in the hard times, Gaius Theodorus, and we'll also be together in the good times."

Uri mused; he had not previously taken into account that his imperfect, much-tormented body might be a vehicle of imperial politics.

"So what happens," he asked, "if all those simple calculations become more complicated? Queen Helena and Izates, who converted to Judaism..."

"Leave them out of it!" expostulated Tija. "They're small fry; their claims to the throne are baseless whatever they do. They won't dare ally with the Parthians because Rome will just overrun them; Adiabene is of no consequence."

"But there are still plenty of other relatives of Herod's, a lot of them living in Rome..."

"It could get complicated," Tija admitted. "Certainly, Agrippa might be snuffed out by the Roman relatives; the gladiators are in combat on Capri and we don't even get to watch the struggle. It could be that they all die, stabbing one another in a circle... The first one pierced jumps up and stabs the last of the killers before dropping dead... If everybody slaughters everybody else, it could even be that Antonia's crippled halfwit of a son, Claudius, is made emperor... It's not beyond the bounds of possibility that I shall become a simple prefect of Judaea and you, my strategos."

"I've got poor eyesight," said Uri. "I can see virtually nothing at a distance; I've had no military training."

"All the better," grinned Tija. "At least you won't see who the soldiers under your command are massacring."

Uri found the taste of the fig to be more sour than the grapefruit he had just eaten. Tija wasn't joking now.

"It's far from certain," he said, "that that's my aim in life."

"Oh, don't be modest!" said Tija. "Why wouldn't it be: everyone longs to be in power. Anyone who denies that is kidding himself."

"What I long for," said Uri, "is to be able to use the Great Library, and if the path to do that lies via the Gymnasium, then what I long for is to be accepted as a student and to complete my studies there."

"Which means you want to receive military training," rejoined Tija, "with your bad eyes. So you want to be my strategos, after all, but you won't admit it to yourself. That's silly! But if that's what you long for, then do something about it."

"I suppose," said Uri equably, "you'll do nothing for me."

"You suppose right," Tija agreed. "In fact I'll do everything within my power to obstruct you. Let's see who's the craftier."

"You're starting with a minor advantage," Uri noted, "seeing that you are already in there, and not purely on account of your brains."

"Let a slave progeny who longs for great things be a genius," announced Tija. "You're a bright boy, but there's no way of knowing what that genius is capable of. If I see you as cut out for great things, I'm not going to shy away from praising your exceptional talents out loud. And I'll trip you up wherever I can, but if you should win through all the same, then I shall have gained a brilliant shield bearer. Is that a deal?"

Uri nodded.

"I'm not going to cram Latin authors down your throat," he said. "Let their knowledge be my shield against you, who doesn't know them."

"I don't need them," said Tija dryly. "Every single Roman poet and historian is ideologically subservient. They're all second-hand annotators, only clever in hindsight, having nothing to do with practical politics. Not one is truly creative, nor is my uncle, in spite of all the brilliant books he writes. I want to be creative."

"An emperor perchance?"

Tija leapt angrily to his feet.

"I can't be emperor!" he yelled. "I can't be emperor because I'm Jewish! That's how the one and only Eternal One castigates all those who were born into His chosen people! A monotheist can never become emperor in Rome!"

Marcus appeared in the atrium, freshly bathed, beaten with birch twigs and massaged with oil.

"Am I intruding?" he asked politely.

"No," growled Tija.

A chill set in.

"You were shouting just before now," said Marcus. "What about?"

Uri gave him a brief outline.

Marcus was hesitant.

Uri chewed it over.

"I don't quite see why a monotheist could not be emperor," he said. "Our God is emperor in Heaven, and everyone serves Him, angels and devils alike, in much the same way as the Senate and Praetorian Guard serve the emperor in Rome. Our other world is just the same as if our ancestors had placed present-day living Rome in Heaven. Polytheism was in keeping with Greek democracy and the Roman republic: peoples and factions competed with each other, the gods did likewise. But for the empire? Might the Romans not be mistaken with their plurality of gods? Might they have a false image of themselves?"

Tija frowned and kept quiet; Uri sensed the coldness he was emanating. He was not pleased that an idea one might call a thought should occur to anyone but himself.

"A monotheistic Roman emperor?" asked Marcus in astonishment.

"Fair enough," said Uri. "Right now that's an impossibility... Rome is very proud of the fact that it welcomes with open arms all the gods of all the peoples it conquers, and it sets up altars to them in Rome... But if the population were to be believers in the emperor... if it were genuinely to become that... why is the Roman population not monotheistic, I wonder? What do they need those countless gods for? That's not truly a religion they have there... All those thousands of gods! Then none of them is a god! But the emperor's power is very real, and all he has is power..."

"So they need a Moses, as my uncle suggests?" Marcus asked. "A divine pharaoh?"

Uri pondered, and a heretical thought crossed his mind. Should he come out with it? But then, logic is logic.

"A Moses who is not Jewish," he said. "A Latin Moses. Greek for that matter. A pagan Moses. That's what is appropriate. The emperor dies, his head is knocked off the statues and replaced by the head of the new emperor... Nothing sacred about that—for all that they are deified after they have died, even somewhat ahead of that. They too need a unique and immortal god."

Tija chuckled:

"So, Jupiter is appointed the one and only god, so the others are sent packing? Pensioned off? Settled in the provinces like veterans? Is that supposed to be a help?"

Uri shrugged his shoulders.

"I don't know," he said, "but something isn't functioning in the world."

"And it's right that the Romans appoint one new high priest after another in Jerusalem?" Tija queried, "Does that sort of high priest have some sort of sanctity?"

"No, he doesn't," Uri admitted. "Of course, I say that with the proviso that I have never seen a high priest in action, and maybe when they officiate at a service the divine spark manifests in them. I only ever met a former high priest in Jerusalem, one by the name of Ananias... He was wearing a white and blue linen robe, but even so there was no sanctity emanating from him—just a politician, a human being."

"All being well, Agrippa with our assistance will be a king," said Tija, "but not much sanctity will emanate from him either—burps and farts are all that emanate from him."

Uri cautiously, almost unnoticeably nodded: it would not do to admit that he had never seen him.

"Do you think that people have any real need at all for religion?" Tija mused, and a note of excitement entered his voice. "Or have they maybe just become used to this tradition of theirs, and they slosh around in it like in a caldarium?"

What came to Uri's mind were some Greek philosophers who attributed so-and-so-many elements to an unmoved mover—four, one, whatever—and cogitated about numbers and ratios but never said anything about gods.

"Is there a need for a religion in Judaea?" Tija asked pressingly.

Uri pondered.

"Is there a need for a religion in Judaea?" Tija asked.

Uri mused.

Alexandria, by giving a person time to think, must be a place that was agreeable to God.

Before his eyes ran images of sects, devotees, idlers, sacrificers, mourners, grieving relatives, mutilated corpses, activists, hustlers, robbers, the ambitious... All were images from his journey as a money carrier, as he had not lived prior to that. He had not lived, just read.

Before his eyes appeared the throng of people he had witnessed on the road from Caesarea to Jerusalem. The people who stood in line at harvest-tide, happily chanting psalms. It was a good feeling to be together. Mourners in the cemetery. Everyone feared dying: better to live in the hope of eternal life than to believe that death was a total extinction—that was unimaginable. There had to be a higher power, but that aside, what was it that drove people to religion? The Sabbath, the feasts, and the rules about cleanliness were subordinate; pagans obeyed rules which had similar functions—Egyptians refused to eat pork, and their priests were circumcised in similar fashion—so those were parts of communal life and had nothing to do with religious piety.

In Rome there were so many shrines and religions that the Roman Jews could make do without raptures.

He glanced up: Tija was sipping wine as he reclined on the couch, Marcus stood with his back against the wall.

"There is a need for an emperor who is present in the soul of all his subjects," said Uri. "Uniformly and exclusively. What a tremendous military power that would make!"

"A pharaoh," said Marcus. "But the pharaohs were thrown out—there has to be a reason for that!"

"You're talking about a Messiah," said Tija.

Uri was surprised.

"Yes," he deliberated. "I may well be talking about a Messiah."

"A pagan Messiah?" said Marcus in astonishment. "Tucked away at the bottom of Uncle Philo's writings there is always a Messiah, but to be honest I can't understand why. He's a clever man, cultivated and does nothing but try to reconcile Hellenism and Judaism yet neither the Greeks nor the Jews read what he writes... I never really understood what in fact he does believe in."

"For one thing," said Tija, "someone who converts to Judaism might be a Messiah. We should explain the Scriptures to make that possible. Along comes a Roman emperor and gets himself circumcised..." he giggled. "That would be some joke!"

"The idea of a pagan Messiah attracts me," said Uri. "A Messiah is the salvation for all peoples, not just for the Jews. At most the Jewish dead will be resurrected half a day earlier..."

"Come off it!" said Marcus. "That's a Pharisaic way of looking at it. In Alexandria everyone is a Sadducee; we don't believe in an other world."

"It doesn't matter what we think," Tija ventured, "it's what the people think. A pagan Messiah... A monotheistic Roman emperor... Good ideas! The only hitch is: why should the Messiah come along while we are alive? Even as an emperor?"

"According to the Scriptures, He may come any time," Marcus suggested, "only the chances are slight..."

"There's no chance at all," said Tija. "History teaches us that people have always been waiting, and He has never come. It is still going on the same today as it has up till now. The coming of the Messiah has been put off, very wisely, to the End of Time. This is not the End of Time—I don't see what would make it that."

Uri nodded.

"Indeed it's not," he said. "There's no sign of it being that. There have to be believers for it to happen. Is there a need for religion in Alexandria?"

Tija laughed out loud, then, after some reflection, said:

"I don't live in Alexandria, only in this house and at the Gymnasium: I haven't the faintest idea what happens in Alexandria because I'm shut off from it. You move around in the city, you ought to know, and in addition you're a newcomer, so you can spot things more clearly than a native."

Uri suddenly had an uncomfortable sense of emptiness in his guts.

I don't make good use of my time: here is this marvelous city, I really ought to concern myself more with it.

Tija had hit on what he was thinking; he broke into a smile.

"If you get into the Gymnasium," he said, "then you won't experience even the little of Alexandria that you have experienced so far. If you want to see anything at all of Alexandria, the Gymnasium will, frankly, be detrimental to you."

Uri laughed.

"I'm onto you!" he said. "You'll do anything to make sure I don't get in, including putting my mind off it."

"I told you before," riposted Tija blithely.

Marcus pushed off the wall to fill himself a cup of wine.

"Politics is all there is," he said. "Jostling for position, hatred, envy— that's all. Only madmen rave nowadays, and they will never lay their hands on power."

URI WAS SO PANIC-STRICKEN AT THE THOUGHT THAT HE WAS LIVING IN Alexandria yet missing out on it that he started to live it up.

He saved enough of his pocket money to be able to go to the better restaurants, and although he was allowed to—and did—make free use of the alabarch's fabulous bathing facilities, with a tepidarium and a caldarium attached to each suite of rooms, he decided that he would also visit the public baths.

In Rome the baths were free of charge, with the emperors donating to their upkeep to curry favor with the population, but in Alexandria one had to pay. In Rome Uri had never been to the baths, but in Alexandria he had time to try them out. It seemed as if the city's entire population swarmed within, hanging around or taking a dip; having themselves massaged with oil; having their nails, hair, or beards clipped; or eating and drinking delicacies. Who, if anyone at all, was doing the work in Alexandria?

Uri was given exactly the same meticulous provision as the rest, among them Hellenes and Hebrews alike, winding their linen towels the same way about their backs, with no detectable segregation between them. Which is not how it was in Rome. A wondrous city, Alexandria, yes indeed. This city was an example of how peoples of disparate religions could peacefully co-exist—a great example, an admirable example, and one day this Alexandrian spirit would spread through the world. Maybe that would be the End of Time.

Uri had already passed through the cold bath, the warm bath, the hot bath, and a renewed cold bath, the oiling, the trimming of his hair, and the snacking, and he was prostrate on a bed on the shady side of the inner garden of the enormous building when one of the bath attendants came up and informed him that one of the rooms had been vacated. Feeling adventurous, Uri readily went after him. A massage was still left, perhaps that was what went on in these many small cubicles tacked next to one another in a back courtyard of the baths complex. On all the doors except one was a sign: OCCUPIED. There was a signboard, but there was no inscription on it, or maybe it was on the reverse side. The baths attendant opened the door, and Uri stepped in; the baths attendant closed the door, and Uri could hear the sign knocking against the door, which suggested that he had indeed reversed the sign and now it too read: OCCUPIED. Jugs full of water, a table laden with wine and fruit, and a conspicuously wide divan, soft blankets on its chalky-white sheet. Order and cleanliness. Uri drank a sip of the wine then clambered onto the high bed and stretched out, loosening his towel at the waist. He lay down, and fell asleep while waiting for the massage.

He awoke to an extremely pleasant sensation. Opening his eyes, he shouted out in alarm: his male member was in one woman's mouth while another woman was stroking his testicles.

"Shush!" said the woman who was stroking, "you'll scare the neighbors!"

The other woman took Uri's penis from her mouth.

"Don't tug, I implore you," she said. "I may bite it off."

"Don't do that," Uri said faintly, without much conviction.

"Still a virgin, are you?" the stroker asked in surprise.

Uri groaned that he was, and please don't stop now, he prayed silently to himself.

"A tool this big, and still a virgin?" the stroker exclaimed indignantly. "What can you be thinking? You should be ashamed of yourself!"

The caressing woman climbed onto the bed, knelt over Uri and slipped his member into her. Uri watched what she was doing in terror, then closed his eyes. It felt as if the sucking were continuing.

That day Uri lost his virginity six times over, one after another, and after the sixth time even the women were satisfied with him.

"Will you be here tomorrow?" Uri asked.

"We usually are," they replied.

"I don't think I've lost enough of my virginity," was Uri's assessment, "so I'll definitely be back tomorrow."

He felt that he would have been capable of a seventh time, but there was a knock on the door, so Uri got down and gave the charming women a kiss on the brow, whereupon one of them tickled his testicles and the other pushed an index finger into his anus, at which Uri was surprised, finding it a singular striking way to say farewell.

He ambled proudly along the streets of Alexandria in the afternoon heat, his back drawn up and on slightly shaking legs, feeling a true hero: a man. Naturally, he turned it over in his mind, it must be harder if a man has to sleep with a woman who is not so proficient in the art of love. He resolved that he was going to try out every single woman in the baths, and then he would pay visits to other baths to gain the necessary technical skill before immersing himself in the Gymnasium.

Sitting on the shore at the Great Harbor, Uri watched the Sun setting and the bustling, and marveled. So that was what women knew about. A signal attainment, major, an experience incomparable with that of discharging semen while asleep. Why didn't poets and philosophers write about it? Of course they did write about it, indirectly, and there were wars that had broken out over a woman's behind, but all that was nothing compared with what a human being's body was able to feel.

He recalled what he had felt on stepping ashore several weeks ago, not far from the place where he happened to be seated. That he would lose his virginity here. He was pleased with himself: he had been right in his presentiment.

Those poor seamen, it came to mind. He snorted with laughter: he could see before his own eyes the way they had raced to that Jewish bordello in Syracusa to get there before the Sun went down. How right they had been.

Alexandria has been a splendid place up till then, but now it was even more splendid. Truly nobody, not even the greatest authors, had a style suited to record this marvel.

Evening drew in. Torches were lit, easy women strolled this way and that, on their own or in groups, as well as men longing to couple, and Uri lost his virginity another three times that evening. True, he had to pay for it each and every time, unlike at the baths where the service was included in the entrance fee, and he also had to accompany one of the women, around daybreak, to a hostelry. That was no longer such fun as it was hard to speak to her about anything, they just ate and drank; Uri got very bored and was glad when he finally managed to get free of her. But then there was room for even such a fleeting poor match in such a marvelous day.

Uri became an assiduous visitor to the baths in Alexandria, and he decided that on returning to Rome he would pay systematic visits on all the baths there. That was forbidden to Jews there, but that ban was unnecessary and ridiculous: being Jewish or not had nothing to do with it. On that basis about a hundred thousand of Alexandria's three hundred thousand Jews could not be that: they were adult men. The way Uri saw it, it was every Alexandrian man's prime duty to keep lovemaking at the baths in mind, and even bonds of marriage would not hold them back from this. After all, the Scriptures did not ban polygamy, and the way he had learned the tradition in Judaea, it only saw fit to punish marital infidelity on the part of a woman, not a man. The complex arguments that were conducted here, in this paradisiac city, over the issue seemed inconsequential; on the whole, everything else seen from here was inconsequential: Rome, Judaea, as well as Jerusalem, where nothing in particular ever happens. Praise be to the Eternal One that He had approvingly taken cognizance of the existence of Alexandria, city of miracles.

It crossed his head from time to time, even during the heady, mind-blowing, sensual days, that he was enjoying all these delights by mistake, illicitly, and there would be all hell to pay if it ever came out that he had never been Agrippa's courier. The decent thing to do would be to admit as much to these sterling individuals, Philo and Tija. But then they would kick him out of the city that was his, indeed more his than theirs, those confoundedly lucky dogs who, through God's unfathomable will, had been born here. They were not in a position to really value the city.

Uri even became infatuated with one or another of the girls, but they always knew what to do to work off such superfluous passions. He even found himself a target for men, but he had no wish for any of that, thank you very much. There must be almost as many homosexuals in Alexandria as there were heterosexuals, it dawned on Uri, and this was probably also true of Rome: that was the only way boatmen were able to stand the months that their voyages took, he reasoned. The way he felt, he supposed he would die if he had to go even a single day without lovemaking from now on, and he now dreaded the very thought of the Gymnasium. Of course, maybe he would be let out at weekends, as was Tija, and he would then be able to race off to the baths, spend the nights there if that were possible, but he kept postponing the entrance interview, even though Philo mentioned that he had now spoken to the head, and he was willing to accept him.

By day Uri frequented the baths, while the nights he spent reading by lamplight in the library of the alabarch's palace, scarcely sleeping a wink. He made up for those vigils during the day, in the intervals between women, on some bench or bed. There were times when he would forget to eat, and he lost weight. Philo cast troubled looks at him:

"There's no need to read at such a pace, dear boy," he said. "Your enrollment is not going to depend on how many dozens more books you read."

"What does it depend on, then?"

Philo shook his head:

"That's just it, I don't know," he said. "It's not even certain that the head is too happy that I'm using my influence to get you in. He had to take Tija on because they get money from us, but you are only our guest. He doesn't like Jews, and that's the truth. For the time being there are still prejudiced people like him in Alexandria, albeit ever fewer of them."

"I have no doubt that similar individuals are also to be found among the Jews," Uri ventured. It took a while for Philo to grasp the jest and he finally snickered. A philosopher, thought Uri; those who cultivate that ability generally have no sense of humor, with the possible exception of Plato, who was a born parodist.

He carried on reading by night, of course, and he wondered whether Philo had frequented the baths in his own younger days, and if so, whether he had ever lost his virginity. On the testimony of the women he got to know on more intimate, conversational terms, not all males were potent, and there were some who made the girls sweat blood to coax something out of them, and there some who dropped off to sleep five times in the process, so Uri should not suppose that they were as virile as him; unfeeling, uninspired, limp dicks could be found in quite substantial numbers among young men too. Of course there were ways of dealing with that too, medicinal herbs, salves, and in extreme cases the tying of a tight ligature with a strong grass stalk, but that was hard physical labor, sometimes as hard as that of those who carried bales. Uri supposed that a very great deal depended on a woman's skills, whereupon they disagreed with a shaking of the head: there were some for whom a flick or two sufficed and who got off at the sight of female breasts, but there were those who could not be roused even by hours of massaging. It was not advisable to have blood let before sexual congress, and in fact they were very angry about the barbers who worked in excessive numbers at the baths and had asked to be settled somewhere else because they were impairing the effectiveness of the good work that the women did, but custom was a hard taskmaster and had a mighty ability to enforce the interests of physicians. Men, on the whole, tended more to be impotent when healthy than potent when sick, that is what they had observed, from which it logically followed that women were much better suited than men to love because a woman was always open.

To his great astonishment, Uri discovered several weeks later that it was possible for interest in even this delight to fade.

It was then that he sought out the Gymnasium.

ISIDOROS, THE GYMNASIARCH, A STOCKY, BALD, GRAVEL-VOICED, middle-aged fellow, received Uri in a cool room to which he had been led by one of the Greek students.

"So it's you," he declared with an unfriendly air, looking Uri—who for this occasion had specially put on a spic-and-span tunic and elegant sandals—up and down. "There are altogether two Jews in all who are studying with us, and that's two too many: you may have heard that I am none too fond of Jews."

"Me neither," said Uri. "I don't see why one should be—any more than of Greeks. I suppose as a community they are pretty awful, but then even among them a few meritorious individuals are to be found."

The head was astonished by this cheeky riposte. He fell silent before asking:

"Why would you want to come here?"

"Because I love reading."

"You can do that on your own anyway."

"I long to have an intellectual guide."

"I can recommend Philo as being worth attention. He is a man of great merit, who has written a lot and read almost as much."

Uri laughed out loud.

Isidoros was not used to seeing people laugh in his presence, though he was highly gratified, needless to say.

"What reasons can you cite in your favor?"

Uri was taken by the man's brusque manner.

"My poor eyesight, perhaps," he said.

Isidoros, marveling, looked him straight in the face.

"At this distance," said Uri, "I can only see outlines but not your features. If you were to pass me in the street, I wouldn't recognize you."

"You consider that to be a virtue?"

"Most recently, yes, I do," said Uri. "Others see well; for me to notice anything of the world, I have to think about it. That is why I like reading: I can lean on the eyes of others, with many eyes I see more."

The head hesitated.

"With us physical sanity is at least as important as mental and spiritual sanity."

"I don't feel disabled," Uri asserted, "just unusual. By being what I am. On long walks my feet and back hurt, my asshole bleeds... If I'm tense or depressed, my stomach knots up and my chest burns... In many respects I'm a coward. That's how my God created me, but he has to have had some purpose in doing so!"

Isidoros got up. There were scrolls and tablets lying about on big shelves, and after some rummaging he pulled one out and put it down on the table.

"Start rendering it into Latin," he said.

Uri picked up the scroll and cautiously unrolled the first written page but then let go of the parchment.

"That's too easy," he declared. "It's the *Odyssey*, and Livy has already translated that."

"Still, have a go."

Uri placed the parchment scroll on the table, at quite some distance from himself, and from memory he slowly, with gusto, in a singing tone began to recite Livy's text. The gymnasiarch impassively listened to him for a while before getting up again and searching out another scroll and putting it down on the table. Uri fell silent.

"This has not yet been translated into Latin," the head said.

Uri unrolled the first page. This too was written in hexameters but gave neither author nor title.

"Who's this by?" Uri asked.

"It doesn't matter. Begin."

Uri first read the Greek text over to himself, but then straightaway ad-libbed a translation into Latin hexameters. He got stuck a bit at times or had to jump back to make a correction, but all the same the translation proceeded smoothly and also kept to the caesuras. Isidoros listened with eyes closed.

"Not bad," he said after a couple of minutes. "Not bad at all. How come you know how to do that sort of thing?"

"It's precisely what I have most practice doing," Uri acknowledged. "In Rome I got a lot of amusement out of it. I would do a lot worse with other exam questions."

"Why amuse yourself doing that in particular? It brings in no money and it's of no interest to anyone."

"Because I was too scared to live," said Uri. "I used to believe that I was a cripple; I needed a substitute."

Isidoros remained silent. He looked at this strange creature in front of him: nothing at all handsome about him, his features were all lopsided, his Jewish nose bent, his chin small and receding, and although his build was slim there were the beginnings of a double chin, barely hidden by the scrawny reddish beard, and on top of everything, he was going bald. The very image of imperfect Jewishness exacerbated by a Germanic strain. And yet there was something winning about him: maybe those small, hazel-green eyes, from which, despite being slit-like from myopic peering, nevertheless blazed the fire of some remote, threatening depth.

"I'll take you on," he finally announced. "But you'll have to be outstanding in sport too."

"I will," Uri promised.

"If you don't excel in any branch of sport, I shall expel you."

"Fair enough."

The gymnasiarch shook his head.

"Are you sure you're Jewish?" he queried.

"So they say," said Uri. "My mother may have been a Syrian slave girl, perhaps, but under no circumstances Jewish... My father is Jewish, but there's no one to say where his mother came from. Or her grandmothers. In Rome Jews, for want of women, wed the daughters of slave people; on my mother's side I might easily be Germanic or Gallic or Illyrian—doesn't it come to the same thing?"

"Here the Jews marry among their own kind," said Isidoros. "They breed like rabbits, and are brazen in their pushiness."

Uri stood up. The suspicion flashed through his mind that the head might perchance have once taken a liking to a Jewish girl, but she had rejected him: a

457

disappointed individual was quite capable of hating an entire people corporatively as a result of such things.

"Report early tomorrow morning at the gate; you will be conducted to the dormitory, and by then I'll have a place designated for you. You may go."

Uri bowed and started off out of the room before turning.

"Who is the author of that piece?"

"I am."

Uri laughed.

"Not bad!" he said. "Not bad at all!"

IF ALEXANDRIA HAD BEEN MARVELOUS UP TILL NOW, IT WAS EVEN MORE marvelous from now on.

Uri was pleased to see that there were no beds in the dormitory, only straw strewn sparsely on the undecorated stone-flagged floor, though that was not cold, because it was heated from below even during the summer. There were no mattresses, no sheets, no blankets—Spartan discipline allied to Asian and Roman comfort.

He was also pleased that the costly robe and elegant sandals he had on were taken away, and in their place he was clothed in coarse linen and simple, stiff-soled sandals. That was what all the students wore, as if they were soldiers in uniform. He was allowed to don own clothes when going out on leave, but not otherwise. The sack in which he had brought a few personal belongings, like a comb that he had been given by one of the prostitutes and some books that he had bought with his savings, was taken off him—he would only be given these back when he finally left the Gymnasium. He was informed that no one here had any personal property and everybody was equal. Just like the Pythagoreans or a Jewish sect, Uri thought. Could that have been where the Essenes got the idea? Meals consisted of communal breakfast, lunch and supper, and conversation was forbidden while dining. Excellent: he liked to engross himself in thought while eating, and he found it disturbing if he also had to make conversation.

He had managed to end up in an Essene community, albeit not in Judaea.

He was most pleased of all that the servants were not hovering constantly around him as in the alabarch's house; he abhorred their officious proximity. He never asked them for anything, but they would keep a look-out for any orders and looked offended any time he managed to get rid of them. Uri had a suspicion that the servants held him in contempt for not giving them orders in the same matter-of-course way as Philo or Marcus or Tija.

Some classes were communal, some individual. Everybody's schedule for the day was written on a tablet, and he was expected to keep to that. His own was already hanging at the entrance to one of the larger rooms, featuring a conspicuously large amount of physical training. Uri counted up the number of tablets: there were twenty-seven of them. So that meant there were that many students along with him. Not a lot. Out of them would come Alexandria's future elite. Twenty-four Greeks and three Jews.

His name was listed simply as Gaius T.

Tija's as Tibjul.

He looked for Apollonos's name, but there were three of them: Alpha, Beta, and Gamma, with no way of telling which was Jewish.

Things would all be very proper.

The tutors were Greek, a mixture of the elderly and middle-aged, along with a lot of young, fit men, the physical instructors. There were almost as many teachers as students. That too was fine.

Matutinal and vespertine prayers were also displayed on the week's timetable but without any indication of who worshiped which god or gods; that was a matter for the individual to settle for himself. Statues of the divinities stood in a separate room, some of them with slightly worn heads or feet, perhaps from being caressed or kissed.

On the first day it became apparent that apart from eating, only the physical training was communal.

They were kept hard at work.

They had to race on foot, throw the discus and javelin, clear hurdles, wrestle, spar with daggers, spears, and staffs, and long-jump from the standing position. Only those in their final year learned horseback riding, it was said, because horses were expensive and there were only a few of them. Physical instruction was held in the Gymnasium's elongated stretch of public park, criss-crossed with paths, which anyone was free to enter, between the columns of the long hall of the stadium, reached from the main thoroughfare, named Arsinoë Avenue, as were many other streets in Alexandria (named after the same Arsinoë, or was it perhaps a different one?). Statues and memorials were scattered throughout the big expanse of grassy, tree-studded parkland, and Uri made special note of a rusted cart that had been placed there once for some reason, perhaps as a sacrificial object. In the middle of the park rose the fir-cone shape of the Paneion, about which the ship's captain had spoken when they arrived: anyone could climb to the summit and glory in the vista. It occurred to Uri that one could sit down at the top without anybody disturbing you, those who visited from city or from outside being so taken up by the view as to pay no notice, so he took to doing his reading there, that was his favorite hiding place, private for all that it was public, though the wind often made his ears ache.

During his weeks in Alexandria, Uri's body had grown slack and he found the running hard, stopping more than once to pant, developing a stitch in his side, so that the others, Tija among them, watched him scornfully as he slowly padded along and sweat, whereas they expertly sauntered around the circuits.

He had difficulty even in throwing the discus: it refused to go off in the direction he wanted, or he released it too early or too late from his hand, so that those around him would run off in real or faked terror lest they be hit, and those who were spectating would simply laugh in derision.

The javelin went half as far for him as it did for the others, but worse still, he regularly pulled his shoulder muscles. A left-hander, a southpaw, the others averred, but Uri did not see why that was important until he grasped that in wrestling it was advantage for a person to be left-handed, though in the beginning he was thrown to the ground by everyone else.

The standing long jump was the most complicated movement of all: identical big bronze weights had to be held in each hand and swung backward and forward, and then, when one judged there was a good rhythm, leading with the weights, both legs would be lifted from the ground. A good few times Uri found the weights flying out of his hands, and it was pure luck that he avoided hitting anyone. The others would grin and scoff.

Oratory was also classed as one of the physical exercises, which was not all that surprising as that was also the case among the wealthy of Rome. What was unusual was that the tutor would set a time limit as well as the subject. Both the subject and the time would be drawn by the student from sets of parchment slips placed face-down on the table; the tutor, holding a larger or smaller hourglass in his hand, would then measure the time allotted for the oration, and if the student did not finish with his topic on time, or finished early, a notch would be scored against his name with a stylus on the wax tablet. This meant the student would have to make a renewed oration on the given subject though he would not know for how long as he would again have to draw a slip. The duration of orations made by lawyers was likewise time-limited in Rome.

If a student succeeded in finishing a nicely rounded address on time, the notch would be omitted. All the orations, however long or short, had to be listened to by the others, and at the end they would have to evaluate every one of them. The topics were varied: an indictment in a murder case, a defense in a case of robbery, prosodic problems, historical problems, astronomy, navigation, the conduct of war, the establishment of military supply lines, *tekhne*—anything at all.

His fellow pupils said that all the best rhetoricians had gone off to Rome, where they were better paid, but Uri was more than happy with Theocritus as his rhetoric tutor, setting high store on his wry, unobtrusive humor.

Their fare was simple: greens, fruit, various kinds of boiled pasta, and meat only on Fridays, which the three Jews did not eat. That was how Uri identified the Jewish Apollonos at lunchtime on the first Friday: he was a stocky, square-headed, insignificant-looking young man who showed no external sign of having a brain. The food they got was simple, but never quite enough as to leave them feeling that they had ate their fill. They were never served wine, only water, and they were allowed no snacks apart from the communal meals. Uri did not notice any attempts to smuggle in anything from outside: he found the slight gnawing of hunger quite easy to take, having known periods of much greater starvation. The others hankered after food, swapping recipes with one another, and meanwhile he read with a gently rumbling stomach: it was possible to borrow scrolls from the Gymnasium's richly stocked library, which contained many rarities.

The mathematics lessons were given by a mad teacher by the name of Demetrius. Ten of them were assigned to him; he explained outrageous laws, writing things down rapidly with his stylus on the board and then, before the class understood what he was talking about, he got to the end of the board and rubbed it clean before carrying on. Uri considered himself lucky to have taught himself the elements of mathematics when still a young boy, on his own at home, because he at least got an inkling of what this fervent fellow—to whom geometry meant everything and who stoutly maintained that Earth was spherical with a circumference of 252,000 stadia—was trying to communicate to them. Uri was already familiar with this fact from reading Eratosthenes, but only now did he learn how this had been calculated: the Sun's angle of incidence was measured simultaneously at the summer solstice in Syene and in Alexandria, five thousand stadia away (the distance was paced out by servants in the traditional fashion); the difference was one fiftieth of a right angle, so five thousand stadia was therefore one fiftieth. Poseidonus had come to a smaller estimate, but the teacher stood firmly by Eratosthenes's result.

The astronomy tutor was Hyperion, a gaunt, slow-speaking man, who could never be asked anything because he would shake his head and continue to say what he had decided in advance to say. Uri imagined this dour man could make a tidy income with astrology outside, in the city, and wondered why he had chosen instead to teach at the Gymnasium. He was surprised, then, when he started to explain the Mithraists' Great Cycles and that the constellations arose from deviations from the earth's orbit that had accumulated over the millennia. The others could grasp nothing of this, but Uri considered that Hyperion knew his business, just not how to communicate it.

For philosophy they—that is to say, the five-strong group that Uri was in—were instructed by a short, chubby old man, who chortled hugely during the lectures. True he could not tell Uri anything new, but it was entertaining that he was able to present the greatest of the Greeks, from first to last, even Aristotle, as parodists, although that was of course taking it a bit far. Uri would gladly have spoken to him, but Antonius Lollas, the uproarious old coot, fended him off and so he restricted himself to listening to the prepared essays and praising them to the skies, as did the others.

The military discipline appealed to Uri, and he was highly discomfited at falling so far behind in the physical exercises. The other students did not pay him much attention in the first week, with Tija acting as if he had never seen him before, in response to which Uri did not speak to him either: it seemed that either Tija was disloyal by nature, or that was the custom.

On the Thursday he asked one of the gymnastics teachers if one could practice alone, and learned that it was permitted. From then on, every evening between supper and the solitary prayer time, he would return to the Gymnasium's stadium and, in the gathering darkness, as the rest spent their free time chatting or lounging about he would run, jump, and throw the discus and javelin.

In the first week he had his sandals stolen, but he did not make the rounds looking for them, nor did he ask who was the culprit, nor did he ask for a new pair. He simply went barefoot.

He could also have obtained a pass at the end of the first week but he decided that he would rather stay back, reading and training: he was well aware by then that his body would be in good shape by the end of the second week, or at most the beginning of the third. That was indeed the case, and the others were amazed. Even the gymnastics instructors noticed that he was hurling the discus and javelin farther and more accurately, and was able to endure longer distances than he had at the start. The other students had not walked as much he had and had less knowledge of what their bodies were capable of when pushed, yet even Uri was pleasantly surprised how well the standing long jump went—so well, in fact, that by the beginning of the third week the gymnasiarch himself, of whom hitherto there had been no trace, took a look. One of the gym masters must have had a word with him, and the rest were astonished too, as the head was not in the habit of dropping in on their physical training lessons; the great scholar, they said to one another, without saying a word to Uri, who did not initiate any conversation with them but could hear what they were saying among themselves, now heard: what on Earth can that exceptional philologist, who hates physical training of any sort, be poking around here for?

But Uri knew: it was him he wanted to take a look at.

They lined up to take their jumps before him. Uri breathed deeply, knowing by now how to regulate his mind to ensure that his body would function at its best.

His turn eventually came, he grasped the weights and stepped up to the line, took one last deep breath, and started to swing them to and fro before giving them a powerful swing forward and jumping with legs flexed.

He had never jumped that far before.

It was measured with a tape. He had leapt over sixteen feet.

A buzz went up when the instructor announced it: pupils did not usually jump that far. Uri stood up straight then put the weights down.

"Once more!" came Isidoros's voice.

Uri picked up the weights, swung them again, and leapt again. He sensed it had not been as good; he was angry with himself: how could he mess up a second jump so badly?

That too was measured, and even so was over fifteen feet.

Isidoros nodded before setting off for the main building.

"I wouldn't mind giving it another go," said Uri.

The head halted and turned around:

"Right, then!"

Uri picked up the weight, concentrated for a long time before swinging the weights then jumping. He sensed immediately that this would be the worst of all his jumps that day.

It was measured, and came to fourteen feet and a bit.

That was not bad either, of course, and the others would have been very happy with it, but Uri was furious.

"That's exactly why I don't like Jews," said Isidoros, and left.

There was a still as people gloated.

"I am a fool!" said Uri to himself. "Why bother jumping around so much?"

A few laughed out loud; the instructor patted him on the shoulder and also snorted a laugh.

That evening at last he was spoken to in the dormitory. He was now accepted because he had not done so well on the second and third attempts: he too was a frail mortal, and the head was no more in favor of him than anyone else, so he was fit to engage in conversation.

I would have been in big trouble, Uri came to realize, if I had jumped even farther on he second attempt, though he knew full well that he had made bigger jumps in the course of his solitary training sessions.

What came to mind was his father's warning not to disclose to others what he knew.

My father could have jumped really far, good Lord, only he realized that it was better not jump at all.

I'll tell him about this; at last he'll be pleased with me.

Uri was counting on being praised by the tutor for physical training, but instead of that he made a total fool of him when he asked the class to list the Olympic victors. Uri had in fact genuinely memorized the huge body of data of who had won what event, going back centuries: a horrendous mass of data of thousands of disciplines, names, and results, and Uri did not get one wrong, yet he failed all the same. He did not get it; the tutor left smugly satisfied. The classmates tittered: Uri had not memorized the corrected register given by Aristotle, but the very first list, which was by the sophist Hippias of Elis.

Uri bit his lip: the classmates had handed him Hippias's list. They had deliberately not let him in on the secret that he ought to have been learning Aristotle's register.

They had gotten their revenge after all.

He did not tell tales on them, just memorized Aristotle's list.

Who would have guessed that Aristotle concerned himself with that sort of thing in his spare time! Mind-boggling! On top of which he had included in his chronology data for the Spartan Games, Olympic Games, even Romulus's genealogy. A big ass, Aristotle too, when it came right down to it.

URI SOON MADE FRIENDS WITH THE JEWISH APOLLONOS, WHO WAS HERE known as Apollonos Gamma, being the third of the Apollonoses. They were brought together by oratory, as in this subject Apollonos proved truly unbeatable, his incredible dodging and weaving, his viewpoint bringing together extremes that were unimaginable to any normal mind, so that Uri listened entranced each and every time he managed to close the arch of his coruscating wittinesses nicely on time. The others had already become used to it and would roar with laughter, applaud and whistle their approval, while Uri had to recognize that he was not going to be able to compete, his brain not being as speedy and imaginative.

Not that his own orations were uninteresting, just more earthbound and objective than Apollonos's. Uri made no use of unusual epithets or memorable similes, but he knew how to project an image of what he was saying, because as his sentences followed one another, he himself could see what he was talking about.

Apollonos set great store on that.

"Your brain is rich, fertile ground," he said to Uri. "You can produce anything on it, whatever it is seeded with. And you have a great eye."

Uri had to laugh: him, a great eye!

"Right you have!" Apollonos avowed. "You can see spatially: depth, distance, proximity, colors, shades, contexts. You may be short-sighted now but you must have seen perfectly at some stage, and you still recall that. It's not your eyes that you see with but something else. You will still see well if you become blinded."

Uri shuddered.

His relationship with Tija took a strange twist.

At the Gymnasium they did not speak much, even avoided each other, as if by agreement. From the fourth weekend, when Uri took advantage of the possibility of a pass, they spent the Sabbath and Sunday, which counted as a free day for the Greeks, together in the alabarch's palace—a full two and a quarter days from sundown on Friday evening, as if to annul the other days of the week, as if they were not students at one and the same Gymnasium. Tija was pleasant, communicative, gossipy, telling witty and cynical tales about the gymnasiarch, the teachers and fellow students, bringing Uri to the realization that Tija was telling the truth. He sensed that Tija was not envious of any of the Greeks, only of Apollonos Gamma—but of him, profoundly. Uri could also sense that because during the week he acted as if he never saw him, Tija was not jealous of him. Uri shrugged his shoulders: that was just the way he was, what could one do? Uri was glad he had the chance to learn much from him.

Things were going well at the Gymnasium: he was accepted, he made good progress in physical training and found the other subjects easy to master, read a vast amount. Despite that, something was still missing.

So, this was the renowned Gymnasium? The tutors so absent-minded, the students so forgetful? His Greek classmates were friendly, Apollonos Gamma too, indeed Apollonos seemed to have taken a real shine to him; Tija would nod if they ran into one another in one of the Gymnasium's rooms or in the garden, whereas Isidoros could not let any encounter pass without throwing out some Judaeophobic jest; yet for all that there was something dreamlike, unserious, about this existence. Uri would willingly have brushed the feeling aside, except that Apollonos confirmed it for him: something was brewing.

This was Apollonos's second year as a pupil at the Gymnasium, and as he saw it the discipline had grown slacker, the teachers more slapdash.

"Everyone has something else going on in the head except precisely the thing he ought to be concerned with," he said in disgruntlement to Uri. "Everyone has his eyes on Rome and the question of who will be the next emperor. My father told me that no one wants to cut any business deal with him, not even his most longstanding clients, who by now have become almost friends. Later, they say, when things settle down again. But the general climate has been settled for decades, all the time that Tiberius was at the height of his power, regardless of Sejanus's purging of the senate and of the bucketfuls of blood shed by Tiberius's men, Macro at their head, when they finally disposed of Sejanus and his gang. In Alexandria no one took such stirrings with any seriousness: it was of no interest to anyone why Tiberius withdrew from Rome and shut himself up on Capri, or why he turned back from the outskirts of Rome the one time he dared to go that far. Rome needed Egypt: Egypt was Rome's granary. Let them unmercifully massacre one another; either way, Rome's internal affairs were no concern of ours. Somehow, though, the situation was different now, as if the constellations had slipped to another place in the firmament. Or rather, as if they were still in their places, one can see that; it's just that some sort of earthquake is getting under way in their souls, and even I can sense that."

At night they would converse in the garden; they were allowed to stay up as the strict order of the Pythagoreans was only upheld formally, for show, but in reality let loose. A fair number of the students would stroll in the Gymnasium's grounds even by night, and at these hours sellers of water, wine, and food would make bargain offers on the goods they carried on their carts. Uri looked up: the stars were out in the sky on the hot summer evening, though he never saw them, just uncertain spots which would sparkle to life every now and then. He tried to picture the figures of his scrolls in the sky, and in the end he knew all the constellations by heart. He envied Apollonos for having sharp eyes and thus for being able to see the stars clearly.

"Many's the time," mused Uri, "that I have felt the whole vault of the sky is weighing down on me with an immense load, and settling on my chest. As if a multitude of gods had come to a decision to let the heavens sink—and straight onto me. I have felt that many times, and the ache in my breast would never stop, and I would get bad heartburn."

Apollonos nodded.

"That's where our fates are written—in the stars," he said. "Rome now imagines it is ruling those stars, and because on every shore of the Great Sea, more out of laziness than conviction, we leave Rome to do as it wishes, and so it rules. If an astrologer whom Tiberius trusts were to come along and kick out Thrasyllus, his current favorite, and the new astrologer were to worm his way into favor by dazzling him with the prospect of eternal life, the weight of the heavenly vault would continue to press on our chests just the same. We would need to know too much to be able to foretell our futures: a person will never know that much, and never has. We would need to live simpler lives, maybe. Not know as much, read as much; the huge amount of superfluous knowledge that we acquire here obscures what is important. This marvelous institution lulls us and dulls us, drives us crazy with all the knowledge we have come by and have yet to come by."

"Why? What's the important thing?"

"I don't know, but it's probably not anything that we happen to have cognizance of. Quite likely what is actually happening on Earth is not that which we see happening, but *something* is quite definitely happening right now, even though it's possible we shall never get to know the truth of the age during which we sojourned with it, temporarily, in our body."

They fell quiet, staring up at the sky. Apollonos could see the stars; Uri could not.

"Something has made life too complicated and profoundly unjust," said Apollonos. "Perhaps there are just too many people, they've overflowed from the little villages, which have been in ferment, though in earlier times they got along fine there. They have settled down in the big cities, been left to themselves, driven crazy. If we, the privileged, feel weighed down, how do you think poor, primitive people manage to bear it? And there are many of them, a great many. You know them better than I do, after all you have lived among them. What is seething in them? You should know. It's frightening what a power would be unleashed if Jewish and Greek poor were to unite in a new Spartacist revolt."

This view surprised Uri, and he set it aside to deliberate more thoroughly.

At weekends the number of spies at the alabarch's palace grew.

Even before, Uri had seen that the alabarch, sometimes accompanied by Philo or Marcus, sometimes without either, would vanish with messengers who had come to Alexandria from all quarters of the world to pay their respects. They came from Adiabene and Commagene and from Syria; they came from Armenia, under Herod's successors; they came from Babylon, the capital city of the Parthian Empire, which was longing to lay its hands on Armenia, and had indeed gone to war for it; and, of course, people came from Judaea, Galilee, Italia and all the bigger cities in Egypt. The world is one big spider's web, and at the center of that web sat the spider, Alabarch Alexander.

It was not certain that Alexander himself financed all these spies, but there was no doubt that he spoke to them. These couriers felt the need to engage closely in his company and whatever they knew—or deemed fit to divulge—they would pass on during these chats. At least that is what Uri supposed, although he was never in a position to hear what the alabarch, the richest Jew in the world, had to discuss with these new arrivals.

Flaccus, the prefect himself, would occasionally turn up at Alabarch Alexander's palace, accompanied by no more than a couple of bodyguards, and he would always bring a gift of some kind, a lovely carpet from the East or a capacious, wine-filled amphora from Rhodes. The amphora, though simple and undecorated, would be gracefully shaped, and the alabarch was always pleased to receive it, though he had many far more decorative amphoras; Uri was later to learn that an amphora like that could be pricier when empty than filled with the finest of wines, because it was made of a special type of pottery that allowed the wine or seeds that it was holding to "breathe," so nothing kept in an amphora from Rhodes would go moldy, even if stored for years. Flaccus was a tall, well-built jovial man—"our Aulus"—who conversed informally with one and all. His parents were reputedly well-known collectors of art; his own palace was likewise full of paintings and sculpture that he had brought over from Rome or acquired since then, including a head of the Gorgon Medusa sculpted by Phidias. He gave Uri a friendly pat on the back when they were introduced, and moved around the alabarch's palace as though at home.

Visits by the prefect were not always announced in advance, but on more than one occasion it had happened that a number of Jewish notabilities (Tija called them his father's bankers) had been waiting at the palace in advance of his arrival.

"What do the bankers deal with?" Uri asked.

"What do you think? They provide lines of credit—what else?" Tija replied.

Uri inferred that the alabarch provided loans at usurious rates of interest, and his men also invested Flaccus's money.

Uri recognized, though not from close acquaintance, the faces of several important figures from Alexandria's Sanhedrin; on the day of the Sabbath, after sunset, these chosen individuals often had supper at the alabarch's home. At one of these dinners, Marcus told one of the council members, a man by the name of Andron, to record Uri among the Alexandrian Jews as a guest of the alabarch; Andron, who ran the Jewish archive, professed his readiness to do so and immediately made a note of Uri's name as well as his mother's and father's names. The records of births and deaths were also in his charge, and he personally made the copies of any changes that were taken to Jerusalem for Passover by the money-carrying delegation. After he had remonstrated that he knew so little about the Roman families, he went on to ask whether there might be a priestly or Levite offshoot in Uri's family; Uri informed him that unfortunately there was none.

At one of the suppers, Flaccus himself honored them with his presence, taking good care to observe all due Jewish prescriptions. He addressed Tryphon, Euodus, Philemon, and the other elders, making polite talk with the middle-aged council members, too, as individuals with whom he had a long and close acquaintance. Tryphon had also brought along his son, Demetrius, who had sensitive equine features with conspicuously large nostrils and thin, buttoned-up lips. Tija conversed with him at length and with obvious respect.

"Who is that Demetrius?" Uri later asked enviously.

Tija laughed.

"An enemy," he said. "They loathe us because our wealth is greater than that of all the elders put together."

Once Uri recognized among the couriers Jehoram, the scrawny interpreter, whom on the way to Samaria he had initially supposed was a thief. Jehoram also spotted Uri but avoided greeting him, turning his head away instead. Uri did not greet him either.

Jehoram may also have reported on me to Alexandria. The interpreter was clearly working for Aaron, the officer, and thus for the Sanhedrin, who had entrapped Pontius Pilate. It was not beyond the bounds of possibility that the idea for the provocation at Mount Gerizim had originated in Alexandria.

Uri again sensed in his nostrils the smell of the mutilated, festering bodies, and he felt sick with disgust.

It was an unclean place in which he was living.

He deliberated on whether he should make it known that he had met Jehoram in Samaria as an agent of the Sanhedrin. However, Uri was not a spy for the alabarch; he was not asked what he knew. Even if they suspected that Jehoram was a double agent, then that was what they suspected; if not, then they did not. I would never work as a paid spy, he reflected, so why should I work for them for nothing?

He did feel, however, that, even without any return, he was in an awkward position, since the alabarch's family had been supporting him for months, and his studies were being paid for by Philo. He would have to recompense them later; they were bound to call in the debt.

How could he escape—not from Alexandria, but from the alabarch's palace?

Despite it being worthwhile to be there.

At irregular intervals, the alabarch would throw a soirée to which Flaccus and the notables of the Greek Gerusia were invited. On these occasions he would put on display the pictures, vases, and statues he had acquired since the last occasion, with harpists and flautists also performing—and, not least, a sumptuous banquet. The alabarch had sole ownership rights over the musicians, and he made a tidy sum of money on them, hiring the group out to wealthy mourners for the compulsory one-week period of burial feast immediately following a funeral.

The alabarch's agents covered the length and breadth of Greece, and if by chance they came across a work of art that was of note, they would send him a message. Not all of his couriers were of discerning taste, but the supervisor whom the alabarch entrusted with organizing the purchases did: he was Greek and a full-time employee of the Musaeum.

This Nicodemus was a smart man, and had started his career as a sculptor but, as he complained to Uri after the two of them had established a friendship, it had been a long time since there were any master sculptors in Alexandria.

"There's too much money around," he explained. "We're able to buy up everything; we're stripping the entire Hellenic world. We're parasites, and we contribute nothing to the arts; there are no significant painters or sculptors here. Phidias had it easy: Athens wanted to put on a good show, both internally and to the outside world; Alexandria, by contrast, does not want to put on a good show because since Cleopatra VII it has had no existence as a sovereign state, and no need to gain acceptance from the world at large."

Uri mentioned to him that he had heard it suggested that Alexandria was poor, though it had a lot of wealthy inhabitants. So how was Nicodemus able to make acquisitions if the library did not have any money?

"Private sources of capital," said Nicodemus. "For instance, whenever I buy an art treasure for the alabarch, he offers the city anything from five to ten percent of the price. That's what the Greek rich also do. It's a good job that the wealthy Greeks and Jews compete with each other, for otherwise the Musaeum would have received nothing for the last eighty years."

The vases, murals, and statues that the alabarch had on display in the atrium were marvelous, and Uri had the luck twice to be able to see them. Flaccus was enraptured by them, and of course by those pictures and statues that he received as gifts, solemnly handed over by the alabarch to claps and cheers. Nor did the Greek guests return home empty handed.

The Greek rich organized similar shows, to which the alabarch and his family would be invited, but not Uri. Thanks to Nicodemus, though, he could gain entry to the Musaeum and even inspect the stores, and he would be amazed at the indomitable imaginative power man could have, if only he were allowed.

AT THE GYMNASIUM WORD WAS SPREAD THAT THEY WOULD BE READY TO put copyists to work in the Library because, they were aiming to collect all the works that had ever been written. He spoke with a few of the Greeks who were accustomed to doing copying work; they were not paid too well, but once a person got into the swing of it, he could make quite a nice sum. They mentioned that in recent times they had not been copying entire scrolls, but a librarian would scan through a scroll and decide what were the important passages, and what were not. It was a deplorable practice because another librarian might decide other passages were important, and who could know what would be of interest centuries from now, but it was all understandable from the point of view of the city's lack of money. They also recounted that most recently the parchment rolls were not copied onto another roll, because then two mistakes in a column were enough to make it necessary to start with a new roll all over again, but now they would copy onto separate leaves which were then fastened back-to-back and collected to produce what was called a book. If the copyists makes an error, only one side of the parchment needed to be rewritten, not the whole roll. Of course, the books of parchment or papyrus could still burn: a way of impregnating the leaves to make them non-flammable had been discovered two generations ago, but it was not utilised because that was expensive.

"Something has ended in Alexandria," said Apollonos Gamma sorrowfully. Tija waggled his head: for three hundred years, since Alexandria's heyday, everything had indeed been decaying, but there was still plenty left to decay.

Uri conceived a big yearning to do some copying, and when it became apparent that rate of pay for copying mathematical treatises, which were considered difficult, was double, he decided to make himself known.

It was just that the Serapeion, in one of whose wings the Great Library was placed, was a temple. Was it possible for him, a Jewish newcomer, to enter such a temple?

Tija chuckled while reassuring him that the Eternal One would not be paying attention to where a Jewish believer was wandering off to in Alexandria: if he were, he would have struck Uri dead long ago. Anyway, Philo went there as well.

It was not easy to enter the Serapeion; Uri was requested for proof that he was a pupil at the Gymnasium, as well as a separate letter of recommendation from Isidoros.

He listed grumpily to Uri's request.

"What do you need money for?" he asked. "The whole Jewish gang is keeping you going."

"It's not the money that's of interest," said Uri, "but the work."

"Try another one. Do you believe you'll come across a scroll of ballistic secrets, which you'll memorize while copying them?"

Uri was astounded. Why ballistic in particular? Siege machines had never interested him.

"We're in a time of peace, gymnasiarch," said Uri. "There will be no war during my lifetime."

Isidoros laughed.

"You're naïve, my child," he said, almost affectionately. "It's a good thing there are some idiots among your generation."

He gave his permission.

Tija went white with anger when he learned of this. Uri was surprised to find out that Apollonos Gamma had also asked about copying work, but Isidoros had refused to give him permission.

His suspicion was roused.

"Are you interested in firing ballista?" he posed the question.

Tija nodded.

"That's the future," he said. "The science of siege machines! My father is a simple exciseman, but I'm going to produce siege machines!"

Tija was especially interested in cannons that worked with compressed air. Experimentation with them had been abandoned a century ago because they had not approached the accuracy of conventional catapults, but still, he believed that the future belonged to compressed air. Uri did some reading up on this in the Gymnasium's library.

Torsion catapults, which threw stone projectiles, had already been in use at the time of Alexander the Great, as were catapults for firing arrows, which remained standard weapons. But despite the attempts of Alexandrian scientists to replace these with compressed-air weapons, they never proved as effective as the torsion catapult. Ctesibius, Philon of Byzantium, and Strato of Lampsacus, that all-around genius of physics, had all excelled at constructing hydraulic machines. Ctesibius devised a torsion catapult that worked with a metallic wire, whereas Dionysius of Alexandria invented a repeating automatic catapult, the only trouble being that it did not fulfill the minimal requirement of being able throw a projectile at least one stadion. All the same, it was an impressive device, because as soon as it fired one arrow it readied itself to shoot again: it worked by virtue of a diminutive cylinder that fed the next arrow from a magazine into the slot.

But if it was possible to compress air, as had been proven, then it must also be possible to rarify it, reasoned Uri. The authors had written nothing about that because it was of no practical significance, and the idea had been promptly forgotten.

Tija was very fond of Philon's book *On Besieging and Defending Towns*, which Uri also took a quick look at. This thorough author recorded notes on how food might be dried and preserved to feed a besieged town, how to ensure the health of its inhabitants, and how to prepare them psychologically. A substantial chapter was devoted to how the drinking water of the besiegers might be poisoned, how it might be possible to send messages from a besieged town to free towns, and to what sort of medicines should be stockpiled, along with observations on undermining the besiegers' self-confidence. In another of the surviving complete parts of the series, the "Treatise on Mechanics," the author dealt with the coding and decoding of reports from spies. It may have been from this source, in part, that the Jews of Judaea developed their use of fire signals. Tija also passed on to Uri a similar book by Aeneas Tacitus, which was less detailed but showed more inventiveness.

Uri was astonished: Why bother studying those works when there was no chance of Alexandria being under siege in the foreseeable future? Tija gaped:

"I read them from the reverse point of view," he declared.

Bit by bit, it dawned on Uri that Tija was preparing to lay siege to cities, and he was studying these means of boosting their defenses to counter them.

"Do you suppose peace-loving Rome is making preparations for a siege?" he asked.

Seeing Uri as hopelessly naïve, Tija made a dismissive flip of the hand.

Uri began copying work in a small cubbyhole at the Serapeion, and he asked specifically to be given scrolls of mathematical works after it had been confirmed that copies of these would be given double pay.

It might well have been even more highly rewarded: a person had to pay great attention so as not to miss the signs for addition, division, squaring or cubing, roots, and so on that were placed beside the Greek script used to symbolize numbers. An *isos* sign used to denote equality, the noun-terminal "*es*" for an unknown quantity, and twice over was the multiple of an unknown; a *dynamis* was the sign for raising to the second power, *kybos* for a cube, a *delta* after a *delta* sign to mark raising to the fourth power, a *delta* and a *kybos* raising to the fifth power, a *kybos* after a *kybos* to indicate raising to the sixth power, and so forth.

The first nine letters of the Greek alphabet were used for the first nine numerals, 1-9; the next nine, to indicate the tens, 10-90, the third three, the hundreds; added to which the signs for the ligature, called a *stigma*, a *qoppa*, and a *sampi*, were taken from obsolete ancient Greek alphabets. To denote thousands a comma was placed before a number, the symbol *M* (for *myriades*) stood for tens of thousands, and in a text a line was written above letters, which stood for numbers (unless it was forgotten). Uri had to transpose into this system a lot of texts written with earlier, divergent alphanumeric designations, and to accomplish this he often had to call upon the assistance of Heron, the supervising librarian, who was conversant with Egyptian and Phoenician scripts but impatient in giving explanations and, as Uri was later to discover, would often go astray in his own calculations. Heron was primarily interested in astronomy, though he did not scrutinize the sky himself, but rather preferred to delve into ancient writings. He was, incidentally, a learned, wise man; it was just that nitpicking, Sisyphean labors were not to his taste.

Copying was hard work, but Uri's eyes were born for the task: he would bend his head close to the manuscript and could see everything perfectly, even better than the others who fiddled about beside him, because he was able to spot even the tiniest signs.

The end of the summer was spent copying; the bonus was that whatever Uri copied he took it upon himself to understand. Uri made an abacus and used that to check calculations; as a result he came to grasp many arithmetic and geometric relationships that previously he had failed to understand. In fact it was the regular mathematical instruction others had received earlier on from their private tutors at home, before going to the Gymnasium, that he missed most. Apollonos Gamma did admit that this was not true mathematics—that had ended two centuries before, during the civil war, with the flight to Cyprus of the legendary head librarian of Alexandria, Aristarchus of Samothrace. Apollonos considered that the Great Library had died intellectually even before Julius Cesar burned it down, adding pensively that perhaps Caesar's flaming arrows would not have set the collection on fire if the spirit had still been alive in Alexandria. Even then, he ventured, the teaching staff were already not creative. Still, Uri could see clearly that there was still a thing or two that might be learned from them, so he defended them: a spirit was still alive in them, to be sure.

Apollonos shook his head in dissent:

"No, it isn't, it hasn't been for eighty-eight years or more, otherwise why would they store nine tenths of the library's stock in flammable premises. Scholarship had no standing even then, because if it had, then the books have been kept in a marble palace and all the works that were lost would still exist today!"

AT SHAVUOT URI ATTENDED A SERVICE AT THE BASILICA BEFORE PRO-
ceeding with the crowds to the island of Pharos. They snaked first toward the palace because tradition had it that the seventy-two elders from Jerusalem were quartered at first in Acra, and it was only after this that, on the initiative of Demetrius of Phaleron, the librarian of Ptolemy II Philadelphus and the Library's leadership in Alexandria at the time, they had moved to the peninsula, where they completed the Septuagint, the Greek version of the Torah or Pentateuch, in seventy-two days. Only now did it occur to Uri how close to the palace lay Delta, where the first Jews to arrive in Alexandria had settled: maybe they were afraid of the indigenous inhabitants and placed their trust in the palace guards coming swiftly to their aid in the event of an attack.

On the island a lot was said by many people, and they also took dips in the marvelously warm sea because it was ritually clean to do so, the very cleanest, so it was extraordinary to see nearly two hundred thousand Jews all together at once in the water, because only the elderly, toddlers and the sick stayed back at home. Uri recalled the mass washing during the feast in Jerusalem, the jostling of some one million shabbily dressed wretches in the filthy, half-dried-out riverbed. The Temple had not been sited well: it would have been better to build it here, in Alexandria. It would really have been better had Moses not felt the need to lead his people out of Egypt.

Uri recalled what Judaeophobic Greek historiographers had written about that exodus, having leafed through some of the ridiculous scribblings that were to be found in the Gymnasium's library: that Pharaoh had banished lepers from the country, and their leader was Moses, a priest, on whom the historian Manetho—who was active during the reign of Ptolemy I Soter and, incidentally, also compiled a serviceable Greek translation of the chronology of dynastic Egypt—bestowed the name Osarseph. At the site of their expulsion in Heliopolis, this priest, himself a leper, is said to have been in league with the Ethiopians in their attacks on Egypt against the pharaoh Amenophis and was supposed to have been the leader of eighty thousand lepers. Later, when the Pharaoh made peace with the Ethiopians, Osarseph was forced to move on with the remaining lepers to Palestine. It is also possible, however, that they were not leprous but afflicted with the plague, the reason being that the same word was used for both diseases by Judaeophobic Greek historians, the more virulent of whom also asserted that Osarseph secretly sent sick people (Jews, that is to say) into Egyptian towns to infect the healthy inhabitants. When Uri questioned Philo about these writings, he dismissed them: there was no need to pay them any attention as no one read them anyway.

Uri copied with great fervor, even to the point of neglecting to bathe. He felt a tense physical dissatisfaction, his body asking his brain why was it wasting its time, to which the brain responded that it too wanted to gain its satisfaction. Uri therefore did the copying with pangs of conscience, reassuring himself that this slave-work, in which one could lose oneself so much, was also part of Alexandria, where in the great freedom that was to be had a person might also permit himself the liberty of not taking part in its turbulent life.

He was able to copy the whole summer through, with the Gymnasium having taken a break, the teachers retiring to their villas in the country, the Greek students going back home to their parents, and Alexandria nearly deserted during the vacation. In the evenings and at night one could still find a big throng of people strolling in the popular places: the taverns down at the harbor were crammed and the crowds who were kept amused by the antics of mime artists in the neighborhood of the Square Stoa meant that there was no fall-off in sales of food and drink from the mobile vendors, although the jostle did ease and there was less reason to fear pickpockets.

Uri copied and read, and he learned that many generations ago there had been a substantial Jewish population in Egypt, in the fortress town on the island of Elephantine; indeed, they had even had their own temple where they made sacrificial offerings of animals and produce. That temple had been demolished, but they had rebuilt it and stayed until they were finally driven out by the Egyptian Greeks, with powerful assistance from the high priests of Jerusalem. As a result it was not just the Samaritans who denied the precedence of the Temple in Jerusalem; moreover, there had also been a Jewish community in Rome at the time of Judah Maccabee, whom the Romans supported in his revolt against the Greeks in Syria, a hundred years before Pompey the Great's conquests of Syria and Jerusalem, and they made sacrificial offerings on their domestic altars! So, it was not true to say that Jews had ended up in Rome for the first time in the wake of Pompey's military expedition; evidence to the contrary could be found in the contemporary decrees of the *praetor peregrinus*, the magistrate charged with the administration of foreign residents, whereby he set limits on the worshipers of the Sabbath Jupiter or Jove—the Iuppiter Sabatinus—residing in Rome and later expelled them. If he expelled them, then they must have been there in the first place, and their faith must have made an impression on the Romans. Uri

attempted to discuss these matters, but Philo had no interest in such triviali-
ties: those historical curiosities were of no philosophical significance, he pronounced, and Uri got a strong sense that the Roman Jews counted for nothing
because they were poor.

At the end of August on Roman reckoning, or the beginning of Elul on
Jewish reckoning, the Greek students and teachers slowly started to filter back
to Alexandria.

Officially, the Egyptian calendar was in force throughout Egypt, including
Alexandria, but no one used it and Uri never learned it. Jews were particularly
sedulous in adhering to the Roman calendar, being much more observant than
the Greeks of the official imperial feast days, which were punctiliously honored
throughout the province. In Alexandria, as Uri saw it, the Jews did everything
possible to put on more splendid celebrations than the Greeks—perhaps fearing
that any negligence on their part would be reported back to Rome.

There was just one official Roman feast day that the Jews of Alexandria
ignored, maybe not officially but through the cautious protest of making themselves conspicuous in their absence: August 1. Whatever day this might fall
on, Jews would always find urgent business to attend to in the country, and
as long as it was not a Sabbath, they would actually travel out of the city. The
Greeks did likewise: anyone who was able would travel out of the city because
it marked the day, sixty-six years ago, on which Alexandria had surrendered to
Augustus. It may not be propitious to celebrate a lost war, but Rome insisted
nonetheless. Flaccus's lifeguards would put on a ceremonial march in the morning of the said day, marching along the harbor before wheeling southward, at
the Western canal, at the tip of the box-shaped harbor known as the Kibotos,
and before the Gymnasium proceeding eastward along Arsinoë Avenue, then
in the district of Makedones (Delta, in other words) turning north to return to
the citadel-like palace of the Akra, their station. They would be accompanied
by large numbers of musicians, and spectators would gawk—that was it. Uri
watched from among the columns of the Gymnasium that faced the street: that
day there was no copying, although the Serapeion was open, and sacrifices were
offered within it to Rome and to the emperor just as they were, compulsorily,
in all shrines to Greek and Egyptian divinities, large and small, of which there
were many thousand in Alexandria. It was also celebrated in Jewish synagogues,
of course, and somewhat more happily than by the Greeks; Uri got the feeling
that Jews, being in the minority, were in their deepest hearts more loyal to the
Roman Empire than the majority Greek population, who would praise their own
loss of independence through gritted teeth. Naturally, Greek notables would

feel obliged to have themselves represented at the celebrations by at least one family member, and the leaders of the Jewish guilds, the *koinon*s, would also make a reluctant appearance.

In the alabarch's family it was Marcus who was deputed to be present at the thanksgiving service at the Basilica. The alabarch himself attended Flaccus's soirée at the palace, where an appearance by the eldest son was also mandatory, so Tija spent that day at Philo's place on the idyllic island on Lake Mareotis, where Uri would willingly have gone, and indeed was invited, but as he had to carry on with the copying work and would not have been able to get back to the city the next day, he stayed back at the alabarch's palace.

He, the guest, was alone in the palace, and though he was a familiar figure to all the servants, and the guards of the alabarch's private army who were assigned to sentry duties would let him come and go as he pleased, Uri still felt uneasy whenever he reached home on his own, wondering each day as he knocked at the door whether he would be admitted or whether the dream had come to an end, the magic spell had faded, and he would once more be an indigent, homeless wanderer. He was home alone, therefore, on the evening and night of this tiresome state celebration, sauntering around the interconnected little inner gardens, which purely for his sake were brightly illuminated with torches fixed to the trees, well aware that his every step was being tracked by the eyes of an invisible Argus. It was swelteringly hot, so he took a dip in the neck-deep water of one of the basins, floating on his back, and by the time he clambered out in his dripping tunic, there was already fruit and wine on the table, and on the couch, a towel along with several clean tunics. Uri dried himself, put on fresh clothes, ate and drank, whereupon it passed through his mind that maybe he was not in full possession of his faculties, but he most decidedly did not want such luxury for himself.

Toward the end of August, the students and teachers slowly started to drift back into Alexandria. Teaching had not recommenced yet—that wouldn't get underway until around mid-September—but the pupils were already snuggling down in the dormitories and in the evenings going to taverns down by the docks, with Uri, Tija, Apollonos Gamma, and even a few of the teachers tagging along. They were regulars at several places, but their favorite was Lysias's tavern because they could get free food and drink in exchange for poetry.

This Lysias, a bald, ruddy-faced man, was a great lover of the arts and could recite the epigrams of Callimachus by heart; it was said that the reason he was so fond of these was that he—like the poet—had a preference for boys. Then again, that had also been the name of an anatomist who'd lived some 250 years before, one of the last masters. That one had performed vivisections—on the model of the great Herophilus—on men who had been condemned to death and were delivered by the orders of Ptolemy I from the Akra, where a prison has been situated ever since. The subjects were dissected alive, for the advancement of science. Also readily cited by Lysias were the maxims of Machon, an author of comedies, which relayed anecdotes about utterances made by famous men while copulating as well as limning the most stupefying positions.

But that was not why the students went there. Rather, it was because almost every evening Lysias held a poetry contest, in which they would be asked to pen the epitaph for an imaginary figure, the name and biography of the fictional character being composed by Lysias himself, with the successful poet being rewarded by being able to order whatever and however much of it he liked, and he would always ask for enough for them all to eat and drink their fill.

It was a genre for which there had been a great vogue in Alexandria three centuries ago, with anyone who harbored pretensions to be a poet modeling himself on Asclepiades, the master of the fictitious epitaph, which traditionally had to be written in distichon or tetrastichon. Lysias rightly valued epigraphic couplets more highly than quadruplets, and if the two-liner was fashioned as Leonine verse, with an internal rhyme, then the winner would be rewarded with a special jug of wine. These impromptu poems then became his property, and it was rumored that he intended to bring out an anthology of them before long and win immortality by being the editor. Telegonus, one of the Greek students who was a dab hand at versifying, claimed to have seen on real tombstones in a cemetery on Samos epitaphs that had first seen light in Lysias's tavern—in other words Lysias was selling the poems wholesale, changing the names of the fictitious persons for real. Monumental masons made good money throughout the Greek world, and while no one reads demanding poetry, but everyone has dead to bury, the other pupils could well believe that Telegonus was telling the truth. For the time being, though, they were more interested in eating suppers than in making money, so they were went avidly to the evening's task.

Tija did not write any epitaphs, but greatly enjoyed listening to the works that were produced; Apollonos Gamma did write, but without much success, as legalistic prose was more his thing; Uri, on the other hand, was inspired and excelled, thereby winning genuine plaudits from (and even the friendship of) a few of the Greek students. One could never tell in advance what outrageous fictitious name and fabulous adventures of fate would occur to Lysias from one day to the next, and Uri was enthused by absurd stories. He liked the idea of a one-armed gravedigger; or a woman with five breasts; the prostitute with elephant tusks; the androgynous whore; the millionaire slave; the crocodilian librarian who, owing to his scaly tail, was unable to sit to do copying work; the faun who sported a penis on his forehead instead of a nose and constantly had to shake his head to clear the testicles from his eyes; and all of the other similarly sterling monstrosities which would spring from Lysias's fertile imagination, and for whom they would have to mourn in appropriately elevated wording.

One evening Lysias, as a jest, set Isidoros, the gymnasiarch, as the target, seeing that epitaphs for living people were not excluded under the rules of the game. Tija snickered, Apollonos Gamma shook his head as that was just not going to work for him, whereas Uri came up with the following couplet:

> You despised us giddy-goat Jews, Isidoros;
> Now God's got His own back by resurrecting you, along with us.

Uri won a big round of applause with that composition, and that day he was delighted to take his turn to order for the whole party.

The next day, Isidoros in person took a seat in Lysias's hostelry.

Uri froze. A trick had been played on him, and he had wandered naïvely into the trap. Isidoros conversed in a pleasant, relaxed manner with all and sundry except he did not so much as blink in Uri's direction. When Lysias announced the subject for that evening, Uri had to nod with a blush: he was the subject. He attempted to invent a witty epitaph about himself, but none came to mind.

Isidoros won:

> While alive he only saw one god, the monotheist;
> Now the myopic Jew can see more in Hades.

Uri joined in the laughter quite happily, and he found occasion more than once to raise a glass to Isidoros, who was wreathed in smiles.

"Hades" was the word used in the Greek Septuagint to translate the Hebrew "Sheol," which meant that Isidoros must be familiar with the Torah. At least Isidoros knew what it was about Judaism that he could not accept, Uri thought with gratitude, and he longed for a world in which his own sympathy for the gymnasiarch (and now he could not doubt that it was mutual) encountered no obstacles.

August 29 marked the Egyptian New Year.

This, in contrast, was a genuine public celebration. Uri roamed around in the city with Sotades. He must have educated and liberal parents; the name he was given came, presumably, from a court jester and writer of obscene satirical poems who had lived in Alexandria 250 years ago.

Popularity must have made that Sotades overconfident, and he met a nasty death on account of a lampoon in which he had mocked Ptolemy II Philadelphus, who had wed his real sister, Arsinoë. "You dipped your wick in an unholy hole," he wrote, and was imprisoned, only to escape and be hunted down on Crete by Admiral Patroclus, who ordered that the poet be given a lead vest and tossed into the sea. About the only recollection of all this which remained in Alexandria was that it had been Arsinoë after whom an unfinished temple and the broad main thoroughfare on which the Gymnasium lay were named, along with Savior Arsinoë, Miracle-working Arsinoë, Immortal Arsinoë, and countless other streets.

No one could say, the student Sotades told Uri, why exactly they had revered this Arsinoë, who had died when young. We always feel a need for someone to whom, for better or worse, we can address our prayers; maybe it is human nature to do so.

Uri's friend Sotades was a pleasant, jolly young man, stocky, with brown hair and dark eyes; he was outstanding at throwing the javelin and sprinting, excelled in military theory, and his own impromptu epitaphs more often than not displayed a finely pointed wit. Uri would have liked to be as jovial, free and easy, and sharp-witted as him, and, above all, he envied his talent as a mathematician, so he could not imagine—and did not dare to inquire—why Sotades took a liking to him. Sotades was the first true Greek friend that he had made in his life, and he was not going to put that friendship at risk over a tactless question. All the Greek students competed for Sotades's friendship, and that was not on account of his family, who had no claims to fame and were not even inhabitants of Alexandria, but purely on his own account; all the same, Sotades good-naturedly brushed them off. Perhaps he is using me as a weapon against them, it occurred to Uri faint-heartedly, yet even so he was thankful that fate had allowed him to acquire a Greek friend in Alexandria.

Sotades towed Uri all around the town on that Egyptian New Year's day; as Uri ascertained in due time from Tija, Jews were not forbidden from taking part in such celebrations.

The biggest throng was at the Great Harbor; among the costumed crowd it was hard to distinguish the professional mimics, who performed on temporary platforms erected for the purpose across the city, and for whose art the public tossed coins into baskets placed in front of these stages. They performed a variety of traditional and improvised sketches, and although Uri could not establish which was which, he was struck by the fact that some of the mimics wore hooked noses and kept on doubling over, bowing to the east and yammering ludicrous nonsense.

"Is that supposed to be us Jews?" he asked.

"Indeed, that's right," Sotades confirmed.

"Why do they hate us?" Uri asked.

"Because you're dangerous," Sotades replied in a friendly fashion.

Uri deferred any further inquiries until later, when a madman known as Carabbas, or "Cabbage-Head," the most popular of the city's fools, climbed onto the stage to a huge ovation. Carabbas was a homeless vagrant, who often slept on the Gymnasium's well-trimmed lawn and so was well known to the students. He was also well known to the women of Alexandria, who were the objects of Carabbas's indiscriminate amatory attentions: any time he saw a shapely woman, he would let out a whoop and, to the delight of bystanders, give pursuit. If the woman turned tail and fled, Carabbas would race for a while alongside her, then stop and drop, panting, to the ground. If the woman halted, Carabbas would roll on his back on the ground and whimper, but he never laid a finger on any of them, never said an improper word. People said that more than once a crowd had beaten up a man who sprang to his woman's defense by way of Carabbas. Carabbas would get free food and drink, both in the Great Harbor and the Western Harbor, but he did not abuse his popularity and consumed only what he needed.

What distinguished him from other destitute homeless was that he would go around stark naked. He minded neither cold nor heat, and never showed the slightest interest in putting on even a sheet: his skin was his clothing, wrinkled and blackened, and it seemed that, every now and again, he'd shed a used-up cabbage-leaf, either dirt that had stuck to him, or maybe the skin itself, and that may have been the source of his nickname. His testicles, which he would scratch unconcernedly, dangled flatly beside his member.

Anyway, it was this Carabbas who scrambled onto the stage as Uri was wondering aloud why the Greeks of Alexandria hated the Jews.

The mimic actors resented the competition, but they did not dare remove him from the stage: they too were familiar with him, and they did not have the nerve to throw any doubt on his vested rights. Carabbas's thick mane dangled in tousled shocks into his eyes. He jumped onto the stage, his testicles flapping as if there were ears growing on the underside of his belly; he beat his chest and shrieked incoherently. The mimics stood by gloomily and waited, while the audience applauded exultantly with much whooping: "Carabbas is singing! Listen to Carabbas!" The musicians tried to blow, bang or pluck a tune under his yells but to no avail. The less sense or rhythm there was to Carabbas's yelling, the more it pleased the public. "Carabbas! Carabbas!" they shouted deliriously.

"The poor wretch," Uri muttered.

Sotades shook his head:

"He's got a great role," he said. "At least he's found himself: with such manifold lack of talent he manages to make a respectable living through his own efforts in the city. Other untalented dopes have to work themselves stupid, practically run themselves into the ground. That man's a genius, our collective genius, Gaius Theodorus."

Uri had much the same thought right then, only he would not have dared to say so. Maybe that was the real difference between Greeks and Jews in the city: the polytheistic Greek admitted it, the monotheistic Jew denied it.

They drifted with the crowds to Arsinoë Avenue, where, to the east of the Gymnasium's grounds, the Sema, the mausoleum of Alexander the Great and the Ptolemies, was located. The building was only opened on Rosh Hashanah, with the priests and priestesses of Alexander the Great (who for the rest of the year made their living at everyday occupations) standing at the entrance in their white robes, their brows wreathed in laurels. A long line of people stood in a queue, waiting to take a look at the dead emperor's alabaster sarcophagus, rattle off a prayer of thanksgiving, and add some coins to the coffers of Alexander's priesthood. It was Ptolemy I Soter who had Alexander's dead body transported to Alexandria, but his golden sarcophagus was looted and melted down by Ptolemy X to pay his mercenaries, and it was he who had replaced it with one of alabaster. The Sema—the mausoleum itself—was raised by Ptolemy IV Philopater, and it was a square, terraced edifice, surprisingly low given the glory of the king resting within. The Hill of The Bodies, the man-made mound somewhat to the south surpassed the Sema in height, as its designer wished to compete with Alexander the Great even in death. Every ruler since had striven to perpetuate his own name with a temple that was taller than the mausoleum.

Uri and Sotades joined the queue to get into the Sema, but for all their standing around they moved no farther forward, so they gave up and went off for a drink instead. Sotades recounted that when Augustus visited Alexandria after the battle of Actium he had Alexander the Great's tomb opened, and the emperor had touched the embalmed body, accidentally knocking off part of the nose. Once the sarcophagus had been hastily resealed, he was offered a view into the tombs of the Ptolemies, which he self-assuredly declined, responding that he had come to see a king, not a motley collection of corpses. Since then, for seventy years, they had not reopened Alexander the Great's coffin for anyone, save for the physicians who every twenty years or so reembalmed the body. Even then nobody else was allowed to look within.

"What became of the nose?" Uri asked.

"Maybe it took on a new, self-sufficient life," Sotades suggested, "and it is roaming about here, down by the harbor."

By then, there were thousands upon thousands roaming about drunkenly down by the harbor, so a nose would hardly have been conspicuous among them. There were also children forlornly wandering around, they worked as porters and stevedores and were also the worse for drink. Uri pitied these ten- and twelve-year-olds: it was they who carried most of the bales of cargo on their scrawny shoulders and necks because they only had to be paid one quarter what an adult would get. There were a lot of them, more than all the donkeys, asses, and adult porters put together. Sotades disapproved of Uri's compassion: the young boys were happy because they were providing for the whole family and because of that they would not be beaten at home.

The Egyptian New Year came to an end that morning. Uri slept the rest of that day because around daybreak he had downed too much honeyed wine at the harbor.

Apart from Lysias's tavern the students also dropped in on a fair number of other places, these enchanting few days of freedom being the best part of the whole school year: they could drink with the catamites, whores, and dockers without ever coming under threat of knife attacks, though they had no trouble spilling one another's guts if they had a difference of opinion on some matter, large or small. In such taverns the students could drink for free, or at least they were never asked for any money, though they were expected to assist with the unloading of the ships at dawn. Whenever possible, Uri would carry the smaller loads, fearing that his back would give out under a bale, and he found it odd that the dockers, who were in such familiar surroundings in the harbor, treated them so politely, even him, although they knew—naturally, they knew full well—that he was Jewish. The Greek students joked with the same condescension with plebs, freedmen, and slaves alike, and they would politely laugh back at being honored. There was no need to ask why: the wealth and power of the families of the Greek students was so exceedingly great that any insult to one of their scions that might be committed would be paid back with interest. For that reason Uri did not relish the dawn unloading work, but he could not wriggle out of it: he labored purely to be considered of equal rank despite his Jewishness, and if he had not done the dock work he would have fallen out of favor with his Greek schoolmates and become a butt of their crude jokes.

There were a lot of Jews from Palestine working as laders of the ships alongside the Greeks and Egyptians, and they could be identified from the fact that several times a day they would pray bowing to the east, having dipped their feet in the sea and sprinkled some water on themselves, as well as the fact that they said their prayer in the Aramaic tongue: *maran 'atha, maran 'atha*, The Lord cometh, they would chant in chorus. They had been driven westward by the land crisis in Judaea: high-priestly families had bought up the land of firstborn sons, leaving them with nothing. They held out hopes of making a fortune in Alexandria, the richest of all Jewish cities. In recent times, in deference to them (since they too, wretches though they might be, were Jewish), speakers in the Basilica had been mixing a few words of Aramaic into the Greek texts. They were particularly loathed by the Egyptian stevedores because they were willing to take on the work at cheaper rates, but they slept in the streets just the same as Greeks and Egyptians, and they too were quick to resort to knives as weapons.

At the beginning of September, Sotades had a visit from his family. They stayed in Alpha district, and Sotades introduced to them Uri as well as two Greek friends. Uri was astonished when he saw Sotades's younger sister: he would never even have imagined a girl could be that pretty. She was tall, slim, with long legs, erect in carriage, with blue eyes and wavy, flowing, waist-length blonde hair: no make-up was used on her eyebrows, eyelids, or lips—none of the cosmetics with which Egyptian women, just as much as the Romans, loved to paint themselves. Every single thing about her was gorgeous, but taken together the overall effect was breathtaking. It was startling to see this Germanic beauty alongside her thickset, brown-haired brother. Sotades's Greek friends were also struck dumb, and the girl blushed before quickly retiring to ease the stupefaction. The whole business was embarrassing for Sotades as he had been given no advance warning that his sister would also be coming to Alexandria, and it seemed to Uri that his friend was not a great fan of the lovely girl.

After the family had departed, Uri asked him again why the Greeks of Egypt did not like the Jews of Alexandria.

"There are too many of you," Sotades declared melancholically. "At least as many as the Latini, but there are a lot of you even in Persia, and through them you snatch up all the trade with China and India from right under our noses."

"No other quarrels?" Uri asked.

Sotades shrugged his shoulders:

"I don't think so," he said. "It's of no consequence how many gods a person is supposed to venerate."

After a brief pause for reflection, he added:

"It might be better, perhaps, if you were very different from us, but in fact you're just the same. That's the trouble."

The statement floored Uri, and he spent a lot of time thinking over what it might mean. He couldn't rid his mind of the figure of Sotades's sister—even trying to summon up the small, swarthy girl whom he would once have gladly purchased in Judaea. He then hurried quickly to one of the baths so that his body at least might be relieved. He fantasized that one day he would come into a fortune and ask for the girl's hand in marriage; that would make Sotades and his family sit up. The girl would decide unexpectedly to convert to Judaism for his sake, and the service would be held in the Basilica. Uri laughed at himself, and especially the question of why he could not just turn around and become Greek. Maybe just because it wasn't customary. Greek women, even Greek men, would marry into rich Jewish families, but it rarely happened the other way around.

Only a few days were left until the return to teaching when Hedylos, one of their classmates, rented out the biggest restaurant on the market square, the Elephant.

The market square was known to one and all as the Agora, although officially it was called the Forum Augusti, and was located on the boundary between Beta and Gamma districts. The Elephant was celebrated for the fact that the uneven, rutted ground of its garden, with walls on three sides, was filled with rickety benches and shaky tables; the tableware was junk, the knives and spoons crooked and blunt, but in the basement they brewed the best beer in Alexandria. The penetrating odor of barley and hops had pervaded the deepest recesses of the market square. On the side where a fourth wall would stand, a canal lapped past the Elephant, somewhere to puke or piss. It was an infernal place, and as it happened extremely fashionable in the circles of the wealthy: to rent—for twenty-some students and one and a half-dozen teachers—for a whole evening a place which normally catered to least five hundred people must have cost a small fortune. Hedylos was not outstanding in his studies, and his family was not known to be especially wealthy, so Uri did not quite understand how his fellow student had so much money to play with.

"He became a Persian," Sotades said disparagingly, though he went to the banquet at the Elephant all the same."

He explained that in Alexandria a person "became Persian" by borrowing money with a letter of credit in which a clause was inserted to say that he had become a Persian subject. A creditor could not recover loan capital, or the interest on it, from an Alexandrian citizen, especially not if the debtor withdrew to some sanctuary or other (which might even be a Jewish house of prayer), because the right of asylum applied to any shrine and any fugitive. Not in the case of a "Persian," however. A "Persian" debtor would seek sanctuary in vain: he would be handed over. No genuine Persian citizen had lived in Alexandria for centuries; they had all assimilated and become Greeks, but it had never been forgotten that in days of old Persia had attacked Egypt, demolishing and desecrating their shrines. Thus, anyone who endorsed a letter of credit by saying that he had become a Persian was exposed to having the loan recovered at any time and by any means—a customary law that was observed by all Alexandrians, including the judiciary, though it was not set down in writing anywhere.

"Hedylos must be crazy," Sotades declared, "If he believes he's going to get into our good books this way."

And he went on, Uri at his side, to gorge himself at Hedylos's expense.

Hedylos was ensconced in the place of honor at the head of a long table, along with his family: his father, mother, and several cousins were also there. The father was a maker of drift-net fishing boats and, as Uri saw it, Hedylos's whole family were delighted. They partook of the overwhelming feast and drank copiously; the tutors sang lustily, the musicians tooted, trilled, and thumped tirelessly. Uri did not much care for the taste of the beer; he ruminated over why the banquet might be worthwhile for Hedylos.

Perhaps it was for the same reason that Agrippa was constantly in debt.

Gymnasium pupils would recall the party even decades later, and if the "Persian" Hedylos or one of his offspring were to look them up with a request of some sort, they would be much readier to oblige.

Toward daybreak a rather shady set of characters arrived, led by a certain Lampo, supposedly a court recorder and a very rich man. They too got plenty to eat and drink, with Hedylos kneeling beside Lampo and reiterating, "You're our man! You're our man!" Hedylos's father was not insulted, and indeed even went so far as to bless them, Greek style.

The other students said later, after they had sobered up, that Lampo was a crafty chap, because judges were always forgetting what had been said previously at a hearing and as the recorder Lampo could write down afterward whatever he wanted. In short, he would falsify the record, and for that reason he was called a papyrus bigshot and quill-killer: he could bend the record to favor or harm who ever he wanted, and absent-minded judges would scrawl their signatures under it, so it was worth greasing Lampo's palm if one wished to avoid coming out badly in a lawsuit. Lampo's reach was long, but it would probably not be such a good thing if he were to become the gymnasiarch, for it was rumored that he had set his heart on that post, but he had not managed to buy over the whole governing body—at least not all of its members. That was just a question of time, according to some, but others claimed Lampo would do no harm: he might be uncultured, but he was smart; perhaps he could tap into more funding for the Gymnasium than the unsociable, standoffish, snooty Isidoros.

Uri was dumbfounded. He recalled now that Isidoros had been present at the start of the banquet, but had left by the time Lampo arrived. May the Eternal One keep Isidoros as gymnasiarch for a long time to come.

Rosh Hashanah was a simple affair: it was announced by a shofar; music was played and there was dancing the whole day long in the Basilica and its surrounds, after which people trooped out to the island of Pharos. It was a dignified, slow stroll along the harbor then the Heptastadion, a demonstrative stroll with the participation of at least two hundred thousand Jews; the Greeks stared at them wherever they passed, and not exactly in a friendly fashion, but nonetheless mutely. Flutes, horns, and twanging harps and lutes accompanied the procession of the mass, which was also joined by processions from other synagogues. At the tip of the peninsula, jostling by the Jewish observatory, pushing one other, they dropped objects into the sea: the carriers of the previous year's sins, so that they might return happily to the city, cleansed, ready for newer sins. Uri had bought himself a cheap earthenware vase for the occasion, and that was what he dropped into the sea. Strangely, he felt that his soul really had been purged.

On Yom Kippur, the Day of Atonement, Uri sat in the Basilica on the first row of benches to the west, which was reserved for the alabarch and his extended family. A huge number of people were packed into the aisles between the rows of benches and by the walls—around 120,000 of them, approximately a third of Alexandria's Jews—with the rest assembling at their own local synagogues. A priest had even come from Jerusalem for the celebration, but he hardly spoke, reciting no more than the benediction. Priests always enjoyed traveling to Alexandria, but they were never able to spend as much time there as they would have liked, as Alexandria's high and mighty had them escorted promptly back to Judaea. One after another, as the alabarch called them in turn to go to the east wall—the leaders of the city's Jewish community would read from the Septuagint. They read, so it was believed, from the original Torah which the seventy-two translators had translated in seventy-two days on the island of Pharos. Every year they would ask the Great Library in the royal palace to borrow the tome, and every year it would be taken back again: this one was authentic, the rest mere copies. After the service had ended, they would all troop out again to the island.

Sukkot was observed even more simply: they did not erect tents, as was done in and around for the throngs of worshipers there, but instead merely set up miniature, tabletop tents fabricated from papyrus and bast, decking them out with fresh leaves; these symbolized the tabernacle which once upon a time was the domicile of God, and until the building of the First Temple had concealed the Ark of the Covenant that the Samaritans had been looking for in the bowels of Mount Gerizim when they were massacred.

Who could say where the Ark of the Covenant was lurking, if indeed it had ever existed.

A FEW WEEKS AFTER THE FESTIVALS, EXCITEMENT BROKE OUT AMONG the Jews of Alexandria: Agrippa had been thrown into prison!

It couldn't have happened more than a fortnight earlier because news—whatever it was—would reach Alexandria from Rome without fail in under nine days. This was even true for events that happened in supposed secret on the island of Capri, where the master of the world, the Roman emperor, resided. News—carried by spies—reached Rome from Capri in about two days, then it took another two days to get to Dikaiarchia (otherwise known to as Puteoli), and from there a ship could reach Alexandria via the most direct route in a week. Uri was angry in retrospect at the frugality of Rome's Jewish community: he could have made the trip to Jerusalem in two and a half weeks if only the would have shelled out for the Puteoli-Alexandria-Caesarea route They would only have had to cover the stretches from Rome to Puteoli and from Caesarea to Jerusalem on foot! He was now in a position to calculate very precisely that the five weeks they would have saved—return journey included—would have cost no more than one thousand two hundred sesterces—an absolutely negligible sum in comparison with the amount of the sacrificial money.

He had a suspicion how things had gone among the Jews of Rome: it would not be such a good idea to return home.

Tiberius had imprisoned Agrippa! His favorite, his friend, the tutor to young Gemellus and Gaius, son of Germanicus—all because in conversation he was reported to have said that Tiberius's days were numbered, and a servant reported this to the emperor.

Philo was devastated.

Tija was unsurprised that Agrippa had ended up in prison, but he was unable to accept the allegations.

"It is quite impossible that Agrippa would have said anything of the sort in the presence of a mere servant," he was convinced. "He might well think it, but he wouldn't say it out loud, not even if he was dead drunk! I bet Tiberius has hidden Agrippa away. Maybe he is worried about his safety—perhaps he fears hired assassins?"

Uri, on the other hand, was of the opinion that autocratic despots had a tendency to carry out these sorts of meaningless, inexplicable acts as no one dared to keep a check on them. He referred to the writings of distinguished historians on similar cases.

Tija shook his head:

"Historians are skilled at portraying everything that has happened as being a matter of necessity, as if nothing else could possibly have happened. They are captive to events, and as a result their brains have shriveled up. Those of us who are alive right now find ourselves amongst a multiplicity of equal chances. I cannot exclude the possibility that a senile Tiberius has gone off his rocker and given credence to a lie by some zealous, exaggerating informer, but for that very reason I can't rule out that this was *not* what happened but rather exactly the opposite. Agrippa has been imprisoned by the emperor, that's what the news says, and let us assume that because it has come from more than one source that the news is true. And yet why should Tiberius have had him imprisoned, given that up till now Agrippa has been so careful and never had a bad word to say about the emperor? If Tiberius really had been angry at him, all he would have had to is nod, and Agrippa would have been stabbed to death. Who would be upset by the death of a man like that? He's only a Jew. He has no wealth: having run through his money long ago he scrapes by on loans; the emperor will not be made a penny richer through his death. Is the death of a peabrain like him going to bring the Roman Empire to its knees? Don't make me laugh! It still leaves plenty of Herod the Great's descendants. But then if Agrippa has been imprisoned, he is alive, so Tiberius has no intention of getting rid of him, though there are individuals in his circle him who can be held to account for any number of murders. The very fact Agrippa was not slain right away but locked up in prison is suspicious. Prison on Capri, where there is no such thing? Or was one set up specially for him?"

Uri admitted that Tija's reasoning was logical.

"A prison is not necessarily a place of punishment," Tija argued. "It is at least as much a place of survival. In the outside world there will be no end of indiscriminate mayhem and murder the moment that news of the emperor's death is made public—but a prison, guarded by sentries, is precisely the place one can be protected from murderers. So it is worth clapping him in irons to ensure his survival, my dear Gaius. Then once things blow over, the prisoner can be brought out and put on show: Alas! He's alive. He survived—and few of you who remained free have. Accept him with good grace. Because he too has suffered. I figure it is better to be imprisoned at the beginning of a period of unrest than later on, by which time a person will inevitably have done things detrimental to the interests of many, things that will never be forgotten—and people are quite capable of taking revenge. Have anyone whom you wish to protect, from others or from himself, locked up in good time!"

Uri mused on whether Matthew might not have had him locked up in prison in Jerusalem for similar reasons. He had indeed told him when they had parted—after that awkward supper they had eaten with Pilate—that he had saved Uri's life, but then again Matthew had said nothing about having him sent to jail with the intention of protecting him.

Uri resolved that one day he would look Matthew up in Ostia and question him directly about it.

Tija's conclusion was diametrically opposite the notions of Alexander and Philo, who were thrown, frankly, into despair on hearing the news. They summoned their chief advisers to the palace and, behind closed doors, went into lengthy sessions to decide on what was to be done. Marcus, experienced politician that he was, expressed no opinion.

One evening, Aulus Flaccus turned up at the alabarch's residence, this time with a large escort and bearing no gifts, which meant that he must have received some unexpected piece of news. Uri just happened to be reading in the atrium as the prefect marched past with his men. It was obviously not all the same to Flaccus what might be happening on Capri or in Rome, and he had come to exchange news with the alabarch.

Tija was invited to attend this discussion and sat through it, and later that night he recounted it with dissatisfaction to Uri:

"They talked such tripe, it made me sick! Just imagine: Agrippa is allowed to write letters from prison, and he even has his own servants with him. I believe my father and the rest are just whimpering: they believe Tiberius has been wound up by Agrippa's ill-wishers, and now Agrippa's life is in danger. At which point I piped up, saying that if Agrippa's life really were at risk, then it would have been ended already. But they just went on whimpering, so I shut up. My father doesn't understand how the empire works. He's a clever man, skilful too, who has risen to become the richest man in Egypt; he understands the art of bribery, but he is a nonentity, not wily enough. Flaccus is wilier. He was not whimpering anywhere near as much, although his life truly is in danger. Whatever happens, my father will remain the alabarch, so I don't know what he is scared of. But when Tiberius dies, whoever his successor, Flaccus will have to be slick in his maneuvering to hold onto his post as prefect."

"Even Pontius Pilate could not manage that," said Uri.

"Pilate was a fool! The moment he learned that Agrippa and Vitellius were plotting against him, he should have agreed with his enemies to resign rather than trying to stand against them. He would then have been able to live out his days in Rome, modestly perhaps, but at least safely. But no, that would not do for the new man, *homo novus*, who had laid hands on a fortune through his wife: he wanted to prove that indeed he was a wily prefect and could hush up any scandal. What became of him? You told me yourself: he was stabbed in the back when he was least expecting it, in Samaria, a place he was quite possibly not even aware fell within his jurisdiction! What was the point of picking a fight with Vitellius, who is perfectly capable of any dirty trick, as he showed when he betrayed his own elder brother in the Sejanus affair ten years ago? Pilate wanted to show the emperor and the Senate that he was an effective prefect as a matter of pride and to keep on getting nice juicy jobs. As though the emperor and Senate cared about anything! The only thing they care about is success, and the only way of achieving that is fraudulently, the same way they did, or at least their forebears had. One has to learn to bend the knee before people who are more powerful: and Flaccus knows how to do that, I think. He bombards Gemellus and Caligula simultaneously with his messengers, even now assuring each of his loyalty. And no doubt he has his men around Macro, with whom he has been on good terms for a long time."

"And who does your father bombard with messengers?" Uri asked. He immediately regretted his impertinence, but it was too late.

Tija was not annoyed, however.

"Herod Antipas," he said. "If anything happens to Agrippa, we're wagering on Antipas. Perhaps not a great choice, as he spoiled his chances by marrying Herodias, to which John the Baptist objected along with us. It's a bad idea to expose oneself to attack on such a broad front—and unforced at that! But if Agrippa is out of it, then we have no option but to plump for him. It's a case of it being six of one and half a dozen of the other."

Uri was unaware what sin Herod Antipas had committed, so Tija sketched the situation quickly: Antipas's first wife had been Phasaelis, a daughter of King

Aretas of Nabatea, but he had repudiated her (which was unseemly, and for that the haughty Arabs would never forgive him—or the Jews in general) in favor of Herodias, the widow of his half-brother Philip. The Galilean preacher John the Baptist, who excoriated incestuous unions and opposed this one in particular, was apprehended for doing so and eventually executed on charges of being a paid agent for Aretas. It hardly mattered whether he had or hadn't been. Incest was not considered a sin in Alexandria, and in the end Rome did not object, as it could stomach a lot; the problem was the subsequent deterioration in relations with Aretas. Rome did not like it when two of its allies were at loggerheads, unless that was its aim, and in this case it was surely not.

"Is that the Philip who, like Antipas, was the ruler of one fourth, a tetrarch?"

Indeed it was, but he had died young, and his former territory had since been annexed to Syria. It was thought, however, that the area could be reannexed to a big Jewish state if—through Rome's goodwill—there were to be a king of the Jews once again.

Tiberius's reform of the banking system to confront an ongoing credit crunch created an even bigger stir: Agrippa was but a single person, whereas any change in the system of borrowing and lending money affected everyone.

The plan was dreamed up by the emperor, bored in his isolation: a crisis in agricultural production was to be addressed by distributing millions of sesterces among specially established banks; these would extend to landowners interest-free three-year state loans, provided the land offered as collateral was worth at least twice the loan.

Of which Uri understood precisely nothing.

Marcus explained it with great passion: it was an incredible step, in effect the emperor's true last will and testament, because it would lead to a slashing of usurious interest rates right across the empire! Of course the emperor was not on his deathbed: his mind was sound—and how!

Tija, irate, in turn added further explanations for Philo and Uri, neither of whom could wrap their minds around the point of the decree. Private banks and sources of credit had been obliged to lower their interest rates, it was curtains for the very juicy profits they had been enjoying because they could not compete with the immense private fortune that the emperor could put behind the scheme, which effectively set up a state banking system at one blow. Everyone would now borrow from these state banks, and usury was finished!

"Which from another angle is not good for us," continued Tija gloomily, "because the Italian farmers are now going to turn to their own kind for loans, and we Egyptians will lose ground."

Uri now began to catch on, while Philo still listened uncomprehendingly.

Uri had a go at explaining it to him. A loan, interest-free for three years, would give Italian landowners breathing room, maybe even put them in a position to produce enough to pay the loan back...

"And then three years later they would be able to apply for another interest-free line of credit!" exclaimed Tija. "That means a scaling back of Egyptian exports of grain! Tiberius is seeking to ruin us by making Rome self-sufficient!"

Marcus interjected soberly: it was going too far to say that! Rome would continue to depend on grain imports from Egypt, albeit rather less than hitherto; the real novelty would be the fall in Italian interest rates as banks across the empire, including those in Egypt, adjusted their own rates. A huge number of Greek and Jewish lenders would be ruined; the Romans, having plenty of capital, would buy them up, so indirectly Tiberius's decree was going to have a favorable impact on Roman banks: that was the true meaning of the gesture, not the rescue of Italian agriculture.

"So what will happen if, despite the injection of capital, the property market is still not righted?" Uri asked.

"That is all the better for Tiberius," Marcus responded. "Since the land is the security for the loans, the bank will acquire it. Once the whole property market is sorted out—and it will be sorted out—land prices will jump, so that any property that has been scooped up to recover unpaid debts is going to be worth more to the banks than it was previously."

"Did Tiberius really think it through in these same terms?" Philo asked in amazement.

"You can be sure of it!" Alabarch Alexander spoke up. "He's a very smart man: I've never met anyone as smart as him. He's wise and also cunning. If the Deified Augustus had been half as smart, India would today lie on the border of the empire."

Uri listened in amazement.

"Tiberius is the true creator of the empire," the alabarch asserted, "not the Deified Augustus... It seems incredible what a dispassionate mind he has... Perhaps because he has suffered so much..."

He recounted how he, a nobody, a Jewish Alexander from Alexandria, had hurried with Antonia to the emperor in Rome bearing the latest Judaean rumors that Germanicus was preparing to travel to Egypt, rumors which, if true, would betoken a renewed war between Rome and Egypt.

Antonia was desperate: Tiberius disliked her cherished first-born son, the heroic commander Germanicus, who had too many supporters in the Senate.

Alexander had tried to convince Antonia to send an envoy to Judaea, where Germanicus remained for the time being, to dissuade him from his plan. Antonia had shaken her head (she was still a strikingly beautiful woman, Drusus's widow, looking much younger than her years): she believed that Germanicus was under a spell, and thinking he could become emperor, would reject envoys.

Antonia had decided that they should instead together report the news to the emperor. That had been a brilliant step: sooner or later Tiberius would come to hear the rumor anyway, so it was better if he learned of it from her. She would betray him, that was true, but it was the only way she could protect her wider kinship.

"That was the first and last occasion on which I saw the emperor," Alexander said. "He is coarse-featured, pockmarked, and scarred, broad-shouldered and strong like a gladiator. His narrow eyes do not give many signs of his intelligence. He heard out what I had to report with a silent Antonia watching. When I had finished, the emperor asked Antonia: one or many? To which she answered: many. Tiberius smiled and told Antonia to pick for herself a territory along the Nile, in the most fertile region, as big a property as she wished. Antonia looked at me, whom she didn't even know, and asked me to make the arrangements, to which Tiberius nodded assent."

They listened to the alabarch in silence—Uri with interest, Philo, Marcus, and Tija with the boredom of having heard the tale many times over. It did occur to Uri, though, that maybe the alabarch should be thinking about his successor, whoever that might be, rather than bothering so much with Tiberius's greatness.

"By taking that step, Antonia was signing her firstborn son's death warrant," the alabarch pronounced solemnly. "She had no choice... Germanicus would in any case have been executed, even if only for prevailing on the high priests in Jerusalem to support him against the emperor, if it came to war. But if Antonia had not hastened to the emperor, her entire family would have been obliterated along with him, perhaps herself as well. By virtue of her decision, everyone else—her second son, her grandsons—was allowed to live, though some of them, Germanicus's deranged widow, Agrippina the Elder, for example, decided to follow her husband into death. At least the choice was left to them... That's how I, a nonentity, was made alabarch, and how Antonia became Tiberius's chief adviser. Tiberius knew exactly what she had sacrificed for the empire; he has never trusted anyone as much as he has Antonia. It is Antonia who has squared everything for us with the emperor ever since. Tiberius could have had a whole host of lovers, but it was Antonia who became his partner. Though after his withdrawal to Capri he never saw her again, and never ordered her to join him. He knew that in Rome there would be a loyal person whom he could trust, a wife in spirit at any rate."

They all fell silent.

"That was not so in my case," said the alabarch, "but then I am not as wise as Tiberius. Antonia asked what the emperor would do to ensure that Germanicus did not travel to Egypt. Tiberius just laughed, saying: Let him! It will only serve as proof against him. He laughed. But then he continued: Let him go to Egypt, that won't serve as proof against him in any case. He was not going to pin the blame for anything on the popular Germanicus, who would die accidentally. He said that to Antonia's face; he was in a position to do so because by then they were allies."

The alabarch jumped up and began to pace around.

"Never saw the likes before! A man takes as a wife in spirit a woman, whose firstborn son he is about to have murdered, with her unquestioning agreement, for the sake of an ideal: for the empire. I was the only witness. My life was in danger from that moment, though I only realized it later on: witnesses like that have a habit of getting snuffed out. Yet that didn't happen: Tiberius was smarter than anyone who has ever been Princeps. He knew that I knew he could do that, even ought to do that, but he left me alive. Ever since then he has had no supporter in Egypt more loyal than me. He knew that from the start. He knows everything in advance..."

"Even so, he might say who was going to be his successor," Tija ventured. "It would save us all a lot of trouble and strife."

Irately, the alabarch waved the notion aside.

AT THE END OF MARCH CAME THE NEWS THAT THE EMPEROR HAD DIED, having reached the age of seventy-eight. It was rumored that he had been killed by Macro, stalwart prefect of his Praetorian Guard, or that Gaius, Germanicus's sole surviving son, had strangled him, or even that Thrasyllus, his favorite seer, had smothered him with a pillow, but these tales were not meant to be taken seriously. The fact is he was old, and even an emperor has to die sometime.

There was commotion in Alexandria, as there was throughout all of the empire along the coast of the Great Sea, then that was overtaken by a deadly hush.

Funeral ceremonies in every shrine. All pennants lowered. Every eagle tipped over. Every shop closed. The baths closed. Every market empty. Prayers for the deceased in all the synagogues. Sports events and theatrical performances postponed. Taverns closed. A ban on all assemblies.

The dockworkers listlessly loaded and unloaded the boats, because even at a time like this the labor of the harbor had to go on. Flaccus's Praetorian Guards prowled around the city, just as listlessly: they had to pick up any drunkards, nor were they free to drink. General gloom and depression set in. Grieving citizens inscribed their names in a huge tome in the Sebasteion that would later be sent to Rome to be placed on public display among similar tomes sent by other cities. In another book were inscribed the names of those, Greeks and Jews alike, who had pledged to contribute money for the erection of a statue to Deified Tiberius. Let there be a statue worthy of him next to the one of Augustus there, in the Sebasteion. A long queue formed in front of the temple entrance, the grieving soldiers ensuring public order in the brilliant sunshine, their helmets and their armor glinting, sweat dripping from beneath it in the heat. The emperor's loyal troops, silently cursing all emperors—dead, existing, and to come—to Hades.

The emperor is dead.

But who would become emperor?

It would be nice to know, because only then could the shops reopen, contests be held, the markets function, and finally, in shrines and houses of prayer, could thanksgiving prayers at last be intoned to welcome the new ruler and to signal that one could again take pleasure in life.

Conjecture spread like wildfire: power was now held by a duumvirate of Gaius, Germanicus's sole surviving son, and Gemellus, the deceased emperor's consanguineous grandson, who had not yet reached the age of majority. But no, that was not right, Gaius had turned down the title. Gaius had been murdered. Gemellus had been murdered, Agrippa as well and that half-wit Claudius too, who, it was certain, could never have become emperor anyway. Everybody had been killed except Macro, the prefect of the Praetorian Guard, who had marched on Rome and taken charge. But no, that couldn't be right either, because peace reigned in Rome. All the same, there must have been some sort of tumult over the succession in Rome, because the *Acta Diurna* had not appeared for a fortnight and when it did resume it would surely greet the new emperor in writing, and at a time like this, in the spring with the shipping season in full swing, the newspaper would reach Alexandria from Rome in ten days.

The first week of April had come and gone by the time when the news arrived from several sources all at once: the new emperor was Gaius, who as a child earned the agnomen Caligula—"Bootikins"—and was straightaway called that, familiarly, by everyone in Alexandria, Greek and Jew alike. As if convinced that the emperor would also look upon his subjects from afar more genially and benignly if his they used his nickname.

Few people in Alexandria—the alabarch's family were among the first—were to learn that considerable wrangling over the succession had in fact broken out in the Senate. In his last will and testament, Tiberius had designated Gaius and Gemellus to be his heirs as co-Principes, and Macro, after racing to Rome with the news of the emperor's death, had immediately set about having the will nullified, primarily on the grounds that designating co-regents, especially when one of them had not yet attained the age of majority, constituted evidence that toward the end of his life the Deified Tiberius—"Augustus" though he might be—had become senile, and a will drawn up by such a man was invalid. The Senate kept dragged the argument out for a while before finally caving in to Macro, who by virtue of having sole command of the army was the most powerful individual in Rome. The will was annulled, and the Senate proclaimed Caligula as sole heir and emperor. It was in much the same way, Uri reflected, that Master Jehuda had attended to that widow's plight in Judaea.

As was proper given his new position, Caligula adopted Gemellus as his son, nominating him as Princeps of Youth. That accomplished, it would have been a good time to relax a little.

Except that the emperor's next step was not to consolidate power in Rome, but to sail the stormy seas to the island of Pandateria, to bring back to Rome the ashes of his mother, Agrippina and his older brother Nero, imprisoned in the Pontines by Tiberius and long dead of starvation.

A fine human gesture.

Caligula sent a message to Rome that from now on the month after August would no longer be September, but Germanicus, after his father. The Assembled Fathers of the Senate instantly rushed to enact the emperor's will and proclaim it throughout the empire: from thenceforth Rosh Hashanah would fall in the month of Germanicus, not September.

The Jews of Alexandria were perturbed at this for they, through the alabarch, had some hand in bumping off Germanicus nineteen years before. What if the new emperor wanted to avenge his father's death on Jewry as a whole? Better if he were to restrict his vengeance to the alabarch himself, with whom, of course they had nothing to do, the alabarch being a Greek citizen, barely Jewish at all. One could smell on the night air that the alabarch was finished in Alexandria. And likewise in Rome, with Agrippa, his main liaison with Roman Jewry, still locked up in the clink.

But then the news came that Emperor Caligula had released Agrippa. The alabarch was a canny man, after all, the scent in the Alexandrian night suggested, and through Agrippa he would arrange with the new emperor that the rights granted to the chosen people by Augustus, never thrown into question by Tiberius, and there engraved on the Jewish stele raised high in front of the Sebasteion for all to see, would henceforth not be thrown into question by anybody.

In a marvelous address that he made Friday evening in the Basilica, the alabarch called upon the city's Jews to express their joy in every possible manner. He praised Emperor Gaius's cultivation, his masculine handsomeness, the sharpness of his intellect, and the martial skill he had inherited from his father, and gave blessings to the Eternal One for picking such a magnificent person to head the empire. Alexandria's Jews were already overjoyed at the beginning of this address, but by the end of it they were even more overjoyed.

The Jews rejoiced, then, celebrating the new emperor and Passover with a gladness that outdid any past gladness as they strove to rejoice in the new emperor more spectacularly than did the Greeks, who were, of course, similarly damned overjoyed. Greeks and Jews and Copts and the members of all the other nations who dwelt in Alexandria competed with one another in joy, and even the beggars were overjoyed. How could anyone not be overjoyed, rich or poor, great or small? Life in Alexandria became one long feast, a veritable revelry, a pageant, with one celebration on top of the other, free eats and free drinks at every turn, and business booming.

The two Egyptian legions were given three hundred sesterces per head from the emperor, with the prefect distributing the funds in person in the grounds of the Gymnasium in front of the Square Stoa. The handout lasted the whole day, music thundering and dancers simpering throughout, with Flaccus calling out each soldier personally by name. The people were for the first time able to see the full strength of the two legions, an imposing spectacle as they stood there in ranks, disciplined, under the blazing sun. Everyone also rejoiced at the Circus, though voices could be heard here and there in the crowd that the plebs in Rome had been given the same, so why was it that the common people of Alexandria never got anything special? Were they all part of one empire or not? Were they any worse than the Romans? Were they—who shipped grain to Rome, after all—inferior to them somehow?

The Greeks offered no end of sacrificial animals in their shrines, feasting royally on them. The Jews of Alexandria were unable to do that, as only the Temple was entitled to make sacrificial offerings of animals, and indeed at the Temple in Jerusalem a huge animal sacrifice was dedicated to the new emperor, over and above the usual morning and evening quotas that had once been paid for in Augustus's day (though he had later forgotten to finance this, and Tiberius had

499

chosen not to support it any longer, it still referred to as the imperial quota). An overwhelming number of animals were sacrificed in honor of Emperor Caligula, and an accurate record was kept: more than 160,000 over the three months of public rejoicing. Uri felt dizzy on hearing that tally. He could almost see before his eyes the wretched villages of Judaea as almost any livestock that remained to them out of the tithe—the firstborn and the pick of the bunch—were herded together by the collectors with military backup and driven off to Jerusalem. There was no need for an animal that was to be sacrificed to the emperor to be ritually clean, intact, and flawless. They would have plundered the villages completely—simply because there was a new emperor, almost nowhere could there have been any meat left for feast days or the Sabbath banquets. Tears sprang to his eyes; for days he would touch no meat, in which Alexandria abounded, and only resumed eating it after he realized that his fasting was not going to assist the wretches of Judaea one bit.

Jewish masons worked from dawn to sundown to engrave hundreds of thanksgiving and laudatory plaques to go on the walls of synagogues to mark the new emperor.

Greek sculptors and painters worked from dawn to sundown carving, casting, and painting Caligulas for several thousand shrines.

The Greeks made out better, as the Jewish engravers who were lining their pockets would moan that more was paid for a statue or a picture than for a plaque, while the Greek craftsmen, if they couldn't find buyers for all of their statues and pictures, could simply throw out whatever was left on their hands and still complain that the Jews had done better yet again.

Uri first encountered a figural representation of the new emperor, one-and-a-half times life sized, at the Serapeion. It portrayed a young, handsome, tall, lean man, with a meditatively sorrowful look on an attractive, girlish face—in fact a statue of Apollos. They also put up a statue of Caligula in the Sebasteion, with harder features, because that one had been carved as a statue of Zeus. Uri could, nevertheless, see a resemblance, from which he concluded that an authentic likeness of Caligula must have been executed, maybe more then one, and sent around the empire.

At least this is one way to see my ruler, he pondered, because there is no chance I'll ever meet the emperor in person.

Philo composed an exquisite letter of salutation to the new emperor on behalf of all the Jews of Alexandria, polishing up a rough draft by Uri, and took it over the prefect at his palace with a request that a Jewish delegation be allowed to sail for Rome to convey the message in person. Flaccus accepted the letter with thanks, but he did not consent to the departure of a Jewish delegation. The sea, he claimed was too stormy. But he would relay the greetings to Rome with the first state express post.

The Jews did not understand why they were not allowed to send a delegation when the Greeks had already sent several.

But, Philo reported to the family, Flaccus had seemed despondent, his expression hollow-eyed; most likely he'd bee suffering many a sleepless night nowadays. There was just a hint of malicious joy in Philo's voice, Uri was astounded to note; Tija said he had his money on Flaccus, "our Aulus," being sacked as soon as the endless round of celebrations ceased and the emperor got around to attending to imperial business in Rome. Flaccus, Tija went on, was well aware of this, for in the final analysis he had been on friendly, even paternal, relations with Gemellus, at least as far as that was possible from a distance, and Caligula was hardly going to forgive him for that. The alabarch shook his head: Macro had made Caligula the absolute ruler, and Flaccus was one of Macro's men so Macro would not let him be replaced. All the same, he must be suffering from sleepless nights, said Philo sardonically. Marcus held his peace, and when his father asked him for his opinion, he shuddered.

"I would not like to live in an Alexandria that had no prefect," he said.

"Flaccus is the prefect for the time being," the alabarch declared. "Rome never had a prefect who was cleverer, more clear-sighted, or cannier than him."

At this Philo merely nodded, then he noted quietly, almost to himself, that Flaccus had been one of the people who had provoked Tiberius to wrath against Agrippina, Germanicus's widow, alleging that the reason Agrippina did not eat at the emperor's banquets was because she was fearful of being poisoned, and anyone who thought that way was capable of being a poisoner herself. That was why Tiberius had started to hate Agrippina, and in the end, of course, he had banished her and had her killed.

"But Flaccus put the centurions in Egypt on their toes," exclaimed the alabarch.

Philo nodded.

"He has the two cohorts eating out of the palm of his hand!" the alabarch continued. "All the judges are under his thumb! He has them all under his control! He has banned Greek shrine fraternities, or placed them under his personal supervision... All within six months! For five years now there has not been one protest, not one riot, not one disturbance of public order in Alexandria! Macro is well aware of that, and he will be able to say so to Caligula if it ever comes to that."

This information surprised Uri, but Tija corroborated it: Alexandria had not always been the tranquil, peaceable city that Uri knew.

Under earlier, weaker-handed prefects street skirmishes, armed robberies, murders, and burglaries had been the order of the day, the greater part of those crimes committed by soldiers of the cohorts, in league with robber gangs funded by wealthy Greeks, because the centurions had systematically skimmed off their weekly pay, and even the rank and file had to live off something. The very first prefect, Arius, was unable to cope with the troops, which is why he retired early to Rome under Maecenas's protection, and that was why Augustus then sent Magius Maximus (who erected the obelisk in the Forum Augusti) back for another spell as prefect, and things remained much the same through the tenure of the prefect prior to Flaccus, the Egyptian-born Hiberus, who had died seven years ago, not entirely by chance soon after Sejanus's fall. Throughout, soldiers had been on the loose, roaming the streets and joining the Greek gangs, all the while making use of weaponry bought by the state, the centurions even paid for the overtime they devoted to robbery, taking a cut as receivers of stolen goods. It even went so far as mercenaries selling their state-owned arms to the riffraff, simply reporting them as stolen once they got back to camp; ordinarily a soldier could normally expect to be demoted, even executed, for such a thing, but instead they were given new weapons from the stores, if they paid, so they paid, and who to but the centurions again? Army accountants hid the losses—again in exchange for a tidy payoff. The whole scam was a neat, nicely rounded system, and it's said that many cohorts and legions in Germania or Gallia go about it in exactly the same way even today.

Uri commented that this was also the case in Judaea. Tija stopped short but then picked up: Flaccus had quickly seen through the game, having quite probably been briefed beforehand in Rome. He cut the number of days of leave that could be granted, and ordered that any weapons in civilian hands be collected, with all articles brought to the harbor to be cataloged and stored in a special warehouse. The investigation went on for more than six months, with many houses searched and several hundred civilians, a dozen soldiers, three book-keepers, and two centurions executed, and ultimately order was restored.

As far as the judges were concerned, it is no surprise that they would favor whoever paid most. In principle, the prefect was the chief justice of the whole of Egypt, exercising the emperor's personal judicial right on his behalf, but before Flaccus came along those functions were not discharged, whether out of laziness or corruption. As soon as he was appointed, Flaccus went around all the koinons, paying particular attention to the judges' guild. He summoned all the judges from all over Egypt and announced that any of them caught engaging in bribery would be executed. The judges ardently nodded their approval, then returned home and had a good laugh. Flaccus followed up by having a few judges of them crucified at random (though not, of course, without any grounds), and the others soon knuckled under. During the first two years of his prefecture, Flaccus made a habit of dropping in unannounced on judicial proceedings and sitting through them to the end without uttering a word. That was enough to set the judges quaking, and they did so to the present day. He achieved all that in Alexandria even without having next to him the ten legal advisers whom Rome usually sends to assist every prefect!

"But that doesn't stop a court recorder from falsifying a judges verdict," said Uri.

"Certainly, Lampo and a few other characters do that," Tija acknowledged, "but the judges are still scared. You can't set up a little Flaccus everywhere; you are never going to have total legal security in Egypt, but then that is also true of Rome when the emperor sticks a paw in... In my view Egypt has never had a prefect who was as well suited for the job as him, nor will there ever be another. Regardless of that, of course, the emperor can replace Flaccus whenever he chooses by hanging some charge of high treason around his neck that even you wouldn't dream up in your worst nightmare. I can quite understand Flaccus having sleepless nights: he dare not sleep for fear of being plagued by such nightmares."

Uri mused. Flaccus was a friend and schoolmate of Augustus's grandsons. Tiberius had begun his own reign by having Augustus's last surviving grandson, Postumus, murdered. Our Aulus cannot ever have considered himself safe. There was no way of knowing how he had done it, but he had wormed his way into Tiberius's graces, even his most intimate circle, which is how he happened to have been there on Capri when the last prefect died, to be nominated by the emperor as Hiberus's successor. Flaccus was no fool.

In the middle of May they learned that Antonia had died on the first day of the month.

She had survived Tiberius by six weeks.

Antonia did not kill herself, it was said; her vital force had simply given out and she followed Tiberius into death, as surely as if she had been his wife. Antonia's birthday, January 31, had been a holiday throughout the empire, including Alexandria, with the Greeks offering sacrifices, and now the day on which she died was proclaimed an official day of mourning. Both had been made state holidays: her birthday would still be celebrated next year, and on

May 1 shops and markets across the empire would be closed to commemorate her, though in her life no statue had ever been erected to her, few even knew her, as for nineteen years she had remained in the background, spinning a web of Roman and Egyptian political threads (she may well have had a role in Sejanus's fall) like a melancholy, wise Fate. Unquestionably, it was fitting to mourn the present emperor's grandmother across the empire.

The death affected the alabarch's family profoundly.

"An era has passed," said the alabarch gloomily. "An era has passed with her death."

Philo said nothing; Tija just shook his head; Marcus, as usual, held his peace. The death was a big blow for the alabarch personally; Antonia's properties in Egypt would revert to the emperor, who was his grandmother's heir personally as well as by virtue of being the Princeps, so that a large chunk of his income, coming as it did from management of the estates, would be lost.

Uri slowly began to catch on: Philo and the others suspected that Antonia might not have simply have died of grief or out of duty in the wake of Tiberius's passing; there had to have been some other factor. Antonia had never been ill a single day, or at least no news of that kind had ever been received via the regular weekly courier service by which Alabarch Alexander had maintained with Antonia. Messengers sped regularly to and fro between Roman senators and wealthy Greeks, the Greek students at the Gymnasium had told him, carrying all manner of nostrums. Not that the old decoctions had been forgotten—authors of popular books of medicine everywhere made sure of that—but whenever, say, an ointment of some kind to banish all boils would become all the rage in Rome, or some herbal remedy that cured all internal maladies would become all the rage in Alexandria, or laserpitium would become all the rage someplace else, it would make its way, inevitably, across the empire.

Antonia's couriers had never been known to carry medicines.

Antonia was not yet seventy, and as Celsus had recorded, people who had reached that age could still have long lives ahead of them. A person of sixty might easily live into their eighties or nineties because that was the kind of stuff they were made of. Had Antonia perchance quarreled with her grandson? Or had Caligula held her responsible for being instrumental in the murder of her own son—his father? Or had she perhaps killed herself after all?

Flaccus, it was reported, had gone into a depression, neglecting his duties, seeing nobody for days on end; even his morning salutations had been canceled.

Previously, Greek and Jewish adherents had hurried over to Flaccus's place in large numbers every morning, and the prefect had invariably received them freshly bathed, in a freshly laundered toga, physically and psychologically fit, mentally prepared. Flaccus would begin attending to business early in the morning, almost at daybreak, involving participants at the salutation to a considerable extent, and he would finish with them by noon, his guests eating their fill, cramming their sportulas full as in Rome, and going back home contentedly for an afternoon snooze. Flaccus, on the other hand, would retire for a mere hour before spending the afternoon driving around the city or galloping off to a parade of the troops in Nicopolis, thirty miles to the east of the city wall, where one of the two legions, the XXII Deotariana, his favorite, was stationed (the other, the III Cyrenaica, was encamped at Marea to the west, south of the lake and some eight miles from the city walls so that soldiers rousting about on leave should not threaten Alexandria's peace too greatly). Nicopolis had been built as a picturesque harbor; Uri had once spent two days there drinking with one of his Greek friends, Timothy, a native. It was at Nicopolis that Augustus had defeated Mark Antony's troops, with Cleopatra being captured and Mark Antony committing suicide—Timothy had pointed out the house. Augustus had founded the town as a memorial to that victory at Actium, as the name indicates, strewing temples all over it, that of Apollos being particularly splendid, with sacred games held there every four years, entrance and food being free and sleeping outdoors a possibility; the event was due to be held that very summer.

Now, it was rumored, Flaccus had ordered that the pavilion in front of the palace in which he resided should have curtains drawn, and he would not emerge the whole day long. He was still mourning Tiberius, some assumed. No, not mourning Tiberius but himself, concluded others.

Something was rotten in Alexandria.

The city had certainly become more malodorous since the news of Tiberius's death: the slaves had ceased cleaning the canals, and rubbish was either not being taken away by the contractors, or if it was, the collection happened only intermittently. People simply threw their rubbish into the water rather than setting out big bags of brown papyrus before the houses for a removal. The removers were no longer removing because it had been the prefect's job to renew their contracts on a half-yearly basis but now he was not willing to see even them to sign the documents. The half-year term had not yet finished, that was true, there were still a few weeks to go, but in the absence of renewed contracts the rubbish removers were working more slowly, if at all, just to let everyone know what an important role they played.

It was not a good thing if rubbish was tossed haphazardly into the canals, because the water, none too clean before, had now become so filthy a person would get colic from drinking it. Yet, as no wells had been bored, the canals supplied Alexandria's drinking water, feeding the aqueducts that served the entire population. Even when the canals had been cleaner it had been necessary to boil the water, and by the end of his first weekend here any foreigner would be certain to suffer from a severe case of the trots; Uri had escaped that, though he himself did not understand why: perhaps his body had become habituated to Roman water, which was most likely about the same quality of that in Alexandria. He was accustomed to picking out dirt and debris by hand, as Rome's municipal administration had denied the inhabitants of Far Side access to the better aqueducts—the difference being that the Jews of Far Side never drank from the Tiber, whereas the Alexandrian populace were dependent on water from the canals.

There were three main canals leading to the Eastern Harbor: the Steganos, the Poseidos, and the Tauros, and two of them, the Steganos and the Tauros were already so chock-full of debris as to be virtually unnavigable, the sailors cursing angrily as their oars did little more than stir the muck around and they made almost no progress, the prows and sides of their craft scratched by all manner of trash, which could lead to great damage. And the beggars who lived off of the rubbish dumps found their very livelihood was under threat—instead of having their pick of the relatively intact goods that usually made their way to the dump (which could be cleaned up and sold at the markets in the suburbs) there was no saving anything tossed into the canals. Any city which does not let its people tidy up is rotten to the core, and it will be stricken with pestilence.

The Poseidos canal, which flowed into the city center, was somewhat cleaner, mostly owing to the fact that for most of its course it ran beside public buildings like the Gymnasium, where less shitting was done and generally less rubbish was produced.

Flaccus had a personal physician, an important individual to whose responsibility the city's hygiene had been delegated, but these days he also could not find the time to attend to it. His name was Strabo (he was supposedly an illegitimate child of the famous geographer, who had left the city a good forty or fifty years before, having spent five or six years in Alexandria, which he had grown very fond of). The physician was an elderly man, so while it wasn't all that likely that he was the geographer's illegitimate child (he had probably adopted the name while roaming around the Greek islands), obviously he was a charlatan, albeit a sage and influential man. Flaccus listened to what he said as he was, not least, a seer, having foreseen, for example, Sejanus's fall from grace. Around that time the wonder doctor had been living in Rome, and that was where Flaccus's father, the art-collecting equestrian, had gotten to know him. It is also quite possible that Strabo stayed on as a healer and soothsayer with the prefect to act a spy for the recently deceased emperor, and Philo, among others, was of the opinion that this fact may well have been revealed in recent days. A change of emperor meant that a lot of secret documents would be brought to light, as those who had been pushed into the background competed for the new emperor's favors. Thus there was every prospect of a rash of unexpected, unexplained suicides. That was how it had been when Augustus died, and that, apparently, was how it would be now that Tiberius had gone.

Uri looked on in amazement: a small, gaunt, silver-haired mannequin, light as a feather. Could he perchance be floating two spans above the ground?

Strabo took the view—this was now the alabarch speaking—that Flaccus's melancholy was only transient, for which he could only prescribe recreation, recreation, and yet more recreation, if he were able, but he was not able to because he could not even get to him. Even the sentries at his palace were loath to let him in, despite that fact they had shown him all humility and respect. Strabo did not reside in the palace but in a fine house on the border of Delta, between the palace and the Jewish quarter, so as to be handy whenever the prefect dispatched a courier for him. In recent times threatening messages had been scrawled and feces daubed on the walls of his house. Alabarch Alexander had offered to let Strabo stay with him until Flaccus came to his senses, but the physician dared not accept the offer in case the prefect took offense if he found out that he had moved farther away.

"The old guy is pretty desperate," said Alexander. "In his place, I would clear out of here, the farther the better."

It occurred to Uri that perhaps one reason why Strabo was still sticking around in the city was so as to call in the various sums of money that he had put out on loan at interest.

Interesting though these matters were, the city's life was not fundamentally altered any more than was Uri's: he studied diligently, practiced a lot on the Gymnasium's grounds, he put on more muscle, his sprint times improved, his lungs expanded; he still did work as a copyist when time allowed, and he lived a merry life. He had now officially entered the age of majority, and when winter came to an end, having turned twenty he was initiated into the joys of paying the tax, the two drachmas (or half a shekel) a year that all grown Jewish men had to pay each year to the Temple in Jerusalem. Observing the transition was a custom among the Jews of Alexandria, and did not exist in Rome, where only the money counted. Admittedly, Uri's ceremony did not take place in the Basilica (that would have been a bit excessive for someone who was not a member of the alabarch's family, merely a newcomer), but in one of the houses of prayer in Beta district. Philo and Tija were present from the alabarch's family, along with several Greek fellow students, who stood throughout without a word of protest: it was not prohibited for Greeks to enter a synagogue in Alexandria, nor indeed could the Jews have placed any ban on it seeing that they were willing to countenance mixed marriages, provided the bride converted. On very rare occasions a groom might convert, but only Greeks who were very much in love or extraordinarily greedy for money were willing to put up with the likely pains of circumcision. Uri also invited Isidoros to his initiation as a taxpayer, but the gymnasiarch did not attend, nor did he excuse himself afterward.

"Good job!" Tija exploded when he learned of that invitation after the event, before adding: "And watch out that my father does not take you for a Greek spy!"

Uri turned furiously on him:

"But it's all right if he takes me to be a spy for Agrippa?"

"Agrippa is just a tool, a fantasy," jeered Tija, "whereas the Greeks are real-life threats!"

The initiation ceremony was held a good nine months after Uri's birthday, largely because he had completely forgotten about it. He had supposed that people only observed anniversaries when things were going badly, and since Jews were accustomed to things going badly, they were insistent in sticking to them. On this occasion he wrote a letter to his father and dispatched it to Rome with a courier of Philo's, who wanted to send several books as a solace to Silanus, the father-in-law of Caligula, in memory of Julia Claudilla (Silanus's daughter and Caligula's wife), who had died during childbirth, along with the baby. Silanus confirmed the receipt of the books, and it was hoped that he had forwarded Uri's letter to Joseph.

On March 16 of the year of Emperor Tiberius's death, the delegation took the sacrificial money to Jerusalem, along with those first two drachmas from Uri. He had earned the money from copying work, and he was proud to have become a member of the mighty community of Jewish males that encompassed half the world. Two years had passed—two years—since he himself had taken the modest holy money of Rome's Jews to Jerusalem. How much he had longed then to meet with the delegates from Alexandria in Caesarea, and how much it had hurt him to find out that his fellow delegates had excluded him.

Now it was the Alexandrian delegation going to Jerusalem, and like every year they carried not just money but also copies of the records of births, marriages, and deaths so that they might be deposited in the safest place. Uri saw them now not so much as powerful men, but as the uninspiring appointees of the hustling, bustling, self-important craft guilds, the Kahals, who had no influence whatsoever. Andron was not a craftsman, of course, but a merchant, and he ran the Jewish archive in Alexandria, but the huge pile of money that was carried by the Alexandrian delegation now seemed like next to nothing in Uri's eyes, accustomed now to the fact that in the alabarch's company one heard talk of talents, not denarii and drachmas.

It occurred to him that he now looked down his nose at those delegates.

Nonetheless, the winter months while Agrippa was in jail had served as a valuable lesson: as the alabarch's esteem declined in Jewish circles, so too did his own in the alabarch's family. Tija made his barbed comment while Agrippa was still in captivity. They can't wait to get rid of me, had been the galling thought on Uri's mind at the time: my fate is tied to that of Agrippa, the "tool." If he falls, so do I. That was a big lesson: fortune is a fickle beast, one misunderstanding is replaced by another, and I would have to go back to Rome if they kicked me out of here.

It is not a healthy development to look down at those delegates.

He had a hunch that his feasting in Alexandria was not going to last much longer, so he tried to enjoy it while he could.

In the Gymnasium there was no hint of tension, or of Lampo's jockeying for Isidoros's post: the teachers taught, fulminating over and over again about whatever was bugging them, with the students soaking up whatever they needed to. Uri preferred the four and a half days that he spent at the Gymnasium to the weekends at the alabarch's palace. He finished the year in early June with distinction. Some of the examinations, such as those in rhetoric and mathematics, were held in public. Uri excelled in rhetoric, while in mathematics, he was lucky, drew theorems he was to tackle, and was able to hold his own. He regretted only that no one from the alabarch's family was present, not even Tija, who had something else on that day.

The performance of the Greek students were celebrated by their families and friends on the grounds of the Gymnasium. Uri sat through all of Apollonos Gamma's exams and was amazed: Gamma reeled off a magnificent oration and even proved capable of turning the geometry of sectors into tropes of rhetorical brilliance. That amazement was shared by Apollonos Gamma's parents and siblings, who had made the trip from Memphis for the occasion. They were simple folk, and they barely understood a word of what their son and brother was saying. They invited Uri to visit them that summer in Memphis: they would show him the pyramids and promised as well to show him the statue of Cornelius Gallus, a Roman poet, orator, and politician who was made prefect of Egypt and had erected a large number of similar statues all around Egypt, all of which had since been demolished except this one. He had even had his glorious achievements inscribed on one of the pyramids; those inscriptions had not been obliterated as yet. He was informed on by his friend Largus, after which Augustus banished him from the empire and the Senate stripped him of his fortune, so in his grief Gallus took his own life. Anyway, it was a statue of this Gallus which was still standing in Memphis.

Uri thanked them kindly for the invitation. He was very sorry that Apollonos Gamma, or Apollos as his parents called him, was not going to be in Alexandria that summer because Uri knew that he would certainly not be able to get to Memphis.

As Uri watched Sotades's exam, crossing his fingers all the while, Isidoros sat down on the grass beside him. Uri respectfully shifted farther away.

"There's no need," said Isidoros.

"But sir!"

Isidoros sat there with his head bowed, cold sweat streaming off him, and said nothing. Uri was unable to pay attention to the answer Sotades was giving.

"The whole thing is cursed," Isidoros finally said.

Uri shuddered.

"Weep for me, my boy, when I'm dead and gone," Isidoros said, clambering to his feet and leaving.

Uri sat numb. He looked for the departing figure of the gymnasiarch but all he could see among the crowd were uncertain outlines. It came to him that he had no idea if Isidoros had a family: he had seen him purely as an intellectual being, albeit his being a man.

The examinations were still in progress when people were again plunged into mourning. Emperor Caligula had fallen ill. Exams were suspended, public baths were closed, a ban was placed on all assemblies, in Greek shrines and Jewish houses of prayer everyone asked or pleaded with their own god or gods for the emperor's recovery; the Serapeion was inundated by worshiping Greeks. Uri went in as usual to work, but the book editors advised him unenthusiastically: maybe in the autumn.

It was a change that Uri could only deeply regret because he was finally making inroads with some of the editors. Among these outwardly gray and dreary figures were some of considerable learning, with whom it was possible to become engrossed in profound discussions connected with the particular problems of his copying work, and maybe they even got to like him. They never disturbed one another as they calmly fiddled around during the prolonged copying sessions. He was fond of the quiet, dry, cool ground floor; the tall windows gave no view outside, the external world existed only in a kind of constant dream. It was a peaceful nook where he worked for money, that is true, but he was also free to vanish into it and daydream at his leisure. Time and peace were necessary to acquire new knowledge through rewriting the knowledge of the ancients, through the spirit that resided in those old texts, delighted to be awoken. Uri would ponder, while he was copying, what kinds of previously unread, unimaginable ideas might form in his brain that day, and that pleased him. The thoughts were like the tiny fish that had scudding around him as he'd waded into the sea up to his knees when they had arrived at Sicily. He did not always manage to catch them; most slipped out of his grasp and vanished without a trace. But sometimes in the morning, when he was half-awake, they would swim back past, and he would make a mental note of them. He found that more fish swam back while he was reading historical works than while he was copying mathematical books, and occasionally, as he mused briefly in his resting place, he had visions that brought together the present age and events long past. Once or twice he saw Alexandria, the whole of it spread out before him, along with its known past and its possible futures, and he would even scare himself, conjuring up an empty desert on the ground where Alexandria had once stood. It must be that Alexandria has not accepted me after all, Uri pondered, and I am seeking my revenge.

Flaccus was nowhere to be seen. Uri had gotten through his exams, but had yet to learn the results. The Gymnasium was deserted. The summer holiday started without the academic year coming to a formal close, though it was usually marked with a big ceremony.

Couriers came and went at the alabarch's palace; Uri knew many of them by sight, but now he noticed some new ones among them. Philo thought it best to retire to his place in the country, with Tija in tow, neither of them offering a date for their return. Uri was not invited. Marcus took part in the discussions held by his father, while Uri was left to his rooms in the alabarch's palace, suddenly all alone.

He should go to Memphis.

He was not on terms with the alabarch to ask directly for permission: that was the sort of thing he could have brought up with Philo—he could even have asked him for the money—but Philo was not there to be asked.

What is the point of staying in Alexandria?

Uri roamed the city, where life went on at the lower ebb of funereal anxiety: the baths were closed, so the girls were unable to pursue their craft at the customary places (though they were said to be hanging around outside the city instead). Taverns were also closed, though the markets were functioning, patrolled by soldiers, on the lookout for any crowd that might gather so they could stroll over and disperse it. No one defied them, but the hatred was plain to see on all sides. At this time of semi-mourning for the ailing emperor, Uri preferred simply to sit around the harbor, his feet dangling above the water; as the lading onto and off of passing ships went on, albeit half-heartedly, because there was no pleasure to be had going ashore in Alexandria.

On Friday evening Uri went to the Basilica, where Sabbath services went ahead as normal; he was allowed to sit next to Alexander and Marcus as before, and said "Amen" along with the congregation at the bidding of the pale red kerchief, but he felt no sense of fellowship. The stargazers no longer thronged around him, though they too were seated as usual on the bench allocated to their profession.

Have I suddenly become a loser—and why?

It dawned on him that in the year and change since his arrival he had not made a single Jewish friend, not even a potential business contact.

Had he just frittered his time away? What would his father say?

He ought to go back home to Rome.

Back, after more than two years' wandering, to his wretched cubbyhole, that dank and dark lair?

There was no way he could go back home.

But all the same, there was no way he could stay.

It would be nice to go to a tavern with Sotades, Hedylos, and the rest to fool around and crack jokes, quote the ancient poets, and improvise parodies, but for some reason that no longer seemed possible. Sotades was happy when the exams were over; he had embraced Uri, and then his Greek admirers, who had likewise sat through all his appearances, after which they had gone down to the harbor to get stinking drunk. That, of course, was when the taverns had still been open, but the moment they closed Sotades had disappeared, gone back home to the country. The Greek students who were resident in Alexandria obviously still looked one another up, but no one came looking for him. But then what business would they have going to the palace of a Jewish chief excise man? It was a pity that the Gymnasium's dormitories were closed over the summer.

During that somber season, every now and again, Uri would climb to the top of the Paneion, the hill with corkscrew paths that stood in the middle of the Gymnasium's grounds, where he had been so fond of reading. Now that he had no scroll or book with him he just stared, seeing very little with his bad eyes. He methodically went around all the parts of the city that he had not yet visited, feeling the walls of the buildings, sniffing around: who could say when he would have to leave, or whether he would ever return. He thought of himself as a traveler without any assigned duties. He mused about that. It occurred to him how free he was. Everyone he knew was proceeding from A to B with some particular goal in mind, all the Greek students, the Jewish ones too, Apollos and Tija. Apollos wanted rights of citizenship as an Alexandrian Greek because his parents were just Jews in Memphis, whereas Tija, who was already a Greek citizen, wanted to set up a business that made military catapults to become even richer than Marcus, who stood to inherit two-thirds of their father's wealth. Everybody had a goal, was pushed or driven by something.

What on Earth is driving me? What is this unholy freedom?

He was gripped by an odd sensation: it was as if this miraculous Alexandria, this prodigious, phenomenal city were somehow unreal, as if the worms of evanescence were diligently at work destroying its imperishable buildings, made as they were of granite and marble, as if the parasites of Time, those invisible deathwatch beetles which feed on stone, had already done their damage, all that was needed was a moderately stiff northerly breeze from the harbor and the whole lot would come crashing down. What would be left, he wondered? Perhaps one or two slim books and pallid scrolls, not in the Serapeion—that sturdy, solid fortress would be blown away with the rest—but in a few private collections about which he had no knowledge.

It was about time he started to think about his own life.

What should he turn his hand to? What should he do to earn a crust of bread, and where?

That mood did not pass after a day or so: his low spirits proved long lasting. He thought of Flaccus, the prefect; he must be feeling something like this nowadays too.

Come to think of it, I might just as well be a prefect somewhere. A strategos in Jerusalem with Tija, serving as his chief of staff in the Roman prefecture. He roared with laughter. He was seated on the top of the Paneion, Greeks lightheartedly chatting all around and among them travelers from distant lands, who were overjoyed to be here and in their delight laughed back at him.

No human occupation held any attraction for him now. How clear he had been when he arrived in Alexandria that he wanted to train as a goldsmith or diamond cutter.

Had he been wasting his time? He had read so many scrolls. Historical works, literature, commentaries on Homer, the poetic theories of amateurish bunglers, dead science. He had done brilliantly on his exams. If his knowledge of geometry had been better, if he had a better grasp of the conical segments, he could find employment as a land surveyor. That was good job, at least in Egypt it was. But then again, in Rome as a Jew?

You'll find no bigger impostor than me in the land of the living! Such a nonsensical gaffe! I was almost executed in Jerusalem as a supposed spy of Agrippa's, whereas here I was pampered and sucked up to as long as that tool, that despicable Agrippa, that quarter-Jewish political vermin whom I never saw in my life, remained alive and heir presumptive of the Great Jewish Kingdom.

THE EMPEROR WAS RESTORED TO HEALTH, THANKS BE TO THE ETERNAL One, to Jupiter, to Zeus, to Serapis, or whoever. The baths reopened, taverns swung their entrances wide open as speedily as the tarts did their legs. Life came roaring back explosively, as after an overlong winter, and rowdy gangs of troopers, among them soldiers of the two legions stationed in Egypt, terrorized the whole city; Flaccus finally dragged himself out of his palace; he was seen carousing here, getting plastered there. No one who braved the streets was safe.

The Greeks mumbled their prayers of thanks in their shrines and the Jews in their synagogues, and there was nothing left of Alexandria. Antonia's death did not just mark the end of an era, but also the end of the most wonderful city that was ever built. Uri could see this, but he kept it to himself. Not that anyone was curious, but even if asked for his opinion, he would not have let on.

He was not in mourning for the Alexandria which had once been, but for the city as he had imagined it on his arrival. In any case, he had not been able to witness the golden age, three centuries before, when poetry and life in Alexandria had been the genuine article, he had only vague notions of what it might have been like.

His illusions had been shattered; his hopes had proved misplaced.

Philo and Tija returned to the city toward the end of the summer, along with the Greek students who returned to whoop it up much as before. Uri hung out with them; he had plenty of time. He read nothing and out of sheer boredom would have gone anywhere, but the wonder had ended. He smiled and nodded as he listened to Sotades, Hedylos, and the others recount their summer adventures, and took no offense at their neglecting to ask him about his own adventures.

Philo acted as if nothing had happened. He told Uri—his favorite mute interlocutor—where he stood with his latest work, which he had spent the summer writing. Uri nodded, occasionally interjecting with a wise comment or suggesting a modification, which Philo would acknowledge, here irately, there with gratitude, just as he had done before, but the matter was no longer genuine: on Uri's part the devoted affection had gone, and he felt that the same was true on Philo's part. Philo was continuing to work on reconciling Greek and Jewish theology, and in this particular work he was assuring his hoped-for readers, the Greeks, that the Messiah would be coming for them too, sooner rather than later.

This is just what it is like, Uri realized, when a marriage goes wrong but neither party wishes to face up to it, delaying for a few months until the inevitable bill of divorce is issued. He also realized that he would be given a bill of divorce as a wife, and that Philo would be issuing it as the husband. A startling thought, but true: he had been used as if he were a young, attractive interlocutress by Philo, the great philosopher, who was seemingly without any sexual allure at all, and he, Uri, had ended up cast in the role of the boring wife, soon to be cast away. As yet a new wife had not appeared in the wings, but one would be before too long, and he would have to play a new part.

Let's see, then, what that new role will be, he concluded obstinately, and continued to converse with Philo, when the latter was so inclined, as if nothing had changed.

In place of Isidoros, a new gymnasiarch was awaiting them at the start of the new academic year—not Lampo, thanks be to the Eternal One, but an eager beaver with angrily flashing eyes who went by the name of Abdaraxus. Tija told him that two centuries ago there had been an engineer of that name in Alexandria who had proven to be an outstanding artificer of military engines, whereas this Abdaraxus occupied himself with researches into Homer, which everybody else found boring. Uri did not inquire after what had happened to Isidoros: he was sure that wherever the old gymnasiarch might be, he had more in common with him than with his fellow students.

I am drifting and drifting, but the Eternal One must have some sort of goal in mind.

He was amazed that this had come to mind. Jews in Alexandria did not live piously, though to some extent they could be said to observe prescriptions of the faith. One could not say even that much about Greek religiosity, just point to widely accepted customs and ceremonies.

He had already experienced a similar atmosphere in that Judaean village whose name, he was surprised to note, he had forgotten. Maybe one day he would similarly forget the name of Alexandria.

Get away from here? But to where? To Rome, back home? What kind of home was that? All the same...

Not just because in the taverns loud-mouthed drunks shouted out that an attempt had been made to choke Emperor Caligula with some Jewish concoctions, but the Roman Jewish pigs had not been able to manage it. Not just because Uri's Greek companions let mindless caterwauling like that go on without offering so much as a word of protest. Uri sensed that some slippery, clammy, disgusting scent was wafting around him in the late summer sunshine. But it could only be emanating from within, he reassured himself, if it was accompanying him everywhere.

The excitements here had become alien.

But with the advent of autumn arrived new excitements. Not much was heard of Agrippa, though plenty was heard regarding the emperor's appointment of Macro, Praetorian commander, as prefect of Egypt and Alexandria. If that news had reached Alexandria the source could only have been the Senate. The alabarch nervously discussed this new piece of information with members of his family and councilors. The number of Jewish councilors around Alabarch Alexander multiplied: a year ago Greek notables were far more prominent among those flocking to his receptions, the prefect at their head. But now Flaccus had again retreated to his palace, it was said. He was a fallen man and he would do better to take refuge somewhere, or even to put an end to his own life.

Was the appointment of Macro good for Alexandria or not? Was it a fall for Macro or not? Had the emperor made the decision because he wanted to be sure he was given an important place or because he wanted to get rid of him? If the latter were the case, then Alexandria had been taken down a peg or two, which was good for neither the local Greeks or the Jews. If the object were to set Macro up as a man of importance, then he would not be left long in this position, and the definitive prefect would only come once he'd moved on. In the meantime an interregnum held sway, and an interregnum was dangerous, Philo averred.

Still, Alabarch Alexander felt optimism was warranted. Macro will be excellent for us because he is a widely experienced statesman of great attainments, and a prefect with a strong grip would be a welcome replacement for Flaccus now that the latter had turned into a weakling. Silanus, Caligula's father-in-law and the main adviser, next to Macro, at the emperor's side, had written that governing was a great burden to a vacillating soul like Caligula (perhaps that was the cause of his recent breakdown), and had it not been for Silanus and Macro standing by him throughout, as far as the physicians were concerned he might well have croaked. Following his recovery, the emperor was obviously going to depend on his advisers even more, so if Macro had been given Egypt, then maybe Silanus would be the next commander of the Praetorian Guard.

Tija did not think that was likely: Silanus was too elderly. Besides, he was only the emperor's former father-in-law, and if the emperor were to wed again, and why not, room would have to be made in the hierarchy for the new father-in-law. Sooner or later, Silanus would become redundant, and if he was on such good terms with Macro as he had indicated in coded language in his letter to the alabarch, then Macro's position could not be all that secure either. Macro's appointment as prefect, it must be acknowledged, was a demotion, Tija added mockingly. That means we, along with him, have slipped down a notch or two.

Marcus, seeing that this line of argument did not go down well with their father, took his side: Caligula wanted to secure his hinterland, so he had sent his most reliable man to Egypt. No doubt he was preparing for a military expedition to follow in his father's glorious footsteps by provoking a local war with the Germani in the hope of pulling off a stupendous victory, and meanwhile he did not want disputes to arise elsewhere. Egypt was the most important of Rome's provinces, Caligula knew that. Macro might even have volunteered for the post, having gotten tired of the constant wrangling in Rome under Tiberius; after all, in practice he had been master in Rome ever since Tiberius had gotten Sejanus out of the way. Up till now Caligula had done what Macro wanted, and presumably that was still the case.

Marcus smiled, the Alabarch and Tija laughed, while Philo turned away so that the others would not see the smile of his face; the Jewish leaders also laughed, but Uri did not pay much attention to the expressions on their faces as they were of no interest. It was after the Kahal leaders, the bosses of the guilds, had departed and the alabarch and Philo had turned in that Marcus let Uri in on a secret: they had Caligula by the balls, with Silanus having given his daughter's hand in marriage, and Macro having forced his wife, Ennia on the emperor about two years ago, and even today Macro's wife was Caligula's lover. The father-in-law and the cuckold could tug Caligula whichever way they wanted, and in that way it was they who had control of the empire.

Uri thought of the endless hills and dales that he had walked through, and the endless seas he had sailed across, and he found it hard to believe that the wills of two such degenerates could prevail over such a huge expanse. Nor even the will of the emperor, whose new coins had already reached Alexandria: the emperor portrayed in profile, a crown on his head from which emanated rays as from a Sun. Isis and Serapis were usually depicted this way on Egyptian money. He had a feeling that if he had coins like that minted, then Caligula must want something from Egypt, though he was not coming out with what it might be, as he never let his own voice be heard in political discussion.

Flaccus was reportedly drinking with his soldiers, being carted back senseless every morning from the houses of wealthy Greeks, but there was no sign of Macro;s arrival, though it was high time he relieved that demented Flaccus, "our Aulus."

Uri reluctantly took part in the poetry competition, as Tija had of late gotten out of the habit of visiting taverns and Apollos failed to appear every now and then. Though Lysias continued to serve him with good humor, Uri nevertheless had the feeling that the cordiality was forced. Sotades would choke back the odd sentence if he noticed that Uri was present. It was not that he had ever said anything offensive about Jews, but lately his sentences struck Uri's keen ear as being unusually clipped. Uri abandoned going out for drinks and focused instead on studying and physical training. He did not meet the new gymnasiarch, merely saw him from a distance. On one occasion he saw Abdaraxus strolling with a tall, well-built man in the Square Stoa; he happened to be sauntering toward the dormitory with Apollos after a sprint when he spotted the two men, and Apollos halted.

"That crook is Dionysius," he said. "He's an evil rabble-rouser, always winding up the crowds against us down in the harbor."

"Why, what sort of things does he say?"

"That we pollute the canals with the plague, and that's why the water stinks so badly," said Apollos. "And anyone who touches a Jew will contract trachoma within the fortnight."

"Who believes that?"

"Well you might ask," Apollos admitted. "People still just laugh it off, but there must be some who see fit to get a hired goon to spout that kind of stuff."

"But who? Apion?"

"I think it's the people who pick up the tab for Apion."

Apion was a historian who had completed the Gymnasium at Alexandria and subsequently moved to Rome; in his most recent works he had recycled Manetho's fables, according to which Moses was expelled from Egypt at the head of a horde of lepers.

Uri shook his head.

"Why spend money on that?" he queried. "Who profits from that? Hardly the masses: they'll still be slaving away at humping stuff around and won't get a penny richer, however hard they applaud."

Apollos sighed.

"If even Isidoros was on their side, they must want something really badly."

"Isidoros on Apion's side?"

Uri could not imagine that a highly cultured man like Isidoros could join forces with such garbage however much he might despise Jews, and in any case the old gymnasiarch did not despise all Jews: he didn't despise Apollos, and he's quite fond of me.

Apollos lowered his voice to say that apparently Isidoros and Lampo had a meeting with Flaccus in the Serapeion, and in secret they had handed over five gold talents.

Five gold talents! That was 120,000 drachmas, or two years' pay for the prefect!

Uri shook his head:

"Who saw that?" he asked. "Who had this information if it was all done in secret?"

Apollos nodded:

"Pure hearsay, of course," he said. "Maybe not one word of it is true, but still: that's what the gossip is. Gossip reveals a lot even when it is untrue."

"Says who?" Uri exclaimed. "There is no way that Isidoros and Flaccus would team up!"

"Unless Lampo was one of Flaccus's drinking pals, and he is that. That's not just idle gossip: plenty of people have seen them together in the Elephant. Hedylos was present on two occasions when Flaccus had a drink with Lampo! Antimachus told the same story: he saw them too!"

It was on the tip of Uri's tongue to mention that he would pump Hedylos for details when it occurred to him that he wouldn't: half a year ago Hedylos would have answered any question he asked, but now? Antimachus was a short, weedy, timid young man, who Uri had never exchanged words with, so it would look odd if he were now to start asking questions.

He shuddered. What was happening in Alexandria?

Apollos said one day to Uri:

"Come along."

There was running that day, which everyone found a bore, and only at the end of the day would there be rhetoric.

Apollos took Uri to an amphitheater.

"I've seen this before," he said, "but I'd like you too to see it and confirm that my eyes are not deceiving me."

It was the second of the three plays that was in question. The author reeled off the story of Dionysus, and when it got to the bit where Dionysus's body was cut into pieces, for which, as in every production, copious amounts of artificial blood were used and the musicians banged the drums with a deafening cacophony, Uri leaned forward, placed his hands in front of his face and peered through the slits between his fingers so he could see better. The actors who were murdering Dionysus on stage wore masks that made them look like Jews—exactly the sort of grotesque figures he'd seen scrawled on the walls of houses. The Jews hated Dionysus, the favorite god of the Alexandrian Greeks. The audience whistled shrilly in the way it did at the Circus when their favorite, the green chariot, did not win a race.

Uri looked at Apollos: Apollos's eyes had not deceived him: they were wide with fear.

"Your eyes are not deceiving you," Uri reassured him.

They did not watch the third play but took a walk in the harbor as Apollos agitatedly, almost stuttering, kept on saying how intolerable it was, it could not be ignored, this was loathsome, vile propaganda against Jews, and someone somewhere should make a speech in which an eminent person, preferably Greek rather than Jew, informed the rabble that in ancient times, when Dionysus is supposed to have lived, there were not yet any Jews anywhere in the world.

"You'll never find any person of that kind," pronounced Uri, who was likewise displeased by the phenomenon but was not as distraught as Apollos; he was frankly amused to see how much artificial blood had been used, and how maladroitly the actor who had played Dionysus had collected his severed legs and arms, taking the view that the miserable drama was a parody of itself, though he was bound to admit that the public had not seen it that way.

In the middle of the autumn Abdaraxus assembled the students and in a lengthy address warned them against getting mixed up in anything. They were standing in the broad, covered peristyle that connected the dormitories with the library, far from the crowds sauntering in the park area. The students should not be duped by the provocations of enemies; they should not let themselves be drawn into brawls because anyone caught taking an active part would be expelled; anyone caught scribbling on walls would be expelled. All of them should confine themselves to studying and keeping physically fit, nothing else. Students were prohibited from entering taverns. Students were also prohibited from going to the baths: the Gymnasium had its own baths, so they should use those. In marketplaces they were to comport themselves with dignity; they should give crowds embroiled in politics a wide berth; anyone asking for their opinion was to be fended off. Anyone on whom any kind of handbill was found would be punished. Everyone would be subject to inspection at all times.

The teaching staff stood somberly behind the gymnasiarch; they must have already gotten it in the neck. The teaching staff had in all likelihood been instructed—maybe even specifically assigned—by Abdaraxus to search through belongings and follow students as they made their way through the city, so it was no surprise that they looked none too happy.

Not that Abdaraxus made any specific threats; he was just doing whatever was necessary to protect the independence and impartiality of his institution. Uri nevertheless felt uncomfortable.

He noticed that nobody was disposed to be his wrestling partner, and nobody wished to stand as an advocate against him in mock court dialogues. It was not that anyone made any objection to him personally, just that nobody put themselves forward. The more decent-minded teachers changed the procedure: Uri, Tija, and Apollos were no longer placed first, but they were supposed to name a Greek student as their partner, though even they did not bother. None of the instructors bade them do it.

"Your Greek pals don't like us," Tija commented at the palace one Sabbath evening when the meal had come to an end.

Uri bridled:

"Who's the Greek citizen, then?" he retorted. "They're your Greek pals!"

"Yours, you mean, you Roman!" hissed Tija. "Your emperor is Caligula, they're his Greeks!"

Uri was astonished.

"What do you mean: Caligula is my emperor?"

"You've even got the same name: Gaius!"

Marcus, who was studying some documents, laughed and looked up:

"Quit that!" he said. "Caligula is the emperor of the Jews of Alexandria, not the Greeks."

Uri was now even more astonished.

Marcus nodded his head as if to say 'Let's get that clear!"

"The emperor in Rome is always the emperor for the Jews here," he declared. "You can be sure of that. That's why the Greeks are nursing such a grudge against us: they are scared, not without good reason, that the Jews will be given more concessions. That's their beef with us. Cleopatra herself loathed us Jews, yet she did nothing to the very end but seek to serve Roman interests. Local minorities always tend to take sides with whoever is the central authority. It's no doubt the same in Judaea in cities where the Greeks are in the minority: there it is they who side more strongly with the emperor in opposition to the Jews."

Uri slowly nodded. That was plain talk if anything was: Marcus must have political talent after all.

Tija was even more infuriated:

"I despise them!" he yelled. "All of them! Sneaky, shifty, foul, furtive brutes! Is that what we're supposed to stuff our money into? Their gymnasium? Let them all choke and be carried away by the plague!"

Uri had not seen Tija in a temper before: there was something truly human in his roar. He was not raging on account of the Greeks, Uri realized; it was his elder brother he hated, being the second in line.

That night, by the light of a luminous full moon, a thought crossed his mind: surely Flaccus, the deposed prefect, couldn't possibly be placing his trust in a plan to stir up the Greeks into fighting a war against Rome? It did at least offer a decidedly greater chance of staying alive than the suggested course of suicide.

War... It had been a long time since Alexandrians had lived through a war, and Uri, never. Even his father and grandfather had lived in times of peace... It would be bizarre if he, Roman citizen that he was, were to take part in a war against Rome.

He resolved that tomorrow he would go to a Jewish restaurant in Delta and put out some feelers to gauge what ordinary Jews were thinking.

He was unable to go the next day, however, because Philo engaged him in a philological discourse, and he only made the trip a week later. The place that came to mind was the very first restaurant he'd visited when he arrived, the one over toward the Basilica, where he had eaten that inexpensive barbel—he had not been back that way since. He looked around but did not find it; he wandered a couple of blocks this way and that, came back and restlessly paced around, but there could be no doubt about it: a fancy leatherware shop was operating where the restaurant used to be.

The Greeks had moved out of the Jewish quarter.

It might have been pure coincidence, but nevertheless they had moved out. He shivered.

There was going to be war.

Around the Basilica there were a lot of bistros still open, with Jews lazing idly on the sidewalk with their extensive families, their children playing around them; a balmy autumn breeze was blowing in from the sea, the edge taken off it by the chain of hills. Tranquility and peace ruled everywhere. Uri sat down on a long bench in front of an equally long table around which a lot of people were chattering away. He dipped a chunk of bread in the salt and chewed on it, gazing about. The conversation next to him was about business and family matters;

his tablemates must have been members of two or three different families. And they paid not the slightest bit of notice to him. The choice of dishes was rather limited, and Uri decided to take the flatfish. He found it a bit odd that it was boneless, as in kosher Jewish restaurants they normally only cooked fish with bones, but this was obviously considered kosher. He was also brought wine and water but there was no mixing bowl so he drank down some of the water and poured in some wine.

The flatfish was good, but it was noticeably flavored with honey, so Uri sprinkled on some salt and ate it like that. He had no idea with whom he should speak, or about what. Those around him were all strangers, as he did not recall ever seeing any of them at the Basilica. Perhaps they did not attend that and instead went to their own synagogues; but then again it was perfectly possible that they did go to the Basilica but were normally seated some distance from him.

"They'll put elephants onto us"—that phrase struck his ear.

Two men were sitting at the end of the table; the words had come from one of them, cutting through the surrounding din.

"They're expensive," said the other.

"They've already gone to Ethiopia to fetch them," the shorter figure insisted.

"Are you kidding? No way!"

"They're trained to pick up human scent trails, human blood," the short one claimed. "When they've done that they trample us down. The next thing is they'll habituate them to Jewish blood..."

A child's cries drowned out the voices, with the infant screaming as if it were being skinned alive. The mother tried to soothe it, but the infant was in the midst a temper tantrum, and eventually the father irately lost his temper too:

"What do you think this Greek gentleman is going to say if you bawl like this?"

The child swiftly fell silent; Uri could only gape in amazement.

He smiled at the infant, but that only set off a fresh wave of panic-stricken howling, prompting the mother to thrust its head into her lap while the father looked apologetically across at Uri.

"Only a tiny tot as yet," he said. "Not used to going out..."

Uri smiled.

They take me for a Greek.

He then realized that the proprietor of the bistro had also assumed he was Greek; they would not have served him boneless fish.

He left half of the fish and almost the entire jug of wine, paid and hurried off. He checked whether his stomach was going to be upset or whether he was going to vomit up the unclean food, but no: he wasn't. He then asked himself whether he wanted to be ill, or rather, was he happy that he could now eat even unclean food? Back at home his mother had frightened her children with the idea that a Jew who ate unclean food would become gravely ill, possibly even die.

Maybe flatfish wasn't so unclean after all, judging by local notions, as it was in Rome. No it couldn't be unclean; in a Jewish restaurant they would not cook unclean food even for Greeks.

On Tuesday he asked Apollos what was known about elephants.

Apollos recounted that Philopator's African elephants had lost the battle against the Indian elephants of Antiochus the Great...

"What else?"

"There's an anecdote about Aristophanes of Byzantium. He grew up in Egypt, unlike Callimachus or Eratosthenes. He was a pupil of Zenodotus, Callimachus, and of Machon, the Jew-hating comic poet, and published an edition of the Iliad based on the work of Zenodotus, the Homeric scholar and first superintendent of the Library of Alexandria, as well as Hesiod, Alcaeus of Messene, Anacreon, and Aristophanes the Comedian. His edition of Pindar was especially important, and he also published Aristotle's *Historia Animalium*... Anyway, Aristophanes of Byzantium is said to have fallen in love with a flower-selling girl who had an elephant as her lover... Maybe not a real elephant, just the nickname for a well-hung fellow. Eumetes II suspected that he wanted to move to Pergamum, which was not too much to peoples' liking at that time because of Byzantium's bitter rivalry with Pergamum, so he had Aristophanes of Byzantium locked up in prison and later strangled..."

Uri sighed. What was there that Apollos did not know? But then he had been able to bury his head in books for much longer than Uri had.

"Anything else?" he asked. "Are Jews afraid of elephants?"

"Yes, they are afraid," said Apollos, "and with good reason. Ptolemy VI Philometor and his consort, his sister Cleopatra II, charged the Jews with the defense of the realm; Onias IV and Dositheos were the two military commanders... His brother, Ptolemy Physkon, set out from Cyrenaica against Cleopatra II, was victorious, had the Jews of Alexandria stripped naked and bound, women and children too, and had them cast before elephants that were made drunk. The elephants did not trample the Jews, however, but instead turned on the king's own people. Physkon took this to be a divine portent and reprieved the Jews; indeed, he raised them to the status of councilors, and this day was for a long time a feast day for the Jews of Alexandria, being held sometime after Shavuot, though already by the time my father was a boy, when he spent three years here, it was no longer being celebrated... In my opinion not a word of it is true."

Uri recounted what he had heard in Delta on Sunday. Apollos just shook his head.

"That's just nonsense. The elephants are not usually brought from Ethiopia but Nubia and the Sudan," he said. "But it's a long time since that happened."

"All the same, that's what people imagine."

"Yes, indeed," said Apollos.

They both fell silent.

ON SUNDAY URI WENT AGAIN WITH APOLLOS TO THE AMPHITHEATER.

There were several theaters in Alexandria, but the most authentic of them was built near the Eastern Harbor and was sited so the open end of the auditorium faced toward the north, maybe to allow for the observation of fleets of ships by the audience. It was this amphitheater that Uri had seen through the gemstone on the day of his arrival in Alexandria. The actors performed mostly comic sketches as tragedies had never had much appeal in Alexandria, even in its heyday. The audience was comprised mostly of Greeks, with exceptionally few Jews: Apollos pointed them out because Uri could not discern them, and not just due to his poor eyesight. The sketches were performed with little in the way of costuming or makeup, the catch-words and accents of the city's famous Greeks parodied in half-baked improvised stories which were purloined from earlier Greek comedies and simplified. Uri recognized barely any of the celebrities. Apollos, who had been living in Alexandria longer, would occasionally mutter the name of the person who happened to be featured at the moment. The stories were trite and the jokes vulgar but the audience lapped it up, and even Uri got the point of a fable about goat-shagging Auillios since Avilius was the middle name of Aulus Flaccus. He and Apollos listened aghast to the tasteless witticisms and the terrified bleats of a genuine goat, which was not exactly keen on a man attempting to couple with it.

"That's Pharoseidon, a stage-name, he's very popular," Apollos—who liked going to the theater—whispered. "He will appear on two or three stages in an afternoon."

"And does he take the goat around with him?"

The mimic left off shagging the goat and stepped to the front of the stage: he was a short, bald, elfin man with a slight speech impediment; odiously perspiring, he began a discourse on the topics of the day, and even responded to questions from the audience—perhaps not entirely unprompted—all the while staying in character as Auillios. How did he, Auillios, see the future of Alexandria? Well, the way he imagined it was that five hundred thousand Jews would be brought in from Judaea, because they eat less than one hundred thousand Greeks and there would be no need to provide shelter for them. Snickers. He imagined changing Greek tarts for Jewish ones because their vaginas were better greased and always wide open. Laughter. He imagined importing loads of pigs from Judaea, because Jews liked them most of all. Whinnies. They like them so much that they don't eat them, suspecting that fellow spirits resided in them. A load of guffaws. He imagined promoting the use of the Syrian language in Alexandria because nobody understood it. Roars of approval, stormy clapping.

Uri felt sick.

Apollos stumbled wanly beside him as they made their way along the harbor among chuckling Greeks.

It was not impossible that there was Jewish blood flowing in that revolting character, the blood of the most gutless Jews who ever lived.

GEMELLUS WAS ASSASSINATED—TIBERIUS'S GRANDSON BY BLOOD, WHOM he had been named co-princeps in his nullified will and whom Caligula had adopted as a son.

Macro was hounded into suicide, together with Ennia, his wife and the emperor's supposed lover. That's why he never arrived in Alexandria to take up his post.

Silanus, the emperor's father-in-law, also took his own life.

It was winter by now, which in Alexandria meant milder weather, with people going about in tunics except for poor Carabbas, who still capered around buck-naked on the Gymnasium grounds, and in the evenings was fed drinks in the harbor area's taverns. Everywhere everybody was wrapped up in politicking, the Greeks and Jews sticking to their own kind.

Uri reached a decision that he would leave: he would finish this year's studies and then go. He had no wish to be seen as Greek among the Jews and Jewish among the Greeks. Alexandria was an attractive city, but he was a Roman and he would have to go home sometime.

The alabarch continued his strong belief in Agrippa's influence, above all confirmed by the fact that the tetrarchate of Philip—which, four years after his death, was amalgamated into Syria—had been awarded to Agrippa by Caligula, so Agrippa had become a king! That is the tip of the iceberg, said Alabarch

Alexander, the rest will come soon enough; and indeed, news came through that Agrippa had also been granted the area around the town of Abilene, Lysanias's former tetrarchy. The second step! Agrippa had been given a golden chain, the weight of his former shackles! "His shackles can't have been all that heavy," remarked Tija sarcastically.

"Agrippa is now by the emperor's side, his adviser!" the alabarch would say as he diligently attended to his business.

Uri waited for the right moment to thank him for his hospitality, but no occasion of that kind arose. Agrippa's domain was only a tiny realm, consisting of no more than a few cities: Auranitis, Paneas, Trachonitis, Gaulanitis and Batanea in northern Transjordan, but even that would do. He sometimes got to deliberating that it might be better than Alexandria if Agrippa were to take up the tetrarchy and he were to be sent there with a message of some kind. It was not far from Decapolis, and there were said to be good libraries in those ten Greek free towns. He would cast himself at Agrippa's feet: my king, he would say, under false apprehension I was regarded as being your delegate; now here I am, I am at your disposal. He pictured a fine, dramatic scene, at the end of which Agrippa appointed him head of his library, one that was to be established, and he would travel far and wide to acquire its stock. In reality, however, Agrippa, had not yet set out for his realm and was still rotting in Rome.

Marcus would say things like: At last! The emperor has dusted himself off and shaken off all the advisers who were leeching off of him. He's had enough of them; Emperor Gaius is all grown up, only now is he really starting to rule. He has been patronized by them, so they deserve their fate. In front of his intimates he called Macro a sermonizer as he fumed against him; now he has no need for a schoolmaster. You'll see soon enough that Caligula will make a great ruler—as if Germanicus were ruling henceforth.

This amounted to open revolt against his father. Before long the alabarch is going to be retired, thought Uri, with Marcus replacing him as the chief exciseman.

No one spoke about Gemellus: his destiny was his undoing, born under a bad star. The dismissed prefect continued to live in his palace, only, it was said, he transferred his seat of government to the citadel of the Akra. It was unclear whether Caligula had rescinded Flaccus's dismissal or reconfirmed him. No one was sent out to replace Flaccus, but then that would have been difficult: the rumor was that Flaccus, wobbling drunkenly on a horse, had held an inspection of the troops at Nicopolis, and his soldiers had hurrahed him lustily and at length. So, the two legions were standing by Flaccus.

Two legions is a lot of soldiers. Where would anyone get the three or four legions that would be needed to face them, and who would lead them?

Uri imagined that Flaccus, to save his own skin, and struggling for Caligula's favor, had declared Jews to be uniformly accountable, one and all, for the denunciation of Germanicus and was expelling them from Alexandria, thereby scoring points with the emperor, who plainly was not in a position himself to make such an order. Signs of this began to multiply: in the harbor Jewish ships were kept waiting longer whereas Greek vessels were admitted before their turn.

Wealthy Jews from the city and across Egypt paid visits to the alabarch to ask for his assistance: their produce was left to rot on board, and delays in the unloading of dry goods were causing them great financial damage. The alabarch would respond cautiously: maybe fallen Flaccus was seeking to foment Jewish turmoil to bravely quell it and keep his position; just let the Jews be patient, trust in the Eternal One and the emperor, keep to the law even if it was not respected on the other side. The Jewish merchants would depart grumbling. It's a pity, one of them remarked agitatedly within earshot of Uri, that there are no major ports in Judaea where Greek ships could be held up in retaliation.

How to respond lies in the alabarch's hands, thought Uri: he supervises commerce on the Nile, and he's got his own private army to boot. All he has to do is hold back a few cargoes, have them meticulously checked to see whether they are, by any chance, rotten, make Greek merchants also suffer from the delays... But the alabarch would do no such thing: his conduct indicated that he had no appetite for a commercial war.

The guard on the alabarch's palace was doubled, Uri was admitted without incident by the older ones but the new recruits continually raised difficulties. It occurred to Uri that his residence permit had expired about a year before, so he had a word with Philo, who brushed the issue aside as being of no importance: anyone would be able to verify that Uri was a student at the Gymnasium, and he had in any case been recorded by the Jews, but that was no reassurance for Uri. All right, said Philo testily as he felt his train of thought slipping away, I'll have a word with the servants.

He did indeed have a word, for one of the servants later declared that he had settled the matter. There you go, said Philo. Uri had his doubts, but he did not go out to the harbor to check: in the end, he was certain, he would simply be burdened with an indifferent Greek official who could not care less whether they had a record of Uri having filed a prolongation but would just as soon have him thrown onto some cargo vessel—as they were in the habit of doing every now and again with illegal immigrants—only to awaken a few weeks later as a slave in Britannia or Hispania—that is, if he did not starve to death en route.

A dark mood hung over the celebration of Passover in Alexandria. It was not that there was any change in the trappings; it was more as if the flesh and bones under peoples' skin had become desiccated. Uri recalled how Antonia's birthday had been celebrated on January 31, dutifully by the Greeks and with conspicuous restraint by the Jews, lest the Greeks report to the emperor that they were overly enthusiastic in honoring the memory of the emperor's grandmother, who had denounced Germanicus, her own son, to Tiberius. Passover was not a festival for the empire but only for the Jews, so the Greeks had nothing to report on.

That Passover also had a shadow cast over it by the fact that Flaccus, in one of his sober moments, at last received the alabarch and once again refused to allow the Jews of Alexandria to send a delegation to Rome to present their grievances. That was when the Jews awoke to the fact that a year had gone by since the prefect had first denied them this right, and they began to doubt whether the emperor had ever received their good wishes. Delegations could only leave the provinces with the permission of the prefect; that was the rule in Alexandria as well. The alabarch irately commented that of course Greek delegations bearing gifts were allowed to travel to the emperor every day; at that Flaccus smiled cynically: those are private individuals, and he could not ban travel by private individuals. Then we'll send private individuals as well, declared the alabarch. All he achieved was that every Jew who set off for Italia thereafter was minutely searched to check if they were carrying any letters, or any article which could be considered a gift; in either case the contraband was impounded. The alabarch's couriers to Agrippa were now forced to take ships bound for Gaza or Tyre, which entailed a detour of several weeks; no more couriers were sent to Silanus, because he was dead.

In June a new tragedy struck: on the eighteenth, Drusilla, the emperor's older sister, died in Rome at the age of twenty-one. Again all baths and all taverns were closed, the Great Library was closed, and once again the Gymnasium ended the academic year without holding a ceremony, thus Uri failed to receive a diploma for a second time. Shops were closed, in workshops no work was done, and only essential supplies could be obtained in the marketplaces. Sombre soldiers, stone-cold sober, patrolled the streets, pulling in any drunks. Shrines and synagogues were preoccupied with grieving for Drusilla: she had been Caligula's favorite sister, so Greeks and Jews competed in their grief, taking care that no one could accuse them of being lax in their mourning. They were reported in any case.

Anyone able to do so left Alexandria, and in the end even the theaters were closed.

The Gymnasium park was not closed, though, and given that it wasn't fenced off the mimics found that they were able to perform there. They started off cautiously, with short sketches, and they did not even ask for money, fearing that a patrol might come along and eject them; but no soldiers came, or rather they did come, but as spectators, and they laughed. The mimics took courage and began parodying the Jews, which put the soldiers in an even better frame of mind, and even made them willing to shell out money.

Why didn't Flaccus eject the mimics? This was a time of mourning! He could have easily prohibited gatherings in the park!

Then it occurred to Uri: it was more comfortable this way. He was pretending that nothing was happening so he did not have to do anything.

The alabarch was quite excessively appalled, and Tija explained why: in recent months, via couriers and Agrippa, his father had built up good relations with Lepidus, Drusilla's second husband, who had stood in as deputy for the childless Caligula at the head of the empire during the emperor's spell of illness, and was now a widower. Should Lepidus be pushed down the hierarchy, Uri reflected sardonically, all those remittances would be lost. And he would be pushed down, one could be sure of that. Tija was still hoping that Agrippina— of the emperor's two surviving older sisters the one whom Caligula listened to, being not at all fond of Julia, perhaps because Agrippina, her name aside, reminded him of his mother—was still as well disposed toward Lepidus as had been alleged.

The mourning went on; the walls were covered with crudely scrawled depictions of big-nosed, crooked-backed figures. That summer was stifling hot Uri moped forlornly in his room. Philo did not retreat to his summer residence but stayed in the palace and, taking over a part of the alabarch's load, received the aggrieved Jewish dignitaries and did what he could to reassure them. Tija likewise went nowhere and was entrusted with control of the palace security. Marcus traveled along the banks of the Nile with his father and a strong escort.

Something was brewing.

Nothing was heard of Isidoros for a long time, but now—it was the talk of the taverns—he had resurfaced in the Gymnasium park, delivering a speech against Flaccus. Exactly what he was accusing the prefect of was unclear, but it had to do with grand theft and fraud. And with the Jews.

The next morning Uri went out into the Gymnasium's grounds.

An expectant crowd was waiting, along with a group of soldiers.

He would have liked to see and hear Isidoros, though he was surely not going to come: the soldiers could not tolerate accusations against Flaccus.

But Isidoros put in an appearance after all, around noon, with a crowd around him like a team of bodyguards. At the Square Stoa, he was offered a platform, thrown together with timber, and Isidoros stepped up onto it.

In shrill tones, he accused Flaccus of having delivered a substantial chunk of Alexandria's trade into Jewish hands. He had stolen the donation that the emperor had sent from Rome for irrigation in Egypt. Flaccus was the reason, Isidoros cried, that interest rates had gone up in Alexandria, though Tiberius's banking reforms had brought rates down throughout the empire. The prefect had a personal stake in all the Jewish banks, and it was with his assistance that Jews had bought out Greek bankrupts and it was they who now dictated terms.

The crowd whooped.

It's your money on which the Jews get fat!

For shame!

You get poorer, they get richer!

Let 'em beat it!

At a signal from their commander, the soldiers of one of the squads tried to push closer to the rostrum, but at that the assembled Greeks produced cudgels. There were a lot of Greeks; the soldiers halted.

Isidoros stepped down from the platform—it wasn't as if his safety were in jeopardy, but he looked anxious to avoid an altercation. He disappeared among his bodyguards.

The Greeks were left in lively discussions about what had been said.

Uri felt it was best if he just went home.

"Is what Isidoros was claiming true?" he asked Tija that evening.

Tija hemmed and hawed.

"So it's true," Uri concluded. "Then why doesn't the prefect intervene?"

"Because he's on the take."

"What do you mean?"

"He's been paid by the Greeks."

"Is that what the five gold talents were?"

Tija looked at Uri in amazement.

"How do you know that?"

"It's one of the things that are being said."

"Well, yes..."

"But apparently Isidoros himself handed it over, despite the fact that he's the one baring his teeth against the prefect!"

"Yes, because he asked for something in return, but Flaccus did not live up to his side of the deal."

"What did he ask for?"

"What do you think? He asked for what he could. That the capital of the Jewish banks be consolidated into that of the Greek banks."

"And how is that done?"

"By decree."

Uri cogitated.

"Then why didn't he do that if he took their money?"

"Because we gave him even more!" Tija cried out. "Even more! If it goes on like this, we'll end up in poverty!"

He's not stupid, this Flaccus, thought Uri. Relieved of his office by the emperor, yet still in place. Back against he wall, he still manages to amass for himself in just a few months at least five years' worth of his salary as prefect in just a few months, and still everyone is on his side—Greeks, Jews, legions! How is the emperor going to untangle that?

When, for the third day running, a large crowd gathered on the Gymnasium's grounds, Isidoros did not put in an appearance. But the soldiers did. They brought along several rostrums, and a series of unknown, loud-voiced Greek speakers yelled out from atop them. An ever-growing number of soldiers arrived and finally, to Uri's astonishment, Flaccus himself showed up, carried on an ornate chariot.

The soldiers cleared a way for him through the crowd, which then closed around him. There must have been at least four cohorts gathered together there, along with a crowd of some twenty thousand people.

Flaccus stepped onto the platform beside the Square Stoa. Four soldiers with shields clambered up beside him, along with a centurion: "Castus! Castus!" was the chant that went up from crowd.

Flaccus bellowed a query as to what their problem was. Not that he was drunk; the crowd fell silent. A Greek orator was hauled out in front of the platform and tugged up onto it.

"Who was it who taught you to slander me?" bellowed Flaccus.

"Isidoros..."

"Louder!"

"Isidoros!"

"Away with him!"

The next speaker was called up.

"Who taught you to spread lies about me?"

"Isidoros..."

They stopped at the fifth speaker. Flaccus declared that not one word of the slander was true: let that be the end of it. Isidoros was being exiled; never again would he be allowed to enter Alexandria. He was also banning assembly on the grounds of the Gymnasium. The crowd should be happy to have been let off that lightly.

Centurion Castus gestured, the soldiers cleared a way through the crowd, and Flaccus's chariot was towed behind, drawn by six horses with an entire cavalry division leading, flanking, and bringing up the rear.

That must have cost the alabarch a pretty penny, Uri supposed.

"It's by no means sure that Isidoros slipped away," Marcus ventured that evening. "He may be hiding somewhere."

Philo shared that view: Shrine leagues, many of which had Isidoros as president, had become conspicuously active, but Flaccus was doing nothing to move against them. Tija explained to Uri that these were groups whose members ate and drank free, for sacrificial purposes, out the money offered by believers. The main thing was that any shrine was also a sacrosanct place of refuge; soldiers were not allowed to enter them—at least hitherto that was unprecedented—and even Flaccus could not contravene the rule because all of Alexandria would be up in arms.

"I don't believe Flaccus will make any effort to capture Isidoros," Marcus commented. "If he were to bring him to trial, Isidoros would spill the beans. It's better that he is not captured..."

Not long after, it was rumored that a substantial shipment of arms had arrived. Bassus was the centurion who was organizing the unloading; on Flaccus's orders, he had collected the arms from all over Egypt, and now the spears, short swords, slingshots, and shields were being packed onto asses and camels, innumerable asses and innumerable camels, and carried from the harbor on Lake Mareotis to the arsenal of the prefect's palace. The harbor was some ten stadia from the palace, and the beasts of burden were touching one another. There were no elephants among them.

Philo asked Uri to take a look to see if the rumor was true. Up till now they had keenly followed Uri's spontaneously offered reports as to what was happening in Alexandria. They would be recognized, but Uri was known solely by students at the Gymnasium so he could go about as freely as he pleased. I've become an official spy for the alabarch in Alexandria, Uri reflected, and laughed at the absurdity.

That evening he reported back: indeed, masses of arms were being delivered to the arsenal: Greeks by the side of the road were gaping and arguing over whether the weapons were going to be used against them or against Rome.

"I'VE HEARD TELL THAT AGRIPPA WILL HAVE NEED OF YOU IN HIS KING-dom," announced Tija one evening as he entered Uri's room.

Uri was agog. It was exactly what he had been wanting to ask but he had never found the right moment.

"But Agrippa's in Rome," Uri noted.

"He's going to have to accede to his throne sooner or later," said Tija. "Let's just hope that you won't forget the two years you spent in Alexandria with us."

Uri nodded. They had come to their decision: he was going to be the alabarch's family spy by Agrippa's side.

He no longer felt any fear with regard to Agrippa. He would simply explain the misunderstanding that had existed from the very beginning and Agrippa would forgive him. Maybe he would not even have to tell him that much: enough people had reported on his actions already.

"When am I to set off?" he queried.

"Not long now, we hope," replied Tija.

It crossed Uri's mind whether or not he ought to take offense at that, but this time Tija was not being sarcastic: he wouldn't be with a matter concerning Agrippa.

Tija was on his way out of the room when he turned back to face him.

"For a long time I really did think that you would be my strategos when I became prefect, but then I came to see that you wouldn't be the right man for that job. I'd lay a claim to you for just about any other position: chief collector, chief archivist, anything."

A devil took hold of Uri.

"And Marcus will be a prefect as well?" he asked sweetly.

Tija's eyes widened only a little in hatred.

"Marcus will be king," he declared with poise and with that was gone.

ON AUGUST 1, THE ANNIVERSARY OF EGYPT'S CONQUEST BY ROME, defamatory graffiti appeared on the walls of houses: "Pig Jews," "Filthy Jews," "Go back to Jerusalem, homeless Jews," "Jewish cat killers," and the like. Big noses and even bigger circumcised sexual organs, meant to signify that the growth of the Jewish population was considered excessive by comparison with the more judicious proliferation of the Greeks. Jews were cursed by drunks in the harbor. Greeks were delighted.

"They'll desist," said Philo nervously. "It's just a fad, it'll blow over."

A few days later the graffiti was washed away; very few new slogans were daubed on the walls thereafter.

In mid-August Uri was wakened at daybreak by a commotion.

In the darkness he reached for a bedside oil lamp; he had been reading by its light late into the night. There was swearing outside. He heard the alabarch's voice as he called out in exasperation: "Failed!"

Philo hushed him.

"It doesn't matter!" he exclaimed, though he was not in the habit of shouting. "That's how it worked out. Never mind! Get a grip on yourself! The Almighty willed that it be so—without blood! He knows best why!"

"Failed!" raged the alabarch.

Marcus was also shouting, calling for the guards.

Uri hazarded a look outside. Armed guards were scrambling toward the gate. An uproar could be heard from the street. Uri listened attentively. A crowd was cheering Agrippa, king of the Jews.

Unfamiliar armed men hurried past him.

A burly, balding, double-chinned, middle-aged man on a palanquin was brought out of one of the rooms. His features were crimson, his head was nodding, he was half asleep.

"No don't! Don't," he shouted. "Put me down!"

The servants put the litter down, and the burly man staggered off the chair and looked around. His eyes caught sight of Uri.

"I'm thirsty," he stated.

Uri hurried to the counter where food and drink was prepared. He filled a beaker with pressed orange juice and took it over to the man, who downed it in one gulp.

"This dry land, even that pitches under my legs," he declared indignantly. "In Egypt even the land is quaking like the sea?"

Uri did not know how to answer. There was shouting from outside.

"Send the riff-raff away!" the man wailed.

"That's not possible now," said Tija, who had appeared from somewhere. "It's too late now."

The man goggled at him.

"And who are you?"

"I'm Tiberius Julius Alexander, Alabarch Alexander's second son."

"Why's it not possible now?"

"Because it's too late!"

He signaled to the bearers who stepped back toward the litter.

"Be so good, Your Majesty, as to be seated in the chair," Tija said in a peremptory tone.

The man sighed and sat in the litter; the servants lifted it up.

"I'm sleepy! I'm tired! I'm hungry! Where are you taking me?" the man asked forlornly.

"To Pharos island!"

The servants set off with him toward the gate.

Tija looked at him as he disappeared.

"What a creep!" he burst out. "The world has never before seen the likes of that pain in the ass!"

Uri looked aghast after the litter. They were carrying Agrippa, king of the Jews, and he was a courier for him. He hadn't even given him a proper look.

"What happened?"

"What happened? He only went and spoiled it, the idiot! Let him die of constipation!"

More armed men trudged by them.

Tija stood there crestfallen.

"Let's go, then," he said. "It behooves us to join the crowd in its happy howling."

URI SLIPPED ON HIS SANDALS AND CAUGHT UP TO TIJA AT THE GATE.

Outside, hordes of people were marching in procession, running, jostling. Word had spread in the Jewish district of Alexandria that the king had arrived.

Tija halted, with Uri beside him.

"His boat got here this afternoon," Tija jeered with repugnance. "He had them anchor a fair distance off shore and waited till evening, as he should have, even got to the shore without being spotted... But then he lost his senses... He'd been told what he should do, but that wasn't good enough for him! He's a king! He knows best! Dickhead! He began screaming at the first Greek squad to arrive to alert the other squads and to seize Flaccus... The emperor had sent him on a special mission, he yelled, and they must seize Flaccus for him immediately! Can you believe the tosspot! King of the Jews! His own bodyguard had trouble protecting him. Even after that he couldn't hold his peace. No wonder the Jews spotted him coming!"

Tija threw himself into the crowd. Uri just stood.

It looked as if they really had messed it up. God Almighty, and how!

Uri stepped out onto the street and was carried off by the crowd. He was being carried in the right direction, toward the Heptastadion. Delirious men, women, old folks, children—all pushed, jostled, joy on faces still puffy from sleep, the king, the king, the king is here!

THE NEXT DAY, AGRIPPA SAILED ON IN A GREAT HURRY WITH HIS ESCORT, headed toward his kingdom with the intention of spending Rosh Hashanah there. The Greeks, putting no obstacles in his way, breathed a sigh of relief. Flaccus did not receive Agrippa, but then Agrippa had no wish to pay him the honor: he had been sent by the emperor to seize the failed prefect and haul him off to Rome.

Agrippa had with him the Jews' congratulatory letter to the emperor, the dispatch of which Flaccus had kept pending for a year. The non-arrival of those congratulations had thrown the emperor into a temper and ever since then he had been disparaging Jews for being so extraordinary arrogant; he is more imperial, if that is possible, than his predecessors. So it was said in Agrippa's own words. He would later on send the congratulatory letter by courier, with the necessary apologies, when he called in at a safe haven on his way to his kingdom. The emperor would surely excuse them; he could not maintain a permanent grudge against the most populous nation in his kingdom.

The king of the Jews had been entrusted with capturing Flaccus; pity he had proved incapable of that, the news went around. But perhaps the Eternal One had willed it so, the more charitable suggested, that our hands should not be stained with blood. After his presence had been detected, there was no choice but to accompany Agrippa in triumph to the holy island; there some people spoke, it was impossible to hear them. He had gaped, open-mouthed; it was impossible to hear him either, and the Jews were deliriously happy, there were around 150,000 of them thronging the island. The Greeks were also roused and stood around gazing at the procession of the Jews. The prefect in turn was unable to move against Agrippa, not having enough men to counter a mass so large; in any case that would have amounted to an open declaration of war.

The Jews exulted, all 150,000 of them, except for those who were in the know, because they raged. Then everyone calmed down. Nothing happened. Flaccus already knew that he was condemned to die, so from his perspective nothing had changed.

It is prohibited to celebrate a triumph at a time of official state mourning, but the Jews did celebrate, and there was no way of pretending it hadn't happened. The Jews had cheered not only Agrippa, but the emperor; the Greeks could send their delegations to the emperor, and Agrippa could send his letter, and the alabarch could dispatch couriers to Rome by roundabout ways.

Agrippa had mentioned that at Caligula's court there was an Alexandrian Greek by the name of Helikon, a dangerous, crafty, and influential man, one of Tiberius's manumitted slaves, who represented Greek interests—and argued against the Jews—with passable vigor and guile. But the Jews of Alexandria were also represented in Rome, since the whole of Far Side, several tens of thousands, was involved with that. We too had our spokesmen!

Let no harm come to Agrippa, though; may he reach his realm intact and act as king, then, if God wills it, his kingdom will flourish and the whole of his grandfather's, Herod the Great's, realm will be his. Then the Jews of Alexandria, along with the other four million Jews—all who live in the Diaspora—will have a strong homeland.

Still, it was a fine gesture on the emperor's part that he had sent a Jew, of all people, to remove the deposed prefect. The emperor could not hate Jews if he was unable to entrust anyone but a Jew with such an important task—no one else but a Jew! The emperor holds us in affection, trusts us; indeed, it is really only us whom he trusts. That is how those who were in the know reassured each another, because ordinary Jews knew nothing of all this, they were just elated to have seen, for the first time in their lives, a genuine, real-life, anointed king of the Jews. But ordinary Jews also supposed that the emperor must hold them in affection if he had, at long last, appointed them a king. Jews had not had a king since the time of Herod the Great, only tetrarchs. There were many who had hated, loathed Herod the Great, that treacherous, bloodthirsty wild beast, always licking Rome's boots and bribing Greeks, building Greek-style towns, aping Greek customs. He had the prime of Jerusalem slaughtered, had the priests murdered and his own people appointed in their place, had the members of the Sanhedrin murdered, had his own wife killed, had his own sons killed, and on top of all that had a Greek stadium constructed in Jerusalem. He had strewn Roman baths all over the city and organized quinquennial Greek games—squandering the dues paid by the Jewish community on such fruitless undertakings. But when all is said and done, he had been the king of the Jews, and even if he had not been entirely Jewish, he was at least half so.

Now there was again a king of the Jews, even if his kingdom was, as yet, tiny. Agrippa may only be one-quarter Jewish, yet he has still become a king of the Jews and is circumcised, and the Eternal One is thereby letting us know that the One and Only Everlasting God has not abandoned his alliance with us, His chosen people, wherever we may live in this pagan-dominated world. Agrippa's flying visit was a heavenly sign that the Messiah, bringing the Last Judgment of the Lord, is nigh. These ideas make their way among the Jews in Delta, and spread through the other districts of Alexandria with Jewish populations, and in their synagogues they offer thanks to the Eternal One, and it is about this that Philo is writing right now, interrupting his other work. As an exception he is not striving to win recognition for the Jews from the Greeks but to boost their diminished self-esteem.

TWO DAYS LATER, SO AS NOT TO COWER THE WHOLE DAY LONG IN THE palace, where the alabarch and his intimates alternately raged and celebrated, Uri headed for the Paneion, in the middle of the Gymnasium's park, to walk the corkscrew paths around it. He took a scroll with him; it would be good to immerse himself in the scandals of some bygone age. But over by the colonnade, more than a stadium long, which marked the limits of the Gymnasium's grounds along Arsinoë Avenue he could see a crowd was forming, so he stopped a little way off to watch, narrowing his eyes to see better. Something must have happened inside the park grounds because the mass was hastening in. Uri followed, slipping between two of the columns. The throng was thicker around the Square Stoa, so Uri strolled that way. Street urchins, dockers and well-dressed citizens alike were all hurrying that way. Could it be someone was delivering a speech? Who, then? Had Isidoros come back?

Someone was standing in the ramshackle, rusty, four-horse chariot that had been placed in the park around a century ago—Cleopatra, the great-grandmother of the last Cleopatra, had been given it as a present. Whoever it was looked as if he had something on his head and was holding something in his hand. Uri came to a stop. He did not have to go closer, in fact, because the chariot lurched forward, pulled by twenty or so people in his very direction; the wheels, having been left ungreased for a hundred years, squeaked loudly. The figure standing in the chariot was naked; on his head was a paper crown, in his right hand was a paper mace: it was Carabbas in his full nudity.

"Here comes the king of the Jews! Render homage to the king of the Jews!" the Greek crowd shouted joyfully.

Carabbas grinned and waved.

"Speech! O king of the Jews. Let's have a ripe fart from you, Carabbas!"

Carabbas grinned and waved; he clutched at the sides and then slipped down onto the floor of the chariot, he pulled himself up again and grinned. A rush mat was draped around his shoulders so that the prick of the mighty king of the Jews should not dangle in full view. The chariot was pulled right by Uri, the crowd pouring after.

"He ought to be circumcised! Otherwise it's not realistic!"

"The king of the Jews is a monkey!"

"To the harbor with him!"

"To the palace!"

People all around to Uri were chortling, yelling, pushing one another, racing after the chariot as it gained momentum on the paved road.

"Recite the Ten Commandments!" came a cry from the crowd. "The Ten Commandments, Carabbas!"

"Get something blue on him! Something blue!"

"Give him a menorah! Make it snappy!"

"Take him through Delta! Let the Jews pay homage!"

"To the palace! The palace!"

"Through Delta! Through Delta! Take him to the Jewish Basilica!"

Uri could hear the sound of his own laughter and stopped. Do I really despise Agrippa that badly?

Yes, that badly.

He pictured Carabbas standing nude on the Basilica's platform and could not avoid laughing.

The throng grew, and he lost sight of the chariot. Next to him the Jews were being reviled with choice profanities, and those he could no longer laugh at. Last night the Jews slaughtered two cats and threw them into the Serapeion, the stinking weasels! They're looking to bring Rome down on us, but they're in for a surprise! A big surprise!

Two fellow students at the Gymnasium appeared beside him, trying to wipe the grins off their faces. Uri did not know what to do, and was so confused that he forgot to greet them, but then they were carried farther along with the procession, so there was no need. Uri was by now trying to drop out of the crowd but was being jostled from all sides. I ought to get to the side of the street, he thought.

He was finally able to extricate himself once they passed under the arcades: the crowd flocked eastward, toward Delta, packing the entire hundred-foot width of the main thoroughfare. Warehousemen clutching cudgels and lugging stone blocks clattered by: the rocks must have come from some building site. This was no longer a joking matter. The Jews living in Delta ought to be alerted, but how?

Uri scurried after the procession, keeping close to the wall. At a crossroad, on the bridge arching above the canal, four or five men had broken from the crowd and were beating up a bearded man.

"I'm not Jewish!" the man was screaming.

They tugged up his tunic and tore off his loincloth.

"See! I'm not Jewish!"

In their disappointment, they set to him with their cudgels anyway, giving him such a sound drubbing that the man was laid out flat, blood streaming from his head. Uri ran off to the right down a street that ran southward by the canal, right into some Greeks who were arriving to join in the fun. They spotted him and slowed down menacingly.

"Carabbas is king!" Uri shouted toward them, and continued running south.

At the next corner he stopped. He was not being followed. He turned left and crossed over the canal to make his way back northward, together with the crowd of Greeks who were heading for Arsinoë Avenue.

The chariot was nowhere to be seen. There were some Jews living in Gamma as well; a carpet shop was on fire, a jeweler's was in the process of being robbed, with boxes flying out of it, ragamuffins scrabbled about, scrambling on all fours for the gemstones that were scattered over the ground. Not one soldier or guard. Stone blocks were hurled at residences of Jews, a menorah was daubed in blue paint on the wall. One of the Greeks in that group, who wasn't doing any painting personally, identified the houses in which Jews lived from a list on a sheet of papyrus he carried.

"The Jews are fighting back!" was heard as the crowd came to a standstill. There was much pushing and shoving as they were unable to proceed farther eastward, so part of the rabble split off and turned to head north toward the harbor.

Uri saw that it was pointless to stick with them, so he once again elbowed his way toward the south to try to disappear in the narrow alleys of Gamma.

Smaller knots of rowdies were breaking into locked Jewish shops with bulky beams of timber: the mourning decreed for Drusilla's death was still being observed, so the owners were not to be found.

Uri turned west, intending to make his way back to the alabarch's palace in Beta.

He saw a mob in one of the squares, visible through a cloud of smoke. There was much shouting, fists being shaken, leaping and whooping, both men and women. Uri squinted and edged closer. A huge bonfire of hastily gathered brushwood was smoking, and in the midst of it he could clearly see some writhing figures, their hands and feet tied. They were small.

"They're not doing a very good job of suffocating, are they!" Uri heard from one side.

He stepped closer. Two women and three children, still alive, were choking in the smoke. Fresh branches were laid on the fire, there were no flames.

"Don't do that!" burst from his lips.

"But they're Jews!" he heard. "They were resisting!"

Someone grabbed him by an arm. Uri tore himself loose and raced off shrieking. He could hear footsteps taking up the pursuit, but they tailed off: over short distances Uri was a quick sprinter.

The alabarch's palace was closed up. He pounded on the door was to no avail. He was watched from the other side of the street by some loitering Greeks. He pounded again. No answer. It was locked up tightly, or maybe everyone had made themselves scarce.

Uri turned around. Several of the Greeks slowly headed toward him. Uri raced off to the east but was not followed.

He had no money, nothing except the sandals, tunic, and loincloth he was wearing. August nights in Alexandria were warm, so it would be perfectly feasible to sleep out under the heavens—only where? Something else he bore was his tribal identification: his sexual organ. He should have left that at home!

Philo's summer residence was a long way off. Anyway, it was far from certain that the guards at the city gates would allow him to leave the city.

I ought to get into the Serapeion, he thought. They know me there.

That was the trouble: they knew him.

He then realized that he had no idea what might be lurking in the mind of any Greek priest, editor, or copyist: they might offer him refuge, but it was just as possible that they would hand him over.

He made his way slowly to the southeast as if he were out taking a stroll. Day was breaking. The neighborhood was peaceful, just like in Alexandria's old days.

He inspected the Serapeion from a distance. The main gate was open, with a couple of people entering, then more arriving either alone or in groups. They were Greeks going to offer prayers—to thank their god that they were able to batter Jews.

HE SPENT THE REST OF THE NIGHT IN THE OLD NECROPOLIS TO THE southwest of the Serapeion, outside the old city wall but inside the present one, where the graves slumbered among the well-trimmed gardens and villas of the rich. Fruit trees bowed over the garden fences above the paths, so that Uri was able to eat his fill and quench his thirst. He sucked at an orange and nibbled olives, then propped his back against a thick tree trunk to catch a nap in the seated position. He clutched a stick that he had found on the ground and stripped of its smaller branches. He tried to calm his racing heartbeat by slowly and rhythmically repeating: "I won't die here! I won't die here!"

He awoke with a start at dawn: a family of four were settling down near him behind a marble gravestone. It was the grave of a dog: the owner must have been very attached to it. The children were so scared they were unable to cry. Jews, no doubt, Uri supposed. He picked up a few oranges, clambered to his feet and went over to the family, offering them the fruit. The woman stared at him in terror, the man looked on warily.

"I'm Jewish too," said Uri.

The children were trembling.

The woman was Jewish, her husband a Greek convert; they had their own house in the south of Gamma, but in the middle of the night it had been set alight by the rioters. They had managed to escape by the garden gate, the children still asleep when they had snatched them up.

"They knew who they were looking for," said the man. "They set alight every single Jewish house, and there aren't many in that neighborhood."

"Sleep now," the woman said to the children. They were still trembling.

"Where will you go next?" the man asked Uri.

"I don't know."

"They'll come for us here," said the man. "I had myself circumcised... Better that I hadn't..."

It had to have been a deep passion. Uri mused that were he to find himself in such a position he would have to have his foreskin sewn back on. He laughed to himself.

"My son is also circumcised," the man groaned.

By the morning another four families had moved to the cemetery—eleven children altogether, wailing, weeping, or mutely trembling. Two of the families had fled from Gamma, one from Delta (they had things to attend to at the harbor and were unable to get back home), one from Beta, where the rabble had also run riot and lit a huge bonfire, though that pyre had smoked rather than burned. On the way, they had seen a heap of charred corpses in the southeastern part of Alpha—probably a whole family. There were stray dogs sniffing around, to say nothing of cats, of course.

"Even the dogs!" wailed one oldster.

Homeless Greek vagrants foraged sleepily amid the graves, pretending that they had not noticed the Jews.

"They'll report that we're here," whispered one of the women.

The young men set off in search of food; returned, bowed to the east to say their prayers, then shared out the fruit. Those who did not pray sternly pointed out that cemeteries were unclean, people should neither eat nor pray there; only after they had left the place. You must not eat, it's not pure! You mustn't eat! Four of the children were immediately forbidden from eating by their parents. An argument then broke out over whether it was permissible to pray in a ritually impure place, and to eat without praying in a cemetery. A few who were already eating stopped doing so. Uri took the view that in an emergency life came before everything else, but others argued that this was no emergency, no one was dying of thirst or starvation, that would only come days later—then it would be permissible. The refugees disputed with revulsion in their hearts.

Uri reasoned that they would be able to stay until midday at the latest for by then the rabble would arrive at the cemetery; they had no doubt been reported on long ago, not necessarily by the homeless but more than likely by their wealthy neighbors for pilfering their fruit. He did not know what to do. A fresh dispute broke out among the fugitives: some disparaged Flaccus, others defended him, saying that he'd always been fond of the Jews, he had almost certainly already mobilized his army to put down the rebels, they were probably already restoring order. Women were sobbing and squabbling. It would be better for him to move on alone.

Uri made a quick count of the people: fourteen adults and thirteen children.

He asked for their attention. He said that he believed they would be safest in Delta, where there were many Jews and would be able to resist even without weapons. They ought to make their way there by the alleyways in the southern part of the district. The mob cannot be everywhere, and anyway they would be likely to approach Delta from their own stronghold down toward the harbor. If they all advanced from the south, the small bands would not dare to attack them, their own group was too large. They should go by the back streets; the mob was rampaging on the main streets, safety in numbers. Together they ought to get to Delta.

That too sparked an argument. The young men were all for leaving the city. Away, away from here. Someone reminded them that there were armed gate-keepers. Well, they'd simply climb over the city wall: eight feet tall, certainly, but they would piggyback for one another. What about the children, then? Throw them over? Yes, throw them over. Would they be any safer outside? But the rumors must already have reached the countryside, they would be hunted down one by one. Just get out of here, out of this damned city!

Uri waited until noon for them to reach a consensus then struck out on his own toward the west. Rachel, the wife of the Greek convert, thanked him with tears for giving them the oranges that morning.

Uri found it easy to climb over the city wall to the west: it was crumbling and the stones jutting out made an easy purchase. He dropped down on the outside without being spotted by anyone. With his eyes screwed up, he spied the shore-line, where and skiffs moored to jetties rocked on the tide; the Western Harbor was a long way from here, some two miles or so to the east.

Uri staggered down to the shore. The sun was blazing hot; it was the time of day people were wont to creep into the shade for a nap. He washed his feet in the sea, noticed some mussels and sighed for the sin he was about to commit before prising them open and slurping up their contents. They tasted wonderful.

He didn't know what to do. Perhaps he should wait until the evening before setting off southward along the city wall until he reached Lake Mareotis and could look for Philo's house there.

Perhaps the alabarch was gathering his private army together and would return. It would be nice to think that, but then again it was clear that the lot of them had run away like cowards. The financial muscle and brains of Alexandria's Jews—to whom he owed a debt of gratitude. He sighed with relief: he owed them nothing, they had deserted him when it came to the crunch.

Late in the afternoon a small group clambered over the city wall; they too ran toward the shore. Uri emerged from a shaded thicket. They were young Jewish men; they related how the previous day a large throng had gathered around noon at the amphitheater in the Eastern Harbor and speakers had demanded that the Jews place statues of the emperor in their synagogues exactly as Greeks did in their own shrines. Jews should observe the laws of Egypt and the empire; there should be an end to exceptionalism.

That was bad news: they had embroiled the emperor in all this. The Greeks were well aware that the Jews were not able to place any graven image in their places of worship. It wasn't they themselves who had dreamed this up: artful ideologues had fed them. Like Isidoros, or Flaccus.

Someone brought up the idea of walking along the lakeshore as far as Marea, where the Third Legion was stationed, to place themselves under their protection. The soldiers would keep them fed and watered. Flaccus would put the revolt down for sure; the prefect would be bound to mobilize the army. Perhaps on the way there they would meet a cohort which was heading for the city.

Uri held his counsel.

At dawn the young Jews set off for the west along the shore. Uri climbed back over the wall in the same spot as before, and made his way back to the cemetery.

There were no Jews there any more. Maybe they'd been caught, but maybe they had just moved on.

He slept lightly, like a wolf, alternately fully alert and sound asleep. In that borderland between the waking state and sleep he was beset by strange visions. He saw himself from the outside: he was lying amid the bushes, but he also had a house, a marvelously splendid, grandiose house in Rome, and he was waiting for his children to get back home from somewhere: he had loads of children and he was rich, but then all at once the walls of the house disappeared, people tramped through the rooms, ate and drank, paying not the least attention to the host, Uri took offense.

I'm curious, that's why I go back, he realized in one of the lucid moments. It doesn't matter if it's dangerous.

In his half-sleep he saw dogs, so he turned into a dog himself so as not to be attacked. He pitied them: being a dog meant canine captivity for life. He ought to change into a stone, but that wasn't any good either: eternal captivity as a rock. Stars twinkle as they struggle in the captivity of their stellar existence. Nothing is able to be anything but what it is. It needs to be said.

That morning Uri got quite far to the south, keeping near the city wall so that in the event he was attacked he could quickly spring back over it. Over that way, too, the wall was neither tall nor fortified everywhere. It would have done no harm if, in the course of his long, solitary exploratory jaunts around Alexandria he had found out some more details. Why did I have no suspicions? I ought to have. The signs were there to be seen.

His thinking was that if he were to be pursued, once over the wall he would untie a boat on the lake and row off to the west: rowing single-handed at sea was not a good idea, but it was perfectly possible on a lake. But no one came along by the wall, so he carried on walking eastward. At the main canal to the east, the Taurus, he turned to the north. He passed by huts and workshops; there were few people out on the streets, and although they looked on him as an intruder, no one set upon him. Some stray dogs sniffed at him mistrustfully, they did not bite, obviously sensing that he would bite back.

Southeast Alexandria was living its own particular everyday life: asses were transporting goods, smiths smithing, cloth dyers dyeing cloth, in the gardens there were women at work in vegetable beds—this was no neighborhood for rabble from the harbor. It crossed Uri's mind to ask to be admitted into one of the workshops; he could offer his labor and spin out the few days it would take before things went back to normal—after all, the prefect could not allow the whole city to go up in flames—but he decided not to take the risk: it would be better in Delta. He may not know anyone who lived there, but at least there were Jews.

He kept on swinging the staff until he finally decided to throw it away. Anyone who lives by weapons dies by them. But he stopped and went back for the stick. It wasn't he who had started the carnage; this was something else.

Now he recalled that he had mislaid the scroll that he had taken to the Paneion. He was annoyed by that. It was a valuable scroll that he had taken from the alabarch's library. Where could he have left it? He could not recall.

The staff at least was a good, strong length of walnut. He carried it in his right hand to give the impression that he was right-handed. Uri loathed all combat sports; he preferred sprinting to any of them them, though he was not too fond of that either. Now, though, he firmly gripped the staff as if he were holding onto the hand of the Eternal One.

He just has to have some goal in mind for me.

No doubt that was also the thought of those who were choked to death on the pyres before they charred peacefully away.

By now he was approaching Delta. He saw a large group drawing near coming from a side street on the left. He narrowed his eyes to get a better look, then stopped. A few characters with cudgels were driving around a dozen people before them, running at the double. As they got near Uri, one of the cudgel wielders yelled over:

"Come on, then! We'll see how these Jews run!"

Uri joined them.

"Where are we headed?"

"Delta!"

It was two or three families they were herding on, from time to time beating them, men, women, old people and young alike. Uri brandished his own staff but did not hit anyone.

"They've all got to be collected," panted one of the cudgel wielders, a large, muscular man with an intelligent look on his face, who was cheerfully, contentedly, almost amicably belaboring the Jews." All to Delta... All... From everywhere..."

Doubts now arose in Uri as to whether it was such a good idea after all to go to Delta, but the pursuers were all strapping young men and would quickly overtake him if he were to make a run for it, so he trotted along with them.

They halted beside a pile of rubbish. Two of them waded in, flailing with their cudgels at the scraps of papyri, rags, and heaped-up debris, treading carefully, slowly, systematically. The site was drying out as the haulers had not picked up garbage for weeks now. Uri squinted first at the Jews, then the Greeks. The Greeks were standing with lowered cudgels. There were eighteen Jews and, from their standpoint, even if Uri was included, just five Greeks, the sixth and seventh still thrashing around with their cudgels in the garbage. The Jews could make a run for it, at least the young and fit could, but they didn't. Instead they stood there, puffing and blowing, disconsolately, a couple of them even mumbling their prayers. Could it be that they, too, supposed that Delta would be a better place to be?

A dump wasn't such a bad idea, Uri considered; better than a cemetery, at any rate.

He looked over at banks of the canal. There was no one down there, no fishermen angling for prey, no fishing boats. Anyone who could swim and could stand the stink would be able to get out of Delta as far as the lake. He regretted not having learned how to swim, but the Tiber, after all, was even filthier than this.

The two Greeks came back; they had not gone far into the trash, but they had not found anybody.

They continued toward Delta, the Jews running resignedly, the Greeks merrily, meticulously whacking them: they were glad the boredom was at an end; they, society's scum, had become important and were fulfilling a lofty purpose.

They saw some burnt-out shops. They ran past a synagogue, its gate open, the bimah strewn with rubble; it had been ransacked. What was there to steal, for God's sake? A Torah—that was worthless to them; the menorah—that might be sold or melted down; lamps—well yes, if it was a silver vessel. The Jews burst out into sobs as they ran.

They had recognized Delta's boundary by the fact that the Greeks had thrown together from beams and stones a makeshift wall across the road; they were taking pains to cement the stones together, lugging over large buckets of sand, mortar and water. The group stopped.

"What's this, then?" queried one of sturdy cudgel wielders.

"It's going to be walled in! All the streets are being shut off!"

The cudgel wielder chortled and amicably smacked on the back of a skinny woman who was bent over by her coughing.

"Right! In with you!"

The Jews scrambled up the stones, and where the wall was still low jumped down, one after the other. Uri clambered after them and took a look behind.

"Drop dead, scumbags!" he yelled before jumping off into Delta.

On the other side several woman and an elderly man lay gasping on the ground. Uri kneeled next to the old man, who shielded his eyes with his hands.

"I too am Jewish," said Uri. "Have you any broken bones?"

They sized him up mistrustfully. Some young men gathered threateningly around him. Uri got to his feet.

"I too am Jewish," he repeated. "Do you want to look?"

"But you ran with the Greeks!"

"Because I wanted to get to Delta! I didn't hit anyone!"

"Liar! You're a spy for the Greeks!"

"Are you nuts?" said Uri, shrugging his shoulders, turning away and slowly starting off northward.

No one followed him.

In Delta, groups of people were standing around, animatedly discussing events; many were marching along with blankets, pots and pans, hammering on tightly shut house doors to no avail; elderly men of distinguished demeanor marched off somewhere or other, perhaps to confer, and firmly, with dignity, brushed off anyone who tried to join them. A long queue of people stood in front of one restaurant, perhaps waiting for food to be doled out; shops were closed, not so much on account of Drusilla's death but because of the conflict. Uri picked up his pace; he knew that Delta had a big population, but not as big as this. He would have liked to get to the Basilica, because he was familiar with that neighborhood, and he would have found it reassuring to find a haven there, only the streets to the north were now sealed off; the industrious Greeks had built walls everywhere, cutting the northern and southern sections of Delta apart.

Uri stood by the northern wall; stonemasons were still working on the far side.

"What are they doing that for?" Uri burst out in Aramaic.

"Because the houses of the rich are to the north," came a response in Aramaic. The man was standing nearby, watching in leisurely fashion, chewing papyrus bark.

"You mean these people here have been thrown out of there?" Uri asked.

"Certainly," said the man. "This makes it easier to rob the houses."

"But you can't do that without the prefect's permission."

"You said it," the man nodded.

Uri took a closer look at him. He had a black beard, black hair, and swarthy features, a fine figure of a man, maybe thirty or so. The man in turn sized Uri up; his eyes narrowed as he was plunged in thought:

"I've seen you somewhere before," he said.

"That could be," said Uri.

"You don't live in Delta."

"No, I don't."

The man pondered, then shrugged his shoulders and turned away, still chewing.

Uri looked around. There was a fever of activity, with each family tugging its belongings after it in a handcart: chairs, pots, blankets, candlesticks. It seemed the Greeks in northern Delta had allowed the Jews to take some things away after all; that meant less resistance than if they had started pillaging everything straightaway.

Uri's stomach was growling. He had not had anything to eat since that morning, and that had only been fruit. I've got out of the habit of doing without food, he thought. It's high time I got used to it again.

"How is it possible to provide for this number of people?" Uri asked.

"There's no way," the man responded.

"So what is going to happen?"

"The Eternal One will come to our aid," said the man.

Uri peered questioningly at his face to see if he was joking, but he found it impossible to tell.

"If a person is hungry and thirsty but has no money," Uri went on, "what is he supposed to do?"

"Croak hungry," the man suggested.

Uri pondered.

"And if that's not to his liking?"

"Steal," the man offered a new suggestion.

Uri guffawed. People were racing about, wailing, beating their breasts or just sitting forlornly, convulsed, on the ground. The man's calm struck Uri as extraordinary.

"You don't live in Delta either, do you," said Uri, more by way of a statement than a question.

"No," said the man. "I have no relatives in Alexandria."

"Neither do I," said Uri.

"Just be glad, then!" the man suggested, "like me."

Uri hemmed.

"I'm called Gaius Theodorus," he said. "I'm from Rome."

The man's eyes glinted.

"I know who you are! You usually sit next to the alabarch in the Basilica."

"That's me."

The man's look turned suspicious at that.

"What are you doing here?" he queried, interrupting his chewing.

"I was sent here by the alabarch to spy out the land for him, and, by the way, so that I should curl up and die as soon as possible."

The man gave Uri's sweat-soaked tunic a once over, thought a moment, and nodded.

"You got there too late, didn't you?"

"Yup."

"They've long since left the city," the man stated. "They've got their own private army; they'll survive. They pay off the Greeks and they're taken care of. But how come you speak Aramaic? People here don't!"

Uri gave a brief explanation.

"My name's Aristarchos," the man said in response. "I'm a seaman; my family lives in Tyre. I've been held up in the port for a week now; I wasn't allowed to unload so I rowed in by dinghy. I've been in negotiation for six days now; they wanted to shift the whole cost of the delay onto my shoulders, as if I had been refusing to unload... They're dead stupid, the Jews here! Very rich, very arrogant, and very stupid. They curse, hint at infractions of the law and meanwhile play tricks, getting me to pay even for my board and lodgings, instead of paying the Greeks a bigger bribe... I'm fairly sure every Jewish boat has been pillaged, mine included. All that was left on it were two of my men; the rest have spent a week drinking in the harbor area... I'm curious as to whether those two men of mine are still alive or have been poleaxed."

"When these here come to be poor, they may come to their senses," Uri ventured.

"They won't!" Aristarchos forecast. "They've been pampered for three hundred years; nothing's going to help them."

At the corner of a nearby street a fight broke out, and many people hurried over to take a look.

"That's something like a storm must be for you," said Uri.

Aristarchos spat.

"Not really," he said. "At sea you at least know what to expect, but not here."

Uri's stomach rumbled again.

"Have you got any money?" he asked.

Aristarchus did not answer straightaway.

"A bit," he said finally.

"So you're not going to starve," Uri suggested.

"I'll ride it out for a while," said Aristarchus.

They stood wordlessly. From the other side of the wall the laughter of the Greeks was audible; a stone block had dropped on someone's toes, that was what they found amusing.

Uri had to concede that the limits of the newly won friendship extended only so far and no farther.

"God be with you!" he said and set off back toward the interior of southern Delta.

THE UPROAR, TERROR, QUARRELING AND WAILING WENT ON. SOME young men broke into a shop and pounced on the food. A dried-out flatbread rolled into Uri's path, as he happened to be poking around the neighborhood, so he wolfed it down. Delta's indigenous inhabitants did what they could to defend their homes against the strange Jews, but some of them realized that this was not going to work and so thought it better to admit a family or two now so that they would have some help later holding off the rest. The dimmer ones proclaimed their rights, shouting from the windows. From the taller buildings lots of people were looking out from the upper floors, reporting what was going on at the far side of the wall. The Greeks were organizing a guard; they might have no military weapons, but they did have cudgels. Uri took this to mean that Flaccus had not opened the arsenals, which was a good sign, but then again he was not scaring off the rabble, which was a bad sign because that was something he could have done a long time ago. Either of the legions could reach the city in less than a day, and the uproar was now in its third day.

That evening Uri lay down on the street; he was tired. He sought out a gateway in which many people were already sleeping in the hope that he'd find safety in numbers. When he awoke the next morning, however, his sandals were missing, even though he had tied the laces tightly to his ankles. They must have been cut off; numbers had given no protection to his sandals. Uri just laughed; a least he would not have to worry about them any more.

The whole of the next day he prowled around south Delta. Others were also prowling around, searching for something to eat and drink; the fine palms and papyrus trees along the broader main thoroughfares were cut down, chopped up and then kindled to boil cauldrons of water brought from the canal to be used in cooking or to drink. Men gestured, yelled, and conferred; children ran around happily and freely; women cooked, cried, shrieked, yelled, and gave orders. The search for shelter went on. Families kept jealous and determined watch on their handcarts, their remaining possessions piled up on them, with the eldest lying on top to protect their belongings with their bodies.

Supposedly yet more new people were being squeezed into Delta. On the north side, the Greeks built a gateway to act as the sole exit; everywhere else the wall was fortified. Flaccus would come to the assistance of the Jews. The Eternal One would assist them. They prayed and pleaded. The alabarch would assist them. But the alabarch was not there, the abject scoundrel; he was in discussions with Flaccus. He was discussing nothing with Flaccus; he had turned tail and run from the city. His army had clashed with the Greeks; there had been no clash. But the alabarch's bankers were in negotiations with the Greeks, seeking to buy them off. We won't negotiate with the Greeks! Everything should be returned to us, and compensation would even be paid! Those who had been murdered could not be given back, and what compensation could make up for them?

Late that afternoon, news spread that the Council of Elders had assembled; there were fifteen of them; and names were given but Uri did not recognize one. Some twenty-five names were bandied about: fifteen of those, then. They wanted order to be kept. That would be good. They would distribute people among the homes. That would also be good. Everyone who had been long established in southern Delta would be compelled to accept at least two families. Or four, even five. But then who's going to make them? The elders would be organizing a guard of fit and strong young men. About time too. The Eternal One can see how we're holding our ground. He won't desert us in this hour of need either.

The elders were getting ready to go to Flaccus and lodge a complaint. What is the point of that? Flaccus is involved in it. No, he's not involved, he doesn't even know what's going on; he's been sprawled in a drunken stupor in the Akra for days. Sure he knows what's going on: he planned the whole thing, paid the Greeks off. How can the emperor permit this? He doesn't! He relieved him of the post, but Flaccus ignored that; he's getting ready to go to war with Rome. Rome will trounce him, but by then we'll be dead. We should dispatch a deputation to the emperor! Fair enough, but who should go? And how? Let the alabarch go! The alabarch won't go: the emperor dislikes him! Why would he dislike him? Because the alabarch informed against the emperor's father, his bankers said as much. Where are those bankers, speaking of that? Not one of them among us? Yes, they are. Several of them have been seen; they too have been squeezed in here. But what are they doing? Lending money at usurious interest rates? They're smarter than that: they're buying up food stocks to sell off at sky-high prices! What food stocks? Where are any food stocks to be found? There's no purchasing of food being done here: more like thieving and pilfering!

I'll have a look at the Council of the Elders, Uri resolved.

That happened sooner than he had supposed.

He was poking around the bank of the Taurus canal, wondering what he could use to catch fish, when someone called out:

"The alabarch's man!"

He was surrounded, pushed around and had his staff wrenched from his grasp.

"The alabarch's spy!" they called out.

Uri tried to pull himself free but was held fast. These people are hacking me to pieces, he realized with astonishment.

"Let's take him to the council," proposed one.

He was pushed and shoved; someone thumped him on the back with a stick, but murmurs went up not to do that. Uri muttered a prayer of thanks.

He was jostled to the upper floor of a pretty house where lots of people were seated, walking around or just standing in the reception room.

"The alabarch's spy!" someone declared. "He always had a seat along with them in the Basilica!"

They let go of him. Uri stood there, breathing heavily. He screwed his eyes up but was unable to make out any faces. His feeling was that these were people he had never seen before, but they could have been in the Basilica for all he knew.

An intelligent-looking man stepped up to him. He was not someone whom Uri remembered seeing.

"What did the alabarch's send you for?" he asked.

Uri held his tongue. He had been Agrippa's messenger, and he had been the alabarch's spy in Greek Alexandria, so now he had turned into the alabarch's spy in the Jewish quarter. Whatever he said, the people here would only believe what they wanted to believe.

"I wasn't sent," he declared after a brief pause. "I came of my own accord."

"What are you after?"

"The Jews are in Delta now, aren't they?"

The man looked at him askance, ran his eye up and down, and shook his head.

"You're the Roman Jew," he surmised. "Philo's favorite. Am I right?"

"Yes, I am a Jew from Rome."

A second man, older and more stubborn-looking, stepped up alongside the first.

"What does the alabarch have in mind?" he asked.

Uri bridled. "Why don't you ask him?" he retorted.

"That's enough of your sauce!" the stubborn-looking man roared.

"I'm not too fond of being manhandled," Uri declared. "My staff was also taken away!"

The two men looked at each other in puzzlement.

"I want my staff back!" Uri cried.

There was silence as everyone in the room looked at him.

"Give it back to him!" the younger man ordered.

One of them offered the staff. Uri took it back and turned away.

"Get them out of here, please."

The younger man gave a nod; there was dignity in the movement.

The escort left the room.

"What do you want?" the younger of the men asked.

"I don't want anything," Uri answered. "They hauled me here. My apologies for disturbing."

He bowed and set off to leave.

"Wait!" the stubborn-looking man exclaimed.

Uri stopped and turned around.

"Where's the alabarch?" came the question from the slit-eyed man with the low forehead.

"How would I know? When I wanted to get back into the palace they were no longer there. I spent two nights in the necropolis, then I came here to Delta. Of my own accord. To my way of thinking it was safer."

They looked at him dumbfounded.

"Do you think that money will smooth over everything?" hissed the narrow-eyed man.

Uri snorted a laugh.

"I haven't got a drachma on me!"

"You buried it!"

"Are you kidding? What use is money here? Tomorrow you won't be able to get even a loaf of bread for one hundred drachmas!"

There was another silence before the younger man said:

"Come over here! Take a seat among us."

Uri looked at him and broke into a smile.

A stool was pushed under him at the table. He sat down.

And they asked him what he thought was to be done.

What ran through Uri's head were all the things he had read in the scrolls Tija had recommended, about the tactics that a town under siege ought to follow. But there wasn't much among the good advice offered by Philon and Aeneas

Tacitus that could be applied here: the Greeks intended not so much to besiege as to starve and humiliate the Jews. Food and water were needed, and those could only be obtained from outside Delta; nothing at all could be grown in this densely inhabited quarter.

"The Greeks need to be prevailed upon to supply us with food," he said, "though I'm aware that will be very costly. All the same, they need to be paid off not to stand guard gratuitously."

"There will be no negotiating with murderers!"

"But there is no choice," Uri countered.

"Let the alabarch negotiate!"

"It may well be that he is doing just that somewhere," said Uri. "But here and now that is what we have to do—even with murderers."

They resumed their argument, red in the face as they began screaming at each other. Uri suddenly realized that they had been discussing this very issue just beforehand. He was fueled by a new hope that maybe it wasn't such a bad thing to be seen as being the alabarch's man; it might even be handy to get them to give him something to eat.

"Your alabarch is a gutless worm," said one of the councilors, whom Uri thought he had seen before: why yes! It was Euodus; one of the guests who had dined at the alabarch's palace. "Why doesn't he come with his army? He would be able to rescue us! It's only riffraff guarding us!"

"I can't imagine why he doesn't come," said Uri. It was all very awkward; the proper thing for him to say would have been that the alabarch was obviously moving Heaven and Earth, but he could not find it in his heart to say so.

A few hours later he was able to eat together with the elders. Looking out of the window he could dimly see figures prowling on the far side of the wall, still equipped only with cudgels.

Uri figured the guards here were staying out of the major pillaging, otherwise they would have been pickled to the gills by now. It was possible, then, that they would be satisfied with a bit of money. It was not their aim that we should die quickly, he reasoned: they'd rather kill us off slowly because that way they would make a tidy profit. The bartering should start low, and we should be grudging in giving any ground; it would be no loss to break off talks at any point, because the Greeks would come hammering on the door for money soon enough.

"They won't deliver anything! It's waste of money! They'll sling their hook straightaway!"

"They will deliver," said Uri. "They've got that much sense."

"Surely you're not counting on this lasting for any length of time?" asked the stubborn-looking man.

"Yes, I am," Uri responded.

That did not go down well with anybody—the elders and the smarter ones really wanted to hear their longings confirmed.

"Flaccus will come to his senses," said one elderly man sitting in a wobbly chair. "He's drunk himself stupid but he'll come to. He's been good to us up till now, partial to us, but he's been led up the garden path, drunk under the table..."

They looked at Uri as if he was the one who knew it all. After all, he lived in the alabarch's palace, knew Flaccus personally, was a student at the Gymnasium...

Uri shook his head.

"Flaccus hasn't taken leave of his senses," he said. "He's very much in command of them, in fact. He's a man who has fallen out of favor. He made a deal beforehand with the Greeks; in my view he took a payment in advance, and he's taking a share of the booty right now. He's amassed a mountain of money so he'll be able to hide out in the Sudan or somewhere... That's his only chance."

"But why at our expense?"

"That's the only way that was open to him! Do you think he would have joined forces with the Jews when he knows that they support whoever is emperor at the moment?"

A protracted and unproductive argument broke out, with the elders getting bogged down in grand politics and history, while Uri sat quietly and thanked the Eternal One that he had been recognized on the bank of the Taurus.

All the members of the council spent the night at the house; the owner, a silk merchant, did well out of it: there was no need for him to accept others in his house, and the freshly organized forces of law and order protected his property along with the councilors. He had a splendid house, with a pool on the ground floor; the two floors above that had eight big rooms, including three with cubicles. There were ten elders, two of them without families, so somehow there was room for them all.

Uri lay on the floor near the pool, along with many others: the noise just would not die down outside, nor would it die down inside, and he turned over in his mind why it had not immediately occurred to him to paint himself as the alabarch's man. It had come down to pure chance that he had ended up here and had been given board and lodging. Am I so helpless? He reflected before coming to the conclusion that he wasn't.

Do I despise the alabarch that much? He was surprised to conclude that he did—as much as he did Agrippa.

Nicolaeus, the most intelligent-looking member of the council, took Uri aside late that evening.

"Where do you think the greatest risk lies?" he asked.

Uri sighed.

"They are going to starve us, come what may. Then an epidemic is going to erupt, and we shall have no way of breaking out."

Nicolaeus nodded.

"They have a big pile of booty now," he said, "but that's just a one-off. Flaccus will not get a share of the real spoils... These wretched little killers will hardly get a thing... You can't loot the same house twice over... The rich Greeks, on the other hand, will pick up our business partners and our contacts... That's the real prize! No one in the wider world gives credence any more to the Jews of Alexandria. We've foolishly allowed ourselves be fleeced; that sort of thing can happen again at any time, we've become unreliable trading partners, that's the problem! A big problem!"

Uri thought about that and decided it was the unadorned truth.

Whatever happened, this was the end of Jewish Alexandria.

THE GREEK RIFFRAFF ON THE OTHER SIDE OF THE WALL MOCKED THE Jews who offered to do deals with them, swearing at them, calling them pestilent, cat-murdering slaves, Moses' leprous people, and then, of course, in the end they took the money and that night brought food and water. The water was not stagnant and though the food might have been less than they asked for, the Jews of Delta were not flagrantly shortchanged. The Greek wretches wanted to make money as best they could.

Late in the afternoon they also hurled over the barricaded walls many copies of a proclamation by Flaccus in which he explained the formation of the Sector as a justified reprisal for countless breaches of the peace by Jews. Hereafter, the document stated, Jews might live within it, but nowhere else in Alexandria. According to the proclamation—and this was what hurt those in Delta most— the Jews counted as newcomers in Alexandria, and the restrictive stipulations that governed foreigners would henceforth be applicable to them as well.

Countless breaches of the peace by Jews? What a hideous lie! We have always observed the law! Our own, God's law, first and foremost, but also whatever was their prevailing law! Even the infamously Judaeophobic debauchee Euergetes III did not think of anything like this in the days when he attacked us!

Foreigners to Alexandria—us? Newcomers? When our rights were graven in stone by king Soter? Those tablets exist to this day in the Museion. Emperor Augustus confirmed and expanded those rights, which are proclaimed for ever and a day by his stele in front of the Sebasteion—that is, if it has not already been toppled. Us, whose Greek Torah, the Pentateuch, was deposited in the Museion of the king's palace as a precious document, the most precious of all, also for ever and a day—that is to say, if they have not incinerated that too! Us, who always scrupulously paid every tax to king and emperor and city? Us, who have been living here for three hundred years? Ever since Alexander the Great paced out the city's boundaries three hundred years ago? We, whose very activities allowed the city to flourish at all?

We have become the foreigners, outlaws, newcomers, slaves?

We were here even before the first Greek simpleton slave set foot in Egypt! We were already here two thousand years ago when Moses led his people out of here! We came home three hundred years ago; we are natives! Homegrown inhabitants!

In spite of which it is now we who are wrongfully burned and massacred!

Uri had to admit it, Aristarchus had been right: these people had been pampered, they were deadly stupid.

The real trouble was not what the proclamation stated—Flaccus's declaration that the Jews were to be foreigners—but what it implied, namely that he was going to set his armed forces against Delta. That was the real problem. Soldiers would be guarding the Sector from now on, not Greek riffraff who were open to bribes. It would become impossible to acquire food, impossible to break out.

Flaccus, "our Aulus," had not gone about things in so stupid a fashion, after all. He had managed to create an internal enemy, and by intervening against it he was going to forge unity between the Greeks and the legions. Rome was going to have a tough nut to crack if it wanted to remove Flaccus. It would come to war, and Flaccus's chances against Rome were not at all bad.

Uri sensed that the sight of the Jews choking to death on the fumes of the pyre had not inspired in him the appropriate sympathy and horror, and he wondered why not. Perhaps because he had already seen that sort of thing at the foot of Mount Gerizim. Thinking back on that scene now, in retrospect, he was astonished to discover that even then he had not been as shocked as he ought to have been. No, not truly shocked.

Ever since he had witnessed the rape and execution of Sejanus's daughter, nothing had surprised him. Then he'd had to vomit, but since then he'd lost the ability to be sick.

For seven years I have been aware of the terrible deeds of which man is capable.

The only difference is that now I'm being hunted too—an important difference, but not one of essence.

He was amazed to consider just how many people had turned out to be scoundrels who he had naïvely thought to be decent and honest. How is it possible for someone who had known the essence of man in general for so long, since he was fifteen, since the Eternal One had blessed or cursed him with the knowledge, had chosen him—how could he still be so mixed up when it came to the details? What was this invincible desire in him, to see created man as better than he was?

Where did this instinct to decency, in him even now, come from? Why had it not entered his head, basking in the light thrown by alabarch's huge presence, to demand that he be given privileges?

He saw before his eyes the figure of his father: he had toiled his whole life long but had never once given up his honesty. Maybe that was how he had been created by the Lord. Still, Uri had not been created from the same mold as his father; he'd had bestowed on him a voluptuous nature, he was indolent and selfish, a hedonist in every way, but even so he had inherited his father's self-tormenting honesty. Tears came to Uri's eyes at the thought of his father having left him to his own devices when his eyesight had deteriorated, yet he had only wanted what was best for his son when he had him squeezed into the delegation.

There was much lamenting in the Sector at this time, and every reason for it, but tears did not come to Uri's eyes on that account. All that was happening in the Sector was what man commits against man. But there was one thing—the fact that his father's honesty had permeated him, through his very flesh and bones, and he could not rid himself of it even when Jew bared fangs against Jew in the Sector, Jew cheated Jew, stealing from and falsely accusing him, even when all Jews were being held in captivity by wretched Greek scum who had been reduced to evil—that did not come simply from what mankind was capable of.

The joy he felt was at past human actions.

Perhaps the Eternal One had not willed it to be so, He who lets let every evil deed be committed in the pursuit of some unknowable higher goal. But there could be no doubt that if He happened to be glancing this way right now, He too was taking delight in this miraculous bond between father and son. He would tell his father as much, find words of some sort for this indescribable miracle, modest and undemonstrative words, and yet his father would understand all the same. Then they would both weep, embracing one another, Father and Son.

For that to happen, of course, he had to live through the Bane, as it was called in the Sector on the model of Onslaught, Attack, Calamity, Sacrifice, Holocaust, Havoc and other similarly inaccurate and idiotic names. He had to live through the Bane, and to get back home to Rome.

NEGOTIATIONS WITH THE GREEKS SLIPPED OUT OF THE HANDS OF THE council members: rebels—a group of young strongmen—drove those who were bargaining for the elders away from the northern gate with cudgels, fists, and knives; they paid the Greeks for two days worth of supplies directly, received the food, and distributed it among their own kith and kin. That shift in power did not last long, however, because the Greek rabble were replaced by legionnaires, and there was no making deals with them.

Jews were still arriving in the Sector from the outside, only now the legionnaires brought them.

The new arrivals related that thirty-eight members of the council of elders had been seized outside Delta and in north Delta, and they had been imprisoned by Flaccus in the Akra. If there were ten councilors in south Delta, then there must still be another twenty-two lying low somewhere. Maybe they were doing something on the outside; maybe they were getting organized, stealing weapons, maybe traipsing around with the alabarch's army somewhere. Wherever they were, council members were nonetheless important people, with authority like mini-pharaohs over the clans and the Kahals, and only they were in a position to protect the Sector against the rebels.

The new arrivals also told them that the Greeks had placed statues or portraits of the emperor in every synagogue that had not been completely trashed. They had desecrated all of the Jewish houses of prayer! There was no longer any place to pray! The largest of the statues had been installed in the Basilica—it was bigger than the statue of Augustus in the Sebasteion. Even there! Yes, even there.

Uri laughed out loud.

"They're dumping their surplus statues on us!"

He would have done better keeping this to himself, because he was almost beaten up for saying so.

In the Basilica Greeks were selling off cheaply the things they had plundered, wailed the new arrivals. One of them had seen his own menorah, a real curiosity, a huge silver piece weighing eight and a half pounds with a lion at its base! The seventy golden chairs no longer had their gilding: that had been prized off and filched by the Greeks!

The members of the council conferred with their confidants; by now there were twelve of them, Tryphon and Andron had by now also turned up. Tryphon had been lying ill in a relative's house; Andron had been picked up by soldiers who had no idea who they were dealing with. Uri was glad that there were now two more councilors, besides Euodus, who had seen him at dinners at the alabarch's palace: they eyed him suspiciously, it is true, but their recognition enhanced his prestige. His relationship with the alabarch was not enough in itself: Uri needed to sing something for his supper.

But then it couldn't be any more difficult to stand his own ground among the Jews here than it had been in the Gymnasium.

He could read Greek authors, the Jews couldn't. In a town under siege autocracy is advisable, and sooner or later that is what will come into being.

Uri proposed that all kitchen knives be rounded up and then used to equip the forces of law and order before the rebels collected them. This was debated by the members of council and accepted. Uri pointed out that under no circumstances should an attack be made on the soldiers guarding them; that may well be precisely what they are waiting for—a genuine *casus belli*.

Andron was astonished.

"I'd never have expected that a myopic bookworm had such a practical head on his shoulders," he said.

"I'm a strategos gone wrong," Uri chuckled.

Families were loathe to hand over their knives, and the bulk of them were hidden away, but they ended up with enough to arm the Gerusia's policemen.

The men applying to be policemen were young and fit; Uri specifically requested that not all of them be taken on, as there were almost certainly some rebels among them. So long as they were in the minority, they would accommodate the will of the majority, unlike their companions who were left out. This too was debated, and not all of them were taken.

Stocks gradually ran down; the local inhabitants still had some flour, salt, and oil on hand, but they only let relatives have any and they tried to conceal their stores, so the council of elders passed a strict decree against hoarding of food. This was displayed, but could not be implemented. Uri proposed that the council ought to requisition all stocks and dole them out in equal rations, but the elders, after prolonged discussion, were unwilling to agree, perhaps because they would do better with things left the way they were, perhaps because they did not feel that their motley forces were strong enough to enforce such a rule.

Uri went with a pair of the new recruits to the southern wall. They found that the soldiers, not considering construction to be their job, had broken off reinforcement work. Uri found several points in the makeshift structure where one could break through. He reported it, proposing that anyone who was very hungry be allowed to make a break for it, on the chance that they might find food somewhere; there was plenty of money within the Sector, but hardly any food. The elders discussed and rejected the proposal. Uri looked around: confidential advisers and young men armed with knives were thronging the room. The idea was going to spread soon enough.

The very next day, Jews broke out at several points, surprising the soldiers, who did not dare leave their sentry posts; whole families, dozens of people rushed out past them. Uri was watching from the upper story of one of the buildings as the Jews raced to the west along deserted streets.

That night a few stole back, reporting that at first the Greeks in the market-places had accepted their money and had given them something to eat in return, but then the mob had attacked, slaughtering many women and children, while elderly people had been bound and taken away. Once again fires were lit and anyone the Greek rioters caught was smoked to death.

Two of them had seen a burned-out synagogue; there were corpses of men littering the ground in front, their heads and genitals cut off. They may well have resisted when Greeks attacked the house of prayer.

In the Sector there was chanting of psalms and prayers.

On the Friday, a Septuagint was brought out of one of the houses and as the Sun went down many hundreds prayed in the street, scattering earth over themselves.

The Greeks patched up and strengthened the walls. They worked slowly, under military supervision, no longer showing the enthusiasm they had when it had been motivated by their own rage.

Infants with bloated stomachs lay in the streets, their emaciated mothers trying in vain to breast-feed them; the men looked straight ahead with madly gleaming eyes.

The elderly went hungry too.

Everyone was famished, but all the same the streets became covered with excreta: people were no longer continent; by now their own tissues were being eaten up.

I need to get out while I still have the strength, Uri thought. He was hunched over on the banks of the canal, his legs drawn up so that his knees were pressing into his stomach to relieve the pain; around him were people chewing on weeds. Uri was not chewing anything but keeping a close eye out in case a mouse or rat that he could swat were to appear.

It was the last week in August. He needed to get out by September at the latest. Which is to say, by Germanicus.

Not yet though: he first needed to weather the Egyptian New Year, then the emperor's birthday. The Greeks were bound to go rabid during the celebrations.

The elders conferred, quite needlessly, but they still conferred. Uri held his peace, feeling only a leaden weariness, his head drooping every now and then.

"What is that spy doing here?" someone called out in a high-pitched voice.

Uri was startled to consciousness.

It was Tryphon's son, Demetrius, who was standing in front of him, his big nostrils pulsating angrily.

Uri got to his feet.

"This is the alabarch's spy!" Demetrius squeaked.

The elders tiredly muttered something; they had no wish for an argument to break out.

"How could you have the nerve to barge your way in here, you scum?" screamed Demetrius.

Uri stood and looked at the handsome, horse-faced boy, who was now skinny like everyone else in Delta.

"If I'm stuck here with you, and not in any position to leave either," said Uri coolly and collectedly, "then I am hardly likely to be the alabarch's spy, am I?"

Demetrius narrowed his eyes to slits in hatred.

"You're Philo's ass-plug, you scum!" he hissed.

Uri was amazed: the boy was jealous.

"That is neither here nor there right now," he noted in a conciliatory tone.

"He's been co-operating nicely with us," said Nikolaeus wearily. "Leave off, both of you."

"He's one of them," hissed Demetrius, flouncing hysterically out of the room.

On the morning of August 29, the Egyptian New Year, a great clamor broke out beyond the northern gate. Squealing piglets were being tossed at the walls, making a big popping noise as they struck, their bellies torn apart, the intestines slithering out, their legs twitching. The northern gate was suddenly thrown open. On the other side of the street facing the gate, a dozen of so crosses were lying on the ground; behind those several ox-drawn carts were standing. The soldiers brought out some well-fed Jewish prisoners, some were tethered to the recumbent crosses, others lashed to the wheels of the carts, which were lifted up by the soldiers. To the sound of cheering from the Greek onlookers, the crosses were slotted into holes that had been excavated where some of the paving stones had been torn up, then they were pulled upright and secured. The carts were then rolled backward, over the prisoners fastened to their wheels, then they slowly set off, the oxen driven around in a circle, over and over, smashing bones, flaying flesh from bodies.

One of the men was tied behind a cart by his legs and dragged until not one shred of flesh was left of the man.

Uri, his eyes screwed up, watched the proceedings from one of the windows and, enthralled, returned again and again to look until the evening. That was how long the biggest Dionysias that Alexandria had ever seen went on. Musicians played their music, drummers drummed, horns were blown, strings plucked, improvised kitchens were set up for the celebrants and a northerly breeze blew the smell of roast meat over to south Delta, along with whiffs of rotting human flesh. Plastered Greeks drank and vomited, vomited and drank. Many more who died on the crosses early that afternoon; they were not taken down by the soldiers. Their relatives gathered at the north gate and called out to the dying, invoked God, and pleaded, sobbing, with the soldiers to be allowed to take down the dead bodies themselves. The soldiers just laughed and ignored them. Or they invited the despairing relatives to come and get them, and anyone who did venture through the gate was bound and then broken on the wheel.

The cries of the dying were heard all day outside the Sector; psalms were sobbed through all day inside the Sector.

A few of those who had been crucified were still alive the next day, some even managed to groan out reassurances to their family, blessing a wife, a little son, a little daughter; the Eternal One would in all certainty have vengeance. We shall rise again and be reunited, they called out, though up till then, being Sadducees, the Jews of Alexandria had not believed in the resurrection of the dead and an afterlife. They spoke Greek, not being able to speak any other language, and the soldiers found it very amusing.

After three days of this it was the turn of another feast: Emperor Gaius's birthday.

The north gate, which had been closed overnight, was opened and three cohorts marched in. They lined up, and a centurion demanded that the elders be brought out.

The elders were rounded up.

The centurion then read out the prefect's decree that the Jews were hiding weapons in their houses—those must be surrendered.

"But we have no weapons," muttered Nikolaeus.

"We are going to carry out a search of the houses," the centurion announced.

They entered the houses, with at least ten soldiers, armed to the teeth, going in together and the remainder standing guard outside, quite unnecessarily as the weakened Jews would not have been able to attack them anyway. Fathers tried to conceal their daughters from the eyes of the soldiers, for which they were dragged out and beaten. A few kitchen knives were recovered and quite a few cudgels, but no other weapons were found. Married women were gathered together, the soldiers taking digs at any husbands who protested, then, along with the girls, they were hustled off through the gate.

The centurion rasped out an order:

"Prefect Flaccus wishes to hear any complaints that you may have. Euodos, Tryphon, and Andron should present themselves and be led to the palace!"

Those who were named presented themselves; they were surrounded by a detachment and led off.

Flaccus had banqueted together with them in the alabarch's palace more than a few times.

That evening a few of the women and girls were allowed to return home.

They were allowed back because that afternoon, in the amphitheater, they had been shepherded onto the stage, where they ate pork in front of a packed auditorium. The pork was roasted in front of them, the half pigs skewered on a big iron rod and diligently rotated over the fire. Some of them retched, because they had been born Jewish, but they ate it anyway; some of them were able to eat it without retching because they had been born pagans and had converted to Judaism for their husbands' sake.

Those who refused to eat were simply torn apart by brute force, also on the stage.

Following this, dancers danced, musicians made music, and mimics mimed in their customary fashion.

Four husbands immediately declared that they would be serving bills of divorce.

On hearing that, one of the wives tore open the vein at her right wrist and bled to death on the street. No one tried to stem the flow of blood.

IT IS AMAZING WHAT WILL BE EATEN WHEN THERE IS NOTHING TO EAT— weeds, cats, rats, mice, hay, refuse. God looks aside, just as he had been looking aside powerlessly for weeks lest he see the enormities wrought on his people.

They were now in the month of Germanicus, time to get out of the Sector: an epidemic had broken out, with debilitated people dying by the dozens in the streets. It was impossible to bury them all promptly in the plot by the canal bank that had been assigned as a temporary cemetery.

There was no longer any point in drumming one's fingers among the elders, so Uri hung around near the south walls, reclining all day long in the shade and weighing up how and where he could make a break for it. He spent the nights out on the streets; the dead bodies in the houses now stank. But he spent most of his time lying down to conserve energy. He was racked by thirst, above all, so he would periodically drag himself off to the canal bank and strain some of the filthy water through his fingers for a drink.

It was strange that his travels should end in this manner, with him dying young.

Joseph would be very sad, but perhaps he would never find out and would live in hope until his last breath that his son was alive somewhere.

Uri was tormented by hallucinations, but all the same it was good to dream, because at least a sort of life awaited him in his dreams.

One night, at the foot of the wall, he dreamed that he was being spoken to.

"I'm Theocritus," the voice said, "From the XXIInds..."

Uri was incapable of making out any faces: he was stretched out among strange animals in a big cave, and they did not speak.

"Theocritus from the XXIInds..."

The cave vanished, the animals vanished, it was dark and a voice was coming from the far side of the wall:

"I'm Theocritus from the XXIInds..."

The voice could be heard coming softly from the outside and directed inward.

"What do you want?" Uri asked.

"I'm going to throw some food over! Watch your head! Don't eat it all in one go..."

Uri sat up. A parcel plopped down on the ground.

"Have you got it?"

"Yes, I have," Uri replied.

He slithered over and undid it. There was a flatbread, honey, and a flask of water inside. Uri ate slowly and not too much; he drank all the water. He pricked up his ears.

"Thank you," he said.

"Theocritus from the XXIInds... Don't forget it!"

He heard steps on the other side of the wall, then silence.

Uri tucked what was left under his tunic and slept a sleep without dreams.

The flatbread and honey kept him going for two days. He continued to recline near the south wall, and on one occasion a group of people were preparing to bury him before he growled "Not yet," at which they took fright and slouched off.

Three evenings later another voice called through the wall. This time it was a man who gave his name as Democritus, also from the XXIInds. He threw over a flatbread, water, and some smoked fish. He asked what Uri's name was, and Uri had to think very hard before it came to mind that he was Gaius Theodorus. He was more pleased by the name than was the mercenary.

"Got that... And don't forget: Democritus from the XXIInds."

"I won't... And now I won't forget my own name either."

This can't go on much longer, Uri reflected, as he again tucked the remainder under his tunic. The legionnaires are beginning to fear reprisals. Theocritus and Democritus, Theocritus and Democritus from the XXIInds... I'll have to bear witness for them when this is all over.

He received food the same way twice more; he divided it up, sat, pondered, and all of a sudden he saw before him the saltcellar—the *salinon*—the geometrical figure consisting of four semicircles. He was able to follow Archimedes's demonstration as never before, as though it were written on a tablet, showing that the area covered by the four quadrants of a circle was pi times the square of the radius.

He even managed to work out how Posidonius of Alexandria, who later settled down on the island of Rhodes, had been able to construct a spherical triangle and suspected, though he was not able to prove conclusively, Archimedes's demonstration that the sum of the angles of a *tripleuron*, a spherical triangle, was greater than two right angles. Demetrius, his mad mathematics master in the Gymnasium, had endeavored in vain to find the proof, had even given it to the students as an assignment, but nobody had been able to crack it. Uri now felt that he could demonstrate it: he saw the signs on his imaginary tablet, deduced it right to the end, and when he succeeded he whooped in delight. Starvation had only diminished his body; none of his brains had gone missing!

The vision soon subsided, but the long demonstration was now lodged somewhere deep in his brain and would remain retrievable, or so he hoped as he lay there without papyrus and ink. Perhaps he would need to eat smoked fish and the memory would be evoked. There was still a bit left of the smoked fish that had been thrown over the wall. It was ritually clean—the pagans were aware of what the Jews were allowed to eat.

It will be Rosh Hashanah tomorrow, someone near him was saying, Tishri 1.

Uri slowly trudged his way northward. He would see how Rosh Hashanah's celebrated so that he could regale his father when he got back home.

Rosh Hashanah was not celebrated in the Sector, however—that was the decision of the remaining elders, and maybe rightly so. They also decided, and posted notices making the decision public, that celebrations of the Day of Atonement and the Feast of Tabernacles would also be canceled: there was nowhere for them to pray in, no house of prayer left for the Jews of Alexandria, and there was no use in pretending. There would also be no fasting, and this too had a certain logic.

So there was no celebration of Rosh Hashanah, no one read out from the Septuagint, no one made any speeches; those who were still alive just sat and stretched out on the road the whole day long, praying to themselves. Uri prayed among them, squatting on his heels and bowing to the east. The quiet, even, constant murmur which emanated from them and enveloped the entire day was soothing and hypnotic. Whenever they noticed that someone had died, they dragged the body to one side so that they might inter it after the holiday, and then they went back to their praying.

Perfect democracy in action, Uri reflected, silently laughing to himself.

On the day after Rosh Hashanah he trudged back to the south wall, his feeding trough, and he waited for his manna from Heaven. It came, moreover, this time it was again faceless Democritus who hurled it over. It never even entered Uri's head to share it with someone else. While he was eating two of his teeth dropped out: two fine, healthy incisors from the lower jaw, bloodied by the gums.

His lower jaw would now be even more receding; he would no longer be recognized. He laughed and carried on happily digesting the food.

EARLY IN THE AFTERNOON OF TISHRI 10, THE FIRST DAY OF THE FEAST of Booths, Uri awoke to the sound of people shuffling past him in a great hurry. He was angry because he had been having a pleasant dream: he was strolling through a marvelous countryside, surrounded by children, his own children, the youngest of whom reminded him of his younger sister, only she did not have a choking cough. The countryside was rather like Campania, with houses of the sort one might find there nestling at the foot of the hills, houses like the one in which he had once been a guest of that jolly family, vociferous in its happiness, not far from Puteoli. He clambered to his feet. He was not even aware that Dikaiarchia and Puteoli were one and the same. The dream was lost, he had been unable to retain it; he greatly regretted that he would not be able to live as a human henceforward. He narrowed his eyes. There was a large gap yawning in the south wall, but that was not the way that people were hurrying. They were headed to the north.

"It's over! Over! Over!"

A throng of men, women, the remaining children and tough oldsters shuffled, tottered, and dashed their way through the wide-open north gate.

To either side stood a line of soldiers, and behind them a crowd of staring, alarmed Greeks.

Uri shuffled along with the crowd, past the ransacked, rubbish-strewn Basilica, then westward. There inside, on the chariot on which Carabbas had been pulled a few weeks before, stood a huge statue—obviously of Caligula. It crossed Uri's head that this was double sacrilege: for one thing, of a Jewish synagogue, for a second, of the emperor, but this was more of a vague suspicion, he would not have been able to cast that into words, his brain was exhausted. Those who tumbled to the ground were considerately helped to their feet by morose soldiers; Uri was surprised to notice that he was too. The crowd shuffled and staggered along the main thoroughfare toward the Heptastadion; farther on, well-fed Jews were joining the procession from side streets; they had not lived through the Bane in the Sector. The Greeks were dumbfounded, looking at the procession, to find that any of these people were still alive.

Uri stopped, panting. He had seen Apollos threading his way through the crowd: he looked to be in fine shape, barely deprived of food.

The Jews marched along the Heptastadion, singing. Some exhausted, emaciated individuals fell to the ground and stayed there—dead. The jubilant living plowed on over them.

On reaching the island of Pharos, they waded into the sea, their arms raised to the heavens, and, as loudly as their throats would bear, sang out their prayers of thanks to the Eternal One for having saved His people again.

Uri was amazed. Around two hundred thousand living skeletons were thronging on the beach and in the water. They were praying in self-abandonment, ecstatically, thankfully, happily. He had the feeling that they had already obliterated their memories of all that had happened.

He spotted Demetrius in the crowd. Panting from the effort, Uri smiled at him.

"You scum!" Demetrius spat out. "Pity you didn't croak!"

"Is your father still alive?" Uri asked in a whisper.

Demetrius gave no answer and disappeared into the crowd.

Uri lay down on the ground and fell asleep.

He awoke to find himself being wrapped in blankets, plied with drink and food. They were Greeks, and did not tell him their names. One begged Uri forgiveness for the horrors that had been committed against his people. Uri grunted: it's not necessary, he wanted to say, but his lips had stuck together.

He reached the palace at daybreak. The sentries admitted him.

His eyes already red from weeping, Philo, on seeing Uri, cried out: "My son! My son!", and embraced the bag of bones. Frail and short though he was, Philo was now able to lift him.

He was given tender meat, a soft milk loaf, and water before being laid down; he slept for two days.

He woke up in his own room with a feeling that he knew again what it felt like to be a baby.

Much attention was lavished on his health; he was supplied with drink and stuffed with endless oranges and light flatbreads, which he would vomit up from time to time. Philo spent several hours each day by his bedside, and while constantly urging him not to talk a lot, not to strain, asked him question after another. Any time Uri started to speak, to give an account of something or other, Philo would interrupt and say what he wanted to say.

We found ourselves in a very difficult position, my dear son, a hellishly difficult position.

On the first day, six weeks ago, the alabarch, with his two sons and elder brother, had withdrawn from the city toward Marea with around 250 excisemen, armed to the teeth. They took refuge in a village was near enough to the city to be able to have a significant effect on events. There was no running water, since there was no aqueduct, just a well, so there was no bath either, and there were no writing implements, no books, no beds—virtually nothing, it was awful, but the villagers had proven to be helpful and kept them fed (though it has to be said they also received generous payment). Every day, the alabarch sent spies into the city to keep an eye on what was happening. There was reason to fear an attack from the legion stationed in Marea, so a watch awas organized, even Marcus had stood guard, so, laudably, had Tija, the boys had dauntlessly held the line. Fortunately, Flaccus had not sent in the III Cyrenaica legion, maybe fearing that Caligula would send warships into the Western Harbor, so he had held them in camp for that eventuality.

We managed to send off couriers to the emperor, my son, thanks to which Caligula has been kept informed about everything since ten days after the Bane got underway. It was not easy for the emperor, truly not, as he was in no position to start a war, but in the end he advocated for the best—the only—option: Caligula sent a crack squad to Alexandria, with the intention of capturing Flaccus. These twelve men were led by Bassus, the centurion under whom Flaccus had all the weapons throughout Egypt collected a while back and who went over to the emperor's side at the right time. Bassus was a magnificent choice due to his local knowledge, and once his boat arrived at the Eastern Harbor he and his men, as Agrippa had beforehand, disembarked undetected; the guards whom Bassus quizzed about Flaccus's whereabouts did recognize him but were not suspicious because the prefect, wisely from his own point of view, had not spread news of Bassus's desertion. At the time, Flaccus happened to be whooping it up with his friends in the house of a man called Stephanion, a freedman of the present emperor—who perhaps was also in on the plan and was sent to Alexandria for that very reason, though there's no way of knowing that for sure. In any event, ten of Bassus's men stood guard outside, waiting for the signal, another two dressed as servants and that was how they got into the room just as Flaccus was getting ready to toast his friends with a drink. At that moment Bassus entered; Flaccus took one look and froze, because he knew immediately that he was finished; and at that moment the signal was given and in rushed the crack troops, bound Flaccus, who showed not the slightest resistance, As the soldiers were made to pledge allegiance to Bassus, the prefect was taken to the Akra, in whose dungeon he has been languishing ever since. The Jewish elders who were being held there—at least those who were left alive—were all released. Bassus called together his bodyguards and gave them a declaration of amnesty to pass along to both legions, an extremely shrewd move on his part because it forestalled any possible revolt. Bassus will stay on as commander in chief of the two legions until the new prefect arrives—Hallelujah!

Philo added tearfully that the emperor had even gone so far as to fulfill the plea that Flaccus be seized on the first day of the Feast of Booths.

"That is, if they couldn't capture him on Rosh Hashanah, as we originally wished and suggested!"

By this noble gesture the emperor had given Jews the chance to continue to trust with good reason in the providence of the Eternal One.

He's a sharp fellow, this Bassus, Uri supposed: he must have received a fair reward from Flaccus for collecting all the weapons in Egypt for him, and now he'll get an even bigger reward. Who knows, he might even make it to the Praetorian Guard in Rome, but even if he doesn't, he will have made his fortune anyway.

Uri chose not to ask why the alabarch's private army had not marched in the Sector's defense. Those 250 excisemen, armed to the teeth, along with the Jews, suitably organized, would have been able to fight successfully against the cudgel-carrying Greek mob and there would have been no occasion for a Sector at all.

Uri did ask about certain details of Flaccus's capture, and Philo unsuspectingly told him what he knew. Uri did some mental counting back and ascertained that Flaccus was not captured at dawn of the Feast of Booths but a day before, only the news had been withheld so that it would have more impact on Jews. On that one day hundreds had died. He did not ask anything more but stretched out voluptuously on his bed.

Theocritus and Democritus, my dear extramural friends among the XXIInds, you fed me to no avail! I shit on standing witness for you since you've been given an amnesty anyway, as have others who were much viler than you were.

Philo made a note of Uri's reticent account, he made notes about the exaggerations in the accounts of those who survived the Bane out of the Sector. Those who'd survived flocked to the alabarch's unscathed palace and demanded revenge, amends, legal redress, retraction of Flaccus's Judaeophobic decree, punishment of the Greeks, punishment of the legions, and compensation for lost income. They also recounted horror stories about one another's deeds during the Bane, their accounts sparing no detail in their prolixity. And of course they painted portraits of their own heroic acts: their unwavering resistance, how they had defended their synagogues as long as they were able to defend them, how many heathens they had strangled with their bare hands, and so on, now that the peace they had mutually longed for so desperately just a few days ago had broken out.

Of the forty-eight elders who had been arrested outside the Sector only thirty-three were left alive, the others having died of the scourging that they suffered for the entertainment of the audience in the amphitheater. It was unprecedented for Jewish social superiors to be humiliated by being punished at the hands of the lowliest slaves! Philo made a note of this for himself, underlining it as one of the most serious crimes. Andron, Tryphon, and Euodos survived. They were not even taken to the amphitheater to be flogged; instead they were confined with the other elders in the Akra, where, to make up for any omissions by the Greeks, they were given a sound thrashing by their cell mates because the cowards showed themselves to be ready to negotiate with Flaccus. Philo, however, noted down in such a manner as to indicate that they too were flogged by the Greeks. Also among those who survived was Nikolaeus, who had just arrived at the head of a delegation to the alabarch and looked, his dark eyes twinkling, at

Uri, who smiled back sardonically and nodded, at which Nikolaeus nodded his acknowledgment. We could be good friends, thought Uri, but it was not to be.

The delegation was visiting the alabarch on the matter of what should happen with regard to Simchat Torah, the ninth and last day of Sukkot, when the annual reading of Torah is completed and recommenced, because observance of Rosh Hashanah, the Day of Atonement, and the Feast of Tabernacles had been omitted this year, the Jews having been left with not one undesecrated synagogue. Now that the Jews were free, what was it to be, given that the festival would soon be upon them?

The alabarch took the common-sense line that the Torah readings should be quickly made up, if necessary over more than one day, on the island of Pharos, the one sacred spot that was left to the Jews. The island of Pharos was doubly holy to Jews as that was the place where the translation of the Septuagint into Greek had been carried out, and that was also where the Jews who had been freed from the Sector were thronging now; sea water was cleaner than the cleanest water from wells or aqueducts, and Jews wanted to give thanks to the Creator for their lives, their deaths, for being the chosen people, and for their salvation, to give thanks to Him for not having deserted them even in the hour of darkest terror, and for making certain those of their loved ones who had been killed during the Bane would be resurrected at the End of Time, which was nigh, the clearest signal for that being the Bane itself. Henceforth until the End of Time they would best be able to give thanks on the island of Pharos, where—and this was no accident—there had been no massacre there even in the worst days of the Bane. The alabarch even went so far as to propose the incredible, almost awesome idea that from now on sacrificial offerings on the island might legitimately be made equally worthy to sacrificial offerings made at the Temple in Jerusalem; indeed, he proposed that a Temple should be erected next to the lighthouse, where it would also be permitted to make sacrificial offerings of animals and produce. On that point the alabarch said warily that it would be necessary to get Jerusalem's agreement, but what was important now was Simhat Torah. Altogether just six Friday evening readings of the Torah had been missed, it should be possible to make this up within two days, and the three hundred thousand surviving Jews of Alexandria would fit on the island.

Others were opposed to this: it was not possible to assimilate that much of the Torah in one go, this was sacrilege, the Torah could not just be rattled off.

Nikolaeus said nothing, neither did Uri; they beheld those arguing on both sides, the bulging veins in their necks, the red faces, their hatred, their thinness—thin themselves and amicably loathing one another.

The alabarch decided that he would make a tour of the Sector, or at least what remained of it. Diligent Greek hands, so it was reported, had largely demolished the walls, and before long not a trace would be left. That day Uri twisted an ankle and was unable to accompany the alabarch to the Sector; he truly regretted that, demonstrating that his right ankle really was swollen, and Philo shook his head: Uri should rest the leg and get cold compresses applied to it. The alabarch clenched his teeth but said nothing, and proceeded on toward the Sector with his sons and elder brother without the hoped-for in-house tour guide, who had personally lived through the Bane there. The remaining elders ceremoniously received them and showed them around the Sector, showing where various events had taken place, where and how many had breathed their last, where the wife who had eaten pork had bled to death, where the Jews had broken through the wall, how they were suffocated to death with smoke and stoned; they showed where the crosses had stood at the north gate and where men had been broken on the wheels of oxcarts. The alabarch was appalled, Philo was appalled, Marcus was pale, Tija livid. Some of the elders had organized a protest against the despised, craven, perfidious alabarch and showered him with abuse to that effect, while the alabarch handed out menorahs as gifts; the heroes prayed and the massed crowd prayed, and Philo shed tears.

All of this was recounted to Uri later by Apollos, who, by chance, had been present, having decided that day to visit the Sector for the first time since the Bane. It turned out he had gotten through those weeks unscathed, if bored stiff, and he had even put on a bit of weight, hiding in the rear part of the house of Pamphilus, a Greek fellow student.

"Tryphon's son is going to make a mark," Apollos said. "He was leading the protest against the alabarch."

"Demetrius?" asked Uri. "How do you mean?"

"He was shouting loudly," said Apollos. "He must want something badly."

The corpses were exhumed from the temporary burial ground and were reinterred with much fuss in the eastern cemetery outside the city wall, with the alabarch in attendance, along with his family, and leading the prayers.

God, for His part, again reminded Jews and Greeks alike that the Jews were His chosen people and of His love for them as well as the validity of their Covenant, because that very day, in the middle of October, as a bound Flaccus was taken on board a ship which was setting off for Rome, the winter winds were unleashed, earlier than ever before, which even the Greeks took to be a heavenly portent.

Uri was also standing in the crowd and watched the erstwhile prefect as he was shoved up the gangplank. Flaccus lurched along like a crushed man, his gaze fixed as if he were no longer among the living. His belongings were taken on board after him in twenty-six large crates, crammed with precious, beautiful gemstones, busts and furniture, according to people who were reliably informed. That will all go to the emperor, wise heads surmised; none of it will be given to Rome. At the head of a squad standing on the shore, looking very bored, was a squat figure of unprepossessing external appearance: that's Bassus, said some, the one who saved the Jews. Uri screwed his eyes up to get a better look: Bassus was balding and looked scruffy. The lanky guy on the horse—that's Castus, Flaccus's favorite centurion, the one who led the detachments that took over the guard of the Sector. He's one of those covered by the amnesty, the shit.

By the middle of October Uri had recuperated sufficiently to go back to the Gymnasium.

His teeth were wobbly but were gradually filling the space left by the two incisors which had fallen out, and his gums had stopped bleeding; his stomach no longer troubled him, having righted itself during the period of starvation.

Abdaraxus received him ruefully. Sadly, Uri had missed a lot of the lessons while he was ill and he was hardly going to be able to make up for it in the current academic year; he was advised that it would be best just to take off the remainder of the year and restart his studies in Germanicus. The gymnasiarch wished him good luck. Uri nodded.

He waited outside the classroom for the mathematics master, Demetrius. The students recoiled at the sight of Uri, who greeted them amiably; then they walked off as quickly as they could.

"I found a solution, sir, to the sum of the angles of a spherical triangle!"

Demetrius paled and whispered:

"Oh, dear!"

"Only I lost track," said Uri. "I had no writing implements in the Sector, so I was unable to get it down in writing and forgot it, and now I can't recall it."

Relieved, Demetrius groaned out again:

"Oh, dear!"

"I was eating smoked fish at the time, and ate smoked fish again yesterday in the hope that it would come back to me, but it didn't. But I'm sure now that there is a proof," Uri said as he departed.

He waited for Apollos and they wound their way up to the top of the Paneion.

"God sees, provided He is looking," Apollos declared. "If He's not looking, He pays no attention to the sacrificial offerings. The incineration of animals and produce at the Temple in Jerusalem should be given up. Judaism should be given up."

Uri rocked pensively on his heels.

"Why do we imagine that we are the only chosen people?" Apollos posed the question. "Our forebears misunderstood something: Moses misheard what the Lord said to him. The Ten Commandments are valid, but nothing apart from that. I am certain that the Lord said that mankind as such was his chosen people, not one people or another; it's wrong that we misappropriated that status for ourselves two thousand years ago. That is why we are so despised, not on account of our monotheism, because others have that kind of thing. We ought to stand out in front of all the heathens and at last announce collectively and ceremoniously that the past two thousand years were a mistake on our part. A dead-end street. Blowing something out of all proportion; a juvenile jape of a scattered slave people. Stuff and nonsense. We are nowadays no longer so small in numbers as we were then, when the Lord sent us a message to keep us going: there are as many of us as there are Latini. We ought to give up this obsolete superstition."

Uri was still rocking back and forth on his heels.

"I'm going back to Rome," he came out with it. "I've had enough of this."

Apollos bit his lips.

"I'll miss you," he said eventually. "Who am I going to fool around with now?"

"There'll be no more fooling around," Uri averred. "A period of frightful gravity is coming, cheerless, humorless, humdrum... Wars of religions, not empires..."

"Those will come to Rome as well," said Apollos.

"I don't think so," said Uri. "The Jewish population there is tiny, it's neither here nor there, it's left to its own devices; the place is swarming with many other, more important peoples. Here, on the other hand, horrors are on the way. Alexandria is a model: it will become fashionable wherever a significant Jewish minority is living, be it in Africa or Asia, anywhere, it is going to be expedited in just the same way. Not so sloppily, slackly, idiotically: for one thing, a Sector will be made with rock-solid walls, properly planned, built for the purpose, not in the hasty, hare-brained way it was here, and only when it's ready will they cram in the Jews. And they will not be released."

"I'm saying the same," Apollos snorted huffily. "Exactly that! If Jews renounce the precept of their being a chosen people, holding on to everything else, then there'll be no reason to massacre them!"

577

"That won't happen," said Uri. "Every blow will only strengthen the belief in their being chosen. A father only thrashes his own son; he doesn't thrash another man's son. My own father turned his back on me when it became clear that my eyesight was bad; he wasn't aggrieved by poor eyesight in another man's son."

"Then an agreement needs to be reached with the Greeks that they too belong to the chosen people!"

"They do without it,"

"But they don't!" Apollos cried out. "They can't stand it either! Any one of them who has any soul can't stand it! That was how I managed to survive! Are you suggesting that I should show no gratitude? I was given shelter, food, and drink, yet before that I hadn't even been on particularly good terms with Pamphilus, and they never tired of apologizing, with pangs of conscience begging me—me! the one who they had given shelter to—to pardon them for all the crimes that they had not themselves committed! Shouldn't I, the Jew, accept them as chosen people? Why not? Who forbids it?"

They were the only two who were shivering in the cold at the top of the Paneion. There were no tourists to bother them since Bassus had closed the harbor to tourist traffic, and neither Greek nor Jewish delegations were permitted to set off for Rome.

PHILO ACQUIRED A NEW FAVORITE, A YOUNG MAN BY THE NAME OF Delphinus. He was introduced by Hippolytus, the young astronomer, who had since turned into a successful astrologer. Delphinus was a sleepy-looking, blue-eyed, girlish young man of about fourteen, all the rest of whose family had been butchered, with the boy only escaping because he had run out to the island of Pharos and had weathered the events in the cellars of the abandoned Jewish observatory among the centuries-old astronomical records; the records had been eaten up by mice, he, like a cat, ate the mice. The boy as a whole had a cat-like look about him, and displayed a certain artlessness in the immature sensuality with which he disported himself in front of the senile Philo.

The first time Uri saw him in Philo's company, he nodded. Philo would undoubtedly have taken him—unlike me—to save him from the Bane; he would not have left the city until he had been found.

Hippolytus had his revenge—it may have taken two and a half years, but he had his revenge.

I can leave Alexandria now.

Uri announced to the alabarch that he wished to go back to Rome; it was time he returned home to his father. Delegations were still not permitted to leave Alexandria, but this did not apply to individuals.

The alabarch did not try to detain him. He provided Uri lavishly with money and entrusted him with a letter to be handed over to Severus, one of the Roman elders. Uri was not familiar with anyone of that name, but had no doubt that he existed and he would find him.

Philo was relieved to be saying farewell; he embraced Uri, tears came to his eyes, and he kept on saying "My son! My son!"

Tija, with a smile, patted the grandson of a slave on the shoulder. Marcus, who was just in the middle of reading a book when Uri announced he was leaving, waved his right hand politely and went on reading.

Uri had a feeling that the missing teeth in his lower jaw gave all of them the shudders. I remind them of the Bane; it's best if they never see me again.

And I'll never see them again, Uri thought happily.

He went down to Lysias's tavern down by the harbor. He found his Greek friends sitting there; the moment they saw him they flinched, but then they invited him over, with extreme courtesy and great pleasure, squeezing together to make room, and ordering a drink which they set down before him. Uri took a seat, sipped the drink and asked about what they happened to be studying, whereupon they started to grumble about the teachers as hey had in the old days, though they were careful to skirt the matter of Abdaraxus. Lysias also came over and gave him a friendly pat of the back, quoting perfectly from memory some of Uri's old impromptu epitaphs, which his old friends received with even greater acclaim than ever; even the new students in attendance laughed in all sincerity.

Sotades, seated at the end of the table, kept on talking to people on his right and left, before finally making up his mind, picking up a beer in one hand, getting to his feet and stepping over. Space was made for him so he could sit down next to Uri, who first asked after the health of his sister, mentioning that he had never seen a lovelier looking woman in his life and nor would he until the end of his days.

Sotades told him that there was at last a suitor whom his proud sister had not rejected out of hand, though their father was still of two minds—the fellow was decent enough, but his family did not have any money, so who knew? Maybe my sister will never get married, he said, and grow into a sour old maid. After that, he launched into what was really on his mind: Agrippa should not have given orders for a procession, that was a mistake, a big mistake, a fatal mistake. The

Greeks had justifiably felt that Jews had become presumptuous, they wanted too much, and no wonder what they did after all that. He regretted hugely what had happened, he deplored it, he had taken no part in anything, but the Jews had plainly brought it upon their own heads, he was involved in nothing, he had sat it out to the end at home, didn't so much as set foot outside the door, he had witnesses that he had never done anything.

Hedylos, who was seated opposite them, seemed to have been waiting for an opening, because he too got to his feet and, leaning over the table, shouted that the Jews could only blame themselves. They had committed many crimes against the Greeks over the centuries, a great many unforgivable crimes, cheated them out of their money, yes, every single Greek, it had been proved, not Uri, of course, who was just a newcomer, but all the same he was a Jew, and in Alexandria the Jews had always betrayed the Greeks, so no wonder they had been on the receiving end this time.

Others told him to can it, don't do that, don't do that, and Pamphilus argued back: What Jewish crimes, Jews are no different from anyone else! You can find white and black sheep in equal proportions among them all! One is like this, another like that! And their religion is just as stupid as anyone else's! Everyone's religion is stupid! Every religion is inhuman and barbarous!

At that a good-looking young boy stood up, presumably a first-year student, and declared that Apion had written that Jews worshiped an ass's head made of gold in their Temple, and he should know, because Apion was a learned rhetorician, a pupil under Theon of Tarsus, none greater than him, and the son of this great Theon was none other than the famous orator Dionysius who was now being unfairly persecuted for his speeches, though he had never lifted a finger against one Jew.

Circling a finger around his head, Pamphilus showed exactly what he thought of the man's mental abilities, sharply questioning in a loud voice just who had been persecuting the stump orator, when he was perfectly free as usual to prowl around wherever he wanted.

Whereupon a man strolled over from another table and declared that the Jews drank Greek blood; in the inner sanctuary of the Temple at Jerusalem they had fattened for a whole year for slaughter a Greek merchant who had innocently dropped by. No lesser a person than King Antiochus Epiphanes had been an eyewitness to this; when he conquered Jerusalem and entered the Temple to pay homage to the Jewish god he found the bloated hapless wretch tied to the altar in the inner sanctuary in the midst of a pile of human bones, and had him released.

"There's nothing in the Holy of Holies!" yelled Pamphilus. "Nothing, nothing at all since the Jews' Ark of the Covenant was stolen! And no humans were ever sacrificed there, or anywhere else!"

The hell they weren't, went through Uri's mind, what about the valley of the Hinnom, in olden times? But he kept quiet.

"Jews are treacherous, it's in their blood," the junior student went on. Uri did not know him. "In the fortress of Pelusium on the Nile the defenders were Jews, notwithstanding which they let in Gabinius, the Roman proconsul of Syria, and his army! They were bribed to do so by Antipater!"

"The Jews resisted the Romans, though, at Leontopolis in the land of Onias. They were alone in fighting for the Greek cause!" shouted Pamphilus.

"And then they switched sides!" came an unexpected contribution from Lysias. "They furnished provisions to the enemy! At Memphis it was they who were the first to assist Mithridates of Pergamum, then us!"

All that had happened a century ago; it was just on the tip of Uri's tongue to call this to their attention when Hedylos bellowed:

"All Jews should be deported! Let them go to Rome! We've offered to pay one thousand sesterces per head for them! That would mean Rome gets three hundred million, but they're not stupid, because they sent back the reply that they weren't wanted even for that much! Well, in that case let them go to their allies among the blacks of Ethiopia!"

Hoots of jubilation followed.

Sotades then added:

"I truly like Jews, and I've given every sign of that, but now they're trying to lord it over us with the idea that they suffered more than anyone else—that's one thing I can't stand about them!"

Someone then called out from the next table that the Jewish word "Sabbath" was derived from the Egyptian word *sabbo*, which Lysimachus had written meant a tumor of the testicles in the slang of the hetaerae—and they should certainly know.

There was a great roar of laughter; Pamphilus sat there palely, Hedylos and Sotades joined in the mirth. Sotades gave Uri a friendly slap on the shoulder. Uri got up and went back to the palace, which had never been his home.

Uri stood at the dock, in brand-new sandals and a tunic of delicate fabric and wrapped in a cloak of even finer angora wool, ruffled by the mild, early-winter northerly breeze. Commercial shipping sailed even during the winter; Uri was pleased to know that he had secured a spot on a powerful bireme with excellent rigging: he would reach Puteoli in two or three weeks, and from there he would soon get to Rome.

In his luggage he had several scrolls, including the *Garland of Great Writers* compiled by Aristophanes of Byzantium and his pupil Aristarchus, as well as the renowned Soros: an anthology of the epigrams of Asclepiades, Poseidippus, and the poet Hedylos, all bound into a bundle, as well as a volume of Leonidas's epigrams about imaginary heroes and stupefying events. An exciseman rifled abstractedly through his sack; soldiers, bored to death, lounged to one side. The exciseman picked up the books and mentioned that Uri's residence permit had expired long ago, so that his embarkation came up against some difficulties. Uri asked whether in that case, seeing that he had apparently been living in Alexandria without permit, would he be permitted, even compelled, to carry on enjoying Alexandrian hospitality henceforth. I'll let you off, said the exciseman, but you cannot take these volumes with you; I am confiscating them in the name of Rome. Uri protested that he had copied these with his own hand; they were his own personal possessions. Right, said the exciseman, then I'll also confiscate your cloak and I'll think about what should happen to the tunic. The soldiers smirked. Uri nodded and slipped off the cloak from around his shoulders. The exciseman, astonished, gestured that Uri should move speedily up the gangplank, and in the end only the books were lost.

Uri looked back, his eyes screwed up, as the boat pulled out of the Eastern Harbor.

The morning sunshine cast a strange light on the buildings. The roofs of the massive, magnificent edifices shone yellowish white; the Sebasteion, the Emporion, and the magnetite vault of the forever-unfinished yawning block of the temple of Arsinoë glistened; the eastern semicircle of the amphitheater was shrouded in a dark shadow from which the western half of the structure emerged, with a reddish tinge, and the buildings beyond looked as if they were covered with snow.

Uri had seen snow once before, in Rome, when he was a little boy, and on that occasion he had laughed all day long.

It was not snowing in Alexandria, of course; the morning was cool, but not cold, yet it still seemed as if the entire city of wonders had been covered by something frozen, definitive, deadly.

IV

ROME

AT PUTEOLI, URI TOOK A LOOK AROUND THE RENOWNED SLAVE MARKET; that is to say, he looked around it in Dikaiarchia, because every inhabitant of the town spoke Greek, and Latin was hardly ever heard. Uri was even a bit apprehensive that he might have forgotten it, since it had been more than two and a half years since he had spoken a word of the language.

The consignment on offer was mediocre: sickly men with dark skin and thick lips and scrawny women, hanging around by the auctioneers' tents; on the stand three people were examining the teeth of a woolly-haired boy, gazing into his mouth, and shaking their heads. Only the cosmetics merchant had attracted a crowd of any size, women carefully studying the varnishes and daubs before making their selections. Uri stood nibbling a lambchop roasted on an open fire (he'd asked for it to be well-done), and as he tucked into his food he found that his stylish cloak was attracting attention. Uri thought it best to make his way back, as quickly as possible, to the port, where he located a ship heading for Ostia, carrying a cargo of wool from Syria. He haggled the fare down by half, not that he couldn't have paid, but he was a grown-up now, quite capable of driving a bargain, and what's more an experienced traveler, and it did a lot for his spirits to show that he couldn't be easily duped. He sold the stylish cloak as a matter of urgency, buying a shabby one instead, and also exchanged his sandals for a secondhand pair. The money he got for those he added to the sum he'd been given by the alabarch, enough to cover the annual salary of a legionnaire for two years: 450 drachmas, to be precise, money that he carried in a linen tube twisted around his waist under his loincloth.

While the ship was being loaded he strolled a bit farther along the wharf, where upon arriving he'd noticed something peculiar. He stepped out onto a bridge, which he saw—even with his poor eyesight he had noticed it—was sagging into the water at one point, though farther off other sections seemed to carry on above the tide.

The bridge—or rather, these pieces of a bridge—crossed the bay between the resort of Baiae and the naval base of Misenum; in place of pilings, ships, acting as pontoons, held girders and planks onto which stones and earth had been hauled in some rough approximation of the Appian Way. Uri strolled over to a building that stood at the other end of the bridge's intact section; it was an inn constructed of timber, and it was in operation. There were no guests in evidence; the innkeeper greeted him jovially in Greek and led him over to a marble relief, the subject of which he started explaining enthusiastically.

Specifically, it was this very bridge.

The plump, ruddy-faced man told him proudly that the bridge had once spanned the entire distance between Puteoli and Baiae, some twenty-six stadia! It had been supported all along its length by ships similar to the few that could still be seen; some were old barks that would otherwise have been scuttled, but many dozens more had either been constructed on the spot, or were grain merchants' crafts that had been pressed into service. But all of them had been taken away, the new ones too, because the shortage of ships had threatened the country with starvation, and now—it had to be admitted, a little late in the day—the entire fleet had been sent to Alexandria. It was a shame this had led to the bridge's collapse because it had been built so exceptionally well: it had been strong enough to last four or five winters.

The emperor surely could not allow a famine this year when last year the Tiber had overflowed and swept away half of Rome.

Let's just hope Far Side wasn't washed away as well, thought Uri.

Uri looked at the relief; it was a splendid work, with much to be seen on it.

The innkeeper pointed out that this, here, was the emperor, and this the Parthian prince Dareios, who was held hostage in Rome, and those there were the senators; that the breastplate on the emperor was not just any breastplate but the very one which had belonged to Alexander the Great; his robes had been of silk, which unfortunately could not be shown on a relief, and they had not been painted as was the case with these carvings—the silk had been dyed a pure purple. And he had worn masses of gemstones on it, which the sculptor had also not represented, but he, the innkeeper, had seen it from very close up—all Indian jewels, no mistake! Also superb were the shield and sword carried by the emperor. He had made sacrificial offerings to Neptune, and to the goddess of Envy, so that no one should be jealous of his acts, and then he rode from the Baiae end onto the bridge, accompanied by the Praetorian guard, storming across it into Puteoli as if he were pursuing an enemy! That was not the end of it, either, because the following day he had returned to the bridge on a war chariot, wearing a gold-hemmed tunic, with famous charioteers riding behind—the innkeeper did not know their names, but they were all very famous—with an immense cargo of war spoils lugged behind! Fully worthy of it, he was as well, because he was the first man in the world who had crossed a sea on foot!

Uri did not interrupt him to mention that an individual by the name of Moses had done just that some time ago.

Well, anyway, the emperor and his entire retinue had remained on the bridge for the whole night, with illumination being provided from the hills that ringed that semicircle of the bay (which if you care to look is like the waning moon), so it was almost as light as day; there was much merrymaking on the skiffs, the emperor also reveling in the bridge, though sad to say not at this inn because a drinking place in the form of a victory arch was built for him in the middle of the bridge, he'd done his celebrating there, he'd even delivered a speech from its roof, with people holding onto him so he didn't get dizzy and fall over. He supposedly mocked Darius I and Xerxes, boasting that he had conquered greater seas than they had; the story goes that the emperor had many of his friends tossed into the sea, though he, the innkeeper could not confirm this because he had been serving guests—there was such a crush at the time, huge it was! There were many who drank in flower-bedecked clothes, and there's no question that Neptune was scared stiff, because the sea was flat as a pancake, and no one drowned in it.

Uri nodded an acknowledgment.

Well, the emperor and his retinue went away, and the bridge stayed up for a while, and lots of people came to see it, so from the business point of view those were boom times: three thousand paces over to the other side, and the same back! (That doesn't come to twenty-six stadia, Uri thought to himself, because that would come to about twenty-two thousand paces.) The reason the bridge was built was because Thrasyllus, the divine Emperor Tiberius's soothsayer, once said that Gaius had about as much chance of assuming power as he did of riding a horse across the Gulf of Baiae. Well, he had become emperor, and he'd ridden a horse across the water, the innkeeper bragged, and he even admitted, after Uri had ordered wine and paid for it, that although the marble relief was placed at the Puteoli end of the bridge, he'd had it moved here so that no harm should come to it; this was a good spot, because all the other innkeepers had picked up and moved on.

The emperor must be a real head case, Uri concluded, and he was glad that he would never have to see him, just as he had never seen Tiberius.

In Ostia, he was tempted to spend a day and have a look at Matthew's four columns, which most probably were buried in the ground somewhere south of the harbor, or perhaps the synagogue was already under construction and the columns were already standing, but then he gave the idea up; it was more important to see his father as soon as he could. He came across a vessel that was sailing right away, but it was carrying a cargo of blocks of desiccated balsam resin. Not a good portent, Uri thought, but then he shrugged his shoulders and booked passage, taking the boat along the Tiber up to Rome. He stood in the prow so that the breeze would spare him the overpowering aroma of balsam. His eyes were narrowed to slits, and he drew the shabby cloak tightly around him as the weather was cool; he had gotten quite unused to cold over the three years he had been away. When the hills of Rome came into sight, he felt an unexpected sensation of joy and triumph.

It was not Alexandria he had to conquer, but Rome.

He did not know how he was going to do that, or for what purpose, but he sensed that he, an experienced, fully grown man, would be able to accomplish anything; the whole of life stood before him, and why should that not be marvelous? His heart beat under his ribs as never before.

The vessel moored at the neglected, moldering docks of Far Side. Uri was delighted that he would soon be home.

It was into the afternoon by then, and on the shore a familiar stench rose from the big leather depots: as a child he had told his father he wanted to work with skins because there were a lot of Jews in that trade, but Joseph had protested that it was a lowly occupation, because the smell was so unpleasant, and besides that tanning ruined the hands. Uri was amazed to be walking on a street he knew, among houses he knew. Nothing had changed. Clearly, people here had experienced nothing new since he had left; perhaps they had not even noticed that two years and ten months had gone by. Yet so much had happened! For example, Alexandria had gone to ruin, and with it whatever had been grand and fine and proud in man—but then again, there were not many Alexandrians who were aware of that; certainly, nobody in Rome had noticed.

He paused before Far Side's inner gate. The neighborhood was so unchanged that what he had lived through during his travels seemed, all at once, improbable, the lengthy, disturbing, all-too-colorful dreams of a single night. He fingered his chin; the prickly touch of the hard bristles of his thick, reddish beard was reassuring. A person doesn't grow a beard overnight.

He tiptoed carefully through the puddles of the inner yard; in front of the houses women were washing in tubs and cooking on open fires, children racing around, filthy, barefooted, and screaming, staring in fright at the newcomer. Reaching his childhood home, Uri halted. Something had happened; the house was ramshackle, and did not use to be in such a dilapidated state. Never mind; he had enough money to repair it. He took a deep breath, pushed aside the carpet hanging over the doorway, and stepped in.

He was struck by the heavy, musty smell and the gloom. There was just one lamp burning indoors, smoking as ever.

A sturdy woman with a shawl over her head was standing with her back to the door, leaning over a tub, while on her right, in his old niche, someone was lying on the floor. The woman turned around and looked at him.

My God! What a hideous woman my mother is!

"I'm back!" said Uri.

The woman stood, scratched her arms, eaten up by contact with lye, while the eldest of his two sisters got sleepily to her feet in the niche.

"Where's Father?" Uri asked.

The woman wrung her hands; the sister clung to him, pressing to him, slobbering over him, sniveling.

"Son," Sarah declared solemnly and severely. "Your father and little sister were taken away by the Lord."

She must have practiced that a lot.

HE WENT TO THE CEMETERY ON HIS OWN. IT WAS RAINING, THERE WAS a cold wind blowing; his shoulders and knees were aching. His mother continued on doing laundry, while his sister did the shopping using Uri's tessera, as she had done for the past two and a half years since their father's death.

Uri stopped at the entrance to the catacomb scooped out of the limestone hillside, just where he had stood with his father all those many years ago, when it had still be hoped that Uri would step into Fortunatus's post at the house of prayer. But Fortunatus's son had become the new grammateus, and since then he too had died. What had the boy been called? Gaudentius! His life had not exactly been blessed with too much joyfulness either.

Uri straightened up and tried to hold back his tears. Then he proceeded down the stairs and entered through the gate. The caretaker's mudbrick cabin lay on the right, lamps alight in it; there were no candles burning in the silver menorah, this not being a feast day. Woken up from his sleep, the guard searched through the sheets of parchment for a long time. Uri helped him out with six asses. Finally the guard located the crypt, unrolling the plan of the catacomb and showing Uri where he had to go. For another four coins he lit a thin torch and thrust it into Uri's hand before settling back on his ledge.

The subterranean passages were wide enough for two or three people to pass. Uri walked straight ahead, then at the fourth junction turned left and continued along the passage. When he guessed he should be close, he brought the torch closer to the walls on his left and right to study the inscriptions on the plates of the rows of burial niches hollowed into them. The air was chilly, but he barely felt it; it was colder outside. He pottered around for a while, looking at marble plates, stone plates, terracotta plates—the material chosen depended on the wealth of the relatives of the deceased—until, finally, on a half-size terracotta plate (the other half of the burial niche still yawned emptily) he spotted his father's name: Ioses Lucius, lived 41 years, three months, and two days. The engraver had scratched the angular, uneven Greek capital letters into the clay while it was still damp; it had so thoroughly dried out that there was barely a gap between the two names. Under the name he could make out the symbols for a menorah, shofar, etrog, and lulav, drawn in the same perfunctory, slapdash fashion.

Tears welled in Uri's eyes.

His father's request that nothing other than a menorah be placed on his gravestone had been to no avail.

His plate may have been cheap, but it was fanciful all the same.

My idiot mother!

Here at last was someone he could hate. He gnashed his teeth, but they wobbled, loosening even further, so he quit.

His limbs were clutched by a cold numbness and he stood motionless, sobbing with despair, and only left once the torch started to flicker.

He trudged back toward the junction, and turned right to reach the gate, where he handed in the torch before going out into the open air.

He realized that he had not even looked for his little sister's resting place above his father's, hadn't even checked to see if her name had been engraved. He deliberated for a while as to whether he should go back, but decided that he was not prepared to pay the caretaker a second time, and kept on walking toward a nearby stretch of the city wall.

A lot of new houses had been built in the neighborhood, near the Appian Way, and before long they would engulf the catacomb itself. The Appian Way was busy, the price of land was bound to go up and the city limits extended. Why wouldn't the entrance to the catacomb be buried and its subterranean passages filled in to allow big houses to be built over them? Jews wouldn't be living here; for them the place would be unclean, forbidden ground, but heathens had no understanding of these matters and would be quite happy to live their lives above the dead until their turn came to depart.

Tears were rolling down his cheeks; he found himself able to cry at last.

It would be nice to believe that all the dead would be resurrected at some point, thanks to the goodwill of the Eternal One. Perhaps—as the peasants in Judaea thought and even the Sadducees of Rome proclaimed—He will hold a Last Judgment when He sees the time is right, with all the dead recalled to life as they were when they was at their finest, completely intact. The dead, brushing off their funeral dress and with it their boniness, their dustiness, their fleshlessness, starting at the resounding strong voices of the shofar and the Anointed, would arise and look around in amazement, happily addressing one another in the resplendent light and benign sweet-scentedness of eternal life. How nice it would be to believe in all that; for then he would be able to tell to his father all that he needed to hear, and Joseph would be amazed and would even praise him, finally glad that his blind-as-a-bat son had successfully managed to grow up into a man.

That notwithstanding, Uri suspected that in the future he would sometimes talk to his father, and within himself might even hear the answers; he would not be able to face what had happened otherwise, because any resurrection was unforeseeably remote, and the state of death was frighteningly protracted.

IT TURNED OUT THAT HE ALREADY HAD A BRIDE LINED UP.

A Roman man had to wed if he had no wish to pay the unmarried man's tax, and that made no sense at all. Nor could he inherit if he remained unmarried.

Sarah eagerly listed her virtues: the girl was from a good family, not merchants it was true, just artisans, her father being a carpenter; she was what you might call sweet; she was over fourteen, her two older sisters were already married, and her younger sisters were still children. There was a firstborn son who was a carpenter like his father, and the second son worked as a docker.

Uri asked if the marriage had been arranged while his father was still alive. For a long time Sarah said nothing. Your father would be very pleased if he knew, she finally answered, after much evasion. It sounded like it was Sarah who had chosen Uri's intended. It was a great honor, she never tired of saying, because Uri's prospective father-in-law earned good money. Very good! "We shall not be left wanting!" she cackled, and persisted in castigating the Jews for not having granted them tzedakah after Joseph died on the grounds that they were able to make use of Uri's tessera to get their monthly rations: "They have nothing to do with it. It's a Roman provision, not a Jewish one!" The carpenter's family lived in a nice house; he had given a decent dowry for the first two girls, and he was very busy with his hands, the prospective father-in-law. She could not, on the spot, off the top of her head, recall the name of Uri's intended. "But she must be called something," she said, before passing gloomily on to other matters: a significant debt had been left after Joseph died. It was impossible to know quite how big, and the bankers had suspended collection, counting on Uri's return. "How on earth would we have paid—out of what?" Now that Uri had finally made an appearance, the debt would most certainly have to be repaid. That was why they had not taken the house away yet; much noise had been made about that, and several of the old houses in the neighborhood had been demolished to make way for new tenements, the foundations had already been dug. "Your father was casual with his money, son," Sarah said. "I can't for the life of me see why he was continually running up debts!" Uri knew but kept quiet about it. "You can't be as casual about things, because from now on you're the man of the house."

"What is the monthly installment to pay off the debt?" Uri queried.

Sarah did not know, but anyway it was irrelevant because she'd had no need to pay it; there was no way for the bankers to recover the sum from her. "But we should have been given the tzedakah! Scum, they are! What scum! You never see such scum anywhere except among Jews!"

Uri asked about how his young sister had died. Sarah told him that she had coughed a lot, always coughing, and finally she had choked, gasping for air. A lot of children in the community suffered from spells of breathlessness, a lot of them died too, growing numbers of them; that must be what God wanted, they were better off close to Him. "She may be an angel by now!" Sarah exclaimed, leaving Uri wondering what training his little sister would have to go through to become an angel in the other world.

Sarah was all for taking Uri straightaway to introduce him to his future in-laws, but Uri dug in his heels: he had business with the elders, he wanted to see to that first of all. Sarah started arguing that marriage was more important, to which Uri responded mildly: "I'm the man of the house, so you'd do better to shut up." Sarah fell into a stupefied silence, then began sobbing hysterically that she had not deserved this, she had always made sacrifices, she had never spared herself, and so on. Finally Uri escaped to the yard, and once he'd settled down he said in a low voice, too low for his mother to hear even if she tried, "I'm not your husband."

He had difficulty tracking Severus down, but finally he succeeded in identifying a senator Severus, who also bore the name Solomon and was able to hand the alabarch's letter over to him.

"Did you read it?" Severus asked.

"No, I didn't," said Uri.

Severus was a plump, wheezy man; he had started out as a weaver and turned himself into a merchant.

"Your father was a smart man," said Severus. "You've got him to thank him for making your fortune."

Uri was of a different opinion about that, but he just nodded politely.

Severus asked about the Bane in Alexandria; there had been horrific reports about it in Far Side. What was the truth of it?

"All of it," Uri replied. "And much more besides."

Severus gave him a cold look, having no sense of humor.

"A large number of Jews were killed, tortured, mutilated, beaten, burgled, robbed, humiliated, raped," stuttered Uri, to satisfy the curiosity of the worthy members of Rome's Gerousia as speedily as possible.

Severus shook his head.

"That sort of thing could never occur in Rome!" he asserted. "The Jews of Alexandria must have upset the Greeks somehow."

Uri was unsure how to respond to that, so by way of encouragement noted.

"It's all the better for us; Rome has thereby gained in importance."

Severus wrinkled his brow and pondered. Lord! What on Earth can the alabarch and his lot want from this dolt? This is Solomon! Uri thought.

Severus broke the seal on the letter, unrolled it in leisurely fashion, read it, and mused. Uri just stood.

"So, when are they coming?" Severus asked.

"I have no idea," answered Uri. It seemed somebody was coming to Rome from Alexandria.

"But one can't just do that at a moment's notice!" Severus exclaimed. "Quarters have to be organized to put them up! It's not as simple as that!"

Uri was on the point of leaving and had even bid farewell, but then Severus asked him where he had gotten through the hard times.

"In the Sector," Uri replied.

"What's that?"

Uri sighed deeply.

"It's a bit like Far Side over here," he answered.

"Then you had luck on your side," Severus declared. "It's better to spend hard times among our kind. Jews always help one another; that is why the Eternal One helps us."

Uri nodded fervently and departed.

AT FIRST, JOSEPH (AND, AFTER HIS DEATH, SARAH) HAD MADE DO BY living off Uri's tessera; that may have been illegal, but it had been overlooked by the municipal administration. Uri suspected that any time the question was raised at the food distribution center as to why the owner of the tessera did not come in person, Sarah would go into hysterics about how he was sick or she was taking care of his business, or would dream up some other excuse, and the officials would simply give up just to get rid of her.

Sarah never tired of weeping and imploring, saying over and over again that he should pay a visit to his bride-to-be, because word would get around soon enough that Uri was back, then they would be offended and call off the marriage. "People like us can't dream of making a better match!"

But Uri first wanted to get a clear idea of where he stood on the matter of the debt.

Three bankers saw him and told him that after his regrettably premature death the repayment of Joseph's loan, out of compassion and respect for the womenfolk he had left behind, had been benevolently suspended until now, but now that his legal heir had returned, they would be compelled to ask him to restart the monthly payments immediately.

That was how Uri got to know, from the bankers rather than his mother, that his father had died four months after Uri had set off from Rome. Now where was I then? I was in Beth Zechariah by then; it must have been around Shavuot. How was it that I felt nothing?

Maybe my Father died because he thought I was no longer alive.

He was jerked back into the present: the numbers were laid out.

His father's debt, at twenty percent interest, came to 240,000 sesterces, which, spread over twelve years, meant 20,000 per year, or 1,666 and two-thirds per month. Of that, Joseph had paid back 6,666 and one-third sesterces, so the remaining debt stood at 233,333 and two-thirds sesterces, with the installments amounting, in round numbers, to 1,620 per month.

Uri breathed a sigh of relief: he made a quick mental calculation of how much it would be at compound interest, as would have been the case had he borrowed from Alexandrian bankers. He came up with an astronomical amount: for a debt maturing in twelve years' time he'd owe 1,780,000 sesterces or, calculating backward, 12,361 sesterces per month. No Roman citizen, even if he were rolling in cash, could afford that.

Thanks be to the Eternal One! These people were, as yet, blissfully ignorant of compound interest.

But he grew despondent nevertheless.

Perhaps it would be better not to get married after all, he speculated, because then he could not legally inherit, which meant the debt could not be inherited either. But then they would take the house away, leaving Sarah and Hermia homeless.

He had been given 450 drachmas by the alabarch, equivalent to 180,000 sesterces—very generous of the cowardly worm, it was—and of that he had spent only 150 sesterces on the journey. One could hardly say he had spent lavishly. But even if he handed over 1,250 sesterces a month he wouldn't be able to cover the monthly repayment on the loan, let alone be left with anything to live on—and who in Far Side earned as much as a legionnaire? Very few, only the wealthiest. The claim was unrealistic, even if the sum his father had managed to pay back over four months had, by some miraculous honesty, been deducted from the total.

Uri sat in front of his judges, the bankers, and felt numb.

He could not have been the first wretch who had sat like this before them, because, after a brief pause, one of them, Julius, spoke up:

"Given that you are just now commencing your independent life, and given that you personally did not incur the debts—although, as we know, you were Joseph's sole beneficiary—we are willing to extend a fresh loan to you, though of course only on condition that you accept the assistance."

Uri understood very well: if he accepted, then he would be in debt to the end of his days. But then again, he was trapped for the rest of his life anyway if he didn't accept it...

It went through his mind that his mother and sister were none of his business; they should be left to their own fates.

But they were his father's business.

From now on they were entrusted to him on that account.

"If you don't accept," Julius continued dispassionately, yet cordially, "your house will be expropriated in lieu of the debt, and you will become homeless. A five-story tenement will be built on the site, and it is solely out of respect for your father's merits and your own prospective future earnings that we did not expropriate it before. In the event that you decide to leave your family to their own devices, we shall have you excluded from Rome's Jewish community and sell you into slavery. If you flee, a wanted poster will go out to the whole of Italia. We held to a firm belief that the favorite of the Jews of Alexandria, who acted as courier for King Agrippa, would return one day to Rome and pay off his father's debt. You've come back; now pay! If you are unable to pay, then take out a loan. You have talents, you have experience, and you can make use of your father's contacts... You have contacts of your own in Alexandria... You were a royal courier... You have capital and acquaintances; at the very worst you have not estimated how much all that is worth. Count it up, deliberate, and give us an answer."

Uri responded instantly:

"How much will you lend me?"

The bankers became friendlier and brought out previously prepared contract for a loan. Fine wine was poured, and Uri signed the contract without hesitation. That accomplished, Uri would, until the end of the year, only have to pay about half the monthly amount he had previously calculated, and the full amount only from January of next year onward, which, with the payments on the new loan tacked on, would come out to around two thousand sesterces per month.

It mattered not, as long as something came up by then.

Purely to tweak the bankers' noses, after the contract had been signed and completed, Uri asked:

"Why is there no *prosbul* in it?"

"We never enter into seven-year contracts, my dear boy," Julius chuckled. "Our planning is long-range. There was no prosbul in the contract we made with your father either."

A prosbul had at one time been employed in Judea, but even there it no longer existed. Under one of the injunctions of Moses, all debts were null and void when they entered a Sabbatical year, but if a prosbul were attached to the debt bill, under the more recent unwritten law, the formula meant there was no such limitation in the seventh year.

In practice, then, the question had no meaning.

However, Uri was feeling impish.

"Might I see my father's contract?"

Julius shook his head.

"It wasn't a written contract that we made," he said. "Word of mouth was enough. We knew your father: he was an honest man, may his memory be blessed."

URI CALCULATED AND RECALCULATED.

He worked out the minimum sum the dowry needed to amount to for him to be able to pay back at least part of the monthly interest for a year or two.

It occurred to him that he ought not to have signed that quite obviously infeasible contract. What if they had tried to get his father to sign it and he had been unwilling? He had paid it back as long as he was able, and he had died doing so.

Uri was dismayed to realize that it had not been due to his absence that Joseph had died, but rather it was the burden of the debt, the sacrifice he had made for his son, that had killed him.

And I signed it! What a dope I have been yet again, my God!

Sarah would hear not a word about the deal that Uri had made. He did try, it has to be said, to get her to understand what it came down to, she protested that she had no interest in any such things, just a good match—a happy future for her firstborn son.

It did occur to Uri that maybe his mother knew more than she was letting on; maybe she knew everything, and only out of obdurate nastiness was she pretending that she understood nothing. In fact, it made no difference whether she understood. He had already decided that he was not going to leave his mother and sister to their own devices.

The carpenter and his family received them with great ceremony that evening, because Sarah, in line with custom, had sent a woman on ahead to act as marriage-broker. The prospective father-in-law's married daughters were not present; they represented the property of their husbands' families and had nothing more to do with their father's family.

Uri gazed at his intended; she had been dolled up, her flat, broad features burning with blushes of shame, and she sat uncomfortably on the couch with her little sisters, who tried to suppress their giggling as they stared impudently, in a prying manner, at Uri. His intended, on the other hand, gazed steadfastly at the floor, a single act of rebellion against a fate she otherwise faced with total resignation.

Before long she will be as hideous as my mother, thought Uri. I'll be saddling myself with two terrible mothers in one go.

Uri cut the courtesies short to ask how much, exactly, was the dowry.

Such frankness took the decent carpenter aback; he played for a bit more time by asking his wife, then hemmed and hawed a bit before stating a disgracefully low sum. Uri burst out laughing, then started to talk about the time he had spent as a cabinetmaker in Judaea. At that his prospective father-in-law perked up and, despite the mute disapproval of his wife, whose forehead was hidden behind a mop of thick hair, he began to ask in detail about aspects of the trade in Judaea, and Uri was able to supply plentiful expert information. The prospective father-in-law asked as to whether Uri was intending to carry on working as a cabinetmaker in Rome, and Uri declared that it was the last thing on his mind; he would be taking over his father's commercial ventures, there was much more money to be made that way. That filled his prospective mother-in-law with boundless hostility, his prospective father-in-law with respect. The play-acting continued until Uri had haggled his way to the necessary dowry.

Sarah sat on a small chair all through the proceedings, her back straight, an occasional severe glance serving to keep a tight hold on her daughter, who was constantly on the verge of a giggling fit.

The wedding was set for mid-February, in two months' time.

Even Uri himself was unsure what he was might hope to accomplish during this two-month respite.

It came to mind that he had a source of an income in mind; it was high time he paid a visit to Gaius Lucius, his patron. By then it was mid-December, however, and on the seventeenth the Saturnalia would bubble over. It was rumored that this year Emperor Caligula had most graciously added on an extra day, so that now the festival would last eight days in total. When a Saturnalia was in progress, the wisest patrons would flee the city, and it was more than likely that Gaius Lucius had already done just that; he could therefore only be expected in early January, after the similarly inebriated New Year festival, when every patrician was obliged to take a fresh oath of loyalty to the present emperor and to Augustus the Divine. (The story went that on the present emperor's orders it was no longer necessary to take an oath to Tiberius but that it was now required to take one to his departed and deified sister, Drusilla.) Since he had returned home, Uri had never once crossed the bridge to the other bank, to Rome proper, and the magnificent processions and events of the Saturnalia were of no interest to him; he had seen enough of those. He sat in his nook, from which his sister, of her own accord and without a word of protest, had moved out, and alternately alert and half asleep he mulled over the problem of how he might be able to provide for his family.

He searched for any documents of his father's relating to the conduct of his business affairs but found nothing. Sarah told him, with surprising respect, "Your father kept it all in his head." Uri could remember that his father had sometimes entered into a ledger his revenues and expenditures, but that was nowhere to be found; indeed, nothing at all of his which had been left behind, not even an item of clothing. He asked his mother if she had thrown everything away, at which Sarah sighed and nodded: "Anything that reminded me of your father was painful to me." Uri ground his wobbling teeth again; his mother had thrown everything away, certainly not out of grief but because she had wanted no trace left behind of a husband with whom she had been obliged to spend those loathsome decades of her life.

There being no documents, Uri had no idea where to start looking for his father's business partners.

Mentally he went through his trips to Judaea and Alexandria in search of business opportunities. There was always silk. That was not used in Judaea— the people there were poor—but in Alexandria it was worn by concubines and catamites, wealthy Greeks and wealthy Jews; despite Tiberius's ban on wearing it in Rome twenty years ago, everyone who could afford it still wore it. Yes, maybe silk. Or was something else, an original idea, needed?

He was, he concluded regretfully, not cut out to be a merchant. The job called for a special instinct, a nose for things that he was incapable of cooking up.

In the middle of January Uri picked up the sportula his father had abandoned—the one thing of his which was left, because his mother and sister had used it along with his own to carry home the food they were given on showing his tessera—and set off to see Gaius Lucius.

Uri was kicking his heels glumly, waiting for the others to finish cramming their sportulas, when Gaius Lucius addressed him.

"Who's this we've got here?"

The patron beamed indulgently at him, his double chin becoming triple, his eyes now barely visible, glowing within the folds of fat.

"I'm Gaius Theodorus, dear patron, the son of Ioses Lucius..."

Gaius Lucius was delighted and embraced him.

"It's a long time since I last saw Ioses. How is he?"

"He died."

"Oh! And you, if I remember right, you traveled off to somewhere..."

"Yes, I traveled a bit."

"Whereabouts?"

"To Judaea, then to Alexandria."

Gaius Lucius nodded appreciatively.

"So, what did you bring from Alexandria?"

Uri went pale and his heart beat fast.

He had bought no gift for his patron; he had forgotten. All at once he heard his father's voice repeatedly warning him not to forget to bring a present for Gaius Lucius, and yet that was exactly what he had done. He needed to make up some excuse quickly! Any excuse!

"I brought you stories, dear patron, interesting and diverting stories. I'll relate them to you as soon as you have the time..."

Gaius Lucius contorted his features.

"Right now you'd better stuff your sportula," he hissed with loathing, "but make sure I don't see you again!"

Uri bowed and immediately withdrew. The only reason he did not chuck the empty sportula in the Tiber was because it was all that was left of his father's things.

THAT WAS A BIG MISTAKE, A SERIOUS ONE! URI WAS DISTRAUGHT.

Losing a generous patron, and in such an incredibly clumsy fashion! He ought to have lied, told him that he had brought a great many gifts, so many that he hadn't been able to carry them, and that the patron should send some bearers over for them later. He could have quickly purchased a million trinkets at any market, claiming that he had brought them from Alexandria, and Gaius Lucius would have been none the wiser.

What absolute stupidity on his part, God in Heaven! What would Joseph have said?

Uri came around to see that, as a matter of fact, he had only said what was incontrovertibly true: his many interesting tales would indeed have been a gift for Gaius Lucius, who loved gossip. But then how was the poor man supposed to know that Uri, in his confusion, really had been offering him a present?

Nothing could be done about that now; Uri and the two women who depended on him—shortly to be three if he counted his intended—had been excluded from enjoying free meals.

He had to find a new patron at once.

It was not against the law or contrary to custom to attach oneself to a new patron, and so that sort of thing happened every now and then, especially if the new patron was an adversary of the previous one. Gaius Lucius no doubt had adversaries, but Uri considered it dishonorable to betray a patron who had fed his father and himself for decades. In any case, gossip that he was, Gaius Lucius would quite likely spread the word across Rome what an ungrateful client Uri was; the patron would brag about discrediting him as a client just as he had with Joseph because of his commercial abilities, and that would be enough to scare off any potential patrons.

Slowly Uri came to see that the real problem was not the empty sportula so much as the fact that by losing favor with Gaius Lucius he had also let the silk market slip away.

What crass stupidity! And there was he, believing he was an experienced and grown-up man.

He stood for a long time on the Jewish Bridge over the island. It was raining; Rome was misty and miserable. Conquer Rome? Some chance! Squeak by somehow, maybe.

The only ones who could help him were the bankers: it was not in their interest that debtors skip town—or starve to death—since in either case they'd never get their money. He would have to pay Julius a visit; he had been the friendliest.

Julius did not receive him, only his secretary. The two of them goggled at each other: Hilarus and Uri, two of the delegates who had carried the ritual dues. Then Hilarus, the former teacher, leapt up and held his arms open to embrace him. Uri patted Hilarus on the back; he had certainly not gotten any slimmer. Matthew had said that he had been an informant for the Roman elders, which might well have been true. Hilarus had wanted to be the deputy leader in Syracusa, and now here he was: secretary to a rich Roman banker. He had gotten what he wanted, and who was to say what else he might still want?

Hilarus grew ever more long-faced as he listened to Uri's concise tale of woe. When he heard how Uri's patron had sent him packing, he sucked a tooth in sympathy.

"Dear, oh, dear," he said. "We really will have to figure something out!"

He then asked about Alexandria, whether Uri knew when the alabarch would be arriving, because Severus had already spread the news that he was coming.

That meant the alabarch really was coming.

As soon as Bassus allowed the Jewish delegations to leave for Rome, Uri guessed. Hilarus informed him that Bassus was no longer in Alexandria; he had returned to Rome to join the Praetorian guard, because the new prefect of Egypt, Vitrasius Pollio, had arrived to take up his post. He was said to be a decent man, and he had ordered a thorough investigation, which would take a while, and it was hardly likely the alabarch would be allowed to leave before it ended.

Uri started to take his leave, but Hilarus detained him further, inquiring about Matthew and Plotius, and he was astonished to hear that Uri had not dropped by when he was in Ostia, where Matthew had charged Plotius with planning a synagogue, which was now under construction and apparently was going to be bigger than the one at Delos. Uri laughed out loud and asked Hilarus to be sure, if he happened to write to Philo, to mention that to him, because he would be glad to know.

"Why don't you write him yourself?" Hilarus wondered.

"I don't like writing," replied Uri.

"Don't give me that," said Hilarus. "You went to the Gymnasium there, and you must have produced orations till they were coming out of your ears!"

"I suppose so," said Uri.

They fell silent.

"Right," said Hilarus. "We'll work something out for you; whatever else we do, we'll figure it out."

That plural was not to Uri's liking, so he set off out before turning around.

"Which of us was carrying the ritual dues?"

Hilarus laughed.

"Didn't you know? We all did, the didrachma tax along with the voluntary contributions—nice and neatly divided. Brazen into the bases of our water flasks."

"Oh, like that!" said Uri, and laughed.

Then he shuddered.

"Remember, that time in Syracusa?" he asked, "when Matthew threatened the customs men that he would dash them all to smithereens."

"Yes," mused Hilarus. "He had his heart in the right place."

Uri trudged home in the mud, reflecting on how he was unable to rid himself of Alexandria, and that was the least of his worries.

TWO DAYS LATER, HILARUS PASSED WORD THAT HE WOULD SET UP A meeting with a few merchants who had too much on their plates and could not cope on their own. Some of them lived in Far Side, others in Rome proper. Uri paid them visits and chatted. They all received him with great respect, and they couldn't praise Joseph's memory highly enough, but Uri had the feeling that it was his Alexandrian past doing the talking. If they only knew! They knew nothing. But then they did have a feel for commerce, and they had money.

By the time the wedding was due to take place, Uri had reached agreement with one of the merchants, a man by the name of Pulcher. This Pulcher was a nephew of the Honoratus whose son had died; his post as grammateus had been left vacant for a son who was due to be born, except there had only been a girl, so one of Pulcher's sons had been given the position, where he had been ever since. Pulcher wanted Uri to take over three ongoing matters, and for a sum that was far from unfavorable; that was how he had gotten his own start, as it had happened alongside Joseph.

"You were still a small boy at the time," said Pulcher. "Did your father never say anything about me?"

"No."

Pulcher chewed a corner of his mouth in regret.

"A pity that Joseph didn't live a bit longer. He took it badly that he heard nothing of you. You really could have sent a message to him."

Uri nodded; as soon as he got the opportunity he had sent word. Matthew had promised that he would let his father know. Well, he didn't. And Joseph had no longer been alive to receive the letters he had sent later on. Who might they have ended up with? Someone had almost certainly read them, and if they had read them, they were likely to use them against him.

He tried to recall what he had written in the two letters. Maybe nothing of any importance. Pray God that was the case.

Between organizing Pulcher's affairs and the impending wedding, Uri rushed into his new life in Rome, glad that he had a lot to do and would not have time for deliberating.

Visiting one of his customers, who had come from Rhodes, he noticed an amphora of exactly the sort he had seen in Alexandria, so he asked where he had obtained it. Well, it was relatives who had sent it. Did he think they might be able to send more? Almost certainly, but wine from Rhodes was not in high repute in Rome.

"I'm very fond of it," said Uri, very excited. "I'm prepared to make an order."

"How much?"

"Fifty amphorae? Or should I make that sixty?"

The merchant, a young man, was astounded.

"Wouldn't it be cheaper by the wine-skin?"

"Why, is that expensive, the amphora?" Uri queried in all ignorance.

"No, it's not expensive, but all the same it costs more. It might break in transit... A wineskin can only puncture, and that can be patched up."

"Never mind," said Uri. "I'll order sixty."

The merchant did a calculation, then handed Uri the total. Uri had a lot of money on him and paid instantly. They drew up a contract, which included the statement that it had been paid for.

"You'll have to pay any customs duty," said the merchant.

"I'll undertake to do that."

That too was put retroactively into the contract.

All the relatives were present at the wedding: from the groom's side, Sarah and Hermia, from the bride's side around twenty people, including all sorts of artisans and suspicious types from the harbor. Uri assumed his sunniest manner and joked with everyone, except his future wife; her family found Uri extremely attractive. During the wedding feast he whispered to his mother to ask his bride's name, at which Sarah frowned disapprovingly. It turned out she still did not know.

"What's your name, sweetheart?" Uri asked his wife once he had taken her back home afterward. Her family was not with them, having themselves gone home straight after the wedding ceremony, glad to have fobbed this daughter off on someone at last so they'd no longer have any need to be concerned about her.

Sarah had cleaned the house in advance, making a place for her own daughter in the nook, now that the sole room would belong to the man and wife.

"I know what you're called," the wife replied grimly.

"So, what's my name, then?" Uri quizzed.

"Gaius."

"Actually, it's Gaius Theodorus," Uri informed her.

The woman gave him a black look:

"Is that what you want—for me to use both names?"

"No, to you I'm just Uri."

"Uri..."

The woman looked at her husband, whom she was supposed to address as Uri.

"Now then, sweetheart, so what's your name?"

"Hagar."

Uri was startled: it was not usual in Rome to give a woman a Hebrew name.

"It's a shame I'm not called Abraham."

Hagar was totally nonplussed.

"Hagar is a woman who bore a son to Abraham," Uri explained, "and from him came another people."

"Which people is that? And who is Abraham?"

Hagar's eyes were blank.

"Don't you know anything about the Scriptures?"

"No."

"And you can't read either?"

"No."

Uri sighed but then said indulgently:

"It's enough that I can."

Uri took the lamp off the table and placed it on the floor, and they undressed in near-total darkness before slipping into bed. Uri pulled over himself the threadbare blanket his father and mother had shared; Hagar was prostrate, unmoving, her eyes wide open. It crossed Uri's mind that in Rome it was not the custom for relatives to inspect the bloodied sheets the next morning, so he could even put it off, but he sensed that this was not an option.

He turned on his side, by which time his eyes had accommodated to the gloom, with the light of the lamp's flame flickering tauntingly across the ceiling. He looked at his wife's face from close up, the shadows now growing, then becoming smaller. His wife closed her eyes, as she still lay there motionless.

"Who gave you the name?"

"I don't know."

This spells big trouble, my Lord, Uri thought to himself as he set about the matter at hand.

"You've been with a woman before," Hagar said when it was nearly dawn.

"Yes."

"A dirty beast, that's what you are! You should be ashamed of yourself! May God curse you!"

Uri was lost in thought.

Abraham's wife was Sarah, and Hagar a concubine; he had a Sarah as his mother and Hagar as his wife. Abraham had the better deal in every respect.

IN THE FIRST MONTH, URI EARNED VERY GOOD MONEY, BUT HE STILL HAD difficulty making the loan payments, which amounted to even more, so he was forced to resort to the dowry. Irrationally, he did not touch the money he had received from the alabarch, as if it mattered from what purse he paid.

When the amphorae arrived at the port, it was spring, and Hagar, still taciturn, was starting to round out. Uri went off to pay the customs duty, calculating the sum beforehand to make certain how much he needed to take. An amphora of that kind was worth at least twenty sesterces, and if the duty was twenty-five percent here as it was in Alexandria, then that would come to three hundred sesterces altogether for the consignment—a lot of money! He needed to haggle that down, and he also needed to rent some warehouse space until he had sold the amphorae.

The excisemen were Roman and so discussed the matter in Latin.

"That's good wine," said the customs official. "That puts it at a value of at least 120 sesterces for the lot."

"Come off it!" said Uri.

"Well, all right, the duty will be twelve sesterces!" said the official. "Or else we'll pour out a bit from each amphora."

Uri breathed a sigh of relief, though he was careful not to let it show. He announced that he was more interested in the latter option.

"But that will make it harder to measure what's left," the customs man pondered more deeply.

"At worst you'll pour out more than a bit," said Uri generously.

"The other way would be to hand over six amphorae to us, and that's that."

"I'd rather you poured some away," said Uri.

"But like I said, it could be that will cost you more."

"So be it."

"You water it down, don't you?" the excise man laughed, "You fill it back up afterward and sell it like that, eh?"

"You could be right about that..." Uri also laughed.

Quite a lot of good wine was poured out of the sixty amphorae into other vessels, leaving Uri with the entire lot. He was very surprised that not even one of the amphorae had been smashed; even the wax seals on the spouts were undamaged, which he considered to be a heavenly portent. He offered the customs official a separate measure on top of the rest, also taking a drink himself; the two of them savored the wine, and the customs man remarked that it wasn't bad, but spit it out and asked, rather amazed:

"There are people who go specifically for that taste?"

"There are."

"Rome's overrun with nutcases," the customs official declared with feeling.

For two sesterces Uri rented from the customs man a warehouse for three weeks, and he and his colleagues carried the sixty amphorae themselves; it was a treasury warehouse, and in principle the customs official had no claim on its use, but then he knew how to open the lock. Uri and he parted on the friendliest possible terms.

They've no idea what an amphora from Rhodes is worth!

The next day he hurried over to his Greek partner and ordered another one hundred amphorae.

A few days later he towed ten empty amphorae on a handcart to Gaius Lucius's house, one of them bearing a small-scale clay medallion of the famous Colossus of Rhodes, which had been toppled several centuries before by an earthquake. He had not needed to empty all the amphorae by himself as the customs men had seen to a few of them, and fortunately only two were broken. In front of Gaius Lucius's house he had asked the guards to take care of them, and made his way to the atrium. Gaius Lucius's eyes darkened on seeing him.

"Your gift has just arrived from Alexandria," said Uri. "Ten amphorae from Rhodes; they are sitting out in front of the house. It pains me that they did not arrive in time."

"Amphorae from Rhodes?" exclaimed Gaius Lucius, and hurried out in front of the house, a few clients toddling in his wake.

Gaius Lucius rapped and smelled at the amphorae, his eyes sparkling. He caressed the diminutive Colossus at particular length.

"Amphorae from Rhodes! Procure more of them! Lots! I'll give fifty sesterces for each one!"

"Your wish is my command, beloved Gaius Lucius," said Uri. "But please accept these as a gift."

Uri had not brought a sportula with him, and as soon as the amphorae had been taken into the house he set off back with his empty handcart. He's given up on running me down all over the place, mused Uri, but he is going to give all his friends amphorae from Rhodes for the next few months, so from his point of view it's worth it.

A BIG FLURRY OF EXCITEMENT BROKE OUT IN FAR SIDE WHEN WORD WENT around that Herod Antipas, together with his wife, Herodias, had arrived in Rome from Galilee. He did not move into quarters in Far Side, but Rome proper. Uri heard about it from Sarah, and his mother was all for Uri paying the ruler a visit and asking for money from him. Uri was flabbergasted:

"Why would he give anything to someone like me of all people?"

"Because your father gave him a loan."

Uri broke out into a laugh.

"That wasn't Antipas, but Agrippa!"

"That makes no difference—they're both kings!"

"Well, he's not king, only a tetrarch! He was granted only a quarter of the kingdom of Herod the Great..."

Sarah was not one to be satisfied.

"All right," said Uri just to shut his mother up. "I'll pay a visit later."

Sarah then asked every day if he had seen the king yet. At first Uri replied that he had not had time, then later on that yes, he had tried but was not admitted. He did not think that one evening Sarah would confront him with the news that she had arranged it: Antipas would see him. Uri thought she must be getting soft in the head, but it transpired that she had kept on pestering Honoratus, having forced her way in to see him; the only thing he could do to get rid of her was to tell Sarah where her son could find Antipas.

"He's staying on Palatine Hill," said Sarah confidently. "You're going there tomorrow morning."

"I'll go," Uri agreed.

"I'll go with you," Sarah announced.

"Me too," said Hagar, who by now was heavily pregnant.

"Your younger sister as well," said Sarah.

Uri had a million other things on his mind and decided to leave it be: let them see that the tetrarch would have him kicked out, then at least they wouldn't keep after him about it.

Sarah, excited and wearing clean clothes, woke him up at daybreak.

In front of the house, he sprinkled himself with water, made a short prayer, and breathed in deeply. Hagar was by then also standing in the doorway, and behind her the female apparition of Hermia, hair neatly combed and looking bewildered.

His mother pressed a clean tunic into his hands and insisted on his wearing his better pair of sandals.

They walked over the Jewish Bridge, the women in hushed silence.

At the far side of the Ponte Fabricius Hagar kneeled and, turning to the east, said a prayer. Uri could not understand why she had done this; he and the others stood waiting until she had finished.

"I've never gone to Rome before," Hagar whispered. "I was giving my thanks to the Eternal One for allowing me to do so..."

Uri was amazed. His mother and sister did not leave Far Side all that often, but it never entered his head to think that his wife had never seen Rome proper.

Tears were rolling down Hagar's face, which was no longer flat but plumped, swollen, marred by a tiny snub of a nose in its middle, a sight that moved Uri to pity.

"I'll show you around Rome," he said almost lovingly.

He chose to go by a very roundabout route to Palatine Hill to show them both the privation and wealth that existed in Rome: he set off north from the riverbank, near the theater of Marcellus, showed them the outside of the theater of Balbus, then they proceeded toward the Campus Martius. The women were unaffected by the sights of destitution, which they were familiar with in Far Side, but stood gazing for a long time at the massive edifices, as Uri told them which was which and what went on inside them. At the Diribitorium, the public voting hall on the Campus Martius, they were astounded to learn that the vast building had a single continuous roof. They dared not enter the rectangular Pantheon, being content to view it from outside, with Uri detailing how many statues of divinities it contained, those of Mars and Venus among many others, and that the vaulted ceiling was fashioned in imitation of the firmament. Inside the Pantheon was a statue of Caesar, and in the vestibule statues of Augustus and Agrippa. They listened incredulously; Sarah, looking suspiciously at her son, asked him how he happened to know so much.

"I've read about them," Uri replied evasively.

Sarah was proud that a statue of the king of the Jews should be there amid the rest, and Uri was of two minds as to whether to point out that this Agrippa was not the king of the Jews but a good friend of Augustus's. He decided it would be better to hold his tongue.

It emerged that none of the women had seen any of the forums, so to start with they went along the Forum of Augustus all the way to the Via Sacra; he did not show them the busy quarter of Subura, which was not fit for women's eyes, and instead doubled back westward with his small female band to the old Forum. There the women marveled at how many colonnaded buildings from different eras were squeezed in next to one other; it was hard to fit between them. They shuddered at the Carcer on hearing that this was where condemned criminals were locked up. The Rostra was of no interest to them, even though Uri explained proudly that this had been enlarged not long ago, nor did the Curia impress them, and Uri found it impossible to distill into a few words what judges and lawyers occupied themselves with. He also showed them the gilded zero milestone, on the base of which the distances to the major imperial cities from Rome were graven, as measured in miles, which is to say units of eight-and-a-half stadia. The womenfolk wondered how far Jerusalem was, and though he bent down closer he could not find that figure inscribed. The women were horrified and felt affronted. Uri recounted that there was a similar stone in the marketplace in Athens which had been set up five centuries ago, but they were unmoved.

Uri then guided them to the stone-girt marker at the site where Julius Caesar had been assassinated. The place had been covered up with the stones of the Temple of Caesar by the Emperor Augustus, Caesar's adopted son, so that no human should set eyes again on that shameful spot.

"So, it was here," said Sarah portentously, and it was evident that she wanted to be moved.

"Who was he?" Hagar asked.

"The first emperor of Rome."

"And he was assassinated?"

"Yes, murdered."

"That's not nice, is it? Who would do such a thing?"

Hagar was utterly bewildered.

"He would have died anyway in the time since then," Uri tried to reassure her. "It happened a long time ago, about eighty years back."

"Still!"

Uri mused whether to take them up with him onto Capitoline Hill, or show them the Temple of Jupiter and the Tarpeian Rock, over which those condemned to die were shoved, under it the one hundred Steps of Tears along which executioners would drag the corpses by meathook to be thrown into the Tiber, but then he decided that would only scare them stiff. If they had not yet woken up to the sort of city they were living in, then far be it from him to teach them.

Hagar made her way up Palatine Hill with considerable difficulty, panting as she clambered up, stopping frequently and using her forearm to mop the sweat off her face. Sarah, for her part, was angry, sure there was a gentler path up; why did they not go that way? She was unwilling to accept Uri's explanation that along the easier route lay the gardens of the wealthy, one could not simply go across that way.

"Look, we'll be at the top very soon," said Uri. "There's no need to hurry."

He pointed out the Temple of Apollo and suggested they take a look inside, but they were afraid that Jews were not permitted to enter. Uri told them that this was where Augustus had held a celebrated assembly to which the ambassadors from Judaea and all the adult Jews then living in Rome, some eight thousand strong, had been invited; they had all gone into the temple. That was, of course, the occasion on which Augustus had divided up the empire of Herod the Great.

"Why wasn't your father invited?" Sarah said indignantly.

"That was a long time ago, when my grandfather was still a slave and my father not even born, and since then assemblies were banned by Tiberius."

Even so the women did not dare enter the Temple of Apollo.

It then occurred to Sarah to ask what they would do if the king—that was what she persisted in calling Antipas—had already left his home.

Uri was quite sure that he was still at home; he was a bit of a voluptuary, and people like him slept until noon.

"How do you know that?" Sarah asked.

"I dined with him once," Uri said abstractedly.

He shouldn't have said that; Sarah's anger flared up.

"You dined with him and didn't look him up immediately! How discourteous can you get! You had dinner with him, a king, and we're still living in poverty! You had dinner with him, and the king doesn't send a litter around for us! Your father would curse you if he were still alive!"

Hermia asked about the details of the supper and what they had eaten, so Uri wisely mentioned matzos and greens, which his meat-eating sister was not very fond of.

At the top of Palatine Hill they wandered among shrines and villas; Sarah had not been given a more exact address. Uri made up his mind to ask a sentinel.

"They were taken away yesterday," the man replied with satisfaction. He had a bush of fine bristles covering his face; his ancestors had most likely come from somewhere in the East.

"Where did they go?"

"I have no idea, but it was the emperor who exiled them."

Sarah started weeping, Hagar was still catching her breath, and Hermia was standing in a half-witted pose.

Uri nodded and sighed.

They went back down, Hagar waddling with even more difficulty than she had been on the way up.

"You messed up there, that's for sure!" hissed Sarah. "If you'd come just two days earlier, you could have carried away bags of money! Just two days!"

The news spread later in Far Side that the emperor had exiled Antipas to Gaul for, as his spies reported, conspiring with the Parthians to launch an attack on Rome; a huge arsenal of weapons had been found in his palace, and he had himself confessed to owning them, though not to preparing to use them against Rome. His wife, Herodias, the good-looking witch of easy virtue, had gone with him (wonders never cease!) to Lugdunum, which was not the worst place on earth to be exiled to, and there was even a chance of returning.

Agrippa had every right to be pleased because now Galilee would fall into his lap! Mind you, he worked for it by spilling the beans that Antipas was hoarding a huge cache of weapons. It's obvious that it had to be him. Antipas could not have been ready for that, this mud-slinging; of course he had no intention of conspiring with the Parthians, though, come to think of it, that wouldn't be such a bad idea. If the Jews were to take sides with the Parthians, then it would all be over for Rome: two million Jews among the Parthians, another two and a half million in the empire! Not a chance! The Jews always had been divided—even back in the time of Moses, since then it's only gotten worse...

It was really something for a Roman emperor to exile a Jewish tetrarch—that was something on which the Jews in Rome proper found themselves being questioned, and they could give their own accounts for it, appraise the situation at length, and while they were the center of attention, they were at last able to feel that they were full-blown, self-respecting Roman citizens, and not just by law.

URI AGAIN WENT TO SEE HILARUS TO ASK FOR AN APPOINTMENT TO SPEAK with Julius in person. Hilarus promised to do what he could, but unfortunately Julius had gone away to the countryside and there was no knowing when he would be back. Uri then asked Hilarus if he could pass on a message. Most certainly, said Hilarus obligingly. Uri had just sat down and started to write when Julius made an appearance from the street. Uri glanced at Hilarus, but he did not return the look.

Julius was ready to see Uri straightaway.

Uri outlined the situation: it was quite obvious that he would only be able to make payments for another month or two before his money ran out, however hard he worked and juggled things. Was there no way that the original loan of two hundred thousand sesterces, which after all had been taken on for Agrippa, could be paid back by his majesty now that he had risen to royal status? No doubt he had the wherewithal. That would leave him—Uri that is—to pay only the interest.

Julius shook his head.

"Agrippa never pays back debts," he declared.

"He didn't before now, but he's got money now; after all, he's a king..."

"He doesn't pay now either."

"To the best of my knowledge, he also owes money to a number of senators. You mean he doesn't pay them back either?"

"Not even them," said Julius.

Uri nodded. Agrippa was not completely stupid; he was expecting his creditors to supplement his minute kingdom. Only when he had been granted the whole territory of Herod the Great's realm would he pay out.

"Right you are!" said Uri. "By the summer I shall be insolvent for sure. What are you going to do, then?"

"We'll take your house away."

"I got married not long ago. We're expecting a first child."

"We never told you to start a family."

"Yes, and then what?" said Uri.

"We shall have you banned from the Jewish community."

"Yes, and then what?"

"We'll spread the word that you are not credit-worthy. We offered you credit that you could pay back your father's debt and the interest on it. You were granted certain concessions. I don't know if you noticed but we did not calculate with compound interest, and that is proof of the exceptional lenience we have shown you. I dare say they taught you in Alexandria what compound interest is."

"They did," said Uri in dismay. "But even so I can't manage!"

"You should not have signed the contract, dear boy."

Uri studied Julius's face: this pleasant, somewhat plump, ruddy-cheeked individual showed not the least trace of cruelty.

"And how is that good for you when it comes down to it?" he queried. "Sooner or later I will have to flee. What are you looking to accomplish?"

Julius snorted a laugh.

"You're a tricky case, not one to be taken lightly," he spelled out genially. "You have excellent contacts both in Judaea and Alexandria. I seem to recall mentioning that already, don't you remember? Anyone in the council of elders might take it into his head to employ you as a secretary, and in so doing he would acquire a substantial advantage over the others. The only way we have of offsetting that is if we have a financial hold on you. After all, if need be, we are in a position to cancel half of your debt, or three-fifths, three-quarters, five-sixths... As the case may be."

Straight talk at long last, Uri was pleased to note.

"If I have acquired a highly respected Jewish patron, does that give me some measure of relief?"

"That's not what I said," Julius said, amused. "I gave no such advice. If I were to give any advice, I might say that we are in a position to remunerate you if you are open to discussion from time to time about where you have been, what you have done... I mean remunerate you in a negative sense... to let you off paying such and such an amount... But then I have not yet given you any advice."

By now Uri was not so pleased.

Like the others, these swine were looking to employ him as a spy.

Father would have said "no, thank you" to that.

But then what would he have said "yes" to?

URI'S SON WAS BORN THREE OR FOUR WEEKS EARLIER THAN EXPECTED, on Germanicus 1, the end of Elul, or to be more precise on Tishri 1, the day before Rosh Hashanah. The child was skinny and long, but healthy; he was given the name Theophilus. Jews who spoke only Greek liked to pronounce Greek names in a Latin manner, and Uri's father-in-law, the carpenter, insisted on that as his grandson's name. It did not matter to Uri; he was just delighted.

A year before he had been groveling in Delta, on the verge of starving to death; he would not have believed at the time that one year on a son would be born to him.

Theo, as he was called for short, was greedy in sucking at the breast, had colic, and was interested in nothing more than sleeping and voiding, and Uri loved him more than any other living soul. His mother, his wife, and his younger sister, on the other hand, conspired against him and would not let him just live.

Hagar was still pregnant when Uri, unable to stand her odor or sleep next to her, moved back into his old cubbyhole, and the three women divided the main room between them. Sarah and Hermia may well have been delighted, and even Hagar was glad. On Friday nights she slept with Uri in the cubbyhole, and after they had discharged the Lord's commandment Hagar was relieved to be able to scuttle back to the main room, where she shared the bed with Sarah, with Hermia sleeping at their feet on a blanket on the ground. Uri was rather surprised that he was still able to comply, to some extent, with the Eternal One's commandment, so greatly had he lost any inclination for women. Once Theo was born, he was placed on the bed, between Hagar and Sarah; Uri was worried about one or the other of the pudgy women rolling over and squashing him flat, but Theo managed to avoid that: the Lord had created him to live.

IN EARLY WINTER, BEFORE THE SATURNALIA, THE DELEGATION OF Alexandrian Jews arrived, with Philo at its head on grounds of seniority, and the alabarch, Marcus and Tija as members (in short, the whole of the alabarch's family, and nobody else) were representing to the emperor the interests of the Jews of Alexandria. It was not usual to make voyages by sea at this time of the year, so there must have been some grave reason for venturing out against winter squalls; no doubt they had set out from Alexandria the moment they were allowed.

Hilarus sent a message to Uri that a reception was being organized in honor of Alabarch Alexander and his family in the house of Honoratus, and Uri should make sure he was there as they had requested his presence. Uri had his best tunic laundered and put on his best pair of sandals (he had two of each).

Honoratus was installed in a big, two-story house between Far Side's old wall and new wall, where some prominent men pressed together among the Roman Jews. Uri did not know many of them. He stopped at the entrance to the atrium and screwed his eyes up. He was greeted by a short, scrawny, hideous fellow: Iustus, the peevish stonemason, whom he had last seen outside the walls of Jerusalem. Iustus was beaming, delighted to be able to see that Uri was in good health; he congratulated him on getting married, having a son, and on his business successes. He good care to remark that he was working as secretary to

Honoratus. Uri smiled in return, was likewise delighted, and meanwhile thought to himself: if I have an enemy here it might easily be Iustus.

"My dear son! My dear son!" Philo called out, and was all over Uri.

The tiny old man hung on, clung to him, kissed him and hugged him, as the crowd cleared the space around them to look on in amazement.

"Our man in Rome!" exclaimed Philo within everyone's hearing. With a spring in his stride, he led Uri across to the alabarch, who patted him in a friendly fashion on the shoulder, then he was embraced with expansive gestures by Marcus and Tija before they introduced him to Honoratus, who likewise embraced him, unleashing a flurry of whispering throughout the big house.

"You'll be our secretary, our interpreter, our factotum!" declared Philo joyfully, tears springing to his eyes.

Philo's tears were sincere, and he had completely forgotten that Uri had been in disfavor before, because now he needed him.

"Tell me all, my son! Tell me all!" Philo drew Uri to one side, but did not take any particular interest in what he was saying and immediately launched into vilifying Uri's successor: "Imagine! He pilfered belongings, that Delphinus, the dirty scum of a rent boy. That's the last time I ever take Hippolytus's word for anything! Even his astrological charts are false!"

He then went on to praise Vitrasius Pollio, the new prefect, who in fact was also the old one because he had led that position twenty-two years earlier, before Flaccus.

Initially, Caligula had appointed Aemilius Rectus, but had not sent him after all, then he appointed Seius Strabo but in the end had not dispatched him either. Although he was the father of Sejanus, even Tiberius hadn't had any problem with Strabo, as he had served as a Praetorian prefect alongside him and had been on an embassy to Alexandria at a time when Tiberius had been afraid that the city would rise up in rebellion against him. As for the physician named Strabo (who had nothing to do with that Strabo), the unfortunate man had been fed deadly poison under Bassus, a pity that. Well, anyway, following him Caligula appointed Macro, but given the way things developed he had him finished off before he could send him off to take up his post, so on the advice of several people he recalled to duty old Pollio, who was loath to leave his property but had allowed himself to be persuaded, obviously with money. Vitrasius had thought carefully about how he was going to get started, working from a real knowledge of local conditions but surprised at how greatly the situation had deteriorated over the past twenty years, and he could do nothing about the fact that only now was he in a position to permit the delegation to set off.

"I've written a lot since then," Philo confided. "I'm curious as to what you will say... You'll live with us, like in the old days! We shall have time again."

Uri remarked timidly that these days he was a married man; his son had been born not long ago, and he was obliged to work as a merchant to sustain his mother, younger sister, wife and son, not to mention pay off a substantial debt that his father had left.

Philo dismissed all that—they would fix everything.

Some prominent Roman Jews introduced themselves to Uri; he did not know them. Hilarus boasted of having been with Uri in the delegation carrying the ritual tax to Jerusalem five years before. Iustus, the other former delegate who was present, again introduced Uri to Honoratus, who greeted him with exceptional cordiality as if he had never seen him before. In truth he may well not have remembered that he had embraced him just shortly beforehand.

What was going through Uri's mind was that the alabarch, along with his whole clan, had long sunk to the floor of the sea, with a thick layer of sand covering them where they lay, under the ruins of Alexandria. Agrippa was also only acting like a king somewhere in the long-distant past, above him a thick layer of silt, from which was growing stunted weeds. It was strange that all these figures had made their way to Rome, but they were no longer what they had once been; indeed, even the Jewish elders of Rome were only Platonic, secondary shadows of their former selves, which were likewise merely shadows of fate. Man is a dream of shadows, Pindar wrote.

Never mind. Why should he not live with the alabarch's family in Rome as well? At least he would not have to live with his own family during that time. He would drop by to see his son later on, cuddle him, play with him, and then rush away from all that physical and mental mess.

If only this equally messy shadow existence would last as long as possible.

IT WAS NO EASY MATTER FINDING SUITABLE ACCOMMODATIONS FOR THE illustrious delegation from Alexandria: the alabarch wanted to live in Rome proper at all costs, whereas Philo wanted to live in Far Side. At first there was a debate on the matter in Honoratus's house, with Marcus and Tija listening begrudgingly and Uri saying nothing either. Alabarch Alexander said that up on Palatine Hill, next to Agrippa's house, was Antonia's, and they could move in there. It was a splendid, imposing house, which he knew well; it was now inhabited by morose Claudius with his wife and their slaves, and he would no doubt be delighted to have some life brought to it. Philo's argument was that they were, after all, a Jewish delegation, and it would be improper for them to ignore the locals by living elsewhere; they would be insulted, and with good reason. The alabarch—who, it had become clear, was no longer the alabarch, having been replaced with a Greek by the new prefect—contended that he could not receive senators in the poverty-stricken Jewish quarter of the city.

"Let them receive you," said Philo. "That's cheaper for us."

"That's not an option!" the alabarch snapped.

Uri was astonished. Before now matters of finance had never been discussed in the alabarch's family, but it was understandable since the alabarch had lost his entire income. Uri tried to reassure himself: they must have a bit of money tucked away to pay off at least part of his debt.

Indeed they did. Philo and Honoratus came to an agreement that, while Uri was working for the delegation, the installments due in the coming months would be considered paid. Uri thought it wise to ask for a written receipt, and what's more—wonders never cease!—was given one. He hoped that in his free time he would be able to do some business on the side, and this gave him an extra reason to pray that Philo's delegation would stay in Rome as long as possible.

There seemed to be every prospect of that happening: the emperor had departed for Gaul, thence to hop over into Germania and relive his father's former victories—or, as malicious political analysts uncharitably suggested, to cross in triumph with a hundred thousand men on a granite-clad, timber bridge over a shallow creek. The alabarch's group was disheartened to hear that: when they had set off from Alexandria the emperor had still been in Rome, and nobody suspected that he was planning a military expedition, but it now looked unlikely that the emperor would be back in the city before spring. Uri was fearful that Philo's party would return to Alexandria for those few months, but that was not how things worked out. Since it was winter, they decided to stay in Rome while they awaited the emperor. They might have other matters to attend to besides cooling their heels as they hung around for Caligula.

By the time the alabarch finally decided to as Claudius for a place to stay at his house, it emerged that he, too, had gone off to Germania, which caused the alabarch no end of amazement. A man that sickly, gone off to war? The word was that the Senate had sent him to congratulate the emperor for crossing the Rhine and trouncing a twenty-strong advance guard. There was more than a touch of mockery in the fact that they chose lame, crackpot Claudius; everyone smirked at that. Claudius's wife, Messalina, received them graciously but did not offer them the house, so the alabarch did not feel he could ask her.

Instead, a tenement under construction in the middle of Far Side was quickly made ready for them—temporarily finished at the fourth story, topped with a roof, and equipped with the most costly furniture and fittings to be had in Rome. The neighborhood was even paved with marble for two thousand cubits in every direction. Over the course of three weeks, six hundred men threw themselves with great fervor into the work, for a day's wage of fifteen asses, with the foremen on two sesterces a day, and even the hod-carrying urchins getting five asses a day—twice as much as the Egyptian Copt children who worked in the harbors and markets of Alexandria.

The ground floor was fashioned into a single enormous atrium. The outer walls' considerable height contrasted with the many shacks that surrounded the house, and Philo had them painted by eight notable (and expensive) painters with murals bearing images from Nature and sights from Egypt. Making their way onto the walls were richly colored papyrus plants, still lifes of the harbor, marvelous make-believe heptaremes, dromedaries, sphinxes, and pyramids— even a phoenix. While it was true that rumors were rife about sightings of that mysterious bird in Lower Egypt at the beginning of that fateful year, Philo had waved them aside, saying it was only a legend. In any case, this harbinger of doom lurked like a winged crocodile on the wall.

The alabarch was given a suite of rooms on the first floor, Philo one on the second, and the two young men separate apartments on the third floor. Even sewerage and under-floor heating were supplied, with several flushable marble water closets installed on the first three floors along with one each for the young men. A host of servants and cooks were hired, and a kitchen installed in a nearby building, which also provided heating for the main house. The plumbing was installed underground, with one pipe carrying hot water upward, another returning the cold water back down. This was an ingenious engineering solution, which did not require a return cistern, as the hot water was sufficient to drive the cold out. Not much warm water reached Marcus and Tija's apartments on the third floor, unfortunately, as it had cooled down by the time it got there, which may explain why they were so dejected upon moving in.

The house had no yard of its own, so a nearby shanty was demolished and the family occupying it rehoused in the worst of the apartments on the fifth floor— the very top—of a nearby tenement building of fairly meager ground plan. The alabarch did ease matters even further with a substantial sum of money, enough to keep a family of sixteen for half a year. They'll somehow manage half a year jostling cheek by jowl with one another, Uri figured, and if they are clever enough to scrimp and save for six months, they might even be in position to buy a nice house in the end. In place of the shanty a Roman bathhouse was built for the alabarch's family, with hot and cold pools, a massage room, and a shallow paddling pool in which ritual ablutions could be taken. Water was supplied by a cistern that was pronounced ritually clean by a group of shochets; it ran through a thin, gently downward sloping lead pipe, supported on sixteen newly erected stone columns, and kept under watch by specially hired guards posted every five hundred yards for a wage of ten asses per day. The moment they noticed that water was being consumed—steaming or burbling sounds—they would sprint uphill with a tubful of fresh water, climb a ladder, and replenish the cistern.

The building looked drab on the outside, but on the inside it came out so well that Honoratus exclaimed that most senators would envy it.

"Let them!" whispered the alabarch darkly, and with his next breath ordered statues to be added to the atrium.

Honoratus's men procured some lovely statues: it was all the rage to acquire any Greek statue that could be moved. One of their finds, this one produced in Rome by a Greek master sculptor, was a superb bust of Germanicus as a handsome young man (after all he was only thirty-two when Tiberius had him murdered). Uri noticed that it bore essentially the same features of Caligula on coins, which was no surprise as sons often tend to resemble their fathers. For that one statue the alabarch paid more than he had for the whole house, including its fixtures. Uri had again gotten used to measuring everything around him in talents rather than sesterces, and it was also rare that a mention of dinars crossed their lips; probably the alabarch's group had little sense of their value, in much the same way he had been in Judaea regarding the value of prutahs.

Awestruck by the sight of the sculpture, Honoratus asked the alabarch whether he would be taking it back with him to Alexandria. The alabarch pondered before saying that if the mission succeeded, then he would donate it to the local Jewish community. There was no end to the gratitude expressed by Honoratus, a sure sign that he had been hoping he could have it.

But it was far from clear what mission the delegation was serving: Who had authorized them, and to what end. No one asked, and Uri refrained from doing so as well.

On the other hand, he did ask Philo how the matter of his own debt was going to be cleared.

Philo was not pleased to be asked, because at that moment, reclining on one side at the leaf of the jacaranda-wood table in his second-floor suite, he happened to be writing about Flaccus, a work on the prefect's deeds and misdeeds, to set these out before Caligula. Having been disturbed, he lost his train of thought and let it slip that the alabarch had reached an agreement with the Roman Jewish bankers exchanging his signature for their underwriting all costs incurred by the delegation while they were in Rome. A promissory note or bill of exchange had long been in use in this type of case, which stated that the Romans would be able to obtain an equivalent sum in cash on demand from the Jewish bankers in Alexandria with whom the alabarch held his own money, or else (and this was the more usual case) they would send a courier to Alexandria with word that they were willing to enter into this or that business transaction for such and such a sum at this or that much interest.

"For them it will be worth it," said Philo darkly, and asked Uri to stick around before he went back to work, because at any time he might have a question that only someone who had lived through the Bane would be able to answer.

Uri dozed while Philo wrote, roused every now and then by the sound of a child's crying, which could be heard above the ordinary noises of Far Side. Tears would come to his eyes, so much would he have preferred to be with his son, but that was not possible because he was being paid to stay away from him. He felt very strongly—indeed knew for sure—that his father had been reborn in his son, and he regretted every minute that he could not spend with him.

URI READ THROUGH THOSE PARTS OF PHILO'S DRAFT THAT HAD BEEN completed, but he did not recognize what had actually happened.

In Philo's outline he blamed Flaccus, with his rabid Judaeophobia, for everything; there was not a word about the Greek business interests who had really been behind the events. Uri did not say anything about that, but he did ask if any estimate had been made of the number of Jews who had been killed in Alexandria during the Bane, since he had seen no information on that.

"It's possible to find out," said Philo.

Uri waited for him to cough up a number, but nothing was forthcoming.

"So how many was it?"

"Not many," Philo replied.

"How many?"

"Three thousand four hundred and fifty-two."

Uri shuddered.

"That many?"

"Not enough to set down before the emperor," said Philo dourly. "It's little more than one percent of the whole Jewish population of Alexandria! The emperor will just laugh it off."

"What, then, would be enough?"

Philo contemplated.

"Two-fifths, four-sevenths? One could get somewhere with that... As it is, we can only plead our case on the severity of the torments... The fact that old people were scourged as if they had been slaves... That Jewish women were made to eat pork... The stress needs to be placed on the quality..."

Uri then asked if Augustus's stele for the Jews was still standing in front of the Sebasteion, to which Philo answered in the affirmative. Perhaps Flaccus had left it standing as a perverse joke, and now it was forbidden; since peace had arrived it was patrolled day and night by guards, and in the event any anti-Jewish obscenity was scrawled on it—which happened often—then it was quickly washed off.

"The sentries themselves do the daubing, so that they have something to do and the sentry duty isn't called off," Philo chortled. "That's how they make their living—and not a bad one at that."

"What happened to Flaccus?" Uri asked.

"He was exiled to Andros," Philo replied. "I'll include that in the book as well! The voyage, how he was taken to sea in the midst of storms, all the while tormented by his guilty conscience and solitude. And if he should die—that too! Sooner or later people like that are killed... My work will be like the choicest Greek tragedy! I'd never have believed the time would come when I would write a tragedy..."

Philo laughed:

"What do you think, my dear Gaius? Who was it who arraigned Flaccus before the Roman courts of law? You'll never believe it: Isidoros and Lampo! Yes, Isidoros and Lampo, his former pals! They accused him of corruption, just imagine! A prefect accused of corruption! Surprise, surprise!"

Philo, who had no sense of humor, chuckled for a long time.

"And what happened to Pilate?" Uri asked.

"I imagine he was also exiled to somewhere."

Uri shook his head. "A risky job it is, governing a country," he commented.

Philo snorted:

"The only bad thing to be is a tyrannical prefect, because they will be punished by the Eternal One for sure," he declared. "Emperors have been mistaken, repeatedly, in their appointments to the posts of prefects of Egypt and Judaea! They ought to appoint Jews: they would know how to serve an emperor faithfully, which would make the Jews themselves accept the emperor. That's what we have to fight for!"

So that was why Marcus and Tija had come to Rome.

Uri figured it was not beyond the bounds of possibility that if Caligula forgave the alabarch, then Marcus would be made the prefect of Egypt and Tija the prefect of Judaea. Before that could happen, of course, he needed to arrange for them to be admitted into the Roman equestrian order. They met the wealth requirement, and the alabarch would no doubt arrange for the senators to be bribed.

Most likely that was the main reason for the whole family being there: if it had simply been a matter of representing the interest of the Jews of Alexandria, it would have been sufficient for the alabarch or Philo to come alone.

A year and a half ago the alabarch's family had been left out of the list of richest families in the provinces on whom the equestrian order was bestowed, but they were here now, uninvited, and that's what they were going to arrange. It might be that Marcus would become prefect of Judaea or Egypt, and Tija might become anything, but the family's prestige in Alexandria—which had taken a tumble in the wake of the Bane—would be restored. The alabarch and his family were providing an escape route, onward and upward.

I might make strategos in Jerusalem yet, thought Uri with amazement, though he was no more thrilled at the prospect than before. Then he dismissed it: Tija avoided him in Rome just as he had among the Greek students of the Gymnasium, as if they had never swapped ideas over drinks.

In his dinner break, which for him lasted from the fifth hour of the afternoon until dusk, Philo would chat with Uri about anything that happened to come to mind, and afterward Uri would go downstairs to the atrium and catch some sleep on a couch while the great philosopher carried on working. There was no end to Philo's censure and bitterness toward the Jews of Alexandria for not appreciating that it was solely the alabarch's strenuous diplomatic efforts that led to Flaccus's arrest, thus bringing the Bane to an end. If the alabarch had not taken action, the killing of Jews in Alexandria would be going on to this day. The morons were constantly complaining that the alabarch had cravenly withdrawn with his private army instead of using them to defend the Sector. What nonsense!

"Customs men are not permitted to undertake military tasks!" Philo groaned. "That would have been unlawful! It behooves us to stick to the law even if our enemies spit on it! We cannot place ammunition against us in their hands!"

He later complained that agitators from Judaea, whipped up into a fervor and disguised as the crews of commercial ships, were arriving in Alexandria and staying. They said the Bane was a warning from God that the end of days was nigh; moreover, they asserted that the Messiah had already been born somewhere in Galilee or Judaea, and they were his disciples, having the audacity to fool the poor congregations to offer sacrifice with water, claiming that it was actually wine! It was an outrageous rebellion against the institution of the priesthood, as only a priest is permitted to make a sacrificial offering of wine during a service; ordinary Jews of nonpriestly descent were arrogating priestly dignity to themselves! That had never happened before in Jewish history! Some believers were so inebriated by this ordinary water that they imagined they really were priests and said the priestly blessing! An abomination! Thank God, subversives like that were now being harried out of Jerusalem, but they were still free to prowl around Alexandria.

Vitrasius Pollio says—and sadly it is true—he cannot interfere in the internal affairs of the Jews, but speaking as a private individual he acknowledges that such subversion is dangerous; it's a good thing that the matter is not to the liking of the more respectable elders either, and any of these subversives caught committing such an act would be flogged.

Not that one needed to worry about the elders: they had put together a list of damages and set this before Pollio, demanding that any injury the Greeks had inflicted on shops, stock, and turnover should be recompensed with interest. Pollio did not have the funds for this (how would he?), and as his investigation had not yet been completed, it would be no easy matter to identify Greek murderers, robbers, and thieves, so from the very outset the task was futile. It would make more sense to find the instigators, who along with their main accomplices had fled to Rome and, in league with the sophist Apion, were trying to worm their way into the emperor's entourage. Meanwhile, some radicals among the elders in Alexandria were voicing demands that the alabarch make compensation from his private wealth to the Jews who had met with misfortune, which was totally absurd.

"Alexandria is not a very nice place to be nowadays," Philo cut off his complaints, only to start up again the next day at supper time.

Uri asked if he knew anything about what had happened to Apollos.

"He won his school certificate," said Philo. "He gained Greek citizenship rights and went off to Corinth."

"Why there in particular?"

"Tija believes it is because the Greeks there will likely also start killing Jews, and Apollos has not yet had enough of it... You know what Tija's like... It's hardly a reason for Apollos to go to Corinth, because there is more likely to be a Bane in Antioch, where Jews now make up two-fifths of the populace. In Corinth they make up only one-quarter and, as such, represent less of a threat to Greek businesses."

Uri looked at Philo in some astonishment. It seemed he knew, after all, what lay behind the Bane in Alexandria. Why then had he not written that down?

"He said farewell before he went," sighed Philo. "He said he never wanted to see the same thing happen again in Alexandria. The two of us together wept greatly over it... He is taking up a post as a teacher of rhetoric in Corinth, and I think there's little prospect of his returning."

Corinth... Go there and leave it all behind... Kidnap his son and take him off to Corinth. Raise him on his own... Teach geometry... Make the rounds of dives and bathhouses...

But it was not possible; certain women were entrusted to his care.

PHILO SPENT A LOT OF TIME GETTING HIMSELF READY IN THE MORNING, relieving himself at least three times and having a bath at least twice before noon. This was when the ideas would come to his head, the ideas that he would set down in the afternoon. Meanwhile Uri would race around town, taking care of his business affairs so he could continue to provide money for his family; so long as he spent his time on that, he wouldn't have to be at home listening to the moans of the womenfolk. They did not give him much chance to pick up and play with his son or talk to him, as those were not very manly things to do. Theo had such lustrous blue eyes that Uri wondered from whom he could have inherited them. He seemed to be a bright and happy child; Uri would try and guess when he would utter his first words and when he could at last have some fun with him. Until then, all he could do was furtively tickle the soles of his feet as long as the women let him.

He had to acquire various scrolls for Philo, and Uri had a glimpse at them as Philo slowly unrolled them. Not one scroll had been in his hands since he had gotten back to Rome: I'll go stupid, he thought. He would either borrow the scrolls from a library or buy them using Philo's money, and on his rounds he came across several genuine rarities. One day, when he was rolling in money, he would amass a marvelous library of his own; he would make a comfortable living from lending, and he would personally teach his children how to letter.

Since the Bane in Alexandria, scrolls on Judaica had become fashionable in Rome, so if time allowed, he might even go into book selling. He stumbled on a surprising number of scrolls in Greek and Aramaic from Judaea and Alexandria. Interest in the Septuagint had grown as people wondered what sort of lone god these heathen Jews could possibly believe in.

"We have become important in their eyes," Philo acknowledged this. "The Latini are starting to realize that there are as many of us in the world as there are of them, and we too have our religion and our history!"

Uri remarked that it was far from certain that this was a good sign: there was considerable Roman interest in the history of Parthia because they considered it to be a hostile power; maybe they view the Jews, too, as a potential enemy.

"Bah!" said Philo, "There's no reason for that. In my opinion, in the depths of their hearts they are starting to understand that the laws of Moses are valid for them too! The Eternal One sees that the time is ripe..."

Uri was heartily fed up with Philo's chatter, but he was better off listening to him that he was once the alabarch set him to work. It turned out that few of the Roman senators spoke any Greek, and even those who did spoke it poorly.

"What an uncultured bunch!" exclaimed the alabarch. "Do they imagine that the whole world is going to learn Latin for their sake?"

The alabarch dragged Uri around with him as interpreter because neither Marcus nor Tija was up to negotiating in Latin. To In the beginning their father had taken them along practically everywhere, but upon realizing that they were mostly staying silent, ordered them to go out every day to the baths, the Circus, and theater, make friends with the sort of people they wouldn't find at home, and practice speaking Latin. Marcus and Tija happily went along with that plan, wound togas around themselves every morning, and left for the day, not to be seen again by Uri.

The alabarch presented everyone he met with some knick-knack that had been picked up since his arrival in Rome, telling the filthy-rich patricians the pieces had been brought from Alexandria. The gifts were received with infantile delight. He is a true politician, pondered Uri, thinking ahead.

Uri found himself pulled in different directions by the alabarch and Philo, and it was useless mumbling that he had his own business that needed attending to.

"Through me you will get to know important people, my son," said the alabarch. "You'll be able to buy up the whole of Rome within a year!"

There was not a word of truth in that: nobody so much as looked at Uri unless he faltered in his interpreting, and then it was only to give him a dirty glare.

At first the interpreting was hard going; the alabarch babbled and never left Uri enough time to translate an entire sentence, so Uri was obliged to anticipate his train of thought and to formulate in Latin the presumed Greek phrase just half a word behind. But within a week or two Uri had learned how the alabarch's mind worked—not that this was terribly difficult. However, he was at last able to do the interpreting automatically, and got to thinking that the alabarch would be better off staying home, leaving him, Uri—serving, as it were, as the extra-long protruded tongue of the alabarch—to do the negotiating with the Romans. But given that the discussions were about nothing specific—no business or politics—Uri came to realize it was not what the two parties said but simply the fact that they were spending a certain amount of time in each other's company that was important.

Still, there were times when meaningful sentences were uttered, and at these moments Uri could scarcely dignify what he was hearing from these senators, the sons of old families of high repute. Among the words he had to interpret into Greek were their opinions about the deeds of the emperors Tiberius and Caligula, including some especially peculiar assertions. He was occasionally tempted to water down his renderings of certain particularly gross Latin words, but he was worried that quizzical senators might in fact know Greek after all and would correct him.

THE SENATORS GOSSIPED ABOUT THE CAPITAL CRIMES THAT TIBERIUS was supposed to have committed.

Over the last two decades of his life Tiberius was known as Caprineus, or he-goat, after Capriae, the ancient name of the island. He would have groups of young girls and catamites make love before him to stimulate his jaded male lust, executing the positions he would point to, one after the other, in the books of Elephantis with their lascivious illustrations. Among the performers could be found the sons and daughters of highly positioned Roman officials—for example, Aulus Vitellius, the eldest son of the dismissed Syrian legate. The youths would cavort in the woods and groves near the emperor's house, disguised as little Pans and scantily clad Nymphs out to lure an innocent passerby—and who would that be except the emperor himself, who was permanently drunk, and known on that account as Biberius.

It was also reported that during a service in a temple Tiberius became so captivated with the form of a young boy of about ten who held a censer that he molested him, along with the boy's brother who had been playing the flute. After the boys related this to their parents, Tiberius had both of their legs broken, and looked on in lascivious delight at their suffering.

In Tiberius's bedchamber there was a famous picture, painted by Parrasius (it hangs there still, as Caligula did not have it removed), in which Atalanta is pictured in the act of satisfying Meleager's lust orally. In his old age, they said, he had unweaned babies brought to him and placed his prick in their mouths to be sucked.

Few friends had traveled with Tiberius to the island of Capri. His favorites, the Greek philosophers, had all committed suicide while the emperor was alive, for reasons they knew best. Nerva starved himself to death because of the emperor's refusal to implement his economic reforms. All the while, Tiberius begged him in vain to eat, but after he had died, he instituted his reforms after all, these forming the foundation of the bank loan scheme that had been the topic of such heated discussion in Alexandria.

Those he had summoned to the island of Capri had been tortured and flung from a cliff overhanging the sea; soldiers were posted at the bottom to check that the unfortunate men had perished, and if not they beat him with oars and wrung his neck.

Thrasyllus, the emperor's favorite astrologer, with whom he had become acquainted in exile and dragged along thereafter, barely survived with his skin. While they were walking together in Rhodes, Tiberius had been at the point of throwing him from a cliff into the sea when Thrasyllus spoke to say that he felt death was near at hand. That made Tiberius shudder; he embraced Thrasyllus and let him live. And, by the way, such is fate: Caligula later had Thrasyllus's granddaughter, Ennia, murdered along with her husband, Macro. Or to be more precise, the couple killed themselves watched by soldiers; all quite lawful, as they had they been planning to murder the emperor.

When Tiberius came to power, it was said, he had his young brother Agrippa dispatched, then the latter's son, Germanicus, and later Germanicus's widow, his daughter-in-law Agrippina, mother of the present emperor. He'd had one of her eyes plucked out, then when she went on a hunger strike he ordered that meat be crammed down her throat until she choked to death. He had anyone more popular than he put to death. The bloodbath staged after Sejanus's plot was discovered was horrible, with hundreds of innocents being killed or driven to take their own lives, with the emperor snatching their estates afterward. Shamefully, the corpses were dragged by meathook down the Steps of Mourning, before being flung into the river Tiber, and on top of that he even had those who dared mourn their relatives themselves killed.

He had no love for anyone: even his very own son, Drusus—whom Livia Drusilla, Augustus's daughter, bore for him—perished in the excesses, poisoned by her and Sejanus. That was when he set about the torturing in earnest: he had Sejanus's two innocent sons starved to death. Nero met his end on the island of Pontia, and Drusus in the deepest dungeon of Augustus's palace on Palatine

Hill, where, in his hunger pangs, he ate his pillow. Perhaps out of a twinge of conscience, he left alive Gaius, our own gracious Emperor Caligula. Anyone whom he became suspicious of on the island of Capri he would have his member bound and then force wine down him until he burst.

Tiberius was a coward: for nine months after Sejanus was murdered he did not dare set foot outside the villa of Jupiter on Capri, which he had rebuilt as a fortress, even though a fleet of warships were stationed in the island's sole tiny harbor. He was terrified by thunder, and would hide whenever a thunderstorm raged; even after the tempest had passed his men had a hard time coaxing him out. Oh, and he confiscated the fortunes of the notabilities of Gaul, Syria, Hispania, and Greece on the most transparent pretexts. And from his youngest days wine was all he quaffed in the camps, and he would go into battle blind drunk, winning only by pure luck.

And you all know the case of Mallonia: a highborn lady who was seduced by Tiberius, but after the first time she never wanted to lie down with him again. He had her called before a court of law, and there he asked her if she had repented. On leaving the court, Mallonia went home, and with a cry of "You brute! Vile old lecher!" she stabbed herself in the heart.

The senators spoke not from memory, but related these sordid tales from scrolls they'd dug up: Caligula, since coming to power, had supposedly unearthed these documents and had them copied in substantial numbers, so that the truth about the misdeeds of Tiberius should be brought to light. "About time," the senators would sigh. "May such things be seen no more! Never again! This must stand as a lesson to us for evermore."

THE ALABARCH SAID NOTHING IN RESPONSE TO ANY OF THESE ACCU-sations, but summarized them later for Philo, who responded with a sage remark:

"What Tiberius actually committed was more than enough by itself. What's the point of spreading stupid legends on top of it?"

Marcus took the view that the crimes ascribed to the dead emperor were merely the offenses that these bullshitters themselves wished they could commit.

The alabarch was thankful that the one person whose name had not crossed anybody's lips was that of the late, lamented Antonia, Tiberius's sister-in-law— possibly because they were well aware that the alabarch had handled Antonia's properties in Egypt, which had since then reverted to the emperor.

There was no end to the praises sung by the same senators for Caligula.

It was a good thing, they said, that the new emperor had managed to get rid of Macro and his father-in-law, Silanus, in time; they had become too big for their britches. They did not go into in any detail regarding the murder of Gemellus, the general opinion being that it had been worth it as the price of peace between Rome and the world at large. They did mention how Gemellus had attempted to take his own life. Since he had just attained the toga of adulthood, and had never fought in a battle, he did not know where to stick the dagger into himself; a centurion had given him some advice, but even so he could not do it—so in the end he was set upon and butchered.

Caligula had been very well advised at the beginning of his rule, and again six months later, to award each and every Roman citizen the sum of three hundred sesterces; that was the way a ruler ought to handle people.

Uri was astonished that no one in Far Side had mentioned such a thing, though citizens there also ought to have been entitled. As soon as he could, he would go off to the municipal administration and ask for his six hundred sesterces.

It was very nice, said the senators and the knights of the equestrian order, that Caligula was in favor of acting, gladiatorial combat, and, in general, everything that Tiberius, in his puritanism, had endeavored to curb. Caligula spent almost all of the immense fortune he had inherited from Tiberius—2,700,000 sesterces; the same immense sum was almost always mentioned—on games, leaving hardly anything for himself. The bare-knuckle contest between the best Campanian and African pugilists, staged not long ago for the gladiatorial games, was quite splendid. Pity you didn't see it! A more selfless, upright, and generous ruler has not been seen since the time of Princeps Julius Caesar. Rome is at last a happy city! In making it so he has more than repaid the Italian people the 160,000 sacrificial oxen that they offered up in their joy at the emperor's accession.

Uri still recalled the jokes that had gone around Alexandria at the time: exactly the same number of animals had been sacrificed in Caligula's honor in three months at Jerusalem. So that was why: the Jews should not be outdone by the Romans, not even by a single animal.

And what huge bears had been slaughtered in the Circus! Four hundred of them, including two white-haired ones! And four hundred wild beasts from Libya, among them lions with colossal manes! And so many gladiators mauled to death! Wonderful!

And how republican the new emperor is in his sentiments: he revived the ancient institution of the popular assembly! (The fact that senators were capable of being pleased by this slightly astonished Uri, even though he had long believed that nothing would surprise him. Maybe they had no real fear of the institution.) And then in Italia he had knocked half a percent off the tax on goods sold at auction! And he had added a fifth judicial division! And he had extended the customary four days of the Saturnalia with a fifth, known as Youth Day! And thrown a banquet for senators and equites, along with their families, personally handing out decorative bands for the women and children! And what a fervor for building! Before long he will have finished the Temple of Divus Augustus and the rebuilding of Pompey's Theater, which had burned down, and refurbished the city wall of Syracusa!

To peals of laughter, it was recounted that when Caligula fell ill many vowed that if only he were to recover... When, indeed, he had done just that, he kept them to their pledges! They were exceedingly surprised, but what could they do? Publius Afranius Potitus, a plebeian, had said before Caligula that he would willingly surrender his own life if only the emperor were to pull through; the emperor recovered, and Afranius was put to death, that he might not forfeit his word. A certain Atanius Secundus, a knight, announced that in the event of a favorable outcome he would fight as a gladiator; he died doing so, with many applauding as he breathed his last—a fine death! These were people who had expected to be rewarded with money; instead the public had a good laugh at their expense.

Uri could not restrain himself from saying to Philo:

"There are lousy times in store for us."

Philo was angered; his scrawny, old little neck flushed bright red as his gaunt, wrinkled face turned purple.

"Every epoch is what we make of it!" he declared. "I can't stand pessimism! The only reason you are not well-enough off is that you are unwilling to trust in yourself! Be hard and purposeful, my dear son!"

Uri said nothing.

The most interesting bit of news was that Caligula had departed all of a sudden to Germania. He wanted to get there before those who were preparing to murder him the moment he reached that country. The conspirators had dedicated the three swords with which they sought to shed his blood in the Temple of Mars Ultor. One of the leaders of the rebels was Lepidus, Drusilla's widower; the other was Gnaeus Cornelius Lentulus Gaetulicus, the prefect of Germany; even Drusilla's younger sisters (that is to say, the emperor's older sisters), Agrippina and Julia, were in on the conspiracy. The emperor exiled his older sisters to Pontia; Agrippina, with the ashes of her executed husband bound to her chest, walked out of the city gate in chains. It had not been long ago that they had enjoyed all the privileges pertaining to the Vestal Virgins: they were prayed to, they could watch races at the Hippodrome from the same section as the emperor, and they had the right to have uttered on their behalf, each year on January 1, the oaths of allegiance.

Lepidus and Gaetulicus were executed. All this had happened not long before the Jewish delegation arrived in Rome; it had not yet been made public knowledge so far but it was high time to do so, because a congratulatory delegation of senators, Claudius at their head, had already set off for Germania, and indeed had already reached there. The more well-informed senators related with chuckles that the emperor had been so angry at his cripple of an uncle leading the delegation that he had him thrown fully clothed into a nearby river.

The alabarch also laughed cheerfully, and only Uri seemed to notice the sound of teeth being gnashed.

Lepidus had become a significant contact for the alabarch after Silanus had been executed, and now he too had been dispatched. Claudius, Antonia's first-born son, was similarly important; only two months ago he had been chosen as fellow-consul by Emperor Caligula, but now he was an object of ridicule.

It wouldn't hurt for the alabarch to find more suitable and less death-prone benefactors, Uri reflected sardonically, as he assiduously continued the mechanical task of interpreting.

ATTENDING THE SERVICE WAS A BURDEN, BECAUSE THERE WERE A LOT of people trying to bribe him to drop a good word for them in the ear of the alabarch or Philo. Among the celebrated relatives who came by was Siculus Sabinus, a smith, who brought a bronze menorah as a gift and requested to be allowed to produce the banisters for the stairs in the alabarch's house, because he had heard that they were still not ready. Uri promised to do so. Distant relatives, acquaintances, even total strangers accosted him; virtually all started by saying how highly they had esteemed Joseph. Indeed, many even mentioned their regard for his grandfather, Tadeus. Some had witnessed Tadeus's manumission, had seen how had jubilantly pressed onto his head the brimless, Phrygian-style liberty cap of soft felt, its top pulled forward.

Come to think of it, where was the cap? Joseph had showed it to him once. Uri must have been three or four. Had Sarah discarded that too? Tadeus had pulled the cap a few times onto his head, and then he died.

The cadgers requested a bridging loan, an insignificant sum of money, a job, a contact, a letter of recommendation—anything. Uri just gave a forced nod and promised them all that he would put in a good word just as soon as he had a chance. He had no intention of saying anything; the situation was never appropriate. As the weeks and months passed a growing number of individuals came by to thank him for having solved their problems, even though Uri protested he had done nothing, which was the truth, and in most cases they would respond with an even more urgent request than the previous one, to which Uri would give exactly the same answer. There were a few among them who had conceived a strong hatred for him, but then they had probably hated him from the beginning.

Philo had finished the introductory part of his work against Flaccus and set it down before Uri, who read it and did not much like it because it was nothing more than a glorification of Augustus and Tiberius, claiming they had always taken Jewish affairs as very much their own and ruled justly. Uri mentioned that Caligula was hardly likely to read a work which started off by lauding his predecessors, and Philo, reluctantly agreeing that was true, with heavy heart dropped the eulogy.

"Right, I'll use it some other time," he said.

Uri outlined his thinking on why Tiberius, at the height of his power, had withdrawn to the island of Capri. By then Tiberius had obviously acquired too many enemies in Rome, but he did not dare put them in check, so he hid himself away, leaving the Praetorian prefect Sejanus effectively in charge of all the machinery of government. Sejanus made full use of his plenipotentiary power and—following Tiberius's instructions—began the bloodshed, for which he was loathed even more than Tiberius. When Tiberius saw that his prefect had become too strong he overthrew him, pinned all the blame on him, and appointed the next plenipotentiary sacrifice in the person of Macro, who arranged for a stupendous bloodbath among Sejanus's supporters but did not have enough time to consolidate power, or rather Tiberius by then did not have the strength to overthrow him; that was left to his successor, Caligula. Uri did not rule out the possibility that if Caligula were an apt pupil, then he would likewise withdraw to some spot, entrusting the next round of slaughter to an intimate who in due time would himself be slaughtered.

Philo chewed that over without enthusiasm before saying no more than, "Emperors are not all that bright, my dear son."

It was a fairly startling opinion given that in the part of his book that had just been ditched Philo had so avidly praised Augustus and Tiberius's peerless mental powers.

"Should you ever come before the emperor, my dear son," Philo added gloomily, "you'd be well advised not to lay bare before him that ungodly notion."

Uri found it amusing that Philo should imagine that a nobody like him could ever end up in the position to offer political advice to an emperor.

Philo suddenly cracked a smile.

"It was Antonia's notion," he divulged the secret. "She sent word to Tiberius, who was then still living in Rome but had already begun to have enough of it, that he should study the life of Solon a little bit, with particular regard to his voluntary exile..."

Uri nodded in acknowledgment: Solon had indeed resorted to that stratagem. How come he had never noticed the parallel before?

"Was Antonia that wise a woman?"

"None wiser than her anywhere," said Philo hoarsely.

There was silence as Philo almost started to weep.

"Did you make her acquaintance?" Uri asked.

"She came once to Alexandria."

He had probably been quite taken by the woman.

"Who were her forebears?" Uri asked.

Philo looked at him in amazement.

"You don't know?"

Uri flushed and shook his head. He didn't.

"Her father was Mark Antony, who else?" Philo stated.

Uri shuddered.

Philo went on to tell him that Augustus had put an end to the many sons sired by Mark Antony who had turned against him, leaving alive only Cleopatra's sons (with an annuity), and Iullus, who had on one occasion organized games at the Circus in Augustus's honor, though ten years later he had him executed as well, because he was among the lovers of the emperor's daughter, Julia. Augustus also spared both Antonias, marrying Antonia the Younger to Drusus, the younger brother of Tiberius, his natural son. Tiberius had then arranged for the murder of his grandson Germanicus, Drusus and Antonia's firstborn son. Germanicus's youngest son, Antonia's grandson, was the current emperor; his older brothers—Antonia's other grandsons, the great-grandsons of Augustus and Mark Antony—had been finished off by Augustus's adopted son, Tiberius.

Antonia must have been nothing short of brilliant to make it unscathed through all that.

Though in the end she did not escape entirely: Caligula awarded his grandmother the honorific Augusta, then harried her into taking her own life.

The only one of Antonia's children left was a son: shiftless, ungainly, sickly, senescent Claudius, who had come to nothing. Uri became interested in him, a grandson of Augustus and Mark Antony in whom a trace of the blood of Marcus Agrippa was still trickling. What if he were to meet him some day, and what if he turned out not to be so inept after all?

It was winter, the weather was rainy and cool; the emperor had taken a boat across to Britannia, had routed a group of fifteen men, and then sailed back to Gaul; back in Rome the alabarch began to display conspicuous signs of weariness, as if he too had been in combat. He was used to the clement air on the banks of the Nile, not the miasmas of Rome, and the foreign food and drink had taken their toll on his belly. Philo remained as shriveled and ageless as before; maybe he had been born that way, and he hardly ate anything.

Firstborn but stunted, Philo had handed over the rights of primogeniture to his younger brother, who was strong at birth, not for a mess of pottage but for the pleasures of dipping into books. Or had their father made the decision? Officially, Philo was the delegation's leader, but he only provoked smiles from the Roman Jews, who sought to curry favor with the alabarch. Uri was alarmed: what if his second child was a son too? He prayed that it be a girl. He imagined what it would be like if he'd had to fight with an envious second-born who was full of hatred, and he shuddered.

When time permitted, Uri threw himself into his own business. The vogue for pitchers from Rhodes declined, and Gaius Lucius ordered no more of them; more to the point, though, he did forgive Uri, who was again able to turn up to the salutations with his sportula. Uri divided his time in such a way that he was the first to arrive at his patron's house, at daybreak, there loaded up his sportula and raced back across the bridge to get back in time for the end of Philo's forenoon preparations. Only in the afternoon would the tired alabarch have pulled it together to have himself carried across by litter, with Uri ambling behind the two sturdy bearers and catching a nap with eyes open.

The atmosphere at home was awful; all three women were unhappy with him, the sole male in the family, for neglecting them. His mother was constantly haranguing and criticizing him as if Uri were her husband; his sister inflicted her silent contempt on him for not being able to get her married; his wife was disgusted by him, as Uri was by his wife. All the same, his wife copulated one Friday night or other. Perhaps it had been the evening when, after a brief coitus, Hagar had stuck around to insist that Uri should ask the alabarch to give them enough money for a new house where she and the infant could have their own room. Uri tried to explain that the assumption of the monthly debt payments was in itself a massive gesture on Philo's part, but Hagar seemed unable to grasp that.

"Where's the money? Who are you squandering it on?" she shrilled. "Everyone envies me for having an eminent husband, but where's the money?"

Uri despaired, not so much at his wife's profound stupidity, but because she had a point. How was it possible that a debt his father had contracted out of necessity and had to pay back to the end of his days was now crippling him, all because Agrippa had laid out a feast for overfed senators? Uri could no longer stand Hagar's cloying; he simply grabbed a blanket and stalked out in the middle of the night. He pulled the blanket over his head, and lay down next to the water tub in front of the house. It was cold, but he managed to fall asleep; he woke up with his nose running and sneezing. When he went back into the house Hagar started hissing again:

"The shame you bring on us! You think no one saw you? Such an embarrassment!"

Uri decided that was it: he would not speak to her again.

"You can't do that!" his mother yelled.

That morning Uri did not so much as look at his son and simply rushed out of the house.

Business was faltering, and in the end he went into the business of trading balsam, which he had been invited to do by men who had really respected his father: The money was paltry but certain, they would say with conviction.

A person is never free from what he has been born into: not from his mother, not from debt, not from balsam.

The Eternal One, however, must have wanted life to sparkle in Rome and for Uri to be temporarily freed of his worries.

The emperor arrived!

IT WAS ALREADY SPRING WHEN THE NEWS ARRIVED, AND SOULS THIS side of the Tiber and beyond were imbued with joyful expectation. Something was happening at last! The least of it was that the emperor would stage a parade and make citizens presents of money, entrances to the Hippodrome, and a banquet.

The news proved to be partially false in that the emperor did not cross the city border but remained outside it, encamped in his favorite Hippodrome, the miraculous gardens his mother Agrippina Major had set out on Vatican Hill. Caligula would amuse himself, receiving embassies there, if he received anyone. It was unclear why he was unwilling to cross the city boundary; Uri's hunch was that he was wrangling with the Senate, a majority of which did not wish to grant him a triumph, at most they could only permit a lesser triumph, which from an emperor's point of view was so insulting that it was better if they granted him nothing at all. Uri shared that suspicion with Marcus, who confirmed that he had heard gossip of that kind; he did not speak to Tija, who continued to avoid him.

Vatican Hill lay close to Far Side, and the members of the Jewish delegation laughed at how, by chance, they had gained a big advantage over other delegations.

Rome was teeming with hundreds of delegations, who had been hanging around the city for months on end on unfinished business, and now they were all racing about, jostling and shoving to be among the first whom the emperor received.

There were many matters on which only an emperor personally could be of assistance. That had been so in the time of Caesar and Augustus and up through the first half of Tiberius's rule: land disputes with neighbors; disputes over authority with degenerate, power-hungry family members; problems with tax and excise remittals; grave religious disputes over major issues of prestige; quarrels over precedence as to which tiny island this or that divinity had originally hailed from, and who had a right to erect a temple in his or her honor; which nation stemmed from which, and which was the more ancient, the more authentic; who owned fishing rights on the sea coasts; and so on and so forth. Any party who won a concession from the emperor could, for at least a decade, exercise arbitrary rule over his own little dunghill back home. In any of these far-reaching matters neither senators nor consuls were competent to reach a decision in place of the emperor, who now had arrived at last—or almost arrived.

Nevertheless, news did arrive that back in winter unrest had broken out in Jamnia, where the largely Jewish population had destroyed a Greek altar erected in Caligula's honor; Herennius Capito had pitched into them with his troops and killed many. This was the same Capito who a while before had captured Agrippa and demanded he pay up on three hundred thousand sesterces of debts, though Agrippa had escaped to Alexandria.

No friend of the Jews was this Capito, supervisor of imperial property for Jamnia and Ashdod, Phasaelis as well as Archelais, with its celebrated groves of palm trees, and also a large palace in Askelon that had at one time belonged to Salome, the sister of Herod the Great. Upon his death Herod had bequeathed these to Livia, Augustus's spouse; Tiberius inherited them after his mother died, and after him they passed to Caligula. The territory was thus a personal property of the emperor's, and it was always the imperial prefect who administered it, with its own special taxation. Herennius Capito had acted as prefect under Livia and Tiberius, and Caligula, exceptionally, had retained him.

Philo lamented: Of all times why did it have to happen now? Why now? The Jews of Jamnia might have waited. What was the purpose of injuring the cause of Alexandria's victims with such idiotic capers?

Tija was sure it had been a provocation, coming directly after the Bane.

"Of course it's a provocation!" The little old man's anger flared. "But why couldn't they wait until the emperor had reached a decision in our case?"

Not knowing any details, Marcus bet that the Greeks had deliberately built the altar too close to a Jewish house of prayer, possibly letting Capito in on the plan. That sort of thing was bound to happen so long as Rome had Greeks and Latini serving as prefects for Jewish territories, he added.

Philo noted that more Philistines than Greeks lived in Jamnia, at which Marcus fumed that it made no difference.

"It serves as a good pretext for the emperor not to intervene in either matter," Tija surmised. "That way he settles the matter in a balanced manner, without bias: Alexandria in one pan of the scales, Jamnia in the other."

Marcus went on:

"Jamnia and the surrounding district are able to raise forty thousand soldiers, compared with none from Alexandria and Egypt... Maybe that was why Jamnia weighed more heavily in the balance."

Philo reproved him too for his cynicism.

Marcus burst out:

"That incident in Jamnia might yet come in very handy! The emperor will have to realize that a Jewish prefect needs to be appointed to govern Jews."

"You're not implying that we set the whole thing up premeditatedly?"

Marcus was miffed.

Tija snickered:

"The Jews are onto a good thing as long as they have Greeks or Latini governing them," he said. "Every time they've had a king of their own kind they've torn each other to pieces."

The alabarch was infuriated, and with good reason; after the Bane he had spent a lot of money sending hundreds of messengers throughout Egypt, Judaea too, with the aim of safeguarding the Jews from Greek provocations. He had cautioned them against responding to provocation with violence, but it had never crossed his mind to send anyone to Jamnia, seeing that it constituted imperial property.

"Where else was I supposed to send an envoy? Athens, Dalmatia, the summit of Mount Ararat, the ruins of Carthage?" the alabarch roared. "Where else? Antioch, Delos, Samos, Cyprus, perchance Rome? What makes the Jews such brainless idiots?"

Uri was now well able to imagine how Pilate, the prefect, in his palace at Caesarea, must have screamed when he learned about the carnage at Mount Gerizim. Would he have sent a cohort there as well to prevent Lucius Vitellius's soldiers from staging a massacre? And where else?

It was on the tip of Uri's tongue to point out that since Jamnia was an imperial property it was unlikely that anything happened there without the emperor's imprimatur, and maybe this was Capito's way of paying for the emperor's confidence, but he swallowed it.

The emperor had arrived and they, the Jewish delegation from Alexandria, had to arrange to be received by the emperor.

Through cordial, unselfish companionship and obscure (though obviously material) promises, Marcus, Tija, and the alabarch had managed to get appropriate senators and equestrians to divulge whom they needed to turn to on the matter of obtaining an interview.

Homilus, some suggested—he was the imperial counselor on matters of delegations, and was the one who saw all delegations first and decided the order in which they would be admitted into the emperor's presence. He was an intelligent man, speaking, in addition to Latin and Greek, Coptic, Aramaic, and one of the Germanic languages.

Not him, others said; Helicon was a better bet.

He was a Greek freedman who alone saw to all Caligula's private affairs, a sort of entertainment chamberlain. Night and day he stayed beside the emperor, and even accompanied him to his bed. A funny man, he instantly comes up with caustic and witty repartee for any situation, having been well instructed by his original master, who gave him to Tiberius; the former emperor freed him from slavery, and he was inherited by Caligula, who supposedly said that this one man had more sense than the whole Senate put together, and only his favorite horse, Incitatus, was cleverer.

The highly ranked informants added regretfully, with much sighing: we were living in such dismal times when a nonentity of a freedman could hold more power than the entire Senate and the whole equestrian order.

Philo was devastated.

Helicon's the one who arranged for Isidoros and Lampo to be Flaccus's public prosecutors. The emperor has received them several times and heaped them with gifts. One could well imagine what sort of things this fellow has whispered into the emperor's ear regarding the Jews of Alexandria.

It was quite certain that only for a huge sum could Helicon be persuaded to call the emperor's attention to the Jewish delegation. It was said that he was not exactly averse to money.

"For all that," the alabarch said angrily, "the emperor appointed Agrippa as king, and for all that Galilee was made Agrippa's!"

Tija threw out the suggestion that it would do no harm to invite Agrippa to Rome.

That incensed the alabarch even more.

"Aren't there enough of us as it is?" he yelled. "Who does Agrippa think he is anyway! It was us who made him king! We stuffed him with money! We still have him eating from the palm of our hand!"

Philo took the line that August 31 was still a long time away; if no triumph went ahead, then Agrippa would only come to Rome for the emperor's birthday, when all the other kings, princes, tribal chiefs, prefects, and legates would make their obligatory pilgrimage to the capital city of the empire, and indeed it would do no harm if he were to arrive early.

Tija waited until his father had calmed down a little before quietly stating:

"It would also do no harm if we were finally to marry into Agrippa's family."

A silence fell; Philo flushed and cleared his throat.

"Marcus," he said.

Marcus, as usual, had been leaning with his back to a wall, but now he broke away and he, too, flushed.

"I don't think there's any need of that!" he exclaimed disconsolately.

The alabarch remained silent.

"That's a practicable proposition," Philo said gloomily. "Agrippa's son Drusus is still a young boy. If anything were to happen to Agrippa—let's say he were to eat himself to death one evening—the kingdom of the Jews would go to the dogs."

Marcus uttered a groan.

"What's Agrippa's eldest daughter named?" he asked mournfully.

"Berenice," said Tija cheerfully. "Soon she'll be twelve... She's said to be pretty. Let's just pray she doesn't grow up ugly."

The next day couriers set off to Agrippa, telling him to leave his fresh acquisition of Galilee and make haste for Rome. The couriers, five in number, were sent by different routes to Galilee with the promise that whoever reached Sepphoris first would earn a special reward.

That was how Uri learned that Agrippa, had moved the capital of Galilee to Sepphoris from Tiberias. By this decision, Agrippa generously and collectively left to Antipas those officials who had been living in the previous capital, and returned to the old adminstrators of the district (or, to be more accurate, to their descendants) as he knew they would serve gratefully and faithfully. Nor could it be said any longer that Galilee's capital city was unclean, as Sepphoris was not built on a cemetery.

CLAUDIUS HAD ALSO RETURNED WITH THE EMPEROR, BUT AS HE HAD NO reason not to cross Rome's *pomerium* he did appear in the city. Philo went to call on him, taking Uri with him.

As they arrived, Claudius was scrambling around, blinking sleepily in a rumpled smock and slippers in a disorderly house full of scrolls, statues, and tapestries. He was glad to see Philo and embraced him; he cast a glance at Uri and muttered something cordially before starting to grumble about his nephew, the beastly fellow, for not letting him live. Uri thought at first that he was still piqued at the emperor for having furiously shoved him into the river, but it turned out that it was not that: Claudius was despondent that he, as Caligula's priest, was forced to take part in all sorts of lunatic ceremonies.

"This whole thing is not for me," wailed this large-bodied, large-headed man, who spoke excellent Greek. "I get myself taken over there in the palanquin, with my guts jolted this way and that; then once I get there I have to sit for hours in the sun, and if I pull my toga over my head, they tell me off, they jabber nonsense, and then sometimes I have to stand up and stutter something, and I'm not even allowed to read or sleep. It'll be the death of me!"

He pulled his left leg a little and spoke a bit oddly: in the middle of sentences his voice began to crack to a higher register, as if his throat were constricting, and he was only able to end the sentence at a squeak.

"This house is no longer mine!" Claudius cried out. "I have had to mortgage it, and my name is still on display in the Forum! Eight million sesterces I had to pay for the unprecedented honor of becoming one of Caligula's priests, which he was so gracious as to offer me! Never in my life did I have more than a hundred thousand! Never! And even that I could never have spent either! It started with my house burning down! Augustus rebuilt it, but apart from that I got no more money from him! I've lived, and still live, off loans! I can be evicted from here at any time! Made homeless! Where will that leave my daughters and servants?"

Philo asked after the emperor's health, at which Claudius—a grandson of

Augustus and Mark Antony, and priest to Emperor Caligula—just shrugged his shoulders.

"He pretends to have gone mad," he said. "But he's just wicked. He's putting on an act. He's testing boundaries just the way an adolescent does."

Philo then asked what sort of reception might Alabarch Alexander encounter with him.

Claudius mused.

"He's unpredictable," he said. "He has one thing and another running through his head, but as to what comes out on top at any moment even the gods cannot say."

Claudius and Philo then started talking about authors and scrolls, mentioning the name of the historian Cordus, and, forgetting about Uri, they wandered off into another room. So Claudius had a copy of Cordus's celebrated scroll, which Augustus himself had ordered be burned. Cordus, having come into conflict with Sejanus, starved himself to death, and the writer's daughter, Marcia, had preserved a copy of the book and was now having it republished. Cordus had eulogized the virtues of Brutus and Cassius, Julius Caesar's assassins, barely concealing his Republican sympathies. Uri gazed longingly in the direction Philo had headed: he would be reading through it right now. Uri was left standing alone in the hall and did not know what he should do.

In stormed a black-haired, plump woman in disarray, wearing a dirty gown and barefooted. She stared at Uri.

"What are you doing here?" she squawked in Latin.

Uri was just about to answer but the woman rushed onward out of the hall.

She might be Messalina, Claudius's wife.

Nothing happened, so Uri strolled over to the window and looked out; a neglected house stood opposite, the shutters on its windows closed; maybe that was Agrippa's house.

Why would the houses of Claudius and Agrippa have been built next to each other?

Was Claudius's house, he wondered, the same as the one whose rebuilding Augustus had financed? Eight hundred thousand sesterces was what Augustus had bequeathed to Claudius, so he had more money now than he remembered. Uri himself had read Augustus's will in some old copy of the *Acta Diurna*; it had caused quite a stir at the time that the emperor should have thought of such an unsuccessful grandson.

A slim, round-shouldered man with a square head and disheveled black hair entered the room and stopped short.

"Who are you?"

"I came with Philo of Alexandria, who has gone off with Claudius to read something," said Uri.

"And?"

"And they left me here," said Uri.

The round-shouldered man pondered.

"If you'd like something to drink or eat, sir, come into the atrium," he said.

Uri thanked him and followed.

It was a big house, with lots of half-empty, barely furnished rooms. The atrium was simply vast.

Two adolescent girls in rumpled dresses were pecking distractedly at food whilst seated on a carpet.

"Claudius's daughters, Antonia and Octavia," the round-shouldered man introduced them; they did not look up. "How should we address you, sir?"

"My name is Gaius Theodorus," said Uri "A Jewish Roman citizen."

"Narcissus, slave," said the round-shouldered man. "What wine may I pour for you?"

"None, thank you."

"Some fruit?"

"Perhaps a bit, yes please..."

Uri ate as he gazed at the girls, who were lazily sprawling and not at all pretty.

A man turned up and set himself down familiarly next to one of the girls. He was followed by three more, all sleepy and rumpled; they must have woken up in one of the rooms somewhere not long before.

"We're going to the baths," one of them threw out to Narcissus. "We'll be back in the afternoon."

"As you wish, sir."

Servants swarmed in. One started to cook, three more carried logs for the fire. A few men, some elderly, some young, also wandered in, and Narcissus poured them glasses of wine. They requested hot water; Narcissus sprinkled spices into the watered wine, which he then placed on the fireplace. Uri lounged in a corner and looked around in amazement at this unusually busy morning traffic in the roomy atrium. Did all these people live here, or had they only come as guests? They were certainly very much at ease, as if the house was theirs. Maybe it was, in fact, theirs, if these were Claudius's creditors.

Narcissus was lying prostrate on the floor and started to copy something, groaning from time to time. Uri crawled over on all fours and took a look before exclaiming:

"That's Aquila's shorthand!"

Narcissus looked up.

"You know it?"

"I learned it when I was a child," said Uri.

"It's very difficult," sighed Narcissus. "This is a speech of Claudius's; he always writes that way, but often he himself can't make it out. It's my job to put it into normal lettering."

"Give it to me, I'll do it," said Uri.

"But, sir..."

"I've nothing to do anyway," said Uri, setting himself on his belly.

Narcissus the slave sat back on his heels and, impressed, held his peace.

Uri could see objects superbly well when they were close to his eyes, and Claudius's shorthand was not unsystematic. A scribe by the name of Tiro, a freedman of Cicero's, was said to have invented a system of shorthand, and this had been refined by Aquila, one of Maecenas's freedmen. Tiro, possibly following an older, discarded, Greek syllabic system of writing, denoted frequent phonetic junctions with specific downward and upward squiggling lines, while Aquila went further by dropping the declined and conjugated endings of nouns and verbs; after all, it makes no difference what function a word serves or what conjugation applies to it as long as a person either knows it anyway or is able to deduce it from the context. On checking his work, a conscientious note taker will also write in the word endings while the original intention is still fresh in his mind, but Claudius had neglected to do that, so Narcissus had good reason for his groaning.

"Just tell me, though, what the speech is about," Uri looked up, screwing his eyes up tightly.

"Virtue and pleasure, in the manner of Democritus," said Narcissus.

"Thanks."

Uri became immersed in working out the text. He quickly realized that Claudius had mixed Greek words in with the Latin, so he was supposed to render these too in Latin.

It was almost ready when Narcissus called him to the table. There were about two dozen people sitting around a huge table, and no one showed any interest in Uri's joining them to eat. It struck him that it was far from easy to tell which of them might be slaves and which senators.

Seated next to him on the right was a quiet young man with broad cheekbones and thin blades for lips who was addressed as Titus; then next to him was a hulking, ruddy-faced fellow who was constantly gabbing even with his mouth full, Sabinus by name, who the signs indicated might be the elder brother of Titus; on his left sat a certain Dexter, a thin man with a protruding Adam's apple; next to each of Claudius's daughters with their unimpressive outer appearances reclined their suitors, one of them answering to the name of Gnaeus, the other, Lucius. Strolling around, a certain Diespiter hacked up the food on a golden platter. A Lupus, Asinus, Celer, and Lusius were listened to with some respect, and Uri dimly recalled that these men had already been consuls. One bashful man was known as Afer, and a fat, elderly gentleman seated at the head of the table was identified as Appius; he was, apparently, the father of the Lucius who was the suitor of one of Claudius's daughters. Posides, a round-faced eunuch, was patted genially on the back by everyone he approached. An old woman, Aelia, was humming loudly and rocking back and forth as she reclined. Slaves called Pallas and Callistus changed the plates, and a young man, Helius, mixed the wine. Everyone knew everyone else, just like one big family. At one point Messalina dashed in, made an excuse that she had lots of things to do, and raced off again. Several of the servants were reclining at the table, a long way from Uri, who therefore could not see their faces, though he was able to hear them addressed as Myron, Polybius and Harpocras. Even though it was past noon by then, Messalina was still not properly dressed. Philo and Claudius had not shown up again, and must have become absorbed in scrolls somewhere, so once the eating had finished Uri went back to work, again lying on his stomach.

Narcissus read through the completed text.

"You've got a nice hand," he said. "I owe you."

"Don't be silly," said Uri. "If I had not had this to do, I would have been bored stiff. Though when it comes down to it Democritus would have been unlikely to agree that 'a person who tramples on the rights of another is unhappier than the person whom he tramples on...'"

Narcissus grinned but said nothing; nor did Uri elaborate. Even so the two of them, Claudius's slave and the Jewish freedman, were able to exchange their opinions of Claudius's lofty excuse for the rights trampling practiced by his nephew, the emperor.

The evening was drawing in by the time Philo and Claudius surfaced. They set to eating the food that the servants had been continually preparing. Claudius introduced Philo to those who were present, whose number had been boosted by the party which returned from the baths. Philo spoke with unfeigned admiration of Claudius's latest work, an eight-volume history of Carthage, which, he said, deserved the most careful attention. Claudius behaved modestly, saying that the history of Etruria that he was working on was more important; he was currently planning for it to stretch to fifteen or twenty volumes, nine of which had already been written.

Narcissus slipped into his hands the speech, and Claudius glanced at it.

"Very nice," he said.

Narcissus pointed out Uri:

"He transcribed it."

"Nifty!" said Claudius. "Who is he?"

Philo piped up.

"He's Gaius Theodorus," he said. "A Roman citizen and my right-hand man. I introduced him this morning."

"Oh, yes!" said Claudius. "It's easy when you have this sort of assistance."

"He was a great help to us in Alexandria," said Philo emotionally. "Along with us he suffered the Bane from start to finish..."

Uri flushed in anger.

"It must have been terrible," said Claudius. "I disapprove of people killing one another. Let people be killed by wild animals."

That evening the alabarch came with Marcus and Tija, as Claudius had sent for them.

By then there were around fifty people eating, drinking, and chatting in the atrium, the nearby rooms, and the garden.

Messalina had finally gotten dressed, and many people paid court to her; she laughed heartily, her massive bosoms heaving. Claudius got plastered and sobered up a second time over.

Messalina was rubbing herself against an ugly, pudgy old woman, who in turn was pressed close to an old man, Appius—all three of them repulsive creatures.

"That is Messalina's mother," Narcissus whispered into Uri's ear, as he looked at the trio aghast. "Not long ago she was wed to Appius Silanus, whose son Lucius is betrothed to Messalina's daughter Octavia..."

A lanky man passed by, loudly joking with several youngsters and a couple of servants in tow.

"Livius Geminius, a senator," Narcissus said. "He was given one million sesterces by the emperor for swearing an oath that he had seen Drusilla ascending unto the heavens and conversing with the gods."

"That's nothing new," Uri growled, racking his brain to remember. "Yes, I read that Deified Livia paid the same amount to Numerius Atticus, who had seen Divus Augustus ascend to the heavens..."

"That's a good memory you have," said Narcissus in acknowledgment.

After being made to vomit, Claudius was immediately hungry, so while Narcissus applied a poultice of cold water to his head Pallas set before him some scrambled eggs.

At that moment, the alabarch and his sons took their places at the dinner table.

"My dear Alexander!" Claudius cried. "Why don't you move into the house across the way? It's standing there empty! You hide away in the Jewish quarter where even a dog is unwilling to look you up! Stay here; Agrippa won't have anything against it... Go on boys, set to opening up the house!"

The keys to Agrippa's house were with Narcissus, who around midnight led the alabarch's party across to the house opposite, with a group of men carrying torches accompanying them. The alabarch decided to accept the offer.

"We have now gotten to the real Rome!" the alabarch put it later, standing in Claudius's atrium. For him, it was an uncharacteristically direct remark.

Not much later Uri fell asleep on the mosaic floor, heated underneath even in the summer, and only woke up around daybreak. Most of the company had changed, but there were still a lot of people around, with newcomers continually supplied with food and drink. Uri made tracks for the larder that was set in a wall in the garden and got a bite to eat. Narcissus laughed at him.

"Do you ever get any sleep?" Uri asked wanly.

"I'm lucky; I can make do with three or four hours."

A familiar figure, after rummaging in the larder, departed with a handful of figs.

"Who is this Dexter?" Uri queried.

"A great man," said Narcissus. "It was he who put Lepidus to the sword."

Uri grunted.

"Lepidus, too, used to visit here after he became a widower," Narcissus clarified. "He was very welcome; after all, he was the emperor brother-in-law and, to put it politely, a bosom friend. That is until the emperor sent Lepidus's friend, Dexter, around to cut him down."

It was not clear what, precisely, Narcissus thought of all this, morally speaking. Uri considered it best not to comment.

"What sort of person was Antonia?" asked Uri.

A shadow passed across Narcissus's eyes.

"No woman ever lived who was cleverer than she," he said with feeling.

That was pretty much what Philo had said.

The alabarch's group had vanished; perhaps they had gone across to Agrippa's house. Uri ruminated that it was time he left, but it was not too safe to toddle about in Rome proper at dawn.

"Go ahead and lie down," Narcissus suggested. "If you have no objection to using a servant's bed, that is."

"I've slept in stranger places than that," said Uri.

There was a glint of uncertainty in Narcissus's eyes, so Uri quickly sketched out his life, after which Narcissus gave a nod of appreciation.

"I would never have thought that of you," he said. "A Jew with bad eyesight..."

Uri chortled.

"And you? What kind of creature are you?"

Narcissus did not know who his parents had been; he had been brought up in a paedagogium, a school for slave children, where he had been handed in as an infant. He did not even know how old he was, but guessed he was around forty-five. He then related that he had been passed from Antonia to Claudius, who wanted to free him but Narcissus had asked him to wait a while.

"He has manumitted virtually all of us," he said, "but all of us stayed with him in any case. The others have the liberty cap of freedmen and I haven't; that's the only difference."

A seemingly paralyzed old man was carried across the garden in a litter.

"That's Barbarus Messala, Messalina's father," said Narcissus. "Claudius's uncle..."

"Wait a minute!" said Uri. "Didn't you give another name for the husband of Messalina's mother?"

"I sure did. She got divorced and married old Silanus, but the ex-husband still comes over for a taste of the food."

"And who pays for all this?"

"The people who chipped in toward the eight million sesterces which allowed Claudius to become an imperial priest... Lots of people... The wealthy kind... Does it matter where they get their fodder, so long as they've paid for it? At home or here? They enjoy it: here at least they can chatter and gossip."

In the atrium servants were tidying up, scrubbing the floor, collecting the remnants of half-eaten meals in large baskets. Those who still wanted to eat and drink were ushered out into the garden and places were laid for them there.

All of a sudden Uri came to a halt.

He had spotted a short, frail, snub-nosed girl with wide eyes, her chestnut hair cut short in a boyish style, who moved toward Narcissus and whispered something to him. Narcissus nodded then turned to Uri.

"Gaius, Caenis; Caenis, Gaius. He's a Roman Jew and a friend of Philo Judaeus, and he's familiar with shorthand."

Narcissus pronounced Caenis's name in the Greek style: Kainis. The girl nodded and looked Uri straight in the eye.

Uri had never seen eyes like that before: big, dark brown, glistening, deeply searching, inwardly directed, with premature wrinkles of sadness under the lower eyelids. Uri was transfixed. A lot of time passed before Kainis averted her gaze and went out into the garden. Uri gazed after her, thunderstruck.

"No woman ever lived who is cleverer than her," Narcissus's voice echoed in his ears.

Uri glanced at him. Narcissus was staring with paternal veneration after Kainis.

"Who is that girl?"

"Antonia's coiffeuse," said Narcissus. "I picked her out at the school for slave children; I paid for her, she was just twelve at the time... Her eyes caught me; I looked into her eyes and was thunderstruck. Antonia bought her release, but she too has stayed on here because Claudius adores her."

Uri sighed deeply.

"He has never touched her," Narcissus blurted. "I'd never allow that! But Claudius couldn't do without her: Kainis has a simply staggeringly good memory."

Kainis came back from the garden, she carried some dew-drenched blankets on her frail shoulders.

Uri stopped in front of her.

"You're said to have a staggeringly good memory," he said hoarsely.

The girl stopped and looked at him.

"You don't look much like a boy," said Uri.

The girl broke into a laugh.

"Bones like a bird, though," she declared.

She had a deep voice.

Uri was nonplussed.

Elatus, she explained, had a daughter called Kainis, who had been raped by Poseidon and in vengeance changed into a man, invulnerable to weaponry, so that she could never be raped again. She vanquished all until people caught on to the fact that they could kill her by by burying her alive. So it came to pass, but she rose up into the heavens in the form of a bird.

Narcissus did not understand the brief parable, after which Uri quietly sighed in Aramaic: Dear God!

"Let not the name of our maker pass your lips," she retorted in Aramaic.

Uri's heart hammered.

"Are you Jewish?" in his confusion he stuttered out the question in Greek.

"I don't know who my parents were," Kainis responded in Greek. "But I can't be Jewish, because they do not abandon a daughter. I can't be Germanic either, because they likewise do not rid themselves of girls. Which means that I could be Latin, Gallic, Hispanic, Copt, Arab, Greek, Punic, Illyrian, Etruscan..."

"How did you come to learn Aramaic?" Uri asked in Aramaic.

"There were people from every nation imaginable in the paedagogium," Kainis replied. "Each spoke in their own language..."

Narcissus growled but it was unnecessary to order Uri away from the girl, because Claudius limped up at great speed, took Kainis by the arm and pulled her away. The girl dropped the blankets and Narcissus leaned down to pick them up.

"The chances on the dice-throwing yet again!" he groused. "They've got a mathematical system; they worked it out together, and it offers quite odds for winning, but only if enough people play for the right length of time... Kainis has explained it twenty times over, but I still don't get it..."

Narcissus set off with Uri following.

"She can remember throws of the dice going back decades," Narcissus declared proudly. "Each game, going back decades! Every throw!"

"That's not possible," said Uri. "She's only a child!"

"She's at least twenty-five years old," said Narcissus, "and I should know because I purchased her!"

URI'S BREAST WAS FILLED WITH A HAPPY, ANGUISHED, ACHING GNAWING that he had never felt before. He wanted to see Kainis every minute of every hour of every day—to at least see her, and to breathe in her fragrance if he could. He saw her wherever he looked; he saw her in Far Side, he saw her on the Jewish Bridge, he saw her in his waking state and in his dreams, and in his imagination he carried on never-ending conversations with her. It was better, but also more painful, to see her in reality. Opportunity to do that was offered by the fact that the alabarch's group only spent any time in Agrippa's cleaned-up house when they returned there to sleep, they spent their days, staying late into the night, across the way at Claudius's house, and though they no longer had any need of Uri, they completely forgot about rescinding his assignment.

Almost all those who hung around at Claudius's place could speak Greek, and if they didn't, then there were plenty of willing voluntary interpreters. Claudius himself never really noticed whether he happened to be speaking Latin or Greek. Uri was terrified that his superfluity would come to light and he would never again be able to see Kainis's gliding figure, so he was particularly diligent in the work that he did for Philo, collecting material for the book that he was writing against Flaccus, even discovering that Caligula had sent a team of assassins after the exiled prefect, and that he had, at last, been slain.

Philo was delighted to write the closing sentences of the book: "Thus he fell, justice righteously inflicting on his own body wounds equal in number to the murdered Jews whom he had unlawfully put to death. And the whole place flowed with blood... Such was the end of Flaccus." Uri also contrived to chase down a few Etruscan sources for Claudius, which Philo and the alabarch were very proud of and Claudius himself praised him for. Uri was thus able to breath a sigh of relief; maybe he would not be sent away for the time being, there was room for him, too, among the many parasites.

Only on Friday afternoons did he return home to spend the Sabbath with his family; he got through the Friday night coupling, and on Saturday evening, as soon as he was free to do so, he raced back to Rome proper, to Claudius's villa on the slopes of Palatine Hill. All he missed was Theo, his son. He consoled himself with the thought that he would spend a lot of time with him later, when it would pay to do so.

Uri conversed with the slaves and the freedmen, doing one favor or another for them, with Narcissus benignly helping him to find acceptance from them. Still, Messalina's servants did not accept him, but ultimately it was better that way; Claudius's and Messalina's servants loathed each other, and Kainis had allied herself to Claudius.

He asked the girl if Claudius had ever tried anything with her. By then he knew that the seemingly innocuous Claudius was lecherous enough to proposition any woman; his first daughter was not in fact a child of his first wife's but of a slave girl known as Boter. When he discarded his first wife, the five-month-old girl—who was not even hers—was set before her front door and, since then, the divorced woman had brought her up.

Kainis chuckled, because she liked nothing more than to laugh:

"Of course he tried it, but I asked him which he would prefer: my pussy or my brains. Claudius weighed his answer carefully and came to the conclusion that since almost every other woman had a pussy he would rather have my brains; since then we have gotten along fine."

Claudius was far from being as stupid as he made out.

Kainis related that Antonia had always run her son down; told everyone left, right, and center that even the dumbest slave was cleverer than that cripple, until in the end people believed her. That way Claudius had managed to stay alive.

A smart woman she must have been.

Kainis smiled.

"Just imagine: you almost get yourself killed for being Mark Antony's daughter, even though your father had abandoned you when you were just a tiny tot, along with your elder sister, your brothers, and your mother, just because he fell in love with an Egyptian whore who just happens to be the queen; your elder brothers are murdered even though innocent, out of gratitude for being spared your life you are forced to marry a dreadful, intolerable man whose father just happens to be the emperor—your father's one-time friend, who had your brothers murdered and on whose account your father took his own life, and so you hate your husband, though you have no choice but to bear him two sons; your husband dies young, and you know that your brother-in-law, now become emperor, whatever else he does, is bound to have your son poisoned... It is hardly surprising that one would learn a thing or two from all that, even if you are a woman."

Uri would pay calls on Kainis in her quarters, and he did not care if the other servants saw him. Kainis got bored with it, though.

"What do you want from me?"

"You."

"You're married."

"That was before I got to know you..."

"I'm older than you."

"That's neither here nor there."

"Get a divorce."

Uri sighed.

"I had to marry for money..."

"So does every man," Kainis said wickedly.

"Fair enough, I'll get a divorce... But I have a son whom the Eternal One entrusted to me... How am I going to raise him on my own? Would you be his mother?"

"I'm not Jewish,"

"Become one."

"I don't believe in your god."

"What god do you believe in?"

"None."

Uri was left not knowing what to say, but he started up again a few days later. Kainis giggled:

"Kill your wife," she suggested.

Uri was far from certain if this was a jest or whether Kainis meant it seriously.

She had once told him that in Claudius's house she felt a bit like she was wandering around a vegetable bed in which rare sorts of magic plants were blooming, though she had no idea what they were.

Kainis finished that off by saying:

"Everyone is a bean, but don't worry: no one will murder you."

Pythagoras, so the popular myth had it, had been killed at the edge of a vast bean field.

It was the sort of thing one would never expect to hear from the mouth of a woman; Uri was entranced, but then again he would have been entranced even if she had been unaware of the legend.

It emerged that Kainis had license to poke about in Claudius's library any time she liked and was free to read whatever she wanted. She could quote from any work of Greek literature or philosophy from memory; once she had cast eyes on anything she was unable to rid her brain of it, but it was not that which Uri marveled at so much as the fact that she was clever, confoundedly clever.

Narcissus told a story of how, around a decade and a half ago, Antonia had dictated a letter to Kainis because no one else happened to be at hand: it was a letter to Tiberius on Capri about matters concerning Sejanus. The mistress had then had second thoughts and ripped the letter up. Kainis, still a young girl, laughed, told her mistress that she had not ripped the letter up in her mind, and went on to quote the letter word for word. Antonia realized what sort of treasure she had found when a week later the girl could still remember every single word. That was when a new type of courier began making the rounds between Rome and Capri, until Sejanus's fall, and indeed beyond: Kainis would set off with Narcissus and the other male servants, with the ostensible aim of overhauling a villa in Campania; beforehand Antonia would dictate her letter to Kainis before tearing it up, once at the villa in Campania Kainis would dictate it back to either Narcissus or Pallas, who would take the letter to Capri. Still at the villa, Kainis would read Tiberius's reply, that too would be torn up, and the group would travel back to Rome. No documents would ever be found on them, though the sentries and Praetorian guards frisked them often enough, as not only Sejanus harbored suspicions but his successor, Macro, too.

Servants are privy to big secrets, and Uri learned about many strange matters. In exchange he told stories about Judaea and Alexandria, talking about the Gymnasium, the drinking dens, Delta and the Bane, spoke about the spread of Greco-Jewish hatred, with Kainis listening out of interest.

"Don't be fooled," she warned Uri once. "Those people don't hate each other."

"Who's that?"

"The alabarch's crowd and the Greek envoys."

She argued that while the Greeks in Caligula's entourage might scheme against the Jews, and they enjoyed the support of Helicon, powerful as he was, the costs of the alabarch's stay in Rome were in reality being funded not by Jewish financiers, but by Isidoros and Lampo.

At first Uri did not understand what Kainis was driving at.

"As long as the alabarch's group are in Rome the Greeks will pick up their expenses," explained Kainis. "They don't live off what they get from the Jews. The alabarch's Jewish bankers in Alexandria pay off Isidoros and Lampo's people in Alexandria. Promissory notes are made out to pay out to the bearer a certain amount, and they pay that out..."

Uri shook his head: there was so much hatred between Greeks and Jews, most especially after the Bane, that it was inconceivable.

"Don't be so stupid!" Kainis admonished him affectionately. "Isidoros and the alabarch made a pact that they were not going to give back the money and gifts that the wealthy Greeks and Jews had granted Flaccus. Bassus brought back to Rome as much as a tenth of Flaccus's fortune, and Caligula could be happy even with that; he has no idea of how much a procurator or prefect steals. The remaining nine-tenths was split between Isidoros and the alabarch, and that is why no compensation will ever be paid in Alexandria. It's a huge fortune, hundreds of millions... They would be mad to give that back. Anyone who seeks to denounce them to the emperor is sent packing. Why do you think the Judaeophobic Apion set off for the Greek islands to bore audiences with his commentaries on Homer? Because he sniffed out the plan and wanted a piece of the action... It's an exile, not a triumphal procession... And why did Flaccus have to be killed in exile? He was no danger to anybody, except for those who had his wealth seized: he would have been able to let drop a thing or two about them..."

Uri blanched. That sounded like sense, but did Philo know about all this, he wondered.

"He knows," Kainis read his silent question. "Has it never occurred to you that Flaccus was never charged with extortion? Neither by the Greeks nor the Jews? Does Philo write anything in his book about the presents Flaccus received from the Greeks and Jews? Or at least about how big a bribe the Greeks paid him?"

He had not written about that, not one word.

653

"Have you read it?" Uri asked.

"I didn't need to to find that out," Kainis replied gleefully.

The eunuch Posides, who was dilly-dallying next to them, nodded that was how it was done, and it usually worked.

"Antonia always tittered when inquiries were made about the money she had inherited from her father," said Posides. "Before making war on Augustus, Cleopatra and Mark Antony ransacked all of Egypt's wealthy, taking away even what was theirs personally—it made no difference whether you were Egyptian, Greek, or Jewish. They piled it up in the palace in Alexandria, but they had no time to make any use of it because as soon as Augustus Divus arrived triumphantly in Alexandria he was sought out by petitioners wanting back the money Cleopatra had stolen, then along came the priests asking for the return of devotional objects, gold... 'Where are all those treasures, then?' Augustus asked in astonishment. 'In the palace cellars,' he was told. Augustus thanked them kindly for the information, loaded up the entire fortune onto a ship and brought it back to Rome."

Posides snickered in pleasure. He was a likable young man, smart, always ready to help, and for some reason he was fond of Uri.

Uri had once asked Posides whether he still had any sexual desire even though he had been castrated. Instead of being offended, Posides answered that he was used to feeling a pleasant tingling in the rectal area when he saw a good-looking woman or man, but that was all that happened, so all in all he probably came out better than anyone who had been left with their gender.

Of Claudius's adult slaves, it was only Pallas with whom Uri did not manage to get on good terms. He was a tall, presentable young man with curly, dark-brown hair, soft-spoken and with an easy sense of humor, constantly larking about and very much a hit with women. Though he was a slave, he was permitted to bow even to ladies of high rank, and while talking with one he would even brush her back, arm or hair, as if by accident. Uri kept a beady eye open to see whether he took such liberties with Kainis, and although he never caught him doing so, he conceived something of a repugnance for the affable, slimy Pallas. His younger brother, Felix, was also one of Claudius's household; he was shorter, did not flirt with women, and assisted Helius with dishing out meals.

Once Kainis asked whether there was not at least one intelligent person among the Jews of Alexandria, and Uri hesitated.

"There is Tija," he said. "That is to say, Tiberius Julius Alexander, the alabarch's second son. He's clever, only cold as ice with it."

Kainis winced as she conceded the point.

There were times when the girl would disappear for a whole day at a time, with Uri waiting and searching desperately for her. Narcissus shrugged his shoulders. Claudius sometimes took her with him as a nomenclator—someone who could prompt him with names—when he went to the Forum, where crowds of people would greet him and Claudius would have no clue who they were. Kainis would know and whisper a reminder; she would hardly forget a name, now, would she?

But then there were times, even when Claudius was there, when Kainis was nowhere to be found in the house.

"Maybe she has a business deal on," Narcissus would say in that case.

It was not befitting for Kainis to be involved in business deals, and in any case where did she get the money to do business?

"Did you receive an inheritance from Antonia?" Uri leveled the question at her.

There was no need for her to answer, but she did:

"Yes, I did: one hundred thousand sesterces."

That was a nice sum to have, provided one had no debts to start with.

"What do you use it for?"

"I bought two tenement houses," she said.

"Where?"

"Somewhere near the statue of Cloelia."

Cloelia was a legendary Roman virgin who was sent as a hostage to the Etruscans, escaped on horseback with a band of her fellow prisoners, and finally swam to safety across the River Tiber. So despite the fact that she was a woman, a statue of her on horseback was set up on the Via Sancta.

"How big are the houses?"

"I don't know. Several floors, I think."

"You mean you don't even look at what you are buying?"

"No, Pallas arranged it; he collects the rent as well."

Uri brooded as he gazed at the dark down on the girl's thin neck; he would have loved to take a gentle bite.

"So what do you do with the money?"

"Nothing. Some day I'll buy another tenement, then another..."

Kainis laughed.

She'll be rolling in it by the time she is old, thought Uri. She has free board and lodging in Claudius's house, and she is irreplaceable: in reality it is she who is being generous to Claudius.

"Don't you intend to get married?"

Kainis stayed silent.

"No. I've no plans," she eventually said.

Diminutive and fragile, she would be able to bear children who might be fine and healthy.

"I'll take you to Zákinthos!" Uri exclaimed.

Kainis laughed.

"What's the need there for another Kainis?" she retorted.

Uri was lost for words. Was there anywhere in Italia another woman who knew that on the island of Zákinthos there was a hill named Kainis?

Though even if she had not known it, there were still no other women like her!

They conversed in Latin, with Kainis guiding him. From time to time she would recommend a more refined word than the one Uri had employed; she sought to make certain that he speak perfect Latin as well. She must have some feelings for me, Uri speculated, hopefully but despondently.

Kainis would sometimes push the servants aside and set to cooking, with Uri prepping the ingredients. She knew a great range of recipes because someone had once chided her about not being able to cook, so in one single night she had leafed through a score of cookery books, committing them to memory. She would even take care that Jewish guests were given ritually clean food.

Uri was just in the middle of rinsing meat in cold water when Titus, of the blade-like lips and broad cheekbones, who was the *aedile* in charge of the roads, came to the fireplace. One story went that a year or so before, while walking in the city with Caligula, the emperor's cloak had been soiled because the street on which the imperial foot was set had been muddy. Claudius's guests would keep coming back to this episode, which was considered hilarious, and no end of jokes about mud followed, with Titus joining in the laughter.

Titus said something to Kainis, who burst out laughing.

A knife went through Uri's chest.

Kainis was forever laughing; she loved laughing, but he had never heard her laugh that way before.

This laugh was neither loud nor soft, neither happy nor sad but something else—a laugh that spoke to one person specifically.

Uri strangled the bloody lump of meat in his hand.

The fellow with the broad cheekbones left.

Kainis fell silent.

She knows that I noticed.

He cautiously made inquiries with other people.

Titus and his brother, Sabinus, came from an equestrian family, their father a well-heeled tax administrator. Sabinus, a rich, stuck-up, garrulous dolt, cannot have cared too much for his younger brother because when Titus found himself strapped for cash he would only lend it to him on the condition that he registered it as a mortgage, and the loan was still outstanding. People sometimes joked about this with Titus, who would simply set his blade-lips in a broad grin and never let up with his assertions that a debtor's fate was better than that of a creditor. On one occasion he ventured to put forward the interesting line of thought that we come into life as a loan at birth, and we pay back everything that was good in it in a single settlement with the agonies of our death throes. For anyone whose life had been rotten death comes as a pleasure: the gods evidently consider life's debt as being settled and so, even-handedly, they spare such a person any death agonies. There was a wise rhetorician named Seneca, whom Caligula, on hearing him plead a neatly turned speech for the defense in the Senate, had ordered put to death. It was said, however, that on being told that Seneca was severely ill, coughing day and night, and having only a few days left to live, the emperor let him go on living. Seneca, who had laughed at Titus's argument, had said that it would be nice to believe that life was equalized by death, but what about those who die in childhood in such a way that they have had no chance to be acquainted either with the value of credit or the importance of paying off of a debt? Uri could not remember what Titus's response was because he was thinking of his little sister, for whom the cost of even her few years of consciousness as a child had been superhuman struggle.

Last year, Uri learned, Titus had taken as his wife a certain Domitilla, about whom little was known, only that she had come with a substantial dowry and that at the very end of December she had given birth to a baby boy, who had likewise been named Titus.

In other words, Titus had married on account of the dowry.

He seemed to recall that Kainis had once referred to that. Her little face had been dark and wicked when she had said that every man marries for money.

Titus made only rare appearances at Claudius's house. Uri would watch closely what he did and with whom he spoke. On those occasions Kainis more often than not did not show herself among the guests, and there were many times when neither Titus nor Kainis were present in Claudius's house.

It was agreed beforehand, Kainis knew in advance when he was not going to come! They must have a rendezvous in the city. They were lovers!

How, he wondered, did they make love? Did Titus lay that hulking, heavy body on the tiny woman and crush her? Or did Kainis ride the monstrous prick of that broad-cheeked character? What sort of things did they get up to with each other?

Uri made an effort to examine his own instincts objectively: what his body sensed when he was picturing Kainis or he stood beside her and breathed in her fragrance. The girl had a Kainis fragrance; she did not use any ointments or grasses, did not pluck hairs from her legs, did not paint her eyebrows or eyelids, did not wear silks or put on a wig. Uri imagined Kainis naked, but his penis did not stiffen, there was only a huge, aching gap in the pit of his stomach as if he did not need to screw the girl but eat her up. He gazed at her long, thin fingers and would have liked to tear them apart and swallow them raw.

On Friday nights he would couple with the now big-bellied Hagar from behind as if he were ejecting his stools through a smarting rectum. He made an effort to think of Kainis but what kept coming to mind was the young Judaean slave girl as she rode on the master's fat belly.

He would try at least to summon up the bodies, faces and odors of the prostitutes in Alexandria, and how they would expertly but lovingly manipulate him but, like the city now sunk to the bottom of the sea, they too had vanished as if they had never been.

I'll go crazy, he thought.

But then he noticed that Titus was spending a growing amount of time talking with Tija; he couldn't hear what they were talking about but they guffawed a lot.

Maybe I have brought them together, he reflected furiously, enviously, jealously, the way only a slave was able to be angry. Kainis's questions had not been nnocuous: she had been spying through me.

Uri cursed the Eternal One for creating him a Jew and debtor who would never be a free man.

BRIBING HELICON WENT MORE SMOOTHLY THAN HAD BEEN ANTICIPATED. An envoy arrived at Agrippa's house on Sunday morning: the emperor would await the Jewish delegation from Alexandria on Monday at noon in the garden on Vatican Hill.

Uri found it awkward that Honoratus's confidant, Iustus, also made an appearance, and it was decided that on an ornamental litter the two of them would have to take a bust of Germanicus that the alabarch was due to present to the emperor on that festive occasion.

The statue was carried under Iustus's direction from Far Side to the gate of the Vatican garden, where they were waiting.

Colonnades and terraces extended along the right bank of the Tiber, with the vast garden reaching its end in a high wall at the foot of Vatican Hill. It was a splendid garden as far as Uri was able to judge through his squinting eyes; in any event the place was a kaleidoscopic mix of shades of green, but he was mostly concentrating on not letting the litter tip and the bust crash down from it. He was carrying the poles at the rear end of the litter, while the shorter Iustus manned the front as his eyesight was all right. Uri kept his eyes fixed on the ground; the path was made up of small, yellow grains and he was concerned that his new sandals might slip on it.

Iustus and Uri also had to carry on their backs sacks containing statuettes, necklaces, pendants, and jewelry made of gold, precious gemstones, and woods, each item a piece of extraordinarily delicate workmanship: they had originated from the pyramids of Egypt, the alabarch's men having seized them from industrious Copt looters.

To the right of the litter walked the alabarch and Philo, Marcus and Tija on the left, each man wearing a beautifully folded, brand-new toga, which they had spent a long time arranging on each other before setting off. The litter bearers also had on new tunics and footwear; Iustus ascribed to that no great significance as he had always been well catered for, but Uri was very pleased because he would never have bought such things for himself.

The master gardeners who had landscaped the garden had cut up the area into parklands and bowers, and before the marble benches stood marble statues, which spouted water. On and around the benches, lazily and leisurely, lingered knots of muscular young men who, according to Iustus were gladiators and actors, the emperor's favorites. It was rumored that one of the emperor's favorite actors was the pantomime artist Mnester, another the tragedian Apelles of Ashkelon; the whispers about the latter held that, like any Greek from Jamnia or Ashkelon, he hated Jews. That might be true, but it was also whispered that Mnester was half-Jewish. Uri would not have recognized them anyway, but Iustus—who usually accompanied theater-mad Honoratus to the theaters and knew all there was to know about the actors—muttered that in his opinion Apelles and Mnester couldn't be there because it was impossible to believe they would have sobered up this early in the day.

It was May and the sun was beating down. Two bodyguards were pacing easily in front, their thighs thick as tree trunks, as was only fitting, though Uri was not awed in the least.

Maybe Bassus was somewhere around; indeed, it would be right for him to be present when the emperor received a delegation from Alexandria.

At one of the bowers the bodyguard signaled, at which Philo and the rest came to a halt, as did Iustus and Uri with a little wobble of the litter. As no one ordered them to put it down, they kept on holding it. One of the guards went into the bower, the other stayed with them. Birds twittered their praises of the Pax Romana.

Uri's palms were sweating. It would be better to set that statue down. He had made a list of all the things they were taking as gifts for the emperor, with the statue being one of the items listed along with the rare Egyptian knick-knacks; by then it was on his lips to say that the notion was none too well-conceived, but he choked that down as he did not want another fruitless dispute with Philo, who was dead set on placing his trust in the emperor's goodwill and never tired of proclaiming what luck it was for the Jewish people that Agrippa had been Caligula's tutor.

The messenger who had informed them of the appointed time for the reception had in the meantime handed back a countersigned copy of the approved list of gifts, though the counter-signatory's name was indecipherable. There was little chance of being able to truly surprise the poor emperor with the imperial administration so assiduously at work.

Uri stared at the nape of the neck of the marble bust; it was gracefully fashioned, the curls of hair painted dark brown. It must be a fine job, being a sculptor: no need to see people or make conversation with clods, just spend the day carving a dumb block of stone and bringing a thing of beauty out of it. One solution would be to enter service as an assistant to a Greek sculptor. Admittedly, Rome was already littered with statues of every kind as the emperors and the wealthy had procured so many splendid pieces from all over the world that there was hardly any space left for the living, and yet new shrines and sculpture parks were always being created—that was really big business, not balsam. It was a pity that sculpting was forbidden for Jews.

Iustus also inspected the head and, just to be on the safe side, blew on it so that not even a single speck of dust should deface it. What ran through Uri's head was that at any moment he would be seeing a real live practicing emperor, the figurehead of a world empire. Then he recollected the bridge that had been built between Puteoli and Baiae; he was sill quite sure that sort of thing would never happen to him. His legs ought to be trembling; he still felt nothing. There's something wrong with me, Uri thought. Startled, he realized that he was no longer like other people.

A tall, slim young man stepped out from between the bushes of the bower; he must be the emperor because the men with him followed at a respectful distance. He was carrying a sword in his left hand, on his right arm a shield, his head helmeted. As he approached Uri got an increasingly clear sight of his facial features. Yes, indeed, he resembled the statue of his father, though it could be the sculptor had exaggerated the resemblance. Emperor Gaius—Caligula—had a handsome face; there was a half-smile playing around his lips, he lifted his dreamy brown eyes, crossed, to the members of the delegation one after the other. His neck, Uri could make out through his slit eyes, was covered in boils. There was something odd about his hair; it had been combed strangely over his ears. He was tall and broad-shouldered, his waist was too long, his thighs disproportionately short, his feet, in contrast, enormous. He seemed to be wearing a silk tunic. Uri did not wait until the emperor looked him in the eyes but cast his look downward; he was just a litter bearer. In retrospect, with his inner eye he noticed that the emperor had on a tight-fitting ornamental breastplate in the middle of which was a round portrait, and his entire get-up seemed to resemble a statue. Yes, the emperor had been dressed for the reception to look like Ares.

"You bring before me my father in stone—you, the one who slew him, filthy Jew?"

Caligula screamed this hysterically, and what followed was a huge stillness. Uri looked up.

The alabarch was stunned, groggy. Philo was trembling. Marcus looked in horror at the statue. Tija stood his ground unperturbed. Iustus dropped the poles at the front of the litter, so Uri swiftly set his down as well and the statue did not fall out.

Caligula flashed his teeth in a grin. He made a sign with his head and four or five bodyguards jumped to grab the alabarch.

"To the dungeons of the Palatine with him!" the emperor ordered.

The alabarch, paralyzed, offered no resistance and staggered away between the bodyguards grasping his arms on either side.

Caligula watched him go before turning to one of his attendants.

"I have no time for them now," he said calmly and collectedly, no longer grimacing. "They should ask for a new appointment."

He turned on his heels and strode back toward the bower.

Philo reeled; Uri jumped across and grasped him under his elbows.

"Take the statue back," he heard in Aramaic. "I'll take over the other gifts."

It was the attendant who had spoken; Uri looked at him. The expression on the face of Homilus, the imperial counselor for delegations, was serious but not hostile; he must have gotten used to scenes like this.

Uri had the presence of mind to repeat this in Greek. Homilus glanced inquisitively at him.

A small table was brought and put down; Uri and Iustus had to unpack all the gifts, with Homilus checking them at length against the list.

Were they afraid that we brought a poisonous snake along?

Marcus and Tija were standing awkwardly, holding Philo by the arm on each side, mutely watching the unpacking. There was something infernally amusing about the whole thing and Uri found it hard to resist the temptation to laugh out loud.

"HE WAS WEARING ALEXANDER THE GREAT'S BREASTPLATE!" MOANED Philo in distress.

So that was a portrait of Alexander the Great decorating the breastplate: he had duplicated himself by wearing himself on his chest. There was another young man who could not have been quite right in the head either; he'd died young, too. It was said of Agrippa that when he had completed his thirty-second year he threw a huge banquet, obviously paid for by a loan, to celebrate the fact that he had lived longer than Alexander the Great.

They were sprawled in the atrium of Agrippa's house, drinking non-stop. Iustus was not there: after he and Uri had lugged the statue back to the servants waiting at the entrance to the garden so that they might transport it back to Far Side, he said his goodbyes and hurried off to his master, Honoratus, to report on the sensational incident and make sure it was spread across Far Side. Philo made no effort to detain him; people would learn about it anyway, the emperor would make sure of that.

Marcus was still seething with anger, whereas Tija sat quietly and pecked at some food. Uri stood coolly next to the statue, thinking that the embassy would soon be returning to Alexandria, while he would be left here with his unpaid and unpayable debt, to die just like his father.

"The fiend was wearing Alexander the Great's breastplate!" exploded Philo again. That was why it looked tight-fitting: it had been made for someone else.

"Are you certain that it was Alexander the Great's?" Uri asked.

"Absolutely!" Philo exclaimed. "I was there when it was lifted up out of the coffin and taken into the prefect's palace! It was a huge honor that a young Jew like me was allowed to be present!"

Philo was guzzling wine, and he painted the scene for them in great detail: they had opened up the alabaster mausoleum, in which the mummified body of Alexander the Great lay. The breastplate alone had been lifted out, then the coffin was resealed. It was surprising how short and scrawny the world's greatest military leader had been.

Philo broke into a laugh.

"What ran through my head at the time was that despite my slight build I too could have been a military leader!"

At the time Alexandria had been expecting a return visit from Emperor Augustus: they were intending to deck him out in the breastplate, and had even provided it with new straps, but Augustus never returned. Maybe it was better that way—this time he could well have knocked an ear off!

"Obviously Bassus brought it back to Rome," Tija said.

"Presumably," said Philo. "It will go astray! It will go astray in Rome!"

Uri was astonished to see that the alabarch's detention, after the initial shock had subsided, did not elicit any undue despondency from members of his family. It was almost as if they were relieved, with the sole exception of Marcus, who kept on reiterating that they ought to have leapt to his defense immediately, though it was true, he added, that they would have been cut down, so that would not have made no difference. He said this again and again and drank steadily.

The emperor had avenged himself for the alabarch's crime, but he seemed willing to receive his family, which implied that the family was absolved of the crime; indeed, it was treated as an official delegation. That meant the delegation might stay in Rome after all.

"We ought to send a courier off to Agrippa straightaway," Marcus chimed in.

"There's no point," said Tija. "If he's en route, the courier will not reach him, and if he hasn't left for Rome anyway, then this piece of news is not going to persuade him either."

No one said anything to this, leaving Uri to deliberate alone in silence: so this is what the life of a powerful, stubborn man who is fighting for prestige comes to?

They had seen that the emperor had dressed up as Ares in their honor, and for a while they debated what the hidden significance of that might be. Philo considered it to be an ominous sign; the emperor was girding for war against the Jews. Though that was better than if he had dressed up as Dionysus, because by showing himself as the favorite god of the Jew-baiting rabble the emperor would unequivocally have been aligning himself with the Greeks. It emerged that they had been informed in advance of the emperor's curious habit of dressing up as a demigod, or even a god, and mincing around in his circle of admirers as if he were an actor; he was fond of dressing up as Apollo or one of the Dioscuri,

Castor or Pollux, though nobody as yet had seen him as Zeus, the father of the Dioscuri—something was holding him back, for the time being, from that sacrilege.

Marcus proposed that whichever pagan god the emperor was clothed as, he had presumably expected the Jewish delegation to fall to its knees, even prostrate themselves in adoration, knowing full well that Jews were forbidden to do this—maybe that had been the entire significance of the costume, nothing to do with whatever god he was dressed up as.

"Yes, of course," Philo growled, "of course, but you saw for yourselves that he did not take it amiss that we did not prostrate ourselves before him!"

Uri had a feeling that Philo did not entirely regret that his younger brother had been placed under lock and key.

"His periwig was putrid," Philo remarked detachedly. "He's got carbuncles on his scalp that no medicament can cure."

"If he left us to go free," Tija mused, nibbling a fig, resting his head on the palm of one hand as he reclined, apparently relieved, "and as I see it that's the case, he must have some aim for us... Nothing would have been easier than to have us all locked up on Palatine Hill or killed... He chose not to... We got off, and we need to work out why he spared our lives."

Uri paid Tija unspoken tribute: beforehand he had not looked like someone who sensed his life was in danger. All the same it troubled him that Tija was displaying such total indifference toward his father.

"Our odds against the Greeks are not completely unfavorable," Philo concluded. "Perhaps he wants to keep them under control through the Jews..."

Tija laughed.

"You'll soon see," he said merrily, "how many people immediately turn away from us... Before long the Jewish bankers will be around to revise the mutual loan contracts." Tija burbled with laughter. "At least we owe them nothing..."

Uri thought it was the right moment to raise the question of whether he might remain in the family's service, and whether his own debt would be repaid by them over that period.

Tija gazed at him, his stare remote, glazed.

"You know too much about us," he remarked laconically. "We can't cut you loose: you're an accessory—that's the word for it."

"Don't worry, my dear son," said Philo affectionately. "We have never yet done away with anybody."

That was a great relief, then, and nobody was proposing that they ought to do anything at all regarding the matter of gaining the alabarch's release.

If that was all the freedom of a powerful alabarch—the world's richest Jew—was worth, then what was the value of the life of an ordinary Jew? Uri wondered, sensing a dreadful taste in his mouth and a spasm in the middle of his chest.

That very evening Julius and Honoratus turned up at Agrippa's residence. They deeply deplored what had happened and expressed their hope that the just Eternal One would intervene, but with all due respect they wished to modify the contracts that the alabarch had signed. Marcus negotiated with them, with Philo and Tija holding their tongues. Not without malice, Marcus referred them to the alabarch: Alexander had signed the contracts and he should also sign any modifications. Julius had a sense of humor and smiled; Honoratus, on the other hand, took a more tragic approach to the suggestion: they were hardly in a position to pay a visit to Alexander in prison, so the firstborn son was beholden to sign instead. Marcus asked what, in fact, the bankers were after. Honoratus replied that from now on they would be unable to provide credit on the same terms as before: instead of issuing banker's drafts they wanted to be given ready money. Marcus instantly agreed with that.

What Kainis had asserted about Greek and Jewish thieves colluding with each other was proving to be true. Uri reflected that Marcus really ought to have been a trifle tougher before going along with it.

The bankers left somewhat dazed; even Julius was taken aback at how easily the task had been accomplished, and in taking leave he exchanged looks with Uri, who bowed respectfully.

"Are you sure there's not going be any bother out of this?" Uri asked.

Tija tittered and Marcus smiled, whereas Philo shook his head.

"You know, my dear son," said Philo, "to a person on whom the Eternal One bestows a fortune He normally also gives a particle of sober common sense as well."

He said nothing more, so Uri again spoke up:

"What about my debt?"

After a brief pause, Philo said:

"We'll pay off six months in advance. Does that satisfy you?"

Uri's throat grew dry and he nodded.

It was late by then. Uri settled down in one corner of the atrium as usual, but he found it difficult to get to sleep.

He had seen a real, live emperor who, like a dramatist, had planned a whole scene in advance and had taken part in it as an actor. He had seen a delegation whose de facto head had been hauled off to jail and, who, so far as he could tell, might well be murdered. And the elder brother and sons of the man who had gotten himself in such hot water—and had amassed the family's wealth in the first place—were not at all concerned about his fate.

They had money: they had swiped one-half of Flaccus's fortune, and he himself, the person whose debt they would repay for a further half-year in one go, would be involved in that theft. And yet he had to accept it, otherwise his family would starve. Tija, as ever, had put it very precisely: he was an accessory.

He entreated the Eternal One that his own children would not become such callous, ungrateful rogues.

NOT THAT NIGHT, BUT THE NEXT AFTERNOON, THEY ADOPTED BEAMING faces and went across to Claudius's house.

The customary throng was milling about and showed no more or less inter-est in them than before. Uri was not clear whether or not they knew about the alabarch's arrest, but he did not feel it incumbent on him to investigate.

Nevertheless, it did seem that they must know something, because Narcissus told him a story about the wealthy Pastor, who a year earlier had been invited to dinner by Caligula, along with a lot of others. Pastor, at the far end of the table, all of a sudden noticed that his son was lying dead, but he had been obliged to sit through the dinner, not daring to ask why his son had been killed—a wise choice because he has another son.

"So why was he killed?" Uri asked.

"Because he was considered too handsome."

Most of the crowd was prattling about an obelisk, or rather the ship that the emperor had ordered to built to transport the obelisk from Egypt to Rome. The massive column was to be found somewhere in the interior of Egypt, and although none of those present knew who had originally commissioned it, or for whom, they all found it in themselves to burst into rapturous odes about the incomparably immense craft that would carry it.

In the atrium Uri spied a familiar figure among the people jostling for food—a burly, elderly, gray-haired man. Uri could not recollect where they had met, until Narcissus identified the man as Lucius Vitellius, the former imperial legate and prefect of Syria, the man who had arrested Pilate at Herod's palace in Jerusalem.

He had initially fallen out of favor under Caligula, Narcissus recounted, but nonetheless had managed to worm his way back into the emperor's graces, and while Caligula had been absent in Germania, had at every session of the Senate had prostrated himself before the empty imperial throne until gradually the whole Senate adopted this newfangled custom, for which the Caesar liked him more than anyone else, and Vitellius even had received some of the shellfish that the armies brought from the sea. That Uri did not follow, so Narcissus explained that on the shores of Gaul Caligula had commanded a military campaign against Britain by drawing his troops up in battle formation facing the English Channel and indicating the target Britannia with a sweep of the hand, at which the soldiers had stormed the water. Because there was no enemy to be seen, they had gone on a hunt for mussel-shells, which the emperor then brought back to Rome as spoils of war.

Uri laughed because he thought Narcissus was putting him on, but Diespiter confirmed that he had heard exactly the same story.

When Diespiter had left, Narcissus did not fail to note that the man had made a fortune by peddling documents of Roman citizenship.

Anyway, there among those scrambling for the best morsels was the ex-consul and ex-legate Vitellius, along with his sons; Uri could not see them close up, so he couldn't figure out which of them was Aulus, who as a boy had allegedly been one of Tiberius's lovers.

As compared with the presence of Vitellius, negotiator of the Roman peace pact with the Parthians, that of Philo and the alabarch's sons was indeed negligible.

They learned from Pallas that among those who had come yesterday evening had been Corbulo, the consul in office who, under orders from the emperor, was nagging the road commissioners about the poor condition of the roads and had demanded they repay the funds they had received from Tiberius for keeping the highways in good repair. It was a large sum of money, and of course the road constructors, according to Narcissus, had embezzled no small amount. Claudius withdrew with Corbulo into one of the library rooms.

Uri sauntered around: he could not see Titus with the broad cheekbones, nor Kainis.

They were making love somewhere.

Another innovation about which there was plenty of gossip was a new imperial dwelling that was being built on the Capitoline because the emperor wanted henceforward to live close to the statue of Jupiter, apparently undisturbed by the noise of the bell fit to the statue.

Philo was speaking at length with a stubby senator with rugged features, who, Uri was told by Pallas, was Aemelius Rectus, the man whom Caligula had initially appointed to take over Flaccus's prefecture before he ended up giving the position to Macro, only to have Macro dispatched. By then the emperor had forgotten about Rectus, though Rectus would have been happy to return to Alexandria to do a bit of extorting.

Messalina's servants led in musicians and offered all some rare fine wines: Messalina herself was very jolly, dancing and whooping it up, and although people did not know the cause of her strikingly high spirits, they gallantly held up their end of the bargain by quaffing what they were offered. Claudius shuffled out with Corbulo, blinked tiredly and stared at his wife, who, shaking her wobbling breasts about, started to screech like a roadside innkeeper's wife "My bleeding has stopped! I'm going to give birth to a son at last!"

Silver-haired Vitellius childishly clapped his hands and in his enthusiasm rolled his eyes back to show their whites.

Claudius forced a grin and put up with a stream of people slapping him on the back or clipping his big mop of a head as if he were a child. Broad-headed, puny idiots also ran up to him, adding their pummeling; these were the sort of people who were kept as domestic pets and taken everywhere by rich folk, that being the fashion, much like the costly monkeys with ropes around their necks who were allowed to run free among the dishes of food. One wise monkey, on seeing what people were doing to Claudius, sprang over and joined in the patting of his head. That garnered the loudest applause of the night, with calls of "Even the monkeys know! Even the monkeys know!" ringing out. The beast's owner, Domitius Afer—he had once sprawled out on the ground and worshiped Caligula after a serious speech for the prosecution which threatened him with the death penalty and, as a result, was not executed but was made a consul—jumped across and stroked the monkey, giving it a nut to stuff in its muzzle. Afer, in turn, was applauded as well. Afer and the tame monkey bowed in acknowledgment of the applause, and more than a few wisecracks were made to the effect that the master increasingly resembled his pet.

Narcissus silently groaned, so Uri sympathetically put an arm his shoulders.

A tall, strikingly beautiful dark-haired woman hugged Claudius in congratulation, while a stocky, bald man shook him by the hand. Uri asked Pallas who they were, because Narcissus had run off angrily.

"She's called Lollia Paulina," Pallas said.

So that good-looking woman had been Caligula's second wife. The emperor had asked for her hand from her former husband, Memmius Regulus, so the betrothal was lawful. So was the stocky chap Memmius Regulus perchance? Pallas confirmed that. The emperor had seen Lollia at her wedding with Memmius Regulus and desired to have her there and then; he may have been imitating Augustus, who had seduced Livia when she was pregnant, but in any case Caligula had lived with Lollia for just two months before getting bored and exiling both her and Memmius Regulus, alleging that they were still in contact; they had, however, finagled it so as to be allowed to stay in Rome while they prepared to travel, and they had been preparing ever since.

"He's always saying 'I do it because I can do it,'" Pallas grumbled softly. "He said the same thing to Antonia, advising her to take her own life as swiftly as possible: 'I do it because I can do it.'"

Uri thought he had passed into depths of Sheol when he noticed a venerable Hindu man beside him. He had handsome, wizened features and a dazzling shock of white hair, but no arms at all; indeed, he had no shoulders either, with his trunk commencing without interruption from the neck downward. Uri shuddered; he looked down and saw that the armless Indian was standing barefoot on the mosaic floor, and that he had conspicuously long toes.

"The Hindu! The Hindu! The Hindu is also here!"

"Fetch a bow and arrows!"

A big circle was formed and the Hindu old man lay on his back on the floor. Messalina placed an apple on the head of her slave Polybius. With his legs kicking up in the air as if they were strong arms and the toes like fingers, the old fellow stretched the bow as he lay there, placed an arrow on the bowstring, and by raising head and trunk slightly he aimed and loosed the arrow. The apple, pierced by the arrow, flew off Polybius's head.

Loud cheering worthy of a tavern broke out among the drunken worthies.

Sixty years ago, Augustus had been presented with this agile crippled man, together with the first tigers, as a gift from an Indian embassy. Back then he had looked like statues of Hermes. He had settled down in Rome, married, and had fourteen children. He was also supposed to be able to play a trumpet with his feet, but there was no trumpet in Claudius's house. Messalina fumed that there wasn't even that much in this tin-pot house and raced off in a flood of tears. Claudius had a shamefaced grin on his face.

CALIGULA TRAVELED INTO CAMPANIA FOR THE SUMMER, WITH THE foreign embassies scrambling after him to carry on their canvassing at the seaside. Political commentators thought it increasingly likely that Caligula would not be holding a triumph and would only enter Rome in ceremonial procession at the end of August: the Senate could not deny him the celebration of his birthday.

Claudius and his household also journeyed into Campania, and they too would only be returning to Rome for Caligula's birthday on August 31 to be present at the ovation.

Uri hoped that these three months would allow him to rid his mind of Kainis—and not only hoped but also vowed to forget her, indeed sealed that vow with a donation of money to the Eternal One. He paid twelve sesterces to the treasury of the Elders; that would travel to Jerusalem for next Passover as part of the voluntary sacrificial offerings—*aparchai* as they were known in Greek—along with the annual didrachma ritual dues payable in February. He felt better after making the donation, though he did not think that the Creator would strive any more assiduously to soothe the pangs of love racking the insides of a believer: indeed, he was amazed that he felt better than he had for several months.

If I eventually end up cursing Kainis, he reflected, maybe I shall feel even more relieved.

He had always been scornful of non-Jews who whispered their wishes into the ears of the statues of divinities that were erected at crossroads and as a preliminary token of gratitude would place a wreath or sacrificial offering of produce at its feet; the withering wreaths and rotting food were repugnant to Uri, making him feel nauseous. He was also disdainful of people who turned to seers and paid substantial sums of money for evil or protective spells of guaranteed, dead-certain efficacy.

Now he had become just as superstitious. It was high time to extricate himself from all this.

There was no news at all about Agrippa. It seemed the king was in no hurry to get to Rome and secure the alabarch's release; he would only reach Rome at the end of August, like everybody else. Philo was bitter in his abuse of the ungrateful Agrippa, whereas Tija hemmed and hawed, and Marcus defended him. Uri noticed that Marcus was now starting to behave like a son-in-law even though his prospective father-in-law was not yet aware that there was a suitor for his eldest daughter.

Philo could not make up his mind whether they should set off after the emperor or stay in Rome. The longer Alexander was imprisoned, the worse the condition into which he would lapse, and it wasn't an extraneous consideration that the status of the Jewish delegation would decline in direct proportion to the length of his captivity. Maybe Caligula would receive them and be in a good mood to be merciful, in which case it might also be possible to secure admittance into the equestrian order for Marcus and Tija. On the other hand, there were things to attend to in Rome, and there were other circles to consider, aside from Claudius's guests; there were the societies that gathered at Sentius Saturninus's, Pomponius Secundus's, or Annius Vinicianus's. These were rich and highly respected senators; one could not treat them so offhandedly as Claudius, at whose place the emperor's unquestioning supporters would usually gather, given that nowadays even they could not gain admittance to the court of the emperor himself. They were also none too well acquainted either with Sanguinius Maximus, the city prefect, who might be able to make life easier for Alexander as he languished in prison.

All that could be learned of the alabarch was the message big-hearted Homilus had sent before the summer break: he had not been consigned to the deepest dungeon, and he was being decently provided for.

That was when Agrippa and his entourage arrived, and Jewish Rome burst into activity.

The king has arrived!

True, he did not take up quarters in Far Side but in Rome proper on the other bank, in his own house on Palatine Hill, which stood beside the house of Antonia, who had passed away two years before, but the Jews of Rome had no other topic of conversation. One spine-chilling detail that was retailed was that the Palatine's cellars reached their deepest point precisely below these two houses, which were interconnected with an exceptionally secret network of underground passageways about which no one knew, and Agrippa was living right above the imprisoned Alabarch Alexander: if the prisoner tapped, then Agrippa could hear him and even tap back. Old people could recall their grandfathers relating that Jews had sent messages from besieged towns to the outside world by tapping and signaling with fires, but then again that had been a long time ago and these days there were no wars, nor were any to be expected, so the tapping code had been forgotten, but maybe Agrippa still knew it because there were many back in the homeland who were acquainted with these things.

Agrippa had become a king; now one could say nothing but good of him, not that anything bad was said about the alabarch, because he was now in prison.

Uri listened to the gossip and said nothing.

Philo, Marcus, and Tija had lengthy talks with Agrippa and his counselors; Agrippa requested that they stay on in his house, so they did just that. Philo merely said they would soon be setting off for Campania on the emperor's trail, and they would most certainly have a need for Uri.

Now Sarah—and even Hagar—was satisfied with him. Sarah let it be known locally that Uri would be the king's archisynagogos; Uri pleaded with her not to use words she did not understand, but as Sarah was unfamiliar with the titles of any other high officials, she continued to prattle on about that to all and sundry.

She also spread word that the emperor had pardoned the king and had recalled him from exile. Uri blushed in shame and tried to get her to understand that was another king, but Sarah was quite sure that one thing she knew was that the Jews had just one king.

"You absolutely must demand that he pay up!" Sarah whispered confidentially into her son's ear one morning, at dawn, as he was setting off to walk across to Rome proper, where he would be joining the king's retinue. "If only your father had lived to see this!" Sarah sobbed as Uri, mortified, got a brisk move on in the early-morning stillness.

Agrippa and his retinue traveled in regal pomp.

The king had his own bodyguard of eight mounted men, to which he had added four of the Praetorian Guard—that much was the due a king who was the emperor's friend. Agrippa sat in the first four-horse carriage with his counselors: a certain Fortunatus, as well as Marsyas and Stoicheus, his manumitted slaves who had been with him back at the time when he was jailed on Capri and who, through forbearance on the part of Tiberius, had been allowed to visit him there. Also traveling with them was Pallas, a fop and the late Antonia's favorite slave, whom Claudius had left behind in his own house. Philo, Marcus, and Tija jolted along in the second coach, while in a third rode the servants with the king's personal effects, their head, Agrippa's favorite cook, and Iustus and Uri.

Philo said of Fortunatus that he had been Agrippa's ambassador to the emperor at the time Antipas had appeared in Rome to demand that he be given Judaea. What Fortunatus had achieved was Antipas's exile to Lugdunum in Gaul, in light of the number and type of weapons that Antipas had amassed in his fortresses, alleged to have been sufficient to arm seventy thousand men to the teeth. This Fortunatus, who now attended to Agrippa's affairs in Rome, was himself a Roman Jew; he had been engaged in his service when Agrippa was living there and had long been his interpreter, as Agrippa had never learned Latin. According to Marcus, the affairs of Agrippa's kingdom and family were entrusted to his friend Silas back home, and that was why they had not come to Rome; it seems that Agrippa was fond of traveling without his family. Philo noted that if Cypron were with her spouse she would have strictly measured out the quantity of what he ate and drank; she herself was on a diet, in fact that was a mania with her, and she checked her children's weights on a daily basis. If she noticed any gain she would hold them to a fast that day lest they ever put on weight as their father had.

It being July, the weather was hot, and Iustus bored Uri stiff with a tale of how Emperor Caligula had made a sacrificial offering on June 1 at the Dea Dei shrine, which they would be reaching any moment now, as it was situated by the five-mile sign. He reported in great detail on the emperor's dress—or rather costume—that day, among other matters; he had not been there, admittedly, but he had been present to hear a report that had been made to Honoratus. Uri deduced something that Iustus had seemingly not recognized: the emperor, on that occasion, must have been dressed up as one of the Dioscuri.

Iustus kept on making stubborn inquiries about Agrippa's schedule, unable to accept that Uri had no idea what the king had planned.

There was no Dea Dei shrine anywhere; Iustus just could not understand. Uri said nothing. The Dea Dei shrine lay to the northwest, on the road to Ostia, not on the Appian Way. Iustus's hearing must not be too sharp; he was no good even as an eavesdropper.

It was still morning when they halted at the first reasonably inviting inn and Agrippa clambered down from his coach. All the others also stopped, with the horsemen dismounting and Philo's group also getting down. Agrippa stretched his back and puffed and blew. Uri got close enough to examine him. Two years ago, when Uri had seen him taken away by litter from the alabarch's palace that early morning August, he had already been corpulent, but he had put on even more weight since then. He was corpulent because he was a king; the wonder was that Caligula had not put on any weight so far.

This being an unplanned break, the inn had received no prior notification of the king's arrival, so seven or eight tables were quickly pulled together to form one long table.

Agrippa sat at the head of the table with his counselors sitting next to him on either side, then Philo and the alabarch's sons, then the Praetorian Guards, the Jewish bodyguards, and, at the far end of the table, Iustus and Uri, who could not see as far as the king. It must be humiliating for Philo's party, the malicious thought struck him, that former slave freedmen had precedence over them, the wealthiest Jews in the world, who even now were supplying the king with money. It then occurred to him that it was unlikely Agrippa had given his blessing to Marcus marrying his daughter, otherwise he would have sat Marcus next to him. They reclined at the table while they waited for food and drink; the quiet buzz of conversation was audible as the bodyguards chatted with one another in subdued voices, the Jewish ones with Jews, the Romans with Romans.

"My sweet Marsyas!" cried the king from the head of the table. "Do excuse me, but please change places with my dear son Marcus!"

A hush fell and one of the counselors, obviously Marsyas, stood up, while Marcus stood up next to Philo. For a brief while they both stood, undecided as to what to do, before Marcus set off toward the king and Marsyas passed behind the king's back to slip into the place that Marcus had vacated. Marcus took up the place on the right of the king.

The king applauded in delight like a child. Fortunatus or Stoicheus seated directly on his left then began to clap, at which the bodyguards also joined in; although they had no idea what they were applauding. Iustus applauded and even Uri struck his hands together.

"What was that about?" Iustus asked quietly.

"I have no idea," said Uri.

"Why did he ask him to swap places?"

"No idea."

"But calling him to take a place right next to him! Why was that?"

Uri found this tedious.

"Because he is going to marry his daughter," he tossed in.

He immediately regretted doing so.

Iustus eyes rounded. There were deep, blue-veined pits under his eyes, his gaunt features slashed by premature wrinkles.

"Marcus? Which daughter? Berenice? Mariamne? Drusilla is too young as yet... Which of them? It's Berenice, isn't it?"

Uri said nothing.

"When?"

"I don't know... I was only joking..."

"Bring us some wine!" the king shouted.

Servants scuttled over with wineskins and mixing dishes.

The king drank greedily, emptying this and the next cup to Marcus, his future son-in-law. Everyone applauded. Marcus in return toasted the king, his future father-in-law, and he in turn was loudly applauded.

Iustus asked in a whisper how much Marcus was due to receive, and whether Agrippa was going to share the kingship with him. It was totally futile for Uri to keep asserting that he did not know because Iustus took it for granted that Uri was privy to everything. Iustus changed tack and began gossiping in a well-informed manner about the wrangling which went on among the Jewish elders of Rome, whereas Uri's head grew heavier as he was drinking on an empty stomach and was soon unable to follow what was being said.

They ate and drank into the evening. Iustus was the only one who attacked his food less than wholeheartedly because he was uncertain if in this place the cooking was ritually clean; the others were not in the least concerned. Iustus, however, asked about each and every item on the menu to determine whether or not he was allowed to eat it, whereas Uri could not repeat often enough that it was permissible.

"I was told in Judaea that nothing the Lord created can be unclean," Uri said.

Iustus was aghast on hearing such dreadful heresy.

Tija popped up beside Uri, holding a long quill feather in one hand.

"Make the king vomit," he instructed Uri.

"Who, me?"

"You're the lowest in rank here!" snapped Tija in a stifled voice.

Uri flushed red, took the feather, unsteadily got to his feet and made his way to the head of the table, stopping on the right-hand side of puce-headed, virtually bald Agrippa and bending forward. The king looked up at him; his eyes were raging.

"What do you want?" he choked.

Uri indicated the feather.

"About time!" muttered the king.

Uri pulled across a mixing dish, knelt, grasped the feather with his right hand, and used his left to cradle the king's hot, sweating head. The king opened his mouth wide and Uri cautiously poked in the plume.

The king vomited prodigiously. Uri closed his eyes and took a deep breath to suppress his own nausea but even so he retched at the horrible, acrid stink. He opened his eyes. No one was looking that their way; they were gorging unconcernedly.

"Thank you," the king gasped as he pushed away the hand holding the feather once he had freed himself of the encumbrance.

Uri tossed the feather into the steaming mess, the unchewed morsels swimming about in the foul-smelling liquid, and picked up the dish.

The king looked up in gratitude and broke into a smile.

"I've seen you somewhere before," he said.

"Yes, your majesty... I gave you a drink of water in Alexandria."

"Really?"

The king knitted his eyebrows.

"Your majesty," Uri quickly interjected. "Two hundred thousand sesterces... You still owe that much! I don't mind paying the interest on it but there is no way that I shall be able to pay back the capital... It was five years this February..."

The king nodded.

"I remember it now," he beamed, proud of his mental capacity. "I remember; it was in Rome! The bankers through a silk merchant!"

He looked at Uri.

"But I already returned the favor!" he said. "I used my influence to get your son into the delegation taking the ritual tax to Jerusalem! I repaid the debt right away! That was what was agreed, don't you recall? I kept my end of the bargain!"

Uri stumbled as he took the dish full of vomit out into the yard.

There he washed his hands and face at length in the cistern before raising his eyes to the firmament. It was evening by then, with dots of indefinite outline twinkling up above.

The king mistook me for my father.

IT WAS NO USE IUSTUS HEAPING HIM WITH QUESTIONS, URI WAS absorbed in his thoughts and did not even hear them.

I've aged fast: I need a pond or slow stream that will allow me to take a look at myself.

Was it then me rather than my son in whom my father was reborn? Have I become my father?

Agrippa had discharged the loan if that really was the agreement, and it may well have been.

I squandered the fortune that he entrusted to me; I did all the wrong things. My father put the capital in my own hands, but I did not invest it well.

This was a new point of view: he would have to think everything through.

He ought to have realized in time; it was quite certain that his father had placed his trust in his son realizing it and acting accordingly.

As Agrippa's courier he had been granted countless opportunities to acquire skills, make his fortune, find a job and acquire prestige in Judaea, Jerusalem, and Alexandria. He had needed only to tell a few white lies, curry a few favors. He should have dropped out of sight, got married in Judaea or Alexandria, learned a trade properly: goldsmithing or diamond cutting—something in which his eyes were an asset, and not get so entangled with his family, neither his father nor the others.

Uri shivered. His father had not known him all that well: he had not supposed that Uri would return home out of love for him.

My father never knew that I loved him!

He was the only one I did love. How come he was unaware of that?

It flashed before him: he needed to endeavor to make his son believe that he really did love him—otherwise Theo, too, would live his life under a misapprehension.

My father did die on my account after all.

He could safely have declined to make the loan to Agrippa; after all, what would have happened? Agrippa would have turned to someone else; he could have gotten a lousy two hundred thousand sesterces from anyone. But his father had requested that Uri be given a place in the delegation, and Agrippa had done just that.

My father wanted to make me happy! He did love me, for all that I am blind as a bat!

He ought to have announced the glad tidings to all and sundry, but he couldn't because he was surrounded by strangers.

AGRIPPA MADE NO SPECIAL EFFORT TO GET TO MEET THE EMPEROR, WHO was shuttling among the villas on the seashore close to Dikaiarchia, spending a few nights in one, then another, possibly out of fear of assassins. Still, if the king was obliged to stay in Italia until the end of September anyway, at least he was going to enjoy spending the time. Perhaps that was why he was in no hurry to secure the alabarch's release, or at least that was how Uri saw it.

The alabarch had assisted Agrippa too much and too often; people did not care to be reminded of their obligations.

In the end they took up quarters in one of the emperor's summer houses on a hill near Puteoli, as Agrippa wished to settle down there for the duration. It was an attractive villa with lots of outhouses where the bodyguards and retinue could also find room; it had some splendid horses, smart hunting hounds, and well-trained servants. Philo, like Agrippa, settled into one of the annexes, setting out his papyruses and scrolls and resuming his work.

Agrippa was fond of hunting and he considered his stay in Italia as a well-deserved break from the burdens of reigning and coexisting with his family.

It was the middle of July by now, and Agrippa managed to persuade even Philo to go hunting with him and the alabarch's sons; Iustus also tagged along. Uri was invited but he declined; as he would not be able to see any game animal that might pop up anyway, he would rather stay behind and clean up Philo's night-time draft.

So everybody rode off, leaving just Uri at home with the servants who had been assigned to Agrippa, aside from the dog handlers, who were out with the dogs on the hunt.

Uri was copying out Philo's scrawl, which he was used to reading (he could read it better than the author himself), when he heard a knock on the door. Uri got up and went to the door; he peered out. A servant was standing there, and behind him Isidoros.

Isidoros entered the room; the servant remained outside. Uri just stood there before eventually speaking:

"Sir!"

The ex-head of the Gymnasium in Alexandria looked around.

"So, this is how we have to meet again, son," said Isidoros with mock emotion. "Parties on opposed sides!"

He quickly cast his eyes over the scroll.

"Would I be right in thinking that the old codger Philo reviles and vilifies us?"

"There's no denying it."

"You write out the first drafts, I suppose?"

"Mostly, yes."

"Well, keep at it, the two of you... I thought I would find him here."

"He went hunting with the king."

"*Your* king! Fine figure of a man... Aren't you his scribe as yet?"

"No, I'm not."

Uri was moved as he stood there.

Isidoros had not changed much, he had only become skinnier, his face more wrinkled.

"When will he get back?" he asked.

"Maybe in the evening... It depends on Agrippa."

"I can't wait for him, I'm in a hurry," said Isidoros. "I've got some important news for him, though."

"Give me the letter; I'll see he gets it."

"It's not a written message."

Isidoros hesitated before adding:

"In that case I'll tell you. You may add that the message is from me."

"Philo is none too fond of you."

"Nor I him—there's smarminess in everything he writes. Despite that we work extremely well together."

Uri nodded. Isidoros looked at him quizzically: what did Uri know, he wondered, before getting back to the reason for his visit.

It wasn't the emperor who had sent him but people in his entourage who kept their eyes on the empire's interest.

In June the emperor had dispatched a letter to Petronius, the Syrian legate in Antioch, asking him to assemble half of the Roman legions stationed on the Euphrates and march with them to Jerusalem, carrying a colossal statue of Zeus, the head of which portrayed the emperor, and to place this in the Temple, in the Holy of Holies.

Uri was dizzy and had to sit down.

"We had managed to get him to believe that it was the Jews alone who did not wish to deify him," Isidoros noted wryly. "Well, that was the result. Even we had not been looking for that... We loathe, absolutely loathe your kind, but not to the extent that we too will perish."

"That's not possible!" Uri whispered.

"Oh, it's quite possible," said Isidoros.

Uri gasped for breath.

"That would mean a stupendously big war! Throughout the Greek-speaking world..."

"Indeed. With that in mind, your king should intercede with Caligula and get him to revoke that order."

Uri was still dizzy.

This was perhaps bigger than any trouble the Jews had ever faced.

"Petronius is a rational chap," said Isidoros. "Ever since he received the letter he has desperately been playing for time because he is well aware what the consequences will be if he attempts to carry out the order. He wrote back that he was worried about withdrawing half of the legions along the border because the Parthians might invade, and he was even more worried that a Jewish revolt would be unavoidable... He made reference to the fact that the Jews were right then in the middle of their harvesting, so if they started to revolt, then a famine would break out, which would make them rebel even more strenuously, and that revolt would spill out over the entire Greek world, wherever Jews are living. Furthermore, he regretted to say that not a single existing statue of Jupiter-Caligula was worthy, so he had urgently ordered one to be made in Sidon. Still, he won't be able to procrastinate for very long if he values his own life, and we can't step in to defend the Jews because news of that will leak out, and when our Jew-hating supporters get to know about that we can look out for ourselves! Your king should work something out as a matter of urgency. Caligula likes him, as he is fond of saying. He is the one decent Jew in the whole world."

Uri snorted with laughter.

"What's wrong?" said Isidoros uneasily.

"An enormous statue of Sejanus was hidden away somewhere in Caesarea." Uri laughed. "All you would have to do is change the head on that..."

"You're nuts," Isidoros blurted out. "I didn't hear that, and don't ever say it to anyone!"

Isidoros went away. Uri's head was splitting and his stomach heaving; he was sweating and felt dizzy.

It spelled trouble, very big trouble.

URI WAS UNABLE TO PASS ON THE NEWS TO PHILO UNTIL AFTER SUPPER, once the bodyguards had carried off an already paralytic Agrippa to bed. He had drunk himself into insensibility so that his body was even more burdensome than usual and three of them could barely manage it.

Philo began to tremble and motioned silently toward the room occupied by the alabarch's two sons. Uri went in and, paying no heed to Tija's protests, ordered them out into Philo's room. Philo was still speechless, so Uri himself stated what Isidoros had told him.

"That can't be true!" Marcus whispered.

Tija glowered mutely.

Uri poured some water and took it over to Philo.

There was a deadly hush.

A warm breeze was drifting into the stuffy room; outside, cicadas stridulated furiously in the pleasant Campanian countryside.

How many times over the last two millennia had Jewish leaders had to confer about such an unexpected grave peril on a glorious summer evening like this?

"He won't dare do it," Marcus said hoarsely.

"Care to bet?" said Tija.

"It makes no sense!" Marcus cried out. "It would result in hundreds of thousands of people dying! No Jew is going to stand for that!"

Philo drank; his teeth were chattering.

"Agrippa is here," he said. "He needs to decide what we should do..."

"He's wasted," Tija noted.

They all held their peace. The cicadas shrilled frantically; what mankind might get up to was a matter of indifference to Nature.

Uri cleared his throat. They looked at him.

"If you wish, I'll tell him in the morning..."

"Don't even consider it!" stormed Philo.

Uri did not understand that.

"He might panic, poor thing," Tija said maliciously. "He would set off for home right away."

Marcus gave a grunt but then said nothing to defend his future father-in-law.

Philo declared that it was all very well this business of Agrippa not wishing to go out on a limb for Alexander, but in this case he was bound to do something, however yellow-bellied he might be. He had to be persuaded to pay a visit to the emperor, but he must not be told anything in advance. Let the emperor cast aspersions straight into his father's friend's face, then let Agrippa do what he liked.

It was a wise proposal; that even Uri could admit.

Tija poured everyone a drink of wine and they all quickly got inebriated enough to get to sleep.

PHILO THREW HIMSELF INTO HIS WORK, HIDING AWAY IN HIS ROOM with Uri as if nothing had happened to labor over the tenth volume of a major history of Etruria that Claudius had generously entrusted to him. Marcus and Tija endeavored to persuade Agrippa to make at least a minimal effort on behalf of their father, because they had their fill of hunting. Tija reasoned that autocrats loved it when people begged them to be merciful, and it was startling how often, in reality, they did exercise clemency, because this way they felt much more at the zenith of their power than if they simply killed indiscriminately. Agrippa listened grumpily.

"It's time you asked to be given Judaea," Marcus said, "before others do."

That was a better tack than the previous one.

"Why would I?" the king was offended. "He banished Antipas and Herodias!"

"It's not as if you don't have enough relatives," Marcus taunted him. "Why do you tolerate his propping up of Marullus? Caligula will believe you have enough on your plate with Galilee!"

A while ago, Vitellius had proposed Marullus as prefect of Judaea, but Tiberius had been unable to give that decision the stamp of approval before he died, leaving the matter of the appointment to Caligula.

Agrippa growled something. He was plainly afraid of the emperor, having heard terrible stories about him over the past half a year, tales of the once taciturn, modest, polite, and helpful Gaius transformed into Caligula, who dressed up as divinities and surrounded himself with actors. What if the emperor were to toss the head of a tiny Jewish kingdom into a dungeon? It would not even be noticed.

Agrippa struggled with himself for a whole day before giving an order that the emperor should be tracked down.

Three days later they found themselves in the garden of a seaside villa. Only the alabarch's sons and Philo went with Agrippa, Uri with Philo; they left Iustus with the bodyguards in a nearby house. Uri tried to get Iustus included but Philo shook his head.

Iustus had never liked me as it was; now he'll loathe me virulently, Uri thought.

Agrippa did not bring any servants along, maybe so that there was no chance of them seeing their master in a humiliating position.

Uri took a scroll of the completed work Philo had written against Flaccus in a linen bag tucked under his arm; he was quite sure that the emperor would not read it.

Uri was at least as tense as Philo or Marcus or Tija. They shouldn't have mentioned this to Agrippa; they were in trouble.

On this occasion they found Caligula in the costume of a tragic actor; a similarly garbed effeminate figure stood next to him, gesticulating. This might be Apelles, who, when he had started, had supported himself as a child prostitute and spoke frankly about it.

Surrounding them was a considerable number of muscular men, charioteers and gladiators, loafing around; Isidoros was there too, standing with Lampo. It looks as if the emperor does not much like being on his own, Uri thought; he has a constant need to be adored.

A tall, intelligent-looking, balding man with a well-kempt beard was the first to come forward; Helicon, presumably.

Agrippa separated from their group and approached the emperor.

Caligula took one look, left Apelles, and set off toward Agrippa with open arms.

In a sharp tone, Helicon cried out:

"The king of the Jews, ho-ho-ho!"

All could see how warmly the emperor embraced the king.

Agrippa looked around as if glorified.

Philo gripped Uri's arm.

The emperor smiled.

Marcus and Tija then stepped closer, with Uri following Philo.

"Hail, my soul's better half!" Caligula called out, clapping his hands. "Hail, hefty king!"

The muscular young men muttered their ovation; Helicon smiled.

"Did you hear the great news, Agrippa?" the emperor asked.

"Since I left Rome I have heard a lot of good news about you," Agrippa replied diplomatically. "Which one specifically did you have in mind?"

"I have become a god! What do you think of that?"

Agrippa became flustered.

"I've become a god," Caligula reiterated, "and everyone recognizes me as a god, only you Jews don't. What would be the reason for that?"

Agrippa remained silent for a while but then found his feet.

"We make as many sacrificial offerings to you as the Latini... Your name has been inscribed on ornamental tablets in all our houses of prayer..."

"But not my statue!"

"That is forbidden by our religion... But we made sacrifices to you for months on end! There is not a Jewish house of prayer in the world in which your name is not inscribed."

Caligula nodded.

"Other nations sacrificed to me as a god," he said. "You on the other hand, made sacrificial offerings to your god for me... Sacrificing for me or to me—that's a fundamental difference, you have to admit."

There was a silence as Agrippa searched for words.

"Never mind," said the emperor mirthfully. "I've already sent instructions to Petronius to march into Jerusalem and set up my statue in the Temple... It's a statue of Zeus, but I'm him as well! The Holy of Holies of your Temple will be known hereafter as 'the sanctum of Gaius embodied as the new Zeus!'"

Agrippa turned purple and clearly wanted to say something; he was about to raise his right hand, possibly in protest, but before he could complete the motion he fell flat on the ground.

AGRIPPA LAY IN BED UNCONSCIOUS FOR TWO DAYS. THE EMPEROR SENT his best physicians to minister to him: they opened his veins to bleed him, slapped him, yanked his tongue out of his mouth, turned him on his side, smeared him with unguents, and induced vomiting—he still refused to come around. His pulse beat, but only feebly and falteringly. Half a dozen physicians were constantly in attendance; Uri and Iustus took turns standing guard at the door while Philo was relieved by Marcus, and Marcus in turn by Tija; Fortunatus, Marsyas and Stoicheus seemed to be present throughout.

Agrippa finally stirred and opened his eyes at the end of the second day.

He drank water only, refusing wine.

He cast his eyes around him and beckoned Philo over.

"Write to him," he whispered, "and I'll sign it..."

Philo grasped Uri by the hand and pulled him out.

"We'll write to him!" Philo declared enthusiastically.

Uri suspected the worst: that meant it would be long.

Philo on this occasion did not rely on Uri to write a draft but, driven by divine inspiration, himself dictated while Uri swiftly scribbled it down in shorthand. Thanks to Narcissus he had already got in some good practice on that, but it was tough work putting into fair copy.

The draft letter to Caligula included all that the emperor needed to know about the Jewish faith, the fidelity of the Jews toward the Roman emperors, and the Creation in general. After a few hours Uri felt that his hand was going to break at the wrist and his eyes were watering so badly that he could no longer see his own scrawl, but Philo would not let him rest. He went on steadily with the dictation, only breaking off now and again to cast a glance at the shorthand and shout out "what's this?" or "what's that?" before resuming. Uri would never have thought that so much energy could reside in the old man's frail frame.

The outline ran to some two scrolls' worth of text, and Uri was well aware that once he had made a fair copy and Philo got a chance to work on that, it would come out much longer.

Uri implored him to stop; the emperor was not going to read thirty lines of it. It was enough to stick to the essentials and there was no need to digress on to so many points. Despite Uri's heeding, Philo's head nodded in the happy heat of inspiration—now the emperor would really learn a thing or two!

Uri told him again that these sort of people, the emperors, never read anything, but Philo never so much as heard him.

"Read it back!" he ordered.

Uri started off. At the second sentence Philo groaned.

"What was that you wrote, you wretch?"

Uri held his tongue: he had only written what Philo had dictated.

"We can't have that! That's impossible!" Philo cried out and, pacing up and down in the room, started dictating the right sentence, out of which grew two long paragraphs.

Uri resigned himself to his fate and went on recording.

Philo put scintillating arguments into Agrippa's mouth in defense of the faith of the Jews, and even Cicero, the celebrated Judaeophobe, could never have written a more rhetorically perfect speech than Philo's. It covered what great friends Caligula's grandfather, Marcus Agrippa, and Agrippa's grandfather, Herod the Great, had been, and how Marcus Agrippa in person had made sacrificial offerings at the Temple (though it did not cover how Augustus had reproved Drusus for doing the same thing). It covered how Augustus and Livia, Caligula's great-grandmother, had donated many splendid gold dishes to the Temple, and it covered how ever since, every day without fail, in the Temple two lambs and an ox were sacrificed to the Roman emperor. It covered how the Jews had never rebelled again Rome's prefects—aside from Pilate, whom Philo set in an extremely unflattering light, inveighing against him for high-handedness, brutality, extortion (which had, of course, been no truer for him than it had been in the case of any prefect), and, on the basis of reports by messengers from Judaea, for having had Jewish prisoners executed without court hearings and sentencing (which was true). It covered Agrippa's gratitude to Caligula for restoring him to liberty, releasing him from his iron shackles (though Philo had forgotten, and Uri did not remind him, about his being given a golden chain the same weight as his former shackles).

Even in that improved manuscript, though, there were still things to correct and that night Uri slumped over the table and fell asleep between two well-turned but lengthy sentences, not responding to any further dictation.

Fortunatus brought news that in the meantime the emperor had set off for Rome.

They pondered what they should do. Agrippa decided that they too would go to Rome.

They got there before the emperor, who had set up camp in a multitude of places along the way, popping in unexpectedly to get avail of the hospitality of total strangers; in one case it turned out to be a place where the banished Agrippina, his mother, had been held prisoner, and he had it demolished.

In Rome Agrippa was placed under treatment by the costliest physicians, not that they had much to do because the king had gotten better of his own accord, albeit he still dragged his left leg.

He ran through Philo's text and approved it. Philo beamed.

Agrippa received emissaries who confirmed that Petronius had departed with legions from the Euphrates and was heading for Galilee; the next day another envoy arrived, according to whom Petronius was already in Galilee. Agrippa raged when he heard that Petronius had invited the elders of Judaea to a conference in Tiberias—Herod Antipas's capital city!

"The bastard is going to bring back Antipas!" he became so apoplectic that it was feared he would have a fit. "Tiberias! And Jews went there to confer! They had no authorization from me but still they went! I'll exterminate them one and all! What does Silas believe he's doing? Or Cypron? Complete idiots!"

The physicians opened a vein again.

The emissaries reassured him that Petronius was playing for time by saying he could not find a suitable statue, that it would take a long time until a worthy one was produced in Sidon, where the master sculptors were slow in their work, as slow as they could possibly be, because Petronius really had no wish to march into Jerusalem.

The physicians opened another vein.

Uri volunteered that he would be very ready to travel anywhere with a message from Agrippa; it would be good to get as far away as he could from Rome, because Kainis would soon be returning with Claudius's household, and it would be good to escape from Sarah and Hagar. He felt that even getting mixed up in a war would be better, but Philo said he would not let him go anywhere.

to spare him, the magnitude of the danger facing Jewry as a whole was not discussed again with Agrippa, nor did they discuss the matter any further among themselves. Uri was astonished.

August 31, the day of the ovation, was approaching when Caligula unexpectedly sent a message that he was awaiting the Jewish delegation in Maecenas's garden.

Agrippa was talked out of going himself; Marcus and Tija were suggested as representatives, but the king decided that Philo and Uri should do the representing.

We're no great loss, Uri thought. He is fond of his own servants, and he has plans for the alabarch's sons, but Philo is already old and I'm a nobody.

THE GARDENS OF MAECENAS AND LAMIA WERE NEAR EACH OTHER, TWO days walking distance from Rome, so they traveled by coach. Once again they took along with them the work Philo had written on Flaccus, adding to it Agrippa's speech. The tiny old man carried out a series of breathing exercises, holding his breath and pulling in his belly, then pushing it out because, he asserted, he could circulate it there too; then he would wriggle, mutter to himself, and sit motionless for a long time—all tricks he had once learned from an Indian magus. He claimed to be able thereby to reduce his pulse rate by two thirds if he wished.

All the things he had heard about Caligula's depravity passed through Uri's head. No doubt he was no more wicked than Divus Augustus or Tiberius, it was just that all of those who surrounded him tolerated his games. "I do it because I can do it," he would say, and indeed he could, because nobody restrained him.

What kind of end could deep-breathing Philo expect?

They entered the garden; Uri blinked. Small houses were set out between small lakes and coppices; servants were scurrying around with spades and rakes. Bodyguards led them to the emperor, who was examining the windows of one of the pavilions and declared that he wanted panes of that translucent white stone he had already talked about. Philo prostrated himself, lying with outspread arms on the ground. Uri followed his example. Caligula glanced at them.

"Augustus Imperator!" Philo bawled out.

Caligula broke into a laugh.

"So, you're the people who detest me, you hardened atheists!" he declared. "The one people who are unwilling to believe that I'm a god. Others can see it straightaway; why can't you? Oh, Yahweh! Oh, Yahweh!" and he raised his arms to the heavens theatrically and mockingly.

Uri shuddered: he had never heard the Name of God pronounced out loud before; now he had heard it, and in so doing he had committed a sin.

A huge guffaw burst out. Uri glanced across. Some Greeks, Isidoros and Lampo among them, were amusing themselves, whirling into a dance as they snickered; they danced around Caligula, addressing him by turns as Zeus, Apollo, Hermes, and Dionysus.

Isidoros came to a stop and said:

"Sire, you will loathe these Jews even more when you learn how little they consider you to be their lord. Every people except theirs make sacrifices to you."

Isidoros made a sweeping gesture to indicate that he meant all of Jewry.

Philo then got up onto one knee and called out:

"It's a lie to say we did not make sacrificial offerings! We did!"

Uri repeated that word for word.

"We made sacrifices three times over!" Philo shouted, waving his thin arms. "The first time was when you became emperor! A second time when you were healed! Then there was a third time when you won your victory in Germania! We sacrificed exactly the same number of animals as the Greeks!"

"Yes," said Caligula, "except it was not to me that you made the offerings: for me, but to your own god!"

That is what he had already said to Agrippa. Could he have forgotten? Was that all he had been taught about the Jews? It wasn't much. How had Agrippa brought him up?

Uri thought the time was ripe for him to produce the two scrolls but the emperor turned on his heels and hastened off, the Greeks after him. Philo and Uri got to their feet, exchanged looks, and raced after them.

The emperor first looked at the women's room in the other pavilion, fired off some comment before tearing up the steps and taking exception to something there too. Pale-faced servants noted down what he said, the Greeks stood around uneasily, and the emperor then bawled:

"Rubbish! Rubbish! Spend more! Spend more!"

He ran down the steps and out of the house, Greeks, servants, and Jews in his wake.

The Greeks let fly a series of jeering comments after the Jews, but Caligula did not hear them.

They tore around five pavilions like this, with Uri panting to keep up; Philo withstood it better.

Then Caligula stopped dead and fixed his eyes on them.

"Why don't you eat pork?" he asked.

The Greeks chortled uproariously, as if they had been struck by a sparkling shaft of wit.

Philo was not ready for a question like that, but Uri had enough presence of mind to respond:

"Many peoples regard various items of food as being prohibited. Many will not eat lamb even though that too is delicious."

"You mean pork is delicious?" the emperor asked.

"Most certainly," said Uri. "Our ancestors banned the eating of it so we would not grow soft."

Caligula was amazed at first before breaking into a laugh. The Greeks did not laugh.

"Right then," said Caligula. "What sorts of political rights do you have?"

He did not wait for an answer, however, nor did he take away the two scrolls he was offered but instead turned to issue an instruction that the windows of this building's large hall should likewise be covered with the same translucent stone panes, and only after that did he turn again to the Jews.

"What do you want anyway?"

He immediately turned away again, indicating place for the curtains.

Caligula pointed toward the Jews and said to Isidoros:

"In my opinion they are not criminals, just sleepwalkers, for not seeing that I am blessed with divinity. Well, in that case I'm not letting my statue be taken into their Temple, but I'll tell you this: every Greek has the right to erect an altar to me anywhere—anywhere at all—and if the Jews demolish it like they did at Jamnia, they will all perish."

On that note, he ran off with the Greeks in train.

Philo and Uri just stood there. The audience had come to an end.

PHILO REMAINED SILENT THROUGHOUT THE COACH RIDE BACK.

Uri was almost ready to believe that the whole thing had never occurred.

Caligula had never sought to have a statue of Zeus taken into the Temple. It was the last thing he wanted; he was not stupid and, having quarrels with the Senate, he would not withstand a general Jewish revolt.

He had wanted to humiliate his father's friend, Agrippa, and place Petronius, the prefect of Syria, in an awkward position lest his favorites get too cocksure. He had gone about things in much the same way as Tiberius had many times. Caligula had studied him mutely for many years and had learned his lessons.

That was all beside the point.

What he had accomplished today was to make them understand that he had rescinded his order.

But then why had he issued it in the first place?

He had rescinded the order merely so that the spirit of the order should live on throughout the Greek world, from Alexandria to Antioch, and what that spirit said to the many millions of Greeks was that the emperor was their divine ruler and not that of the Jews. He had humiliated the Jews, terrified and threatened them, and that was enough, because the Greeks had a problem only with their close rivals, the Jews, in the part of the world in which they dwelt, not with the Latini, who lived far away and for whom they had no regard at all.

Fleet-footed messengers (Jews themselves who had taken fright) would be doing the work of spreading the emperor's true message throughout the Hellenic world—free of charge at that.

Jamnia had been a provocation on the part of the emperor—now he had admitted as much.

Caligula wanted to be a Pharaoh, not just a simple Princeps. And through that rescinded order he had not only achieved that pharaonization in the minds of Egyptians, but also in the minds of Greeks: they hadn't noticed that they had been degraded to the status of Copt slaves.

The Senate, reluctant? Unwilling to grant him a triumph? The Greeks across the empire would stand by him and smash the Senate's power from the outside.

Caligula was counting on Alexandria taking side against Rome. That was why he had Alexander the Great's breastplate brought to him. It was not out of some megalomania, a delusion of grandeur, but a clear political calculation. That was why he dressed up as Dionysus: once upon a time the Athenian Assembly had granted Alexander the Great the honor of Dionysiac divinity. That was why Caligula had surrounded himself with Greek counselors, and that was why he had not sent relief troops to Alexandria as soon as the Bane erupted. It was not beyond the bounds of possibility that he had sent a message to Flaccus—though the prefect had already been dismissed by then—to allow the city's Greeks to let off steam for a while.

He had aligned himself with the Greeks, ostensibly against the Jews, but in reality against Rome.

Caligula had comprehended what Flaccus had placed trust in; the emperor himself had continued his desperate undertaking with a substantially higher chance of success. Like a second Mark Antony, in alliance with Egypt and the Greek world, he was girding for a war against Rome, and Rome had no other allies—only the paltry Jews. This community did not fully appreciate their position and did not understand that by remaining faithful to Rome, they were fatefully consigning themselves to standing alone wherever they were living, alienating themselves in the villages and towns with mixed Greek and Jewish population.

That had been a fateful error on the part of the Jews: they needed to come to terms with their Greek neighbors, not place their trust in faraway imperial help. The Jews had made exactly the same mistake under the Persians, likewise under the Ptolemies, and now it was going to be repeated yet again, for a third time.

Who should he speak to? To Philo, who as it was had spent his life urging Greco-Jewish conciliation?

The emperor was also a descendant not only of Agrippa and Augustus, but of Mark Antony. Philo would have been better advised to refer to this heritage in the lengthy self-justification they'd never had the opportunity to hand over. Caligula really did want to be a second—and this time successful—Mark Antony. That was his plan.

The moment in which Uri drew this wide-ranging conclusion was exceptionally clear; he had a sense that he had gotten a glimpse into Caligula's head.

If Kainis were here she would ponder a little, her marvelous deep eyes gazing at a point in the far distance, then she would break into a smile and nod.

There was nobody else but her whom he could tell.

No one else would understand.

Even if they could comprehend, they would not dare agree. Cultured, clever, political, shrewd they might be—Philo for sure, Tija even more so, and Marcus was no dimwit either—but still they would not understand it. Maybe Tija... possibly he also saw it, because he was a second son. But he would not be pleased to be told something that he himself suspected; he might even decide to have his revenge.

Though he was not sure that Tija saw it. Something was clouding the eyes of the Jewish aristocracy—prejudice, perhaps—but more likely personal goals for what they wanted to achieve; that is what prevented them from seeing clearly. The Jews felt that they were the chosen people, and that was what made them so blind; Apollos had already said as much. They placed their trust in the Creator, and Philo did so especially. He was confident that the Eternal One would soon send down a Messiah; decent, dotty old man that he was, he made a habit of referring to this in his works.

Maybe that was what he was deliberating about right now, staring vacantly ahead, absorbed in himself, jolting along in the coach.

A shocking thought flashed into Uri's head: polytheism pictured the human world more realistically—more immorally anyway, closer to the way things are—than did faith in a remote, faceless God.

He banished the thought.

Isidoros knows, it occurred to Uri, and he would be far from pleased if the emperor were to become a pharaoh because then Isidoros would lose the leading position he holds in Alexandria. He must fear that he—along with Lampo, Helicon, and all the other Greek favorites—will be executed by the pharaoh-emperor the moment his plan of shifting the seat of the empire to Alexandria succeeds. Isidoros was not defending the Jews but himself.

A clever man, cultivated, he had read a lot of historical works; he was not seized by ideas as Philo was but by politics—he saw things more clearly.

Uri wondered what he himself still wanted from life.

He did not want anything. He wanted to live out his days somehow, seeing that the Creator had bestowed life on him, and he wanted to raise his son, and he would like it if his son were present when he died.

That was all, nothing else.

BY THEN THE NEWS HAD REACHED EVEN NON-JEWISH ROME THAT Petronius had marched into Galilee at the head of the legions, taking a statue of Zeus with him, the Temple in Jerusalem being the destination. What they were unaware of was that the emperor had withdrawn his order—or maybe he hadn't after all. His stipulation that the Greeks were free to erect their shrines anywhere they pleased, and the Jews were not permitted to obstruct this, would stand as *casus belli* in every place where Greek and Jewish communities co-existed, which was true of all the Greek islands, Syria, Armenia, Palestine, and Egypt, the entire eastern half of the Roman Empire. From now on it would be possible, in principle, for the Greeks to raise altars even in Far Side, or anywhere, in the direct neighborhood of the synagogues. Altars and statues—just as they had done in Jamnia.

Agrippa recovered nicely, and as he had lost weight from dieting his human features reemerged; the physicians heartened him that he would be able to take part in Caligula's ovation, which was his most fervent wish, and they announced to him that the emperor had retracted his order.

"A real friend he is!" Agrippa burst out ecstatically. "My friend and pupil! I'm the only one who can exert an influence on him!"

He asked for meat.

It was in this period that a fire broke out in the alabarch's unoccupied house in Far Side. The watchmen, the vigiles, not being Jewish, were unenthusiastic about turning up, as was the rule for fires in the XIVth District, and the house burned to the ground. The only object to escape harm was a statue of Germanicus, only the paint was burned off, and that was easily fixed. The statue was taken into Honoratus's house. Pure accident, said the elders, but people talked of arson. Sarah even knew who had done it: demons, but Uri did not ask who they might be.

The guard on Agrippa's house on the Palatine was strengthened.

Uri had the feeling things were not looking good.

He spent little time in Far Side but he could not avoid seeing that homeless Jews were crammed into the alleyways, lying in the mud and muck, their infants crawling about on all fours on borrowed blankets, the elderly begging, their emaciated, trembling arms stretched out.

These were Jewish refugees from Alexandria, and they did not stop coming. They had envied the wealthy Jews of Alexandria who had been left with enough cash to bribe the authorities and boatmen at home as well as the Romans in Puteoli or Ostia. Even those who'd had the money to buy fake relatives in Far Side found that these relatives would not support them once they'd arrived. The Jews of Alexandria, not so long ago still rich and so high and mighty, were now floundering, praying and cursing in the Far Side mud, reviling the alabarch and his family for stealing their money.

They did not starve, at least: they could count on the fund—to which all members of Rome's Jewish community coughed up, though with much groaning—to provide minimal assistance for the poor and visitors, but that could not cover the cost of a residence. Several dozen families had installed themselves between the warehouses in the harbor area, while others had moved in among the non-Jewish homeless on the island in the Tiber, subject to flooding every other month.

Uri wanted neither to hear nor see them, but they were there, and in ever-greater numbers at that, and they were right. However many families he might accept, they did not have enough room for themselves in the first place, and soon enough another child would be born.

News spread in Far Side that peace had not been restored in Alexandria; one time it would be the Greeks demonstrating, another the Jews, and the prefect could not cope with breaking them up. The still-imprisoned alabarch was barely spoken of at all in Far Side; if he was mentioned, it was only in terms of the widely shunned new arrivals.

When he took his son out for some fresh air, the boy would burble as he pointed in terror at the homeless people, and Uri could not comfort him.

"We won't be homeless," he whispered in Theo's ear, following with a gentle nip in the hope that it would lighten the mood, and Theo did laugh.

The presence of the immigrants was not taken kindly in Far Side. The newcomers surged to the synagogues because on the Sabbath they too had a need to worship, and the house of prayer that Uri's family attended could not accommodate half of the congregation, so on the Sabbath they would set out trestle tables in front of the temple, just as had been done in the village in Judaea, but the celebration of the communal meal here went on in low spirits, surly and dejected, with everyone receiving a great deal less food and wine than they had in former times. The immigrants did no work; they expected fellow Jews in Rome to provide for them. The most resolute of them toiled in the harbor, some of these had been wealthy artisans for whose craftsmanship there was no demand in Rome or wealthy tradesmen who had no network of contacts here, but they kept their income quiet and they paid no tithes or dues to the communities of the synagogues here.

The mood in Far Side had never been at such a low ebb.

It was at this point that Julius, the banker, asked Uri to pay him a visit.

After a brief exchange of the customary courtesies, he got down to business: would Uri, being Philo's right-hand man, see to it that the alabarch dug into his fortune to make some sacrifice for the upkeep of the new arrivals, and also to secure support from Agrippa, seeing that Uri was his confidant.

Uri said nothing.

Julius acknowledged that it would be no easy matter, of course, but then again it could not go on as it was.

Uri nodded.

Julius then asked what Uri was up to in Claudius's house.

"I help with the cooking," Uri replied laconically.

Julius could not get over his astonishment.

"A lot of high-ups go there, sir," said Uri. "My place is among the servants."

"But cooking?"

"So it can be guaranteed that Philo and the alabarch's two sons receive food that is ritually clean."

Julius nodded.

If reports are being made about me, thought Uri, and they are surely being made, they must have seen me bustling around next to Kainis at the fireplace.

"So when will Marcus and Berenice be wed?"

It was Iustus's prime duty to report that.

"It's not been made any of my business to know, sir."

Uri's answers were not at all to Julius's liking.

"Before I forget completely," the banker added, "Philo has not been covering your debt for months."

Uri turned pale.

"But he promised me that he would pay half a year in advance!" he howled.

"Well, he didn't," Julius declared. "Press him, my son, and keep your ears open harder in Claudius's house in case any tidbit of interest to us comes your way from the servants. You do realize, of course, that we could move three or four refugee families in with yours."

Uri said nothing.

THE OVATION TOOK PLACE, WITH THE EMPEROR RIDING INTO ROME IN the presence of the dignitaries, though not of Uri. The emperor's third wife, Caesonia, had given birth to a girl to whom he gave the name Drusilla in memory of his late sister: he took the infant up to the Capitoline and placed her on the knee of Jupiter, entrusting her to the care of Minerva. He himself, he ordered, had to be referred to as "Jupiter" in the official documents.

At the beginning of his rule he had strictly forbidden that images of him be produced, but now, the story went, he himself had begun sculpting, and the leading Greek master sculptors gushed what a marvelous feel he had.

He took it into his head now to make it a capital offense to have been amused or bathed during the period of public mourning at his sister Drusilla's demise. There were retrospective reports a-plenty, and heads rolled.

Two shrines to the emperor were constructed as well, one voted on by the Senate, the second he himself had built on the Palatine, not far from Claudius's house: "So Claudius does not have far to walk," it was said. It was well known that with his lame leg Claudius rarely walked and had himself taken everywhere by litter. It was also said that Caligula's house on the Capitoline would soon be completed. He had his palace annexed to the temple to Castor and Pollux so that their statues should stand guard over the entrance. He also decided to construct yet another temple next to the Temple of Jupiter, and to have Phidias's statue of Zeus transported there from Olympia, remodeled with his own likeness. A vast ship intended to bring the statue was built (another huge boat was constructed to bring the obelisk from Egypt), but it was caught in a storm and sank, so the emperor ordered that the statue be copied in Rome.

To celebrate the landing of the obelisk the Far Side warehouses were rebuilt and tidied up, at least externally; all Rome jostled for a place there, though Uri stayed at home to sort out the source materials for the twelfth volume of Claudius's history of the Etruscans. Sarah and Hagar went off to the riverbank and on their return babbled on about what a marvelous column the obelisk was. It was going to be trundled on rollers to the Circus Maximus and set up in front of that. Had Uri seen any columns when he was in Egypt? He replied that he had not, as he had never visited the country. The women were confused and Uri suddenly understood that they thought of Egypt as a single city like Rome or Alexandria—a city consisting of districts like Far Side in Rome.

Uri's second son was premature. At Hagar's request he was named Marcellus. He looked exactly like her as well, with his round, flat, and witless features. Uri went along with the name but did ask her why she'd settled on that in particular; Hagar answered that it was because it was Latin and meant warrior. Uri sighed: his wife did not know one word of Latin, so how would she happen to know what Marcellus meant? He quietly noted that if anything its meaning lay closer to "feeble" or "drooping," but Hagar shook her head: no, she had been told that Marcellus came from Mars, and it meant a warrior.

If the child were to take after his mother, then a lot of grief would come to this Marcellus.

Theo, by contrast, was marvelous: fair-haired, blue-eyed, and even though he didn't talk yet he seemed to understand everything, and he adored chuckling.

Uri just prayed that the boy's eyesight would stay sharp; hopefully the German or Gaul from whom he had inherited the eye-color was also eagle-eyed.

Caligula announced that he was going to travel to Alexandria, an old dream of his, but then he stayed in Rome after all because the twenty-third of September marked the birthday of Deified Augustus and the beginning of a week-long Augustalia, which he could not miss. All delegations in Rome were invited. By now completely recuperated, Agrippa was keen to see the gladiators slaying one another and the wild beasts, and he made arrangements for Philo and the alabarch's sons also to be allowed to go to the Circus.

Philo now promised to cover the interest on Uri's debt for one whole year, not just six months, and sent him off with a letter to deliver to Isidoros. Uri was astonished to be the one chosen.

"Who else should I send?" Philo retorted. "He was your gymnasiarch; it won't attract any attention."

The two were cooking something up.

Isidoros lived at the eastern end of the old Forum in a tiny, old house on the Via Sacra, famed for its goldsmiths, with a jeweler working in half of the building. He took the letter, broke the seal and held it at a distance, throwing his head back before shaking his head resignedly: he couldn't make it out so he requested Uri read it aloud. Uri did so. Philo was inquiring whether Isidoros happened to know of any book collection in Rome where he might get access to the works of Archilocus.

The letter covered nothing more.

Isidoros shook his head; he had no time for reading in recent years, and he had no knowledge of Rome.

"Do you want to dictate an answer?"

Isidoros declined.

"You can say as much," he declared.

There was a silence. Uri would have quite liked to chat with the former head of his school, and it seemed Isidoros was not against it either. They said nothing.

After some reflection, Isidoros broke the silence: "Tell him that Caligula is planning to sail to Alexandria in the winter."

Uri was astounded.

"In between he is going to make many pronouncements that he is setting off soon," said Isidoros. "He will keep on repeating that and putting it off to the point that no one believes he is actually preparing to go. But Caligula is very cunning; it would be a mistake to underestimate him. There is a space of a few days around the middle of January when it is somewhat less risky than usual to set sail in winter. It will be organized so that ships are standing by in Brindisium to make the voyage to the Greek coast, but Caligula will not be going on them. Meanwhile a decrepit-looking merchant ship will arrive in Ostia—he'll travel with that, with no accompanying flotilla, straight to Alexandria. If I'm still alive, I'll give a signal when the ship arrives; if I happen no longer to be living, keep your ears to the ground for word that a man called Apollonius of Tyana, an Egyptian soothsayer, has appeared in the emperor's entourage."

Musing further, Isidoros added:

"Caligula is dangerous," he said, "not out of political premeditation, I don't think, but genuinely dangerous. It's incredible how a man as cunning and calculating as he is can be so faint-hearted; he's boundlessly insecure. He is seeking to prove, to himself first and foremost, that he is able to successfully confront even Poseidon."

Uri shivered.

"I think," Isidoros said, "that Alexander the Great may well have been a similarly uptight, unfortunate, pocket-sized tyrant. He was oppressed by his father's greatness, oppressed by Aristotle's greatness, oppressed by his midget size, and that's why he threw himself into his lunatic military ventures, which, quite by chance, happened to work out."

"Who should I give that message to?" Uri asked.

Isidoros again pondered.

"To Tija," he said finally. "Let him decide who to pass it on to, but he mustn't forget: it's a message from me."

Isidoros appeared to be weary. Uri watched him. Isidoros smiled and recited:

> *You despised us giddy-goat Jews, Isidoros;*
> *Now God has His own back by resurrecting you, along with us.*

Uri almost broke into tears as he was so honored.

Isidoros shook his head.

"There in the tavern at the time I did not notice that the caesura in the hexameters is not observed. You should correct that when you get a chance."

IT IS NOT DONE TO INFORM ON ONE'S BREAD-GIVER, EVEN IF ONE TAKES side against him and is in agreement with those who have been robbed. Uri did not keep his ears open. He passed on to Philo the request Julius had made, and Philo sighed; he too was taken by the wretched fates of the many immigrants, indeed it was with their interests in mind that the delegation was doing all it could with the emperor. There needed to be a full restitution of the rights of the Jews of Alexandria, then the immigrants could go back to their homes.

"It's not worth trying to press Agrippa; he's got no money," said Philo. "Up until now he has been living off credit; he has hardly any revenue from his kingdom, and he was only given Galilee a short while ago. Once he is granted Judaea, that will be the time to turn to him."

Philo also promised that he really would make Uri's loan payments for one year in advance.

Caligula spent his time attending competitions, and the Jewish delegation followed suit. The senators and knights of the equestrian order idled away their days at the Hippodrome or at the Diribitorium, if the sun was particularly severe. There instead of outside in the amphitheater, they could organize fights in the Diribitorium, which was covered with canvas and furnished with benches, and they even stretched a canvas roof over the Forum. The reason for their idling was because Caligula would turn up at whatever time his fancy dictated and if he found that any one of the nobles was not there, be it dawn or late in the evening, he would take revenge. It became customary for the Senators to wear a cap, Thessalian fashion, to avoid distress from the sun's rays, and Caligula permitted them to set their behinds upon cushions instead of the bare boards.

One day there were not enough prisoners who had been condemned to die by being cast before the wild animals, so the emperor looked around the upper rows and had some of the spectators picked out of the crowd and led away, their tongues sliced off so that they could not yell out. All were devoured by the animals.

Among the charioteers he was strongly attached to the party that wore the green, which was also called the Party of the Leek, and hated all the others. He no longer drove a chariot himself as he had done two years before, but even today the place where he used to practice was named the Gaianum, after him.

Uri had a slight breather as he was not invited to the races and was able to get on with his own business affairs. He raced around the city, which carried on with its normal daily business, until he came to the realization—something his father had never been able to see—that it was not worth seeking out merchants in their homes, walking seven or eight miles a day; it was simpler for him to arrange all his transactions at the Forum, because anyone who had any business at all worth mentioning would eventually put in an appearance.

There they made deals and gossiped about actors, charioteers, and gladiators as they had always done; they were far from affairs of state and Uri had a strong suspicion that more than one of his business partners had no idea who happened to be the current emperor.

That warm autumn many people met far from pretty ends.

Caligula had Sextus Papinius—whose father, Anicius Cerealius, had been a senator and was an ex-consul—tortured and put to death, though nobody ever found out what he had been charged with.

Titius Rufus took his own life after being charged with having declared that the members of the Senate were cowardly.

Scribonius Proculus was heard daring to criticize the emperor whereupon the others who were present in the Senate, so it was said, surrounded their fellow senator and tore him to pieces.

Calvisius Sabinus, a former legate to Pannonia, and his wife committed suicide before standing trial. Caligula, possibly recalling the heroism of his own mother Agrippina, could not stand the thought that Sabinus's wife had visited some military outposts and had done sentry duty, so sentenced her to death. Sabinus's crime, on the other hand, had been buying slaves—one to know Homer by heart, another to know Hesiod, and a special slave for each of the nine lyric poets.

Carrinus Secundus was banished because an informer claimed he had made a comment about the emperor.

Protogenes, one of Caligula's slaves, used to walk around with two large books to the Senate's sessions even though under the law non-senators should not have been present in the room; in the books were bound each and every denunciation that senators and knights of the equestrian order had sent to Tiberius during the emperor's rule. At the beginning of his reign Caligula had pretended ceremonially to have these burned but they had, strangely, survived, or perhaps it was only copies that had been burned, or else these were copies, though they were authenticated by the Sphinx used already by Augustus on his seal, and on the basis of these documents Caligula sentenced to death or exile those at whose fortune his mouth watered, and the Senate tolerated it.

One night, upon returning from an orgy, very lightly dressed and in sandals, and being noticed by a group strolling into the garden on Vatican Hill, the emperor had them all—men and women alike—slaughtered, and that same night his murderers searched out the relatives of the dead and murdered them too.

Betilienus Bassus was kept in the stocks for two days and then tortured to death, first in a violin and then on the horse. The violin was a crafty system of ropes, constructed so a person struggling to get free would instead strangle himself, whereas the horse was a variant of impalement on a stake—both awful ways of dying. Betilienus Bassus had been the emperor's personal *quaestor*, and there was no way of knowing what had caused Caligula to be angry at him. He forced the man's father, Betilienus Capito, to be present at his son's execution. Capito asked to be allowed to shut his eyes, whereupon Caligula ordered him to be slain likewise. Capito tried to save himself by saying that he would uncover a conspiracy and he named some of Caligula's closest cronies, including Callistus and even Caesonia, the emperor's wife; nonetheless he was also executed.

One of the alleged conspirators whom Caligula did have liquidated was Julius Canus, a friend with whom he had fallen out. The story went that up to the moment of his execution the condemned was calmly playing chess. He went to his execution saying that he would make his next move from the hereafter.

None of these things was much discussed in the Forum: people had more important matters to talk about: they simply did deals and litigated. Nor were they touched on in Claudius's house, just as the imprisoned alabarch was not mentioned. Uri learned many things from Philo and, exceptionally, Tija, who nowadays occasionally deigned to converse with him. Tija was interested in the mood on Far Side, and Uri reported detachedly, without any display of emotion, on the wretchedness faced by the newcomers.

Uri showed up in Claudius's house as little as possible, more particularly only at times when Philo requested him; he had no wish to see Kainis.

Visitors made their appearances at Claudius's house much as before, though Uri sensed there had been some subtle changes, though perhaps that was only because he knew full well that something was up. Claudius had lost weight and looked pale. He personally attributed it to the fact that the continual Circus attendances meant that he was not getting adequate sleep. It was true that he would keep nodding off in the rows given over to senators in the Circus, and on those occasions he would be pelted with fruit and pebbles by his infantile aristocratic neighbors or the even more infantile plebes in the upper rows.

Agrippa also made appearances with his servants at Claudius's place, with Stentorian-voiced, ruddy-faced Sabinus, the elder brother of Titus, greeting the king like an old friend, roaring in Greek:

"Damn that province! You'll only rot there! Come back to Rome! This is your home!"

Agrippa chuckled.

Uri noticed that Agrippa was not on speaking terms with Claudius. They had been boyhood friends because Antonia had been on good terms with Agrippa's mother, Berenice, who was Salome's daughter and thus a niece of Herod the

Great. Since Herod had his son, Berenice's husband, Aristobulus, strangled to death, she wanted at all costs to live in Rome. Claudius and Agrippa had grown up together; they had shared the same teachers, yet nevertheless they no longer engaged in conversation with each other in public.

Claudius had no need to address Agrippa: all necessary communications were seen to by their servants. Uri was certain that Tija had passed on Isidoros's message to the king, and he in turn to Claudius. He wondered with which members of the Senate Claudius had discussed it. Innumerable people swilled and guzzled at Claudius's house, with gangs of them arriving from contests or baths and then disappearing in gangs bound somewhere else. If Caligula were to make an escape to Alexandria, that would mean civil war; Rome would lose its most important province, famine would break out, and sooner or later Hispania, Gaul, Moesia, and Pannonia would also secede, to say nothing of ever-unreliable Germania.

Did the senators still wish to have a vast Roman world empire?

Every two or three weeks Caligula announced that this time he really was setting sail for Alexandria, yet he stayed in Rome, just as Isidoros had said.

An increasingly tubby Messalina wearied the company by relating each day that she was sacrificing to another god that at long last she might bear a son, and she was given plenty of good advice on which gods she should sacrifice to.

Writings by Cordus were circulated and hotly debated, because Cordus, in his own cautious manner, had propounded the advantages of a Republican form of government instead of an autocracy. Seneca, the pale, constantly coughing praetor, had on one occasion even brought along Marcia, Cordus's daughter; she and her husband, Metilius, were greeted with great respect. It was out of love for his daughter, it was said, that Cordus had opted not to open a vein to kill himself but rather starved himself to death.

"You're avoiding me," Kainis challenged Uri.

Uri looked at her and felt an enormous pang in his stomach.

"I'm avoiding you," he said and staggered off.

As the emperor stayed in Rome for the Saturnalia, senators, knights of the equestrian order, and embassies were also unable to depart. Vows now only had to be taken to Augustus, Caligula, and Drusilla, not to Tiberius, Agrippina, and Julia, but even after that holiday nobody could go away because mid-January marked the commencement of the games on the Palatine, in which anyone who was anybody had to take part.

It was nighttime when torchbearers came to order Uri from his place in bed next to Hagar. Philo had made no demands on his services for two whole days, on both of which Uri had rushed to and fro from early morning till late at night; he had a feeling that people were looking to cut him out of the trade in balsam, and at the time he had no other source of income. The unfamiliar torchbearers claimed that King Agrippa had summoned him, and they ordered him to put on his best set of clothes. Uri dressed hastily, with Hagar moaning, Sarah snoring, and Marcellus sleeping; Theo propped himself on one elbow on the floor, where he had been moved once his younger brother was born. Uri placed a finger on his lips to make a silent plea to keep quiet; Theo had nodded mutely and kept staring with interest as he watched the light of the torches recede.

Fortunatus was waiting outside Honoratus's house.

"We're going to the games," he said.

Fortunatus, the thickset, bucktoothed, snub-nosed middle-aged man with receding red hair who attended to Agrippa's affairs in Rome, seemed depressed.

They sat in a litter, with four servants carrying them, and were whisked over the Jewish bridge.

"What's this all about?" Uri asked.

He got no response from Fortunatus.

Uri had the feeling that he had already been through something similar before. He tried to recollect when that had been. It had been in Jerusalem, he finally realized, when he was taken to dine with Pilate, but that time there had been no one sitting opposite him in the litter.

The Palatine palace comprised several buildings of various sizes and shapes on the hillside, the structures interconnected by passages and colonnades and each given its own name. The travelers were set down at the back, where slaves were already unloading a shipment of fresh food. Fortunatus knew the way; he had clearly accompanied Agrippa there many times before, and with a torch in one hand he hastened ahead down the winding corridors, with Uri after him. At some places sentries asked for the password, which Fortunatus gave as "Jupiter," at which they were allowed to go farther.

At the head of a staircase, Fortunatus suddenly switched to saying something else: "One more," and there that watchword got them through.

They reached an exit; here Fortunatus stopped and looked down.

Uri squinted.

It was growing light. They were standing on the roof of a temporary timber theater on the eastern flank of the hill, with rows of seats set out in semicircles below. It was the Palatine theater, which was constructed every year in mid-January in Augustus's honor and then pulled down again when the games were over. The building of the temporary theater was a well-paying job, with entrepreneurs ready to kill to get the business. Between the theater stage and the audience stood a square block whose function Uri was unable to divine.

"We'll wait here," said Fortunatus.

Uri's stomach rumbled.

"Quiet!" enjoined Fortunatus.

A few sentries were loafing in the theater; Uri felt weak in his legs from hunger but he did not dare squat down on his heels.

After a while some servants materialized with fresh cushions, gave them a thorough patting, and placed a tray laden with with wine and water, fruit and cold meat beside each cushion. Uri's stomach and throat were gnawing with hunger. Dancers who were not yet wearing costumes now sauntered out onto the far side of the stage; musicians were loafing about, grabbing a bite to eat, plucking strings, yawning. Uri snuck back to the wall by the entrance, leaned back, and slept with his eyes open; Fortunatus said nothing.

It was well into the morning by the time the theater filled with notables, who, accompanied by bodyguards and wives and children, searched for their places, chatted, and set about eating. Screw his eyes up as he might, instead of faces Uri could only discern lighter and darker blotches as he glanced to either side. Fortunatus's face was nearby and showed tense attention. Perhaps Agrippa would come by here, and he was after something, Uri pondered, but Agrippa did not come.

Caligula, his wife and, in her arms, his daughter took to the stage as if they were actors. The senators rose to their feet to applaud and cheer, and it was at this that Uri realized it was the emperor. Caligula, the figure dressed in the purple-edged toga, even took a bow before bounding into the imperial box over which a canvas canopy had been stretched. Grandees jumped onto the stage and assisted Caesonia down, the sleeping infant in her arms. The number of bodyguards at the entrances grew, with two now placed at the one where Uri was standing, one of them fairly normal in appearance, though grim in features, the other, however, was distinctly odd, wearing a long cloak and having what seemed to be a very short torso. He was rocking on his legs, and Uri noticed that he was wearing footwear with elevated soles, that was what made his figure look so peculiar, as if he were going about in buskins. He said something to the other officer in a surprisingly high-pitched voice; the other responded with a gruff grunt. Fortunatus looked at them, and they at him, and although they exchanged no words, Uri had the feeling that Fortunatus knew who they were.

All the spectators again rose to their feet, and Uri could see nothing so he stood on tiptoe. Some priestly figure was fiddling around at the stone block.

Uri peered and could make out on the forehead a band of the ribbon that gave priests immunity from taxes and legal obligations. A four-legged animal was brought and laid on the block of stone. Uri now grasped that he was watching some sort of ceremony: at the start of every day of the Games a sacrifice was offered to Divus Augustus. It was a spectacle which was strictly forbidden to him, as a Jew, but then again Fortunatus was also present and he too was Jewish. I saw much the same in Jerusalem and now I am seeing it in Rome, it ran through his mind, and he smiled. A chanting was heard from a chorus. Uri could not see how the priest dispatched the animal. Now the public chanted something—Uri could not make out the words—before contentedly taking their seats.

Then servants emerged in the upper tiers and tossed killed birds into the crowd. People jumped up, senators and knights in just the same fashion as the plebs, snatching for and squabbling over the rare birds, each carcass probably worth a small fortune, feathers flying and floating around, children and women screaming. As Uri saw it, Caligula popped his head out from under the canopy and gazed up delightedly at the wrangling. Gradually the spectators calmed down, musicians and dancers came on, and the day's games commenced.

Someone among the spectators sitting in the upper tiers said:

"The emperor has added a few days!"

In other words (or so Uri took it), that day would normally have been the last day of the games but Caligula had prolonged the feast.

He saw only the multiple, blurred outlines of the dancers, but the music was not unpleasant.

After them a man came out leading two immense white beasts. The public whooped and hollered, and Uri screwed his eyes: they were white bears of an immense size and were led in free, without any restraints, and then reared up on their hind legs and danced around in time with the music. The public applauded. The sound of an infant crying was heard somewhere down below—possibly the emperor's baby daughter, Drusilla. A golden potty was brought, and the empress got her daughter to pee into it, which was of greater interest to the crowd than the bears as they leapt to their feet once more. Uri took a few paces forward in order to peek between shoulders and heads, but was only able to get a glimpse of the canvas canopy. He stepped back and looked at Fortunatus, who seemed to be angry, bit his lips, and said nothing.

Uri leaned against the wall again, allowing himself to be lulled by the music, and in fact he did drop off to sleep with the thought that it was better to nap when one was hungry than to stay awake.

He awoke to someone shaking him by the shoulder.

The dancers were still twirling down below. It must have been past noon. He looked around: Fortunatus was still standing, paying attention to the stage, but the two officers were no longer there. Uri's stomach was rumbling loudly, Fortunatus snarled at him.

"Sorry!" Uri muttered.

In the upper tiers and down below, to the extent that Uri was able to see with any tolerable clarity, the spectators were stretched out, eating, drinking, chatting. Large trays lay on the benches, half-full or still full of all kinds of delectables. The nearest big brass tray was lying just five paces away on the floor of the semicircle of the upper aisle; all he needed to do was step over, snatch up something in the blink of an eye, and step back. No one would notice.

Uri marveled at how he could feel so famished: he had gone hungry for days, even weeks on end not so long ago, two and a half years earlier to be exact, and he had eaten a normal supper the previous evening. He must be getting soft, he thought, but all the same his hunger was suspicious. Maybe his nerves were getting to him.

Today the emperor would be assassinated.

He was staggered that such a thought should come to mind. He looked around. Spectators were unconcernedly chortling and nibbling, some even snoring at full stretch; children were plucking out feathers from the carcasses of birds, throwing them up in the air and squealing as they floated down.

He wondered if among the spectators could be found Apollonius, the Egyptian soothsayer to whom Isidoros had referred.

It was now that he became fully awake. He took another glance at Fortunatus, who was leaning resolutely against the wall, his lips clenched tightly.

It must have been past the sixth hour of the day once the musicians suddenly stopped. A pantomime in Greek was then performed, with the leader of a troupe of thieves being crucified for some reason, dripping lavish quantities of artificial blood as the soldiers prodded his hanging body. Floods of artificial blood had likewise flowed in Alexandria when the murderers in Jewish masks had hacked Dionysus to bits in the theater, and Uri was curious as to whether the bandit chief would be resurrected in the same way as Dionysus had recovered, and stuck together the various severed limbs, but at this point the performance was interrupted. The spectators also went quiet. A figure was springing upward, from row to row, like a lurching gazelle. The emperor. The spectators swiveled to look. The emperor was striving to reach the exit by which Uri and the others were leaning on the wall, and he raced past them.

"Let's go," Fortunatus muttered.

Uri followed him.

Bodyguards peeled themselves off the wall and hurried after the emperor. He raced along the corridor and turned left. The room was crowded with elaborately dressed children, some fighting with wooden swords, others rolling on the ground. Upon seeing the emperor, their leader, a gangly young man, commanded them to pay their respects, at which the children lined up. Caligula inspected them, casting a fond eye over their ranks.

"The anthem!" shouted the gangly figure.

He hummed the starting note, and on a count of his raised hands the children launched into the song.

Standing among the bodyguards at the back, Uri noticed that they included the buskin-wearing officer and the other.

It all happened in a flash of a second: the figure in buskins smashed a fist into the back of the emperor's neck and yelled "To it!" The other sprang in front of the dazed emperor and slipped a dagger into his belly. Caligula slumped to the ground; the figure in buskins kicked him in the jaw.

"I'm still alive!" the emperor yelled.

Screaming, the children scattered in all directions. The gangly figure yelled "Back!"

At this point the mass of the bodyguards joined in the killing, roaring:

"One more! One more!"

Guardsmen of the Germanic corps and litter bearers, poles in hand, rushed in and clashed with the Latin bodyguards. Squads of them were cut down. Some senators also attacked from the rear, and several of them too were cut down. The majority of the Germanic guardsmen ran into the theater without spotting the corpse of the slain emperor.

"Follow him before he's burned!" Fortunatus bellowed and raced away.

Uri was rooted to the spot; he did not understand.

He then stepped back, his heart pounding. A woman ran in with a child in her arms but a centurion stabbed her; another grabbed the infant from her and dashed its head against a wall until it had become mere tatters of flesh. Blood spattered over the wall. So much blood from such a tiny child.

Uri was transfixed, standing stock-still, not knowing what he was supposed to do. Who was he supposed to be following? Who was going to be burned? He came to the realization that Fortunatus could only have meant Caligula's dead body. Once that was burned then the emperor would be dead for sure. Obviously that was what he had to report to Agrippa.

The three corpses lay there. Many people came to stare. The assassins had vanished. Spectators jostled in the corridor, some running one way, others in the opposite direction. Then they too dwindled. Four or five bodyguards were left by the bodies, standing there, not one knowing what to do, waiting for orders.

A soldier appeared at the other end of the room, at the foot of a staircase, dragging someone down after him.

"I don't want it! I don't want it!" Claudius wailed.

Uri stepped forward before coming to a stop. What would he be able to do, one solitary figure without a weapon?

Some guardsmen were aiding the soldier.

"He was hiding on a terrace of the Hermaeum!" the soldier shouted. "I've found him! I noticed his feet sticking out from the curtains hanging before the door!"

"Let's take him! Carry him!"

Claudius was grabbed by arms and legs, but the old man was heavy and they were unable to lift him.

"I don't want it!" screeched Claudius.

"Imperator! We're swearing an oath of loyalty to you, don't you see that?" the soldier yelled. The others stopped.

"Are we taking an oath of loyalty?"

"Claudius is emperor!" yelled the soldier.

"Claudius is emperor! Claudius is emperor!"

They hoisted the flailing Claudius onto their shoulders.

"I don't want it! I've already said so: I don't want it!" he squealed.

"To the camp with him!"

"To the camp!"

Five of them carried the protesting Claudius.

The dead bodies were also picked up and carried out, with Uri hurrying behind. They got to an internal courtyard where a small pyre had already been built, with more branches of wood still being added. Caligula's body was dropped on this, with his wig now slipping off. The pyre was now lit with a torch, and flames were soon licking the corpse.

They watched in silence, respectfully, as it burned before a centurion snapped:

"There's not much wood. We'll burn him later on, outside!"

The half-charred corpse was tossed onto a cart, his wife and the remaining tatters of the five-month-old daughter on top, and then hauled out of the yard.

URI GOT TO AGRIPPA'S HOUSE WITHOUT MISHAP.

Everyone was there but Claudius, whom they had learned had been taken to the guards' barracks beyond the Porta Nomentana.

"He's in a good place there," Agrippa asserted.

Sabinus, the corpulent, ruddy-faced prattler, declared that the consuls, Sentius and Secundus, had occupied and closed the Forum and the Capitol. Titus had it on good authority that immediately before doing so they had transferred the funds from the treasuries to the Capitol. Fortunatus reported that all of Caligula's images and statues throughout the city had been torn down and smashed. Valerius Asiaticus, an ex-consul, was quoted as exclaiming: "I only wish I had killed him!" They also recalled one of Caligula's notorious sayings: "How I wish all you Romans had only one neck to throttle!" in retorting "He had but one neck, but many hands throttled him!"

The Senate had convoked by then.

The Germanic guards were apparently still in the theater, having closed all exits, believing that the emperor was still there somewhere, and would let no one out.

Agrippa nodded.

"We'll have to wait a few days," he said. "It's likely that before the day is out the Republic will be reinstated and the killers will be rewarded, but by tomorrow they will be in such great conflict that as far as they are concerned anyone at all will do as emperor!"

Uri was amazed at this pudgy, soft man. A widely experienced politician, Agrippa was smiling mockingly.

"They might even elect Vicinianus," said a strong, serious man. "He is well-respected."

"That's precisely the problem, prefect," said Agrippa. "They don't want a strong emperor over them if the Republic does not work. Vicinianus is too powerful a personality."

The serious man (undoubtedly Sanguinius Maximus, the consular prefect who had also been privy to Caligula's assassination) shook his head.

"Enough, gentlemen!" Agrippa exclaimed. "Everybody considers Claudius a halfwit! He's the only man in Rome whom no one fears! We just have to wait and see."

Sabinus proposed that a delegation be sent to the Senate.

"Let's at least spy and see how the land lies!"

Agrippa shook his head.

"There's no need."

Sabinus was agitated and fearful.

"We still need a few more of the Praetorian Guard," he said. "We haven't got everyone on our side yet!"

Agrippa waved that aside.

"I told Claudius to offer all the guardsmen fifteen thousand sesterces. Provided Claudius doesn't forget, that'll win them over, but he's so scared that he won't forget!"

"Where is Claudius going to get hold of that much money?" Marcus queried in amazement.

Agrippa grinned broadly:

"From you."

CASSIUS CHAEREA WAS THE BUSKINED OFFICER WITH THE HIGH-PITCHED voice who had been the first to lay hands on Caligula, and Cornelius Sabinus was the first to stab him. The Senate acknowledged their imperishable merits and enshrined these in law. There was furious argument in the Senate over who had been the author of the tyrannicide, with yesterday's cowards all competing. Others, such as Aemilius Regulus and Annius Minucianus, had also had the idea of slaying Caligula but Chaerea had beaten them to the punch. Papinius and Clemens alleged that Chaerea had initiated them too in the plan, while Chaerea said that Callistus, Caligula's freed slave, had also assisted, whereupon the Senate decided that Callistus could retain the fortune he had raked together, with the rumor going around that Chaerea would be getting at least a half of Callistus's wealth.

Once the soldiers of the Germanic corps learned that their efforts in locking those many hundreds of people in the theater were too late to be of service they became exasperated and slew a lot of innocent spectators.

Things then happened just the way Agrippa had said they would: after they'd won over the Praetorian Guard the Senate elected Claudius emperor, and on his orders Chaerea was executed as a regicide whereas Cornelius Sabinus took his own life.

The story went that Chaerea, otherwise a placid man, had endured years of teasing by Caligula, who had constantly addressed him, owing to his falsetto voice, as his "peasant girl," referring to his supposed effeminacy when there was no doubt over his gender, and commonly giving the watchwords "Venus" and "Priapus" when he was on duty.

Uri considered that to be quite credible. If Caligula had avoided making that sort of mistake, then presumably he would have made good his escape and the Roman Empire would have broken up.

Indeed, there had been ships standing by at Brindisium (the Senate's emissaries had already organized their burning) and just one solitary trading vessel which was beyond suspicion had set off from Ostia for Alexandria. The tale told about Apollonius, the Egyptian soothsayer, was that he had arrived in Rome that very day because he had prophesied Caligula's death would occur on January 24, and the emperor had been of a mind to have him executed but had been assassinated himself before that could be done. The soothsayer never came forward, and it was assumed he had escaped, but Uri suspecting that his name had more likely been a password rather than that of a real person.

Claudius freed the alabarch, enrolled Marcus and Tija in the equestrian order, and gave the rank of consul to Agrippa, even permitting him to make his maiden speech in the Senate in Greek. He went on to bestow Judaea on him, thus restoring Herod the Great's kingdom. Agrippa's elder brother, Herod, who had been living in Rome all along and took no part in public affairs, was installed by Claudius as a member of the Praetorian Guard, the two of them having presumably been close friends when they were young.

Isidoros and Lampo became new imperial counselors, that being the new emperor's way of thanking them for their outstanding services.

Two weeks after Claudius took power, Messalina gave birth to a son, who was named Germanicus.

Claudius then sent Titus to the Second Legion in Britannia; he left with his family, while Kainis stayed in Rome.

Uri could not work out what Kainis was hoping for by associating with him but, all the same, could not stand not to see her once or twice a week. Through Philo, who wished to expand Agrippa's apologia, with an addition regarding the Alexandrian embassy's maneuvering with Caligula, into a major treatise on virtues for Claudius's edification, and for this he needed Uri, so that Uri continued to be able to visit Claudius's house, the only difference being that the guards thoroughly frisked him to check that he was not concealing a dagger or asp under his cloak. Narcissus in fact gave them an order to let Uri into the house whenever he might come; by now Narcissus's lips were clenched self-importantly tight.

"Are you their boss now?" Uri asked in jest, gesturing toward the guards.

Narcissus did not laugh, though he should have done so; instead he nodded and clenched his jaw even more tightly. Uri was introduced to the guards' reliefs, then a couple of weeks later Narcissus assembled all the visitors, Uri included, in front of the house, and after an increasingly protracted wait he appeared, his eyes narrowed to slits, surveyed the multitude, beckoned to those whom he deemed worthy of being admitted, and whispered in their ear individually the day's password, the rest traipsed dejectedly away. It went through Uri's mind that Narcissus ought to be renamed Cerberus, but he did not mention this to anyone else; a few weeks earlier he would have said it out loud.

"They tolerated anything," Kainis said of the senators, "until Caligula swooped down on them; all hoped that even if fate did not spare the others, it would somehow miss them. But corporately they could not countenance the thought that Alexandria should become the capital city of the empire and Rome a province of Egypt. Now they have settled down and, lords of the world as they are, they are back to their old game of telling tales on each other to the emperor."

She also related that Agrippa had spent a long time persuading Claudius to take over the reins of government, with Claudius desperately balking at first, just as he had later on once the bodyguards hauled him out into the palace and lifted him onto their shoulders. He had no interest in Rome, he had protested to Agrippa; let Italia be a province of Alexandria for all he cared, it deserved no more; let the empire go hang, let every present-day and future empire go hang, just leave him in peace, he wanted at last to be able to live out his own life, there wasn't much left anyway. Agrippa's one strong argument was that now Caligula had been done away with, Claudius and his entire family would otherwise instantly be slaughtered, so it would be better if he were the one doing the killing. Claudius bellowed that he was not going to be anyone's murderer however much people might want that, and in fact he had never agreed with Agrippa's plan; he had desperately tried proposing other candidates for emperor, running through half the Senate and extolling their merits, but Agrippa, Marcus, and the consuls had found all of them unsuitable.

Kainis chuckled; she still liked chuckling, but now she did so more dolefully than before.

"What is it about him that you are still in love with?" Uri asked her bluntly, meaning Titus.

"I don't know," she replied. "He's a selfish beast, but he's clever. He is good to have a laugh with, and that in itself is something."

"He left you, didn't he? What did you hope for? That he would get a divorce and marry you? He already has two sons."

Kainis bit her lips and did not answer.

One afternoon she said to him:

"Come with me."

They went across to Agrippa's house.

Agrippa had by then moved out with his servants: as king of Judaea, Samaria, Galilee, Peraea and Trachonitis, he was now ensconced in Caesarea like the Roman prefects before him. Marcus had gone with him to wed Agrippa's eldest daughter, Berenice. The bridegroom's father, the former alabarch, pale, thin, and now reduced to silence, also went with them, hoping that the climate of Judaea would restore his broken health. Tija sailed back to Alexandria, at Claudius's request, to bring order to the rioting Jews, while Philo alone stayed in Rome.

Kainis took Uri's hand and pulled him into one of the smaller rooms, stopping in front of a bed.

"Here you are!" she said.

Uri trembled.

She pulled off her clothes.

She had a fragrant, frail, delicate body, diminutive with small, pert breasts, a slim waist, her hipbones slightly jutting out under the skin, her thighs long and thin, with soft fluff between them. Uri got to his knees, kissed and stroked her, but he sensed no desire. Kainis lay on her back on the bed and pulled up her legs. Uri kissed her breasts, her neck, her shoulders, her arms, her flat stomach—still nothing. Tears came to his eyes. Kainis stroked his head and neck, kissed his ears, embraced him, and hugged him tight.

"I don't know why I can't," Uri said.

"It doesn't matter," Kainis whispered.

"I've never loved a woman so much before! I just don't understand!"

"It doesn't matter."

"Maybe I'll never again be a full man!"

"Of course you will!" Kainis whispered as she kissed his brow. "Of course you will! The problem's with me. I love you like a twin brother. It's me who needs to be excused."

Tears were by now flooding Kainis's face.

Uri never again went back to Claudius's house, and from then on he also avoided the small room in Agrippa's house.

IN AGRIPPA'S HOUSE HE WORKED ON A ROUGH DRAFT FOR PHILO OF A work about Caligula's transgressions. Philo included many other details, including passages that disparaged Isidoros and Lampo as due warning to Claudius for rewarding, and retaining in his entourage, the Greeks who had betrayed Caligula. Uri also drafted a plan for Claudius's decree restoring to the Jews of Alexandria all rights that had previously been recognized by Augustus and

Tiberius. Philo also added to the fair copy a clause that stated, henceforth, that Jews and Greeks carried equal right of citizenship, but Claudius without comment had this deleted before the proclamation. Even so it was a major achievement, which left Philo beaming and planning further projects.

In Far Side Uri was no longer pestered or called on to spy on his benefactors; it was tacitly understood that their hands would always slip off him, as they would trying to hold a wrestler who had prepared by oiling himself (which was precisely why the practice of oiling was forbidden at the Gymnasium in Alexandria). The big items had been decided: Claudius, Agrippa's childhood friend, had become emperor, Philo had covered the interest payments on Uri's loan one year in advance, and it would not do to touch one of Agrippa's confidants.

All the same, Uri was fearful. Philo's energies did not seem to be diminishing, but his coughing worsened and he had a fever. It may have been malaria, which virtually every stranger to Rome acquired, or maybe something else. If he were to die, there would no longer be anybody supporting Uri, and the elders of Far Side would take their revenge. Not that he had ever done them any harm, but he had found himself close to the center of power, and they would not forgive him for that. It was assumed that he had influence on the emperor, and they believed his connection with Agrippa had remained intact—that was enough for them to make his life impossible.

It was high time to break out of Far Side.

One thing that came to mind was to become a teacher at the Gymnasium in Rome: they paid well, so he would no longer be dependent on Jews. If Apollos could make it as a teacher of rhetoric in Corinth, then perhaps he could find something similar in Rome. He mentioned it to Philo, who was delighted.

"It's a great idea, dear son! You'll be able to carry on my work!"

Uri had no wish to persuade the youth of Rome that the Jewish faith was an ancestor and more perfect version of their own; all he wanted was a livelihood. Still, Philo's delight made him consider the possibility; it seemed he might still feel some twinge of conscience on account of him.

Philo suggested that he look up Isidoros.

Isidoros shook his head.

"I can't intervene on your behalf," he said. "Even as it is I'm accused of being a Jewish stooge. Let the Jews help; there are enough of them."

After numerous tries, Uri managed to get an interview with the director of the Gymnasium. He was a bearded, bristle-haired, burly Greek, a third-rate commentator on Homer, more doltish than even Apion, but then again he always managed to beg, borrow, and steal the money needed for the school's upkeep and thus enjoyed universal esteem. After a brief introduction he returned to studying a scroll, barely glancing at Uri. Uri outlined the purpose of his visit and held out the prospect that if the director wished he could obtain testimonials to his studies on Alexandria, which would take a couple of months to reach Rome.

"That won't be necessary," the director said affably.

Uri also proposed that initially, if need be, he would be willing to offer his teaching services without salary, in the hope of obtaining a future job.

"I have no wish for that sort of thing from anybody," said the director even more affably.

Uri fell silent.

"Things are not yet so bad," the director said, lifting his eyes from the scroll, "that we should have a Jew teaching Greek rhetoric in Rome."

"It happens in Corinth," said Uri, trying his best to swallow the insult.

"Then they must be in a bad way."

Uri paid his respects and left.

Philo did not ask how Uri had done, and he did not say.

Claudius gave an amnesty to all prisoners except for common thieves, reviewing each case personally. He went on to administer justice every day in the Forum, either with the entire Senate or alone, with counselors sitting by; the public was happy to wander by and gawk. Quaestors and praetors accompanied the new emperor whenever the business concerned an investigation of financial affairs, and for doing that he was praised by the people. He had the poisons that he had found in Caligula's effects destroyed, as well as the books of Protogenes, and the freedman was also disposed of to the great relief of many. Claudius's grandmother Livia was deified, and a statue of her was placed in the temple of Augustus; sculptors could again be envied, while in the text of any vow they took women were compelled to mention her too.

Equestrian games were held on Claudius's birthday, August 1, but, because the temple of Mars had been dedicated officially on the same day, the event also marked that anniversary. Claudius objected to being worshiped and prayed to, making efforts to get the number of statues and images in shrines cut down because nowadays there was barely any room for the living, and also abolished many feast days and holidays because so few days were left for work. He was praised for that too, by people who did not work anyway.

Hagar became pregnant again.

That summer Far Side burst into activity: the Alexandrian refugees, who had multiplied in the meantime, thronged onto synagogue pulpits to lash out at the Jewish elders of Rome, cursing them bitterly for being unwilling to get the emperor to back the return to the goods that the Greek rabble had stolen from them, or at least to seek monetary compensation. In the synagogues, with the permission of the archisynagogos, anyone who wished was allowed to speak, and no archisynagogos dared risk provoking a brawl by objecting. Even as it was, a brawl would break out each and every time the indigenous Roman faithful tired of the newcomers' complaints and those would end with the Alexandrian preachers being hauled off the pulpit. In the beginning the quarrels were limited to specific houses of prayer as the elders made an effort to distribute the refugees evenly among all the synagogues, regardless of their place of residence (though the refugees generally lacked that in any case), but as time went by refugees assembled in Far Side's larger spaces to make their demands. The younger hotheads among them pelted the larger houses with stones, while desperate womenfolk lay down in the entrances to houses of the rich, refusing to move out of the way. The elders made some effort to restore order, but as they had no Jewish police force at their disposal they would call out the night watch, who turned out to be just as reluctant to keep the peace as as they were to put out fires, and the situation became so acrimonious that the magistracy sent over officials from Rome proper, but they got nowhere either, as few of them knew even a word of Greek.

Anyone able to do so locked himself in. Uri was not able to do that since he had only a curtain hanging in front of his door. On more than one occasion he returned home to find the house occupied by beggars, indeed whole bands would force their way in, young and old alike displaying their gangrenous legs and ulcerated bellies. Theo would stare with a startled look, Sarah and Hagar scream, Hermia hide away in her recess, while Uri would try to speak to them in a decent tone but to no avail. There was little of any value in the house, but even so any articles that could be carried away were taken, and anything immovable was damaged. The refugees were unaware that Uri had survived the Bane in Delta, and Uri did not bother to mention it, as words seemed to have no effect on them.

Theo had owned an inflatable ball made from a cow's rumen—even that was stolen. Uri promised to buy him a new one, though Theo was glad that the old ball would now belong to a poor child, and even took the view that his next ball also ought to be given to another poor child. A wooden doll with flexible limbs which had belonged to Marcellus also went missing, but he was not yet able to articulate any opinion on this. The womenfolk complained endlessly, moving Uri at first to replace missing pots and pans, carpets and blankets.

He did wonder, though, whether he had seen any of the intruders before in Delta, but of course his eyesight had already been poor then and it had not improved since.

In the autumn the whole matter was passed up to Claudius, who, for simplicity's sake, passed an outright ban on Jews assembling anywhere at all. The night watch was charged with checking that the decree was adhered to.

That was a harsh decision. Jews were not allowed to assemble even in synagogues on the Sabbath or for other feasts. The Jews of Rome had never experienced a blow as severe as this, for even the very first slaves had managed to win for themselves the right to free practice of their religion, and no one since had thrown any doubt on this. The sentinels of the night watch guarded the synagogues, both within and outside Far Side; since no more than three Jews were allowed to enter the building at the same time, there was no longer the possibility of conducting collective public prayers, as at least ten males were required for that. Even at a funeral, in principle, only three family members could be present.

The elders made the rounds of the civic authorities and made appeals to the legal warranty that all Roman citizens were guaranteed freedom to practice their religion, which the officials acknowledged—though at the same time they referred to an obscure ancient law which applied to associations of craftsmen, under which both the Jews and Egyptian faiths were classed. The Jews strenuously protested that their faith was not a craft, but the officials were unmoved.

It was not possible that the Jews of Rome should be left unable to pray to the Lord when they had been praying to Him for two millennia wherever they might be living. The elders then had no choice but to order that the refugees immediately withdraw from Rome, and, because they had no means for enforcing the decision, they asked the civic authorities, those turned to the night watch, and the night watch in turn sought help from the guardsmen.

Carrying Marcellus in his arms, Uri stood at the door of their house, a frightened Theo clinging to his legs, with Sarah, Hermia, and pregnant Hagar shifting from leg to leg in front of them. They saw a long line of Alexandrian refugees, carrying small bundles of possessions on their heads or backs and under an escort of night watch and soldiers, approach the Far Side gate. Marching along were old people, children, women, men, Jews with eyes downcast, fixed on the ground. The Roman Jews stood by, mute and inactive, whether they watched indifferently, or with hostility, or even sympathetically.

"We won't be driven out, will we?" Theo whispered.

"No, not us," Uri replied.

"Not ever?"

"Never."

The refugees filed by in a long row; the civic authorities had promised that they would be escorted to the border not just of Far Side but Rome, and they would not be permitted to return. No one asked what would become of them in Italia: let them make do as best they could.

"If our house were able to swell," Theo whispered, "and it could grow as big as, or even bigger than, Far Side, we would let them stay, wouldn't we?"

"Yes, we would," said Uri.

"Then I'm going to pray that our house should swell," announced Theo determinedly.

Uri held back his tears: his firstborn son was barely three years old yet was already saying things like that. A marvel, he was. He could already count up to sixty and do addition and multiplication, and he had grasped in an instant the principle of squares and within a further five seconds that of deriving a square root. Barely three years old—and he still had a heart!

The elders had reaped a major victory: the public disorder ceased and the Jews of Rome were able to celebrate Rosh Hashanah peacefully in their synagogues.

PHILO BREATHED HIS LAST FOUR YEARS AFTER THE DELEGATION'S arrival in Rome. Life departed unnoticed from his slight body: he shivered slightly and then it was all over. Uri and a servant were with him. Uri called physicians to the bedside and they stuffed herbal remedies into him. Philo was rational to the end and was unwilling to discuss neither illness nor death; he would only talk about how Greek philosophy, for the sake of the poor Greeks, had to be filled with the spirit of the only Everlasting One.

Months before, Uri had written letters to Caesarea and Alexandria, but he got no answer from either Marcus or Tija. By then the alabarch had expired, his health broken by the spell in prison. Then news arrived that Marcus had died unexpectedly and without child. Tija did not reply to his letter but Uri was informed that he was alive. News of the death of his younger brother had reached Philo, but Uri had no wish to add to his sorrows with the news of Marcus's demise.

The young widow, Berenice, did not wait out a year of mourning before marrying her uncle, Agrippa's elder brother, Herod, Claudius's friend, who was vested rule of the kingdom of Chalcis, north of Judaea, that he too have his minute royal territory.

When the seal on Philo's last will and testament was broken, Uri was flabbergasted to learn that Philo had bequeathed him two hundred thousand sesterces; even when he had been sick he had still remembered the size of the debt being carried by his amanuensis. The payments made to date had only covered the interest; now Uri would not only be able to pay back the whole amount of the loan, he would even have a few thousand sesterces left.

Philo loved me like a son, Uri reflected, and he was assailed by remorse. It was true he had taken faithful care of him and had been by his side until he died; he had in fact even been rather fond of him, but he could not say he had loved him. He had recited a blessing for him and made a tear in his own garments, but he had no felt no emotion except pity.

The library that Philo had brought with him and had added to since, together with his manuscripts, Philo willed to Rome's Jewish community. Uri was annoyed that everything would go missing but he did not have the nerve not to carry out Philo's last wish. Nevertheless he made copies of all the works Philo had written in Rome, partly out of respect but also because he had written out the original drafts, and it was only after making the copies that he handed over the library to Honoratus, who was only interested in the statue of Germanicus that had been standing in his house since the fire.

Philo was laid to rest with great pomp, at the expense of the community, by the Appian Way, with many speeches being made during the procession and at the entrance to the catacomb, with nobody failing to sprinkle their eulogy with quotations from Philo. Uri himself was asked whether he wished to speak, but he declined.

Given that Philo had no relatives living in Rome, Uri arranged a funeral banquet in the house that had been built for the delegation, and in which Philo had died. The house was bought by bankers, the banquet paid for out of the selling price, and what remained was paid in to the community *aparchai*. Admittedly, it would have been proper for him also to observe a week of mourning but because he was not a relative this was not expected of him. Uri asked Iustus to put together a list of VIPs, and some fifty prominent members of Rome's Jewish community mourned the great philosopher's passing by eating and drinking an excellent meal.

Uri counted out the sum of his debt into Julius's hand. Julius wrote a receipt and raised his hand over Uri's head in a blessing.

"It's a pity you have managed to repay," the banker chuckled. "We no longer have you in our power!"

"What use was that to you anyway?"

"You never can tell. We're not fond of people who are not debtors. That's also true of people in general—they won't like you for it."

Uri joined in his chuckling.

When it comes down to it, I was able to travel halfway around the world for free, he thought, and only my father died of it.

It then occurred to him that the two hundred thousand sesterces was money that belonged to the Jews of Alexandria.

I have been besmirched.

HAGAR GAVE BIRTH TO A DAUGHTER, THEN TO ANOTHER DAUGHTER.

At that point Uri decided that he would bring a halt to his reproductive functions, and even though Hagar might have objected she chose not to. A tolerable existence came into being: Uri went about his business affairs, Sarah, Hagar, and Hermia managed the household, and the children fulfilled the Lord's will by eagerly growing up.

Each morning Uri would hurry off to his patron with his sportula, and every month he would bring back the food due him given his tessera (though no longer from the Field of Mars but at a new distribution center that had been put up next to the hutments of Far Side, given the growing number of Jews), and what was left of his time he divided between Theo and the Forum. With Theo he acted as teacher, and he did his business in the old Forum, listening to the gossip of the day with pleasure. The womenfolk hardly ever upbraided him. They had a better-than-average living standard in Far Side—much better than at any time in the past, even they could admit that much.

Uri's upper incisors also dropped out, his remaining teeth ached, and his gums often hurt and bled, but there was also a good side: at least this way he was no longer so deplorably bucktoothed as he had been and, as he discovered by accident, through the gap that had been left in their place he was, with the help of his lower lip, able to produce a whistle that sounded like a flute, and indeed he taught himself to whistle two flute lines at once. He got into the habit of whistling to himself in the Forum, and a growing number of people gathered around to listen with amazement, as a result of which more than one business deal came his way that he had not counted on obtaining. He was advised to make an appearance in the Circus or as a musician at the imperial court, but Uri just laughed that off and continued to whistle free of charge for his colleagues.

He enjoyed whistling. He enjoyed recalling melodies that he had heard in Judaea and Alexandria, and he enjoyed figuring out new melodies. He liked amusing others, but most of all he liked whistling to his solitary self, or to the gulls and pigeons as he strolled over the Jewish bridge on his walk home to Far

Side as evening drew in. He was sorry that he could not grow wings like the legendary Kainis, who had flown while being buried.

These were tranquil years: Uri did his business in the Forum with the other traders, buying and selling, signing commissions and paying those who executed them. All this became an everyday routine, of no interest but at least certain, and Theo was growing up by leaps and bounds.

The merchants would turn up at the Forum in the company of their servants, who would set down in writing the more important clauses of the contracts they made. Uri was at last in a position to hire servants but he preferred to jot down his own short notes on scraps of papyrus, which in turn became popular in Rome and started to displace the use of wax tablets. These were reminders, not strictly worded documents, and anyone involved in a deal could have evaded its terms, objecting that no legally enforceable contract existed, and they might even win a lawsuit—but anyone who tried such a thing would have been mercilessly blacklisted by the others, and there were precedents for that.

Life at the Forum and in its surroundings was at its liveliest in the morning and toward dusk, with speakers hoisting themselves onto the Rostra to cheer people up with their views; these were times when Uri chose to flee, having taken a dislike to crowds since Alexandria. From time to time Claudius himself would put in an appearance, whether to administer justice or to deliver a speech publicly (or to be more precise, that his speech be read out by someone while he sat through it in a closed litter). On such occasions Claudius would be besieged by petitioners and Uri would pull back: he had seen Claudius plenty of times before.

There was a lot of gossip about the emperor. When he invited back from exile those whom Caligula had banished, he was praised. Among those who were summoned back were Caligula's older sisters, Agrippina and Julia. He was even praised for bringing back the old name of September for the month of Germanicus. (One joke that made the rounds went: "What was Claudius's older brother called?—'September!'") People thought they knew everything there was to be known about him: he was henpecked, and it was Messalina who wore the trousers and governed Rome; Pallas his cashier and Narcissus his secretary were the real force behind the scenes, and castrated Posides, the one whom he loved best. Uri kept his ears open, but the name Kainis never came up: no one knew of her existence, and it was better that her name was not spread around.

Claudius at last got started on the problem of the overcrowding of the harbor of Ostia, a move that proved very popular. Delegations had already pestered Caligula on the matter but that had been the least of his problems. Now Rome would at last have a usable harbor close by, rather than in faraway Puteoli, and the volume of trade would be even bigger. Uri had enough presence of mind to get in on the expansion of the hutments on the left bank of the Tiber, close to the walls of Far Side. The new harbor was to be be constructed around two miles north of Ostia, and would bear the proud name of Portus Romanus. Preliminary work was already being commenced to accommodate larger ships entering Rome. Uri did not inspect either the site or the materials; that was what engineers were paid for.

By then roughly five years had gone by since he had come ashore on returning home from Alexandria, and he recalled what he had felt then: that he had to conquer Rome. He may not have conquered it, but he had at least to some degree made himself at home there.

It was really the Forum that had become Uri's home, that vast, bustling debating space, which by now had become a true stock market, although people did not know as yet that this was what such a thing should be called. He had his favorite Jewish eating-houses, where he had a regular table, in the alleyways near the Forum, behind the Via Sacra, in the shady Subura district. It was not so much Jews who frequented the places as Greeks, Latini, Persians, Syrians, Gauls, Hispanics, and Ethiopians; the Jews for the most part still did their business in Far Side, though they too had their dealings with the whole world.

In the Forum it did not matter that Uri was Jewish; all that counted was his creditworthiness. On occasions he participated in wagers as to whether or not a commercial item would return, or whether or not some large shipment would reach its destination in time; people liked to make bets, to take risks, and that they did, or played chess and checkers, or they took a siesta early in the afternoon in one of Subura's bustling hostelries and narrow alleys, where the sun never shone.

And they chattered and chattered and chattered. They adored gossiping about charioteers, gladiators, and actors and knew everything there was to be known about them.

Since returning to Rome Uri had not bothered to read a single issue of the *Acta Diurna*. But even so he was well informed about everything he needed to know. In Rome one had to know Rome; the world only mattered from a commercial perspective, and Uri sensed no loss at hearing nothing said about Egypt or Judaea. It crossed his mind to purchase an inn in the neighborhood of the Forum, and in fact he was in a position to do that. He would be concerned primarily with providing a place for his business partners to snooze; he was thinking of a daytime dosshouse of the sort that had not yet been invented, but he rejected the idea as it was not something he could run on his own, and he could not rely on help from the womenfolk.

So, the Forum became home to him, and otherwise his home was with his son Theo, whom he would take out for walks and instruct as they chatted.

By the time he was six Theo had a better knowledge of arithmetic and geometry than Uri had ever possessed, and there were times when he posed questions that Uri was not only unable to answer but did not even fully understand. When that was the case Theo would impatiently lay hands on a twig and would sketch out in one of the puddles of mud—which never completely dried in Far Side even in the summer—what he was talking about, as if he were a pocket Archimedes. Please don't let him be killed by some numbskull mercenary... He was growing into a strong, well-developed boy, who could jump superbly, turn somersaults, and run fast and over long distances, plus he was fair-haired and blue-eyed like a Teutonic god. Uri was constantly offering an earnest prayer, entreating the Creator that Theo's eyes should not fail in his adolescent years.

"With this boy you have compensated me for everything, Lord!" he would murmur softly in the synagogue on the Sabbath, and there he was even permitted to shed a tear or two.

Uri lived as if he had been castrated, and he even began to look the part outwardly: he put on weight, his legs hurt; he ate more and more, and he drank more and more, especially beer, which enabled him to burp loudly and relieve the continual biting, burning pain in his chest. In the market one could purchase metal mirrors, and Uri would sometimes pick one up as if he were thinking of buying it (he never did, neither for himself nor for Hagar, even though she asked him for one) and would take a look at himself. He had turned into a balding, broadly jowled, double-chinned, clean-shaven, slit-eyed figure, with a lower jawline that was barely visible and an upper one badly sunken due to the loss of his teeth. Ugly enough, in fact, to be elected emperor.

Still, there were plenty of businessmen in the Forum who were even uglier customers, and more generally: such was this era of peace that nearly everyone was overweight.

There was no war. Claudius traveled to make war in the far-off country of Britannia as there was no chance of a quarrel closer to hand. Vitellius stood in for him in Rome; he did not make any laws and did not make decisions, and he would still always prostrate himself before Claudius seat, just as he had done previously before Caligula's seat. Supposedly Claudius won some sort of victory in Britannia, at which point he changed his son's name from Germanicus to Britannicus. He was praised in the Forum; it was peace in their time. Big celebrations were held in both theaters, with ten chariot races every day, and in the intermissions bears and other wild beasts were slain—a great many of them, three hundred bears alone—and athletes competed.

One of Claudius's daughters, Claudia Octavia, was betrothed to Lucius Junius Silanus, the other, Claudia Antonia, was married to Gnaeus Pompeius, but Claudius did not let the event be celebrated with any particular fuss as the Senate was in session that day and he was present in the chamber. Both sons-in-law quickly became prefects. He restored to Pompeius the cognomen "Magnus," of which Caligula had stripped him.

Claudius began to dress in the Greek fashion, wearing a cloak and high boots, and at the Gymnasium's competitions he dressed in a purple coat and wore a golden crown. Uri was displeased upon hearing news like that. The emperor was praised because he did not ask others for contributions toward the competitions but paid for them himself. He passed one especially upright law forbidding anyone who had a dependent from naming the emperor as his heir, and he handed back fortunes that Tiberius and Caligula had taken away.

He then did something stupid, banning taverns in which unduly large crowds assembled, and also forbade them to sell roast meat or hot water (which was the name for mulled wine). People grumbled and Uri fumed inwardly: never mind the meat but one did not forbid Romans their favorite drink of hot water. There was no way of enforcing that anyway!

Claudius returned the various statues that Caligula had collected from other towns, but the people were not happy even about that: if the gods had so decided once that the statues should be brought to Rome, then they should stay there!

Next Julia, the emperor's niece and a granddaughter of Tiberius, was banished, supposedly because Messalina was jealous of her beauty and feared she might be replaced as Claudius's wife, and hoarse Seneca was also banished, still unable to die but still delivering speeches that were far too clever for his own good.

The emperor put on ever more gladiatorial contests, with relatively few wild beasts being sacrificed but with many human victims—people who, it turned out, had allegedly been squealers to Tiberius or Caligula. The statue of Augustus that had stood in the Circus Maximus was taken away so that it did not have to survey the ceaseless bloodshed. Though Rome's population was amused, Uri began to think that maybe it was time to get away.

Then the emperor settled accounts with Gaius Appius Silanus, the man who had wed Messalina's mother. Claudius had held him in high esteem, but then suddenly he had him put to death. It was whispered that it was Messalina, who supposedly had wanted to sleep with him but found him unwilling, who did away with him. It was also whispered that Narcissus had persuaded the emperor, claiming that both he and Messalina had dreamed that Appius had raised a hand against him, so alarming Claudius that he had Appius summarily executed.

That was quite certainly untrue, Uri knew: Narcissus loathed Messalina and Messalina loathed him; he would hardly have cooperated with her. And yet they really did have Appius Silanus murdered, along with his son. Claudius's son-in-law did not raise a murmur of protest.

He'll make an emperor yet, will Claudius, thought Uri, and it again crossed his mind that he should get out of Rome, but he stayed because that was where all his ties were.

Before long senator Annius Vinicianus and Furius Camillus Scribonianus, the prefect of Dalmatia, were said to have conspired together. Vinicianus, of course, was among those who had been put forward as candidates for the imperial office by the other factions following the death of Caligula. The matter never reached a court of law because Vinicianus took his own life beforehand. Many were tortured, in spite of the fact that Claudius, at the very beginning of his reign, had sworn not to torture any free citizen. The victims were generally taken to the Gemonian Stairs; those who were executed elsewhere only had their heads taken there out of propriety. The individuals who had bribed Messalina and Narcissus got off scot-free—Uri could only imagine how much they must have paid.

The emperor returned to the road commissioners the fines that Caligula and Corbulo had taken from them on the pretext that they had not been maintaining the highways, and he had Corbulo executed. He also attempted to claw back from the former supporters of Caligula the gifts of which they had been beneficiaries: any who did not speak Latin had their citizenship rights revoked, though some paid for it, with the money shared out among Messalina and her freedmen, who were bribed. In the beginning, the franchise was costly, but after a while the price went down. People grumbled, probably because they saw their own free status coming under threat: "The next thing you know a person will become a citizen for just handing over some broken glassware!"

For the right money it was even possible, word went around, to buy a prefecture or monopoly from Messalina and her freedmen.

Uri was amused when advertisements for "Latin teaching" started going up in Far Side. Some Jews, seriously worried that they might lose their citizenship, began to bone up on their Latin, but then they dropped it once the whole thing fell apart.

Terror gradually began to take hold again, and the price of basic consumer goods rose as if a war was on the horizon, with Claudius being compelled, ultimately, to fix prices in the Field of Mars, with men reading out the cost of goods for hours on end and traders listening with woeful faces at the prospect of going to the wall.

Nothing happened, however; it remained a time of peace, and only a few aristocrats were touched by the cleanup. Augustus, in the early days of his reign, had conducted an almost annual cleanup, and that was what it had been called at the time, except that was a long time ago.

The rumors gave way to outright fantasy. It was said that Messalina was encouraging decent women of rank to commit adultery, compelling their husbands to watch them coupling with charioteers and actors. Claudius was unaware of this, it was added charitably, but then others retorted that it was only because he did not wish to be aware of it: Messalina just sent him over one servant girl after another to sleep with.

For one thing, it was true—as anybody could check—that Messalina had bronze statues made of Mnester, the actor. She was enamored with him, it was whispered. She was supposed to have cajoled her husband to order Mnester to do whatever she asked; up until then Mnester had been disinclined to have any dalliance with her, but if the emperor had so ordered, then he had no choice.

Uri did not believe all he was told, but even he was forced to see that the *carpentum*—the two-wheeled carriage, the use of which was only allowed for matrons, the Vestal Virgins, and priests within the territory of Rome on extraordinary occasions such as feasts—was used to transport Messalina all over the city on a daily basis. She herself, in her black wig and almost overflowing from the carriage, waved to the masses as if she were their emperor.

Supposedly it was Messalina who got rid of Catonius Justus, the commander of the Praetorian Guard; the new commander—her favorite, Rufrius Pollio—was, exceptionally, granted a seat and image in the Senate. It was said that Laco, prefect of the night watch, was so incensed by this that in the end he too was granted the same mark of esteem.

Some word of this must have filtered through to Claudius because he raised the number of chariot races to twenty-four per day and thereby regained a measure of popularity.

After that Claudius had Asiaticus and Magnus executed; Asiaticus had too much property, and Magnus was the emperor's son-in-law and a good friend. After his death the emperor gave away for a second time his daughter Antonia to Cornelius Sulla Faustus, who by pure chance happened to be Messalina's elder brother.

In no way could that be regarded any more as just an unfounded rumor.

An end was also put to the life of Silanus, Claudius's other son-in-law, who had kept so conspicuously quiet when his father was butchered.

Also disposed of was his secretary, the freedman Polybius, who was said to have been a lover of Messalina's, only he had quarreled with her.

Messalina was not going to last long at this rate, Uri figured, and he went on doing his deals at the Forum.

He came to realize that he felt sorry for the emperor.

The unfortunate man had wanted to do so much good, and indeed still did: he removed the prefect of one of Rome's provinces on account of the money the man had been extorting; he forbade any prefects who returned to Rome from appointment from accepting a prefecture in another province within the space of five years; he distributed to the Rome's populace a dole of three hundred sesterces per head (which came in handy for Uri, as he was able to put it aside). People still complained that previous emperors had always distributed votive monies in a ceremony lasting for several days, with some two hundred thousand plebeians being granted the favor on each occasion, while Claudius did not even appear in person. Uri, though, was glad of that, as he would not have liked to look Claudius in the eye.

Claudius still wanted to do good: he had it announced that a solar eclipse was expected to take place on his birthday, and he had stargazers explain to the people in advance the way in which the moon covered up the sun instead of using the occasion to gain the acceptance of the superstitious rabble for some unfavorable law.

Slaves were forbidden from giving evidence against any former master, because in recent times it had become fashionable for interrogators to force people to sell their slaves as a way of getting them to testify against their existing master, which had already been deemed unlawful.

Claudius had not wished to become emperor; how strenuously he had resisted when Caligula's dead body had been still warm and yet he had been elected all the same.

Strange are the ways of fate: Agrippa, who had put Claudius in power, repaying the three hundred thousand sesterces that Antonia had once given him, was now dead.

After a reign of three years, he had stuffed himself to death, and Herod the Great's kingdom once again became a Roman province. Over that three years the king had acquired a personal fortune of twelve million dinars, paying back everything he had owed, with the interest, to all those who were still alive;

obviously Tija had gotten back any money that his father and Marcus had even lent. Uri was the only one who had received nothing, but then that was not part of the agreement he had made with Joseph.

Agrippa the Younger was only seventeen years old, so he had been sent to Rome to complete his education, and Judaea was once again governed by a prefect. Initially Cuspius Fadus was appointed to the position, but Claudius replaced him a year later, because he had begun embezzling the day after he arrived. News of that only reached Rome slowly, but once it did Tija, by now a renegade, was appointed prefect of Judaea.

Tiberius Julius Alexander became the first Jew to govern Judaea, Galilee, and Samaria as a Roman prefect.

HE OUGHT TO MOVE TO JUDAEA.

Uri sounded out the plan on the womenfolk, who would on no account entertain the idea.

Uri spelled out that he was worried that Eulogia, the younger of his daughters, often had a cough, and he had no wish to see her meet the same end as his own little sister; Rome's air was burdensome and the ground swampy, there were lots of mosquitoes. But Sarah was unwilling to leave the house, which Uri had remodeled, adding two small rooms on the roof, one for his mother and the other for himself; these could be reached by two separate outside ladders and had no door between them.

"People also get coughs in Judaea," Sarah declared.

It was useless for Uri to explain that the climate was better there, and people as a rule did not get persistent fevers for no apparent reason, because the way Sarah had heard it the climate was just the same as in Rome.

Uri told them that the present prefect of Judaea, Tiberius Julius Alexander, was a close acquaintance, more or less a friend, and he was sure of being able to get an important post from him.

"And what would that be?" Hagar asked.

Uri took a deep breath:

"It's possible I could be the strategos," he announced.

He did not assume Tija would have any recollection of this passing notion, but he would undoubtedly offer him some lucrative post, at least in the early days of his prefecture as he was still finding his feet, though later on he would be bound to manage—he was clever enough.

The word had been pronounced but there was no reaction.

727

"What's a strategos?" Hagar asked.

"A commander-in-chief."

Hagar did not believe him.

The womenfolk had their vengeance in refusing anything he desired and in desiring anything he refused.

Uri gave up on the idea of Judaea.

Two weeks later he was invited over by Honoratus.

"Our prefect has sent for you," he said to Uri with a friendly smile on his face. "Tiberius Julius Alexander has requested that you travel out to Caesarea and offer him your services. We, for our part, are willing to give you any support you require. If you wish to take your family, we'll provide an escort seeing that you also have children to think of."

Uri went pale and then blushed.

Honoratus went on to chat about this and that, and even embraced him before taking his leave.

Uri went home and made another attempt—futile—to bring the womenfolk around.

He could not say that he was starting to get itchy feet in Rome: if they had failed to grasp that before, they would grasp it even less now. Nor was it advisable to let on to the gossipy women anything he knew about the imperial family's internal affairs because they would start spreading it around and it would all be over.

God in Heaven! Why did you not give me Kainis?

Hagar was opposed to the matter because they spoke Aramaic there.

"Everyone speaks Greek there!" Uri protested.

Hagar did not believe that, but the offer of an "escort" must have hit some nail in her silly head. What would that mean?

Uri went into enthusiastic detail about how they would have armed guards accompanying them just like the richest, most eminent Jews had! Even the delegation that delivered the ritual dues to Jerusalem did not get that! And they would have servants in Judaea, lots of them, they would do everything: cook, sew, weave, wash, shop, and they would take their orders from Hagar.

She went pink with delight.

Hermia also warmed to the idea. Only Sarah proved intransigent.

"The Creator led us to Rome," she declared, "and it's our duty to fulfill his wish."

"It could be that now he is leading us to Judaea!" Uri shouted. "I got a call from the prefect, who is just like a king!"

"Only he's not Jewish," Sarah argued.

"But he is! He's the first Jewish prefect that Rome has had in Judaea! He's a Jewish king, only he's not called that!"

"There's only one king," Sarah said with total conviction.

"But he died!"

"He's been banished and will return."

"That was Herod Antipas, not Agrippa!"

Uri was slowly forced to realize that Sarah was frightened of any change; she did not dare move out of Far Side on her own. She was old, and now her mind was simply not up to seeing the world from another angle.

Uri was tempted to leave the women to their own devices, his other children too, and just take Theo to Judaea, but then he had to concede that he was not free to do that. Theo loved his younger brother and sisters, and Hagar was his mother.

They are all entrusted to me, and perhaps the Creator gave me Theo that I might able to carry the others on my back.

But if he were to reject an offer like this, what could he count on in Far Side from now on?

Honoratus was flabbergasted to hear Uri's excuses.

"That's a serious mistake you're making," he said. "I'll send the message to Judaea."

He did not embrace Uri when he left.

EMPEROR CLAUDIUS HAD HIS WIFE, MESSALINA, DISPATCHED ALONG with her lover, Gaius Silius, whose father, Publius Silius, had been slain on the orders of Tiberius, and he also had the actor Mnester put to death.

The tale went around that Narcissus had run in haste to Ostia, where Claudius had gone to inspect the grain supply, and sought to persuade the emperor to return quickly to Rome because Messalina, despite being wed to the emperor, was celebrating her marriage to Silius. Incredulous though he was, Claudius went back with Narcissus and caught them in the act; Messalina fled and retreated into the gardens of Asiaticus, who had been executed on her account. She was hauled out and cut to shreds, or that was how rumor had it. Uri did not put any credence in the story because not long after Claudius married his niece Agrippina, Caligula's still good-looking elder sister, and he adopted her son Domitius, in whom flowed the blood of Marcus Agrippa and, through Antonia the Elder, of Mark Antony.

Poor Britannicus, Claudius's son by Messalina!

Claudius had wearied of Messalina becoming so powerful.

Now Agrippina would get to become powerful.

It had been prohibited to marry one's niece in Rome from the very start, *ab urbe condita*. Vitellius delivered a big speech in the Senate, proclaiming that it was a matter of public interest that the emperor should be able to marry his niece, and the Senate unanimously changed the law.

"I'd marry my niece as well, if only I had one!" traders joked on greeting one another in the Forum.

"It won't be long before one's allowed to marry one's nephew!"

"Not just allowed but obligated!"

Agrippina made a start by putting to death Lollia Paulina, who had been Caligula's wife, because she had been flirting with the newly married Claudius. Lollia Paulina's head was so mangled, it was said, that Agrippina herself only recognized it after prying open the mouth with her own hands and inspecting the teeth. Lollia had teeth like a horse; Uri recollected them well.

From then onward, Agrippina used the carpentum.

Otherwise life, as ever, went on in the Forum.

Then strange news began to come in from Judaea: a famine had broken out. Queen Helena of Adiabene had shipments of grain transported there from Egypt, but evidently not enough because a rebellion broke out under the leadership of a certain Judas the Galilean when Quirinius, the prefect of Syria, sought to tax them. The rebels were called Zealots, just like their predecessors of a number of generations before, and Tija, so the news went, had crucified their leaders Jacob and Simon, the sons of said Judas.

Maybe it wasn't such a bad thing that we stayed in Rome, Uri thought.

Those who reigned over Adiabene still sought to become Jewish rulers. He was reminded of the palace that was being built in Jerusalem for the queen and her son Izates. Agrippa I's son was still small, as fate would have it, Helena, the Jewish convert, might still be made queen of Judaea.

Of course, Tija would take steps to see that did not happen. Maybe what he did was justified, but Uri was none too happy about the chosen method of execution: it was not right for a Jew to crucify another Jew, even if he were a rebel. Have him burned at the stake, stoned to death, throttled, or beheaded, but not crucified. It then crossed his mind that if he had happened to be strategos, then he would have been an accomplice in this crime. He shuddered. Maybe the Lord really had designated Rome as the place in which he was to live.

JULIUS INVITED URI TO SEE HIM.

The banker had a grim look on his face, and also present were an anxious-looking Iustus, the secretary to Honoratus, and an older, somewhat flabby gentleman, whom Uri had difficulty in recognizing as Fortunatus, Agrippa's confidant. Evidently he had returned to Rome after the king had died; maybe he was serving the younger Agrippa, it ran through Uri's head, and with his eyes narrowed he took a glance at him. He was still ginger-haired, freckled, and snub-nosed, but somehow more resolute than he had been when they were waiting for Caligula to be killed: his forehead seemed wider, his eyebrows bushier, and his eyes more deeply set. Uri felt uncomfortable.

"Tell us what you know about the Nazarenes," Julius requested.

Uri did not understand.

"Don't tell us you never heard of them," said Julius.

Uri shook his head as if he were trying to free his ears from being plugged; he did not even understand the word itself.

"There is a sect from Nazareth," Iustus said. "Surely you know where that is located."

Uri tried to recollect it from Strabo's maps.

"Did you not pass by that way?" Fortunatus asked.

"No."

"But you did spend time in Judaea?"

"You know very well that I did! But I never went to Nazareth! I believe it's in Galilee anyway, and I never went to Galilee!"

"Nazareth is in Judaea," Iustus corrected.

Uri swallowed hard. He was now quite certain that Nazareth was situated in Galilee—he could see the map in his mind's eye, but he couldn't prove it, most especially if they knew exactly where it was.

"Anyway, I have no idea who the Nazarenes are!"

There was a silence.

"Why did you not go to Judaea when the prefect invited you to do so?"

The tone of Julius's voice was serious.

"Because I was unable to persuade the women in my family," Uri sighed. "They're the ones who didn't want to go. I personally would have gone with great pleasure! My wife... my wife is not too bright... My mother is old and tired, afraid to go out on her own even to the market..."

There was silence.

"It must have been a rather serious reason," Fortunatus remarked, "to turn down a request like that."

"That was the reason. What possible purpose could I have for lying to you?"

It crossed Uri's mind that perhaps Fortunatus was jealous; maybe he had heard some unfounded rumor about him, Uri, being Agrippa's courier, and now, even though Agrippa was no longer alive, the jealousy lived on. He might also be jealous that Uri had been present when Caligula was slain; Fortunatus had been present too, but so was Uri. That was enough reason to hate him. How could he placate him?

"A real man doesn't hide behind a hysterical woman," Iustus asserted. "What is the true reason for your staying in Rome? It wasn't the Nazarenes who instructed you by any chance? After all, you might have gotten to know them during the time you were staying in Judaea, after we came back. Two years you spent in Judaea, and that was when they were getting organized! You then spent a whole year in Jerusalem, and they were there by then!"

Uri almost broke out laughing. First I was a spy for Agrippa, then for the alabarch. Who am I spying for now? Maybe I ought to at least know who they're talking about!

"Tell us what you know about the Nazarenes," Julius repeated the request.

"You tell me what you know about them," Uri asked respectfully.

Iustus and Julius exchanged glances—this was one hell of a stubborn man.

URI WOKE UP TO THE FACT THAT HE HAD AGAIN BLUNDERED BADLY. HE had neglected the Jews of Rome, had not built up friendships or mutually binding business contacts among them, did not even have a person whom he could ask what he was suspected of.

He had thought that he, being a person with full rights of Roman citizenship, could pursue his business and quietly subsist, spending his days in the Forum and his nights in Far Side freely and with impunity.

He asked his wife and mother if they had heard anything about any Nazarenes, but they declared that they hadn't, they had not heard anything. Perhaps that was so, but perhaps they were not telling him what they knew. Uri had been increasingly prone to venting his anger when they nagged him with their nonsense, so even he had recognized that maybe they were afraid to say anything.

That left the Forum, where a few other Jews apart from himself moved about, but he did not make inquiries with them but rather among the Syrians and Greeks.

Yes, they had picked up on something.

Jews with fierce eyes had made an appearance there claiming that someone had been killed somewhere and had risen again.

Risen again? What did they mean?

Much the same as Dionysus. At some point he gathered the limbs that had been ripped off him and put himself together again.

Others had heard that the person the Jews had always been awaiting made an appearance.

Who was that? The Anointed?

Someone the Jews have always been waiting for. So say the bringers of glad tidings, which is the name used by the people themselves, who, before they came to Rome, had been spreading the word in some of the Greek cities in Syria. Now they were here in Rome.

Who appeared? The Messiah?

The Greeks were unfamiliar with the word, deriving from the Aramaic for "Anointed," but the Syrians nodded.

Yes, the Messiah.

So, when did this resurrection occur?

Some ten or twelve years ago, toward the end of Tiberius's rule.

But if the Anointed had arrived then the world ought to have changed radically! Had they seen any change in the world?

The world had not changed—on that the gossipers in the Forum could agree.

It was from Theo that Uri learned the most.

The boy was eight years old, and old man, Eusebius, who had once been Uri's teacher, was unwilling to instruct him.

"The boy knows more than I do," said Eusebius, moved when Uri took Theo to him and he recommended instead that he be allowed to frequent libraries. Uri thought that was sound advice and introduced Theo to two librarians. They found it odd that a boy so young would be seeking their services, but they had no objection provided he did not chew or tear the scrolls or scrawl anything in them. Theo almost burst into tears: what did they think he was? So he did regularly go the libraries to read. Uri did not have time to interrogate him about what he happened to be reading; Theo just told him that he read all sorts of things.

Theo had heard Uri interrogating his grandmother and mother, and a few days later he came out with what he had picked up about the Nazarenes from other youngsters in Far Side.

They would come from Greek-inhabited towns in Syria either alone or in small groups and attach themselves to families who had relatives or acquaintances in the East, after which they would go back, only for new people to show up in their places a few months later. Most of them were men. But there were a few women as well; they had permanent smiles on their faces, would constantly stroke children, and they had prodigious appetites. The smiling women would say that the Anointed had been born by the grace of the Eternal One, and he had lived for a long time in obscurity, but on the orders of the Creator he had revealed himself and had kept on curing people until it became manifest that he was the one for whom they had been waiting, but the evil people had crucified him, yet on the third day he had risen, his disciples had seen him and spoken with him, they had been able to touch his bleeding wounds and he had not even felt it, just laughed, then he ascended into Heaven, promising to come back. The women also said that with him they too had died and risen again, and all those who believed in the resurrection of the Anointed would live forever, and anyone who did not believe in him would come off badly. Children were scared of them because that meant they were not living people but spirits who had assumed bodily form, but they didn't understand why, in that case, they ate so much.

Theo also mentioned that the way the other children told it, the first thing the smiling women spoke of in any sentence they uttered was the Anointed. If they were asked "Was the food to your taste?" they would answer: "The Anointed would say at times like these that it was to his taste," or if asked "Will the weather tomorrow be good?" would answer: "The Anointed would say 'Yes.'" And their prayers were not for the Lord to give them that day their daily bread, but to give them tomorrow's bread already today, and they would add: again.

They spoke about a new Melchizedek who would convert both Jews and Greeks in Syria, and the Anointed's speaking had been written down and spread, and there was something about his life in these books.

"Get hold of them for me," Uri requested.

"I've already tried," Theo responded, "but they won't hand them out to nonbelievers. They gather together in their homes, and someone reads them out and someone explains them, and in the meantime they eat in honor of him."

Uri was amazed.

"Do they by any chance bury their shit with a trowel?" he asked.

Theo laughed in astonishment; they had said nothing about that to him.

"The new Melchizedek," he related a few days later, "was not acquainted with the Anointed; indeed, he persecuted his brothers and disciples, but he went somewhere and all at once heard a voice, and the Anointed appeared to him, like the burning bush to Moses, to ask him what he was up to with his believers. And at this he had been converted, and now he went through the town proclaiming his word, saying he had been blinded; the persecutor had turned into a believer, and his eyesight was restored by his faith."

Uri was dubious.

Melchizedek, high priest and king of Jerusalem in the time of Abraham, was a puzzling figure of the Scripture, it was not even clear that he was Jewish, but he had blessed the nomadic Abraham as Abram of the most high God, possessor of Heaven and Earth, who gave him tithes of all, as it was written in The First Book of Moses.

"What are they after? Are they after a rebellion?"

"I don't know," said Theo.

After a brief pause Theo asked:

"Father, are you able to believe in any of this?"

Uri smiled:

"No, I'm not."

"Why not?"

"Because if the Anointed were to come, then everything would change radically, and that would be obvious to us. If he came and was killed and yet everything did not change, then he can't have been the Anointed."

"And he didn't rise again?"

"If he was the Anointed, then he would have no need to rise again because it would be impossible to kill him. If he was just a man, then he would not rise again—only at the same time as everyone shall rise again."

"They say that he allowed himself to be captured and killed to set an example."

"Surely not!"

"They say that he took our sins upon himself, that is why he died deliberately, in place of us, and anyone who believes in him shall become without sin..."

"That's sheer paganism!" Uri spluttered in rage. "That's not Jewish thinking! There's something of the kind among the Greeks when Apollo is celebrated: two scapegoats are chosen and expelled from town, and they carry with them all the sins of the others..."

"I've read about them," said Theo. "They're what are called *pharmakoi*."

"There you are, see! We don't have anything like that in our sacred writings."

Theo then added details.

"They proclaim that heathens and those who as heathens believe in the Crucified One are permitted to eat ritually unclean food, but those who are Jewish, or believe in him as Jews, are not permitted to eat ritually unclean food. If a heathen believes in him, he is not required to be circumcised and yet can still be Judaized."

"That's stuff and nonsense!" said Uri. "There have been uncircumcised God-fearers up till now, but they can't eat unclean food."

"They say that the Anointed was born in Bethlehem."

"Not Nazareth?"

"No."

"I was told it was Nazareth. Isn't that what they're called: Nazarenes?"

"That's right... All the same, they say he was born in Bethlehem when the star appeared fifty years ago."

"Is that so?"

Uri explained to Theo that people are superstitious and they like nothing better than to tie signs in the celestial Heaven to events here on earth even though they have nothing to do with each other.

"I know that," said Theo. "That's what astrology is about."

Uri tried to recollect when it had been, according to the stargazers in Jerusalem, that a comet had last appeared in the southern firmament: it had been about twenty years before he was born. On that basis the supposed Anointed must have been getting on forty when he was killed. What had been his occupation, he wondered, if he was not changing the world?

Eventually Theo managed to borrow a sheet of papyrus on which the smiling missionaries had written down the essential things that had to known about the Anointed. His whole life and deeds fit onto that single sheet. The Anointed had been called Jesus, and his father was Joseph. He had become a carpenter, like his father, and John the Baptist had immersed him too in water. He had accomplished miraculous cures, shown much wisdom in what he said, and he had proclaimed love. He was killed but resurrected before rising up into Heaven.

Uri looked at the sheet with disapproval. It plainly served as a prompt for missionaries, who were able to explain all the short statements at great length. There were many in Judaea and Galilee who practiced cures by laying on hands, and the things the man had said were pretty much what the Pharisee masters said anyway: "Do not unto others that which you would not do unto yourself"; "Love thy neighbor as thyself"; "If someone smiteth thee in the face, turn the other cheek"; "Render unto the Lord that which is the Lord's, and render unto Caesar the things which are Caesar's"; "Let he that is without sin cast the first stone."

There was just one of Jesus's saying on the sheet that Uri had not heard before: "There is neither Jew nor Greek, there is neither master nor bondman, there is neither male nor female: for ye are all one in the Lord. There is no family any more, only fellowship."

That's not a bad way of thinking, Uri deliberated; Philo would be pleased with that.

There was little on the sheet about torture, resurrection, and ascension into Heaven. It was odd who had noticed that he was not in the grave where he ought to have been: two women, both of them by the name of Mariamne, one of them from Magdala. At first the Resurrected One was not recognized, his external appearance having changed, but then they did recognize him, and the Anointed said unto them: "You are blessed because thou hast seen me and believed; but more blessed are they that have not seen and yet have believed."

Those women must have adored that man to an extraordinary degree if they were so unable to reconcile themselves to his having died. He can have been no ordinary prophet, and no ordinary man. There were many who orated in Jerusalem in the Women's Chamber, in the shade of the eastern colonnade of the Temple; maybe he was among them when I passed that way, Uri reflected. He could recollect none of the faces: he had not been standing close enough, and nothing was said on the sheet about his appearance.

He pressed the sheet into Theo's hand, asking him to return it to whomever he had gotten it from. He should not copy it, or bring it into the house, because the house was subject to being searched at any time and it would not look good if they were able to turn up any evidence that could be used against them. Theo promised not to copy it.

Uri then chatted with his son about astronomy, about Ages, and about Mithras, who, legend had it, was likewise able to resurrect; he talked about the observatory in Jerusalem, which had been used more for spying on people down below than gazing at the skies up above, and he also talked about the astronomers in Alexandria. He spoke about how the earth was spherical and how its circumference had been calculated by a simple but superb method. Theo immediately grasped it: the deviance between the angles of incidence of the Sun in the two wells fascinated him, and the only thing that gave him pause was how it was possible to measure the distance between Alexandria and Syene, how it was organized, and who checked that they had not just made a guess at the result. Theo considered five thousand stadia to be a suspiciously round number, and Uri grinned happily to hear his reasoning. He remarked that a pedometer device had been invented at Alexandria, possibly at the very time of Eratosthenes's measurement.

Theo asked how it was that if the earth was spherical we did not fall off its surface or live at the bottom of the sphere and not its top, and why, if one lived on the side, we did not slide down on our behind. Uri thought that was a logical question, and he had to admit that he hadn't a clue.

Theo pondered.

"Father, when you were in Alexandria did you stand just as upright as you do in Rome?"

"Yes, I did," said Uri, caught by surprise. "Why do you ask?"

"Because if you stand upright in Rome, then that has to be the top of the sphere, and under the earth there has to be a tray on which the earth stands, like a ball, and you are standing upright relative to that. If I know the earth's circumference, which is 252,000 stadia, and I know the distance from Rome to Alexandria, then I could work out your angle of inclination."

Uri acknowledged that this was so, but neither he nor anyone else had been leaning at an angle in Alexandria.

"Then there cannot be a tray under the earth and the earth just floats," Theo reasoned. "But how can that be? Are our legs pointing everywhere to the center of the earth?"

"Presumably," Uri deliberated.

"Why's that?"

Uri racked his brains but he could not recall a single work that dealt with that subject.

Theo decided that he was going to throw himself into astronomy. He wanted to calculate his father's nonexistent angle of inclination in Alexandria, and Uri promised him that the next time he was in the Forum he would take a look at the foot of the gilded zero milestone to check how far Alexandria was from Rome. Uri was quite surprised that he had never before looked, but then it occurred to him that it was because one cannot walk on the sea, and he was only interested in distances that he personally had tramped.

THEY HAD THOUGHT THAT THE GILDED MILESTONE COULD BE INSPECTED any time.

Only the elders had decided to expel the Nazarenes. They did not have the right to do that but they had at least gotten it made an imperial edict: Claudius signed a document empowering the Roman Jewish elders to place the Nazarenes on the list of the sacrilegious and to eject them. The emperor did not wish for the same sort of unrest as eight years before, when Jews had to be banned from assembling due to the influx of refugees from Alexandria. Through mishearing, or more likely as a deliberate toning-down, the decree spoke of the followers of a certain Chrestos ("The One You Need" rather than Christos, "the Anointed"), but it was an edict, and it had to be put into effect.

Uri was asked to see Honoratus, who had aged considerably and now used a stick to support himself even when seated.

"The Nazarene missionaries will have to leave Rome," he said.

"So I've heard."

"You will also have to leave Rome."

Uri felt dizzy.

"But I'm not a Nazarene!" he cried out.

Behind Honoratus Iustus stood mute and unflinching; it was clear that he would jump to his master's defense if Uri were to assail him.

"The word is that you are a Nazarene," said Honoratus. "I'm sorry."

"And what if I say that I'm not?"

"That's what a lot of them say," said Honoratus.

"So what's the proof?"

"I'm not prepared to argue. You have two days to pack up and go."

Uri stood there.

The Eternal One does not wish for me to be able to raise my children peacefully.

Two days.

Uri rushed to a Latin lawyer whom he had already made use of in smaller business transactions and who was both conscientious and successful in what he had done.

"I don't take on that sort of case."

"But it's unlawful! I'm a Roman citizen!"

"But you're Jewish. This is a religious matter; the Jews are the competent authorities."

"But how can it be a purely religious matter if they're expelling me, who always adhered to the letter of Roman laws and the prescriptions of the Jewish faith—expelling me, together with my guiltless infants, on the basis of an unfounded, unproven, false accusation! They haven't even raised formal charges against me! How is it possible to expel a family like that?"

"I can't do anything because it is an edict."

"What does that mean, 'edict?' How can an edict have greater force than the law in general? Is this what the famed Roman rule of law amounts to?"

"That's right."

He would have to go higher: to the very top.

Uri hastened to Claudius's house; it was surrounded by a large detachment of the Praetorian Guard, with several cordons and infantry.

"The emperor is not seeing anyone."

"I didn't come to see the emperor but Narcissus," Uri yelled.

"What did you bring?"

"Nothing; I simply want to speak with him!"

"He's got even less time than the emperor."

"I have to speak with him right away. Send word to him that Gaius is asking for him, Gaius the Jew."

The bodyguards roared with laughter.

Uri became incensed.

"He will punish you if you don't tell him! Don't get mad at me when that happens!"

There was an edge to Uri's voice that led one of the bodyguards eventually to stroll away inside.

Uri moved to one side and squatted on his heels. He felt queasy, and shooting pains shook his rectum so brutally that he feared he would defecate. He stood up and clenched the muscles of his posterior like the lips on his face.

They let him in.

Two guards gripped him on either side and marched him through the familiar house.

At the back, by a wall of the garden into which the atrium opened, where once a chamber had been situated, a cabin had been built—that was where he was led. They stopped at the door; two fully armed guards were on sentry duty. One went into the house then came out and beckoned; Uri stepped forward and the two guards set to frisking him.

"You can go."

Uri stepped into the cabin behind one of the guards.

Narcissus was reclining on a couch beside a table, clutching one arm to his brow as if he had a headache. He motioned for the guard to go. Uri stepped closer but remained at a respectful distance.

"Well, then," said Narcissus, rising from his prone position. "What wind has brought you here?"

Narcissus's black hair was as ruffled as it used to be, but two deep wrinkles had formed at the corners of his mouth and spoiled his appearance.

Uri gave him a brief summary.

Narcissus shook his head:

"I can't intervene in what Jews decide among themselves."

"But I'm not a Nazarene!"

"So what? That's what they've decided, and that's that."

Narcissus looked around, then went to a coffer and opened it.

"How much do you need?" he asked, dipping one hand into the chest and then scattering a shower of coins onto the floor.

"But it wasn't money I was after..."

"Take as much as you can."

Uri squatted down and grasped a fistful of coins but did not know where to put them.

"Do I have to give you a sack as well?" Narcissus snapped irately and then dissolved in laughter. "Still the same old clot!"

Narcissus again looked around then pulled up the hem of his tunic, bit into it and with his hand ripped off a quite sizable piece, which he handed to Uri.

"I'm sorry!" said Uri.

"I'll get them to bring another later."

Uri bundled up a heap of coins in the strip of linen, twisted it together, raised his tunic, and squeezed it under his loincloth. He felt his skin creeping at the touch and was overtaken again by an urge to defecate.

"Come over here a moment," said Narcissus by the chest.

It was a good three-quarters full of coins and gemstones.

"That's two days' output!" Narcissus said proudly. "They forgot to empty it yesterday. That's quite something, huh?" He snickered. "Have you any idea how much I'm worth? No? Take a guess! A wild guess."

Uri thought of the figure brought in by census of the equestrian order and ventured:

"Six hundred thousand sesterces?"

"Try three hundred million! It's already up to three hundred million, and there will be plenty more!"

Uri clucked his tongue politely in wonderment.

Narcissus kicked the treasure under his bed from the middle of the room.

"Weren't you worried about coming to see me?" he asked.

"No, why should I be?"

"There's the matter of my notoriety as a devourer of human flesh!" said Narcissus with a grin. "It would be right to be frightened of me. I'm the emperor's mass murderer, haven't you heard?"

Uri held his peace. The wrinkles on either side of Narcissus's mouth were absorbing his attention.

"Now get lost!" said Narcissus listlessly, clutching his temples with his hands. "And don't let me see you here ever again."

URI WAS CAUGHT SHORT AT THE BOTTOM OF PALATINE HILL, WITH A light brown fluid trickling down his leg.

He waded into the Tiber at the foot of the Fabricius Bridge: the water was dirty anyway, and so were the coins, which burned to the touch despite being twisted up in the sweaty piece of linen Narcissus had given him. He waded into the water up to his waist; it was cold, and he was overwhelmed by a feeling of having experienced it all sometime before. Superstitious people believe that means a similar event must have happened in a previous life. What came to Uri's mind was a vision of the sea in which he had gamboled happily as a young man before the crossing to Sicily. If a wave had swept over him and carried him off, none of this would have happened.

What was the point of living?

Why was the Eternal One afflicting him with a new misery?

What more did he have to learn that he would carry silently to the grave along with all his other abominable experiences?

He peered over from beside the island to the opposite bank. Far Side. Why had he been obliged to live there up until now? Why had he been born there?

It would be better to leave the damned place forever.

The womenfolk wailed when Uri told them the next day of the decision, and it was evident that they didn't get it. Theo just stood there mutely, horrified, Marcellus shrieked, and the girls blubbered, understanding absolutely nothing of it all. Uri ordered everyone to pack their things, forbidding them to take with them anything other than a small dish, a spoon, and the clothes in which they were standing. It wasn't a good idea to wander around with a big burden, he said, but they did not grasp what he meant, looking at him as if he were Satan personified. The children were each allowed to bring one toy of their choosing, the girls picked out wooden dolls with flexible limbs, Marcellus a pair of bone dice, and Theo his new ball, deflated.

Uri then ordered the women to carry everything they could out of the house and set it down before the door. They carried the articles out, blubbering but sedulously as they were scared of him, seeing some glint in his eyes. Uri searched through the articles, setting aside the scrolls, which he was going to leave with somebody in Far Side. He pondered what he should take with him before deciding that he needed nothing.

As he was rummaging he picked up a small, soft object wrapped in linen, which he undid. It was an old Phrygian cap—the liberty cap of his grandfather, Taddeus.

He would take that, seeing that nothing at all of his father's had remained.

Theo took the scrolls to one of the libraries and handed them over, saying that they would come by some day to pick them up. The owner of the library, a weaver, bit his lip and held a hand in blessing over Theo's head.

That evening Uri set alight the pile that had been assembled in front of the house—beds, blankets, clothes. People from the neighborhood gathered around and watched it all burn in silence. He poked at the still-glowing embers with a pole to make sure it would all burn completely. Anything that would not burn—the pottery, for instance—he smashed: the metal objects he hammered beyond recognition. That exertion was just what his spirits needed, with Theo and Marcellus joining in the angry demolition work. The others looked on and were excited as well, but propriety held them back from giving way to their destructive instincts.

They slept on the bare floor of the main room, all of them together. Everybody was tired, blubbering, sniffing, coughing, clearing their throats, but Uri could hear how sleep nevertheless eventually came over them. They didn't believe that they were leaving Rome.

The next morning they sprinkled water on themselves from the tub and recited the Sh'ma; by the time they finished a group of men were standing by, hammers and pickaxes in hand, along with eight of the *vigiles*. They should also have smashed the water tub apart.

Fortunatus was with them.

"I'm deeply sorry," he said. "There is much injustice done in cases like this, but what is one to do? I personally am convinced that you are being victimized despite being blameless! Others too. I'm going to seek a review of all your cases—as soon as I can."

Uri smiled at him pleasantly and nodded. Fortunatus held his tongue.

Uri then took down the mezuzah from above the door post and put it in his sack. He rolled up his tefillin and placed that too in his sack; he was of a mind to throw it away but decided he'd let the Jews see it and feel ashamed of themselves. They looked on but did not feel ashamed of themselves.

The vigiles stepped closer. One of them handed over a papyrus.

"This is the expulsion order," he said. "It has your name on it and the others. Put it away: it will also serve to ensure your safe conduct."

Uri did not examine it but rolled it up and slipped it next to the Torah scroll in a fine, expensive leather satchel he had recently bought, and put that too in the sack.

"Let's go, then," he said.

They set off with the vigiles straggling behind.

They heard a rumbling sound and stooped to look back.

The men with the pickaxes had started with the two new rooms on the top.

The women burst into tears.

"It's better this way," said Uri. "We can be grateful that thanks to their impatience we are able to see it. Let's get the mourning over with now, then it won't be necessary any more."

The vigiles escorted them to the southeastern gate of Far Side but did not go onto the bridge with them. Uri had specifically asked to be allowed to exit that way as he wanted to get onto the road to Ostia as soon as possible. They could have gone by way of the new road that was just under construction, which could be reached from the west by turning south off the Via Aurelia across the Monteverde, where a start had been made on a new Jewish catacomb, but then they would have ended up at Portus, the new harbor on the right of the Tiber, and not at Ostia, because there was no bridge across the Tiber.

They trudged along, sunk in themselves, the women and children thoroughly alarmed.

"Father," said Theo quietly, "have we just been ostracized?"

Uri laughed. Theo had evidently been reading about how they used to vote by potsherds in the assembly of Athens to expel for ten years those who were too upright, too talented, or too powerful for their own good.

"Something like that," said Uri. "Only there's no way of knowing who exactly cast a vote against us."

"If it's a voting by potsherds, then we can go back after ten years, can't we?"

Uri patted Theo on the head.

"This isn't Athens," he said. "Maybe before that."

"But, father, if you have been expelled through voting by potsherds, that means you must be an important person!"

"Quite possibly I am," Uri chuckled, "but I'm the only one who doesn't know."

The answer tickled Theo. Marcellus bored his way between them, and Uri also patted him on the head, though he felt bad, realizing that this was the first time he had given the boy a pat on the head.

He started to tell them about how many important men had been subject to ostracism.

Among those expelled from Athens had been Phidias, the greatest sculptor the world had ever seen or was likely to see, who had been accused of pilfering the gold that had been used to cover an ivory statue of Athena in the Parthenon. Phidias had deliberately put on easily removable gold leaves, perhaps counting on the malice in advance; when it was stripped off and weighed none was found missing, but even so he was forced to flee.

Another who had to leave his hometown was Diogenes, who was loathed in Sinope because he invariably told the truth. He was accused falsely of forging the Sinopean currency, but all the same he was driven out. His was not an easy voyage: he settled for a while in Athens, but on a trip to Aegina he was captured by pirates and sold as a slave in Crete. He was lucky to be bought by a decent family; he tutored the children and managed to get to Corinth. He even ridiculed Alexander the Great and the Athenian assembly; upon hearing Alexander had been identified with Dionysus, he is said to have replied, "Then call me Serapis."

Diogenes came in very handy as an example for Uri since the philosopher had voluntarily made a virtue of extreme poverty, practiced it with a view to spiritual improvement, and attained the considerable age of eighty, at which he was only able to die by holding his breath.

"Does that mean we have become dogs?" Marcellus asked.

Uri told him that no, they were not dogs, nor was Diogenes, he was a fine, upstanding man and a great thinker, and the term cynic, derived from the Greek word for "doggie," was just a term of derision, which sounded phonetically similar to the place Antisthenes, supposedly Diogenes's master, favored for his lectures.

Uri was able to tell many tales like that, and they talked and talked as they made their way, small bundles on their backs, along the busy, noisy streets toward the city gate west of the obelisk that towered proudly in front of the Circus Maximus.

THEY LEFT THE CITY AND TOOK THE ROAD TO OSTIA; THOSE GOING ON foot did not need to pay any toll, only mounted messengers or those traveling on carts. They made slow progress on account of the women and children; Uri's legs and back hurt, he was overweight. A spot of starvation would do wonders for that.

The money was no longer burning his skin under his loincloth; he had thrown Narcissus's rag out that evening and instead tied up the cone in one of his own cloths. He had not counted it, but figured it must be a tidy sum: it was mostly dinars, but there were some aurei as well. The jangling protrusion under his paunch would not be apparent to anyone else.

He chirpily related how on good days with the delegation, fourteen years before, he had covered a distance equal to two marathon runs; it had been hard to begin with but one got used to it.

Then he let them in on a big secret: the reason they were heading for Ostia was because he had acquaintances there. He would be able to conduct his business from there, probably more successfully than from Rome, and anyway Ostia had a much better climate than Rome.

Marcellus was fearful of robbers, but Uri reassured him that they were not going to be slaughtered for the sake of a pair of dice.

"It's better to have nothing, then they leave you alone."

Theo cogitated.

"We didn't have all that much and we were still expelled. Why was that?"

"We have a lot of things that can't be seen," Uri said.

"What have you got?" Marcellus asked.

Uri pondered.

"Knowledge—that's what I've got," he responded, "that's what they envy me."

"Still you didn't know beforehand that we were going to be thrown out!"

Marcellus is not so dim after all, Uri was delighted to note.

"No one is clever enough to be able to foresee the future."

"Soothsayers see ahead!" yelled Marcellus.

"But soothsayers tell lies."

"No they don't!" Marcellus protested. "I'm going to be a soothsayer!"

They walked, stopping from time to time when the girls needed to pee, then Hagar needed to pee, then Sarah, then Hermia; then the boys felt hungry and Uri kept their spirits up with the idea that they would stop for a meal at a hostelry. Hagar was carrying the rest of the family's money tied to her waist under her smock.

"Let's go back!" Marcellus wailed. "I want to go back home!"

"Our house is no longer standing," said Uri.

"But it is!" Marcellus bawled. "We've done enough walking. Let's go home!"

Uri sighed:

"We'll have a pretty house in Ostia, much prettier than the one we had."

Theo tried to calm his brother:

"This is the first time we have been out walking, the first time we have been outside Rome. Now we have a chance to see a bit of the world!"

"But I don't want to see a bit of the world!" Marcellus howled. "I don't want a prettier house! I want our own house!"

Out of exhaustion he finally went silent, lay down on the road, and fell asleep. They pulled the boy aside so that he would not be trampled on by carts or mules.

They sat under the shade of a tree; it was midsummer and stifling hot. The two girls, Irene and Eulogia, were crying and thirsty. Uri and Hagar stood by the roadside hunting for a carriage which was delivering food, and finally along came a cart drawn by a pair of oxen from which they were able to buy for a few asses a flatbread which was split up among them.

"Let's go home, son," Sarah chimed in. "The children are tired."

Uri looked at his mother. A knot of matted hair was dangling over her unprepossessing face—cloddish features, hook nose, the bristles poking out of her chin, her dull eyes.

It was because of her, her dumb stubbornness, that we didn't go to Caesarea. Now she had lost what little brains she had.

He looked at Hermia, her mouth agape, snoring as she slept on her back, with Theo brushing away the flies. How hideous and old she looked: her mother's daughter. For what purpose are people like her brought into the world, he wondered? What pleasure does the Creator find in them? How come He does not inspect the womb? That should be His job.

Theo snuggled up to his father. He, by contrast, is marvelous, and smart, Uri meditated. One sound individual to seven relatives—but no, that was not right, because Joseph's looks had been pleasant enough, and he had also been smart. The ratio was more like eight to two. The Lord must have some intention behind that.

"We need to go more quickly," whispered Theo. "That way we get there and they settle down sooner."

Uri stroked the boy's golden locks.

Get there? But where?

"I owe you an apology," Uri said softly. "I promised you that we would never be banished."

Theo looked at him uncomprehendingly.

"When was that?"

Uri could see that he genuinely had no recollection of how scared he had been when the refugees had been driven out.

"You said that if our house were able to swell, we would take in all the refugees," he reminded him.

Theo, who had a capacious memory, shook his head: he did not remember.

He had been born with a healthy mind and did not retain memories of the bad.

WITH MUCH EFFORT, THEY REACHED OSTIA IN FOUR DAYS. THERE WAS A look of obtuse idiocy in Sarah's eyes; Hagar resigned herself to her fate; Hermia whimpered but said nothing. The children worked their way into tramping along, with Uri tapping the girls' backs to straighten up: being round-shouldered did not look nice, he didn't want them to be so slack in their deportment that no one would marry them.

He spoke about the sea to Marcellus, and as the boy wanted to hear about monsters, he invented a string of marine creatures: some on whose backs one could ride; others who, when there was a storm, would gobble a man up so he would live in their belly while the tempest raged and afterward would then spit him out intact, like the whale did with Jonah. He promised Marcellus to seat him on the back of a charming monster like that as soon as they reached the sea, though in all truth they seldom showed up.

They got into Ostia without any trouble, with no guards anywhere to be seen. Uri's recollection was that Matthew had once told him that he planned to build the synagogue by the seashore, to the south of the city wall, next to shrines of some kind, so he struck off southward as if he knew where he was going.

Theo looked at the nice big tidy houses and pledged to his sisters: "We're also going to have a multistory house with a roof garden!"

Marcellus stopped in front of one such house, fringed with cypresses, and wanted to go in.

"We don't live here," said Theo.

"But this is where I want to live!" Marcellus howled.

They dragged him onward.

Uri found the city wall and also the gate leading to the sea.

They spotted a big shrine to the right, intersecting colonnaded roads, an orderly line of trees, and farther away, directly by the seashore, a very tall, strange L-shaped building. Evening was drawing in, and the building threw a shadow northwestward onto a long two-story house.

Uri hurried ahead. He went around the building and looked back on it from the sea.

The entrance, set to look southeast, had been installed between two tall columns. On the left ran a long wall, where a line of tiny windows ran above the height of a man, and there was a roof over the columns much higher than that of the building. Off to the right, set at right angles and running in a northeasterly direction, ran another long wall topped with tiny windows placed at a similar height. Above that northeasterly wall could be seen two more columns.

748

So there were four columns supporting an exceptionally high, gabled roof. This had to be it.

Uri was astounded. He had not seen a Jewish house of prayer this big except for the Basilica at Alexandria, and that had been constructed as a market hall. There was something ungainly and exaggerated about the building; it was like no other. Perhaps that was because the columns had existed first and they had to be incorporated at all costs.

The entrance was locked. By now his family had caught up.

"Wait here!" said Uri and then walked along by the northeastern wall toward the terraced housing.

The two walls of the synagogue and the line of the terrace formed what was in effect a regular square, lacking only a wall to the southwest, and in that direction a line of palm trees had been planted by way of a fencing. There was no fence or plants between the northeasterly wall of the synagogue and the terrace.

This had to be the house which Matthew lived in.

As he got nearer, Uri saw that the two-story terrace was not a single building but three houses attached to one another, which must mean that two of them were servants' quarters or let out to guests.

On a terrace in front of the upstairs windows, which was presumably shared between the three houses, a line of washing was hanging.

Uri knocked on the door on the left, the one which did not have the shadow of the synagogue falling in it. He knocked again.

A burly, completely grizzled man stepped out of the door, blinking as the setting sun hit him straight in the yes.

"We're full up," he said by way of a greeting.

"Plotius!" Uri exclaimed.

Plotius narrowed his eyes and stepped closer.

"Don't you recognize me?" Uri asked.

"The voice is familiar... Hang on a moment! Don't tell me! Your voice... You always had a cold... Gaius? Surely not!"

Plotius embraced him.

"Come in," he said. "We'll have something to eat and drink and you can tell me all about yourself."

"I'm here with my family; they're waiting on the beach..."

"Let them wait! Come in!"

Uri found himself entering a spacious room with furnishings that pointed to an affluent lifestyle. They took seats on stools.

"How many years has it been?" Plotius asked.

"Fourteen."

"Well, I never!"

Plotius brought out some wine and a mixing dish.

"Matthew?" Uri asked.

Plotius poured carefully.

"He got a hankering to be at sea," he said, "so he went back to sailing."

Uri nodded.

Plotius had built the synagogue with Matthew's money then driven Matthew out, together with his family, and gone on to steal his house.

They quaffed the wine.

"We are having golden days in Ostia," Plotius whooped. He had become corpulent, his face flabbily filled-out. "This is the biggest synagogue in the Diaspora—a span's width taller than the one at Delos, a bigger mikveh as well, that's inside, under the columns... It will take fifty people at one go! And the harbor too—Portus—is a marvel! Some of that construction work is mine! In large part, one could say. Yes, mine!"

He poured some more and took a drink.

"Just imagine," he leaned forward as he said this, "it was me who worked out what to do with that immense boat used to bring the obelisk from Heliopolis, because they had no idea what to do with it next: pile it full of fist-sized pieces of rock and sink it opposite the harbor entrance, then build up on that an artificial western bank to give protection against the winds... Next to it piles need to be driven into the water with baskets of puteolanum sling between them, and on that build up deep-water moles... Puteolanum—that's the concrete which hardens in water that I was doing research on in Caesarea... Remember? Anyway, it was accepted," Plotius bellowed. "It was completed in just eighteen months! Claudius congratulated me personally! It'll last several centuries! Several centuries!"

A tall, slender, bearded young man came into the room and stared disapprovingly at them.

"My son," said Plotius hoarsely. "He'll be the archisynagogos after me."

"Hold on a minute!" said Uri. "I remember what he's called... Fortunatus, isn't it?"

Plotius stiffened.

"Yes, Plotius Fortunatus... Do you remember everything?"

"Pretty much."

Plotius Fortunatus picked up the mixing bowl and went out with it.

Plotius chortled.

"He doesn't like it when I drink. That kind of son... He's married now... I've got three grandsons... They live here, next door... The terrace is shared."

Uri drank a sip of water before asking:

"We need somewhere to stay."

Plotius shut his trap.

"There are eight of us," Uri went on. "Four adults and four children. The synagogue is a guesthouse also, isn't it?"

"It happens to be full up right now."

"There's nobody there," said Uri. "The front door is closed."

"There are a bunch of people coming first thing tomorrow."

"We've been four days on the road from Rome," said Uri. "Except for me they're women and children."

Plotius stood up, stretched his back, and looked away over Uri's head.

"We are not allowed to give lodgings to Nazarenes," he blurted out.

Uri felt faint and fell silent.

"People in Ostia don't take kindly to Nazarenes," said Plotius, taking his seat again. He tried to pull a friendly face. "No one will put Nazarenes up. You're frozen out. I'd never have believed that you are one too!"

"We aren't Nazarenes," said Uri. "I don't even know what they stand for!"

"Scum!" growled Plotius. "The Jews in Rome are scum... But what can we do? The news has preceded you."

They fell silent. Plotius Fortunatus had not taken the water out, so Uri drank that. He had not eaten or drunk anything all day, and his stomach was rumbling very audibly.

"This room would do for us overnight."

Plotius sighed.

"I'm ready to put anyone up!" he protested. "I put up refugees from Alexandria, gave them food free of charge... I did the same for the Nazarenes at first, but they're intolerable: they keep on pressing and trying to convert you. They do it even when they're asleep. Totally mad! The Alexandrians at least did nothing more than wail and curse, that's quite in order... But not Nazarenes—never again."

"But I've told you: we aren't Nazarenes," said Uri.

"They believe you are!"

"Who's they?"

"The Jews of Ostia! They got a clip on the ear from Rome; they even dropped a word with me. You have no idea how hard it was to come to terms with them! They wanted to demolish my house of prayer just when it was ready! There was a battle raging here on the shorefront—you've got no idea what they're like! I enticed the faithful from the synagogue in the town—that was what I was charged with! There was something in that. I barely got through it!"

"We haven't eaten all day."

Plotius stood up and paced up and down.

"They're on the beach," Uri said. "Come and have a look. Mother's gone crazy, my younger sister is a bit crazy as it is, my wife dumb as a dead person... I have two sons and two daughters."

"With your describing them so nicely, what I am supposed to look at them for?"

Plotius went on with his pacing. Uri remained seated.

"Go to Puteoli," Plotius suggested, taking his seat again. "I doubt they would have sent a messenger that far from Rome. They're too lazy. You might even get work there: everyone is getting out right now, so if only because of that..."

It was dark by now, with a cold draft coming through the window.

"Just one night..."

"You can't!" Plotius yelled. "They come to check! Take it from me that you can't!"

"At least give us some food and drink! You've got that much."

"All right, but you'll have to leave and go as far away as you can."

Uri got to his feet.

"We'll do that," he said with a smile. "We'll leave and go as fast and as far as we can, don't you worry!"

He reached under his tunic, pulled out the linen bag from under his loincloth, took out a sesterce, and plonked that down on the table. He then retied the bag, pushed it back under his loincloth, and smoothed his tunic. Plotius stared without a word.

"Matthew gave me that at Syracusa," Uri explained. "Pass it on to him when you next see him."

Plotius held his peace.

IT WOULD HAVE BEEN SIMPLEST TO TAKE A BOAT TO PUTEOLI, BUT THAT would have cost a fortune, and Uri was unwilling to reveal that they were not exactly penniless. Let them get used to it—and to going by foot.

He took Irene and Eulogia, by turns, on his shoulders; the others carried on their backs a bag he had obtained from Plotius for the purpose of carrying what was left of their dried provisions. They had spent the night in the open air next to the synagogue as Plotius had not allowed them to come inside. The flask of water was entrusted by Uri to Hagar with the exhortation that water was the most precious of all: she should make sure not one drop was spilled. He had hoped that he would be able to coax a drop of solidarity out of Hagar by this display of trust, but her eyes remained blank, keeping her feelings to herself and resigned to enduring whatever she had to endure.

It was fine, it was summer; an exhausted person could have a marvelous sleep wrapped up in a blanket.

That was how Uri tried to buoy their spirits: Puteoli was a nice city, he had been there before, and by the winter they would have their own house there.

Theo was happy to walk, and with his hungry eyes he took in the whole spectacle; he even said expressly that at last they were taking part in a great adventure, and he reassured everyone that he could not care less about Rome. Marcellus no longer cried but marched, clutching his dice and looking straight ahead, doing whatever Uri told him. The women stumbled on; they did not quarrel and did what Uri ordered them to do.

Uri endeavored to spell out the advantages of a vagrant life: the whole thing would be a shared experience for the children, which would serve to bond them together even when had grown up and were left on their own; they would learn about wandering and doing without; they would count their blessings even more when the opportunity arose.

Uri led them southward across the meadows, away from the more obstructed coast; his goal was to get onto the roads in Campania that he had walked on fourteen years before.

He gave them permission to steal fruit from deserted orchards. The womenfolk said nothing; not even Sarah raised a peep in protest.

The blisters on their feet burst, but the skin on the soles of the feet gradually hardened. By then all of them were walking with their sandals slung around their neck. At times the girls would race ahead and set themselves in the grass and weeds, squealing with excitement, as they awaited the others. Marcellus would be in eager pursuit of them.

On the Sabbath it was forbidden to do work of any kind, including journeying by foot, so Uri marked out a distance of one hundred paces beyond which the children were not allowed to move, but the girls cried so hard that he allowed two hundred. Irene then went off two hundred paces from the bush under which they had settled and climbed up into a tree, on a branch of which she obstinately spent the rest of the day. Uri tried to coax her down by whistling to her but the rebellion was in earnest, with Marcellus and Eulogia jumping with joy and Hagar irately asserting that making music was also forbidden on the Sabbath, though Uri was of the opinion that whistling did not amount to working but was rather a prayer without words, and that was allowed. Hagar grouchily stomped off to one side.

They resumed marching until Uri all of a sudden sensed rather than saw that they were proceeding on what seemed like familiar soil. He halted.

That agreeable family with whom the delegation had been given lodging lived somewhere near there. He told his own family so: he had acquaintances there: happy, friendly people who made everything for themselves—sowing the soil, tending fruit-trees, shearing sheep, as well as spinning and weaving—he was quite sure they would be put up there.

Some buildings could be seen at the foot of the hill they had just summited: Uri shouted out that this was it.

Theo raced down the hill, with Marcellus hurrying after him. Uri and the women slowly caught up.

Four big, burnt-out houses stood next to one another, and sooty stones were all that was left; there was no sign of any roofing and the main beams were all charred. Any furniture had either been removed or had been burned to ashes. Where the stables had stood the ground was dark and greasy; in the former gardens only weeds pushed up through the soil.

"Jews were living in just one of the houses," said Uri, by way of indicating that it was not only Jews who had been overtaken by the same fate.

"Was it robbers?" Marcellus asked in a whisper.

"Probably," said Uri.

"Are we too going be burned out?"

"We've got nothing," Theo reminded his brother, "so they let us live."

Uri just stood, tears flowing.

The children and women looked on horrified. Never before had they seen him cry.

They spent the night sleeping amidst the ruins.

"Why did you cry, Papa?" Theo asked quietly.

Uri sighed.

"I would have liked to have a family just like theirs," he said. "They laughed incessantly! Played jokes on one another! Talked nineteen to the dozen, everybody at the same time! They loved each other! I thought about them every now and then both in Judaea and in Alexandria... Hoping that one day I would have a family like that."

"And didn't you?" Theo asked.

Uri hugged him, kissed his cheek, and pulled him close.

"Yes, I did, thanks be to the Eternal One."

On the wider highways they'd encounter freight carts; from them it was possible to buy greens, water, and flatbread; occasionally groups of suspicious characters would hurry past. Perhaps escaped slaves or highwaymen, but they did not bother them: the family was too big and they quite obviously had nothing.

The children got used to constantly being on the move, with even the girls discovering the advantages of the lifestyle, with their grandmother and aunt never in a position to continually dress them down. With a vacant look on her face, Sarah would wash their clothes in a stream and hang them out to dry on tree branches; she would divide up the food and wash the dishes, complaining of neither heat nor cold. Hagar even gave up on her constant sniveling when she saw it made no sense, while Hermia whenever possible would lie down and escape into sleep.

With a knife Uri cut himself a staff and so too did Theo, along with a slender one for Marcellus after he, naturally, demanded his own. Uri demonstrated to Theo how to fight with a staff, and Marcellus wanted to join in and learn. The womenfolk and the girls gaped to see Uri fighting, prancing forward and backward, brandishing the staff, somersaulting, feinting to trick his invisible opponent. Hagar was amazed and even Sarah came out of her semi-stupor.

"Where did you learn that?" she asked.

"At the Gymnasium," said Uri. "I also learned how to throw the javelin, shoot with a bow and arrow, and fight with a sword."

Marcellus's father immediately grew in his eyes, and while his elder brother and father practiced face to face, he set about tree trunks, whacking them over and over again until his own stick broke, at which he burst into floods of tears and Uri had to cut him a new one.

The knife he carried under his tunic, tied to his back on the left, so that he could produce it quickly if they ever came under attack. No one attacked them, however, among the wonderful hills of the Campanian countryside, where so much tasty fruit was growing in the wild. Uri still remembered what was edible, steering clear of the mushrooms, being unfamiliar with them.

He lost weight, his paunch vanishing and his muscles becoming satisfactorily toned, and much to his sons' joy he found he could leap from a standing position almost as far as he had been able to back in Alexandria. Theo would leap, Marcellus would leap, and the girls also leapt with much screaming. Uri's chest no longer ached, nor his rectum, nor his remaining teeth, and his heart beat nice and slowly.

During the day they got into the practice of padding along southward, quietly satisfied that they would not die of hunger, with odd scraps of poems coming to Uri's mind.

He recalled just one line from a poem by Archilochus: "He wanders unhinged on the path of his bleak, vagrant existence." That had already been known to men many centuries before.

Another line, from Gorgias, came to mind: "Why should we lead happier lives than those, the beautiful ones?"

These were the sort of lines Uri crooned to himself. Theo asked where they came from, and this father enlightened him.

"That's what poetry is good for," Uri brooded. "Lines come to mind when you find yourself in situations similar to those of which poets once sang, and it makes you feel at ease. If something already happened to them, then it's quite all right! You're wandering, and people who died a long time ago wander with you."

He added in some amazement that it was strange how short poems were worth much more than epic verse.

Common prayer was worth even more.

The family prayed aloud both in the morning and the evening. When he had been at home in Far Side Uri had generally missed both, because he left early to attend to business rather than waking up with his family and, whenever possible, he got home when they were already asleep. Now, following Uri's lead, they prayed and lay down to sleep together. Experience had shown that yesterday they had not died of starvation, they had not been devoured by wolves, nor had they frozen last night, so in all likelihood the Almighty was protectively watching over them, and since they had committed no sin, either against Him or against other people, it would be no different tomorrow.

Theo noticed that in reciting his prayers his father said something in a different way than he was familiar with. Before they ate their meal, he would say a grace customarily used in Judaea: "Give us tomorrow's bread today." This was not something the Roman Jews said, nor indeed did it make much sense, as they would usually pray for the Lord to give their daily bread today, so Uri was slightly surprised when Theo asked him what he meant: he was not aware that it had slipped out.

"I rather think," he said, "that it is a reference to the Messiah's coming."

"The thing that the Nazarenes talk about as coming 'again'?"

"Quite probably."

The others adopted the same wording.

After supper and before they turned in for the night, Uri, with help from Theo, would teach Marcellus and the girls a little Latin. The girls were none too happy, but Uri encouraged them by saying that they would find better husbands that way. Marcellus did not need encouraging as he always wanted to know whatever his brother knew, the only trouble being that he wanted everything right away, without having to work for it. At these times Sarah and Hagar would draw their blanket up over their head and pretend to sleep, while Hermia would stare glassy-eyed into the air.

To go to sleep they would wrap up in their blankets with the small ones in the inside, rather like a wolf pack.

"Papa," said Theo one evening. "It's true, isn't it, that you love us more than you used to?"

Uri was moved.

Musing, he said:

"Maybe it's more a case of liking myself a little better."

"Yourself?"

"It seems that I prefer being an outlaw to anything else. Maybe the Eternal One created us all to be outlaws, that's our natural state, only he forgot to engrave into our souls that we should want to remain outlaws."

PUTEOLI, WHERE THEY WERE GOING TO LIVE, HAD TO BE CLOSE, AS NOW they found they had to go westward, toward the sea.

There was no road any longer, only gardens—some tidy, some derelict—with narrow, weed-covered paths between them, and Hermia one day stepped on a thorn. It went deep into the sole of her right foot, and Uri and Hagar and Sarah all took turns attempting to extract it, Uri with his knife, the others with their nails. Hermia wailed; it was hurting a lot. They waited a while and Uri gave it another try, but it was in vain.

"Just leave me here!" Hermia pleaded. "You all just go on."

Uri shook his head.

The children went off to steal fruit, the adults stayed with her. It grew dark and they slept under some bushes.

By the next day Hermia's leg had swollen up to the knee and turned purple. Uri, thinking back to Judaea, tried to get her to understand that he would have to cut the foot open with his knife to release the pus otherwise it would lead to real problems, but Hermia would not agree, and Sarah also protested that to thrust a knife into living flesh was against the Law. Hagar, for her part, lay there and dropped off to sleep, wailing every now and then, while the children chased after one another.

By the evening the leg had swollen up as far as the thigh.

Uri could see before his eyes the medical tables they had learned in Alexandria. A swelling like this would spread farther until it reached the lungs, where it would be fatal. It was now imperative to cut off part of his sister's foot, and not with the knife he had but with a sharp scalpel.

Hermia died at daybreak, having been in agony for hours, rasping and choking with the whole of her tumid right side burning. Her eyes rolled back hideously, she was slack-jawed, she tossed and turned, and in the end her back was frozen, arched taut in a spasm.

The family scratched at the earth, Uri with his knife, the children and the two women with their hands, and when the pit was deep enough they slipped in the dead body. It was no easy task as they were unable to break the corpse's rigid back. They scattered earth over her, but could not cover her entirely, so they had to dig elsewhere, carrying that dirt over to add to what they'd excavated. Theo rambled a fair distance in search of a decently sized stone and with much effort located and brought one back on his own. Uri put on grandfather's liberty cap, the women knitted a shawl, and the children pulled their little cloaks over their heads. Uri uttered a mourners' Kaddish, the others added muttered "Amens," and they all rent their ragged clothes.

They then ate all that they had; they had no wine or even water but swallowed their tears.

They sprinkled soil on themselves, their heads and clothes, washed their hands and feet in earth, then, bowing to the southeast and seated on their heels, they glorified the Eternal One. Uri glorified Him fervently and drunkenly until he suddenly realized that he was unable to recall his sister's features—neither her face when she had been alive nor the face she'd displayed after her death.

That day they did not move on. Uri went off a little way and started sketching with a twig in the ground. He sketched portraits of all the people he had known who were now dead. Joseph, Philo, Marcus, a few of the Jews who died of starvation in Alexandria and whom he had seen once only—all except Hermia. The remaining two women and the children did not disturb him, thinking he was praying.

"He's writing a letter to the Lord," Hagar told the children with an air of mystery.

"Me too! Me too!"

All the children wanted to write letters, and they kept on pestering Theo until he had written down their wishes in the dust. They asked the Eternal One for their aunt to become an angel on the other side, to give her nice clothes, to get her a lot of honeyed flatbread to eat, and for her to be boundlessly happy, though none of them asked the Lord to guide her back to Earth.

THERE WAS NO WORK TO BE HAD IN PUTEOLI, WITH CLAUDIUS HAVING done such a good job on developing the large harbor at Ostia, so much nearer Rome.

Uri paid rent on a dwelling in a suburb some distance from the port, at the foot of a hill not far from the villa at which Caligula had given an audience to the Jewish delegation, when Agrippa had suffered a stroke and all but expired. Cheap though it was, the dwelling was of course expensive for them, but Uri could not countenance leaving his own family without a roof and having to sleep out on the streets like true beggars. They got two rooms, with the children happily taking possession of theirs—after all, it had beds in it, real beds! They bounced on them and, try as Uri might to discipline them, he found that even Theo would not obey him. Uri had to concede that his paternal authority had dwindled since he had proven unable to drive death away from Hermia.

Hagar, sensing she was finally and permanently installed in a dwelling, now livened up and started to nag and nag at a husband who had kept quiet about carrying a fortune around on him. Uri let her rant, but the children took notice. "What a liar you are!" Uri went with Sarah to the market and bought everything the children needed, including sweets. Sarah asked a neighbor for a live coal to light their own fire then set to work happily cooking and washing, as cooking and washing were all she could do.

Theo had the job of calming his mother down, but even he was unable to stem the flood:

"You killed Hermia, you brute! We could have hired a boat and she would still be alive to this day!" Hagar shrieked.

"You never liked my sister," Uri retorted.

"You don't like anyone, you selfish beast!"

Uri looked for work, but no one was taking on anybody.

He would have preferred to avoid the company of Jews, but that was not possible on account of the Sabbaths and feast days; it was true they could offer no work, but they did send around a three-man team to assess the circumstances in which all newcomers were living. They sniffed around in the rented dwelling

759

then, after a certain amount of whispered consultation, they announced how much Uri would have to contribute to the synagogue's half-shekel Temple tax: two sesterces a month.

This was a stupefying amount.

"You have a large family," was their explanation.

"But we don't even have a menorah! Not even a crummy little lamp!" Uri expostulated.

"That we can give you," was their answer.

They did not ask why they had turned up in Puteoli from Rome: the Jews of Rome had evidently not sent a courier out this far from Rome, so it seemed Plotius had been right about that. They didn't inquire because it was not in their interest to do so. After all, unless they had good reason no one would withdraw from Rome to a declining town like Puteoli.

There was no work.

Uri tried to capitalize on his tessera, but the local magistrate did not wish to get involved even though he had a duty to do so: Romans were envied by the inhabitants of Puteoli even though most of them made their livelihood from letting summer cottages to them. Instead they asked for all manner of identification papers that could only be obtained in Rome, so Uri gave up trying. Only services catering to vacationers operated in the town, and even those only during the summer: whores, boatmen, bath attendants, restauranteurs, masseurs, musicians, and singers made a good living, but they ran closed shops, and never took in newcomers.

He took his children out to the coast to show them where Caligula's bridge had once stood; now that no trace of it was left. The children were astounded and did not believe a word of what he said; Theo took a dip in the sea while the others, not daring to follow him, collected sea shells and took them home to make into necklaces.

Three whole months went by without any work; by autumn he was left with money for just two more weeks.

Uri even tried to sign up on a ship, asking for half the money to be paid in advance so that he could leave it to his family during the months he would be absent, but he was judged by his toothlessness to be too old.

The Jews had no need of a scribe or cleaner in the synagogue; they needed taxpayers.

"This is not a good place to come to," grumbled an elderly, half-blind dyer. "This is a place that people escape from. My children and grandchildren have scattered in all directions across the big wide world. My own legs are too poor."

"If I learn how to dye cloth, will you take me on?"

"No."

There was not enough money to get them to Alexandria or Judaea.

There were Jewish merchants in town, but they would not open their doors.

On the first Sabbath the newcomers had been received with great joy at the synagogue. It was a dilapidated little building with a crumbling roof, and food on offer was skimpy. Uri took his whole family, resplendent in freshly laundered clothes. Uri spoke pleasantly to the unknown congregation, but they only had eyes for Theo, because he was a good-looking, slender boy of a type they themselves did not produce. I ought to have kept him hidden, thought Uri; already they are jealous of me here as well. Total strangers patted Uri and Theo on the back and hastened to load up plates for them at the table that had been laid in front of the house of prayer, but it was impossible to strike up any conversation because they spent all their time talking with each other.

There was wine to be had, and Uri permitted the girls to drink a little.

"It's good here," said Eulogia confidentially to her father. "We're staying, aren't we?"

"We're staying," Uri said.

He mended the broken dolls' legs then went off to putter on his own around the harbor, gazing at one of the stones there.

Not long ago he had been a well-off Roman merchant with a dozen superb, reliable contacts and a comfortable existence. He had been improvident: instead of investing his money in gold he had put it into new ventures, which were gone with the wind. He had put blind faith in the future. If it were just him alone, the admonition from the Lord would stand him in good stead. He had been too cocksure: he was not where he should have been, he had been affluent. The time had come for him to be poor.

The thing is, God help me! I have a family. How is it that you don't see us? Why do you afflict others because of my conceitedness?

He was reminded of "Sisyphus," a comedy by Critias and Cinesias of Athens and Diagoras of Melos, who were known as atheists even though they were not Jews. As Prodicus of Ceos was supposed to have said, "Man makes precisely the god he needs." Those things had come to mind after the Bane in Alexandria.

Alexandria would not pass; it was coming.

THEO WANTED TO RAMBLE WITH URI, CONCERNED ABOUT HIS FATHER'S growing increasingly despondent; the womenfolk could keep their eyes on the young ones.

"I can do many things," Uri told him as he mooched around the harbor. "The trouble is that these people have no need for the things I can do."

"But there was a need for them in Rome!"

"Not very much even there, and not at all in Puteoli. This city is dead."

"So let's move on!"

"Where to?"

"It doesn't matter. We'll stick it out! We've learned how to roam around. It was not all that long ago that all Jews wandered. In the Scriptures everyone is constantly fleeing. Let's just move on. I genuinely enjoy it."

One evening Uri raised with Hagar and Sarah the suggestion that they should go farther south. Syracusa wasn't too bad a city; even now it no doubt bubbled with life, and, what's more, it had become safer since Caligula had ordered that its walls be repaired.

Maybe he had wanted to stop there on the way to Alexandria, it occurred to Uri. Caligula had been so cunning in forestalling everything except his own assassination.

Sarah remained quiet: she did not grasp it at all, just peacefully went on darning one of the children's tunics by the light of a lamp. It was not the Jews who provided the lamp; Uri had bought one.

"We're not going anywhere," Hagar stated scathingly. "You're going to have to dig into the remaining money."

"But there is no money left!"

"Sure there is, you lying dog!"

There really was no more than five sesterces left, but it was useless for Uri to say so.

He got up at dawn and tiptoed out of the house in which, besides themselves, lived three families of Latini, two on the upper floor.

He set off for the harbor. Theo caught up.

"I'm going with you," he said.

"Go home!"

"I'm not leaving you alone!"

Uri stopped at the edge of still sleeping, auroral Puteoli.

"How did we end up here, Theo?" he asked.

"The Eternal One guided us here," said his son.

"For what purpose?"

"So that we may fulfill his will."

Uri could have countered that but instead chose to remain silent.

When they reached the harbor area, Uri turned toward the slave market.

They arrived too early; day had hardly broken, so they sat down and waited.

The vendors stole out of the alleyways to open their stalls. Uri bought a flat-bread and some wine for eight asses, which they both ate and drank.

"What do you intend to do, father?" Theo asked.

Uri said nothing before pressing the remaining four sesterces and four asses into Theo's hand.

"It's better you have it," he said.

"But that's a lot of money!"

"Better it's with you."

By the time the sun was up, several slave-traders and a few black slaves had arrived. An awn was stretched over the timber scaffold, on which the people who were for sale would be stood. The traders then set about their breakfast, eating with a will.

Alongside the platform, a small booth was opened, in which sat a man from the local authority, a pint-sized pipsqueak who was supposed to collect the tax due on each slave who was sold. Tiberius had decreed that a two percent tax was payable to the treasury on the sale of any slave, and that had remained in force ever since. A vendor would always do his best to offset the burden of the tax on the purchaser, and the purchaser in his turn would protest against that but in the end, of course, would always pay up.

The fifth of the black slaves had just clambered down from the platform when Uri, youthful and fresh jumped up. Theo was thunderstruck.

"Hey there, people!" Uri called out merrily. "I'm selling myself!"

SIX PEOPLE IN SUCCESSION PEERED INTO HIS MOUTH AND CLAMBERED down from the scaffold without a word. Uri took off his tunic, standing in just a loincloth and flexing his arms and legs as he stiffened in the pose of the statue of a discus thrower, then in the pose of a javelin thrower statue, and then in the pose of Phidias's statue of Athene, taking a few long standing-jumps and scanning some lines of Virgil in Latin, before being pushed off by surly-faced vendors.

"Father, that was silly," said a shamefaced Theo.

Uri panted.

"That's all I could come up with," he remonstrated, pulling his tunic back over his head.

"Let's go," Theo said.

They had set off when a tall, brawny chap clapped a hand on Uri's shoulder.

"I'm interested," he said.

Uri came to a stop and stuttered:

"I'm fluent in three languages, have a passing familiarity with another four, I can take shorthand, wrestle, shoot a bow and arrow, use a sling, smooth wood with a plane, reap with a sickle..."

"It's your son I'm interested in."

Uri fell silent before giving a laugh:

"Only I am for sale," he said.

"Two thousand sesterces for your son," said the buyer.

"Get lost!"

"Ten thousand," Theo spoke.

Uri goggled at him.

"Don't be stupid!" he exclaimed. "Are you mad?"

"Deal," said the buyer. "I'll give that."

Uri laughed.

"He's not for sale," he said blithely. "He's a Roman citizen, just like me."

By then there were six bruisers standing in a circle around them.

"Ten thousand," the buyer repeated. "And I'll pay the tax."

"He's not for sale," Uri repeated.

"I've agreed to the terms. He'll have a fine time with me."

"I said no!"

The bruisers grabbed hold of Theo. Uri roared in fury and flung himself on one of them but simply rebounded off his rock-hard abdomen. People looked their way: at last something was happening.

"He's not for sale!" Uri bawled.

The buyer stuffed money and a written document into a sack and threw that on the ground. Uri's hands were twisted behind his back and he was kicking and shouting inarticulately; the onlookers found it uproariously funny.

Theo was then bundled onto a cart.

"Don't worry, father! Take care of yourself!" he shouted as he looked back.

The bruisers took off after the cart. Uri would have run after them but he was tripped up by a bystander, to great applause.

Uri lay flat on his face on the ground, panting, the nape of his neck throbbing.

"You bastards!" he yelled.

People around about snickered and then dispersed. No one spoke to him or touched the sack that lay beside him on the ground. Someone began gesticulating and shouting from the platform, attracting the attention of the idle onlookers given that Uri could not be expected to be the source of any further amusement.

Uri himself sat up and stared dully at the sack. He opened it, poured out the money and started to count it.

Squatting on his heels, dizzy, he counted 1,960 seterces.

He was left to scrape the money together and stuff it back in the sack. Also lying there on the ground was a written contract regarding two thousand sesterces, signed by someone called Maronius, which had been given a stamp of state approval, above which was an official text that read that the buyer had deducted tax from the price paid for the slave, signed with some illegible scrawl.

URI RELATED TO HAGAR WHAT HAD HAPPENED.

Hagar was not too upset: she had never liked Theo, because she could see how much Uri loved him; she loved Marcellus, whom Uri had not liked.

She told the children that Theo had run away.

Uri protested that he had not run away but been kidnapped as a slave!

"It's my fault!" Uri cried out. "I wanted to sell myself, though not out of self-sacrifice, I know that now, but simply because I was seeking to escape from my responsibility—for you all! And the Lord is punishing me for my dishonesty by hitting me where it hurts hardest: he's taken Theo away!"

This was too much for the children to take in; they whimpered and batted their eyes dutifully but they took what Hagar had said as being the truth. They understood that he had simply run away, and they secretly cursed him and envied him.

They then rented a dwelling in the center of Puteoli because the women and children did not dare go to the harbor on their own; to some extent they were justified because public safety in Puteoli had become atrocious as the town had become impoverished, with unemployed youths tearing about the place with cudgels, robbing women and battering children. Only in the port area was there some degree of order as the municipal authority had posted vigiles in that part of town.

The dwelling space they obtained consisted of two unfurnished rooms, one for the women, the other for children, without even a curtain between them. Uri resumed his search for work. He rambled around unsteadily, his eyesight even worse than ever, in the grip of insomnia as he was unable to sleep, continually going over in his mind what had happened: if he had been in good shape he would have decked at least one of the six bruisers.

"Anything precious is wrecked!" he kept reiterating obsessively at night. "We wreck anything at all!"

Half-asleep, the children would grumble; they wanted to sleep.

It became autumnal, with the vacationers moving back to Rome. The house was unheated and Uri's back throbbed painfully; water had only been installed on the ground floor and so had to be carried up from there. Uri bought a water jug, a basin, and some pots and pans at a nearby market.

Sarah washed, cooked, and carried up water from the tap downstairs, but one day she had a dizzy spell, slipped, and rolled down the stairs, breaking her neck.

"She did not want to live any more, and the stairs sensed that," Hagar whispered into the children's ears. Uri reddened but said nothing.

The funeral was expensive: Uri was unable to haggle for a price reduction and the Jews of Puteoli were unsympathetic, requiring him to install a gravestone, saying they would not bury her unless there was one (the stonemason must have had an arrangement to get a commission). In Puteoli there were no catacombs in which to carry out burials; the Jews had a plot of land at the foot of the hill.

On the stone, Uri had engraved Sarah's name and the fact that she had lived forty-five years; the Italian stonemason kept reminding him that it would cost a bare ten sesterces more to engrave an etrog, lulav, and menorah, but there Uri drew the line. It was not nice to take revenge on a dead person, but that was what he did to his mother for having engraved on his father's grave marker all the things he had expressly asked not be there.

Sarah was buried. They ran out of money; Uri finally took a job as a fuller.

He might have found better work, but his soul wanted to do penance.

Fulling consisted of walking all day long on clothes that had been thrown into huge tubs of human urine—nothing more. Among the people who did this were convicted prisoners, drunken wretches, lonely madmen, deserters, bankrupt businessmen, vagrant peasants, all kinds of reprobates, but not a single slave. Uri was astonished that only freedmen were permitted to perform such a menial task, but when one of them—while drunk—slipped, fell, and broke his arm it became clear why: being a freedman, he was not entitled to any compensation, however much he pleaded. A freedman's body was also free; it was at his disposal and so had no value. A slave's body, by contrast, did have a value because it did not belong to him, so if he was injured, his owner was entitled to be compensated.

Uri trampled clothes in the urine, rinsed them, then mangled them with a rolling pin—backbreaking labor. Urine was a disinfectant—that was known back in the time of Hippocrates but what was not known—or maybe it had just been kept under wraps—was that urine attacks the feet. It corroded Uri's skin, sometimes to the point of making it hard to drag himself back home, where he would find that Hagar had not left him any supper, having ensured that the children eat up everything by the time he got back. Uri would rub fish oil onto the bone-deep abscesses on his feet and moan in pain.

"You stink!" Hagar averred.

"You stink!" averred Marcellus, with Irene and Eulogia following suit.

Uri might have wondered whether his wife or children were more repelled, but he did not wonder at all, just existed, in a light sleep that reeked of piss. He had dreadful dreams: he would be the owner of a nice big house on a hillside but it would be open on all sides and people would walk through as if he were not even there. In another recurring dream he would be residing on the top floor of a building and would want to go home but the stairs had been replaced by a rickety ladder and that had broken, so he needed to clamber up on a narrow plank, but he was dizzy and his feet slipped, leaving him hanging between ground and sky, unable to reach his dwelling. He hated most of all a dream in which long, thin worms crawled out of his toes; he would grab them and keep on pulling at them, but they were seemingly endless.

Marcellus, being his mother's darling, gained ascendancy over the others. He remained stubby-faced and hook-nosed, with dark hair and skin; there was no knowing what strains of African or Asian tribes had spitefully taken up residence in him. Uri did not have the strength to give any instruction either to him or to his daughters, who had turned out ugly, with buck teeth, gaunt features, and hooked noses; they had picked up a smattering of kitchen Latin while roaming unsupervised about in the harbor quarter, but they never read anything. Uri also read nothing, and they had no scrolls apart from the Torah, so that the kids spent their time hanging around the harbor. Hagar now did the washing and cooking, not moving from the third floor except to shop. She was frightened of the unknown town and unable herself to get straight in her mind even which way was north or south. She had never learned to speak a word of Latin because everyone in the markets spoke Greek, and here she was unable to talk with the neighbors because they did not speak a word of Greek, coming from Latium as they did. My so-called loved ones are all going to be stupid, Uri thought. Dear God, this was Your wish.

Uri stuck with the fulling work until spring and then quit. He had collected enough money to be able to spend another few months looking for work. He bet on the tourists, hoping someone would have need for a scrivener, or something of the kind.

He ought to have taken on the job as a fuller earlier, not out of penance, but because then Theo would still be free and with them. How could he have been so insane? How could he have so completely taken leave of his senses?

He spent the entire day, day after day, on his own at the pier conversing with his father or with Theo.

He would ask Joseph why he had to stick it out with his so-called family, and Joseph would answer mournfully that he had to because he, Uri's father, had set the miserable example.

You're different in character from me, the father would say to the daydreaming Uri. You were a born a hedonist; it's my fault that you are forced to be an ascetic.

But who was there to set an example for you, seeing as your father, Taddeus, died young and you never even knew him?

The Eternal One, Joseph mournfully declared, who hates His chosen people but has never abandoned them, no matter how unfaithful, wretched, selfish, extortionist, profiteering, narrow-minded, stupid, cowardly, swaggering, and blind, or how many times He might be gravely disappointed.

"Would the Lord have done better to abandon us?" Uri would ask his father.

Joseph pondered but gave no answer.

It would have been better, Uri concluded. Then the Jewish community, the Kahal, would not have banished me; I could have been a free Greek or Roman.

Joseph looked on him: My dear boy, the Greek polis operates in exactly the same way; all societies work that way. Do you think that's why I let you stuff so many letters into that mind of yours?

There at the water's edge Uri was overcome with shame. Even with my eyesight being so poor my father could have set me to work and yet he did not. He allowed me to read so that I might gain knowledge, may his name be blessed!

Uri asked of Theo what he was to do with his younger brother, sisters, and mother. Theo eagerly explained that no person was hopeless; a lot could be achieved with education.

So what should I turn my hand to, dear son.

Theo, the easy-going, handsome boy that he was, puckered his brow and thought very hard before saying: You know what, Father, not everyone in Dikaiarchia is literate. Sell them what you know best and you yourself enjoy doing. It was stupid that in penance for me you sold the one thing that you haven't got: your health.

Theo also said that insanity was not a punishment; the punishment was meted out by the Almighty on a person for driving himself mad out of cowardice. Uri begged his son's pardon because he had even gotten his penance wrong.

Theo chuckled in his usual way; he was always forgiving of everything.

PASSOVER SABBATH WAS CELEBRATED AT THE SYNAGOGUE. THE LOCAL Jews arrived in high spirits; Uri and his family skulked about aimlessly in the garden.

Uri took particular notice of an ancient woman with her back bent at a right angle, who was talking aloud to herself as she gnawed with her toothless gums at chunks of bread she had dunked in her wine. Uri edged closer: the crone was cursing in Aramaic as she rocked her head left and right, not being able to look up as her rigid spine did not allow that.

"What's the matter?" Uri asked her in Aramaic.

"That I'm still alive," wheezed the crone, unable to look at him.

"It won't last much longer, never fear," Uri assured her.

"The hell it won't, God damn it to Hell and back," she shrilled. "My only problem is my back! Why could I never manage to get leprosy or the plague!"

Uri laughed.

"How old are you, granny?"

"What the hell do I know!" the old woman spluttered. "My grandsons are already starting to die out on me, but I'm still here without any teeth!"

"Your gums must be good and hard by now," Uri ventured.

"The Lord punishes me by still making it possible for me to guzzle and shit. And I still pee so tidily that I could write my name with it."

Uri guffawed.

A plump man came over, amazed.

"You're able to talk to her?" he asked in Greek.

"Yes, I can."

"She's my great-grandma. She's been dumped on me from over there, but no one can make a word out of what she burbles on about."

"She's a very nice old lady," Uri reassured him.

"She's a nice old lady who's been dumped on me from over-there; she wheezes on all day to the point we can stand it no longer."

"This overfed donkey is one of my great-grandsons," the crone said in Aramaic. "He doesn't understand a word of what I say, just spouts like all the other idiots here, things like 'Hey!' and 'Whoa!' that even the dimmest ordinary beast understands—he can't even latch on to things like that. I gave birth to a whole pack of them, may the Eternal One damn them all!"

"What's that she's saying?" the tubby man asked.

Uri interpreted her as saying:

"She regrets that she can't speak Greek and so is unable to discourse with you about exalted matters."

The flabby fellow looked askance at Uri.

"She said that?"

"That's what she said."

"Just among her grandsons—she has around twenty, and who knows how many great-grandsons—they chose me of all people to pass her on to!"

Jason, the flabby fellow, asked Uri how much he would ask for per week to take over looking after the old woman.

Uri specified a huge sum.

"Done!" Jason breathed a sigh of relief. "Blessed be Passover! I feel right now as if I had just escaped from Egypt."

Auntie Milka was not easy to get along with. Uri was greatly entertained for a few weeks, but then less and less, only to pack it in two months later, just after Shavuot, which was only observed nominally in Puteoli since it had no agricultural connotations.

"I can't take any more," he admitted shamefacedly. "The money's very necessary, but I'm being driven mad by how she endlessly repeats herself. She's a sweet old thing, but I'm afraid that I'll throttle her one day!"

Milka was not present when this came under discussion.

"I'm amazed you stuck at it as long as you did," Jason said. "I secretly rather hoped you would do away with her!"

"That wasn't part of the agreement," Uri riposted. "I'm open to offers though."

Jason could not decide whether Uri was joking or meant that seriously, so he chose to respond with a laugh or two. Uri was counting on his savings from the money he had received being enough to last until early winter.

At this point Jason offered him quite another deal. He had a horrible wife, compared with whom Auntie Milka was an angel, and she had gotten it into her head to follow up her family tree.

"She's hoping that some of her forebears were priests," said Jason. "I told her that it doesn't make the slightest bit of difference now she's married to me, seeing that I'm not a Kohen or from the tribe of Levi, but she's gotten it into her head and she's neglecting the kids, neglecting me, not prepared to do any cooking, and now she's not willing to nurse the seventh child, who was born only four months ago! If the baby's not a Kohen, she won't nurse him! And if he were a Levite, would she suckle him from one tit?"

The proposition was that Uri should track down the ancestors of Jason's wife and draw up a family tree, which would then be sent to Jerusalem to be verified.

"You want me to unearth a Kohen ancestor?" Uri asked.

"Yes, dig one up."

Jason had money, so Uri again accepted the deal.

The documentation in Puteoli was sketchy because Neapolis was the older port and a Jewish colony had been established there earlier than anywhere else in Italia; indeed, for a long time every Jewish document in the whole of Campania had to be taken there. Free Jewish merchants had set up a Neapolitan community many centuries ago, long before Far Side emerged in Rome; they were making the voyage from Alexandria to Magna Graecia, and many settled down there. But even their descendants never mixed with the later Jews of Rome, who had always been considered by them to be just the progeny of wretched slaves, and so purely on this account they regarded Uri condescendingly. However, since Uri had paid plenty of money to inspect the archives they let him browse, and he conscientiously foraged in the archives; Jason paid enough to allow Uri, on the pretext of earning his income, to travel away from his family for weeks on end. Neapolis lay near Puteoli and could be reached in under a day by boat, cart, or even on foot, but it was still another city, making it reasonable to claim it was too far away for him to return home for the night.

In one fell swoop, Jason was able to calm down the hysterics of both his own abhorred wife and Uri's Hagar.

Uri took his time with his work in the Neapolitan archives, happily wandering around the town, eating and drinking a lot, and meanwhile his family also enjoyed a good life—without him. I've managed to escape from them at least for a while, Uri reflected; it may be a sin but the Lord will surely forgive me.

Milka finally died, but not Jason's wife, who continued her nagging at him thanks be to the Eternal One, who was unchanging in her hatred for her husband.

Uri came across some interesting documents in the Jewish archive at Neapolis and also visited some of the Greek libraries now that he was again free to spend his time reading. It was like being a student all over again, but he was free to learn whatever he wanted, unencumbered with stupid teachers. He knew nobody in Naples and, what's more, did not want to get to know anybody, being pleased to have his time to himself.

Naples had become a glittering, boring, and quiet town under Caligula, and became even more so under Claudius. Both emperors had spent considerable sums of money on it and the surrounding area that when they took summer holidays they would find suitably distinguished shrines and theaters of Roman standards for them to visit; they had also given generously toward the restoration of Greek relics. There were few bordellos and taverns in the town, with Puteoli offering more in that line. The volumes held by one of the larger Greek libraries had been housed in one of the annexes of an enormous new temple to Castor and Pollux; construction had been started by Caligula given his infatuation with the Dioscuri, and completed by Claudius, seeing that it had been started. Uri befriended the librarian there, a man called Daphnos, who also produced some of the rarities for Uri to inspect. He was middle-aged and a freedman, initially fearful that Uri was seeking to oust him from his position, but Uri brought the matter up of his own accord, without any prompting, telling him that he had no need to worry as Uri had no wish to live in Naples. In gratitude, the librarian took a day off to bring Uri to see Virgil's nearby grave; later, after they had drunk themselves into a fine state in one of the nearby taverns, they tried to outdo each other in reciting from his poems. Uri recounted tales about Alexandria, Daphnos, for his part, about Tarsus, from which he originally hailed.

"They loathe Jews there," Daphnos said, "but no one can say why. There even the Jews hate themselves and denounce one another to the Greeks; it's been like that for generations and no one can say why that should be. All Greeks from Tarsus are terrible, and the Jews no less."

"So, does that make you terrible, too?" Uri queried.

Daphnos mused on that:

"I would have been so if I had not been taken away from there as a child."

Daphnos was all for taking Uri over to the island of Capri now that it was possible; for enough money anyone could inspect Tiberius's pavilions with their erotic pictures. Uri was not interested; he could well imagine them.

It turned out that Daphnos's wife was a converted Jew. Uri told some stories about how in Alexandria Jewish wives who were converted Greeks were made to eat pork in the theater during the Bane, and how those who were unwilling to do so had been flogged, and about the ensuing tragedies that had resulted in Delta.

In return, Daphnos told Uri about how his father's Greek owner, along with his parents, grandparents, and children in Tarsus, had been wiped out by Greek enemies. They had even set fire to his house only because he had been a decent man; all his slaves had been set adrift at sea. Then they had traversed Thrace, Dalmatia, and even Pannonia, which is inhabited by particularly wild tribes. In Germania, Daphnos's father had become a Germanic warrior and had eventually fallen in battle and taken prisoner by the Romans; he found it useless trying to explain to them in choice Greek that he came from Tarsus. Indeed, there was not a single person in the Roman army who understood a single word of Greek—or even Latin, for that matter—because they too were Germans and only spoke other dialects of that, though by then Daphnos spoke six varieties of Germanic. There were countless Germanic tribes, some of which were called Gauls or Sarmatians, though that was mistaken, they were all Germanic, and they all hated each other and hacked one another to pieces. He went on to give a list of the fabulous and fanciful names borne by the various tribes: Usipi, Tencteri, Chatti, Langobardi, Angrivarii, Chamavi, Frisians, Chauci, Cherusci, Cimbri, Suebi, Hermunduri, Naristi, Marcomanni or Manimi, Quadi, Marsigni, Cotini, Osi, Buri, Lugii, Harii, Helveconae, Helisii, Naharvali, Gotones, Suiones, Aestii, Sitones, Peucini, Venedi, Fenni, and so on. Daphnos told Uri about their origins and mythology, and meanwhile Uri found himself nodding off from time to time as they drank on inside the library in a small room where this pleasant chap hid his drink, because his wife would not stand for any drunkenness.

Over eighteen months of work Uri had still not come up with a Kohen Levite ancestor for Jason's wife, but just when the situation was starting to become insupportable he came up with one. Jason's wife had a copy of all the documents sent to Jerusalem, and it took a year for the ancestor to be corroborated by them, and nobody was more surprised that Uri: seemingly they were slapdash about their work there as well. Jason's wife was happy, though the find had no practical consequence save for the fact that hereafter she could justifiably reproach her husband with not even being a Levite.

Jason had provided Uri with a sinecure for four complete years, and his children were thus able to grow up in a fairly well-to-do manner, albeit often in his absence, but then the benefactor suffered a stroke from which he died immediately, thanks be to the Eternal One, who, it seemed, did not wish that this decent man suffer for any length of time.

Jason's wife was all for engaging Uri as a secretary but he politely declined.

He paid one last visit to Naples to take leave of his friend. They went off for a drink. Daphnos told him that people had come from Alexandria with books, saying that Claudius had put a considerable sum of money into expanding the Mouseion, with new rooms added onto the wing of the royal palace housing the old Great Library so that it would now be U-shaped, rather like a small covered amphitheater, with room for five hundred readers, and in the middle a long table on which reciters could set out their scrolls.

"Every blessed day," said Daphnos, "orators with the finest voices read aloud from the works of Claudius! They read through his history of Etruria, and once they get to the end, they start all over again from the beginning."

"Just like the Torah!" said Uri, screaming with laughter. "I swear to you that I wrote one of the volumes: Philo didn't make a single correction."

They drank until they were truly drunk; Uri was still dizzy when he took a boat back to Puteoli the next day.

They had enough money to last for a year or so. Uri soon became bored with Naples: the aimless walking, the dropping into taverns, the life-endangering glare, the patched-up boats, the dull-witted boatmen who would steer their craft into the paths of the big freighters, only avoiding head-on collisions at the last second with much screaming, and having nothing to read anyway.

Something would have to come along.

FIVE YEARS AFTER HE HAD THE NAZARENES EXPELLED FROM ROME, Claudius was assassinated.

Prior to that the emperor had his Greek counselors, Isidoros and Lampo, beheaded. The boatmen in the harbor of Puteoli, who did nothing much beyond boasting and swilling, knew the two characters well because they had been obliged to cut them in on a portion of every consignment—a percentage which had grown steadily over the years. Isidoros, so the story went, made a disrespectful comment about the emperor, apparently calling him, in a fit of pique, the illegitimate son of Salome, the old Jewish king's younger sister, who was well known as a whore; some negotiations at which they were present happened to be under way, Claudius gave a sign, and the heads of Isidoros and Lampo fell in one swish of a blade.

Uri remembered what Isidoros had requested of him in Alexandria, namely to mourn his passing when it came. He was unable to mourn him: why, precisely?

If anything, he was angry at him. Clever man that he was, why had he not slinked away with his millions to the countryside? There he could have gotten by, but he had wanted to be at the center of things. Maybe he had been infuriated that the emperor was a man who knew a lot less than he did. Isidoros had not been such a wise man after all.

Claudius had been poisoned with mushrooms by his wife, Agrippina; that was the way she killed him. There's no way of knowing how people had gotten hold of that idea, but it spread the length and breadth of Italia.

It wasn't as if they were sorry for Claudius, who—as was well known since someone had kept a careful tally and circulated many copies in Puteoli as well as elsewhere—inflicted the death penalty on 35 senators and 224 Roman equites at the urging of Narcissus or Messalina. Uri had even seen a scandal-sheet of this kind, with many familiar names on the list, including each and every slave who belonged to Messalina—they were presumably condemned to death by

Narcissus. No women's names appeared on the list, though in many cases their husbands or fathers had died in their stead. He did not see Kainis's name listed anywhere either.

Domitius, a son of Agrippina, the sister of emperor Caligula, whom Claudius had adopted and who called himself Nero, was installed as the new emperor. His father, the first husband of Agrippina, was reportedly a cheat and an overbearing character in general. The young emperor was just seventeen, so Annaeus Seneca, who was already a senator, was recalled by Agrippina from banishment and appointed as his tutor, so thus as far as internal affairs were concerned he became de facto supreme ruler, sharing rule with Burrus, the Praetorian Prefect, who saw to Nero's correspondence in Greek, which is to say he saw to all foreign affairs.

Poor Britannicus, was the general view.

Narcissus was captured at his house in Baiae; he was dragged to Messalina's grave and there stabbed to death, and by then had amassed four hundred million sesterces, all of which now passed to Nero.

It occurred to Uri that if he had known Narcissus lived so close to Puteoli he would have paid him a visit and tapped him for more money.

Nero came in for much praise from the people: what a nice, smart boy he is, he'll make a great emperor.

Nero did indeed make a good start, declaring, on the advice of Seneca and Burrus, an amnesty for all of those who had not been convicted for crimes against public morality by Claudius and his board of judges, and Uri was unexpectedly realized that he was now free to return to Rome if he still had a copy of the expulsion order.

He still had it in the leather satchel, next to the Torah scroll.

There were many who were unable to go back to Rome right away because over the intervening years they had lost their expulsion orders.

Uri was amazed that the Nazarenes had also been accorded an amnesty. He remembered how in Claudius's house Seneca had often warned Rome against new conquerors, saying, "Those we vanquish today will subjugate us tomorrow," and in saying that he included the Jews; indeed, he meant them first and foremost. Perhaps we do not add up to a large number of souls, Uri supposed; we do not count as a source of real danger.

They managed to get back to Rome in two weeks, along the way sleeping in beds in hostelries and eating splendid meals. The children and Hagar were all excited, we're going home, we're going home, they kept on repeating, though Uri was well aware the children in particular could have no clear memories of Far Side.

He had a big argument with Hagar, who wanted to return to Far Side, but Uri dug his heels in.

"Our house was pulled down, and I hated it anyway!" he said. "And I'm not prepared to live among Jews any more!"

"But we're Jews ourselves!" Hagar protested.

"There are four and a half million Jews in the world," said Uri, "but only forty thousand of them live in Far Side! We have the right to live wherever we please!"

Hagar had no arguments, no matter how much she shouted at him at the top of her voice, but for once that made no impression on Uri. The children did not voice an opinion, not even Mama's favorite.

Uri rented a dwelling on the Via Nomentana, or at least the very end of it, in an ill-reputed eastern suburb of true Rome. The place was on the fifth floor of an unplastered timber tenement building; the rent—cheap though it had to be paid a year in advance—was collected, in return for a regular receipt, by a caretaker, a boozy, bossy busybody who yammered on incessantly, to which the other residents would respond in kind. He was in charge of nine tenement buildings in the area, and once he'd made his rounds taciturn collectors would take the money from him to the landlord, though who that was even the caretaker did not know.

Uri said to Marcellus:

"Life for many people is little more than being born in Far Side, padding around all the time by foot and getting as far as the Via Nomentana, a mere mile and a half from where they were born!"

Marcellus gave an inane stare.

Theo would have understood him.

The house may even belong to Kainis, Uri speculated, and laughed to himself in the way he had been doing recently: cryptically and mirthlessly.

It was the sort of tenement in which the largest and most expensive dwelling was situated on the ground floor, and the higher one had to climb up the narrow, creaking, rickety, wooden steps without a railing, constantly at risk of tumbling down, the cheaper and more cramped they were.

Their dwelling consisted of a single room, in which the cooking was done, the smoke and steam let out by holding the shutter out wide, and in which they also slept, on the floor.

There were three more dwellings on the fifth floor, the others even more cramped, and without even curtains over their doorways. It was impossible to tell exactly how many people lived in them, despite Uri's efforts to ferret that out.

At the foot of the staircase was the always-closed front door of the best of the dwellings, occupying the entire ground floor, said to be inhabited by a prosperous Thracian wine merchant. Before this stood an enormous uncovered wooden pail into which the occupants emptied the slops of their chamber pots; the contents of the filled pail was taken away each day by fullers, after the turds were taken out by shovel or by hand in front and scattered on the street in front of the entrance to the building. Only the urine was valuable, as that was used to launder the clothes and blankets that the idle Romans had no wish to trouble themselves with cleaning. The house stank throughout all five floors of shit, piss, food, smoke—the stench of human effluvia.

What would the Essenes have made of all this?

The tenement building had been constructed, along with many others, in a street that had previously burned down to the ground, and it was to be hoped that it would last a few years before it either burned down itself or simply collapsed, as was often the case with the hastily built Roman tenement buildings. As a counter against the common outbreaks of fire, by one of Nero's decrees, it was required that a porch be erected in front of any tenement building, from the flat roof of which the vigiles were able to fight a blaze more effectively. The landlords of such buildings invariably passed the cost on to the tenants and Uri too soon received a demand to contribute, although no doubt the previous tenant had already paid it. Uri fumed and asked to be allowed to pay it in installments, and the caretaker eventually consented.

Uri made an appearance in Far Side at the premises of its Jewish officials, who were not interested where he lived but only in whether or not he had proof that he fulfilled his obligation to pay the sacrificial money to his Jewish community over the past five years. He did not have this so, reluctantly, he had to pay for a second time around five years' worth of the annual didrachma of dues, deliberately cursing at a stage whisper so that he would be heard (though he knew this would happen to him, and brought along the correct sum). Having paid, he was informed that insofar as confirmation of having paid it was received from Puteoli, then he would get the ten denarii back. Uri then asked for a receipt for the ten denarii, which, reluctantly, they gave him. A fresh problem arose when he registered the members of his family, as it was noted that Theo ought to have held his bar mitzvah, and they asked for confirmation that it had taken place. Uri reported that Theo had been pressed into slavery, and he had no idea where he might be, which the officials did not like one bit, so they called in a superior, who asked for written verification; Uri had, in fact, put the signed contract in his satchel, alongside the Torah scroll, but he had not brought that with him, only the expulsion order, which posters put up all over Rome advised should be presented. All the officials were young men and they sternly enjoined him to present that too. Uri promised. They even caviled at the fact that Uri was unable to show any written confirmation that Sarah's grave was in Puteoli even though that had no financial implication at all. Uri was just beginning to detest them heartily, when who should materialize but an abominably obese Hilarus, who had evidently worked his way up to become some sort of potentate, as he was greeted with great respect. Hilarus drew their attention to the need to take special care in handling Uri's case, which they duly promised.

"Has he signed a disclaimer yet?" Hilarus asked.

It turned out that he had not. Hilarus shook his head then invited Uri to go with him into a separate room, asking to be given all the documentation, which they respectfully handed to him, while making big smiles at Uri: it was clearly a rare event for one of the bigwigs personally to take over a case.

"It was not a pretty business," Hilarus wheezed after examining the assembled documentation, "not nice at all, but then what could we do? It was an imperial edict and had to be carried out to the letter..."

Uri nodded.

"I'm glad to see you are in such splendid condition!" Hilarus declared. "Sadly, there are all too many who are in rather poor shape... Not the Nazarenes: they stuck together, they're in good spirits, but those who were accused groundlessly... Anyway, what are your plans?"

"Well, perhaps I wouldn't mind being able to make a living somehow," Uri answered modestly.

Hilarus enthusiastically approved.

"The disclaimer from seeking compensation," Hilarus said, "is unfortunately required from you... Everyone who has now been allowed to return has to surrender any right of compensation. One can understand the thinking behind it, the houses now being lived in by others who had committed no crime. Personal articles have since been scattered or were distributed by the community to the needy; we have no legal basis for asking for these to be returned. It's because of that we cannot register anyone who doesn't waive the rights to compensation and they are not permitted to reside in Rome."

Uri nodded in acknowledgment.

"Where are you going to live?" Hilarus asked.

"Somewhere across the way."

"Yes, of course, of course," muttered Hilarus. "Your house was demolished, wasn't it? A fine six-story tenement building was built in its place. Do you want to take a look?"

Uri mentioned his readiness to see it on some other occasion.

"We could maybe get two families to move in together. We have ways of making that happen, and that would give you a room," Hilarus offered in friendly fashion. "You would have to pay rent, of course," he added.

Uri had no wish to meddle with the lives of two innocent families as Hilarus so blithely suggested. The potentate asked for an already prepared letter of disclaimer to be brought in and waited in person while Uri read through it and signed. He then contentedly placed it in with the rest of the documentation.

"So what happens with people who have lost their notice of expulsion?" Uri asked. "Does that mean they can't come back?"

"Not at all," said Hilarus, "because we have kept a copy, but then we have to get witnesses who live here to verify that they really were the people referred to... In the meantime they will have gotten older, changed, won't they? It's a somewhat torturous procedure, which is hard to arrange from a distance, so it may take a while, but it's not beyond the bounds of the possible."

Uri nodded.

"These are bleak times; bleak times, indeed," Hilarus sighed, even biting into his lower lip. "But we'll put on a splendid bar mitzvah for your second son—just you wait and see!"

Seeing that he was in Far Side anyway, Uri also paid a visit to the library where five years previously Theo had placed his scrolls on deposit. The weaver who had run the library then was no longer alive; his place had been taken over by his son.

"Yes, indeed," said the gangly, hollow-chested, dark-haired young man, highly strung and blinking. "Right away."

He soon reappeared with some twenty scrolls, though Uri had thought there were fewer.

"Remarkable works they are," the young man said deferentially. "Most instructive!"

Uri looked the young man over; he must have been around twenty years old. He really has read them; pity he's not my own son.

"They're in very good condition," he commented.

"Naturally."

Uri wavered:

"I'm prepared to let them stay on here," he finally declared. "Let others read them."

There was a brief pause.

"Your trust is highly flattering," the young man said, clearly touched. "I'll give you a receipt, so you can take them back any time you wish."

"That'll be fine."

Uri had no idea how he was going to make a living. He calculated that they had sufficient money to last them another two or three months; something would surely turn up by then.

One morning he was approached by the caretaker, who was somewhat afraid of him had been trying to get on his good side after finding that he could not simply blather on for any length of time with him as he could with the other residents; the man asked whether he was by any chance interested in a job as a tiler on a construction project. Uri was interested.

At the time large-scale festivities were being held no more than seven or eight stadia away from the Via Nomentana on the Field of Mars, where Nero had ordered a new timber amphitheater to be built. Uri merrily tiled away while these were going on, being not the slightest bit curious about what the new emperor looked like. Marcellus, Hagar, and the girls attended the celebrations since all Rome was going, and they did not feel apprehensive about being in the crowd as now they could at last feel that they were true Romans. Uri went on tiling and kept on sniffing himself; the other laborers noticed nothing, but he felt he could not get rid of a stench of urine.

In his spare time he used broken tiles that were being discarded as rejects to build up portraits of Kainis and others. This was noticed by the foreman, who eventually asked him if he wanted a job as a painter. Uri was reminded of Judaea, and Hiskiyya, who had painted all those fantastic birds in the palace that was being built for Queen Helena of Adiabene, so he took on a job as a painter.

After he had finished painting his first wall, Uri was offered a higher wage, and he accepted it.

Once again he was making money.

He had waited nineteen years for the chance to be a painter.

If only he could now stick to that as a trade.

He was well aware that he was not really cut out for painting murals, more for painting panels; those were small and needed to be looked at from close at hand. Mural decorations he would have to look at from a distance, and his pictures did not show up well from that perspective because he himself could only see shadowy blotches if he stepped back, and even that was something. Like the others, he painted in tempera, applying pigment ground to a paste in water to a solvent of egg yolk, milk, honey, and vegetable oil, onto a gesso ground, just as he had learned in Jerusalem. The alternative way, the encaustic technique (which employed a binder of molten beeswax into which the pigments were applied with a metal spatula, burned into grooves on the drawing), he knew only from written descriptions. In any case, this was used in Rome only in the houses of the very richest people, and they only painted the residences of the parvenu middle class in the eastern part of Rome proper, on the Viminal ridge and the hills around there.

He painted, gossiped, talked politics, and drank with the other painters and tilers, them drinking wine and he sticking to beer. Many a time they got so sloshed that after the noon siesta they would not wake up until the evening. He would hand one-third of his wages to Hagar, which in itself was no small amount, hiding the remaining two-thirds under one of the tiles in the villa that was under construction.

He took a fancy to one of the water carriers, a slim, young, firm-bodied, black girl with curly raven locks called Flora, and one afternoon seduced her, having no idea why the girl was willing to go to bed with him, and any time he asked she just giggled. Flora wasn't brainy, but she was pleasant, and would fondle Uri's male organ, amazed that it had no foreskin even when it just dangled limply, as she had never encountered its like before. He was cautious when making love to the girl, which he did in one of the remote nooks of the residence that was rising around them, taking particular care not to impregnate her. For the first time in many years he became a man again, poking her in any number of ways. The girl would playfully tweak the graying hairs on his chest and stroke the bald pate of his head, imagining, as she put it herself, that it was crowned with a thick head of hair.

Life, in short, acquired richness, but then one day at dawn the tenement building burned down.

THE VIGILES DID NOT MAKE AN APPEARANCE, AND URI AND HIS FAMILY had to run down a flaming, alarmingly crackling staircase dressed in no more than their tunics; it was a miracle none of them was consumed in the blaze, for the moment they got out the stairs collapsed and two of the other families on the fifth story, some twenty people all told, young and old, women and men, all perished.

The entire block of buildings in this slum area along the Via Nomentana caught fire and burned to the ground, rather as if it had been set alight at several places simultaneously, and presumably that is what really did happen. Uri hugged his trembling daughters, Marcellus wailed hysterically, and Hagar just sat staring vacantly. Frightfully burned people were lying on the ground, screaming; water was thrown over them, and they writhed and rasped until they passed away in dreadful agonies. Uri looked at them and was astounded because he could see that in fact they were choking to death, and it crossed his mind that perhaps we do not only breathe with our lungs, as one is taught, but in some other way, only we don't know what that is.

They lost not only their personal possessions but also six months' rent that they had paid in advance, but would never be able to use.

That too was a cause of the fire, Uri realized, because the insurer would pay out damages to the landlord, who would then have a new building thrown up in under two months and would then again have the brazen cheek to demand a whole year's rent in advance from the new tenants. Uri seethed: he should have seen it coming. He would never grow a head on his shoulders; he was still always surprised at how evil people were.

The scum had us pay for the fire roofs before they set fire to the whole street!

They had to find somewhere to live.

They moved to a peasant dwelling which lay just within the city walls, close to the Porta Nomentana. Part of Uri's secret cache of two-thirds of his wages went toward this; he told Hagar a fib about having been granted a loan, but then they also needed to eat, for the tessera did not bring in enough and Uri's patron, Gaius Lucius, had died while they were away. Uri went once to his patron's house, having bought a brand-new sportula for the occasion, but the deceased man's sons had him chased off, having no wish to support a Jewish client. Afterward Uri had not gone in search of a new patron, hoping that he would be able to earn enough from painting. Marcellus had a prodigious appetite, and Irene too could pack it away; only Eulogia pecked at her food. When Marcellus turned fourteen he would be able to put on the *toga virilis* of a Roman citizen and he too would be entitled to a tessera, but they could not go hungry until then.

Uri then recalled that he had not taken advantage of the two bounties of three hundred sesterces that Caligula had distributed in person to the population, nor the one that Claudius had ordered to be distributed while they were in Puteoli, and this latter was the larger amount, because those with large families were entitled to receive one thousand sesterces, and Uri could prove he had three children. At cockcrow one day, before anybody was up, he went off to do his mural painting work and, around midday, rushed off to the local authority to assert his right to receive these. He was asked for all manner of verification, for which he had to go back once more to Far Side, and now it was with Iustus that he spoke. He had likewise become one of the superiors in the office of the Jewish community, no longer working as secretary to Honoratus but having secretaries work for him. Iustus put on an act as if Uri had never been ostracized, embracing him, patting him on the back, exulting greatly, and promising to collect all that was necessary to support Uri's impeccable right of citizenship as a Roman Jew, for there were copies of all the documents in the archives, though it was quite obvious that he would do nothing.

Unexpectedly, however, Uri was judged retrospectively to have qualified to be granted four hundred sesterces, the amount Nero distributed to the plebs when he attained power, though the authorities would hear nothing further about any other monies. Uri hid that four hundred sesterces for even grimmer times to come.

They puffed and blew, snored and squabbled in the peasant dwelling, and they went hungry. The peasant himself, who moved out into the stable with his family, did not provide any fare, which had to be purchased separately. Hagar moaned and so did the girls, but the worst was when they did not moan, just sat there staring mournfully, accusingly. Marcellus would say nothing, not even to complain, but there were times when he would vanish for days on end and would not say where he had been, for all the clouts he was given by Hagar, who doted on him. Uri was reduced to screaming:

"Go out and get some work, or at least beg! It's always me alone who does the work! At least save me, with my bad back, from having to lug the bread that we get for the tessera all the way from the Campus Martius—half a day that takes!"

Hagar had by then switched off, with the look in her eyes suggesting that Uri was an intolerable character for continually yelling without any reason at all, whereas the children were amazed because why should they too have to work and lug things around.

"You've all been spoiled rotten!" Uri yelled, which was true, though right then they happened to be living in dire poverty and were starving, so they loathed their father all the more.

Why should I be making all of the sacrifices for them? Why don't I just leave them to stew in their own juices? I'm going to clear off, move in somewhere with Flora, pay the fee for her manumission and give her a string of uncircumcised Ethiopian metoicosts!

Uri found out where Aristobulus lived; he was the elder brother of Agrippa and kept his distance both from Jews and from politics. Uri had to rap on the door for a long time before it was opened. Aristobulus was an old man with an intelligent, lined face; he listened with amazement to Uri's request.

"I don't get it," he said. "If your father gave Agrippa a loan why didn't he ask him for the money to be paid?"

"Because my father died prematurely."

"You were in a position to ask, though."

"I did, but he didn't give it back."

"So what am I supposed to do? Pay off a debt incurred by my elder brother, who's no longer alive? On what grounds? It's not me who became king! Ask Herod, Agrippa's other elder brother; at least he's got some pathetic little kingdom..."

This was the Herod who had married Marcus's widowed wife, Berenice, his sister; his kingdom really was tiny, but then again Claudius had granted him oversight of the Temple's affairs, including the appointment of high priests. But that Herod was far away.

Aristobulus, a grandson of Herod the Great, owned a large, splendid residence on Quirinal Hill, and he lived there on his own with his servants. He could see that Uri must be in trouble and suggested that he make contact with the young Agrippa, his nephew, who also lived in Rome: he was the heir to Agrippa's fortune and also to his debts, as he was also the heir apparent to the throne of Judaea.

Uri mentioned that, as far as he knew, Cumanus had for quite some time been the prefect of Galilee, whereas the prefect of Judaea and Samaria was Felix, a one-time slave of Claudius's who had wed Drusilla, Agrippa's younger daughter, and if Nero had left them in those positions, then it was rather unlikely that Agrippa the Younger would become king.

Aristobulus gave a gloating laugh: the story had gone around that the circumcision had been extremely painful for Felix, as in his case they had not only removed the foreskin but also a fair chunk of the penis—so much for Felix and Drusilla. Aristobulus grumbled on a bit and then referred him to his firstborn daughter, Jotape, on the off chance that she would take pity on him.

"It's been a long time since any soul moved my heart to pity," said Aristobulus gloomily. "In my opinion it serves anyone who is born human right to toil to the end of his days and can only expire in dreadful agony. At least I'm fond of animals, though I do nothing for them, and have been in the habit of praying that a new deluge should come upon us, and this time with no Noah and no ark."

Jotape was a spinster who resided in a magnificent house near the Porta Capena; she was said to gaze at the passing traffic all day long from behind a curtain, she could never have enough of that, though she was also a passionate collector of original Greek statues and pictures. Jotape was very tall, a hump-backed, bony-faced, hook-nosed amazon who looked as if she'd started developing as a man but on the way ended up in a woman's body.

She heard Uri out, shook her head and expressed her sympathies in a deep drawl. But she regretted there was nothing she could do for him as she had no money herself.

"My father sent you here, didn't he?"

"Yes."

"That's his way of signaling his unshakable distaste. He refers to me anyone he does not consider to be agreeable, and he never considers anyone so."

Uri was transfixed by a panel painting propped up against a leather couch.

"Zeuxis?" he asked in wonder.

It was Jotape's turn to be amazed:

"How do you know that?"

"I saw a copy of one of his works in Alexandria. It must have cost a fortune!"

"Six hundred thousand sesterces."

"It's worth at least three times that! Not that Zeuxis wasn't reduced to giving his pictures away for free at the end of his life..."

"I bought that from its fourth owner; each of them made a fair bit of money on it."

The picture was of fauns playing with one another, each with a human face full of character.

"Those fauns are architects!" Uri remarked to the present owner. "He completed it when the protracted planning work on the Erechtheun in Athens was in progress. I once knew their names but off the top of my head I can't recall them right now... For a long time it was thought that the one on the far left was Phidias, but it can't be him because then he'd have to be bald..."

Jotape pointed to another panel.

"Who do you think that is?" she asked.

Uri went closer, bent down, and inspected it. It was a picture of Hermes, he could see that now.

"How much did it cost?"

"Two million."

Uri was silent.

"Don't you know?"

Uri sighed.

"Not bad, but it's a copy," he said. "An imitation Parrhasius. The face is the painter's, but the folds of the drapery are weak... Even his pupils did better work than that..."

"It's an original," Jotape snorted.

"I suppose that's possible."

They fell silent. Jotape took stock of Uri.

"What did you actually want from me?" she eventually asked.

Uri himself was not rightly sure. Several dozens of millions of sesterces in value was amassed in the house in the form of pictures and sculptures. Herod the Great had misappropriated the money back then by blood and iron, and his descendants were able to spend it on whatever they fancied.

"I'm going to sell off the collection," Jotape announced. "There's no sense in just me having the pleasure. I've got no heir; I'll have a Greek-Jewish shrine put up the like of which has never been seen before, and I'll have the collection carried over."

Uri nodded. Philo would have been delighted by the idea.

"There's no money I can give you," said Jotape. "Truly not! I scarcely eat a thing, barely more than a sparrow."

"That's one of the secrets of a long life," Uri said approvingly.

Jotape was interested in that subject and talked about special seeds and buds which simulate meat and pasta, indeed are healthier than anything else, and she warmly recommended to Uri that he consume these, living off them every blessed day: he would feel phenomenally well. Uri refrained from pointing out to the lady that Jews were not permitted to eat seeds on feast days, but politely thanked her for the advice and took his leave.

There were hordes of beggars in the neighborhood of the Porta Capena, including as usual a lot of grubby children from Far Side.

I will not send my children out begging; it'll never get so bad that I'm reduced to that!

He went to pick up the four hundred sesterces that he had hidden on the building site, but his colleagues must have spied on him, because the money was nowhere to be found under the tile. They did not starve to death, but they continued to go to bed with their empty stomachs rumbling.

MARCELLUS TURNED THIRTEEN. HE CRAMMED ALL HE NEEDED, AND went for his bar mitzvah at the synagogue; Hagar wept and the girls stood there inanely, then they went back home.

Uri carried on with the painting; it was fairly well paid but the peasant raised the rent, and Hagar had no wish to move. They had to think twice what to spend the money on.

A heavy, leaden-gray year ensued, the only point of light in which was Flora. Uri spent little time at home. Marcellus hung around town, sometimes only getting back the next day; the girls did nothing and Uri was occasionally provoked into bawling that they ought to read something, but they never did.

Marcellus turned fourteen, the age at which he could assume the garb of manhood, when was entered into the register of full Roman citizens, and also when he was granted his own tessera.

Uri was touched to examine the lead token on its leather thong when he slipped this over Marcellus's neck in front of the municipal authority's building.

"You've become a breadwinner, an equal member of the family," he told him, raising his right hand over his head in benediction. "Lord Almighty! To have lived to see this at last!"

Hagar wept, the girls blubbered and recited a thanksgiving prayer to the Eternal One that they would no longer go hungry.

Marcellus said his prayers with them, then vanished. Uri raged with anger.

Marcellus strolled into the peasant dwelling only two weeks later in the evening and asked for his supper. Hagar clung to him and kept on endlessly asking:

"Did you come to any harm? Did anything bad happen to you?"

Uri could see that there was nothing wrong with the boy and bottled up his indignation.

"Where were you, then, young man?" he asked cordially.

"In Far Side," said Marcellus, squatting back on his heels as he got to work on a meat dumpling.

Uri digested the information.

"So, what goes on in Far Side these days?" he asked.

"Nothing in particular."

Marcellus smugly tucked in with Uri looking on. Hagar wept in happiness and the girls withdrew to one of the corners, knowing a storm was brewing.

There was no tessera around Marcus's neck.

"So what did you do with your tessera?" Uri asked, also squatting, eye-to-eye with Marcellus.

"I handed it over to them," Marcellus answered calmly.

A big stillness fell. Even Hagar stopped her weeping.

"And to just who did you hand it over, young man?" Uri asked.

"To my real family," announced Marcellus, looking stubbornly at his father.

"So, who makes up your real family?" he asked in a hushed tone.

"There are many," said Marcellus, "and there will be ever greater numbers!"

Uri was now certain, and he suppressed his temptation to swear.

"That wouldn't by any chance be the Nazarenes, would it, young man?"

"I'm also one," Marcellus declared proudly.

Hagar began to shriek but then thought it best to keep her mouth shut. The girls cowered.

"So you've become a Nazarene, my darling boy?"

Marcellus nodded, and a self-confident grin appeared on his lips.

Hagar hurried outside with the girls to leave the two of them together.

"How come? How did it happen?"

"I was inspired by the Holy Ghost," declared Marcellus, looking his father steadily in the eye.

"And what's that?"

"The Lord's Breath, which permeates all things."

"Do you perchance mean the Shekinah?"

Marcellus shook his head and resolutely reiterated:

"I was inspired by the Holy Ghost, which he breathed into the disciples at Shavuot."

"Who? The Eternal One? And what's Shavuot?"

"Not the Eternal One but the Lord! That's when He ascended into Heaven."

For them the Lord was not the Creator but the Anointed.

Uri looked at his son. His features were at once prematurely aged and puerile; one could make out the moronic features of Sarah and also Hagar along with everything else. The blood of a lot of my loopy ancestors runs together in that boy, Uri reflected; Plato would be glad to see it: there in front of his eyes a clear example of the idea of a pan-human imbecility.

"So, what did you have to do to be inspired by the Holy Ghost?" Uri politely asked. "Is that why you handed over your tessera?"

Marcellus shook his head, and said as though he were reciting a lesson:

"The Holy Ghost is blowing in all places and can confer its grace on anyone it wishes, the good and the evil alike, and it purifies their soul."

Uri nodded.

"Can the Holy Ghost enter me?" he asked.

Marcellus became flustered; the sound of interconnected pulleys creaking in his brain was almost audible.

"Anyone," he finally stammered out, flushing with irritation at having to show mercy to his father in the spirit of the Teaching.

"Eat it up nicely," Uri urged. "Your mother cooks tasty dumplings."

Unable to eat, Marcellus was silent.

Uri tried to recall the wording on the sheet that Theo had acquired from the Nazarenes more than five years ago, just before their expulsion.

"There is no family any more, only fellowship," he muttered.

Marcellus gave a start.

"This Messiah of yours preaches fine ideals," said Uri, "and I have no doubt he was a good healer."

"A fisher of souls," Marcellus proclaimed.

Uri was startled by this combination of words, so he asked his son to explain. Marcellus gathered his wits and related that the Jesus of Nazareth in question had converted fishermen as his first disciples, and they had then been sent out to heal the souls of others.

The Nazarene evangelists fish for suitable souls, Uri supposed, and Marcellus was one such. Quite probably any second-born son had a soul that was suitable; it would be interesting to know if there happened to be any first-born sons among them.

Uri tried not to think of Theo, and he regarded as a success any day at the end of which, before falling asleep, he could tell himself that he had not thought once about him the whole day, as he was thinking of him now. He thought it unlikely Theo would join a sect to be loved; Marcellus had joined one. It's because I have shown him no love, Uri reflected, and however nit-witted he may be, he has sensed that.

He felt a strange prickling on the nape of his neck: relief. Let Marcellus's new family take him away, along with his tessera; his half-baked, hangdog features would not be missed. What would the loss of him be compared with the loss of Theo? He would somehow scrape along with just Hagar and their unsightly daughters.

No one could have been more amazed at himself than Uri when he heard his voice sounding sympathetic, almost affectionate:

"Well, now! And is property communal with your people?"

There was a sincere expression of interest in his tone; Marcellus could sense that his father's exasperation had melted away, and he was taken aback because he could not fathom what had happened in a few brief moments.

"Communal property?" Uri repeated, smiling at his son.

It was a dispassionate, distant smile.

Marcellus snorted and shook his head:

"No, not that."

"So, they didn't actually ask you for your tessera?"

"No, they didn't, I offered it myself. But they loved me before I did that!"

Uri was moved to genuine pity for his son.

"A vow of poverty?"

Marcellus shook his head.

"A vow of silence?"

Marcellus did not understand what he was driving at.

"Where is it that you gather?" Uri asked, tacking on after that to reassure him: "I don't want to know the address or the names of any individuals. I've got no desire to inform on them, but do they live in Rome?"

"Of course, they do," said Marcellus. "They live in Far Side: after all, they're Jews."

Uri shook his head.

"But for them, as best I know, there is nothing to choose between a Greek or a Jew."

"Nor is there! No such thing a man or woman, Greek or Jew, master or servant..."

"There are also women?"

"There are! My own priest is a woman..."

Uri was staggered.

"A woman? As a priest?"

Marcellus elaborated in his relief:

"Any of us can become a priest! Man or woman, servant or master, provided their soul is pure enough!"

He recounted that at the supper that was put on every Saturday in honor of the Messiah (the Friday evening they would devote to the Sabbath like regular Jews) water would be served but it would be partaken of by way of wine because the Anointed had turned water into wine, and that miracle was repeated in all places where His faithful gathered together, and the supper itself was also consecrated to him.

Uri dimly recalled hearing something of the kind before; possibly Philo had mentioned that cranks of a similar stripe had arrived in Alexandria. They had presumably made a start on their evangelism earlier there than in Rome; it would also have been more fertile ground after the Bane.

"Do you have supper and pray?"

"Yes, we do!" exclaimed Marcellus enthusiastically. "We drink water on which the priestess has given the priestly benediction and through that it turns into wine, becomes holy water, and we partake of that, thinking of Him, and his Spirit invades us, and we pray to Him, who was killed but rose again from the dead to come among us a second time, and the Lord will surely come again because he has promised to do so!"

Uri nodded. Holy water was used by Greeks in their rites; the Jews had nothing equivalent, and it was forbidden for anyone who was not a born Cohen to utter the priestly blessing. This was some hybrid of Greek and Jewish religious notions in much the same way as in Alexandria Serapis was a blend of Greek and Egyptian traditions.

Out of that could only come a religious war of Jew against Jew.

"Did your Messiah who rose again from the dead have twelve disciples, by any chance?" Uri asked.

Flabbergasted, Marcellus said: yes, there had been. The twelve were his first apostles.

"Have you already been snooping on us?" he asked mistrustfully.

"No, I haven't," Uri replied. "It's just that Mithras had that number of disciples. Well, and don't you suppose that the Anointed happened to be born to a virgin? Mithras's disciples make that claim about him."

Marcellus protested: no, of course not, what nonsense! He had a regular father, Joseph by name, and his mother was Mariamne.

Uri helped himself to a dumpling, whereupon Marcellus resumed with a will. They peacefully dug in, and Uri meanwhile asked whether there were any Greeks in the group. Marcellus said there weren't—just masters and servants, men and women. However, there were already Greek believers in Asia, and a lot of god-fearing Greeks in Syrian and Greek towns had converted to belief in the Messiah, who in any case believed in the God of Israel, only they had not been circumcised, and now did not need to anyway. Indeed, his own priestess had become a Nazarene there because both she and her husband were Roman, but they too had been driven out of Far Side under Claudius; they too had traipsed around in Italia but then sailed to Corinth, where had found employment in tent-making. It was then that the Holy Ghost had touched them, and since then, they were happy. The priestess's husband had died shortly before; he had died happy, and Priscilla, the widow, was also happy in the knowledge that her husband was sitting in Light on the right hand of the Creator, next to the Anointed, who had expunged death for evermore.

Expunged death! God in Heaven!

Sitting in Light! The light of Enoch!

Priestess!

Uri gazed at the broad, flat face and the long, down-turned hook of the nose under which a straggle of black wisps of hair had begun to arise. The child not only had no father but no mother either, or so he felt.

Hagar and the girls cautiously edged in from the stairwell and were witnesses to the miracle that Uri and Marcellus were peacefully eating and conversing with each other; they did not know what to make of the transformation.

Uri looked at them.

If they understood, Uri reflected, I would say that I could finally be through with humanity.

URI REQUESTED THAT MARCELLUS ASK HIS PRIESTESS IF HE COULD ALSO take part in a supper on Saturday. Marcellus was reluctant, but it was clearly something he could not refuse: they were willing to make a convert of anyone, Uri thought, and that was explicitly laid down.

The priestess sent word that the congregation was willing to accept Uri.

The believers did not seem any more lunatic or wretched than people do generally; indeed, their dress betrayed a degree of affluence, which came as a bit of an unwelcome surprise to Uri, though he himself could not have said why. They assembled in a secluded cottage, not far from the southern border of Far Side; it was where Priscilla had lived since she lost her husband. They had purchased the cottage with the money they had made in Corinth, with Priscilla explaining to Uri, as the newcomer, that they had made tents for nomadic tribes, since all the Jews there lived in towns and had nothing to do with agriculture.

Priscilla was of medium height, silver-haired, with a good physique, with strongly marked but not unpleasant features and a hint of a self-confident smile playing around her lips. She did not wear clothes of mourning, which Uri interpreted as meaning that they had expunged death, and anyone who had died was living.

They must be horribly afraid of death.

They must be horribly unable to bear being on their own, and ultimately unable to bear not being loved. They were unable to bear the human condition.

On Saturday evening, with the Sabbath over, sixteen of them sat on stools around a long table, with Uri as the seventeenth. I'm a prime number, he thought, being somehow very pleased with the idea.

Priscilla had a few innocuous words for each and every one, addressing them by name, and their faces would light up as if tears were glittering in their eyes, tears of hope, and she proceeded to break the bread and cut it into slices. They gazed reverentially before leaping up and distributing the bread, and then she poured water into the beakers from a jug.

"We are assembled here, my brothers," intoned Priscilla, and a great stillness descended, "to give remembrance unto our Lord, who died for our sake and rose again from the dead for our sake, and who gave the gift of immortality to those of us who believe in Him, and ours has become the kingdom of Heaven here on Earth, because we are simple souls and we gained admission for that reason."

The faithful mumbled an "Amen," passed the beakers along the table, drank the water, then wept. Uri looked down at his beaker, sniffed it, and had a taste: it was water.

Then they partook of the bread, which was ordinary bread, and Priscilla said that the food was the last supper that the Lord, the Resurrected Anointed, ate on the evening before his death; this was repeated by the faithful throughout the world in whom New Life had taken root through the Holy Ghost that the Anointed had inspired into believers here on Earth.

Priscilla then recited the usual Sabbath prayer that had to be delivered on the Friday evening, but added on a priestly blessing.

Everyone shuddered, including Uri, who had seldom heard the blessing from any priest.

They all said "Amen" and took another draft from their beaker.

Priscilla then asked in almost a conversational tone what news the faithful had brought of the big wide world, and a quiet, informal conversation followed; their faces became animated, they took on life rather as if the Motionless, that dormant primitive substance about which Zeno writes, had been set in motion by the second, deeper substance, the Spirit. They spoke about Philippi, Thessalonica, and Ephesus, from which they had heard good things about their brothers and sisters. Priscilla was asked for news from Corinth, and with a slightly gloomy face she said that she had received a letter that there had been some debate between the apostles, but the matter seemed to have been resolved; for her own part, she added that some of these brothers were not without their vanity. Not that this was a problem, because it was our business in life to perfect our souls, there was a little time still left for that, not much but still a bit, before the Lord again appeared among us, but it would be unfortunate if this were to lead to strife among believers. The Lord took no pleasure in that.

A pudgy, comically snub-nosed man asked Priscilla whether she would read out the letter, to which Priscilla said that she would gladly read it out, if it were up to her, but the apostle had asked her to delay doing so because he was preparing to travel to Rome in person. Before that he wanted to send yet another long letter to the Romans among the faithful; indeed, it was rumored that the successor and vicar on Earth of Him who was Resurrected was also planning to make a trip from Jerusalem to Rome in person at much the same time. This generated a flurry of excited whispers among the believers, who clearly knew what persons were being referred to.

Uri cast a stealthy glance at Marcellus, who was sitting next to him in rapt devotion; he wondered if he too was aware, but he could not tell from the doltish expression on his face.

That was how the initiates talked, not so much on account of Uri, the stranger, at whom they flashed occasional smiles, but (or so Uri felt) because that was their usual way. At the end Priscilla blessed on behalf of the crucified and risen-again Anointed; the faithful had tears in their eyes, Marcellus too, Uri just bowed his head. To finish, the priestess reminded the believers never to forget that they were now saints and should lead their lives accordingly. The faithful, weeping and joyous, solemnly pledged their word.

"Your son is a great asset for us," Priscilla said to Uri when they had broken up to stand around and chat in smaller groups, with Marcellus politely poised three paces to the side.

Uri nodded and then switched to another subject.

"I was once also very desirous to see Corinth," he noted, "but I never managed to get there."

"We ourselves only went there out of necessity," chuckled Priscilla, who seemed to be a very sane, sober-minded individual. "That was where a boat was headed from Brindisi, when it looked like we would starve to death if we had stayed in Italia."

"A good friend of mine lives there," said Uri. "We were in the same year at the Gymnasium in Alexandria."

Priscilla gave a jolt.

"He wasn't named Apollos, was he?" she asked shrewdly.

Uri was in turn shaken.

"Yes, that's him!"

They sized each other up, and Uri went on:

"I envied him for getting a post as a teacher of rhetoric at the Gymnasium in Corinth."

"He left that post a long time ago," said Priscilla.

There was a silence; Marcellus drew closer.

"Do you happen to know what he is doing now?" Uri asked.

Priscilla hesitated.

"He is supported by the faithful," she disclosed finally. "He's one of our apostles who is involved in the dispute..."

"Whose apostle is that?"

"The Lord Jesus, our Lord and Messiah, who rose again from the dead."

Uri sighed.

Had Apollos deluded himself willingly, like these people? That just was not possible. Apollos had a sharp mind and had always looked trouble head on.

"Are you sure that isn't another Apollos?" he asked and in hope provided a thumbnail sketch of his friend's appearance.

"That's him!" Priscilla exclaimed in amazement, batting her eyelids both in panic and happiness. "He's a marvelous orator, and that was his trouble, but he is now learning humility and is commendably cutting back on those oratorical skills... There was some tension between him and our dear friend, the father of our souls; he is not as eloquent as Apollos but his fortitude is unsurpassed: there's an incredible strength packed into his paltry small frame, and he is able to speak in the simplest language, such that even dimmer souls should understand, because our Lord said that 'Only the truly foolish shall enter into the kingdom of Heaven.' It is hard to train ourselves to be simple-minded; we have been spoiled by the oh-so-slick smartness that we have inevitably picked up over the course of our sinful lives, and that is why we are flawed in our faith... That dispute, however, has blown over, thanks be to our Lord and Messiah who died for us and was resurrected for our sake!"

URI TRAMPED WITH MARCELLUS TOWARD ROME PROPER ACROSS THE Cestius Bridge, arching over on the western side of Tiber Island on the way back from Far Side, and making their way toward the Fabricius Bridge on the eastern side.

If only he could amble along like this with Theo.

Uri's mind was uneasy. Apollos! Impossible! What on Earth did he see in these fanatics?

Marcellus, walking beside him, was unforthcoming; obviously he too was at a loss for what to make of the events of that evening, though Uri suspected that he did not have any cause for rejoicing. He had been wanting to break off relations with his father at all costs, and his his father had the cheek to join in a gathering of his new family, where not only was he greeted decently but cherished by them, as they visibly clasped him to their bosom. It must have been a big blow for the boy to feel that his father was butting into his life. He needed to find a way to reassure him.

Uri felt sorry for his son, but the news of Apollos's conversion had hit him hard.

Apollos had been an extremely clever boy. He must have seen something in the sect that Uri was missing.

Uri therefore tried to look at the fanatics through Apollos's eyes, and he had to admit that they preached their doctrine from a purely rational point of view. It was a message that every cowardly Greek and Jew in any city with a mixed population (most of them, in other words) desired: that Greeks and Jews should not kill each other as in Alexandria or Jamnia. Let not the powerful (in other words, Roman government) play them against one another; let them join forces in a common religion that preached equality between all men, whatever station they had been born into, exactly like the Stoics and Epicureans, or the most humanitarian of the minds borne out of Greek philosophy.

Philo had sought to communicate that same idea, in his own fashion. But he did not get through to the masses—how could he have, as his works were purely academic, full of complex intellectual material?

Perhaps it was more clearly visible from Corinth what had to be attained, and maybe also how. All that evening the references had been solely to Greek cities in which sizable Jewish minorities resided—those were the places inhabited by the adherents of the sect. They were trying desperately to invite the Greeks and the Jews into one camp before they set to slaughtering each other, which could happen any moment.

Jews who were living in minority communities or in mixed marriages in Greek towns were terrified that Alexandria's Bane was going to reach them, and they were doing everything they could to forestall it. It could not be done from a position of power, as the Greeks were wealthier; it also could not be done by cultivation, for they themselves did not possess it, which left only the spiritual route.

A pity, though, to do it by way of such a demented faith! If there is a Messiah, there ought to be a radical change, too. If there is none, then the well-intentioned faith will simply crumble!

Uri came to a halt on the Fabricius Bridge, and Marcellus followed suit. Uri looked down into the darkness, where the Tiber flowed even more darkly below them.

This risen-again Messiah was not such a good idea. Only crackpots would believe in that—the weak, the feeble, the born losers. Those people would never become strong.

"Is the Anointed of the House of David?" Uri turned unexpectedly toward Marcellus.

Marcellus, startled, pondered a while.

"Isn't that what you proclaim: that the Anointed is of the House of David?"

Apologetically, Marcellus explained:

"I haven't been with them long, so I haven't heard that."

Uri shook his head and then went on to ask another question:

"How did that resurrection occur?"

Marcellus was relieved, because that he knew.

"Well, the way it happened was that the Messiah was accused of proclaiming that he was the Anointed, the king of Israel, so he was taken before the prefect, who interrogated him, then he was scourged and crucified."

"And who was the prefect?"

"Pontius Pilate."

Uri shuddered.

"A Roman prefect has no authority in religious affairs," he said. "The Jewish court has jurisdiction! It should have been dealt with by the Sanhedrin."

Marcellus knew nothing of the legal niceties, but he did say that as he was dying the Anointed had managed to convert one of the malefactors.

"Who was that?"

"Two malefactors, two thieves, were crucified together with him, so one of them."

Uri broke out in a sweat and felt faint.

"What sort of thieves?"

Marcellus did not know: just some malefactors.

"Did Pilate sentence them too?"

"Yes."

"They too were Jews?"

"Yes."

"But the Roman prefect does not pass sentence on Jewish miscreants; no way does he waste his time with piddling matters like that! They are dealt with by the local Jewish courts, but then again the Jews don't use crucifixion! Nor do they hand common criminals over to the Romans!"

Feeling very awkward, Marcellus kept quiet.

"When did it happen?" Uri asked.

Marcellus knew that.

"He was crucified just before Passover, on Friday afternoon, at the third hour, and the Messiah yielded up the ghost to the Creator in the sixth hour."

Uri wiped off the sweat, which despite a cold breeze blowing from the west was trickling from his neck and the crown of his head.

He could picture his cell in Jerusalem. There were four of them: himself and three others.

"Dear son," said Uri, "in the end, what is it that your people preach about the Anointed: is He a man or is He God?"

Marcellus closed his eyes and concentrated.

"He existed before the Creation," he stuttered, "but that became manifest after His resurrection... Everything that the Lord has hidden from view becomes manifest sooner or later..."

"If the Anointed was there even before the Creator created the world," Uri noted sharply, "then He could hardly have hidden Him from view."

Marcellus yelled out:

"He has existed from the beginning of time, but only now has He manifested Himself!"

"Does He have an existence over and above the Creation?"

"Yes!"

"The Anointed is the Creator's emissary, isn't He?"

"He is!"

"Don't you see a contradiction here? If the Anointed is subject to the Creator, then He couldn't have existed before the Creation!"

His lips pressed tightly together, Marcellus obstinately said nothing.

Uri groaned:

"What is it that your people claim?" he asked. "Was the Messiah born a man? Did He have a mother and father?"

"He did!"

"Joseph and Mariamne, you said."

"Joseph and Mariamne!"

"How is it possible then, that He was born to them when He existed before the Creation?"

"He's the Messiah; for Him anything is possible! He's the one for whom we have been waiting! And He came among us!"

Uri studied the face of his second-born son in the moonlight. Was it right to open his eyes?

"My dear son," he said. "Are you aware of any other cases when Pilate had other Jews executed in the same way?"

"No, we aren't," Marcellus stated firmly. "The Eternal One marked Him out for this one and only offense."

"Let me tell you something," said Uri. "There was a time once when I was held in a prison cell in Jerusalem. Two rogues were locked up with me; they had not been sentenced... That Thursday night, late in the night, a new prisoner was brought in... He had overthrown the tables of the moneychangers, those who bought and sold in Temple square..."

Marcellus was horrified, shuddering, Uri could see.

"Did this Messiah of yours do anything of the kind?"

Marcellus groaned:

"Yes."

"Did He kick up a fuss?"

"Yes, He did, but that's not why He was crucified!"

"Did He get into a brawl in Temple square?"

"He drove them out with a whip, but that was not why He was executed."

"Of course it was! I saw Him, I spoke with Him! He was human just like you or me! But He did not say He was the Messiah because He wasn't! He was a man, a wretched, decent, and honest man like you or me! He was getting on, His beard turning gray, His face a bit puffy; He prayed and then they came for Him on the Friday at daybreak, took Him off and later on the two rogues as well, who had also not been sentenced!"

Marcellus listened aghast.

"The only reason I wasn't executed was because I'm a Roman citizen! And after that I had dinner at Pilate's place!" Uri declared. "He executed Jewish prisoners as a deterrent, and specifically at Passover, so it would be witnessed by the multitudes and they wouldn't get any ideas about rising in rebellion. Because they had done so not long before! He had no idea who exactly he was putting to death! He wasn't interested either! Pilate was afraid of provocation back then and also of Vitellius, with good reason, too, because it was Vitellius who got rid of him in the end!"

Marcellus held his peace.

"Herod Antipas was also there!" Uri affirmed. "He just happened to be there... He wasn't in the habit of making pilgrimages to Jerusalem; Galilee falls outside the area where making the pilgrimage is compulsory, but he happened to be there because Vitellius had been threatening him, too, and he wanted to ally with Pilate! What do your people have to say about that? What were you told?"

Marcellus kept a strained silence before finally speaking:

"Antipas also interrogated the Messiah and referred Him back to Pilate..."

Uri groaned out loud.

"Your Anointed hero was a man! A man! I was jailed with Him, saw Him from an arm's length away!"

Overcome with hatred, Marcellus hissed:

"You never did time in prison! You never even traveled to Jerusalem! You never dined with Pilate!"

ONE OF SOPHOCLES'S DICTUMS IS THAT THERE IS NOTHING WORSE THAN man.

Carneades, on the other hand, wrote that notions about nonexistent objects come into being in the same way as those regarding existing ones, and they are just as effective as the latter, the proof being that they result in real acts. Men therefore act according to what they believe in; whether those beliefs are true or not makes no difference.

Flora did not turn up for a few days. That happened every now and again; she took water to other places and obviously made love to other men, but Uri asked no questions about what had happened, setting high store on the fact that she never asked for money in return. When she next brought water Uri was not as chipper as usual, and indeed she asked him what the matter was.

"I had a meeting with my son," Uri muttered. "It was rather depressing."

Flora still did not understand, but she did not ask for further details, preferring to pump him about whether or not he would prefer her hair long and straight, because there was an ointment available which straightens curly hair. Uri did his best to talk her out of the nostrum. The lovemaking ensued eventually but was not as sweet as it had been previously, and Uri had a feeling that this had also reached its end.

Marcellus lounged about at home, eating the whole day long, doing what he had done as a boy in Puteoli, only now he had an ideology to wheel out in its defense. Uri would politely inquire whether he might wish, by any chance, to earn a bit toward covering the cost of his upkeep, to which Marcellus would respond with deep conviction that he was now a holy man, the Holy Ghost was laboring inside him and a New World was here, it would spread, gradually perhaps, to take in the entire world, and then everything would change: everything that had been on high would be set down low, and everything that had been lower down would be set on high, and there would no longer be any need to labor.

"You might at least ask to be given back your tessera!" Uri would growl.

Marcellus would be offended:

"I endowed that on the congregation! I can't ask for it back! It's my gift!"

"Endowments are for the rich to make! You're poor!"

"No, I'm not poor! I became rich through giving it to them!"

Uri was silenced; there was some truth in that dialectic.

"You're just Jews who've gotten taken for a ride, my dear son," he eventually grumbled irately. "You don't even know what you're scared of!"

"Of what, then?" Marcellus riposted insolently.

"Of Rome, my dear son!"

That was far over Marcellus's head. He blinked at his father. The old fool! He's a captive of the old, invalidated world, ripe for dying! Such a pity that he too would be resurrected.

URI WAS QUITE SURE THAT HE HAD BEEN INVITED BACK TO THE ASSEM-blies of the Nazarenes, but apparently they had sent their messages via Marcellus, who had chosen not to pass them on. Uri would not have gone among them another time anyway, but he was grateful to his son for making it possible to have visited the one time, and he pondered why it was that he viewed these pleasant, pure, noble-spirited people as frightening.

He tried to discount Marcellus, but even so they remained frightening.

Idolizing an emperor who is setting himself up as a god is very human because it holds out the promise of any number of advantages, and so everyone at least pretends to believe in it. An emperor is like his currency: a real object given in return for simulated belief.

It is superstitious to believe in the succor of a pagan deity, but what is a bewildered person, left on his own and terrified of death, supposed to do if he gets into trouble, or if a fatal disease afflicts him or one of those whom he loves? He will race over to a statue of the deity, embrace its feet, and whisper his wishes into its ear, and if by any chance these should be fulfilled, he will put up a plaque of thanksgiving.

Believing in an Eternal One who does not have a human face and demon-strably has had no hand in human affairs for millenia is also not foolish: a person thereby belongs to a community that protects him in direst need with the alms and pe'ah, nurses them in the event of illness, and does not even cast aside unwanted children, irrespective of whether a person is a Sadducee, a Pharisee, or an Essene. All these systems of belief, as Uri now saw it, were in fact mutually exclusive in a radical fashion, and it was merely out of laziness that believers in these various religions were all called Jews. They believed themselves to be the chosen people of a one and only God; fair enough, but so did the Samaritans, who slaughtered other Jews because they had in turn slaughtered them.

The religion of the Jews had long not been one religion; maybe there never had been just one, not even when Moses led them out of Egypt.

There were still Jews only among those living in minority communities, threatened and hard-pressed, like in Alexandria. Wherever they were in the majority—as in large parts of Judaea and Galilee—there were no longer any Jews, though no one had put it into words, and the Jews themselves were not aware of it either yet.

In the rural villages, Jews were still Jews, and there, they were ignorant of any other faith; although their naïve faith was not that of the priests, they were not aware of this and they were happy to offer ritual dues to the Temple.

The religion of the Jews of Rome was also faithless—like every Roman religion. Customs and ceremonies half-heartedly adhered to, strictly supervised. The Kahal as an institution operated in an earthly fashion, committing earthly crimes; just like any other community, its true god was Mammon. The Jews of Rome were wrong to protest that the ancient laws of crafts did not apply to them—the Jew-hating officials of Rome saw that much more clearly.

But to believe in a man who was killed and rose again from the dead, and to say that He is the Anointed, even though there had been no drastic change in the world—that was more grievous than any superstition.

Maybe it was a folly sprung from the general lack of belief.

He pictured the million-strong mass thronging toward Jerusalem, and all of a sudden being converted and becoming followers of the Anointed. He shuddered.

It was fortunate that the Judaean peasants were conservative; it was quite impossible to drive anything new into their skulls.

He had already encountered narrow looks like Marcellus's; he had seen blind fanatics before. The ecstatic looks in Beth Zechariah as they had waited for the First Fruits to be collected had been like that; the expressions of the pilgrims going to Jerusalem had been like that; the faces of the Judaeophobic Greek rabble in Alexandria had been like that. He tried to picture who among his seemingly normal acquaintances he could imagine turning blindly irrational. He could not imagine such blindness in Kainis's eyes, nor Theo's—but in Narcissus's, Claudius's, and Philo's he could. He wondered if Tija's eyes could turn into those of a fanatic. Hardly: in his eyes there was a glint that from the outset had something inhuman, distant, cold about it.

He also tried to picture how Apollos, a skilled orator, would speak to a congregation of ecstatic believers. He just couldn't; he could not see the new eyes, only the old, rational ones. Apollos did not believe in this folly; he just hoped that Greeks and Jews might be able to approach one another via this resurrected Anointed, in the same way that Philo had wanted this to happen, the hatred driven from their hearts and minds in the same way as wise men like Simon the Magus exorcised demons from the sick.

Priscilla's eyes were rational eyes; she was no ecstatic believer, just pretending to be profoundly convinced of something that had no reality at all. She was lying. What was going on in her mind, he wondered? Was she resolving the loneliness of widowhood by extending hospitality to believers? Maybe she was unable to mourn her husband. Had she never loved him anyway, and so was feeling guilt on that account, persuading herself that he had not actually died? Had she committed serious offenses against her husband, and instead of being repentant was she declaring the offenses nonexistent because there was no wrong if there was no death? Why did they have no children? Were there never any? It might easily have been a dreadful marriage.

Otherwise nothing happened. Marcellus ate, drank, slept, and loafed around; Hagar cooked, with the girls helping her out of sheer boredom, and Uri did his job. The murals he painted were met with general approval. Construction work on a new house took them to Quirinal Hill, and while the walls were raised he worked on tiling the floor and, if any time was left, familiarized himself with the encaustic technique.

There were practitioners of this ancient Oriental technique in Rome, and it was possible to obtain the pigments and tools needed for it in their small boutiques, the most important tool being a metal implement, with a spoon at one end and a spatula at the other, offering a cold surface for applying the pigments to the molten binder without working away the thickness, thereby producing what were almost relief paintings, with it added the possibility of mixing all the primary colors—red, yellow, white, black—according to taste, on one palette, producing innumerable shades. A well-executed work was not just a colored drawing as it would have been made centuries ago but a genuine painting that almost vied with sculpture, with the advantage over tempera that there was no need to treat the finished surface, and air would not harm it.

In those same small boutiques it was also possible to obtain original Greek pictures, and Uri was fascinated by their depiction of perspective, which despite having been discovered long ago by the Greek masters had never become prevalent in Rome. Uri could see that the masters were guided by the painterly depiction of eminent buildings in that they came to realize that parallel lines converged in the distance to come together at a point on an imaginary horizon; in Nature there were no parallel lines, they were a construct of man, interfering in Nature, further elaborating on God's work. Without man there would be no parallels. Perhaps there were many things not present in the Creation that man had introduced; the Creator may wonder as He pleases at what has come out of this creature's imagination.

People had begun to use the geometric deception, which gave a picture a three-dimensional appearance that recorded the sight of living beings, as a result of which the viewpoint of a viewer standing outside the picture had become decisive, Uri could recognize, and he contemplated where he should place himself if he wished to sneak into the picture.

He outlined that problem to one of the picture-dealers, a pleasant and wise man, who was skilled at his line of business but simply could not grasp what Uri was driving at.

"In paintings of the present day," Uri explained, "what I see is a separate world from that in which I, the viewer, exist. But then what is the world from which I am looking? Another world?"

The picture-dealer was stumped.

"If it's not another world," said Uri, "and there is only one world, then I too should be in the picture... But in that case what is it that I'm seeing and how?"

There were shoppers in the boutique, themselves painters, and they drifted over and started to argue, talking indiscriminately until eventually one of them stated that the problem had already been solved by their painting rooms, which spread a continuous picture over the four walls, the floor and ceiling; the rooms of Augustus and Livia had been painted along that principle, and if a person stood in the middle of the room, whichever way he turned he would be in the picture.

"It's a problem for architects, not painters," an individual opined in a falsetto voice from the door of the shop. "The most logical building is a hemisphere."

"Why a hemisphere?" someone asked.

"Because we always stand on something... If that were not the case, then we ought to be hovering in the center of a complete sphere, anchored from every angle."

Several people laughed.

The falsetto-voiced individual stepped farther into the shop. Uri cast a look at him. He was a young, plump person, his belly quivering, who moved with the limpness of the castrated, his beady eyes shining, brilliant and blue, from a puffy, whiskerless face.

The eunuch looked at Uri.

"Father!" he cried.

THEY WERE SITTING ON THE TERRACE OF A TAVERN, SIPPING HOT WATER. Uri, trying to choke back his tears of pain and of joy, was shivering.

Little remained of the old Theo, just the eyes and the intelligence; he was just another eunuch.

"Is your eyesight all right?" Uri asked.

Theo was surprised by the question.

"Of course."

They fell silent.

"I don't really know why I should be angry at them," Theo made a start. "I had no sexual desire at the time I was castrated so I have no way of knowing what I might have missed."

"Don't you feel something of the kind? Doesn't your rectum tingle?"

Theo was again surprised.

"Yes, it does... If I see a good-looking woman or man, there is some tingling thereabouts... Not much, but I distinctly feel it. It's more an aesthetic pleasure than anything else... A fine picture has the same effect."

"Why did you have to be castrated?"

"Because that fellow who bought me used me as a lover. I reminded him of his dead wife."

Uri was unable to hold back his tears.

"He was a decent man," Theo tried to reassure him. "He genuinely loved me: he taught me and looked after me."

"What did he do with you—poke you in the ass?"

"How many openings does a man have? Not a lot. He used those."

"And is he still...?"

"He was stabbed one night; I have no idea why... I mourned him."

Theo related that he was living in Pompeii. It was an attractive, wealthy town; he built and decorated villas there, had no intentions of moving away; he was highly regarded, despite his youth, being handed on from one customer to the next.

"I soon picked up substantial wealth, and was able to buy my release," he said. "The ear tag has already grown over. Look here! I would have sent you money if I had known where to find you..."

"Is it quite certain that you can have no child?" Uri asked.

"Yes, quite sure," Theo tinkled a laugh in his high falsetto. "But I've got a family: boys, girls, men, women... My household... I have bought them all and obtained their release from servitude but they all chose to stay at my place, every single one... There are dogs and cats as well... I have often pondered why blood-relationship is so important. People go to war and kill on account of it, but why? I have considered what I'd do if I found you, if I could join you... But it's far from certain that you'd be pleased, seeing what's become of me..."

Uri did not speak.

"Marcellus and the girls will make you grandchildren," said Theo.

Uri remained silent.

"There was a time," said Theo, laughing, "when I calculated your precise angle of inclination in Alexandria... I noted it down somewhere..."

Theo then went on to recount disconnectedly about all sorts of things, Uri listening mutely.

Men were amazed that he had no foreskin on his sexual organ, women too, who would return oral favors, though without any effect. As he had not celebrated his bar mitzvah, and now was not permitted to, being a eunuch, he ate all the things which were forbidden to Jews; thus, the various types of seafood were delicious, and he had developed a great liking for pork, being himself in the habit of roasting seasoned pork chops, and also organizing big dinner parties for sittings of one hundred heads in his garden. He was loud in his praise of Pompeii for its location, its climate, the marvelous gardens and buildings. He was in the habit of coming up to Rome for materials, doing the purchasing himself but leaving others to see to transporting them. He did painting, not just construction work, his illustrations of plants being particularly well known.

"I also tailor dresses!" he boasted, "from silk and muslin... I make more doing that than I do from building work!"

By way of reassurance, he added that he had played no part in the gladiatorial display that a certain Livincius Regulus had organized in the amphitheater at Pompeii, news of which had gotten back to Rome. The day had ended in a general brawl between the inhabitants of Nuceria and Pompeii, who had backed different gladiators, and frightful bloodshed had ensued. That sort of thing would not happen again, however: the inhabitants of Pompeii had been forbidden to hold any public games for ten years, thanks be to the Eternal One.

Uri held his peace, thinking to himself that at least this one way of livin was better than being killed.

Theo showed no interest in his siblings or his mother, yet there had been a time when he loved them; Uri said nothing about them. Theo repeated that he would be glad to see them in Pompeii but had no intention of moving away from there; he wanted to grow old and eventually die there.

"I'm easily found. Everyone knows me and is fond of me," he said contentedly. "Theophilus the eunuch!"

Theo paid and then beckoned his four servants, who ran over with a litter. With some effort he wedged in his ample body and blew a kiss to his father.

URI FELT THAT SOMETHING HAD DEFINITELY BROKEN INSIDE HIMSELF.

He said nothing at home about having met Theo.

Some time after that Irene broke the news that she was pregnant.

"And who is the happy father of my grandchild?" Uri asked cordially.

He snorted when he heard that it was a water-carrying slave.

"My dear, sweet daughter!" he cried out in alarm.

Irene bit her lower lip under her protruding incisors, looking determinedly yet fearfully and dumbly at her father.

Water carriers were well known for taking advantage of any widow and virgin they could lay hands on. Uri knew that he was going to have to pay the price to obtain the manumission of this slave. He was a puny, pint-sized fellow, swarthy-skinned and with a sneaky look—Heaven knows where she had found him.

Uri informed him with a certain glee:

"You'll have to get circumcised, my dear boy, which will be pretty painful. A fair chunk may be cut out of your prick, at least I hope so. That's the price for my paying up."

The prospective son-in-law slyly held his tongue in assent.

I had a water-carrier as a lover, Uri reflected, and my daughter's husband will be a water-carrier. Pure poetic justice on the part of the Eternal One.

What had to be done came to pass, and the former slave took the name Isaac. Hagar pretended to be happy, baking and cooking for the wedding feast though there were not many present.

Irene had imagined a more glittering affair and upbraided her father for being stingy even though obtaining her husband's release had not cost all that much.

"Maybe not," Uri agreed, "but obtaining Roman citizenship for my grandson will cost an arm and a leg."

Irene did not understand: if the father was a freedman, and he himself had been born free, why would their son not be free?

Uri sighed before launching into an explanation that he wouldn't be because Pallas—Claudius's slave, the younger brother of Marcus Antonius Felix, who was prefect of Judaea and Samaria—had deviously conceived an amendment to the law whereby if a free woman married a slave she too would acquire the status of a slave. That had been ratified during Claudius's reign and was still in force.

"But Isaac is a freedman now!" Irene protested.

"And so you too only have freedman status, and your child too! Only his or her child, your grandchild, will be able to gain citizenship rights and a tessera."

Irene burst out sobbing; she had not been aware of that; if she had known beforehand, if anyone had drawn her attention to that, if her father had told her in advance, if her father had instructed her—no way would she have gotten mixed up with someone like that...

Uri got tired of this.

"He'll be a citizen, don't get so upset! It's just that it will cost a fortune!" he shouted. "The law was passed so that exceptions could be made to its provisions—at a price! It was driven through the Senate, and Pallas received a reward of five million sesterces from Claudius for doing it. The bastard knew very well that it would be very remunerative! That is why it has remained in force under Nero—because they also get a cut! The exceptions are the essence of any law—that's where the money is to be made! That's the only reason any law gets passed!"

Irene kept on sobbing; she could not follow this basic principle of political science. Uri left her and set off to find out exactly who had to be paid because even though Pallas had not been put to death like Narcissus, and had even been left with his many hundreds of millions, he had nevertheless been booted out of office.

Uri could not stand the sight of the shifty look on Isaac's face, once he had moved in with them, and the man's body odor made him ill, so he purchased for them a shanty on the edge of Far Side, where it was unlikely any tenement buildings would be envisaged, and that was where Uri's first grandchild was born, a boy of unprepossessing appearance but healthy. It cost a lot to get him the rights of citizenship, but that was arranged.

Uri looked now to Eulogia, the younger of his two daughters, who was no more attractive; she was barely past twelve when she made her own catch, a numbskull lunk of a Jewish boy from Far Side. It turned out that this ordinary boy was related to Siculus Sabinus, that wealthy imbecile of a smith who had also traveled to Jerusalem, in fact he was a nephew of his, and was employed in his uncle's workshop. Once the wedding had been solemnized, Eulogia moved to Far Side, wanting to be rid of her unbearable parents just as soon as she could. Uri bestowed a decent dowry, glad that they were not going to leech off of him.

He was left with no money and had to ask for a loan, so he took on even more work.

Marcellus finally slunk off with his congregation, moving into the house of one of the faithful brethren, where they were going to wait the return of the Anointed.

"Just wait, son! Hang on tight!"

Him he gave no money.

Uri was left with Hagar in the peasant cottage on the Via Nomentana. He bought it outright for what was, in fact, a rock-bottom price, but the peasant was happy to move out. It was a mud brick house, prone to damp and to mold, and no money was left for renovations. But it would be good for as long as it lasted before falling about their ears.

Uri let his wife know that he wouldn't mind her moving in with one of their daughters on Far Side, but Hagar chose to commute: twice a week she would walk over to Far Side, cook for Eulogia, then walk back to Via Nomentana. On these days Irene would go over to Eulogia's place to pick up half of the food. The lazy old bag, thought Uri. Hagar is working more for her daughters than she ever did for me. There was no need to cook for Uri as servants brought lunch for those employed on the construction site at a fairly cheap price; it may not have been ritually pure, but then neither was painting men and beasts on walls in accord with Mosaic law.

Looking at Hagar's dim, ugly, lackluster features, Uri was amazed. How much the two of them had been through at each other's sides and yet not together. If Uri said something, Hagar did not understand, and even if she did happen to, she pretended not to. For sure the Lord had not created them for each other, so it was a miracle that they had children nonetheless. How could that be?

These were years of peace, with the world governed by Burrus, the one-armed Praetorian prefect, and the wise Seneca, with people just nodding when Britannicus, the natural-born son of Claudius, was killed: that was the price of tranquility. Seneca had allegedly warned Nero against killing by cautioning: "However many people you slaughter you cannot kill your successor." In his wise letters of a Stoic to Marcia, the daughter of Cordus, Seneca preached poverty and humility, meanwhile amassing three hundred million sesterces for himself in four years; people nodded and read his book with that in mind.

There was a flurry of excitement when Nero divorced Octavia, Claudius's daughter, whom he had wed when he was sixteen, and married Poppaea Sabina, who had been the lover and wife of his friend Otho. Otho was sent to be prefect of Lusitania; it was a miracle he was not killed. Nero then took Octavia back, but had second thoughts and chose instead to have her dispatched; Claudius's ugly daughter was just twenty, yet she had to die. Tales went around that Nero even made love to his mother in the closed carriage, the stains were there to be seen in the coach and on their garments, and after that Nero deprived her of all her bodyguards and had her board a boat with a collapsible cabin, designed to fall in on top of her and sink at Bauli. The ceiling of her cabin did indeed collapse, but she managed to swim free; only her lady-in-waiting, Acerronia Polla, perished, wounded in the wreck and stabbed to death by the oarsmen. The emperor finally managed to have his mother slaughtered, with Agrippina commanding Herculeius, the ship's captain who was her assassin: "Strike it in my womb!" When he viewed her undraped corpse Nero was said to have remarked: "I had so beautiful a mother!" and went on to organize a big funeral for her.

Otherwise nothing noteworthy happened; business went on. Wars with the Brits and Germani proceeded, but those events were far afield; Nero negotiated a spectacular détente with the Parthians, greeting their king and ambassadors with kisses and games. In the Forum there was excited discussion about how the emperor had ordered that henceforth it would be necessary to pay to lodge an appeal with the Senate, in effect a new form of tax.

In Far Side excitement was aroused by the visit paid on the elders by Tiberius Julius Alexander and an equine-featured character, the new alabarch of Alexandria, who was being introduced by Tiberius Julius Alexander to the city prefects.

It was Demetrius, it dawned on Uri, son of Tryphon, the Alexandrian elder.

He had postured against the alabarch and his family until, in the end, he had made his peace with the hated figure of Tija. He had wanted it badly; how astute Apollos had been to spot it.

What has become of Apollos?

Nero put on many games. Seawater was piped into a wooden amphitheater erected on the Campus Martius, along with genuine sea monsters, with gladiators struggling in an underwater battle with them. The emperor also established the Neronia, a contest in three parts, which was planned to be quinquennial, with music and literature, gymnastics and wrestling, horse and chariot racing on the program. Nero thus ran through his inherited fortune even quicker than Caligula had, so that the Seneca-Burrus duo introduced new taxes, and even forbade the sale of any kind of cooked viands in the taverns, with the exception of beans. That was not at all to the liking of the populace, who of course marveled at the games, and had no end of enjoyment at seeing a lady in her eighties shaking a leg among the high-born women who were led onto the stage: she was Aelia, who had also continually danced and crooned in Claudius's house although she was already old then. A concession brought in by Cladius under which a full menu had been provided for plebeians was rescinded, and they went back to distributing only food parcels; that was also not to people's liking either, but money was also scattered into the crowds, along with wooden balls, inscribed as if they were coins, which could be redeemed for foodstuffs, drinks, clothes, or knick-knacks—people liked those, scrimmaging and getting into fights over them.

In the center of Agrippina's lake Tigellinus, a favorite of Nero's, had built a great raft, which was towed around by boats. The raft was decorated with gold and ivory, like Phidias's statues, and he had wild animals, birds, and sea creatures brought from distant lands; onto the shore of the lake were led high-born women who offered themselves like courtesans, all naked, many thousands of them, and numerous men of rank and plebeian riffraff were also invited to the debauchery. In the course of this Nero had himself given in marriage to a character by the name of Pythagoras playing the role of husband, with himself wearing the bridal vein, people handing over real money as a dowry to the couple, with witnesses to the marriage and even priests being found, and ending in chain copulations, in which a special corps of Augustans, as they called themselves, an impudent bunch selected by Nero from the young men of the order of knights and sturdy young commoners, led the field. It was the talk of the town for weeks.

It was then that the conflagration broke out.

It started in the Circus among the booths; it is possible that the sausage grillers had been careless, or at least it was said, but with the wind it spread quickly, sweeping over to the Palatine; the buildings along the narrow streets clinging to the side of the hill went up in flames, the area around the Forum, the emperor's palace, a great many temples, shrines, storehouses, hutments, and tenement buildings caught fire, with the shrine to Luna, the statue to Hercules, the Temple of Jupiter Stator, the shrine to Romulus, the residence of King Numa Pompilius, the temple of Vesta, and the Subura district burned down, as did the libraries with their irreplaceable scrolls. The fire did not spread as far as the outer part of the Via Nomentana, but did reach the inner part, with the tall tenement buildings catching fire. Either the wind carried sparks, or the landlords kept their wits about them and set their own houses alight, knowing the insurers would pay out. It became a conflagration and the vigiles were rushed off their feet. Fire had also broken out on Aventine Hill, said people who rushed over there to find a good spot from which to watch the magnificent spectacle. The fire fanned out to the whole city; Esquiline Hill was ablaze, possibly kindled by sharp-witted plebeians of the lowest class because while the vigiles were busy fighting the fire they had license to rob. Uri trudged toward the inner city on the second day but did not see much, just glowing patches. People were racing around with water or stolen livestock, soldiers trotting by as well as groups of vigiles with their wagons; there was a shortage of water, maybe because the aqueducts had been cut off. A mad panic had overcome the city, so Uri went back home.

The conflagration burned for six days, with many priceless treasures lost. The fire eventually burned out, and sighs of relief were heaved, but then the flames sprang up again from beneath the ashes on the property of Tigellinus, of all people, and smoke again covered the sky.

The emperor was in Antium when the fire broke out and only returned when it had reached his own palace, which lay between Palatine Hill and the gardens of Maecenas, but there was nothing he could do either, and the imperial palace as well as all its surroundings burned down.

Four districts were untouched, three burned down to the ground, and the other seven suffered severe damage.

The great fire started on July 17—the same date as the Senones had torched an as yet tiny Rome. Uri lay low in his cottage and blessed the Eternal One that he had bought poultry and goats, which the peasant had not been keen to bother with; now he drove them into a pen, on which he placed a strong lock as there was going to be a food shortage. He had his own well, for which he also gave blessings to the Eternal One. On the following day, the third after the outbreak had started, Hagar came back from Far Side, where she has hurried when the fire broke out. Nothing at all had burned there as the fire had not jumped from one bank of the Tiber to the other, and nobody there would dream of igniting a blaze.

"The city, though, the city!" Hagar wailed, as if Rome had become her place of residence, and she scattered ashes over herself.

Not long after Hagar, Marcellus also showed up.

"He is coming for the second time, He is coming!" he proclaimed. "It's all true! The prophets have been preaching the truth, His prophets! He sent Satan on ahead, as it is written, and Nero cleared the way for Him! This fire is His fire! He is nigh! He'll be here at any moment! It has started, it has started! Get down on your knees and pray!"

"You nitwit!" Uri bellowed. "Don't do these things! It's dangerous!"

"This is the proof!" Marcellus yelled. "Even the infidels can see! Even the pagans can see! This is His doing!"

"You numskull, do you want people to think the Jews were the arsonists?"

"The unfaithful will end up in Hell!" yelled Marcellus. "You'll be the first! That's what you deserve!"

He called on his mother to join them, because they were praying over in Far Side; a lot of people had been joining in, and in a great fever of excitement they were awaiting the Anointed, who had sent a message with the fire and would be coming with a sword. Sustained by the faith of His believers, He was treading on clouds, the smoke was His smoke, the flames—His flames. Hagar, however, felt too tired to entertain any wish to traipse back over there.

"You too will be consigned to Hell!" said Marcellus, baring his lips in derision at his mother before he raced off.

Uri uttered a groan.

He could see this spelled big trouble.

The ruins were still smoking when from the Rostra, which had been kept intact, Nero announced with due imperial dignity that he would rebuild a Rome more splendid than it had ever been, saying that the fire had been a blessing in disguise, because now he could have an even bigger royal palace erected, replete with the loveliest imaginable gardens for the glory of Rome. He promised to have a navigable canal cut from Lake Avernus to the mouth of the Tiber which could supply enough water for fighting fires; Rome would be turned into an orderly city, not a dirty hole of narrow, dark, unfathomable alleyways—more orderly than Alexandria. He decreed that debris and rubbish should be transported down the Tiber by ships and tipped onto the marshes of Ostia. As for the buildings themselves, he ordered that up to the second story they were to be solidly constructed, without wooden beams, of hard rock from the cliffs of Alba. In addition, every building was to be enclosed by its own proper wall, not by one common to others. He asked the populace to propitiate the gods by offering prayers to Vulcanus, Ceres, and Proserpina, while Juno in the Capitol, which the fire had left intact, was to be entreated by matrons. Nero also pronounced that he had heard there were rumors he himself had set fire to Rome! He, the emperor! What an unrivaled, loathsome, fanciful insinuation! What base slander! He was therefore giving the order to arrest all those sinister, conspiratorial, lunatic, evil Jews who say that the Great Fire was the vengeance of their God, who damned Rome, cast an evil spell on Rome, to befuddle, stupefy and pollute the minds of the Roman populace. They are the ones who caused the fire and occasioned Rome's misery, and they are guilty of causing the deaths of hundreds of innocent citizens as many saw and can give witness.

The citizens catcalled and whistled, cursing the Jews, and they rushed to take revenge.

The Nazarenes, and anyone who was alleged to be such, were seized and tortured, and they readily admitted to being incendiary and named their accomplices. Many Jews were denounced, by way of preemptive exculpation, by other Jews who thus avoided torture, this being a simple way to rid oneself of rivals and enemies. The Augustans even detained and stripped guiltless passersby, and anyone found lacking a foreskin was hacked to pieces, though anyone who did possess one was beaten to death in fury anyway. It was not advisable to be out on Rome's remaining streets during those days.

It was not just Jews who had fled from Alexandria to Italia but also a fair number of Greeks, and they brought with them their own tales of horror. Superstitions which had grown up in Alexandria during the Bane were also propagated in Rome: on the Sabbath Jews drank the blood of non-Jews; they slaughtered Greek children and roasted them, which is why they did not eat pork. The most watertight accusation against Jews was one of black magic: the Jews were able by muttering their curses anywhere to set anything ablaze, they had no need for a spark or tinder. Most of those who were tortured confessed that this charge was well-founded before their skulls were cracked by the wheel. It was a highly credible charge too, the political commentators recalled: at the time of Germanicus's death Piso had been accused first and foremost of black magic, and he had admitted as much by the fact that he had gone on to commit suicide even while the trial was still in progress. He, too, had been perverted by the Jews.

Seeing that they had betrayed mother Rome, so read the charge, those who were to be executed were first sewed into the hides of wild animals together with monkeys, rats and dogs like matricides, and they were then cast into the Tiber. But then they ran out of monkeys, so then those sewed into the skins were cast to packs of dogs. But then there was a shortage of skins and the dog-owners began to object because they had trained their animals to run, but once they had eaten human flesh they would never again be obedient, as a result of which Nero had the Nazarenes thrown to wild beasts in the wooden amphitheater on the Field of Mars, dressing up himself as a charioteer and watching the proceedings from close at hand in the arena, but those animals eventually had their fill and there were not enough of them anyway, so Nero had the remainder crucified in his gardens which had been consumed by the fire, giving free entrance.

When Uri heard what was happening, he hurried over to the gardens. He had engendered Marcellus; let him at least witness his death, assuming the dogs or tigers had not already devoured him. He was not worried about being recognized or being crucified because, so he felt, he had already seen enough of life.

Many hundreds of people were hanging on crosses, some head downward: some were still living, others were already dead. Horsemen kept order, relatives, water jugs in hand or on their head, searched forlornly and were not molested; a multitude of gawkers enjoyed the spectacle, which beat any entertainment put on at the Circus. Not since the Spartacus revolt had been suppressed had so many people been crucified, and that had been a long time ago.

Uri trod methodically; he had to walk up close to every single cross to see the face of the crucified person. It was a tiring procedure as he was constantly being jostled and shoved. The living moaned, pleading for water, writhing, choking, the shit trickling down their legs, blood dribbling from the mouths and ears of those who had been crucified upside down; the stronger ones, young men with their heads dangling down, could still flex their muscles and even as they hung there could bring their upper bodies into a horizontal position before dropping back down again.

Uri recognized many acquaintances from Far Side, but he would never have believed that they too would have joined this mad, fanatical sect. Either they had not joined, or the persons denouncing them were eager to lay their hands on their wealth. He was astounded when he discovered the dead body of aging Honoratus, as his left leg was missing; that must have been chopped off earlier. He quite certainly had not been a Nazarene, but a revolution was taking place in Far Side, with new people stepping into the places of the old elders, who were not equipped to do away with the Nazarenes. Many of the faces he considered to be Judaean; they had presumably come over as missionaries. He stood for a long time by one of the aged men who had been hanged head down: no longer alive, his long, silvery beard was fluttering in the breeze and as far as it was possible to make out from the inverted head, he had a smile on his face. He must have cheerfully gotten some big sins off his chest as he had been dying.

Uri spent the whole day walking around in the garden because new individuals were constantly being brought for crucifixion, but Marcellus was not among them. Had he escaped? Had he come to his senses in time? Had he been killed earlier?

At twilight Nero had the crucified set aflame so that they should provide light and the crowds would be able to see them: straw was heaped at the foot of the crosses and sprinkled with oil that it would burn with a lot of smoke. The dead sizzled mutely, the living screamed as they burned.

Alexandria had come to Rome. Until then, in Rome Jews had merely been scorned or laughed at; the Nazarene zealots had at last made them hated.

Marcellus clambered out from among the goats when Uri returned late that night.

"I didn't see you crucified, dear son," Uri greeted him unemotionally.

Marcellus was mopping goat droppings from his legs.

"Did you betray them, dear son?" Uri asked genially. "Did you race to inform against them? Was that how you saved your skin?"

Marcellus kept quiet; Hagar, as prescribed, wrung her hands.

"I don't think I would have betrayed them," Uri contemplated. "They were your family, your brothers and sisters..."

"They lied," Marcellus hissed viciously.

"It took this long for you to realize? When they are being murdered? What kind of faith is that?"

"He will come," Marcellus muttered, "only He will come by night, stealthily, like a thief... By the morning the world will be different... And wrongdoers will be the first to be pardoned!"

Uri fell silent.

There are still things I need to learn, he thought as he laughed. He howled with laughter for a long time, unable to help it.

Hagar looked at him in horror, Marcellus with hatred. Hagar then plucked a chicken, cooked; they said prayers for the dead and ate heartily without a word.

A CONSTRUCTION FEVER LIKE NEVER BEFORE BROKE OUT IN ROME. NERO announced that he was having a statue built, bigger than the Colossus of Rhodes had been, to be made of gold, raised in front of his palace, and he was applauded.

A lot of new housing on the Alta Semita and Vicus Longus, north of the Viminal, had burned down, and Uri's murals were destroyed with them. This was a stroke of luck because the owners set to rebuilding their houses; their money had not been reduced to ashes. Uri had more work than ever before, so he was able to repay his debts.

He stayed outside of the hunt after Nazarenes; he was not counted as being a Jew—he was not a factor in people's eyes and no one envied him his ramshackle mud-brick cottage, indeed, people were unaware of where he resided.

He brooded over the fact that people nowadays were no longer modest and humble enough.

They thought that no one before them had suffered, and nobody had thought about anything. People thought that they alone, like no one before, had an entitlement to survive death. They sneered at the tens and hundreds of millions who had lived before them—they had been imbeciles, they imagined, just for allowing themselves to die. They imagined that the Lord was singling them out, of all people, with His infinite grace, that they would be the first generation which was going to escape death, and that today's world was the most dreadful of worlds in which to live and for that reason ripe for change.

These people had not read any historical works, or if they had, they grasped nothing from them.

Nor had they read the Holy Writ, as they should.

Uri ran through his own life in his mind and found that there had been innumerable occasions when he might easily have thought that no one had experienced worse things than he had—yet all the same he never thought that.

What made me so forbearing? What made me so meek? Did I imagine, perhaps, that I would be granted a second life? That if I endured this one, then I would get another one as a reward?

Maybe because I indulged in dreaming, I did acquire a second life? I daydreamed while I was reading, and I daydreamed while I was walking. I have had more than just one life.

The time had come to muse about that sort of thing because he had married off his daughters, his first grandson had been born, his sons had grown up and were not starving to death—what had become of them was quite another matter—and the Lord could not expect him to work on the survival of the species. Let his children look after themselves as best they could.

As he grew older, Uri felt a sweeping dismissive wave of the hand taking hold in his mind. Perhaps the Eternal One was exercising mercy to facilitate the departure of a believer from this world by bestowing on him, in due time, a mighty distaste for life. He was losing his teeth, his joints were losing their resilience, his back was losing its straightness, food and drink were losing their flavor, he was losing his virility, all so that there would be nothing for him to regret.

He did still want to read. Which reminded him that there had once been a time when he had wanted to build up a library for himself. Why not?

One Sunday he sauntered over into Far Side, where he had not been for a long time. Nothing had changed except that a few ugly tenement buildings had been thrown up. He turned into the house where Theo, before he had been castrated, had placed his scrolls on deposit. Over the intervening years the sympathetic young man's back had grown crooked and gray hairs now flecked his hair; he expressed his willingness to return the scrolls that had been entrusted to him.

"I haven't come for them," said Uri. "I would like to invest money in your library."

The young man was left speechless.

"I haven't come to take anything away but to give!"

"I understand," he managed to croak.

He was called Salutius; he was amazed.

"Everything is going to the dogs," Uri explained. "Tablets of stone are being smashed, tablets of bronze melted down, columns are being demolished. They might well wish to set light to any archives as well. Scrolls nevertheless have some chance of surviving."

IT ENTERED SALUTIUS'S HEAD TO INVITE URI INTO THE HOUSE AND introduce him to the family. But Uri made a face:

"I have no interest in families," he said emphatically. "I'd rather go somewhere and have a drink."

They went to the Far Side docks where a pulsing life went on among the new hutments and tall loading cranes working on a pulley system. Uri picked one of the more shaded terraces.

"Well?" he said, and Salutius smiled.

Caught up in his own thoughts, Salutius held his peace. He did not tender any thanks, nor did he pander to Uri; he was disconcerted and did not disguise it.

"Wine?" Uri asked him.

"I don't usually drink."

"Me neither."

Consequently, they drank wine undiluted as the water that was brought to the table looked turbid.

"I earn good money," said Uri. "I have heaps of work, and the more atrocious the pictures I paint, the more money I am paid. I paint whatever I'm asked: nymphs, satyrs, gods, monsters, glades, boats, an idyll or a battle scene or a Trojan horse..."

Salutius nodded. He did not object that Uri, despite being Jewish, daubed representations of the human form.

"Why specifically books, though?" he asked.

"I want to invest in Jewish rarities," said Uri. "I have a hunch that anything Jewish will soon prove to be a rarity."

Salutius pondered.

"Why don't you buy jewels instead?" he asked. "They're easier to shift."

"I don't want to make a business," Uri said. "I would like to preserve something that would otherwise be lost."

They sipped their wine; it was no better than the wine from Rhodes that Uri had once stored in the amphorae, not so far from this terrace.

"To give an example," Uri said, "to this day in Alexandria there still stands a Jewish stele inscribed on which are all the rights of the Jews there stemming from the time of Augustus. It ought to be copied and brought over here."

Salutius was taken aback.

"You don't see the future in too bright a light," he remarked.

"To me the entire basin of the Great Sea, along with all its coasts, just stinks," said Uri. "Nowadays all the things I have seen are starting to cohere in my head. I managed to come through one calamity in Alexandria, and that stele also survived it, but it won't survive the next one."

"Why do you think that the trouble will strike Alexandria in particular?"

"Not just there—everywhere."

They sipped their wine. Around them buzzed the clamor of cheerful life; there were lots of high-class ladies, seamen, dockers, seers, fortune-tellers, whores, tradesmen, staring pedestrians, street musicians, vendors, beggars.

"Rome as well?" Salutius checked.

Uri pondered.

"Maybe not so badly," he said. "There are not many Jews here, and nowadays they're cowed, so they're not going to kick up any fuss. I have a pretty good idea how things are going on with your people here."

"With us?"

It was an appropriate question; Uri nodded.

"With you Jews," he confirmed. "I say my prayers in the morning and evening, I find it gratifying, but I am not a member of any congregation. I celebrate the Sabbath on my own; I have a bite to eat, stretch out, ruminate, and nod off to sleep. On Friday afternoon my wife comes over here to see her daughters and stays until Sunday. They don't miss me; it's enough to feed them with money. I also pay the didrachma; that's Jewish enough for me. I can't regrow a foreskin, but I might well do it if I could."

Salutius posed the logical question:

"Have you become a Nazarene?"

"No," said Uri. "I haven't become blinded, though I'm not sure why; perhaps the Eternal One does not wish it."

They sipped their wine. Around them merrily abounded senseless life.

"What's your idea of how it would work?" Salutius asked.

"When I've got some money, I'll bring it here and you'll concern yourself with acquisitions. I don't need any receipts, I don't want to interfere in any way: you buy whatever you choose. At most I'll give you advice, but you won't have to accept it."

"I won't have to copy the stele?"

That was the first time a note of irony had crept into Salutius's voice; Uri was delighted.

"No, dear boy," he said. "You won't have to."

Salutius chuckled.

They ordered a new round of wine. Uri let Salutius pay this time. He was an odd character, quite out of place in a drinking place down by the harbor. He rapidly blinked his dark eyes, he had a thin face and thin lips, his eyes were deep set—a complete ascetic, the whole man, with long limbs and hairy hands. He was seated with his back bowed. A real bookworm, but then he had a good eye; he had not started reading out of necessity.

"To give you one example," Salutius broke the silence, "there is the matter of the legacy of poor Honoratus."

"Would you ever!"

"His house was robbed, needless to say. The Germanicus statue was carried off right away, and they also took his furniture, jewels, dining service, glassware... His family had scattered, the house was left empty... But so far as I know nobody needed his collection of scrolls... Philo's entire library is still in his cellar, as well as a lot else that he collected in his younger days, when he was just an archisynagogos... He was already stealing back then."

"Let's buy them!"

"There's no one to buy from."

"What, then?"

"We can steal them," Salutius suggested, "but I can't cope with them on my own."

Uri reached under his tunic and produced his money pouch, which with great difficulty he detached from a chain around his neck and offered it to Salutius.

"Hire men to do it," he said.

Salutius accepted the pouch and weighed it up in his hand.

"I haven't counted," said Uri, "but it'll be a good sum."

Salutius was not sure where to hide the pouch, so Uri handed over the neck chain. Both pouch and neck chain disappeared under Salutius's tunic.

LATE THAT EVENING URI MADE HIS WAY BACK FROM FAR SIDE TO THE VIA Nomentana both happy and half-drunk with the feeling that a heavy load had slipped from his shoulders.

That boy understands, he does.

He may not know it, but he understands.

I'm going to have a son.

It's interesting that men have an instinct like that. To have a son. Those lunatics will find out one day that the Anointed in whom they pin their beliefs is actually the Creator's own son.

Careful now, Uri cautioned himself, avoiding two drunks who were staggering along, clutching to each other. Just don't lean too heavily on the kid. Don't get too close; leave him his freedom. After all, he's an adult.

IN ACCORDANCE WITH NERO'S PLANS, A SITE WAS MARKED OUT FOR A new imperial palace ornamented with parks, glades, and lakes, in front of which was quickly raised a colossal statue, something like one hundred feet high, of bronze covered with gold. The best master sculptors were unable to equal Phidias's command of perspective, and it was only from a distance that it could be seen to have human form, but then it was not possible to view it from a distance on account of the nearby houses and a tall, multistory aqueduct, whereas seen from close at hand, from below, the head looked tiny and was dominated by the jaw. They haven't got a clue, Uri decided smugly.

Nero, so tongues wagged, had kicked his pregnant wife, Poppaea Sabina, in the belly, killing both mother-to-be and fetus. According to Salutius, the Jews were in mourning because Sabina was pious and had procured for them many concessions from the emperor, which was why not all Jews had been exterminated, only the Nazarenes.

Nero regretted this deed, calling the deceased Venus and setting up a shrine to her, then took a boy who strongly resembled her, castrated him, and treated him as his wife, appearing in public with him from then on. The boy's name was Sporus. It was said that Nero married him with all due legal ceremonies, but he kept another likeness of Sabina in the form of a slave girl, with whom the young emperor also lived, as well as another slave girl who bore a striking resemblance to his mother.

The emperor also had his cousin Julia executed, along with all kinds of other relatives; he also wanted to marry the freedwoman, Acte, but was talked out of that, and he later debauched one of the Vestal Virgins, Rubria, who was made to disappear. Nero also devised a kind of game, in which, dressed in a tiger skin, he was let loose from a cage and regularly had himself taken from behind by his freedman Doryphorus while he took Sporus, and meanwhile they licked and bit the private parts of men and women tied to stakes—which is to say there was peace and quiet in Rome, so the people were free to gossip leisurely about such abominations, business blossomed, and the imperial city was reconstructed at breakneck speed.

Eventually the emperor had his two freedmen, Pallas and Doryphorus, dispatched, Pallas because he had been a lover of the lovely mother, Doryphorus because he thought that he could do anything with impunity just because the emperor was in the habit of screwing him in the backside.

The emperor made his first public appearance as a lute player and singer in the amphitheater of Naples but then, in view of his triumphant success, in Rome too. He was encouraged and praised by Seneca, but then the emperor sent his tutor a message to slit his veins, reasoning that two years previously the Brits, under the leadership of a giantess by the name of Boudicca, had rebelled because Seneca had compelled them to take on massive loans at usurious interest rates, it was out of this that he made his enormous fortune, but the Brits had gotten fed up with it. Admittedly, Boudicca and the Iceni had been put down two years previously, before the Great Fire, but the reasons for the rebellion only came out later. A conspiracy was also talked about, of which Calpurnius Piso was supposed to be the leader, and Seneca had been implicated in it, along with several other writers. Seneca willed his fortune to the emperor and with his young wife Paulina, who was determined to go with him, severed several veins, but she was saved, her arms being bandaged to check the bleeding. She eked out a few more years, though the pallor of her face showed the drain upon her vital powers. Imperial Rome shot up at a mad pace, providing Uri with immense opportunities to work, so that every two or three weeks he would take a pouch of money to Salutius, who soon reached a point when he did not know where to store the scrolls and books assembled from gluing pages together.

A storehouse had to be found.

Again they sat down by the dockyard in Far Side, drinking another kind of wine, though in truth that was not particularly good either.

"It needs to be somewhere secure," said Salutius.

Uri grunted.

"If it's true that the Jews are in danger," said Salutius, "then it ought to be somewhere on the left bank of the Tiber."

"But then again, it's just possible that the Jewish quarter will be the safest place... There's nothing here to offend the eyes of any future ruler."

"You mean there won't be any persecution of the Jews after all?"

"That there will," said Uri with conviction, "most certainly, but there is also going to be civil war. In Rome there's no knowing what will burn down, or why. The holiest shrines will be the very first things to be set alight. In my mind's eye I sometimes see even the Capitoline in flames."

"You could get yourself a job at Delphi," Salutius remarked mischievously.

"It's too far away," Uri complained. "My legs hurt and walking is difficult for me."

"But there's been a huge demand for sibylline prophets ever since Augustus annihilated them..."

Uri laughed.

"It's a great business," he acknowledged. "Only one can soon get bored with the wording."

Salutius was interested in specific details of the civil war, so Uri sketched it out: Nero would be assassinated, in the same way as Caligula and Claudius had been dispatched, and this would mark an end of the descendants of Aeneas, as even Nero's little daughter had died and he had not managed to sire a boy, so as a result innumerable self-appointed warlords would go after one another, with Rome, sooner or later, being the battlefield.

"You have an unrivaled talent for prophecy," Salutius teased.

"I only tell it as I see it."

"Where's the warlord who has ever won anywhere? There isn't a war in sight! Nero reached peace with the Parthians on such terms that they worship him even more stoutly than they do their own king!"

"Local wars will be sparked so that victories will be obtained in big battles."

"That will require large loss of blood."

"There will be immense bloodshed."

Uri recounted what had happened with Pilate.

"Perhaps on the suggestion of a Jew, Vitellius engaged a false prophet who worked the Samaritans up into thinking that the Ark of the Covenant was buried in Mount Gerizim. The faithful assembled there and were butchered by Vitellius's men, after which it was reported that Pilate had given the order. That was the downfall of Pilate. Cooped up idly in the tower of Phasael in Jerusalem I had a nightmare vision of a devilishly cunning prefect of Syria who stirred up such a huge revolt among the Jews that it could only be quashed by the concentration of huge armies, and he marched into Rome as a great commander by the Porta Triumphalis. It's been a long time since Rome has celebrated a real triumph. It's been a long time since Rome has had a military commander who has slaughtered hundreds of thousands. If anyone wants to become a successful warlord in one of the provinces or even has a wish to be emperor he need do no more than get provocateurs to egg on the devout populace and then mercilessly put down the agitation... Jews are eminently suitable for that."

Salutius shook his head:

"A war of the Jews? There'll never be such a thing; there are just too many different kinds of Jews. They have different interests, a different status, in every

Syrian and Greek city. The Jews of Judaea will not go into a frenzy like they did in Samaria. You're too fond of seeing spooks, Gaius Theodorus."

Uri extended his mud-brick house at the end of the Via Nomentana, on the outskirts of the city, with an inconspicuous, sturdy, cement-floored building that no one would imagine stored valuables, and most particularly that no one would imagine a storeroom for books.

Meanwhile the two developed a close friendship. There were times when Salutius was on the verge of talking about his family, but Uri headed that off. He had no wish to hear about the troubles his adopted son was having with his wife and children: it was of no importance. There were also times when Salutius asked about Uri's experiences, and Uri would respond curtly and listlessly: it was of no importance. There were also times when Salutius would start to talk about the incomparable treasures he had acquired in recent weeks, ancient prophecies written on linen like the Scroll of the Lamb, the Oracle of the Potter, and rare sibylline books, but Uri did not wish to hear about them since he had no time to read them anyway.

Most likely this was what friendships with the great Greeks had been like, Uri considered: a friendship between the highly experienced man and the clever young man—it was on that they set the highest store.

Their own children had probably also been no great shakes.

It was around this time, just as he was feeling himself to be a father figure, that he also regained his virility: he procured a plump, dim young girl who cleaned the houses that were under construction and was willing to open her legs for him any time at all.

HOUSING AND HALLS WERE CONSTRUCTED, IMPERIAL BUILDINGS WENT up on the sites of the narrow streets of old; the sun now blazed down on broad streets, and Romans, used to the tight, murky alleyways, were astonished and donned hats to protect their heads. Aqueducts were constructed, and the emperor introduced new, heavy taxation, though this did not affect the plebes. By now the emperor was also singing in Rome and, indeed, he set off with his lovers and most faithful supporters that the cities of Greece might also share in the enjoyment of his unsurpassed art, and also to complete the Great Circuit, and emerge victor at the four major festivals. The imperial freedman Helius, formerly a slave who had been chief steward in Claudius's household, remained in Rome as the representative of imperial power: it was to him that one needed to apply for permission or to appeal in the event of a dispute, and also his palm construction bosses had to grease when they wanted to move in on ground that was contested. Nobody supposed that Uri might know Helius personally, and he did not so much as mention this to Salutius.

"It does not look good if things carry on like this," Salutius brooded. "Rome has really come down in the world."

Uri nodded.

Gaul, under the leadership of Vindex, a knight, broke out in revolt, and there were further battles somewhere in Britannia. Salutius related to Uri that he'd heard in Far Side about other things happening in Judaea.

Already under Felix large crowds had tramped out into the wilderness, where they did nothing, just prayed and fasted, but even that was enough for Felix to attack them, killing many in the process.

"Were they Nazarenes?" Uri asked.

Salutius was not sure.

Under Felix there had been a prophet of some kind who had attracted large crowds in Judaea. The man said he was from Alexandria and preached that these were the last days; he had prayed together with them on the Mount of Olives, and he was supposed to want to capture Jerusalem. He claimed that at one word from him the walls of Jerusalem would come tumbling down and at one word would rise again.

"Was he a Nazarene?"

"He might have been," said Salutius.

Salutius did not know what he was called except that he sometimes referred to himself as a second Elijah and sometimes asserted that he was the second rock. An old man by the name of Simon had been called the first rock: he had been crucified in Rome after the Great Fire and counted as a sort of high priest among the Nazarenes, having supposedly been named to the position by their Anointed personally before he had been executed.

The assembly on the Mount of Olives had been attacked; four hundred were killed and two hundred seized, but the prophet and his friends had escaped.

Disaffected men prowled from village to village banding into gangs, and if they spotted a non-Jewish person they would murder him.

Greeks and Jews regularly clashed and ran each other down in Caesarea; Felix had wanted to disperse the Jews who had come out best in one of the minor frays in the market square but they had resisted, at which many of them had been cut down. Nero had therefore sent out Festus to Judaea as a replacement for Felix, and he must have been a good soldier because he wiped out the rebels wherever he encountered them and restored peace. This was at a time when

Poppaea Sabina was still living; she supported Festus, but then the emperor kicked her in the belly, and Festus also died, though there is no knowing what caused his death; he was followed as prefect by Albinus, who was violent, insulting to Jews, embezzled from the treasury, released common criminals from prison if they were able to pay him, and generally behaved more like a robber chief than a prefect. Nero replaced him after the Great Fire because he had not warned him about the Nazarenes and instead sent Gessius Florus, who, rumor had it, was even more barbarous than Albinus. At the recent Passover holiday a crowd of one million had pleaded unanimously for him to be more humane, even pushing their way into his palace to plead; Cestius Gallus, the prefect of Syria, had also been there, Florus had promised all they asked, then after the holiday, after Cestius had set sail back to Antioch, he had carried on perpetrating acts of cruelty.

"What do you mean: pushed their way into his palace?" Uri snorted. "That's nonsense! You can't just push your way into Herod's palace: there's a guard and high fencing around it."

"That's what they say," Salutius said apologetically.

"There's a stone platform in front of the palace," said Uri. "From that they usually read out announcements of public interest so that passersby in the market can see and hear, but it's not possible to defend a prefect on it from the masses so he could not possibly have been standing there! Vitellius used it to announce that he has restored to the Temple the right to safeguard the high-priestly vestments, but then that was good news!"

Salutius also related that before Nero had set off on his tour of Greece he had received an embassy from the Greeks of Caesarea and, so it was being said in Far Side, he had recognized them as being in control of the city, whereas he revoked the Jews' rights of citizenship.

"But in Caesarea there are more Jews than Greeks," said Uri. "It's not like in Alexandria."

"Still, that's what they say, and also that the Greeks sacrificed a chicken on an earthen vessel set bottom upward at the entrance to the Jewish synagogue, which inflamed the Jews because that ritually polluted the entire synagogue, as a result of which many, many thousands of them marched to Narbata, saying that they were not willing to go back to Caesarea."

"Is that also untrue?" Salutius asked.

"It may well be true," said Uri. "The largest synagogue there lies on an isolated plot of land; at the time I was passing through there a Greek owner had been unwilling to sell to the Jews the land they needed to get proper access to it."

He went on:

"It's a recipe for another Jamnia."

Salutius gave him an inquisitive look, but Uri waved it aside: it was of no importance.

Salutius related that Iustus and the other Jewish leaders had forbidden the Jews of Rome from taking sides on Judaean matters; they should leave all that to Agrippa II, who shuttled between Caesarea and Rome as a kind of honorary king even if in reality it was the prefects who saw to things. And indeed no one in Far Side did take up positions; everyone was lying low. There was neither hide nor hair of any Nazarenes: either they had all been put to death, or they were in hiding. The big wheel next to Iustus was a shoemaker by the name of Annius; planted among the elders by the impoverished leatherworkers and dockers, he was a forceful, impatient man who was intent on having any remaining Nazarenes unmasked and banished from Italia—that was what he blared out in every forum.

"*Ceterum censeo*? A Jewish Cato?"

"Something like that," Salutius laughed.

Uri pondered.

"People like that usually have a skeleton in the cupboard. I wouldn't be surprised if he had been a Nazarene himself earlier on."

"Your son-in-law Isaac is on good terms with him."

"He was converted not so long ago, so he's a bit zealous."

"I get the impression your son is working as a secretary for Iustus these days," Salutius remarked.

"Marcellus?"

"That's his name."

Uri held his tongue then went on:

"Take care with him. I rather think he's been caught."

They turned to speaking about scrolls.

Salutius had gotten the text on the stele in Alexandria copied and also many important scrolls in Caesarea, where there was no Jewish library but a considerable number of private collectors. Among these were Essene texts, including some in Aramaic from Jerusalem, Qumran, and Masada, as well as scores from the unwritten law books; none of them was complete and in some cases there were startling differences in their assessments of comparable states of affairs. Salutius had read them with great interest and made marginal notes. He had acquired from Naples stacks of copies of the rolls that Uri had considered were of interest. Among these were a whole lot of treaties between states from times prior to Alexander the Great, along with a cache of private documents and a pre-Septuagint Greek fragment from the Torah. He had arranged for a copy to be made in Syracusa of a Greek text of the Book of Enoch. Uri took a glance at it: it was not exactly the same as the version he had read out in Beth Zechariah, but it was a fine, comprehensive text. One thing that had come to light in Far Side was a lengthy Aramaic text about the life and deeds of the Nazarenes' Jesus; there had been no need to copy that as the owner had been glad to be rid of it for a rock-bottom price.

"It's a pity I know no Aramaic," said Salutius. "Would you take a look?"

Uri sighed.

"I have a lot of work," he said. "Some day, when I find the time for it."

Out of his own money Salutius had acquired all forty-two volumes of the *Satyricon* of Petronius Arbiter, who had felt obliged to take his own life not long before, at much the same time as Lucanus and Seneca. Since they had died the prices of their works had shot up, and they could be expected to go even higher. Lucanus's epic poems and Seneca's letters and plays were already present in Salutius's library; he had taken a great deal of enjoyment from the *Satyricon* and warmly recommended it, but Uri waved that too aside—some day, when he found the time.

"He writes about us, you should know," said Salutius. "We're referred to as Gauls in general, but the Roman Jews specifically as Gauls of Massilia to give us no grounds for complaint! The Nazarenes also get short shrift... It refers to the 'Anointed One' as 'Sacra' and invents all sorts of weird and wonderful things about him... He ends with a conflagration which covers the entire world, going into such exquisite details as how all the species die, especially man, and how the cockroaches and rats flee into the Flood, soon to become human and carry on where they left off."

"Yes, okay! Some day, when I find the time," said Uri. "That business with the Flood sounds not a bad idea. I'm going to paint that."

He did not have time for painting either, because he was entrusted with guiding the construction work on half a dozen or more buildings at any one time: he contracted the painters, he stipulated the where, what, and how of the painting, and he made very good money, but he himself did no painting. He had an extensible ladder carried around after him so that he could inspect from close range pictures painted high up on walls or on the ceiling. He was held in high regard by the painters, but if they praised him to his face in the hope of getting further commissions, he was in the habit of saying:

"I know a thing or two, but if I could see properly!"

That was taken to be a joke, so they would guffaw obsequiously.

He was even entrusted with decorating ceilings in the imperial palace. Uri protested that he had no skills: that was waved aside. People knew he had attended the Gymnasium in Alexandria, they were told by Helius himself, who bore the responsibility for the palace being finished by the time Nero returned from the Greek islands.

It was ticklish, but he had to accept. His name had come to the ears of Helius, and it had struck a chord with Helius, the former chief steward in Claudius's household and now master of Rome.

Uri cursed himself. Helius had most likely heard by pure chance on a single occasion in Claudius's house that he could boast of having attended the Gymnasium in Alexandria; the only person he could have bragged to about it was Kainis, whom he had adored. Better not to have done that either.

He conceived a plan to use for the vast ceiling contiguous hexagonal panels of gilded ivory; an elaborate contraption worked with a pulley system would be able to slip these aside simultaneously in such a way that pipes running across the ceiling could sprinkle down scented spray—not merely one variety but three, delivered by parallel sets of pipes.

Once that was ready and the spraying was working impressively, he was then assigned to work on three fountains beside the lake in the imperial garden, the requirement being that it should be unique in the world. Uri asked Salutius to get hold of any works dealing with mechanics and hydraulics, tipping him off with the titles of a few which he had examined in Alexandria, and he succeeded in hunting down a few of these.

Uri did not go home for weeks on end, spending his nights in the palace as it was being completed, sketching, designing, and calculating sizes by torchlight on wax tablets and papyrus scrolls. He was lavishly remunerated and handed it all over to Salutius to expand the library. After a while he thought it best to rent a room on the Via Sacra near the site on which the palace was under construction. After his very first night there, Uri came to the realization that this was the same room that Isidoros had once lived in, with the same jeweler still working in the other half of the house. Now how many years ago had Isidoros passed away? At least thirteen.

It was good being alone in that room in that tiny, old house, one of a few of which were still standing in that area; it was good not to have to see Hagar's misshapen, baggy face, varicose legs, and unhinged expression, not to hear her incoherent muttering. Hagar would upbraid him for grievances from ten or fifteen years back; for example, in Puteoli she had pleaded in vain for them to move to Capua, where cabbages were cheaper, or that he had not smeared his feet with that fat the wise-woman had recommended when they had been covered in sores from fulling. She would insist that she used to meet Theo, who had gotten married, had fathered several sons, and now lived in Far Side. Uri would make an occasional attempt to intervene, but he was unable to halt her insane monologues. Hagar's breath smelled of wine, and it was quite common for her to nod off to sleep in the middle of a confused and interminable sentence; she was sober only when she set off to see her daughters in Far Side. Uri was quite sure from certain signs that she was also in the habit of meeting Marcellus, though she never said a word about him, but every now and again she would spout something about the Anointed who would one day, when he returned, be the judge of the quick and the dead and until then the sparks would preserve themselves as one day a column of fire would arise from them.

Uri engaged the best Greek sculptors Rome offered and, working with them, devised a way of making the fountains harmonize with one another to resonate like a water organ. They were delighted with the idea, though one sculptor did remark that Nero had himself designed an organ, only he had not yet put it on show. Uri took fright and broached with his commissioners the matter of Nero's plans, which, as it turned out, had been produced by an old Syrian slave, so he manumitted him and pulled him into the planning work. He conversed with him in Aramaic, and they took a liking to one another. The old Syrian had never read in his life, but had at his disposal incredible talents for mathematics and music; Uri while at work would whistle two-part melodies, with the old Syrian joining in with his deep and hoarse voice. Their performances would be entirely ad libbed, but they still always managed to stay in harmony; the other foremen would gather around to listen and applaud.

The fountains were completed, but the music they made was jumbled, as Uri could hear; he was not at all happy with that. The old Syrian then hit on a way of regulating the pressure in the water pipes that ran in the garden, allowing the three fountains to play a melody as if they were parts of a single flute. Uri had the pipes relaid, and on the fourth attempt it worked. He made sure it was engraved on the pedestals of the statues that the water organ had been the invention of divine Nero.

So much was Uri involved in planning that his mind would not rest, and just coincidentally he worked out how it would be possible to lift beams and marble tablets several stories high with minimal human exertion. His first effort was by hydraulics: cylinders filled with water and linked together underneath by parallel tubes, and the screw devised for raising water by Archimedes of Syracusa helped somewhat, but this needed a lot of water and the tube would always puncture somewhere, resulting in a minor local flood. He was then reminded of the principle of a device that used compressed air to project missiles, developed by military engineers in Alexandria, which fired all right but usually inaccurately.

Air may be invisible but if it is compressible it must be present. But then an idea he had entertained a long time ago came again to mind: if it was possible to compress air, it must also be possible to rarify it. If it is rarefied, then it will be pressurized by the surrounding air. What if that idea could be used for raising weights? Heavy weights might be packed into a tube resting on the ground, and a second tube, which ended high up, would lift the building materials if an appropriate quantity of air could be sucked out. The only question was how accurately the cylinders could be manufactured, so that air did not leak back in. He even made drawings but then he found had no need for them because in the meantime work on the palace had been finished and he did not get the chance to build the special crane. He therefore took the plans to the library and got Salutius to enter them in the catalogue under the heading "Gaius Theodurus's Pneumatic Crane."

What would Plotius say to that? Not the drunken, sick-minded beast he had become but the individual with whom he had once drunk wine in a tavern in Syracusa.

When Nero took up occupation in the palace a big housewarming was held, those leading the architects and builders were granted huge bonuses and banqueted with the emperor. Uri got nothing and was not even invited to the celebrations. The fountains did not make music: the tubes had been sawn through the day before.

By then the Jewish War was in full swing.

UNBELIEVABLE STORIES WERE TOLD THROUGHOUT ROME PROPER AND Far Side; it was hard to tell what was exaggeration and what was outright fabrication, but then a stream of refugees arrived in Ostia and made their way by foot to Rome and Far Side. At first the elders only accepted those with money, but the pressure grew so great that the others had to be admitted too. The municipal authority placed on the Jews the entire burden of responsibility for keeping discipline, so the elders recruited a Jewish volunteer police force. Iustus issued an order for them to put a lid on the talk, and that they did, only somehow or other news continued to get around. Salutius used to walk out to Uri's place from Far Side to take the air, as he put it, and he would relate what had been going on in Far Side.

Uri now lived on his own in the Via Sacra, having bought the whole house; he now took rent from the jeweler. He got no more commissions from the state, but private builders passed him on by word of mouth and he could take on just as much as he wanted. Hagar eventually moved back to Far Side into Eulogia's place, solemnly swearing that she would drink no more; Uri gave them money to extend the house.

The story that went around Far Side was that the war broke out when on the Day of Atonement one of Gessius Florus's soldiers bared his prick to a crowd of Jews from the roof of the Temple colonnade. As a matter of fact it had broke out when the Greeks of Caesarea assailed the Jews and massacred ten thousand of them in the course of a single night. That marked the start of a general slaughter in the cities of Syria, with Sebaste and Askelon being razed to the ground; at Scythopolis the Jews wisely came to an agreement with the Greeks that they would not harm each other, then during the night of the third day of the compact, as they lay unguarded and asleep, all the Jews—more than thirteen thousand persons—had their throats cut.

The number of victims was doubted: it was far too high.

Those who had fled from Caesarea asserted that many high priests, such as Jonathan and John, the alabarch of Caesarea, had been slain. Florus was a poor commander, constantly losing against Jewish troops who were led either by the scions of high priests or robber chiefs of peasant parentage. Eleazar, son of the high priest Ananias, had acquired a considerable name for himself as a military leader, it was said, permitting his soldiers to commit all kinds of cruelties. At breakneck speeds, the Jews of Jerusalem were digging tunnels beneath the Temple with their exits at the Sheep's Pool or Bethesda, but no, that could not be right, because it was past even the northern wall and anyway those passages have existed for a thousand years and more. This was the northern wall that Agrippa I was so assiduous about having built, but construction on which he was forced to halt on strict orders from his friend Claudius.

Then news came through that in clashes between pro- and anti-Roman Jews the house of Ananias the high priest, Herod's palace, the palace of the Hasmoneans, and the Antonia fortress had been set fire to, along with the repository of the archives—indeed, that had been the very first target, including all contracts belonging to creditors.

That was quite credible.

The list of the edifices did not hold any great significance for most of Rome's Jews, as few of them had ever been to Jerusalem.

There was also great turmoil in Alexandria; Tuscus, the prefect in Egypt, was not master of the situation, with constant clashes occurring between Greeks and Jews. Nero had Tuscus replaced and executed for bathing in the bath that had been specially constructed for the emperor's intended visit to Alexandria. That visit did not come about, and Alexandria was left without a prefect for a while before Nero finally appointed Tija prefect of Egypt.

Alexandria at last had a Jewish prefect at its head!

The Jews of Far Side were ecstatic, although there were the eternal whiners and gripers who insisted that in his time as prefect of Galilee Tiberius Julius Alexander had executed Jewish malcontents, though to no avail because a certain Menahem—the son of a crucified rebel leader called Judas the Galilean, who was said to be literate—had taken up his father's generalship and broken open the armory at Masada and given arms not only to his own people but to other robbers. Then he had entered Jerusalem with his hordes, had the high priest Ananias pulled out of his hiding place in the aqueduct, and killed him along with his younger brother Ezekiel. All the same, Far Siders were on the whole delighted that at last Rome had a Jewish prefect of Egypt, and in any case since then Menahem had been captured, tortured, and slain by the men of his rival Eleazar.

News then came that Tiberius Julius Alexander had quelled sedition on the part of the Jews; his legions had entered Delta by force and cut down fifty thousand of them.

Hang on! That must be an exaggeration!

A further wave of refugees arrived from Alexandria and declared that it was not an exaggeration. The legions had staged terrible bloodshed on the orders of Tiberius Julius Alexander. He was a Roman, and had not been Jewish for a long time.

Uri was reminded of Philo: he would have been very happy with that number—one-fifth of the Jews of Alexandria, though if one took into account the fall in population due to the exodus of refugees, something like one-quarter had been lost. Still, the fact that it was his nephew, of all people, who had been responsible for this carnage? Compared with him Flaccus had been an innocent lamb.

In Antioch a commotion erupted in the Hippodrome over the Greeks of the "Green" faction demanding that Jews of the "Blue" faction also cheer for the "Green" charioteers, which the Jews were unwilling to do, at which they were cut down, along with another fifty thousand across the rest of the city so as Rome would not be bested by Alexandria.

833

However, most Jews were killed by other Jews in military actions, with anti-Romans killing pro-Romans and vice-versa. Agrippa II and his sisters sided with Rome and the high priests, with the priests and people of the land rising and fighting against them; impromptu bands of robbers pillaged everywhere, even fighting against each other. Nero dispatched Vespasian from Greece but there was no way of knowing where his legion was. Vespasian was supposed to have been sent to Judaea as a punishment for falling asleep in the auditorium during one of the emperor's lengthy singing performances.

"Who is this Vespasian?"

"He was the commander in Britannia."

Salutius knew nothing more about him.

"Everyone in Far Side is placing their trust in the Parthians," he noted, "with one commercial traveler after the other heading for Babylon. If the Parthians kick aside the peace there is nothing to stop them reaching Egypt, and Syria will just fall into their lap. Without one mortar to their name they would be able to expand their empire to three times the size!"

Uri shook his head:

"The Parthians won't disturb the peace; there hasn't been a foreign delegation received in greater splendor in Rome than the Parthians by Nero. Nero's not stupid. At the time there was as yet no war but he made a pact with the Parthians with the aim of their being good enough to stay calm whatever happens."

"Was Nero banking on a revolt of the Jews?" Salutius asked in amazement.

"It's Caligula's recipe," said Uri. "It's not so much that they expect a revolt as provoke one."

"But what interest would Nero have in the Jews being beaten down? They're just as much his subjects as anybody else! He's only interested in singing!"

"The impartial Athenian judges cannot have been too choosy in setting their criteria before awarding all the crowns and laurels to Nero as well as the title of *victor ludorum*... Still, I'll stake my life on it that he nevertheless requested with the deepest possible respect that the Jews be given a mighty walloping. Nero would have assented with a breezy flick of a wrist: why not, if that's the price?"

"But you weren't there!"

"I was as good as there."

A stillness fell before Salutius confessed that as a Roman he was deeply attached to her provinces, yet as a Jew he wanted the Parthians to win.

"The Parthians will remain neutral," Uri reiterated. "There are too many Jews living there. If it were to annex Judaea, Galilean and Syrian Jews would become the majority population within their empire and would displace the non-Jewish Parthians. If the Persians have a grain of good sense, then out of consideration for their own Jews they will promise our Jews anything at all but in the meantime the years will pass and Rome will slaughter its own Jews."

"So how many Jews will lose their lives, do you imagine?"

"Two or three million," Uri estimated. "We were late in starting to collect the books together. Everything and everyone will be lost."

Salutius could not believe that.

"You're a born pessimist: you see the negative side of everything!" he exclaimed irately. "As quick as hatred flickers up so too it will die down from one day to the next!" He lowered his voice. "After Nero there will be an emperor in full possession of his faculties and he'll establish order."

"That's when you really need to get worried, but let's hope you're right!" said Uri, who was already bored with the subject and began to inquire about the Nazarenes.

"They're also keeping quiet," said Salutius. "Anyway they are not supposed to express opinions on earthly matters; they are meant to strive for their heavenly bliss. The way they see it every horror is a certain sign of the Anointed's drawing nigh—the worse it is, the better."

"What about my son?"

All Salutius knew about Marcellus was that he was occupied with questioning and sounding out the refugees. He had some influence because it mattered how he judged them.

Uri nodded. It was clear that Marcellus was on the take for writing the most favorable reports possible about them; Marcellus would make a pile.

Salutius informed Uri that Iustus was in charge of the collection of the money for relief.

Uri nodded. That meant Iustus would embezzle at least half of it.

Lately Iustus had been pushing the municipal authority for an expansion of the catacombs on Monteverde and the Appian Way. The passageways now being planned for them were from the outset too narrow, because before long the numbers of the dead would be twice as high as they had used to be.

In recent times a certain tension had grown up between Salutius and Uri, so Uri sensed and no doubt his adopted son as well. True, he had not officially adopted him, but the relationship between them had come to the same thing; now, however, something had been upset. Uri noticed that he was colder and more savage in his manner of expressing himself when Salutius was around than he was when he was on his own.

At nights he rolled about restlessly on his bed. In the olden days the din of the Subura could be heard as far as the Via Sacra, and Uri had liked that clamorous, bustling, dirty, cheerful neighborhood the best of all Rome, but after the Great Fire the district had been cleaned up. Now it was spic-and-span and life had been squeezed out of it; it was now still as a grave on the Via Sacra in the evening and Uri would increasingly catch himself with tears in his eyes.

He mourned Beth Zechariah, which some group or other had sacked and put to the torch, raping the women, clubbing the elderly to death, pressing the younger men into army service, and dashing the heads of the infants against walls or throwing them into wells. He mourned Master Jehuda and the black-haired young girl. He mourned the Jews of Caesarea, cool, stand-offish, and wealthy as they had been, not having the least suspicion that they would all be killed. He mourned Delta, where Tija's soldiers were now on a killing spree: he had repaid with interest the Alexandrian Jews who had said a word against his father's cowardice and brazen thievery. Tija was cruel and calculating, but he too had feelings; a non-Jewish prefect would have been happy with a few hundred dead. There was no human way of speaking about this, though.

He ought to write it down.

NERO WAS ASSASSINATED AT LONG LAST: HE HAD LIVED THIRTY AND A half years. He was succeeded as emperor by aged Galba, the prefect of Hispania; after the announcement the Romans all bought liberty caps and slapped them on their noggins—that was their way of celebrating it. Dress shops ran the caps up overnight and sold them at triple the price. Galba had the ashes of the murdered progeny of Augustus placed in the Mausoleum; surprisingly he only had Helius and a few of his closest cronies executed after they had been tortured somewhat in public, but he spared the lives of both Sporus and Tigellinus, the prefect of the Praetorian Guard, despite the calls of the populace for them to be punished. He did not commit acts of cruelty, so he was laughed at as he walked with a stooped back, white hair, and a broadsword by his side. When the legions in Lower Germany shouted for Aulus Vitellius, their prefect, to be made emperor, Galba adopted Lucius Piso, appointing him imperial heir. This enraged Marcus Silvius Otho, who, expecting to be chosen, had returned from Lusitania (it was he who had passed on his wife, Poppaea Sabina, to Nero), and he turned against Galba. A messenger reported to Galba that Otho had been killed. Believing this, and expressing his sorrow, Galba then set out for the Capitoline to offer sacrifice, but he was met on the way by horsemen and footsoldiers who cut him down. His last words were "What harm have I done?" He was in his seventy-third year and had ruled nine months. Otho was then named emperor. A false Nero amassed an army and he was killed; Piso, who did not rule for even one day, was killed; Aulus Vitellius's armies approached Rome and joined the battle with Otho's army at Cremona, with forty thousand men falling in the fight. Otho went to meet Vitellius, resigned, then took his own life in his thirty-seventh year, after a rule of just three months. He was succeeded as emperor by Vitellius, the emperor Tiberius's one-time catamite. His father had wanted to be the emperor, but it was the son who did so. He banqueted and caroused; Nero's Golden House was not fine enough for him so he had an even bigger palace built for himself on the Palatine. He held games, had only Otho's few supporters finished off, not even confiscating any fortunes. Evil omens occurred: on the Capitoline many huge footprints were seen; a comet was seen at noon. The Temple of Jupiter had opened of its own accord with great clangor. Vitellius's days were numbered, it was whispered.

Meanwhile the Jewish war lingered on, with Vespasianus heading the legions in Galilee, but upon hearing about the commotion in Rome he refrained from the conflict.

Who, then, is this Vespasianus?

Well, the younger brother of Sabinus Flavius, the prefect of Rome.

When Uri heard this he thought he had misheard it. He reeled.

It was Kainis's lover, Titus of the blade-like lips and broad cheekbones.

He laughed immoderately.

"There may be some reason to hope," he spluttered, choking with laughter, "that I have some influence at court!"

He burst out in a fresh fit of laughing.

Salutius looked at him with a pitying stare: poor Gaius Theodorus was getting on in years; he too was beginning to lose his wits.

"The two of them," whispered Uri, "are going to exterminate the entire Jewish race."

"Which two?"

"Vespasianus and Tiberius Julius Alexander, that's who! Vespasianus will be emperor... But don't say a word to anybody! Let people believe that there is still an Eternal One!"

Salutius cast his eyes down and studied the floor.

It was uncomfortable to see a dearly loved person reduced to ruins.

CIVIL WAR WAS RAGING IN GALILEE, SAMARIA, AND JUDAEA; ANYONE might become a military leader be he a priestly scion or one of the "people of the land," an am ha'aretz; anyone could be robbed, anyone murdered—the Roman legions avoided getting involved. The more prosperous Jews fled to Italia or Babylon. Rome was not too keen to receive, but Babylon even less so: Jewish robber chiefs with residency in Parthia mustered armies of peasants there too, slew non-Jews and rich Jews alike and robbed them of their money until, with great difficulty, they had disposed of the last one. Like the Judaean gangs, they had started with hostage-taking but by the end they only killed.

New refugees from Alexandria said that Vespasianus had arrived there, leaving the command of Legio V and Legio X to his son, Titus, and that he had applied himself to the magic arts with great expertise: curing the blind and the crippled and even raising the dead by the laying-on of hands, a kiss, or fine words. Tiberius Julius Alexander was the other favorite of the Greeks, being heaped with gifts.

The two legions in Alexandria swore an oath of obedience to Vespasianus and acclaimed him as emperor; he brought in new taxes, purloined the treasures of the shrines, and halted grain shipments to Rome, threatening it with famine. Legio V and X waged war in Judaea, with Tiberius Julius Alexander becoming commander-in-chief of Titus's forces, taking care of their support lines, their provisioning, their weaponry, mortars, and ballistics. Many Jews were anxious to side with the Romans, sending emissaries to meet them, but the Romans had more than enough Jewish fighters already and they were not after homage but a splendid victory and an even more splendid triumphal parade.

At Cremona the forces that were loyal to Vitellius clashed with those that had pledged their allegiance to Vespasianus, with his older brother, Sabinus, and the younger of his sons, Domitian, at their head. Rome went up in flames, with the opposing forces fighting on Capitoline Hill, which even the oldest historians could not recall as having happened before. The Temple of Jupiter and much else burned down. The dead on the field of battle included Sabinus, that hulking, ruddy-faced loudmouth, and fifty thousand more. Vitellius was seized and dragged along the Via Sacra, with people taunting him, especially for his huge paunch, then he was locked up in a dungeon deep down in Palatine Hill along with statues of him that had been hastily overturned and brought there. For all that he called out "And yet I was once your emperor," he was mocked further, then he was tortured on the Stairs of Mourning and rolled down to the foot of them before being decapitated and dragged off to the Tiber. Vespasianus, who was still in Alexandria, was elected by the Senate as emperor, with Domitian governing on his behalf.

Judaea, Samaria, and Galilee were put to the torch, towns and villages being sacked; their defenders fought to the end before stabbing to death their wives and children and finally themselves. Jerusalem was laid siege to for a long time by Titus's legions, among which were some Jewish detachments, just as in the time of Herod the Great. Toward the end of this Great Revolt one million people fled to the city from the surrounding countryside, defending it as long as they were able and even beyond. They died of hunger and thirst in the tens of thousands, opposing factions slaughtered one another in their tens of thousands, mothers ate their children, sons their fathers, until finally the Romans occupied the city and slew everyone, then ransacked and then demolished the Temple. The Ark of the Covenant, it was whispered, was still there, buried under the ashes, for it had come to light during the siege and it was now in the best possible place because no one would unearth it and that is how it would stay.

It was said that there had never been a war as momentous as this. On virtually every house wall in Rome the riff-raff had scrawled the tag "HEP," an abbreviation for *Hierolosyma est perduta*, meaning "Jerusalem is lost"; also popular was the shorter "HC": *Hierolosyma est capta*. Mobs of young men would disrobe old men in the street and if one was found to be circumcised, he would be beaten to death. The vigiles looked the other way.

Ninety-four thousand Jewish captives were driven through the streets of Rome in the triumphal procession that was held jointly by Vespasianus and Titus, the likes of which had never been seen by Rome's inhabitants. The procession entered Rome by the Porta Triumphalis and snaked across the city, taking in all the jam-packed theaters en route. It stopped at the Forum, where the chief leaders of the Jews were tortured and then executed, and then continued to the Temple of Jupiter on the Capitoline, where Vespasianus and Titus made sacrifices, completing them with the customary prayers. Spoils in inconceivable abundance were carried along and also wheeled by were huge floats, some three or four stories high, bearing tableaux which gave the crowds of onlookers a good indication of the various aspects of what had happened. The gawkers of Rome had their fill of eating, drinking, and shouting their lungs off. Later on fifty thousand more Jewish captives arrived.

Vespasianus set to the construction of an enormous amphitheater on the site of Nero's former palace, with the glittering gilded bronze colossus of that emperor of such unhappy memory left intact alongside it. With him the Julio-Claudian dynasty had come to an end; now it was the turn of the Flavian dynasty.

One hundred thousand Jewish slaves and forty thousand Roman plebs built the Colosseum, as the Flavian amphitheater was named by the people of Rome, after Nero's statue; the construction was financed by the treasures that had been plundered from the Temple in Jerusalem. The plans were drawn up by the best Greek architects, to the chagrin of Roman builders, who were at best hired as subcontractors and suppliers.

A Jewish tax was introduced in Rome under which the didrachma, the annual tribute that all Jewish males between the ages of twenty and fifty had paid by ancestral custom to the Temple in Jerusalem was henceforth to be collected for the Temple of Jupiter on the Capitoline, and it was made compulsory for all Jews between the ages of three and seventy, including children and women. Even so there was not enough money, and along with other measures Vespasianus introduced a tax upon urine. Even Titus, his son, found that excessive, in response to which the emperor held a sestertius coin to his son's nose, wittily asking: "Why, does that stink?"

For the amphitheater a vast oval pit, with a circumference of almost one thousand six hundred feet, was dug up precisely on the spot where Nero's artificial lakes had once been situated. Uri had not been sorry to see them go, as the fountains had never been allowed to make music.

The Jewish slave laborers working on the Colosseum spent their nights chained up next to it in unheated military tents, which, with them sleeping on four racks and on the ground, were dark inside and stank so badly that they found it hard to breathe. Uri went among them every day, handing out blankets and clothes he had bought and taking them evening meals; the slave drivers raised no objection as he had softened them with money.

The prisoners received the gifts with gratitude and told stories in return.

Uri found it hard to order in his mind all that had happened, and when and how it had happened, with each person telling his own story and not knowing too precisely about other events.

Vespasianus had spared Gadara because it surrendered to him.

But then Vespasianus had also wiped out the entire population of cities which had sent emissaries to him to surrender.

Vespasianus had sent six thousand handpicked young captives to the city of Achaea when Nero had driven chariots and sung in the Isthmaean Games; some five hundred of these where thrown into work on building the Colosseum, the rest sold in Greek cities. These young men were despised by the other prisoners because they had fallen into captivity at a good time, when the war had only just begun, and so had managed to steer clear of torture.

In Jerusalem during the siege there had been two factions, later three, with self-appointed dictators and their supporters firing catapults and ballistae at one another and setting fire to each other's camps. The Zealots, led by Johanan, were in the upper camp, raising towers in three corners of Temple Square and setting up their catapults on the roof of the Temple; Eleazar set up camp in Temple Square; while Simon occupied the Upper City, attacking from there. No, not the Romans who were besieging the city but the others, and no, it was not Johanan but Eleazar. But how could it have been Eleazar, as he arrived later on at the head of the Idumaes?

More Jews were killed by Jews than by Romans. Anyone who wanted to invite the Romans to enter the city for the sake of restoring peace was cut down by the Jews; anyone who managed to get out because he had paid off the Zealots guarding the gates was cut down by the Romans. There was no escape and they were not even buried. Even Ananias, the high priest, was slain by the Jews for wanting peace.

Izates of Adiabene fought against Rome but he obtained none of the assistance from the Parthian Empire on which he had counted; in truth, the Parthian Empire was in no position to render assistance because much the same sort of Jewish robber chieftains were pillaging there as in Judaea and Galilee, funded by the Romans. Well, no, there was no need to fund them: the lead shown by Judaea was enough. All the same, a lot of Babylonian Jews flooded into Galilee to fight against Rome, and all fell in the struggles like Silas, a former deputy to Agrippa II. The treacherous king took Rome's side all along, while his sister, that whore Berenice, the three-time widow, became the lover of Titus.

Samaria was ravaged by the Romans just the same as if it had been Judaea or Galilee: the Romans had no clue as to who was a true Jew and who not. The Romans also staged a bloodbath at Mount Gerizim, where at least ten thousand lost their lives; the Samaritans, the swine, must have deserved it as their holy mountain offered them no protection.

It was a war of everyone against everyone; pity and sympathy was extinguished in them all. Victims were shot from the roof of the Temple, with countless priests and pilgrims dying, having been admitted even while the fighting was in progress; even the altar was smashed by the Jewish catapults.

The way it started was that the high priests had filched the tithe from the threshing-floors for themselves, leaving the priests hungry. That was the cause of the civil strife.

The way it started was when construction work on the Temple was finished; thirty thousand men were left unemployed. It was they who started the unruliness.

Corpses floated down the river as far as the Dead Sea, and there they have lain ever since in the thousands, among the blocks of pitch.

Bodies lay five feet high at the pyramids.

The pyramids? Uri was amazed, but it turned out that Helena had raised three pyramids for the Adiabene dynasty outside the walls of Jerusalem.

The first to be demolished was the palace of Agrippa. Uri could not figure that out either until it emerged that it had been put up by Agrippa II in front of the old palace of the Hasmoneans, opposite Herod's palace in the market square of the Upper Town, and a splendid building it had been too.

Where, then, were the towers that the rebels had put up? Well, one was above the Chystos, the Chamber of Hewn Stone, and another two on the east, by the ravine. What did they mean by above the Chystos? A wall stretched all the way there, from the Antonia fortress to the bridge, said Uri; it's possible to walk along the top of it. He was laughed at because that western wall had been pulled down back when it was still almost peacetime.

He asked questions, making notes when he got back home, but then the prisoners were informed that Uri was an unclean person, whereupon they grew cool toward him.

Uri asked about the reason for hostile turn in their attitude. Those who deigned even to answer said: you are a Nazarene madman, the whole thing was your fault. Others stated: you've been putting on the feedbag here in Edom all the time we've been shedding blood for the freedom of the Jews. They said: you're Jewish like Tiberius Julius Alexander is Jewish. They declared: you're a rotten traitor. Whatever they said, a look of boundless hatred flashed from their slaves' eyes. Uri noted this, but as long as he was able to afford it he continued to pay for the gifts, though he personally no longer went out among them.

It was better so because the mood in the tents was frightful; the prisoners loathed one another even more intensely than they did the Romans; there were at least twenty factions, each of which loathed the other nineteen with an undying passion, and they squealed on and denounced one another to the Jews of Rome, who lost no chance—as they had during the Jewish War over the past four years—to distance themselves from everything which was happening in Judaea and Galilee. Uri once made the mistake of inquiring after the fate of Beth Zechariah, which led to it being spread around that in fact he himself was from Beth Zechariah, and one after the other reported that everything and everybody in Beth Zechariah was just fine, even claiming to be personally acquainted with Uri's relatives there, they were all alive and well: it was awkward.

The money ran out; he had to do something for the wretches. The elders among the Roman Jews organized a collection for the slaves and asked the municipal authority to assist them in distributing it: they did not wish to take sides in the domestic squabbles of the prisoners. Everyone could well imagine how much of that money actually got to the slaves. The native Jews of Rome made sporadic donations, but in moderation; they had no money themselves as the Jewish tax had taken it all.

A vast palace was built for the emperor's darling, a certain Antonia, next to the barracks of the Praetorian Guard past the Via Nomentana. That just has to be Kainis, Uri thought to himself; after what seemed like the hundredth time of trying, and at the cost of a tidy sum of money, he eventually arranged for a letter to be handed over to her.

TWO DAYS BEFORE THE TIME HE HAD INDICATED, IT SPRANG TO URI'S mind that he ought to take Kainis a gift. A nice scroll of some kind. He went out to the unoccupied peasant cottage; the cement storehouse in the yard was untouched. He opened the door and entered.

It was empty, not one scroll remaining.

Uri sank to the ground and remained sitting there for a long time.

The lock had not been broken; Salutius was the only other one with a key. It had to be him who had taken the scrolls.

He trudged over to Far Side. Salutius had grown a long beard and his hair had turned white since they had last met, six months before; his look was agitated, he was even more round-shouldered than ever. The atmosphere in Far Side must have been straining his nerves.

"I'm glad to see you," he said.

"Where are the scrolls?"

Salutius went red in the face.

"I tried to alert you," he stammered, "but you're constantly caught up running around on matters connected with your prisoners. Half of it is yours."

"Half of what?"

"The money."

Uri thought he was going to choke.

"You've sold the books?"

"I got a superb price for them," Salutius protested. "Thanks to your brilliant business flair! They paid a fortune for the lot!"

"Who's they?"

"The imperial library! They're collecting all scrolls on Judaica; they're buying up anything Jewish!"

Uri stared blankly.

"They paid three hundred thousand sesterces!" Salutius rhapsodized. "Half of it's yours!"

Uri took a few deep breaths in the same way as he had seen Philo do.

"Keep it!" he muttered, getting up from his seat and staggering out.

IT WAS POSSIBLE TO GET THEM BACK; HE HAD TO GET THEM BACK.

He needed to record what had happened; that could not be done without the source materials.

By the time he set off to see Kainis it was no longer money he wanted to ask for, but help in reclaiming his library.

He peered shortsightedly as he walked along the Via Nomentana but there was no way he could miss the massive block of the Praetorian Guard's barracks. Kainis's palace had to be nearby.

The palace had a long, tall, whitewashed wall; it must be enormous inside.

Uri would have liked to think that Kainis had arranged for her palace to be built not far from his own cottage with the aim of being close to him, but he could not entertain any such thoughts: Kainis had put herself under the constant supervision of bodyguards.

Uri gave his name, and a guard went inside; Uri waited. The way in which permission to enter had to be asked for was the same as it had been with Narcissus. This time he was not stricken by an urge to defecate: back then he had still been fretting over his family.

After a thorough frisking, three guards escorted him through a vestibule then across an immense, lushly verdant garden in which a brook was babbling and fountains were splashing. A circular pavilion of alabaster stood at the bottom of the garden; the guards came to a halt and one of them indicated the way with a nod of his head. Uri went up the three steps and entered the pavilion.

Kainis got up from a couch and walked toward Uri.

Uri blinked. Kainis had on a short, beautifully pleated white tunic with a maroon silk belt; her hair was now completely silvery. She came to a stop and Uri approached closer to see her better. Her features were wrinkled, her slight, slim body wizened, her legs spindly, but that did not bother Uri: she had carefully made up her eyelids and lips.

She's titivated herself in my honor, it occurred to Uri, and he smiled.

The deep pools of Kainis's eyes, even now wonderful to look at, flickered. Just a flash, but Uri noticed.

She wants to conceal her pity for me, he thought.

Uri had hardly any teeth and his mouth had crumpled; he was also now totally bald.

They studied each other at length before a tubby individual darted out and flung his arms around Uri's neck.

"Gaius! Gaius!" the eunuch Posides exclaimed.

Uri sighed: he might have guessed that he was not going to be spared a head-to-head with Kainis. He patted Posides's round cheeks.

"You haven't aged a day!" he said.

"We don't usually. Now give Kainis a peck! She's been waiting so long to meet you!"

Uri halted.

Kainis turned to go back into the pavilion, followed by Uri and Posides.

Magnificent statues, paintings, furniture, rugs.

Kainis seated herself on a stool without a back. Posides indicated to Uri to take a seat on a comfortable leather armchair facing her, while he plopped down at his mistress's feet.

"How are your protégés, the Jewish slaves?" Kainis asked. She had the same marvelously deep voice as she had of old.

"They are happy and proud to be helping build the Colosseum," Uri replied.

Kainis chuckled. She still liked to do that.

Posides also chortled.

"My firstborn son was also castrated," Uri tossed an aside to Posides.

"Consider yourself lucky!" he cried out merrily. "At least he's happy!"

"He lives in Pompeii."

"Pompeii's divine!" said Posides. "Ten years ago there was an earthquake in Naples and the amphitheater was slightly damaged, almost burying the emperor, but the astronomers all say that there won't be another tremor for a hundred years, and it's true that Vesuvius has hardly been discharging any smoke!"

Uri looked at Kainis. It did not matter that Posides was present.

"It would have been nice to grow old together with you," he said.

Kainis's eyelids fluttered again.

"I would not have been a good wife to you, Uri," she said. "I would never have been able to stand what I could have had to undergo beside you."

"Certainly you could have," Uri responded. "A person is able to take a lot. You can regret not having lived with me: I've had an interesting life; I learned a lot."

"I too have had an interesting life," said Kainis.

Uri was silent. Only now had it registered that Kainis had called him Uri; she had never done that before, it had always been Gaius. Did I mention it to her that I was called Uri at home? Most probably if she had said it.

"She's still got an interesting life!" Posides exclaimed. "Every morning it is her who gives the password!"

"What password?" Uri asked.

"The guards' password, of course! They come over in the tunnel and Kainis makes one up on the spot! Sometimes a devil gets into her and she spouts whole lines of poetry, but the dopes can't remember those!"

"Are you the prefect of the Praetorian Guard, then?" Uri was astounded.

"Nominally Tija is," said Kainis, "but the poor fellow has picked up so many ailments that in practice I substitute for him..."

"And how is our friend Titus these days?"

"He's growing old too," said Kainis, "but he's still got the old sense of humor... The three of us have loads of laughs—him, Tija, and me."

"Has his wife died, then?"

"She died fairly early on in Britannia," Kainis said. "Not being loved can kill, and I can't deny it, my Titus did not love his wife. After she died he sent me a message that I should hotfoot it to Britannia, but I chose not to. I was deeply offended," Kainis giggled. "I sent him a message that he should come back here. He wasn't able to do that for a fair time, what with having adventures with all sorts of British amazons... But then when he was made proconsul for Africa I went with him... I also followed him to Alexandria... You had told me such a lot about it, Uri, that I rather fancied having a look around myself..."

Uri laughed.

"I've heard that he healed by a laying on of hands."

"I was there too! That was something to see!" Posides squealed. "I was standing there on the platform next to the Square Stoa, in the gardens of the Gymnasium, a tremendous crowd around it, Tija was also there on the platform, and the astrologers Barbillus and Seleucus in their ornamental cloaks... 'Healer! Healer!' the people were roaring, and he was healing all kinds of maladies: the blind saw again, the maimed started to run, the deaf to hear... With his own hands he draped a cloak over naked, jabbering, babbling lunatics and they instantly began to extol him eloquently... A superb to-do it was! Tija organized it marvelously... He even went so far as sending genuinely sick people up before Titus, not just the pretend-sick. Not knowing that they were genuine, he went through exactly the same hocus pocus for them too—and now listen to this!—he cured several of them as well! Not all, but some for sure! Those he didn't went on making a fuss, and there was nothing he could do about it! He raged afterward that he would rip out Tija's guts with his own bare hands, have him broken on the wheel! We just roared with laughter."

"It must have been fun," Uri acknowledged.

"But then of course when he raised the taxes, the people switched soon enough to detesting him... They found it hard to swallow the tax of one drachma per capita... but what they took to worst was that he sold them the imperial properties in Egypt—that was also Tija's wheeze—which meant that they were made to pay a staggering amount—forty million sesterces Titus squeezed out of them, but they didn't dare resist: if Tija is capable of having fifty thousand Jews slain, then he can put easily dispatch five times as many Greeks... They weren't calling him 'Healer' then, but 'Salted Fish Vendor.'"

"We had a lot of laughs," said Kainis dispassionately. "We were still in Egypt and we got news that Domitianus was behaving excessively like an emperor in Rome, so Titus wrote him a very polite letter which was full of sentences like: 'Many thanks, son, for not dethroning me yet!'"

Uri laughed out loud.

"Tiberius also had a wit," he said. "There was the time a Greek delegation that was visiting him about a year after his mother's death expressed condolences, to which he responded by expressing condolences to them on the death of Helena."

All three of them chuckled.

Posides clambered to his feet.

"Would you like anything to eat or drink, my dear Gaius?"

Uri gestured that he didn't. Posides shook his head to indicate that he would very much prefer to leave them to their own devices but squatted back down at Kainis's feet, with her patting the crown of his head.

"What do you need my help with?" Kainis asked.

Uri kept silent for a while before sighing:

"Originally I wanted to ask for money for the Jewish captives," he said, "but something has come up in the meantime... I've had my library sold off behind my back... It was an extensive library with a great many books of rare Judaica..."

Kainis's eyes grew darker; she remained still before saying:

"What do you need the library for?"

"I want to write an account of what happened, and also why it happened."

"We already have a Jewish historian," said Kainis. "He's from a family of high priests and was also a military leader; he came across to our side at the right time... What he is writing is the official account."

"You mean no one else may write one?"

"One of them is plenty."

There was a pause.

"But who checks that he has dressed it up in the right language? Who carries out the role of censor? The emperor in person?"

"My dear Titus hasn't read a thing in a long while," Kainis brushed that aside. "I run through everything."

She chuckled.

"Just imagine, most recently I read that our legions were besieging Jotapata, and what should I see in it but that Titus—my Titus's son Titus—was the very first to scale the walls!"

Posides giggled with her.

In the textbook literature there did not exist a commander who did not direct a siege from the rear. Uri joined in the laughter.

"Do you scratch out anything like that?" he asked.

"No way do I scratch it out," Kainis chortled. "Readers like adventure-story twists. I even showed it to young Titus. He was delighted to be portrayed as such a big hero!"

Posides snickered.

"Kainis showed me the passage where this Jewish leader of priestly descent writes about how he hid himself in a certain deep pit, adjoining a large den, along with the remaining defenders after the castle has been occupied. He wanted to defect, but his Jews wouldn't let him, so he hit upon the idea of drawing lots to determine who should kill the others. This proposal prevailed, so they drew lots, but by the providence of the Jewish god each time this priestly leader drew a lot to be left alive to the very last... Now, Kainis calculated the probability of that happening..."

"Yes," said Kainis, "because earlier on he had written that sixty persons of eminence remained alive, so doing it that way, the probability of his remaining alive would have been so near zero that I told him at least to leave out the numbers..."

They all laughed.

"And have the casualties been added up?" Uri asked.

"Most certainly!" Kainis replied. "Two million Jews died—that was the number I agreed with the author in advance, but the funny thing is that there must have been roughly that number in reality. It does not lie in Rome's interest to decrease the number of victims. On the contrary."

Other nations would quake even more. Smart thinking.

"And what is the emperor doing?" Uri asked.

"Everything. He can do whatever he wants, but it's me who gives the orders."

Uri looked at the fragile old lady, mistress of the empire of the world, and was amazed.

"Ask for anything else," Kainis crooned softly. "Anything you want you'll get—though not me, of course."

Posides giggled.

"Ask for some monopoly!" he prompted in a loud whisper. "That's the best! An absolutely safe bet! You can't imagine how much people are prepared to pay us for a good monopoly! We'll give you one for free!"

Uri held his tongue.

"That's what Kainis dreamed up for you," said Posides, "because she's extremely bright, brighter than even me—giving you a monopoly on the importation of Jewish oil."

Uri was dizzy.

Importing ritually pure oil from Judaea for a Jewish Roman population that had grown to two hundred thousand! A huge business! It ran through his head that an amphora of oil cost one drachma in Judaea, and in Rome it sold for eight or nine times that price. About half of that would go to procurement and transport costs, but the rest was clear profit. Many millions of sesterces per year. In the first year one would have to invest it all, but any banker would willingly provide a loan.

Uri held his tongue, just sighing.

"Who had the rights up till now?" he asked.

Kainis chuckled. Uri startled: it was the first time she had laughed sincerely.

"What did I tell you!" she spoke triumphantly to Posides, who growled like a dog.

"He'll still want it!" he growled. "You'll see!"

"Who holds the rights now?" Uri repeated the question.

"What do you care?" barked Posides. "I have on me solicitations from Jews for that very thing—three of them. They've shelled out to us in advance a total of forty million sesterces!"

"If I'm granted it, then I'll have to pay them back, won't I?"

"No way!" exclaimed Posides. "I'm not talking about loans! Not even backhanders! The money was given as a pure token of devotion; they know very well that if they are not granted that monopoly specifically they'll get another one instead and purely because by sheer chance their names come to our mind..."

"You won't harm anyone," said Kainis. "Anyone who has money can invest it in something anyway."

Uri remained quiet. The blood was starting to rush to his head.

"I don't want any monopoly from you," he said. "I didn't fall in love with you so that one day you would make me a millionaire."

There was a silence.

"I have an invention," he went on. "It's a lifting device. There are drawings, but they're in my library, somewhere in the possession of your people... I could sketch it if you give me a pen and papyrus... It could replace the work of hundreds. I didn't come here on that account but if you would buy it, that would make me very happy."

Kainis nudged Posides on the head, and he scrambled to his feet and rolled out of the room.

There was silence.

"Was this wonder palace worth the death of two million people?" Uri asked with a nod of his head all around them to indicate what he was referring to.

"If that is the price..."

"It's a pretty steep price!"

"They would have died whether or not we were around."

"That's not true."

Kainis's face darkened, her wonderful eyes narrowed; she jumped up.

"You weren't born a slave," she said shrilly. "You don't have the faintest idea about people!"

There was a silence. The guards rushed in, at which Kainis angrily dismissed them and they rushed out again.

Uri did not take fright, merely felt a profound sorrow and pity.

"All the same," he murmured softly, "you would have been better off living with me."

Kainis held her peace; she was pacing in the hall. Uri watched her: from a distance she still had the figure of a young girl. She had borne no children.

She was a miracle the Eternal One had created to ruin, and sooner than kill.

My everlasting love out of whom grew the master of Rome.

They remained hushed until Posides returned with a wax tablet and stylus.

"It'll soon be ready," said Uri, sketching the lift. Underneath linked by a tube there were two cylinders, one open, upon the other a weight with a suction pump connected to the latter (he wrote underneath the word "vacuum"). He also designated the position after the suction, with the weight being lifted.

He handed it to Posides, who took it and gave it to Kainis, who snatched a look.

"You can leave," she said.

Posides bowed and glided out.

Kainis resumed her place on the stool, sitting with a straight back as before, laying the lovely, long, thin fingers of her hands in her lap, looking at Uri with her fathomless gaze.

"Clever," said Kainis. "Air is like water; it's just that one can't see it... But what blacksmith can produce cylinders as tight as that?"

"I know some good sculptors," said Uri, "who are able to make high-precision castings."

They fell silent.

"You've grown ugly," said Kainis. "Your mouth looks terrible like that with all your teeth gone... but your personality is unchanged. I liked your personality a great deal."

"You were the only love of my life," said Uri.

"Good," said Kainis, "that's how it goes. Maybe in another life."

"There is no other life."

"No resurrection?"

"That least of all."

"I never thought that you'd become a Nazarene at the time you were expelled," Kainis noted.

So, she had known about it. Uri was thrilled.

"Ordinary Jews are just as vile as anyone else; the Nazarenes are crazy," he said. "I'm not even a Jew any more."

"You never were," said Kainis. "I'm not an empress either; I just sham it. Titus isn't an emperor; he's only shamming it. His son Titus is also only shamming it. We do it to stop being bored. The other son, Domitianus, isn't shamming; he is going to commit wholesale carnage."

"Your own Titus did that too."

"That's true, but he only did what all of them after Tiberius wanted. Vitellius wanted that, so did Caligula, so did Nero... Titus actually did it. Someone would manage it, anyway."

Uri looked at Kainis's wrinkled face.

"How much we would have quarreled!" said Uri wistfully. "How we would have yelled at each other! It would have been superb!"

Kainis laughed.

"So what is going to happen to my library?" Uri asked.

Kainis grew solemn.

"Our man is writing his work, taking from the source materials whatever he needs, then he burns them. After all, he's a historian."

Uri nodded: that was indeed the way history was usually written.

"What did you want to write about?" Kainis asked.

"Something about the Nazarenes."

Kainis nodded.

"It's a simple religion," she said. "It will win through."

Uri was astounded.

"You know about it too?"

"If you know," Kainis said heatedly, "why wouldn't I? Anything that calls for insight we know just the same. I'm in the habit of conversing with you in my imagination... You give such fine answers... joking, teasing..."

She left off.

Tears welled up in Uri's eyes, and he turned away.

"It's a dangerous religion," he said. "It's going to cause hideous problems."

"Yes," said Kainis. "It's a brilliant idea that there should be someone, a human, who was resurrected and it's necessary to wait until he comes back again. It's also a good touch for it to be immaterial who's a Jew and who isn't—anyone can be chosen, the only thing which has to be accepted is the resurrection... You don't need to be able to do anything, neither read nor write, nor does one have to stick to any prescriptions, and anyone can become a priest, everybody is sacred who believes in the Resurrected One, and by doing so one they will gain everlasting life! There aren't even any ceremonies! They eat, praise his name, they are together, and that's the solution to loneliness, to immortality... There is no religion more simple-minded than that on the market! Unholy strife will come of this within the Jewish world; that's going to be the real war of the Jews, and a madness will be set loose out of Judaism, a madness of the losers, and it is going to prevail, because the losers are in the majority... If only Spartacus had a religion like that! The only trouble they will have is that he's not going to come again, he doesn't want to, and they are impatient—that is what will sow disorder among them..."

"They'll find a solution," Uri considered. "They will find a solution for everything as long as the faith remains. From now on they'll lie about everything."

"They lied up till now."

"But not as eagerly as this."

They fell silent.

"But if you knew all that... What was the point of demolishing the Temple? Why bring so many prisoners here to Rome?"

Kainis sighed.

"Titus—the son of my Titus, that is—held a war council when Jerusalem was already in their hands as to what should become of the Temple. Tija argued against destroying it, the others were for... Young Titus supposed that as long as the Temple was standing the Jews wouldn't be able to rest, whether they remained faithful to their old prophets or became followers of this Messiah. Tija said that if there was no ritual center for the religion any more, it would not mean the end of it, as new centers would spring up wherever Jews live."

"Tija, the scoundrel, will be proved right," Uri concluded after some reflection.

"That's my view as well," said Kainis. "Tija also disagreed with bringing the Jewish captives to Rome... He said that Rome may have won the war but the Jews will win the peace. He concluded that on this occasion they ought to have gone about it the other way around: Rome's Jews ought to have been repatriated to Judaea, rather than bringing Judea's Jews over here, because in thirty years time half of Rome's plebs will be Jewish, and half of them in turn will be Nazarene."

"So why did that not happen?" Uri asked, his flesh creeping.

Kainis gave a peel of laughter.

"Because it would have been expensive! It was cheaper to demolish the Temple... To say nothing of a matter of vanity, as usual... My Titus would only have brought a few Jewish captives over but his son was all for a triumphal procession of an immensity such as had never been seen before with as many prisoners as possible... My Titus in the end went along with it because he is fonder of young Titus than he is of his second son. Domitianus was almost eaten up with envy to see that his brother was granted a triumphal procession as big as that because it's one that people will remember for years to come. I warned my Titus, so it did not just come from Tija, that the Jews would be the cause of a lot of trouble in Rome, but he just waved it off airily: that was not something we would live to see, let those who are alive worry about them..."

"And your historian is going to write about that?"

Kainis laughed:

"Near enough."

Two days later Uri went back to the palace to get an answer. A guard again went inside. Uri waited a long time. Then the gate opened and the elderly woman herself stood there in a shimmering, iridescent silk tunic, ribbons in her silvery hair, a dour armed man on either side.

"It's a no go," Kainis said regretfully. "The emperor was furious about it. He said that a lifting device like that would rob people of work and it would not pay to keep them on a daily wage."

"I suppose I must be thankful that he didn't have me executed," Uri said, bowed his head, and went away.

A PERSON DID NOT NEED A LIBRARY TO WRITE A BOOK. ONE NEEDED nothing more than papyrus and ink.

What was it, in fact, that he wanted to write? Maybe things that had never been written down before, and if they had not been written down earlier, then they were new. Still, there was something different from previous ages about the present age, he supposed, and maybe it wasn't an accident that the Anointed had not come earlier, or so the deranged zealots believed, but nowadays.

There was no necessity to write a bulky historical work replete with facts. It was possible to write, without any facts at all, letters about things of importance, or figures of importance, like Seneca's letters to Marcia. It was just that writing like that would not provide a morally ennobling solace but quite the reverse. People should quake in their boots with fear, as Aristotle wrote.

"Letters to Kainis."

There were a number of ongoing construction projects that he was head of; they paid well and he was able to set aside enough to support the total costs of keeping himself for a year. His daughters, even though he was supporting them, were continually asking for more; nothing was enough for them, but now they would have to make do with what they had. He ought to be able to get the essence down in one year, he supposed.

He tingled with a pleasant sense of excitement; he was about to embark on a new life.

It is hard getting going with writing; Uri would lie on his bed at night and try to figure out what to start with—who and what should he write about to Kainis.

One evening he had two visitors, Iustus and a Latin. Uri scrambled to his feet. Iustus did the talking: Uri was requested to become a member of the committee on the *fiscus Judaicus*—this nice man of the equestrian order was the praetor and he represented the state. With due regard to his experience and wisdom, Uri could be offered the sum of one hundred thousand sesterces for his cooperation; the other Jewish members worked for free.

Kainis is reaching a hand out for me, it crossed Uri's mind, and he smiled.

He thanked them for asking but, given so many existing calls on his time he would have to decline. This was noted with relief by Iustus and uneasily by the praetor: obviously it was him who would be hauled over the coals by Kainis or Posides. Though he did what he could to convince Uri, the latter politely showed him the door.

The first night on which he sat down to write he found the light shed by the oil lamp to be inadequate. He needed to buy another. Nerves, perhaps, he thought.

It is hard getting going.

There were now three lamps burning on the table but still he could not see any letters. He bent his head down closer, pulled it back farther, but the contours were still uncertain, and precisely in between there seemed to be nothing. What the devil?

By day he would have to peer on the building site, examining the murals, and he noticed that in the middle of his visual field he could see nothing, only if he looked at them sideways, but if he moved on he could still see something there. His right eye had always been the worse but with that he could at least vaguely see something in the center; his left eye was the better one, but with that he could see nothing in the center.

That night he strained his eyes mightily to see his own handwriting on the sheet of papyrus but then it began to hurt and burn, and they became dried out.

Drat! There was no need to get so excited!

He took out one of his scrolls but he had a hard job making out the letters on that either. He had been semi-blind nearly all his livelong days, but at least he had been able to read. It was no use holding it closer, no use holding it farther away.

I need a long rest, Uri thought. I've been working too hard.

He couldn't sleep, and it was getting on for daybreak, when he perceived the first rays of light, before he regained his composure. He tested which eye he could see better with: there was no doubt the sight in his right eye was better. Maybe it was starting to improve. It is said that the very short-sighted begin to see things at a distance more clearly as they get on in years, and people who had good eyesight find they can see nothing close at hand.

At the building site he went up close to a wall, then farther away, then he peered at it askew. He had the impression that he saw it more clearly that way. Perhaps from now on slantwise was how he ought to read as well.

That night at home he went to bed; it was a moonlit night. He closed his eyes and then opened them: he could still see light. It had been a transient dysfunction; he needed to get a good night's sleep.

In his dreams he could see well; pictures had been sharp in his dreams all along. When he woke up and could see only vague outlines, and only out of the corners of the eyes, he groaned.

Good God! Is this blindness?

He had to wait several weeks for true blindness. Just enough time to make some necessary arrangements. He acquired a sharp scalpel to open his veins any time. He went out to see his daughters and inform them that soon he would be unable to see anything at all, so would they be so kind as to see to his daily needs if they had a wish to receive any inheritance: there would be more or less according to how they conducted themselves.

Irene wailed and cried crocodile tears; swarthy-skinned Isaac, her husband, the one-time water-carrier but more recently a tax collector, maintained his silence. Isaac, it was said, had worked his way onto the committee which assessed and collected the Jewish tax—a *consilium*, as it was called, with powers to search houses and a Latin praetor at its head. Uri congratulated him. They did not understand why he was not more enthusiastic.

It's more than possible that this Isaac will be an executioner should the occasion arise, Uri contemplated, cursing Kainis for her munificence. The stupid woman might at least leave my grandchildren out of it if she was unwilling to bear me any children.

He repeated: would they be so good as to nurse him as he would be unable to see anything. They promised.

Eulogia, the younger daughter, looked at him dopily, glancing at her mother, who lived there. Hagar muttered angrily: "Your father acting up again, is he?" They had two children there.

Uri picked up his pay at all three building sites. At home he had devised ingenious hiding-places in the floor, and he split the coins between them. What a stroke of good luck it had been to learn tiling. With great difficulty he wrote out a final will and testimony, leaving blanks for the names.

He took a deep breath, then cautiously, staying close to walls, he stumbled his way over to Salutius's place and asked for his share.

"Certainly," said Salutius. "Of course."

Only he did not have it as ready money because he had invested Uri's share so it would earn a decent return, but there was no rush to take it out now because they could get it back later on at a nice interest.

"I need it now," Uri said.

Not now—that was the agreement.

Salutius grubbed together slightly more than 3,000 sesterces; that was all he had at home of the 150,000. Uri counted it and had Salutius sign an acknowledgment of receipt.

"What did you invest it in?" he asked.

Salutius swallowed hard.

"Don't be shy! I won't bite your head off."

Salutius still wavered, looking over Uri's shoulder. Uri smiled encouragingly.

"They're collecting for a Third Temple," he whispered.

"Who are they—the lunatics?"

"Well, it's Iustus and the elders. Your son dropped in personally to ask me for a donation..."

"And what if someone refuses to give?"

"People give—even those who have difficulty shelling out the Jewish tax. They take out a loan, and at a very low interest rate, I have to say."

"Just who's behind the money that's being loaned, my dear son?"

Salutius did not know.

Uri snorted a laugh:

"So when is this Temple of theirs going to be built, dear son, and where exactly?"

"The promise is that if it hasn't been built up in Jerusalem five years from now, the money will be returned with interest... They don't take kindly at all if anyone refuses."

Uri sighed even as he snorted:

"But every last penny of our money, dear son? A small amount would have done the trick!"

Salutius said nothing before beginning to yammer out that although the Eternal One had singled Rome out to punish the Jews for their sins, He would not abandon His people providing the people gave proof of their fidelity, and it happened that precisely in these fraught times a new alliance, more complete and deeper than ever before, was being struck between God and His people.

Uri shook his head and like a bird looked sideways at Salutius's features, tortured as they were by heartburn and a bum heartbeat, and gave a nod.

"I'll send around for my money in five years' time," he said and went off.

He wanted to find a servant.

Homer had also been blind; he dictated his *Iliad* to a servant, so tradition had it.

It is not true that one can't live with blindness.

If one couldn't, there was always the scalpel.

IT WAS BETTER TO SLEEP BECAUSE IN HIS DREAMS HE COULD SEE.

He knew he was awake by the fact that he couldn't see. In the early days he could still make out a few patches and rejoiced that he could still see light, but after a while there was not even that.

He felt around for his hiding-places: the tiles were in place and not wobbling. Under one of them was the scalpel.

His daughters took turns visiting the Via Sacra, bringing him his meals and water and taking away the dirty things; they spent a little time with their father but they had nothing to talk about as Uri had no interest in how his grandchildren were progressing and mixed up their names.

He asked them to round him up a servant who was knew how to write, and they promised earnestly to try, but did not manage to find one.

He ought to have found one for himself earlier. Uri asked for a dog. Stray dogs, outcasts, roamed around in packs in Rome and would attach themselves to any living soul, but Uri's daughters did not get him a dog, implying that they were scared to.

Uri sat by an open window, which faced southward, with the sunlight warming his face and imagined he could see the light. He imagined that he had the dog that had been on the ship: if he tried hard to imagine a thing, it was as if he were seeing it.

He made up stories about the dog: that it had been with him in Beth Zechariah, and with him in Alexandria, playing with him in the Gymnasium garden; he imagined the fuss the dog would kick up in the alabarch's palace; he imagined making a present of it to Kainis, the young Kainis in Claudius's house, and how sometimes the dog would run away to return to him in the Via Sacra and describe in a human voice the reign of the Flavian dynasty. It was a smart dog: Kainis's intelligence and wit had rubbed off.

Uri would snicker to himself and bless the Eternal One for bestowing man with imagination when He created him.

He made up stories for himself, or dreamed them, and he laughed.

As he chewed with his toothless gums the dry flatbread that his daughters brought him he imagined he was eating barbel in Alexandria, and he could sense its aroma in his nose.

The Eternal One, may He be blessed, had also bestowed memory on man.

If a person lived long enough, his dead acquaintances cavorted like fish in silt and there was no knowing which of them might rise to the surface at any one time—maybe that was what was meant by the spirit world. Master Jehuda emerged, grumbled and laughed; appearing separately was the young, black-haired girl, and because she had been invoked by Uri she became his wife, and she lived out with him the rest of his days, and Uri sired a brood of children who miraculously were untouched by war and were even now living nicely in their village, all of them prosperous farmers. Uri also married Sotades's younger sister, the devastatingly pretty Greek girl, slim, blue-eyed, and with the long blonde hair, and lived happily with her in Alexandria.

Theo was a frequent visitor, the trouble being that he was ruled over by a eunuch; Uri would admonish, plead, order him to be released from the eunuch's power, to work and get himself manumitted, and Theo, a blue-eyed, slender, handsome adolescent would pledge to do everything he could: "Don't worry about me, father!" Theo would say and chuckle.

There were many visitors, muttering and moving around the room, sampling the food on his plate, tucking him in if he fell asleep. Uri would send his little sister away to Naples: the climate was better there and she would not cough, and he gave her a lot of money to take with her. Joseph also visited, listening with amazement to Uri's tales about Jerusalem and Alexandria, and was reassured that it was not as bad as all that in Rome either for that matter.

Sometimes Uri would have revenge: he would jab a thorn into Agrippa's neck, trip Tija as he was running, or give the alabarch a cheeky riposte. "No need for that, dear son," Philo would yammer. Uri had no idea that he was not sleeping on such occasions because in his dreams he was incapable of taking vengeance, and he could not control his dreams, but he was glad of them, even though they were oppressive, because at least he could see.

His daughters also paid visits, bringing him food, and Uri would tear them off a strip for not getting married, to which they would either laugh or lie that they were already married. Uri's daughters also brought along children, maintaining that they were his grandchildren, and the children would blubber out something. The women would tell them to stroke their grandfather's cheek, while Uri would try to nibble at their tiny hands, would bark and curse them, as a result of which they did not come again. It was cold, and Uri was freezing and demanded that they put Tadeus's liberty cap on his head, but the evil-minded people just would not understand him so Uri pulled his tunic over his head, which the women pulled off, leaving Uri to bellow that he had to have the liberty cap on him at all times! But they refused to understand and wouldn't hear a word about Tadeus. It was appalling to be at the whim of women like that.

Nor would the women read back to him what he had dictated to the servant. Though there were times when a light went on in his head and he was able to compose marvelous passages, by the next day he would have forgotten what these were and he needed to have it reread so that he could pick up where he had left off, but the women couldn't read however much he yelled, and the servant would just hide away.

Joseph often visited and talked about business matters with Uri. He had changed his voice and his odor, and occasionally he said he was a physician, but Uri still recognized him. Joseph wanted to open a vein to bleed him but Uri was not prepared to allow this; he was held down but managed to free himself because every day he undertook many hours of physical exercise that could also be done blind—they had not anticipated that and so gave up.

Uri provided his father some superb bits of advice, and Joseph was increasingly proud of his son. They jointly went into a machine-making business in which Uri designed lifting devices and even learned how to cast statues, which they shipped to all the ports. One time they traveled to Syracusa for discussions and to meet Matthew, who was working as harbor master. He had not aged one bit and immediately ordered three lifting machines. Uri reminded him that he had given to Plotius what he owed, and Matthew said that Plotius had indeed passed it on.

When Hermia brought him his meal, Uri ordered barbel, but she moaned that it was horrendously expensive, whereupon Uri tipped her off that he had money, only he had hidden it. That greatly intrigued Hermia, but Uri would not reveal where the money was hidden.

He complained about the food, shouting at the women who brought him meals, after which they did not bring any more. Good thing I'm used to starving, the thought entered Uri's mind. It stank in the room; Uri defecated besides the chamber-pot, smearing it on the floor, and he laughed when he found there was no water in the pitcher.

Joseph sat beside Uri's bed and told him stories. He knew some fabulous tales, and Uri listened spellbound.

"Tell them to Theo as well," he asked his father.

"Who's Theo?"

Uri deliberated.

"I'll be him when I grow up."

Joseph promised.

At dawn one day, Uri woke up feeling like he was choking. Joseph was not to be found anywhere. Uri coughed but it did not relieve the pressure in his chest. He called out, but no one came. His stomach hurt, his chest was painful, the nape of his neck was racked with stabbing pains. He was gasping for air, his arms flailed and his legs churned but he could only choke, his muscles would not function, they just burned. Uri's struggled mightily.

I still want to live, he thought to himself, and was lost in wonder.

ABOUT THE AUTHOR
AND TRANSLATOR

Born in 1946 in Budapest, award-winning dramatist, novelist, and translator GYÖRGY SPIRÓ has earned a reputation as one of post-war Hungary's most prominent and prolific literary figures..He teaches at ELTE University of Budapest, where he specializes in Slavic literatures.

TIM WILKINSON gave up his job in the pharmaceutical industry to translate Hungarian literature and history. He is the primary translator of Nobel Prize-winner Imre Kertész. Wilkinson's translation of Kertész's *Fatelessness* won the PEN/Book of the Month Club Translation Prize in 2005.

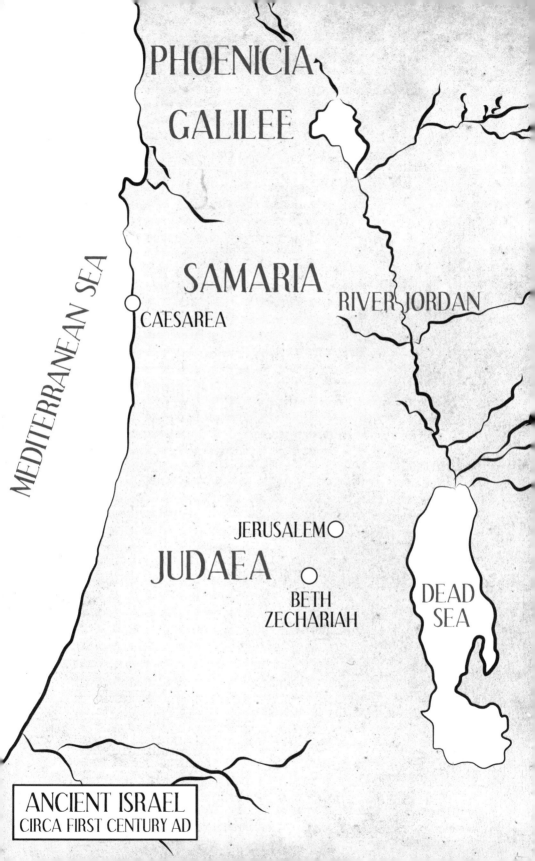

PHOENICIA

GALILEE

MEDITERRANEAN SEA

SAMARIA

CAESAREA

RIVER JORDAN

JERUSALEM○

JUDAEA   ○

BETH
ZECHARIAH

DEAD
SEA

ANCIENT ISRAEL
CIRCA FIRST CENTURY AD